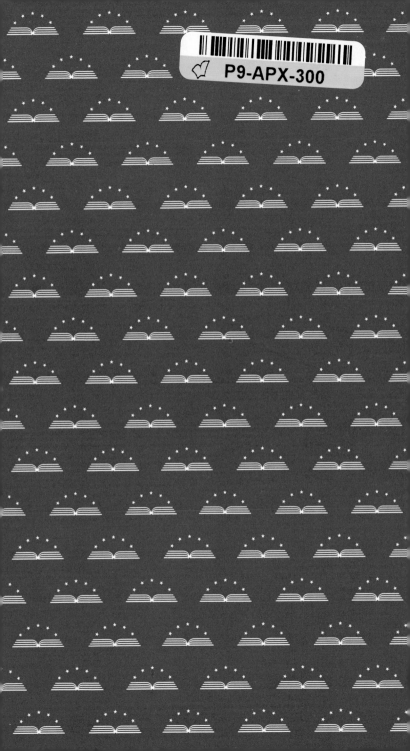

MARK TWAIN

MARK TWAIN

MISSISSIPPI WRITINGS

The Adventures of Tom Sawyer
Life on the Mississippi
Adventures of Huckleberry Finn
Pudd'nhead Wilson

THE LIBRARY OF AMERICA

The Iowa-California text of *The Adventures of Tom Sawyer*
here reprinted was correctly established from the authoritative
documents published and copyrighted © in 1980 by
The Regents of the University of California.
Reprinted by permission of the University of California Press.
The name "Mark Twain" is used by permission of Harper & Row.

The paper used in this publication meets the
minimum requirements of the American National Standard
for Information Sciences—Permanence of Paper for
Printed Library Materials, ANSI Z39.48–1984.

Distributed to the trade in the United States
and Canada by the Viking Press.

Library of Congress Catalog Card Number: 82-9917
For Cataloging in Publication Data, see end of *Notes* section.
ISBN 0-940450-07-0

Eighth Printing
The Library of America—5

GUY CARDWELL
WROTE THE NOTES AND CHRONOLOGY
AND SELECTED THE TEXTS
FOR THIS VOLUME

The text of The Adventures of Tom Sawyer was established from the authoritative documents by Paul Baender in cooperation with his associates, John C. Gerber and Terry Firkins, and is reprinted here from The Works of Mark Twain published by the Iowa Center for Textual Studies and the University of California Press.

Grateful acknowledgement is made to the National Endowment for the Humanities and the Ford Foundation for their generous financial support of this series.

Contents

THE ADVENTURES OF
TOM SAWYER

TO

MY WIFE

This Book is
Affectionately Dedicated.

Preface

MOST OF the adventures recorded in this book really occurred; one or two were experiences of my own, the rest those of boys who were schoolmates of mine. Huck Finn is drawn from life; Tom Sawyer also, but not from an individual—he is a combination of the characteristics of three boys whom I knew, and therefore belongs to the composite order of architecture.

The odd superstitions touched upon were all prevalent among children and slaves in the West at the period of this story—that is to say, thirty or forty years ago.

Although my book is intended mainly for the entertainment of boys and girls, I hope it will not be shunned by men and women on that account, for part of my plan has been to try to pleasantly remind adults of what they once were themselves, and of how they felt and thought and talked, and what queer enterprises they sometimes engaged in.

THE AUTHOR.

Hartford, 1876.

Contents

I

"Tom!"

No answer.

"Tom!"

No answer.

"What's gone with that boy, I wonder? You TOM!"

No answer.

The old lady pulled her spectacles down and looked over them, about the room; then she put them up and looked out under them. She seldom or never looked *through* them for so small a thing as a boy; they were her state pair, the pride of her heart, and were built for "style," not service;—she could have seen through a pair of stove lids just as well. She looked perplexed for a moment, and then said, not fiercely, but still loud enough for the furniture to hear:

"Well, I lay if I get hold of you I'll—"

She did not finish, for by this time she was bending down and punching under the bed with the broom—and so she needed breath to punctuate the punches with. She resurrected nothing but the cat.

"I never did see the beat of that boy!"

She went to the open door and stood in it and looked out among the tomato vines and "jimpson" weeds that constituted the garden. No Tom. So she lifted up her voice at an angle calculated for distance, and shouted:

"Y-o-u-u *Tom!*"

There was a slight noise behind her and she turned just in time to seize a small boy by the slack of his roundabout and arrest his flight.

"There! I might 'a' thought of that closet. What you been doing in there?"

"Nothing."

"Nothing! Look at your hands. And look at your mouth. What *is* that truck?"

"*I* don't know, aunt."

"Well *I* know. It's jam—that's what it is. Forty times I've said if you didn't let that jam alone I'd skin you. Hand me that switch."

The switch hovered in the air—the peril was desperate—

"My! Look behind you, aunt!"

The old lady whirled around, and snatched her skirts out of danger. The lad fled, on the instant, scrambled up the high board fence, and disappeared over it.

His aunt Polly stood surprised a moment, and then broke into a gentle laugh.

"Hang the boy, can't I never learn anything? Ain't he played me tricks enough like that for me to be looking out for him by this time? But old fools is the biggest fools there is. Can't learn an old dog new tricks, as the saying is. But my goodness, he never plays them alike, two days, and how is a body to know what's coming? He 'pears to know just how long he can torment me before I get my dander up, and he knows if he can make out to put me off for a minute or make me laugh, it's all down again and I can't hit him a lick. I ain't doing my duty by that boy, and that's the Lord's truth, good-ness knows. Spare the rod and spile the child, as the Good Book says. I'm a-laying up sin and suffering for us both, *I* know. He's full of the Old Scratch, but laws-a-me! he's my own dead sister's boy, poor thing, and I ain't got the heart to lash him, somehow. Every time I let him off my conscience does hurt me so, and every time I hit him my old heart most breaks. Well-a-well, man that is born of woman is of few days and full of trouble, as the Scripture says, and I reckon it's so. He'll play hookey this evening,* and I'll just be obleeged to make him work, to-morrow, to punish him. It's mighty hard to make him work Saturdays, when all the boys is having holiday, but he hates work more than he hates anything else, and I've *got* to do some of my duty by him, or I'll be the ruination of the child."

Tom did play hookey, and he had a very good time. He got back home barely in season to help Jim, the small colored boy, saw next day's wood and split the kindlings, before sup-per—at least was there in time to tell his adventures to Jim while Jim did three-fourths of the work. Tom's younger brother, (or rather, half-brother) Sid, was already through

*South-western for "afternoon."

with his part of the work (picking up chips,) for he was a quiet boy and had no adventurous, troublesome ways.

While Tom was eating his supper, and stealing sugar as opportunity offered, aunt Polly asked him questions that were full of guile, and very deep—for she wanted to trap him into damaging revealments. Like many other simple-hearted souls, it was her pet vanity to believe she was endowed with a talent for dark and mysterious diplomacy and she loved to contemplate her most transparent devices as marvels of low cunning. Said she:

"Tom, it was middling warm in school, warn't it?"

"Yes'm."

"Powerful warm, warn't it?"

"Yes'm."

"Didn't you want to go in a-swimming, Tom?"

A bit of a scare shot through Tom—a touch of uncomfortable suspicion. He searched aunt Polly's face, but it told him nothing. So he said:

"No'm—well, not very much."

The old lady reached out her hand and felt Tom's shirt, and said:

"But you ain't too warm now, though." And it flattered her to reflect that she had discovered that the shirt was dry without anybody knowing that that was what she had in her mind. But in spite of her, Tom knew where the wind lay, now. So he forestalled what might be the next move:

"Some of us pumped on our heads—mine's damp yet. See?"

Aunt Polly was vexed to think she had overlooked that bit of circumstantial evidence, and missed a trick. Then she had a new inspiration:

"Tom, you didn't have to undo your shirt collar where I sewed it to pump on your head, did you? Unbutton your jacket!"

The trouble vanished out of Tom's face. He opened his jacket. His shirt collar was securely sewed.

"Bother! Well, go 'long with you. I'd made sure you'd played hookey and been a-swimming. But I forgive ye, Tom. I reckon you're a kind of a singed cat, as the saying is—better'n you look. *This* time."

She was half sorry her sagacity had miscarried, and half
glad that Tom had stumbled into obedient conduct for once.

But Sidney said:

"Well, now, if I didn't think you sewed his collar with
white thread, but it's black."

"Why, I did sew it with white! Tom!"

But Tom did not wait for the rest. As he went out at the
door he said:

"Siddy, I'll lick you for that."

In a safe place Tom examined two large needles which were
thrust into the lappels of his jacket, and had thread bound
about them—one needle carried white thread and the other
black. He said:

"She'd never noticed, if it hadn't been for Sid. Consound
it! sometimes she sews it with white and sometimes she sews
it with black. I wish to geeminy she'd stick to one or
t'other—*I* can't keep the run of 'em. But I bet you I'll lam
Sid for that. I'll learn him!"

He was not the Model Boy of the village. He knew the
model boy very well though—and loathed him.

Within two minutes, or even less, he had forgotten all his
troubles. Not because his troubles were one whit less heavy
and bitter to him than a man's are to a man, but because a
new and powerful interest bore them down and drove them
out of his mind for the time—just as men's misfortunes are
forgotten in the excitement of new enterprises. This new interest was a valued novelty in whistling, which he had just
acquired from a negro, and he was suffering to practice it
undisturbed. It consisted in a peculiar bird-like turn, a sort of
liquid warble, produced by touching the tongue to the roof
of the mouth at short intervals in the midst of the music—
the reader probably remembers how to do it if he has ever
been a boy. Diligence and attention soon gave him the knack
of it, and he strode down the street with his mouth full of
harmony and his soul full of gratitude. He felt much as an
astronomer feels who has discovered a new planet. No doubt,
as far as strong, deep, unalloyed pleasure is concerned, the
advantage was with the boy, not the astronomer.

The summer evenings were long. It was not dark, yet. Presently Tom checked his whistle. A stranger was before him—

a boy a shade larger than himself. A new-comer of any age or either sex was an impressive curiosity in the poor little shabby village of St. Petersburg. This boy was well dressed, too—well dressed on a week-day. This was simply astounding. His cap was a dainty thing, his close-buttoned blue cloth round-about was new and natty, and so were his pantaloons. He had shoes on—and yet it was only Friday. He even wore a necktie, a bright bit of ribbon. He had a citified air about him that ate into Tom's vitals. The more Tom stared at the splendid marvel, the higher he turned up his nose at his finery and the shabbier and shabbier his own outfit seemed to him to grow. Neither boy spoke. If one moved, the other moved—but only sidewise, in a circle; they kept face to face and eye to eye all the time. Finally Tom said:

"I can lick you!"

"I'd like to see you try it."

"Well, I can do it."

"No you can't, either."

"Yes I can."

"No you can't."

"I can."

"You can't."

"Can!"

"Can't!"

An uncomfortable pause. Then Tom said:

"What's your name?"

" 'Tisn't any of your business, maybe."

"Well I 'low I'll *make* it my business."

"Well why don't you?"

"If you say much I will."

"Much—much—*much*! There now."

"Oh, you think you're mighty smart, *don't* you? I could lick you with one hand tied behind me, if I wanted to."

"Well why don't you do it? You *say* you can do it."

"Well I *will*, if you fool with me."

"Oh yes—I've seen whole families in the same fix."

"Smarty! You think you're *some*, now, *don't* you? Oh what a hat!"

"You can lump that hat if you don't like it. I dare you to knock it off—and anybody that'll take a dare will suck eggs."

"You're a liar!"

"You're another."

"You're a fighting liar and dasn't take it up."

"Aw—take a walk!"

"Say—if you gimme much more of your sass I'll take and bounce a rock off'n your head."

"Oh, of *course* you will."

"Well I *will*."

"Well why don't you *do* it then? What do you keep *saying* you will, for? Why don't you *do* it? It's because you're afraid."

"I *ain't* afraid."

"You are."

"I ain't."

"You are."

Another pause, and more eyeing and sidling around each other. Presently they were shoulder to shoulder. Tom said:

"Get away from here!"

"Get away yourself!"

"I won't."

"*I* won't either."

So they stood, each with a foot placed at an angle as a brace, and both shoving with might and main, and glowering at each other with hate. But neither could get an advantage. After struggling till both were hot and flushed, each relaxed his strain with watchful caution, and Tom said:

"You're a coward and a pup. I'll tell my big brother on you, and he can thrash you with his little finger, and I'll make him do it, too."

"What do I care for your big brother? I've got a brother that's bigger than he is—and what's more, he can throw him over that fence, too." [Both brothers were imaginary.]

"That's a lie."

"*Your* saying so don't make it so."

Tom drew a line in the dust with his big toe, and said:

"I dare you to step over that, and I'll lick you till you can't stand up. Anybody that'll take a dare will steal a sheep."

The new boy stepped over promptly, and said:

"Now you said you'd do it, now let's see you do it."

"Don't you crowd me, now; you better look out."

"Well you *said* you'd do it—why don't you do it?"

"By jingo! for two cents I *will* do it."

The new boy took two broad coppers out of his pocket and held them out with derision. Tom struck them to the ground. In an instant both boys were rolling and tumbling in the dirt, gripped together like cats; and for the space of a minute they tugged and tore at each other's hair and clothes, punched and scratched each other's noses, and covered themselves with dust and glory. Presently the confusion took form, and through the fog of battle Tom appeared, seated astride the new boy and pounding him with his fists.

"Holler 'nuff!" said he.

The boy only struggled to free himself. He was crying,— mainly from rage.

"Holler 'nuff!"—and the pounding went on.

At last the stranger got out a smothered "Nuff!" and Tom let him up and said:

"Now that'll learn you. Better look out who you're fooling with, next time."

The new boy went off brushing the dust from his clothes, sobbing, snuffling, and occasionally looking back and shaking his head and threatening what he would do to Tom the "next time he caught him out." To which Tom responded with jeers, and started off in high feather; and as soon as his back was turned the new boy snatched up a stone, threw it and hit him between the shoulders and then turned tail and ran like an antelope. Tom chased the traitor home, and thus found out where he lived. He then held a position at the gate for some time, daring the enemy to come outside, but the enemy only made faces at him through the window and declined. At last the enemy's mother appeared, and called Tom a bad, vicious, vulgar child, and ordered him away. So he went away; but he said he "'lowed" to "lay" for that boy.

He got home pretty late, that night, and when he climbed cautiously in at the window, he uncovered an ambuscade, in the person of his aunt; and when she saw the state his clothes were in her resolution to turn his Saturday holiday into captivity at hard labor became adamantine in its firmness.

II

S ATURDAY MORNING was come, and all the summer world
was bright and fresh, and brimming with life. There was
a song in every heart; and if the heart was young the music
issued at the lips. There was cheer in every face and a spring
in every step. The locust trees were in bloom and the fragrance of the blossoms filled the air. Cardiff Hill, beyond the
village and above it, was green with vegetation, and it lay just
far enough away to seem a Delectable Land, dreamy, reposeful and inviting.

Tom appeared on the sidewalk with a bucket of whitewash
and a long-handled brush. He surveyed the fence, and all
gladness left him and a deep melancholy settled down upon
his spirit. Thirty yards of board fence, nine feet high. Life to
him seemed hollow, and existence but a burden. Sighing, he
dipped his brush and passed it along the topmost plank; repeated the operation; did it again; compared the insignificant
whitewashed streak with the far-reaching continent of un-
whitewashed fence, and sat down on a tree-box discouraged.
Jim came skipping out at the gate with a tin pail, and singing "Buffalo Gals." Bringing water from the town pump
had always been hateful work in Tom's eyes, before, but
now it did not strike him so. He remembered that there
was company at the pump. White, mulatto and negro boys
and girls were always there waiting their turns, resting,
trading playthings, quarreling, fighting, skylarking. And he
remembered that although the pump was only a hundred
and fifty yards off, Jim never got back with a bucket of water
under an hour—and even then somebody generally had to go
after him. Tom said:

"Say, Jim, I'll fetch the water if you'll whitewash some."

Jim shook his head and said:

"Can't, Mars Tom. Ole missis, she tole me I got to go an'
git dis water an' not stop foolin' roun' wid anybody. She say
she spec' Mars Tom gwyne to ax me to whitewash, an' so she
tole me go 'long an' 'tend to my own business—she 'lowed
she'd 'tend to de whitewashin'."

"Oh, never you mind what she said, Jim. That's the way she always talks. Gimme the bucket—I won't be gone only a minute. *She* won't ever know."

"Oh, I dasn't, Mars Tom. Ole missis she'd take an' tar de head off'n me. 'Deed she would."

"*She!* She never licks anybody—whacks 'em over the head with her thimble—and who cares for that, I'd like to know. She talks awful, but talk don't hurt—anyways it don't if she don't cry. Jim, I'll give you a marvel. I'll give you a white alley!"

Jim began to waver.

"White alley, Jim! And it's a bully taw."

"My! Dat's a mighty gay marvel, *I* tell you! But Mars Tom I's powerful 'fraid ole missis—"

"And besides, if you will I'll show you my sore toe."

Jim was only human—this attraction was too much for him. He put down his pail, took the white alley, and bent over the toe with absorbing interest while the bandage was being unwound. In another moment he was flying down the street with his pail and a tingling rear, Tom was whitewashing with vigor, and aunt Polly was retiring from the field with a slipper in her hand and triumph in her eye.

But Tom's energy did not last. He began to think of the fun he had planned for this day, and his sorrows multiplied. Soon the free boys would come tripping along on all sorts of delicious expeditions, and they would make a world of fun of him for having to work—the very thought of it burnt him like fire. He got out his worldly wealth and examined it—bits of toys, marbles and trash; enough to buy an exchange of *work*, maybe, but not half enough to buy so much as half an hour of pure freedom. So he returned his straightened means to his pocket and gave up the idea of trying to buy the boys. At this dark and hopeless moment an inspiration burst upon him! Nothing less than a great, magnificent inspiration!

He took up his brush and went tranquilly to work. Ben Rogers hove in sight presently—the very boy, of all boys, whose ridicule he had been dreading. Ben's gait was the hop-skip-and-jump—proof enough that his heart was light and his anticipations high. He was eating an apple, and giving a long, melodious whoop, at intervals, followed by a deep-toned ding-dong-dong, ding-dong-dong, for he was person-ating a steamboat. As he drew near, he slackened speed, took the middle of the street, leaned far over to starboard and rounded to ponderously and with laborious pomp and cir-cumstance—for he was personating the "Big Missouri," and considered himself to be drawing nine feet of water. He was boat and captain and engine-bells combined, so he had to imagine himself standing on his own hurricane deck giving the orders and executing them:

"Stop her, sir! Ting-a-ling-ling!" The headway ran almost out and he drew up slowly toward the side-walk.

"Ship up to back! Ting-a-ling-ling!" His arms straightened and stiffened down his sides.

"Set her back on the stabboard! Ting-a-ling-ling! Chow! ch-chow-wow! Chow!" His right hand, meantime, describing stately circles,—for it was representing a forty-foot wheel.

"Let her go back on the labbord! Ting-a-ling-ling! Chow-ch-chow-chow!" The left hand began to describe circles.

"Stop the stabboard! Ting-a-ling-ling! Stop the labbord! Come ahead on the stabboard! Stop her! Let your outside turn over slow! Ting-a-ling-ling! Chow-ow-ow! Get out that head-line! *Lively*, now! Come—out with your spring-line—what're you about there! Take a turn round that stump with the bight of it! Stand by that stage, now—let her go! Done with the engines, sir! Ting-a-ling-ling! *Sh't! s'sh't! sh't!*" (trying the gauge-cocks.)

Tom went on whitewashing—paid no attention to the steamboat. Ben stared a moment and then said:

"Hi-*yi! You're* up a stump, ain't you!"

No answer. Tom surveyed his last touch with the eye of an artist; then he gave his brush another gentle sweep and sur-veyed the result, as before. Ben ranged up alongside of him. Tom's mouth watered for the apple, but he stuck to his work. Ben said:

"Hello, old chap, you got to work, hey?"

Tom wheeled suddenly and said:

"Why it's you, Ben! I warn't noticing."

"Say—*I'm* going in a-swimming, *I* am. Don't you wish

you could? But of course you'd druther *work*—wouldn't you? 'Course you would!"

Tom contemplated the boy a bit, and said:

"What do you call work?"

"Why, ain't *that* work?"

Tom resumed his whitewashing, and answered carelessly:

"Well, maybe it is, and maybe it ain't. All I know, is, it suits Tom Sawyer."

"Oh come, now, you don't mean to let on that you *like* it?"

The brush continued to move.

"Like it? Well I don't see why I oughtn't to like it. Does a boy get a chance to whitewash a fence every day?"

That put the thing in a new light. Ben stopped nibbling his apple. Tom swept his brush daintily back and forth—stepped back to note the effect—added a touch here and there—criticised the effect again—Ben watching every move and getting more and more interested, more and more absorbed. Presently he said:

"Say, Tom, let *me* whitewash a little."

Tom considered; was about to consent; but he altered his mind:

"No—no—I reckon it wouldn't hardly do, Ben. You see, aunt Polly's awful particular about this fence—right here on the street, you know—but if it was the back fence I wouldn't mind and *she* wouldn't. Yes, she's awful particular about this fence; it's got to be done very careful; I reckon there ain't one boy in a thousand, maybe two thousand, that can do it the way it's got to be done."

"No—is that so? Oh come, now—lemme just try. Only just a little—I'd let *you*, if you was me, Tom."

"Ben, I'd like to, honest injun; but aunt Polly—well Jim wanted to do it, but she wouldn't let him; Sid wanted to do it, and she wouldn't let Sid. Now don't you see how I'm fixed? If you was to tackle this fence and anything was to happen to it—"

"Oh, shucks, I'll be just as careful. Now lemme try. Say—I'll give you the core of my apple."

"Well, here—. No, Ben, now don't. I'm afeard—"

"I'll give you *all* of it!"

Tom gave up the brush with reluctance in his face but alacrity in his heart. And while the late steamer "Big Missouri" worked and sweated in the sun, the retired artist sat on a barrel in the shade close by, dangled his legs, munched his apple, and planned the slaughter of more innocents. There was no lack of material; boys happened along every little while; they came to jeer, but remained to whitewash. By the time Ben was fagged out, Tom had traded the next chance to Billy Fisher for a kite, in good repair; and when *he* played out Johnny Miller bought in for a dead rat and a string to swing it with—and so on, and so on, hour after hour. And when the middle of the afternoon came, from being a poor poverty-stricken boy in the morning, Tom was literally rolling in wealth. He had, beside the things before mentioned, twelve marbles, part of a jewsharp, a piece of blue bottle-glass to look through, a spool cannon, a key that wouldn't unlock anything, a fragment of chalk, a glass stopper of a decanter, a tin soldier, a couple of tadpoles, six fire-crackers, a kitten with only one eye, a brass door-knob, a dog collar—but no dog—the handle of a knife, four pieces of orange peel, and a dilapidated old window sash.

He had had a nice, good, idle time all the while—plenty of company—and the fence had three coats of whitewash on it! If he hadn't run out of whitewash, he would have bankrupted every boy in the village.

Tom said to himself that it was not such a hollow world, after all. He had discovered a great law of human action, without knowing it—namely, that in order to make a man or a boy covet a thing, it is only necessary to make the thing difficult to attain. If he had been a great and wise philosopher, like the writer of this book, he would now have comprehended that Work consists of whatever a body is *obliged* to do and that Play consists of whatever a body is not obliged to do. And this would help him to understand why constructing artificial flowers or performing on a treadmill is work, while rolling ten-pins or climbing Mont Blanc is only amusement. There are wealthy gentlemen in England who drive four-horse passenger-coaches twenty or thirty miles on a daily line, in the summer, because the privilege costs them considerable money; but if they were offered wages for the service, that would turn it into work and then they would resign.

The boy mused a while over the substantial change which had taken place in his worldly circumstances, and then wended toward head-quarters to report.

III

Tom presented himself before aunt Polly, who was sitting by an open window in a pleasant rearward apartment which was bed-room, breakfast-room, dining room and library combined. The balmy summer air, the restful quiet, the odor of the flowers, and the drowsing murmur of the bees had had their effect, and she was nodding over her knitting—for she had no company but the cat, and it was asleep in her lap. Her spectacles were propped up on her gray head for safety. She had thought that of course Tom had deserted long ago, and she wondered to see him place himself in her power again in this intrepid way. He said:

"Mayn't I go and play now, aunt?"

"What, a'ready? How much have you done?"

"It's all done, aunt."

"Tom, don't lie to me—I can't bear it."

"I ain't, aunt; it *is* all done."

Aunt Polly placed small trust in such evidence. She went out to see for herself; and she would have been content to find twenty per cent of Tom's statement true. When she found the entire fence whitewashed, and not only whitewashed but elaborately coated and recoated, and even a streak added to the ground, her astonishment was almost unspeakable. She said:

"Well, I never! There's no getting around it, you *can* work when you're a mind to, Tom." And then she diluted the compliment by adding, "But it's powerful seldom you're a mind to, I'm bound to say. Well, go 'long and play; but mind you get back some time in a week, or I'll tan you."

She was so overcome by the splendor of his achievement that she took him into the closet and selected a choice apple and delivered it to him, along with an improving lecture upon the added value and flavor a treat took to itself when it came without sin through virtuous effort. And while she closed with a happy Scriptural flourish, he "hooked" a doughnut.

Then he skipped out, and saw Sid just starting up the outside stairway that led to the back rooms on the second floor.

Clods were handy and the air was full of them in a twinkling. They raged around Sid like a hail-storm; and before aunt Polly could collect her surprised faculties and sally to the rescue, six or seven clods had taken personal effect and Tom was over the fence and gone. There was a gate, but as a general thing he was too crowded for time to make use of it. His soul was at peace, now that he had settled with Sid for calling attention to his black thread and getting him into trouble.

Tom skirted the block and came around into a muddy alley that led by the back of his aunt's cow-stable; he presently got safely beyond the reach of capture and punishment, and hasted toward the public square of the village, where two "military" companies of boys had met for conflict, according to previous appointment. Tom was General of one of these armies, Joe Harper (a bosom friend,) General of the other. These two great commanders did not condescend to fight in person—that being better suited to the still smaller fry—but sat together on an eminence and conducted the field operations by orders delivered through aides-de-camp. Tom's army won a great victory, after a long and hard-fought battle. Then the dead were counted, prisoners exchanged, the terms of the next disagreement agreed upon and the day for the necessary battle appointed; after which the armies fell into line and marched away, and Tom turned homeward alone.

As he was passing by the house where Jeff Thatcher lived, he saw a new girl in the garden—a lovely little blue-eyed creature with yellow hair plaited into two long tails, white summer frock and embroidered pantalettes. The fresh-crowned hero fell without firing a shot. A certain Amy Lawrence vanished out of his heart and left not even a memory of herself behind. He had thought he loved her to distraction, he had regarded his passion as adoration; and behold it was only a poor little evanescent partiality. He had been months winning her; she had confessed hardly a week ago; he had been the happiest and the proudest boy in the world only seven short days, and here, in one instant of time she had gone out of his heart like a casual stranger whose visit is done.

He worshipped this new angel with furtive eye, till he saw that she had discovered him; then he pretended he did not

know she was present, and began to "show off" in all sorts
of absurd boyish ways in order to win her admiration. He
kept up this grotesque foolishness for some time; but by and
by, while he was in the midst of some dangerous gymnastic
performances, he glanced aside and saw that the little girl was
wending her way toward the house. Tom came up to the
fence and leaned on it, grieving, and hoping she would tarry
yet a while longer. She halted a moment on the steps and
then moved toward the door. Tom heaved a great sigh as she
put her foot on the threshold. But his face lit up, right away,
for she tossed a pansy over the fence a moment before she
disappeared.

The boy ran around and stopped within a foot or two of
the flower, and then shaded his eyes with his hand and began
to look down street as if he had discovered something of interest going on in that direction. Presently he picked up a
straw and began trying to balance it on his nose, with his
head tilted far back; and as he moved from side to side, in his
efforts, he edged nearer and nearer toward the pansy; finally
his bare foot rested upon it, his pliant toes closed upon it and
he hopped away with the treasure, and disappeared around
the corner. But only for a minute—only while he could button the flower inside his jacket, next his heart—or next his
stomach, possibly, for he was not much posted in anatomy,
and not hypercritical anyway.

He returned, now, and hung about the fence till nightfall,
"showing off," as before; but the girl never exhibited herself
again, though Tom comforted himself a little with the hope
that she had been near some window, meantime, and been
aware of his attentions. Finally he went home reluctantly,
with his poor head full of visions.

All through supper his spirits were so high that his aunt
wondered "what had got into the child." He took a good
scolding about clodding Sid, and did not seem to mind it in
the least. He tried to steal sugar under his aunt's very nose,
and got his knuckles rapped for it. He said:

"Aunt, you don't whack Sid when he takes it."

"Well, Sid don't torment a body the way you do. You'd be
always into that sugar if I warn't watching you."

Presently she stepped into the kitchen, and Sid, happy in

his immunity, reached for the sugar-bowl—a sort of glorying over Tom which was well-nigh unbearable. But Sid's fingers slipped and the bowl dropped and broke. Tom was in ecstasies. In such ecstasies that he even controlled his tongue and was silent. He said to himself that he would not speak a word, even when his aunt came in, but would sit perfectly still till she asked who did the mischief; and then he would tell and there would be nothing so good in the world as to see that pet model "catch it." He was so brim-full of exultation that he could hardly hold himself when the old lady came back and stood above the wreck discharging lightnings of wrath from over her spectacles. He said to himself, "Now it's coming!" And the next instant he was sprawling on the floor! The potent palm was uplifted to strike again when Tom cried out:

"Hold on, now, what 're you belting *me*, for?—Sid broke it!"

Aunt Polly paused, perplexed, and Tom looked for healing pity. But when she got her tongue again, she only said:

"Umf! Well, you didn't get a lick amiss, I reckon. You been into some other owdacious mischief when I wasn't around, like enough."

Then her conscience reproached her, and she yearned to say something kind and loving; but she judged that this would be construed into a confession that she had been in the wrong, and discipline forbade that. So she kept silence, and went about her affairs with a troubled heart. Tom sulked in a corner and exalted his woes. He knew that in her heart his aunt was on her knees to him, and he was morosely gratified by the consciousness of it. He would hang out no signals, he would take notice of none. He knew that a yearning glance fell upon him, now and then, through a film of tears, but he refused recognition of it. He pictured himself lying sick unto death and his aunt bending over him beseeching one little forgiving word, but he would turn his face to the wall, and die with that word unsaid. Ah, how would she feel then? And he pictured himself brought home from the river, dead, with his curls all wet, and his poor hands still forever, and his sore heart at rest. How she would throw herself upon him, and how her tears would fall like rain, and her lips pray

God to give her back her boy and she would never never abuse him any more! But he would lie there cold and white and make no sign—a poor little sufferer whose griefs were at an end. He so worked upon his feelings with the pathos of these dreams that he had to keep swallowing, he was so like to choke; and his eyes swam in a blur of water, which overflowed when he winked, and ran down and trickled from the end of his nose. And such a luxury to him was this petting of his sorrows, that he could not bear to have any worldly cheeriness or any grating delight intrude upon it; it was too sacred for such contact; and so, presently, when his cousin Mary danced in, all alive with the joy of seeing home again after an age-long visit of one week to the country, he got up and moved in clouds and darkness out at one door as she brought song and sunshine in at the other.

He wandered far from the accustomed haunts of boys, and sought desolate places that were in harmony with his spirit. A log raft in the river invited him, and he seated himself on its outer edge and contemplated the dreary vastness of the stream, wishing, the while. that he could only be drowned, all at once and unconsciously, without undergoing the uncomfortable routine devised by nature. Then he thought of his flower. He got it out, rumpled and wilted, and it mightily increased his dismal felicity. He wondered if *she* would pity him if she knew? Would she cry, and wish that she had a right to put her arms around his neck and comfort him? Or would she turn coldly away like all the hollow world? This picture brought such an agony of pleasurable suffering that he worked it over and over again in his mind and set it up in new and varied lights till he wore it threadbare. At last he rose up sighing, and departed in the darkness.

About half past nine or ten o'clock, he came along the deserted street to where the Adored Unknown lived; he paused a moment; no sound fell upon his listening ear; a candle was casting a dull glow upon the curtain of a second-story window. Was the sacred presence there? He climbed the fence, threaded his stealthy way through the plants, till he stood under that window; he looked up at it long, and with emotion; then he laid him down on the ground under it, disposing himself upon his back, with his hands clasped upon his breast and holding his poor wilted flower. And thus he would die—out in the cold world, with no shelter over his homeless head, no friendly hand to wipe the death-damps from his brow, no loving face to bend pityingly over him when the great agony came. And thus *she* would see him when she looked out upon the glad morning—and Oh! would she drop one little tear upon his poor lifeless form, would she heave one little sigh to see a bright young life so rudely blighted, so untimely cut down?

The window went up, a maid-servant's discordant voice profaned the holy calm, and a deluge of water drenched the prone martyr's remains!

The strangling hero sprang up with a relieving snort, there was a whiz as of a missile in the air, mingled with the murmur of a curse, a sound as of shivering glass followed, and a small vague form went over the fence and shot away in the gloom.

Not long after, as Tom, all undressed for bed, was surveying his drenched garments by the light of a tallow dip, Sid woke up; but if he had any dim idea of making any "references to allusions," he thought better of it and held his peace—for there was danger in Tom's eye.

Tom turned in without the added vexation of prayers, and Sid made mental note of the omission.

IV

THE SUN ROSE upon a tranquil world, and beamed down upon the peaceful village like a benediction. Breakfast over, aunt Polly had family worship; it began with a prayer built from the ground up of solid courses of Scriptural quotations welded together with a thin mortar of originality; and from the summit of this she delivered a grim chapter of the Mosaic Law, as from Sinai.

Then Tom girded up his loins, so to speak, and went to work to "get his verses." Sid had learned his lesson days before. Tom bent all his energies to the memorizing of five verses; and he chose part of the Sermon on the Mount because he could find no verses that were shorter. At the end of half an hour Tom had a vague general idea of his lesson, but no more, for his mind was traversing the whole field of human thought, and his hands were busy with distracting recreations. Mary took his book to hear him recite, and he tried to find his way through the fog:

"Blessed are the—a—a—"

"Poor—"

"Yes—poor; blessed are the poor—a—a—"

"In spirit—"

"In spirit; blessed are the poor in spirit, for they—they—"

"*Theirs*—"

"For *theirs*. Blessed are the poor in spirit, for *theirs*—is the kingdom of heaven. Blessed are they that mourn, for they—they—"

"Sh—"

"For they—a—"

"S, H, A—"

"For they S, H—Oh I don't know what it is!"

"*Shall!*"

"Oh, *shall!* for they shall—for they shall—a—a—shall mourn—a—a—blessed are they that shall—they that—a—they that shall mourn, for they shall—a—shall *what?* Why

28

don't you tell me, Mary?—what do you want to be so mean, for?"

"Oh, Tom, you poor thick-headed thing, I'm not teasing you. I wouldn't do that. You must go and learn it again. Don't you be discouraged, Tom, you'll manage it—and if you do, I'll give you something ever so nice. There, now, that's a good boy."

"All right! What is it, Mary, tell me what it is."

"Never you mind, Tom. You know if I say it's nice, it *is* nice."

"You bet you that's so, Mary. All right, I'll tackle it again."

And he did "tackle it again"—and under the double pressure of curiosity and prospective gain, he did it with such spirit that he accomplished a shining success. Mary gave him a bran-new "Barlow" knife worth twelve and a half cents; and the convulsion of delight that swept his system shook him to his foundations. True, the knife would not cut anything, but it was a "sure-enough" Barlow, and there was inconceivable grandeur in that—though where the western boys ever got the idea that such a weapon could possibly be counterfeited to its injury, is an imposing mystery and will always remain so, perhaps. Tom contrived to scarify the cupboard with it and was arranging to begin on the bureau, when he was called off to dress for Sunday-school.

Mary gave him a tin basin of water and a piece of soap, and he went outside the door and set the basin on a little bench there; then he dipped the soap in the water and laid it down; turned up his sleeves; poured out the water on the ground, gently, and then entered the kitchen and began to wipe his face diligently on the towel behind the door. But Mary removed the towel and said:

"Now ain't you ashamed, Tom. You mustn't be so bad. Water won't hurt you."

Tom was a trifle disconcerted. The basin was refilled, and this time he stood over it a little while, gathering resolution; took in a big breath and began. When he entered the kitchen presently, with both eyes shut, and groping for the towel with his hands, an honorable testimony of suds and water was dripping from his face. But when he emerged from the towel, he was not yet satisfactory; for the clean territory stopped short at his chin and his jaws, like a mask; below and beyond this line there was a dark expanse of unirrigated soil that spread downward in front and backward around his neck. Mary took him in hand, and when she was done with him he was a man and a brother, without distinction of color, and his saturated hair was neatly brushed, and its short curls wrought into a dainty and symmetrical general effect. [He privately smoothed out the curls, with labor and difficulty, and plastered his hair close down to his head; for he held curls to be effeminate, and his own filled his life with bitterness.] Then Mary got out a suit of his clothing that had been used only on Sundays during two years—they were simply called his "other clothes"—and so by that we know the size of his wardrobe. The girl "put him to rights" after he had dressed himself; she buttoned his neat roundabout up to his chin, turned his vast shirt collar down over his shoulders, brushed him off and crowned him with his speckled straw hat. He now looked exceedingly improved and uncomfortable. And he was fully as uncomfortable as he looked; for there was a restraint about whole clothes and cleanliness that galled him. He hoped that Mary would forget his shoes, but the hope was blighted; she coated them thoroughly with tallow, as was the custom, and brought them out. He lost his temper and said he was always being made to do everything he didn't want to do. But Mary said, persuasively:

"Please, Tom—that's a good boy."

So he got into the shoes, snarling. Mary was soon ready, and the three children set out for Sunday-school—a place that Tom hated with his whole heart; but Sid and Mary were fond of it.

Sabbath-school hours were from nine to half past ten; and then church service. Two of the children always remained for the sermon, voluntarily; and the other always remained, too—for stronger reasons. The church's high-backed, uncushioned pews would seat about three hundred persons; the edifice was but a small, plain affair, with a sort of pine board tree-box on top of it for a steeple. At the door Tom dropped back a step and accosted a Sunday-dressed comrade:

"Say, Billy, got a yaller ticket?"

"Yes."

"What'll you take for her?"

"What'll you give?"

"Piece of lickrish and a fish-hook."

"Less see 'em."

Tom exhibited. They were satisfactory, and the property changed hands. Then Tom traded a couple of white alleys for three red tickets, and some small trifle or other for a couple of blue ones. He waylaid other boys as they came, and went on buying tickets of various colors ten or fifteen minutes longer. He entered the church, now, with a swarm of clean and noisy boys and girls, proceeded to his seat and started a quarrel with the first boy that came handy. The teacher, a grave, elderly man, interfered; then turned his back a moment and Tom pulled a boy's hair in the next bench, and was absorbed in his book when the boy turned around; stuck a pin in another boy, presently, in order to hear him say "Ouch!" and got a new reprimand from his teacher. Tom's whole class were of a pattern—restless, noisy and troublesome. When they came to recite their lessons, not one of them knew his verses perfectly, but had to be prompted all along. However, they worried through, and each got his reward—in small blue tickets, each with a passage of Scripture on it; each blue ticket was pay for two verses of the recitation. Ten blue tickets equaled a red one, and could be exchanged for it; ten red tickets equaled a yellow one; for ten yellow tickets the Superintendent gave a very plainly bound Bible, (worth forty cents in those easy times,) to the pupil. How many of my readers would have the industry and the application to memorize two thousand verses, even for a Doré Bible? And yet Mary had acquired two Bibles in this way—it was the patient work of two years; and a boy of German parentage had won four or five. He once recited three thousand verses without stopping; but the strain upon his mental faculties was too great, and he was little better than an idiot from that day forth—a grievous misfortune for the school, for on great occasions, before company, the Superintendent (as Tom expressed it) had always made this boy come out and "spread himself." Only the older pupils managed to keep their tickets and stick to their tedious work long enough to get a Bible, and so the delivery of one of these prizes was a rare and noteworthy circumstance; the successful pupil was so great and conspicuous for that day that on the spot every scholar's breast was fired with a fresh ambition that often lasted a couple of weeks. It is possible that Tom's mental stomach had never really hungered for one of those prizes, but unquestionably his entire being had for many a day longed for the glory and the eclat that came with it.

In due course the Superintendent stood up in front of the pulpit, with a closed hymn-book in his hand and his forefinger inserted between its leaves, and commanded attention. When a Sunday-school Superintendent makes his customary little speech, a hymn-book in the hand is as necessary as is the inevitable sheet of music in the hand of a singer who stands forward on the platform and sings a solo at a concert—though why, is a mystery: for neither the hymn-book nor the sheet of music is ever referred to by the sufferer. This superintendent was a slim creature of thirty-five, with a sandy goatee and short sandy hair; he wore a stiff standing-collar whose upper edge almost reached his ears and whose sharp points curved forward abreast the corners of his mouth—a fence that compelled a straight lookout ahead, and a turning of the whole body when a side view was required; his chin was propped on a spreading cravat which was as broad and as long as a bank note, and had fringed ends; his boot toes were turned sharply up, in the fashion of the day, like sleigh-runners—an effect patiently and laboriously produced by the young men by sitting with their toes pressed against a wall for hours together. Mr. Walters was very earnest of mien, and very sincere and honest at heart; and he held sacred things and places in such reverence, and so separated them from worldly matters, that unconsciously to himself his Sunday-school voice had acquired a peculiar intonation which was wholly absent on week-days. He began, after this fashion:

"Now children, I want you all to sit up just as straight and pretty as you can and give me all your attention for a minute or two. There—that is it. That is the way good little boys and girls should do. I see one little girl who is looking out of the window—I am afraid she thinks I am out there somewhere—perhaps up in one of the trees making a speech to the little birds. [Applausive titter.] I want to tell you how good it makes me feel to see so many bright, clean little faces assembled in a place like this, learning to do right and be good."

And so forth and so on. It is not necessary to set down the rest of the oration. It was of a pattern which does not vary, and so it is familiar to us all.

The latter third of the speech was marred by the resumption of fights and other recreations among certain of the bad boys, and by fidgetings and whisperings that extended far and wide, washing even to the bases of isolated and incorruptible rocks like Sid and Mary. But now every sound ceased suddenly, with the subsidence of Mr. Walters's voice, and the conclusion of the speech was received with a burst of silent gratitude.

A good part of the whispering had been occasioned by an event which was more or less rare—the entrance of visitors; lawyer Thatcher, accompanied by a very feeble and aged man; a fine, portly, middle-aged gentleman with iron-gray hair; and a dignified lady who was doubtless the latter's wife. The lady was leading a child. Tom had been restless and full of chafings and repinings; conscience-smitten, too—he could not meet Amy Lawrence's eye, he could not brook her loving gaze. But when he saw this small new-comer his soul was all ablaze with bliss in a moment. The next moment he was "showing off" with all his might—cuffing boys, pulling hair, making faces—in a word, using every art that seemed likely to fascinate a girl and win her applause. His exaltation had but one alloy—the memory of his humiliation in this angel's garden—and that record in sand was fast washing out, under the waves of happiness that were sweeping over it now.

The visitors were given the highest seat of honor, and as soon as Mr. Walters's speech was finished, he introduced them to the school. The middle-aged man turned out to be a prodigious personage—no less a one than the county judge—altogether the most august creation these children had ever looked upon—and they wondered what kind of material he was made of—and they half wanted to hear him roar, and were half afraid he might, too. He was from Constantinople, twelve miles away—so he had traveled, and seen the world—these very eyes had looked upon the county court house—which was said to have a tin roof. The awe which these reflections inspired was attested by the impressive silence and the ranks of staring eyes. This was the great Judge Thatcher, brother of their own lawyer. Jeff Thatcher immediately went forward, to be familiar with the great man and be envied by the school. It would have been music to his soul to hear the whisperings:

"Look at him, Jim! He's a-going up there. Say—look! he's a-going to shake hands with him—he *is* a-shaking hands with him! By jings, don't you wish you was Jeff?"

Mr. Walters fell to "showing off," with all sorts of official bustlings and activities, giving orders, delivering judgments, discharging directions here, there, everywhere that he could find a target. The librarian "showed off"—running hither and thither with his arms full of books and making a deal of the splutter and fuss that insect authority delights in. The young lady teachers "showed off"—bending sweetly over pupils that were lately being boxed, lifting pretty warning fingers at bad little boys and patting good ones lovingly. The young gentlemen teachers "showed off" with small scoldings and other little displays of authority and fine attention to discipline—and most of the teachers, of both sexes, found business up at the library, by the pulpit; and it was business that frequently had to be done over again two or three times, (with much seeming vexation.) The little girls "showed off" in various ways, and the little boys "showed off" with such diligence that the air was thick with paper wads and the murmur of scufflings. And above it all the great man sat and beamed a majestic judicial smile upon all the house, and warmed himself in the sun of his own grandeur—for he was "showing off," too.

There was only one thing wanting, to make Mr. Walters's ecstasy complete, and that was, a chance to deliver a Bible-prize and exhibit a prodigy. Several pupils had a few yellow tickets, but none had enough—he had been around among the star pupils inquiring. He would have given worlds, now, to have that German lad back again with a sound mind.

And now at this moment, when hope was dead, Tom Sawyer came forward with nine yellow tickets, nine red tickets, and ten blue ones, and demanded a Bible. This was a thunderbolt out of a clear sky. Walters was not expecting an application from this source for the next ten years. But there was no getting around it—here were the certified checks, and they were good for their face. Tom was therefore elevated to a place with the Judge and the other elect, and the great news was announced from head-quarters. It was the most stunning surprise of the decade; and so profound was the sensation that it lifted the new hero up to the judicial one's altitude, and the school had two marvels to gaze upon in place of one. The boys were all eaten up with envy—but those that suffered the bitterest pangs were those who perceived too late that they themselves had contributed to this hated splendor by trading tickets to Tom for the wealth he had amassed in selling whitewashing privileges. These despised themselves, as being the dupes of a wily fraud, a guileful snake in the grass.

The prize was delivered to Tom with as much effusion as the Superintendent could pump up under the circumstances; but it lacked somewhat of the true gush, for the poor fellow's instinct taught him that there was a mystery here that could not well bear the light, perhaps; it was simply preposterous that *this* boy had warehoused two thousand sheaves of Scriptural wisdom on his premises—a dozen would strain his capacity, without a doubt.

Amy Lawrence was proud and glad, and she tried to make Tom see it in her face—but he wouldn't look. She wondered; then she was just a grain troubled; next a dim suspicion came and went—came again; she watched; a furtive glance told her worlds—and then her heart broke, and she was jealous, and angry, and the tears came and she hated everybody: Tom most of all, (she thought.)

Tom was introduced to the Judge; but his tongue was tied, his breath would hardly come, his heart quaked—partly because of the awful greatness of the man, but mainly because he was *her* parent. He would have liked to fall down and worship him, if it were in the dark. The Judge put his hand on Tom's head and called him a fine little man, and asked him what his name was. The boy stammered, gasped, and got it out:

"Tom."

"Oh, no, not Tom—it is—"

"Thomas."

"Ah, that's it. I thought there was more to it, maybe. That's very well. But you've another one I daresay, and you'll tell it to me, won't you?"

"Tell the gentleman your other name, Thomas," said Walters, "and say *sir.*—You mustn't forget your manners."

"Thomas Sawyer—sir."

"That's it! That's a good boy. Fine boy. Fine, manly little fellow. Two thousand verses is a great many—very, very great many. And you never can be sorry for the trouble you took to learn them; for knowledge is worth more than anything there is in the world; it's what makes great men and good men; you'll be a great man and a good man yourself, someday, Thomas, and then you'll look back and say, It's all owing to the precious Sunday-school privileges of my boyhood—it's all owing to my dear teachers that taught me to learn—it's all owing to the good Superintendent, who encouraged me, and watched over me, and gave me a beautiful Bible—a splendid elegant Bible, to keep and have it all for my own, always—it's all owing to right bringing up! That is what you will say, Thomas—and you wouldn't take any money for those two thousand verses then—no indeed you wouldn't. And now you wouldn't mind telling me and this lady some of the things you've learned—no, I know you wouldn't—for we are proud of little boys that learn. Now no doubt you know the names of all the twelve disciples. Won't you tell us the names of the first two that were appointed?"

Tom was tugging at a button and looking sheepish. He blushed, now, and his eyes fell. Mr. Walters's heart sank within him. He said to himself, It is not possible that the boy can answer the simplest question—why *did* the Judge ask him? Yet he felt obliged to speak up and say:

"Answer the gentleman, Thomas—don't be afraid."

Tom still hung fire.

"Now I know you'll tell *me*," said the lady. "The names of the first two disciples were—"

"DAVID AND GOLIAH!"

Let us draw the curtain of charity over the rest of the scene.

V

ABOUT HALF PAST TEN the cracked bell of the small church began to ring, and presently the people began to gather for the morning sermon. The Sunday-school children distributed themselves about the house and occupied pews with their parents, so as to be under supervision. Aunt Polly came, and Tom and Sid and Mary sat with her—Tom being placed next the aisle, in order that he might be as far away from the open window and the seductive outside summer scenes as possible. The crowd filed up the aisles: the aged and needy postmaster, who had seen better days; the mayor and his wife—for they had a mayor there, among other unnecessaries; the justice of the peace; the widow Douglas, fair, smart and forty, a generous, good-hearted soul and well-to-do, her hill mansion the only palace in the town, and the most hospitable and much the most lavish in the matter of festivities that St. Petersburg could boast; the bent and venerable Major and Mrs. Ward; lawyer Riverson, the new notable from a distance; next the belle of the village, followed by a troop of lawn-clad and ribbon-decked young heart-breakers; then all the young clerks in town in a body—for they had stood in the vestibule sucking their cane-heads, a circling wall of oiled and simpering admirers, till the last girl had run their gauntlet; and last of all came the Model Boy, Willie Mufferson, taking as heedful care of his mother as if she were cut glass. He always brought his mother to church, and was the pride of all the matrons. The boys all hated him, he was so good. And besides, he had been "thrown up to them" so much. His white handkerchief was hanging out of his pocket behind, as usual on Sundays—accidentally. Tom had no handkerchief, and he looked upon boys who had, as snobs.

The congregation being fully assembled, now, the bell rang once more, to warn laggards and stragglers, and then a solemn hush fell upon the church which was only broken by the tittering and whispering of the choir in the gallery. The choir always tittered and whispered all through service. There was once a church choir that was not ill-bred, but I have forgotten where it was, now. It was a great many years ago, and I can scarcely remember anything about it, but I think it was in some foreign country.

The minister gave out the hymn, and read it through with a relish, in a peculiar style which was much admired in that part of the country. His voice began on a medium key and climbed steadily up till it reached a certain point, where it bore with strong emphasis upon the topmost word and then plunged down as if from a spring-board:

Shall I be car-ri-ed toe the skies, on flow'ry *beds*
of ease,
Whilst others fought to win the prize, and sailed thro' *blood-*
-y seas?

He was regarded as a wonderful reader. At church "sociables" he was always called upon to read poetry; and when he was through, the ladies would lift up their hands and let them fall helplessly in their laps, and "wall" their eyes, and shake their heads, as much as to say, "Words cannot express it; it is too beautiful, *too* beautiful for this mortal earth."

After the hymn had been sung, the Rev. Mr. Sprague turned himself into a bulletin board and read off "notices" of meetings and societies and things till it seemed that the list would stretch out to the crack of doom—a queer custom which is still kept up in America, even in cities, away here in this age of abundant newspapers. Often, the less there is to justify a traditional custom, the harder it is to get rid of it.

And now the minister prayed. A good, generous prayer, it was, and went into details: it pleaded for the church, and the little children of the church; for the other churches of the village; for the village itself; for the county; for the State; for the State officers; for the United States; for the churches of the United States; for Congress; for the President; for the officers of the government; for poor sailors, tossed by stormy seas; for the oppressed millions groaning under the heel of European monarchies and Oriental despotisms; for such as have the light and the good tidings, and yet have not eyes to see nor ears to hear withal; for the heathen in the far islands of the sea; and closed with a supplication that the words he was about to speak might find grace and favor, and be as seed sown in fertile ground, yielding in time a grateful harvest of good. Amen.

There was a rustling of dresses, and the standing congregation sat down. The boy whose history this book relates, did not enjoy the prayer, he only endured it—if he even did that much. He was restive, all through it; he kept tally of the details of the prayer, unconsciously—for he was not listening, but he knew the ground of old, and the clergyman's regular route over it—and when a little trifle of new matter was interlarded, his ear detected it and his whole nature resented it; he considered additions unfair, and scoundrelly. In the midst of the prayer a fly had lit on the back of the pew in front of him and tortured his spirit by calmly rubbing its hands together; embracing its head with its arms and polishing it so vigorously that it seemed to almost part company with the body, and the slender thread of a neck was exposed to view; scraping its wings with its hind legs and smoothing them to its body as if they had been coat tails; going through its whole toilet as tranquilly as if it knew it was perfectly safe. As indeed it was; for as sorely as Tom's hands itched to grab for it they did not dare—he believed his soul would be instantly destroyed if he did such a thing while the prayer was going on. But with the closing sentence his hand began to curve and steal forward; and the instant the "Amen" was out the fly was a prisoner of war. His aunt detected the act and made him let it go.

The minister gave out his text and droned along monotonously through an argument that was so prosy that many a head by and by began to nod—and yet it was an argument that dealt in limitless fire and brimstone and thinned the predestined elect down to a company so small as to be hardly worth the saving. Tom counted the pages of the sermon; after church he always knew how many pages there had been, but he seldom knew anything else about the discourse. However, this time he was really interested for a little while. The minister made a grand and moving picture of the assembling together of the world's hosts at the millennium when the lion and the lamb should lie down together and a little child should lead them. But the pathos, the lesson, the moral of the

great spectacle were lost upon the boy; he only thought of
the conspicuousness of the principal character before the on-
looking nations; his face lit with the thought, and he said to
himself that he wished he could be that child, if it was a tame
lion.

Now he lapsed into suffering again, as the dry argument
was resumed. Presently he bethought him of a treasure he
had and got it out. It was a large black beetle with formidable
jaws—a "pinch-bug," he called it. It was in a percussion-cap
box. The first thing the beetle did was to take him by the
finger. A natural fillip followed, the beetle went floundering
into the aisle and lit on its back, and the hurt finger went into
the boy's mouth. The beetle lay there working its helpless
legs, unable to turn over. Tom eyed it, and longed for it; but
it was safe out of his reach. Other people uninterested in the
sermon, found relief in the beetle, and they eyed it too. Presently a vagrant poodle dog came idling along, sad at heart,
lazy with the summer softness and the quiet, weary of captivity, sighing for change. He spied the beetle; the drooping tail
lifted and wagged. He surveyed the prize; walked around it;
smelt at it from a safe distance; walked around it again; grew
bolder, and took a closer smell; then lifted his lip and made
a gingerly snatch at it, just missing it; made another, and another; began to enjoy the diversion; subsided to his stomach
with the beetle between his paws, and continued his experiments; grew weary at last, and then indifferent and absent-
minded. His head nodded, and little by little his chin descended and touched the enemy, who seized it. There was a
sharp yelp, a flirt of the poodle's head, and the beetle fell a
couple of yards away, and lit on its back once more. The
neighboring spectators shook with a gentle inward joy, several faces went behind fans and handkerchiefs, and Tom was
entirely happy. The dog looked foolish, and probably felt so;
but there was resentment in his heart, too, and a craving for
revenge. So he went to the beetle and began a wary attack on
it again; jumping at it from every point of a circle, lighting
with his forepaws within an inch of the creature, making even
closer snatches at it with his teeth, and jerking his head till
his ears flapped again. But he grew tired once more, after a
while; tried to amuse himself with a fly but found no relief;

followed an ant around, with his nose close to the floor, and quickly wearied of that; yawned, sighed, forgot the beetle entirely, and sat down on it! Then there was a wild yelp of agony and the poodle went sailing up the aisle; the yelps continued, and so did the dog; he crossed the house in front of the altar; he flew down the other aisle; he crossed before the doors; he clamored up the home-stretch; his anguish grew with his progress, till presently he was but a woolly comet moving in its orbit with the gleam and the speed of light. At last the frantic sufferer sheered from its course, and sprang into its master's lap; he flung it out of the window, and the voice of distress quickly thinned away and died in the distance.

By this time the whole church was red-faced and suffocating with suppressed laughter, and the sermon had come to a dead stand-still. The discourse was resumed presently, but it went lame and halting, all possibility of impressiveness being at an end; for even the gravest sentiments were constantly being received with a smothered burst of unholy mirth, under cover of some remote pew-back, as if the poor parson had said a rarely facetious thing. It was a genuine relief to the whole congregation when the ordeal was over and the benediction pronounced.

Tom Sawyer went home quite cheerful, thinking to himself that there was some satisfaction about divine service when there was a bit of variety in it. He had but one marring thought; he was willing that the dog should play with his pinch-bug, but he did not think it was upright in him to carry it off.

VI

MONDAY MORNING found Tom Sawyer miserable. Monday morning always found him so—because it began another week's slow suffering in school. He generally began that day with wishing he had had no intervening holiday, it made the going into captivity and fetters again so much more odious.

Tom lay thinking. Presently it occurred to him that he wished he was sick; then he could stay home from school. Here was a vague possibility. He canvassed his system. No ailment was found, and he investigated again. This time he thought he could detect colicky symptoms, and he began to encourage them with considerable hope. But they soon grew feeble, and presently died wholly away. He reflected further. Suddenly he discovered something. One of his upper front teeth was loose. This was lucky; he was about to begin to groan, as a "starter," as he called it, when it occurred to him that if he came into court with that argument, his aunt would pull it out, and that would hurt. So he thought he would hold the tooth in reserve for the present, and seek further. Nothing offered for some little time, and then he remembered hearing the doctor tell about a certain thing that laid up a patient for two or three weeks and threatened to make him lose a finger. So the boy eagerly drew his sore toe from under the sheet and held it up for inspection. But now he did not know the necessary symptoms. However, it seemed well worth while to chance it, so he fell to groaning with considerable spirit.

But Sid slept on unconscious.

Tom groaned louder, and fancied that he began to feel pain in the toe.

No result from Sid.

Tom was panting with his exertions by this time. He took a rest and then swelled himself up and fetched a succession of admirable groans.

Sid snored on.

Tom was aggravated. He said, "Sid, Sid!" and shook him.

This course worked well, and Tom began to groan again. Sid yawned, stretched, then brought himself up on his elbow with a snort, and began to stare at Tom. Tom went on groaning. Sid said:

"Tom! Say, Tom!" [No response.] "Here, Tom! *Tom!* What is the matter, Tom?" And he shook him, and looked in his face anxiously.

Tom moaned out:

"O don't, Sid. Don't joggle me."

"Why what's the matter, Tom? I must call auntie."

"No—never mind. It'll be over by and by, maybe. Don't call anybody."

"But I must! *Don't* groan so, Tom, it's awful. How long you been this way?"

"Hours. Ouch! O don't stir so, Sid, you'll kill me."

"Tom, why didn't you wake me sooner? O, Tom, *don't*! It makes my flesh crawl to hear you. Tom, what is the matter?"

"I forgive you everything, Sid. [Groan.] Everything you've ever done to me. When I'm gone—"

"Oh, Tom, you ain't dying, are you? Don't, Tom—O, don't. Maybe—"

"I forgive everybody, Sid. [Groan.] Tell 'em so, Sid. And Sid, you give my window-sash and my cat with one eye to that new girl that's come to town, and tell her—"

But Sid had snatched his clothes and gone. Tom was suffering in reality, now, so handsomely was his imagination working, and so his groans had gathered quite a genuine tone.

Sid flew down stairs and said:

"O, aunt Polly, come! Tom's dying!"

"Dying!"

"Yes'm. Don't wait—come quick!"

"Rubbage! I don't believe it!"

But she fled up stairs, nevertheless, with Sid and Mary at her heels. And her face grew white, too, and her lip trembled. When she reached the bedside she gasped out:

"You Tom! Tom, what's the matter with you!"

"O, auntie, I'm—"

"What's the matter with you—what *is* the matter with you, child!"

"O, auntie, my sore toe's mortified!"

The old lady sank down into a chair and laughed a little, then cried a little, then did both together. This restored her and she said:

"Tom, what a turn you did give me. Now you shut up that nonsense and climb out of this."

The groans ceased and the pain vanished from the toe. The boy felt a little foolish, and he said:

"Aunt Polly it *seemed* mortified, and it hurt so I never minded my tooth at all."

"Your tooth, indeed! What's the matter with your tooth?"

"One of them's loose, and it aches perfectly awful."

"There, there, now, don't begin that groaning again. Open your mouth. Well—your tooth *is* loose, but you're not going to die about that. Mary, get me a silk thread, and a chunk of fire out of the kitchen."

Tom said:

"O, please auntie, don't pull it out. It don't hurt any more. I wish I may never stir if it does. Please don't, auntie. *I* don't want to stay home from school."

"Oh, you don't, don't you? So all this row was because you thought you'd get to stay home from school and go a-fishing? Tom, Tom, I love you so, and you seem to try every way you can to break my old heart with your outrageousness."

By this time the dental instruments were ready. The old lady made one end of the silk thread fast to Tom's tooth with a loop and tied the other to the bedpost. Then she seized the chunk of fire and suddenly thrust it almost into the boy's face. The tooth hung dangling by the bedpost, now.

But all trials bring their compensations. As Tom wended to school after breakfast, he was the envy of every boy he met because the gap in his upper row of teeth enabled him to expectorate in a new and admirable way. He gathered quite a following of lads interested in the exhibition; and one that had cut his finger and had been a centre of fascination and homage up to this time, now found himself suddenly without an adherent, and shorn of his glory. His heart was heavy, and he said with a disdain which he did not feel, that it wasn't anything to spit like Tom Sawyer;

but another boy said "Sour grapes!" and he wandered away a dismantled hero.

Shortly Tom came upon the juvenile pariah of the village, Huckleberry Finn, son of the town drunkard. Huckleberry was cordially hated and dreaded by all the mothers of the town, because he was idle, and lawless, and vulgar and bad— and because all their children admired him so, and delighted in his forbidden society, and wished they dared to be like him. Tom was like the rest of the respectable boys, in that he envied Huckleberry his gaudy outcast condition, and was under strict orders not to play with him. So he played with him every time he got a chance. Huckleberry was always dressed in the cast-off clothes of full-grown men, and they were in perennial bloom and fluttering with rags. His hat was a vast ruin with a wide crescent lopped out of its brim; his coat, when he wore one, hung nearly to his heels and had the rear-ward buttons far down the back; but one suspender supported his trousers; the seat of the trousers bagged low and contained nothing; the fringed legs dragged in the dirt when not rolled up.

Huckleberry came and went, at his own free will. He slept on doorsteps in fine weather and in empty hogsheads in wet; he did not have to go to school or to church, or call any being master or obey anybody; he could go fishing or swimming when and where he chose, and stay as long as it suited him; nobody forbade him to fight; he could sit up as late as he pleased; he was always the first boy that went barefoot in the spring and the last to resume leather in the fall; he never had to wash, nor put on clean clothes; he could swear wonderfully. In a word, everything that goes to make life precious, that boy had. So thought every harassed, hampered, respectable boy in St. Petersburg.

Tom hailed the romantic outcast:

"Hello, Huckleberry!"

"Hello yourself, and see how you like it."

"What's that you got?"

"Dead cat."

"Lemme see him, Huck. My, he's pretty stiff. Where'd you get him?"

"Bought him off'n a boy."

"What did you give?"

"I give a blue ticket and a bladder that I got at the slaughter house."

"Where'd you get the blue ticket?"

"Bought it off'n Ben Rogers two weeks ago for a hoop-stick."

"Say—what is dead cats good for, Huck?"

"Good for? Cure warts with."

"No! Is that so? I know something that's better."

"I bet you don't. What is it?"

"Why, spunk-water."

"Spunk-water! I wouldn't give a dern for spunk-water."

"You wouldn't, wouldn't you? D'you ever try it?"

"No, I hain't. But Bob Tanner did."

"Who told you so!"

"Why he told Jeff Thatcher, and Jeff told Johnny Baker, and Johnny told Jim Hollis, and Jim told Ben Rogers, and Ben told a nigger, and the nigger told me. There, now!"

"Well, what of it? They'll all lie. Leastways all but the nigger. I don't know *him*. But I never see a nigger that *wouldn't* lie. Shucks! Now you tell me how Bob Tanner done it, Huck."

"Why he took and dipped his hand in a rotten stump where the rain water was."

"In the daytime?"

"Cert'nly."

"With his face to the stump?"

"Yes. Least I reckon so."

"Did he *say* anything?"

"I don't reckon he did. I don't know."

"Aha! Talk about trying to cure warts with spunk-water such a blame fool way as that! Why that ain't a-going to do any good. You got to go all by yourself, to the middle of the woods, where you know there's a spunk-water stump, and just as it's midnight you back up against the stump and jam your hand in and say:

> "Barley-corn, barley-corn, injun-meal shorts,
>   Spunk-water, spunk-water, swaller these warts;"

and then walk away quick, eleven steps, with your eyes shut, and then turn around three times and walk home without speaking to anybody. Because if you speak the charm's busted."

"Well that sounds like a good way; but that ain't the way Bob Tanner done."

"No, sir, you can bet he didn't; becuz he's the wartiest boy in this town; and he wouldn't have a wart on him if he'd knowed how to work spunk-water. I've took off thousands of warts off of my hands that way, Huck. I play with frogs so much that I've always got considerable many warts. Sometimes I take 'em off with a bean."

"Yes, bean's good. I've done that."

"Have you? What's your way?"

"You take and split the bean, and cut the wart so as to get some blood, and then you put the blood on one piece of the bean and take and dig a hole and bury it 'bout midnight at the cross-roads in the dark of the moon, and then you burn up the rest of the bean. You see that piece that's got the blood on it will keep drawing and drawing, trying to fetch the other piece to it, and so that helps the blood to draw the wart, and pretty soon off she comes."

"Yes, that's it, Huck—that's it; though when you're burying it, if you say 'Down bean; off, wart; come no more to bother me!' it's better. That's the way Joe Harper does, and he's ben nearly to Constantinople and most everywheres. But say—how do you cure 'em with dead cats?"

"Why you take your cat and go and get in the graveyard 'long about midnight when somebody that was wicked has been buried; and when it's midnight a devil will come, or maybe two or three, but you can't see 'em, you can only hear something like the wind, or maybe hear 'em talk; and when they're taking that feller away, you heave your cat after 'em and say 'Devil follow corpse, cat follow devil, warts follow cat, *I*'m done with ye!' That'll fetch *any* wart."

"Sounds right. D'you ever try it, Huck?"

"No, but old Mother Hopkins told me."

"Well I reckon it's so, then. Becuz they say she's a witch."

"Say! Why, Tom, I *know* she is. She witched pap. Pap says so his own self. He come along one day, and he see she was

a-witching him, so he took up a rock, and if she hadn't
dodged he'd a got her. Well that very night he rolled off'n a
shed wher' he was a-layin' drunk, and broke his arm."

"Why that's awful. How did he know she was a-witching
him."

"Lord, pap can tell, easy. Pap says when they keep looking
at you right stiddy, they're a-witching you. Specially if they
mumble. Becuz when they mumble they're a-saying the
Lord's Prayer back'ards."

"Say, Huck, when you going to try the cat?"

"To-night. I reckon they'll come after old Hoss Williams
to-night."

"But they buried him Saturday, Huck. Didn't they get him
Saturday night?"

"Why how you talk! How could their charms work till
midnight?—and *then* it's Sunday. Devils don't slosh around
much of a Sunday, I don't reckon."

"I never thought of that. That's so. Lemme go with you?"

"Of course—if you ain't afeard."

"Afeard! 'Tain't likely. Will you meow?"

"Yes—and you meow back, if you get a chance. Last time,
you kep' me a-meowing around till old Hays went to throwing rocks at me and says 'Dern that cat!' and so I hove a brick
through his window—but don't you tell."

"I won't. I couldn't meow that night, becuz auntie was
watching me, but I'll meow this time. Say, Huck, what's
that?"

"Nothing but a tick."

"Where'd you get him?"

"Out in the woods."

"What'll you take for him?"

"I don't know. I don't want to sell him."

"All right. It's a mighty small tick, anyway."

"O, anybody can run a tick down that don't belong to
them. I'm satisfied with it. It's a good enough tick for me."

"Sho, there's ticks a plenty. I could have a thousand of 'em
if I wanted to."

"Well why don't you? Becuz you know mighty well you
can't. This is a pretty early tick, I reckon. It's the first one I've
seen this year."

"Say Huck—I'll give you my tooth for him."

"Less see it."

Tom got out a bit of paper and carefully unrolled it. Huckleberry viewed it wistfully. The temptation was very strong. At last he said:

"Is it genuwyne?"

Tom lifted his lip and showed the vacancy.

"Well, all right," said Huckleberry, "it's a trade."

Tom enclosed the tick in the percussion-cap box that had lately been the pinch-bug's prison, and the boys separated, each feeling wealthier than before.

When Tom reached the little isolated frame school-house, he strode in briskly, with the manner of one who had come with all honest speed. He hung his hat on a peg and flung himself into his seat with business-like alacrity. The master, throned on high in his great splint-bottom arm-chair, was dozing, lulled by the drowsy hum of study. The interruption roused him:

"Thomas Sawyer!"

Tom knew that when his name was pronounced in full, it meant trouble.

"Sir!"

"Come up here. Now sir, why are you late again, as usual?"

Tom was about to take refuge in a lie, when he saw two long tails of yellow hair hanging down a back that he recognized by the electric sympathy of love; and by that form was *the only vacant place* on the girl's side of the school-house. He instantly said:

"I STOPPED TO TALK WITH HUCKLEBERRY FINN!"

The master's pulse stood still, and he stared helplessly. The buzz of study ceased. The pupils wondered if this fool-hardy boy had lost his mind. The master said:

"You—you did what?"

"Stopped to talk with Huckleberry Finn."

There was no mistaking the words.

"Thomas Sawyer, this is the most astounding confession I have ever listened to. No mere ferule will answer for this offense. Take off your jacket."

The master's arm performed until it was tired and the stock of switches notably diminished. Then the order followed:

"Now sir, go and sit with the *girls*! And let this be a warning to you."

The titter that rippled around the room appeared to abash the boy, but in reality that result was caused rather more by his worshipful awe of his unknown idol and the dread pleasure that lay in his high good fortune. He sat down upon the end of the pine bench and the girl hitched herself away from him with a toss of her head. Nudges and winks and whispers traversed the room, but Tom sat still, with his arms upon the long, low desk before him, and seemed to study his book. By and by attention ceased from him, and the accustomed school murmur rose upon the dull air once more. Presently the boy began to steal furtive glances at the girl. She observed it, "made a mouth" at him and gave him the back of her head for the space of a minute. When she cautiously faced around again, a peach lay before her. She thrust it away. Tom gently put it back. She thrust it away, again, but with less animosity. Tom patiently returned it to its place. Then she let it remain. Tom scrawled on his slate, "Please take it— I got more." The girl glanced at the words, but made no sign. Now the boy began to draw something on the slate, hiding his work with his left hand. For a time the girl refused to notice; but her human curiosity presently began to manifest itself by hardly perceptible signs. The boy worked on, apparently unconscious. The girl made a sort of non-committal attempt to see, but the boy did not betray that he was aware of it. At last she gave in and hesitatingly whispered:

"Let me see it."

Tom partly uncovered a dismal caricature of a house with two gable ends to it and a cork-screw of smoke issuing from the chimney. Then the girl's interest began to fasten itself upon the work and she forgot everything else. When it was finished, she gazed a moment, then whispered:

"It's nice—make a man."

The artist erected a man in the front yard, that resembled a derrick. He could have stepped over the house; but the girl was not hypercritical; she was satisfied with the monster, and whispered:

"It's a beautiful man—now make me coming along."

Tom drew an hour-glass with a full moon and straw limbs

TOM AS AN ARTIST

to it and armed the spreading fingers with a portentous fan. The girl said:

"It's ever so nice—I wish I could draw."

"It's easy," whispered Tom, "I'll learn you."

"O, will you? When?"

"At noon. Do you go home to dinner?"

"I'll stay, if you will."

"Good,—that's a whack. What's your name?"

"Becky Thatcher. What's yours? Oh, I know. It's Thomas Sawyer."

"That's the name they lick me by. I'm Tom, when I'm good. You call me Tom, will you?"

"Yes."

Now Tom began to scrawl something on the slate, hiding the words from the girl. But she was not backward this time. She begged to see. Tom said:

"Oh it ain't anything."

"Yes it is."

"No it ain't. You don't want to see."

"Yes I do, indeed I do. Please let me."

"You'll tell."

"No I won't—deed and deed and double deed I won't."

"You won't tell anybody at all?—Ever, as long as you live?"

"No, I won't ever tell *any*body. Now let me."

"Oh, *you* don't want to see!"

"Now that you treat me so, I *will* see." And she put her small hand upon his and a little scuffle ensued, Tom pretending to resist in earnest but letting his hand slip by degrees till these words were revealed: *"I love you."*

"O, you bad thing!" And she hit his hand a smart rap, but reddened and looked pleased, nevertheless.

Just at this juncture the boy felt a slow, fateful grip closing on his ear, and a steady, lifting impulse. In that vise he was borne across the house and deposited in his own seat, under a peppering fire of giggles from the whole school. Then the master stood over him during a few awful moments, and finally moved away to his throne without saying a word. But although Tom's ear tingled, his heart was jubilant.

As the school quieted down Tom made an honest effort to study, but the turmoil within him was too great. In turn he took his place in the reading class and made a botch of it; then in the geography class and turned lakes into mountains, mountains into rivers, and rivers into continents, till chaos was come again; then in the spelling class, and got "turned down," by a succession of mere baby words till he brought up at the foot and yielded up the pewter medal which he had worn with ostentation for months.

VII

THE HARDER Tom tried to fasten his mind on his book, the more his ideas wandered. So at last, with a sigh and a yawn, he gave it up. It seemed to him that the noon recess would never come. The air was utterly dead. There was not a breath stirring. It was the sleepiest of sleepy days. The drowsing murmur of the five and twenty studying scholars soothed the soul like the spell that is in the murmur of bees. Away off in the flaming sunshine, Cardiff Hill lifted its soft green sides through a shimmering veil of heat, tinted with the purple of distance; a few birds floated on lazy wing high in the air; no other living thing was visible but some cows, and they were asleep.

Tom's heart ached to be free, or else to have something of interest to do to pass the dreary time. His hand wandered into his pocket and his face lit up with a glow of gratitude that was prayer, though he did not know it. Then furtively the percussion-cap box came out. He released the tick and put him on the long flat desk. The creature probably glowed with a gratitude that amounted to prayer, too, at this moment, but it was premature: for when he started thankfully to travel off, Tom turned him aside with a pin and made him take a new direction.

Tom's bosom friend sat next him, suffering just as Tom had been, and now he was deeply and gratefully interested in this entertainment in an instant. This bosom friend was Joe Harper. The two boys were sworn friends all the week, and embattled enemies on Saturdays. Joe took a pin out of his lappel and began to assist in exercising the prisoner. The sport grew in interest momently. Soon Tom said that they were interfering with each other, and neither getting the fullest benefit of the tick. So he put Joe's slate on the desk and drew a line down the middle of it from top to bottom.

"Now," said he, "as long as he is on your side you can stir him up and I'll let him alone; but if you let him get away and get on my side, you're to leave him alone as long as I can keep him from crossing over."

"All right—go ahead—start him up."

The tick escaped from Tom, presently, and crossed the equator. Joe harassed him a while and then he got away and crossed back again. This change of base occurred often. While one boy was worrying the tick with absorbing interest, the other would look on with interest as strong, the two heads bowed together over the slate, and the two souls dead to all things else. At last luck seemed to settle and abide with Joe. The tick tried this, that, and the other course, and got as excited and as anxious as the boys themselves, but time and again just as he would have victory in his very grasp, so to speak, and Tom's fingers would be twitching to begin, Joe's pin would deftly head him off and keep possession. At last Tom could stand it no longer. The temptation was too strong. So he reached out and lent a hand with his pin. Joe was angry in a moment. Said he:

"Tom, you let him alone."

"I only just want to stir him up a little, Joe."

"No, sir, it ain't fair; you just let him alone."

"Blame it, I ain't going to stir him much."

"Let him alone, I tell you!"

"I won't!"

"You shall—he's on my side of the line."

"Look here, Joe Harper, whose is that tick?"

"*I* don't care whose tick he is—he's on my side of the line, and you shan't touch him."

"Well I'll just bet I will, though. He's my tick and I'll do what I blame please with him, or die!"

A tremendous whack came down on Tom's shoulders, and its duplicate on Joe's; and for the space of two minutes the dust continued to fly from the two jackets and the whole school to enjoy it. The boys had been too absorbed to notice the hush that had stolen upon the school a while before when the master came tip-toeing down the room and stood over them. He had contemplated a good part of the performance before he contributed his bit of variety to it.

When school broke up at noon, Tom flew to Becky Thatcher, and whispered in her ear:

"Put on your bonnet and let on you're going home; and when you get to the corner, give the rest of 'em the slip, and turn down through the lane and come back. I'll go the other way and come it over 'em the same way."

So the one went off with one group of scholars, and the other with another. In a little while the two met at the bottom of the lane, and when they reached the school they had it all to themselves. Then they sat together, with a slate before them, and Tom gave Becky the pencil and held her hand in his, guiding it, and so created another surprising house. When the interest in art began to wane, the two fell to talking. Tom was swimming in bliss. He said:

"Do you love rats?"

"No! I hate them!"

"Well, I do too—*live* ones. But I mean dead ones, to swing round your head with a string."

"No, I don't care for rats much, anyway. What *I* like, is chewing-gum."

"O, I should say so! I wish I had some now."

"Do you? I've got some. I'll let you chew it a while, but you must give it back to me."

That was agreeable, so they chewed it turn about, and dangled their legs against the bench in excess of contentment.

"Was you ever at a circus?" said Tom.

"Yes, and my pa's going to take me again some time, if I'm good."

"I been to the circus three or four times—lots of times. Church ain't shucks to a circus. There's things going on at a circus all the time. I'm going to be a clown in a circus when I grow up."

"O, are you! That will be nice. They're so lovely, all spotted up."

"Yes, that's so. And they get slathers of money—most a dollar a day, Ben Rogers says. Say, Becky, was you ever engaged?"

"What's that?"

"Why engaged to be married."

"No."

"Would you like to?"

"I reckon so. I don't know. What is it like?"

"Like? Why it ain't like anything. You only just tell a boy

you won't ever have anybody but him, ever ever *ever*, and then you kiss and that's all. Anybody can do it."

"Kiss? What do you kiss for?"

"Why that, you know, is to—well, they always do that."

"Everybody?"

"Why yes, everybody that's in love with each other. Do you remember what I wrote on the slate?"

"Ye-yes."

"What was it?"

"I shan't tell you."

"Shall I tell *you*?"

"Ye-Yes—but some other time."

"No, now."

"No, not now—to-morrow."

"O, no, *now*. Please Becky—I'll whisper it. I'll whisper it ever so easy."

Becky hesitating, Tom took silence for consent, and passed his arm about her waist and whispered the tale ever so softly, with his mouth close to her ear. And then he added:

"Now you whisper it to me—just the same."

She resisted, for a while, and then said:

"You turn your face away so you can't see, and then I will. But you mustn't ever tell anybody— *will* you, Tom? Now you won't, *will* you?"

"No, indeed indeed I won't. Now, Becky."

He turned his face away. She bent timidly around till her breath stirred his curls and whispered, "I—love—you!"

Then she sprang away and ran around and around the desks and benches, with Tom after her, and took refuge in a corner at last, with her little white apron to her face. Tom clasped her about her neck and pleaded:

"Now Becky, it's all done—all over but the kiss. Don't you be afraid of that—it ain't anything at all. Please, Becky." And he tugged at the apron and the hands.

By and by she gave up, and let her hands drop; her face, all glowing with the struggle, came up and submitted. Tom kissed the red lips and said:

"Now it's all done, Becky. And always after this, you know, you ain't ever to love anybody but me, and you ain't ever to marry anybody but me, never never and forever. Will you?"

"No, I'll never love anybody but you, Tom, and I'll never marry anybody but you—and you ain't to ever marry anybody but me, either."

"Certainly. Of course. That's *part* of it. And always coming to school or when we're going home, you're to walk with me, when there ain't anybody looking—and you choose me and I choose you at parties, because that's the way you do when you're engaged."

"It's so nice. I never heard of it before."

"Oh it's ever so gay! Why me and Amy Lawrence—"

The big eyes told Tom his blunder and he stopped, confused.

"O, Tom! Then I ain't the first you've ever been engaged to!"

The child began to cry. Tom said:

"O don't cry, Becky. I don't care for her any more."

"Yes you do, Tom—you know you do."

Tom tried to put his arm about her neck, but she pushed him away and turned her face to the wall, and went on crying. Tom tried again, with soothing words in his mouth, and was repulsed again. Then his pride was up, and he strode away and went outside. He stood about, restless and uneasy, for a while, glancing at the door, every now and then, hoping she would repent and come to find him. But she did not. Then he began to feel badly and fear that he was in the wrong. It was a hard struggle with him to make new advances, now, but he nerved himself to it and entered. She was still standing back there in the corner, sobbing, with her face to the wall. Tom's heart smote him. He went to her and stood a moment, not knowing exactly how to proceed. Then he said hesitatingly:

"Becky, I—I don't care for anybody but you."

No reply—but sobs.

"Becky,"—pleadingly. "Becky, won't you say something?"

More sobs.

Tom got out his chiefest jewel, a brass knob from the top of an andiron, and passed it around her so that she could see it, and said:

"Please, Becky, won't you take it?"

She struck it to the floor. Then Tom marched out of the

house and over the hills and far away, to return to school no more that day. Presently Becky began to suspect. She ran to the door; he was not in sight; she flew around to the play-yard; he was not there. Then she called:

"Tom! Come back Tom!"

She listened intently, but there was no answer. She had no companions but silence and loneliness. So she sat down to cry again and upbraid herself; and by this time the scholars began to gather again, and she had to hide her griefs and still her broken heart and take up the cross of a long, dreary, aching afternoon, with none among the strangers about her to exchange sorrows with.

VIII

Tom dodged hither and thither through lanes until he was well out of the track of returning scholars, and then fell into a moody jog. He crossed a small "branch" two or three times, because of a prevailing juvenile superstition that to cross water baffled pursuit. Half an hour later he was disappearing behind the Douglas mansion on the summit of Cardiff Hill, and the school-house was hardly distinguishable away off in the valley behind him. He entered a dense wood, picked his pathless way to the centre of it, and sat down on a mossy spot under a spreading oak. There was not even a zephyr stirring; the dead noonday heat had even stilled the songs of the birds; nature lay in a trance that was broken by no sound but the occasional far-off hammering of a woodpecker, and this seemed to render the pervading silence and sense of loneliness the more profound. The boy's soul was steeped in melancholy; his feelings were in happy accord with his surroundings. He sat long with his elbows on his knees and his chin in his hands, meditating. It seemed to him that life was but a trouble, at best, and he more than half envied Jimmy Hodges, so lately released; it must be very peaceful, he thought, to lie and slumber and dream forever and ever, with the wind whispering through the trees and caressing the grass and the flowers over the grave, and nothing to bother and grieve about, ever any more. If he only had a clean Sunday-school record he could be willing to go, and be done with it all. Now as to this girl. What had he done? Nothing. He had meant the best in the world, and been treated like a dog—like a very dog. She would be sorry some day—maybe when it was too late. Ah, if he could only die *temporarily*!

But the elastic heart of youth cannot be kept compressed into one constrained shape long at a time. Tom presently began to drift insensibly back into the concerns of this life again. What if he turned his back, now, and disappeared mysteriously? What if he went away—ever so far away, into unknown countries beyond the seas—and never came back any more! How would she feel then! The idea of being a clown

recurred to him now, only to fill him with disgust. For friv-
olity, and jokes, and spotted tights were an offense, when
they intruded themselves upon a spirit that was exalted into
the vague august realm of the romantic. No, he would be a
soldier, and return, after long years, all war-worn and illustrious. No—better still, he would join the Indians, and hunt
buffaloes and go on the war-path in the mountain ranges and
the trackless great plains of the Far West, and away in the
future come back a great chief, bristling with feathers, hideous with paint, and prance into Sunday-school, some drowsy
summer morning, with a blood-curdling war-whoop, and sear
the eye-balls of all his companions with unappeasable envy.
But no, there was something gaudier even than this. He
would be a pirate! That was it! *Now* his future lay plain before him, and glowing with unimaginable splendor. How his
name would fill the world, and make people shudder! How
gloriously he would go plowing the dancing seas, in his long,
low, black-hulled racer, the "Spirit of the Storm," with his
grisly flag flying at the fore! And at the zenith of his fame,
how he would suddenly appear at the old village and stalk
into church, all brown and weather-beaten, in his black velvet
doublet and trunks, his great jack-boots, his crimson sash, his
belt bristling with horse-pistols, his crime-rusted cutlass at his
side, his slouch hat with waving plumes, his black flag unfurled, with the skull and cross-bones on it, and hear with
swelling ecstasy the whisperings, "It's Tom Sawyer the Pirate!—the Black Avenger of the Spanish Main!"

Yes, it was settled; his career was determined. He would
run away from home and enter upon it. He would start the
very next morning. Therefore he must now begin to get
ready. He would collect his resources together. He went to a
rotten log near at hand and began to dig under one end of it
with his Barlow knife. He soon struck wood that sounded
hollow. He put his hand there and uttered this incantation
impressively:

"What hasn't come here, *come*! What's here, *stay* here!"

Then he scraped away the dirt, and exposed a pine shingle.
He took it up and disclosed a shapely little treasure-house
whose bottom and sides were of shingles. In it lay a marble.

Tom's astonishment was boundless! He scratched his head with a perplexed air, and said:

"Well, that beats anything!"

Then he tossed the marble away pettishly, and stood cogitating. The truth was, that a superstition of his had failed, here, which he and all his comrades had always looked upon as infallible. If you buried a marble with certain necessary incantations, and left it alone a fortnight, and then opened the place with the incantation he had just used, you would find that all the marbles you had ever lost had gathered themselves together there, meantime, no matter how widely they had been separated. But now, this thing had actually and unquestionably failed. Tom's whole structure of faith was shaken to its foundations. He had many a time heard of this thing succeeding, but never of its failing before. It did not occur to him that he had tried it several times before, himself, but could never find the hiding places afterwards. He puzzled over the matter some time, and finally decided that some witch had interfered and broken the charm. He thought he would satisfy himself on that point; so he searched around till he found a small sandy spot with a little funnel-shaped depression in it. He laid himself down and put his mouth close to this depression and called:

"Doodle-bug, doodle-bug, tell me what I want to know! Doodle-bug, doodle-bug tell me what I want to know!"

The sand began to work, and presently a small black bug appeared for a second and then darted under again in a fright.

"He dasn't tell! So it *was* a witch that done it. I just knowed it."

He well knew the futility of trying to contend against witches, so he gave up, discouraged. But it occurred to him that he might as well have the marble he had just thrown away, and therefore he went and made a patient search for it. But he could not find it. Now he went back to his treasure-house and carefully placed himself just as he had been standing when he tossed the marble away; then he took another marble from his pocket and tossed it in the same way, saying:

"Brother go find your brother!"

He watched where it stopped, and went there and looked.

But it must have fallen short or gone too far; so he tried twice more. The last repetition was successful. The two marbles lay within a foot of each other.

Just here the blast of a toy tin trumpet came faintly down the green aisles of the forest. Tom flung off his jacket and trousers, turned a suspender into a belt, raked away some brush behind the rotten log, disclosing a rude bow and arrow, a lath sword and a tin trumpet and in a moment had seized these things and bounded away, bare-legged, with fluttering shirt. He presently halted under a great elm, blew an answering blast, and then began to tip-toe and look warily out, this way and that. He said cautiously—to an imaginary company:

"Hold, my merry men! Keep hid till I blow."

Now appeared Joe Harper, as airily clad and elaborately armed as Tom. Tom called:

"Hold! Who comes here into Sherwood Forest without my pass?"

"Guy of Guisborne wants no man's pass. Who are thou that—that—"

—"Dares to hold such language," said Tom, prompting— for they talked "by the book," from memory.

"Who art thou that dares to hold such language?"

"I, indeed! I am Robin Hood, as thy caitiff carcase soon shall know."

"Then art thou indeed that famous outlaw? Right gladly will I dispute with thee the passes of the merry wood. Have at thee!"

They took their lath swords, dumped their other traps on the ground, struck a fencing attitude, foot to foot, and began a grave, careful combat, "two up and two down." Presently Tom said:

"Now if you've got the hang, go it lively!"

So they "went it lively," panting and perspiring with the work. By and by Tom shouted:

"Fall! fall! Why don't you fall?"

"I shan't! Why don't you fall yourself? You're getting the worst of it."

"Why that ain't anything. *I* can't fall; that ain't the way it is in the book. The book says 'Then with one back-handed stroke he slew poor Guy of Guisborne.' You're to turn around and let me hit you in the back."

There was no getting around the authorities, so Joe turned, received the whack, and fell.

"Now," said Joe, getting up, "you got to let me kill *you*. That's fair."

"Why I can't do that. It ain't in the book."

"Well it's blamed mean,—that's all."

"Well, say, Joe—you can be Friar Tuck, or Much the miller's son and lam me with a quarter-staff; or I'll be the Sheriff of Nottingham and you be Robin Hood a little while and kill me."

This was satisfactory, and so these adventures were carried out. Then Tom became Robin Hood again, and was allowed by the treacherous nun to bleed his strength away through his neglected wound. And at last Joe, representing a whole tribe of weeping outlaws, dragged him sadly forth, gave his bow into his feeble hands, and Tom said, "Where this arrow falls, there bury poor Robin Hood under the greenwood tree." Then he shot the arrow and fell back and would have died but he lit on a nettle and sprang up too gaily for a corpse.

The boys dressed themselves, hid their accoutrements, and went off grieving that there were no outlaws any more, and wondering what modern civilization could claim to have done to compensate for their loss. They said they would rather be outlaws a year in Sherwood Forest than President of the United States forever.

IX

AT HALF PAST NINE, that night, Tom and Sid were sent to bed, as usual. They said their prayers, and Sid was soon asleep. Tom lay awake and waited, in restless impatience. When it seemed to him that it must be nearly daylight, he heard the clock strike ten! This was despair. He would have tossed and fidgeted, as his nerves demanded, but he was afraid he might wake Sid. So he lay still, and stared up into the dark. Everything was dismally still. By and by, out of the stillness little scarcely perceptible noises began to emphasize themselves. The ticking of the clock began to bring itself into notice. Old beams began to crack mysteriously. The stairs creaked faintly. Evidently spirits were abroad. A measured, muffled snore issued from Aunt Polly's chamber. And now the tiresome chirping of a cricket that no human ingenuity could locate, began. Next the ghastly ticking of a death-watch in the wall at the bed's head made Tom shudder—it meant that somebody's days were numbered. Then the howl of a far-off dog rose on the night air and was answered by a fainter howl from a remoter distance. Tom was in an agony. At last he was satisfied that time had ceased and eternity begun; he began to doze, in spite of himself; the clock chimed eleven but he did not hear it. And then there came mingling with his half-formed dreams, a most melancholy caterwauling. The raising of a neighboring window disturbed him. A cry of "S'cat! you devil!" and the crash of an empty bottle against the back of his aunt's woodshed brought him wide awake, and a single minute later he was dressed and out of the window and creeping along the roof of the "ell" on all fours. He "meow'd" with caution once or twice, as he went; then jumped to the roof of the woodshed and thence to the ground. Huckleberry Finn was there, with his dead cat. The boys moved off and disappeared in the gloom. At the end of half an hour they were wading through the tall grass of the graveyard.

It was a graveyard of the old-fashioned western kind. It was on a hill, about a mile and a half from the village. It had a crazy board fence around it, which leaned inward in places, and outward the rest of the time, but stood upright nowhere. Grass and weeds grew rank over the whole cemetery. All the old graves were sunken in. There was not a tombstone on the place; round-topped, worm-eaten boards staggered over the graves, leaning for support and finding none. "Sacred to the Memory of" So-and-so had been painted on them once, but it could no longer have been read, on the most of them, now, even if there had been light.

A faint wind moaned through the trees, and Tom feared it might be the spirits of the dead complaining at being disturbed. The boys talked little, and only under their breath, for the time and the place and the pervading solemnity and silence oppressed their spirits. They found the sharp new heap they were seeking, and ensconced themselves within the protection of three great elms that grew in a bunch within a few feet of the grave.

Then they waited in silence for what seemed a long time. The hooting of a distant owl was all the sound that troubled the dead stillness. Tom's reflections grew oppressive. He must force some talk. So he said in a whisper:

"Hucky, do you believe the dead people like it for us to be here?"

Huckleberry whispered:

"I wisht I knowed. It's awful solemn like, *ain't* it?"

"I bet it is."

There was a considerable pause, while the boys canvassed this matter inwardly. Then Tom whispered:

"Say, Hucky—do you reckon Hoss Williams hears us talking?"

"O' course he does. Least his sperrit does."

Tom, after a pause:

"I wish I'd said *Mister* Williams. But I never meant any harm. Everybody calls him Hoss."

"A body can't be too partic'lar how they talk 'bout these-yer dead people, Tom."

This was a damper, and conversation died again. Presently Tom seized his comrade's arm and said:

"Sh!"

"What is it, Tom?" And the two clung together with beating hearts.

"Sh! There 'tis again! Didn't you hear it?"

"I—"

"There! Now you hear it."

"Lord, Tom they're coming! They're coming, sure. What'll we do?"

"I dono. Think they'll see us?"

"O, Tom, they can see in the dark, same as cats. I wisht I hadn't come."

"O, don't be afeard. *I* don't believe they'll bother us. We ain't doing any harm. If we keep perfectly still, maybe they won't notice us at all."

"I'll try to, Tom, but Lord I'm all of a shiver."

"Listen!"

The boys bent their heads together and scarcely breathed. A muffled sound of voices floated up from the far end of the graveyard.

"Look! See there!" whispered Tom. "What is it?"

"It's devil-fire. O, Tom, this is awful."

Some vague figures approached through the gloom, swinging an old-fashioned tin lantern that freckled the ground with innumerable little spangles of light. Presently Huckleberry whispered with a shudder:

"It's the devils sure enough. Three of 'em! Lordy, Tom, we're goners! Can you pray?"

"I'll try, but don't you be afeard. They ain't going to hurt us. Now I lay me down to sleep, I—"

"Sh!"

"What is it, Huck?"

"They're *humans*! One of 'em is, anyway. One of 'em's old Muff Potter's voice."

"No—'tain't so, is it?"

"I bet I know it. Don't you stir nor budge. *He* ain't sharp enough to notice us. Drunk, same as usual, likely—blamed old rip!"

"All right, I'll keep still. Now they're stuck. Can't find it. Here they come again. Now they're hot. Cold again. Hot again. Red hot! They're p'inted right, this time. Say Huck, I know another o' them voices; it's Injun Joe."

"That's so—that murderin' half-breed! I'd druther they was devils, a dern sight. What kin they be up to?"

The whispers died wholly out, now, for the three men had reached the grave and stood within a few feet of the boys' hiding place.

"Here it is," said the third voice; and the owner of it held the lantern up and revealed the face of young Dr. Robinson.

Potter and Injun Joe were carrying a handbarrow with a rope and a couple of shovels on it. They cast down their load and began to open the grave. The doctor put the lantern at the head of the grave and came and sat down with his back against one of the elm trees. He was so close the boys could have touched him.

"Hurry, men!" he said in a low voice; "the moon might come out at any moment."

They growled a response and went on digging. For some time there was no noise but the grating sound of the spades discharging their freight of mould and gravel. It was very monotonous. Finally a spade struck upon the coffin with a dull woody accent, and within another minute or two the men had hoisted it out on the ground. They pried off the lid with their shovels, got out the body and dumped it rudely on the ground. The moon drifted from behind the clouds and exposed the pallid face. The barrow was got ready and the corpse placed on it, covered with a blanket, and bound to its place with the rope. Potter took out a large spring-knife and cut off the dangling end of the rope and then said:

"Now the cussed thing's ready, Sawbones, and you'll just out with another five, or here she stays."

"That's the talk!" said Injun Joe.

"Look here, what does this mean?" said the doctor. "You required your pay in advance, and I've paid you."

"Yes, and you done more than that," said Injun Joe, approaching the doctor, who was now standing. "Five year ago you drove me away from your father's kitchen one night, when I come to ask for something to eat, and you said I warn't there for any good; and when I swore I'd get even with you if it took a hundred years, your father had me jailed for a vagrant. Did you think I'd forget? The Injun blood ain't in me for nothing. And now I've *got* you, and you got to *settle*, you know!"

He was threatening the doctor, with his fist in his face, by this time. The doctor struck out suddenly and stretched the ruffian on the ground. Potter dropped his knife, and exclaimed:

"Here, now, don't you hit my pard!" And the next moment he had grappled with the doctor and the two were struggling with might and main, trampling the grass and tearing the ground with their heels. Injun Joe sprang to his feet, his eyes flaming with passion, snatched up Potter's knife, and went creeping, catlike and stooping, round and round about the combatants, seeking an opportunity. All at once the doctor flung himself free, seized the heavy headboard of Williams's grave and felled Potter to the earth with it—and in the same instant the half-breed saw his chance and drove the knife to the hilt in the young man's breast. He reeled and fell partly upon Potter, flooding him with his blood, and in the same moment the clouds blotted out the dreadful spectacle and the two frightened boys went speeding away in the dark.

Presently, when the moon emerged again, Injun Joe was standing over the two forms, contemplating them. The doctor murmured inarticulately, gave a long gasp or two and was still. The half-breed muttered:

"*That* score is settled—damn you."

Then he robbed the body. After which he put the fatal knife in Potter's open right hand, and sat down on the dismantled coffin. Three—four—five minutes passed, and then Potter began to stir and moan. His hand closed upon the knife; he raised it, glanced at it, and let it fall, with a shudder. Then he sat up, pushing the body from him, and gazed at it, and then around him, confusedly. His eyes met Joe's.

"Lord, how is this, Joe?" he said.

"It's a dirty business," said Joe, without moving. "What did you do it for?"

"I! I never done it!"

"Look here! That kind of talk won't wash."

Potter trembled and grew white.

"I thought I'd got sober. I'd no business to drink to-night. But it's in my head yet—worse'n when we started here. I'm all in a muddle; can't recollect anything of it hardly. Tell me, Joe—*honest*, now, old feller—did I do it? Joe, I never meant to—'pon my soul and honor I never meant to, Joe. Tell me how it was Joe. O, it's awful—and him so young and promising."

"Why you two was scuffling, and he fetched you one with the head-board and you fell flat; and then up you come, all reeling and staggering, like, and snatched the knife and jammed it into him, just as he fetched you another awful clip—and here you've laid, dead as a wedge till now."

"O, I didn't know what I was a-doing. I wish I may die this minute if I did. It was all on accounts of the whisky; and the excitement, I reckon. I never used a weepon in my life before, Joe. I've fought, but never with weepons. They'll all say that. Joe, don't tell! Say you won't tell, Joe—that's a good feller. I always liked you Joe, and stood up for you, too. Don't you remember? You *won't* tell, *will* you Joe?" And the poor creature dropped on his knees before the stolid murderer, and clasped his appealing hands.

"No, you've always been fair and square with me, Muff Potter, and I won't go back on you.—There, now, that's as fair as a man can say."

"O, Joe, you're an angel. I'll bless you for this the longest day I live." And Potter began to cry.

"Come, now, that's enough of that. This ain't any time for blubbering. You be off yonder way and I'll go this. Move, now, and don't leave any tracks behind you."

Potter started on a trot that quickly increased to a run. The half-breed stood looking after him. He muttered:

"If he's as much stunned with the lick and fuddled with the rum as he had the look of being, he won't think of the knife till he's gone so far he'll be afraid to come back after it to such a place by himself—chicken-heart!"

Two or three minutes later the murdered man, the blanketed corpse, the lidless coffin and the open grave were under no inspection but the moon's. The stillness was complete again, too.

X

THE TWO BOYS flew on and on, toward the village, speechless with horror. They glanced backward over their shoulders from time to time, apprehensively, as if they feared they might be followed. Every stump that started up in their path seemed a man and an enemy, and made them catch their breath; and as they sped by some outlying cottages that lay near the village, the barking of the aroused watch-dogs seemed to give wings to their feet.

"If we can only get to the old tannery, before we break down!" whispered Tom, in short catches between breaths, "I can't stand it much longer."

Huckleberry's hard pantings were his only reply, and the boys fixed their eyes on the goal of their hopes and bent to their work to win it. They gained steadily on it, and at last, breast to breast they burst through the open door and fell grateful and exhausted in the sheltering shadows beyond. By and by their pulses slowed down, and Tom whispered:

"Huckleberry, what do you reckon 'll come of this?"

"If Dr. Robinson dies, I reckon hanging 'll come of it."

"Do you though?"

"Why I *know* it, Tom."

Tom thought a while, then he said:

"Who'll tell? We?"

"What are you talking about? S'pose something happened and Injun Joe *didn't* hang? Why he'd kill us some time or other, just as dead sure as we're a-laying here."

"That's just what I was thinking to myself, Huck."

"If anybody tells, let Muff Potter do it, if he's fool enough. He's generally drunk enough."

Tom said nothing—went on thinking. Presently he whispered:

"Huck, Muff Potter don't *know* it. How can he tell?"

"What's the reason he don't know it?"

"Because he'd just got that whack when Injun Joe done it. D' you reckon he could see anything? D' you reckon he knowed anything?"

"By hokey, that's so Tom!"

"And besides, look-a-here—maybe that whack done for *him*!"

"No, 'tain't likely Tom. He had liquor in him; I could see that; and besides, he always has. Well when pap's full, you might take and belt him over the head with a church and you couldn't phase him. He says so, his own self. So it's the same with Muff Potter, of course. But if a man was dead sober, I reckon maybe that whack might fetch him; I dono."

After another reflective silence, Tom said:

"Hucky, you sure you can keep mum?"

"Tom, we *got* to keep mum. *You* know that. That Injun devil wouldn't make any more of drownding us than a couple of cats, if we was to squeak 'bout this and they didn't hang him. Now look-a-here, Tom, less take and swear to one another—that's what we got to do—swear to keep mum."

"I'm agreed, Huck. It's the best thing. Would you just hold hands and swear that we—"

"O, no, that wouldn't do for this. That's good enough for little rubbishy common things—specially with gals, 'cuz *they* go back on you anyway, and blab if they get in a huff—but there orter be writing 'bout a big thing like this. And blood."

Tom's whole being applauded this idea. It was deep, and dark, and awful; the hour, the circumstances, the surroundings, were in keeping with it. He picked up a clean pine shingle that lay in the moonlight, took a little fragment of "red keel" out of his pocket, got the moon on his work, and painfully scrawled these lines, emphasizing each slow down-stroke by clamping his tongue between his teeth, and letting up the pressure on the up-strokes:

> Huck Finn and
> Tom Sawyer swears
> they will keep mum
> about this and they
> wish they may Drop
> down dead in their
> tracks if they ever
> tell and Rot.

Huckleberry was filled with admiration of Tom's facility in writing, and the sublimity of his language. He at once took a pin from his lappel and was going to prick his flesh, but Tom said:

"Hold on! Don't do that. A pin's brass. It might have verdigrease on it."

"What's verdigrease?"

"It's p'ison. That's what it is. You just swaller some of it once—you'll see."

So Tom unwound the thread from one of his needles, and each boy pricked the ball of his thumb and squeezed out a drop of blood. In time, after many squeezes, Tom managed to sign his initials, using the ball of his little finger for a pen. Then he showed Huckleberry how to make an H and an F, and the oath was complete. They buried the shingle close to the wall, with some dismal ceremonies and incantations, and the fetters that bound their tongues were considered to be locked and the key thrown away.

A figure crept stealthily through a break in the other end of the ruined building, now, but they did not notice it.

"Tom," whispered Huckleberry, "does this keep us from *ever* telling—*always?*"

"Of course it does. It don't make any difference *what* happens, we got to keep mum. We'd drop down dead—don't *you* know that?"

"Yes, I reckon that's so."

They continued to whisper for some little time. Presently a dog set up a long, lugubrious howl just outside—within ten feet of them. The boys clasped each other suddenly, in an agony of fright.

"Which of us does he mean?" gasped Huckleberry.

"I dono—peep through the crack. Quick!"

"No, *you*, Tom!"

"I can't—I can't *do* it, Huck!"

"Please, Tom. There 'tis again!"

"O, lordy, I'm thankful!" whispered Tom. "I know his voice. It's Bull Harbison."*

---

*If Mr. Harbison had owned a slave named Bull, Tom would have spoken of him as "Harbison's Bull;" but a son or a dog of that name was "Bull Harbison."

"O, that's good—I tell you, Tom, I was most scared to death; I'd a bet anything it was a *stray* dog."

The dog howled again. The boys' hearts sank once more.

"O, my! that ain't no Bull Harbison!" whispered Huckleberry. "*Do*, Tom!"

Tom, quaking with fear, yielded, and put his eye to the crack. His whisper was hardly audible when he said:

"O, Huck, IT'S A STRAY DOG!"

"Quick, Tom, quick! Who does he mean?"

"Huck, he must mean us both—we're right together."

"O, Tom, I reckon we're goners. I reckon there ain't no mistake 'bout where *I*'ll go to. I been so wicked."

"Dad fetch it! This comes of playing hookey and doing everything a feller's told *not* to do. I might a been good, like Sid, if I'd a tried—but no, I wouldn't, of course. But if ever I get off this time, I lay I'll just *waller* in Sunday-schools!" And Tom began to snuffle a little.

"*You* bad!" and Huckleberry began to snuffle, too. "Consound it, Tom Sawyer, you're just old pie, 'longside o' what *I* am. O, *lordy*, lordy, lordy, I wisht I only had half your chance."

Tom choked off and whispered:

"Look, Hucky, look! He's got his *back* to us!"

Hucky looked, with joy in his heart.

"Well he has, by jingoes! Did he before?"

"Yes, he did. But I, like a fool, never thought. O, this is bully, you know. *Now*, who can he mean?"

The howling stopped. Tom pricked up his ears.

"Sh! What's that?" he whispered.

"Sounds like—like hogs grunting. No—it's somebody snoring, Tom."

"That *is* it? Where 'bouts is it, Huck?"

"I bleeve it's down at t'other end. Sounds so, anyway. Pap used to sleep there, sometimes, 'long with the hogs, but laws bless you, he just lifts things when *he* snores. Besides, I reckon he ain't ever coming back to this town any more."

The spirit of adventure rose in the boys' souls once more.

"Hucky, do you das't to go if I lead?"

"I don't like to, much. Tom, s'pose it's Injun Joe!"

Tom quailed. But presently the temptation rose up strong

again and the boys agreed to try, with the understanding that they would take to their heels if the snoring stopped. So they went tip-toeing stealthily down, the one behind the other. When they had got to within five steps of the snorer, Tom stepped on a stick, and it broke with a sharp snap. The man moaned, writhed a little, and his face came into the moonlight. It was Muff Potter. The boys' hearts had stood still, and their bodies too, when the man moved, but their fears passed away now. They tip-toed out, through the broken weatherboarding, and stopped at a little distance to exchange a parting word. That long, lugubrious howl rose on the night air again! They turned and saw the strange dog standing within a few feet of where Potter was lying, and *facing* Potter, with his nose pointing heavenward.

"O, geeminy, it's *him!*" exclaimed both boys, in a breath.

"Say, Tom—they say a stray dog come howling around Johnny Miller's house, 'bout midnight, as much as two weeks ago; and a whipporwill come in and lit on the bannisters and sung, the very same evening; and there ain't anybody dead there yet."

"Well I know that. And suppose there ain't. Didn't Gracie Miller fall in the kitchen fire and burn herself terrible the very next Saturday?"

"Yes, but she ain't *dead*. And what's more, she's getting better, too."

"All right, you wait and see. She's a goner, just as dead sure as Muff Potter's a goner. That's what the niggers say, and they know all about these kind of things, Huck."

Then they separated, cogitating. When Tom crept in at his bedroom window, the night was almost spent. He undressed with excessive caution, and fell asleep congratulating himself that nobody knew of his escapade. He was not aware that the gently-snoring Sid was awake, and had been so for an hour.

When Tom awoke, Sid was dressed and gone. There was a late look in the light, a late sense in the atmosphere. He was startled. Why had he not been called—persecuted till he was up, as usual? The thought filled him with bodings. Within five minutes he was dressed and down stairs, feeling sore and drowsy. The family were still at table, but they had finished breakfast. There was no voice of rebuke; but there were averted eyes; there was a silence and an air of solemnity that struck a chill to the culprit's heart. He sat down and tried to seem gay, but it was up-hill work; it roused no smile, no response, and he lapsed into silence and let his heart sink down to the depths.

After breakfast his aunt took him aside, and Tom almost brightened in the hope that he was going to be flogged; but it was not so. His aunt wept over him and asked him how he could go and break her old heart so; and finally told him to go on, and ruin himself and bring her gray hairs with sorrow to the grave, for it was no use for her to try any more. This was worse than a thousand whippings, and Tom's heart was sorer now than his body. He cried, he pleaded for forgiveness, promised reform over and over again and then received his dismissal feeling that he had won but an imperfect forgiveness and established but a feeble confidence.

He left the presence too miserable to even feel vengeful toward Sid; and so the latter's prompt retreat through the back gate was unnecessary. He moped to school gloomy and sad, and took his flogging, along with Joe Harper, for playing hookey the day before, with the air of one whose heart was busy with heavier woes and wholly dead to trifles. Then he betook himself to his seat, rested his elbows on his desk and his jaws in his hands and stared at the wall with the stony stare of suffering that has reached the limit and can no further go. His elbow was pressing against some hard substance. After a long time he slowly and sadly changed his position, and took up this object with a sigh. It was in a paper. He unrolled it. A long, lingering, colossal sigh followed, and his heart broke. It was his brass andiron knob!

This final feather broke the camel's back.

XI

CLOSE UPON THE HOUR of noon the whole village was suddenly electrified with the ghastly news. No need of the as yet undreamed-of telegraph; the tale flew from man to man, from group to group, from house to house with little less than telegraphic speed. Of course the schoolmaster gave holiday for that afternoon; the town would have thought strangely of him if he had not.

A gory knife had been found close to the murdered man, and it had been recognized by somebody as belonging to Muff Potter—so the story ran. And it was said that a belated citizen had come upon Potter washing himself in the "branch" about one or two o'clock in the morning, and that Potter had at once sneaked off—suspicious circumstances, especially the washing, which was not a habit with Potter. It was also said that the town had been ransacked for this "murderer" (the public are not slow in the matter of sifting evidence and arriving at a verdict,) but that he could not be found. Horsemen had departed down all the roads in every direction, and the Sheriff "was confident" that he would be captured before night.

All the town was drifting toward the graveyard. Tom's heart-break vanished and he joined the procession, not because he would not a thousand times rather go anywhere else, but because an awful, unaccountable fascination drew him on. Arrived at the dreadful place, he wormed his small body through the crowd and saw the dismal spectacle. It seemed to him an age since he was there before. Somebody pinched his arm. He turned, and his eyes met Huckleberry's. Then both looked elsewhere at once, and wondered if anybody had noticed anything in their mutual glance. But everybody was talking, and intent upon the grisly spectacle before them.

"Poor fellow!" "Poor young fellow!" "This ought to be a lesson to grave-robbers!" "Muff Potter'll hang for this if they catch him!" This was the drift of remark; and the minister said, "It was a judgment; His hand is here."

Now Tom shivered from head to heel; for his eye fell upon

the stolid face of Injun Joe. At this moment the crowd began to sway and struggle, and voices shouted, "It's him! it's him! he's coming himself!"

"Who? Who?" from twenty voices.

"Muff Potter!"

"Hallo, he's stopped!—Look out, he's turning! Don't let him get away!"

People in the branches of the trees over Tom's head, said he wasn't trying to get away—he only looked doubtful and perplexed.

"Infernal impudence!" said a bystander; "wanted to come and take a quiet look at his work, I reckon—didn't expect any company."

The crowd fell apart, now, and the Sheriff came through, ostentatiously leading Potter by the arm. The poor fellow's face was haggard, and his eyes showed the fear that was upon him. When he stood before the murdered man, he shook as with a palsy, and he put his face in his hands and burst into tears.

"I didn't do it, friends," he sobbed; " 'pon my word and honor I never done it."

"Who's accused you?" shouted a voice.

This shot seemed to carry home. Potter lifted his face and looked around him with a pathetic hopelessness in his eyes. He saw Injun Joe, and exclaimed:

"O, Injun Joe, you promised me you'd never—"

"Is that your knife?"—and it was thrust before him by the Sheriff.

Potter would have fallen if they had not caught him and eased him to the ground. Then he said:

"Something *told* me 't if I didn't come back and get—" He shuddered; then waved his nerveless hand with a vanquished gesture and said, "Tell 'em, Joe, tell 'em—it ain't any use any more."

Then Huckleberry and Tom stood dumb and staring, and heard the stony-hearted liar reel off his serene statement, they expecting every moment that the clear sky would deliver God's lightnings upon his head, and wondering to see how long the stroke was delayed. And when he had finished and still stood alive and whole, their wavering impulse to break

their oath and save the poor betrayed prisoner's life faded and
vanished away, for plainly this miscreant had sold himself to
Satan and it would be fatal to meddle with the property of
such a power as that.

"Why didn't you leave? What did you want to come here
for?" somebody said.

"I couldn't help it—I couldn't help it," Potter moaned. "I
wanted to run away, but I couldn't seem to come anywhere
but here." And he fell to sobbing again.

Injun Joe repeated his statement, just as calmly, a few minutes afterward on the inquest, under oath; and the boys,
seeing that the lightnings were still withheld, were confirmed
in their belief that Joe had sold himself to the devil. He was
now become, to them, the most balefully interesting object
they had ever looked upon, and they could not take their fas-
cinated eyes from his face. They inwardly resolved to watch
him, nights, when opportunity should offer, in the hope of
getting a glimpse of his dread master.

Injun Joe helped to raise the body of the murdered man
and put it in a wagon for removal; and it was whispered
through the shuddering crowd that the wound bled a little!
The boys thought that this happy circumstance would turn
suspicion in the right direction; but they were disappointed,
for more than one villager remarked:

"It was within three feet of Muff Potter when it done it."

Tom's fearful secret and gnawing conscience disturbed his
sleep for as much as a week after this; and at breakfast one
morning Sid said:

"Tom, you pitch around and talk in your sleep so much
that you keep me awake about half the time."

Tom blanched and dropped his eyes.

"It's a bad sign," said Aunt Polly, gravely. "What you got
on your mind, Tom?"

"Nothing. Nothing 't I know of." But the boy's hand
shook so that he spilled his coffee.

"And you do talk such stuff," Sid said. "Last night you said
'it's blood, it's blood, that's what it is!' You said that over
and over. And you said 'Don't torment me so—I'll tell.' Tell
what? What is it you'll tell?"

Everything was swimming before Tom. There is no telling what might have happened, now, but luckily the concern passed out of Aunt Polly's face and she came to Tom's relief without knowing it. She said:

"Sho! It's that dreadful murder. I dream about it most every night myself. Sometimes I dream it's me that done it."

Mary said she had been affected much the same way. Sid seemed satisfied. Tom got out of the presence as quickly as he plausibly could, and after that he complained of toothache for a week and tied up his jaws every night. He never knew that Sid lay nightly watching, and frequently slipped the bandage free and then leaned on his elbow listening a good while at a time, and afterward slipped the bandage back to its place again. Tom's distress of mind wore off gradually and the toothache grew irksome and was discarded. If Sid really managed to make anything out of Tom's disjointed mutterings, he kept it to himself.

It seemed to Tom that his schoolmates never would get done holding inquests on dead cats, and thus keeping his trouble present to his mind. Sid noticed that Tom never was coroner at one of these inquiries, though it had been his habit to take the lead in all new enterprises; he noticed, too, that Tom never acted as a witness,—and that was strange; and Sid did not overlook the fact that Tom even showed a marked aversion to these inquests, and always avoided them when he could. Sid marveled, but said nothing. However, even inquests went out of vogue at last, and ceased to torture Tom's conscience.

Every day or two, during this time of sorrow, Tom watched his opportunity and went to the little grated jail-window and smuggled such small comforts through to the "murderer" as he could get hold of. The jail was a trifling little brick den that stood in a marsh at the edge of the village, and no guards were afforded for it; indeed it was seldom occupied. These offerings greatly helped to ease Tom's conscience.

The villagers had a strong desire to tar-and-feather Injun Joe and ride him on a rail, for body-snatching, but so formidable was his character that nobody could be found who was willing to take the lead in the matter, so it was dropped. He had been careful to begin both of his inquest-statements with the fight, without confessing the grave-robbery that preceded it; therefore it was deemed wisest not to try the case in the courts at present.

XII

ONE OF THE REASONS why Tom's mind had drifted away from its secret troubles was, that it had found a new and weighty matter to interest itself about. Becky Thatcher had stopped coming to school. Tom had struggled with his pride a few days, and tried to "whistle her down the wind," but failed. He began to find himself hanging around her father's house, nights, and feeling very miserable. She was ill. What if she should die! There was distraction in the thought. He no longer took an interest in war, nor even in piracy. The charm of life was gone; there was nothing but dreariness left. He put his hoop away, and his bat; there was no joy in them any more. His aunt was concerned. She began to try all manner of remedies on him. She was one of those people who are infatuated with patent medicines and all new-fangled methods of producing health or mending it. She was an inveterate experimenter in these things. When something fresh in this line came out she was in a fever, right away, to try it; not on herself, for she was never ailing, but on anybody else that came handy. She was a subscriber for all the "Health" periodicals and phrenological frauds; and the solemn ignorance they were inflated with was breath to her nostrils. All the "rot" they contained about ventilation, and how to go to bed, and how to get up, and what to eat, and what to drink, and how much exercise to take, and what frame of mind to keep one's self in, and what sort of clothing to wear, was all gospel to her, and she never observed that her health-journals of the current month customarily upset everything they had recommended the month before. She was as simple-hearted and honest as the day was long, and so she was an easy victim. She gathered together her quack periodicals and her quack medicines, and thus armed with death, went about on her pale horse, metaphorically speaking, with "hell following after." But she never suspected that she was not an angel of healing and the balm of Gilead in disguise, to the suffering neighbors.

The water treatment was new, now, and Tom's low con-

dition was a windfall to her. She had him out at daylight
every morning, stood him up in the woodshed and drowned
him with a deluge of cold water; then she scrubbed him
down with a towel like a file, and so brought him to; then
she rolled him up in a wet sheet and put him away under
blankets till she sweated his soul clean and "the yellow stains
of it came through his pores"—as Tom said.

Yet notwithstanding all this, the boy grew more and more
melancholy and pale and dejected. She added hot baths, sitz
baths, shower baths and plunges. The boy remained as dismal
as a hearse. She began to assist the water with a slim oatmeal
diet and blister plasters. She calculated his capacity as she
would a jug's, and filled him up every day with quack cure-
alls.

Tom had become indifferent to persecution, by this time.
This phase filled the old lady's heart with consternation. This
indifference must be broken up at any cost. Now she heard
of Pain-Killer for the first time. She ordered a lot at once. She
tasted it and was filled with gratitude. It was simply fire in a
liquid form. She dropped the water treatment and everything
else, and pinned her faith to Pain-Killer. She gave Tom a tea-
spoonful and watched with the deepest anxiety for the result.
Her troubles were instantly at rest, her soul at peace again;
for the "indifference" was broken up. The boy could not have
shown a wilder, heartier interest, if she had built a fire under
him.

Tom felt that it was time to wake up; this sort of life might
be romantic enough, in his blighted condition, but it was getting to have too little sentiment and too much distracting variety about it. So he thought over various plans for relief, and
finally hit upon that of professing to be fond of Pain-Killer.
He asked for it so often that he became a nuisance, and his
aunt ended by telling him to help himself and quit bothering
her. If it had been Sid, she would have had no misgivings to
alloy her delight; but since it was Tom, she watched the bottle clandestinely. She found that the medicine did really di-
minish, but it did not occur to her that the boy was mending
the health of a crack in the sitting-room floor with it.

One day Tom was in the act of dosing the crack when his

aunt's yellow cat came along, purring, eyeing the tea-spoon avariciously, and begging for a taste. Tom said:

"Don't ask for it unless you want it, Peter."

But Peter signified that he did want it.

"You better make sure."

Peter was sure.

"Now you've asked for it, and I'll give it to you, because there ain't anything mean about *me*; but if you find you don't like it, you mustn't blame anybody but your own self."

Peter was agreeable. So Tom pried his mouth open and poured down the Pain-Killer. Peter sprang a couple of yards into the air, and then delivered a war-whoop and set off round and round the room, banging against furniture, upsetting flower pots and making general havoc. Next he rose on his hind feet and pranced around, in a frenzy of enjoyment, with his head over his shoulder and his voice proclaiming his unappeasable happiness. Then he went tearing around the house again spreading chaos and destruction in his path. Aunt Polly entered in time to see him throw a few double summersets, deliver a final mighty hurrah, and sail through the open window, carrying the rest of the flower-pots with him. The old lady stood petrified with astonishment, peering over her glasses; Tom lay on the floor expiring with laughter.

"Tom, what on earth ails that cat?"

"*I* don't know, aunt," gasped the boy.

"Why I never see anything like it. What *did* make him act so?"

"Deed I don't know aunt Polly; cats always act so when they're having a good time."

"They do, do they?" There was something in the tone that made Tom apprehensive.

"Yes'm. That is, I believe they do."

"You *do?*"

"Yes'm."

The old lady was bending down, Tom watching, with interest emphasized by anxiety. Too late he divined her "drift." The handle of the tell-tale tea-spoon was visible under the bed-valance. Aunt Polly took it, held it up. Tom winced, and dropped his eyes. Aunt Polly raised him by the usual handle—his ear—and cracked his head soundly with her thimble.

"Now, sir, what did you want to treat that poor dumb beast so, for?"

"I done it out of pity for him—because he hadn't any aunt."

"Hadn't any aunt!—you numscull. What has that got to do with it?"

"Heaps. Because if he'd a had one she'd a burnt him out herself! She'd a roasted his bowels out of him 'thout any more feeling than if he was a human!"

Aunt Polly felt a sudden pang of remorse. This was putting the thing in a new light; what was cruelty to a cat *might* be cruelty to a boy, too. She began to soften; she felt sorry. Her eyes watered a little, and she put her hand on Tom's head and said gently:

"I was meaning for the best, Tom. And Tom, it *did* do you good."

Tom looked up in her face with just a perceptible twinkle peeping through his gravity:

"I know you was meaning for the best, aunty, and so was I with Peter. It done *him* good, too. I never seen him get around so since—"

"O, go 'long with you, Tom, before you aggravate me again. And you try and see if you can't be a good boy, for once, and you needn't take any more medicine."

Tom reached school ahead of time. It was noticed that this strange thing had been occurring every day latterly. And now, as usual of late, he hung about the gate of the school yard instead of playing with his comrades. He was sick, he said; and he looked it. He tried to seem to be looking everywhere but whither he really was looking—down the road. Presently Jeff Thatcher hove in sight, and Tom's face lighted; he gazed a moment, and then turned sorrowfully away. When Jeff arrived, Tom accosted him, and "led up" warily to opportunities for remark about Becky, but the giddy lad never could see the bait. Tom watched and watched, hoping whenever a frisking frock came in sight, and hating the owner of it as soon as he saw she was not the right one. At last frocks ceased to appear, and he dropped hopelessly into the dumps; he entered the empty school house and sat down to suffer. Then one more frock passed in at the gate, and Tom's heart gave a great bound. The next instant he was out, and "going on" like an Indian; yelling, laughing, chasing boys, jumping over the fence at risk of life and limb, throwing hand-springs, standing on his head—doing all the heroic things he could conceive of, and keeping a furtive eye out, all the while, to see if Becky Thatcher was noticing. But she seemed to be unconscious of it all; she never looked. Could it be possible that she was not aware that he was there? He carried his exploits to her immediate vicinity; came war-whooping around, snatched a boy's cap, hurled it to the roof of the schoolhouse, broke through a group of boys, tumbling them in every direction, and fell sprawling, himself, under Becky's nose, almost upsetting her—and she turned, with her nose in the air, and he heard her say, "Mf! some people think they're mighty smart—always showing off!"

Tom's cheeks burned. He gathered himself up and sneaked off, crushed and crestfallen.

XIII

Tom's mind was made up, now. He was gloomy and desperate. He was a forsaken, friendless boy, he said; nobody loved him; when they found out what they had driven him to, perhaps they would be sorry; he had tried to do right and get along, but they would not let him; since nothing would do them but to be rid of him, let it be so; and let them blame *him* for the consequences—why shouldn't they? what right had the friendless to complain? Yes, they had forced him to it at last: he would lead a life of crime. There was no choice.

By this time he was far down Meadow Lane, and the bell for school to "take up" tinkled faintly upon his ear. He sobbed, now, to think he should never, never hear that old familiar sound any more—it was very hard, but it was forced on him; since he was driven out into the cold world, he must submit—but he forgave them. Then the sobs came thick and fast.

Just at this point he met his soul's sworn comrade, Joe Harper—hard-eyed, and with evidently a great and dismal purpose in his heart. Plainly here were "two souls with but a single thought." Tom, wiping his eyes with his sleeve, began to blubber out something about a resolution to escape from hard usage and lack of sympathy at home by roaming abroad into the great world never to return; and ended by hoping that Joe would not forget him.

But it transpired that this was a request which Joe had just been going to make of Tom, and had come to hunt him up for that purpose. His mother had whipped him for drinking some cream which he had never tasted and knew nothing about; it was plain that she was tired of him and wished him to go; if she felt that way, there was nothing for him to do but succumb; he hoped she would be happy, and never regret having driven her poor boy out into the unfeeling world to suffer and die.

As the two boys walked sorrowing along, they made a new compact to stand by each other and be brothers and never separate till death relieved them of their troubles. Then they began to lay their plans. Joe was for being a hermit, and living on crusts in a remote cave, and dying, some time, of cold, and want, and grief; but after listening to Tom, he conceded that there were some conspicuous advantages about a life of crime, and so he consented to be a pirate.

Three miles below St. Petersburg, at a point where the Mississippi river was a trifle over a mile wide, there was a long, narrow, wooded island, with a shallow bar at the head of it, and this offered well as a rendezvous. It was not inhabited; it lay far over toward the further shore, abreast a dense and almost wholly unpeopled forest. So Jackson's Island was chosen. Who were to be the subjects of their piracies, was a matter that did not occur to them. Then they hunted up Huckleberry Finn, and he joined them promptly, for all careers were one to him; he was indifferent. They presently separated to meet at a lonely spot on the river bank two miles above the village at the favorite hour—which was midnight. There was a small log raft there which they meant to capture. Each would bring hooks and lines, and such provision as he could steal in the most dark and mysterious way—as became outlaws. And before the afternoon was done, they had all managed to enjoy the sweet glory of spreading the fact that pretty soon the town would "hear something." All who got this vague hint were cautioned to "be mum and wait."

About midnight Tom arrived with a boiled ham and a few trifles, and stopped in a dense undergrowth on a small bluff overlooking the meeting-place. It was starlight, and very still. The mighty river lay like an ocean at rest. Tom listened a moment, but no sound disturbed the quiet. Then he gave a low, distinct whistle. It was answered from under the bluff. Tom whistled twice more; these signals were answered in the same way. Then a guarded voice said:

"Who goes there?"

"Tom Sawyer, the Black Avenger of the Spanish Main. Name your names."

"Huck Finn the Red-Handed, and Joe Harper the Terror of the Seas." Tom had furnished these titles, from his favorite literature.

" 'Tis well. Give the countersign."

Two hoarse whispers delivered the same awful word simultaneously to the brooding night:

"BLOOD!"

Then Tom tumbled his ham over the bluff and let himself down after it, tearing both skin and clothes to some extent in the effort. There was an easy, comfortable path along the shore under the bluff, but it lacked the advantages of difficulty and danger so valued by a pirate.

The Terror of the Seas had brought a side of bacon, and had about worn himself out with getting it there. Finn the Red-Handed had stolen a skillet, and a quantity of half cured leaf tobacco, and had also brought a few corn-cobs to make pipes with. But none of the pirates smoked or "chewed" but himself. The Black Avenger of the Spanish Main said it would never do to start without some fire. That was a wise thought; matches were hardly known there in that day. They saw a fire smouldering upon a great raft a hundred yards above, and they went stealthily thither and helped themselves to a chunk. They made an imposing adventure of it, saying "Hist!" every now and then and suddenly halting with finger on lip; moving with hands on imaginary dagger-hilts; and giving orders in dismal whispers that if "the foe" stirred to "let him have it to the hilt," because "dead men tell no tales." They knew well enough that the raftsmen were all down at the village laying in stores or having a spree, but still that was no excuse for their conducting this thing in an unpiratical way.

They shoved off, presently, Tom in command, Huck at the after oar and Joe at the forward. Tom stood amidships, gloomy-browed, and with folded arms, and gave his orders in a low, stern whisper:

"Luff, and bring her to the wind!"

"Aye-aye, sir!"

"Steady, stead-y-y-y!"

"Steady it is, sir!"

"Let her go off a point!"

"Point it is, sir!"

As the boys steadily and monotonously drove the raft toward mid-stream, it was no doubt understood that these orders were given only for "style," and were not intended to mean anything in particular.

"What sail's she carrying?"

"Courses, tops'ls and flying-jib, sir."

"Send the r'yals up! Lay out aloft, there, half a dozen of ye,—foretopmast-stuns'l! Lively, now!"

"Aye-aye, sir!"

"Shake out that maintogalans'l! Sheets and braces! *Now*, my hearties!"

"Aye-aye, sir!"

"Hellum-a-lee—hard a port! Stand by to meet her when she comes! Port, port! *Now*, men! With a will! Stead-y-y-y!"

"Steady it is, sir!"

The raft drew beyond the middle of the river; the boys pointed her head right, and then lay on their oars. The river was not high, so there was not more than a two- or three-mile current. Hardly a word was said during the next three-quarters of an hour. Now the raft was passing before the distant town. Two or three glimmering lights showed where it lay, peacefully sleeping, beyond the vague vast sweep of star-gemmed water, unconscious of the tremendous event that was happening. The Black Avenger stood, still with folded arms, "looking his last" upon the scene of his former joys and his later sufferings, and wishing "she" could see him now, abroad on the wild sea, facing peril and death with dauntless heart, going to his doom with a grim smile on his lips. It was but a small strain on his imagination to remove Jackson's Island beyond eye-shot of the village, and so he "looked his last" with a broken and satisfied heart. The other pirates were looking their last, too; and they all looked so long that they came near letting the current drift them out of the range of the island. But they discovered the danger in time, and made shift to avert it. About two o'clock in the morning the raft grounded on the bar two hundred yards above the head of the island, and they waded back and forth until they had landed their freight. Part of the little raft's belongings consisted of an old sail, and this they spread over a nook in the bushes for a tent to shelter their provisions; but they themselves would sleep in the open air in good weather, as became outlaws.

They built a fire against the side of a great log twenty or thirty steps within the sombre depths of the forest, and then cooked some bacon in the frying pan for supper, and used up half of the corn "pone" stock they had brought. It seemed glorious sport to be feasting in that wild free way in the virgin forest of an unexplored and uninhabited island, far from the haunts of men, and they said they never would return to civilization. The climbing fire lit up their faces and threw its ruddy glare upon the pillared tree trunks of their forest temple, and upon the varnished foliage and festooning vines.

When the last crisp slice of bacon was gone, and the last allowance of corn pone devoured, the boys stretched themselves out on the grass, filled with contentment. They could have found a cooler place, but they would not deny themselves such a romantic feature as the roasting camp-fire.

"*Ain't* it gay?" said Joe.

"It's *nuts!*" said Tom. "What would the boys say if they could see us?"

"Say? Well they'd just die to be here—hey Hucky?"

"I reckon so," said Huckleberry; "anyways *I*'m suited. I don't want nothing better'n this. I don't ever get enough to eat, gen'ally—and here they can't come and pick at a feller and bullyrag him so."

"It's just the life for me," said Tom. "You don't have to get up, mornings, and you don't have to go to school, and wash, and all that blame foolishness. You see a pirate don't have to do *anything*, Joe, when he's ashore, but a hermit *he* has to be praying considerable, and then he don't have any fun, anyway, all by himself that way."

"O yes, that's so," said Joe, "but I hadn't thought much about it, you know. I'd a good deal ruther be a pirate, now that I've tried it."

"You see," said Tom, "people don't go much on hermits, now-a-days, like they used to in old times, but a pirate's always respected. And a hermit's got to sleep on the hardest place he can find, and put sack-cloth and ashes on his head, and stand out in the rain, and—"

"What does he put sack-cloth and ashes on his head for?" inquired Huck.

"*I* dono. But they've *got* to do it. Hermits always do. You'd have to do that if you was a hermit."

"Dern'd if I would," said Huck.

"Well what would you do?"

"I dono. But I wouldn't do that."

"Why Huck you'd *have* to. How'd you get around it?"

"Why I just wouldn't stand it. I'd run away."

"Run away! Well you *would* be a nice old slouch of a her-mit. You'd be a disgrace."

The Red-Handed made no response, being better em-ployed. He had finished gouging out a cob, and now he fitted a weed stem to it, loaded it with tobacco, and was pressing a coal to the charge and blowing a cloud of fragrant smoke— he was in the full bloom of luxurious contentment. The other pirates envied him this majestic vice, and secretly resolved to acquire it shortly. Presently Huck said:

"What does pirates have to do?"

Tom said:

"Oh they have just a bully time—take ships, and burn them, and get the money and bury it in awful places in their island where there's ghosts and things to watch it, and kill everybody in the ships—make 'em walk a plank."

"And they carry the women to the island," said Joe; "they don't kill the women."

"No," assented Tom, "they don't kill the women—they're too noble. And the women's always beautiful, too."

"And don't they wear the bulliest clothes! Oh, no! All gold and silver and di'monds," said Joe, with enthusiasm.

"Who?" said Huck.

"Why the pirates."

Huck scanned his own clothing forlornly.

"I reckon I ain't dressed fitten for a pirate," said he, with a regretful pathos in his voice; "but I ain't got none but these."

But the other boys told him the fine clothes would come fast enough, after they should have begun their adventures. They made him understand that his poor rags would do to begin with, though it was customary for wealthy pirates to start with a proper wardrobe.

Gradually their talk died out and drowsiness began to steal upon the eyelids of the little waifs. The pipe dropped from the fingers of the Red-Handed, and he slept the sleep of the conscience-free and the weary. The Terror of the Seas and the Black Avenger of the Spanish Main had more difficulty in getting to sleep. They said their prayers inwardly, and lying down, since there was nobody there with authority to make them kneel and recite aloud; in truth they had a mind not to say them at all, but they were afraid to proceed to such lengths as that, lest they might call down a sudden and special thunderbolt from Heaven. Then at once they reached and hovered upon the imminent verge of sleep—but an intruder came, now, that would not "down." It was conscience. They began to feel a vague fear that they had been doing wrong to run away; and next they thought of the stolen meat, and then the real torture came. They tried to argue it away by reminding conscience that they had purloined sweetmeats and apples scores of times; but conscience was not to be appeased by such thin plausibilities. It seemed to them, in the end, that there was no getting around the stubborn fact that taking sweetmeats was only "hooking," while taking bacon and hams and such valuables was plain simple *stealing*—and there was a command against that in the Bible. So they inwardly resolved that so long as they remained in the business, their piracies should not again be sullied with the crime of stealing. Then conscience granted a truce, and these curiously inconsistent pirates fell peacefully to sleep.

XIV

WHEN TOM AWOKE in the morning, he wondered where he was. He sat up and rubbed his eyes and looked around. Then he comprehended. It was the cool gray dawn, and there was a delicious sense of repose and peace in the deep pervading calm and silence of the woods. Not a leaf stirred; not a sound obtruded upon great Nature's meditation. Beaded dew-drops stood upon the leaves and grasses. A white layer of ashes covered the fire, and a thin blue breath of smoke rose straight into the air. Joe and Huck still slept.

Now, far away in the woods a bird called; another answered; presently the hammering of a woodpecker was heard. Gradually the cool dim gray of the morning whitened, and as gradually sounds multiplied and life manifested itself. The marvel of Nature shaking off sleep and going to work unfolded itself to the musing boy. A little green worm came crawling over a dewy leaf, lifting two-thirds of his body into the air from time to time and "sniffing around," then proceeding again—for he was measuring, Tom said; and when the worm approached him, of its own accord, he sat as still as a stone, with his hopes rising and falling, by turns, as the creature still came toward him or seemed inclined to go elsewhere; and when at last it considered a painful moment with its curved body in the air and then came decisively down upon Tom's leg and began a journey over him, his whole heart was glad—for that meant that he was going to have a new suit of clothes—without the shadow of a doubt a gaudy piratical uniform. Now a procession of ants appeared, from nowhere in particular, and went about their labors; one struggled manfully by with a dead spider five times as big as itself in its arms, and lugged it straight up a tree-trunk. A brown spotted lady-bug climbed the dizzy height of a grass-blade, and Tom bent down close to it and said, "Lady-bug, lady-bug, fly away home, your house is on fire, your children's alone," and she took wing and went off to see about it—which did not surprise the boy, for he knew of old that this insect was credulous about conflagrations and he had prac-

ticed upon its simplicity more than once. A tumble-bug came
next, heaving sturdily at its ball, and Tom touched the creature, to see it shut its legs against its body and pretend to be
dead. The birds were fairly rioting, by this time. A cat-bird,
the northern mocker, lit in a tree over Tom's head, and trilled
out her imitations of her neighbors in a rapture of enjoyment;
then a shrill jay swept down, a flash of blue flame, and
stopped on a twig almost within the boy's reach, cocked his
head to one side and eyed the strangers with a consuming
curiosity; a gray squirrel and a big fellow of the "fox" kind
came skurrying along, sitting up at intervals to inspect and
chatter at the boys, for the wild things had probably never
seen a human being before and scarcely knew whether to be
afraid or not. All Nature was wide awake and stirring, now;
long lances of sunlight pierced down through the dense foliage far and near, and a few butterflies came fluttering upon
the scene.

Tom stirred up the other pirates and they all clattered away
with a shout, and in a minute or two were stripped and chasing after and tumbling over each other in the shallow limpid
water of the white sand-bar. They felt no longing for the little
village sleeping in the distance beyond the majestic waste of
water. A vagrant current or a slight rise in the river had carried off their raft, but this only gratified them, since its going
was something like burning the bridge between them and civilization.

They came back to camp wonderfully refreshed, glad-
hearted, and ravenous; and they soon had the camp-fire blazing up again. Huck found a spring of clear cold water close
by, and the boys made cups of broad oak or hickory leaves,
and felt that water, sweetened with such a wild-wood charm
as that, would be a good enough substitute for coffee. While
Joe was slicing bacon for breakfast, Tom and Huck asked him
to hold on a minute; they stepped to a promising nook in the
river bank and threw in their lines; almost immediately they
had reward. Joe had not had time to get impatient before
they were back again with some handsome bass, a couple of
sun-perch and a small catfish—provision enough for quite a
family. They fried the fish with the bacon and were astonished; for no fish had ever seemed so delicious before. They

did not know that the quicker a fresh water fish is on the fire after he is caught the better he is; and they reflected little upon what a sauce open air sleeping, open air exercise, bathing, and a large ingredient of hunger makes, too.

They lay around in the shade, after breakfast, while Huck had a smoke, and then went off through the woods on an exploring expedition. They tramped gaily along, over decaying logs, through tangled underbrush, among solemn monarchs of the forest, hung from their crowns to the ground with a drooping regalia of grape-vines. Now and then they came upon snug nooks carpeted with grass and jeweled with flowers.

They found plenty of things to be delighted with but nothing to be astonished at. They discovered that the island was about three miles long and a quarter of a mile wide, and that the shore it lay closest to was only separated from it by a narrow channel hardly two hundred yards wide. They took a swim about every hour, so it was close upon the middle of the afternoon when they got back to camp. They were too hungry to stop to fish, but they fared sumptuously upon cold ham, and then threw themselves down in the shade to talk. But the talk soon began to drag, and then died. The stillness, the solemnity that brooded in the woods, and the sense of loneliness, began to tell upon the spirits of the boys. They fell to thinking. A sort of undefined longing crept upon them. This took dim shape, presently—it was budding home-sickness. Even Finn the Red-Handed was dreaming of his doorsteps and empty hogsheads. But they were all ashamed of their weakness, and none was brave enough to speak his thought.

For some time, now, the boys had been dully conscious of a peculiar sound in the distance, just as one sometimes is of the ticking of a clock which he takes no distinct note of. But now this mysterious sound became more pronounced, and forced a recognition. The boys started, glanced at each other, and then each assumed a listening attitude. There was a long silence, profound and unbroken; then a deep, sullen boom came floating down out of the distance.

"What is it!" exclaimed Joe, under his breath.

"I wonder," said Tom in a whisper.

" 'Tain't thunder," said Huckleberry, in an awed tone, "be-cuz thunder—"

"Hark!" said Tom. "Listen—don't talk."

They waited a time that seemed an age, and then the same muffled boom troubled the solemn hush.

"Let's go and see."

They sprang to their feet and hurried to the shore toward the town. They parted the bushes on the bank and peered out over the water. The little steam ferry boat was about a mile below the village, drifting with the current. Her broad deck seemed crowded with people. There were a great many skiffs rowing about or floating with the stream in the neighbor-hood of the ferry boat, but the boys could not determine what the men in them were doing. Presently a great jet of white smoke burst from the ferry-boat's side, and as it ex-panded and rose in a lazy cloud, that same dull throb of sound was borne to the listeners again.

"I know now!" exclaimed Tom; "somebody's drownded!"

"That's it!" said Huck; "they done that last summer, when Bill Turner got drownded; they shoot a cannon over the wa-ter, and that makes him come up to the top. Yes, and they take loaves of bread and put quicksilver in 'em and set 'em afloat, and wherever there's anybody that's drownded, they'll float right there and stop."

"Yes, I've heard about that," said Joe. "I wonder what makes the bread do that."

"Oh it ain't the bread, so much," said Tom; "I reckon it's mostly what they *say* over it before they start it out."

"But they don't say anything over it," said Huck. "I've seen 'em, and they don't."

"Well that's funny," said Tom. "But maybe they say it to themselves. Of *course* they do. Anybody might know that."

The other boys agreed that there was reason in what Tom said, because an ignorant lump of bread, uninstructed by an incantation, could not be expected to act very intelligently when sent upon an errand of such gravity.

"By jings I wish I was over there, now," said Joe.

"I do too," said Huck. "I'd give heaps to know who it is."

The boys still listened and watched. Presently a revealing thought flashed through Tom's mind, and he exclaimed:

"Boys, I know who's drownded—it's us!"

They felt like heroes in an instant. Here was a gorgeous triumph; they were missed; they were mourned; hearts were breaking on their account; tears were being shed; accusing memories of unkindnesses to these poor lost lads were rising up, and unavailing regrets and remorse were being indulged; and best of all, the departed were the talk of the whole town, and the envy of all the boys, as far as this dazzling notoriety was concerned. This was fine. It was worth while to be a pirate, after all.

As twilight drew on, the ferry boat went back to her accustomed business and the skiffs disappeared. The pirates returned to camp. They were jubilant with vanity over their new grandeur and the illustrious trouble they were making. They caught fish, cooked supper and ate it, and then fell to guessing at what the village was thinking and saying about them; and the pictures they drew of the public distress on their account were gratifying to look upon—from their point of view. But when the shadows of night closed them in, they gradually ceased to talk, and sat gazing into the fire, with their minds evidently wandering elsewhere. The excitement was gone, now, and Tom and Joe could not keep back thoughts of certain persons at home who were not enjoying this fine frolic as much as they were. Misgivings came; they grew troubled and unhappy; a sigh or two escaped, unawares. By and by Joe timidly ventured upon a round-about "feeler" as to how the others might look upon a return to civilization—not right now, but—

Tom withered him with derision! Huck, being uncommitted, as yet, joined in with Tom, and the waverer quickly "explained," and was glad to get out of the scrape with as little taint of chicken-hearted home-sickness clinging to his garments as he could. Mutiny was effectually laid to rest for the moment.

As the night deepened, Huck began to nod, and presently to snore. Joe followed next. Tom lay upon his elbow motionless, for some time, watching the two intently. At last he got up cautiously, on his knees, and went searching among the grass and the flickering reflections flung by the camp-fire. He picked up and inspected several large semi-cylinders of the thin white bark of a sycamore, and finally chose two which seemed to suit him. Then he knelt by the fire and painfully wrote something upon each of these with his "red keel;" one he rolled up and put in his jacket pocket, and the other he put in Joe's hat and removed it to a little distance from the owner. And he also put into the hat certain school-boy treasures of almost inestimable value—among them a lump of chalk, an India rubber ball, three fish-hooks, and one of that kind of marbles known as a "sure 'nough crystal." Then he tip-toed his way cautiously among the trees till he felt that he was out of hearing, and straightway broke into a keen run in the direction of the sand-bar.

XV

A FEW MINUTES later Tom was in the shoal water of the bar, wading toward the Illinois shore. Before the depth reached his middle he was half-way over; the current would permit no more wading, now, so he struck out confidently to swim the remaining hundred yards. He swam quartering up stream, but still was swept downward rather faster than he had expected. However, he reached the shore finally, and drifted along till he found a low place and drew himself out. He put his hand on his jacket pocket, found his piece of bark safe, and then struck through the woods, following the shore, with streaming garments. Shortly before ten o'clock he came out into an open place opposite the village, and saw the ferry boat lying in the shadow of the trees and the high bank. Everything was quiet under the blinking stars. He crept down the bank, watching with all his eyes, slipped into the water, swam three or four strokes and climbed into the skiff that did "yawl" duty at the boat's stern. He laid himself down under the thwarts and waited, panting.

Presently the cracked bell tapped and a voice gave the order to "cast off." A minute or two later the skiff's head was standing high up, against the boat's swell, and the voyage was begun. Tom felt happy in his success, for he knew it was the boat's last trip for the night. At the end of a long twelve or fifteen minutes the wheels stopped, and Tom slipped overboard and swam ashore in the dusk, landing fifty yards down stream, out of danger of possible stragglers.

He flew along unfrequented alleys, and shortly found himself at his aunt's back fence. He climbed over, approached the "ell" and looked in at the sitting-room window, for a light was burning there. There sat Aunt Polly, Sid, Mary, and Joe Harper's mother, grouped together, talking. They were by the bed, and the bed was between them and the door. Tom went to the door and began to softly lift the latch; then he pressed gently and the door yielded a crack; he continued pushing cautiously, and quaking every time it creaked, till he judged he might squeeze through on his knees; and so he put his head through and began, warily.

"What makes the candle blow so?" said Aunt Polly. Tom hurried up. "Why that door's open, I believe. Why of course it is. No end of strange things now. Go 'long and shut it, Sid."

Tom disappeared under the bed just in time. He lay and "breathed" himself for a time, and then crept to where he could almost touch his aunt's foot.

"But as I was saying," said aunt Polly, "he warn't *bad*, so to say—only misch*ee*vous. Only just giddy, and harum-scarum, you know. He warn't any more responsible than a colt. *He* never meant any harm, and he was the best-hearted boy that ever was"—and she began to cry.

"It was just so with my Joe—always full of his devilment, and up to every kind of mischief, but he was just as unselfish and kind as he could be—and laws bless me, to think I went and whipped him for taking that cream, never once recollecting that I throwed it out myself because it was sour, and I never to see him again in this world, never, never, never, poor abused boy!" And Mrs. Harper sobbed as if her heart would break.

"I hope Tom's better off where he is," said Sid, "but if he'd been better in some ways—"

"*Sid!*" Tom felt the glare of the old lady's eye, though he could not see it. "Not a word against my Tom, now that he's gone! God'll take care of *him*—never you trouble *your*self, sir! Oh, Mrs. Harper, I don't know how to give him up, I don't know how to give him up! He was such a comfort to me, although he tormented my old heart out of me, 'most."

"The Lord giveth and the Lord hath taken away. Blessed be the name of the Lord! But it's *so* hard—Oh, it's so hard! Only last Saturday my Joe busted a fire-cracker right under my nose and I knocked him sprawling. Little did I know then, how soon—O, if it was to do over again I'd hug him and bless him for it."

"Yes, yes, yes, I know just how you feel, Mrs. Harper, I know just exactly how you feel. No longer ago than yesterday noon, my Tom took and filled the cat full of Pain-Killer, and

I did think the cretur would tear the house down. And God forgive me, I cracked Tom's head with my thimble, poor boy, poor dead boy. But he's out of all his troubles now. And the last words I ever heard him say was to reproach—"

But this memory was too much for the old lady, and she broke entirely down. Tom was snuffling, now, himself—and more in pity of himself than anybody else. He could hear Mary crying, and putting in a kindly word for him from time to time. He began to have a nobler opinion of himself than ever before. Still he was sufficiently touched by his aunt's grief to long to rush out from under the bed and overwhelm her with joy—and the theatrical gorgeousness of the thing appealed strongly to his nature, too, but he resisted and lay still.

He went on listening, and gathered, by odds and ends that it was conjectured at first that the boys had got drowned while taking a swim; then the small raft had been missed; next, certain boys said the missing lads had promised that the village should "hear something" soon; the wise-heads had "put this and that together" and decided that the lads had gone off on that raft and would turn up at the next town below, presently; but toward noon the raft had been found, lodged against the Missouri shore some five or six miles be-low the village,—and then hope perished; they must be drowned, else hunger would have driven them home by nightfall if not sooner. It was believed that the search for the bodies had been a fruitless effort merely because the drown-ing must have occurred in mid-channel, since the boys, being good swimmers, would otherwise have escaped to shore. This was Wednesday night. If the bodies continued missing until Sunday, all hope would be given over, and the funerals would be preached on that morning. Tom shuddered.

Mrs. Harper gave a sobbing good-night and turned to go. Then with a mutual impulse the two bereaved women flung themselves into each other's arms and had a good, consoling cry, and then parted. Aunt Polly was tender far beyond her wont, in her good-night to Sid and Mary. Sid snuffled a bit and Mary went off crying with all her heart.

Aunt Polly knelt down and prayed for Tom so touchingly,

so appealingly, and with such measureless love in her words and her old trembling voice, that he was weltering in tears again, long before she was through.

He had to keep still long after she went to bed, for she kept making broken-hearted ejaculations from time to time, tossing unrestfully, and turning over. But at last she was still, only moaning a little in her sleep. Now the boy stole out, rose gradually by the bedside, shaded the candle-light with his hand, and stood regarding her. His heart was full of pity for her. He took out his sycamore scroll and placed it by the candle. But something occurred to him, and he lingered, considering. His face lighted with a happy solution of his thought; he put the bark hastily in his pocket. Then he bent over and kissed the faded lips, and straightway made his stealthy exit, latching the door behind him.

He threaded his way back to the ferry landing, found nobody at large there, and walked boldly on board the boat, for he knew she was tenantless except that there was a watchman, who always turned in and slept like a graven image. He untied the skiff at the stern, slipped into it, and was soon rowing cautiously up stream. When he had pulled a mile above the village, he started quartering across and bent himself stoutly to his work. He hit the landing on the other side neatly, for this was a familiar bit of work to him. He was moved to capture the skiff, arguing that it might be considered a ship and therefore legitimate prey for a pirate, but he knew a thorough search would be made for it and that might end in revelations. So he stepped ashore and entered the wood.

He sat down and took a long rest, torturing himself meantime to keep awake, and then started wearily down the homestretch. The night was far spent. It was broad daylight before he found himself fairly abreast the island bar. He rested again until the sun was well up and gilding the great river with its splendor, and then he plunged into the stream. A little later he paused, dripping, upon the threshold of the camp, and heard Joe say:

"No, Tom's true-blue, Huck, and he'll come back. He won't desert. He knows that would be a disgrace to a pirate, and Tom's too proud for that sort of thing. He's up to something or other. Now I wonder what?"

"Well, the things is ours, anyway, ain't they?"

"Pretty near, but not yet, Huck. The writing says they are if he ain't back here to breakfast."

"Which he is!" exclaimed Tom, with fine dramatic effect, stepping grandly into camp.

A sumptuous breakfast of bacon and fish was shortly provided, and as the boys set to work upon it, Tom recounted (and adorned) his adventures. They were a vain and boastful company of heroes when the tale was done. Then Tom hid himself away in a shady nook to sleep till noon, and the other pirates got ready to fish and explore.

XVI

After dinner all the gang turned out to hunt for turtle eggs on the bar. They went about poking sticks into the sand, and when they found a soft place they went down on their knees and dug with their hands. Sometimes they would take fifty or sixty eggs out of one hole. They were perfectly round white things a trifle smaller than an English walnut. They had a famous fried-egg feast that night, and another on Friday morning.

After breakfast they went whooping and prancing out on the bar, and chased each other round and round, shedding clothes as they went, until they were naked, and then continued the frolic far away up the shoal water of the bar, against the stiff current, which latter tripped their legs from under them from time to time and greatly increased the fun. And now and then they stooped in a group and splashed water in each other's faces with their palms, gradually approaching each other, with averted faces to avoid the strangling sprays, and finally gripping and struggling till the best man ducked his neighbor, and then they all went under in a tangle of white legs and arms and came up blowing, sputtering, laughing and gasping for breath at one and the same time.

When they were well exhausted, they would run out and sprawl on the dry, hot sand, and lie there and cover themselves up with it, and by and by break for the water again and go through the original performance once more. Finally it occurred to them that their naked skin represented flesh-colored "tights" very fairly; so they drew a ring in the sand and had a circus—with three clowns in it, for none would yield this proudest post to his neighbor.

Next they got their marbles and played "knucks" and "ring-taw" and "keeps" till that amusement grew stale. Then Joe and Huck had another swim, but Tom would not venture, because he found that in kicking off his trousers he had kicked his string of rattlesnake rattles off his ankle, and he wondered how he had escaped cramp so long without the protection of this mysterious charm. He did not venture again until he had found it, and by that time the other boys were tired and ready to rest. They gradually wandered apart, dropped into the "dumps," and fell to gazing longingly across the wide river to where the village lay drowsing in the sun. Tom found himself writing "BECKY" in the sand with his big toe; he scratched it out, and was angry with himself for his weakness. But he wrote it again, nevertheless; he could not help it. He erased it once more and then took himself out of temptation by driving the other boys together and joining them.

But Joe's spirits had gone down almost beyond resurrection. He was so homesick that he could hardly endure the misery of it. The tears lay very near the surface. Huck was melancholy, too. Tom was down-hearted, but tried hard not to show it. He had a secret which he was not ready to tell, yet, but if this mutinous depression was not broken up soon, he would have to bring it out. He said, with a great show of cheerfulness:

"I bet there's been pirates on this island before, boys. We'll explore it again. They've hid treasures here somewhere. How'd you feel to light on a rotten chest full of gold and silver—hey?"

But it roused only a faint enthusiasm, which faded out, with no reply. Tom tried one or two other seductions; but they failed, too. It was discouraging work. Joe sat poking up the sand with a stick and looking very gloomy. Finally he said:

"O, boys, let's give it up. I want to go home. It's so lonesome."

"Oh, no, Joe, you'll feel better by and by," said Tom. "Just think of the fishing that's here."

"I don't care for fishing. I want to go home."

"But Joe, there ain't such another swimming place anywhere."

"Swimming's no good. I don't seem to care for it, somehow, when there ain't anybody to say I shan't go in. I mean to go home."

"O, shucks! Baby! You want to see your mother, I reckon."

"Yes, I *do* want to see my mother—and you would too, if

you had one. I ain't any more baby than you are." And Joe snuffled a little.

"Well, we'll let the cry-baby go home to his mother, *won't* we Huck? Poor thing—does it want to see its mother? And so it shall. You like it here, *don't* you Huck? We'll stay, won't we?"

Huck said "Y-e-s"—without any heart in it.

"I'll never speak to you again as long as I live," said Joe, rising. "There, now!" And he moved moodily away and began to dress himself.

"Who cares!" said Tom. "Nobody wants you to. Go 'long home and get laughed at. O, you're a nice pirate. Huck and me ain't cry-babies. We'll stay, won't we Huck? Let him go if he wants to. I reckon we can get along without him, per'aps."

But Tom was uneasy, nevertheless, and was alarmed to see Joe go sullenly on with his dressing. And then it was discomforting to see Huck eyeing Joe's preparations so wistfully, and keeping up such an ominous silence. Presently, without a parting word, Joe began to wade off toward the Illinois shore. Tom's heart began to sink. He glanced at Huck. Huck could not bear the look, and dropped his eyes. Then he said:

"I want to go, too, Tom. It was getting so lonesome anyway, and now it'll be worse. Let's us go too, Tom."

"I won't! You can all go, if you want to. I mean to stay."

"Tom, I better go."

"Well go 'long—who's hendering you."

Huck began to pick up his scattered clothes. He said:

"Tom, I wisht you'd come too. Now you think it over. We'll wait for you when we get to shore."

"Well you'll wait a blame long time, that's all."

Huck started sorrowfully away, and Tom stood looking after him, with a strong desire tugging at his heart to yield his pride and go along too. He hoped the boys would stop, but they still waded slowly on. It suddenly dawned on Tom that it was become very lonely and still. He made one final struggle with his pride, and then darted after his comrades, yelling:

"Wait! Wait! I want to tell you something!"

They presently stopped and turned around. When he got to where they were, he began unfolding his secret, and they listened moodily till at last they saw the "point" he was driving at, and then they set up a war-whoop of applause and said it was "splendid!" and said if he had told them that at first, they wouldn't have started away. He made a plausible excuse; but his real reason had been the fear that not even the secret would keep them with him any very great length of time, and so he had meant to hold it in reserve as a last seduction.

The lads came gaily back and went at their sports again with a will, chattering all the time about Tom's stupendous plan and admiring the genius of it. After a dainty egg and fish dinner, Tom said he wanted to learn to smoke, now. Joe caught at the idea and said he would like to try, too. So Huck made pipes and filled them. These novices had never smoked anything before but cigars made of grape-vine, and they "bit" the tongue and were not considered manly, anyway.

Now they stretched themselves out on their elbows and began to puff, charily, and with slender confidence. The smoke had an unpleasant taste, and they gagged a little, but Tom said:

"Why it's just as easy! If I'd a knowed *this* was all, I'd a learnt long ago."

"So would I," said Joe. "It's just nothing."

"Why many a time I've looked at people smoking, and thought well I wish I could do that; but I never thought I could," said Tom.

"That's just the way with me, hain't it Huck? You've heard me talk just that away—haven't you Huck? I'll leave it to Huck if I haven't."

"Yes—heaps of times," said Huck.

"Well I have too," said Tom; "O, hundreds of times. Once down there by the slaughter-house. Don't you remember, Huck? Bob Tanner was there, and Johnny Miller, and Jeff Thatcher, when I said it. Don't you remember Huck, 'bout me saying that?"

"Yes, that's so," said Huck. "That was the day after I lost a white alley. No, 'twas the day before."

"There—I told you so," said Tom. "Huck recollects it."

"I bleeve I could smoke this pipe all day," said Joe. "*I* don't feel sick."

"Neither do I," said Tom. "*I* could smoke it all day. But I bet you Jeff Thatcher couldn't."

"Jeff Thatcher! Why he'd keel over just with two draws. Just let him try it once. *He'd* see!"

"I bet he would. And Johnny Miller—I wish I could see Johnny Miller tackle it once."

"O, don't *I*!" said Joe. "Why I bet you Johnny Miller couldn't any more do this than nothing. Just one little snifter would fetch *him*."

"Deed it would, Joe. Say—I wish the boys could see us now."

"So do I."

"Say,—boys, don't say anything about it, and some time when they're around, I'll come up to you and say 'Joe, got a pipe? I want a smoke.' And you'll say, kind of careless like, as if it warn't anything, you'll say, 'Yes, I got my *old* pipe, and another one, but my tobacker ain't very good.' And I'll say, 'Oh, that's all right, if it's *strong* enough.' And then you'll out with the pipes, and we'll light up just as ca'm, and then just see 'em look!"

"By jings that'll be gay, Tom! I wish it was *now*!"

"So do I! And when we tell 'em we learned when we was off pirating, won't they wish they'd been along?"

"O, I reckon not! I'll just *bet* they will!"

So the talk ran on. But presently it began to flag a trifle, and grow disjointed. The silences widened; the expectoration marvelously increased. Every pore inside the boys' cheeks became a spouting fountain; they could scarcely bail out the cellars under their tongues fast enough to prevent an inundation; little overflowings down their throats occurred in spite of all they could do, and sudden retchings followed every time. Both boys were looking very pale and miserable, now. Joe's pipe dropped from his nerveless fingers. Tom's followed. Both fountains were going furiously and both pumps bailing with might and main. Joe said feebly:

"I've lost my knife. I reckon I better go and find it."

Tom said, with quivering lip and halting utterance:

"I'll help you. You go over that way and I'll hunt around by the spring. No, you needn't come, Huck—we can find it."

So Huck sat down again, and waited an hour. Then he

found it lonesome, and went to find his comrades. They were wide apart in the woods, both very pale, both fast asleep. But something informed him that if they had had any trouble they had got rid of it.

They were not talkative at supper that night. They had a humble look; and when Huck prepared his pipe after the meal and was going to prepare theirs, they said no, they were not feeling very well—something they ate at dinner had disagreed with them.

About midnight Joe awoke, and called the boys. There was a brooding oppressiveness in the air that seemed to bode something. The boys huddled themselves together and sought the friendly companionship of the fire, though the dull dead heat of the breathless atmosphere was stifling. They sat still, intent and waiting. The solemn hush continued. Beyond the light of the fire everything was swallowed up in the blackness of darkness. Presently there came a quivering glow that vaguely revealed the foliage for a moment and then vanished. By and by another came, a little stronger. Then another. Then a faint moan came sighing through the branches of the forest and the boys felt a fleeting breath upon their cheeks, and shuddered with the fancy that the Spirit of the Night had gone by. There was a pause. Now a weird flash turned night into day and showed every little grass-blade, separate and distinct, that grew about their feet. And it showed three white, startled faces, too. A deep peal of thunder went rolling and tumbling down the heavens and lost itself in sullen rumblings in the distance. A sweep of chilly air passed by, rustling all the leaves and snowing the flaky ashes broadcast about the fire. Another fierce glare lit up the forest and an instant crash followed that seemed to rend the tree-tops right over the boys' heads. They clung together in terror, in the thick gloom that followed. A few big rain-drops fell pattering upon the leaves.

"Quick! boys, go for the tent!" exclaimed Tom.

They sprang away, stumbling over roots and among vines in the dark, no two plunging in the same direction. A furious blast roared through the trees, making everything sing as it went. One blinding flash after another came, and peal on peal of deafening thunder. And now a drenching rain poured down and the rising hurricane drove it in sheets along the ground. The boys cried out to each other, but the roaring wind and the booming thunder-blasts drowned their voices utterly. However, one by one they straggled in at last and took shelter under the tent, cold, scared, and streaming with water; but to have company in misery seemed something to be grateful for. They could not talk, the old sail flapped so furiously, even if the other noises would have allowed them. The tempest rose higher and higher, and presently the sail tore loose from its fastenings and went winging away on the blast. The boys seized each others' hands and fled, with many tumblings and bruises, to the shelter of a great oak that stood upon the river bank. Now the battle was at its highest. Under the ceaseless conflagration of lightnings that flamed in the skies, everything below stood out in clean-cut and shadowless distinctness: the bending trees, the billowy river, white with foam, the driving spray of spume-flakes, the dim outlines of the high bluffs on the other side, glimpsed through the drifting cloud-rack and the slanting veil of rain. Every little while some giant tree yielded the fight and fell crashing through the younger growth; and the unflagging thunder-peals came now in ear-splitting explosive bursts, keen and sharp, and unspeakably appalling. The storm culminated in one matchless effort that seemed likely to tear the island to pieces, burn it up, drown it to the tree tops, blow it away, and deafen every creature in it, all at one and the same moment. It was a wild night for homeless young heads to be out in.

But at last the battle was done, and the forces retired with weaker and weaker threatenings and grumblings, and peace resumed her sway. The boys went back to camp, a good deal awed; but they found there was still something to be thankful for, because the great sycamore, the shelter of their beds, was a ruin, now, blasted by the lightnings, and they were not under it when the catastrophe happened.

Everything in camp was drenched, the camp-fire as well; for they were but heedless lads, like their generation, and had made no provision against rain. Here was matter for dismay, for they were soaked through and chilled. They were eloquent in their distress; but they presently discovered that the fire had eaten so far up under the great log it had been built against, (where it curved upward and separated itself from the ground,) that a hand-breadth or so of it had escaped wetting; so they patiently wrought until, with shreds and bark gathered from the under sides of sheltered logs, they coaxed the fire to burn again. Then they piled on great dead boughs till they had a roaring furnace and were glad-hearted once more. They dried their boiled ham and had a feast, and after that they sat by the fire and expanded and glorified their midnight adventure until morning, for there was not a dry spot to sleep on, anywhere around.

As the sun began to steal in upon the boys, drowsiness came over them and they went out on the sand-bar and lay down to sleep. They got scorched out, by and by, and drearily set about getting breakfast. After the meal they felt rusty, and stiff-jointed, and a little homesick once more. Tom saw the signs, and fell to cheering up the pirates as well as he could. But they cared nothing for marbles, or circus, or swimming, or anything. He reminded them of the imposing secret, and raised a ray of cheer. While it lasted, he got them interested in a new device. This was to knock off being pirates, for a while, and be Indians for a change. They were attracted by this idea; so it was not long before they were stripped, and striped from head to heel with black mud, like so many zebras,—all of them chiefs, of course—and then they went tearing through the woods to attack an English settlement.

By and by they separated into three hostile tribes, and darted upon each other from ambush with dreadful war-whoops, and killed and scalped each other by thousands. It was a gory day. Consequently it was an extremely satisfactory one.

They assembled in camp toward supper time, hungry and happy; but now a difficulty arose—hostile Indians could not break the bread of hospitality together without first making peace, and this was a simple impossibility without smoking a pipe of peace. There was no other process that ever they had heard of. Two of the savages almost wished they had remained pirates. However, there was no other way: so with such show of cheerfulness as they could muster they called for the pipe and took their whiff as it passed, in due form.

And behold they were glad they had gone into savagery,

for they had gained something; they found that they could now smoke a little without having to go and hunt for a lost knife; they did not get sick enough to be seriously uncomfortable. They were not likely to fool away this high promise for lack of effort. No, they practiced cautiously, after supper, with right fair success, and so they spent a jubilant evening. They were prouder and happier in their new acquirement than they would have been in the scalping and skinning of the Six Nations. We will leave them to smoke and chatter and brag, since we have no further use for them at present.

XVII

B UT THERE WAS no hilarity in the little town that same tranquil Saturday afternoon. The Harpers, and Aunt Polly's family, were being put into mourning, with great grief and many tears. An unusual quiet possessed the village, although it was ordinarily quiet enough, in all conscience. The villagers conducted their concerns with an absent air, and talked little; but they sighed often. The Saturday holiday seemed a burden to the children. They had no heart in their sports, and gradually gave them up.

In the afternoon Becky Thatcher found herself moping about the deserted school-house yard, and feeling very melancholy. But she found nothing there to comfort her. She soliloquised:

"Oh, if I only had his brass andiron-knob again! But I haven't got anything now to remember him by." And she choked back a little sob.

Presently she stopped, and said to herself:

"It was right here. O, if it was to do over again, I wouldn't say that—I wouldn't say it for the whole world. But he's gone now; I'll never never never see him any more."

This thought broke her down and she wandered away, with the tears rolling down her cheeks. Then quite a group of boys and girls,—playmates of Tom's and Joe's—came by, and stood looking over the paling fence and talking in reverent tones of how Tom did so-and-so, the last time they saw him, and how Joe said this and that small trifle (pregnant with awful prophecy, as they could easily see now!)—and each speaker pointed out the exact spot where the lost lads stood at the time, and then added something like "and I was a-standing just so—just as I am now, and as if you was him—I was as close as that—and he smiled, just this way—and then something seemed to go all over me, like,—awful, you know—and I never thought what it meant, of course, but I can see now!"

Then there was a dispute about who saw the dead boys last in life, and many claimed that dismal distinction, and offered evidences, more or less tampered with by the witness; and when it was ultimately decided who *did* see the departed last, and exchanged the last words with them, the lucky parties took upon themselves a sort of sacred importance, and were gaped at and envied by all the rest. One poor chap, who had no other grandeur to offer, said with tolerably manifest pride in the remembrance:

"Well, Tom Sawyer he licked me once."

But that bid for glory was a failure. Most of the boys could say that, and so that cheapened the distinction too much. The group loitered away, still recalling memories of the lost heroes, in awed voices.

When the Sunday-school hour was finished, the next morning, the bell began to toll, instead of ringing in the usual way. It was a very still Sabbath, and the mournful sound seemed in keeping with the musing hush that lay upon nature. The villagers began to gather, loitering a moment in the vestibule to converse in whispers about the sad event. But there was no whispering in the house; only the funereal rustling of dresses as the women gathered to their seats, disturbed the silence there. None could remember when the little church had been so full before. There was finally a waiting pause, an expectant dumbness, and then Aunt Polly entered, followed by Sid and Mary, and they by the Harper family, all in deep black, and the whole congregation, the old minister as well, rose reverently and stood, until the mourners were seated in the front pew. There was another communing silence, broken at intervals by muffled sobs, and then the minister spread his hands abroad and prayed. A moving hymn was sung, and the text followed: "I am the resurrection and the life."

As the service proceeded, the clergyman drew such pictures of the graces, the winning ways and the rare promise of the lost lads, that every soul there, thinking he recognized these pictures, felt a pang in remembering that he had persistently blinded himself to them, always before, and had as persistently seen only faults and flaws in the poor boys. The minister related many a touching incident in the lives of the departed, too, which illustrated their sweet, generous natures, and the people could easily see, now, how noble and beautiful those episodes were, and remembered with grief that at the time they occurred they had seemed rank rascalities, well deserving of the cowhide. The congregation became more and more moved, as the pathetic tale went on, till at last the whole company broke down and joined the weeping mourners in a chorus of anguished sobs, the preacher himself giving way to his feelings, and crying in the pulpit.

There was a rustle in the gallery, which nobody noticed; a moment later the church door creaked; the minister raised his streaming eyes above his handkerchief, and stood transfixed! First one and then another pair of eyes followed the minister's, and then almost with one impulse the congregation rose and stared while the three dead boys came marching up the aisle, Tom in the lead, Joe next, and Huck, a ruin of drooping rags, sneaking sheepishly in the rear! They had been hid in the unused gallery listening to their own funeral sermon!

Aunt Polly, Mary and the Harpers threw themselves upon their restored ones, smothered them with kisses and poured out thanksgivings, while poor Huck stood abashed and uncomfortable, not knowing exactly what to do or where to hide from so many unwelcoming eyes. He wavered, and started to slink away, but Tom seized him and said:

"Aunt Polly, it ain't fair. Somebody's got to be glad to see Huck."

"And so they shall. *I*'m glad to see him, poor motherless thing!" And the loving attentions Aunt Polly lavished upon him were the one thing capable of making him more uncomfortable than he was before.

Suddenly the minister shouted at the top of his voice:

"Praise God from whom all blessings flow—SING!—and put your hearts in it!"

And they did. Old Hundred swelled up with a triumphant burst, and while it shook the rafters Tom Sawyer the Pirate looked around upon the envying juveniles about him and confessed in his heart that this was the proudest moment of his life.

As the "sold" congregation trooped out they said they

would almost be willing to be made ridiculous again to hear Old Hundred sung like that once more.

Tom got more cuffs and kisses that day—according to Aunt Polly's varying moods—than he had earned before in a year; and he hardly knew which expressed the most gratefulness to God and affection for himself.

XVIII

THAT WAS TOM'S great secret—the scheme to return home with his brother pirates and attend their own funerals. They had paddled over to the Missouri shore on a log, at dusk on Saturday, landing five or six miles below the village; they had slept in the woods at the edge of town till nearly daylight, and had then crept through back lanes and alleys and finished their sleep in the gallery of the church among a chaos of invalided benches.

At breakfast, Monday morning, Aunt Polly and Mary were very loving to Tom, and very attentive to his wants. There was an unusual amount of talk. In the course of it Aunt Polly said:

"Well, I don't say it wasn't a fine joke, Tom, to keep everybody suffering 'most a week so you boys had a good time, but it is a pity you could be so hard-hearted as to let *me* suffer so. If you could come over on a log to go to your funeral, you could have come over and give me a hint some way that you warn't *dead*, but only run off."

"Yes, you could have done that, Tom," said Mary; "and I believe you would if you had thought of it."

"Would you Tom?" said Aunt Polly, her face lighting wistfully. "Say, now, would you, if you'd thought of it?"

"I—well I don't know. 'Twould a spoiled everything."

"Tom, I hoped you loved me that much," said Aunt Polly, with a grieved tone that discomforted the boy. "It would been something if you'd cared enough to *think* of it, even if you didn't *do* it."

"Now auntie, that ain't any harm," pleaded Mary; "it's only Tom's giddy way—he is always in such a rush that he never thinks of anything."

"More's the pity. Sid would have thought. And Sid would have come and *done* it, too. Tom, you'll look back, some day, when it's too late, and wish you'd cared a little more for me when it would have cost you so little."

"Now auntie, you know I do care for you," said Tom.

"I'd know it better if you acted more like it."

"I wish now I'd thought," said Tom, with a repentant tone; "but I dreamed about you anyway. That's something, ain't it?"

"It ain't much—a cat does that much—but it's better than nothing. What did you dream?"

"Why Wednesday night I dreamt that you was sitting over there by the bed, and Sid was sitting by the wood-box, and Mary next to him."

"Well, so we did. So we always do. I'm glad your dreams could take even that much trouble about us."

"And I dreamt that Joe Harper's mother was here."

"Why, she *was* here! Did you dream any more?"

"O, lots. But it's so dim, now."

"Well, *try* to recollect—can't you?"

"Somehow it seems to me that the wind—the wind blowed the—the—"

"Try harder, Tom! The wind did blow something. Come!"

Tom pressed his fingers on his forehead an anxious minute, and then said:

"I've got it now! I've got it now! It blowed the candle!"

"Mercy on us! Go on, Tom—go on!"

"And it seems to me that you said, 'Why I believe that that door—' "

"Go *on*, Tom!"

"Just let me study a moment—just a moment. Oh, yes— you said you believed the door was open."

"As I'm a-sitting here, I did! Didn't I, Mary? Go on!"

"And then—and then—well I won't be certain, but it seems like as if you made Sid go and—and—"

"Well? Well? What did I make him do, Tom? What did I make him do?"

"You made him—you—O, you made him shut it."

"Well for the land's sake! I never heard the beat of that in all my days! Don't tell *me* there ain't anything in dreams, any more. Sereny Harper shall know of this before I'm an hour older. I'd like to see her get around *this* with her rubbage 'bout superstition. Go on, Tom!"

"Oh, it's all getting just as bright as day, now. Next you said I warn't *bad*, only mischeevous and harum-scarum, and not any more responsible than—than—I think it was a colt, or something."

"And so it was! Well, goodness gracious! Go on, Tom!"

"And then you began to cry."

"So I did. So I did. Not the first time, neither. And then—"

"Then Mrs. Harper she began to cry, and said Joe was just the same and she wished she hadn't whipped him for taking cream when she'd throwed it out her own self—"

"Tom! The sperrit was upon you! You was a-prophecying—that's what you was doing! Land alive, go on, Tom!"

"Then Sid he said—he said—"

"I don't think I said anything," said Sid.

"Yes you did, Sid," said Mary.

"Shut your heads and let Tom go on! What did he say, Tom?"

"He said—I *think* he said he hoped I was better off where I was gone to, but if I'd been better sometimes—"

"*There*, d'you hear that! It was his very words!"

"And you shut him up sharp."

"I lay I did! There must a been an angel there. There *was* an angel there, somewheres!"

"And Mrs. Harper told about Joe scaring her with a firecracker, and you told about Peter and the Pain-Killer—"

"Just as true as I live!"

"And then there was a whole lot of talk 'bout dragging the river for us, and 'bout having the funeral Sunday, and then you and old Miss Harper hugged and cried, and she went."

"It happened just so! It happened just so, as sure as I'm a-sitting in these very tracks. Tom you couldn't told it more like, if you'd a seen it! And *then* what? Go on, Tom?"

"Then I thought you prayed for me—and I could see you and hear every word you said. And you went to bed, and I was so sorry that I took and wrote on a piece of sycamore bark, *'We ain't dead— we are only off being pirates,'* and put it on the table by the candle; and then you looked so good, laying there asleep, that I thought I went and leaned over and kissed you on the lips."

"Did you, Tom, *did* you! I just forgive you everything for that!" And she seized the boy in a crushing embrace that made him feel like the guiltiest of villains.

"It was very kind, even though it was only a—dream," Sid soliloquised just audibly.

"Shut up, Sid! A body does just the same in a dream as he'd do if he was awake. Here's a big Milum apple I've been saving for you Tom, if you was ever found again—now go 'long to school. I'm thankful to the good God and Father of us all I've got you back, that's long-suffering and merciful to them that believe on Him and keep His word, though goodness knows I'm unworthy of it, but if only the worthy ones got His blessings and had His hand to help them over the rough places, there's few enough would smile here or ever enter into His rest when the long night comes. Go 'long Sid, Mary, Tom—take yourselves off—you've hendered me long enough."

The children left for school, and the old lady to call on Mrs. Harper and vanquish her realism with Tom's marvelous dream. Sid had better judgment than to utter the thought that was in his mind as he left the house. It was this: "Pretty thin—as long a dream as that, without any mistakes in it!"

What a hero Tom was become, now! He did not go skipping and prancing, but moved with a dignified swagger as became a pirate who felt that the public eye was on him. And indeed it was; he tried not to seem to see the looks or hear the remarks as he passed along, but they were food and drink to him. Smaller boys than himself flocked at his heels, as proud to be seen with him and tolerated by him as if he had been the drummer at the head of a procession or the elephant leading a menagerie into town. Boys of his own size pretended not to know he had been away at all; but they were consuming with envy, nevertheless. They would have given anything to have that swarthy sun-tanned skin of his, and his glittering notoriety; and Tom would not have parted with either for a circus.

At school the children made so much of him and of Joe, and delivered such eloquent admiration from their eyes, that the two heroes were not long in becoming insufferably "stuck-up." They began to tell their adventures to hungry listeners—but they only began; it was not a thing likely to have an end, with imaginations like theirs to furnish material. And finally, when they got out their pipes and went serenely puffing around, the very summit of glory was reached.

Tom decided that he could be independent of Becky

Thatcher now. Glory was sufficient. He would live for glory. Now that he was distinguished, maybe she would be wanting to "make up." Well, let her—she should see that he could be as indifferent as some other people. Presently she arrived. Tom pretended not to see her. He moved away and joined a group of boys and girls and began to talk. Soon he observed that she was tripping gayly back and forth with flushed face and dancing eyes, pretending to be busy chasing school-mates, and screaming with laughter when she made a capture; but he noticed that she always made her captures in his vicin-ity, and that she seemed to cast a conscious eye in his direc-tion at such times, too. It gratified all the vicious vanity that was in him; and so, instead of winning him it only "set him up" the more and made him the more diligent to avoid be-traying that he knew she was about. Presently she gave over skylarking, and moved irresolutely about, sighing once or twice and glancing furtively and wistfully toward Tom. Then she observed that now Tom was talking more particularly to Amy Lawrence than to any one else. She felt a sharp pang and grew disturbed and uneasy at once. She tried to go away, but her feet were treacherous, and carried her to the group instead. She said to a girl almost at Tom's elbow—with sham vivacity:

"Why Mary Austin! you bad girl, why didn't you come to Sunday-school?"

"I did come—didn't you see me?"

"Why no! Did you? Where did you sit?"

"I was in Miss Peters's class, where I always go. I saw *you*."

"Did you? Why it's funny I didn't see you. I wanted to tell you about the pic-nic."

"O, that's jolly. Who's going to give it?"

"My ma's going to let me have one."

"O, goody; I hope she'll let *me* come."

"Well she will. The pic-nic's for me. She'll let anybody come that I want, and I want you."

"That's ever so nice. When is it going to be?"

"By and by. Maybe about vacation."

"O, won't it be fun! You going to have all the girls and boys?"

"Yes, every one that's friends to me—or wants to be;" and

she glanced ever so furtively at Tom, but he talked right along
to Amy Lawrence about the terrible storm on the island, and
how the lightning tore the great sycamore tree "all to flin-
ders" while he was "standing within three feet of it."

"O, may I come?" said Gracie Miller.

"Yes."

"And me?" said Sally Rogers.

"Yes."

"And me, too?" said Susy Harper. "And Joe?"

"Yes."

And so on, with clapping of joyful hands till all the group
had begged for invitations but Tom and Amy. Then Tom
turned coolly away, still talking, and took Amy with him.
Becky's lip trembled and the tears came to her eyes; she hid
these signs with a forced gayety and went on chattering, but
the life had gone out of the pic-nic, now, and out of everything else; she got away as soon as she could and hid herself
and had what her sex call "a good cry." Then she sat moody,
with wounded pride till the bell rang. She roused up, now,
with a vindictive cast in her eye, and gave her plaited tails a
shake and said she knew what *she*'d do.

At recess Tom continued his flirtation with Amy with jubilant self-satisfaction. And he kept drifting about to find
Becky and lacerate her with the performance. At last he spied
her, but there was a sudden falling of his mercury. She was
sitting cosily on a little bench behind the school-house looking at a picture book with Alfred Temple—and so absorbed
were they, and their heads so close together over the book
that they did not seem to be conscious of anything in the
world beside. Jealousy ran red hot through Tom's veins. He
began to hate himself for throwing away the chance Becky
had offered for a reconciliation. He called himself a fool, and
all the hard names he could think of. He wanted to cry with
vexation. Amy chatted happily along, as they walked, for her
heart was singing, but Tom's tongue had lost its function.
He did not hear what Amy was saying, and whenever she
paused expectantly he could only stammer an awkward assent,
which was as often misplaced as otherwise. He kept drifting
to the rear of the school-house, again and again, to sear his
eye-balls with the hateful spectacle there. He could not help

it. And it maddened him to see, as he thought he saw, that Becky Thatcher never once suspected that he was even in the land of the living. But she did see, nevertheless; and she knew she was winning her fight, too, and was glad to see him suffer as she had suffered.

Amy's happy prattle became intolerable. Tom hinted at things he had to attend to; things that must be done; and time was fleeting. But in vain—the girl chirped on. Tom thought, "O hang her, ain't I ever going to get rid of her?" At last he *must* be attending to those things; she said artlessly that she would be "around" when school let out. And he hastened away, hating her for it.

"Any other boy!" Tom thought, grating his teeth. "Any boy in the whole town but that Saint Louis smarty that thinks he dresses so fine and is aristocracy! O, all right, I licked you the first day you ever saw this town, mister, and I'll lick you again! You just wait till I catch you out! I'll just take and—"

And he went through the motions of thrashing an imaginary boy—pummeling the air, and kicking and gouging. "Oh, you do, do you? You holler 'nough, do you? Now, then, let that learn you!" And so the imaginary flogging was finished to his satisfaction.

Tom fled home at noon. His conscience could not endure any more of Amy's grateful happiness, and his jealousy could bear no more of the other distress. Becky resumed her picture-inspections with Alfred, but as the minutes dragged along and no Tom came to suffer, her triumph began to cloud and she lost interest; gravity and absent-mindedness followed, and then melancholy; two or three times she pricked up her ear at a footstep, but it was a false hope; no Tom came. At last she grew entirely miserable and wished she hadn't carried it so far. When poor Alfred, seeing that he was losing her, he did not know how, and kept exclaiming: "O here's a jolly one! look at this!" she lost patience at last, and said, "Oh, don't bother me! I don't care for them!" and burst into tears, and got up and walked away.

Alfred dropped alongside and was going to try to comfort her, but she said:

"Go away and leave me alone, can't you! I hate you!"

So the boy halted, wondering what he could have done—

for she had said she would look at pictures all through the
nooning—and she walked on, crying. Then Alfred went musing into the deserted school-house. He was humiliated and
angry. He easily guessed his way to the truth—the girl had
simply made a convenience of him to vent her spite upon
Tom Sawyer. He was far from hating Tom the less when this
thought occurred to him. He wished there was some way to
get that boy into trouble without much risk to himself.
Tom's spelling book fell under his eye. Here was his opportunity. He gratefully opened to the lesson for the afternoon
and poured ink upon the page.

Becky, glancing in at a window behind him at the moment,
saw the act, and moved on, without discovering herself. She
started homeward, now, intending to find Tom and tell him;
Tom would be thankful and their troubles would be healed.
Before she was half way home, however, she had changed her
mind. The thought of Tom's treatment of her when she was
talking about her pic-nic came scorching back and filled her
with shame. She resolved to let him get whipped on the damaged spelling-book's account, and to hate him forever, into
the bargain.

XIX

Tom arrived at home in a dreary mood, and the first thing his aunt said to him showed him that he had brought his sorrows to an unpromising market:

"Tom, I've a notion to skin you alive!"

"Auntie, what have I done?"

"Well, you've done enough. Here I go over to Sereny Harper, like an old softy, expecting I'm going to make her believe all that rubbage about that dream, when lo and behold you she'd found out from Joe that you was over here and heard all the talk we had that night. Tom I don't know what is to become of a boy that will act like that. It makes me feel so bad to think you could let me go to Sereny Harper and make such a fool of myself and never say a word."

This was a new aspect of the thing. His smartness of the morning had seemed to Tom a good joke before, and very ingenious. It merely looked mean and shabby now. He hung his head and could not think of anything to say for a moment. Then he said:

"Auntie, I wish I hadn't done it—but I didn't think."

"O, child you never think. You never think of anything but your own selfishness. You could think to come all the way over here from Jackson's Island in the night to laugh at our troubles, and you could think to fool me with a lie about a dream; but you couldn't ever think to pity us and save us from sorrow."

"Auntie, I know now it was mean, but I didn't mean to be mean. I didn't, honest. And besides I didn't come over here to laugh at you that night."

"What did you come for, then?"

"It was to tell you not to be uneasy about us, because we hadn't got drowned."

"Tom, Tom, I would be the thankfullest soul in this world if I could believe you ever had as good a thought as that, but you know you never did—and I know it, Tom."

"Indeed and 'deed I did, auntie—I wish I may never stir if I didn't."

"O, Tom, don't lie—don't do it. It only makes things a hundred times worse."

"It ain't a lie, auntie, it's the truth. I wanted to keep you from grieving—that was all that made me come."

"I'd give the whole world to believe that—it would cover up a power of sins Tom. I'd 'most be glad you'd run off and acted so bad. But it ain't reasonable; because, why didn't you tell me, child?"

"Why, you see, auntie, when you got to talking about the funeral, I just got all full of the idea of our coming and hiding in the church, and I couldn't somehow bear to spoil it. So I just put the bark back in my pocket and kept mum."

"What bark?"

"The bark I had wrote on to tell you we'd gone pirating. I wish, now, you'd waked up when I kissed you—I do, honest."

The hard lines in his aunt's face relaxed and a sudden tenderness dawned in her eyes.

"*Did* you kiss me, Tom?"

"Why yes I did."

"Are you sure you did, Tom?"

"Why yes I did, auntie—certain sure."

"What did you kiss me for, Tom?"

"Because I loved you so, and you laid there moaning and I was so sorry."

The words sounded like truth. The old lady could not hide a tremor in her voice when she said:

"Kiss me again, Tom!—and be off with you to school, now, and don't bother me any more."

The moment he was gone, she ran to a closet and got out the ruin of a jacket which Tom had gone pirating in. Then she stopped, with it in her hand, and said to herself:

"No, I don't dare. Poor boy, I reckon he's lied about it—but it's a blessed, blessed lie, there's such comfort come from it. I hope the Lord—I *know* the Lord will forgive him, because it was such goodheartedness in him to tell it. But I don't want to find out it's a lie. I won't look."

She put the jacket away, and stood by musing a minute. Twice she put out her hand to take the garment again, and twice she refrained. Once more she ventured, and this time she fortified herself with the thought: "It's a good lie—it's a good lie—I won't let it grieve me." So she sought the jacket pocket. A moment later she was reading Tom's piece of bark through flowing tears and saying "I could forgive the boy, now, if he'd committed a million sins!"

XX

THERE WAS SOMETHING about aunt Polly's manner, when she kissed Tom, that swept away his low spirits and made him light-hearted and happy again. He started to school and had the luck of coming upon Becky Thatcher at the head of Meadow Lane. His mood always determined his manner. Without a moment's hesitation he ran to her and said:

"I acted mighty mean to-day, Becky, and I'm so sorry. I won't ever, ever do that way again, as long as ever I live—please make up, won't you?"

The girl stopped and looked him scornfully in the face:

"I'll thank you to keep yourself *to* yourself, Mr. Thomas Sawyer. I'll never speak to you again."

She tossed her head and passed on. Tom was so stunned that he had not even presence of mind enough to say "Who cares, Miss Smarty?" until the right time to say it had gone by. So he said nothing. But he was in a fine rage, nevertheless. He moped into the school-yard wishing she were a boy, and imagining how he would trounce her if she were. He presently encountered her and delivered a stinging remark as he passed. She hurled one in return, and the angry breach was complete. It seemed to Becky, in her hot resentment, that she could hardly wait for school to "take in," she was so impatient to see Tom flogged for the injured spelling-book. If she had had any lingering notion of exposing Alfred Temple, Tom's offensive fling had driven it entirely away.

Poor girl, she did not know how fast she was nearing trouble herself. The master, Mr. Dobbins, had reached middle age with an unsatisfied ambition. The darling of his desires was, to be a doctor, but poverty had decreed that he should be nothing higher than a village schoolmaster. Every day he took a mysterious book out of his desk and absorbed himself in it at times when no classes were reciting. He kept that book under lock and key. There was not an urchin in school but was perishing to have a glimpse of it, but the chance never came. Every boy and girl had a theory about the nature of that book; but no two theories were alike, and there was no way of getting at the facts in the case. Now, as Becky was passing by the desk, which stood near the door, she noticed that the key was in the lock! It was a precious moment. She glanced around; found herself alone, and the next instant she had the book in her hands. The title-page—Professor somebody's "Anatomy"—carried no information to her mind; so she began to turn the leaves. She came at once upon a handsomely engraved and colored frontispiece—a human figure, stark naked. At that moment a shadow fell on the page and Tom Sawyer stepped in at the door, and caught a glimpse of the picture. Becky snatched at the book to close it, and had the hard luck to tear the pictured page half down the middle. She thrust the volume into the desk, turned the key, and burst out crying with shame and vexation:

"Tom Sawyer, you are just as mean as you can be, to sneak up on a person and look at what they're looking at."

"How could *I* know you was looking at anything?"

"You ought to be ashamed of yourself Tom Sawyer; you know you're going to tell on me, and O, what shall I do, what shall I do! I'll be whipped, and I never was whipped in school."

Then she stamped her little foot and said:

"*Be* so mean if you want to! *I* know something that's going to happen. You just wait and you'll see! Hateful, hateful, hateful!"—and she flung out of the house with a new explosion of crying.

Tom stood still, rather flustered by this onslaught. Presently he said to himself:

"What a curious kind of a fool a girl is. Never been licked in school! Shucks, what's a licking! That's just like a girl—they're so thin-skinned and chicken-hearted. Well, of course *I* ain't going to tell old Dobbins on this little fool, because there's other ways of getting even on her, that ain't so mean; but what of it? Old Dobbins will ask who it was tore his book. Nobody'll answer. Then he'll do just the way he always does—ask first one and then t'other, and when he comes to the right girl he'll know it, without any telling. Girls' faces always tell on them. They ain't got any backbone. She'll get licked. Well, it's a kind of a tight place for Becky Thatcher, because there ain't any way out of it." Tom conned the thing a moment longer, and then added: "All right, though; she'd like to see me in just such a fix—let her sweat it out!"

Tom joined the mob of skylarking scholars outside. In a few moments the master arrived and school "took in." Tom did not feel a strong interest in his studies. Every time he stole a glance at the girls' side of the room Becky's face troubled him. Considering all things, he did not want to pity her, and yet it was all he could do to help it. He could get up no exultation that was really worthy the name. Presently the spelling-book discovery was made, and Tom's mind was entirely full of his own matters for a while after that. Becky roused up from her lethargy of distress and showed good interest in the proceedings. She did not expect that Tom could get out of his trouble by denying that he spilt the ink on the book himself; and she was right. The denial only seemed to make the thing worse for Tom. Becky supposed she would be glad of that, and she tried to believe she was glad of it, but she found she was not certain. When the worst came to the worst, she had an impulse to get up and tell on Alfred Temple, but she made an effort and forced herself to keep still—because, said she to herself, "he'll tell about me tearing the picture, sure—I wouldn't say a word, not to save his life!"

Tom took his whipping and went back to his seat not at all broken-hearted, for he thought it was possible that he had unknowingly upset the ink on the spelling-book himself, in some skylarking bout—he had denied it for form's sake and because it was custom, and had stuck to the denial from principle.

A whole hour drifted by; the master sat nodding in his throne, the air was drowsy with the hum of study. By and by, Mr. Dobbins straightened himself up, yawned, then unlocked his desk, and reached for his book, but seemed undecided whether to take it out or leave it. Most of the pupils glanced up languidly, but there were two among them that watched his movements with intent eyes. Mr. Dobbins fingered his book absently for a while, then took it out and settled himself in his chair to read! Tom shot a glance at Becky. He had seen a hunted and helpless rabbit look as she did, with a gun leveled at its head. Instantly he forgot his quarrel with her. Quick—something must be done!—done in a flash, too! But

the very imminence of the emergency paralyzed his invention.
Good!—he had an inspiration! He would run and snatch the
book, spring through the door and fly! But his resolution
shook for one little instant, and the chance was lost—the
master opened the volume. If Tom only had the wasted opportunity back again! Too late; there was no help for Becky
now, he said. The next moment the master faced the school.
Every eye sunk under his gaze. There was that in it which
smote even the innocent with fear. There was silence while
one might count ten; the master was gathering his wrath.
Then he spoke:

"Who tore this book?"

There was not a sound. One could have heard a pin drop.
The stillness continued; the master searched face after face for
signs of guilt.

"Benjamin Rogers, did you tear this book?"

A denial. Another pause.

"Joseph Harper, did you?"

Another denial. Tom's uneasiness grew more and more intense under the slow torture of these proceedings. The master
scanned the ranks of boys—considered a while, then turned
to the girls:

"Amy Lawrence?"

A shake of the head.

"Gracie Miller?"

The same sign.

"Susan Harper, did you do this?"

Another negative. The next girl was Becky Thatcher. Tom
was trembling from head to foot with excitement and a sense
of the hopelessness of the situation.

"Rebecca Thatcher," [Tom glanced at her face—it was
white with terror,]—"did you tear—no, look me in the
face"—[her hands rose in appeal]—"did you tear this book?"

A thought shot like lightning through Tom's brain. He
sprang to his feet and shouted—

"*I* done it!"

The school stared in perplexity at this incredible folly. Tom
stood a moment, to gather his dismembered faculties; and
when he stepped forward to go to his punishment the surprise, the gratitude, the adoration that shone upon him out

of poor Becky's eyes seemed pay enough for a hundred flog-
gings. Inspired by the splendor of his own act, he took without an outcry the most merciless flaying that even Mr. Dobbins had ever administered; and also received with
indifference the added cruelty of a command to remain two
hours after school should be dismissed—for he knew who
would wait for him outside till his captivity was done, and
not count the tedious time as loss, either.

Tom went to bed that night planning vengeance against
Alfred Temple; for with shame and repentance Becky had
told him all, not forgetting her own treachery; but even the
longing for vengeance had to give way, soon, to pleasanter
musings, and he fell asleep at last with Becky's latest words
lingering dreamily in his ear—

"Tom, how *could* you be so noble!"

XXI

VACATION was approaching. The schoolmaster, always severe, grew severer and more exacting than ever, for he wanted the school to make a good showing on "Examination" day. His rod and his ferule were seldom idle now—at least among the smaller pupils. Only the biggest boys, and young ladies of eighteen and twenty escaped lashing. Mr. Dobbins's lashings were very vigorous ones, too; for although he carried, under his wig, a perfectly bald and shiny head, he had only reached middle age and there was no sign of feebleness in his muscle. As the great day approached, all the tyranny that was in him came to the surface; he seemed to take a vindictive pleasure in punishing the least shortcomings. The consequence was, that the smaller boys spent their days in terror and suffering and their nights in plotting revenge. They threw away no opportunity to do the master a mischief. But he kept ahead all the time. The retribution that followed every vengeful success was so sweeping and majestic that the boys always retired from the field badly worsted. At last they conspired together and hit upon a plan that promised a dazzling victory. They swore-in the sign-painter's boy, told him the scheme, and asked his help. He had his own reasons for being delighted, for the master boarded in his father's family and had given the boy ample cause to hate him. The master's wife would go on a visit to the country in a few days, and there would be nothing to interfere with the plan; the master always prepared himself for great occasions by getting pretty well fuddled, and the sign-painter's boy said that when the dominie had reached the proper condition on Examination Evening he would "manage the thing" while he napped in his chair; then he would have him awakened at the right time and hurried away to school.

In the fulness of time the interesting occasion arrived. At eight in the evening the schoolhouse was brilliantly lighted, and adorned with wreaths and festoons of foliage and flowers. The master sat throned in his great chair upon a raised platform, with his blackboard behind him. He was looking tolerably mellow. Three rows of benches on each side and six rows in front of him were occupied by the dignitaries of the town and by the parents of the pupils. To his left, back of the rows of citizens, was a spacious temporary platform upon which were seated the scholars who were to take part in the exercises of the evening; rows of small boys, washed and dressed to an intolerable state of discomfort; rows of gawky big boys; snow-banks of girls and young ladies clad in lawn and muslin and conspicuously conscious of their bare arms, their grandmothers' ancient trinkets, their bits of pink and blue ribbon and the flowers in their hair. All the rest of the house was filled with non-participating scholars.

The exercises began. A very little boy stood up and sheepishly recited, "You'd scarce expect one of my age to speak in public on the stage, etc."—accompanying himself with the painfully exact and spasmodic gestures which a machine might have used—supposing the machine to be a trifle out of order. But he got through safely, though cruelly scared, and got a fine round of applause when he made his manufactured bow and retired.

A little shame-faced girl lisped "Mary had a little lamb, etc.," performed a compassion-inspiring curtsy, got her meed of applause, and sat down flushed and happy.

Tom Sawyer stepped forward with conceited confidence and soared into the unquenchable and indestructible "Give me liberty or give me death" speech, with fine fury and frantic gesticulation, and broke down in the middle of it. A ghastly stage-fright seized him, his legs quaked under him and he was like to choke. True, he had the manifest sympathy of the house—but he had the house's silence, too, which was even worse than its sympathy. The master frowned, and this completed the disaster. Tom struggled a while and then retired, utterly defeated. There was a weak attempt at applause, but it died early.

"The Boy Stood on the Burning Deck" followed; also "The Assyrian Came Down," and other declamatory gems. Then there were reading exercises, and a spelling fight. The meagre Latin class recited with honor. The prime feature of the evening was in order, now—original "compositions" by the young ladies. Each in her turn stepped forward to the

edge of the platform, cleared her throat, held up her manuscript (tied with dainty ribbon), and proceeded to read, with
labored attention to "expression" and punctuation. The
themes were the same that had been illuminated upon similar
occasions by their mothers before them, their grandmothers,
and doubtless all their ancestors in the female line clear back
to the Crusades. "Friendship" was one; "Memories of Other
Days;" "Religion in History;" "Dream Land;" "The Advantages of Culture;" "Forms of Political Government Compared
and Contrasted;" "Melancholy;" "Filial Love;" "Heart Longings," etc., etc.

A prevalent feature in these compositions was a nursed and
petted melancholy; another was a wasteful and opulent gush
of "fine language;" another was a tendency to lug in by the
ears particularly prized words and phrases until they were
worn entirely out; and a peculiarity that conspicuously
marked and marred them was the inveterate and intolerable
sermon that wagged its crippled tail at the end of each and
every one of them. No matter what the subject might be, a
brain-racking effort was made to squirm it into some aspect
or other that the moral and religious mind could contemplate
with edification. The glaring insincerity of these sermons was
not sufficient to compass the banishment of the fashion from
the schools, and it is not sufficient to-day; it never will be
sufficient while the world stands, perhaps. There is no school
in all our land where the young ladies do not feel obliged to
close their compositions with a sermon; and you will find that
the sermon of the most frivolous and least religious girl in the
school is always the longest and the most relentlessly pious.
But enough of this. Homely truth is unpalatable.

Let us return to the "Examination." The first composition
that was read was one entitled "Is this, then, Life?" Perhaps
the reader can endure an extract from it:

"In the common walks of life, with what delightful emotions does the youthful mind look forward to some antici-
pated scene of festivity! Imagination is busy sketching rose-
tinted pictures of joy. In fancy, the voluptuous votary of
fashion sees herself amid the festive throng, 'the observed
of all observers.' Her graceful form, arrayed in snowy

robes, is whirling through the mazes of the joyous dance; her eye is brightest, her step is lightest in the gay assembly.

"In such delicious fancies time quickly glides by, and the welcome hour arrives for her entrance into the elysian world, of which she has had such bright dreams. How fairy-like does every thing appear to her enchanted vision! each new scene is more charming than the last. But after a while she finds that beneath this goodly exterior, all is vanity: the flattery which once charmed her soul, now grates harshly upon her ear; the ball-room has lost its charms; and with wasted health and imbittered heart, she turns away with the conviction that earthly pleasures cannot satisfy the longings of the soul!"

And so forth and so on. There was a buzz of gratification from time to time during the reading, accompanied by whispered ejaculations of "How sweet!" "How eloquent!" "So true!" etc., and after the thing had closed with a peculiarly afflicting sermon the applause was enthusiastic.

Then arose a slim, melancholy girl, whose face had the "interesting" paleness that comes of pills and indigestion, and read a "poem." Two stanzas of it will do:

A MISSOURI MAIDEN'S FAREWELL TO ALABAMA.

ALABAMA, good-bye! I love thee well!
    But yet for awhile do I leave thee now!
Sad, yes, sad thoughts of thee my heart doth swell,
    And burning recollections throng my brow!
For I have wandered through thy flowery woods;
    Have roamed and read near Tallapoosa's stream;
Have listened to Tallassee's warring floods,
    And wooed on Coosa's side Aurora's beam.

Yet shame I not to bear an o'er-full heart,
    Nor blush to turn behind my tearful eyes;
'Tis from no stranger land I now must part,
    'Tis to no strangers left I yield these sighs.
Welcome and home were mine within this State,
    Whose vales I leave—whose spires fade fast from me;

And cold must be mine eyes, and heart, and tête,
   When, dear Alabama! they turn cold on thee!

There were very few there who knew what *"tête"* meant, but the poem was very satisfactory, nevertheless.

Next appeared a dark complexioned, black eyed, black haired young lady, who paused an impressive moment, assumed a tragic expression and began to read in a measured, solemn tone:

A VISION.

DARK and tempestuous was night. Around the throne on high not a single star quivered; but the deep intonations of the heavy thunder constantly vibrated upon the ear; whilst the terrific lightning revelled in angry mood through the cloudy chambers of heaven, seeming to scorn the power exerted over its terror by the illustrious Franklin! Even the boisterous winds unanimously came forth from their mystic homes, and blustered about as if to enhance by their aid the wildness of the scene.

At such a time, so dark, so dreary, for human sympathy my very spirit sighed; but instead thereof,

"My dearest friend, my counsellor, my comforter and
   guide—
My joy in grief, my second bliss in joy," came to my
   side.

She moved like one of those bright beings pictured in the sunny walks of fancy's Eden by the romantic and young, a queen of beauty unadorned save by her own transcendent loveliness. So soft was her step, it failed to make even a sound, and but for the magical thrill imparted by her genial touch, as other unobtrusive beauties, she would have glided away unperceived—unsought. A strange sadness rested upon her features, like icy tears upon the robe of December, as she pointed to the contending elements without, and bade me contemplate the two beings presented.

This nightmare occupied some ten pages of manuscript and wound up with a sermon so destructive of all hope to non-

Presbyterians that it took the first prize. This composition was considered to be the very finest effort of the evening. The mayor of the village, in delivering the prize to the author of it, made a warm speech in which he said that it was by far the most "eloquent" thing he had ever listened to, and that Daniel Webster himself might well be proud of it.

It may be remarked, in passing, that the number of compositions in which the word "beauteous" was over-fondled, and human experience referred to as "life's page," was up to the usual average.

Now the master, mellow almost to the verge of geniality, put his chair aside, turned his back to the audience, and began to draw a map of America on the blackboard, to exercise the geography class upon. But he made a sad business of it with his unsteady hand, and a smothered titter rippled over the house. He knew what the matter was, and set himself to right it. He sponged out lines and re-made them; but he only distorted them more than ever, and the tittering was more pronounced. He threw his entire attention upon his work, now, as if determined not to be put down by the mirth. He felt that all eyes were fastened upon him; he imagined he was succeeding, and yet the tittering continued; it even manifestly increased. And well it might. There was a garret above, pierced with a scuttle over his head; down through this scuttle came a cat, suspended around the haunches by a string; she had a rag tied about her head and jaws to keep her from mewing; as she slowly descended she curved upward and clawed at the string, she swung downward and clawed at the intangible air. The tittering rose higher and higher—the cat was within six inches of the absorbed teacher's head—down, down, a little lower, and she grabbed his wig with her desperate claws, clung to it and was snatched up into the garret in an instant with her trophy still in her possession! And how the light did blaze abroad from the master's bald pate—for the sign-painter's boy had *gilded* it!

That broke up the meeting. The boys were avenged. Vacation had come.

NOTE—The pretended "compositions" quoted in this chapter are taken without alteration from a volume entitled "Prose and Poetry, by a Western Lady"—but they are exactly and precisely after the school-girl pattern and hence are much happier than any mere imitations could be.

XXII

Tom joined the new order of Cadets of Temperance, being attracted by the showy character of their "regalia." He promised to abstain from smoking, chewing and profanity as long as he remained a member. Now he found out a new thing—namely, that to promise not to do a thing is the surest way in the world to make a body want to go and do that very thing. Tom soon found himself tormented with a desire to drink and swear; the desire grew to be so intense that nothing but the hope of a chance to display himself in his red sash kept him from withdrawing from the order. Fourth of July was coming; but he soon gave that up—gave it up before he had worn his shackles over forty-eight hours—and fixed his hopes upon old Judge Frazer, justice of the peace, who was apparently on his death-bed and would have a big public funeral, since he was so high an official. During three days Tom was deeply concerned about the Judge's condition and hungry for news of it. Sometimes his hopes ran high—so high that he would venture to get out his regalia and practice before the looking-glass. But the Judge had a most discouraging way of fluctuating. At last he was pronounced upon the mend—and then convalescent. Tom was disgusted; and felt a sense of injury, too. He handed in his resignation at once—and that night the Judge suffered a relapse and died. Tom resolved that he would never trust a man like that again. The funeral was a fine thing. The Cadets paraded in a style calculated to kill the late member with envy. Tom was a free boy again, however—there was something in that. He could drink and swear, now—but found to his surprise that he did not want to. The simple fact that he could, took the desire away, and the charm of it.

Tom presently wondered to find that his coveted vacation was beginning to hang a little heavily on his hands.

He attempted a diary—but nothing happened during three days, and so he abandoned it.

The first of all the negro minstrel shows came to town, and

made a sensation. Tom and Joe Harper got up a band of performers and were happy for two days.

Even the Glorious Fourth was in some sense a failure, for it rained hard, there was no procession in consequence, and the greatest man in the world (as Tom supposed) Mr. Benton, an actual United States Senator, proved an overwhelming disappointment—for he was not twenty-five feet high, nor even anywhere in the neighborhood of it.

A circus came. The boys played circus for three days afterward in tents made of rag carpeting—admission, three pins for boys, two for girls—and then circusing was abandoned.

A phrenologist and a mesmerizer came—and went again and left the village duller and drearier than ever.

There were some boys-and-girls' parties, but they were so few and so delightful that they only made the aching voids between ache the harder.

Becky Thatcher was gone to her Constantinople home to stay with her parents during vacation—so there was no bright side to life anywhere.

The dreadful secret of the murder was a chronic misery. It was a very cancer for permanency and pain.

Then came the measles.

During two long weeks Tom lay a prisoner, dead to the world and its happenings. He was very ill, he was interested in nothing. When he got upon his feet at last and moved feebly down town, a melancholy change had come over everything and every creature. There had been a "revival," and everybody had "got religion;" not only the adults, but even the boys and girls. Tom went about, hoping against hope for the sight of one blessed sinful face, but disappointment crossed him everywhere. He found Joe Harper studying a Testament, and turned sadly away from the depressing spectacle. He sought Ben Rogers, and found him visiting the poor with a basket of tracts. He hunted up Jim Hollis, who called his attention to the precious blessing of his late measles as a warning. Every boy he encountered added another ton to his depression; and when, in desperation, he flew for refuge at last to the bosom of Huckleberry Finn and was received with a Scriptural quotation, his heart broke and he crept home and to bed realizing that he alone of all the town was lost, forever and forever.

And that night there came on a terrific storm, with driving rain, awful claps of thunder and blinding sheets of lightning. He covered his head with the bedclothes and waited in a horror of suspense for his doom; for he had not the shadow of a doubt that all this hubbub was about him. He believed he had taxed the forbearance of the powers above to the extremity of endurance and that this was the result. It might have seemed to him a waste of pomp and ammunition to kill a bug with a battery of artillery, but there seemed nothing incongruous about the getting up such an expensive thunderstorm as this to knock the turf from under an insect like himself.

By and by the tempest spent itself and died without accomplishing its object. The boy's first impulse was to be grateful, and reform. His second was to wait—for there might not be any more storms.

The next day the doctors were back; Tom had relapsed. The three weeks he spent on his back this time seemed an entire age. When he got abroad at last he was hardly grateful that he had been spared, remembering how lonely was his estate, how companionless and forlorn he was. He drifted listlessly down the street and found Jim Hollis acting as judge in a juvenile court that was trying a cat for murder, in the presence of her victim, a bird. He found Joe Harper and Huck Finn up an alley eating a stolen melon. Poor lads! they—like Tom—had suffered a relapse.

XXIII

AT LAST the sleepy atmosphere was stirred—and vigorously: the murder trial came on in the court. It became the absorbing topic of village talk immediately. Tom could not get away from it. Every reference to the murder sent a shudder to his heart, for his troubled conscience and his fears almost persuaded him that these remarks were put forth in his hearing as "feelers;" he did not see how he could be suspected of knowing anything about the murder, but still he could not be comfortable in the midst of this gossip. It kept him in a cold shiver all the time. He took Huck to a lonely place to have a talk with him. It would be some relief to unseal his tongue for a little while; to divide his burden of distress with another sufferer. Moreover, he wanted to assure himself that Huck had remained discreet.

"Huck, have you ever told anybody about—that?"

"'Bout what?"

"You know what."

"Oh—'course I haven't."

"Never a word?"

"Never a solitry word, so help me. What makes you ask?"

"Well, I was afeard."

"Why Tom Sawyer, we wouldn't be alive two days if that got found out. *You* know that."

Tom felt more comfortable. After a pause:

"Huck, they couldn't anybody get you to tell, could they?"

"Get me to tell? Why if I wanted that half-breed devil to drownd me they could get me to tell. They ain't no different way."

"Well, that's all right, then. I reckon we're safe as long as we keep mum. But let's swear again, anyway. It's more surer."

"I'm agreed."

So they swore again with dread solemnities.

"What is the talk around, Huck? I've heard a power of it."

"Talk? Well, it's just Muff Potter, Muff Potter, Muff Potter all the time. It keeps me in a sweat, constant, so's I want to hide som'ers."

"That's just the same way they go on round me. I reckon he's a goner. Don't you feel sorry for him, sometimes?"

"Most always—most always. He ain't no account; but then he hain't ever done anything to hurt anybody. Just fishes a little, to get money to get drunk on—and loafs around considerable; but lord we all do that—leastways most of us,—preachers and such like. But he's kind of good—he give me half a fish, once, when there warn't enough for two; and lots of times he's kind of stood by me when I was out of luck."

"Well, he's mended kites for me, Huck, and knitted hooks on to my line. I wish we could get him out of there."

"My! we couldn't get him out Tom. And besides 'twouldn't do any good; they'd ketch him again."

"Yes—so they would. But I hate to hear 'em abuse him so like the dickens when he never done—that."

"I do too, Tom. Lord, I hear 'em say he's the bloodiest looking villain in this country, and they wonder he wasn't ever hung before."

"Yes, they talk like that, all the time. I've heard 'em say that if he was to get free they'd lynch him."

"And they'd do it, too."

The boys had a long talk, but it brought them little comfort. As the twilight drew on, they found themselves hanging about the neighborhood of the little isolated jail, perhaps with an undefined hope that something would happen that might clear away their difficulties. But nothing happened; there seemed to be no angels or fairies interested in this luckless captive.

The boys did as they had often done before—went to the cell grating and gave Potter some tobacco and matches. He was on the ground floor and there were no guards.

His gratitude for their gifts had always smote their consciences before—it cut deeper than ever, this time. They felt cowardly and treacherous to the last degree when Potter said:

"You've ben mighty good to me, boys—better'n anybody else in this town. And I don't forget it, I don't. Often I says to myself, says I, 'I used to mend all the boys' kites and things, and show 'em where the good fishin' places was, and

befriend 'em what I could, and now they've all forgot old
Muff when he's in trouble; but Tom don't, and Huck don't—
they don't forget him,' says I, 'and I don't forget them.' Well,
boys, I done an awful thing—drunk and crazy at the time—
that's the only way I account for it—and now I got to swing
for it, and it's right. Right, and *best*, too I reckon—hope so,
anyway. Well, we won't talk about that. I don't want to make
you feel bad; you've befriended me. But what I want to say,
is, don't *you* ever get drunk—then you won't ever get here.
Stand a little furder west—so—that's it; it's a prime comfort
to see faces that's friendly when a body's in such a muck of
trouble,—and there don't none come here but yourn. Good
friendly faces—good friendly faces. Git up on one another's
backs and let me touch 'em. That's it. Shake hands—yourn'll
come through the bars, but mine's too big. Little hands, and
weak—but they've helped Muff Potter a power, and they'd
help him more if they could."

Tom went home miserable, and his dreams that night were
full of horrors. The next day and the day after, he hung about
the court room, drawn by an almost irresistible impulse to go
in, but forcing himself to stay out. Huck was having the same
experience. They studiously avoided each other. Each wandered away, from time to time, but the same dismal fascination always brought them back presently. Tom kept his ears
open when idlers sauntered out of the court room, but invari-
ably heard distressing news—the toils were closing more and
more relentlessly around poor Potter. At the end of the second day the village talk was to the effect that Injun Joe's evidence stood firm and unshaken, and that there was not the
slightest question as to what the jury's verdict would be.

Tom was out late, that night, and came to bed through the
window. He was in a tremendous state of excitement. It was
hours before he got to sleep. All the village flocked to the
Court house the next morning, for this was to be the great
day. Both sexes were about equally represented in the packed
audience. After a long wait the jury filed in and took their
places; shortly afterward, Potter, pale and haggard, timid and
hopeless, was brought in, with chains upon him, and seated
where all the curious eyes could stare at him; no less conspicuous was Injun Joe, stolid as ever. There was another pause,

and then the judge arrived and the sheriff proclaimed the opening of the court. The usual whisperings among the lawyers and gathering together of papers followed. These details and accompanying delays worked up an atmosphere of preparation that was as impressive as it was fascinating.

Now a witness was called who testified that he found Muff Potter washing in the brook, at an early hour of the morning that the murder was discovered, and that he immediately sneaked away. After some further questioning, counsel for the prosecution said—

"Take the witness."

The prisoner raised his eyes for a moment, but dropped them again when his own counsel said—

"I have no questions to ask him."

The next witness proved the finding of the knife near the corpse. Counsel for the prosecution said:

"Take the witness."

"I have no questions to ask him," Potter's lawyer replied.

A third witness swore he had often seen the knife in Potter's possession.

"Take the witness."

Counsel for Potter declined to question him. The faces of the audience began to betray annoyance. Did this attorney mean to throw away his client's life without an effort?

Several witnesses deposed concerning Potter's guilty behavior when brought to the scene of the murder. They were allowed to leave the stand without being cross-questioned.

Every detail of the damaging circumstances that occurred in the graveyard upon that morning which all present remembered so well, was brought out by credible witnesses, but none of them were cross-examined by Potter's lawyer. The perplexity and dissatisfaction of the house expressed itself in murmurs and provoked a reproof from the bench. Counsel for the prosecution now said:

"By the oaths of citizens whose simple word is above suspicion, we have fastened this awful crime beyond all possibility of question, upon the unhappy prisoner at the bar. We rest our case here."

A groan escaped from poor Potter, and he put his face in his hands and rocked his body softly to and fro, while a painful silence reigned in the court room. Many men were moved, and many women's compassion testified itself in tears. Counsel for the defence rose and said:

"Your honor, in our remarks at the opening of this trial, we foreshadowed our purpose to prove that our client did this fearful deed while under the influence of a blind and irresponsible delirium produced by drink. We have changed our mind. We shall not offer that plea." [Then to the clerk]: "Call Thomas Sawyer!"

A puzzled amazement awoke in every face in the house, not even excepting Potter's. Every eye fastened itself with wondering interest upon Tom as he rose and took his place upon the stand. The boy looked wild enough, for he was badly scared. The oath was administered.

"Thomas Sawyer, where were you on the seventeenth of June, about the hour of midnight?"

Tom glanced at Injun Joe's iron face and his tongue failed him. The audience listened breathless, but the words refused to come. After a few moments, however, the boy got a little of his strength back, and managed to put enough of it into his voice to make part of the house hear:

"In the graveyard!"

"A little bit louder, please. Don't be afraid. You were—"

"In the graveyard."

A contemptuous smile flitted across Injun Joe's face.

"Were you anywhere near Horse Williams's grave?"

"Yes, sir."

"Speak up—just a trifle louder. How near were you?"

"Near as I am to you."

"Were you hidden, or not?"

"I was hid."

"Where?"

"Behind the elms that's on the edge of the grave."

Injun Joe gave a barely perceptible start.

"Any one with you?"

"Yes, sir. I went there with—"

"Wait—wait a moment. Never mind mentioning your companion's name. We will produce him at the proper time. Did you carry anything there with you?"

Tom hesitated and looked confused.

"Speak out my boy—don't be diffident. The truth is always respectable. What did you take there?"

"Only a—a—dead cat."

There was a ripple of mirth, which the court checked.

"We will produce the skeleton of that cat. Now my boy, tell us everything that occurred—tell it in your own way—don't skip anything, and don't be afraid."

Tom began—hesitatingly at first, but as he warmed to his subject his words flowed more and more easily; in a little while every sound ceased but his own voice; every eye fixed itself upon him; with parted lips and bated breath the audience hung upon his words, taking no note of time, rapt in the ghastly fascinations of the tale. The strain upon pent emotion reached its climax when the boy said—

"—and as the doctor fetched the board around and Muff Potter fell, Injun Joe jumped with the knife and—"

Crash! quick as lightning the half-breed sprang for a window, tore his way through all opposers, and was gone!

XXIV

Tom was a glittering hero once more—the pet of the old, the envy of the young. His name even went into immortal print, for the village paper magnified him. There were some that believed he would be President, yet, if he escaped hanging.

As usual, the fickle, unreasoning world took Muff Potter to its bosom and fondled him as lavishly as it had abused him before. But that sort of conduct is to the world's credit; therefore it is not well to find fault with it.

Tom's days were days of splendor and exultation to him, but his nights were seasons of horror. Injun Joe infested all his dreams, and always with doom in his eye. Hardly any temptation could persuade the boy to stir abroad after nightfall. Poor Huck was in the same state of wretchedness and terror, for Tom had told the whole story to the lawyer the night before the great day of the trial, and Huck was sore afraid that his share in the business might leak out, yet, notwithstanding Injun Joe's flight had saved him the suffering of testifying in court. The poor fellow had got the attorney to promise secrecy, but what of that? Since Tom's harassed conscience had managed to drive him to the lawyer's house by night and wring a dread tale from lips that had been sealed with the dismalest and most formidable of oaths, Huck's confidence in the human race was well nigh obliterated. Daily Muff Potter's gratitude made Tom glad he had spoken; but nightly he wished he had sealed up his tongue.

Half the time Tom was afraid Injun Joe would never be captured; the other half he was afraid he would be. He felt sure he never could draw a safe breath again until that man was dead and he had seen the corpse.

Rewards had been offered, the country had been scoured, but no Injun Joe was found. One of those omniscient and awe-inspiring marvels, a detective, came up from St. Louis, moused around, shook his head, looked wise, and made that sort of astounding success which members of that craft usually achieve. That is to say, he "found a clew." But you can't hang a "clew" for murder, and so after that detective had got through and gone home, Tom felt just as insecure as he was before.

The slow days drifted on, and each left behind it a slightly lightened weight of apprehension.

XXV

THERE COMES A TIME in every rightly constructed boy's life when he has a raging desire to go somewhere and dig for hidden treasure. This desire suddenly came upon Tom one day. He sallied out to find Joe Harper, but failed of success. Next he sought Ben Rogers; he had gone fishing. Presently he stumbled upon Huck Finn the Red-Handed. Huck would answer. Tom took him to a private place and opened the matter to him confidentially. Huck was willing. Huck was always willing to take a hand in any enterprise that offered entertainment and required no capital, for he had a troublesome superabundance of that sort of time which is *not* money.

"Where'll we dig?" said Huck.

"O, most anywhere."

"Why, is it hid all around?"

"No indeed it ain't. It's hid in mighty particular places, Huck—sometimes on islands, sometimes in rotten chests under the end of a limb of an old dead tree, just where the shadow falls at midnight; but mostly under the floor in ha'nted houses."

"Who hides it?"

"Why robbers, of course—who'd you reckon? Sunday-school sup'rintendents?"

"I don't know. If 'twas mine I wouldn't hide it; I'd spend it and have a good time."

"So would I. But robbers don't do that way. They always hide it and leave it there."

"Don't they come after it any more?"

"No, they think they will, but they generally forget the marks, or else they die. Anyway it lays there a long time and gets rusty; and by and by somebody finds an old yellow paper that tells how to find the marks—a paper that's got to be ciphered over about a week because it's mostly signs and hy'rogliphics."

"Hyro—which?"

"Hy'rogliphics—pictures and things, you know, that don't seem to mean anything."

"Have you got one of them papers, Tom?"

"No."

"Well then, how you going to find the marks?"

"I don't want any marks. They always bury it under a ha'nted house or on an island, or under a dead tree that's got one limb sticking out. Well, we've tried Jackson's Island a little, and we can try it again some time; and there's the old ha'nted house up the Still-House branch, and there's lots of dead-limb trees—dead loads of 'em."

"Is it under all of them?"

"How you talk! No!"

"Then how you going to know which one to go for?"

"Go for all of 'em!"

"Why Tom, it'll take all summer."

"Well, what of that? Suppose you find a brass pot with a hundred dollars in it, all rusty and gay, or a rotten chest full of di'monds. How's that?"

Huck's eyes glowed.

"That's bully. Plenty bully enough for me. Just you gimme the hundred dollars and I don't want no di'monds."

"All right. But I bet you *I* ain't going to throw off on di'monds. Some of 'em's worth twenty dollars apiece—there ain't any, hardly, but's worth six bits or a dollar."

"No! Is that so?"

"Cert'nly—anybody'll tell you so. Hain't you ever seen one, Huck?"

"Not as I remember."

"O, kings have slathers of them."

"Well, I don't know no kings, Tom."

"I reckon you don't. But if you was to go to Europe you'd see a raft of 'em hopping around."

"Do they hop?"

"Hop?—your granny! No!"

"Well what did you say they did, for?"

"Shucks, I only meant you'd *see* 'em—not hopping, of course—what do they want to hop for?—but I mean you'd just see 'em—scattered around, you know, in a kind of a general way. Like that old hump-backed Richard."

"Richard? What's his other name?"

"He didn't have any other name. Kings don't have any but a given name."

"No?"

"But they don't."

"Well, if they like it, Tom, all right; but I don't want to be a king and have only just a given name, like a nigger. But say—where you going to dig first?"

"Well, I don't know. S'pose we tackle that old dead-limb tree on the hill t'other side of Still-House branch?"

"I'm agreed."

So they got a crippled pick and a shovel, and set out on their three-mile tramp. They arrived hot and panting, and threw themselves down in the shade of a neighboring elm to rest and have a smoke.

"I like this," said Tom.

"So do I."

"Say, Huck, if we find a treasure here, what you going to do with your share?"

"Well I'll have pie and a glass of soda every day, and I'll go to every circus that comes along. I bet I'll have a gay time."

"Well ain't you going to save any of it?"

"Save it? What for?"

"Why so as to have something to live on, by and by."

"O, that ain't any use. Pap would come back to thish-yer town some day and get his claws on it if I didn't hurry up, and I tell you he'd clean it out pretty quick. What you going to do with yourn, Tom?"

"I'm going to buy a new drum, and a sure-'nough sword, and a red neck-tie and a bull pup, and get married."

"Married!"

"That's it."

"Tom, you—why you ain't in your right mind."

"Wait—you'll see."

"Well that's the foolishest thing you could do, Tom. Look at pap and my mother. Fight? Why they used to fight all the time. I remember, mighty well."

"That ain't anything. The girl I'm going to marry won't fight."

"Tom, I reckon they're all alike. They'll all comb a body.

Now you better think 'bout this a while. I tell you you better. What's the name of the gal?"

"It ain't a gal at all—it's a girl."

"It's all the same, I reckon; some says gal, some says girl—both's right, like enough. Anyway, what's her name, Tom?"

"I'll tell you some time—not now."

"All right—that'll do. Only if you get married I'll be more lonesomer than ever."

"No you won't. You'll come and live with me. Now stir out of this and we'll go to digging."

They worked and sweated for half an hour. No result. They toiled another half hour. Still no result. Huck said:

"Do they always bury it as deep as this?"

"Sometimes—not always. Not generally. I reckon we haven't got the right place."

So they chose a new spot and began again. The labor dragged a little, but still they made progress. They pegged away in silence for some time. Finally Huck leaned on his shovel, swabbed the beaded drops from his brow with his sleeve, and said:

"Where you going to dig next, after we get this one?"

"I reckon maybe we'll tackle the old tree that's over yonder on Cardiff Hill back of the widow's."

"I reckon that'll be a good one. But won't the widow take it away from us, Tom? It's on her land."

"*She* take it away! Maybe she'd like to try it once. Whoever finds one of these hid treasures, it belongs to him. It don't make any difference whose land it's on."

That was satisfactory. The work went on. By and by Huck said—

"Blame it, we must be in the wrong place again. What do you think?"

"It *is* mighty curious Huck. I don't understand it. Sometimes witches interfere. I reckon maybe that's what's the trouble now."

"Shucks, witches ain't got no power in the daytime."

"Well, that's so. I didn't think of that. Oh, *I* know what the matter is! What a blamed lot of fools we are! You got to find out where the shadow of the limb falls at midnight, and that's where you dig!"

"Then consound it, we've fooled away all this work for nothing. Now hang it all, we got to come back in the night. It's an awful long way. Can you get out?"

"I bet I will. We've got to do it to-night, too, because if somebody sees these holes they'll know in a minute what's here and they'll go for it."

"Well, I'll come around and maow to-night."

"All right. Let's hide the tools in the bushes."

The boys were there that night, about the appointed time. They sat in the shadow waiting. It was a lonely place, and an hour made solemn by old traditions. Spirits whispered in the rustling leaves, ghosts lurked in the murky nooks, the deep baying of a hound floated up out of the distance, an owl answered with his sepulchral note. The boys were subdued by these solemnities, and talked little. By and by they judged that twelve had come; they marked where the shadow fell, and began to dig. Their hopes commenced to rise. Their interest grew stronger, and their industry kept pace with it. The hole deepened and still deepened, but every time their hearts jumped to hear the pick strike upon something, they only suffered a new disappointment. It was only a stone or a chunk. At last Tom said—

"It ain't any use, Huck, we're wrong again."

"Well but we *can't* be wrong. We spotted the shadder to a dot."

"I know it, but then there's another thing."

"What's that?"

"Why we only guessed at the time. Like enough it was too late or too early."

Huck dropped his shovel.

"That's it," said he. "That's the very trouble. We got to give this one up. We can't ever tell the right time, and besides this kind of thing's too awful, here this time of night with witches and ghosts a-fluttering around so. I feel as if something's behind me all the time; and I'm afeard to turn around, becuz maybe there's others in front a-waiting for a chance. I been creeping all over, ever since I got here."

"Well, I've been pretty much so, too, Huck. They most always put in a dead man when they bury a treasure under a tree, to look out for it."

"Lordy!"

"Yes, they do. I've always heard that."

"Tom I don't like to fool around much where there's dead people. A body's bound to get into trouble with 'em, sure."

"I don't like to stir 'em up, either, Huck. S'pose this one here was to stick his skull out and say something!"

"Don't, Tom! It's awful."

"Well it just is. Huck, I don't feel comfortable a bit."

"Say, Tom, let's give this place up, and try somewheres else."

"All right, I reckon we better."

"What'll it be?"

Tom considered a while; and then said—

"The ha'nted house. That's it!"

"Blame it, I don't like ha'nted houses, Tom. Why they're a dern sight worse'n dead people. Dead people might talk, maybe, but they don't come sliding around in a shroud, when you ain't noticing, and peep over your shoulder all of a sudden and grit their teeth, the way a ghost does. I couldn't stand such a thing as that, Tom—nobody could."

"Yes, but Huck, ghosts don't travel around only at night— they won't hender us from digging there in the daytime."

"Well that's so. But you know mighty well people don't go about that ha'nted house in the day nor the night."

"Well, that's mostly because they don't like to go where a man's been murdered, anyway—but nothing's ever been seen around that house except in the night—just some blue lights slipping by the windows—no regular ghosts."

"Well where you see one of them blue lights flickering around, Tom, you can bet there's a ghost mighty close behind it. It stands to reason. Becuz *you* know that they don't anybody but ghosts use 'em."

"Yes, that's so. But anyway they don't come around in the daytime, so what's the use of our being afeard?"

"Well, all right. We'll tackle the ha'nted house if you say so—but I reckon it's taking chances."

They had started down the hill by this time. There in the middle of the moonlit valley below them stood the "ha'nted" house, utterly isolated, its fences gone long ago, rank weeds smothering the very doorstep, the chimney crumbled to ruin,

the window-sashes vacant, a corner of the roof caved in. The
boys gazed a while, half expecting to see a blue light flit past
a window; then talking in a low tone, as befitted the time and
the circumstances, they struck far off to the right, to give the
haunted house a wide berth, and took their way homeward
through the woods that adorned the rearward side of Cardiff
Hill.

XXVI

ABOUT NOON the next day the boys arrived at the dead tree; they had come for their tools. Tom was impatient to go to the haunted house; Huck was measurably so, also— but suddenly said—

"Lookyhere, Tom, do you know what day it is?"

Tom mentally ran over the days of the week, and then quickly lifted his eyes with a startled look in them—

"My! I never once thought of it, Huck!"

"Well I didn't neither, but all at once it popped onto me that it was Friday."

"Blame it, a body can't be too careful, Huck. We might a got into an awful scrape, tackling such a thing on a Friday."

"*Might!* Better say we *would*! There's some lucky days, maybe, but Friday ain't."

"Any fool knows that. I don't reckon *you* was the first that found it out, Huck."

"Well, I never said I was, did I? And Friday ain't all, nei- ther. I had a rotten bad dream last night—dreampt about rats."

"No! Sure sign of trouble. Did they fight?"

"No."

"Well that's good, Huck. When they don't fight it's only a sign that there's trouble around, you know. All we got to do is to look mighty sharp and keep out of it. We'll drop this thing for to-day, and play. Do you know Robin Hood, Huck?"

"No. Who's Robin Hood?"

"Why he was one of the greatest men that was ever in En- gland—and the best. He was a robber."

"Cracky, I wisht I was. Who did he rob?"

"Only sheriffs and bishops and rich people and kings, and such like. But he never bothered the poor. He loved 'em. He always divided up with 'em—perfectly square."

"Well, he must 'a' ben a brick."

"I bet you he was, Huck. Oh, he was the noblest man that ever was. They ain't any such men now, I can tell you. He could lick any man in England, with one hand tied behind him; and he could take his yew bow and plug a ten cent piece every time, a mile and a half."

"What's a *yew* bow?"

"*I* don't know. It's some kind of a bow, of course. And if he hit that dime only on the edge he would set down and cry—and curse. But we'll play Robin Hood—it's noble fun. I'll learn you."

"I'm agreed."

So they played Robin Hood all the afternoon, now and then casting a yearning eye down upon the haunted house and passing a remark about the morrow's prospects and possibilities there. As the sun began to sink into the west they took their way homeward athwart the long shadows of the trees and soon were buried from sight in the forests of Cardiff Hill.

On Saturday, shortly after noon, the boys were at the dead tree again. They had a smoke and a chat in the shade, and then dug a little in their last hole, not with great hope, but merely because Tom said there were so many cases where people had given up a treasure after getting down within six inches of it, and then somebody else had come along and turned it up with a single thrust of a shovel. The thing failed this time, however, so the boys shouldered their tools and went away feeling that they had not trifled with fortune but had fulfilled all the requirements that belong to the business of treasure-hunting.

When they reached the haunted house there was something so weird and grisly about the dead silence that reigned there under the baking sun, and something so depressing about the loneliness and desolation of the place, that they were afraid, for a moment, to venture in. Then they crept to the door and took a trembling peep. They saw a weed-grown, floorless room, unplastered, an ancient fireplace, vacant windows, a ruinous staircase; and here, there, and everywhere, hung ragged and abandoned cobwebs. They presently entered, softly, with quickened pulses, talking in whispers, ears alert to catch the slightest sound, and muscles tense and ready for instant retreat.

In a little while familiarity modified their fears and they

gave the place a critical and interested examination, rather admiring their own boldness, and wondering at it, too. Next they wanted to look up stairs. This was something like cutting off retreat, but they got to daring each other, and of course there could be but one result—they threw their tools into a corner and made the ascent. Up there were the same signs of decay. In one corner they found a closet that promised mystery, but the promise was a fraud—there was nothing in it. Their courage was up, now, and well in hand. They were about to go down and begin work when—

"Sh!" said Tom.

"What is it?" whispered Huck, blanching with fright.

"Sh! . . . . . . There! . . . . Hear it?"

"Yes! . . . . O, my! Let's run!"

"Keep still! Don't you budge! They're coming right toward the door."

The boys stretched themselves upon the floor with their eyes to knot holes in the planking, and lay waiting, in a misery of fear.

"They've stopped . . . . No—coming . . . . . . Here they are. Don't whisper another word, Huck. My goodness, I wish I was out of this!"

Two men entered. Each boy said to himself: "There's the old deef and dumb Spaniard that's been about town once or twice lately—never saw t'other man before."

"T'other" was a ragged, unkempt creature, with nothing very pleasant in his face. The Spaniard was wrapped in a *serape*; he had bushy white whiskers; long white hair flowed from under his sombrero, and he wore green goggles. When they came in, "t'other" was talking in a low voice; they sat down on the ground, facing the door, with their backs to the wall, and the speaker continued his remarks. His manner became less guarded and his words more distinct as he proceeded:

"No," said he, "I've thought it all over, and I don't like it. It's dangerous."

"Dangerous!" grunted the "deaf and dumb" Spaniard,—to the vast surprise of the boys. "Milksop!"

This voice made the boys gasp and quake. It was Injun Joe's! There was silence for some time. Then Joe said:

"What's any more dangerous than that job up yonder—but nothing's come of it."

"That's different. Away up the river so, and not another house about. 'Twon't ever be known that we tried, anyway, long as we didn't succeed."

"Well, what's more dangerous than coming here in the daytime?—anybody would suspicion us that saw us."

"*I* know that. But there warn't any other place as handy after that fool of a job. I want to quit this shanty. I wanted to yesterday, only it warn't any use trying to stir out of here, with those infernal boys playing over there on the hill right in full view."

"Those infernal boys" quaked again under the inspiration of this remark, and thought how lucky it was that they had remembered it was Friday and concluded to wait a day. They wished in their hearts they had waited a year.

The two men got out some food and made a luncheon. After a long and thoughtful silence, Injun Joe said:

"Look here, lad—you go back up the river where you belong. Wait there till you hear from me. I'll take the chances on dropping into this town just once more, for a look. We'll do that 'dangerous' job after I've spied around a little and think things look well for it. Then for Texas! We'll leg it together!"

This was satisfactory. Both men presently fell to yawning, and Injun Joe said:

"I'm dead for sleep! It's your turn to watch."

He curled down in the weeds and soon began to snore. His comrade stirred him once or twice and he became quiet. Presently the watcher began to nod; his head drooped lower and lower; both men began to snore now.

The boys drew a long, grateful breath. Tom whispered—

"Now's our chance—come!"

Huck said:

"I can't—I'd die if they was to wake."

Tom urged—Huck held back. At last Tom rose slowly and softly, and started alone. But the first step he made wrung such a hideous creak from the crazy floor that he sank down almost dead with fright. He never made a second attempt. The boys lay there counting the dragging moments till it seemed to them that time must be done and eternity growing gray; and then they were grateful to note that at last the sun was setting.

Now one snore ceased. Injun Joe sat up, stared around—smiled grimly upon his comrade, whose head was drooping upon his knees—stirred him up with his foot and said—

"Here! *You're* a watchman, ain't you! All right, though—nothing's happened."

"My! Have I been asleep?"

"Oh, partly, partly. Nearly time for us to be moving, pard. What'll we do with what little swag we've got left?"

"I don't know—leave it here as we've always done, I reckon. No use to take it away till we start south. Six hundred and fifty in silver's something to carry."

"Well—all right—it won't matter to come here once more."

"No—but I'd say come in the night as we used to do—it's better."

"Yes; but look here; it may be a good while before I get the right chance at that job; accidents might happen; 'tain't in such a very good place; we'll just regularly bury it—and bury it deep."

"Good idea," said the comrade, who walked across the room, knelt down, raised one of the rearward hearthstones and took out a bag that jingled pleasantly. He subtracted from it twenty or thirty dollars for himself and as much for Injun Joe and passed the bag to the latter, who was on his knees in the corner, now, digging with his bowie knife.

The boys forgot all their fears, all their miseries in an instant. With gloating eyes they watched every movement. Luck!—the splendor of it was beyond all imagination! Six hundred dollars was money enough to make half a dozen boys rich! Here was treasure-hunting under the happiest auspices—there would not be any bothersome uncertainty as to where to dig. They nudged each other every moment—eloquent nudges and easily understood, for they simply meant "O, but ain't you glad *now* we're here!"

Joe's knife struck upon something.

"Hello!" said he.

"What is it?" said his comrade.

"Half-rotten plank—no it's a box, I believe. Here—bear a
hand and we'll see what it's here for. Never mind, I've broke
a hole."

He reached his hand in and drew it out—

"Man, it's money!"

The two men examined the handful of coins. They were
gold. The boys above were as excited as themselves, and as
delighted.

Joe's comrade said—

"We'll make quick work of this. There's an old rusty pick
over amongst the weeds in the corner the other side of the
fire-place—I saw it a minute ago."

He ran and brought the boys' pick and shovel. Injun Joe
took the pick, looked it over critically, shook his head, muttered something to himself, and then began to use it. The box
was soon unearthed. It was not very large; it was iron bound
and had been very strong before the slow years had injured
it. The men contemplated the treasure a while in blissful silence.

"Pard, there's thousands of dollars here," said Injun Joe.

" 'Twas always said that Murrel's gang used around here
one summer," the stranger observed.

"I know it," said Injun Joe; "and this looks like it, I should
say."

"*Now* you won't need to do that job."

The half-breed frowned. Said he—

"You don't know me. Least you don't know all about that
thing. 'Tain't robbery altogether—it's *revenge!*" and a wicked
light flamed in his eyes. "I'll need your help in it. When it's
finished—then Texas. Go home to your Nance, and your
kids, and stand by till you hear from me."

"Well—if you say so. What'll we do with this—bury it
again?"

"Yes." [Ravishing delight overhead.] "*No!* by the great
Sachem, no!" [Profound distress overhead.] "I'd nearly forgot. That pick had fresh earth on it!" [The boys were sick
with terror in a moment.] "What business has a pick and a
shovel here? What business with fresh earth on them? Who
brought them here—and where are they gone? Have you
heard anybody?—seen anybody? What! bury it again and

leave them to come and see the ground disturbed? Not exactly—not exactly. We'll take it to my den."

"Why of course! Might have thought of that before. You
mean Number One?"

"No—Number Two—under the cross. The other place is
bad—too common."

"All right. It's nearly dark enough to start."

Injun Joe got up and went about from window to window
cautiously peeping out. Presently he said:

"Who could have brought those tools here? Do you reckon
they can be up stairs?"

The boys' breath forsook them. Injun Joe put his hand on
his knife, halted a moment, undecided, and then turned toward the stairway. The boys thought of the closet, but their
strength was gone. The steps came creaking up the stairs—
the intolerable distress of the situation woke the stricken resolution of the lads—they were about to spring for the closet,
when there was a crash of rotten timbers and Injun Joe
landed on the ground amid the debris of the ruined stairway.
He gathered himself up cursing, and his comrade said:

"Now what's the use of all that? If it's anybody, and
they're up there, let them *stay* there—who cares? If they want
to jump down, now, and get into trouble, who objects? It
will be dark in fifteen minutes—and then let them follow us
if they want to. I'm willing. In my opinion, whoever hove
those things in here caught a sight of us and took us for
ghosts or devils or something. I'll bet they're running yet."

Joe grumbled a while; then he agreed with his friend that
what daylight was left ought to be economised in getting
things ready for leaving. Shortly afterward they slipped out of
the house in the deepening twilight, and moved toward the
river with their precious box.

Tom and Huck rose up, weak but vastly relieved, and
stared after them through the chinks between the logs of the
house. Follow? Not they. They were content to reach ground
again without broken necks, and take the townward track
over the hill. They did not talk much. They were too much
absorbed in hating themselves—hating the ill luck that made
them take the spade and the pick there. But for that, Injun
Joe never would have suspected. He would have hidden the

silver with the gold to wait there till his "revenge" was satisfied, and then he would have had the misfortune to find that
money turn up missing. Bitter, bitter luck that the tools were
ever brought there!

They resolved to keep a lookout for that Spaniard when he
should come to town spying out for chances to do his re-
vengeful job, and follow him to "Number Two," wherever
that might be. Then a ghastly thought occurred to Tom:

"Revenge? What if he means *us*, Huck!"

"O, don't!" said Huck, nearly fainting.

They talked it all over, and as they entered town they
agreed to believe that he might possibly mean somebody
else—at least that he might at least mean nobody but Tom,
since only Tom had testified.

Very, very small comfort it was to Tom to be alone in danger! Company would be a palpable improvement, he thought.

"That's what I've found out, Huck. I reckon that's the very No. 2 we're after."

"I reckon it is, Tom. Now what you going to do?"

"Lemme think."

Tom thought a long time. Then he said:

"I'll tell you. The back door of that No. 2 is the door that comes out into that little close alley between the tavern and the old rattle-trap of a brick store. Now you get hold of all the door-keys you can find, and I'll nip all of Auntie's and the first dark night we'll go there and try 'em. And mind you keep a lookout for Injun Joe, because he said he was going to drop into town and spy around once more for a chance to get his revenge. If you see him, you just follow him; and if he don't go to that No. 2, that ain't the place."

"Lordy I don't want to foller him by myself!"

"Why it'll be night, sure. He mightn't ever see you—and if he did, maybe he'd never think anything."

"Well, if it's pretty dark I reckon I'll track him. I dono—I dono. I'll try."

"You bet *I'll* follow him, if it's dark, Huck! Why he might 'a' found out he couldn't get his revenge, and be going right after that money."

"It's so, Tom, it's so. I'll foller him; I will, by jingoes!"

"Now you're *talking*! Don't you ever weaken, Huck, and I won't."

XXVIII

THAT NIGHT Tom and Huck were ready for their adventure. They hung about the neighborhood of the tavern until after nine, one watching the alley at a distance and the other the tavern door. Nobody entered the alley or left it; nobody resembling the Spaniard entered or left the tavern door. The night promised to be a fair one; so Tom went home, with the understanding that if a considerable degree of darkness came on, Huck was to come and "maow," whereupon he would slip out and try the keys. But the night remained clear, and Huck closed his watch and retired to bed in an empty sugar-hogshead about twelve.

Tuesday the boys had the same ill luck. Also Wednesday. But Thursday night promised better. Tom slipped out in good season with his aunt's old tin lantern, and a large towel to blindfold it with. He hid the lantern in Huck's sugar hogshead and the watch began. An hour before midnight the tavern closed up and its lights (the only ones thereabouts) were put out. No Spaniard had been seen. Nobody had entered or left the alley. Everything was auspicious. The blackness of darkness reigned, the perfect stillness was interrupted only by occasional mutterings of distant thunder.

Tom got his lantern, lit it in the hogshead, wrapped it closely in the towel, and the two adventurers crept in the gloom toward the tavern. Huck stood sentry and Tom felt his way into the alley. Then there was a season of waiting anxiety that weighed upon Huck's spirits like a mountain. He began to wish he could see a flash from the lantern—it would frighten him, but it would at least tell him that Tom was alive yet. It seemed hours since Tom had disappeared. Surely he must have fainted; maybe he was dead; maybe his heart had burst under terror and excitement. In his uneasiness Huck found himself drawing closer and closer to the alley; fearing all sorts of dreadful things, and momentarily expecting some catastrophe to happen that would take away his breath. There was not much to take away, for he seemed only able to inhale it by thimblefuls, and his heart would soon wear itself out, the way it was beating. Suddenly there was a flash of light and Tom came tearing by him:

"Run!" said he; "run, for your life!"

He needn't have repeated it; once was enough; Huck was making thirty or forty miles an hour before the repetition was uttered. The boys never stopped till they reached the shed of a deserted slaughter-house at the lower end of the village. Just as they got within its shelter the storm burst and the rain poured down. As soon as Tom got his breath he said:

"Huck, it was awful! I tried two of the keys, just as soft as I could; but they seemed to make such a power of racket that I couldn't hardly get my breath I was so scared. They wouldn't turn in the lock, either. Well, without noticing what I was doing, I took hold of the knob, and open comes the door! It warn't locked! I hopped in, and shook off the towel, and, *great Caesar's ghost!*"

"What!—what'd you see, Tom!"

"Huck, I most stepped onto Injun Joe's hand!"

"No!"

"Yes! He was laying there, sound asleep on the floor, with his old patch on his eye and his arms spread out."

"Lordy, what did you do? Did he wake up?"

"No, never budged. Drunk, I reckon. I just grabbed that towel and started!"

"I'd never 'a' thought of the towel, I bet!"

"Well, *I* would. My aunt would make me mighty sick if I lost it."

"Say, Tom, did you see that box?"

"Huck, I didn't wait to look around. I didn't see the box, I didn't see the cross. I didn't see anything but a bottle and a tin cup on the floor by Injun Joe; yes, and I saw two barrels and lots more bottles in the room. Don't you see, now, what's the matter with that ha'nted room?"

"How?"

"Why it's ha'nted with whisky! Maybe *all* the Temperance Taverns have got a ha'nted room, hey Huck?"

"Well I reckon maybe that's so. Who'd 'a' thought such a thing? But say, Tom, now's a mighty good time to get that box, if Injun Joe's drunk."

"It is, that! You try it!"

Huck shuddered.

"Well, no—I reckon not."

"And *I* reckon not, Huck. Only one bottle alongside of Injun Joe ain't enough. If there'd been three, he'd be drunk enough and I'd do it."

There was a long pause for reflection, and then Tom said:

"Lookyhere, Huck, less not try that thing any more till we know Injun Joe's not in there. It's too scary. Now if we watch every night, we'll be dead sure to see him go out, some time or other, and then we'll snatch that box quicker'n lightning."

"Well, I'm agreed. I'll watch the whole night long, and I'll do it every night, too, if you'll do the other part of the job."

"All right, I will. All you got to do is to trot up Hooper street a block and maow—and if I'm asleep, you throw some gravel at the window and that'll fetch me."

"Agreed, and good as wheat!"

"Now Huck, the storm's over, and I'll go home. It'll begin to be daylight in a couple of hours. You go back and watch that long, will you?"

"I said I would, Tom, and I will. I'll ha'nt that tavern every night for a year! I'll sleep all day and I'll stand watch all night."

"That's all right. Now where you going to sleep?"

"In Ben Rogers's hayloft. He lets me, and so does his pap's nigger man, Uncle Jake. I tote water for Uncle Jake whenever he wants me to, and any time I ask him he gives me a little something to eat if he can spare it. That's a mighty good nigger, Tom. He likes me, becuz I don't ever act as if I was above him. Sometimes I've set right down and eat *with* him. But you needn't tell that. A body's got to do things when he's awful hungry he wouldn't want to do as a steady thing."

"Well, if I don't want you in the daytime, Huck, I'll let you sleep. I won't come bothering around. Any time you see something's up, in the night, just skip right around and maow."

XXIX

THE FIRST THING Tom heard on Friday morning was a glad piece of news—Judge Thatcher's family had come back to town the night before. Both Injun Joe and the treasure sunk into secondary importance for a moment, and Becky took the chief place in the boy's interest. He saw her and they had an exhausting good time playing "hi-spy" and "gully-keeper" with a crowd of their schoolmates. The day was completed and crowned in a peculiarly satisfactory way: Becky teased her mother to appoint the next day for the long-promised and long-delayed pic-nic, and she consented. The child's delight was boundless; and Tom's not more moderate. The invitations were sent out before sunset, and straightway the young folks of the village were thrown into a fever of preparation and pleasurable anticipation. Tom's excitement enabled him to keep awake until a pretty late hour, and he had good hopes of hearing Huck's "maow," and of having his treasure to astonish Becky and the pic-nickers with, next day; but he was disappointed. No signal came that night.

Morning came, eventually, and by ten or eleven o'clock a giddy and rollicking company were gathered at Judge Thatcher's, and everything was ready for a start. It was not the custom for elderly people to mar pic-nics with their presence. The children were considered safe enough under the wings of a few young ladies of eighteen and a few young gentlemen of twenty-three or thereabouts. The old steam ferry boat was chartered for the occasion; presently the gay throng filed up the main street laden with provision baskets. Sid was sick and had to miss the fun; Mary remained at home to entertain him. The last thing Mrs. Thatcher said to Becky, was—

"You'll not get back till late. Perhaps you'd better stay all night with some of the girls that live near the ferry landing, child."

"Then I'll stay with Susy Harper, mamma."

"Very well. And mind and behave yourself and don't be any trouble."

Presently, as they tripped along, Tom said to Becky:

"Say—I'll tell you what we'll do. 'Stead of going to Joe Harper's, we'll climb right up the hill and stop at widow Douglas's. She'll have ice cream! She has it 'most every day—dead loads of it. And she'll be awful glad to have us."

"O, that will be fun!"

Then Becky reflected a moment and said:

"But what will mamma say?"

"How'll she ever know?"

The girl turned the idea over in her mind, and said reluctantly:

"I reckon it's wrong—but—"

"But shucks! Your mother won't know, and so what's the harm? All she wants is that you'll be safe; and I bet you she'd 'a' said go there if she'd 'a' thought of it. I know she would!"

The widow Douglas's splendid hospitality was a tempting bait. It and Tom's persuasions presently carried the day. So it was decided to say nothing to anybody about the night's programme. Presently it occurred to Tom that maybe Huck might come this very night and give the signal. The thought took a deal of the spirit out of his anticipations. Still he could not bear to give up the fun at widow Douglas's. And why should he give it up, he reasoned—the signal did not come the night before, so why should it be any more likely to come to-night? The sure fun of the evening outweighed the uncertain treasure; and boy like, he determined to yield to the stronger inclination and not allow himself to think of the box of money another time that day.

Three miles below town the ferry boat stopped at the mouth of a woody hollow and tied up. The crowd swarmed ashore and soon the forest distances and craggy heights echoed far and near with shoutings and laughter. All the different ways of getting hot and tired were gone through with, and by and by the rovers straggled back to camp fortified with responsible appetites, and then the destruction of the good things began. After the feast there was a refreshing season of rest and chat in the shade of spreading oaks. By and by somebody shouted—

"Who's ready for the cave?"

Everybody was. Bundles of candles were produced, and

straightway there was a general scamper up the hill. The mouth of the cave was high up the hillside—an opening shaped like a letter A. Its massive oaken door stood unbarred. Within was a small chamber, chilly as an ice-house, and walled by Nature with solid limestone that was dewy with a cold sweat. It was romantic and mysterious to stand here in the deep gloom and look out upon the green valley shining in the sun. But the impressiveness of the situation quickly wore off, and the romping began again. The moment a candle was lighted there was a general rush upon the owner of it; a struggle and a gallant defense followed, but the candle was soon knocked down or blown out, and then there was a glad clamor of laughter and a new chase. But all things have an end. By and by the procession went filing down the steep descent of the main avenue, the flickering rank of lights dimly revealing the lofty walls of rock almost to their point of junction sixty feet overhead. This main avenue was not more than eight or ten feet wide. Every few steps other lofty and still narrower crevices branched from it on either hand—for McDougal's cave was but a vast labyrinth of crooked aisles that ran into each other and out again and led nowhere. It was said that one might wander days and nights together through its intricate tangle of rifts and chasms, and never find the end of the cave; and that he might go down, and down, and still down, into the earth, and it was just the same—labyrinth underneath labyrinth, and no end to any of them. No man "knew" the cave. That was an impossible thing. Most of the young men knew a portion of it, and it was not customary to venture much beyond this known portion. Tom Sawyer knew as much of the cave as any one.

The procession moved along the main avenue some three quarters of a mile, and then groups and couples began to slip aside into branch avenues, fly along the dismal corridors, and take each other by surprise at points where the corridors joined again. Parties were able to elude each other for the space of half an hour without going beyond the "known" ground.

By and by, one group after another came straggling back to the mouth of the cave, panting, hilarious, smeared from head to foot with tallow drippings, daubed with clay, and entirely delighted with the success of the day. Then they were astonished to find that they had been taking no note of time and that night was about at hand. The clanging bell had been calling for half an hour. However, this sort of close to the day's adventures was romantic and therefore satisfactory. When the ferry-boat with her wild freight pushed into the stream, nobody cared sixpence for the wasted time but the captain of the craft.

Huck was already upon his watch when the ferry-boat's lights went glinting past the wharf. He heard no noise on board, for the young people were as subdued and still as people usually are who are nearly tired to death. He wondered what boat it was, and why she did not stop at the wharf—and then he dropped her out of his mind and put his attention upon his business. The night was growing cloudy and dark. Ten o'clock came, and the noise of vehicles ceased, scattered lights began to wink out, all straggling foot passengers disappeared, the village betook itself to its slumbers and left the small watcher alone with the silence and the ghosts. Eleven o'clock came, and the tavern lights were put out; darkness everywhere, now. Huck waited what seemed a weary long time, but nothing happened. His faith was weakening. Was there any use? Was there really any use? Why not give it up and turn in?

A noise fell upon his ear. He was all attention in an instant. The alley door closed softly. He sprang to the corner of the brick store. The next moment two men brushed by him, and one seemed to have something under his arm. It must be that box! So they were going to remove the treasure. Why call Tom now? It would be absurd—the men would get away with the box and never be found again. No, he would stick to their wake and follow them; he would trust to the darkness for security from discovery. So communing with himself, Huck stepped out and glided along behind the men, cat-like, with bare feet, allowing them to keep just far enough ahead not to be invisible.

They moved up the river street three blocks, then turned to the left up a cross street. They went straight ahead, then, until they came to the path that led up Cardiff Hill; this they took. They passed by the old Welchman's house, half way up the hill, without hesitating, and still climbed upward. Good, thought Huck, they will bury it in the old quarry. But they never stopped at the quarry. They passed on, up the summit. They plunged into the narrow path between the tall sumach bushes, and were at once hidden in the gloom. Huck closed up and shortened his distance, now, for they would never be able to see him. He trotted along a while; then slackened his pace, fearing he was gaining too fast; moved on a piece, then stopped altogether; listened; no sound; none, save that he seemed to hear the beating of his own heart. The hooting of an owl came from over the hill—ominous sound! But no footsteps. Heavens, was everything lost! He was about to spring with winged feet, when a man cleared his throat not four feet from him! Huck's heart shot into his throat, but he swallowed it again; and then he stood there shaking as if a dozen agues had taken charge of him at once, and so weak that he thought he must surely fall to the ground. He knew where he was. He knew he was within five steps of the stile leading into widow Douglas's grounds. Very well, he thought, let them bury it there; it won't be hard to find.

Now there was a voice—a very low voice—Injun Joe's:

"Damn her, maybe she's got company—there's lights, late as it is."

"I can't see any."

This was that stranger's voice—the stranger of the haunted house. A deadly chill went to Huck's heart—this, then, was the "revenge" job! His thought was, to fly. Then he remembered that the widow Douglas had been kind to him more than once, and maybe these men were going to murder her. He wished he dared venture to warn her; but he knew he didn't dare—they might come and catch him. He thought all this and more in the moment that lapsed between the stranger's remark and Injun Joe's next—which was—

"Because the bush is in your way. Now—this way—now you see, don't you?"

"Yes. Well there *is* company there, I reckon. Better give it up."

"Give it up, and I just leaving this country forever! Give it up and maybe never have another chance. I tell you again, as I've told you before, I don't care for her swag—you may have

it. But her husband was rough on me—many times he wa
rough on me—and mainly he was the justice of the peac
that jugged me for a vagrant. And that ain't all. It ain't th
millionth part of it! He had me *horsewhipped*!—horsewhippe
in front of the jail, like a nigger!—with all the town lookin
on! HORSEWHIPPED!—do you understand? He took advan
tage of me and died. But I'll take it out of *her*."

"Oh, don't kill her! Don't do that!"

"Kill? Who said anything about killing? I would kill *him* i
he was here; but not her. When you want to get revenge or
a woman you don't kill her—bosh! you go for her looks. You
slit her nostrils—you notch her ears, like a sow's!"

"By God, that's—"

"Keep your opinion to yourself! It will be safest for you
I'll tie her to the bed. If she bleeds to death, is that my fault
I'll not cry, if she does. My friend, you'll help in this thing—
for *my* sake—that's why you're here—I mightn't be able
alone. If you flinch, I'll kill you. Do you understand that
And if I have to kill you, I'll kill her—and then I reckon
nobody'll ever know much about who done this business."

"Well, if it's got to be done, let's get at it. The quicker the
better—I'm all in a shiver."

"Do it *now*? And company there? Look here—I'll get suspicious of you, first thing you know. No—we'll wait till the
lights are out—there's no hurry."

Huck felt that a silence was going to ensue—a thing still
more awful than any amount of murderous talk; so he held
his breath and stepped gingerly back; planted his foot carefully and firmly, after balancing, one-legged, in a precarious
way and almost toppling over, first on one side and then on
the other. He took another step back, with the same elabo-
ration and the same risks; then another and another, and—a
twig snapped under his foot! His breath stopped and he listened. There was no sound—the stillness was perfect. His
gratitude was measureless. Now he turned in his tracks, between the walls of sumach bushes—turned himself as carefully as if he were a ship—and then stepped quickly but
cautiously along. When he emerged at the quarry he felt
secure, and so he picked up his nimble heels and flew. Down,
down he sped, till he reached the Welchman's. He banged at

the door, and presently the heads of the old man and his two stalwart sons were thrust from windows.

"What's the row there? Who's banging? What do you want?"

"Let me in—quick! I'll tell everything."

"Why who are you?"

"Huckleberry Finn—quick, let me in!"

"Huckleberry Finn, indeed! It ain't a name to open many doors, I judge! But let him in, lads, and let's see what's the trouble."

"Please don't ever tell *I* told you," were Huck's first words when he got in. "Please don't—I'd be killed, sure—but the widow's been good friends to me sometimes, and I want to tell—I *will* tell if you'll promise you won't ever say it was me."

"By George he *has* got something to tell, or he wouldn't act so!" exclaimed the old man; "out with it and nobody here'll ever tell, lad."

Three minutes later the old man and his sons, well armed, were up the hill, and just entering the sumach path on tip-toe, their weapons in their hands. Huck accompanied them no further. He hid behind a great boulder and fell to listening. There was a lagging, anxious silence, and then all of a sudden there was an explosion of firearms and a cry.

Huck waited for no particulars. He sprang away and sped down the hill as fast as his legs could carry him.

XXX

As the earliest suspicion of dawn appeared on Sunday morning, Huck came groping up the hill and rapped gently at the old Welchman's door. The inmates were asleep but it was a sleep that was set on a hair-trigger, on account of the exciting episode of the night. A call came from a window—

"Who's there!"

Huck's scared voice answered in a low tone:

"Do please let me in! It's only Huck Finn!"

"It's a name that can open this door night or day, lad!—and welcome!"

These were strange words to the vagabond boy's ears, and the pleasantest he had ever heard. He could not recollect that the closing word had ever been applied in his case before. The door was quickly unlocked, and he entered. Huck was given a seat and the old man and his brace of tall sons speedily dressed themselves.

"Now my boy I hope you're good and hungry, because breakfast will be ready as soon as the sun's up, and we'll have a piping hot one, too—make yourself easy about that! I and the boys hoped you'd turn up and stop here last night."

"I was awful scared," said Huck, "and I run. I took out when the pistols went off, and I didn't stop for three mile. I've come now becuz I wanted to know about it, you know; and I come before daylight becuz I didn't want to run acrost them devils, even if they was dead."

"Well, poor chap, you do look as if you'd had a hard night of it—but there's a bed here for you when you've had your breakfast. No, they ain't dead, lad—we are sorry enough for that. You see we knew right where to put our hands on them, by your description; so we crept along on tip-toe till we got within fifteen feet of them—dark as a cellar that sumach path was—and just then I found I was going to sneeze. It was the meanest kind of luck! I tried to keep it back, but no use—'twas bound to come, and it did come! I was in the lead, with my pistol raised, and when the sneeze started those scoundrels a-rustling to get out of the path, I sung out, 'Fire, boys!' and blazed away at the place where the rustling was. So did the boys. But they were off in a jiffy, those villains, and we after them, down through the woods. I judge we never touched them. They fired a shot apiece as they started, but their bullets whizzed by and didn't do us any harm. As soon as we lost the sound of their feet we quit chasing, and went down and stirred up the constables. They got a posse together, and went off to guard the river bank, and as soon as it is light the sheriff and a gang are going to beat up the woods. My boys will be with them presently. I wish we had some sort of description of those rascals—'twould help a good deal. But you couldn't see what they were like, in the dark, lad, I suppose?"

"O, yes, I saw them down town and follered them."

"Splendid! Describe them—describe them, my boy!"

"One's the old deef and dumb Spaniard that's ben around here once or twice, and t'other's a mean looking ragged—"

"That's enough, lad, we know the men! Happened on them in the woods back of the widow's one day, and they slunk away. Off with you, boys, and tell the sheriff—get your breakfast to-morrow morning!"

The Welchman's sons departed at once. As they were leaving the room Huck sprang up and exclaimed:

"Oh, please don't tell *any*body it was me that blowed on them! Oh, please!"

"All right if you say it, Huck, but you ought to have the credit of what you did."

"Oh, no, no! Please don't tell!"

When the young men were gone, the old Welchman said—

"They won't tell—and I won't. But why don't you want it known?"

Huck would not explain, further than to say that he already knew too much about one of those men and would not have the man know that he knew anything against him for the whole world—he would be killed for knowing it, sure.

The old man promised secrecy once more, and said:

"How did you come to follow these fellows, lad? Were they looking suspicious?"

Huck was silent while he framed a duly cautious reply. Then he said:

"Well, you see, I'm a kind of a hard lot,—least everybody says so, and I don't see nothing agin it—and sometimes I can't sleep much, on accounts of thinking about it and sort of trying to strike out a new way of doing. That was the way of it last night. I couldn't sleep, and so I come along up street 'bout midnight, a-turning it all over, and when I got to that old shackly brick store by the Temperance Tavern, I backed up agin the wall to have another think. Well, just then along comes these two chaps slipping along close by me, with something under their arm and I reckoned they'd stole it. One was a-smoking, and t'other one wanted a light; so they stopped right before me and the cigars lit up their faces and I see that the big one was the deef and dumb Spaniard, by his white whiskers and the patch on his eye, and t'other one was a rusty, ragged looking devil."

"Could you see the rags by the light of the cigars?"

This staggered Huck for a moment. Then he said:

"Well, I don't know—but somehow it seems as if I did."

"Then they went on, and you—"

"Follered 'em—yes. That was it. I wanted to see what was up—they sneaked along so. I dogged 'em to the widder's stile, and stood in the dark and heard the ragged one beg for the widder, and the Spaniard swear he'd spile her looks just as I told you and your two—"

"What! The *deaf and dumb* man said all that!"

Huck had made another terrible mistake! He was trying his best to keep the old man from getting the faintest hint of who the Spaniard might be, and yet his tongue seemed determined to get him into trouble in spite of all he could do. He made several efforts to creep out of his scrape, but the old man's eye was upon him and he made blunder after blunder. Presently the Welchman said:

"My boy, don't be afraid of me. I wouldn't hurt a hair of your head for all the world. No—I'd protect you—I'd protect you. This Spaniard is not deaf and dumb; you've let that slip without intending it; you can't cover that up now. You know something about that Spaniard that you want to keep dark. Now trust me—tell me what it is, and trust me—I won't betray you."

Huck looked into the old man's honest eyes a moment, then bent over and whispered in his ear—

" 'Tain't a Spaniard—it's Injun Joe!"

The Welchman almost jumped out of his chair. In a moment he said:

"It's all plain enough, now. When you talked about notching ears and slitting noses I judged that that was your own embellishment, because white men don't take that sort of revenge. But an Injun! That's a different matter, altogether."

During breakfast the talk went on, and in the course of it the old man said that the last thing which he and his sons had done, before going to bed, was to get a lantern and examine the stile and its vicinity for marks of blood. They found none, but captured a bulky bundle of—

"Of WHAT!"

If the words had been lightning they could not have leaped with a more stunning suddenness from Huck's blanched lips. His eyes were staring wide, now, and his breath suspended— waiting for the answer. The Welchman started—stared in return—three seconds—five seconds—ten—then replied—

"Of burglar's tools. Why what's the *matter* with you?"

Huck sank back, panting gently, but deeply, unutterably grateful. The Welchman eyed him gravely, curiously—and presently said—

"Yes, burglar's tools. That appears to relieve you a good deal. But what did give you that turn? What were *you* expecting we'd found?"

Huck was in a close place—the inquiring eye was upon him—he would have given anything for material for a plausible answer—nothing suggested itself—the inquiring eye was boring deeper and deeper—a senseless reply offered— there was no time to weigh it, so at a venture he uttered it— feebly:

"Sunday-school books, maybe."

Poor Huck was too distressed to smile, but the old man laughed loud and joyously, shook up the details of his anatomy from head to foot, and ended by saying that such a laugh was money in a man's pocket, because it cut down the doctor's bills like everything. Then he added:

"Poor old chap, you're white and jaded—you ain't well a bit—no wonder you're a little flighty and off your balance But you'll come out of it. Rest and sleep will fetch you al right, I hope."

Huck was irritated to think he had been such a goose and betrayed such a suspicious excitement, for he had dropped the idea that the parcel brought from the tavern was the treasure as soon as he had heard the talk at the widow's stile. He had only *thought* it was not the treasure, however—he had not known that it wasn't—and so the suggestion of a captured bundle was too much for his self-possession. But on the whole he felt glad the little episode had happened, for now he knew beyond all question that that bundle was not *the* bundle, and so his mind was at rest and exceedingly comfortable. In fact everything seemed to be drifting just in the right direction, now; the treasure must be still in No. 2, the men would be captured and jailed that day, and he and Tom could seize the gold that night without any trouble or any fear of interruption.

Just as breakfast was completed there was a knock at the door. Huck jumped for a hiding place, for he had no mind to be connected even remotely with the late event. The Welch-man admitted several ladies and gentlemen, among them the widow Douglas, and noticed that groups of citizens were climbing the hill—to stare at the stile. So the news had spread.

The Welchman had to tell the story of the night to the visitors. The widow's gratitude for her preservation was out-spoken.

"Don't say a word about it, madam. There's another that you're more beholden to than you are to me and my boys, maybe, but he don't allow me to tell his name. We wouldn't ever have been there but for him."

Of course this excited a curiosity so vast that it almost be-littled the main matter—but the Welchman allowed it to eat into the vitals of his visitors, and through them be transmit-ted to the whole town, for he refused to part with his secret. When all else had been learned, the widow said:

"I went to sleep reading in bed and slept straight through all that noise. Why didn't you come and wake me?"

"We judged it warn't worth while. Those fellows warn't likely to come again—they hadn't any tools left to work with, and what was the use of waking you up and scaring you to death? My three negro men stood guard at your house all the rest of the night. They've just come back."

More visitors came, and the story had to be told and re-told for a couple of hours more.

There was no Sabbath school during day-school vacation, but everybody was early at church. The stirring event was well canvassed. News came that not a sign of the two villains had been yet discovered. When the sermon was finished, Judge Thatcher's wife dropped alongside of Mrs. Harper as she moved down the aisle with the crowd and said:

"Is my Becky going to sleep all day? I just expected she would be tired to death."

"Your Becky?"

"Yes,"—with a startled look,—"didn't she stay with you last night?"

"Why, no."

Mrs. Thatcher turned pale, and sank into a pew, just as aunt Polly, talking briskly with a friend, passed by. Aunt Polly said:

"Good morning, Mrs. Thatcher. Good morning Mrs. Harper. I've got a boy that's turned up missing. I reckon my Tom staid at your house last night—one of you. And now he's afraid to come to church. I've got to settle with him."

Mrs. Thatcher shook her head feebly and turned paler than ever.

"He didn't stay with us," said Mrs. Harper, beginning to look uneasy. A marked anxiety came into Aunt Polly's face.

"Joe Harper, have you seen my Tom this morning?"

"No'm."

"When did you see him last?"

Joe tried to remember, but was not sure he could say. The people had stopped moving out of church. Whispers passed along, and a boding uneasiness took possession of every countenance. Children were anxiously questioned, and young teachers. They all said they had not noticed whether Tom and Becky were on board the ferry-boat on the homeward trip; it was dark; no one thought of inquiring if any one was missing. One young man finally blurted out his fear that they were still in the cave! Mrs. Thatcher swooned away; Aunt Polly fell to crying and wringing her hands.

The alarm swept from lip to lip, from group to group, from street to street, and within five minutes the bells were wildly clanging and the whole town was up! The Cardiff Hill episode sank into instant insignificance, the burglars were forgotten, horses were saddled, skiffs were manned, the ferry boat ordered out, and before the horror was half an hour old, two hundred men were pouring down high-road and river toward the cave.

All the long afternoon the village seemed empty and dead. Many women visited Aunt Polly and Mrs. Thatcher and tried to comfort them. They cried with them, too, and that was still better than words. All the tedious night the town waited for news; but when the morning dawned at last, all the word that came was, "Send more candles—and send food." Mrs. Thatcher was almost crazed; and aunt Polly also. Judge Thatcher sent messages of hope and encouragement from the cave, but they conveyed no real cheer.

The old Welchman came home toward daylight, spattered with candle grease, smeared with clay, and almost worn out. He found Huck still in the bed that had been provided for him, and delirious with fever. The physicians were all at the cave, so the widow Douglas came and took charge of the patient. She said she would do her best by him, because, whether he was good, bad, or indifferent, he was the Lord's, and nothing that was the Lord's was a thing to be neglected. The Welchman said Huck had good spots in him, and the widow said—

"You can depend on it. That's the Lord's mark. He don't leave it off. He never does. Puts it somewhere on every creature that comes from His hands."

Early in the forenoon parties of jaded men began to straggle into the village, but the strongest of the citizens continued searching. All the news that could be gained was that remotenesses of the cavern were being ransacked that had never been visited before; that every corner and crevice was going to be thoroughly searched; that wherever one wandered through the maze of passages, lights were to be seen flitting hither and thither in the distance, and shoutings and pistol shots sent their hollow reverberations to the ear down the sombre aisles. In one place, far from the section usually traversed by tourists, the names "BECKY & TOM" had been found traced upon the rocky wall with candle smoke, and near at hand a grease-soiled bit of ribbon. Mrs. Thatcher recognized the ribbon and cried over it. She said it was the last relic she should ever have of her child; and that no other memorial of her could ever be so precious, because this one parted latest from the living body before the awful death came. Some said that now and then, in the cave, a far-away speck of light would glimmer, and then a glorious shout would burst forth and a score of men go trooping down the echoing aisle—and then a sickening disappointment always followed; the children were not there; it was only a searcher's light.

Three dreadful days and nights dragged their tedious hours along, and the village sank into a hopeless stupor. No one had heart for anything. The accidental discovery, just made, that the proprietor of the Temperance Tavern kept liquor on his premises, scarcely fluttered the public pulse, tremendous as the fact was. In a lucid interval, Huck feebly led up to the subject of taverns, and finally asked—dimly dreading the worst—if anything had been discovered at the Temperance Tavern since he had been ill?

"Yes," said the widow.

Huck started up in bed, wild-eyed:

"What! What was it!"

"Liquor!—and the place has been shut up. Lie down, child—what a turn you did give me!"

"Only tell me one thing—only just one—please! Was it Tom Sawyer that found it?"

The widow burst into tears.

"Hush, hush, child, hush! I've told you before, you must *not* talk. You are very, very sick!"

Then nothing but liquor had been found; there would have been a great pow-wow if it had been the gold. So the treasure was gone forever—gone forever! But what could she be crying about? Curious that she should cry.

These thoughts worked their dim way through Huck's mind, and under the weariness they gave him he fell asleep. The widow said to herself:

"There—he's alseep, poor wreck. Tom Sawyer find it! Pity but somebody could find Tom Sawyer! Ah, there ain't many left, now, that's got hope enough, or strength enough, either, to go on searching."

XXXI

NOW TO RETURN to Tom and Becky's share in the pic-
nic. They tripped along the murky aisles with the rest
of the company, visiting the familiar wonders of the cave—
wonders dubbed with rather over-descriptive names, such as
"The Drawing Room," "The Cathedral," "Aladdin's Palace,"
and so on. Presently the hide-and-seek frolicking began, and
Tom and Becky engaged in it with zeal until the exertion began to grow a trifle wearisome; then they wandered down a
sinuous avenue holding their candles aloft and reading the
tangled web-work of names, dates, post-office addresses and
mottoes with which the rocky walls had been frescoed (in
candle smoke.) Still drifting along and talking, they scarcely
noticed that they were now in a part of the cave whose walls
were not frescoed. They smoked their own names under an
overhanging shelf and moved on. Presently they came to a
place where a little stream of water, trickling over a ledge and
carrying a limestone sediment with it, had, in the slow-drag-
ging ages, formed a laced and ruffled Niagara in gleaming
and imperishable stone. Tom squeezed his small body behind
it in order to illuminate it for Becky's gratification. He found
that it curtained a sort of steep natural stairway which was
enclosed between narrow walls, and at once the ambition to
be a discoverer seized him. Becky responded to his call, and
they made a smoke-mark for future guidance and started
upon their quest. They wound this way and that, far down
into the secret depths of the cave, made another mark, and
branched off in search of novelties to tell the upper world
about. In one place they found a spacious cavern, from whose
ceiling depended a multitude of shining stalactites of the
length and circumference of a man's leg; they walked all
about it, wondering and admiring, and presently left it by
one of the numerous passages that opened into it. This
shortly brought them to a bewitching spring, whose basin
was encrusted with a frost work of glittering crystals; it
was in the midst of a cavern whose walls were supported
by many fantastic pillars which had been formed by the

joining of great stalactites and stalagmites together, the result of the ceaseless water-drip of centuries. Under the roof
vast knots of bats had packed themselves together, thousands in a bunch; the lights disturbed the creatures and
they came flocking down by hundreds, squeaking and dart-
ing furiously at the candles. Tom knew their ways and the
danger of this sort of conduct. He seized Becky's hand and
hurried her into the first corridor that offered; and none
too soon, for a bat struck Becky's light out with its wing
while she was passing out of the cavern. The bats chased
the children a good distance; but the fugitives plunged into
every new passage that offered, and at last got rid of the
perilous things. Tom found a subterranean lake, shortly,
which stretched its dim length away until its shape was lost
in the shadows. He wanted to explore its borders, but concluded that it would be best to sit down and rest a while,
first. Now, for the first time, the deep stillness of the place
laid a clammy hand upon the spirits of the children. Becky
said—

"Why, I didn't notice, but it seems ever so long since I
heard any of the others."

"Come to think, Becky, we are away down below them—
and I don't know how far away north, or south, or east, or
whichever it is. We couldn't hear them here."

Becky grew apprehensive.

"I wonder how long we've been down here, Tom. We better start back."

"Yes, I reckon we better. P'raps we better."

"Can you find the way, Tom? It's all a mixed-up crookedness to me."

"I reckon I could find it—but then the bats. If they put
both our candles out it will be an awful fix. Let's try some
other way, so as not to go through there."

"Well. But I hope we won't get lost. It would be so awful!"
and the child shuddered at the thought of the dreadful possibilities.

They started through a corridor, and traversed it in silence
a long way, glancing at each new opening, to see if there was
anything familiar about the look of it; but they were all
strange. Every time Tom made an examination, Becky would

watch his face for an encouraging sign, and he would say cheerily—

"Oh, it's all right. This ain't the one, but we'll come to it right away!"

But he felt less and less hopeful with each failure, and presently began to turn off into diverging avenues at sheer random, in the desperate hope of finding the one that was wanted. He still said it was "all right," but there was such a leaden dread at his heart, that the words had lost their ring and sounded just as if he had said, "All is lost!" Becky clung to his side in an anguish of fear, and tried hard to keep back the tears, but they would come. At last she said:

"O, Tom, never mind the bats, let's go back that way! We seem to get worse and worse off all the time."

Tom stopped.

"Listen!" said he.

Profound silence; silence so deep that even their breathings were conspicuous in the hush. Tom shouted. The call went echoing down the empty aisles and died out in the distance in a faint sound that resembled a ripple of mocking laughter.

"Oh, don't do it again, Tom, it is too horrid," said Becky.

"It is horrid, but I better, Becky; they *might* hear us, you know;" and he shouted again.

The "might" was even a chillier horror than the ghostly laughter, it so confessed a perishing hope. The children stood still and listened; but there was no result. Tom turned upon the back track at once, and hurried his steps. It was but a little while before a certain indecision in his manner revealed another fearful fact to Becky—he could not find his way back!

"O, Tom, you didn't make any marks!"

"Becky I was such a fool! Such a fool! I never thought we might want to come back! No—I can't find the way. It's all mixed up."

"Tom, Tom, we're lost! we're lost! We never never can get out of this awful place! O, why *did* we ever leave the others!"

She sank to the ground and burst into such a frenzy of crying that Tom was appalled with the idea that she might die, or lose her reason. He sat down by her and put his arms around her; she buried her face in his bosom, she clung to him, she poured out her terrors, her unavailing regrets, and the far echoes turned them all to jeering laughter. Tom begged her to pluck up hope again, and she said she could not. He fell to blaming and abusing himself for getting her into this miserable situation; this had a better effect. She said she would try to hope again, she would get up and follow wherever he might lead if only he would not talk like that any more. For he was no more to blame than she, she said.

So they moved on, again—aimlessly—simply at random— all they could do was to move, keep moving. For a little while, hope made a show of reviving—not with any reason to back it, but only because it is its nature to revive when the spring has not been taken out of it by age and familiarity with failure.

By and by Tom took Becky's candle and blew it out. This economy meant so much! Words were not needed. Becky understood, and her hope died again. She knew that Tom had a whole candle and three or four pieces in his pockets—yet he must economise.

By and by, fatigue began to assert its claims; the children tried to pay no attention, for it was dreadful to think of sitting down when time was grown to be so precious; moving, in some direction, in any direction, was at least progress and might bear fruit; but to sit down was to invite death and shorten its pursuit.

At last Becky's frail limbs refused to carry her farther. She sat down. Tom rested with her, and they talked of home, and the friends there, and the comfortable beds and above all, the light! Becky cried, and Tom tried to think of some way of comforting her, but all his encouragements were grown threadbare with use, and sounded like sarcasms. Fatigue bore so heavily upon Becky that she drowsed off to sleep. Tom was grateful. He sat looking into her drawn face and saw it grow smooth and natural under the influence of pleasant dreams; and by and by a smile dawned and rested there. The peaceful face reflected somewhat of peace and healing into his own spirit, and his thoughts wandered away to bygone times and dreamy memories. While he was deep in his musings, Becky woke up with a breezy little laugh—but it was stricken dead upon her lips, and a groan followed it.

"Oh, how *could* I sleep! I wish I never never had waked! No, no, I don't, Tom! Don't look so! I won't say it again."

"I'm glad you've slept, Becky; you'll feel rested, now, and we'll find the way out."

"We can try, Tom; but I've seen such a beautiful country in my dream. I reckon we are going there."

"Maybe not, maybe not. Cheer up, Becky, and let's go on trying."

They rose up and wandered along, hand in hand and hopeless. They tried to estimate how long they had been in the cave, but all they knew was that it seemed days and weeks, and yet it was plain that this could not be, for their candles were not gone yet.

A long time after this—they could not tell how long—Tom said they must go softly and listen for dripping water—they must find a spring. They found one presently, and Tom said it was time to rest again. Both were cruelly tired, yet Becky said she thought she could go a little farther. She was surprised to hear Tom dissent. She could not understand it. They sat down, and Tom fastened his candle to the wall in front of them with some clay. Thought was soon busy; nothing was said for some time. Then Becky broke the silence:

"Tom, I am so hungry!"

Tom took something out of his pocket.

"Do you remember this?" said he.

Becky almost smiled.

"It's our wedding cake, Tom."

"Yes—I wish it was as big as a barrel, for it's all we've got."

"I saved it from the pic-nic for us to dream on, Tom, the way grown-up people do with wedding cake—but it'll be our—"

She dropped the sentence where it was. Tom divided the cake and Becky ate with good appetite, while Tom nibbled at his moiety. There was abundance of cold water to finish the feast with. By and by Becky suggested that they move on again. Tom was silent a moment. Then he said:

"Becky, can you bear it if I tell you something?"

Becky's face paled, but she said she thought she could.

"Well then, Becky, we must stay here, where there's water to drink. That little piece is our last candle!"

Becky gave loose to tears and wailings. Tom did what he could to comfort her but with little effect. At length Becky said:

"Tom!"

"Well, Becky?"

"They'll miss us and hunt for us!"

"Yes, they will! Certainly they will!"

"Maybe they're hunting for us now, Tom?"

"Why I reckon maybe they are. I hope they are."

"When would they miss us, Tom?"

"When they get back to the boat, I reckon."

"Tom, it might be dark, then—would they notice we hadn't come?"

"I don't know. But anyway, your mother would miss you as soon as they got home."

A frightened look in Becky's face brought Tom to his senses and he saw that he had made a blunder. Becky was not to have gone home that night! The children became silent and thoughtful. In a moment a new burst of grief from Becky showed Tom that the thing in his mind had struck hers also—that the Sabbath morning might be half spent before Mrs. Thatcher discovered that Becky was not at Mrs. Harper's.

The children fastened their eyes upon the bit of candle and watched it melt slowly and pitilessly away; saw the half inch of wick stand alone at last; saw the feeble flame rise and fall, rise and fall, climb the thin column of smoke, linger at its top a moment, and then—the horror of utter darkness reigned!

How long afterward it was that Becky came to a slow consciousness that she was crying in Tom's arms, neither could tell. All that they knew was, that after what seemed a mighty stretch of time, both awoke out of a dead stupor of sleep and resumed their miseries once more. Tom said it might be Sunday, now—maybe Monday. He tried to get Becky to talk, but her sorrows were too oppressive, all her hopes were gone. Tom said that they must have been missed long ago, and no doubt the search was going on. He would shout, and maybe some one would come. He tried it; but in the darkness the distant echoes sounded so hideously that he tried it no more.

The hours wasted away, and hunger came to torment the captives again. A portion of Tom's half of the cake was left; they divided and ate it. But they seemed hungrier than before. The poor morsel of food only whetted desire.

By and by Tom said:

"*Sh!* Did you hear that?"

Both held their breath and listened. There was a sound like the faintest, far-off shout. Instantly Tom answered it, and leading Becky by the hand, started groping down the corridor in its direction. Presently he listened again; again the sound was heard, and apparently a little nearer.

"It's them!" said Tom; "they're coming! Come along, Becky—we're all right now!"

The joy of the prisoners was almost overwhelming. Their speed was slow, however, because pitfalls were somewhat common, and had to be guarded against. They shortly came to one and had to stop. It might be three feet deep, it might be a hundred—there was no passing it, at any rate. Tom got down on his breast and reached as far down as he could. No bottom. They must stay there and wait until the searchers came. They listened; evidently the distant shoutings were growing more distant! a moment or two more and they had gone altogether. The heart-sinking misery of it! Tom whooped until he was hoarse, but it was of no use. He talked hopefully to Becky; but an age of anxious waiting passed and no sounds came again.

The children groped their way back to the spring. The weary time dragged on; they slept again, and awoke famished and woe-stricken. Tom believed it must be Tuesday by this time.

Now an idea struck him. There were some side passages near at hand. It would be better to explore some of these than bear the weight of the heavy time in idleness. He took a kite-line from his pocket, tied it to a projection, and he and Becky started, Tom in the lead, unwinding the line as he groped along. At the end of twenty steps the corridor ended in a "jumping-off place." Tom got down on his knees and felt be-

low, and then as far around the corner as he could reach with
his hands conveniently; he made an effort to stretch yet a little
further to the right, and at that moment, not twenty yards
away, a human hand, holding a candle, appeared from behind
a rock! Tom lifted up a glorious shout, and instantly that
hand was followed by the body it belonged to—Injun Joe's!
Tom was paralyzed; he could not move. He was vastly gratified, the next moment, to see the "Spaniard" take to his heels
and get himself out of sight. Tom wondered that Joe had not
recognized his voice and come over and killed him for testifying in court. But the echoes must have disguised the voice.
Without doubt, that was it, he reasoned. Tom's fright weakened every muscle in his body. He said to himself that if he
had strength enough to get back to the spring he would stay
there, and nothing should tempt him to run the risk of meeting Injun Joe again. He was careful to keep from Becky what
it was he had seen. He told her he had only shouted "for
luck."

But hunger and wretchedness rise superior to fears in the
long run. Another tedious wait at the spring and another long
sleep brought changes. The children awoke tortured with a
raging hunger. Tom believed it must be Wednesday or Thursday or even Friday or Saturday, now, and that the search had
been given over. He proposed to explore another passage. He
felt willing to risk Injun Joe and all other terrors. But Becky
was very weak. She had sunk into a dreary apathy and would
not be roused. She said she would wait, now, where she was,
and die—it would not be long. She told Tom to go with the
kite-line and explore if he chose; but she implored him to
come back every little while and speak to her; and she made
him promise that when the awful time came, he would stay
by her and hold her hand until all was over.

Tom kissed her, with a choking sensation in his throat, and
made a show of being confident of finding the searchers or an
escape from the cave; then he took the kite-line in his hand
and went groping down one of the passages on his hands and
knees, distressed with hunger and sick with bodings of coming doom.

XXXII

TUESDAY AFTERNOON came, and waned to the twilight. The village of St. Petersburg still mourned. The lost children had not been found. Public prayers had been offered up for them, and many and many a private prayer that had the petitioner's whole heart in it; but still no good news came from the cave. The majority of the searchers had given up the quest and gone back to their daily avocations, saying that it was plain the children could never be found. Mrs. Thatcher was very ill, and a great part of the time delirious. People said it was heart-breaking to hear her call her child, and raise her head and listen a whole minute at a time, then lay it wearily down again with a moan. Aunt Polly had drooped into a settled melancholy, and her gray hair had grown almost white. The village went to its rest on Tuesday night, sad and forlorn.

Away in the middle of the night a wild peal burst from the village bells, and in a moment the streets were swarming with frantic half-clad people, who shouted, "Turn out! turn out! they're found! they're found!" Tin pans and horns were added to the din, the population massed itself and moved toward the river, met the children coming in an open carriage drawn by shouting citizens, thronged around it, joined its homeward march, and swept magnificently up the main street roaring huzzah after huzzah!

The village was illuminated; nobody went to bed again; it was the greatest night the little town had ever seen. During the first half hour a procession of villagers filed through Judge Thatcher's house, seized the saved ones and kissed them, squeezed Mrs. Thatcher's hand, tried to speak but couldn't— and drifted out raining tears all over the place.

Aunt Polly's happiness was complete, and Mrs. Thatcher's nearly so. It would be complete, however, as soon as the messenger dispatched with the great news to the cave should get the word to her husband. Tom lay upon a sofa with an eager auditory about him and told the history of the wonderful adventure, putting in many striking additions to adorn it withal; and closed with a description of how he left Becky and went on an exploring expedition; how he followed two avenues as far as his kite-line would reach; how he followed a third to the fullest stretch of the kite-line, and was about to turn back when he glimpsed a far-off speck that looked like daylight; dropped the line and groped toward it, pushed his head and shoulders through a small hole and saw the broad Mississippi rolling by! And if it had only happened to be night he would not have seen that speck of daylight and would not have explored that passage any more! He told how he went back for Becky and broke the good news and she told him not to fret her with such stuff, for she was tired, and knew she was going to die, and wanted to. He described how he labored with her and convinced her; and how she almost died for joy when she had groped to where she actually saw the blue speck of daylight; how he pushed his way out at the hole and then helped her out; how they sat there and cried for gladness; how some men came along in a skiff and Tom hailed them and told them their situation and their famished condition; how the men didn't believe the wild tale at first, "because," said they "you are five miles down the river below the valley the cave is in"—then took them aboard, rowed to a house, gave them supper, made them rest till two or three hours after dark and then brought them home.

Before day-dawn, Judge Thatcher and the handful of searchers with him were tracked out, in the cave, by the twine clews they had strung behind them, and informed of the great news.

Three days and nights of toil and hunger in the cave were not to be shaken off at once, as Tom and Becky soon discovered. They were bedridden all of Wednesday and Thursday, and seemed to grow more and more tired and worn, all the time. Tom got about, a little, on Thursday, was down town Friday, and nearly as whole as ever Saturday; but Becky did not leave her room until Sunday, and then she looked as if she had passed through a wasting illness.

Tom learned of Huck's sickness and went to see him on Friday, but could not be admitted to the bedroom; neither could he on Saturday or Sunday. He was admitted daily after that, but was warned to keep still about his adventure and introduce no exciting topic. The widow Douglas staid by to see that he obeyed. At home Tom learned of the Cardiff Hill event; also that the "ragged man's" body had eventually been found in the river near the ferry landing; he had been drowned while trying to escape, perhaps.

About a fortnight after Tom's rescue from the cave, he started off to visit Huck, who had grown plenty strong enough, now, to hear exciting talk, and Tom had some that would interest him, he thought. Judge Thatcher's house was on Tom's way, and he stopped to see Becky. The Judge and some friends set Tom to talking, and some one asked him ironically if he wouldn't like to go to the cave again. Tom said yes, he thought he wouldn't mind it. The Judge said:

"Well, there are others just like you, Tom, I've not the least doubt. But we have taken care of that. Nobody will get lost in that cave any more."

"Why?"

"Because I had its big door sheathed with boiler iron two weeks ago, and triple-locked—and I've got the keys."

Tom turned as white as a sheet.

"What's the matter, boy! Here, run, somebody! Fetch a glass of water!"

The water was brought and thrown into Tom's face.

"Ah, now you're all right. What was the matter with you, Tom?"

"Oh, Judge, Injun Joe's in the cave!"

XXXIII

WITHIN A FEW MINUTES the news had spread, and a dozen skiff-loads of men were on their way to McDougal's cave, and the ferry-boat, well filled with passengers, soon followed. Tom Sawyer was in the skiff that bore Judge Thatcher.

When the cave door was unlocked, a sorrowful sight presented itself in the dim twilight of the place. Injun Joe lay stretched upon the ground, dead, with his face close to the crack of the door, as if his longing eyes had been fixed, to the latest moment, upon the light and the cheer of the free world outside. Tom was touched, for he knew by his own experience how this wretch had suffered. His pity was moved, but nevertheless he felt an abounding sense of relief and security, now, which revealed to him in a degree which he had not fully appreciated before, how vast a weight of dread had been lying upon him since the day he lifted his voice against this bloody-minded outcast.

Injun Joe's bowie knife lay close by, its blade broken in two. The great foundation-beam of the door had been chipped and hacked through, with tedious labor; useless labor, too, it was, for the native rock formed a sill outside it, and upon that stubborn material the knife had wrought no effect; the only damage done was to the knife itself. But if there had been no stony obstruction there the labor would have been useless still, for if the beam had been wholly cut away Injun Joe could not have squeezed his body under the door, and he knew it. So he had only hacked that place in order to be doing something—in order to pass the weary time—in order to employ his tortured faculties. Ordinarily one could find half a dozen bits of candle stuck around in the crevices of this vestibule, left there by tourists; but there were none now. The prisoner had searched them out and eaten them. He had also contrived to catch a few bats, and these, also, he had eaten, leaving only their claws. The poor unfortunate had starved to death. In one place near at hand, a stalagmite had been slowly growing up from the ground for ages, builded by the water-drip from a stalactite overhead. The captive had broken off the stalagmite, and upon the stump had placed a stone wherein he had scooped a shallow hollow to catch the precious drop that fell once in every three minutes with the dreary regularity of a clock-tick—a dessert spoonful once in four and twenty hours. That drop was falling when the Pyramids were new; when Troy fell; when the foundations of Rome were laid; when Christ was crucified; when the Conqueror created the British empire; when Columbus sailed; when the massacre at Lexington was "news." It is falling now; it will still be falling when all these things shall have sunk down the afternoon of history, and the twilight of tradition, and been swallowed up in the thick night of oblivion. Has everything a purpose and a mission? Did this drop fall patiently during five thousand years to be ready for this flitting human insect's need? and has it another important object to accomplish ten thousand years to come? No matter. It is many and many a year since the hapless half-breed scooped out the stone to catch the priceless drops, but to this day the tourist stares longest at that pathetic stone and that slow dropping water when he comes to see the wonders of McDougal's cave. Injun Joe's Cup stands first in the list of the cavern's marvels; even "Aladdin's Palace" cannot rival it.

Injun Joe was buried near the mouth of the cave; and people flocked there in boats and wagons from the town and from all the farms and hamlets for seven miles around; they brought their children, and all sorts of provisions, and confessed that they had had almost as satisfactory a time at the funeral as they could have had at the hanging.

This funeral stopped the further growth of one thing—the petition to the Governor for Injun Joe's pardon. The petition had been largely signed; many tearful and eloquent meetings had been held, and a committee of sappy women been appointed to go in deep mourning and wail around the governor and implore him to be a merciful ass and trample his duty under foot. Injun Joe was believed to have killed five citizens of the village, but what of that? If he had been Satan himself there would have been plenty of weaklings ready to scribble their names to a pardon-petition and drip a tear on it from their permanently impaired and leaky water-works.

The morning after the funeral Tom took Huck to a private place to have an important talk. Huck had learned all about Tom's adventure from the Welchman and the widow Douglas, by this time, but Tom said he reckoned there was one thing they had not told him; that thing was what he wanted to talk about now. Huck's face saddened. He said:

"I know what it is. You got into No. 2 and never found anything but whisky. Nobody told me it was you; but I just knowed it must 'a' ben you, soon as I heard 'bout that whisky business; and I knowed you hadn't got the money becuz you'd 'a' got at me some way or other and told me even if you was mum to everybody else. Tom, something's always told me we'd never get holt of that swag."

"Why Huck, *I* never told on that tavern-keeper. *You* know his tavern was all right the Saturday I went to the pic-nic. Don't you remember you was to watch there that night?"

"Oh, yes! Why it seems 'bout a year ago. It was that very night that I follered Injun Joe to the widder's."

"*You* followed him?"

"Yes—but you keep mum. I reckon Injun Joe's left friends behind him, and I don't want 'em souring on me and doing me mean tricks. If it hadn't ben for me he'd be down in Texas now, all right."

Then Huck told his entire adventure in confidence to Tom, who had only heard of the Welchmen's part of it before.

"Well," said Huck, presently, coming back to the main question, "whoever nipped the whisky in No. 2, nipped the money too, I reckon—anyways it's a goner for us, Tom."

"Huck, that money wasn't ever in No. 2!"

"What!" Huck searched his comrade's face keenly. "Tom, have you got on the track of that money again?"

"Huck, it's in the cave!"

Huck's eyes blazed.

"Say it again, Tom!"

"The money's in the cave!"

"Tom,—honest injun, now—is it fun, or earnest?"

"Earnest, Huck—just as earnest as ever I was in my life. Will you go in there with me and help get it out?"

"I bet I will! I will if it's where we can blaze our way to it and not get lost."

"Huck, we can do that without the least little bit of trouble in the world."

"Good as wheat! What makes you think the money's—"

"Huck, you just wait till we get in there. If we don't find it I'll agree to give you my drum and everything I've got in the world. I will, by jings."

"All right—it's a whiz. When do you say?"

"Right now, if you say it. Are you strong enough?"

"Is it far in the cave? I ben on my pins a little, three or four days, now, but I can't walk more'n a mile, Tom—least I don't think I could."

"It's about five mile into there the way anybody but me would go, Huck, but there's a mighty short cut that they don't anybody but me know about. Huck, I'll take you right to it in a skiff. I'll float the skiff down there, and I'll pull it back again all by myself. You needn't ever turn your hand over."

"Less start right off, Tom."

"All right. We want some bread and meat, and our pipes, and a little bag or two, and two or three kite-strings, and some of these new-fangled things they call lucifer matches. I tell you many's the time I wished I had some when I was in there before."

A trifle after noon the boys borrowed a small skiff from a citizen who was absent, and got under way at once. When they were several miles below "Cave Hollow," Tom said:

"Now you see this bluff here looks all alike all the way down from the cave hollow—no houses, no wood-yards, bushes all alike. But do you see that white place up yonder where there's been a land-slide? Well, that's one of my marks. We'll get ashore, now."

They landed.

"Now Huck, where we're a-standing you could touch that hole I got out of with a fishing-pole. See if you can find it."

Huck searched all the place about, and found nothing. Tom proudly marched into a thick clump of sumach bushes and said—

"Here you are! Look at it, Huck; it's the snuggest hole in this country. You just keep mum about it. All along I've been wanting to be a robber, but I knew I'd got to have a thing like this, and where to run across it was the bother. We've got it now, and we'll keep it quiet, only we'll let Joe Harper and Ben Rogers in—because of course there's got to be a Gang, or else there wouldn't be any style about it. Tom Sawyer's Gang—it sounds splendid, don't it, Huck?"

"Well it just does, Tom. And who'll we rob?"

"Oh, most anybody. Waylay people—that's mostly the way."

"And kill them?"

"No—not always. Hive them in the cave till they raise a ransom."

"What's a ransom?"

"Money. You make them raise all they can, off'n their friends; and after you've kept them a year, if it ain't raised then you kill them. That's the general way. Only you don't kill the women. You shut up the women, but you don't kill them. They're always beautiful and rich, and awfully scared. You take their watches and things, but you always take your hat off and talk polite. They ain't anybody as polite as robbers—you'll see that in any book. Well the women get to loving you, and after they've been in the cave a week or two weeks they stop crying and after that you couldn't get them to leave. If you drove them out they'd turn right around and come back. It's so in all the books."

"Why it's real bully, Tom. I b'lieve it's better'n to be a pirate."

"Yes, it's better in some ways, because it's close to home and circuses and all that."

By this time everything was ready and the boys entered the hole, Tom in the lead. They toiled their way to the farther end of the tunnel, then made their spliced kite-strings fast and moved on. A few steps brought them to the spring and Tom felt a shudder quiver all through him. He showed Huck the fragment of candle-wick perched on a lump of clay against the wall, and described how he and Becky had watched the flame struggle and expire.

The boys began to quiet down to whispers, now, for the stillness and gloom of the place oppressed their spirits. They went on, and presently entered and followed Tom's other corridor until they reached the "jumping-off place." The candles revealed the fact that it was not really a precipice, but only a steep clay hill twenty or thirty feet high. Tom whispered—

"Now I'll show you something, Huck."

He held his candle aloft and said—

"Look as far around the corner as you can. Do you see that? There—on the big rock over yonder—done with candle smoke."

"Tom, it's a *cross!*"

"*Now* where's your Number Two? '*Under the cross,*' hey? Right yonder's where I saw Injun Joe poke up his candle, Huck!"

Huck stared at the mystic sign a while, and then said with a shaky voice—

"Tom, less git out of here!"

"What! and leave the treasure?"

"Yes—leave it. Injun Joe's ghost is round about there, certain."

"No it ain't, Huck, no it ain't. It would ha'nt the place where he died—away out at the mouth of the cave—five mile from here."

"No, Tom, it wouldn't. It would hang round the money. I know the ways of ghosts, and so do you."

Tom began to fear that Huck was right. Misgivings gathered in his mind. But presently an idea occurred to him—

"Lookyhere, Huck, what fools we're making of ourselves! Injun Joe's ghost ain't a-going to come around where there's a cross!"

The point was well taken. It had its effect.

"Tom I didn't think of that. But that's so. It's luck for us, that cross is. I reckon we'll climb down there and have a hunt for that box."

Tom went first, cutting rude steps in the clay hill as he descended. Huck followed. Four avenues opened out of the small cavern which the great rock stood in. The boys examined three of them with no result. They found a small recess in the one nearest the base of the rock, with a pallet of blankets spread down in it; also an old suspender, some bacon rhind, and the well gnawed bones of two or three fowls. But there was no money box. The lads searched and re-searched this place, but in vain. Tom said:

"He said *under* the cross. Well, this comes nearest to being under the cross. It can't be under the rock itself, because that sets solid on the ground."

They searched everywhere once more, and then sat down discouraged. Huck could suggest nothing. By and by Tom said:

"Lookyhere, Huck, there's footprints and some candle grease on the clay about one side of this rock, but not on the other sides. Now what's that for? I bet you the money *is* under the rock. I'm going to dig in the clay."

"That ain't no bad notion, Tom!" said Huck with animation.

Tom's "real Barlow" was out at once, and he had not dug four inches before he struck wood.

"Hey, Huck!—you hear that?"

Huck began to dig and scratch now. Some boards were soon uncovered and removed. They had concealed a natural chasm which led under the rock. Tom got into this and held his candle as far under the rock as he could, but said he could not see to the end of the rift. He proposed to explore. He stooped and passed under; the narrow way descended gradually. He followed its winding course, first to the right, then to the left, Huck at his heels. Tom turned a short curve, by and by, and exclaimed—

"My goodness, Huck, lookyhere!"

It was the treasure box, sure enough, occupying a snug little cavern, along with an empty powder keg, a couple of guns in leather cases, two or three pairs of old moccasins, a leather belt, and some other rubbish well soaked with the water-drip.

"Got it at last!" said Huck, plowing among the tarnished coins with his hand. "My, but we're rich, Tom!"

"Huck, I always reckoned we'd get it. It's just too good to believe, but we *have* got it, sure! Say—let's not fool around here. Let's snake it out. Lemme see if I can lift the box."

It weighed about fifty pounds. Tom could lift it, after an awkward fashion, but could not carry it conveniently.

"I thought so," he said; "*they* carried it like it was heavy, that day at the ha'nted house. I noticed that. I reckon I was right to think of fetching the little bags along."

The money was soon in the bags and the boys took it up to the cross-rock.

"Now less fetch the guns and things," said Huck.

"No, Huck—leave them there. They're just the tricks to have when we go to robbing. We'll keep them there all the time, and we'll hold our orgies there, too. It's an awful snug place for orgies."

"What's orgies?"

"*I* dono. But robbers always have orgies, and of course we've got to have them, too. Come along, Huck, we've been in here a long time. It's getting late, I reckon. I'm hungry, too. We'll eat and smoke when we get to the skiff."

They presently emerged into the clump of sumach bushes, looked warily out, found the coast clear, and were soon lunching and smoking in the skiff. As the sun dipped toward the horizon they pushed out and got under way. Tom skimmed up the shore through the long twilight, chatting cheerily with Huck, and landed shortly after dark.

"Now Huck," said Tom, "we'll hide the money in the loft of the widow's wood-shed, and I'll come up in the morning and we'll count it and divide, and then we'll hunt up a place out in the woods for it where it will be safe. Just you lay quiet here and watch the stuff till I run and hook Benny Taylor's little wagon; I won't be gone a minute."

He disappeared, and presently returned with the wagon, put the two small sacks into it, threw some old rags on top of them, and started off, dragging his cargo behind him. When the boys reached the Welchman's house, they stopped to rest. Just as they were about to move on, the Welchman stepped out and said:

"Hallo, who's that?"

"Huck and Tom Sawyer."

"Good! Come along with me, boys, you are keeping everybody waiting. Here—hurry up, trot ahead—I'll haul the wagon for you. Why, it's not as light as it might be. Got bricks in it?—or old metal?"

"Old metal," said Tom.

"I judged so; the boys in this town will take more trouble and fool away more time, hunting up six bits worth of old iron to sell to the foundry than they would to make twice the money at regular work. But that's human nature—hurry along, hurry along!"

The boys wanted to know what the hurry was about.

"Never mind; you'll see, when we get to the widow Douglas's."

Huck said with some apprehension—for he was long used to being falsely accused—

"Mr. Jones, *we* haven't been doing nothing."

The Welchman laughed.

"Well, I don't know, Huck, my boy. I don't know about that. Ain't you and the widow good friends?"

"Yes. Well, she's ben good friends to me, any ways."

"All right, then. What do you want to be afraid for?"

This question was not entirely answered in Huck's slow mind before he found himself pushed, along with Tom, into Mrs. Douglas's drawing room. Mr. Jones left the wagon near the door and followed.

The place was grandly lighted, and everybody that was of any consequence in the village was there. The Thatchers were there, the Harpers, the Rogerses, Aunt Polly, Sid, Mary, the minister, the editor, and a great many more, and all dressed in their best. The widow received the boys as heartily as any one could well receive two such looking beings. They were covered with clay and candle grease. Aunt Polly blushed crimson with humiliation, and frowned and shook her head at Tom. Nobody suffered half as much as the two boys did, however. Mr. Jones said:

"Tom wasn't at home, yet, so I gave him up; but I stumbled on him and Huck right at my door, and so I just brought them along in a hurry."

"And you did just right," said the widow: "Come with me, boys."

She took them to a bed chamber and said:

"Now wash and dress yourselves. Here are two new suits of clothes—shirts, socks, everything complete. They're Huck's—no, no thanks Huck—Mr. Jones bought one and I the other. But they'll fit both of you. Get into them. We'll wait—come down when you are slicked up enough."

Then she left.

XXXIV

HUCK SAID:

"Tom, we can slope, if we can find a rope. The window ain't high from the ground."

"Shucks, what do you want to slope for?"

"Well I ain't used to that kind of a crowd. I can't stand it. I ain't going down there, Tom."

"O, bother! It ain't anything. I don't mind it a bit. I'll take care of you."

Sid appeared.

"Tom," said he, "Auntie has been waiting for you all the afternoon. Mary got your Sunday clothes ready, and everybody's been fretting about you. Say—ain't this grease and clay, on your clothes?"

"Now Mr. Siddy, you jist 'tend to your own business. What's all this blow-out about, anyway?"

"It's one of the widow's parties that she's always having. This time it's for the Welchman and his sons, on account of that scrape they helped her out of the other night. And say— I can tell you something, if you want to know."

"Well, what?"

"Why old Mr. Jones is going to try to spring something on the people here to-night, but I overheard him tell auntie to-day about it, as a secret, but I reckon it's not much of a secret *now*. Everybody knows—the widow, too, for all she tries to let on she don't. Oh, Mr. Jones was bound Huck should be here—couldn't get along with his grand secret without Huck, you know!"

"Secret about what, Sid?"

"About Huck tracking the robbers to the widow's. I reckon Mr. Jones was going to make a grand time over his surprise, but I bet you it will drop pretty flat."

Sid chuckled in a very contented and satisfied way.

"Sid, was it you that told?"

"O, never mind who it was. *Somebody* told—that's enough."

"Sid, there's only one person in this town mean enough to

do that, and that's you. If you had been in Huck's place you'd 'a' sneaked down the hill and never told anybody on the robbers. You can't do any but mean things, and you can't bear to see anybody praised for doing good ones. There—no thanks, as the widow says"—and Tom cuffed Sid's ears and helped him to the door with several kicks. "Now go and tell auntie if you dare—and to-morrow you'll catch it!"

Some minutes later the widow's guests were at the supper table, and a dozen children were propped up at little side tables in the same room, after the fashion of that country and that day. At the proper time Mr. Jones made his little speech, in which he thanked the widow for the honor she was doing himself and his sons, but said that there was another person whose modesty—

And so forth and so on. He sprung his secret about Huck's share in the adventure in the finest dramatic manner he was master of, but the surprise it occasioned was largely counterfeit and not as clamorous and effusive as it might have been under happier circumstances. However, the widow made a pretty fair show of astonishment, and heaped so many compliments and so much gratitude upon Huck that he almost forgot the nearly intolerable discomfort of his new clothes in the entirely intolerable discomfort of being set up as a target for everybody's gaze and everybody's laudations.

The widow said she meant to give Huck a home under her roof and have him educated; and that when she could spare the money she would start him in business in a modest way. Tom's chance was come. He said:

"Huck don't need it. Huck's rich!"

Nothing but a heavy strain upon the good manners of the company kept back the due and proper complimentary laugh at this pleasant joke. But the silence was a little awkward. Tom broke it—

"Huck's got money. Maybe you don't believe it, but he's got lots of it. Oh, you needn't smile—I reckon I can show you. You just wait a minute."

Tom ran out of doors. The company looked at each other with a perplexed interest—and inquiringly at Huck, who was tongue-tied.

"Sid, what ails Tom?" said aunt Polly. "He—well, there ain't ever any making of that boy out. I never—"

Tom entered, struggling with the weight of his sacks, and Aunt Polly did not finish her sentence. Tom poured the mass of yellow coin upon the table and said—

"There—what did I tell you? Half of it's Huck's and half of it's mine!"

The spectacle took the general breath away. All gazed, nobody spoke for a moment. Then there was a unanimous call for an explanation. Tom said he could furnish it, and he did. The tale was long, but brim full of interest. There was scarcely an interruption from any one to break the charm of its flow. When he had finished, Mr. Jones said—

"I thought I had fixed up a little surprise for this occasion, but it don't amount to anything now. This one makes it sing mighty small, I'm willing to allow."

The money was counted. The sum amounted to a little over twelve thousand dollars. It was more than any one present had ever seen at one time before, though several persons were there who were worth considerably more than that in property.

XXXV

THE READER may rest satisfied that Tom's and Huck's windfall made a mighty stir in the poor little village of St. Petersburg. So vast a sum, all in actual cash, seemed next to incredible. It was talked about, gloated over, glorified, until the reason of many of the citizens tottered under the strain of the unhealthy excitement. Every "haunted" house in St. Petersburg and the neighboring villages was dissected, plank by plank, and its foundations dug up and ransacked for hidden treasure—and not by boys, but men—pretty grave, unromantic men, too, some of them. Wherever Tom and Huck appeared they were courted, admired, stared at. The boys were not able to remember that their remarks had possessed weight before; but now their sayings were treasured and repeated; everything they did seemed somehow to be regarded as remarkable; they had evidently lost the power of doing and saying commonplace things; moreover, their past history was raked up and discovered to bear marks of conspicuous originality. The village paper published biographical sketches of the boys.

The widow Douglas put Huck's money out at six per cent., and Judge Thatcher did the same with Tom's at aunt Polly's request. Each lad had an income, now, that was simply prodigious—a dollar for every week-day in the year and half of the Sundays. It was just what the minister got—no, it was what he was promised—he generally couldn't collect it. A dollar and a quarter a week would board, lodge and school a boy in those old simple days—and clothe him and wash him, too, for that matter.

Judge Thatcher had conceived a great opinion of Tom. He said that no commonplace boy would ever have got his daughter out of the cave. When Becky told her father, in strict confidence, how Tom had taken her whipping at school, the Judge was visibly moved; and when she pleaded grace for the mighty lie which Tom had told in order to shift that whipping from her shoulders to his own, the Judge said with a fine outburst that it was a noble, a generous, a magnanimous lie—a lie that was worthy to hold up its head and march down through history breast to breast with George Washington's lauded Truth about the hatchet! Becky thought her father had never looked so tall and so superb as when he walked the floor and stamped his foot and said that. She went straight off and told Tom about it.

Judge Thatcher hoped to see Tom a great lawyer or a great soldier some day. He said he meant to look to it that Tom should be admitted to the National military academy and afterwards trained in the best law school in the country, in order that he might be ready for either career or both.

Huck Finn's wealth and the fact that he was now under the widow Douglas's protection, introduced him into society—no, dragged him into it, hurled him into it—and his sufferings were almost more than he could bear. The widow's servants kept him clean and neat, combed and brushed, and they bedded him nightly in unsympathetic sheets that had not one little spot or stain which he could press to his heart and know for a friend. He had to eat with knife and fork; he had to use napkin, cup and plate; he had to learn his book, he had to go to church; he had to talk so properly that speech was become insipid in his mouth; whithersoever he turned, the bars and shackles of civilization shut him in and bound him hand and foot.

He bravely bore his miseries three weeks, and then one day turned up missing. For forty-eight hours the widow hunted for him everywhere in great distress. The public were profoundly concerned; they searched high and low, they dragged the river for his body. Early the third morning Tom Sawyer wisely went poking among some old empty hogsheads down behind the abandoned slaughter-house, and in one of them he found the refugee. Huck had slept there; he had just breakfasted upon some stolen odds and ends of food, and was lying off, now, in comfort with his pipe. He was unkempt, uncombed, and clad in the same old ruin of rags that had made him picturesque in the days when he was free and happy. Tom routed him out, told him the trouble he had been causing, and urged him to go home. Huck's face lost its tranquil content, and took a melancholy cast. He said:

"Don't talk about it, Tom. I've tried it, and it don't work;

it don't work, Tom. It ain't for me; I ain't used to it. The widder's good to me, and friendly; but I can't stand them ways. She makes me git up just at the same time every morning; she makes me wash, they comb me all to thunder; she won't let me sleep in the wood-shed; I got to wear them blamed clothes that just smothers me, Tom; they don't seem to any air git through 'em, somehow; and they're so rotten nice that I can't set down, nor lay down, nor roll around anywhers; I hain't slid on a cellar-door for—well, it 'pears to be years; I got to go to church and sweat and sweat—I hate them ornery sermons! I can't ketch a fly in there, I can't chaw, I got to wear shoes all Sunday. The widder eats by a bell; she goes to bed by a bell; she gits up by a bell—everything's so awful reglar a body can't stand it."

"Well, everybody does that way, Huck."

"Tom, it don't make no difference. I ain't everybody, and I can't *stand* it. It's awful to be tied up so. And grub comes too easy—I don't take no interest in vittles, that way. I got to ask, to go a-fishing; I got to ask, to go in a-swimming— dern'd if I hain't got to ask to do everything. Well, I'd got to talk so nice it wasn't no comfort—I'd got to go up in the attic and rip out a while, every day, to git a taste in my mouth, or I'd a died, Tom. The widder wouldn't let me smoke; she wouldn't let me yell, she wouldn't let me gape, nor stretch, nor scratch, before folks—" [Then with a spasm of special irritation and injury],— "And dad fetch it, she prayed all the time! I never *see* such a woman! I *had* to shove, Tom—I just had to. And besides, that school's going to open, and I'd a had to go to it—well, I wouldn't stand *that*, Tom. Lookyhere, Tom, being rich ain't what it's cracked up to be. It's just worry and worry, and sweat and sweat, and a-wishing you was dead all the time. Now these clothes suits me, and this bar'l suits me, and I ain't ever going to shake 'em any more. Tom, I wouldn't ever got into all this trouble if it hadn't 'a' ben for that money; now you just take my sheer of it along with yourn, and gimme a ten-center sometimes— not many times, becuz I don't give a dern for a thing 'thout it's tollable hard to git—and you go and beg off for me with the widder."

"Oh, Huck, you know I can't do that. 'Tain't fair; and besides if you'll try this thing just a while longer you'll come to like it."

"Like it! Yes—the way I'd like a hot stove if I was to set on it long enough. No, Tom, I won't be rich, and I won't live in them cussed smothery houses. I like the woods, and the river, and hogsheads, and I'll stick to 'em, too. Blame it all! just as we'd got guns, and a cave, and all just fixed to rob, here this dern foolishness has got to come up and spile it all!"

Tom saw his opportunity—

"Lookyhere, Huck, being rich ain't going to keep me back from turning robber."

"No! Oh, good-licks, are you in real dead-wood earnest, Tom?"

"Just as dead earnest as I'm a-sitting here. But Huck, we can't let you into the gang if you ain't respectable, you know."

Huck's joy was quenched.

"Can't let me in, Tom? Didn't you let me go for a pirate?"

"Yes, but that's different. A robber is more high-toned than what a pirate is—as a general thing. In most countries they're awful high up in the nobility—dukes and such."

"Now Tom, hain't you always ben friendly to me? You wouldn't shet me out, would you, Tom? You wouldn't do that, now, *would* you, Tom?"

"Huck, I wouldn't want to, and I *don't* want to—but what would people say? Why they'd say, 'Mph! Tom Sawyer's Gang! pretty low characters in it!' They'd mean you, Huck. You wouldn't like that, and I wouldn't."

Huck was silent for some time, engaged in a mental struggle. Finally he said:

"Well, I'll go back to the widder for a month and tackle it and see if I can come to stand it, if you'll let me b'long to the gang, Tom."

"All right, Huck, it's a whiz! Come along, old chap, and I'll ask the widow to let up on you a little, Huck."

"Will you Tom—now will you? That's good. If she'll let up on some of the roughest things, I'll smoke private and cuss private, and crowd through or bust. When you going to start the gang and turn robbers?"

"Oh, right off. We'll get the boys together and have the initiation to-night, maybe."

"Have the which?"

"Have the initiation."

"What's that?"

"It's to swear to stand by one another, and never tell the gang's secrets, even if you're chopped all to flinders, and kill anybody and all his family that hurts one of the gang."

"That's gay—that's mighty gay, Tom, I tell you."

"Well I bet it is. And all that swearing's got to be done at midnight, in the lonesomest, awfulest place you can find—a ha'nted house is the best, but they're all ripped up, now."

"Well, midnight's good, anyway, Tom."

"Yes, so it is. And you've got to swear on a coffin, and sign it with blood."

"Now that's something *like*! Why it's a million times bullier than pirating. I'll stick to the widder till I rot, Tom; and if I git to be a reglar ripper of a robber, and everybody talking 'bout it, I reckon she'll be proud she snaked me in out of the wet."

CONCLUSION

S O ENDETH this chronicle. It being strictly a history of a
boy, it must stop here; the story could not go much further without becoming the history of a *man*. When one
writes a novel about grown people, he knows exactly where
to stop—that is, with a marriage; but when he writes of juveniles, he must stop where he best can.

Most of the characters that perform in this book still live,
and are prosperous and happy. Some day it may seem worth
while to take up the story of the younger ones again and see
what sort of men and women they turned out to be; therefore
it will be wisest not to reveal any of that part of their lives at
present.

THE END.

LIFE ON THE MISSISSIPPI

The "Body of the Nation"

But the basin of the Mississippi is the BODY OF THE NATION. All the other parts are but members, important in themselves, yet more important in their relations to this. Exclusive of the Lake basin and of 300,000 square miles in Texas and New Mexico, which in many aspects form a part of it, this basin contains about 1,250,000 square miles. In extent it is the second great valley of the world, being exceeded only by that of the Amazon. The valley of the frozen Ob approaches it in extent; that of the La Plata comes next in space, and probably in habitable capacity, having about ⁸/₉ of its area; then comes that of the Yenisei, with about ⁷/₉; the Lena, Amoor, Hoang-ho, Yang-tse-kiang, and Nile, ⁵/₉; the Ganges, less than ¹/₂; the Indus, less than ¹/₃; the Euphrates, ¹/₅; the Rhine, ¹/₁₅. It exceeds in extent the whole of Europe, exclusive of Russia, Norway, and Sweden. *It would contain Austria four times, Germany or Spain five times, France six times, the British Islands or Italy ten times.* Conceptions formed from the river-basins of Western Europe are rudely shocked when we consider the extent of the valley of the Mississippi; nor are those formed from the sterile basins of the great rivers of Siberia, the lofty plateaus of Central Asia, or the mighty sweep of the swampy Amazon more adequate. Latitude, elevation, and rainfall all combine to render every part of the Mississippi Valley capable of supporting a dense population. *As a dwelling-place for civilized man it is by far the first upon our globe.*—EDITOR'S TABLE, *Harper's Magazine,* February, 1863.

Contents.

CONTENTS

I.

The River and Its History

THE MISSISSIPPI is well worth reading about. It is not a commonplace river, but on the contrary is in all ways remarkable. Considering the Missouri its main branch, it is the longest river in the world—four thousand three hundred miles. It seems safe to say that it is also the crookedest river in the world, since in one part of its journey it uses up one thousand three hundred miles to cover the same ground that the crow would fly over in six hundred and seventy-five. It discharges three times as much water as the St. Lawrence, twenty-five times as much as the Rhine, and three hundred and thirty-eight times as much as the Thames. No other river has so vast a drainage-basin: it draws its water supply from twenty-eight States and Territories; from Delaware, on the Atlantic seaboard, and from all the country between that and Idaho on the Pacific slope—a spread of forty-five degrees of longitude. The Mississippi receives and carries to the Gulf water from fifty-four subordinate rivers that are navigable by steamboats, and from some hundreds that are navigable by flats and keels. The area of its drainage-basin is as great as the combined areas of England, Wales, Scotland, Ireland, France, Spain, Portugal, Germany, Austria, Italy, and Turkey; and almost all this wide region is fertile; the Mississippi valley, proper, is exceptionally so.

It is a remarkable river in this: that instead of widening toward its mouth, it grows narrower; grows narrower and deeper. From the junction of the Ohio to a point half way down to the sea, the width averages a mile in high water: thence to the sea the width steadily diminishes, until, at the "Passes," above the mouth, it is but little over half a mile. At the junction of the Ohio the Mississippi's depth is eighty-seven feet; the depth increases gradually, reaching one hundred and twenty-nine just above the mouth.

The difference in rise and fall is also remarkable—not in the upper, but in the lower river. The rise is tolerably uniform down to Natchez (three hundred and sixty miles above the mouth)—about fifty feet. But at Bayou La Fourche the river rises only twenty-four feet; at New Orleans only fifteen, and just above the mouth only two and one half.

An article in the New Orleans "Times-Democrat," based upon reports of able engineers, states that the river annually empties four hundred and six million tons of mud into the Gulf of Mexico—which brings to mind Captain Marryat's rude name for the Mississippi—"the Great Sewer." This mud, solidified, would make a mass a mile square and two hundred and forty-one feet high.

The mud deposit gradually extends the land—but only gradually; it has extended it not quite a third of a mile in the two hundred years which have elapsed since the river took its place in history. The belief of the scientific people is, that the mouth used to be at Baton Rouge, where the hills cease, and that the two hundred miles of land between there and the Gulf was built by the river. This gives us the age of that piece of country, without any trouble at all—one hundred and twenty thousand years. Yet it is much the youthfulest batch of country that lies around there anywhere.

The Mississippi is remarkable in still another way—its disposition to make prodigious jumps by cutting through narrow necks of land, and thus straightening and shortening itself. More than once it has shortened itself thirty miles at a single jump! These cut-offs have had curious effects: they have thrown several river towns out into the rural districts, and built up sand bars and forests in front of them. The town of Delta used to be three miles below Vicksburg: a recent cut-off has radically changed the position, and Delta is now *two miles above* Vicksburg.

Both of these river towns have been retired to the country by that cut-off. A cut-off plays havoc with boundary lines and jurisdictions: for instance, a man is living in the State of Mississippi to-day, a cut-off occurs to-night, and to-morrow the man finds himself and his land over on the other side of the river, within the boundaries and subject to the laws of the State of Louisiana! Such a thing, happening in the upper river in the old times, could have transferred a slave from Missouri to Illinois and made a free man of him.

The Mississippi does not alter its locality by cut-offs alone:

it is always changing its habitat *bodily*—is always moving bodily *sidewise*. At Hard Times, La., the river is two miles west of the region it used to occupy. As a result, the original *site* of that settlement is not now in Louisiana at all, but on the other side of the river, in the State of Mississippi. *Nearly the whole of that one thousand three hundred miles of old Mississippi River which La Salle floated down in his canoes, two hundred years ago, is good solid dry ground now.* The river lies to the right of it, in places, and to the left of it in other places.

Although the Mississippi's mud builds land but slowly, down at the mouth, where the Gulf's billows interfere with its work, it builds fast enough in better protected regions higher up: for instance, Prophet's Island contained one thousand five hundred acres of land thirty years ago; since then the river has added seven hundred acres to it.

But enough of these examples of the mighty stream's eccentricities for the present—I will give a few more of them further along in the book.

Let us drop the Mississippi's physical history, and say a word about its historical history—so to speak. We can glance briefly at its slumbrous first epoch in a couple of short chapters; at its second and wider-awake epoch in a couple more; at its flushest and widest-awake epoch in a good many succeeding chapters; and then talk about its comparatively tranquil present epoch in what shall be left of the book.

The world and the books are so accustomed to use, and over-use, the word "new" in connection with our country, that we early get and permanently retain the impression that there is nothing old about it. We do of course know that there are several comparatively old dates in American history, but the mere figures convey to our minds no just idea, no distinct realization, of the stretch of time which they represent. To say that De Soto, the first white man who ever saw the Mississippi River, saw it in 1542, is a remark which states a fact without interpreting it: it is something like giving the dimensions of a sunset by astronomical measurements, and cataloguing the colors by their scientific names;—as a result, you get the bald fact of the sunset, but you don't see the sunset. It would have been better to paint a picture of it.

The date 1542, standing by itself, means little or nothing to us; but when one groups a few neighboring historical dates and facts around it, he adds perspective and color, and then realizes that this is one of the American dates which is quite respectable for age.

For instance, when the Mississippi was first seen by a white man, less than a quarter of a century had elapsed since Francis I.'s defeat at Pavia; the death of Raphael; the death of Bayard, *sans peur et sans reproche*; the driving out of the Knights-Hospitallers from Rhodes by the Turks; and the placarding of the Ninety-Five Propositions,—the act which began the Reformation. When De Soto took his glimpse of the river, Ignatius Loyola was an obscure name; the order of the Jesuits was not yet a year old; Michael Angelo's paint was not yet dry on the Last Judgment in the Sistine Chapel; Mary Queen of Scots was not yet born, but would be before the year closed. Catherine de Medici was a child; Elizabeth of England was not yet in her teens; Calvin, Benvenuto Cellini, and the Emperor Charles V. were at the top of their fame, and each was manufacturing history after his own peculiar fashion; Margaret of Navarre was writing the "Heptameron" and some religious books,—the first survives, the others are forgotten, wit and indelicacy being sometimes better literature-preservers than holiness; lax court morals and the absurd chivalry business were in full feather, and the joust and the tournament were the frequent pastime of titled fine gentlemen who could fight better than they could spell, while religion was the passion of their ladies, and the classifying their offspring into children of full rank and children by brevet their pastime. In fact, all around, religion was in a peculiarly blooming condition: the Council of Trent was being called; the Spanish Inquisition was roasting, and racking, and burning, with a free hand; elsewhere on the continent the nations were being persuaded to holy living by the sword and fire; in England, Henry VIII. had suppressed the monasteries, burnt Fisher and another bishop or two, and was getting his English reformation and his harem effectively started. When De Soto stood on the banks of the Mississippi, it was still two years before Luther's death; eleven years before the burning of Servetus; thirty years before the St. Bartholomew slaughter; Rabelais was not yet published; "Don Quixote" was not yet written; Shakspeare was not yet born; a hundred long years must still elapse before Englishmen would hear the name of Oliver Cromwell.

Unquestionably the discovery of the Mississippi is a datable fact which considerably mellows and modifies the shiny new-ness of our country, and gives her a most respectable outside-aspect of rustiness and antiquity.

De Soto merely glimpsed the river, then died and was bur-ied in it by his priests and soldiers. One would expect the priests and the soldiers to multiply the river's dimensions by ten—the Spanish custom of the day—and thus move other adventurers to go at once and explore it. On the contrary, their narratives when they reached home, did not excite that amount of curiosity. The Mississippi was left unvisited by whites during a term of years which seems incredible in our energetic days. One may "sense" the interval to his mind, af-ter a fashion, by dividing it up in this way: After De Soto glimpsed the river, a fraction short of a quarter of a century elapsed, and then Shakspeare was born; lived a trifle more than half a century, then died; and when he had been in his grave considerably more than half a century, the *second* white man saw the Mississippi. In our day we don't allow a hundred and thirty years to elapse between glimpses of a marvel. If somebody should discover a creek in the county next to the one that the North Pole is in, Europe and America would start fifteen costly expeditions thither: one to explore the creek, and the other fourteen to hunt for each other.

For more than a hundred and fifty years there had been white settlements on our Atlantic coasts. These people were in intimate communication with the Indians: in the south the Spaniards were robbing, slaughtering, enslaving and convert-ing them; higher up, the English were trading beads and blankets to them for a consideration, and throwing in civili-zation and whiskey, "for lagniappe;"[1] and in Canada the French were schooling them in a rudimentary way, mission-arying among them, and drawing whole populations of them at a time to Quebec, and later to Montreal, to buy furs of them. Necessarily, then, these various clusters of whites must have heard of the great river of the far west; and indeed, they

[1]See page 489.

did hear of it vaguely,—so vaguely and indefinitely, that its course, proportions, and locality were hardly even guessable. The mere mysteriousness of the matter ought to have fired curiosity and compelled exploration; but this did not occur. Apparently nobody happened to want such a river, nobody needed it, nobody was curious about it; so, for a century and a half the Mississippi remained out of the market and undisturbed. When De Soto found it, he was not hunting for a river, and had no present occasion for one; consequently he did not value it or even take any particular notice of it.

But at last La Salle the Frenchman conceived the idea of seeking out that river and exploring it. It always happens that when a man seizes upon a neglected and important idea, people inflamed with the same notion crop up all around. It happened so in this instance.

Naturally the question suggests itself, Why did these people want the river now when nobody had wanted it in the five preceding generations? Apparently it was because at this late day they thought they had discovered a way to make it useful; for it had come to be believed that the Mississippi emptied into the Gulf of California, and therefore afforded a short cut from Canada to China. Previously the supposition had been that it emptied into the Atlantic, or Sea of Virginia.

II.

The River and Its Explorers

L A SALLE himself sued for certain high privileges, and they were graciously accorded him by Louis XIV. of inflated memory. Chief among them was the privilege to explore, far and wide, and build forts, and stake out continents, and hand the same over to the king, and pay the expenses himself; receiving, in return, some little advantages of one sort or another; among them the monopoly of buffalo hides. He spent several years and about all of his money, in making perilous and painful trips between Montreal and a fort which he had built on the Illinois, before he at last succeeded in getting his expedition in such a shape that he could strike for the Mississippi.

And meantime other parties had had better fortune. In 1673 Joliet the merchant, and Marquette the priest, crossed the country and reached the banks of the Mississippi. They went by way of the Great Lakes; and from Green Bay, in canoes, by way of Fox River and the Wisconsin. Marquette had solemnly contracted, on the feast of the Immaculate Conception, that if the Virgin would permit him to discover the great river, he would name it Conception, in her honor. He kept his word. In that day, all explorers travelled with an outfit of priests. De Soto had twenty-four with him. La Salle had several, also. The expeditions were often out of meat, and scant of clothes, but they always had the furniture and other requisites for the mass; they were always prepared, as one of the quaint chroniclers of the time phrased it, to "explain hell to the salvages."

On the 17th of June, 1673, the canoes of Joliet and Marquette and their five subordinates reached the junction of the Wisconsin with the Mississippi. Mr. Parkman says: "Before them a wide and rapid current coursed athwart their way, by the foot of lofty heights wrapped thick in forests." He continues: "Turning southward, they paddled down the stream, through a solitude unrelieved by the faintest trace of man."

A big cat-fish collided with Marquette's canoe, and startled

233

him; and reasonably enough, for he had been warned by the Indians that he was on a foolhardy journey, and even a fatal one, for the river contained a demon "whose roar could be heard at a great distance, and who would engulf them in the abyss where he dwelt." I have seen a Mississippi cat-fish that was more than six feet long, and weighed two hundred and fifty pounds; and if Marquette's fish was the fellow to that one, he had a fair right to think the river's roaring demon was come.

"At length the buffalo began to appear, grazing in herds on the great prairies which then bordered the river; and Marquette describes the fierce and stupid look of the old bulls as they stared at the intruders through the tangled mane which nearly blinded them."

The voyagers moved cautiously: "Landed at night and made a fire to cook their evening meal; then extinguished it, embarked again, paddled some way farther, and anchored in the stream, keeping a man on the watch till morning."

They did this day after day and night after night; and at the end of two weeks they had not seen a human being. The river was an awful solitude, then. And it is now, over most of its stretch.

But at the close of the fortnight they one day came upon the footprints of men in the mud of the western bank—a Robinson Crusoe experience which carries an electric shiver with it yet, when one stumbles on it in print. They had been warned that the river Indians were as ferocious and pitiless as the river demon, and destroyed all comers without waiting for provocation; but no matter, Joliet and Marquette struck into the country to hunt up the proprietors of the tracks. They found them, by and by, and were hospitably received and well treated—if to be received by an Indian chief who has taken off his last rag in order to appear at his level best is to be received hospitably; and if to be treated abundantly to fish, porridge, and other game, including dog, and have these things forked into one's mouth by the ungloved fingers of Indians is to be well treated. In the morning the chief and six hundred of his tribesmen escorted the Frenchmen to the river and bade them a friendly farewell.

On the rocks above the present city of Alton they found

some rude and fantastic Indian paintings, which they describe. A short distance below "a torrent of yellow mud
rushed furiously athwart the calm blue current of the Mississippi, boiling and surging and sweeping in its course logs,
branches, and uprooted trees." This was the mouth of the
Missouri, "that savage river," which "descending from its mad
career through a vast unknown of barbarism, poured its turbid floods into the bosom of its gentle sister."

By and by they passed the mouth of the Ohio; they passed
canebrakes; they fought mosquitoes; they floated along, day
after day, through the deep silence and loneliness of the river,
drowsing in the scant shade of makeshift awnings, and broil-
ing with the heat; they encountered and exchanged civilities
with another party of Indians; and at last they reached the
mouth of the Arkansas (about a month out from their starting-point), where a tribe of war-whooping savages swarmed
out to meet and murder them; but they appealed to the Virgin for help; so in place of a fight there was a feast, and plenty
of pleasant palaver and fol-de-rol.

They had proved to their satisfaction, that the Mississippi
did not empty into the Gulf of California, or into the Atlantic. They believed it emptied into the Gulf of Mexico. They
turned back, now, and carried their great news to Canada.

But belief is not proof. It was reserved for La Salle to furnish the proof. He was provokingly delayed, by one misfortune after another, but at last got his expedition under way at
the end of the year 1681. In the dead of winter he and Henri
de Tonty, son of Lorenzo Tonty, who invented the tontine,
his lieutenant, started down the Illinois, with a following of
eighteen Indians brought from New England, and twenty-
three Frenchmen. They moved in procession down the surface of the frozen river, on foot, and dragging their canoes
after them on sledges.

At Peoria Lake they struck open water, and paddled thence
to the Mississippi and turned their prows southward. They
ploughed through the fields of floating ice, past the mouth of
the Missouri; past the mouth of the Ohio, by and by; "and,
gliding by the wastes of bordering swamp, landed on the 24th
of February near the Third Chickasaw Bluffs," where they
halted and built Fort Prudhomme.

"Again," says Mr. Parkman, "they embarked; and with every stage of their adventurous progress, the mystery of this vast new world was more and more unveiled. More and more they entered the realms of spring. The hazy sunlight, the warm and drowsy air, the tender foliage, the opening flowers, betokened the reviving life of nature."

Day by day they floated down the great bends, in the shadow of the dense forests, and in time arrived at the mouth of the Arkansas. First, they were greeted by the natives of this locality as Marquette had before been greeted by them—with the booming of the war drum and the flourish of arms. The Virgin composed the difficulty in Marquette's case; the pipe of peace did the same office for La Salle. The white man and the red man struck hands and entertained each other during three days. Then, to the admiration of the savages, La Salle set up a cross with the arms of France on it, and took possession of the whole country for the king—the cool fashion of the time—while the priest piously consecrated the robbery with a hymn. The priest explained the mysteries of the faith "by signs," for the saving of the savages; thus compensating them with possible possessions in Heaven for the certain ones on earth which they had just been robbed of. And also, by signs, La Salle drew from these simple children of the forest acknowledgments of fealty to Louis the Putrid, over the water. Nobody smiled at these colossal ironies.

These performances took place on the site of the future town of Napoleon, Arkansas, and there the first confiscation-cross was raised on the banks of the great river. Marquette's and Joliet's voyage of discovery ended at the same spot—the site of the future town of Napoleon. When De Soto took his fleeting glimpse of the river, away back in the dim early days, he took it from that same spot—the site of the future town of Napoleon, Arkansas. Therefore, three out of the four memorable events connected with the discovery and exploration of the mighty river occurred, by accident, in one and the same place. It is a most curious distinction, when one comes to look at it and think about it. France stole that vast country on that spot, the future Napoleon; and by and by Napoleon himself was to give the country back again!—make restitution, not to the owners, but to their white American heirs.

The voyagers journeyed on, touching here and there; "passed the sites, since become historic, of Vicksburg and Grand Gulf;" and visited an imposing Indian monarch in the Teche country, whose capital city was a substantial one of sun-baked bricks mixed with straw—better houses than many that exist there now. The chief's house contained an audience room forty feet square; and there he received Tonty in State, surrounded by sixty old men clothed in white cloaks. There was a temple in the town, with a mud wall about it ornamented with skulls of enemies sacrificed to the sun.

The voyagers visited the Natchez Indians, near the site of the present city of that name, where they found a "religious and political despotism, a privileged class descended from the sun, a temple and a sacred fire." It must have been like getting home again; it was home with an advantage, in fact, for it lacked Louis XIV.

A few more days swept swiftly by, and La Salle stood in the shadow of his confiscating cross, at the meeting of the waters from Delaware, and from Itaska, and from the mountain ranges close upon the Pacific, with the waters of the Gulf of Mexico, his task finished, his prodigy achieved. Mr. Parkman, in closing his fascinating narrative, thus sums up:

"On that day, the realm of France received on parchment a stupendous accession. The fertile plains of Texas; the vast basin of the Mississippi, from its frozen northern springs to the sultry borders of the Gulf; from the woody ridges of the Alleghanies to the bare peaks of the Rocky Mountains—a region of savannas and forests, sun-cracked deserts and grassy prairies, watered by a thousand rivers, ranged by a thousand warlike tribes, passed beneath the sceptre of the Sultan of Versailles; and all by virtue of a feeble human voice, inaudible at half a mile."

III.

Frescoes from the Past

APPARENTLY the river was ready for business, now. But no, the distribution of a population along its banks was as calm and deliberate and time-devouring a process as the discovery and exploration had been.

Seventy years elapsed, after the exploration, before the river's borders had a white population worth considering; and nearly fifty more before the river had a commerce. Between La Salle's opening of the river and the time when it may be said to have become the vehicle of anything like a regular and active commerce, seven sovereigns had occupied the throne of England, America had become an independent nation, Louis XIV. and Louis XV. had rotted and died, the French monarchy had gone down in the red tempest of the revolution, and Napoleon was a name that was beginning to be talked about. Truly, there were snails in those days.

The river's earliest commerce was in great barges—keelboats, broadhorns. They floated and sailed from the upper rivers to New Orleans, changed cargoes there, and were tediously warped and poled back by hand. A voyage down and back sometimes occupied nine months. In time this commerce increased until it gave employment to hordes of rough and hardy men; rude, uneducated, brave, suffering terrific hardships with sailor-like stoicism; heavy drinkers, coarse frolickers in moral sties like the Natchez-under-the-hill of that day, heavy fighters, reckless fellows, every one, elephantinely jolly, foul-witted, profane; prodigal of their money, bankrupt at the end of the trip, fond of barbaric finery, prodigious braggarts; yet, in the main, honest, trustworthy, faithful to promises and duty, and often picturesquely magnanimous.

By and by the steamboat intruded. Then, for fifteen or twenty years, these men continued to run their keelboats down-stream, and the steamers did all of the up-stream business, the keelboatmen selling their boats in New Orleans, and returning home as deck passengers in the steamers.

But after a while the steamboats so increased in number and

in speed that they were able to absorb the entire commerce; and then keelboating died a permanent death. The keelboatman became a deck hand, or a mate, or a pilot on the steamer; and when steamer-berths were not open to him, he took a berth on a Pittsburgh coal-flat, or on a pine-raft constructed in the forests up toward the sources of the Mississippi.

In the heyday of the steamboating prosperity, the river from end to end was flaked with coal-fleets and timber rafts, all managed by hand, and employing hosts of the rough characters whom I have been trying to describe. I remember the annual processions of mighty rafts that used to glide by Hannibal when I was a boy,—an acre or so of white, sweet-smelling boards in each raft, a crew of two dozen men or more, three or four wigwams scattered about the raft's vast level space for storm-quarters,—and I remember the rude ways and the tremendous talk of their big crews, the ex-keelboatmen and their admiringly patterning successors; for we used to swim out a quarter or third of a mile and get on these rafts and have a ride.

By way of illustrating keelboat talk and manners, and that now-departed and hardly-remembered raft-life, I will throw in, in this place, a chapter from a book which I have been working at, by fits and starts, during the past five or six years, and may possibly finish in the course of five or six more. The book is a story which details some passages in the life of an ignorant village boy, Huck Finn, son of the town drunkard of my time out west, there. He has run away from his persecuting father, and from a persecuting good widow who wishes to make a nice, truth-telling, respectable boy of him; and with him a slave of the widow's has also escaped. They have found a fragment of a lumber raft (it is high water and dead summer time), and are floating down the river by night, and hiding in the willows by day,—bound for Cairo,—whence the negro will seek freedom in the heart of the free States. But in a fog, they pass Cairo without knowing it. By and by they begin to suspect the truth, and Huck Finn is persuaded to end the dismal suspense by swimming down to a huge raft which they have seen in the distance ahead of them, creeping aboard under cover of the darkness, and gathering the needed information by eavesdropping:—

But you know a young person can't wait very well when he is impatient to find a thing out. We talked it over, and by and by Jim said it was such a black night, now, that it would n't be no risk to swim down to the big raft and crawl aboard and listen,—they would talk about Cairo, because they would be calculating to go ashore there for a spree, maybe, or anyway they would send boats ashore to buy whiskey or fresh meat or something. Jim had a wonderful level head, for a nigger: he could most always start a good plan when you wanted one.

I stood up and shook my rags off and jumped into the river, and struck out for the raft's light. By and by, when I got down nearly to her, I eased up and went slow and cautious. But everything was all right—nobody at the sweeps. So I swum down along the raft till I was most abreast the camp fire in the middle, then I crawled aboard and inched along and got in amongst some bundles of shingles on the weather side of the fire. There was thirteen men there—they was the watch on deck of course. And a mighty rough-looking lot, too. They had a jug, and tin cups, and they kept the jug moving. One man was singing—roaring, you may say; and it was n't a nice song—for a parlor anyway. He roared through his nose, and strung out the last word of every line very long. When he was done they all fetched a kind of Injun war-whoop, and then another was sung. It begun:—

> "There was a woman in our towdn,
>   In our towdn did dwed'l (dwell,)
> She loved her husband dear-i-lee,
>   But another man twyste as wed'l.

> Singing too, riloo, riloo, riloo,
>   Ri-too, riloo, rilay - - - e,
> She loved her husband dear-i-lee,
>   But another man twyste as wed'l."

And so on—fourteen verses. It was kind of poor, and when he was going to start on the next verse one of them said it was the tune the old cow died on; and another one

said, "Oh, give us a rest." And another one told him to
take a walk. They made fun of him till he got mad and
jumped up and begun to cuss the crowd, and said he could
lam any thief in the lot.

They was all about to make a break for him, but the
biggest man there jumped up and says: —

"Set whar you are, gentlemen. Leave him to me; he 's
my meat."

Then he jumped up in the air three times and cracked his
heels together every time. He flung off a buckskin coat that
was all hung with fringes, and says, "You lay thar tell the
chawin-up 's done;" and flung his hat down, which was all
over ribbons, and says, "You lay thar tell his sufferins is
over."

Then he jumped up in the air and cracked his heels together again and shouted out: —

"Whoo-oop! I 'm the old original iron-jawed, brass-
mounted, copper-bellied corpse-maker from the wilds of
Arkansaw! — Look at me! I 'm the man they call Sudden
Death and General Desolation! Sired by a hurricane, dam'd
by an earthquake, half-brother to the cholera, nearly related
to the small-pox on the mother's side! Look at me! I take
nineteen alligators and a bar'l of whiskey for breakfast
when I 'm in robust health, and a bushel of rattlesnakes and
a dead body when I 'm ailing! I split the everlasting rocks
with my glance, and I squench the thunder when I speak!
Whoo-oop! Stand back and give me room according to my
strength! Blood 's my natural drink, and the wails of the
dying is music to my ear! Cast your eye on me, gentlemen! — and lay low and hold your breath, for I 'm bout to
turn myself loose!"

All the time he was getting this off, he was shaking his
head and looking fierce, and kind of swelling around in a
little circle, tucking up his wrist-bands, and now and then
straightening up and beating his breast with his fist, saying,
"Look at me, gentlemen!" When he got through, he
jumped up and cracked his heels together three times, and
let off a roaring "whoo-oop! I 'm the bloodiest son of a
wildcat that lives!"

Then the man that had started the row tilted his old

slouch hat down over his right eye; then he bent stooping
forward, with his back sagged and his south end sticking
out far, and his fists a-shoving out and drawing in in front
of him, and so went around in a little circle about three
times, swelling himself up and breathing hard. Then he
straightened, and jumped up and cracked his heels together
three times before he lit again (that made them cheer), and
he begun to shout like this:—

"Whoo-oop! bow your neck and spread, for the kingdom of sorrow 's a-coming! Hold me down to the earth,
for I feel my powers a-working! whoo-oop! I 'm a child of
sin, *don't* let me get a start! Smoked glass, here, for all!
Don't attempt to look at me with the naked eye, gentlemen! When I 'm playful I use the meridians of longitude
and parallels of latitude for a seine, and drag the Atlantic
Ocean for whales! I scratch my head with the lightning and
purr myself to sleep with the thunder! When I 'm cold, I
bile the Gulf of Mexico and bathe in it; when I 'm hot
I fan myself with an equinoctial storm; when I 'm thirsty I
reach up and suck a cloud dry like a sponge; when I range
the earth hungry, famine follows in my tracks! Whoo-oop!
Bow your neck and spread! I put my hand on the sun's face
and make it night in the earth; I bite a piece out of the
moon and hurry the seasons; I shake myself and crumble
the mountains! Contemplate me through leather—*don't*
use the naked eye! I 'm the man with a petrified heart and
biler-iron bowels! The massacre of isolated communities is
the pastime of my idle moments, the destruction of nationalities the serious business of my life! The boundless vastness of the great American desert is my enclosed property,
and I bury my dead on my own premises!" He jumped up
and cracked his heels together three times before he lit
(they cheered him again), and as he come down he shouted
out: "Whoo-oop! bow your neck and spread, for the pet
child of calamity 's a-coming!"

Then the other one went to swelling around and blowing again—the first one—the one they called Bob; next,
the Child of Calamity chipped in again, bigger than ever;
then they both got at it at the same time, swelling round
and round each other and punching their fists most into

each other's faces, and whooping and jawing like Injuns; then Bob called the Child names, and the Child called him names back again: next, Bob called him a heap rougher names and the Child come back at him with the very worst kind of language; next, Bob knocked the Child's hat off, and the Child picked it up and kicked Bob's ribbony hat about six foot; Bob went and got it and said never mind, this war n't going to be the last of this thing, because he was a man that never forgot and never forgive, and so the Child better look out, for there was a time a-coming, just as sure as he was a living man, that he would have to answer to him with the best blood in his body. The Child said no man was willinger than he was for that time to come, and he would give Bob fair warning, *now*, never to cross his path again, for he could never rest till he had waded in his blood, for such was his nature, though he was sparing him now on account of his family, if he had one.

Both of them was edging away in different directions, growling and shaking their heads and going on about what they was going to do; but a little black-whiskered chap skipped up and says:—

"Come back here, you couple of chicken-livered cowards, and I 'll thrash the two of ye!"

And he done it, too. He snatched them, he jerked them this way and that, he booted them around, he knocked them sprawling faster than they could get up. Why, it war n't two minutes till they begged like dogs—and how the other lot did yell and laugh and clap their hands all the way through, and shout "Sail in, Corpse-Maker!" "Hi! at him again, Child of Calamity!" "Bully for you, little Davy!" Well, it was a perfect pow-wow for a while. Bob and the Child had red noses and black eyes when they got through. Little Davy made them own up that they was sneaks and cowards and not fit to eat with a dog or drink with a nigger; then Bob and the Child shook hands with each other, very solemn, and said they had always respected each other and was willing to let bygones be bygones. So then they washed their faces in the river; and just then there was a loud order to stand by for a crossing, and some of them

went forward to man the sweeps there, and the rest went
aft to handle the after-sweeps.

I laid still and waited for fifteen minutes, and had a
smoke out of a pipe that one of them left in reach; then the
crossing was finished, and they stumped back and had a
drink around and went to talking and singing again. Next
they got out an old fiddle, and one played, and another
patted juba, and the rest turned themselves loose on a regular old-fashioned keel-boat break-down. They couldn't
keep that up very long without getting winded, so by and
by they settled around the jug again.

They sung "jolly, jolly raftsman's the life for me," with a
rousing chorus, and then they got to talking about differences betwixt hogs, and their different kind of habits; and
next about women and their different ways; and next about
the best ways to put out houses that was afire; and next
about what ought to be done with the Injuns; and next
about what a king had to do, and how much he got; and
next about how to make cats fight; and next about what to
do when a man has fits; and next about differences betwixt
clear-water rivers and muddy-water ones. The man they
called Ed said the muddy Mississippi water was wholesomer to drink than the clear water of the Ohio; he said if
you let a pint of this yaller Mississippi water settle, you
would have about a half to three quarters of an inch of
mud in the bottom, according to the stage of the river, and
then it war n't no better then Ohio water—what you
wanted to do was to keep it stirred up—and when the river
was low, keep mud on hand to put in and thicken the water
up the way it ought to be.

The Child of Calamity said that was so; he said there was
nutritiousness in the mud, and a man that drunk Mississippi water could grow corn in his stomach if he wanted
to. He says:—

"You look at the graveyards; that tells the tale. Trees
won't grow worth shucks in a Cincinnati graveyard, but in
a Sent Louis graveyard they grow upwards of eight
hundred foot high. It 's all on account of the water the
people drunk before they laid up. A Cincinnati corpse don't
richen a soil any."

And they talked about how Ohio water did n't like to mix with Mississippi water. Ed said if you take the Mississippi on a rise when the Ohio is low, you'll find a wide band of clear water all the way down the east side of the Mississippi for a hundred mile or more, and the minute you get out a quarter of a mile from shore and pass the line, it is all thick and yaller the rest of the way across. Then they talked about how to keep tobacco from getting mouldy, and from that they went into ghosts and told about a lot that other folks had seen; but Ed says:—

"Why don't you tell something that you 've seen yourselves? Now let me have a say. Five years ago I was on a raft as big as this, and right along here it was a bright moonshiny night, and I was on watch and boss of the stabboard oar forrard, and one of my pards was a man named Dick Allbright, and he come along to where I was sitting, forrard—gaping and stretching, he was—and stooped down on the edge of the raft and washed his face in the river, and come and set down by me and got out his pipe, and had just got it filled, when he looks up and says,—

" 'Why looky-here,' he says, 'ain't that Buck Miller's place, over yander in the bend?'

" 'Yes,' says I, 'it is—why?' He laid his pipe down and leant his head on his hand, and says,—

" 'I thought we 'd be furder down.' I says,—

" 'I thought it too, when I went off watch'—we was standing six hours on and six off—'but the boys told me,' I says, 'that the raft didn't seem to hardly move, for the last hour,'—says I, 'though she 's a slipping along all right, now,' says I. He give a kind of a groan, and says,—

" 'I 've seed a raft act so before, along here,' he says, ' 'pears to me the current has most quit above the head of this bend durin' the last two years,' he says.

"Well, he raised up two or three times, and looked away off and around on the water. That started me at it, too. A body is always doing what he sees somebody else doing, though there may n't be no sense in it. Pretty soon I see a black something floating on the water away off to stabboard and quartering behind us. I see he was looking at it, too. I says,—

" 'What 's that?' He says, sort of pettish,—

" 'Tain't nothing but an old empty bar'l.'

" 'An empty bar'l!' says I, 'why,' says I, 'a spy-glass is a fool to *your* eyes. How can you tell it 's an empty bar'l?' He says,—

" 'I don't know; I reckon it ain't a bar'l, but I thought it might be,' says he.

" 'Yes,' I says, 'so it might be, and it might be anything else, too; a body can't tell nothing about it, such a distance as that,' I says.

"We had n't nothing else to do, so we kept on watching it. By and by I says,—

" 'Why looky-here, Dick Allbright, that thing 's a-gaining on us, I believe.'

"He never said nothing. The thing gained and gained, and I judged it must be a dog that was about tired out. Well, we swung down into the crossing, and the thing floated across the bright streak of the moonshine, and, by George, it *was* a bar'l. Says I,—

" 'Dick Allbright, what made you think that thing was a bar'l, when it was a half a mile off,' says I. Says he,—

" 'I don't know.' Says I,—

" 'You tell me, Dick Allbright.' He says,—

" 'Well, I knowed it was a bar'l; I 've seen it before; lots has seen it; they says it 's a hanted bar'l.'

"I called the rest of the watch, and they come and stood there, and I told them what Dick said. It floated right along abreast, now, and did n't gain any more. It was about twenty foot off. Some was for having it aboard, but the rest did n't want to. Dick Allbright said rafts that had fooled with it had got bad luck by it. The captain of the watch said he did n't believe in it. He said he reckoned the bar'l gained on us because it was in a little better current than what we was. He said it would leave by and by.

"So then we went to talking about other things, and we had a song, and then a breakdown; and after that the captain of the watch called for another song; but it was clouding up, now, and the bar'l stuck right thar in the same place, and the song did n't seem to have much warm-up to it, somehow, and so they did n't finish it, and there war n't any cheers, but it sort of dropped flat, and nobody said anything for a minute. Then everybody tried to talk at once, and one chap got off a joke, but it war n't no use, they did n't laugh, and even the chap that made the joke did n't laugh at it, which ain't usual. We all just settled down glum, and watched the bar'l, and was oneasy and oncomfortable. Well, sir, it shut down black and still, and then the wind begin to moan around, and next the lightning begin to play and the thunder to grumble. And pretty soon there was a regular storm, and in the middle of it a man that was running aft stumbled and fell and sprained his ankle so that he had to lay up. This made the boys shake their heads. And every time the lightning come, there was that bar'l with the blue lights winking around it. We was always on the look-out for it. But by and by, towards dawn, she was gone. When the day come we could n't see her anywhere, and we war n't sorry, neither.

"But next night about half-past nine, when there was songs and high jinks going on, here she comes again, and took her old roost on the stabboard side. There war n't no more high jinks. Everybody got solemn; nobody talked; you could n't get anybody to do anything but set around moody and look at the bar'l. It begun to cloud up again. When the watch changed, the off watch stayed up, 'stead of turning in. The storm ripped and roared around all night, and in the middle of it another man tripped and sprained his ankle, and had to knock off. The bar'l left towards day, and nobody see it go.

"Everybody was sober and down in the mouth all day. I don't mean the kind of sober that comes of leaving liquor alone,—not that. They was quiet, but they all drunk more than usual,—not together,—but each man sidled off and took it private, by himself.

"After dark the off watch did n't turn in; nobody sung, nobody talked; the boys did n't scatter around, neither; they sort of huddled together, forrard; and for two hours they set there, perfectly still, looking steady in the one direction, and heaving a sigh once in a while. And then, here comes the bar'l again. She took up her old place. She staid there all night; nobody turned in. The storm come on again, after midnight. It got awful dark; the rain poured down; hail, too; the thunder boomed and roared and bellowed; the wind blowed a hurricane; and the lightning spread over everything in big sheets of glare, and showed the whole raft as plain as day; and the river lashed up white as milk as far as you could see for miles, and there was that bar'l jiggering along, same as ever. The captain ordered the watch to man the after sweeps for a crossing, and nobody would go,—no more sprained ankles for them, they said. They would n't even *walk* aft. Well then, just then the sky split wide open, with a crash, and the lightning killed two men of the after watch, and crippled two more. Crippled them how, says you? Why, *sprained their ankles!*

"The bar'l left in the dark betwixt lightnings, towards dawn. Well, not a body eat a bite at breakfast that morning. After that the men loafed around, in twos and threes, and talked low together. But none of them herded with Dick Allbright. They all give him the cold shake. If he come around where any of the men was, they split up and sidled away. They would n't man the sweeps with him. The captain had all the skiffs hauled up on the raft, alongside of his wigwam, and would n't let the dead men be took ashore to be planted; he did n't believe a man that got ashore would come back; and he was right.

"After night come, you could see pretty plain that there was going to be trouble if that bar'l come again; there was such a muttering going on. A good many wanted to kill Dick Allbright, because he'd seen the bar'l on other trips, and that had an ugly look. Some wanted to put him ashore. Some said, let's all go ashore in a pile, if the bar'l comes again.

"This kind of whispers was still going on, the men being bunched together forrard watching for the bar'l, when, lo and behold you, here she comes again. Down she comes, slow and steady, and settles into her old tracks. You could a heard a pin drop. Then up comes the captain, and says:—

" 'Boys, don't be a pack of children and fools; I don't want this bar'l to be dogging us all the way to Orleans, and *you* don't; well, then, how 's the best way to stop it?

Burn it up,—that 's the way. I'm going to fetch it aboard,' he says. And before anybody could say a word, in he went.

"He swum to it, and as he come pushing it to the raft, the men spread to one side. But the old man got it aboard and busted in the head, and there was a baby in it! Yes sir, a stark naked baby. It was Dick Allbright's baby; he owned up and said so.

" 'Yes,' he says, a-leaning over it, 'yes, it is my own lamented darling, my poor lost Charles William Allbright deceased,' says he,—for he could curl his tongue around the bulliest words in the language when he was a mind to, and lay them before you without a jint started, anywheres. Yes, he said he used to live up at the head of this bend, and one night he choked his child, which was crying, not intending to kill it,—which was prob'ly a lie,—and then he was scared, and buried it in a bar'l, before his wife got home, and off he went, and struck the northern trail and went to rafting; and this was the third year that the bar'l had chased him. He said the bad luck always begun light, and lasted till four men was killed, and then the bar'l did n't come any more after that. He said if the men would stand it one more night,—and was a-going on like that,—but the men had got enough. They started to get out a boat to take him ashore and lynch him, but he grabbed the little child all of a sudden and jumped overboard with it hugged up to his breast and shedding tears, and we never see him again in this life, poor old suffering soul, nor Charles William neither."

"*Who* was shedding tears?" says Bob; "was it Allbright or the baby?"

"Why, Allbright, of course; didn't I tell you the baby was dead? Been dead three years—how could it cry?"

"Well, never mind how it could cry—how could it *keep* all that time?" says Davy. "You answer me that."

"I don't know how it done it," says Ed. "It done it though—that 's all I know about it."

"Say—what did they do with the bar'l?" says the Child of Calamity.

"Why, they hove it overboard, and it sunk like a chunk of lead."

"Edward, did the child look like it was choked?" says one.

"Did it have its hair parted?" says another.

"What was the brand on that bar'l, Eddy?" says a fellow they called Bill.

"Have you got the papers for them statistics, Edmund?" says Jimmy.

"Say, Edwin, was you one of the men that was killed by the lightning?" says Davy.

"Him? O, no, he was both of 'em," says Bob. Then they all haw-hawed.

"Say, Edward, don't you reckon you 'd better take a pill? You look bad—don't you feel pale?" says the Child of Calamity.

"O, come, now, Eddy," says Jimmy, "show up; you must a kept part of that bar'l to prove the thing by. Show us the bunghole—*do*—and we'll all believe you."

"Say, boys," says Bill, "less divide it up. Thar 's thirteen of us. I can swaller a thirteenth of the yarn, if you can worry down the rest."

Ed got up mad and said they could all go to some place which he ripped out pretty savage, and then walked off aft cussing to himself, and they yelling and jeering at him, and roaring and laughing so you could hear them a mile.

"Boys, we 'll split a watermelon on that," says the Child of Calamity; and he come rummaging around in the dark amongst the shingle bundles where I was, and put his hand on me. I was warm and soft and naked; so he says "Ouch!" and jumped back.

"Fetch a lantern or a chunk of fire here, boys—there 's a snake here as big as a cow!"

So they run there with a lantern and crowded up and looked in on me.

"Come out of that, you beggar!" says one.

"Who are you?" says another.

"What are you after here? Speak up prompt, or overboard you go."

"Snake him out, boys. Snatch him out by the heels."

I began to beg, and crept out amongst them trembling.

They looked me over, wondering, and the Child of Calamity says:—

"A cussed thief! Lend a hand and less heave him overboard!"

"No," says Big Bob, "less get out the paint-pot and paint him a sky blue all over from head to heel, and *then* heave him over!"

"Good! that 's it. Go for the paint, Jimmy."

When the paint come, and Bob took the brush and was just going to begin, the others laughing and rubbing their hands, I begun to cry, and that sort of worked on Davy, and he says:—

" 'Vast there! He 's nothing but a cub. I 'll paint the man that tetches him!"

So I looked around on them, and some of them grumbled and growled, and Bob put down the paint, and the others did n't take it up.

"Come here to the fire, and less see what you 're up to here," says Davy. "Now set down there and give an account of yourself. How long have you been aboard here?"

"Not over a quarter of a minute, sir," says I.

"How did you get dry so quick?"

"I don't know, sir. I 'm always that way, mostly."

"Oh, you are, are you? What 's your name?"

I war n't going to tell my name. I did n't know what to say, so I just says:

"Charles William Allbright, sir."

Then they roared—the whole crowd; and I was mighty glad I said that, because maybe laughing would get them in a better humor.

When they got done laughing, Davy says:—

"It won't hardly do, Charles William. You could n't have growed this much in five year, and you was a baby when you come out of the bar'l, you know, and dead at that. Come, now, tell a straight story, and nobody 'll hurt you, if you ain't up to anything wrong. What *is* your name?"

"Aleck Hopkins, sir. Aleck James Hopkins."

"Well, Aleck, where did you come from, here?"

"From a trading scow. She lays up the bend yonder. I was born on her. Pap has traded up and down here all his life; and he told me to swim off here, because when you went by he said he would like to get some of you to speak to a Mr. Jonas Turner, in Cairo, and tell him—"

"Oh, come!"

"Yes, sir, it 's as true as the world; Pap he says—"

"Oh, your grandmother!"

They all laughed, and I tried again to talk, but they broke in on me and stopped me.

"Now, looky-here," says Davy; "you 're scared, and so you talk wild. Honest, now, do you live in a scow, or is it a lie?"

"Yes, sir, in a trading scow. She lays up at the head of the bend. But I war n't born in her. It 's our first trip."

"Now you 're talking! What did you come aboard here, for? To steal?"

"No, sir, I did n't.—It was only to get a ride on the raft. All boys does that."

"Well, I know that. But what did you hide for?"

"Sometimes they drive the boys off."

"So they do. They might steal. Looky-here; if we let you off this time, will you keep out of these kind of scrapes hereafter?"

" 'Deed I will, boss. You try me."

"All right, then. You ain't but little ways from shore. Overboard with you, and don't you make a fool of yourself another time this way.—Blast it, boy, some raftsmen would rawhide you till you were black and blue!"

I did n't wait to kiss good-bye, but went overboard and broke for shore. When Jim come along by and by, the big raft was away out of sight around the point. I swum out and got aboard, and was mighty glad to see home again.

The boy did not get the information he was after, but his adventure has furnished the glimpse of the departed raftsman and keelboatman which I desire to offer in this place.

I now come to a phase of the Mississippi River life of the flush times of steamboating, which seems to me to warrant full examination—the marvellous science of piloting, as displayed there. I believe there has been nothing like it elsewhere in the world.

IV.

The Boys' Ambition

WHEN I WAS a boy, there was but one permanent ambition among my comrades in our village[1] on the west
bank of the Mississippi River. That was, to be a steamboatman. We had transient ambitions of other sorts, but they
were only transient. When a circus came and went, it left us
all burning to become clowns; the first negro minstrel show
that came to our section left us all suffering to try that kind
of life; now and then we had a hope that if we lived and were
good, God would permit us to be pirates. These ambitions
faded out, each in its turn; but the ambition to be a steamboatman always remained.

Once a day a cheap, gaudy packet arrived upward from St.
Louis, and another downward from Keokuk. Before these
events, the day was glorious with expectancy; after them, the
day was a dead and empty thing. Not only the boys, but the
whole village, felt this. After all these years I can picture that
old time to myself now, just as it was then: the white town
drowsing in the sunshine of a summer's morning; the streets
empty, or pretty nearly so; one or two clerks sitting in front
of the Water Street stores, with their splint-bottomed chairs
tilted back against the wall, chins on breasts, hats slouched
over their faces, asleep—with shingle-shavings enough
around to show what broke them down; a sow and a litter of
pigs loafing along the sidewalk, doing a good business in watermelon rinds and seeds; two or three lonely little freight
piles scattered about the "levee;" a pile of "skids" on the slope
of the stone-paved wharf, and the fragrant town drunkard
asleep in the shadow of them; two or three wood flats at the
head of the wharf, but nobody to listen to the peaceful lapping of the wavelets against them; the great Mississippi, the
majestic, the magnificent Mississippi, rolling its mile-wide
tide along, shining in the sun; the dense forest away on the
other side; the "point" above the town, and the "point" be-

[1] Hannibal, Missouri.

low, bounding the river-glimpse and turning it into a sort of sea, and withal a very still and brilliant and lonely one. Presently a film of dark smoke appears above one of those remote "points;" instantly a negro drayman, famous for his quick eye and prodigious voice, lifts up the cry, "S-t-e-a-m-boat a-comin'!" and the scene changes! The town drunkard stirs, the clerks wake up, a furious clatter of drays follows, every house and store pours out a human contribution, and all in a twinkling the dead town is alive and moving. Drays, carts, men, boys, all go hurrying from many quarters to a common centre, the wharf. Assembled there, the people fasten their eyes upon the coming boat as upon a wonder they are seeing for the first time. And the boat *is* rather a handsome sight, too. She is long and sharp and trim and pretty; she has two tall, fancy-topped chimneys, with a gilded device of some kind swung between them; a fanciful pilot-house, all glass and "gingerbread," perched on top of the "texas" deck behind them; the paddle-boxes are gorgeous with a picture or with gilded rays above the boat's name; the boiler deck, the hurricane deck, and the texas deck are fenced and ornamented with clean white railings; there is a flag gallantly flying from the jack-staff; the furnace doors are open and the fires glaring bravely; the upper decks are black with passengers; the captain stands by the big bell, calm, imposing, the envy of all; great volumes of the blackest smoke are rolling and tumbling out of the chimneys—a husbanded grandeur created with a bit of pitch pine just before arriving at a town; the crew are grouped on the forecastle; the broad stage is run far out over the port bow, and an envied deck-hand stands picturesquely on the end of it with a coil of rope in his hand; the pent steam is screaming through the gauge-cocks; the captain lifts his hand, a bell rings, the wheels stop; then they turn back, churning the water to foam, and the steamer is at rest. Then such a scramble as there is to get aboard, and to get ashore, and to take in freight and to discharge freight, all at one and the same time; and such a yelling and cursing as the mates facilitate it all with! Ten minutes later the steamer is under way again, with no flag on the jack-staff and no black smoke issuing from the chimneys. After ten more minutes the town is dead again, and the town drunkard asleep by the skids once more.

My father was a justice of the peace, and I supposed he possessed the power of life and death over all men and could hang anybody that offended him. This was distinction enough for me as a general thing; but the desire to be a steamboatman kept intruding, nevertheless. I first wanted to be a cabin-boy, so that I could come out with a white apron on and shake a table-cloth over the side, where all my old comrades could see me; later I thought I would rather be the deck-hand who stood on the end of the stage-plank with the coil of rope in his hand, because he was particularly conspicuous. But these were only day-dreams,—they were too heavenly to be contemplated as real possibilities. By and by one of our boys went away. He was not heard of for a long time. At last he turned up as apprentice engineer or "striker" on a steamboat. This thing shook the bottom out of all my Sunday-school teachings. That boy had been notoriously worldly, and I just the reverse; yet he was exalted to this eminence, and I left in obscurity and misery. There was nothing generous about this fellow in his greatness. He would always manage to have a rusty bolt to scrub while his boat tarried at our town, and he would sit on the inside guard and scrub it, where we could all see him and envy him and loathe him. And whenever his boat was laid up he would come home and swell around the town in his blackest and greasiest clothes, so that nobody could help remembering that he was a steamboatman; and he used all sorts of steamboat technicalities in his talk, as if he were so used to them that he forgot common people could not understand them. He would speak of the "labboard" side of a horse in an easy, natural way that would make one wish he was dead. And he was always talking about "St. Looy" like an old citizen; he would refer casually to occasions when he "was coming down Fourth Street," or when he was "passing by the Planter's House," or when there was a fire and he took a turn on the brakes of "the old Big Missouri;" and then he would go on and lie about how many towns the size of ours were burned down there that day. Two or three of the boys had long been persons of consideration among us because they had been to St. Louis once and had a vague general knowledge of its wonders, but the day of their glory was over now. They lapsed into a humble silence, and learned to disappear when the ruthless "cub"-engineer approached. This fellow had money, too, and hair oil. Also an ignorant silver watch and a showy brass watch chain. He wore a leather belt and used no suspenders. If ever a youth was cordially admired and hated by his comrades, this one was. No girl could withstand his charms. He "cut out" every boy in the village. When his boat blew up at last, it diffused a tranquil contentment among us such as we had not known for months. But when he came home the next week, alive, renowned, and appeared in church all battered up and bandaged, a shining hero, stared at and wondered over by everybody, it seemed to us that the partiality of Providence for an undeserving reptile had reached a point where it was open to criticism.

This creature's career could produce but one result, and it speedily followed. Boy after boy managed to get on the river. The minister's son became an engineer. The doctor's and the post-master's sons became "mud clerks;" the wholesale liquor dealer's son became a bar-keeper on a boat; four sons of the chief merchant, and two sons of the county judge, became pilots. Pilot was the grandest position of all. The pilot, even in those days of trivial wages, had a princely salary—from a hundred and fifty to two hundred and fifty dollars a month, and no board to pay. Two months of his wages would pay a preacher's salary for a year. Now some of us were left disconsolate. We could not get on the river—at least our parents would not let us.

So by and by I ran away. I said I never would come home again till I was a pilot and could come in glory. But somehow I could not manage it. I went meekly aboard a few of the boats that lay packed together like sardines at the long St. Louis wharf, and very humbly inquired for the pilots, but got only a cold shoulder and short words from mates and clerks. I had to make the best of this sort of treatment for the time being, but I had comforting day-dreams of a future when I should be a great and honored pilot, with plenty of money, and could kill some of these mates and clerks and pay for them.

V.

I Want to Be a Cub-Pilot

MONTHS AFTERWARD the hope within me struggled to a reluctant death, and I found myself without an ambition. But I was ashamed to go home. I was in Cincinnati, and I set to work to map out a new career. I had been reading about the recent exploration of the river Amazon by an expedition sent out by our government. It was said that the expedition, owing to difficulties, had not thoroughly explored a part of the country lying about the head-waters, some four thousand miles from the mouth of the river. It was only about fifteen hundred miles from Cincinnati to New Orleans, where I could doubtless get a ship. I had thirty dollars left; I would go and complete the exploration of the Amazon. This was all the thought I gave to the subject. I never was great in matters of detail. I packed my valise, and took passage on an ancient tub called the "Paul Jones," for New Orleans. For the sum of sixteen dollars I had the scarred and tarnished splendors of "her" main saloon principally to myself, for she was not a creature to attract the eye of wiser travellers.

When we presently got under way and went poking down the broad Ohio, I became a new being, and the subject of my own admiration. I was a traveller! A word never had tasted so good in my mouth before. I had an exultant sense of being bound for mysterious lands and distant climes which I never have felt in so uplifting a degree since. I was in such a glorified condition that all ignoble feelings departed out of me, and I was able to look down and pity the untravelled with a compassion that had hardly a trace of contempt in it. Still, when we stopped at villages and wood-yards, I could not help lolling carelessly upon the railings of the boiler deck to enjoy the envy of the country boys on the bank. If they did not seem to discover me, I presently sneezed to attract their attention, or moved to a position where they could not help seeing me. And as soon as I knew they saw me I gaped and stretched, and gave other signs of being mightily bored with travelling.

I kept my hat off all the time, and stayed where the wind and the sun could strike me, because I wanted to get the bronzed and weather-beaten look of an old traveller. Before the second day was half gone, I experienced a joy which filled me with the purest gratitude; for I saw that the skin had begun to blister and peel off my face and neck. I wished that the boys and girls at home could see me now.

We reached Louisville in time—at least the neighborhood of it. We stuck hard and fast on the rocks in the middle of the river, and lay there four days. I was now beginning to feel a strong sense of being a part of the boat's family, a sort of infant son to the captain and younger brother to the officers. There is no estimating the pride I took in this grandeur, or the affection that began to swell and grow in me for those people. I could not know how the lordly steamboatman scorns that sort of presumption in a mere landsman. I particularly longed to acquire the least trifle of notice from the big stormy mate, and I was on the alert for an opportunity to do him a service to that end. It came at last. The riotous powwow of setting a spar was going on down on the forecastle, and I went down there and stood around in the way— or mostly skipping out of it—till the mate suddenly roared a general order for somebody to bring him a capstan bar. I sprang to his side and said: "Tell me where it is—I 'll fetch it!"

If a rag-picker had offered to do a diplomatic service for the Emperor of Russia, the monarch could not have been more astounded than the mate was. He even stopped swearing. He stood and stared down at me. It took him ten seconds to scrape his disjointed remains together again. Then he said impressively: "Well, if this don't beat hell!" and turned to his work with the air of a man who had been confronted with a problem too abstruse for solution.

I crept away, and courted solitude for the rest of the day. I did not go to dinner; I stayed away from supper until everybody else had finished. I did not feel so much like a member of the boat's family now as before. However, my spirits returned, in instalments, as we pursued our way down the river. I was sorry I hated the mate so, because it was not in (young) human nature not to admire him. He was huge and muscular, his face was bearded and whiskered all over; he had a red woman and a blue woman tattooed on his right arm,— one on each side of a blue anchor with a red rope to it; and in the matter of profanity he was sublime. When he was getting out cargo at a landing, I was always where I could see and hear. He felt all the majesty of his great position, and made the world feel it, too. When he gave even the simplest order, he discharged it like a blast of lightning, and sent a long, reverberating peal of profanity thundering after it. I could not help contrasting the way in which the average landsman would give an order, with the mate's way of doing it. If the landsman should wish the gang-plank moved a foot farther forward, he would probably say: "James, or William, one of you push that plank forward, please;" but put the mate in his place, and he would roar out: "Here, now, start that gang-plank for'ard! Lively, now! *What* 're you about! Snatch it! *snatch* it! There! there! Aft again! aft again! Don't you hear me? Dash it to dash! are you going to *sleep* over it! 'Vast heaving. 'Vast heaving, I tell you! Going to heave it clear astern? WHERE 're you going with that barrel! *for'ard* with it 'fore I make you swallow it, you dash-dash-dash-*dashed* split between a tired mud-turtle and a crippled hearse-horse!"

I wished I could talk like that.

When the soreness of my adventure with the mate had somewhat worn off, I began timidly to make up to the humblest official connected with the boat—the night watchman. He snubbed my advances at first, but I presently ventured to offer him a new chalk pipe, and that softened him. So he allowed me to sit with him by the big bell on the hurricane deck, and in time he melted into conversation. He could not well have helped it, I hung with such homage on his words and so plainly showed that I felt honored by his notice. He told me the names of dim capes and shadowy islands as we glided by them in the solemnity of the night, under the winking stars, and by and by got to talking about himself. He seemed over-sentimental for a man whose salary was six dollars a week—or rather he might have seemed so to an older person than I. But I drank in his words hungrily, and with a faith that might have moved mountains if it had been applied judiciously. What was it to me that he was soiled and seedy and fragrant with gin? What was it to me that his grammar was bad, his construction worse, and his profanity so void of art that it was an element of weakness rather than strength in his conversation? He was a wronged man, a man who had seen trouble, and that was enough for me. As he mellowed into his plaintive history his tears dripped upon the lantern in his lap, and I cried, too, from sympathy. He said he was the son of an English nobleman—either an earl or an alderman, he could not remember which, but believed was both; his father, the nobleman, loved him, but his mother hated him from the cradle; and so while he was still a little boy he was sent to "one of them old, ancient colleges"—he couldn't remember which; and by and by his father died and his mother seized the property and "shook" him, as he phrased it. After his mother shook him, members of the nobility with whom he was acquainted used their influence to get him the position of "lob-lolly-boy in a ship;" and from that point my watchman threw off all trammels of date and locality and branched out into a narrative that bristled all along with incredible adventures; a narrative that was so reeking with bloodshed and so crammed with hair-breadth escapes and the most engaging and unconscious personal villanies, that I sat speechless, enjoying, shuddering, wondering, worshipping.

It was a sore blight to find out afterwards that he was a low, vulgar, ignorant, sentimental, half-witted humbug, an untravelled native of the wilds of Illinois, who had absorbed wildcat literature and appropriated its marvels, until in time he had woven odds and ends of the mess into this yarn, and then gone on telling it to fledglings like me, until he had come to believe it himself.

VI.

A Cub-Pilot's Experience

WHAT WITH LYING on the rocks four days at Louisville, and some other delays, the poor old "Paul Jones" fooled away about two weeks in making the voyage from Cincinnati to New Orleans. This gave me a chance to get acquainted with one of the pilots, and he taught me how to steer the boat, and thus made the fascination of river life more potent than ever for me.

It also gave me a chance to get acquainted with a youth who had taken deck passage—more 's the pity; for he easily borrowed six dollars of me on a promise to return to the boat and pay it back to me the day after we should arrive. But he probably died or forgot, for he never came. It was doubtless the former, since he had said his parents were wealthy, and he only travelled deck passage because it was cooler.[1]

I soon discovered two things. One was that a vessel would not be likely to sail for the mouth of the Amazon under ten or twelve years; and the other was that the nine or ten dollars still left in my pocket would not suffice for so imposing an exploration as I had planned, even if I could afford to wait for a ship. Therefore it followed that I must contrive a new career. The "Paul Jones" was now bound for St. Louis. I planned a siege against my pilot, and at the end of three hard days he surrendered. He agreed to teach me the Mississippi River from New Orleans to St. Louis for five hundred dollars, payable out of the first wages I should receive after graduating. I entered upon the small enterprise of "learning" twelve or thirteen hundred miles of the great Mississippi River with the easy confidence of my time of life. If I had really known what I was about to require of my faculties, I should not have had the courage to begin. I supposed that all a pilot had to do was to keep his boat in the river, and I did not consider that that could be much of a trick, since it was so wide.

The boat backed out from New Orleans at four in the af-

[1] "Deck" passage—*i.e.*, steerage passage.

ternoon, and it was "our watch" until eight. Mr. Bixby, my
chief, "straightened her up," plowed her along past the sterns
of the other boats that lay at the Levee, and then said, "Here
take her; shave those steamships as close as you 'd peel an
apple." I took the wheel, and my heart-beat fluttered up into
the hundreds; for it seemed to me that we were about to
scrape the side off every ship in the line, we were so close. I
held my breath and began to claw the boat away from the
danger; and I had my own opinion of the pilot who had
known no better than to get us into such peril, but I was too
wise to express it. In half a minute I had a wide margin of
safety intervening between the "Paul Jones" and the ships;
and within ten seconds more I was set aside in disgrace, and
Mr. Bixby was going into danger again and flaying me alive
with abuse of my cowardice. I was stung, but I was obliged
to admire the easy confidence with which my chief loafed
from side to side of his wheel, and trimmed the ships so
closely that disaster seemed ceaselessly imminent. When he
had cooled a little he told me that the easy water was close
ashore and the current outside, and therefore we must hug
the bank, up-stream, to get the benefit of the former, and stay
well out, down-stream, to take advantage of the latter. In my
own mind I resolved to be a down-stream pilot and leave the
up-streaming to people dead to prudence.

Now and then Mr. Bixby called my attention to certain
things. Said he, "This is Six-Mile Point." I assented. It was
pleasant enough information, but I could not see the bearing
of it. I was not conscious that it was a matter of any interest
to me. Another time he said, "This is Nine-Mile Point." Later
he said, "This is Twelve-Mile Point." They were all about
level with the water's edge; they all looked about alike to me;
they were monotonously unpicturesque. I hoped Mr. Bixby
would change the subject. But no; he would crowd up
around a point, hugging the shore with affection, and then
say: "The slack water ends here, abreast this bunch of China-
trees; now we cross over." So he crossed over. He gave me
the wheel once or twice, but I had no luck. I either came near
chipping off the edge of a sugar plantation, or I yawed too
far from shore, and so dropped back into disgrace again and
got abused.

The watch was ended at last, and we took supper and went to bed. At midnight the glare of a lantern shone in my eyes, and the night watchman said:—

"Come! turn out!"

And then he left. I could not understand this extraordinary procedure; so I presently gave up trying to, and dozed off to sleep. Pretty soon the watchman was back again, and this time he was gruff. I was annoyed. I said:

"What do you want to come bothering around here in the middle of the night for? Now as like as not I 'll not get to sleep again to-night."

The watchman said:—

"Well, if this an't good, I 'm blest."

The "off-watch" was just turning in, and I heard some brutal laughter from them, and such remarks as "Hello, watchman! an't the new cub turned out yet? He 's delicate, likely. Give him some sugar in a rag and send for the chambermaid to sing rock-a-by-baby to him."

About this time Mr. Bixby appeared on the scene. Something like a minute later I was climbing the pilot-house steps with some of my clothes on and the rest in my arms. Mr. Bixby was close behind, commenting. Here was something fresh—this thing of getting up in the middle of the night to go to work. It was a detail in piloting that had never occurred to me at all. I knew that boats ran all night, but somehow I had never happened to reflect that somebody had to get up out of a warm bed to run them. I began to fear that piloting was not quite so romantic as I had imagined it was; there was something very real and work-like about this new phase of it.

It was a rather dingy night, although a fair number of stars were out. The big mate was at the wheel, and he had the old tub pointed at a star and was holding her straight up the middle of the river. The shores on either hand were not much more than half a mile apart, but they seemed wonderfully far away and ever so vague and indistinct. The mate said:—

"We 've got to land at Jones's plantation, sir."

The vengeful spirit in me exulted. I said to myself, I wish you joy of your job, Mr. Bixby; you 'll have a good time finding Mr. Jones's plantation such a night as this; and I hope you never *will* find it as long as you live.

Mr. Bixby said to the mate: —

"Upper end of the plantation, or the lower?"

"Upper."

"I can't do it. The stumps there are out of water at thi stage. It 's no great distance to the lower, and you 'll have to get along with that."

"All right, sir. If Jones don't like it he 'll have to lump it, reckon."

And then the mate left. My exultation began to cool and my wonder to come up. Here was a man who not only pro posed to find this plantation on such a night, but to find ei ther end of it you preferred. I dreadfully wanted to ask a question, but I was carrying about as many short answers a my cargo-room would admit of, so I held my peace. All desired to ask Mr. Bixby was the simple question whether he was ass enough to really imagine he was going to find tha plantation on a night when all plantations were exactly alike and all the same color. But I held in. I used to have fine inspirations of prudence in those days.

Mr. Bixby made for the shore and soon was scraping it just the same as if it had been daylight. And not only that but singing—

"Father in heaven, the day is declining," etc.

It seemed to me that I had put my life in the keeping of a peculiarly reckless outcast. Presently he turned on me and said: —

"What's the name of the first point above New Orleans?"

I was gratified to be able to answer promptly, and I did. I said I did n't know.

"Don't *know?*"

This manner jolted me. I was down at the foot again, in a moment. But I had to say just what I had said before.

"Well, you 're a smart one," said Mr. Bixby. "What 's the name of the *next* point?"

Once more I did n't know.

"Well, this beats anything. Tell me the name of *any* point or place I told you."

I studied a while and decided that I could n't.

"Look here! What do you start out from, above Twelve-Mile Point, to cross over?"

"I—I—don't know."

"You—you—don't know?" mimicking my drawling manner of speech. "What *do* you know?"

"I—I—nothing, for certain."

"By the great Cæsar's ghost, I believe you! You 're the stupidest dunderhead I ever saw or ever heard of, so help me Moses! The idea of *you* being a pilot—*you*! Why, you don't know enough to pilot a cow down a lane."

Oh, but his wrath was up! He was a nervous man, and he shuffled from one side of his wheel to the other as if the floor was hot. He would boil a while to himself, and then overflow and scald me again.

"Look here! What do you suppose I told you the names of those points for?"

I tremblingly considered a moment, and then the devil of temptation provoked me to say:—

"Well—to—to—be entertaining, I thought."

This was a red rag to the bull. He raged and stormed so (he was crossing the river at the time) that I judge it made him blind, because he ran over the steering-oar of a trading-scow. Of course the traders sent up a volley of red-hot profanity. Never was a man so grateful as Mr. Bixby was: because he was brim full, and here were subjects who would *talk back*. He threw open a window, thrust his head out, and such an irruption followed as I never had heard before. The fainter and farther away the scowmen's curses drifted, the higher Mr. Bixby lifted his voice and the weightier his adjectives grew. When he closed the window he was empty. You could have drawn a seine through his system and not caught curses enough to disturb your mother with. Presently he said to me in the gentlest way:—

"My boy, you must get a little memorandum-book, and every time I tell you a thing, put it down right away. There 's only one way to be a pilot, and that is to get this entire river by heart. You have to know it just like A B C."

That was a dismal revelation to me; for my memory was never loaded with anything but blank cartridges. However, I did not feel discouraged long. I judged that it was best to make some allowances, for doubtless Mr. Bixby was "stretch-ing." Presently he pulled a rope and struck a few strokes on the big bell. The stars were all gone now, and the night was as black as ink. I could hear the wheels churn along the bank, but I was not entirely certain that I could see the shore. The voice of the invisible watchman called up from the hurricane deck: —

"What 's this, sir?"

"Jones's plantation."

I said to myself, I wish I might venture to offer a small bet that it is n't. But I did not chirp. I only waited to see. Mr. Bixby handled the engine bells, and in due time the boat's nose came to the land, a torch glowed from the forecastle, a man skipped ashore, a darky's voice on the bank said, "Gimme de k'yarpet-bag, Mars' Jones," and the next moment we were standing up the river again, all serene. I reflected deeply a while, and then said,—but not aloud,—Well, the finding of that plantation was the luckiest accident that ever happened; but it could n't happen again in a hundred years. And I fully believed it *was* an accident, too.

By the time we had gone seven or eight hundred miles up the river, I had learned to be a tolerably plucky upstream steersman, in daylight, and before we reached St. Louis I had made a trifle of progress in night-work, but only a trifle. I had a note-book that fairly bristled with the names of towns, "points," bars, islands, bends, reaches, etc.; but the informa-tion was to be found only in the note-book—none of it was in my head. It made my heart ache to think I had only got half of the river set down; for as our watch was four hours off and four hours on, day and night, there was a long four-hour gap in my book for every time I had slept since the voyage began.

My chief was presently hired to go on a big New Orleans boat, and I packed my satchel and went with him. She was a grand affair. When I stood in her pilot-house I was so far above the water that I seemed perched on a mountain; and her decks stretched so far away, fore and aft, below me, that I wondered how I could ever have considered the little "Paul Jones" a large craft. There were other differences, too. The "Paul Jones's" pilot-house was a cheap, dingy, battered rattle-

trap, cramped for room: but here was a sumptuous glass temple; room enough to have a dance in; showy red and gold
window-curtains; an imposing sofa; leather cushions and a
back to the high bench where visiting pilots sit, to spin yarns
and "look at the river;" bright, fanciful "cuspadores" instead
of a broad wooden box filled with sawdust; nice new oil-cloth
on the floor; a hospitable big stove for winter; a wheel as
high as my head, costly with inlaid work; a wire tiller-rope;
bright brass knobs for the bells; and a tidy, white-aproned,
black "texas-tender," to bring up tarts and ices and coffee during mid-watch, day and night. Now this was "something
like;" and so I began to take heart once more to believe that
piloting was a romantic sort of occupation after all. The moment we were under way I began to prowl about the great
steamer and fill myself with joy. She was as clean and as
dainty as a drawing-room; when I looked down her long,
gilded saloon, it was like gazing through a splendid tunnel;
she had an oil-picture, by some gifted sign-painter, on every
state-room door; she glittered with no end of prism-fringed
chandeliers; the clerk's office was elegant, the bar was marvellous, and the bar-keeper had been barbered and upholstered
at incredible cost. The boiler deck (*i.e.*, the second story of
the boat, so to speak), was as spacious as a church, it seemed
to me; so with the forecastle; and there was no pitiful handful
of deck-hands, firemen, and roust-abouts down there, but a
whole battalion of men. The fires were fiercely glaring from
a long row of furnaces, and over them were eight huge boilers! This was unutterable pomp. The mighty engines—but
enough of this. I had never felt so fine before. And when I
found that the regiment of natty servants respectfully "sir'd"
me, my satisfaction was complete.

VII.

A Daring Deed

W̲HEN I RETURNED to the pilot-house St. Louis was gone and I was lost. Here was a piece of river which was all down in my book, but I could make neither head nor tail of it: you understand, it was turned around. I had seen it when coming up-stream, but I had never faced about to see how it looked when it was behind me. My heart broke again, for it was plain that I had got to learn this troublesome river *both ways*.

The pilot-house was full of pilots, going down to "look at the river." What is called the "upper river" (the two hundred miles between St. Louis and Cairo, where the Ohio comes in) was low; and the Mississippi changes its channel so constantly that the pilots used to always find it necessary to run down to Cairo to take a fresh look, when their boats were to lie in port a week; that is, when the water was at a low stage. A deal of this "looking at the river" was done by poor fellows who seldom had a berth, and whose only hope of getting one lay in their being always freshly posted and therefore ready to drop into the shoes of some reputable pilot, for a single trip, on account of such pilot's sudden illness, or some other necessity. And a good many of them constantly ran up and down inspecting the river, not because they ever really hoped to get a berth, but because (they being guests of the boat) it was cheaper to "look at the river" than stay ashore and pay board. In time these fellows grew dainty in their tastes, and only infested boats that had an established reputation for setting good tables. All visiting pilots were useful, for they were always ready and willing, winter or summer, night or day, to go out in the yawl and help buoy the channel or assist the boat's pilots in any way they could. They were likewise welcome because all pilots are tireless talkers, when gathered together, and as they talk only about the river they are always understood and are always interesting. Your true pilot cares nothing about anything on earth but the river, and his pride in his occupation surpasses the pride of kings.

We had a fine company of these river-inspectors along, this trip. There were eight or ten; and there was abundance of room for them in our great pilot-house. Two or three of them wore polished silk hats, elaborate shirt-fronts, diamond breastpins, kid gloves, and patent-leather boots. They were choice in their English, and bore themselves with a dignity proper to men of solid means and prodigious reputation as pilots. The others were more or less loosely clad, and wore upon their heads tall felt cones that were suggestive of the days of the Commonwealth.

I was a cipher in this august company, and felt subdued, not to say torpid. I was not even of sufficient consequence to assist at the wheel when it was necessary to put the tiller hard down in a hurry; the guest that stood nearest did that when occasion required—and this was pretty much all the time, because of the crookedness of the channel and the scant water. I stood in a corner; and the talk I listened to took the hope all out of me. One visitor said to another:—

"Jim, how did you run Plum Point, coming up?"

"It was in the night, there, and I ran it the way one of the boys on the 'Diana' told me; started out about fifty yards above the wood pile on the false point, and held on the cabin under Plum Point till I raised the reef—quarter less twain—then straightened up for the middle bar till I got well abreast the old one-limbed cotton-wood in the bend, then got my stern on the cotton-wood and head on the low place above the point, and came through a-booming—nine and a half."

"Pretty square crossing, an't it?"

"Yes, but the upper bar 's working down fast."

Another pilot spoke up and said:—

"I had better water than that, and ran it lower down; started out from the false point—mark twain—raised the second reef abreast the big snag in the bend, and had quarter less twain."

One of the gorgeous ones remarked:—

"I don't want to find fault with your leadsmen, but that 's a good deal of water for Plum Point, it seems to me."

There was an approving nod all around as this quiet snub dropped on the boaster and "settled" him. And so they went on talk-talk-talking. Meantime, the thing that was running in my mind was, "Now if my ears hear aright, I have not only to get the names of all the towns and islands and bends, and so on, by heart, but I must even get up a warm personal acquaintanceship with every old snag and one-limbed cotton-wood and obscure wood pile that ornaments the banks of this river for twelve hundred miles; and more than that, I must actually know where these things are in the dark, unless these guests are gifted with eyes that can pierce through two miles of solid blackness; I wish the piloting business was in Jericho and I had never thought of it."

At dusk Mr. Bixby tapped the big bell three times (the signal to land), and the captain emerged from his drawing-room in the forward end of the texas, and looked up inquiringly. Mr. Bixby said:—

"We will lay up here all night, captain."

"Very well, sir."

That was all. The boat came to shore and was tied up for the night. It seemed to me a fine thing that the pilot could do as he pleased, without asking so grand a captain's permission. I took my supper and went immediately to bed, discouraged by my day's observations and experiences. My late voyage's note-booking was but a confusion of meaningless names. It had tangled me all up in a knot every time I had looked at it in the daytime. I now hoped for respite in sleep; but no, it revelled all through my head till sunrise again, a frantic and tireless nightmare.

Next morning I felt pretty rusty and low-spirited. We went booming along, taking a good many chances, for we were anxious to "get out of the river" (as getting out to Cairo was called) before night should overtake us. But Mr. Bixby's partner, the other pilot, presently grounded the boat, and we lost so much time getting her off that it was plain the darkness would overtake us a good long way above the mouth. This was a great misfortune, especially to certain of our visiting pilots, whose boats would have to wait for their return, no matter how long that might be. It sobered the pilot-house talk a good deal. Coming up-stream, pilots did not mind low water or any kind of darkness; nothing stopped them but fog. But down-stream work was different; a boat was too nearly helpless, with a stiff current pushing behind her; so it was not customary to run down-stream at night in low water.

There seemed to be one small hope, however: if we could get through the intricate and dangerous Hat Island crossing before night, we could venture the rest, for we would have plainer sailing and better water. But it would be insanity to attempt Hat Island at night. So there was a deal of looking at watches all the rest of the day, and a constant ciphering upon the speed we were making; Hat Island was the eternal subject; sometimes hope was high and sometimes we were delayed in a bad crossing, and down it went again. For hours all hands lay under the burden of this suppressed excitement; it was even communicated to me, and I got to feeling so solicitous about Hat Island, and under such an awful pressure of responsibility, that I wished I might have five minutes on shore to draw a good, full, relieving breath, and start over again. We were standing no regular watches. Each of our pilots ran such portions of the river as he had run when coming up-stream, because of his greater familiarity with it; but both remained in the pilot-house constantly.

An hour before sunset, Mr. Bixby took the wheel and Mr. W—— stepped aside. For the next thirty minutes every man held his watch in his hand and was restless, silent, and uneasy. At last somebody said, with a doomful sigh,—

"Well yonder 's Hat Island—and we can't make it."

All the watches closed with a snap, everybody sighed and muttered something about its being "too bad, too bad—ah, if we could *only* have got here half an hour sooner!" and the place was thick with the atmosphere of disappointment. Some started to go out, but loitered, hearing no bell-tap to land. The sun dipped behind the horizon, the boat went on. Inquiring looks passed from one guest to another; and one who had his hand on the door-knob and had turned it, waited, then presently took away his hand and let the knob turn back again. We bore steadily down the bend. More looks were exchanged, and nods of surprised admiration—but no words. Insensibly the men drew together behind Mr. Bixby, as the sky darkened and one or two dim stars came out. The dead silence and sense of waiting became oppressive. Mr. Bixby pulled the cord, and two deep, mellow notes from the big bell floated off on the night. Then a pause, and one more note was struck. The watchman's voice followed, from the hurricane deck:—

"Labboard lead, there! Stabboard lead!"

The cries of the leadsmen began to rise out of the distance, and were gruffly repeated by the word-passers on the hurricane deck.

"M-a-r-k three! . . . . M-a-r-k three! . . . . Quarter-less-three! . . . . Half twain! . . . . Quarter twain! . . . . M-a-r-k twain! . . . . Quarter-less"—

Mr. Bixby pulled two bell-ropes, and was answered by faint jinglings far below in the engine room, and our speed slackened. The steam began to whistle through the gauge-cocks. The cries of the leadsmen went on—and it is a weird sound, always, in the night. Every pilot in the lot was watching now, with fixed eyes, and talking under his breath. Nobody was calm and easy but Mr. Bixby. He would put his wheel down and stand on a spoke, and as the steamer swung into her (to me) utterly invisible marks—for we seemed to be in the midst of a wide and gloomy sea—he would meet and fasten her there. Out of the murmur of half-audible talk, one caught a coherent sentence now and then—such as:

"There; she 's over the first reef all right!"

After a pause, another subdued voice:—

"Her stern 's coming down just *exactly* right, by *George*!"

"Now she 's in the marks; over she goes!"

Somebody else muttered:—

"Oh, it was done beautiful— *beautiful*!"

Now the engines were stopped altogether, and we drifted with the current. Not that I could see the boat drift, for I could not, the stars being all gone by this time. This drifting was the dismalest work; it held one's heart still. Presently I discovered a blacker gloom than that which surrounded us. It was the head of the island. We were closing right down upon it. We entered its deeper shadow, and so imminent seemed the peril that I was likely to suffocate; and I had the strongest impulse to do *something*, anything, to save the vessel. But still Mr. Bixby stood by his wheel, silent, intent as a cat, and all the pilots stood shoulder to shoulder at his back.

"She 'll not make it!" somebody whispered.

The water grew shoaler and shoaler, by the leadsman's cries, till it was down to—

"Eight-and-a-half! . . . . E-i-g-h-t feet! . . . . E-i-g-h-t feet! . . . . Seven-and"—

Mr. Bixby said warningly through his speaking tube to the engineer:—

"Stand by, now!"

"Aye-aye, sir!"

"Seven-and-a-half! Seven feet! *Six*-and"—

We touched bottom! Instantly Mr. Bixby set a lot of bells ringing, shouted through the tube, "*Now*, let her have it— every ounce you 've got!" then to his partner, "Put her hard down! snatch her! snatch her!" The boat rasped and ground her way through the sand, hung upon the apex of disaster a single tremendous instant, and then over she went! And such a shout as went up at Mr. Bixby's back never loosened the roof of a pilot-house before!

There was no more trouble after that. Mr. Bixby was a hero that night; and it was some little time, too, before his exploit ceased to be talked about by river men.

Fully to realize the marvellous precision required in laying the great steamer in her marks in that murky waste of water, one should know that not only must she pick her intricate way through snags and blind reefs, and then shave the head of the island so closely as to brush the overhanging foliage with her stern, but at one place she must pass almost within arm's reach of a sunken and invisible wreck that would snatch the hull timbers from under her if she should strike it, and destroy a quarter of a million dollars' worth of steamboat and cargo in five minutes, and maybe a hundred and fifty human lives into the bargain.

The last remark I heard that night was a compliment to Mr. Bixby, uttered in soliloquy and with unction by one of our guests. He said:—

"By the Shadow of Death, but he 's a lightning pilot!"

VIII.

Perplexing Lessons

AT THE END of what seemed a tedious while, I had managed to pack my head full of islands, towns, bars, "points," and bends; and a curiously inanimate mass of lumber it was, too. However, inasmuch as I could shut my eyes and reel off a good long string of these names without leaving out more than ten miles of river in every fifty, I began to feel that I could take a boat down to New Orleans if I could make her skip those little gaps. But of course my complacency could hardly get start enough to lift my nose a trifle into the air, before Mr. Bixby would think of something to fetch it down again. One day he turned on me suddenly with this settler: —

"What is the shape of Walnut Bend?"

He might as well have asked me my grandmother's opinion of protoplasm. I reflected respectfully, and then said I did n't know it had any particular shape. My gunpowdery chief went off with a bang, of course, and then went on loading and firing until he was out of adjectives.

I had learned long ago that he only carried just so many rounds of ammunition, and was sure to subside into a very placable and even remorseful old smooth-bore as soon as they were all gone. That word "old" is merely affectionate; he was not more than thirty-four. I waited. By and by he said, —

"My boy, you 've got to know the *shape* of the river perfectly. It is all there is left to steer by on a very dark night. Everything else is blotted out and gone. But mind you, it has n't the same shape in the night that it has in the day-time."

"How on earth am I ever going to learn it, then?"

"How do you follow a hall at home in the dark? Because you know the shape of it. You can't see it."

"Do you mean to say that I 've got to know all the million trifling variations of shape in the banks of this interminable river as well as I know the shape of the front hall at home?"

"On my honor, you 've got to know them *better* than any man ever did know the shapes of the halls in his own house."

"I wish I was dead!"

"Now I don't want to discourage you, but"—

"Well, pile it on me; I might as well have it now as another time."

"You see, this has got to be learned; there is n't any getting around it. A clear starlight night throws such heavy shadows that if you did n't know the shape of a shore perfectly you would claw away from every bunch of timber, because you would take the black shadow of it for a solid cape; and you see you would be getting scared to death every fifteen minutes by the watch. You would be fifty yards from shore all the time when you ought to be within fifty feet of it. You can't see a snag in one of those shadows, but you know exactly where it is, and the shape of the river tells you when you are coming to it. Then there 's your pitch-dark night; the river is a very different shape on a pitch-dark night from what it is on a starlight night. All shores seem to be straight lines, then, and mighty dim ones, too; and you 'd *run* them for straight lines only you know better. You boldly drive your boat right into what seems to be a solid, straight wall (you knowing very well that in reality there is a curve there), and that wall falls back and makes way for you. Then there 's your gray mist. You take a night when there 's one of these grisly, drizzly, gray mists, and then there is n't *any* particular shape to a shore. A gray mist would tangle the head of the oldest man that ever lived. Well, then, different kinds of *moonlight* change the shape of the river in different ways. You see"—

"Oh, don't say any more, please! Have I got to learn the shape of the river according to all these five hundred thousand different ways? If I tried to carry all that cargo in my head it would make me stoop-shouldered."

"*No!* you only learn *the* shape of the river; and you learn it with such absolute certainty that you can always steer by the shape that 's *in your head*, and never mind the one that 's before your eyes."

"Very well, I'll try it; but after I have learned it can I depend on it? Will it keep the same form and not go fooling around?"

Before Mr. Bixby could answer, Mr. W——— came in to take the watch, and he said,—

"Bixby, you 'll have to look out for President's Island and all that country clear away up above the Old Hen and Chickens. The banks are caving and the shape of the shores changing like everything. Why, you would n't know the point above 40. You can go up inside the old sycamore snag, now."[1]

So that question was answered. Here were leagues of shore changing shape. My spirits were down in the mud again. Two things seemed pretty apparent to me. One was, that in order to be a pilot a man had got to learn more than any one man ought to be allowed to know; and the other was, that he must learn it all over again in a different way every twenty-four hours.

That night we had the watch until twelve. Now it was an ancient river custom for the two pilots to chat a bit when the watch changed. While the relieving pilot put on his gloves and lit his cigar, his partner, the retiring pilot, would say something like this:—

"I judge the upper bar is making down a little at Hale's Point; had quarter twain with the lower lead and mark twain[2] with the other."

"Yes, I thought it was making down a little, last trip. Meet any boats?"

"Met one abreast the head of 21, but she was away over hugging the bar, and I could n't make her out entirely. I took her for the 'Sunny South'—had n't any skylights forward of the chimneys."

And so on. And as the relieving pilot took the wheel his partner[3] would mention that we were in such-and-such a bend, and say we were abreast of such-and-such a man's wood-yard or plantation. This was courtesy; I supposed it was *necessity*. But Mr. W—— came on watch full twelve minutes late on this particular night,—a tremendous breach of etiquette; in fact, it is the unpardonable sin among pilots. So Mr. Bixby gave him no greeting whatever, but simply surren-

---

[1] It may not be necessary, but still it can do no harm to explain that "inside" means between the snag and the shore.—M. T.

[2] Two fathoms. Quarter twain is 2¼ fathoms, 13½ feet. Mark three is three fathoms.

[3] "Partner" is technical for "the other pilot."

dered the wheel and marched out of the pilot-house without
a word. I was appalled; it was a villanous night for blackness,
we were in a particularly wide and blind part of the river,
where there was no shape or substance to anything, and it
seemed incredible that Mr. Bixby should have left that poor
fellow to kill the boat trying to find out where he was. But I
resolved that I would stand by him any way. He should find
that he was not wholly friendless. So I stood around, and
waited to be asked where we were. But Mr. W—— plunged
on serenely through the solid firmament of black cats that
stood for an atmosphere, and never opened his mouth. Here
is a proud devil, thought I; here is a limb of Satan that would
rather send us all to destruction than put himself under obligations to me, because I am not yet one of the salt of the
earth and privileged to snub captains and lord it over everything dead and alive in a steamboat. I presently climbed up
on the bench; I did not think it was safe to go to sleep while
this lunatic was on watch.

However, I must have gone to sleep in the course of time,
because the next thing I was aware of was the fact that day
was breaking, Mr. W—— gone, and Mr. Bixby at the
wheel again. So it was four o'clock and all well—but me; I
felt like a skinful of dry bones and all of them trying to ache
at once.

Mr. Bixby asked me what I had stayed up there for. I confessed that it was to do Mr. W—— a benevolence,—tell him
where he was. It took five minutes for the entire preposter-
ousness of the thing to filter into Mr. Bixby's system, and
then I judge it filled him nearly up to the chin; because he
paid me a compliment—and not much of a one either. He
said,—

"Well, taking you by-and-large, you do seem to be more
different kinds of an ass than any creature I ever saw before.
What did you suppose he wanted to know for?"

I said I thought it might be a convenience to him.

"Convenience! D-nation! Did n't I tell you that a man 's
got to know the river in the night the same as he 'd know his
own front hall?"

"Well, I can follow the front hall in the dark if I know it *is*
the front hall; but suppose you set me down in the middle of

it in the dark and not tell me which hall it is; how am *I* to know?"

"Well, you 've *got* to, on the river!"

"All right. Then I 'm glad I never said anything to Mr. W——"

"I should say so. Why, he 'd have slammed you through the window and utterly ruined a hundred dollars' worth of window-sash and stuff."

I was glad this damage had been saved, for it would have made me unpopular with the owners. They always hated any-body who had the name of being careless, and injuring things.

I went to work now to learn the shape of the river; and of all the eluding and ungraspable objects that ever I tried to get mind or hands on, that was the chief. I would fasten my eyes upon a sharp, wooded point that projected far into the river some miles ahead of me, and go to laboriously photographing its shape upon my brain; and just as I was beginning to suc-ceed to my satisfaction, we would draw up toward it and the exasperating thing would begin to melt away and fold back into the bank! If there had been a conspicuous dead tree standing upon the very point of the cape, I would find that tree inconspicuously merged into the general forest, and oc-cupying the middle of a straight shore, when I got abreast of it! No prominent hill would stick to its shape long enough for me to make up my mind what its form really was, but it was as dissolving and changeful as if it had been a mountain of butter in the hottest corner of the tropics. Nothing ever had the same shape when I was coming down-stream that it had borne when I went up. I mentioned these little difficul-ties to Mr. Bixby. He said,—

"That 's the very main virtue of the thing. If the shapes did n't change every three seconds they would n't be of any use. Take this place where we are now, for instance. As long as that hill over yonder is only one hill, I can boom right along the way I 'm going; but the moment it splits at the top and forms a V, I know I 've got to scratch to starboard in a hurry, or I 'll bang this boat's brains out against a rock; and then the moment one of the prongs of the V swings behind the other, I 've got to waltz to larboard again, or I 'll have a misunderstanding with a snag that would snatch the keelson out of this steamboat as neatly as if it were a sliver in your hand. If that hill did n't change its shape on bad nights there would be an awful steamboat grave-yard around here inside of a year."

It was plain that I had got to learn the shape of the river in all the different ways that could be thought of,—upside down, wrong end first, inside out, fore-and-aft, and "thort-ships,"—and then know what to do on gray nights when it had n't any shape at all. So I set about it. In the course of time I began to get the best of this knotty lesson, and my self-complacency moved to the front once more. Mr. Bixby was all fixed, and ready to start it to the rear again. He opened on me after this fashion:—

"How much water did we have in the middle crossing at Hole-in-the-Wall, trip before last?"

I considered this an outrage. I said:—

"Every trip, down and up, the leadsmen are singing through that tangled place for three quarters of an hour on a stretch. How do you reckon I can remember such a mess as that?"

"My boy, you 've got to remember it. You 've got to re-member the exact spot and the exact marks the boat lay in when we had the shoalest water, in every one of the five hundred shoal places between St. Louis and New Orleans; and you must n't get the shoal soundings and marks of one trip mixed up with the shoal soundings and marks of another, either, for they 're not often twice alike. You must keep them separate."

When I came to myself again, I said,—

"When I get so that I can do that, I 'll be able to raise the dead, and then I won't have to pilot a steamboat to make a living. I want to retire from this business. I want a slush-bucket and a brush; I 'm only fit for a roustabout. I have n't got brains enough to be a pilot; and if I had I would n't have strength enough to carry them around, unless I went on crutches."

"Now drop that! When I say I 'll learn[1] a man the river, I mean it. And you can depend on it, I'll learn him or kill him."

[1] "Teach" is not in the river vocabulary.

IX.

Continued Perplexities

THERE WAS no use in arguing with a person like this. I promptly put such a strain on my memory that by and by even the shoal water and the countless crossing-marks began to stay with me. But the result was just the same. I never could more than get one knotty thing learned before another presented itself. Now I had often seen pilots gazing at the water and pretending to read it as if it were a book; but it was a book that told me nothing. A time came at last, however, when Mr. Bixby seemed to think me far enough advanced to bear a lesson on water-reading. So he began:—

"Do you see that long slanting line on the face of the water? Now, that 's a reef. Moreover, it 's a bluff reef. There is a solid sand-bar under it that is nearly as straight up and down as the side of a house. There is plenty of water close up to it, but mighty little on top of it. If you were to hit it you would knock the boat's brains out. Do you see where the line fringes out at the upper end and begins to fade away?"

"Yes, sir."

"Well, that is a low place; that is the head of the reef. You can climb over there, and not hurt anything. Cross over, now, and follow along close under the reef—easy water there—not much current."

I followed the reef along till I approached the fringed end. Then Mr. Bixby said,—

"Now get ready. Wait till I give the word. She won't want to mount the reef: a boat hates shoal water. Stand by—wait—*wait*—keep her well in hand. *Now* cramp her down! Snatch her! snatch her!"

He seized the other side of the wheel and helped to spin it around until it was hard down, and then we held it so. The boat resisted, and refused to answer for a while, and next she came surging to starboard, mounted the reef, and sent a long, angry ridge of water foaming away from her bows.

"Now watch her; watch her like a cat, or she 'll get away from you. When she fights strong and the tiller slips a little, n a jerky, greasy sort of way, let up on her a trifle; it is the way she tells you at night that the water is too shoal; but keep edging her up, little by little, toward the point. You are well up on the bar, now; there is a bar under every point, because the water that comes down around it forms an eddy and allows the sediment to sink. Do you see those fine lines on the face of the water that branch out like the ribs of a fan? Well, those are little reefs; you want to just miss the ends of them, but run them pretty close. Now look out—look out! Don't you crowd that slick, greasy-looking place; there ain't nine feet there; she won't stand it. She begins to smell it; look sharp, I tell you! Oh blazes, there you go! Stop the starboard wheel! Quick! Ship up to back! Set her back!"

The engine bells jingled and the engines answered promptly, shooting white columns of steam far aloft out of the 'scape pipes, but it was too late. The boat had "smelt" the bar in good earnest; the foamy ridges that radiated from her bows suddenly disappeared, a great dead swell came rolling forward and swept ahead of her, she careened far over to larboard, and went tearing away toward the other shore as if she were about scared to death. We were a good mile from where we ought to have been, when we finally got the upper hand of her again.

During the afternoon watch the next day, Mr. Bixby asked me if I knew how to run the next few miles. I said:—

"Go inside the first snag above the point, outside the next one, start out from the lower end of Higgins's wood-yard, make a square crossing and"—

"That 's all right. I 'll be back before you close up on the next point."

But he was n't. He was still below when I rounded it and entered upon a piece of river which I had some misgivings about. I did not know that he was hiding behind a chimney to see how I would perform. I went gayly along, getting prouder and prouder, for he had never left the boat in my sole charge such a length of time before. I even got to "setting" her and letting the wheel go, entirely, while I vaingloriously turned my back and inspected the stern marks and hummed a tune, a sort of easy indifference which I had prodigiously admired in Bixby and other great pilots. Once I inspected rather long, and when I faced to the front again my heart flew into my mouth so suddenly that if I had n't clapped my teeth together I should have lost it. One of those frightful bluff reefs was stretching its deadly length right across our bows! My head was gone in a moment; I did not know which end I stood on; I gasped and could not get my breath; I spun the wheel down with such rapidity that it wove itself together like a spider's web; the boat answered and turned square away from the reef, but the reef followed her! I fled, and still it followed still it kept—right across my bows! I never looked to see where I was going, I only fled. The awful crash was imminent—why did n't that villain come! If I committed the crime of ringing a bell, I might get thrown overboard. But better that than kill the boat. So in blind desperation I started such a rattling "shivaree" down below as never had astounded an engineer in this world before, I fancy. Amidst the frenzy of the bells the engines began to back and fill in a furious way, and my reason forsook its throne—we were about to crash into the woods on the other side of the river. Just then Mr. Bixby stepped calmly into view on the hurricane deck. My soul went out to him in gratitude. My distress vanished, I would have felt safe on the brink of Niagara, with Mr. Bixby on the hurricane deck. He blandly and sweetly took his tooth-pick out of his mouth between his fingers, as if it were a cigar,—we were just in the act of climbing an overhanging big tree, and the passengers were scudding astern like rats,—and lifted up these commands to me ever so gently:—

"Stop the starboard. Stop the larboard. Set her back on both."

The boat hesitated, halted, pressed her nose among the boughs a critical instant, then reluctantly began to back away.

"Stop the larboard. Come ahead on it. Stop the starboard. Come ahead on it. Point her for the bar."

I sailed away as serenely as a summer's morning. Mr. Bixby came in and said, with mock simplicity,—

"When you have a hail, my boy, you ought to tap the big bell three times before you land, so that the engineers can get ready."

I blushed under the sarcasm, and said I had n't had any hail.

"Ah! Then it was for wood, I suppose. The officer of the watch will tell you when he wants to wood up."

I went on consuming, and said I was n't after wood.

"Indeed? Why, what could you want over here in the bend, then? Did you ever know of a boat following a bend upstream at this stage of the river?"

"No, sir,—and *I* was n't trying to follow it. I was getting away from a bluff reef."

"No, it was n't a bluff reef; there is n't one within three miles of where you were."

"But I saw it. It was as bluff as that one yonder."

"Just about. Run over it!"

"Do you give it as an order?"

"Yes. Run over it."

"If I don't, I wish I may die."

"All right; I am taking the responsibility."

I was just as anxious to kill the boat, now, as I had been to save her before. I impressed my orders upon my memory, to be used at the inquest, and made a straight break for the reef. As it disappeared under our bows I held my breath; but we slid over it like oil.

"Now don't you see the difference? It was n't anything but a *wind* reef. The wind does that."

"So I see. But it is exactly like a bluff reef. How am I ever going to tell them apart?"

"I can't tell you. It is an instinct. By and by you will just naturally *know* one from the other, but you never will be able to explain why or how you know them apart."

It turned out to be true. The face of the water, in time, became a wonderful book—a book that was a dead language to the uneducated passenger, but which told its mind to me without reserve, delivering its most cherished secrets as clearly as if it uttered them with a voice. And it was not a book to be read once and thrown aside, for it had a new story to tell every day. Throughout the long twelve hundred miles there was never a page that was void of interest, never one that you could leave unread without loss, never one that you would want to skip, thinking you could find higher enjoyment in some other thing. There never was so wonderful a book written by man; never one whose interest was so absorbing, so unflagging, so sparklingly renewed with every re-perusal. The passenger who could not read it was charmed with a peculiar sort of faint dimple on its surface (on the rare occasions when he did not overlook it altogether); but to the pilot that was an *italicized* passage; indeed, it was more than that, it was a legend of the largest capitals, with a string of shouting exclamation points at the end of it; for it meant that a wreck or a rock was buried there that could tear the life out of the strongest vessel that ever floated. It is the faintest and simplest expression the water ever makes, and the most hideous to a pilot's eye. In truth, the passenger who could not read this book saw nothing but all manner of pretty pictures in it painted by the sun and shaded by the clouds, whereas to the trained eye these were not pictures at all, but the grimmest and most dead-earnest of reading-matter.

Now when I had mastered the language of this water and had come to know every trifling feature that bordered the great river as familiarly as I knew the letters of the alphabet, I had made a valuable acquisition. But I had lost something, too. I had lost something which could never be restored to me while I lived. All the grace, the beauty, the poetry had gone out of the majestic river! I still keep in mind a certain wonderful sunset which I witnessed when steamboating was new to me. A broad expanse of the river was turned to blood; in the middle distance the red hue brightened into gold, through which a solitary log came floating, black and conspicuous; in one place a long, slanting mark lay sparkling upon the water; in another the surface was broken by boiling, tumbling rings, that were as many-tinted as an opal; where the ruddy flush was faintest, was a smooth spot that was covered with graceful circles and radiating lines, ever so delicately traced; the shore on our left was densely wooded, and the sombre shadow that fell from this forest was broken in one place by a long, ruffled trail that shone like silver; and high above the forest wall a clean-stemmed dead tree waved a single leafy bough that glowed like a flame in the unobstructed splendor that was flowing from the sun. There were graceful curves, reflected images, woody heights, soft distances; and over the whole scene, far and near, the dissolving lights drifted steadily, enriching it, every passing moment, with new marvels of coloring.

I stood like one bewitched. I drank it in, in a speechless rapture. The world was new to me, and I had never seen anything like this at home. But as I have said, a day came when I began to cease from noting the glories and the charms which the moon and the sun and the twilight wrought upon the river's face; another day came when I ceased altogether to note them. Then, if that sunset scene had been repeated, I should have looked upon it without rapture, and should have commented upon it, inwardly, after this fashion: This sun means that we are going to have wind to-morrow; that floating log means that the river is rising, small thanks to it; that slanting mark on the water refers to a bluff reef which is going to kill somebody's steamboat one of these nights, if it keeps on stretching out like that; those tumbling "boils" show a dissolving bar and a changing channel there; the lines and circles in the slick water over yonder are a warning that that troublesome place is shoaling up dangerously; that silver streak in the shadow of the forest is the "break" from a new snag, and he has located himself in the very best place he could have found to fish for steamboats; that tall dead tree, with a single living branch, is not going to last long, and then how is a body ever going to get through this blind place at night without the friendly old landmark?

No, the romance and the beauty were all gone from the river. All the value any feature of it had for me now was the amount of usefulness it could furnish toward compassing the safe piloting of a steamboat. Since those days, I have pitied doctors from my heart. What does the lovely flush in a beauty's cheek mean to a doctor but a "break" that ripples above some deadly disease? Are not all her visible charms sown thick with what are to him the signs and symbols of hidden decay? Does he ever see her beauty at all, or does n't he simply view her professionally, and comment upon her unwholesome condition all to himself? And does n't he sometimes wonder whether he has gained most or lost most by learning his trade?

X.

Completing My Education

WHOSOEVER HAS DONE me the courtesy to read m[y] chapters which have preceded this may possibly won[der] that I deal so minutely with piloting as a science. It wa[s] the prime purpose of those chapters; and I am not quite don[e] yet. I wish to show, in the most patient and painstaking way what a wonderful science it is. Ship channels are buoyed an[d] lighted, and therefore it is a comparatively easy undertakin[g] to learn to run them; clear-water rivers, with gravel bottom[s] change their channels very gradually, and therefore one need[s] to learn them but once; but piloting becomes another matte[r] when you apply it to vast streams like the Mississippi and th[e] Missouri, whose alluvial banks cave and change constantly whose snags are always hunting up new quarters, whose sand bars are never at rest, whose channels are forever dodging an[d] shirking, and whose obstructions must be confronted in a[ll] nights and all weathers without the aid of a single light-hous[e] or a single buoy; for there is neither light nor buoy to b[e] found anywhere in all this three or four thousand miles [of] villanous river.[1] I feel justified in enlarging upon this grea[t] science for the reason that I feel sure no one has ever ye[t] written a paragraph about it who had piloted a steamboa[t] himself, and so had a practical knowledge of the subject. I[f] the theme were hackneyed, I should be obliged to deal gentl[y] with the reader; but since it is wholly new, I have felt at lib[b]erty to take up a considerable degree of room with it.

When I had learned the name and position of every visibl[e] feature of the river; when I had so mastered its shape that [I] could shut my eyes and trace it from St. Louis to New Or[leans]; when I had learned to read the face of the water as on[e] would cull the news from the morning paper; and finally when I had trained my dull memory to treasure up an endles[s] array of soundings and crossing-marks, and keep fast hold o[f] them, I judged that my education was complete: so I got t[o]

[1] True at the time referred to; not true now (1882).

tilting my cap to the side of my head, and wearing a tooth-
pick in my mouth at the wheel. Mr. Bixby had his eye on
these airs. One day he said,—

"What is the height of that bank yonder, at Burgess's?"

"How can I tell, sir? It is three quarters of a mile away."

"Very poor eye—very poor. Take the glass."

I took the glass, and presently said,—

"I can't tell. I suppose that that bank is about a foot and a
half high."

"Foot and a half! That 's a six-foot bank. How high was
the bank along here last trip?"

"I don't know; I never noticed."

"You did n't? Well, you must always do it hereafter."

"Why?"

"Because you 'll have to know a good many things that
it tells you. For one thing, it tells you the stage of the river—
tells you whether there 's more water or less in the river along
here than there was last trip."

"The leads tell me that." I rather thought I had the advantage of him there.

"Yes, but suppose the leads lie? The bank would tell you
so, and then you 'd stir those leadsmen up a bit. There was a
ten-foot bank here last trip, and there is only a six-foot bank
now. What does that signify?"

"That the river is four feet higher than it was last trip."

"Very good. Is the river rising or falling?"

"Rising."

"No it ain't."

"I guess I am right, sir. Yonder is some drift-wood floating
down the stream."

"A rise *starts* the drift-wood, but then it keeps on floating
a while after the river is done rising. Now the bank will tell
you about this. Wait till you come to a place where it shelves
a little. Now here; do you see this narrow belt of fine sediment? That was deposited while the water was higher. You
see the drift-wood begins to strand, too. The bank helps in
other ways. Do you see that stump on the false point?"

"Ay, ay, sir."

"Well, the water is just up to the roots of it. You must
make a note of that."

"Why?"

"Because that means that there 's seven feet in the chute of 103."

"But 103 is a long way up the river yet."

"That 's where the benefit of the bank comes in. There i water enough in 103 *now*, yet there may not be by the tim we get there; but the bank will keep us posted all along. You don't run close chutes on a falling river, up-stream, and there are precious few of them that you are allowed to run at al down-stream. There 's a law of the United States against it The river may be rising by the time we get to 103, and in tha case we 'll run it. We are drawing—how much?"

"Six feet aft,—six and a half forward."

"Well, you do seem to know something."

"But what I particularly want to know is, if I have got t keep up an everlasting measuring of the banks of this river twelve hundred miles, month in and month out?"

"Of course!"

My emotions were too deep for words for a while. Pres ently I said,—

"And how about these chutes? Are there many of them?"

"I should say so. I fancy we shan't run any of the river thi trip as you 've ever seen it run before—so to speak. If th river begins to rise again, we 'll go up behind bars that you 've always seen standing out of the river, high and dry lik the roof of a house; we 'll cut across low places that you 'v never noticed at all, right through the middle of bars tha cover three hundred acres of river; we 'll creep through crack where you 've always thought was solid land; we 'll dar through the woods and leave twenty-five miles of river off t one side; we 'll see the hind-side of every island between New Orleans and Cairo."

"Then I 've got to go to work and learn just as much mor river as I already know."

"Just about twice as much more, as near as you can com at it."

"Well, one lives to find out. I think I was a fool when went into this business."

"Yes, that is true. And you are yet. But you 'll not be whe you 've learned it."

"Ah, I never can learn it."

"I will see that you *do*."

By and by I ventured again:—

"Have I got to learn all this thing just as I know the rest of he river—shapes and all—and so I can run it at night?"

"Yes. And you 've got to have good fair marks from one nd of the river to the other, that will help the bank tell ou when there is water enough in each of these countless)laces,—like that stump, you know. When the river first be-;ins to rise, you can run half a dozen of the deepest of them; vhen it rises a foot more you can run another dozen; the next oot will add a couple of dozen, and so on: so you see you 1ave to know your banks and marks to a dead moral cer-ainty, and never get them mixed; for when you start through)ne of those cracks, there 's no backing out again, as there is n the big river; you 've got to go through, or stay there six nonths if you get caught on a falling river. There are about ifty of these cracks which you can't run at all except when :he river is brim full and over the banks."

"This new lesson is a cheerful prospect."

"Cheerful enough. And mind what I 've just told you; when you start into one of those places you 've got to go through. They are too narrow to turn around in, too crooked to back out of, and the shoal water is always *up at the head*; never elsewhere. And the head of them is always likely to be filling up, little by little, so that the marks you reckon their depth by, this season, may not answer for next."

"Learn a new set, then, every year?"

"Exactly. Cramp her up to the bar! What are you standing up through the middle of the river for?"

The next few months showed me strange things. On the same day that we held the conversation above narrated, we met a great rise coming down the river. The whole vast face of the stream was black with drifting dead logs, broken boughs, and great trees that had caved in and been washed away. It required the nicest steering to pick one's way through this rushing raft, even in the day-time, when crossing from point to point; and at night the difficulty was mightily increased; every now and then a huge log, lying deep in the water, would suddenly appear right under our bows, coming

head-on; no use to try to avoid it then; we could only stop
the engines, and one wheel would walk over that log from
one end to the other, keeping up a thundering racket and
careening the boat in a way that was very uncomfortable to
passengers. Now and then we would hit one of these sunken
logs a rattling bang, dead in the centre, with a full head of
steam, and it would stun the boat as if she had hit a continent. Sometimes this log would lodge, and stay right across
our nose, and back the Mississippi up before it; we would
have to do a little craw-fishing, then, to get away from the
obstruction. We often hit *white* logs, in the dark, for we could
not see them till we were right on them; but a black log is a
pretty distinct object at night. A white snag is an ugly customer when the daylight is gone.

Of course, on the great rise, down came a swarm of prodigious timber-rafts from the head waters of the Mississippi,
coal barges from Pittsburgh, little trading scows from everywhere, and broad-horns from "Posey County," Indiana,
freighted with "fruit and furniture"—the usual term for describing it, though in plain English the freight thus aggran-
dized was hoop-poles and pumpkins. Pilots bore a mortal
hatred to these craft; and it was returned with usury. The law
required all such helpless traders to keep a light burning, but
it was a law that was often broken. All of a sudden, on a
murky night, a light would hop up, right under our bows
almost, and an agonized voice, with the backwoods "whang"
to it, would wail out:—

"Whar 'n the —— you goin' to! Cain't you see nothin',
you dash-dashed aig-suckin', sheep-stealin', one-eyed son of a
stuffed monkey!"

Then for an instant, as we whistled by, the red glare from
our furnaces would reveal the scow and the form of the ges-
ticulating orator as if under a lightning-flash, and in that instant our firemen and deck-hands would send and receive a
tempest of missiles and profanity, one of our wheels would
walk off with the crashing fragments of a steering-oar, and
down the dead blackness would shut again. And that flat-
boatman would be sure to go into New Orleans and sue our
boat, swearing stoutly that he had a light burning all the time,
when in truth his gang had the lantern down below to sing

and lie and drink and gamble by, and no watch on deck. Once, at night, in one of those forest-bordered crevices (behind an island) which steamboatmen intensely describe with the phrase "as dark as the inside of a cow," we should have eaten up a Posey County family, fruit, furniture, and all, but that they happened to be fiddling down below and we just caught the sound of the music in time to sheer off, doing no serious damage, unfortunately, but coming so near it that we had good hopes for a moment. These people brought up their lantern, then, of course; and as we backed and filled to get away, the precious family stood in the light of it—both sexes and various ages—and cursed us till everything turned blue. Once a coal-boatman sent a bullet through our pilot-house, when we borrowed a steering-oar of him in a very narrow place.

XI.

The River Rises

D URING THIS BIG RISE these small-fry craft were an
intolerable nuisance. We were running chute after
chute,—a new world to me,—and if there was a particularly
cramped place in a chute, we would be pretty sure to meet a
broad-horn there; and if he failed to be there, we would find
him in a still worse locality, namely, the head of the chute, on
the shoal water. And then there would be no end of profane
cordialities exchanged.

Sometimes, in the big river, when we would be feeling our
way cautiously along through a fog, the deep hush would
suddenly be broken by yells and a clamor of tin pans, and all
in an instant a log raft would appear vaguely through the
webby veil, close upon us; and then we did not wait to swap
knives, but snatched our engine bells out by the roots and
piled on all the steam we had, to scramble out of the way!
One does n't hit a rock or a solid log raft with a steamboat
when he can get excused.

You will hardly believe it, but many steamboat clerks always carried a large assortment of religious tracts with them
in those old departed steamboating days. Indeed they did.
Twenty times a day we would be cramping up around a bar,
while a string of these small-fry rascals were drifting down
into the head of the bend away above and beyond us a couple
of miles. Now a skiff would dart away from one of them, and
come fighting its laborious way across the desert of water. It
would "ease all," in the shadow of our forecastle, and the
panting oarsmen would shout, "Gimmee a pa-a-per!" as the
skiff drifted swiftly astern. The clerk would throw over a file
of New Orleans journals. If these were picked up *without comment*, you might notice that now a dozen other skiffs had
been drifting down upon us without saying anything. You
understand, they had been waiting to see how No. 1 was
going to fare. No. 1 making no comment, all the rest would
bend to their oars and come on, now; and as fast as they
came the clerk would heave over neat bundles of religious

tracts, tied to shingles. The amount of hard swearing which twelve packages of religious literature will command when impartially divided up among twelve raftsmen's crews, who have pulled a heavy skiff two miles on a hot day to get them, is simply incredible.

As I have said, the big rise brought a new world under my vision. By the time the river was over its banks we had forsaken our old paths and were hourly climbing over bars that had stood ten feet out of water before; we were shaving stumpy shores, like that at the foot of Madrid Bend, which I had always seen avoided before; we were clattering through chutes like that of 82, where the opening at the foot was an unbroken wall of timber till our nose was almost at the very spot. Some of these chutes were utter solitudes. The dense, untouched forest overhung both banks of the crooked little crack, and one could believe that human creatures had never intruded there before. The swinging grape-vines, the grassy nooks and vistas glimpsed as we swept by, the flowering creepers waving their red blossoms from the tops of dead trunks, and all the spendthrift richness of the forest foliage, were wasted and thrown away there. The chutes were lovely places to steer in; they were deep, except at the head; the current was gentle; under the "points" the water was absolutely dead, and the invisible banks so bluff that where the tender willow thickets projected you could bury your boat's broadside in them as you tore along, and then you seemed fairly to fly.

Behind other islands we found wretched little farms, and wretcheder little log-cabins; there were crazy rail fences sticking a foot or two above the water, with one or two jeans-clad, chills-racked, yellow-faced male miserables roosting on the top-rail, elbows on knees, jaws in hands, grinding tobacco and discharging the result at floating chips through crevices left by lost teeth; while the rest of the family and the few farm-animals were huddled together in an empty wood-flat riding at her moorings close at hand. In this flatboat the family would have to cook and eat and sleep for a lesser or greater number of days (or possibly weeks), until the river should fall two or three feet and let them get back to their log-cabin and their chills again—chills being a merciful provision of an all-wise Providence to enable them to take exercise without exertion. And this sort of watery camping out was a thing which these people were rather liable to be treated to a couple of times a year: by the December rise out of the Ohio, and the June rise out of the Mississippi. And yet these were kindly dispensations, for they at least enabled the poor things to rise from the dead now and then, and look upon life when a steamboat went by. They appreciated the blessing, too, for they spread their mouths and eyes wide open and made the most of these occasions. Now what *could* these banished creatures find to do to keep from dying of the blues during the low-water season!

Once, in one of these lovely island chutes, we found our course completely bridged by a great fallen tree. This will serve to show how narrow some of the chutes were. The passengers had an hour's recreation in a virgin wilderness, while the boat-hands chopped the bridge away; for there was no such thing as turning back, you comprehend.

From Cairo to Baton Rouge, when the river is over its banks, you have no particular trouble in the night, for the thousand-mile wall of dense forest that guards the two banks all the way is only gapped with a farm or wood-yard opening at intervals, and so you can't "get out of the river" much easier than you could get out of a fenced lane; but from Baton Rouge to New Orleans it is a different matter. The river is more than a mile wide, and very deep—as much as two hundred feet, in places. Both banks, for a good deal over a hundred miles, are shorn of their timber and bordered by continuous sugar plantations, with only here and there a scattering sapling or row of ornamental China-trees. The timber is shorn off clear to the rear of the plantations, from two to four miles. When the first frost threatens to come, the planters snatch off their crops in a hurry. When they have finished grinding the cane, they form the refuse of the stalks (which they call *bagasse*) into great piles and set fire to them, though in other sugar countries the bagasse is used for fuel in the furnaces of the sugar mills. Now the piles of damp bagasse burn slowly, and smoke like Satan's own kitchen.

An embankment ten or fifteen feet high guards both banks of the Mississippi all the way down that lower end of the river, and this embankment is set back from the edge of the shore from ten to perhaps a hundred feet, according to circumstances; say thirty or forty feet, as a general thing. Fill that whole region with an impenetrable gloom of smoke from a hundred miles of burning bagasse piles, when the river is over the banks, and turn a steamboat loose along there at midnight and see how she will feel. And see how you will feel, too! You find yourself away out in the midst of a vague dim sea that is shoreless, that fades out and loses itself in the murky distances; for you cannot discern the thin rib of embankment, and you are always imagining you see a straggling tree when you don't. The plantations themselves are transformed by the smoke, and look like a part of the sea. All through your watch you are tortured with the exquisite misery of uncertainty. You hope you are keeping in the river, but you do not know. All that you are sure about is that you are likely to be within six feet of the bank *and* destruction, when you think you are a good half-mile from shore. And you are sure, also, that if you chance suddenly to fetch up against the embankment and topple your chimneys overboard, you will have the small comfort of knowing that it is about what you were expecting to do. One of the great Vicksburg packets darted out into a sugar plantation one night, at such a time, and had to stay there a week. But there was no novelty about it; it had often been done before.

I thought I had finished this chapter, but I wish to add a curious thing, while it is in my mind. It is only relevant in that it is connected with piloting. There used to be an excellent pilot on the river, a Mr. X., who was a somnambulist. It was said that if his mind was troubled about a bad piece of river, he was pretty sure to get up and walk in his sleep and do strange things. He was once fellow-pilot for a trip or two with George Ealer, on a great New Orleans passenger packet. During a considerable part of the first trip George was uneasy, but got over it by and by, as X. seemed content to stay in his bed when asleep. Late one night the boat was approaching Helena, Arkansas; the water was low, and the crossing above the town in a very blind and tangled condition. X. had seen the crossing since Ealer had, and as the night was particularly drizzly, sullen, and dark, Ealer was con-

sidering whether he had not better have X. called to assist in
running the place, when the door opened and X. walked in.
Now on very dark nights, light is a deadly enemy to piloting;
you are aware that if you stand in a lighted room, on such a
night, you cannot see things in the street to any purpose; but
if you put out the lights and stand in the gloom you can make
out objects in the street pretty well. So, on very dark nights,
pilots do not smoke; they allow no fire in the pilot-house
stove if there is a crack which can allow the least ray to escape; they order the furnaces to be curtained with huge tar-
paulins and the sky-lights to be closely blinded. Then no light
whatever issues from the boat. The undefinable shape that
now entered the pilot-house had Mr. X.'s voice. This said,—

"Let me take her, George; I 've seen this place since you
have, and it is so crooked that I reckon I can run it myself
easier than I could tell you how to do it."

"It is kind of you, and I swear *I* am willing. I have n't got
another drop of perspiration left in me. I have been spinning
around and around the wheel like a squirrel. It is so dark I
can't tell which way she is swinging till she is coming around
like a whirligig."

So Ealer took a seat on the bench, panting and breathless.
The black phantom assumed the wheel without saying anything, steadied the waltzing steamer with a turn or two, and
then stood at ease, coaxing her a little to this side and then to
that, as gently and as sweetly as if the time had been noonday.
When Ealer observed this marvel of steering, he wished he
had not confessed! He stared, and wondered, and finally
said,—

"Well, I thought I knew how to steer a steamboat, but that
was another mistake of mine."

X. said nothing, but went serenely on with his work. He
rang for the leads; he rang to slow down the steam; he
worked the boat carefully and neatly into invisible marks,
then stood at the centre of the wheel and peered blandly out
into the blackness, fore and aft, to verify his position; as the
leads shoaled more and more, he stopped the engines entirely,
and the dead silence and suspense of "drifting" followed;
when the shoalest water was struck, he cracked on the steam,
carried her handsomely over, and then began to work her

arily into the next system of shoal marks; the same patient, ceedful use of leads and engines followed, the boat slipped through without touching bottom, and entered upon the third and last intricacy of the crossing; imperceptibly she moved through the gloom, crept by inches into her marks, drifted tediously till the shoalest water was cried, and then, under a tremendous head of steam, went swinging over the reef and away into deep water and safety!

Ealer let his long-pent breath pour out in a great, relieving sigh, and said:—

"That 's the sweetest piece of piloting that was ever done on the Mississippi River! I would n't believed it could be done, if I had n't seen it."

There was no reply, and he added:—

"Just hold her five minutes longer, partner, and let me run down and get a cup of coffee."

A minute later Ealer was biting into a pie, down in the "texas," and comforting himself with coffee. Just then the night watchman happened in, and was about to happen out again, when he noticed Ealer and exclaimed,—

"Who is at the wheel, sir?"

"X."

"Dart for the pilot-house, quicker than lightning!"

The next moment both men were flying up the pilot-house companion-way, three steps at a jump! Nobody there! The great steamer was whistling down the middle of the river at her own sweet will! The watchman shot out of the place again; Ealer seized the wheel, set an engine back with power, and held his breath while the boat reluctantly swung away from a "towhead" which she was about to knock into the middle of the Gulf of Mexico!

By and by the watchman came back and said,—

"Did n't that lunatic tell you he was asleep, when he first came up here?"

"No."

"Well, he was. I found him walking along on top of the railings, just as unconcerned as another man would walk a pavement; and I put him to bed; now just this minute there he was again, away astern, going through that sort of tight-rope deviltry the same as before."

"Well, I think I 'll stay by, next time he has one of thos« fits. But I hope he 'll have them often. You just ought to have seen him take this boat through Helena crossing. *I* never saw anything so gaudy before. And if he can do such gold-leaf kid-glove, diamond-breastpin piloting when he is sound asleep, what *could n't* he do if he was dead!"

XII.

Sounding

WHEN THE RIVER is very low, and one's steamboat is "drawing all the water" there is in the channel,—or a few inches more, as was often the case in the old times,—one must be painfully circumspect in his piloting. We used to have to "sound" a number of particularly bad places almost every trip when the river was at a very low stage.

Sounding is done in this way. The boat ties up at the shore, just above the shoal crossing; the pilot not on watch takes his "cub" or steersman and a picked crew of men (sometimes an officer also), and goes out in the yawl—provided the boat has not that rare and sumptuous luxury, a regularly-devised "sounding-boat"—and proceeds to hunt for the best water, the pilot on duty watching his movements through a spy-glass, meantime, and in some instances assisting by signals of the boat's whistle, signifying "try higher up" or "try lower down;" for the surface of the water, like an oil-painting, is more expressive and intelligible when inspected from a little distance than very close at hand. The whistle signals are seldom necessary, however; never, perhaps, except when the wind confuses the significant ripples upon the water's surface. When the yawl has reached the shoal place, the speed is slackened, the pilot begins to sound the depth with a pole ten or twelve feet long, and the steersman at the tiller obeys the order to "hold her up to starboard;" or "let her fall off to larboard;"[1] or "steady—steady as you go."

When the measurements indicate that the yawl is approaching the shoalest part of the reef, the command is given to "ease all!" Then the men stop rowing and the yawl drifts with the current. The next order is, "Stand by with the buoy!" The moment the shallowest point is reached, the pilot delivers the order, "Let go the buoy!" and over she goes. If the pilot is not satisfied, he sounds the place again; if he finds better

---

[1] The term "larboard" is never used at sea, now, to signify the left hand; but was always used on the river in my time.

water higher up or lower down, he removes the buoy to th[e]
place. Being finally satisfied, he gives the order, and all th[e]
men stand their oars straight up in the air, in line; a bla[st]
from the boat's whistle indicates that the signal has bee[n]
seen; then the men "give way" on their oars and lay the yaw[l]
alongside the buoy; the steamer comes creeping carefull[y]
down, is pointed straight at the buoy, husbands her powe[r]
for the coming struggle, and presently, at the critical momen[t]
turns on all her steam and goes grinding and wallowing ov[er]
the buoy and the sand, and gains the deep water beyond. O[r]
maybe she does n't; maybe she "strikes and swings." Then sh[e]
has to while away several hours (or days) sparring herself of[f]

Sometimes a buoy is not laid at all, but the yawl go[es]
ahead, hunting the best water, and the steamer follows alon[g]
in its wake. Often there is a deal of fun and excitement abou[t]
sounding, especially if it is a glorious summer day, or a blu[s]
tering night. But in winter the cold and the peril take mo[re]
of the fun out of it.

A buoy is nothing but a board four or five feet long, wit[h]
one end turned up; it is a reversed school-house bench, wit[h]
one of the supports left and the other removed. It is anchore[d]
on the shoalest part of the reef by a rope with a heavy ston[e]
made fast to the end of it. But for the resistance of th[e]
turned-up end of the reversed bench, the current would pu[ll]
the buoy under water. At night, a paper lantern with a cand[le]
in it is fastened on top of the buoy, and this can be seen [a]
mile or more, a little glimmering spark in the waste of black[-]
ness.

Nothing delights a cub so much as an opportunity to g[o]
out sounding. There is such an air of adventure about it; of[-]
ten there is danger; it is so gaudy and man-of-war-like to s[it]
up in the stern-sheets and steer a swift yawl; there is some[-]
thing fine about the exultant spring of the boat when an ex[-]
perienced old sailor crew throw their souls into the oars; it [is]
lovely to see the white foam stream away from the bows[;]
there is music in the rush of the water; it is deliciously exhil[-]
arating, in summer, to go speeding over the breezy expanse[s]
of the river when the world of wavelets is dancing in the sun[.]
It is such grandeur, too, to the cub, to get a chance to giv[e]
an order; for often the pilot will simply say, "Let her g[o]

about!" and leave the rest to the cub, who instantly cries, in his sternest tone of command, "Ease starboard! Strong on the larboard! Starboard give way! With a will, men!" The cub enjoys sounding for the further reason that the eyes of the passengers are watching all the yawl's movements with absorbing interest if the time be daylight; and if it be night he knows that those same wondering eyes are fastened upon the yawl's lantern as it glides out into the gloom and dims away in the remote distance.

One trip a pretty girl of sixteen spent her time in our pilot-house with her uncle and aunt, every day and all day long. I fell in love with her. So did Mr. Thornburg's cub, Tom G——. Tom and I had been bosom friends until this time; but now a coolness began to arise. I told the girl a good many of my river adventures, and made myself out a good deal of a hero; Tom tried to make himself appear to be a hero, too, and succeeded to some extent, but then he always had a way of embroidering. However, virtue is its own reward, so I was a barely perceptible trifle ahead in the contest. About this time something happened which promised handsomely for me: the pilots decided to sound the crossing at the head of 21. This would occur about nine or ten o'clock at night, when the passengers would be still up; it would be Mr. Thornburg's watch, therefore my chief would have to do the sounding. We had a perfect love of a sounding-boat—long, trim, graceful, and as fleet as a greyhound; her thwarts were cushioned; she carried twelve oarsmen; one of the mates was always sent in her to transmit orders to her crew, for ours was a steamer where no end of "style" was put on.

We tied up at the shore above 21, and got ready. It was a foul night, and the river was so wide, there, that a landsman's uneducated eyes could discern no opposite shore through such a gloom. The passengers were alert and interested; everything was satisfactory. As I hurried through the engine-room, picturesquely gotten up in storm toggery, I met Tom, and could not forbear delivering myself of a mean speech:—

"Ain't you glad *you* don't have to go out sounding?"

Tom was passing on, but he quickly turned, and said,—

"Now just for that, you can go and get the sounding-pole

yourself. I was going after it, but I 'd see you in Halifax, now before I 'd do it."

"Who wants you to get it? *I* don't. It 's in the sounding boat."

"It ain't, either. It 's been new-painted; and it 's been up on the ladies cabin guards two days, drying."

I flew back, and shortly arrived among the crowd of watching and wondering ladies just in time to hear the command:

"Give way, men!"

I looked over, and there was the gallant sounding-boat booming away, the unprincipled Tom presiding at the tiller and my chief sitting by him with the sounding-pole which had been sent on a fool's errand to fetch. Then that young girl said to me,—

"Oh, how awful to have to go out in that little boat on such a night! Do you think there is any danger?"

I would rather have been stabbed. I went off, full of venom, to help in the pilot-house. By and by the boat's lantern disappeared, and after an interval a wee spark glimmered upon the face of the water a mile away. Mr. Thornburg blew the whistle, in acknowledgment, backed the steamer out, and made for it. We flew along for a while, then slackened steam and went cautiously gliding toward the spark. Presently Mr. Thornburg exclaimed,—

"Hello, the buoy-lantern's out!"

He stopped the engines. A moment or two later he said,—

"Why, there it is again!"

So he came ahead on the engines once more, and rang for the leads. Gradually the water shoaled up, and then began to deepen again! Mr. Thornburg muttered:—

"Well, I don't understand this. I believe that buoy has drifted off the reef. Seems to be a little too far to the left. No matter, it is safest to run over it, anyhow."

So, in that solid world of darkness we went creeping down on the light. Just as our bows were in the act of plowing over it, Mr. Thornburg seized the bell-ropes, rang a startling peal, and exclaimed,—

"My soul, it 's the sounding-boat!"

A sudden chorus of wild alarms burst out far below—a

pause—and then a sound of grinding and crashing followed.
Mr. Thornburg exclaimed,—

"There! the paddle-wheel has ground the sounding-boat to
lucifer matches! Run! See who is killed!"

I was on the main deck in the twinkling of an eye. My chief
and the third mate and nearly all the men were safe. They had
discovered their danger when it was too late to pull out of
the way; then, when the great guards overshadowed them a
moment later, they were prepared and knew what to do; at
my chief's order they sprang at the right instant, seized the
guard, and were hauled aboard. The next moment the sound-
ing-yawl swept aft to the wheel and was struck and splintered
to atoms. Two of the men and the cub Tom, were missing—
a fact which spread like wild-fire over the boat. The passengers came flocking to the forward gangway, ladies and all,
anxious-eyed, white-faced, and talked in awed voices of the
dreadful thing. And often and again I heard them say, "Poor
fellows! poor boy, poor boy!"

By this time the boat's yawl was manned and away, to
search for the missing. Now a faint call was heard, off to the
left. The yawl had disappeared in the other direction. Half
the people rushed to one side to encourage the swimmer with
their shouts; the other half rushed the other way to shriek to
the yawl to turn about. By the callings, the swimmer was approaching, but some said the sound showed failing strength.
The crowd massed themselves against the boiler-deck railings,
leaning over and staring into the gloom; and every faint and
fainter cry wrung from them such words as "Ah, poor fellow,
poor fellow! is there *no* way to save him?"

But still the cries held out, and drew nearer, and presently
the voice said pluckily,—

"I can make it! Stand by with a rope!"

What a rousing cheer they gave him! The chief mate took
his stand in the glare of a torch-basket, a coil of rope in his
hand, and his men grouped about him. The next moment the
swimmer's face appeared in the circle of light, and in another
one the owner of it was hauled aboard, limp and drenched,
while cheer on cheer went up. It was that devil Tom.

The yawl crew searched everywhere, but found no sign of

the two men. They probably failed to catch the guard, tum
bled back, and were struck by the wheel and killed. Tom ha
never jumped for the guard at all, but had plunged head-firs
into the river and dived under the wheel. It was nothing;
could have done it easy enough, and I said so; but everybod
went on just the same, making a wonderful to-do over tha
ass, as if he had done something great. That girl could n
seem to have enough of that pitiful "hero" the rest of the trip
but little I cared; I loathed her, any way.

The way we came to mistake the sounding-boat's lanter
for the buoy-light was this. My chief said that after laying th
buoy he fell away and watched it till it seemed to be secure
then he took up a position a hundred yards below it and
little to one side of the steamer's course, headed the sound
ing-boat up-stream, and waited. Having to wait some time
he and the officer got to talking; he looked up when h
judged that the steamer was about on the reef; saw that th
buoy was gone, but supposed that the steamer had alread
run over it; he went on with his talk; he noticed that th
steamer was getting very close down on him, but that was th
correct thing; it was her business to shave him closely, fo
convenience in taking him aboard; he was expecting her t
sheer off, until the last moment; then it flashed upon him tha
she was trying to run him down, mistaking his lantern for th
buoy-light; so he sang out, "Stand by to spring for the guard
men!" and the next instant the jump was made.

XIII.

A Pilot's Needs

BUT I AM WANDERING from what I was intending to do, that is, make plainer than perhaps appears in the previous chapters, some of the peculiar requirements of the science of piloting. First of all, there is one faculty which a pilot must incessantly cultivate until he has brought it to absolute perfection. Nothing short of perfection will do. That faculty is memory. He cannot stop with merely thinking a thing is so and so; he must *know* it; for this is eminently one of the "exact" sciences. With what scorn a pilot was looked upon, in the old times, if he ever ventured to deal in that feeble phrase "I think," instead of the vigorous one "I know!" One cannot easily realize what a tremendous thing it is to know every trivial detail of twelve hundred miles of river and know it with absolute exactness. If you will take the longest street in New York, and travel up and down it, conning its features patiently until you know every house and window and door and lamp-post and big and little sign by heart, and know them so accurately that you can instantly name the one you are abreast of when you are set down at random in that street in the middle of an inky black night, you will then have a tolerable notion of the amount and the exactness of a pilot's knowledge who carries the Mississippi River in his head. And then if you will go on until you know every street crossing, the character, size, and position of the crossing-stones, and the varying depth of mud in each of those numberless places, you will have some idea of what the pilot must know in order to keep a Mississippi steamer out of trouble. Next, if you will take half of the signs in that long street, and *change their places* once a month, and still manage to know their new positions accurately on dark nights, and keep up with these repeated changes without making any mistakes, you will understand what is required of a pilot's peerless memory by the fickle Mississippi.

I think a pilot's memory is about the most wonderful thing in the world. To know the Old and New Testaments by heart, and be able to recite them glibly, forward or backward, or be gin at random anywhere in the book and recite both ways an never trip or make a mistake, is no extravagant mass of know edge, and no marvellous facility, compared to a pilot's masse knowledge of the Mississippi and his marvellous facility in th handling of it. I make this comparison deliberately, and believ I am not expanding the truth when I do it. Many will think m figure too strong, but pilots will not.

And how easily and comfortably the pilot's memory doe its work; how placidly effortless is its way; how *unconscious* it lays up its vast stores, hour by hour, day by day, and neve loses or mislays a single valuable package of them all! Take a instance. Let a leadsman cry, "Half twain! half twain! ha twain! half twain! half twain!" until it becomes as monoto nous as the ticking of a clock; let conversation be going o all the time, and the pilot be doing his share of the talking and no longer consciously listening to the leadsman; and i the midst of this endless string of half twains let a sing "quarter twain!" be interjected, without emphasis, and the the half twain cry go on again, just as before: two or thre weeks later that pilot can describe with precision the boat position in the river when that quarter twain was uttered, an give you such a lot of head-marks, stern-marks, and side marks to guide you, that you ought to be able to take th boat there and put her in that same spot again yourself! Th cry of "quarter twain" did not really take his mind from hi talk, but his trained faculties instantly photographed the bear ings, noted the change of depth, and laid up the importan details for future reference without requiring any assistanc from *him* in the matter. If you were walking and talking wit a friend, and another friend at your side kept up a monoto nous repetition of the vowel sound A, for a couple of blocks and then in the midst interjected an R, thus, A, A, A, A, A R, A, A, A, etc., and gave the R no emphasis, you would no be able to state, two or three weeks afterward, that the R ha been put in, nor be able to tell what objects you were passin at the moment it was done. But you could if your memor had been patiently and laboriously trained to do that sort o thing mechanically.

Give a man a tolerably fair memory to start with, and pi

loting will develop it into a very colossus of capability. But *only in the matters it is daily drilled in*. A time would come when the man's faculties could not help noticing landmarks and soundings, and his memory could not help holding on to them with the grip of a vice; but if you asked that same man at noon what he had had for breakfast, it would be ten chances to one that he could not tell you. Astonishing things can be done with the human memory if you will devote it faithfully to one particular line of business.

At the time that wages soared so high on the Missouri River, my chief, Mr. Bixby, went up there and learned more than a thousand miles of that stream with an ease and rapidity that were astonishing. When he had seen each division *once* in the daytime and *once* at night, his education was so nearly complete that he took out a "daylight" license; a few trips later he took out a full license, and went to piloting day and night,—and he ranked A 1, too.

Mr. Bixby placed me as steersman for a while under a pilot whose feats of memory were a constant marvel to me. However, his memory was born in him, I think, not built. For instance, somebody would mention a name. Instantly Mr. Brown would break in:—

"Oh, I knew *him*. Sallow-faced, red-headed fellow, with a little scar on the side of his throat, like a splinter under the flesh. He was only in the Southern trade six months. That was thirteen years ago. I made a trip with him. There was five feet in the upper river then; the 'Henry Blake' grounded at the foot of Tower Island drawing four and a half; the 'George Elliott' unshipped her rudder on the wreck of the 'Sunflower' "—

"Why, the 'Sunflower' did n't sink until"—

"*I* know when she sunk; it was three years before that, on the 2d of December; Asa Hardy was captain of her, and his brother John was first clerk; and it was his first trip in her, too; Tom Jones told me these things a week afterward in New Orleans; he was first mate of the 'Sunflower.' Captain Hardy stuck a nail in his foot the 6th of July of the next year, and died of the lockjaw on the 15th. His brother John died two years after,—3d of March,—erysipelas. I never saw either of the Hardys,—they were Alleghany River men,—but people who knew them told me all these things. And they said Captain Hardy wore yarn socks winter and summer just the same, and his first wife's name was Jane Shook,—she was from New England,—and his second one died in a lunatic asylum. It was in the blood. She was from Lexington, Kentucky. Name was Horton before she was married."

And so on, by the hour, the man's tongue would go. He could *not* forget any thing. It was simply impossible. The most trivial details remained as distinct and luminous in his head, after they had lain there for years, as the most memorable events. His was not simply a pilot's memory; its grasp was universal. If he were talking about a trifling letter he had received seven years before, he was pretty sure to deliver you the entire screed from memory. And then without observing that he was departing from the true line of his talk, he was more than likely to hurl in a long-drawn parenthetical biography of the writer of that letter; and you were lucky indeed if he did not take up that writer's relatives, one by one, and give you their biographies, too.

Such a memory as that is a great misfortune. To it, all occurrences are of the same size. Its possessor cannot distinguish an interesting circumstance from an uninteresting one. As a talker, he is bound to clog his narrative with tiresome details and make himself an insufferable bore. Moreover, he cannot stick to his subject. He picks up every little grain of memory he discerns in his way, and so is led aside. Mr. Brown would start out with the honest intention of telling you a vastly funny anecdote about a dog. He would be "so full of laugh" that he could hardly begin; then his memory would start with the dog's breed and personal appearance; drift into a history of his owner; of his owner's family, with descriptions of weddings and burials that had occurred in it, together with recitals of congratulatory verses and obituary poetry provoked by the same; then this memory would recollect that one of these events occurred during the celebrated "hard winter" of such and such a year, and a minute description of that winter would follow, along with the names of people who were frozen to death, and statistics showing the high figures which pork and hay went up to. Pork and hay would suggest corn and fodder; corn and fodder would sug-

gest cows and horses; cows and horses would suggest the circus and certain celebrated bare-back riders; the transition
from the circus to the menagerie was easy and natural; from
the elephant to equatorial Africa was but a step; then of
course the heathen savages would suggest religion; and at the
end of three or four hours' tedious jaw, the watch would
change, and Brown would go out of the pilot-house muttering extracts from sermons he had heard years before about
the efficacy of prayer as a means of grace. And the original
first mention would be all you had learned about that dog,
after all this waiting and hungering.

A pilot must have a memory; but there are two higher
qualities which he must also have. He must have good and
quick judgment and decision, and a cool, calm courage that
no peril can shake. Give a man the merest trifle of pluck to
start with, and by the time he has become a pilot he cannot
be unmanned by any danger a steamboat can get into; but
one cannot quite say the same for judgment. Judgment is a
matter of brains, and a man must *start* with a good stock of
that article or he will never succeed as a pilot.

The growth of courage in the pilot-house is steady all the
time, but it does not reach a high and satisfactory condition
until some time after the young pilot has been "standing his
own watch," alone and under the staggering weight of all the
responsibilities connected with the position. When an apprentice has become pretty thoroughly acquainted with the river,
he goes clattering along so fearlessly with his steamboat,
night or day, that he presently begins to imagine that it is *his*
courage that animates him; but the first time the pilot steps
out and leaves him to his own devices he finds out it was the
other man's. He discovers that the article has been left out of
his own cargo altogether. The whole river is bristling with
exigencies in a moment; he is not prepared for them; he does
not know how to meet them; all his knowledge forsakes him;
and within fifteen minutes he is as white as a sheet and scared
almost to death. Therefore pilots wisely train these cubs by
various strategic tricks to look danger in the face a little more
calmly. A favorite way of theirs is to play a friendly swindle
upon the candidate.

Mr. Bixby served me in this fashion once, and for years

afterward I used to blush even in my sleep when I thought of
it. I had become a good steersman; so good, indeed, that
had all the work to do on our watch, night and day; Mr
Bixby seldom made a suggestion to me; all he ever did was to
take the wheel on particularly bad nights or in particularly
bad crossings, land the boat when she needed to be landed
play gentleman of leisure nine tenths of the watch, and collect
the wages. The lower river was about bank-full, and if any
body had questioned my ability to run any crossing between
Cairo and New Orleans without help or instruction, I should
have felt irreparably hurt. The idea of being afraid of any
crossing in the lot, in the *day-time*, was a thing too prepos
terous for contemplation. Well, one matchless summer's day
I was bowling down the bend above island 66, brimful of
self-conceit and carrying my nose as high as a giraffe's, when
Mr. Bixby said,—

"I am going below a while. I suppose you know the next
crossing?"

This was almost an affront. It was about the plainest and
simplest crossing in the whole river. One could n't come to
any harm, whether he ran it right or not; and as for depth
there never had been any bottom there. I knew all this, per
fectly well.

"Know how to *run* it? Why, I can run it with my eyes
shut."

"How much water is there in it?"

"Well, that is an odd question. I could n't get bottom there
with a church steeple."

"You think so, do you?"

The very tone of the question shook my confidence. That
was what Mr. Bixby was expecting. He left, without saying
anything more. I began to imagine all sorts of things. Mr
Bixby, unknown to me, of course, sent somebody down to
the forecastle with some mysterious instructions to the leadsmen, another messenger was sent to whisper among the officers, and then Mr. Bixby went into hiding behind a smoke-
stack where he could observe results. Presently the captain
stepped out on the hurricane deck; next the chief mate appeared; then a clerk. Every moment or two a straggler was
added to my audience; and before I got to the head of the

island I had fifteen or twenty people assembled down there under my nose. I began to wonder what the trouble was. As I started across, the captain glanced aloft at me and said, with a sham uneasiness in his voice,—

"Where is Mr. Bixby?"

"Gone below, sir."

But that did the business for me. My imagination began to construct dangers out of nothing, and they multiplied faster than I could keep the run of them. All at once I imagined I saw shoal water ahead! The wave of coward agony that surged through me then came near dislocating every joint in me. All my confidence in that crossing vanished. I seized the bell-rope; dropped it, ashamed; seized it again; dropped it once more; clutched it tremblingly once again, and pulled it so feebly that I could hardly hear the stroke myself. Captain and mate sang out instantly, and both together,—

"Starboard lead there! and quick about it!"

This was another shock. I began to climb the wheel like a squirrel; but I would hardly get the boat started to port before I would see new dangers on that side, and away I would spin to the other; only to find perils accumulating to starboard, and be crazy to get to port again. Then came the leadsman's sepulchral cry:—

"D-e-e-p four!"

Deep four in a bottomless crossing! The terror of it took my breath away.

"M-a-r-k three! . . . M-a-r-k three . . . Quarter less three! . . . Half twain!"

This was frightful! I seized the bell-ropes and stopped the engines.

"Quarter twain! Quarter twain! *Mark* twain!"

I was helpless. I did not know what in the world to do. I was quaking from head to foot, and I could have hung my hat on my eyes, they stuck out so far.

"Quarter *less* twain! Nine and a *half*!"

We were *drawing* nine! My hands were in a nerveless flutter. I could not ring a bell intelligibly with them. I flew to the speaking-tube and shouted to the engineer,—

"Oh, Ben, if you love me, *back* her! Quick, Ben! Oh, back the immortal *soul* out of her!"

I heard the door close gently. I looked around, and there stood Mr. Bixby, smiling a bland, sweet smile. Then the audience on the hurricane deck sent up a thundergust of humiliating laughter. I saw it all, now, and I felt meaner than the meanest man in human history. I laid in the lead, set the boat in her marks, came ahead on the engines, and said:—

"It was a fine trick to play on an orphan, *was n't* it? I suppose I 'll never hear the last of how I was ass enough to heave the lead at the head of 66."

"Well, no, you won't, maybe. In fact I hope you won't; for I want you to learn something by that experience. Did n't you *know* there was no bottom in that crossing?"

"Yes, sir, I did."

"Very well, then. You should n't have allowed me or anybody else to shake your confidence in that knowledge. Try to remember that. And another thing: when you get into a dangerous place, don't turn coward. That is n't going to help matters any."

It was a good enough lesson, but pretty hardly learned. Yet about the hardest part of it was that for months I so often had to hear a phrase which I had conceived a particular distaste for. It was, "Oh, Ben, if you love me, back her!"

XIV.

Rank and Dignity of Piloting

IN MY PRECEDING CHAPTERS I have tried, by going into the minutiæ of the science of piloting, to carry the reader step by step to a comprehension of what the science consists of; and at the same time I have tried to show him that it is a very curious and wonderful science, too, and very worthy of his attention. If I have seemed to love my subject, it is no surprising thing, for I loved the profession far better than any I have followed since, and I took a measureless pride in it. The reason is plain: a pilot, in those days, was the only unfettered and entirely independent human being that lived in the earth. Kings are but the hampered servants of parliament and people; parliaments sit in chains forged by their constituency; the editor of a newspaper cannot be independent, but must work with one hand tied behind him by party and patrons, and be content to utter only half or two thirds of his mind; no clergyman is a free man and may speak the whole truth, regardless of his parish's opinions; writers of all kinds are manacled servants of the public. We write frankly and fearlessly, but then we "modify" before we print. In truth, every man and woman and child has a master, and worries and frets in servitude; but in the day I write of, the Mississippi pilot had *none.* The captain could stand upon the hurricane deck, in the pomp of a very brief authority, and give him five or six orders while the vessel backed into the stream, and then that skipper's reign was over. The moment that the boat was under way in the river, she was under the sole and unquestioned control of the pilot. He could do with her exactly as he pleased, run her when and whither he chose, and tie her up to the bank whenever his judgment said that that course was best. His movements were entirely free; he consulted no one, he received commands from nobody, he promptly resented even the merest suggestions. Indeed, the law of the United States forbade him to listen to commands or suggestions, rightly considering that the pilot necessarily knew better how to handle the boat than anybody could tell him. So here was the novelty of a king without a keeper, an absolute monarch who was absolute in sober truth and not by a fiction of words. I have seen a boy of eighteen taking a great steamer serenely into what seemed almost certain destruction, and the aged captain standing mutely by, filled with apprehension but powerless to interfere. His interference, in that particular instance, might have been an excellent thing, but to permit it would have been to establish a most pernicious precedent. It will easily be guessed, considering the pilot's boundless authority, that he was a great personage in the old steamboating days. He was treated with marked courtesy by the captain and with marked deference by all the officers and servants; and this deferential spirit was quickly communicated to the passengers, too. I think pilots were about the only people I ever knew who failed to show, in some degree, embarrassment in the presence of travelling foreign princes. But then, people in one's own grade of life are not usually embarrassing objects.

By long habit, pilots came to put all their wishes in the form of commands. It "gravels" me, to this day, to put my will in the weak shape of a request, instead of launching it in the crisp language of an order.

In those old days, to load a steamboat at St. Louis, take her to New Orleans and back, and discharge cargo, consumed about twenty-five days, on an average. Seven or eight of these days the boat spent at the wharves of St. Louis and New Orleans, and every soul on board was hard at work, except the two pilots; *they* did nothing but play gentleman up town, and receive the same wages for it as if they had been on duty. The moment the boat touched the wharf at either city, they were ashore; and they were not likely to be seen again till the last bell was ringing and everything in readiness for another voyage.

When a captain got hold of a pilot of particularly high reputation, he took pains to keep him. When wages were four hundred dollars a month on the Upper Mississippi, I have known a captain to keep such a pilot in idleness, under full pay, three months at a time, while the river was frozen up. And one must remember that in those cheap times four hundred dollars was a salary of almost inconceivable splendor. Few men on shore got such pay as that, and when they did they were mightily looked up to. When pilots from either end of the river wandered into our small Missouri village, they were sought by the best and the fairest, and treated with exalted respect. Lying in port under wages was a thing which many pilots greatly enjoyed and appreciated; especially if they belonged in the Missouri River in the heyday of that trade (Kansas times), and got nine hundred dollars a trip, which was equivalent to about eighteen hundred dollars a month. Here is a conversation of that day. A chap out of the Illinois River, with a little stern-wheel tub, accosts a couple of ornate and gilded Missouri River pilots:—

"Gentlemen, I 've got a pretty good trip for the up-country, and shall want you about a month. How much will it be?"

"Eighteen hundred dollars apiece."

"Heavens and earth! You take my boat, let me have your wages, and I 'll divide!"

I will remark, in passing, that Mississippi steamboatmen were important in landsmen's eyes (and in their own, too, in a degree) according to the dignity of the boat they were on. For instance, it was a proud thing to be of the crew of such stately craft as the "Aleck Scott" or the "Grand Turk." Negro firemen, deck hands, and barbers belonging to those boats were distinguished personages in their grade of life, and they were well aware of that fact, too. A stalwart darkey once gave offence at a negro ball in New Orleans by putting on a good many airs. Finally one of the managers bustled up to him and said,—

"Who *is* you, any way? Who *is* you? dat 's what *I* wants to know!"

The offender was not disconcerted in the least, but swelled himself up and threw that into his voice which showed that he knew he was not putting on all those airs on a stinted capital.

"Who *is* I? Who *is* I? I let you know mighty quick who I is! I want you niggers to understan' dat I fires de middle do'[1] on de 'Aleck Scott!'"

That was sufficient.

The barber of the "Grand Turk" was a spruce young negro,

[1] Door.

who aired his importance with balmy complacency, and was greatly courted by the circle in which he moved. The young colored population of New Orleans were much given to flirting, at twilight, on the banquettes of the back streets. Somebody saw and heard something like the following, one evening, in one of those localities. A middle-aged negro woman projected her head through a broken pane and shouted (very willing that the neighbors should hear and envy), "You Mary Ann, come in de house dis minute! Stannin' out dah foolin' 'long wid dat low trash, an' heah's de barber off 'n de 'Gran' Turk' wants to conwerse wid you!"

My reference, a moment ago, to the fact that a pilot's peculiar official position placed him out of the reach of criticism or command, brings Stephen W—— naturally to my mind. He was a gifted pilot, a good fellow, a tireless talker, and had both wit and humor in him. He had a most irreverent independence, too, and was deliciously easy-going and comfortable in the presence of age, official dignity, and even the most august wealth. He always had work, he never saved a penny, he was a most persuasive borrower, he was in debt to every pilot on the river, and to the majority of the captains. He could throw a sort of splendor around a bit of harum-scarum, devil-may-care piloting, that made it almost fascinating—but not to everybody. He made a trip with good old Captain Y —— once, and was "relieved" from duty when the boat got to New Orleans. Somebody expressed surprise at the discharge. Captain Y—— shuddered at the mere mention of Stephen. Then his poor, thin old voice piped out something like this: —

"Why, bless me! I would n't have such a wild creature on my boat for the world—not for the whole world! He swears, he sings, he whistles, he yells—I never saw such an Injun to yell. All times of the night—it never made any difference to him. He would just yell that way, not for anything in particular, but merely on account of a kind of devilish comfort he got out of it. I never could get into a sound sleep but he would fetch me out of bed, all in a cold sweat, with one of those dreadful war-whoops. A queer being,—very queer being; no respect for anything or anybody. Sometimes he called me 'Johnny.' And he kept a fiddle, and a cat. He played execrably. This seemed to distress the cat, and so the cat would howl. Nobody could sleep where that man—and his family—was. And reckless? There never was anything like it. Now you may believe it or not, but as sure as I am sitting here, he brought my boat a-tilting down through those awful snags at Chicot under a rattling head of steam, and the wind a-blowing like the very nation, at that! My officers will tell you so. They saw it. And, sir, while he was a-tearing right down through those snags, and I a-shaking in my shoes and praying, I wish I may never speak again if he did n't pucker up his mouth and go to *whistling*! Yes, sir; whistling 'Buffalo gals, can't you come out to-night, can't you come out to-night, can't you come out to-night;' and doing it as calmly as if we were attending a funeral and were n't related to the corpse. And when I remonstrated with him about it, he smiled down on me as if I was his child, and told me to run in the house and try to be good, and not be meddling with my superiors!"[1]

Once a pretty mean captain caught Stephen in New Orleans out of work and as usual out of money. He laid steady siege to Stephen, who was in a very "close place," and finally persuaded him to hire with him at one hundred and twenty-five dollars per month, just half wages, the captain agreeing not to divulge the secret and so bring down the contempt of all the guild upon the poor fellow. But the boat was not more than a day out of New Orleans before Stephen discovered that the captain was boasting of his exploit, and that all the officers had been told. Stephen winced, but said nothing. About the middle of the afternoon the captain stepped out on the hurricane deck, cast his eye around, and looked a good deal surprised. He glanced inquiringly aloft at Stephen, but Stephen was whistling placidly, and attending to business. The captain stood around a while in evident discomfort, and once or twice seemed about to make a suggestion; but the etiquette of the river taught him to avoid that sort of rashness, and so he managed to hold his peace. He chafed and puzzled a few min-

[1] Considering a captain's ostentatious but hollow chieftainship, and a pilot's real authority, there was something impudently apt and happy about that way of phrasing it.

utes longer, then retired to his apartments. But soon he was out again, and apparently more perplexed than ever. Presently he ventured to remark, with deference,—

"Pretty good stage of the river now, ain't it, sir?"

"Well, I should say so! Bank-full *is* a pretty liberal stage."

"Seems to be a good deal of current here."

"Good deal don't describe it! It 's worse than a millrace."

"Is n't it easier in toward shore than it is out here in the middle?"

"Yes, I reckon it is; but a body can't be too careful with a steamboat. It 's pretty safe out here; can't strike any bottom here, you can depend on that."

The captain departed, looking rueful enough. At this rate, he would probably die of old age before his boat got to St. Louis. Next day he appeared on deck and again found Stephen faithfully standing up the middle of the river, fighting the whole vast force of the Mississippi, and whistling the same placid tune. This thing was becoming serious. In by the shore was a slower boat clipping along in the easy water and gaining steadily; she began to make for an island chute; Stephen stuck to the middle of the river. Speech was *wrung* from the captain. He said,—

"Mr. W——, don't that chute cut off a good deal of distance?"

"I think it does, but I don't know."

"Don't know! Well, is n't there water enough in it now to go through?"

"I expect there is, but I am not certain."

"Upon my word this is odd! Why, those pilots on that boat yonder are going to try it. Do you mean to say that you don't know as much as they do?"

"*They!* Why, *they* are two-hundred-and-fifty-dollar pilots! But don't you be uneasy; I know as much as any man can afford to know for a hundred and twenty-five!"

The captain surrendered.

Five minutes later Stephen was bowling through the chute and showing the rival boat a two-hundred-and-fifty-dollar pair of heels.

XV.

The Pilots' Monopoly

O NE DAY, on board the "Aleck Scott," my chief, Mr. Bixby, was crawling carefully through a close place at Cat Island, both leads going, and everybody holding his breath. The captain, a nervous, apprehensive man, kept still as long as he could, but finally broke down and shouted from the hurricane deck, —

"For gracious' sake, give her steam, Mr. Bixby! give her steam! She 'll never raise the reef on this headway!"

For all the effect that was produced upon Mr. Bixby, one would have supposed that no remark had been made. But five minutes later, when the danger was past and the leads laid in, he burst instantly into a consuming fury, and gave the captain the most admirable cursing I ever listened to. No bloodshed ensued; but that was because the captain's cause was weak; for ordinarily he was not a man to take correction quietly.

Having now set forth in detail the nature of the science of piloting, and likewise described the rank which the pilot held among the fraternity of steamboatmen, this seems a fitting place to say a few words about an organization which the pilots once formed for the protection of their guild. It was curious and noteworthy in this, that it was perhaps the com-pactest, the completest, and the strongest commercial organi-zation ever formed among men.

For a long time wages had been two hundred and fifty dol-lars a month; but curiously enough, as steamboats multiplied and business increased, the wages began to fall little by little. It was easy to discover the reason of this. Too many pilots were being "made." It was nice to have a "cub," a steersman, to do all the hard work for a couple of years, gratis, while his master sat on a high bench and smoked; all pilots and cap-tains had sons or nephews who wanted to be pilots. By and by it came to pass that nearly every pilot on the river had a steersman. When a steersman had made an amount of prog-ress that was satisfactory to any two pilots in the trade, they could get a pilot's license for him by signing an application directed to the United States Inspector. Nothing further was needed; usually no questions were asked, no proofs of capacity required.

Very well, this growing swarm of new pilots presently began to undermine the wages, in order to get berths. Too late—apparently—the knights of the tiller perceived their mistake. Plainly, something had to be done, and quickly; but what was to be the needful thing? A close organization. Nothing else would answer. To compass this seemed an impossibility; so it was talked, and talked, and then dropped. It was too likely to ruin whoever ventured to move in the matter. But at last about a dozen of the boldest—and some of them the best—pilots on the river launched themselves into the enterprise and took all the chances. They got a special charter from the legislature, with large powers, under the name of the Pilots' Benevolent Association; elected their officers, completed their organization, contributed capital, put "association" wages up to two hundred and fifty dollars at once—and then retired to their homes, for they were promptly discharged from employment. But there were two or three unnoticed trifles in their by-laws which had the seeds of propagation in them. For instance, all idle members of the association, in good standing, were entitled to a pension of twenty-five dollars per month. This began to bring in one straggler after another from the ranks of the new-fledged pilots, in the dull (summer) season. Better have twenty-five dollars than starve; the initiation fee was only twelve dollars, and no dues required from the unemployed.

Also, the widows of deceased members in good standing could draw twenty-five dollars per month, and a certain sum for each of their children. Also, the said deceased would be buried at the association's expense. These things resurrected all the superannuated and forgotten pilots in the Mississippi Valley. They came from farms, they came from interior villages, they came from everywhere. They came on crutches, on drays, in ambulances,—any way, so they got there. They paid in their twelve dollars, and straightway began to draw out twenty-five dollars a month and calculate their burial bills.

By and by, all the useless, helpless pilots, and a dozen first-class ones, were in the association, and nine tenths of the best pilots out of it and laughing at it. It was the laughing-stock of the whole river. Everybody joked about the by-law requiring members to pay ten per cent of their wages, every month, into the treasury for the support of the association, whereas all the members were outcast and tabooed, and no one would employ them. Everybody was derisively grateful to the association for taking all the worthless pilots out of the way and leaving the whole field to the excellent and the deserving; and everybody was not only jocularly grateful for that, but for a result which naturally followed, namely, the gradual advance of wages as the busy season approached. Wages had gone up from the low figure of one hundred dollars a month to one hundred and twenty-five, and in some cases to one hundred and fifty; and it was great fun to enlarge upon the fact that this charming thing had been accomplished by a body of men not one of whom received a particle of benefit from it. Some of the jokers used to call at the association rooms and have a good time chaffing the members and offering them the charity of taking them as steersmen for a trip, so that they could see what the forgotten river looked like. However, the association was content; or at least it gave no sign to the contrary. Now and then it captured a pilot who was "out of luck," and added him to its list; and these later additions were very valuable, for they were good pilots; the incompetent ones had all been absorbed before. As business freshened, wages climbed gradually up to two hundred and fifty dollars—the association figure—and became firmly fixed there; and still without benefiting a member of that body, for no member was hired. The hilarity at the association's expense burst all bounds, now. There was no end to the fun which that poor martyr had to put up with.

However, it is a long lane that has no turning. Winter approached, business doubled and trebled, and an avalanche of Missouri, Illinois, and Upper Mississippi River boats came pouring down to take a chance in the New Orleans trade. All of a sudden, pilots were in great demand, and were correspondingly scarce. The time for revenge was come. It was a bitter pill to have to accept association pilots at last, yet captains and owners agreed that there was no other way. But none of these outcasts offered! So there was a still bitterer pill to be swallowed: they must be sought out and asked for their services. Captain—— was the first man who found it necessary to take the dose, and he had been the loudest derider of the organization. He hunted up one of the best of the association pilots and said,—

"Well, you boys have rather got the best of us for a little while, so I 'll give in with as good a grace as I can. I 've come to hire you; get your trunk aboard right away. I want to leave at twelve o'clock."

"I don't know about that. Who is your other pilot?"

"I 've got I. S——. Why?"

"I can't go with him. He don't belong to the association."

"What!"

"It 's so."

"Do you mean to tell me that you won't turn a wheel with one of the very best and oldest pilots on the river because he don't belong to your association?"

"Yes, I do."

"Well, if this is n't putting on airs! I supposed I was doing you a benevolence; but I begin to think that I am the party that wants a favor done. Are you acting under a law of the concern?"

"Yes."

"Show it to me."

So they stepped into the association rooms, and the secretary soon satisfied the captain, who said,—

"Well, what am I to do? I have hired Mr. S—— for the entire season."

"I will provide for you," said the secretary. "I will detail a pilot to go with you, and he shall be on board at twelve o'clock."

"But if I discharge S——, he will come on me for the whole season's wages."

"Of course that is a matter between you and Mr. S——, captain. We cannot meddle in your private affairs."

The captain stormed, but to no purpose. In the end he had to discharge S——, pay him about a thousand dollars, and take an association pilot in his place. The laugh was beginning to turn the other way, now. Every day, thenceforward, a new victim fell; every day some outraged captain discharged a non-association pet, with tears and profanity, and installed a hated association man in his berth. In a very little while, idle non-associationists began to be pretty plenty, brisk as business was, and much as their services were desired. The laugh was shifting to the other side of their mouths most palpably. These victims, together with the captains and owners, presently ceased to laugh altogether, and began to rage about the revenge they would take when the passing business "spurt" was over.

Soon all the laughers that were left were the owners and crews of boats that had two non-association pilots. But their triumph was not very long-lived. For this reason: It was a rigid rule of the association that its members should never, under any circumstances whatever, give information about the channel to any "outsider." By this time about half the boats had none but association pilots, and the other half had none but outsiders. At the first glance one would suppose that when it came to forbidding information about the river these two parties could play equally at that game; but this was not so. At every good-sized town from one end of the river to the other, there was a "wharf-boat" to land at, instead of a wharf or a pier. Freight was stored in it for transportation; waiting passengers slept in its cabins. Upon each of these wharf-boats the association's officers placed a strong box, fastened with a peculiar lock which was used in no other service but one—the United States mail service. It was the letter-bag lock, a sacred governmental thing. By dint of much beseeching the government had been persuaded to allow the association to use this lock. Every association man carried a key which would open these boxes. That key, or rather a peculiar way of holding it in the hand when its owner was asked for river information by a stranger,—for the success of the St. Louis and New Orleans association had now bred tolerably thriving branches in a dozen neighboring steamboat trades,—was the association man's sign and diploma of membership; and if the stranger did not respond by producing a similar key and holding it in a certain manner duly prescribed, his question was politely ignored. From the association's secretary each member received a package of more or less gorgeous blanks, printed like a bill-head, on handsome paper, properly ruled in columns; a bill-head worded something like this: —

STEAMER GREAT REPUBLIC.
JOHN SMITH, MASTER.
Pilots, John Jones and Thomas Brown.

CROSSINGS.	SOUNDINGS.	MARKS.	REMARKS.

These blanks were filled up, day by day, as the voyage progressed, and deposited in the several wharf-boat boxes. For instance, as soon as the first crossing, out from St. Louis, was completed, the items would be entered upon the blank, under the appropriate headings, thus: —

"St. Louis. Nine and a half (feet). Stern on court-house, head on dead cottonwood above wood-yard, until you raise the first reef, then pull up square." Then under head of Remarks: "Go just outside the wrecks; this is important. New snag just where you straighten down; go above it."

The pilot who deposited that blank in the Cairo box (after adding to it the details of every crossing all the way down from St. Louis) took out and read half a dozen fresh reports (from upward-bound steamers) concerning the river between Cairo and Memphis, posted himself thoroughly, returned them to the box, and went back aboard his boat again so armed against accident that he could not possibly get his boat into trouble without bringing the most ingenious carelessness to his aid.

Imagine the benefits of so admirable a system in a piece of river twelve or thirteen hundred miles long, whose channel was shifting every day! The pilot who had formerly been obliged to put up with seeing a shoal place once or possibly twice a month, had a hundred sharp eyes to watch it for him, now, and bushels of intelligent brains to tell him how to run it. His information about it was seldom twenty-four hours old. If the reports in the last box chanced to leave any misgivings on his mind concerning a treacherous crossing, he had his remedy; he blew his steam-whistle in a peculiar way as soon as he saw a boat approaching; the signal was answered in a peculiar way if that boat's pilots were association men;

ınd then the two steamers ranged alongside and all uncertain-
ies were swept away by fresh information furnished to the
ınquirer by word of mouth and in minute detail.

The first thing a pilot did when he reached New Orleans
ər St. Louis was to take his final and elaborate report to the
ıssociation parlors and hang it up there,—*after* which he was
free to visit his family. In these parlors a crowd was always
gathered together, discussing changes in the channel, and the
moment there was a fresh arrival, everybody stopped talking
ill this witness had told the newest news and settled the latest
ıncertainty. Other craftsmen can "sink the shop," sometimes,
ınd interest themselves in other matters. Not so with a pilot;
ıe must devote himself wholly to his profession and talk of
ıothing else; for it would be small gain to be perfect one day
ınd imperfect the next. He has no time or words to waste if
ıe would keep "posted."

But the outsiders had a hard time of it. No particular place
to meet and exchange information, no wharf-boat reports,
ıone but chance and unsatisfactory ways of getting news. The
consequence was that a man sometimes had to run five
ıundred miles of river on information that was a week or ten
days old. At a fair stage of the river that might have answered; but when the dead low water came it was destructive.

Now came another perfectly logical result. The outsiders
ɔegan to ground steamboats, sink them, and get into all sorts
ɔf trouble, whereas accidents seemed to keep entirely away
from the association men. Wherefore even the owners and
captains of boats furnished exclusively with outsiders, and
previously considered to be wholly independent of the association and free to comfort themselves with brag and laughter, began to feel pretty uncomfortable. Still, they made a
show of keeping up the brag, until one black day when every
captain of the lot was formally ordered to immediately discharge his outsiders and take association pilots in their stead.
And who was it that had the dashing presumption to do that?
Alas, it came from a power behind the throne that was greater
than the throne itself. It was the underwriters!

It was no time to "swap knives." Every outsider had to take
his trunk ashore at once. Of course it was supposed that there
was collusion between the association and the underwriters,

but this was not so. The latter had come to comprehend the excellence of the "report" system of the association and the safety it secured, and so they had made their decision among themselves and upon plain business principles.

There was weeping and wailing and gnashing of teeth in the camp of the outsiders now. But no matter, there was but one course for them to pursue, and they pursued it. They came forward in couples and groups, and proffered their twelve dollars and asked for membership. They were surprised to learn that several new by-laws had been long ago added. For instance, the initiation fee had been raised to fifty dollars; that sum must be tendered, and also ten per cent of the wages which the applicant had received each and every month since the founding of the association. In many cases this amounted to three or four hundred dollars. Still, the association would not entertain the application until the money was present. Even then a single adverse vote killed the application. Every member had to vote yes or no in person and before witnesses; so it took weeks to decide a candidacy, because many pilots were so long absent on voyages. However, the repentant sinners scraped their savings together, and one by one, by our tedious voting process, they were added to the fold. A time came, at last, when only about ten remained outside. They said they would starve before they would apply. They remained idle a long while, because of course nobody could venture to employ them.

By and by the association published the fact that upon a certain date the wages would be raised to five hundred dollars per month. All the branch associations had grown strong, now, and the Red River one had advanced wages to seven hundred dollars a month. Reluctantly the ten outsiders yielded, in view of these things, and made application. There was *another* new by-law, by this time, which required them to pay dues not only on all the wages they had received since the association was born, but also on what they would have received if they had continued at work up to the time of their application, instead of going off to pout in idleness. It turned out to be a difficult matter to elect them, but it was accomplished at last. The most virulent sinner of this batch had stayed out and allowed "dues" to accumulate against him so ong that he had to send in six hundred and twenty-five dollars with his application.

The association had a good bank account now, and was very strong. There was no longer an outsider. A by-law was added forbidding the reception of any more cubs or apprentices for five years; after which time a limited number would be taken, not by individuals, but by the association, upon these terms: the applicant must not be less than eighteen years old, and of respectable family and good character; he must pass an examination as to education, pay a thousand dollars in advance for the privilege of becoming an apprentice, and must remain under the commands of the association until a great part of the membership (more than half, I think) should be willing to sign his application for a pilot's license.

All previously-articled apprentices were now taken away from their masters and adopted by the association. The president and secretary detailed them for service on one boat or another, as they chose, and changed them from boat to boat according to certain rules. If a pilot could show that he was in infirm health and needed assistance, one of the cubs would be ordered to go with him.

The widow and orphan list grew, but so did the association's financial resources. The association attended its own funerals in state, and paid for them. When occasion demanded, it sent members down the river upon searches for the bodies of brethren lost by steamboat accidents; a search of this kind sometimes cost a thousand dollars.

The association procured a charter and went into the insurance business, also. It not only insured the lives of its members, but took risks on steamboats.

The organization seemed indestructible. It was the tightest monopoly in the world. By the United States law, no man could become a pilot unless two duly licensed pilots signed his application; and now there was nobody outside of the association competent to sign. Consequently the making of pilots was at an end. Every year some would die and others become incapacitated by age and infirmity; there would be no new ones to take their places. In time, the association could put wages up to any figure it chose; and as long as it should be wise enough not to carry the thing too far and provoke the national government into amending the licensing system, steamboat owners would have to submit, since there would be no help for it.

The owners and captains were the only obstruction that lay between the association and absolute power; and at last this one was removed. Incredible as it may seem, the owners and captains deliberately did it themselves. When the pilots' association announced, months beforehand, that on the first day of September, 1861, wages would be advanced to five hundred dollars per month, the owners and captains instantly put freights up a few cents, and explained to the farmers along the river the necessity of it, by calling their attention to the burdensome rate of wages about to be established. It was a rather slender argument, but the farmers did not seem to detect it. It looked reasonable to them that to add five cents freight on a bushel of corn was justifiable under the circumstances, overlooking the fact that this advance on a cargo of forty thousand sacks was a good deal more than necessary to cover the new wages.

So, straightway the captains and owners got up an association of their own, and proposed to put captains' wages up to five hundred dollars, too, and move for another advance in freights. It was a novel idea, but of course an effect which had been produced once could be produced again. The new association decreed (for this was before all the outsiders had been taken into the pilots' association) that if any captain employed a non-association pilot, he should be forced to discharge him, and also pay a fine of five hundred dollars. Several of these heavy fines were paid before the captains' organization grew strong enough to exercise full authority over its membership; but that all ceased, presently. The captains tried to get the pilots to decree that no member of their corporation should serve under a non-association captain; but this proposition was declined. The pilots saw that they would be backed up by the captains and the underwriters anyhow, and so they wisely refrained from entering into entangling alliances.

As I have remarked, the pilots' association was now the compactest monopoly in the world, perhaps, and seemed simply indestructible. And yet the days of its glory were numbered. First, the new railroad stretching up through Mississippi, Tennessee, and Kentucky, to Northern railway centres, began to divert the passenger travel from the steamers; next the war came and almost entirely annihilated the steamboating industry during several years, leaving most of the pilots idle, and the cost of living advancing all the time; then the treasurer of the St. Louis association put his hand into the till and walked off with every dollar of the ample fund; and finally, the railroads intruding everywhere, there was little for steamers to do, when the war was over, but carry freights; so straightway some genius from the Atlantic coast introduced the plan of towing a dozen steamer cargoes down to New Orleans at the tail of a vulgar little tug-boat; and behold, in the twinkling of an eye, as it were, the association and the noble science of piloting were things of the dead and pathetic past!

XVI.

Racing Days

IT WAS ALWAYS the custom for the boats to leave New Orleans between four and five o'clock in the afternoon. From
three o'clock onward they would be burning rosin and pitch
pine (the sign of preparation), and so one had the picturesque
spectacle of a rank, some two or three miles long, of tall,
ascending columns of coal-black smoke; a colonnade which
supported a sable roof of the same smoke blended together
and spreading abroad over the city. Every outward-bound
boat had its flag flying at the jack-staff, and sometimes a duplicate on the verge staff astern. Two or three miles of mates
were commanding and swearing with more than usual emphasis; countless processions of freight barrels and boxes were
spinning athwart the levee and flying aboard the stage-planks;
belated passengers were dodging and skipping among these
frantic things, hoping to reach the forecastle companion way
alive, but having their doubts about it; women with reticules
and bandboxes were trying to keep up with husbands
freighted with carpet-sacks and crying babies, and making a
failure of it by losing their heads in the whirl and roar and
general distraction; drays and baggage-vans were clattering
hither and thither in a wild hurry, every now and then getting
blocked and jammed together, and then during ten seconds
one could not see them for the profanity, except vaguely and
dimly; every windlass connected with every fore-hatch, from
one end of that long array of steamboats to the other, was
keeping up a deafening whiz and whir, lowering freight into
the hold, and the half-naked crews of perspiring negroes that
worked them were roaring such songs as "De Las' Sack! De
Las' Sack!"—inspired to unimaginable exaltation by the
chaos of turmoil and racket that was driving everybody else
mad. By this time the hurricane and boiler decks of the steamers would be packed and black with passengers. The "last
bells" would begin to clang, all down the line, and then the
powwow seemed to double; in a moment or two the final
warning came,—a simultaneous din of Chinese gongs, with

the cry, "All dat ain't goin', please to git asho'!"—and behold, the powwow quadrupled! People came swarming ashore, overturning excited stragglers that were trying to swarm aboard. One more moment later a long array of stage-planks was being hauled in, each with its customary latest passenger clinging to the end of it with teeth, nails, and everything else, and the customary latest procrastinator making a wild spring shoreward over his head.

Now a number of the boats slide backward into the stream, leaving wide gaps in the serried rank of steamers. Citizens crowd the decks of boats that are not to go, in order to see the sight. Steamer after steamer straightens herself up, gathers all her strength, and presently comes swinging by, under a tremendous head of steam, with flag flying, black smoke rolling, and her entire crew of firemen and deck-hands (usually swarthy negroes) massed together on the forecastle, the best "voice" in the lot towering from the midst (being mounted on the capstan), waving his hat or a flag, and all roaring a mighty chorus, while the parting cannons boom and the multitudinous spectators swing their hats and huzza! Steamer after steamer falls into line, and the stately procession goes winging its flight up the river.

In the old times, whenever two fast boats started out on a race, with a big crowd of people looking on, it was inspiring to hear the crews sing, especially if the time were night-fall, and the forecastle lit up with the red glare of the torch-baskets. Racing was royal fun. The public always had an idea that racing was dangerous; whereas the opposite was the case—that is, after the laws were passed which restricted each boat to just so many pounds of steam to the square inch. No engineer was ever sleepy or careless when his heart was in a race. He was constantly on the alert, trying gauge-cocks and watching things. The dangerous place was on slow, plodding boats, where the engineers drowsed around and allowed chips to get into the "doctor" and shut off the water supply from the boilers.

In the "flush times" of steamboating, a race between two notoriously fleet steamers was an event of vast importance. The date was set for it several weeks in advance, and from that time forward, the whole Mississippi Valley was in a state

of consuming excitement. Politics and the weather were
dropped, and people talked only of the coming race. As the
time approached, the two steamers "stripped" and got ready.
Every incumbrance that added weight, or exposed a resisting
surface to wind or water, was removed, if the boat could possibly do without it. The "spars," and sometimes even their supporting derricks, were sent ashore, and no means left to set the
boat afloat in case she got aground. When the "Eclipse" and the
"A.L. Shotwell" ran their great race many years ago, it was said
that pains were taken to scrape the gilding off the fanciful device
which hung between the "Eclipse's" chimneys, and that for that
one trip the captain left off his kid gloves and had his head
shaved. But I always doubted these things.

If the boat was known to make her best speed when drawing five and a half feet forward and five feet aft, she was carefully loaded to that exact figure—she would n't enter a dose
of homœopathic pills on her manifest after that. Hardly any
passengers were taken, because they not only add weight but
they never will "trim boat." They always run to the side when
there is anything to see, whereas a conscientious and experienced steamboatman would stick to the centre of the boat
and part his hair in the middle with a spirit level.

No way-freights and no way-passengers were allowed, for
the racers would stop only at the largest towns, and then it
would be only "touch and go." Coal flats and wood flats were
contracted for beforehand, and these were kept ready to hitch
on to the flying steamers at a moment's warning. Double
crews were carried, so that all work could be quickly done.

The chosen date being come, and all things in readiness,
the two great steamers back into the stream, and lie there
jockeying a moment, and apparently watching each other's
slightest movement, like sentient creatures; flags drooping,
the pent steam shrieking through safety-valves, the black
smoke rolling and tumbling from the chimneys and darkening
all the air. People, people everywhere; the shores, the house-
tops, the steamboats, the ships, are packed with them, and
you know that the borders of the broad Mississippi are going
to be fringed with humanity thence northward twelve
hundred miles, to welcome these racers.

Presently tall columns of steam burst from the 'scape-pipes

of both steamers, two guns boom a good-by, two red-shirted heroes mounted on capstans wave their small flags above the massed crews on the forecastles, two plaintive solos linger on the air a few waiting seconds, two mighty choruses burst forth—and here they come! Brass bands bray Hail Columbia, huzza after huzza thunders from the shores, and the stately creatures go whistling by like the wind.

Those boats will never halt a moment between New Orleans and St. Louis, except for a second or two at large towns, or to hitch thirty-cord wood-boats alongside. You should be on board when they take a couple of those wood-boats in tow and turn a swarm of men into each; by the time you have wiped your glasses and put them on, you will be wondering what has become of that wood.

Two nicely matched steamers will stay in sight of each other day after day. They might even stay side by side, but for the fact that pilots are not all alike, and the smartest pilots will win the race. If one of the boats has a "lightning" pilot, whose "partner" is a trifle his inferior, you can tell which one is on watch by noting whether that boat has gained ground or lost some during each four-hour stretch. The shrewdest pilot can delay a boat if he has not a fine genius for steering. Steering is a very high art. One must not keep a rudder dragging across a boat's stern if he wants to get up the river fast.

There is a great difference in boats, of course. For a long time I was on a boat that was so slow we used to forget what year it was we left port in. But of course this was at rare intervals. Ferry-boats used to lose valuable trips because their passengers grew old and died, waiting for us to get by. This was at still rarer intervals. I had the documents for these occurrences, but through carelessness they have been mislaid. This boat, the "John J. Roe," was so slow that when she finally sunk in Madrid Bend, it was five years before the owners heard of it. That was always a confusing fact to me, but it is according to the record, any way. She was dismally slow; still, we often had pretty exciting times racing with islands, and rafts, and such things. One trip, however, we did rather well. We went to St. Louis in sixteen days. But even at this rattling gait I think we changed watches three times in Fort Adams reach, which is five miles long. A "reach" is a piece of straight river, and of course the current drives through such a place in a pretty lively way.

That trip we went to Grand Gulf, from New Orleans, in four days (three hundred and forty miles); the "Eclipse" and "Shotwell" did it in one. We were nine days out, in the chute of 63 (seven hundred miles); the "Eclipse" and "Shotwell" went there in two days. Something over a generation ago, a boat called the "J. M. White" went from New Orleans to Cairo in three days, six hours, and forty-four minutes. In 1853 the "Eclipse" made the same trip in three days, three hours, and twenty minutes.[1] In 1870 the "R. E. Lee" did it in three days and *one* hour. This last is called the fastest trip on record. I will try to show that it was not. For this reason: the distance between New Orleans and Cairo, when the "J. M. White" ran it, was about eleven hundred and six miles; consequently her average speed was a trifle over fourteen miles per hour. In the "Eclipse's" day the distance between the two ports had become reduced to one thousand and eighty miles; consequently her average speed was a shade under fourteen and three eighths miles per hour. In the "R. E. Lee's" time the distance had diminished to about one thousand and thirty miles; consequently her average was about fourteen and one eighth miles per hour. Therefore the "Eclipse's" was conspicuously the fastest time that has ever been made.

THE RECORD OF SOME FAMOUS TRIPS.

[From Commodore Rollingpin's Almanac.]

FAST TIME ON THE WESTERN WATERS.

FROM NEW ORLEANS TO NATCHEZ—268 MILES.

				D.	H.	M.						H.	M.
1814.	Orleans	made the run in	6	6	40	1844.	Sultana . .	made the run in			19	45
1814.	Comet	"	"	5	10	1851.	Magnolia	"	"		19	50
1815.	Enterprise	"	"	4	11	20	1853.	A. L. Shotwell	"	"		19	49
1817.	Washington	"	"	4			1853.	Southern Belle	"	"		20	3
1817.	Shelby	"	"	3	20	1853.	Princess (No. 4)	"	"		20	26
1819.	Paragon	"	"	3	8	1853.	Eclipse	"	"		19	47
1828.	Tecumseh	"	"	3	1	20	1855.	Princess (New)	"	"		18	53
1834.	Tuscarora	"	"	1	21	1855.	Natchez (New)	"	"		17	30
1838.	Natchez	"	"	1	17	1856.	Princess (New)	"	"		17	30
1840.	Ed. Shippen	"	"	1	8	1870.	Natchez	"	"		17	17
1842.	Belle of the West	"	1	18	1870.	R. E. Lee	"	"		17	11

[1] Time disputed. Some authorities add 1 hour and 16 minutes to this.

Time Tables—*Continued*

FROM NEW ORLEANS TO CAIRO—1,024 MILES.

		D.	H.	M.			D.	H.	M.
844.	J. M. White made the run in	3	6	44	1869.	Dexter . . made the run in	3	6	20
852.	Reindeer " "	3	12	45	1870.	Natchez " "	3	4	34
853.	Eclipse "	3	4	4	1870.	R. E. Lee " "	3	1	
853.	A. L. Shotwell " "	3	3	40					

FROM NEW ORLEANS TO LOUISVILLE—1,440 MILES.

		D.	H.	M.			D.	H.	M.
815.	Enterprise made the run in	25	2	40	1840.	Ed. Shippen made the run in	5	14	
817.	Washington " "	25			1842.	Belle of the West "	6	14	
817.	Shelby " "	20	4	20	1843.	Duke of Orleans "	5	23	
819.	Paragon " "	18	10		1844.	Sultana " "	5	12	
828.	Tecumseh " "	8	4		1849.	Bostona " "	5	8	
834.	Tuscarora " "	7	16		1851.	Belle Key " "	4	23	
837.	Gen. Brown " "	6	22		1852.	Reindeer " "	4	20	45
837.	Randolph " "	6	22		1852.	Eclipse " "	4	19	
837.	Empress " "	6	17		1853.	A. L. Shotwell " "	4	10	20
837.	Sultana " "	6	15		1853.	Eclipse " "	4	9	30

FROM NEW ORLEANS TO DONALDSVILLE—78 MILES.

		H.	M.			H.	M.
852.	A. L. Shotwell made the run in	5	42	1860.	Atlantic . . . made the run in	5	11
852.	Eclipse " "	5	42	1860.	Gen. Quitman " "	5	6
854.	Sultana " "	5	12	1865.	Ruth " "	4	43
856.	Princess " "	4	51	1870.	R. E. Lee " "	4	59

FROM NEW ORLEANS TO ST. LOUIS—1,218 MILES.

		D.	H.	M.			D.	H.	M.
844.	J. M. White made the run in	3	23	9	1870.	Natchez . . made the run in	3	21	58
849.	Missouri " "	4	19		1870.	R. E. Lee " "	3	18	14
869.	Dexter " "	4	9						

FROM LOUISVILLE TO CINCINNATI—141 MILES.

		D.	H.	M.			D.	H.	M.
819.	Gen. Pike made the run in	1	16		1843.	Congress made the run in		12	20
819.	Paragon " "	1	14	20	1846.	Ben Franklin (No. 6) "		11	45
822.	Wheeling Packet " "	1	10		1852.	Alleghaney " "		10	38
837.	Moselle " "		12		1852.	Pittsburgh " "		10	23
843.	Duke of Orleans " "		12		1853.	Telegraph No. 3 "		9	52

FROM LOUISVILLE TO ST. LOUIS—750 MILES.

		D.	H.	M.			D.	H.	M.
1843.	Congress made the run in	2	1		1854.	Northerner made the run in	1	22	30
854.	Pike " "	1	23		1855.	Southerner " "	1	19	

FROM CINCINNATI TO PITTSBURGH—490 MILES.

		D.	H.			D.	H.
850.	Telegraph No. 2 made the run in	1	17	1852.	Pittsburgh made the run in	1	15
851.	Buckeye State " "	1	16				

FROM ST. LOUIS TO ALTON—30 MILES.

		H.	M.			H.	M.
853.	Altona . . . made the run in	1	35	1876.	War Eagle . . made the run in	1	37
876.	Golden Eagle " "	1	37				

Time Tables—*Continued*

MISCELLANEOUS RUNS.

In June, 1859, the St. Louis and Keokuk Packet, City of Louisiana, made the run from St. Louis to Keokuk (214 miles) in 16 hours and 20 minutes, the best time on record.

In 1868 the steamer Hawkeye State, of the Northern Line Packet Company, made the run from St. Louis to St. Paul (800 miles) in 2 days and 20 hours. Never was beaten.

In 1853 the steamer Polar Star made the run from St. Louis to St. Joseph, on the Missouri River, in 64 hours. In July, 1856, the steamer Jas. H. Lucas, Andy Wineland, Master, made the same run in 60 hours and 57 minutes. The distance between the ports is 600 miles, and when the difficulties of navigating the turbulent Missouri are taken into consideration, the performance of the Lucas deserves especial mention.

The time made by the R. E. Lee from New Orleans to St. Louis in 1870, in her famous race with the Natchez, is the best on record, and, inasmuch as the race created a national interest, we give below her time table from port to port.

Left New Orleans, Thursday, June 30th, 1870, at 4 o'clock and 55 minutes, p.m.; reached

	D.	H.	M.			D.	H.	M.
Carrollton			27½	Vicksburg		1		38
Harry Hills		1	00½	Milliken's Bend		1	2	37
Red Church		1	39	Bailey's		1	3	48
Bonnet Carre		2	38	Lake Providence		1	5	47
College Point		3	50½	Greenville		1	10	55
Donaldsonville		4	59	Napoleon		1	16	22
Plaquemine		7	05½	White River		1	16	56
Baton Rouge		8	25	Australia		1	19	
Bayou Sara		10	26	Helena		1	23	25
Red River		12	56	Half Mile Below St. Francis		2		
Stamps		13	56	Memphis		2	6	9
Bryaro		15	51½	Foot of Island 37		2	9	
Hinderson's		16	29	Foot of Island 26		2	13	30
Natchez		17	11	Tow-head, Island 14		2	17	23
Cole's Creek		19	21	New Madrid		2	19	50
Waterproof		18	53	Dry Bar No. 10		2	20	37
Rodney		20	45	Foot of Island 8		2	21	25
St. Joseph		21	02	Upper Tow-head—Lucas Bend		3		
Grand Gulf		22	06	Cairo		3	1	
Hard Times		22	18	St. Louis		3	18	14
Half Mile Below Warrenton	1							

The Lee landed at St. Louis at 11:25 A.M., on July 4th, 1870—six hours and thirty-six minutes ahead of the Natchez. The officers of the Natchez claimed seven hours and one minute stoppage on account of fog and repairing machinery. The R. E. Lee was commanded by Captain John W. Cannon, and the Natchez was in charge of that veteran Southern boatman, Captain Thomas P. Leathers.

XVII.

Cut-Offs and Stephen

THESE DRY DETAILS are of importance in one particular.
They give me an opportunity of introducing one of the
Mississippi's oddest peculiarities, — that of shortening its
length from time to time. If you will throw a long, pliant
apple-paring over your shoulder, it will pretty fairly shape itself into an average section of the Mississippi River; that is,
the nine or ten hundred miles stretching from Cairo, Illinois,
southward to New Orleans, the same being wonderfully
crooked, with a brief straight bit here and there at wide intervals. The two-hundred-mile stretch from Cairo northward to
St. Louis is by no means so crooked, that being a rocky country which the river cannot cut much.

The water cuts the alluvial banks of the "lower" river into
deep horseshoe curves; so deep, indeed, that in some places if
you were to get ashore at one extremity of the horseshoe and
walk across the neck, half or three quarters of a mile, you
could sit down and rest a couple of hours while your steamer
was coming around the long elbow, at a speed of ten miles
an hour, to take you aboard again. When the river is rising
fast, some scoundrel whose plantation is back in the country,
and therefore of inferior value, has only to watch his chance,
cut a little gutter across the narrow neck of land some dark
night, and turn the water into it, and in a wonderfully short
time a miracle has happened: to wit, the whole Mississippi
has taken possession of that little ditch, and placed the coun-
tryman's plantation on its bank (quadrupling its value), and
that other party's formerly valuable plantation finds itself
away out yonder on a big island; the old water-course around
it will soon shoal up, boats cannot approach within ten miles
of it, and down goes its value to a fourth of its former worth.
Watches are kept on those narrow necks, at needful times,
and if a man happens to be caught cutting a ditch across
them, the chances are all against his ever having another opportunity to cut a ditch.

Pray observe some of the effects of this ditching business.

337

Once there was a neck opposite Port Hudson, Louisiana, which was only half a mile across, in its narrowest place. You could walk across there in fifteen minutes; but if you made the journey around the cape on a raft, you travelled thirty-five miles to accomplish the same thing. In 1722 the river darted through that neck, deserted its old bed, and thus shortened itself thirty-five miles. In the same way it shortened itself twenty-five miles at Black Hawk Point in 1699. Below Red River Landing, Raccourci cut-off was made (forty or fifty years ago, I think). This shortened the river twenty-eight miles. In our day, if you travel by river from the southernmost of these three cut-offs to the northernmost, you go only seventy miles. To do the same thing a hundred and seventy-six years ago, one had to go a hundred and fifty-eight miles!—a shortening of eighty-eight miles in that trifling distance. At some forgotten time in the past, cut-offs were made above Vidalia, Louisiana; at island 92; at island 84; and at Hale's Point. These shortened the river, in the aggregate, seventy-seven miles.

Since my own day on the Mississippi, cut-offs have been made at Hurricane Island; at island 100; at Napoleon, Arkansas; at Walnut Bend; and at Council Bend. These shortened the river, in the aggregate, sixty-seven miles. In my own time a cut-off was made at American Bend, which shortened the river ten miles or more.

Therefore, the Mississippi between Cairo and New Orleans was twelve hundred and fifteen miles long one hundred and seventy-six years ago. It was eleven hundred and eighty after the cutoff of 1722. It was one thousand and forty after the American Bend cut-off. It has lost sixty-seven miles since. Consequently its length is only nine hundred and seventy-three miles at present.

Now, if I wanted to be one of those ponderous scientific people, and "let on" to prove what had occurred in the remote past by what had occurred in a given time in the recent past, or what will occur in the far future by what has occurred in late years, what an opportunity is here! Geology never had such a chance, nor such exact data to argue from! Nor "development of species," either! Glacial epochs are great things, but they are vague—vague. Please observe:—

In the space of one hundred and seventy-six years the Lower Mississippi has shortened itself two hundred and forty-two miles. That is an average of a trifle over one mile and a third per year. Therefore, any calm person, who is not blind or idiotic, can see that in the Old Oölitic Silurian Period, just a million years ago next November, the Lower Mississippi River was upwards of one million three hundred thousand miles long, and stuck out over the Gulf of Mexico like a fishing-rod. And by the same token any person can see that seven hundred and forty-two years from now the Lower Mississippi will be only a mile and three quarters long, and Cairo and New Orleans will have joined their streets together, and be plodding comfortably along under a single mayor and a mutual board of aldermen. There is something fascinating about science. One gets such wholesale returns of conjecture out of such a trifling investment of fact.

When the water begins to flow through one of those ditches I have been speaking of, it is time for the people thereabouts to move. The water cleaves the banks away like a knife. By the time the ditch has become twelve or fifteen feet wide, the calamity is as good as accomplished, for no power on earth can stop it now. When the width has reached a hundred yards, the banks begin to peel off in slices half an acre wide. The current flowing around the bend travelled formerly only five miles an hour; now it is tremendously increased by the shortening of the distance. I was on board the first boat that tried to go through the cut-off at American Bend, but we did not get through. It was toward midnight, and a wild night it was—thunder, lightning, and torrents of rain. It was estimated that the current in the cut-off was making about fifteen or twenty miles an hour; twelve or thirteen was the best our boat could do, even in tolerably slack water, therefore perhaps we were foolish to try the cut-off. However, Mr. Brown was ambitious, and he kept on trying. The eddy running up the bank, under the "point," was about as swift as the current out in the middle; so we would go flying up the shore like a lightning express train, get on a big head of steam, and "stand by for a surge" when we struck the current that was whirling by the point. But all our preparations were useless. The instant the current hit us it spun us around

like a top, the water deluged the forecastle, and the boat careened so far over that one could hardly keep his feet. The
next instant we were away down the river, clawing with
might and main to keep out of the woods. We tried the ex-
periment four times. I stood on the forecastle companion way
to see. It was astonishing to observe how suddenly the boat
would spin around and turn tail the moment she emerged
from the eddy and the current struck her nose. The sounding
concussion and the quivering would have been about the
same if she had come full speed against a sand-bank. Under
the lightning flashes one could see the plantation cabins and
the goodly acres tumble into the river; and the crash they
made was not a bad effort at thunder. Once, when we spun
around, we only missed a house about twenty feet, that had
a light burning in the window; and in the same instant that
house went overboard. Nobody could stay on our forecastle;
the water swept across it in a torrent every time we plunged
athwart the current. At the end of our fourth effort we
brought up in the woods two miles below the cut-off; all the
country there was overflowed, of course. A day or two later
the cut-off was three quarters of a mile wide, and boats passed
up through it without much difficulty, and so saved ten miles.

The old Raccourci cut-off reduced the river's length
twenty-eight miles. There used to be a tradition connected
with it. It was said that a boat came along there in the night
and went around the enormous elbow the usual way, the pilots not knowing that the cut-off had been made. It was a
grisly, hideous night, and all shapes were vague and distorted.
The old bend had already begun to fill up, and the boat got
to running away from mysterious reefs, and occasionally hitting one. The perplexed pilots fell to swearing, and finally
uttered the entirely unnecessary wish that they might never
get out of that place. As always happens in such cases, that
particular prayer was answered, and the others neglected. So
to this day that phantom steamer is still butting around in
that deserted river, trying to find her way out. More than one
grave watchman has sworn to me that on drizzly, dismal
nights, he has glanced fearfully down that forgotten river as
he passed the head of the island, and seen the faint glow of
the spectre steamer's lights drifting through the distant

gloom, and heard the muffled cough of her 'scape-pipes and the plaintive cry of her leads-men.

In the absence of further statistics, I beg to close this chapter with one more reminiscence of "Stephen."

Most of the captains and pilots held Stephen's note for borrowed sums, ranging from two hundred and fifty dollars upward. Stephen never paid one of these notes, but he was very prompt and very zealous about renewing them every twelve month.

Of course there came a time, at last, when Stephen could no longer borrow of his ancient creditors; so he was obliged to lie in wait for new men who did not know him. Such a victim was good-hearted, simple-natured young Yates (I use a fictitious name, but the real name began, as this one does, with a Y). Young Yates graduated as a pilot, got a berth, and when the month was ended and he stepped up to the clerk's office and received his two hundred and fifty dollars in crisp new bills, Stephen was there! His silvery tongue began to wag, and in a very little while Yates's two hundred and fifty dollars had changed hands. The fact was soon known at pilot headquarters, and the amusement and satisfaction of the old creditors were large and generous. But innocent Yates never suspected that Stephen's promise to pay promptly at the end of the week was a worthless one. Yates called for his money at the stipulated time; Stephen sweetened him up and put him off a week. He called then, according to agreement, and came away sugar-coated again, but suffering under another postponement. So the thing went on. Yates haunted Stephen week after week, to no purpose, and at last gave it up. And then straightway Stephen began to haunt Yates! Wherever Yates appeared, there was the inevitable Stephen. And not only there, but beaming with affection and gushing with apologies for not being able to pay. By and by, whenever poor Yates saw him coming, he would turn and fly, and drag his company with him, if he had company; but it was of no use; his debtor would run him down and corner him. Panting and red-faced, Stephen would come, with outstretched hands and eager eyes, invade the conversation, shake both of Yates's arms loose in their sockets, and begin: —

"My, what a race I 've had! I saw you did n't see me, and

so I clapped on all steam for fear I 'd miss you entirely. And here you are! there, just stand so, and let me look at you! Just the same old noble countenance." [To Yates's friend:] "Just look at him! *Look* at him! Ain't it just *good* to look at him! *Ain't* it now? Ain't he just a picture! *Some* call him a picture; *I* call him a panorama! That 's what he is—an entire panorama. And now I 'm reminded! How I do wish I could have seen you an hour earlier! For twenty-four hours I 've been saving up that two hundred and fifty dollars for you; been looking for you everywhere. I waited at the Planter's from six yesterday evening till two o'clock this morning, without rest or food; my wife says, 'Where have you been all night?' I said, 'This debt lies heavy on my mind.' She says, 'In all my days I never saw a man take a debt to heart the way you do.' I said, 'It 's my nature; how can *I* change it?' She says, 'Well, do go to bed and get some rest.' I said, 'Not till that poor, noble young man has got his money.' So I set up all night, and this morning out I shot, and the first man I struck told me you had shipped on the 'Grank Turk' and gone to New Orleans. Well, sir, I had to lean up against a building and cry. So help me goodness, I could n't help it. The man that owned the place come out cleaning up with a rag, and said he did n't like to have people cry against his building, and then it seemed to me that the whole world had turned against me, and it was n't any use to live any more; and coming along an hour ago, suffering no man knows what agony, I met Jim Wilson and paid him the two hundred and fifty dollars on account; and to think that here you are, now, and I have n't got a cent! But as sure as I am standing here on this ground on this particular brick,—there, I 've scratched a mark on the brick to remember it by,—I 'll borrow that money and pay it over to you at twelve o'clock sharp, to-morrow! Now, stand so; let me look at you just once more."

And so on. Yates's life became a burden to him. He could not escape his debtor and his debtor's awful sufferings on account of not being able to pay. He dreaded to show himself in the street, lest he should find Stephen lying in wait for him at the corner.

Bogart's billiard saloon was a great resort for pilots in those days. They met there about as much to exchange river news as to play. One morning Yates was there; Stephen was here, too, but kept out of sight. But by and by, when about all the pilots had arrived who were in town, Stephen suddenly appeared in the midst, and rushed for Yates as for a long-lost brother.

"*Oh*, I am so glad to see you! Oh my soul, the sight of you is such a comfort to my eyes! Gentlemen, I owe all of you money; among you I owe probably forty thousand dollars. I want to pay it; I intend to pay it—every last cent of it. You all know, without my telling you, what sorrow it has cost me to remain so long under such deep obligations to such patient and generous friends; but the sharpest pang I suffer—by far the sharpest—is from the debt I owe to this noble young man here; and I have come to this place this morning especially to make the announcement that I have at last found a method whereby I can pay off all my debts! And most especially I wanted *him* to be here when I announced it. Yes, my faithful friend,—my benefactor, I 've found the method! I 've found the method to pay off *all* my debts, and you 'll get your money!" Hope dawned in Yates's eye; then Stephen, beaming benignantly, and placing his hand upon Yates's head, added, "I am going to pay them off in alphabetical order!"

Then he turned and disappeared. The full significance of Stephen's "method" did not dawn upon the perplexed and musing crowd for some two minutes; and then Yates murmured with a sigh:—

"Well, the Y's stand a gaudy chance. He won't get any further than the C's in *this* world, and I reckon that after a good deal of eternity has wasted away in the next one, I 'll still be referred to up there as 'that poor, ragged pilot that came here from St. Louis in the early days!'"

XVIII.

I Take a Few Extra Lessons

DURING THE TWO or two and a half years of my appren
ticeship, I served under many pilots, and had experience
of many kinds of steamboatmen and many varieties of steam
boats; for it was not always convenient for Mr. Bixby to have
me with him, and in such cases he sent me with somebody
else. I am to this day profiting somewhat by that experience
for in that brief, sharp schooling, I got personally and famil
iarly acquainted with about all the different types of human
nature that are to be found in fiction, biography, or history
The fact is daily borne in upon me, that the average shore
employment requires as much as forty years to equip a man
with this sort of an education. When I say I am still profiting
by this thing, I do not mean that it has constituted me a
judge of men—no, it has not done that; for judges of men
are born, not made. My profit is various in kind and degree.
but the feature of it which I value most is the zest which that
early experience has given to my later reading. When I find a
well-drawn character in fiction or biography, I generally take
a warm personal interest in him, for the reason that I have
known him before—met him on the river.

The figure that comes before me oftenest, out of the shadows of that vanished time, is that of Brown, of the steamer
"Pennsylvania"—the man referred to in a former chapter.
whose memory was so good and tiresome. He was a middle-
aged, long, slim, bony, smooth-shaven, horse-faced, ignorant.
stingy, malicious, snarling, fault-hunting, mote-magnifying
tyrant. I early got the habit of coming on watch with dread
at my heart. No matter how good a time I might have been
having with the off-watch below, and no matter how high
my spirits might be when I started aloft, my soul became lead
in my body the moment I approached the pilot-house.

I still remember the first time I ever entered the presence of
that man. The boat had backed out from St. Louis and was
"straightening down;" I ascended to the pilot-house in high
feather, and very proud to be semi-officially a member of the

xecutive family of so fast and famous a boat. Brown was at
ne wheel. I paused in the middle of the room, all fixed to
nake my bow, but Brown did not look around. I thought he
ook a furtive glance at me out of the corner of his eye, but
s not even this notice was repeated, I judged I had been
nistaken. By this time he was picking his way among some
angerous "breaks" abreast the wood-yards; therefore it
would not be proper to interrupt him; so I stepped softly to
ne high bench and took a seat.

There was silence for ten minutes; then my new boss
urned and inspected me deliberately and painstakingly from
ead to heel for about—as it seemed to me—a quarter of an
our. After which he removed his countenance and I saw it
o more for some seconds; then it came around once more,
nd this question greeted me:—

"Are you Horace Bigsby's cub?"

"Yes, sir."

After this there was a pause and another inspection. Then:

"What's your name?"

I told him. He repeated it after me. It was probably the
only thing he ever forgot; for although I was with him many
nonths he never addressed himself to me in any other way
han "Here!" and then his command followed.

"Where was you born?"

"In Florida, Missouri."

A pause. Then:—

"Dern sight better staid there!"

By means of a dozen or so of pretty direct questions, he
oumped my family history out of me.

The leads were going now, in the first crossing. This interrupted the inquest. When the leads had been laid in, he resumed:—

"How long you been on the river?"

I told him. After a pause:—

"Where 'd you get them shoes?"

I gave him the information.

"Hold up your foot!"

I did so. He stepped back, examined the shoe minutely and
contemptuously, scratching his head thoughtfully, tilting his
nigh sugar-loaf hat well forward to facilitate the operation,

then ejaculated, "Well, I 'll be dod derned!" and returned t his wheel.

What occasion there was to be dod derned about it is thing which is still as much of a mystery to me now as it w then. It must have been all of fifteen minutes—fifteen min utes of dull, homesick silence—before that long horse-fac swung round upon me again—and then, what a change! was as red as fire, and every muscle in it was working. No came this shriek:

"Here!—You going to set there all day?"

I lit in the middle of the floor, shot there by the electr suddenness of the surprise. As soon as I could get m voice I said, apologetically:—"I have had no orders, sir "You 've had no *orders*! My, what a fine bird we are! W must have *orders*! Our father was a *gentleman*—owne slaves—and *we 've* been to *school*. Yes, *we* are a gentlema *too*, and got to have *orders*! ORDERS, is it? ORDERS what you want! Dod dern my skin, *I 'll* learn you to swe yourself up and blow around *here* about your dod-derne *orders*! G' way from the wheel!" (I had approached it withou knowing it.)

I moved back a step or two, and stood as in a dream, a my senses stupefied by this frantic assault.

"What you standing there for? Take that ice-pitcher dow to the texas-tender—come, move along, and don't you be a day about it!"

The moment I got back to the pilot-house, Brown said:—

"Here! What was you doing down there all this time?"

"I could n't find the texas-tender; I had to go all the wa to the pantry."

"Derned likely story! Fill up the stove."

I proceeded to do so. He watched me like a cat. Presentl he shouted:—

"Put down that shovel! Derndest numskull I ever saw— ain't even got sense enough to load up a stove."

All through the watch this sort of thing went on. Yes, an the subsequent watches were much like it, during a stretch o months. As I have said, I soon got the habit of coming o duty with dread. The moment I was in the presence, even i he darkest night, I could feel those yellow eyes upon me, and knew their owner was watching for a pretext to spit out some venom on me. Preliminarily he would say:—

"Here! Take the wheel."

Two minutes later:—

"*Where* in the nation you going to? Pull her down! pull her down!"

After another moment:—

"Say! You going to hold her all day? Let her go—meet her! meet her!"

Then he would jump from the bench, snatch the wheel from me, and meet her himself, pouring out wrath upon me all the time.

George Ritchie was the other pilot's cub. He was having good times now; for his boss, George Ealer, was as kind-hearted as Brown was n't. Ritchie had steered for Brown the season before; consequently he knew exactly how to entertain himself and plague me, all by the one operation. Whenever I took the wheel for a moment on Ealer's watch, Ritchie would sit back on the bench and play Brown, with continual ejaculations of "Snatch her! snatch her! Derndest mud-cat I ever saw!" "Here! Where you going *now*? Going to run over that snag?" "Pull her *down*! Don't you hear me? Pull her *down*!" "There she goes! *Just* as I expected! I *told* you not to cramp that reef. G' way from the wheel!"

So I always had a rough time of it, no matter whose watch it was; and sometimes it seemed to me that Ritchie's good-natured badgering was pretty nearly as aggravating as Brown's dead-earnest nagging.

I often wanted to kill Brown, but this would not answer. A cub had to take everything his boss gave, in the way of vigorous comment and criticism; and we all believed that there was a United States law making it a penitentiary offence to strike or threaten a pilot who was on duty. However, I could *imagine* myself killing Brown; there was no law against that; and that was the thing I used always to do the moment I was abed. Instead of going over my river in my mind as was my duty, I threw business aside for pleasure, and killed Brown. I killed Brown every night for months; not in old,

stale, commonplace ways, but in new and picturesque ones,—
ways that were sometimes surprising for freshness of desig
and ghastliness of situation and environment.

Brown was *always* watching for a pretext to find fault; an
if he could find no plausible pretext, he would invent one. H
would scold you for shaving a shore, and for not shaving it
for hugging a bar, and for not hugging it; for "pulling down"
when not invited, and for *not* pulling down when not invited
for firing up without orders, and for waiting *for* orders. In
word, it was his invariable rule to find fault with *everything*
you did; and another invariable rule of his was to throw a
his remarks (to you) into the form of an insult.

One day we were approaching New Madrid, bound dow
and heavily laden. Brown was at one side of the wheel, steer
ing; I was at the other, standing by to "pull down" or "shov
up." He cast a furtive glance at me every now and then. I ha
long ago learned what that meant; viz., he was trying to in
vent a trap for me. I wondered what shape it was going t
take. By and by he stepped back from the wheel and said i
his usual snarly way:—

"Here!—See if you 've got gumption enough to roun
her to."

This was simply *bound* to be a success; nothing could pre
vent it; for he had never allowed me to round the boat t
before; consequently, no matter how I might do the thing
he could find free fault with it. He stood back there with hi
greedy eye on me, and the result was what might have bee
foreseen: I lost my head in a quarter of a minute, and did n
know what I was about; I started too early to bring the boa
around, but detected a green gleam of joy in Brown's eye
and corrected my mistake; I started around once more whil
too high up, but corrected myself again in time; I made othe
false moves, and still managed to save myself; but at last
grew so confused and anxious that I tumbled into the ver
worst blunder of all—I got too far *down* before beginning t
fetch the boat around. Brown's chance was come.

His face turned red with passion; he made one bound
hurled me across the house with a sweep of his arm, spun th
wheel down, and began to pour out a stream of vituperatio
upon me which lasted till he was out of breath. In the cours

of this speech he called me all the different kinds of hard names he could think of, and once or twice I thought he was even going to swear—but he had never done that, and he didn't this time. "Dod dern" was the nearest he ventured to the luxury of swearing, for he had been brought up with a wholesome respect for future fire and brimstone.

That was an uncomfortable hour; for there was a big audience on the hurricane deck. When I went to bed that night, I killed Brown in seventeen different ways—all of them new.

XIX.

Brown and I Exchange Compliments

Two trips later, I got into serious trouble. Brown was steering; I was "pulling down." My younger brother appeared on the hurricane deck, and shouted to Brown to stop at some landing or other a mile or so below. Brown gave no intimation that he had heard anything. But that was his way; he never condescended to take notice of an under clerk. The wind was blowing; Brown was deaf (although he always pretended he was n't), and I very much doubted if he had heard the order. If I had had two heads, I would have spoken; but as I had only one, it seemed judicious to take care of it; so I kept still.

Presently, sure enough, we went sailing by that plantation. Captain Klinefelter appeared on the deck, and said:—

"Let her come around, sir, let her come around. Did n't Henry tell you to land here?"

"*No*, sir!"

"I sent him up to do it."

"He *did* come up; and that 's all the good it done, the dod derned fool. He never said anything."

"Did n't *you* hear him?" asked the captain of me.

Of course I did n't want to be mixed up in this business; but there was no way to avoid it; so I said:—

"Yes, sir."

I knew what Brown's next remark would be, before he uttered it; it was:—

"Shut your mouth! you never heard anything of the kind."

I closed my mouth according to instructions. An hour later Henry entered the pilot-house, unaware of what had been going on. He was a thoroughly inoffensive boy, and I was sorry to see him come, for I knew Brown would have no pity on him. Brown began, straightway:—

"Here! why did n't you tell me we 'd got to land at that plantation?"

"I did tell you, Mr. Brown."

"It 's a lie!"

I said:—

"You lie, yourself. He did tell you."

Brown glared at me in unaffected surprise; and for as much as a moment he was entirely speechless; then he shouted to me:—

"I'll attend to your case in a half a minute!" then to Henry, "And you leave the pilot-house; out with you!"

It was pilot law, and must be obeyed. The boy started out, and even had his foot on the upper step outside the door, when Brown, with a sudden access of fury, picked up a ten-pound lump of coal and sprang after him; but I was between, with a heavy stool, and I hit Brown a good honest blow which stretched him out.

I had committed the crime of crimes,—I had lifted my hand against a pilot on duty! I supposed I was booked for the penitentiary sure, and could n't be booked any surer if I went on and squared my long account with this person while I had the chance; consequently I stuck to him and pounded him with my fists a considerable time,—I do not know how long, the pleasure of it probably made it seem longer than it really was;—but in the end he struggled free and jumped up and sprang to the wheel: a very natural solicitude, for, all this time, here was this steamboat tearing down the river at the rate of fifteen miles an hour and nobody at the helm! However, Eagle Bend was two miles wide at this bank-full stage, and correspondingly long and deep; and the boat was steering herself straight down the middle and taking no chances. Still, that was only luck—a body *might* have found her charging into the woods.

Perceiving, at a glance, that the "Pennsylvania" was in no danger, Brown gathered up the big spy-glass, war-club fashion, and ordered me out of the pilot-house with more than Comanche bluster. But I was not afraid of him now; so, instead of going, I tarried, and criticised his grammar; I reformed his ferocious speeches for him, and put them into good English, calling his attention to the advantage of pure English over the bastard dialect of the Pennsylvanian collieries whence he was extracted. He could have done his part to admiration in a cross-fire of mere vituperation, of course; but he was not equipped for this species of controversy; so he presently laid aside his glass and took the wheel, muttering and shaking his head; and I retired to the bench. The racket had brought everybody to the hurricane deck, and I trembled when I saw the old captain looking up from the midst of the crowd. I said to myself, "Now I *am* done for!"—For although, as a rule, he was so fatherly and indulgent toward the boat's family, and so patient of minor shortcomings, he could be stern enough when the fault was worth it.

I tried to imagine what he *would* do to a cub pilot who had been guilty of such a crime as mine, committed on a boat guard-deep with costly freight and alive with passengers. Our watch was nearly ended. I thought I would go and hide somewhere till I got a chance to slide ashore. So I slipped out of the pilot-house, and down the steps, and around to the texas door,—and was in the act of gliding within, when the captain confronted me! I dropped my head, and he stood over me in silence a moment or two, then said impressively,—

"Follow me."

I dropped into his wake; he led the way to his parlor in the forward end of the texas. We were alone, now. He closed the after door; then moved slowly to the forward one and closed that. He sat down; I stood before him. He looked at me some little time, then said,—

"So you have been fighting Mr. Brown?"

I answered meekly:—

"Yes, sir."

"Do you know that that is a very serious matter?"

"Yes, sir."

"Are you aware that this boat was ploughing down the river fully five minutes with no one at the wheel?"

"Yes, sir."

"Did you strike him first?"

"Yes, sir."

"What with?"

"A stool, sir."

"Hard?"

"Middling, sir."

"Did it knock him down?"

"He—he fell, sir."

"Did you follow it up? Did you do anything further?"

"Yes, sir."

"What did you do?"

"Pounded him, sir."

"Pounded him?"

"Yes, sir."

"Did you pound him much?—that is, severely?"

"One might call it that, sir, maybe."

"I 'm deucéd glad of it! Hark ye, never mention that I said that. You have been guilty of a great crime; and don't you ever be guilty of it again, on this boat. *But*—lay for him ashore! Give him a good sound thrashing, do you hear? I 'll pay the expenses. Now go—and mind you, not a word of this to anybody. Clear out with you!—you 've been guilty of a great crime, you whelp!"

I slid out, happy with the sense of a close shave and a mighty deliverance; and I heard him laughing to himself and slapping his fat thighs after I had closed his door.

When Brown came off watch he went straight to the captain, who was talking with some passengers on the boiler deck, and demanded that I be put ashore in New Orleans— and added:—

"I 'll never turn a wheel on this boat again while that cub stays."

The captain said:—

"But he need n't come round when you are on watch, Mr. Brown."

"I won't even stay on the same boat with him. *One* of us has got to go ashore."

"Very well," said the captain, "let it be yourself;" and resumed his talk with the passengers.

During the brief remainder of the trip, I knew how an emancipated slave feels; for I was an emancipated slave myself. While we lay at landings, I listened to George Ealer's flute; or to his readings from his two bibles, that is to say, Goldsmith and Shakspeare; or I played chess with him—and would have beaten him sometimes, only he always took back his last move and ran the game out differently.

XX.

A Catastrophe

WE LAY three days in New Orleans, but the captain di not succeed in finding another pilot; so he propose that I should stand a daylight watch, and leave the nigh watches to George Ealer. But I was afraid; I had never stoo a watch of any sort by myself, and I believed I should be sur to get into trouble in the head of some chute, or ground th boat in a near cut through some bar or other. Brown re mained in his place; but he would not travel with me. So th captain gave me an order on the captain of the "A. T. Lacey, for a passage to St. Louis, and said he would find a new pilo there and my steersman's berth could then be resumed. Th "Lacey" was to leave a couple of days after the "Penn sylvania."

The night before the "Pennsylvania" left, Henry and I sa chatting on a freight pile on the levee till midnight. The sub ject of the chat, mainly, was one which I think we had no exploited before — steamboat disasters. One was then on it way to us, little as we suspected it; the water which was to make the steam which should cause it, was washing past som point fifteen hundred miles up the river while we talked; — but it would arrive at the right time and the right place. W doubted if persons not clothed with authority were of muc use in cases of disaster and attendant panic; still, they migh be of *some* use; so we decided that if a disaster ever fell withi our experience we would at least stick to the boat, and giv such minor service as chance might throw in the way. Henr remembered this, afterward, when the disaster came, and acted accordingly.

The "Lacey" started up the river two days behind th "Pennsylvania." We touched at Greenville, Mississippi, a cou ple of days out, and somebody shouted: —

"The 'Pennsylvania' is blown up at Ship Island, and hundred and fifty lives lost!"

At Napoleon, Arkansas, the same evening, we got an extra

ssued by a Memphis paper, which gave some particulars. It mentioned my brother, and said he was not hurt.

Further up the river we got a later extra. My brother was again mentioned; but this time as being hurt beyond help. We did not get full details of the catastrophe until we reached Memphis. This is the sorrowful story: —

It was six o'clock on a hot summer morning. The "Pennsylvania" was creeping along, north of Ship Island, about sixty miles below Memphis on a half-head of steam, towing a wood-flat which was fast being emptied. George Ealer was in the pilot-house—alone, I think; the second engineer and a striker had the watch in the engine room; the second mate had the watch on deck; George Black, Mr. Wood, and my brother, clerks, were asleep, as were also Brown and the head engineer, the carpenter, the chief mate, and one striker; Capt. Klinefelter was in the barber's chair, and the barber was preparing to shave him. There were a good many cabin passengers aboard, and three or four hundred deck passengers—so it was said at the time—and not very many of them were astir. The wood being nearly all out of the flat now, Ealer rang to "come ahead" full steam, and the next moment four of the eight boilers exploded with a thunderous crash, and the whole forward third of the boat was hoisted toward the sky! The main part of the mass, with the chimneys, dropped upon the boat again, a mountain of riddled and chaotic rubbish—and then, after a little, fire broke out.

Many people were flung to considerable distances, and fell in the river; among these were Mr. Wood and my brother, and the carpenter. The carpenter was still stretched upon his mattress when he struck the water seventy-five feet from the boat. Brown, the pilot, and George Black, chief clerk, were never seen or heard of after the explosion. The barber's chair, with Captain Klinefelter in it and unhurt, was left with its back overhanging vacancy—everything forward of it, floor and all, had disappeared; and the stupefied barber, who was also unhurt, stood with one toe projecting over space, still stirring his lather unconsciously, and saying not a word.

When George Ealer saw the chimneys plunging aloft in

front of him, he knew what the matter was; so he muffled his
face in the lapels of his coat, and pressed both hands there
tightly to keep this protection in its place so that no steam
could get to his nose or mouth. He had ample time to attend
to these details while he was going up and returning. He
presently landed on top of the unexploded boilers, forty feet
below the former pilot-house, accompanied by his wheel and
a rain of other stuff, and enveloped in a cloud of scalding
steam. All of the many who breathed that steam, died; none
escaped. But Ealer breathed none of it. He made his way to
the free air as quickly as he could; and when the steam cleared
away he returned and climbed up on the boilers again, and
patiently hunted out each and every one of his chessmen and
the several joints of his flute.

By this time the fire was beginning to threaten. Shrieks and
groans filled the air. A great many persons had been scalded,
a great many crippled; the explosion had driven an iron crow-
bar through one man's body—I think they said he was a
priest. He did not die at once, and his sufferings were very
dreadful. A young French naval cadet, of fifteen, son of a
French admiral, was fearfully scalded, but bore his tortures
manfully. Both mates were badly scalded, but they stood to
their posts, nevertheless. They drew the wood-boat aft, and
they and the captain fought back the frantic herd of frightened immigrants till the wounded could be brought there and
placed in safety first.

When Mr. Wood and Henry fell in the water, they struck
out for shore, which was only a few hundred yards away; but
Henry presently said he believed he was not hurt, (what an
unaccountable error!) and therefore would swim back to the
boat and help save the wounded. So they parted, and Henry
returned.

By this time the fire was making fierce headway, and several
persons who were imprisoned under the ruins were begging
piteously for help. All efforts to conquer the fire proved fruitless; so the buckets were presently thrown aside and the officers fell-to with axes and tried to cut the prisoners out. A
striker was one of the captives; he said he was not injured,
but could not free himself; and when he saw that the fire was
likely to drive away the workers, he begged that some one

would shoot him, and thus save him from the more dreadful death. The fire did drive the axemen away, and they had to listen, helpless, to this poor fellow's supplications till the flames ended his miseries.

The fire drove all into the wood-flat that could be accommodated there; it was cut adrift, then, and it and the burning steamer floated down the river toward Ship Island. They moored the flat at the head of the island, and there, unsheltered from the blazing sun, the half-naked occupants had to remain, without food or stimulants, or help for their hurts, during the rest of the day. A steamer came along, finally, and carried the unfortunates to Memphis, and there the most lavish assistance was at once forthcoming. By this time Henry was insensible. The physicians examined his injuries and saw that they were fatal, and naturally turned their main attention to patients who could be saved.

Forty of the wounded were placed upon pallets on the floor of a great public hall, and among these was Henry. There the ladies of Memphis came every day, with flowers, fruits, and dainties and delicacies of all kinds, and there they remained and nursed the wounded. All the physicians stood watches there, and all the medical students; and the rest of the town furnished money, or whatever else was wanted. And Memphis knew how to do all these things well; for many a disaster like the "Pennsylvania's" had happened near her doors, and she was experienced, above all other cities on the river, in the gracious office of the Good Samaritan.

The sight I saw when I entered that large hall was new and strange to me. Two long rows of prostrate forms—more than forty, in all—and every face and head a shapeless wad of loose raw cotton. It was a grewsome spectacle. I watched there six days and nights, and a very melancholy experience it was. There was one daily incident which was peculiarly depressing: this was the removal of the doomed to a chamber apart. It was done in order that the *morale* of the other patients might not be injuriously affected by seeing one of their number in the death-agony. The fated one was always carried out with as little stir as possible, and the stretcher was always hidden from sight by a wall of assistants; but no matter: everybody knew what that cluster of bent forms, with its muffled step and its slow movement meant; and all eyes watched it wistfully, and a shudder went abreast of it like a wave.

I saw many poor fellows removed to the "death-room," and saw them no more afterward. But I saw our chief mate carried thither more than once. His hurts were frightful, especially his scalds. He was clothed in linseed oil and raw cotton to his waist, and resembled nothing human. He was often out of his mind; and then his pains would make him rave and shout and sometimes shriek. Then, after a period of dumb exhaustion, his disordered imagination would suddenly transform the great apartment into a forecastle, and the hurrying throng of nurses into the crew; and he would come to a sitting posture and shout, "Hump yourselves, *hump* yourselves, you petrifactions, snail-bellies, pall-bearers! going to be all *day* getting that hatful of freight out?" and supplement this explosion with a firmament-obliterating irruption of profanity which nothing could stay or stop till his crater was empty. And now and then while these frenzies possessed him, he would tear off handfuls of the cotton and expose his cooked flesh to view. It was horrible. It was bad for the others, of course— this noise and these exhibitions; so the doctors tried to give him morphine to quiet him. But, in his mind or out of it, he would not take it. He said his wife had been killed by that treacherous drug, and he would die before he would take it. He suspected that the doctors were concealing it in his ordinary medicines and in his water—so he ceased from putting either to his lips. Once, when he had been without water during two sweltering days, he took the dipper in his hand, and the sight of the limpid fluid, and the misery of his thirst, tempted him almost beyond his strength; but he mastered himself and threw it away, and after that he allowed no more to be brought near him. Three times I saw him carried to the death-room, insensible and supposed to be dying; but each time he revived, cursed his attendants, and demanded to be taken back. He lived to be mate of a steamboat again.

But he was the only one who went to the death-room and returned alive. Dr. Peyton, a principal physician, and rich in all the attributes that go to constitute high and flawless character, did all that educated judgment and trained skill could

lo for Henry; but, as the newspapers had said in the beginning, his hurts were past help. On the evening of the sixth
day his wandering mind busied itself with matters far away,
and his nerveless fingers "picked at his coverlet." His hour
had struck; we bore him to the death-room, poor boy.

XXI.

A Section in My Biography

IN DUE COURSE I got my license. I was a pilot now, full fledged. I dropped into casual employments; no misfortunes resulting, intermittent work gave place to steady and protracted engagements. Time drifted smoothly and prosperously on, and I supposed—and hoped—that I was going to follow the river the rest of my days, and die at the wheel when my mission was ended. But by and by the war came, commerce was suspended, my occupation was gone.

I had to seek another livelihood. So I became a silver miner in Nevada; next, a newspaper reporter; next, a gold miner, in California; next, a reporter in San Francisco; next, a special correspondent in the Sandwich Islands; next, a roving correspondent in Europe and the East; next, an instructional torch-bearer on the lecture platform; and, finally, I became a scribbler of books, and an immovable fixture among the other rocks of New England.

In so few words have I disposed of the twenty-one slow-drifting years that have come and gone since I last looked from the windows of a pilot-house.

Let us resume, now.

XXII.

I Return to My Muttons

A FTER TWENTY-ONE years' absence, I felt a very strong desire to see the river again, and the steamboats, and such of the boys as might be left; so I resolved to go out there. I enlisted a poet for company, and a stenographer to "take him down," and started westward about the middle of April.

As I proposed to make notes, with a view to printing, I took some thought as to methods of procedure. I reflected that if I were recognized, on the river, I should not be as free to go and come, talk, inquire, and spy around, as I should be if unknown; I remembered that it was the custom of steamboatmen in the old times to load up the confiding stranger with the most picturesque and admirable lies, and put the sophisticated friend off with dull and ineffectual facts: so I concluded, that, from a business point of view, it would be an advantage to disguise our party with fictitious names. The idea was certainly good, but it bred infinite bother; for although Smith, Jones, and Johnson are easy names to remember when there is no occasion to remember them, it is next to impossible to recollect them when they are wanted. How do criminals manage to keep a brand-new *alias* in mind? This is a great mystery. I was innocent; and yet was seldom able to lay my hand on my new name when it was needed; and it seemed to me that if I had had a crime on my conscience to further confuse me, I could never have kept the name by me at all.

We left per Pennsylvania Railroad, at 8 A.M. April 18.

"*Evening.* Speaking of dress. Grace and picturesqueness drop gradually out of it as one travels away from New York."

I find that among my notes. It makes no difference which direction you take, the fact remains the same. Whether you move north, south, east, or west, no matter: you can get up in the morning and guess how far you have come, by noting

what degree of grace and picturesqueness is by that time lack
ing in the costumes of the new passengers;—I do not mean
of the women alone, but of both sexes. It may be that *car
riage* is at the bottom of this thing; and I think it is; for there
are plenty of ladies and gentlemen in the provincial cities
whose garments are all made by the best tailors and dressmak
ers of New York; yet this has no perceptible effect upon the
grand fact: the educated eye never mistakes those people for
New-Yorkers. No, there is a godless grace, and snap, and
style about a born and bred New-Yorker which mere clothing
cannot effect.

"*April* 19. This morning, struck into the region of full
goatees—sometimes accompanied by a moustache, but
only occasionally."

It was odd to come upon this thick crop of an obsolete and
uncomely fashion; it was like running suddenly across a for
gotten acquaintance whom you had supposed dead for a gen
eration. The goatee extends over a wide extent of country
and is accompanied by an iron-clad belief in Adam and the
biblical history of creation, which has not suffered from the
assaults of the scientists.

"*Afternoon*. At the railway stations the loafers carry *both*
hands in their breeches pockets; it was observable, hereto
fore, that one hand was sometimes out of doors,—here
never. This is an important fact in geography."

If the loafers determined the character of a country, it
would be still more important, of course.

"Heretofore, all along, the station-loafer has been often
observed to scratch one shin with the other foot; here
these remains of activity are wanting. This has an ominous
look."

By and by, we entered the tobacco-chewing region. Fifty
years ago, the tobacco-chewing region covered the Union. It
is greatly restricted now.

Next, boots began to appear. Not in strong force, however
Later—away down the Mississippi—they became the rule.
They disappeared from other sections of the Union with the

mud; no doubt they will disappear from the river villages, also, when proper pavements come in.

We reached St. Louis at ten o'clock at night. At the counter of the hotel I tendered a hurriedly-invented fictitious name, with a miserable attempt at careless ease. The clerk paused, and inspected me in the compassionate way in which one inspects a respectable person who is found in doubtful circumstances; then he said,—

"It's all right; I know what sort of a room you want. Used to clerk at the St. James, in New York."

An unpromising beginning for a fraudulent career. We started to the supper room, and met two other men whom I had known elsewhere. How odd and unfair it is: wicked impostors go around lecturing under my *nom de guerre*, and nobody suspects them; but when an honest man attempts an imposture, he is exposed at once.

One thing seemed plain: we must start down the river the next day, if people who could not be deceived were going to crop up at this rate: an unpalatable disappointment, for we had hoped to have a week in St. Louis. The Southern was a good hotel, and we could have had a comfortable time there. It is large, and well conducted, and its decorations do not make one cry, as do those of the vast Palmer House, in Chicago. True, the billiard-tables were of the Old Silurian Period, and the cues and balls of the Post-Pliocene; but there was refreshment in this, not discomfort; for there is rest and healing in the contemplation of antiquities.

The most notable absence observable in the billiard room, was the absence of the river man. If he was there he had taken in his sign, he was in disguise. I saw there none of the swell airs and graces, and ostentatious displays of money, and pompous squanderings of it, which used to distinguish the steamboat crowd from the dry-land crowd in the bygone days, in the thronged billiard-rooms of St. Louis. In those times, the principal saloons were always populous with river men; given fifty players present, thirty or thirty-five were likely to be from the river. But I suspected that the ranks were thin now, and the steamboatmen no longer an aristocracy. Why, in my time they used to call the "barkeep" Bill, or Joe, or Tom, and slap him on the shoulder; I watched for that.

But none of these people did it. Manifestly a glory that onc
was had dissolved and vanished away in these twenty-on
years.

When I went up to my room, I found there the young ma
called Rogers, crying. Rogers was not his name; neither wa
Jones, Brown, Dexter, Ferguson, Bascom, nor Thompsor
but he answered to either of these that a body found hand
in an emergency; or to any other name, in fact, if he perceive
that you meant him. He said:—

"What is a person to do here when he wants a drink c
water?—drink this slush?"

"Can't you drink it?"

"I could if I had some other water to wash it with."

Here was a thing which had not changed; a score of year
had not affected this water's mulatto complexion in the least
a score of centuries would succeed no better, perhaps. I
comes out of the turbulent, bank-caving Missouri, and ever
tumblerful of it holds nearly an acre of land in solution. I go
this fact from the bishop of the diocese. If you will let you
glass stand half an hour, you can separate the land from th
water as easy as Genesis; and then you will find them botl
good: the one good to eat, the other good to drink. The lan
is very nourishing, the water is thoroughly wholesome. Th
one appeases hunger; the other, thirst. But the natives do no
take them separately, but together, as nature mixed them
When they find an inch of mud in the bottom of a glass, the
stir it up, and then take the draught as they would gruel. It i
difficult for a stranger to get used to this batter, but onc
used to it he will prefer it to water. This is really the case. I
is good for steamboating, and good to drink; but it is worth
less for all other purposes, except baptizing.

Next morning, we drove around town in the rain. The cit
seemed but little changed. It *was* greatly changed, but it di
not seem so; because in St. Louis, as in London and Pitts
burgh, you can't persuade a new thing to look new; the coa
smoke turns it into an antiquity the moment you take you
hand off it. The place had just about doubled its size, since
was a resident of it, and was now become a city of 400,00
inhabitants; still, in the solid business parts, it looked abou
as it had looked formerly. Yet I am sure there is not as mucl

smoke in St. Louis now as there used to be. The smoke used to bank itself in a dense billowy black canopy over the town, and hide the sky from view. This shelter is very much thinner now; still, there is a sufficiency of smoke there, I think. I heard no complaint.

However, on the outskirts changes were apparent enough; notably in dwelling-house architecture. The fine new homes are noble and beautiful and modern. They stand by themselves, too, with green lawns around them; whereas the dwellings of a former day are packed together in blocks, and are all of one pattern, with windows all alike, set in an arched frame-work of twisted stone; a sort of house which was handsome enough when it was rarer.

There was another change—the Forest Park. This was new to me. It is beautiful and very extensive, and has the excellent merit of having been made mainly by nature. There are other parks, and fine ones, notably Tower Grove and the Botanical Gardens; for St. Louis interested herself in such improvements at an earlier day than did the most of our cities.

The first time I ever saw St. Louis, I could have bought it for six million dollars, and it was the mistake of my life that I did not do it. It was bitter now to look abroad over this domed and steepled metropolis, this solid expanse of bricks and mortar stretching away on every hand into dim, measure-defying distances, and remember that I had allowed that opportunity to go by. Why I should have allowed it to go by seems, of course, foolish and inexplicable to-day, at a first glance; yet there were reasons at the time to justify this course.

A Scotchman, Hon. Charles Augustus Murray, writing some forty-five or fifty years ago, said: "The streets are narrow, ill paved and ill lighted." Those streets are narrow still, of course; many of them are ill paved yet; but the reproach of ill lighting cannot be repeated, now. The "Catholic New Church" was the only notable building then, and Mr. Murray was confidently called upon to admire it, with its "species of Grecian portico, surmounted by a kind of steeple, much too diminutive in its proportions, and surmounted by sundry ornaments" which the unimaginative Scotchman found himself "quite unable to describe;" and therefore was grateful when a German tourist helped him out with the exclamation: "By—, they look exactly like bed-posts!" St. Louis is well equipped with stately and noble public buildings now, and the little church, which the people used to be so proud of, lost its importance a long time ago. Still, this would not surprise Mr. Murray, if he could come back; for he prophesied the coming greatness of St. Louis with strong confidence.

The further we drove in our inspection-tour, the more sensibly I realized how the city had grown since I had seen it last; changes in detail became steadily more apparent and frequent than at first, too: changes uniformly evidencing progress, energy, prosperity.

But the change of changes was on the "levee." This time, a departure from the rule. Half a dozen sound-asleep steamboats where I used to see a solid mile of wide-awake ones! This was melancholy, this was woful. The absence of the pervading and jocund steamboatman from the billiard-saloon was explained. He was absent because he is no more. His occupation is gone, his power has passed away, he is absorbed into the common herd, he grinds at the mill, a shorn Samson and inconspicuous. Half a dozen lifeless steamboats, a mile of empty wharves, a negro fatigued with whiskey stretched asleep, in a wide and soundless vacancy, where the serried hosts of commerce used to contend![1] Here was desolation, indeed.

> "The old, old sea, as one in tears,
>   Comes murmuring, with foamy lips,
> And knocking at the vacant piers,
>   Calls for his long-lost multitude of ships."

The towboat and the railroad had done their work, and done it well and completely. The mighty bridge, stretching along over our heads, had done its share in the slaughter and spoliation. Remains of former steamboatmen told me, with wan satisfaction, that the bridge does n't pay. Still, it can be no sufficient compensation to a corpse, to know that the dy-

[1] Capt. Marryat, writing forty-five years ago, says: "St. Louis has 20,000 inhabitants. *The river abreast of the town is crowded with steamboats, lying in two or three tiers.*"

namite that laid him out was not of as good quality as it had been supposed to be.

The pavements along the river front were bad; the sidewalks were rather out of repair; there was a rich abundance of mud. All this was familiar and satisfying; but the ancient armies of drays, and struggling throngs of men, and mountains of freight, were gone; and Sabbath reigned in their stead. The immemorial mile of cheap foul doggeries remained, but business was dull with them; the multitudes of poison-swilling Irishmen had departed, and in their places were a few scattering handfuls of ragged negroes, some drinking, some drunk, some nodding, others asleep. St. Louis is a great and prosperous and advancing city; but the river-edge of it seems dead past resurrection.

Mississippi steamboating was born about 1812; at the end of thirty years, it had grown to mighty proportions; and in less than thirty more, it was dead! A strangely short life for so majestic a creature. Of course it is not absolutely dead; neither is a crippled octogenarian who could once jump twenty-two feet on level ground; but as contrasted with what it was in its prime vigor, Mississippi steamboating may be called dead.

It killed the old-fashioned keel-boating, by reducing the freight-trip to New Orleans to less than a week. The railroads have killed the steamboat passenger traffic by doing in two or three days what the steamboats consumed a week in doing; and the towing-fleets have killed the through-freight traffic by dragging six or seven steamer-loads of stuff down the river at a time, at an expense so trivial that steamboat competition was out of the question.

Freight and passenger way-traffic remains to the steamers. This is in the hands—along the two thousand miles of river between St. Paul and New Orleans—of two or three close corporations well fortified with capital; and by able and thoroughly business-like management and system, these make a sufficiency of money out of what is left of the once prodigious steamboating industry. I suppose that St. Louis and New Orleans have not suffered materially by the change, but alas for the wood-yard man!

He used to fringe the river all the way; his close-ranked

merchandise stretched from the one city to the other, along the banks, and he sold uncountable cords of it every year for cash on the nail; but all the scattering boats that are left burn coal now, and the seldomest spectacle on the Mississippi to-day is a wood-pile. Where now is the once wood-yard man?

XXIII.

Travelling Incognito

M<small>Y IDEA</small> was, to tarry a while in every town between St. Louis and New Orleans. To do this, it would be necessary to go from place to place by the short packet lines. It was an easy plan to make, and would have been an easy one to follow, twenty years ago—but not now. There are wide intervals between boats, these days.

I wanted to begin with the interesting old French settlements of St. Genevieve and Kaskaskia, sixty miles below St. Louis. There was only one boat advertised for that section—a Grand Tower packet. Still, one boat was enough; so we went down to look at her. She was a venerable rackheap, and a fraud to boot; for she was playing herself for personal property, whereas the good honest dirt was so thickly caked all over her that she was righteously taxable as real estate. There are places in New England where her hurricane deck would be worth a hundred and fifty dollars an acre. The soil on her forecastle was quite good—the new crop of wheat was already springing from the cracks in protected places. The companionway was of a dry sandy character, and would have been well suited for grapes, with a southern exposure and a little subsoiling. The soil of the boiler deck was thin and rocky, but good enough for grazing purposes. A colored boy was on watch here—nobody else visible. We gathered from him that this calm craft would go, as advertised, "if she got her trip;" if she did n't get it, she would wait for it.

"Has she got any of her trip?"

"Bless you, no, boss. She ain't unloadened, yit. She only come in dis mawnin'."

He was uncertain as to when she might get her trip, but thought it might be to-morrow or maybe next day. This would not answer at all; so we had to give up the novelty of sailing down the river on a farm. We had one more arrow in our quiver: a Vicksburg packet, the "Gold Dust," was to leave at 5 P.M. We took passage in her for Memphis, and gave up the idea of stopping off here and there, as being impracti-

cable. She was neat, clean, and comfortable. We camped c
the boiler deck, and bought some cheap literature to kill tin
with. The vender was a venerable Irishman with a benevole
face and a tongue that worked easily in the socket, and fro
him we learned that he had lived in St. Louis thirty-four yea
and had never been across the river during that period. The
he wandered into a very flowing lecture, filled with class
names and allusions, which was quite wonderful for fluenc
until the fact became rather apparent that this was not th
first time, nor perhaps the fiftieth, that the speech had bee
delivered. He was a good deal of a character, and much bett
company than the sappy literature he was selling. A rando
remark, connecting Irishmen and beer, brought this nugg
of information out of him:—

"They don't drink it, sir. They *can't* drink it, sir. Give a
Irishman lager for a month, and he 's a dead man. An Irish
man is lined with copper, and the beer corrodes it. But whi
key polishes the copper and is the saving of him, sir."

At eight o'clock, promptly, we backed out and—crosse
the river. As we crept toward the shore, in the thick darknes
a blinding glory of white electric light burst suddenly fror
our forecastle, and lit up the water and the warehouses a
with a noon-day glare. Another big change, this,—no mo
flickering, smoky, pitch-dripping, ineffectual torch-basket
now: their day is past. Next, instead of calling out a score c
hands to man the stage, a couple of men and a hatful of stean
lowered it from the derrick where it was suspended, launche
it, deposited it in just the right spot, and the whole thing wa
over and done-with before a mate in the olden time coul
have got his profanity-mill adjusted to begin the preparator
services. Why this new and simple method of handling th
stages was not thought of when the first steamboat was built
is a mystery which helps one to realize what a dull-witted slu
the average human being is.

We finally got away at two in the morning, and when
turned out at six, we were rounding to at a rocky point wher
there was an old stone warehouse—at any rate, the ruins o
it; two or three decayed dwelling-houses were near by, in th
shelter of the leafy hills; but there were no evidences of hu
man or other animal life to be seen. I wondered if I had for

gotten the river; for I had no recollection whatever of this place; the shape of the river, too, was unfamiliar; there was nothing in sight, anywhere, that I could remember ever having seen before. I was surprised, disappointed, and annoyed.

We put ashore a well-dressed lady and gentleman, and two well-dressed, lady-like young girls, together with sundry Russia-leather bags. A strange place for such folk! No carriage was waiting. The party moved off as if they had not expected any, and struck down a winding country road afoot.

But the mystery was explained when we got under way again; for these people were evidently bound for a large town which lay shut in behind a tow-head (*i.e.,* new island) a couple of miles below this landing. I could n't remember that town; I could n't place it, could n't call its name. So I lost part of my temper. I suspected that it might be St. Genevieve—and so it proved to be. Observe what this eccentric river had been about: it had built up this huge useless tow-head directly in front of this town, cut off its river communications, fenced it away completely, and made a "country" town of it. It is a fine old place, too, and deserved a better fate. It was settled by the French, and is a relic of a time when one could travel from the mouths of the Mississippi to Quebec and be on French territory and under French rule all the way.

Presently I ascended to the hurricane deck and cast a longing glance toward the pilot-house.

XXIV.

My Incognito Is Exploded

A FTER A CLOSE STUDY of the face of the pilot on watch, I was satisfied that I had never seen him before; so I went up there. The pilot inspected me; I re-inspected the pilot. These customary preliminaries over, I sat down on the high bench, and he faced about and went on with his work. Every detail of the pilot-house was familiar to me, with one exception,—a large-mouthed tube under the breast-board. I puzzled over that thing a considerable time; then gave up and asked what it was for.

"To hear the engine-bells through."

It was another good contrivance which ought to have been invented half a century sooner. So I was thinking, when the pilot asked,—

"Do you know what this rope is for?"

I managed to get around this question, without committing myself.

"Is this the first time you were ever in a pilot-house?"

I crept under that one.

"Where are you from?"

"New England."

"First time you have ever been West?"

I climbed over this one.

"If you take an interest in such things, I can tell you what all these things are for."

I said I should like it.

"This," putting his hand on a backing-bell rope, "is to sound the fire-alarm; this," putting his hand on a go-a-head bell, "is to call the texas-tender; this one," indicating the whistle-lever, "is to call the captain"—and so he went on, touching one object after another, and reeling off his tranquil spool of lies.

I had never felt so like a passenger before. I thanked him, with emotion, for each new fact, and wrote it down in my note-book. The pilot warmed to his opportunity, and proceeded to load me up in the good old-fashioned way. At times I was afraid he was going to rupture his invention; but it always stood the strain, and he pulled through all right. He drifted, by easy stages, into revealments of the river's marvellous eccentricities of one sort and another, and backed them up with some pretty gigantic illustrations. For instance,—

"Do you see that little bowlder sticking out of the water yonder? well, when I first came on the river, that was a solid ridge of rock, over sixty feet high and two miles long. All washed away but that." [This with a sigh.]

I had a mighty impulse to destroy him, but it seemed to me that killing, in any ordinary way, would be too good for him.

Once, when an odd-looking craft, with a vast coal-scuttle slanting aloft on the end of a beam, was steaming by in the distance, he indifferently drew attention to it, as one might to an object grown wearisome through familiarity, and observed that it was an "alligator boat."

"An alligator boat? What 's it for?"

"To dredge out alligators with."

"Are they so thick as to be troublesome?"

"Well, not now, because the government keeps them down. But they used to be. Not everywhere; but in favorite places, here and there, where the river is wide and shoal— like Plum Point, and Stack Island, and so on—places they call alligator beds."

"Did they actually impede navigation?"

"Years ago, yes, in very low water; there was hardly a trip, then, that we did n't get aground on alligators."

It seemed to me that I should certainly have to get out my tomahawk. However, I restrained myself and said,—

"It must have been dreadful."

"Yes, it was one of the main difficulties about piloting. It was so hard to tell anything about the water; the damned things shift around so—never lie still five minutes at a time. You can tell a wind-reef, straight off, by the look of it; you can tell a break; you can tell a sand-reef—that 's all easy; but an alligator reef does n't show up, worth anything. Nine times in ten you can't tell where the water is; and when you *do* see where it is, like as not it ain't there when *you* get there, the devils have swapped around so, meantime. Of course

there were some few pilots that could judge of alligator wate
nearly as well as they could of any other kind, but they ha
to have natural talent for it; it was n't a thing a body coul
learn, you had to be born with it. Let me see: there was Be
Thornburg, and Beck Jolly, and Squire Bell, and Horac
Bixby, and Major Downing, and John Stevenson, and Bill
Gordon, and Jim Brady, and George Ealer, and Billy Young
blood—all A 1 alligator pilots. *They* could tell alligator wate
as far as another Christian could tell whiskey. Read it?—Ah
could n't they, though! I only wish I had as many dollars a
they could read alligator water a mile and a half off. Yes, an
it paid them to do it, too. A good alligator pilot could alway
get fifteen hundred dollars a month. Nights, other people ha
to lay up for alligators, but those fellows never laid up fo
alligators; they never laid up for anything but fog. They coul
smell the best alligator water—so it was said; I don't knov
whether it was so or not, and I think a body 's got his hand
full enough if he sticks to just what he knows himself, with
out going around backing up other people's say-so's, thoug
there 's a plenty that ain't backward about doing it, as long a
they can roust out something wonderful to tell. Which is no
the style of Robert Styles, by as much as three fathom—
maybe quarter-*less*."

[My! Was this Rob Styles?—This moustached and statel
figure?—A slim enough cub, in my time. How he has im
proved in comeliness in five and twenty years—and in th
noble art of inflating his facts.] After these musings, I sai
aloud,—

"I should think that dredging out the alligators would n'
have done much good, because they could come back agai
right away."

"If you had had as much experience of alligators as I have
you would n't talk like that. You dredge an alligator once an
he 's *convinced*. It 's the last you hear of *him*. He would n'
come back for pie. If there 's one thing that an alligator i
more down on than another, it 's being dredged. Besides
they were not simply shoved out of the way; the most of th
scoopful were scooped aboard; they emptied them into th
hold; and when they had got a trip, they took them to Or
leans to the Government works."

"What for?"

"Why, to make soldier-shoes out of their hides. All the Government shoes are made of alligator hide. It makes the best shoes in the world. They last five years, and they won't absorb water. The alligator fishery is a Government monopoly. All the alligators are Government property—just like the live-oaks. You cut down a live-oak, and Government fines you fifty dollars; you kill an alligator, and up you go for misprision of treason—lucky duck if they don't hang you, too. And they will, if you 're a Democrat. The buzzard is the sacred bird of the South, and you can't touch him; the alligator is the sacred bird of the Government, and you 've got to let him alone."

"Do you ever get aground on the alligators now?"

"Oh, no! it has n't happened for years."

"Well, then, why do they still keep the alligator boats in service?"

"Just for police duty—nothing more. They merely go up and down now and then. The present generation of alligators know them as easy as a burglar knows a roundsman; when they see one coming, they break camp and go for the woods."

After rounding-out and finishing-up and polishing-off the alligator business, he dropped easily and comfortably into the historical vein, and told of some tremendous feats of half a dozen old-time steamboats of his acquaintance, dwelling at special length upon a certain extraordinary performance of his chief favorite among this distinguished fleet—and then adding:—

"That boat was the 'Cyclone,'—last trip she ever made—she sunk, that very trip—captain was Tom Ballou, the most immortal liar that ever I struck. He could n't ever seem to tell the truth, in *any* kind of weather. Why, he would make you fairly shudder. He *was* the most scandalous liar! I left him, finally; I could n't stand it. The proverb says, 'like master, like man;' and if you stay with that kind of a man, you 'll come under suspicion by and by, just as sure as you live. He paid first-class wages; but said I, What 's wages when your reputation 's in danger? So I let the wages go, and froze to my reputation. And I 've never regretted it. Reputation 's worth everything, ain't it? That 's the way I look at it. He had more selfish organs than any seven men in the world—all packed in the stern-sheets of his skull, of course, where they belonged. They weighed down the back of his head so that it made his nose tilt up in the air. People thought it was vanity, but it was n't, it was malice. If you only saw his foot, you 'd take him to be nineteen feet high, but he was n't; it was because his foot was out of drawing. He was intended to be nineteen feet high, no doubt, if his foot was made first, but he did n't get there; he was only five feet ten. That 's what he was, and that 's what he is. You take the lies out of him, and he 'll shrink to the size of your hat; you take the malice out of him, and he 'll disappear. That 'Cyclone' was a rattler to go, and the sweetest thing to steer that ever walked the waters. Set her amidships, in a big river, and just let her go; it was all you had to do. She would hold herself on a star all night, if you let her alone. You could n't ever feel her rudder. It was n't any more labor to steer her than it is to count the Republican vote in a South Carolina election. One morning, just at daybreak, the last trip she ever made, they took her rudder aboard to mend it; I did n't know anything about it, I backed her out from the wood-yard and went a-weaving down the river all serene. When I had gone about twenty-three miles, and made four horribly crooked crossings—"

"Without any rudder?"

"Yes—old Capt. Tom appeared on the roof and began to find fault with me for running such a dark night—"

"Such a *dark night*?—Why, you said—"

"Never mind what I said,—'t was as dark as Egypt *now*, though pretty soon the moon began to rise, and—"

"You mean the *sun*—because you started out just at break of—look here! Was this *before* you quitted the captain on account of his lying, or—"

"It was before—oh, a long time before. And as I was saying, he—"

"But was this the trip she sunk, or was—"

"Oh, no!—months afterward. And so the old man, he—"

"Then she made *two* last trips, because you said—"

He stepped back from the wheel, swabbing away his perspiration, and said—

"Here!" (calling me by name), "*you* take her and lie a

while—you 're handier at it than I am. Trying to play yourself for a stranger and an innocent!—why, I knew you before
you had spoken seven words; and I made up my mind to find
out what was your little game. It was to *draw me out*. Well,
I let you, did n't I? Now take the wheel and finish the watch;
and next time play fair, and you won't have to work your
passage."

Thus ended the fictitious-name business. And not six hours
out from St. Louis! but I had gained a privilege, anyway, for
I had been itching to get my hands on the wheel, from the
beginning. I seemed to have forgotten the river, but I had n't
forgotten how to steer a steamboat, nor how to enjoy it,
either.

XXV.

From Cairo to Hickman

THE SCENERY, from St. Louis to Cairo—two hundred miles—is varied and beautiful. The hills were clothed in the fresh foliage of spring now, and were a gracious and worthy setting for the broad river flowing between. Our trip began auspiciously, with a perfect day, as to breeze and sunshine, and our boat threw the miles out behind her with satisfactory despatch.

We found a railway intruding at Chester, Illinois; Chester has also a penitentiary now, and is otherwise marching on. At Grand Tower, too, there was a railway; and another at Cape Girardeau. The former town gets its name from a huge, squat pillar of rock, which stands up out of the water on the Missouri side of the river—a piece of nature's fanciful handiwork—and is one of the most picturesque features of the scenery of that region. For nearer or remoter neighbors, the Tower has the Devil's Bake Oven—so called, perhaps, because it does not powerfully resemble anybody else's bake oven; and the Devil's Tea Table—this latter a great smooth-surfaced mass of rock, with diminishing wine-glass stem, perched some fifty or sixty feet above the river, beside a be-flowered and garlanded precipice, and sufficiently like a tea-table to answer for anybody, Devil or Christian. Away down the river we have the Devil's Elbow and the Devil's Race-course, and lots of other property of his which I cannot now call to mind.

The town of Grand Tower was evidently a busier place than it had been in old times, but it seemed to need some repairs here and there, and a new coat of whitewash all over. Still, it was pleasant to me to see the old coat once more. "Uncle" Mumford, our second officer, said the place had been suffering from high water and consequently was not looking its best now. But he said it was not strange that it did n't waste whitewash on itself, for more lime was made there, and of a better quality, than anywhere in the West; and added,—
"On a dairy farm you never can get any milk for your coffee,

nor any sugar for it on a sugar plantation; and it is against sense to go to a lime town to hunt for whitewash." In my own experience I knew the first two items to be true; and also that people who sell candy don't care for candy; therefore there was plausibility in Uncle Mumford's final observation that "people who make lime run more to religion than white-wash." Uncle Mumford said, further, that Grand Tower was a great coaling centre and a prospering place.

Cape Girardeau is situated on a hillside, and makes a hand-some appearance. There is a great Jesuit school for boys at the foot of the town by the river. Uncle Mumford said it had as high a reputation for thoroughness as any similar institu-tion in Missouri. There was another college higher up on an airy summit,—a bright new edifice, picturesquely and pecu-liarly towered and pinnacled—a sort of gigantic casters, with the cruets all complete. Uncle Mumford said that Cape Gir-ardeau was the Athens of Missouri, and contained several col-leges besides those already mentioned; and all of them on a religious basis of one kind or another. He directed my atten-tion to what he called the "strong and pervasive religious look of the town," but I could not see that it looked more religious than the other hill towns with the same slope and built of the same kind of bricks. Partialities often make people see more than really exists.

Uncle Mumford has been thirty years a mate on the river. He is a man of practical sense and a level head; has observed; has had much experience of one sort and another; has opin-ions; has, also, just a perceptible dash of poetry in his com-position, an easy gift of speech, a thick growl in his voice, and an oath or two where he can get at them when the exi-gencies of his office require a spiritual lift. He is a mate of the blessed old-time kind; and goes gravely damning around, when there is work to the fore, in a way to mellow the ex-steamboatman's heart with sweet soft longings for the van-ished days that shall come no more. "*Git* up, there,—— —— you! Going to be all day? Why d'n't you *say* you was petrified in your hind legs, before you shipped!"

He is a steady man with his crew; kind and just, but firm; so they like him, and stay with him. He is still in the slouchy garb of the old generation of mates; but next trip the Anchor

Line will have him in uniform—a natty blue naval uniform, with brass buttons, along with all the officers of the line— and then he will be a totally different style of scenery from what he is now.

Uniforms on the Mississippi! It beats all the other changes put together, for surprise. Still, there is another surprise— that it was not made fifty years ago. It is so manifestly sensible, that it might have been thought of earlier, one would suppose. During fifty years, out there, the innocent passenger in need of help and information, has been mistaking the mate for the cook, and the captain for the barber—and being roughly entertained for it, too. But his troubles are ended now. And the greatly improved aspect of the boat's staff is another advantage achieved by the dress-reform period.

Steered down the bend below Cape Girardeau. They used to call it "Steersman's Bend;" plain sailing and plenty of water in it, always; about the only place in the Upper River that a new cub was allowed to take a boat through, in low water.

Thebes, at the head of the Grand Chain, and Commerce at the foot of it, were towns easily rememberable, as they had not undergone conspicuous alteration. Nor the Chain, either—in the nature of things; for it is a chain of sunken rocks admirably arranged to capture and kill steamboats on bad nights. A good many steamboat corpses lie buried there, out of sight; among the rest my first friend the "Paul Jones;" she knocked her bottom out, and went down like a pot, so the historian told me—Uncle Mumford. He said she had a gray mare aboard, and a preacher. To me, this sufficiently accounted for the disaster; as it did, of course, to Mumford, who added,—

"But there are many ignorant people who would scoff at such a matter, and call it superstition. But you will always notice that they are people who have never travelled with a gray mare and a preacher. I went down the river once in such company. We grounded at Bloody Island; we grounded at Hanging Dog; we grounded just below this same Commerce; we jolted Beaver Dam Rock; we hit one of the worst breaks in the 'Graveyard' behind Goose Island; we had a roustabout killed in a fight; we burnt a boiler; broke a shaft; collapsed a flue; and went into Cairo with nine feet of water in the

1old—may have been more, may have been less. I remember
it as if it were yesterday. The men lost their heads with terror.
They painted the mare blue, in sight of town, and threw the
preacher overboard, or we should not have arrived at all. The
preacher was fished out and saved. He acknowledged, himself, that he had been to blame. I remember it all, as if it were
yesterday."

That this combination—of preacher and gray mare—
should breed calamity, seems strange, and at first glance unbelievable; but the fact is fortified by so much unassailable
proof that to doubt is to dishonor reason. I myself remember
a case where a captain was warned by numerous friends
against taking a gray mare and a preacher with him, but persisted in his purpose in spite of all that could be said; and the
same day,—it may have been the next, and some say it was,
though I think it was the same day,—he got drunk and fell
down the hatchway and was borne to his home a corpse. This
is literally true.

No vestige of Hat Island is left now; every shred of it is
washed away. I do not even remember what part of the river
it used to be in, except that it was between St. Louis and
Cairo somewhere. It was a bad region—all around and about
Hat Island, in early days. A farmer who lived on the Illinois
shore there, said that twenty-nine steamboats had left their
bones strung along within sight from his house. Between St.
Louis and Cairo the steamboat wrecks average one to the
mile;—two hundred wrecks, altogether.

I could recognize big changes from Commerce down. Beaver Dam Rock was out in the middle of the river now, and
throwing a prodigious "break;" it used to be close to the
shore, and boats went down outside of it. A big island that
used to be away out in mid-river, has retired to the Missouri
shore, and boats do not go near it any more. The island called
Jacket Pattern is whittled down to a wedge now, and is
booked for early destruction. Goose Island is all gone but a
little dab the size of a steamboat. The perilous "Graveyard,"
among whose numberless wrecks we used to pick our way so
slowly and gingerly, is far away from the channel now, and a
terror to nobody. One of the islands formerly called the Two
Sisters is gone entirely; the other, which used to lie close to

the Illinois shore, is now on the Missouri side, a mile away; it is joined solidly to the shore, and it takes a sharp eye to see where the seam is—but it is Illinois ground yet, and the people who live on it have to ferry themselves over and work the Illinois roads and pay Illinois taxes: singular state of things!

Near the mouth of the river several islands were missing—washed away. Cairo was still there—easily visible across the long, flat point upon whose further verge it stands; but we had to steam a long way around to get to it. Night fell as we were going out of the "Upper River" and meeting the floods of the Ohio. We dashed along without anxiety; for the hidden rock which used to lie right in the way has moved up stream a long distance out of the channel; or rather, about one county has gone into the river from the Missouri point, and the Cairo point has "made down" and added to its long tongue of territory correspondingly. The Mississippi is a just and equitable river; it never tumbles one man's farm overboard without building a new farm just like it for that man's neighbor. This keeps down hard feelings.

Going into Cairo, we came near killing a steamboat which paid no attention to our whistle and then tried to cross our bows. By doing some strong backing, we saved him; which was a great loss, for he would have made good literature.

Cairo is a brisk town now; and is substantially built, and has a city look about it which is in noticeable contrast to its former estate, as per Mr. Dickens's portrait of it. However, it was already building with bricks when I had seen it last—which was when Colonel (now General) Grant was drilling his first command there. Uncle Mumford says the libraries and Sunday-schools have done a good work in Cairo, as well as the brick masons. Cairo has a heavy railroad and river trade, and her situation at the junction of the two great rivers is so advantageous that she cannot well help prospering.

When I turned out, in the morning, we had passed Columbus, Kentucky, and were approaching Hickman, a pretty town, perched on a handsome hill. Hickman is in a rich tobacco region, and formerly enjoyed a great and lucrative trade in that staple, collecting it there in her warehouses from a large area of country and shipping it by boat; but Uncle Mumford says she built a railway to facilitate this commerce a little more, and he thinks it facilitated it the wrong way—took the bulk of the trade out of her hands by "collaring it along the line without gathering it at her doors."

XXVI.

Under Fire

TALK BEGAN to run upon the war now, for we were getting down into the upper edge of the former battle-stretch by this time. Columbus was just behind us, so there was a good deal said about the famous battle of Belmont. Several of the boat's officers had seen active service in the Mississippi war-fleet. I gathered that they found themselves sadly out of their element in that kind of business at first, but afterward got accustomed to it, reconciled to it, and more or less at home in it. One of our pilots had his first war experience in the Belmont fight, as a pilot on a boat in the Confederate service. I had often had a curiosity to know how a green hand might feel, in his maiden battle, perched all solitary and alone on high in a pilot house, a target for Tom, Dick and Harry, and nobody at his elbow to shame him from showing the white feather when matters grew hot and perilous around him; so, to me his story was valuable—it filled a gap for me which all histories had left till that time empty.

THE PILOT'S FIRST BATTLE

He said:—

It was the 7th of November. The fight began at seven in the morning. I was on the "R. H. W. Hill." Took over a load of troops from Columbus. Came back, and took over a battery of artillery. My partner said he was going to see the fight; wanted me to go along. I said, no, I was n't anxious, I would look at it from the pilot-house. He said I was a coward, and left.

That fight was an awful sight. General Cheatham made his men strip their coats off and throw them in a pile, and said, "Now follow me to hell or victory!" I heard him say that from the pilot-house; and then he galloped in, at the head of his troops. Old General Pillow, with his white hair, mounted on a white horse, sailed in, too, leading his troops as lively as a boy. By and by the Federals chased the rebels back, and here they came! tearing along, everybody for himself and Devil take the hindmost! and down under the bank they scrambled, and took shelter. I was sitting with my legs hanging out of the pilot-house window. All at once I noticed a whizzing sound passing my ear. Judged it was a bullet. I did n't stop to think about anything, I just tilted over backwards and landed on the floor, and staid there. The balls came booming around. Three cannon-balls went through the chimney; one ball took off the corner of the pilot-house; shells were screaming and bursting all around. Mighty warm times—I wished I had n't come. I lay there on the pilot-house floor, while the shots came faster and faster. I crept in behind the big stove, in the middle of the pilot-house. Presently a minie-ball came through the stove, and just grazed my head, and cut my hat. I judged it was time to go away from there. The captain was on the roof with a red-headed major from Memphis—a fine-looking man. I heard him say he wanted to leave here, but "that pilot is killed." I crept over to the starboard side to pull the bell to set her back; raised up and took a look, and I saw about fifteen shot holes through the window panes; had come so lively I had n't noticed them. I glanced out on the water, and the spattering shot were like a hail-storm. I thought best to get out of that place. I went down the pilot-house guy, head first—not feet first but head first—slid down—before I struck the deck, the captain said we must leave there. So I climbed up the guy and got on the floor again. About that time, they collared my partner and were bringing him up to the pilot-house between two soldiers. Somebody had said I was killed. He put his head in and saw me on the floor reaching for the backing bells. He said, "Oh, hell, he ain't shot," and jerked away from the men who had him by the collar, and ran below. We were there until three o'clock in the afternoon, and then got away all right.

The next time I saw my partner, I said, "Now, come out, be honest, and tell me the truth. Where did you go when you went to see that battle?" He says, "I went down in the hold."

All through that fight I was scared nearly to death. I hardly knew anything, I was so frightened; but you see, nobody knew that but me. Next day General Polk sent for me, and praised me for my bravery and gallant conduct.

I never said anything, I let it go at that. I judged it was n't so, but it was not for me to contradict a general officer.

Pretty soon after that I was sick, and used up, and had to go off to the Hot Springs. When there, I got a good many letters from commanders saying they wanted me to come back. I declined, because I was n't well enough or strong enough; but I kept still, and kept the reputation I had made.

A plain story, straightforwardly told; but Mumford told me that that pilot had "gilded that scare of his, in spots;" that his subsequent career in the war was proof of it.

We struck down through the chute of Island No. 8, and I went below and fell into conversation with a passenger, a handsome man, with easy carriage and an intelligent face. We were approaching Island No. 10, a place so celebrated during the war. This gentleman's home was on the main shore in its neighborhood. I had some talk with him about the war times; but presently the discourse fell upon "feuds," for in no part of the South has the vendetta flourished more briskly, or held out longer between warring families, than in this particular region. This gentleman said:—

"There 's been more than one feud around here, in old times, but I reckon the worst one was between the Darnells and the Watsons. Nobody don't know now what the first quarrel was about, it 's so long ago; the Darnells and the Watsons don't know, if there 's any of them living, which I don't think there is. Some says it was about a horse or a cow—anyway, it was a little matter; the money in it was n't of no consequence—none in the world—both families was rich. The thing could have been fixed up, easy enough; but no, that would n't do. Rough words had been passed; and so, nothing but blood could fix it up after that. That horse or cow, whichever it was, cost sixty years of killing and crip-pling! Every year or so somebody was shot, on one side or the other; and as fast as one generation was laid out, their sons took up the feud and kept it a-going. And it 's just as I say; they went on shooting each other, year in and year out—

making a kind of a religion of it, you see—till they 'd done forgot, long ago, what it was all about. Wherever a Darnell caught a Watson, or a Watson caught a Darnell, one of 'em was going to get hurt—only question was, which of them got the drop on the other. They 'd shoot one another down, right in the presence of the family. They did n't *hunt* for each other, but when they happened to meet, they pulled and begun. Men would shoot boys, boys would shoot men. A man shot a boy twelve years old—happened on him in the woods, and did n't give him no chance. If he *had* 'a' given him a chance, the boy 'd 'a' shot *him*. Both families belonged to the same church (everybody around here is religious); through all this fifty or sixty years' fuss, both tribes was there every Sunday, to worship. They lived each side of the line, and the church was at a landing called Compromise. Half the church and half the aisle was in Kentucky, the other half in Tennessee. Sundays you 'd see the families drive up, all in their Sunday clothes, men, women, and children, and file up the aisle, and set down, quiet and orderly, one lot on the Tennessee side of the church and the other on the Kentucky side; and the men and boys would lean their guns up against the wall, handy, and then all hands would join in with the prayer and praise; though they say the man next the aisle did n't kneel down, along with the rest of the family; kind of stood guard. I don't know; never was at that church in my life; but I remember that that 's what used to be said.

"Twenty or twenty-five years ago, one of the feud families caught a young man of nineteen out and killed him. Don't remember whether it was the Darnells and Watsons, or one of the other feuds; but anyway, this young man rode up—steamboat laying there at the time—and the first thing he saw was a whole gang of the enemy. He jumped down behind a wood-pile, but they rode around and begun on him, he firing back, and they galloping and cavorting and yelling and banging away with all their might. Think he wounded a couple of them; but they closed in on him and chased him into the river; and as he swum along down stream, they followed along the bank and kept on shooting at him; and when he struck shore he was dead. Windy Marshall told me about it. He saw it. He was captain of the boat.

"Years ago, the Darnells was so thinned out that the old man and his two sons concluded they'd leave the country. They started to take steamboat just above No. 10; but the Watsons got wind of it; and they arrived just as the two young Darnells was walking up the companion-way with their wives on their arms. The fight begun then, and they never got no further—both of them killed. After that, old Darnell got into trouble with the man that run the ferry, and the ferry-man got the worst of it—and died. But his friends shot old Darnell through and through—filled him full of bullets, and ended him."

The country gentleman who told me these things had been reared in ease and comfort, was a man of good parts, and was college bred. His loose grammar was the fruit of careless habit, not ignorance. This habit among educated men in the West is not universal, but it is prevalent—prevalent in the towns, certainly, if not in the cities; and to a degree which one cannot help noticing, and marvelling at. I heard a Westerner who would be accounted a highly educated man in any country, say "never mind, it *don't make no difference*, anyway." A life-long resident who was present heard it, but it made no impression upon her. She was able to recall the fact afterward when reminded of it; but she confessed that the words had not grated upon her ear at the time—a confession which suggests that if educated people can hear such blasphemous grammar, from such a source, and be unconscious of the deed, the crime must be tolerably common—so common that the general ear has become dulled by familiarity with it, and is no longer alert, no longer sensitive to such affronts.

No one in the world speaks blemishless grammar; no one has ever written it—*no* one, either in the world or out of it (taking the Scriptures for evidence on the latter point); therefore it would not be fair to exact grammatical perfection from the peoples of the Valley; but they and all other peoples may justly be required to refrain from *knowingly* and *purposely* debauching their grammar.

I found the river greatly changed at Island No. 10. The island which I remembered was some three miles long and a quarter of a mile wide, heavily timbered, and lay near the

Kentucky shore—within two hundred yards of it, I should say. Now, however, one had to hunt for it with a spy-glass. Nothing was left of it but an insignificant little tuft, and this was no longer near the Kentucky shore; it was clear over against the opposite shore, a mile away. In war times the island had been an important place, for it commanded the situation; and, being heavily fortified, there was no getting by it. It lay between the upper and lower divisions of the Union forces, and kept them separate, until a junction was finally effected across the Missouri neck of land; but the island being itself joined to that neck now, the wide river is without obstruction.

In this region the river passes from Kentucky into Tennessee, back into Missouri, then back into Kentucky, and thence into Tennessee again. So a mile or two of Missouri sticks over into Tennessee.

The town of New Madrid was looking very unwell; but otherwise unchanged from its former condition and aspect. Its blocks of frame-houses were still grouped in the same old flat plain, and environed by the same old forests. It was as tranquil as formerly, and apparently had neither grown nor diminished in size. It was said that the recent high water had invaded it and damaged its looks. This was surprising news; for in low water the river bank is very high there (fifty feet), and in my day an overflow had always been considered an impossibility. This present flood of 1882 will doubtless be celebrated in the river's history for several generations before a deluge of like magnitude shall be seen. It put all the unprotected low lands under water, from Cairo to the mouth; it broke down the levees in a great many places, on both sides of the river; and in some regions south, when the flood was at its highest, the Mississippi was *seventy miles* wide! A number of lives were lost, and the destruction of property was fearful. The crops were destroyed, houses washed away, and shelterless men and cattle forced to take refuge on scattering elevations here and there in field and forest, and wait in peril and suffering until the boats put in commission by the national and local governments and by newspaper enterprise could come and rescue them. The properties of multitudes of

people were under water for months, and the poorer one
must have starved by the hundred if succor had not bee
promptly afforded.[1] The water had been falling during a con
siderable time now, yet as a rule we found the banks sti
under water.

[1]For a detailed and interesting description of the great flood, written o
board of the New Orleans "Times-Democrat's" relief-boat, see Appendix A

XXVII.

Some Imported Articles

WE MET TWO STEAMBOATS at New Madrid. Two steamboats in sight at once! an infrequent spectacle now in the lonesome Mississippi. The loneliness of this solemn, stupendous flood is impressive—and depressing. League after league, and still league after league, it pours its chocolate tide along, between its solid forest walls, its almost untenanted shores, with seldom a sail or a moving object of any kind to disturb the surface and break the monotony of the blank, watery solitude; and so the day goes, the night comes, and again the day—and still the same, night after night and day after day,—majestic, unchanging sameness of serenity, repose, tranquillity, lethargy, vacancy,—symbol of eternity, realization of the heaven pictured by priest and prophet, and longed for by the good and thoughtless!

Immediately after the war of 1812, tourists began to come to America, from England; scattering ones at first, then a sort of procession of them—a procession which kept up its plodding, patient march through the land during many, many years. Each tourist took notes, and went home and published a book—a book which was usually calm, truthful, reasonable, kind; but which seemed just the reverse to our tender-footed progenitors. A glance at these tourist-books shows us that in certain of its aspects the Mississippi has undergone no change since those strangers visited it, but remains to-day about as it was then. The emotions produced in those foreign breasts by these aspects were not all formed on one pattern, of course; they *had* to be various, along at first, because the earlier tourists were obliged to originate their emotions, whereas in older countries one can always borrow emotions from one's predecessors. And, mind you, emotions are among the toughest things in the world to manufacture out of whole cloth; it is easier to manufacture seven facts than one emotion. Captain Basil Hall, R. N., writing fifty-five years ago, says:—

"Here I caught the first glimpse of the object I had so

long wished to behold, and felt myself amply repaid at that moment for all the trouble I had experienced in coming so far; and stood looking at the river flowing past till it was too dark to distinguish anything. But it was not till I had visited the same spot a dozen times, that I came to a right comprehension of the grandeur of the scene."

Following are Mrs. Trollope's emotions. She is writing a few months later in the same year, 1827, and is coming in at the mouth of the Mississippi: —

"The first indication of our approach to land was the appearance of this mighty river pouring forth its muddy mass of waters, and mingling with the deep blue of the Mexican Gulf. I never beheld a scene so utterly desolate as this entrance of the Mississippi. Had Dante seen it, he might have drawn images of another Bolgia from its horrors. One only object rears itself above the eddying waters; this is the mast of a vessel long since wrecked in attempting to cross the bar, and it still stands, a dismal witness of the destruction that has been, and a boding prophet of that which is to come."

Emotions of Hon. Charles Augustus Murray (near St. Louis), seven years later: —

"It is only when you ascend the mighty current for fifty or a hundred miles, and use the eye of imagination as well as that of nature, that you begin to understand all his might and majesty. You see him fertilizing a boundless valley, bearing along in his course the trophies of his thousand victories over the shattered forest—here carrying away large masses of soil with all their growth, and there forming islands, destined at some future period to be the residence of man; and while indulging in this prospect, it is then time for reflection to suggest that the current before you has flowed through two or three thousand miles, and has yet to travel one thousand three hundred more before reaching its ocean destination."

Receive, now, the emotions of Captain Marryat, R. N., author of the sea tales, writing in 1837, three years after Mr. Murray: —

"Never, perhaps, in the records of nations, was there an instance of a century of such unvarying and unmitigated crime as is to be collected from the history of the turbulent and blood-stained Mississippi. The stream itself appears as if appropriate for the deeds which have been committed. It is not like most rivers, beautiful to the sight, bestowing fertility in its course; not one that the eye loves to dwell upon as it sweeps along, nor can you wander upon its bank, or trust yourself without danger to its stream. It is a furious, rapid, desolating torrent, loaded with alluvial soil; and few of those who are received into its waters ever rise again,[1] or can support themselves long upon its surface without assistance from some friendly log. It contains the coarsest and most uneatable of fish, such as the cat-fish and such genus, and as you descend, its banks are occupied with the fetid alligator, while the panther basks at its edge in the cane-brakes, almost impervious to man. Pouring its impetuous waters through wild tracks covered with trees of little value except for firewood, it sweeps down whole forests in its course, which disappear in tumultuous confusion, whirled away by the stream now loaded with the masses of soil which nourished their roots, often blocking up and changing for a time the channel of the river, which, as if in anger at its being opposed, inundates and devastates the whole country round; and as soon as it forces its way through its former channel, plants in every direction the uprooted monarchs of the forest (upon whose branches the bird will never again perch, or the raccoon, the opossum, or the squirrel climb) as traps to the adventurous navigators of its waters by steam, who, borne down upon these concealed dangers which pierce through the planks, very often have not time to steer for and gain the shore before they sink to the bottom. There are no pleasing associations connected with the great common sewer of the Western America, which pours out its mud into the Mexican Gulf, polluting the clear blue sea for many miles beyond its mouth. It is a river of desolation; and instead of reminding

[1] There was a foolish superstition of some little prevalence in that day, that the Mississippi would neither buoy up a swimmer, nor permit a drowned person's body to rise to the surface.

you, like other beautiful rivers, of an angel which has descended for the benefit of man, you imagine it a devil, whose energies have been only overcome by the wonderful power of steam."

It is pretty crude literature for a man accustomed to handling a pen; still, as a panorama of the emotions sent weltering through this noted visitor's breast by the aspect and traditions of the "great common sewer," it has a value. A value, though marred in the matter of statistics by inaccuracies; for the catfish is a plenty good enough fish for anybody, and there are no panthers that are "impervious to man."

Later still comes Alexander Mackay, of the Middle Temple, Barrister at Law, with a better digestion, and no catfish dinner aboard, and feels as follows: —

"The Mississippi! It was with indescribable emotions that I first felt myself afloat upon its waters. How often in my school-boy dreams, and in my waking visions afterwards, had my imagination pictured to itself the lordly stream, rolling with tumultuous current through the boundless region to which it has given its name, and gathering into itself, in its course to the ocean, the tributary waters of almost every latitude in the temperate zone! Here it was then in its reality, and I, at length, steaming against its tide. I looked upon it with that reverence with which every one must regard a great feature of external nature."

So much for the emotions. The tourists, one and all, remark upon the deep, brooding loneliness and desolation of the vast river. Captain Basil Hall, who saw it at flood-stage, says: —

"Sometimes we passed along distances of twenty or thirty miles without seeing a single habitation. An artist, in search of hints for a painting of the deluge, would here have found them in abundance."

The first shall be last, etc. Just two hundred years ago, the old original first and gallantest of all the foreign tourists, pioneer, head of the procession, ended his weary and tedious discovery-voyage down the solemn stretches of the great river—La Salle, whose name will last as long as the river itself shall last. We quote from Mr. Parkman:—

"And now they neared their journey's end. On the sixth of April, the river divided itself into three broad channels. La Salle followed that of the west, and D'Autray that of the east; while Tonty took the middle passage. As he drifted down the turbid current, between the low and marshy shores, the brackish water changed to brine, and the breeze grew fresh with the salt breath of the sea. Then the broad bosom of the great Gulf opened on his sight, tossing its restless billows, limitless, voiceless, lonely as when born of chaos, without a sail, without a sign of life."

Then, on a spot of solid ground, La Salle reared a column "bearing the arms of France; the Frenchmen were mustered under arms; and while the New England Indians and their squaws looked on in wondering silence, they chanted the *Te Deum*, the *Exaudiat*, and the *Domine salvum fac regem*."

Then, whilst the musketry volleyed and rejoicing shouts burst forth, the victorious discoverer planted the column, and made proclamation in a loud voice, taking formal possession of the river and the vast countries watered by it, in the name of the King. The column bore this inscription:—

LOUIS LE GRAND, ROY DE FRANCE ET DE NAVARRE, REGNE;
LE NEUVIEME AVRIL, 1682.

New Orleans intended to fittingly celebrate, this present year, the bicentennial anniversary of this illustrious event; but when the time came, all her energies and surplus money were required in other directions, for the flood was upon the land then, making havoc and devastation everywhere.

XXVIII.

Uncle Mumford Unloads

ALL DAY we swung along down the river, and had the stream almost wholly to ourselves. Formerly, at such a stage of the water, we should have passed acres of lumber rafts, and dozens of big coal barges; also occasional little trading-scows, peddling along from farm to farm, with the peddler's family on board; possibly, a random scow, bearing a humble Hamlet and Co. on an itinerant dramatic trip. But these were all absent. Far along in the day, we saw one steamboat; just one, and no more. She was lying at rest in the shade, within the wooded mouth of the Obion River. The spy-glass revealed the fact that she was named for me—or *he* was named for me, whichever you prefer. As this was the first time I had ever encountered this species of honor, it seems excusable to mention it, and at the same time call the attention of the authorities to the tardiness of my recognition of it.

Noted a big change in the river, at Island 21. It was a very large island, and used to lie out toward mid-stream; but it is joined fast to the main shore now, and has retired from business as an island.

As we approached famous and formidable Plum Point, darkness fell, but that was nothing to shudder about—in these modern times. For now the national government has turned the Mississippi into a sort of two-thousand-mile torchlight procession. In the head of every crossing, and in the foot of every crossing, the government has set up a clear-burning lamp. You are never entirely in the dark, now; there is always a beacon in sight, either before you, or behind you, or abreast. One might almost say that lamps have been squandered there. Dozens of crossings are lighted which were not shoal when they were created, and have never been shoal since; crossings so plain, too, and also so straight, that a steamboat can take herself through them without any help, after she has been through once. Lamps in such places are of course not wasted; it is much more convenient and comfortable for a pilot to hold on them than on a spread of formless blackness that won't stay still; and money is saved to the boat, at the same time, for she can of course make more miles with her rudder amidships than she can with it squared across her stern and holding her back.

But this thing has knocked the romance out of piloting, to a large extent. It and some other things together, have knocked all the romance out of it. For instance, the peril from snags is not now what it once was. The government's snag-boats go patrolling up and down, in these matter-of-fact days, pulling the river's teeth; they have rooted out all the old clusters which made many localities so formidable; and they allow no new ones to collect. Formerly, if your boat got away from you, on a black night, and broke for the woods, it was an anxious time with you; so was it also, when you were groping your way through solidified darkness in a narrow chute; but all that is changed now,—you flash out your electric light, transform night into day in the twinkling of an eye, and your perils and anxieties are at an end. Horace Bixby and George Ritchie have charted the crossings and laid out the courses by compass; they have invented a lamp to go with the chart, and have patented the whole. With these helps, one may run in the fog now, with considerable security, and with a confidence unknown in the old days.

With these abundant beacons, the banishment of snags, plenty of daylight in a box and ready to be turned on whenever needed, and a chart and compass to fight the fog with, piloting, at a good stage of water, is now nearly as safe and simple as driving stage, and is hardly more than three times as romantic.

And now in these new days, these days of infinite change, the Anchor Line have raised the captain above the pilot by giving him the bigger wages of the two. This was going far, but they have not stopped there. They have decreed that the pilot shall remain at his post, and stand his watch clear through, whether the boat be under way or tied up to the shore. We, that were once the aristocrats of the river, can't go to bed now, as we used to do, and sleep while a hundred tons of freight are lugged aboard; no, we must sit in the pilot-house; and keep awake, too. Verily we are being treated like a parcel of mates and engineers. The Government has taken away the romance of our calling; the Company has taken away its state and dignity.

Plum Point looked as it had always looked by night, with the exception that now there were beacons to mark the crossings, and also a lot of other lights on the Point and along its shore; these latter glinting from the fleet of the United States River Commission, and from a village which the officials have built on the land for offices and for the employés of the service. The military engineers of the Commission have taken upon their shoulders the job of making the Mississippi over again,—a job transcended in size by only the original job of creating it. They are building wing-dams here and there, to deflect the current; and dikes to confine it in narrower bounds; and other dikes to make it stay there; and for unnumbered miles along the Mississippi, they are felling the timber-front for fifty yards back, with the purpose of shaving the bank down to low-water mark with the slant of a house-roof, and ballasting it with stones; and in many places they have protected the wasting shores with rows of piles. One who knows the Mississippi will promptly aver—not aloud, but to himself—that ten thousand River Commissions, with the mines of the world at their back, cannot tame that lawless stream, cannot curb it or confine it, cannot say to it, Go here, or Go there, and make it obey; cannot save a shore which it has sentenced; cannot bar its path with an obstruction which it will not tear down, dance over, and laugh at. But a discreet man will not put these things into spoken words; for the West Point engineers have not their superiors anywhere; they know all that can be known of their abstruse science; and so, since they conceive that they can fetter and handcuff that river and boss him, it is but wisdom for the unscientific man to keep still, lie low, and wait till they do it. Captain Eads, with his jetties, has done a work at the mouth of the Mississippi which seemed clearly impossible; so we do not feel full confidence now to prophesy against like impossibilities. Otherwise one would pipe out and say the Commission might as well bully the comets in their courses and undertake to make them behave, as try to bully the Mississippi into right and reasonable conduct.

I consulted Uncle Mumford concerning this and cognate matters; and I give here the result, stenographically reported, and therefore to be relied on as being full and correct; except that I have here and there left out remarks which were addressed to the men, such as "*where* in blazes are you going with that barrel now?" and which seemed to me to break the flow of the written statement, without compensating by adding to its information or its clearness. Not that I have ventured to strike out all such interjections; I have removed only those which were obviously irrelevant; wherever one occurred which I felt any question about, I have judged it safest to let it remain.

UNCLE MUMFORD'S IMPRESSIONS

Uncle Mumford said:—

"As long as I have been mate of a steamboat,—thirty years—I have watched this river and studied it. Maybe I could have learnt more about it at West Point, but if I believe it I wish I may be WHAT *are you sucking your fingers there for?—Collar that kag of nails!* Four years at West Point, and plenty of books and schooling, will learn a man a good deal, I reckon, but it won't learn him the river. You turn one of those little European rivers over to this Commission, with its hard bottom and clear water, and it would just be a holiday job for them to wall it, and pile it, and dike it, and tame it down, and boss it around, and make it go wherever they wanted it to, and stay where they put it, and do just as they said, every time. But this ain't that kind of a river. They have started in here with big confidence, and the best intentions in the world; but they are going to get left. What does Ecclesiastes vii. 13 say? Says enough to knock *their* little game galley-west, don't it? Now you look at their methods once. There at Devil's Island, in the Upper River, they wanted the water to go one way, the water wanted to go another. So they put up a stone wall. But what does the river care for a stone wall? When it got ready, it just bulged through it. Maybe they can build another that will stay; that is, up there—but not down here they can't. Down here in the Lower River, they drive some pegs to turn the water away

from the shore and stop it from slicing off the bank; very
well, don't it go straight over and cut somebody else's bank?
Certainly. Are they going to peg *all* the banks? Why, they
could buy ground and build a new Mississippi cheaper. They
are pegging Bulletin Tow-head now. It won't do any good.
If the river has got a mortgage on that island, it will foreclose
sure, pegs or no pegs. Away down yonder, they have driven
two rows of piles straight through the middle of a dry bar
half a mile long, which is forty foot out of the water when
the river is low. What do you reckon that is for? If I know, I
wish I may land in—HUMP *yourself, you son of an undertaker!—out with that coal-oil, now, lively,* LIVELY! And just
look at what they are trying to do down there at Milliken's
Bend. There 's been a cut-off in that section, and Vicksburg
is left out in the cold. It 's a country town now. The river
strikes in below it; and a boat can't go up to the town except
in high water. Well, they are going to build wing-dams in the
bend opposite the foot of 103, and throw the water over and
cut off the foot of the island and plow down into an old ditch
where the river used to be in ancient times; and they think
they can persuade the water around that way, and get it to
strike in above Vicksburg, as it used to do, and fetch the town
back into the world again. That is, they are going to take this
whole Mississippi, and twist it around and make it run several
miles *up stream.* Well, you 've got to admire men that deal in
ideas of that size and can tote them around without crutches
but you have n't got to believe they can *do* such miracles
have you? And yet you ain't absolutely obliged to believe they
can't. I reckon the safe way, where a man can afford it, is to
copper the operation, and at the same time buy enough property in Vicksburg to square you up in case they win. Government is doing a deal for the Mississippi, now—spending
loads of money on her. When there used to be four thousand
steamboats and ten thousand acres of coal-barges, and rafts
and trading scows, there was n't a lantern from St. Paul to
New Orleans, and the snags were thicker than bristles on a
hog's back; and now when there 's three dozen steamboats
and nary barge or raft, Government has snatched out all the
snags, and lit up the shores like Broadway, and a boat 's as
safe on the river as she 'd be in heaven. And I reckon that by

the time there ain't any boats left at all, the Commission will have the old thing all reorganized, and dredged out, and fenced in, and tidied up, to a degree that will make navigation just simply perfect, and absolutely safe and profitable; and all the days will be Sundays, and all the mates will be Sunday-school suWHAT-*in-the-nation-you-fooling-around-there-for, you sons of unrighteousness, heirs of perdition! Going to be a* YEAR *getting that hogshead ashore?*"

During our trip to New Orleans and back, we had many conversations with river men, planters, journalists, and offi-cers of the River Commission—with conflicting and confus-ing results. To wit:—

1. Some believed in the Commission's scheme to arbitrarily and permanently confine (and thus deepen) the channel, pre-serve threatened shores, etc.

2. Some believed that the Commission's money ought to be spent only on building and repairing the great system of levees.

3. Some believed that the higher you build your levee, the higher the river's bottom will rise; and that consequently the levee system is a mistake.

4. Some believed in the scheme to relieve the river, in flood-time, by turning its surplus waters off into Lake Borgne, etc.

5. Some believed in the scheme of northern lake-reservoirs to replenish the Mississippi in low-water seasons.

Wherever you find a man down there who believes in one of these theories you may turn to the next man and frame your talk upon the hypothesis that he does *not* believe in that theory; and after you have had experience, you do not take this course doubtfully, or hesitatingly, but with the confi-dence of a dying murderer—converted one, I mean. For you will have come to know, with a deep and restful certainty, that you are not going to meet two people sick of the same theory, one right after the other. No, there will always be one or two with the other diseases along between. And as you proceed, you will find out one or two other things. You will find out that there is no distemper of the lot but is contagious; and you cannot go where it is without catching it. You may vaccinate yourself with deterrent facts as much as you please—it will do no good; it will seem to "take," but it does n't; the moment you rub against any one of those theorists, make up your mind that it is time to hang out your yellow flag.

Yes, you are his sure victim: yet his work is not all to your hurt—only part of it; for he is like your family physician, who comes and cures the mumps, and leaves the scarlet-fever behind. If your man is a Lake-Borgne-relief theorist, for instance, he will exhale a cloud of deadly facts and statistics which will lay you out with that disease, sure; but at the same time he will cure you of any other of the five theories that may have previously got into your system.

I have had all the five; and had them "bad;" but ask me not, in mournful numbers, which one racked me hardest, or which one numbered the biggest sick list, for I do not know. In truth, no one can answer the latter question. Mississippi Improvement is a mighty topic, down yonder. Every man on the river banks, south of Cairo, talks about it every day, during such moments as he is able to spare from talking about the war; and each of the several chief theories has its host of zealous partisans; but, as I have said, it is not possible to determine which cause numbers the most recruits.

All were agreed upon one point, however: if Congress would make a sufficient appropriation, a colossal benefit would result. Very well; since then the appropriation has been made—possibly a sufficient one, certainly not too large a one. Let us hope that the prophecy will be amply fulfilled.

One thing will be easily granted by the reader; that an opinion from Mr. Edward Atkinson, upon any vast national commercial matter, comes as near ranking as authority, as can the opinion of any individual in the Union. What he has to say about Mississippi River Improvement will be found in the Appendix.[1]

Sometimes, half a dozen figures will reveal, as with a lightning-flash, the importance of a subject which ten thousand labored words, with the same purpose in view, had left at last

[1]See Appendix B.

but dim and uncertain. Here is a case of the sort—paragraph from the "Cincinnati Commercial:"—

"The towboat 'Jos. B. Williams' is on her way to New Orleans with a tow of thirty-two barges, containing six hundred thousand bushels (seventy-six pounds to the bushel) of coal exclusive of her own fuel, being the largest tow ever taken to New Orleans or anywhere else in the world. Her freight bill, at 3 cents a bushel, amounts to $18,000. It would take eighteen hundred cars, of three hundred and thirty-three bushels to the car, to transport this amount of coal. At $10 per ton, or $100 per car, which would be a fair price for the distance by rail, the freight bill would amount to $180,000, or $162,000 more by rail than by river. The tow will be taken from Pittsburg to New Orleans in fourteen or fifteen days. It would take one hundred trains of eighteen cars to the train to transport this one tow of six hundred thousand bushels of coal, and even if it made the usual speed of fast freight lines, it would take one whole summer to put it through by rail."

When a river in good condition can enable one to save $162,000 and a whole summer's time, on a single cargo, the wisdom of taking measures to keep the river in good condition is made plain to even the uncommercial mind.

XXIX.

A Few Specimen Bricks

WE PASSED through the Plum Point region, turned
Craighead's Point, and glided unchallenged by what
was once the formidable Fort Pillow, memorable because of
the massacre perpetrated there during the war. Massacres are
sprinkled with some frequency through the histories of several Christian nations, but this is almost the only one that can
be found in American history; perhaps it is the only one
which rises to a size correspondent to that huge and sombre
title. We have the "Boston Massacre," where two or three
people were killed; but we must bunch Anglo-Saxon history
together to find the fellow to the Fort Pillow tragedy; and
doubtless even then we must travel back to the days and the
performances of Cœur de Lion, that fine "hero," before we
accomplish it.

More of the river's freaks. In times past, the channel used
to strike above Island 37, by Brandywine Bar, and down towards Island 39. Afterward, changed its course and went from
Brandywine down through Vogelman's chute in the Devil's
Elbow, to Island 39—part of this course reversing the old
order; the river running *up* four or five miles, instead of
down, and cutting off, throughout, some fifteen miles of distance. This in 1876. All that region is now called Centennial
Island.

There is a tradition that Island 37 was one of the principal
abiding places of the once celebrated "Murel's Gang." This
was a colossal combination of robbers, horse-thieves, negro-
stealers, and counterfeiters, engaged in business along the
river some fifty or sixty years ago. While our journey across
the country towards St. Louis was in progress we had had no
end of Jesse James and his stirring history; for he had just
been assassinated by an agent of the Governor of Missouri,
and was in consequence occupying a good deal of space in
the newspapers. Cheap histories of him were for sale by train
boys. According to these, he was the most marvellous creature of his kind that had ever existed. It was a mistake. Murel

was his equal in boldness; in pluck; in rapacity; in cruelty, brutality, heartlessness, treachery, and in general and comprehensive vileness and shamelessness; and very much his superior in some larger aspects. James was a retail rascal; Murel, wholesale. James's modest genius dreamed of no loftier flight than the planning of raids upon cars, coaches, and country banks; Murel projected negro insurrections and the capture of New Orleans; and furthermore, on occasion, this Murel could go into a pulpit and edify the congregation. What are James and his half-dozen vulgar rascals compared with this stately old-time criminal, with his sermons, his meditated insurrections and city-captures, and his majestic following of ten hundred men, sworn to do his evil will!

Here is a paragraph or two concerning this big operator, from a now forgotten book which was published half a century ago:—

He appears to have been a most dexterous as well as consummate villain. When he travelled, his usual disguise was that of an itinerant preacher; and it is said that his discourses were very "soul-moving"—interesting the hearers so much that they forgot to look after their horses, which were carried away by his confederates while he was preaching. But the stealing of horses in one State, and selling them in another, was but a small portion of their business; the most lucrative was the enticing slaves to run away from their masters, that they might sell them in another quarter. This was arranged as follows; they would tell a negro that if he would run away from his master, and allow them to sell him, he should receive a portion of the money paid for him, and that upon his return to them a second time they would send him to a free State, where he would be safe. The poor wretches complied with this request, hoping to obtain money and freedom; they would be sold to another master, and run away again to their employers; sometimes they would be sold in this manner three or four times, until they had realized three or four thousand dollars by them; but as, after this, there was fear of detection, the usual custom was to get rid of the only witness that could be produced against them, which was the negro himself, by murdering him, and throwing his body into the Mississippi. Even if it was established that they had stolen a negro, before he was murdered, they were always prepared to evade punishment; for they concealed the negro who had run away, until he was advertised, and a reward offered to any man who would catch him. An advertisement of this kind warrants the person to take the property, if found. And then the negro becomes a property in trust, when, therefore, they sold the negro, it only became a breach of trust, not stealing; and for a breach of trust, the owner of the property can only have redress by a civil action, which was useless, as the damages were never paid. It may be inquired, how it was that Murel escaped Lynch law under such circumstances? This will be easily understood when it is stated that he had *more than a thousand sworn confederates,* all ready at a moment's notice to support any of the gang who might be in trouble. The names of all the principal confederates of Murel were obtained from himself, in a manner which I shall presently explain. The gang was composed of two classes: the Heads or Council, as they were called, who planned and concerted, but seldom acted; they amounted to about four hundred. The other class were the active agents, and were termed strikers, and amounted to about six hundred and fifty. These were the tools in the hands of the others; they ran all the risk, and received but a small portion of the money; they were in the power of the leaders of the gang, who would sacrifice them at any time by handing them over to justice, or sinking their bodies in the Mississippi. The general rendezvous of this gang of miscreants was on the Arkansas side of the river, where they concealed their negroes in the morasses and canebrakes.

The depredations of this extensive combination were severely felt; but so well were their plans arranged, that although Murel, who was always active, was everywhere suspected, there was no proof to be obtained. It so happened, however, that a young man of the name of Stewart, who was looking after two slaves which Murel had decoyed away, fell in with him and obtained his confidence, took the oath, and was admitted into the gang as one of the

General Council. By this means all was discovered; for Stewart turned traitor, although he had taken the oath, and having obtained every information, exposed the whole concern, the names of all the parties, and finally succeeded in bringing home sufficient evidence against Murel, to procure his conviction and sentence to the Penitentiary (Murel was sentenced to fourteen years' imprisonment); so many people who were supposed to be honest, and bore a respectable name in the different States, were found to be among the list of the Grand Council as published by Stewart, that every attempt was made to throw discredit upon his assertions—his character was vilified, and more than one attempt was made to assassinate him. He was obliged to quit the Southern States in consequence. It is, however, now well ascertained to have been all true; and although some blame Mr. Stewart for having violated his oath, they no longer attempt to deny that his revelations were correct. I will quote one or two portions of Murel's confessions to Mr. Stewart, made to him when they were journeying together. I ought to have observed, that the ultimate intentions of Murel and his associates were, by his own account, on a very extended scale; having no less an object in view than *raising the blacks against the whites, taking possession of, and plundering New Orleans, and making themselves possessors of the territory.* The following are a few extracts:—

"I collected all my friends about New Orleans at one of our friends' houses in that place, and we sat in council three days before we got all our plans to our notion; we then determined to undertake the rebellion at every hazard, and make as many friends as we could for that purpose. Every man's business being assigned him, I started to Natchez on foot, having sold my horse in New Orleans,—with the intention of stealing another after I started. I walked four days, and no opportunity offered for me to get a horse. The fifth day, about twelve, I had become tired, and stopped at a creek to get some water and rest a little. While I was sitting on a log, looking down the road the way that I had come, a man came in sight riding on a good-looking horse. The very moment I saw him, I was determined to have his horse, if he was in the garb of a traveller. He rode

up, and I saw from his equipage that he was a traveller.
arose and drew an elegant rifle pistol on him and ordered
him to dismount. He did so, and I took his horse by the
bridle and pointed down the creek, and ordered him to
walk before me. He went a few hundred yards and stopped.
I hitched his horse, and then made him undress himself, all
to his shirt and drawers, and ordered him to turn his back
to me. He said, 'If you are determined to kill me, let me
have time to pray before I die.' I told him I had no time to
hear him pray. He turned around and dropped on his
knees, and I shot him through the back of the head. .
ripped open his belly and took out his entrails, and sunk
him in the creek. I then searched his pockets, and found
four hundred dollars and thirty seven cents, and a number
of papers that I did not take time to examine. I sunk the
pocket-book and papers and his hat, in the creek. His boots
were bran-new, and fitted me genteelly; and I put them on
and sunk my old shoes in the creek, to atone for them.
rolled up his clothes and put them into his portmanteau, a.
they were bran-new cloth of the best quality. I mounted a.
fine a horse as ever I straddled, and directed my course for
Natchez in much better style than I had been for the las
five days.

"Myself and a fellow by the name of Crenshaw gathered
four good horses and started for Georgia. We got in com
pany with a young South Carolinian just before we got to
Cumberland Mountain, and Crenshaw soon knew all about
his business. He had been to Tennessee to buy a drove o
hogs, but when he got there pork was dearer than he cal
culated, and he declined purchasing. We concluded he was
a prize. Crenshaw winked at me; I understood his idea
Crenshaw had travelled the road before, but I never had
we had travelled several miles on the mountain, when he
passed near a great precipice; just before we passed it Cren
shaw asked me for my whip, which had a pound of lead in
the butt; I handed it to him, and he rode up by the side o
the South Carolinian, and gave him a blow on the side o
the head and tumbled him from his horse; we lit from our
horses and fingered his pockets; we got twelve hundred and
sixty-two dollars. Crenshaw said he knew a place to hide

him, and he gathered him under his arms, and I by his feet, and conveyed him to a deep crevice in the brow of the precipice, and tumbled him into it, and he went out of sight; we then tumbled in his saddle, and took his horse with us, which was worth two hundred dollars.

"We were detained a few days, and during that time our friend went to a little village in the neighborhood and saw the negro advertised (a negro in our possession), and a description of the two men of whom he had been purchased, and giving his suspicions of the men. It was rather squally times, but any port in a storm: we took the negro that night on the bank of a creek which runs by the farm of our friend, and Crenshaw shot him through the head. We took out his entrails and sunk him in the creek.

"He had sold the other negro the third time on Arkansaw River for upwards of five hundred dollars; and then stole him and delivered him into the hand of his friend, who conducted him to a swamp, and veiled the tragic scene, and got the last gleanings and sacred pledge of secrecy; as a game of that kind will not do unless it ends in a mystery to all but the fraternity. He sold the negro, first and last, for nearly two thousand dollars, and then put him forever out of the reach of all pursuers; and they can never graze him unless they can find the negro; and that they cannot do, for his carcass has fed many a tortoise and catfish before this time, and the frogs have sung this many a long day to the silent repose of his skeleton."

We were approaching Memphis, in front of which city, and witnessed by its people, was fought the most famous of the river battles of the Civil War. Two men whom I had served under, in my river days, took part in that fight: Mr. Bixby, head pilot of the Union fleet, and Montgomery, Commodore of the Confederate fleet. Both saw a great deal of active service during the war, and achieved high reputations for pluck and capacity.

As we neared Memphis, we began to cast about for an excuse to stay with the "Gold Dust" to the end of her course—Vicksburg. We were so pleasantly situated, that we did not wish to make a change. I had an errand of considerable im-

portance to do at Napoleon, Arkansas, but perhaps I cou[...]
manage it without quitting the "Gold Dust." I said as muc[...]
so we decided to stick to present quarters.

The boat was to tarry at Memphis till ten the next mor[...]
ing. It is a beautiful city, nobly situated on a commandin[...]
bluff overlooking the river. The streets are straight and sp[...]
cious, though not paved in a way to incite distempered a[...]
miration. No, the admiration must be reserved for the town
sewerage system, which is called perfect; a recent reform
however, for it was just the other way, up to a few yea[...]
ago—a reform resulting from the lesson taught by a desola[...]
ing visitation of the yellow-fever. In those awful days the pe[...]
ple were swept off by hundreds, by thousands; and so gre[...]
was the reduction caused by flight and by death together, tha[...]
the population was diminished three-fourths, and so r[...]
mained for a time. Business stood nearly still, and the stree[...]
bore an empty Sunday aspect.

Here is a picture of Memphis, at that disastrous tim[...]
drawn by a German tourist who seems to have been an ey[...]
witness of the scenes which he describes. It is from Chapt[...]
VII., of his book, just published, in Leipzig, "Mississipp[...]
Fahrten, von Ernst von Hesse-Wartegg:"—

"In August the yellow-fever had reached its extreme[...]
height. Daily, hundreds fell a sacrifice to the terrible ep[...]
demic. The city was become a mighty graveyard, two-thir[...]
of the population had deserted the place, and only th[...]
poor, the aged and the sick, remained behind, a sure pre[...]
for the insidious enemy. The houses were closed: litt[...]
lamps burned in front of many—a sign that here death ha[...]
entered. Often, several lay dead in a single house; from th[...]
windows hung black crape. The stores were shut up, fo[...]
their owners were gone away or dead.

"Fearful evil! In the briefest space it struck down an[...]
swept away even the most vigorous victim. A slight indis[...]
position, then an hour of fever, then the hideous deliriur[...]
then—the Yellow Death! On the street corners, and in th[...]
squares, lay sick men, suddenly overtaken by the disease
and even corpses, distorted and rigid. Food failed. Mea[...]

spoiled in a few hours in the fetid and pestiferous air, and turned black.

"Fearful clamors issue from many houses; then after a season they cease, and all is still: noble, self-sacrificing men come with the coffin, nail it up, and carry it away, to the graveyard. In the night stillness reigns. Only the physicians and the hearses hurry through the streets; and out of the distance, at intervals, comes the muffled thunder of the railway train, which with the speed of the wind, and as if hunted by furies, flies by the pest-ridden city without halting."

But there is life enough there now. The population exceeds orty thousand and is augmenting, and trade is in a flourishng condition. We drove about the city; visited the park and he sociable horde of squirrels there; saw the fine residences, ose-clad and in other ways enticing to the eye; and got a ;ood breakfast at the hotel.

A thriving place is the Good Samaritan City of the Missisippi: has a great wholesale jobbing trade; foundries, machine hops; and manufactories of wagons, carriages, and cottoned oil; and is shortly to have cotton mills and elevators.

Her cotton receipts reached five hundred thousand bales ast year—an increase of sixty thousand over the year before.)ut from her healthy commercial heart issue five trunk lines)f railway; and a sixth is being added.

This is a very different Memphis from the one which the anished and unremembered procession of foreign tourists ised to put into their books long time ago. In the days of the 10w forgotten but once renowned and vigorously hated Mrs. Trollope, Memphis seems to have consisted mainly of one ong street of log-houses, with some outlying cabins sprinkled around rearward toward the woods; and now and then a pig, and no end of mud. That was fifty-five years ago. She stopped at the hotel. Plainly it was not the one which gave us our breakfast. She says:—

"The table was laid for fifty persons, and was nearly full. They ate in perfect silence, and with such astonishing rapidity that their dinner was over literally before ours was

begun; the only sounds heard were those produced by tl
knives and forks, with the unceasing chorus of coughin,
etc."

"Coughing, *etc.*" The "etc." stands for an unpleasant wor
there, a word which she does not always charitably cover u
but sometimes prints. You will find it in the following d
scription of a steamboat dinner which she ate in compar
with a lot of aristocratic planters; wealthy, well-born, ign
rant swells they were, tinselled with the usual harmless mil
tary and judicial titles of that old day of cheap shams an
windy pretence:—

"The total want of all the usual courtesies of the tabl
the voracious rapidity with which the viands were seize
and devoured; the strange uncouth phrases and pronunc
ation; the loathsome spitting, from the contamination (
which it was absolutely impossible to protect our dresse
the frightful manner of feeding with their knives, till tl
whole blade seemed to enter into the mouth; and the st
more frightful manner of cleaning the teeth afterward wi
a pocket knife, soon forced us to feel that we were n
surrounded by the generals, colonels, and majors of the o
world; and that the dinner hour was to be anything rath
than an hour of enjoyment."

XXX.

Sketches by the Way

I<small>T WAS</small> a big river, below Memphis; banks brimming full, everywhere, and very frequently more than full, the waters pouring out over the land, flooding the woods and fields for miles into the interior; and in places, to a depth of fifteen feet; signs, all about, of men's hard work gone to ruin, and all to be done over again, with straitened means and a weakened courage. A melancholy picture, and a continuous one;—hundreds of miles of it. Sometimes the beacon lights stood in water three feet deep, in the edge of dense forests which extended for miles without farm, wood-yard, clearing, or break of any kind; which meant that the keeper of the light must come in a skiff a great distance to discharge his trust,—and often in desperate weather. Yet I was told that the work is faithfully performed, in all weathers; and not always by men, sometimes by women, if the man is sick or absent. The Government furnishes oil, and pays ten or fifteen dollars a month for the lighting and tending. A Government boat distributes oil and pays wages once a month.

The Ship Island region was as woodsy and tenantless as ever. The island has ceased to be an island; has joined itself compactly to the main shore, and wagons travel, now, where the steamboats used to navigate. No signs left of the wreck of the "Pennsylvania." Some farmer will turn up her bones with his plow one day, no doubt, and be surprised.

We were getting down now into the migrating negro region. These poor people could never travel when they were slaves; so they make up for the privation now. They stay on a plantation till the desire to travel seizes them; then they pack up, hail a steamboat, and clear out. Not for any particular place; no, nearly any place will answer; they only want to be moving. The amount of money on hand will answer the rest of the conundrum for them. If it will take them fifty miles, very well; let it be fifty. If not, a shorter flight will do.

During a couple of days, we frequently answered these hails. Sometimes there was a group of high-water-stained, tumble-down cabins, populous with colored folk, and no whites visible; with grassless patches of dry ground here and there; a few felled trees, with skeleton cattle, mules, and horses, eating the leaves and gnawing the bark—no other food for them in the flood-wasted land. Sometimes there was a single lonely landing-cabin; near it the colored family that had hailed us; little and big, old and young, roosting on the scant pile of household goods; these consisting of a rusty gun, some bedticks, chests, tinware, stools, a crippled looking-glass, a venerable arm-chair, and six or eight base-born and spiritless yellow curs, attached to the family by strings. They must have their dogs; can't go without their dogs. Yet the dogs are never willing; they always object; so, one after another, in ridiculous procession, they are dragged aboard; all four feet braced and sliding along the stage, head likely to be pulled off; but the tugger marching determinedly forward, bending to his work, with the rope over his shoulder for better purchase. Sometimes a child is forgotten and left on the bank; but never a dog.

The usual river-gossip going on in the pilot-house. Island No. 63—an island with a lovely "chute," or passage, behind it in the former times. They said Jesse Jamieson, in the "Skylark," had a visiting pilot with him one trip—a poor old broken-down, superannuated fellow—left him at the wheel, at the foot of 63, to run off the watch. The ancient mariner went up through the chute, and down the river outside; and up the chute and down the river again; and yet again and again; and handed the boat over to the relieving pilot, at the end of three hours of honest endeavor, at the same old foot of the island where he had originally taken the wheel! A darkey on shore who had observed the boat go by, about thirteen times, said, " 'clar to gracious, I would n't be s'prised if dey 's a whole line o' dem Sk'ylarks!"

Anecdote illustrative of influence of reputation in the changing of opinion. The "Eclipse" was renowned for her swiftness. One day she passed along; an old darkey on shore, absorbed in his own matters, did not notice what steamer it was. Presently some one asked:—

"Any boat gone up?"

"Yes, sah."

"Was she going fast?"

"Oh, so-so—loafin' along."

"Now, do you know what boat that was?"

"No, sah."

"Why, uncle, that was the 'Eclipse.' "

"No! Is dat so? Well, I bet it was—cause she jes' went by here a-*sparklin'*!"

Piece of history illustrative of the violent style of some of the people down along here. During the early weeks of high water, A's fence rails washed down on B's ground, and B's rails washed up in the eddy and landed on A's ground. A said, "Let the thing remain so; I will use your rails, and you use mine." But B objected—would n't have it so. One day, A came down on B's ground to get his rails. B said, "I 'll kill you!" and proceeded for him with his revolver. A said, "I 'm not armed." So B, who wished to do only what was right, threw down his revolver; then pulled a knife, and cut A's throat all around, but gave his principal attention to the front, and so failed to sever the jugular. Struggling around, A managed to get his hands on the discarded revolver, and shot B dead with it—and recovered from his own injuries.

Further gossip;—after which, everybody went below to get afternoon coffee, and left me at the wheel, alone. Something presently reminded me of our last hour in St. Louis, part of which I spent on this boat's hurricane deck, aft. I was joined there by a stranger, who dropped into conversation with me—a brisk young fellow, who said he was born in a town in the interior of Wisconsin, and had never seen a steamboat until a week before. Also said that on the way down from La Crosse he had inspected and examined his boat so diligently and with such passionate interest that he had mastered the whole thing from stem to rudder-blade. Asked me where I was from. I answered, New England. "Oh, a Yank!" said he; and went chatting straight along, without waiting for assent or denial. He immediately proposed to take me all over the boat and tell me the names of her different parts, and teach me their uses. Before I could enter protest or excuse, he was already rattling glibly away at his benevolent work; and when I perceived that he was misnaming the things, and inhospitably amusing himself at the expense of an

innocent stranger from a far country, I held my peace, and let
him have his way. He gave me a world of misinformation,
and the further he went, the wider his imagination expanded,
and the more he enjoyed his cruel work of deceit. Sometimes,
after palming off a particularly fantastic and outrageous lie
upon me, he was so "full of laugh" that he had to step aside
for a minute, upon one pretext or another, to keep me from
suspecting. I staid faithfully by him until his comedy was finished. Then he remarked that he had undertaken to "learn"
me all about a steamboat, and had done it; but that if he had
overlooked anything, just ask him and he would supply the
lack. "Anything about this boat that you don't know the
name of or the purpose of, you come to me and I'll tell you."
I said I would, and took my departure; disappeared, and approached him from another quarter, whence he could not see
me. There he sat, all alone, doubling himself up and writhing
this way and that, in the throes of unappeasable laughter. He
must have made himself sick; for he was not publicly visible
afterward for several days. Meantime, the episode dropped
out of my mind.

The thing that reminded me of it now, when I was alone
at the wheel, was the spectacle of this young fellow standing
in the pilot-house door, with the knob in his hand, silently
and severely inspecting me. I don't know when I have seen
anybody look so injured as he did. He did not say anything—
simply stood there and looked; reproachfully looked and pon-
dered. Finally he shut the door, and started away; halted on
the texas a minute; came slowly back and stood in the door
again, with that grieved look in his face; gazed upon me a
while in meek rebuke, then said:—

"You let me learn you all about a steamboat, *did n't* you?"

"Yes," I confessed.

"Yes, you did—*did n't* you?"

"Yes."

"*You* are the feller that—that—"

Language failed. Pause—impotent struggle for further
words—then he gave it up, choked out a deep, strong oath,
and departed for good. Afterward I saw him several times
below during the trip; but he was cold—would not look at
me. Idiot, if he had not been in such a sweat to play his

witless practical joke upon me, in the beginning, I would have persuaded his thoughts into some other direction, and saved him from committing that wanton and silly impoliteness.

I had myself called with the four o'clock watch, mornings, for one cannot see too many summer sunrises on the Mississippi. They are enchanting. First, there is the eloquence of silence; for a deep hush broods everywhere. Next, there is the haunting sense of loneliness, isolation, remoteness from the worry and bustle of the world. The dawn creeps in stealthily; the solid walls of black forest soften to gray, and vast stretches of the river open up and reveal themselves; the water is glass-smooth, gives off spectral little wreaths of white mist, there is not the faintest breath of wind, nor stir of leaf; the tranquillity is profound and infinitely satisfying. Then a bird pipes up, another follows, and soon the pipings develop into a jubilant riot of music. You see none of the birds; you simply move through an atmosphere of song which seems to sing itself. When the light has become a little stronger, you have one of the fairest and softest pictures imaginable. You have the intense green of the massed and crowded foliage near by; you see it paling shade by shade in front of you; upon the next projecting cape, a mile off or more, the tint has lightened to the tender young green of spring; the cape beyond that one has almost lost color, and the furthest one, miles away under the horizon, sleeps upon the water a mere dim vapor, and hardly separable from the sky above it and about it. And all this stretch of river is a mirror, and you have the shadowy reflections of the leafage and the curving shores and the receding capes pictured in it. Well, that is all beautiful; soft and rich and beautiful; and when the sun gets well up, and distributes a pink flush here and a powder of gold yonder and a purple haze where it will yield the best effect, you grant that you have seen something that is worth remembering.

We had the Kentucky Bend country in the early morning— scene of a strange and tragic accident in the old times. Captain Poe had a small stern-wheel boat, for years the home of himself and his wife. One night the boat struck a snag in the head of Kentucky Bend, and sank with astonishing suddenness; water already well above the cabin floor when the captain got aft. So he cut into his wife's stateroom from above with an axe; she was asleep in the upper berth, the roof a flimsier one than was supposed; the first blow crashed down through the rotten boards and clove her skull.

This bend is all filled up now—result of a cut-off; and the same agent has taken the great and once much-frequented Walnut Bend, and set it away back in a solitude far from the accustomed track of passing steamers.

Helena we visited, and also a town I had not heard of before, it being of recent birth—Arkansas City. It was born of a railway; the Little Rock, Mississippi River and Texas Railroad touches the river there. We asked a passenger who belonged there what sort of a place it was. "Well," said he, after considering, and with the air of one who wishes to take time and be accurate, "It's a hell of a place." A description which was photographic for exactness. There were several rows and clusters of shabby frame-houses, and a supply of mud sufficient to insure the town against a famine in that article for a hundred years; for the overflow had but lately subsided. There were stagnant ponds in the streets, here and there, and a dozen rude scows were scattered about, lying aground wherever they happened to have been when the water drained off and people could do their visiting and shopping on foot once more. Still, it is a thriving place, with a rich country behind it, an elevator in front of it, and also a fine big mill for the manufacture of cotton-seed oil. I had never seen this kind of a mill before.

Cotton-seed was comparatively valueless in my time; but it is worth $12 or $13 a ton now, and none of it is thrown away. The oil made from it is colorless, tasteless, and almost if not entirely odorless. It is claimed that it can, by proper manipulation, be made to resemble and perform the office of any and all oils, and be produced at a cheaper rate than the cheapest of the originals. Sagacious people shipped it to Italy, doctored it, labelled it, and brought it back as olive oil. This trade grew to be so formidable that Italy was obliged to put a prohibitory impost upon it to keep it from working serious injury to her oil industry.

Helena occupies one of the prettiest situations on the Mississippi. Her perch is the last, the southernmost group of hills which one sees on that side of the river. In its normal condition it is a pretty town; but the flood (or possibly the seepage) had lately been ravaging it; whole streets of houses had been invaded by the muddy water, and the outsides of the buildings were still belted with a broad stain extending upwards from the foundations. Stranded and discarded scows lay all about; plank sidewalks on stilts four feet high were still standing; the board sidewalks on the ground level were loose and ruinous,—a couple of men trotting along them could make a blind man think a cavalry charge was coming; everywhere the mud was black and deep, and in many places malarious pools of stagnant water were standing. A Mississippi inundation is the next most wasting and desolating infliction to a fire.

We had an enjoyable time here, on this sunny Sunday: two full hours' liberty ashore while the boat discharged freight. In the back streets but few white people were visible, but there were plenty of colored folk—mainly women and girls; and almost without exception upholstered in bright new clothes of swell and elaborate style and cut—a glaring and hilarious contrast to the mournful mud and the pensive puddles.

Helena is the second town in Arkansas, in point of population—which is placed at five thousand. The country about it is exceptionally productive. Helena has a good cotton trade; handles from forty to sixty thousand bales annually; she has a large lumber and grain commerce; has a foundry, oil mills, machine shops and wagon factories—in brief has $1,000,000 invested in manufacturing industries. She has two railways, and is the commercial centre of a broad and prosperous region. Her gross receipts of money, annually, from all sources, are placed by the New Orleans "Times-Democrat" at $4,000,000.

XXXI.

A Thumb-Print and What Came of It

W<small>E WERE</small> approaching Napoleon, Arkansas. So I began to think about my errand there. Time, noonday; and bright and sunny. This was bad—not best, anyway; for mine was not (preferably) a noonday kind of errand. The more I thought, the more that fact pushed itself upon me— now in one form, now in another. Finally, it took the form of a distinct question: is it good common sense to do the errand in daytime, when, by a little sacrifice of comfort and inclination, you can have night for it, and no inquisitive eyes around? This settled it. Plain question and plain answer make the shortest road out of most perplexities.

I got my friends into my stateroom, and said I was sorry to create annoyance and disappointment, but that upon reflection it really seemed best that we put our luggage ashore and stop over at Napoleon. Their disapproval was prompt and loud; their language mutinous. Their main argument was one which has always been the first to come to the surface, in such cases, since the beginning of time: "But you decided and *agreed* to stick to this boat, etc.;" as if, having determined to do an unwise thing, one is thereby bound to go ahead and make *two* unwise things of it, by carrying out that determination.

I tried various mollifying tactics upon them, with reasonably good success: under which encouragement, I increased my efforts; and, to show them that *I* had not created this annoying errand, and was in no way to blame for it, I presently drifted into its history—substantially as follows:

Toward the end of last year, I spent a few months in Munich, Bavaria. In November I was living in Fräulein Dahlweiner's *pension*, 1*a*, Karlstrasse; but my working quarters were a mile from there, in the house of a widow who supported herself by taking lodgers. She and her two young children used to drop in every morning and talk German to me— by request. One day, during a ramble about the city, I visited one of the two establishments where the Government keeps and watches corpses until the doctors decide that they are permanently dead, and not in a trance state. It was a grisly place, that spacious room. There were thirty-six corpses of adults in sight, stretched on their backs on slightly slanted boards, in three long rows—all of them with wax-white, rigid faces, and all of them wrapped in white shrouds. Along the sides of the room were deep alcoves, like bay windows; and in each of these lay several marble-visaged babes, utterly hidden and buried under banks of fresh flowers, all but their faces and crossed hands. Around a finger of each of these fifty still forms, both great and small, was a ring; and from the ring a wire led to the ceiling, and thence to a bell in a watch-room yonder, where, day and night, a watchman sits always alert and ready to spring to the aid of any of that pallid company who, waking out of death, shall make a movement—for any even the slightest movement will twitch the wire and ring that fearful bell. I imagined myself a death-sentinel drowsing there alone, far in the dragging watches of some wailing, gusty night, and having in a twinkling all my body stricken to quivering jelly by the sudden clamor of that awful summons! So I inquired about this thing; asked what resulted usually? if the watchman died, and the restored corpse came and did what it could to make his last moments easy? But I was rebuked for trying to feed an idle and frivolous curiosity in so solemn and so mournful a place; and went my way with a humbled crest.

Next morning I was telling the widow my adventure, when she exclaimed—

"Come with me! I have a lodger who shall tell you all you want to know. He has been a night watchman there."

He was a living man, but he did not look it. He was abed, and had his head propped high on pillows; his face was wasted and colorless, his deep-sunken eyes were shut; his hand, lying on his breast, was talon-like, it was so bony and long-fingered. The widow began her introduction of me. The man's eyes opened slowly, and glittered wickedly out from the twilight of their caverns; he frowned a black frown; he lifted his lean hand and waved us peremptorily away. But the widow kept straight on, till she had got out the fact that I was a stranger and an American. The man's face changed at once; brightened, became even eager—and the next moment he and I were alone together.

I opened up in cast-iron German; he responded in quite flexible English; thereafter we gave the German language a permanent rest.

This consumptive and I became good friends. I visited him every day, and we talked about everything. At least, about everything but wives and children. Let anybody's wife or anybody's child be mentioned, and three things always followed: the most gracious and loving and tender light glimmered in the man's eyes for a moment; faded out the next, and in its place came that deadly look which had flamed there the first time I ever saw his lids unclose; thirdly, he ceased from speech, there and then for that day; lay silent, abstracted, and absorbed; apparently heard nothing that I said; took no notice of my good-byes, and plainly did not know, by either sight or hearing, when I left the room.

When I had been this Karl Ritter's daily and sole intimate during two months, he one day said, abruptly,—

"I will tell you my story."

A DYING MAN'S CONFESSION

Then he went on as follows:—

I have never given up, until now. But now I have given up. I am going to die. I made up my mind last night that it must be, and very soon, too. You say you are going to revisit your river, by and by, when you find opportunity. Very well; that, together with a certain strange experience which fell to my lot last night, determines me to tell you my history—for you will see Napoleon, Arkansas; and for my sake you will stop there, and do a certain thing for me—a thing which you will willingly undertake after you shall have heard my narrative.

Let us shorten the story wherever we can, for it will need it, being long. You already know how I came to go to America, and how I came to settle in that lonely region in the South. But you do not know that I had a wife. My wife was young, beautiful, loving, and oh, so divinely good and blameless and gentle! And our little girl was her mother in miniature. It was the happiest of happy households.

One night—it was toward the close of the war—I woke up out of a sodden lethargy, and found myself bound and gagged, and the air tainted with chloroform! I saw two men in the room, and one was saying to the other, in a hoarse whisper, "I *told* her I would, if she made a noise, and as for the child—"

The other man interrupted in a low, half-crying voice—

"You said we'd only gag them and rob them, not hurt them; or I would n't have come."

"Shut up your whining; *had* to change the plan when they waked up; you done all *you* could to protect them, now let that satisfy you; come, help rummage."

Both men were masked, and wore coarse, ragged "nigger" clothes; they had a bull's-eye lantern, and by its light I noticed that the gentler robber had no thumb on his right hand. They rummaged around my poor cabin for a moment; the head bandit then said, in his stage whisper,—

"It 's a waste of time—*he* shall tell where it 's hid. Undo his gag, and revive him up."

The other said—

"All right—provided no clubbing."

"No clubbing it is, then—provided he keeps still."

They approached me; just then there was a sound outside; a sound of voices and trampling hoofs; the robbers held their breath and listened; the sounds came slowly nearer and nearer; then came a shout—

"*Hello*, the house! Show a light, we want water."

"The captain's voice, by G—!" said the stage-whispering ruffian, and both robbers fled by the way of the back door, shutting off their bull's-eye as they ran.

The strangers shouted several times more, then rode by— there seemed to be a dozen of the horses—and I heard nothing more.

I struggled, but could not free myself from my bonds. I tried to speak, but the gag was effective; I could not make a sound. I listened for my wife's voice and my child's—listened long and intently, but no sound came from the other end of the room where their bed was. This silence became more and more awful, more and more ominous, every moment. Could you have endured an hour of it, do you think? Pity me, then, who had to endure three. Three hours?—it was three ages! Whenever the clock struck, it seemed as if years had gone by since I had heard it last. All this time I was struggling in my bonds; and at last, about dawn, I got myself free, and rose up and stretched my stiff limbs. I was able to distinguish details pretty well. The floor was littered with things thrown there by the robbers during their search for my savings. The first object that caught my particular attention was a document of mine which I had seen the rougher of the two ruffians glance at and then cast away. It had blood on it! I staggered to the other end of the room. Oh, poor unoffending, helpless ones, there they lay, their troubles ended, mine begun!

Did I appeal to the law—I? Does it quench the pauper's thirst if the King drink for him? Oh, no, no, no—I wanted no impertinent interference of the law. Laws and the gallows could not pay the debt that was owing to me! Let the laws leave the matter in my hands, and have no fears: I would find the debtor and collect the debt. How accomplish this, do you say? How accomplish it, and feel so sure about it, when I had neither seen the robbers' faces, nor heard their natural voices, nor had any idea who they might be? Nevertheless, I *was* sure—quite sure, quite confident. I had a clue—a clue which you would not have valued—a clue which would not have greatly helped even a detective, since he would lack the secret of how to apply it. I shall come to that, presently—you shall see. Let us go on, now, taking things in their due order. There was one circumstance which gave me a slant in a definite direction to begin with: Those two robbers were manifestly soldiers in tramp disguise; and not new to military service, but old in it—regulars, perhaps; they did not acquire their soldierly attitude, gestures, carriage, in a day, nor a month, nor yet in a year. So I thought, but said nothing. And one of them had said, "the captain's voice, by G—!"—the one whose life I would have. Two miles away, several regiments were in camp, and two companies of U. S. cavalry. When I learned that Captain Blakely, of Company C had passed our way, that night, with an escort, I said nothing, but in that company I resolved to seek my man. In conversation I studiously and persistently described the robbers as tramps,

ımp followers; and among this class the people made useless
:arch, none suspecting the soldiers but me.

Working patiently, by night, in my desolated home, I made
disguise for myself out of various odds and ends of cloth-
ıg; in the nearest village I bought a pair of blue goggles. By
nd by, when the military camp broke up, and Company C
ʹas ordered a hundred miles north, to Napoleon, I secreted
ıy small hoard of money in my belt, and took my departure
ı the night. When Company C arrived in Napoleon, I was
lready there. Yes, I was there, with a new trade—fortune-
:ller. Not to seem partial, I made friends and told fortunes
mong all the companies garrisoned there; but I gave Com-
any C the great bulk of my attentions. I made myself limit-
:ssly obliging to these particular men; they could ask me no
ıvor, put upon me no risk, which I would decline. I became
he willing butt of their jokes; this perfected my popularity;
became a favorite.

I early found a private who lacked a thumb—what joy it
ʹas to me! And when I found that he alone, of all the com-
ʹany, had lost a thumb, my last misgiving vanished; I was
ure I was on the right track. This man's name was Kruger, a
Ǧerman. There were nine Germans in the company. I
ʹatched, to see who might be his intimates; but he seemed
o have no especial intimates. But *I* was his intimate; and I
ook care to make the intimacy grow. Sometimes I so hun-
ʒered for my revenge that I could hardly restrain myself from
ʒoing on my knees and begging him to point out the man
ʹho had murdered my wife and child; but I managed to bri-
ile my tongue. I bided my time, and went on telling fortunes,
ıs opportunity offered.

My apparatus was simple: a little red paint and a bit of
ʹhite paper. I painted the ball of the client's thumb, took a
ɔrint of it on the paper, studied it that night, and revealed his
ʹortune to him next day. What was my idea in this nonsense?
[t was this: When I was a youth, I knew an old Frenchman
ʹho had been a prison-keeper for thirty years, and he told me
:hat there was one thing about a person which never changed,
rrom the cradle to the grave—the lines in the ball of the
:humb; and he said that these lines were never exactly alike in

the thumbs of any two human beings. In these days, we photograph the new criminal, and hang his picture in the Rogues
Gallery for future reference; but that Frenchman, in his day
used to take a print of the ball of a new prisoner's thumb and
put that away for future reference. He always said that pictures were no good—future disguises could make them useless; "The thumb 's the only sure thing," said he; "you can'
disguise that." And he used to prove his theory, too, on my
friends and acquaintances; it always succeeded.

I went on telling fortunes. Every night I shut myself in, all
alone, and studied the day's thumb-prints with a magnifying
glass. Imagine the devouring eagerness with which I pored
over those mazy red spirals, with that document by my side
which bore the right-hand thumb- and finger-marks of that
unknown murderer, printed with the dearest blood—to
me—that was ever shed on this earth! And many and many
a time I had to repeat the same old disappointed remark
"will they *never* correspond!"

But my reward came at last. It was the print of the thumb
of the forty-third man of Company C whom I had experimented on—private Franz Adler. An hour before, I did not
know the murderer's name, or voice, or figure, or face, or
nationality; but now I knew all these things! I believed I
might feel sure; the Frenchman's repeated demonstrations
being so good a warranty. Still, there was a way to *make* sure.
I had an impression of Kruger's left thumb. In the morning
I took him aside when he was off duty; and when we were
out of sight and hearing of witnesses, I said, impressively:—

"A part of your fortune is so grave, that I thought it would
be better for you if I did not tell it in public. You and another
man, whose fortune I was studying last night,—private Adler,—have been murdering a woman and a child! You are
being dogged: within five days both of you will be assassinated."

He dropped on his knees, frightened out of his wits; and
for five minutes he kept pouring out the same set of words,
like a demented person, and in the same half-crying way
which was one of my memories of that murderous night in
my cabin:—

"I did n't do it; upon my soul I did n't do it; and I tried to

keep *him* from doing it; I did, as God is my witness. He did
t alone."

This was all I wanted. And I tried to get rid of the fool;
out no, he clung to me, imploring me to save him from the
assassin. He said,—

"I have money—ten thousand dollars—hid away, the fruit
of loot and thievery; save me—tell me what to do, and you
shall have it, every penny. Two thirds of it is my cousin Adler's; but you can take it all. We hid it when we first came
here. But I hid it in a new place yesterday, and have not told
him—shall not tell him. I was going to desert, and get away
with it all. It is gold, and too heavy to carry when one is
running and dodging; but a woman who has been gone over
the river two days to prepare my way for me is going to follow me with it; and if I got no chance to describe the hiding-
place to her I was going to slip my silver watch into her hand,
or send it to her, and she would understand. There's a piece
of paper in the back of the case, which tells it all. Here, take
the watch—tell me what to do!"

He was trying to press his watch upon me, and was exposing the paper and explaining it to me, when Adler appeared
on the scene, about a dozen yards away. I said to poor
Kruger:—

"Put up your watch, I don't want it. You shan't come to
any harm. Go, now; I must tell Adler his fortune. Presently I
will tell you how to escape the assassin; meantime shall have
to examine your thumb-mark again. Say nothing to Adler
about this thing—say nothing to anybody."

He went away filled with fright and gratitude, poor devil.
I told Adler a long fortune,—purposely so long that I could
not finish it; promised to come to him on guard, that night,
and tell him the really important part of it—the tragical part
of it, I said,—so must be out of reach of eavesdroppers. They
always kept a picket-watch outside the town,—mere discipline and ceremony,—no occasion for it, no enemy around.

Toward midnight I set out, equipped with the countersign,
and picked my way toward the lonely region where Adler was
to keep his watch. It was so dark that I stumbled right on a
dim figure almost before I could get out a protecting word.
The sentinel hailed and I answered, both at the same mo-

ment. I added, "It 's only me—the fortune-teller." Then
slipped to the poor devil's side, and without a word I drov
my dirk into his heart! *Ja wohl*, laughed I, it *was* the traged
part of his fortune, indeed! As he fell from his horse, h
clutched at me, and my blue goggles remained in his han
and away plunged the beast dragging him, with his foot i
the stirrup.

I fled through the woods, and made good my escape, leav
ing the accusing goggles behind me in that dead man's han

This was fifteen or sixteen years ago. Since then I hav
wandered aimlessly about the earth, sometimes at worl
sometimes idle; sometimes with money, sometimes wit
none; but always tired of life, and wishing it was done, fc
my mission here was finished, with the act of that night; an
the only pleasure, solace, satisfaction I had, in all those t
dious years, was in the daily reflection, "I have killed him!"

Four years ago, my health began to fail. I had wandere
into Munich, in my purposeless way. Being out of money,
sought work, and got it; did my duty faithfully about a yea
and was then given the berth of night watchman yonder i
that dead-house which you visited lately. The place suited m
mood. I liked it. I liked being with the dead—liked bein
alone with them. I used to wander among those rigid corpse
and peer into their austere faces, by the hour. The later th
time, the more impressive it was; I preferred the late tim
Sometimes I turned the lights low: this gave perspective, yo
see; and the imagination could play; always, the dim recedin
ranks of the dead inspired one with weird and fascinating fan
cies. Two years ago—I had been there a year then—I wa
sitting all alone in the watch-room, one gusty winter's nigh
chilled, numb, comfortless; drowsing gradually into uncon
sciousness; the sobbing of the wind and the slamming of dis
tant shutters falling fainter and fainter upon my dulling ea
each moment, when sharp and suddenly that dead-bell ran
out a blood-curdling alarum over my head! The shock of i
nearly paralyzed me; for it was the first time I had eve
heard it.

I gathered myself together and flew to the corpse-room
About midway down the outside rank, a shrouded figure wa
sitting upright, wagging its head slowly from one side to th

other—a grisly spectacle! Its side was toward me. I hurried to it and peered into its face. Heavens, it was Adler!

Can you divine what my first thought was? Put into words, it was this: "It seems, then, you escaped me once: there will be a different result this time!"

Evidently this creature was suffering unimaginable terrors. Think what it must have been to wake up in the midst of that voiceless hush, and look out over that grim congregation of the dead! What gratitude shone in his skinny white face when he saw a living form before him! And how the fervency of this mute gratitude was augmented when his eyes fell upon the life-giving cordials which I carried in my hands! Then imagine the horror which came into this pinched face when I put the cordials behind me, and said mockingly,—

"Speak up, Franz Adler—call upon these dead. Doubtless they will listen and have pity; but here there is none else that will."

He tried to speak, but that part of the shroud which bound his jaws, held firm and would not let him. He tried to lift imploring hands, but they were crossed upon his breast and tied. I said—

"Shout, Franz Adler; make the sleepers in the distant streets hear you and bring help. Shout—and lose no time, for there is little to lose. What, you cannot? That is a pity; but it is no matter—it does not always bring help. When you and your cousin murdered a helpless woman and child in a cabin in Arkansas—my wife, it was, and my child!—they shrieked for help, you remember; but it did no good; you remember that it did no good, is it not so? Your teeth chatter—then why cannot you shout? Loosen the bandages with your hands—then you can. Ah, I see—your hands are tied, they cannot aid you. How strangely things repeat themselves, after long years; for *my* hands were tied, that night, you remember? Yes, tied much as yours are now—how odd that is. I could not pull free. It did not occur to you to untie me; it does not occur to me to untie you. Sh——! there's a late footstep. It is coming this way. Hark, how near it is! One can count the footfalls—one—two—three. There—it is just outside. Now is the time! Shout, man, shout!—it is the one sole chance between you and eternity! Ah, you see you have de-

layed too long—it is gone by. There—it is dying out. It is
gone! Think of it—reflect upon it—you have heard a human
footstep for the last time. How curious it must be, to listen
to so common a sound as that, and know that one will never
hear the fellow to it again."

Oh, my friend, the agony in that shrouded face was ecstasy
to see! I thought of a new torture, and applied it—assisting
myself with a trifle of lying invention:—

"That poor Kruger tried to save my wife and child, and
did him a grateful good turn for it when the time came. I
persuaded him to rob you; and I and a woman helped him to
desert, and got him away in safety."

A look as of surprise and triumph shone out dimly through
the anguish in my victim's face. I was disturbed, disquieted.
I said—

"What, then,—did n't he escape?"

A negative shake of the head.

"No? What happened, then?"

The satisfaction in the shrouded face was still plainer. The
man tried to mumble out some words—could not succeed;
tried to express something with his obstructed hands—failed;
paused a moment, then feebly tilted his head, in a meaning
way, toward the corpse that lay nearest him.

"Dead?" I asked. "Failed to escape?—caught in the act and
shot?"

Negative shake of the head.

"How, then?"

Again the man tried to do something with his hands. I
watched closely, but could not guess the intent. I bent over
and watched still more intently. He had twisted a thumb
around and was weakly punching at his breast with it.

"Ah—stabbed, do you mean?"

Affirmative nod, accompanied by a spectral smile of such
peculiar devilishness, that it struck an awakening light
through my dull brain, and I cried—

"Did I stab him, mistaking him for you?—for that stroke
was meant for none but you."

The affirmative nod of the re-dying rascal was as joyous as
his failing strength was able to put into its expression.

"O, miserable, miserable me, to slaughter the pitying soul

that stood a friend to my darlings when they were helpless, and would have saved them if he could! miserable, oh, miserable, miserable me!"

I fancied I heard the muffled gurgle of a mocking laugh. I took my face out of my hands, and saw my enemy sinking back upon his inclined board.

He was a satisfactory long time dying. He had a wonderful vitality, an astonishing constitution. Yes, he was a pleasant long time at it. I got a chair and a newspaper, and sat down by him and read. Occasionally I took a sip of brandy. This was necessary, on account of the cold. But I did it partly because I saw, that along at first, whenever I reached for the bottle, he thought I was going to give him some. I read aloud: mainly imaginary accounts of people snatched from the grave's threshold and restored to life and vigor by a few spoonsful of liquor and a warm bath. Yes, he had a long, hard death of it—three hours and six minutes, from the time he rang his bell.

It is believed that in all these eighteen years that have elapsed since the institution of the corpse-watch, no shrouded occupant of the Bavarian dead-houses has ever rung its bell. Well, it is a harmless belief. Let it stand at that.

The chill of that death-room had penetrated my bones. It revived and fastened upon me the disease which had been afflicting me, but which, up to that night, had been steadily disappearing. That man murdered my wife and my child; and in three days hence he will have added me to his list. No matter—God! how delicious the memory of it!—I caught him escaping from his grave, and thrust him back into it!

After that night, I was confined to my bed for a week; but as soon as I could get about, I went to the dead-house books and got the number of the house which Adler had died in. A wretched lodging-house, it was. It was my idea that he would naturally have gotten hold of Kruger's effects, being his cousin; and I wanted to get Kruger's watch, if I could. But while I was sick, Adler's things had been sold and scattered, all except a few old letters, and some odds and ends of no value. However, through those letters, I traced out a son of Kruger's, the only relative he left. He is a man of thirty, now, a shoemaker by trade, and living at No. 14 Königstrasse,

Mannheim—widower, with several small children. Withou explaining to him why, I have furnished two thirds of hi support, ever since.

Now, as to that watch—see how strangely things happen I traced it around and about Germany for more than a year at considerable cost in money and vexation; and at last I go it. Got it, and was unspeakably glad; opened it, and foun nothing in it! Why, I might have known that that bit of pape was not going to stay there all this time. Of course I gave u that ten thousand dollars then; gave it up, and dropped it ou of my mind: and most sorrowfully, for I had wanted it fo Kruger's son.

Last night, when I consented at last that I must die, I be gan to make ready. I proceeded to burn all useless papers and sure enough, from a batch of Adler's, not previously ex amined with thoroughness, out dropped that long-desirec scrap! I recognized it in a moment. Here it is—I will trans late it:

> "Brick livery stable, stone foundation, middle of town corner of Orleans and Market. Corner toward Court-house Third stone, fourth row. Stick notice there, saying how many are to come."

There—take it, and preserve it. Kruger explained that tha stone was removable; and that it was in the north wall of the foundation, fourth row from the top, and third stone fron the west. The money is secreted behind it. He said the closing sentence was a blind, to mislead in case the paper should fal into wrong hands. It probably performed that office fo Adler.

Now I want to beg that when you make your intendec journey down the river, you will hunt out that hidden money and send it to Adam Kruger, care of the Mannheim addres which I have mentioned. It will make a rich man of him, anc I shall sleep the sounder in my grave for knowing that I have done what I could for the son of the man who tried to save my wife and child—albeit my hand ignorantly struck him down, whereas the impulse of my heart would have been to shield and serve him.

XXXII.

The Disposal of a Bonanza

"Such was Ritter's narrative," said I to my two friends. There was a profound and impressive silence, which lasted a considerable time; then both men broke into a fusillade of excited and admiring ejaculations over the strange incidents of the tale; and this, along with a rattling fire of questions, was kept up until all hands were about out of breath. Then my friends began to cool down, and draw off, under shelter of occasional volleys, into silence and abysmal reverie. For ten minutes now, there was stillness. Then Rogers said dreamily:—

"Ten thousand dollars."

Adding, after a considerable pause,—

"Ten thousand. It is a heap of money."

Presently the poet inquired,—

"Are you going to send it to him right away?"

"Yes," I said. "It is a queer question."

No reply. After a little, Rogers asked, hesitatingly:

"*All* of it?—That is—I mean—"

"*Certainly*, all of it."

I was going to say more, but stopped,—was stopped by a train of thought which started up in me. Thompson spoke, but my mind was absent and I did not catch what he said. But I heard Rogers answer,—

"Yes, it seems so to me. It ought to be quite sufficient; for I don't see that *he* has done anything."

Presently the poet said,—

"When you come to look at it, it is *more* than sufficient. Just look at it—five thousand dollars! Why, he could n't spend it in a lifetime! And it would injure him, too; perhaps ruin him—you want to look at that. In a little while he would throw his last away, shut up his shop, maybe take to drinking, maltreat his motherless children, drift into other evil courses, go steadily from bad to worse—"

"Yes, that 's it," interrupted Rogers, fervently, "I 've seen it a hundred times—yes, more than a hundred. You put

money into the hands of a man like that, if you want to de
stroy him, that 's all; just put money into his hands, it 's a
you 've got to do; and if it don't pull him down, and take a
the usefulness out of him, and all the self-respect and every
thing, then I don't know human nature—ain't that s
Thompson? And even if we were to give him a *third* of i
why, in less than six months—"

"Less than six *weeks*, you 'd better say!" said I, warming u
and breaking in. "Unless he had that three thousand dolla
in safe hands where he could n't touch it, he would no mo
last you six weeks than—"

"Of *course* he would n't," said Thompson; "I 've edite
books for that kind of people; and the moment they get the
hands on the royalty—maybe it 's three thousand, maybe
's two thousand—"

"What business has that shoemaker with two thousand do
lars, I should like to know?" broke in Rogers, earnestly. "
man perhaps perfectly contented now, there in Mannhein
surrounded by his own class, eating his bread with the app
tite which laborious industry alone can give, enjoying hi
humble life, honest, upright, pure in heart; and *blest!*—ye
I say blest! blest above all the myriads that go in silk attir
and walk the empty artificial round of social folly—but jus
you put *that* temptation before him once! just you lay fiftee
hundred dollars before a man like that, and say—"

"Fifteen hundred devils!" cried I, "*five* hundred would ro
his principles, paralyze his industry, drag him to the rumshop
thence to the gutter, thence to the almshouse, thence to—"

"*Why* put upon ourselves this crime, gentlemen?" inter
rupted the poet earnestly and appealingly. "He is happ
where he is, and *as* he is. Every sentiment of honor, ever
sentiment of charity, every sentiment of high and sacred be
nevolence warns us, beseeches us, commands us to leave hin
undisturbed. That is real friendship, that is true friendship
We could follow other courses that would be more showy
but none that would be so truly kind and wise, depen
upon it."

After some further talk, it became evident that each of us
down in his heart, felt some misgivings over this settlemen
of the matter. It was manifest that we all felt that we ough

to send the poor shoemaker *something*. There was long and thoughtful discussion of this point; and we finally decided to send him a chromo.

Well, now that everything seemed to be arranged satisfactorily to everybody concerned, a new trouble broke out: it transpired that these two men were expecting to share equally in the money with me. That was not my idea. I said that if they got half of it between them they might consider themselves lucky. Rogers said: —

"Who would have had *any* if it had n't been for me? I flung out the first hint—but for that it would all have gone to the shoemaker."

Thompson said that he was thinking of the thing himself at the very moment that Rogers had originally spoken.

I retorted that the idea would have occurred to me plenty soon enough, and without anybody's help. I was slow about thinking, maybe, but I was sure.

This matter warmed up into a quarrel; then into a fight; and each man got pretty badly battered. As soon as I had got myself mended up after a fashion, I ascended to the hurricane deck in a pretty sour humor. I found Captain McCord there, and said, as pleasantly as my humor would permit: —

"I have come to say good-bye, captain. I wish to go ashore at Napoleon."

"Go ashore where?"

"Napoleon."

The captain laughed; but seeing that I was not in a jovial mood, stopped that and said, —

"But are you serious?"

"Serious? I certainly am."

The captain glanced up at the pilot-house and said, —

"He wants to get off at Napoleon!"

"*Napoleon?*"

"That's what he says."

"Great Cæsar's ghost!"

Uncle Mumford approached along the deck. The captain said, —

"Uncle, here 's a friend of yours wants to get off at Napoleon!"

"Well, by—!"

I said,—

"Come, what is all this about? Can't a man go ashore at Napoleon if he wants to?"

"Why, hang it, don't you know? There *is n't* any Napoleon any more. Has n't been for years and years. The Arkansas River burst through it, tore it all to rags, and emptied it into the Mississippi!"

"Carried the *whole* town away?—banks, churches, jails, newspaper-offices, court-house, theatre, fire department, livery stable,—*everything*?"

"Everything. Just a fifteen-minute job, or such a matter. Did n't leave hide nor hair, shred nor shingle of it, except the fag-end of a shanty and one brick chimney. This boat is paddling along right now, where the dead-centre of that town used to be; yonder is the brick chimney,—all that 's left of Napoleon. These dense woods on the right used to be a mile back of the town. Take a look behind you—up-stream—now you begin to recognize this country, don't you?"

"Yes, I do recognize it now. It is the most wonderful thing I ever heard of; by a long shot the most wonderful—and unexpected."

Mr. Thompson and Mr. Rogers had arrived, meantime, with satchels and umbrellas, and had silently listened to the captain's news. Thompson put a half-dollar in my hand and said softly:—

"For my share of the chromo."

Rogers followed suit.

Yes, it was an astonishing thing to see the Mississippi rolling between unpeopled shores and straight over the spot where I used to see a good big self-complacent town twenty years ago. Town that was county-seat of a great and important county; town with a big United States marine hospital; town of innumerable fights—an inquest every day; town where I had used to know the prettiest girl, and the most accomplished in the whole Mississippi Valley; town where we were handed the first printed news of the "Pennsylvania's" mournful disaster a quarter of a century ago; a town no more—swallowed up, vanished, gone to feed the fishes; nothing left but a fragment of a shanty and a crumbling brick chimney!

XXXIII.

Refreshments and Ethics

IN REGARD to Island 74, which is situated not far from the former Napoleon, a freak of the river here has sorely perplexed the laws of men and made them a vanity and a jest. When the State of Arkansas was chartered, she controlled "to the centre of the river"—a most unstable line. The State of Mississippi claimed "to the channel"—another shifty and unstable line. No. 74 belonged to Arkansas. By and by a cut-off threw this big island out of Arkansas, and yet not *within* Mississippi. "Middle of the river" on one side of it, "channel" on the other. That is as I understand the problem. Whether I have got the details right or wrong, this *fact* remains: that here is this big and exceedingly valuable island of four thousand acres, thrust out in the cold, and belonging to neither the one State nor the other; paying taxes to neither, owing allegiance to neither. One man owns the whole island, and of right is "the man without a country."

Island 92 belongs to Arkansas. The river moved it over and joined it to Mississippi. A chap established a whiskey shop there, without a Mississippi license, and enriched himself upon Mississippi custom under Arkansas protection (where no license was in those days required).

We glided steadily down the river in the usual privacy—steamboat or other moving thing seldom seen. Scenery as always: stretch upon stretch of almost unbroken forest, on both sides of the river; soundless solitude. Here and there a cabin or two, standing in small openings on the gray and grassless banks—cabins which had formerly stood a quarter or half-mile farther to the front, and gradually been pulled farther and farther back as the shores caved in. As at Pilcher's Point, for instance, where the cabins had been moved back three hundred yards in three months, so we were told; but the caving banks had already caught up with them, and they were being conveyed rearward once more.

Napoleon had but small opinion of Greenville, Mississippi, in the old times; but behold, Napoleon is gone to the cat-

fishes, and here is Greenville full of life and activity, and mak
ing a considerable flourish in the Valley; having three thou
sand inhabitants, it is said, and doing a gross trade o
$2,500,000 annually. A growing town.

There was much talk on the boat about the Calhoun Lanc
Company, an enterprise which is expected to work whole
some results. Colonel Calhoun, a grandson of the statesman
went to Boston and formed a syndicate which purchasec
a large tract of land on the river, in Chicot County
Arkansas,—some ten thousand acres—for cotton-growing
The purpose is to work on a cash basis: buy at first hands
and handle their own product; supply their negro laborer:
with provisions and necessaries at a trifling profit, say 8 or 1c
per cent; furnish them comfortable quarters, etc., and encourage them to save money and remain on the place. If thi:
proves a financial success, as seems quite certain, they propose
to establish a banking-house in Greenville, and lend money a1
an unburdensome rate of interest—6 per cent is spoken of.

The trouble heretofore has been—I am quoting remarks o1
planters and steamboatmen—that the planters, althougl
owning the land, were without cash capital; had to hypothe-
cate both land and crop to carry on the business. Consequently, the commission dealer who furnishes the money
takes some risk and demands big interest—usually 10 pei
cent, and $2^{1/2}$ per cent for negotiating the loan. The plantei
has also to buy his supplies through the same dealer, paying
commissions and profits. Then when he ships his crop, the
dealer adds his commissions, insurance, etc. So, taking it by
and large, and first and last, the dealer's share of that crop is
about 25 per cent.[1]

A cotton-planter's estimate of the average margin of profit
on planting, in his section: One man and mule will raise ten
acres of cotton, giving ten bales cotton, worth, say, $500; cost
of producing, say $350; net profit, $150, or $15 per acre. There
is also a profit now from the cotton-seed, which formerly had

---

[1] "But what can the State do where the people are under subjection to rates
of interest ranging from 18 to 30 per cent, and are also under the necessity of
purchasing their crops in advance even of planting, at these rates, for the
privilege of purchasing all their supplies at 100 per cent profit?"—*Edward
Atkinson.*

little value—none where much transportation was necessary. In sixteen hundred pounds crude cotton, four hundred are lint, worth, say, ten cents a pound; and twelve hundred pounds of seed, worth $12 or $13 per ton. Maybe in future even the *stems* will not be thrown away. Mr. Edward Atkinson says that for each bale of cotton there are fifteen hundred pounds of stems, and that these are very rich in phosphate of lime and potash; that when ground and mixed with ensilage or cotton-seed meal (which is too rich for use as fodder in large quantities), the stem mixture makes a superior food, rich in all the elements needed for the production of milk, meat, and bone. Heretofore the stems have been considered a nuisance.

Complaint is made that the planter remains grouty toward the former slave, since the war; will have nothing but a chill business relation with him, no sentiment permitted to intrude; will not keep a "store" himself, and supply the negro's wants and thus protect the negro's pocket and make him able and willing to stay on the place and an advantage to him to do it, but lets that privilege to some thrifty Israelite, who encourages the thoughtless negro and wife to buy all sorts of things which they could do without,—buy on credit, at big prices, month after month, credit based on the negro's share of the growing crop; and at the end of the season, the negro's share belongs to the Israelite, the negro is in debt besides, is discouraged, dissatisfied, restless, and both he and the planter are injured; for he will take steamboat and migrate, and the planter must get a stranger in his place who does not know him, does not care for him, will fatten the Israelite a season, and follow his predecessor per steamboat.

It is hoped that the Calhoun Company will show, by its humane and protective treatment of its laborers, that its method is the most profitable for both planter and negro; and it is believed that a general adoption of that method will then follow.

And where so many are saying their say, shall not the barkeeper testify? He is thoughtful, observant, never drinks; endeavors to earn his salary, and *would* earn it if there were custom enough. He says the people along here in Mississippi and Louisiana will send up the river to buy vegetables rather

than raise them, and they will come aboard at the landing
and buy fruits of the barkeeper. Thinks they "don't know any
thing but cotton;" believes they don't know how to raise veg
etables and fruit—"at least the most of them." Says "a nigge
will go to H for a watermelon" ("H" is all I find in the ste
nographer's report—means Halifax probably, though tha
seems a good way to go for a watermelon). Barkeeper buy
watermelons for five cents up the river, brings them dowi
and sells them for fifty. "Why does he mix such elaborate anc
picturesque drinks for the nigger hands on the boat?" Becaus
they won't have any other. "They want a *big* drink; don"
make any difference what you make it of, they want the wortl
of their money. You give a nigger a plain gill of half-a-dolla
brandy for five cents—will he touch it? No. Ain't size enougl
to it. But you put up a pint of all kinds of worthless rubbish
and heave in some red stuff to make it beautiful—red 's the
main thing—and he would n't put down that glass to go tc
a circus." All the bars on this Anchor Line are rented anc
owned by one firm. They furnish the liquors from their owi
establishment, and hire the barkeepers "on salary." Good li
quors? Yes, on some of the boats, where there are the kind o
passengers that want it and can pay for it. On the other boats
No. Nobody but the deck hands and firemen to drink it
"Brandy? Yes, I 've got brandy, plenty of it; but you don'
want any of it unless you 've made your will." It is n't as i
used to be in the old times. Then everybody travelled b
steamboat, everybody drank, and everybody treated every
body else. "Now most everybody goes by railroad, and th
rest don't drink." In the old times, the barkeeper owned th
bar himself, "and was gay and smarty and talky and all jew
elled up, and was the toniest aristocrat on the boat; used tc
make $2,000 on a trip. A father who left his son a steamboa
bar, left him a fortune. Now he leaves him board and lodg
ing; yes, and washing, if a shirt a trip will do. Yes, indeedy
times are changed. Why, do you know, on the principal lin
of boats on the Upper Mississippi, they don't have any bar a
all! Sounds like poetry, but it 's the petrified truth."

XXXIV.

Tough Yarns

S TACK ISLAND. I remembered Stack Island; also Lake
Providence, Louisiana—which is the first distinctly
Southern-looking town you come to, downward-bound; lies
level and low, shade-trees hung with venerable gray beards of
Spanish moss; "restful, pensive, Sunday aspect about the
place," comments Uncle Mumford, with feeling—also with
truth.

A Mr. H. furnished some minor details of fact concerning
this region which I would have hesitated to believe if I had
not known him to be a steamboat mate. He was a passenger
of ours, a resident of Arkansas City, and bound to Vicksburg
to join his boat, a little Sunflower packet. He was an austere
man, and had the reputation of being singularly unworldly,
for a river man. Among other things, he said that Arkansas
had been injured and kept back by generations of exaggera-
tions concerning the mosquitoes there. One may smile, said
he, and turn the matter off as being a small thing; but when
you come to look at the effects produced, in the way of discouragement of immigration, and diminished values of property, it was quite the opposite of a small thing, or thing in
any wise to be coughed down or sneered at. These mosquitoes had been persistently represented as being formidable
and lawless; whereas "the truth is, they are feeble, insignificant in size, diffident to a fault, sensitive"—and so on, and so
on; you would have supposed he was talking about his family. But if he was soft on the Arkansas mosquitoes, he was
hard enough on the mosquitoes of Lake Providence to make
up for it—"those Lake Providence colossi," as he finely called
them. He said that two of them could whip a dog, and that
four of them could hold a man down; and except help come,
they would kill him—"butcher him," as he expressed it. Referred in a sort of casual way—and yet significant way—to
"the fact that the life policy in its simplest form is unknown
in Lake Providence—they take out a mosquito policy besides." He told many remarkable things about those lawless

insects. Among others, said he had seen them try to *vote*. Noticing that this statement seemed to be a good deal of a strain on us, he modified it a little: said he might have been mistaken, as to that particular, but knew he had seen them around the polls "canvassing."

There was another passenger—friend of H.'s—who backed up the harsh evidence against those mosquitoes, and detailed some stirring adventures which he had had with them. The stories were pretty sizable, merely pretty sizable; yet Mr. H. was continually interrupting with a cold, inexorable "Wait—knock off twenty-five per cent of that; now go on;" or, "Wait—you are getting that too strong; cut it down, cut it down—you get a leetle too much costumery on to your statements: always dress a fact in tights, never in an ulster;" or, "Pardon, once more: if you are going to load anything more on to that statement, you want to get a couple of lighters and tow the rest, because it's drawing all the water there is in the river already; stick to facts—just stick to the cold facts; what these gentlemen want for a book is the frozen truth—ain't that so, gentlemen?" He explained privately that it was necessary to watch this man all the time, and keep him within bounds; it would not do to neglect this precaution, as he, Mr. H., "knew to his sorrow." Said he, "I will not deceive you; he told me such a monstrous lie once, that it swelled my left ear up, and spread it so that I was actually not able to see out around it; it remained so for months, and people came miles to see me fan myself with it."

XXXV.

Vicksburg during the Trouble

W E USED to plough past the lofty hill-city, Vicksburg, down-stream; but we cannot do that now. A cut-off has made a country town of it, like Osceola, St. Genevieve, and several others. There is currentless water—also a big island—in front of Vicksburg now. You come down the river the other side of the island, then turn and come up to the town; that is, in high water: in low water you can't come up, but must land some distance below it.

Signs and scars still remain, as reminders of Vicksburg's tremendous war-experiences; earthworks, trees crippled by the cannon balls, cave-refuges in the clay precipices, etc. The caves did good service during the six weeks' bombardment of the city—May 18 to July 4, 1863. They were used by the non-combatants—mainly by the women and children; not to live in constantly, but to fly to for safety on occasion. They were mere holes, tunnels, driven into the perpendicular clay bank, then branched Y shape, within the hill. Life in Vicksburg, during the six weeks was perhaps—but wait; here are some materials out of which to reproduce it:—

Population, twenty-seven thousand soldiers and three thousand non-combatants; the city utterly cut off from the world—walled solidly in, the frontage by gunboats, the rear by soldiers and batteries; hence, no buying and selling with the outside; no passing to and fro; no God-speeding a parting guest, no welcoming a coming one; no printed acres of world-wide news to be read at breakfast, mornings—a tedious dull absence of such matter, instead; hence, also, no running to see steamboats smoking into view in the distance up or down, and ploughing toward the town—for none came, the river lay vacant and undisturbed; no rush and turmoil around the railway station, no struggling over bewildered swarms of passengers by noisy mobs of hackmen—all quiet there; flour two hundred dollars a barrel, sugar thirty, corn ten dollars a bushel, bacon five dollars a pound, rum a hundred dollars a gallon; other things in proportion: consequently, no roar and racket of drays and carriages tearing along the streets; nothing for them to do, among that handful of non-combatants of exhausted means; at three o'clock in the morning, silence; silence so dead that the measured tramp of a sentinel can be heard a seemingly impossible distance; out of hearing of this lonely sound, perhaps the stillness is absolute: all in a moment come ground-shaking thunder-crashes of artillery, the sky is cobwebbed with the criss-crossing red lines streaming from soaring bomb-shells, and a rain of iron fragments descends upon the city; descends upon the empty streets: streets which are not empty a moment later, but mottled with dim figures of frantic women and children skurrying from home and bed toward the cave dungeons—encouraged by the humorous grim soldiery, who shout "Rats, to your holes!" and laugh.

The cannon-thunder rages, shells scream and crash overhead, the iron rain pours down, one hour, two hours, three, possibly six, then stops; silence follows, but the streets are still empty; the silence continues; by and by a head projects from a cave here and there and yonder, and reconnoitres, cautiously; the silence still continuing, bodies follow heads, and jaded, half-smothered creatures group themselves about, stretch their cramped limbs, draw in deep draughts of the grateful fresh air, gossip with the neighbors from the next cave; maybe straggle off home presently, or take a lounge through the town, if the stillness continues; and will skurry to the holes again, by and by, when the war-tempest breaks forth once more.

There being but three thousand of these cave-dwellers—merely the population of a village—would they not come to know each other, after a week or two, and familiarly; insomuch that the fortunate or unfortunate experiences of one would be of interest to all?

Those are the materials furnished by history. From them might not almost anybody reproduce for himself the life of that time in Vicksburg? Could you, who did not experience it, come nearer to reproducing it to the imagination of another non-participant than could a Vicksburger who *did* experience it? It seems impossible; and yet there are reasons why it might not really be. When one makes his first voyage in a ship, it is an experience which multitudinously bristles with striking novelties; novelties which are in such sharp contrast with all this person's former experiences that they take a seemingly deathless grip upon his imagination and memory. By tongue or pen he can make a landsman live that strange and stirring voyage over with him; make him see it all and feel it all. But if he wait? If he make ten voyages in succession—what then? Why, the thing has lost color, snap, surprise; and has become commonplace. The man would have nothing to tell that would quicken a landsman's pulse.

Years ago, I talked with a couple of the Vicksburg non-combatants—a man and his wife. Left to tell their story in their own way, those people told it without fire, almost without interest.

A week of their wonderful life there would have made their tongues eloquent forever perhaps; but they had six weeks of it, and that wore the novelty all out; they got used to being bomb-shelled out of home and into the ground; the matter became commonplace. After that, the possibility of their ever being startlingly interesting in their talks about it was gone. What the man said was to this effect:—

"It got to be Sunday all the time. Seven Sundays in the week—to us, anyway. We had n't anything to do, and time hung heavy. Seven Sundays, and all of them broken up at one time or another, in the day or in the night, by a few hours of the awful storm of fire and thunder and iron. At first we used to shin for the holes a good deal faster than we did afterwards. The first time, I forgot the children, and Maria fetched them both along. When she was all safe in the cave she fainted. Two or three weeks afterwards, when she was running for the holes, one morning, through a shell-shower, a big shell burst near her and covered her all over with dirt, and a piece of the iron carried away her game-bag of false hair from the back of her head. Well, she stopped to get that game-bag before she shoved along again! Was getting used to things already, you see. We all got so that we could tell a good deal about shells; and after that we did n't always go under shelter if it was a light shower. Us men would loaf around and talk; and a man would say, 'There she goes!' and name the kind of shell it was from the sound of it, and go on talking—if there was n't any danger from it. If a shell was bursting close over us, we stopped talking and stood still;—uncomfortable, yes, but it was n't safe to move. When it let go, we went on talking again, if nobody hurt—maybe saying, 'That was a ripper!' or some such commonplace comment before we resumed; or, maybe, we would see a shell poising itself away high in the air overhead. In that case, every fellow just whipped out a sudden, 'See you again, gents!' and shoved. Often and often I saw gangs of ladies promenading the streets, looking as cheerful as you please, and keeping an eye canted up watching the shells; and I 've seen them stop still when they were uncertain about what a shell was going to do, and wait and make certain; and after that they s'antered along again, or lit out for shelter, according to the verdict. Streets in some towns have a litter of pieces of paper, and odds and ends of one sort or another lying around. Ours had n't; they had *iron* litter. Sometimes a man would gather up all the iron fragments and unbursted shells in his neighborhood, and pile them into a kind of monument in his front yard—a ton of it, sometimes. No glass left; glass could n't stand such a bombardment; it was all shivered out. Windows of the houses vacant—looked like eye-holes in a skull. *Whole* panes were as scarce as news.

"We had church Sundays. Not many there, along at first; but by and by pretty good turnouts. I 've seen service stop a minute, and everybody sit quiet—no voice heard, pretty funeral-like then—and all the more so on account of the awful boom and crash going on outside and overhead; and pretty soon, when a body could be heard, service would go on again. Organs and church-music mixed up with a bombardment is a powerful queer combination—along at first. Coming out of church, one morning, we had an accident— the only one that happened around me on a Sunday. I was just having a hearty hand-shake with a friend I had n't seen for a while, and saying, 'Drop into our cave to-night, after bombardment; we 've got hold of a pint of prime wh—.' Whiskey, I was going to say, you know, but a shell interrupted. A chunk of it cut the man's arm off, and left it dangling in my hand. And do you know the thing that is going to stick the longest in my memory, and outlast everything else, little and big, I reckon, is the mean thought I had then? It was 'the whiskey *is saved*.' And yet, don't you know, it was kind of excusable; because it was as scarce as diamonds, and we had only just that little; never had another taste during the siege.

"Sometimes the caves were desperately crowded, and always hot and close. Sometimes a cave had twenty or twenty-five people packed into it; no turning-room for anybody; air so foul, sometimes, you could n't have made a candle burn in it. A child was born in one of those caves one night. Think of that; why, it was like having it born in a trunk.

"Twice we had sixteen people in our cave; and a number of times we had a dozen. Pretty suffocating in there. We always had eight; eight belonged there. Hunger and misery and sickness and fright and sorrow, and I don't know what all, got so loaded into them that none of them were ever rightly their old selves after the siege. They all died but three of us within a couple of years. One night a shell burst in front of the hole and caved it in and stopped it up. It was lively times, for a while, digging out. Some of us came near smothering. After that we made two openings—ought to have thought of it at first.

"Mule meat? No, we only got down to that the last day or two. Of course it was good; anything is good when you are starving."

This man had kept a diary during—six weeks? No, only the first six days. The first day, eight close pages; the second, five; the third, one—loosely written; the fourth, three or four lines; a line or two the fifth and sixth days; seventh day, diary abandoned; life in terrific Vicksburg having now become commonplace and matter of course.

The war history of Vicksburg has more about it to interest the general reader than that of any other of the river-towns. It is full of variety, full of incident, full of the picturesque. Vicksburg held out longer than any other important river-town, and saw warfare in all its phases, both land and water—the siege, the mine, the assault, the repulse, the bombardment, sickness, captivity, famine.

The most beautiful of all the national cemeteries is here. Over the great gateway is this inscription:—

> "HERE REST IN PEACE 16,600 WHO DIED FOR THEIR
> COUNTRY IN THE YEARS 1861 TO 1865."

The grounds are nobly situated; being very high and commanding a wide prospect of land and river. They are tastefully laid out in broad terraces, with winding roads and paths; and there is profuse adornment in the way of semi-tropical shrubs and flowers; and in one part is a piece of native wild-wood, left just as it grew, and, therefore, perfect in its charm. Everything about this cemetery suggests the hand of the national Government. The Government's work is always conspicuous for excellence, solidity, thoroughness, neatness. The Government does its work well in the first place, and then takes care of it.

By winding-roads—which were often cut to so great a depth between perpendicular walls that they were mere roofless tunnels—we drove out a mile or two and visited the monument which stands upon the scene of the surrender of Vicksburg to General Grant by General Pemberton. Its metal will preserve it from the hackings and chippings which so defaced its predecessor, which was of marble; but the brick foundations are crumbling, and it will tumble down by and by. It overlooks a picturesque region of wooded hills and ravines; and is not unpicturesque itself, being well smothered in flowering weeds. The battered remnant of the marble monument has been removed to the National Cemetery.

On the road, a quarter of a mile townward, an aged colored man showed us, with pride, an unexploded bomb-shell which has lain in his yard since the day it fell there during the siege.

"I was a-stannin' heah, an' de dog was a-stannin' heah; de dog he went for de shell, gwine to pick a fuss wid it; but I did n't; I says, 'Jes' make youseff at home heah; lay still whah you is, or bust up de place, jes' as you 's a mind to, but *I* 's got business out in de woods, *I* has!' "

Vicksburg is a town of substantial business streets and pleasant residences; it commands the commerce of the Yazoo and Sunflower Rivers; is pushing railways in several directions, through rich agricultural regions, and has a promising future of prosperity and importance.

Apparently, nearly all the river towns, big and little, have made up their minds that they must look mainly to railroads for wealth and upbuilding, henceforth. They are acting upon this idea. The signs are, that the next twenty years will bring about some noteworthy changes in the Valley, in the direction of increased population and wealth, and in the intellectual advancement and the liberalizing of opinion which go naturally with these. And yet, if one may judge by the past, the river towns will manage to find and use a chance, here and there, to cripple and retard their progress. They kept themselves back in the days of steamboating supremacy, by a system of wharfage-dues so stupidly graded as to prohibit what may be called small *retail* traffic in freights and passengers. Boats were charged such heavy wharfage that they could not afford to land for one or two passengers or a light lot of freight. Instead of encouraging the bringing of trade to their doors, the towns diligently and effectively discouraged it. They could have had many boats and low rates; but their policy rendered few boats and high rates compulsory. It was a policy which extended—and extends—from New Orleans to St. Paul.

We had a strong desire to make a trip up the Yazoo and the Sunflower—an interesting region at any time, but additionally interesting at this time, because up there the great inundation was still to be seen in force,—but we were nearly sure to have to wait a day or more for a New Orleans boat on our return; so we were obliged to give up the project.

Here is a story which I picked up on board the boat that night. I insert it in this place merely because it is a good story, not because it belongs here—for it does n't. It was told by a passenger—a college professor—and was called to the surface in the course of a general conversation which began with talk about horses, drifted into talk about astronomy, then into talk about the lynching of the gamblers in Vicksburg half a century ago, then into talk about dreams and superstitions; and ended, after midnight, in a dispute over free trade and protection.

XXXVI.

The Professor's Yarn

IT WAS in the early days. I was not a college professor then. I was a humble-minded young land-surveyor, with the world before me—to survey, in case anybody wanted it done. I had a contract to survey a route for a great mining-ditch in California, and I was on my way thither, by sea—a three or four weeks' voyage. There were a good many passengers, but I had very little to say to them; reading and dreaming were my passions, and I avoided conversation in order to indulge these appetites. There were three professional gamblers on board—rough, repulsive fellows. I never had any talk with them, yet I could not help seeing them with some frequency, for they gambled in an upper-deck state-room every day and night, and in my promenades I often had glimpses of them through their door, which stood a little ajar to let out the surplus tobacco smoke and profanity. They were an evil and hateful presence, but I had to put up with it, of course.

There was one other passenger who fell under my eye a good deal, for he seemed determined to be friendly with me, and I could not have gotten rid of him without running some chance of hurting his feelings, and I was far from wishing to do that. Besides, there was something engaging in his countrified simplicity and his beaming good-nature. The first time I saw this Mr. John Backus, I guessed, from his clothes and his looks, that he was a grazier or farmer from the back woods of some western State—doubtless Ohio—and afterward when he dropped into his personal history and I discovered that he *was* a cattle-raiser from interior Ohio, I was so pleased with my own penetration that I warmed toward him for verifying my instinct.

He got to dropping alongside me every day, after breakfast, to help me make my promenade; and so, in the course of time, his easy-working jaw had told me everything about his business, his prospects, his family, his relatives, his politics— in fact everything that concerned a Backus, living or dead. And meantime I think he had managed to get out of me everything I knew about my trade, my tribe, my purposes, my prospects, and myself. He was a gentle and persuasive genius, and this thing showed it; for I was not given to talking about my matters. I said something about triangulation, once; the stately word pleased his ear; he inquired what it meant; I explained; after that he quietly and inoffensively ignored my name, and always called me Triangle.

What an enthusiast he was in cattle! At the bare name of a bull or a cow, his eye would light and his eloquent tongue would turn itself loose. As long as I would walk and listen, he would walk and talk; he knew all breeds, he loved all breeds, he caressed them all with his affectionate tongue. I tramped along in voiceless misery whilst the cattle question was up; when I could endure it no longer, I used to deftly insert a scientific topic into the conversation; then my eye fired and his faded; my tongue fluttered, his stopped; life was a joy to me, and a sadness to him.

One day he said, a little hesitatingly, and with somewhat of diffidence: —

"Triangle, would you mind coming down to my stateroom a minute, and have a little talk on a certain matter?"

I went with him at once. Arrived there, he put his head out, glanced up and down the saloon warily, then closed the door and locked it. We sat down on the sofa, and he said: —

"I'm a-going to make a little proposition to you, and if it strikes you favorable, it'll be a middling good thing for both of us. You ain't a-going out to Californy for fun, nuther am I—it's *business*, ain't that so? Well, you can do me a good turn, and so can I you, if we see fit. I've raked and scraped and saved, a considerable many years, and I've got it all here." He unlocked an old hair trunk, tumbled a chaos of shabby clothes aside, and drew a short stout bag into view for a moment, then buried it again and relocked the trunk. Dropping his voice to a cautious low tone, he continued, "She's all there—a round ten thousand dollars in yellow-boys; now this is my little idea: What I don't know about raising cattle, ain't worth knowing. There's mints of money in it, in Californy. Well, I know, and you know, that all along a line that's being surveyed, there's little dabs of land that they call 'gores,' that fall to the surveyor free gratis for nothing. All you 've got to do, on your side, is to survey in such a way that the 'gores' will fall on good fat land, then you turn 'em over to me, I stock 'em with cattle, *in* rolls the cash, plank out your share of the dollars regular, right along, and—

I was sorry to wither his blooming enthusiasm, but it could not be helped. I interrupted, and said severely,—

"I am not that kind of a surveyor. Let us change the subject, Mr. Backus."

It was pitiful to see his confusion and hear his awkward and shamefaced apologies. I was as much distressed as he was—especially as he seemed so far from having suspected that there was anything improper in his proposition. So I hastened to console him and lead him on to forget his mishap in a conversational orgy about cattle and butchery. We were lying at Acapulco; and, as we went on deck, it happened luckily that the crew were just beginning to hoist some beeves aboard in slings. Backus's melancholy vanished instantly, and with it the memory of his late mistake.

"Now only look at that!" cried he; "My goodness, Triangle, what *would* they say to it in *Ohio*? Would n't their eyes bug out, to see 'em handled like that?—would n't they, though?"

All the passengers were on deck to look—even the gamblers—and Backus knew them all, and had afflicted them all with his pet topic. As I moved away, I saw one of the gamblers approach and accost him; then another of them; then the third. I halted; waited; watched; the conversation continued between the four men; it grew earnest; Backus drew gradually away; the gamblers followed, and kept at his elbow. I was uncomfortable. However, as they passed me presently, I heard Backus say, with a tone of persecuted annoyance:—

"But it ain't any use, gentlemen; I tell you again, as I 've told you a half a dozen times before, I war n't raised to it, and I ain't a-going to resk it."

I felt relieved. "His level head will be his sufficient protection," I said to myself.

During the fortnight's run from Acapulco to San Francisco I several times saw the gamblers talking earnestly with Backus, and once I threw out a gentle warning to him. He chuckled comfortably and said,—

"Oh, yes! they tag around after me considerable—want me

) play a little, just for amusement, they say—but laws-a-me,
my folks have told me once to look out for that sort of live-
tock, they 've told me a thousand times, I reckon."

By and by, in due course, we were approaching San Fran-
isco. It was an ugly black night, with a strong wind blowing,
ut there was not much sea. I was on deck, alone. Toward
en I started below. A figure issued from the gamblers' den,
nd disappeared in the darkness. I experienced a shock, for I
vas sure it was Backus. I flew down the companion-way,
ooked about for him, could not find him, then returned to
he deck just in time to catch a glimpse of him as he re-
ntered that confounded nest of rascality. Had he yielded at
ast? I feared it. What had he gone below for?—His bag of
oin? Possibly. I drew near the door, full of bodings. It was
-crack, and I glanced in and saw a sight that made me bit-
erly wish I had given my attention to saving my poor cattle-
riend, instead of reading and dreaming my foolish time
way. He was gambling. Worse still, he was being plied with
hampagne, and was already showing some effect from it. He
raised the "cider," as he called it, and said now that he had
ot a taste of it he almost believed he would drink it if it was
pirits, it was so good and so ahead of anything he had ever
un across before. Surreptitious smiles, at this, passed from
ne rascal to another, and they filled all the glasses, and whilst
Backus honestly drained his to the bottom they pretended to
o the same, but threw the wine over their shoulders.

I could not bear the scene, so I wandered forward and tried
o interest myself in the sea and the voices of the wind. But
o, my uneasy spirit kept dragging me back at quarter-hour
ntervals; and always I saw Backus drinking his wine—fairly
nd squarely, and the others throwing theirs away. It was the
ainfulest night I ever spent.

The only hope I had was that we might reach our anchor-
ge with speed—that would break up the game. I helped the
hip along all I could with my prayers. At last we went boom-
ng through the Golden Gate, and my pulses leaped for joy.
I hurried back to that door and glanced in. Alas, there was
mall room for hope—Backus's eyes were heavy and blood-
shot, his sweaty face was crimson, his speech maudlin and
thick, his body sawed drunkenly about with the weaving

motion of the ship. He drained another glass to the dreg
whilst the cards were being dealt.

He took his hand, glanced at it, and his dull eyes lit up fc
a moment. The gamblers observed it, and showed their gra
ification by hardly perceptible signs.

"How many cards?"

"None!" said Backus.

One villain—named Hank Wiley—discarded one card, th
others three each. The betting began. Heretofore the bets ha
been trifling—a dollar or two; but Backus started off with a
eagle now, Wiley hesitated a moment, then "saw it" an
"went ten dollars better." The other two threw up the
hands.

Backus went twenty better. Wiley said,—

"I see that, and go you a *hundred* better!" then smiled an
reached for the money.

"Let it alone," said Backus, with drunken gravity.

"What! you mean to say you 're going to cover it?"

"Cover it? Well I reckon I am—and lay another hundre
on top of it, too."

He reached down inside his overcoat and produced the re
quired sum.

"Oh, that 's your little game, is it? I see your raise, an
raise it five hundred!" said Wiley.

"Five hundred *better*!" said the foolish bull-driver, an
pulled out the amount and showered it on the pile. The thre
conspirators hardly tried to conceal their exultation.

All diplomacy and pretence were dropped now, and th
sharp exclamations came thick and fast, and the yellow pyra
mid grew higher and higher. At last ten thousand dollars la
in view. Wiley cast a bag of coin on the table, and said wit
mocking gentleness,—

"Five thousand dollars better, my friend from the rural dis
tricts—what do you say *now*?"

"I *call* you!" said Backus, heaving his golden shot-bag o
the pile. "What have you got?"

"Four kings, you d—d fool!" and Wiley threw down hi
cards and surrounded the stakes with his arms.

"Four *aces*, you ass!" thundered Backus, covering his ma

with a cocked revolver. "*I 'm a professional gambler myself, and 've been laying for you duffers all this voyage!*"

Down went the anchor, rumbledy-dum-dum! and the long trip was ended.

Well—well, it is a sad world. One of the three gamblers was Backus's "pal." It was he that dealt the fateful hands. According to an understanding with the two victims, he was to have given Backus four queens, but alas, he did n't.

A week later, I stumbled upon Backus—arrayed in the height of fashion—in Montgomery Street. He said, cheerily, as we were parting,—

"Ah, by-the-way, you need n't mind about those gores. I don't really know anything about cattle, except what I was able to pick up in a week's apprenticeship over in Jersey just before we sailed. My cattle-culture and cattle-enthusiasm have served their turn—I shan't need them any more."

Next day we reluctantly parted from the "Gold Dust" and her officers, hoping to see that boat and all those officers again, some day. A thing which the fates were to render tragically impossible!

XXXVII.

The End of the "Gold Dust"

F OR, three months later, August 8, while I was writing on of these foregoing chapters, the New York pape brought this telegram:—

A TERRIBLE DISASTER

Seventeen Persons Killed by an Explosion on the Steamer "Gold Dust."

"NASHVILLE, Aug. 7.—A despatch from Hickman, Ky says:—

"The steamer 'Gold Dust' exploded her boilers at thre o'clock to-day, just after leaving Hickman. Forty-seven per sons were scalded and seventeen are missing. The boat wa landed in the eddy just above the town, and through th exertions of the citizens the cabin passengers, officers, an part of the crew and deck passengers were taken ashore an removed to the hotels and residences. Twenty-four of th injured were lying in Holcomb's dry-goods store at on time, where they received every attention before being re moved to more comfortable places."

A list of the names followed, whereby it appeared that c the seventeen dead, one was the barkeeper; and among th forty-seven wounded, were the captain, chief mate, secon mate, and second and third clerks; also Mr. Lem. S. Gra pilot, and several members of the crew.

In answer to a private telegram, we learned that none c these was severely hurt, except Mr. Gray. Letters received af terward confirmed this news, and said that Mr. Gray was im proving and would get well. Later letters spoke less hopefull of his case; and finally came one announcing his death. *i* good man, a most companionable and manly man, and wor thy of a kindlier fate.

XXXVIII.

The House Beautiful

WE TOOK PASSAGE in a Cincinnati boat for New Orleans; or on a Cincinnati boat—either is correct; the former is the eastern form of putting it, the latter the western.

Mr. Dickens declined to agree that the Mississippi steamboats were "magnificent," or that they were "floating palaces,"—terms which had always been applied to them; terms which did not over-express the admiration with which the people viewed them.

Mr. Dickens's position was unassailable, possibly; the people's position was certainly unassailable. If Mr. Dickens was comparing these boats with the crown jewels; or with the Taj, or with the Matterhorn; or with some other priceless or wonderful thing which he had seen, they were not magnificent—he was right. The people compared them with what *they* had seen; and, thus measured, thus judged, the boats were magnificent—the term was the correct one, it was not at all too strong. The people were as right as was Mr. Dickens. The steamboats were finer than anything on shore. Compared with superior dwelling-houses and first class hotels in the Valley, they were indubitably magnificent, they were "palaces." To a few people living in New Orleans and St. Louis, they were not magnificent, perhaps; not palaces; but to the great majority of those populations, and to the entire populations spread over both banks between Baton Rouge and St. Louis, they were palaces; they tallied with the citizen's dream of what magnificence was, and satisfied it.

Every town and village along that vast stretch of double river-frontage had a best dwelling, finest dwelling, mansion,—the home of its wealthiest and most conspicuous citizen. It is easy to describe it: large grassy yard, with paling fence painted white—in fair repair; brick walk from gate to door; big, square, two-story "frame" house, painted white and porticoed like a Grecian temple—with this difference, that the imposing fluted columns and Corinthian capitals were a pathetic sham, being made of white pine, and painted;

iron knocker; brass door knob—discolored, for lack of pol
ishing. Within, an uncarpeted hall, of planed boards; opening
out of it, a parlor, fifteen feet by fifteen—in some instance
five or ten feet larger; ingrain carpet; mahogany centre-table
lamp on it, with green-paper shade—standing on a gridiron
so to speak, made of high-colored yarns, by the young ladie
of the house, and called a lamp-mat; several books, piled and
disposed, with cast-iron exactness, according to an inherited
and unchangeable plan; among them, Tupper, much pen
cilled; also, "Friendship's Offering," and "Affection'
Wreath," with their sappy inanities illustrated in die-awa
mezzotints; also, Ossian; "Alonzo and Melissa;" maybe "Ivan
hoe;" also "Album," full of original "poetry" of the Thou
hast-wounded-the-spirit-that-loved-thee breed; two or three
goody-goody works—"Shepherd of Salisbury Plain," etc.
current number of the chaste and innocuous Godey's "Lady'
Book," with painted fashion-plate of wax-figure women with
mouths all alike—lips and eyelids the same size—each five
foot woman with a two-inch wedge sticking from under he
dress and letting-on to be half of her foot. Polished air-tigh
stove (new and deadly invention), with pipe passing through
a board which closes up the discarded good old fireplace. On
each end of the wooden mantel, over the fireplace, a large
basket of peaches and other fruits, natural size, all done in
plaster, rudely, or in wax, and painted to resemble the origi
nals—which they don't. Over middle of mantel, engraving—
Washington Crossing the Delaware; on the wall by the door
copy of it done in thunder-and-lightning crewels by one of
the young ladies—work of art which would have made
Washington hesitate about crossing, if he could have foreseen
what advantage was going to be taken of it. Piano—kettle in
disguise—with music, bound and unbound, piled on it, and
on a stand near by: Battle of Prague; Bird Waltz; Arkansas
Traveller; Rosin the Bow; Marseilles Hymn; On a Lone Barren Isle (St. Helena); The Last Link is Broken; She wore a
Wreath of Roses the Night when last we met; Go, forget me,
Why should Sorrow o'er that Brow a Shadow fling; Hours
there were to Memory Dearer; Long, Long Ago; Days of
Absence; A Life on the Ocean Wave, a Home on the Rolling
Deep; Bird at Sea; and spread open on the rack, where the

plaintive singer has left it, *Ro*-holl on, silver *moo*-hoon, guide the *trav*-el-lerr his *way*, etc. Tilted pensively against the piano, a guitar—guitar capable of playing the Spanish Fandango by itself, if you give it a start. Frantic work of art on the wall—pious motto, done on the premises, sometimes in colored yarns, sometimes in faded grasses: progenitor of the "God Bless Our Home" of modern commerce. Framed in black mouldings on the wall, other works of art, conceived and committed on the premises, by the young ladies; being grim black-and-white crayons; landscapes, mostly: lake, solitary sail-boat, petrified clouds, pre-geological trees on shore, anthracite precipice; name of criminal conspicuous in the corner. Lithograph, Napoleon Crossing the Alps. Lithograph, The Grave at St. Helena. Steel-plates, Trumbull's Battle of Bunker Hill, and the Sally from Gibraltar. Copper-plates, Moses Smiting the Rock, and Return of the Prodigal Son. In big gilt frame, slander of the family in oil: papa holding a book ("Constitution of the United States"); guitar leaning against mamma, blue ribbons fluttering from its neck; the young ladies, as children, in slippers and scalloped pantelettes, one embracing toy horse, the other beguiling kitten with ball of yarn, and both simpering up at mamma, who simpers back. These persons all fresh, raw, and red—apparently skinned. Opposite, in gilt frame, grandpa and grandma, at thirty and twenty-two, stiff, old-fashioned, high-collared, puff-sleeved, glaring pallidly out from a background of solid Egyptian night. Under a glass French clock dome, large bouquet of stiff flowers done in corpsy white wax. Pyramidal what-not in the corner, the shelves occupied chiefly with bric-a-brac of the period, disposed with an eye to best effect: shell, with the Lord's Prayer carved on it; another shell—of the long-oval sort, narrow, straight orifice, three inches long, running from end to end—portrait of Washington carved on it; not well done; the shell had Washington's mouth, originally—artist should have built to that. These two are memorials of the long-ago bridal trip to New Orleans and the French Market. Other bric-a-brac: Californian "specimens"—quartz, with gold wart adhering; old Guinea-gold locket, with circlet of ancestral hair in it; Indian arrow-heads, of flint; pair of bead moccasins, from uncle who crossed the Plains;

three "alum" baskets of various colors—being skeleton-frame
of wire, clothed-on with cubes of crystallized alum in the
rock-candy style—works of art which were achieved by the
young ladies; their doubles and duplicates to be found upon
all what-nots in the land; convention of desiccated bugs and
butterflies pinned to a card; painted toy-dog, seated upon bel-
lows-attachment—drops its under jaw and squeaks when
pressed upon; sugar-candy rabbit—limbs and features
merged together, not strongly defined; pewter presidential-
campaign medal; miniature card-board wood-sawyer, to be
attached to the stove-pipe and operated by the heat; small
Napoleon, done in wax; spread-open daguerreotypes of dim
children, parents, cousins, aunts, and friends, in all attitudes
but customary ones; no templed portico at back, and manufactured landscape stretching away in the distance—that came
in later, with the photograph; all these vague figures lavishly
chained and ringed—metal indicated and secured from doubt
by stripes and splashes of vivid gold bronze; all of them too
much combed, too much fixed up; and all of them uncomfortable in inflexible Sunday-clothes of a pattern which the
spectator cannot realize could ever have been in fashion; husband and wife generally grouped together—husband sitting,
wife standing, with hand on his shoulder—and both preserv-
ing, all these fading years, some traceable effect of the da-
guerreotypist's brisk "Now smile, if you please!" Bracketed
over what-not—place of special sacredness—an outrage in
water-color, done by the young niece that came on a visit
long ago, and died. Pity, too; for she might have repented of
this in time. Horse-hair chairs, horse-hair sofa which keeps
sliding from under you. Window shades, of oil stuff, with
milk-maids and ruined castles stencilled on them in fierce colors. Lambrequins dependent from gaudy boxings of beaten
tin, gilded. Bedrooms with rag carpets; bedsteads of the
"corded" sort, with a sag in the middle, the cords needing
tightening; snuffy feather-bed—not aired often enough;
cane-seat chairs, splint-bottomed rocker; looking-glass on
wall, school-slate size, veneered frame; inherited bureau;
wash-bowl and pitcher, possibly—but not certainly; brass
candlestick, tallow candle, snuffers. Nothing else in the room.

Not a bathroom in the house; and no visitor likely to come along who has ever seen one.

That was the residence of the principal citizen, all the way from the suburbs of New Orleans to the edge of St. Louis. When he stepped aboard a big fine steamboat, he entered a new and marvellous world: chimney-tops cut to counterfeit a spraying crown of plumes—and maybe painted red; pilot-house, hurricane deck, boiler-deck guards, all garnished with white wooden filagree work of fanciful patterns; gilt acorns topping the derricks; gilt deer-horns over the big bell; gaudy symbolical picture on the paddle-box, possibly; big roomy boiler-deck, painted blue, and furnished with Windsor arm-chairs; inside, a far receding snow-white "cabin;" porcelain knob and oil-picture on every state-room door; curving patterns of filagree-work touched up with gilding, stretching overhead all down the converging vista; big chandeliers every little way, each an April shower of glittering glass-drops; lovely rainbow-light falling everywhere from the colored glazing of the skylights; the whole a long-drawn, resplendent tunnel, a bewildering and soul-satisfying spectacle! in the ladies' cabin a pink and white Wilton carpet, as soft as mush, and glorified with a ravishing pattern of gigantic flowers. Then the Bridal Chamber—the animal that invented that idea was still alive and unhanged, at that day—Bridal Chamber whose pretentious flummery was necessarily overawing to the now tottering intellect of that hosannahing citizen. Every state-room had its couple of cosy clean bunks, and perhaps a look-ing-glass and a snug closet; and sometimes there was even a wash-bowl and pitcher, and part of a towel which could be told from mosquito netting by an expert—though generally these things were absent, and the shirt-sleeved passengers cleansed themselves at a long row of stationary bowls in the barber shop, where were also public towels, public combs, and public soap.

Take the steamboat which I have just described, and you have her in her highest and finest, and most pleasing, and comfortable, and satisfactory estate. Now cake her over with a layer of ancient and obdurate dirt, and you have the Cincinnati steamer awhile ago referred to. Not all over—only inside; for she was ably officered in all departments except the steward's.

But wash that boat and repaint her, and she would be about the counterpart of the most complimented boat of the old flush times: for the steamboat architecture of the West has undergone no change; neither has steamboat furniture and ornamentation undergone any.

XXXIX.

Manufactures and Miscreants

WHERE THE RIVER, in the Vicksburg region, used to be
corkscrewed, it is now comparatively straight—made
o by cut-off; a former distance of seventy miles is reduced to
hirty-five. It is a change which threw Vicksburg's neighbor,
Delta, Louisiana, out into the country and ended its career as
a river town. Its whole river-frontage is now occupied by a
vast sand-bar, thickly covered with young trees—a growth
which will magnify itself into a dense forest, by and by, and
completely hide the exiled town.

In due time we passed Grand Gulf and Rodney, of war
fame, and reached Natchez, the last of the beautiful hill-
cities—for Baton Rouge, yet to come, is not on a hill, but
only on high ground. Famous Natchez-under-the-hill has not
changed notably in twenty years; in outward aspect—judging
by the descriptions of the ancient procession of foreign tourists—it has not changed in sixty; for it is still small, straggling, and shabby. It had a desperate reputation, morally, in
the old keel-boating and early steamboating times—plenty of
drinking, carousing, fisticuffing, and killing there, among the
riff-raff of the river, in those days. But Natchez-on-top-of-the-
hill is attractive; has always been attractive. Even Mrs. Trollope (1827) had to confess its charms:

"At one or two points the wearisome level line is relieved
by *bluffs*, as they call the short intervals of high ground.
The town of Natchez is beautifully situated on one of those
high spots. The contrast that its bright green hill forms
with the dismal line of black forest that stretches on every
side, the abundant growth of the paw-paw, palmetto and
orange, the copious variety of sweet-scented flowers that
flourish there, all make it appear like an oasis in the desert.
Natchez is the furthest point to the north at which oranges
ripen in the open air, or endure the winter without shelter.
With the exception of this sweet spot, I thought all the

little towns and villages we passed wretched-looking in the extreme."

Natchez, like her near and far river neighbors, has railways now, and is adding to them—pushing them hither and thither into all rich outlying regions that are naturally tributary to her. And like Vicksburg and New Orleans, she has her ice-factory; she makes thirty tons of ice a day. In Vicksburg and Natchez, in my time, ice was jewelry; none but the rich could wear it. But anybody and everybody can have it now. I visited one of the ice-factories in New Orleans, to see what the polar regions might look like when lugged into the edge of the tropics. But there was nothing striking in the aspect of the place. It was merely a spacious house, with some innocent steam machinery in one end of it and some big porcelain pipes running here and there. No, not porcelain—they merely seemed to be; they were iron, but the ammonia which was being breathed through them had coated them to the thickness of your hand with solid milk-white ice. It ought to have melted; for one did not require winter clothing in that atmosphere: but it did not melt; the inside of the pipe was too cold.

Sunk into the floor were numberless tin boxes, a foot square and two feet long, and open at the top end. These were full of clear water; and around each box, salt and other proper stuff was packed; also, the ammonia gases were applied to the water in some way which will always remain a secret to me, because I was not able to understand the process. While the water in the boxes gradually froze, men gave it a stir or two with a stick occasionally—to liberate the air-bubbles, I think. Other men were continually lifting out boxes whose contents had become hard frozen. They gave the box a single dip into a vat of boiling water, to melt the block of ice free from its tin coffin, then they shot the block out upon a platform car, and it was ready for market. These big blocks were hard, solid, and crystal-clear. In certain of them, big bouquets of fresh and brilliant tropical flowers had been frozen-in; in others, beautiful silken-clad French dolls, and other pretty objects. These blocks were to be set on end in a platter, in the centre of dinner-tables, to cool the tropical air;

and also to be ornamental, for the flowers and things imprisoned in them could be seen as through plate glass. I was told
that this factory could retail its ice, by wagon, throughout
New Orleans, in the humblest dwelling house quantities, at
six or seven dollars a ton, and make a sufficient profit. This
being the case, there is business for ice factories in the North;
for we get ice on no such terms there, if one take less than
three hundred and fifty pounds at a delivery.

The Rosalie Yarn Mill, of Natchez, has a capacity of 6,000
spindles and 160 looms, and employs 100 hands. The Natchez
Cotton Mills Company began operations four years ago in a
two-story building of 50 × 190 feet, with 4,000 spindles and
128 looms; capital $105,000, all subscribed in the town. Two
years later, the same stockholders increased their capital to
$225,000; added a third story to the mill, increased its length
to 317 feet; added machinery to increase the capacity to 10,300
spindles and 304 looms. The company now employ 250 op-
eratives, many of whom are citizens of Natchez. "The mill
works 5,000 bales of cotton annually and manufactures the
best standard quality of brown shirtings and sheetings and
drills, turning out 5,000,000 yards of these goods per year."[1]
A close corporation—stock held at $5,000 per share, but
none in the market.

The changes in the Mississippi River are great and strange,
yet were to be expected; but I was not expecting to live to
see Natchez and these other river towns become manufacturing strongholds and railway centres.

Speaking of manufactures reminds me of a talk upon that
topic which I heard—which I overheard—on board the Cincinnati boat. I awoke out of a fretted sleep, with a dull
confusion of voices in my ears. I listened—two men were
talking; subject, apparently, the great inundation. I looked
out through the open transom. The two men were eating a
late breakfast; sitting opposite each other; nobody else
around. They closed up the inundation with a few words—
having used it, evidently, as a mere ice-breaker and acquaint-
anceship-breeder—then they dropped into business. It soon
transpired that they were drummers—one belonging in Cincinnati, the other in New Orleans. Brisk men, energetic of

[1] "New Orleans Times-Democrat," Aug. 26, 1882.

movement and speech; the dollar their god, how to get it their religion.

"Now as to this article," said Cincinnati, slashing into the ostensible butter and holding forward a slab of it on his knife-blade, "it 's from our house; look at it—smell of it—taste it. Put any test on it you want to. Take your own time—no hurry—make it thorough. There now—what do you say? butter, ain't it? Not by a thundering sight—it's oleomarga-rine! Yes, sir, that 's what it is—oleomargarine. You can't tell it from butter; by George, an *expert* can't. It 's from our house. We supply most of the boats in the West; there 's hardly a pound of butter on one of them. We are crawling right along—*jumping* right along is the word. We are going to have that entire trade. Yes, and the hotel trade, too. You are going to see the day, pretty soon, when you can't find an ounce of butter to bless yourself with, in any hotel in the Mississippi and Ohio Valleys, outside of the biggest cities. Why, we are turning out oleomargarine *now* by the thousands of tons. And we can sell it so dirt-cheap that the whole coun-try has *got* to take it—can't get around it you see. Butter don't stand any show—there ain't any chance for competi-tion. Butter 's had its *day*—and from this out, butter goes to the wall. There 's more money in oleomargarine than—why, you can't imagine the business we do. I 've stopped in every town, from Cincinnati to Natchez; and I 've sent home big orders from every one of them."

And so-forth and so-on, for ten minutes longer, in the same fervid strain. Then New Orleans piped up and said:—

"Yes, it 's a first-rate imitation, that 's a certainty; but it ain't the only one around that 's first-rate. For instance, they make olive-oil out of cotton-seed oil, now-a-days, so that you can't tell them apart."

"Yes, that 's so," responded Cincinnati, "and it was a tip-top business for a while. They sent it over and brought it back from France and Italy, with the United States custom-house mark on it to indorse it for genuine, and there was no end of cash in it; but France and Italy broke up the game—of course they naturally would. Cracked on such a rattling impost that cotton-seed olive-oil could n't stand the raise; had to hang up and quit."

"Oh, it *did*, did it? You wait here a minute."

Goes to his state-room, brings back a couple of long bottles, and takes out the corks—says:—

"There now, smell them, taste them, examine the bottles, inspect the labels. One of 'm 's from Europe, the other 's never been out of this country. One 's European olive-oil, the other 's American cotton-seed olive-oil. Tell 'm apart? 'Course you can't. Nobody can. People that want to, can go to the expense and trouble of shipping their oils to Europe and back—it 's their privilege; but our firm knows a trick worth six of that. We turn out the whole thing—clean from the word go—in our factory in New Orleans: labels, bottles, oil, everything. Well, no, not labels: been buying *them* abroad—get them dirt-cheap there. You see, there 's just one little wee speck, essence, or whatever it is, in a gallon of cotton-seed oil, that gives it a smell, or a flavor, or something—get that out, and you 're all right—perfectly easy then to turn the oil into any kind of oil you want to, and there ain't anybody that can detect the true from the false. Well, we know how to get that one little particle out—and we 're the only firm that does. And we turn out an olive-oil that is just simply perfect—undetectable! We are doing a ripping trade, too—as I could easily show you by my order-book for this trip. Maybe you 'll butter everybody's bread pretty soon, but we 'll cotton-seed his salad for him from the Gulf to Canada, and that 's a dead-certain thing."

Cincinnati glowed and flashed with admiration. The two scoundrels exchanged business-cards, and rose. As they left the table, Cincinnati said,—

"But you have to have custom-house marks, don't you? How do you manage that?"

I did not catch the answer.

We passed Port Hudson, scene of two of the most terrific episodes of the war—the night-battle there between Farragut's fleet and the Confederate land batteries, April 14th, 1863; and the memorable land battle, two months later, which lasted eight hours—eight hours of exceptionally fierce and stubborn fighting—and ended, finally, in the repulse of the Union forces with great slaughter.

XL.

Castles and Culture

BATON ROUGE was clothed in flowers, like a bride—no, much more so; like a greenhouse. For we were in the absolute South now—no modifications, no compromises, no half-way measures. The magnolia-trees in the Capitol grounds were lovely and fragrant, with their dense rich foliage and huge snow-ball blossoms. The scent of the flower is very sweet, but you want distance on it, because it is so powerful. They are not good bedroom blossoms—they might suffocate one in his sleep. We were certainly in the South at last; for here the sugar region begins, and the plantations—vast green levels, with sugar-mill and negro quarters clustered together in the middle distance—were in view. And there was a tropical sun overhead and a tropical swelter in the air.

And at this point, also, begins the pilot's paradise: a wide river hence to New Orleans, abundance of water from shore to shore, and no bars, snags, sawyers, or wrecks in his road.

Sir Walter Scott is probably responsible for the Capitol building; for it is not conceivable that this little sham castle would ever have been built if he had not run the people mad, a couple of generations ago, with his mediæval romances. The South has not yet recovered from the debilitating influence of his books. Admiration of his fantastic heroes and their grotesque "chivalry" doings and romantic juvenilities still survives here, in an atmosphere in which is already perceptible the wholesome and practical nineteenth-century smell of cotton-factories and locomotives; and traces of its inflated language and other windy humbuggeries survive along with it. It is pathetic enough, that a whitewashed castle, with turrets and things—materials all ungenuine within and without, pretending to be what they are not—should ever have been built in this otherwise honorable place; but it is much more pathetic to see this architectural falsehood undergoing restoration and perpetuation in our day, when it would have been so easy to let dynamite finish what a charitable fire began, and

468

then devote this restoration-money to the building of something genuine.

Baton Rouge has no patent on imitation castles, however, and no monopoly of them. Here is a picture from the advertisement of the "Female Institute" of Columbia, Tennessee. The following remark is from the same advertisement:—

"The Institute building has long been famed as a model of striking and beautiful architecture. Visitors are charmed with its resemblance to the old castles of song and story, with its towers, turreted walls, and ivy-mantled porches."

Keeping school in a castle is a romantic thing; as romantic as keeping hotel in a castle.

By itself the imitation castle is doubtless harmless, and well enough; but as a symbol and breeder and sustainer of maudlin Middle-Age romanticism here in the midst of the plainest and sturdiest and infinitely greatest and worthiest of all the centuries the world has seen, it is necessarily a hurtful thing and a mistake.

Here is an extract from the prospectus of a Kentucky "Female College." Female college sounds well enough; but since the phrasing it in that unjustifiable way was done purely in the interest of brevity, it seems to me that she-college would have been still better—because shorter, and means the same thing: that is, if either phrase means anything at all:—

"The president is southern by birth, by rearing, by education, and by sentiment; the teachers are all southern in sentiment, and with the exception of those born in Europe were born and raised in the south. Believing the southern to be the highest type of civilization this continent has seen,[1] the young ladies are trained according to the south-

[1] Illustrations of it thoughtlessly omitted by the advertiser:

KNOXVILLE, Tenn., October 19.—This morning a few minutes after ten o'clock, General Joseph A. Mabry, Thomas O'Connor, and Joseph A. Mabry, Jr., were killed in a shooting affray. The difficulty began yesterday afternoon by General Mabry attacking Major O'Connor and threatening to kill him. This was at the fair grounds, and O'Connor told Mabry that it was not the place to settle their difficulties. Mabry then told O'Connor he should not live. It seems that Mabry was armed and O'Connor was not. The cause of the difficulty was an old feud about the transfer of some property from Mabry to O'Connor. Later in the afternoon Mabry sent word to O'Connor that

ern ideas of delicacy, refinement, womanhood, religion, and propriety; hence we offer a first-class female college for the south and solicit southern patronage."

What, warder, ho! the man that can blow so complacent a blast as that, probably blows it from a castle.

From Baton Rouge to New Orleans, the great sugar plantations border both sides of the river all the way, and stretch their league-wide levels back to the dim forest-walls of bearded cypress in the rear. Shores lonely no longer. Plenty of dwellings all the way, on both banks—standing so close together, for long distances, that the broad river lying be-

---

he would kill him on sight. This morning Major O'Connor was standing in the door of the Mechanics' National Bank, of which he was president. General Mabry and another gentleman walked down Gay Street on the opposite side from the bank. O'Connor stepped into the bank, got a shot gun, took deliberate aim at General Mabry and fired. Mabry fell dead, being shot in the left side. As he fell O'Connor fired again, the shot taking effect in Mabry's thigh. O'Connor then reached into the bank and got another shot gun. About this time Joseph A. Mabry, Jr., son of General Mabry, came rushing down the street, unseen by O'Connor until within forty feet, when the young man fired a pistol, the shot taking effect in O'Connor's right breast, passing through the body near the heart. The instant Mabry shot, O'Connor turned and fired, the load taking effect in young Mabry's right breast and side. Mabry fell pierced with twenty buckshot, and almost instantly O'Connor fell dead without a struggle. Mabry tried to rise, but fell back dead. The whole tragedy occurred within two minutes, and neither of the three spoke after he was shot. General Mabry had about thirty buckshot in his body. A bystander was painfully wounded in the thigh with a buckshot, and another was wounded in the arm. Four other men had their clothing pierced by buckshot. The affair caused great excitement, and Gay Street was thronged with thousands of people. General Mabry and his son Joe were acquitted only a few days ago of the murder of Moses Lusby and Don Lusby, father and son, whom they killed a few weeks ago. Will Mabry was killed by Don Lusby last Christmas. Major Thomas O'Connor was President of the Mechanics' National Bank here, and was the wealthiest man in the State.—*Associated Press Telegram.*

One day last month, Professor Sharpe, of the Somerville, Tenn., Female College, "a quiet and gentlemanly man," was told that his brother-in-law, a Captain Burton, had threatened to kill him. Burton, it seems, had already killed one man and driven his knife into another. The Professor armed himself with a double-barrelled shot gun, started out in search of his brother-in-law, found him playing billiards in a saloon, and blew his brains out. The

tween the two rows, becomes a sort of spacious street. A most home-like and happy-looking region. And now and then you see a pillared and porticoed great manor-house, embowered in trees. Here is testimony of one or two of the procession of foreign tourists that filed along here half a century ago. Mrs. Trollope says:—

"The unbroken flatness of the banks of the Mississippi continued unvaried for many miles above New Orleans; but the graceful and luxuriant palmetto, the dark and noble ilex, and the bright orange, were everywhere to be seen, and it was many days before we were weary of looking at them."

Captain Basil Hall:—

"The district of country which lies adjacent to the Mississippi, in the lower parts of Louisiana, is everywhere thickly peopled by sugar planters, whose showy houses, gay piazzas, trig gardens, and numerous slave-villages, all clean and neat, gave an exceedingly thriving air to the river scenery."

"Memphis Avalanche" reports that the Professor's course met with pretty general approval in the community; knowing that the law was powerless, in the actual condition of public sentiment, to protect him, he protected himself.

About the same time, two young men in North Carolina quarrelled about a girl, and "hostile messages" were exchanged. Friends tried to reconcile them, but had their labor for their pains. On the 24th the young men met in the public highway. One of them had a heavy club in his hand, the other an axe. The man with the club fought desperately for his life, but it was a hopeless fight from the first. A well-directed blow sent his club whirling out of his grasp, and the next moment he was a dead man.

About the same time, two "highly connected" young Virginians, clerks in a hardware store at Charlottesville, while "skylarking," came to blows. Peter Dick threw pepper in Charles Roads's eyes; Roads demanded an apology; Dick refused to give it, and it was agreed that a duel was inevitable, but a difficulty arose; the parties had no pistols, and it was too late at night to procure them. One of them suggested that butcher-knives would answer the purpose, and the other accepted the suggestion; the result was that Roads fell to the floor with a gash in his abdomen that may or may not prove fatal. If Dick has been arrested, the news has not reached us. He "expressed deep regret," and we are told by a Staunton correspondent of the "Philadelphia Press" that "every effort has been made to hush the matter up."—*Extracts from the Public Journals.*

All the procession paint the attractive picture in the same way. The descriptions of fifty years ago do not need to have a word changed in order to exactly describe the same region as it appears to-day—except as to the "trigness" of the houses. The whitewash is gone from the negro cabins now; and many, possibly most, of the big mansions, once so shining white, have worn out their paint and have a decayed, neglected look. It is the blight of the war. Twenty-one years ago everything was trim and trig and bright along the "coast," just as it had been in 1827, as described by those tourists.

Unfortunate tourists! People humbugged them with stupid and silly lies, and then laughed at them for believing and printing the same. They told Mrs. Trollope that the alligators—or crocodiles, as she calls them—were terrible creatures; and backed up the statement with a blood-curdling account of how one of these slandered reptiles crept into a squatter cabin one night, and ate up a woman and five children. The woman, by herself, would have satisfied any ordinarily-impossible alligator; but no, these liars must make him gorge the five children besides. One would not imagine that jokers of this robust breed would be sensitive—but they were. It is difficult, at this day, to understand, and impossible to justify, the reception which the book of the grave, honest, intelligent, gentle, manly, charitable, well-meaning Capt. Basil Hall got. Mrs. Trollope's account of it may perhaps entertain the reader; therefore I have put it in the Appendix.[1]

[1] See Appendix C.

XLI.

The Metropolis of the South

THE APPROACHES to New Orleans were familiar; general aspects were unchanged. When one goes flying through London along a railway propped in the air on tall arches, he may inspect miles of upper bedrooms through the open windows, but the lower half of the houses is under his level and out of sight. Similarly, in high-river stage, in the New Orleans region, the water is up to the top of the enclosing levee-rim, the flat country behind it lies low—representing the bottom of a dish—and as the boat swims along, high on the flood, one looks down upon the houses and into the upper windows. There is nothing but that frail breastwork of earth between the people and destruction.

The old brick salt-warehouses clustered at the upper end of the city looked as they had always looked; warehouses which had had a kind of Aladdin's lamp experience, however, since I had seen them; for when the war broke out the proprietor went to bed one night leaving them packed with thousands of sacks of vulgar salt, worth a couple of dollars a sack, and got up in the morning and found his mountain of salt turned into a mountain of gold, so to speak, so suddenly and to so dizzy a height had the war news sent up the price of the article.

The vast reach of plank wharves remained unchanged, and there were as many ships as ever: but the long array of steamboats had vanished; not altogether, of course, but not much of it was left.

The city itself had not changed—to the eye. It had greatly increased in spread and population, but the look of the town was not altered. The dust, waste-paper-littered, was still deep in the streets; the deep, trough-like gutters alongside the curb-stones were still half full of reposeful water with a dusty surface; the sidewalks were still—in the sugar and bacon region—incumbered by casks and barrels and hogsheads; the great blocks of austerely plain commercial houses were as dusty-looking as ever.

Canal Street was finer, and more attractive and stirring than formerly, with its drifting crowds of people, its several processions of hurrying street-cars, and—toward evening—its broad second-story verandas crowded with gentlemen and ladies clothed according to the latest mode.

Not that there is any "architecture" in Canal Street: to speak in broad, general terms, there is no architecture in New Orleans, except in the cemeteries. It seems a strange thing to say of a wealthy, far-seeing, and energetic city of a quarter of a million inhabitants, but it is true. There is a huge granite U. S. Custom-house—costly enough, genuine enough, but as a decoration it is inferior to a gasometer. It looks like a state prison. But it was built before the war. Architecture in America may be said to have been born since the war. New Orleans, I believe, has had the good luck—and in a sense the bad luck—to have had no great fire in late years. It must be so. If the opposite had been the case, I think one would be able to tell the "burnt district" by the radical improvement in its architecture over the old forms. One can do this in Boston and Chicago. The "burnt district" of Boston was commonplace before the fire; but now there is no commercial district in any city in the world that can surpass it—or perhaps even rival it—in beauty, elegance, and tastefulness.

However, New Orleans has begun—just this moment, as one may say. When completed, the new Cotton Exchange will be a stately and beautiful building; massive, substantial, full of architectural graces; no shams or false pretenses or uglinesses about it anywhere. To the city, it will be worth many times its cost, for it will breed its species. What has been lacking hitherto, was a model to build toward; something to educate eye and taste; a *suggester*, so to speak.

The city is well outfitted with progressive men—thinking, sagacious, long-headed men. The contrast between the spirit of the city and the city's architecture is like the contrast between waking and sleep. Apparently there is a "boom" in everything but that one dead feature. The water in the gutters used to be stagnant and slimy, and a potent disease-breeder; but the gutters are flushed now, two or three times a day, by powerful machinery; in many of the gutters the water never stands still, but has a steady current. Other sanitary improvements have been made; and with such effect that New Orleans claims to be (during the long intervals between the occasional yellow-fever assaults) one of the healthiest cities in the Union. There 's plenty of ice now for everybody, manufactured in the town. It is a driving place commercially, and has a great river, ocean, and railway business. At the date of our visit, it was the best lighted city in the Union, electrically speaking. The New Orleans electric lights were more numerous than those of New York, and very much better. One had this modified noonday not only in Canal and some neighboring chief streets, but all along a stretch of five miles of river frontage. There are good clubs in the city now—several of them but recently organized—and inviting modern-style pleasure resorts at West End and Spanish Fort. The telephone is everywhere. One of the most notable advances is in journalism. The newspapers, as I remember them, were not a striking feature. Now they are. Money is spent upon them with a free hand. They get the news, let it cost what it may. The editorial work is not hack-grinding, but literature. As an example of New Orleans journalistic achievement, it may be mentioned that the "Times-Democrat" of August 26, 1882, contained a report of the year's business of the towns of the Mississippi Valley, from New Orleans all the way to St. Paul—two thousand miles. That issue of the paper consisted of *forty* pages; seven columns to the page; two hundred and eighty columns in all; fifteen hundred words to the column; an aggregate of four hundred and twenty thousand words. That is to say, not much short of three times as many words as there are in this book. One may with sorrow contrast this with the architecture of New Orleans.

I have been speaking of public architecture only. The domestic article in New Orleans is reproachless, notwithstanding it remains as it always was. All the dwellings are of wood—in the American part of the town, I mean—and all have a comfortable look. Those in the wealthy quarter are spacious; painted snow-white usually, and generally have wide verandas, or double-verandas, supported by ornamental columns. These mansions stand in the centre of large grounds, and rise, garlanded with roses, out of the midst of swelling masses of shining green foliage and many-colored

blossoms. No houses could well be in better harmony with
their surroundings, or more pleasing to the eye, or more
home-like and comfortable-looking.

One even becomes reconciled to the cistern presently; this
is a mighty cask, painted green, and sometimes a couple of
stories high, which is propped against the house-corner on
stilts. There is a mansion-and-brewery suggestion about the
combination which seems very incongruous at first. But the
people cannot have wells, and so they take rain-water. Neither
can they conveniently have cellars, or graves;[1] the town being
built upon "made" ground; so they do without both, and few
of the living complain, and none of the others.

[1] The Israelites are buried in graves—by permission, I take it, not require-
ment; but none else, except the destitute, who are buried at public expense
The graves are but three or four feet deep.

XLII.

Hygiene and Sentiment

THEY BURY their dead in vaults, above the ground.
These vaults have a resemblance to houses—sometimes to temples; are built of marble, generally; are architecturally graceful and shapely; they face the walks and driveways of the cemetery; and when one moves through the midst of a thousand or so of them and sees their white roofs and gables stretching into the distance on every hand, the phrase "city of the dead" has all at once a meaning to him. Many of the cemeteries are beautiful, and are kept in perfect order. When one goes from the levee or the business streets near it, to a cemetery, he observes to himself that if those people down there would live as neatly while they are alive as they do after they are dead, they would find many advantages in it; and besides, their quarter would be the wonder and admiration of the business world. Fresh flowers, in vases of water, are to be seen at the portals of many of the vaults: placed there by the pious hands of bereaved parents and children, husbands and wives, and renewed daily. A milder form of sorrow finds its inexpensive and lasting remembrancer in the coarse and ugly but indestructible "immortelle"—which is a wreath or cross or some such emblem, made of rosettes of black linen, with sometimes a yellow rosette at the conjunction of the cross's bars,—kind of sorrowful breast-pin, so to say. The immortelle requires no attention: you just hang it up, and there you are; just leave it alone, it will take care of your grief for you, and keep it in mind better than you can; stands weather first-rate, and lasts like boiler-iron.

On sunny days, pretty little chameleons—gracefullest of leggéd reptiles—creep along the marble fronts of the vaults, and catch flies. Their changes of color—as to variety—are not up to the creature's reputation. They change color when a person comes along and hangs up an immortelle; but that is nothing: any right-feeling reptile would do that.

I will gradually drop this subject of graveyards. I have been trying all I could to get down to the sentimental part of it,

but I cannot accomplish it. I think there is no genuinely sen
timental part to it. It is all grotesque, ghastly, horrible. Grave
yards may have been justifiable in the bygone ages, wher
nobody knew that for every dead body put into the ground
to glut the earth and the plant-roots and the air with disease
germs, five or fifty, or maybe a hundred, persons must die
before their proper time; but they are hardly justifiable now
when even the children know that a dead saint enters upon a
century-long career of assassination the moment the earth
closes over his corpse. It is a grim sort of a thought. The
relics of St. Anne, up in Canada, have now, after nineteen
hundred years, gone to curing the sick by the dozen. But it is
merest matter-of-course that these same relics, within a gen
eration after St. Anne's death and burial, *made* several thou
sand people sick. Therefore these miracle-performances are
simply compensation, nothing more. St. Anne is somewha
slow pay, for a Saint, it is true; but better a debt paid after
nineteen hundred years, and outlawed by the statute of limi
tations, than not paid at all; and most of the knights of the
halo do not pay at all. Where you find one that pays—like
St. Anne—you find a hundred and fifty that take the benefi
of the statute. And none of them pay any more than the prin
cipal of what they owe—they pay none of the interest either
simple or compound. A Saint can never *quite* return the prin
cipal, however; for his dead body *kills* people, whereas his
relics *heal* only—they never restore the dead to life. That par
of the account is always left unsettled.

"Dr. F. Julius Le Moyne, after fifty years of medical prac
tice, wrote: 'The inhumation of human bodies, dead from
infectious diseases, results in constantly loading the atmo
sphere, and polluting the waters, with not only the germs
that rise from simply putrefaction, but also with the *specifi*
germs of the diseases from which death resulted.'

"The gases (from buried corpses) will rise to the surface
through eight or ten feet of gravel, just as coal-gas will do
and there is practically no limit to their power of escape.

"During the epidemic in New Orleans in 1853, Dr. E. H
Barton reported that in the Fourth District the mortality
was four hundred and fifty-two per thousand—more than

double that of any other. In this district were three large cemeteries, in which during the previous year more than three thousand bodies had been buried. In other districts the proximity of cemeteries seemed to aggravate the disease.

"In 1828 Professor Bianchi demonstrated how the fearful reappearance of the plague at Modena was caused by excavations in ground where, *three hundred years previously* the victims of the pestilence had been buried. Mr. Cooper, in explaining the causes of some epidemics, remarks that the opening of the plague burial-grounds at Eyam resulted in an immediate outbreak of disease."—*North American Review, No.* 3, *Vol.* 135.

In an address before the Chicago Medical Society, in advocacy of cremation, Dr. Charles W. Purdy made some striking comparisons to show what a burden is laid upon society by the burial of the dead:—

"One and one-fourth times more money is expended annually in funerals in the United States than the Government expends for public-school purposes. Funerals cost this country in 1880 enough money to pay the liabilities of all the commercial failures in the United States during the same year, and give each bankrupt a capital of $8,630 with which to resume business. Funerals cost annually more money than the value of the combined gold and silver yield of the United States in the year 1880! These figures do not include the sums invested in burial-grounds and expended in tombs and monuments, nor the loss from depreciation of property in the vicinity of cemeteries."

For the rich, cremation would answer as well as burial; for the ceremonies connected with it could be made as costly and ostentatious as a Hindoo *suttee*; while for the poor, cremation would be better than burial, because so cheap[1]—so cheap until the poor got to imitating the rich, which they would do by and by. The adoption of cremation would relieve us of a muck of threadbare burial-witticisms; but, on the other hand, it would resurrect a lot of mildewed old cremation-jokes that have had a rest for two thousand years.

[1] Four or five dollars is the minimum cost.

I have a colored acquaintance who earns his living by odd jobs and heavy manual labor. He never earns above four hundred dollars in a year, and as he has a wife and several young children, the closest scrimping is necessary to get him through to the end of the twelve months debtless. To such a man a funeral is a colossal financial disaster. While I was writing one of the preceding chapters, this man lost a little child. He walked the town over with a friend, trying to find a coffin that was within his means. He bought the very cheapest one he could find, plain wood, stained. It cost him *twenty-six dollars*. It would have cost less than four, probably, if it had been built to put something useful into. He and his family will feel that outlay a good many months.

XLIII.

The Art of Inhumation

ABOUT THE SAME TIME, I encountered a man in the street, whom I had not seen for six or seven years; and something like this talk followed. I said,—

"But you used to look sad and oldish; you don't now. Where did you get all this youth and bubbling cheerfulness? Give me the address."

He chuckled blithely, took off his shining tile, pointed to a notched pink circlet of paper pasted into its crown, with something lettered on it, and went on chuckling while I read, "J. B——, UNDERTAKER." Then he clapped his hat on, gave it an irreverent tilt to leeward, and cried out,—

"That 's what 's the matter! It used to be rough times with me when you knew me—insurance-agency business, you know; mighty irregular. Big fire, all right—brisk trade for ten days while people scared; after that, dull policy-business till next fire. Town like this don't have fires often enough—a fellow strikes so many dull weeks in a row that he gets discouraged. But you bet you, *this* is the business! People don't wait for examples to *die*. No, sir, they drop off right along—there ain't any dull spots in the undertaker line. I just started in with two or three little old coffins and a hired hearse, and *now* look at the thing! I 've worked up a business here that would satisfy any man, don't care who he is. Five years ago, lodged in an attic; live in a swell house now, with a mansard roof, and all the modern inconveniences."

"Does a coffin pay so well? Is there much profit on a coffin?"

"*Go*-way! How you talk!" Then, with a confidential wink, a dropping of the voice, and an impressive laying of his hand on my arm; "Look here; there 's one thing in this world which is n't ever cheap. That 's a coffin. There 's one thing in this world which a person don't ever try to jew you down on. That 's a coffin. There 's one thing in this world which a person don't say,—'I 'll look around a little, and if I find I can't do better I 'll come back and take it.' That 's a coffin.

481

There 's one thing in this world which a person won't take i
pine if he can go walnut; and won't take in walnut if he ca
go mahogany; and won't take in mahogany if he can go a
iron casket with silver door-plate and bronze handles. That
a coffin. And there 's one thing in this world which you don
have to worry around after a person to get him to pay fo
And *that* 's a coffin. Undertaking?—why it 's the dead-sure
business in Christendom, and the nobbiest.

"Why, just look at it. A rich man won't have anything bu
your very best; and you can just pile it on, too—pile it o
and sock it to him—he won't ever holler. And you take in
poor man, and if you work him right he 'll bust himself on
single lay-out. Or especially a woman. F'r instance: Mr
O'Flaherty comes in—widow—wiping her eyes and kind c
moaning. Unhandkerchiefs one eye, bats it around tearfull
over the stock; says,—

" 'And fhat might ye ask for that wan?'

" 'Thirty-nine dollars, madam,' says I.

" 'It 's a foine big price, sure, but Pat shall be buried like
gintleman, as he was, if I have to work me fingers off for i
I 'll have that wan, sor.'

" 'Yes, madam,' says I, 'and it is a very good one, too; nc
costly, to be sure, but in this life we must cut our garment t
our clothes, as the saying is.' And as she starts out, I heave ir
kind of casually, 'This one with the white satin lining is
beauty, but I am afraid—well, sixty-five dollars *is* a rather–
rather—but no matter, I felt obliged to say to Mr
O'Shaughnessy,—'

" 'D' ye mane to soy that Bridget O'Shaughnessy bough
the mate to that joo-ul box to ship that dhrunken divil t
Purgatory in?'

" 'Yes, madam.'

" 'Then Pat shall go to heaven in the twin to it, if it take
the last rap the O'Flaherties can raise; and moind you, stic
on some extras, too, and I 'll give ye another dollar.'

"And as I lay-in with the livery stables, of course I don
forget to mention that Mrs. O'Shaughnessy hired fifty-fou
dollars' worth of hacks and flung as much style into Dennis'
funeral as if he had been a duke or an assassin. And of cours
she sails in and goes the O'Shaughnessy about four hacks an

an omnibus better. That *used* to be, but that 's all played now; that is, in this particular town. The Irish got to piling up hacks so, on their funerals, that a funeral left them ragged and hungry for two years afterward; so the priest pitched in and broke it all up. He don't allow them to have but two hacks now, and sometimes only one."

"Well," said I, "if you are so light-hearted and jolly in ordinary times, what *must* you be in an epidemic?"

He shook his head.

"No, you 're off, there. We don't like to see an epidemic. An epidemic don't pay. Well, of course I don't mean that, exactly; but it don't pay in proportion to the regular thing. Don't it occur to you, why?"

"No."

"Think."

"I can't imagine. What is it?"

"It 's just two things."

"Well, what *are* they?"

"One 's Embamming."

"And what 's the other?"

"Ice."

"How is that?"

"Well, in ordinary times, a person dies, and we lay him up in ice; one day, two days, maybe three, to wait for friends to come. Takes a lot of it—melts fast. We charge jewelry rates for that ice, and war-prices for attendance. Well, don't you know, when there 's an epidemic, they rush 'em to the cemetery the minute the breath 's out. No market for ice in an epidemic. Same with Embamming. You take a family that 's able to embam, and you 've got a soft thing. You can mention sixteen different ways to do it—though there *ain't* only one or two ways, when you come down to the bottom facts of it—and they 'll take the highest-priced way, every time. It 's human nature—human nature in grief. It don't reason, you see. 'Time being, it don't care a dam. All it wants is physical immortality for deceased, and they 're willing to pay for it. All you 've got to do is to just be ca'm and stack it up—they 'll stand the racket. Why, man, you can take a defunct that you could n't *give* away; and get your embamming traps around you and go to work; and in a couple of hours he is worth a cool six hundred—that 's what *he* 's worth. There ain't anything equal to it but trading rats for di'monds in time of famine. Well, don't you see, when there 's an epidemic, people don't wait to embam. No, indeed they don't; and it hurts the business like hellth, as we say—hurts it like hell-th, *health*, see?—Our little joke in the trade. Well, I must be going. Give me a call whenever you need any—I mean, when you 're going by, sometime."

In his joyful high spirits, he did the exaggerating himself, if any has been done. I have not enlarged on him.

With the above brief references to inhumation, let us leave the subject. As for me, I hope to be cremated. I made that remark to my pastor once, who said, with what he seemed to think was an impressive manner,—

"I would n't worry about that, if I had your chances."

Much he knew about it—the family all so opposed to it.

XLIV.

City Sights

THE OLD FRENCH PART of New Orleans—anciently the Spanish part—bears no resemblance to the American end of the city: the American end which lies beyond the intervening brick business-centre. The houses are massed in blocks; are austerely plain and dignified; uniform of pattern, with here and there a departure from it with pleasant effect; all are plastered on the outside, and nearly all have long, iron-railed verandas running along the several stories. Their chief beauty is the deep, warm, varicolored stain with which time and the weather have enriched the plaster. It harmonizes with all the surroundings, and has as natural a look of belonging there as has the flush upon sunset clouds. This charming decoration cannot be successfully imitated; neither is it to be found elsewhere in America.

The iron railings are a specialty, also. The pattern is often exceedingly light and dainty, and airy and graceful—with a large cipher or monogram in the centre, a delicate cobweb of baffling, intricate forms, wrought in steel. The ancient railings are hand-made, and are now comparatively rare and proportionately valuable. They are become bric-a-brac.

The party had the privilege of idling through this ancient quarter of New Orleans with the South's finest literary genius, the author of "the Grandissimes." In him the South has found a masterly delineator of its interior life and its history. In truth, I find by experience, that the untrained eye and vacant mind can inspect it and learn of it and judge of it more clearly and profitably in his books than by personal contact with it.

With Mr. Cable along to see for you, and describe and explain and illuminate, a jog through that old quarter is a vivid pleasure. And you have a vivid *sense* as of unseen or dimly seen things—vivid, and yet fitful and darkling; you glimpse salient features, but lose the fine shades or catch them imperfectly through the vision of the imagination: a case, as it were, of ignorant near-sighted stranger traversing the rim of wide vague horizons of Alps with an inspired and enlightened long-sighted native.

We visited the old St. Louis Hotel, now occupied by municipal offices. There is nothing strikingly remarkable about it; but one can say of it as of the Academy of Music in New York, that if a broom or a shovel has ever been used in it there is no circumstantial evidence to back up the fact. It is curious that cabbages and hay and things do not grow in the Academy of Music; but no doubt it is on account of the interruption of the light by the benches, and the impossibility of hoeing the crop except in the aisles. The fact that the ushers grow their buttonhole-bouquets on the premises shows what might be done if they had the right kind of an agricultural head to the establishment.

We visited also the venerable Cathedral, and the pretty square in front of it; the one dim with religious light, the other brilliant with the worldly sort, and lovely with orange trees and blossomy shrubs; then we drove in the hot sun through the wilderness of houses and out on to the wide dead level beyond, where the villas are, and the water wheels to drain the town, and the commons populous with cows and children; passing by an old cemetery where we were told lie the ashes of an early pirate; but we took him on trust, and did not visit him. He was a pirate with a tremendous and sanguinary history; and as long as he preserved unspotted, in retirement, the dignity of his name and the grandeur of his ancient calling, homage and reverence were his from high and low; but when at last he descended into politics and became a paltry alderman, the public "shook" him, and turned aside and wept. When he died, they set up a monument over him; and little by little he has come into respect again; but it is respect for the pirate, not the alderman. To-day the loyal and generous remember only what he was, and charitably forget what he became.

Thence, we drove a few miles across a swamp, along a raised shell road, with a canal on one hand and a dense wood on the other; and here and there, in the distance, a ragged and angular-limbed and moss-bearded cypress, top standing out, clear cut against the sky, and as quaint of form as the apple-trees in Japanese pictures—such was our course and the surroundings of it. There was an occasional alligator swimming comfortably along in the canal, and an occasional picturesque colored person on the bank, flinging his statue-rigid reflection upon the still water and watching for a bite.

And by and by we reached the West End, a collection of hotels of the usual light summer-resort pattern, with broad verandas all around, and the waves of the wide and blue Lake Pontchartrain lapping the thresholds. We had dinner on a ground-veranda over the water—the chief dish the renowned fish called the pompano, delicious as the less criminal forms of sin.

Thousands of people come by rail and carriage to West End and to Spanish Fort every evening, and dine, listen to the bands, take strolls in the open air under the electric lights, go sailing on the lake, and entertain themselves in various and sundry other ways.

We had opportunities on other days and in other places to test the pompano. Notably, at an editorial dinner at one of the clubs in the city. He was in his last possible perfection there, and justified his fame. In his suite was a tall pyramid of scarlet cray-fish—large ones; as large as one's thumb; delicate, palatable, appetizing. Also devilled whitebait; also shrimps of choice quality; and a platter of small soft-shell crabs of a most superior breed. The other dishes were what one might get at Delmonico's, or Buckingham Palace; those I have spoken of can be had in similar perfection in New Orleans only, I suppose.

In the West and South they have a new institution,—the Broom Brigade. It is composed of young ladies who dress in a uniform costume, and go through the infantry drill, with broom in place of musket. It is a very pretty sight, on private view. When they perform on the stage of a theatre, in the blaze of colored fires, it must be a fine and fascinating spectacle. I saw them go through their complex manual with grace, spirit, and admirable precision. I saw them do everything which a human being can possibly do with a broom, except sweep. I did not see them sweep. But I know they could learn. What they have already learned proves that. And if they ever should learn, and should go on the war-path down Tchoupitoulas or some of those other streets around there, those thoroughfares would bear a greatly improved aspect in a very few minutes. But the girls themselves would n't; so nothing would be really gained, after all.

The drill was in the Washington Artillery building. In this building we saw many interesting relics of the war. Also a fine oil-painting representing Stonewall Jackson's last interview with General Lee. Both men are on horseback. Jackson has just ridden up, and is accosting Lee. The picture is very valuable, on account of the portraits, which are authentic. But, like many another historical picture, it means nothing without its label. And one label will fit it as well as another:—

First Interview between Lee and Jackson.

Last Interview between Lee and Jackson.

Jackson Introducing Himself to Lee.

Jackson Accepting Lee's Invitation to Dinner.

Jackson Declining Lee's Invitation to Dinner—with Thanks.

Jackson Apologizing for a Heavy Defeat.

Jackson Reporting a Great Victory.

Jackson Asking Lee for a Match.

It tells *one* story, and a sufficient one; for it says quite plainly and satisfactorily, "Here are Lee and Jackson together." The artist would have made it tell that this is Lee and Jackson's last interview if he could have done it. But he could n't, for there was n't any way to do it. A good legible label is usually worth, for information, a ton of significant attitude and expression in a historical picture. In Rome, people with fine sympathetic natures stand up and weep in front of the celebrated "Beatrice Cenci the Day before her Execution." It shows what a label can do. If they did not know the picture, they would inspect it unmoved, and say, "Young girl with hay fever; young girl with her head in a bag."

I found the half-forgotten Southern intonations and elisions as pleasing to my ear as they had formerly been. A Southerner talks music. At least it is music to me, but then I was born in the South. The educated Southerner has no use for an *r*, except at the beginning of a word. He says "honah," and "dinnah," and "Gove'nuh," and "befo' the waw," and so on. The words may lack charm to the eye, in print, but they have it to the ear. When did the *r* disappear from Southern

peech, and how did it come to disappear? The custom of
dropping it was not borrowed from the North, nor inherited
from England. Many Southerners—most Southerners—put
a _y_ into occasional words that begin with the _k_ sound. For
instance, they say Mr. K'yahtah (Carter) and speak of playing
k'yahds or of riding in the k'yahs. And they have the pleasant
custom—long ago fallen into decay in the North—of frequently employing the respectful "Sir." Instead of the curt
Yes, and the abrupt No, they say "Yes, Suh"; "No, Suh."

But there are some infelicities. Such as "like" for "as," and
the addition of an "at" where it is n't needed. I heard an
educated gentleman say, "Like the flag-officer did." His cook
or his butler would have said, "Like the flag-officer done."
You hear gentlemen say, "Where have you been at?" And
here is the aggravated form—heard a ragged street Arab say
it to a comrade: "I was a-ask'n' Tom whah you was a-sett'n'
at." The very elect carelessly say "will" when they mean
"shall"; and many of them say, "I did n't go to do it," meaning "I did n't mean to do it." The Northern word "guess"—
imported from England, where it used to be common, and
now regarded by satirical Englishmen as a Yankee original—
is but little used among Southerners. They say "reckon." They
have n't any "does n't" in their language; they say "don't"
instead. The unpolished often use "went" for "gone." It is
nearly as bad as the Northern "had n't ought." This reminds
me that a remark of a very peculiar nature was made here in
my neighborhood (in the North) a few days ago: "He had n't
ought to have went." How is that? Is n't that a good deal of
a triumph? One knows the orders combined in this half-
breed's architecture without inquiring: one parent Northern,
the other Southern. To-day I heard a school-mistress ask,
"Where is John gone?" This form is so common—so
nearly universal, in fact—that if she had used "whither" instead of "where," I think it would have sounded like an affectation.

We picked up one excellent word—a word worth travelling to New Orleans to get; a nice limber, expressive, handy
word—"Lagniappe." They pronounce it lanny-_yap_. It is
Spanish—so they said. We discovered it at the head of a column of odds and ends in the Picayune, the first day; heard

twenty people use it the second; inquired what it meant the third; adopted it and got facility in swinging it the fourth. It has a restricted meaning, but I think the people spread it out a little when they choose. It is the equivalent of the thirteenth roll in a "baker's dozen." It is something thrown in, gratis, for good measure. The custom originated in the Spanish quarter of the city. When a child or a servant buys something in a shop—or even the mayor or the governor, for aught I know—he finishes the operation by saying,—

"Give me something for lagniappe."

The shopman always responds; gives the child a bit of liquorice-root, gives the servant a cheap cigar or a spool of thread, gives the governor—I don't know what he gives the governor; support, likely.

When you are invited to drink,—and this does occur now and then in New Orleans,—and you say, "What, again?—no, I 've had enough;" the other party says, "But just this one time more,—this is for lagniappe." When the beau perceives that he is stacking his compliments a trifle too high, and sees by the young lady's countenance that the edifice would have been better with the top compliment left off, he puts his "I beg pardon,—no harm intended," into the briefer form of "Oh, that 's for lagniappe." If the waiter in the restaurant stumbles and spills a gill of coffee down the back of your neck, he says, "For lagniappe, sah," and gets you another cup without extra charge.

XLV.

Southern Sports

IN THE NORTH one hears the war mentioned, in social conversation, once a month; sometimes as often as once a week; but as a distinct subject for talk, it has long ago been relieved of duty. There are sufficient reasons for this. Given a dinner company of six gentlemen to-day, it can easily happen that four of them—and possibly five—were not in the field at all. So the chances are four to two, or five to one, that the war will at no time during the evening become the topic of conversation; and the chances are still greater that if it become the topic it will remain so but a little while. If you add six ladies to the company, you have added six people who saw so little of the dread realities of the war that they ran out of talk concerning them years ago, and now would soon weary of the war topic if you brought it up.

The case is very different in the South. There, every man you meet was in the war; and every lady you meet saw the war. The war is the great chief topic of conversation. The interest in it is vivid and constant; the interest in other topics is fleeting. Mention of the war will wake up a dull company and set their tongues going, when nearly any other topic would fail. In the South, the war is what A.D. is elsewhere: they date from it. All day long you hear things "placed" as having happened since the waw; or du'in' the waw; or befo' the waw; or right aftah the waw; or 'bout two yeahs or five yeahs or ten yeahs befo' the waw or aftah the waw. It shows how intimately every individual was visited, in his own person, by that tremendous episode. It gives the inexperienced stranger a better idea of what a vast and comprehensive calamity invasion is than he can ever get by reading books at the fireside.

At a club one evening, a gentleman turned to me and said, in an aside:—

"You notice, of course, that we are nearly always talking about the war. It is n't because we have n't anything else to talk about, but because nothing else has so strong an interest for us. And there is another reason: In the war, each of us, in his own person, seems to have sampled all the different varieties of human experience; as a consequence, you can't mention an outside matter of any sort but it will certainly remind some listener of something that happened during the war,—and out he comes with it. Of course that brings the talk back to the war. You may try all you want to, to keep other subjects before the house, and we may all join in and help, but there can be but one result: the most random topic would load every man up with war reminiscences, and *shut* him up too; and talk would be likely to stop presently, because you can't talk pale inconsequentialities when you 've got a crimson fact or fancy in your head that you are burning to fetch out.

The poet was sitting some little distance away; and presently he began to speak—about the moon.

The gentleman who had been talking to me remarked in an "aside:" "There, the moon is far enough from the seat of war, but you will see that it will suggest something to somebody about the war; in ten minutes from now the moon, as a topic, will be shelved."

The poet was saying he had noticed something which was a surprise to him; had had the impression that down here toward the equator, the moonlight was much stronger and brighter than up North; had had the impression that when he visited New Orleans, many years ago, the moon—

Interruption from the other end of the room:—

"Let me explain that. Reminds me of an anecdote. Every thing is changed since the war, for better or for worse; but you 'll find people down here born grumblers, who see no change except the change for the worse. There was an old negro woman of this sort. A young New-Yorker said in her presence, 'What a wonderful moon you have down here!' She sighed and said, 'Ah, bless yo' heart, honey, you ought to seen dat moon befo' de waw!' "

The new topic was dead already. But the poet resurrected it, and gave it a new start.

A brief dispute followed, as to whether the difference between Northern and Southern moonlight really existed or was only imagined. Moonlight talk drifted easily into talk about artificial methods of dispelling darkness. Then somebody remembered that when Farragut advanced upon Port Hudson on a dark night—and did not wish to assist the aim of the Confederate gunners—he carried no battle-lanterns, but painted the decks of his ships white, and thus created a dim but valuable light, which enabled his own men to grope their way around with considerable facility. At this point the war got the floor again—the ten minutes not quite up yet.

I was not sorry, for war talk by men who have been in a war is always interesting; whereas moon talk by a poet who has not been in the moon is likely to be dull.

We went to a cockpit in New Orleans on a Saturday afternoon. I had never seen a cock-fight before. There were men and boys there of all ages and all colors, and of many languages and nationalities. But I noticed one quite conspicuous and surprising absence: the traditional brutal faces. There were no brutal faces. With no cock-fighting going on, you could have played the gathering on a stranger for a prayer-meeting; and after it began, for a revival,—provided you blindfolded your stranger,—for the shouting was something prodigious.

A negro and a white man were in the ring; everybody else outside. The cocks were brought in in sacks; and when time was called, they were taken out by the two bottle-holders, stroked, caressed, poked toward each other, and finally liberated. The big black cock plunged instantly at the little gray one and struck him on the head with his spur. The gray responded with spirit. Then the Babel of many-tongued shoutings broke out, and ceased not thenceforth. When the cocks had been fighting some little time, I was expecting them momently to drop dead, for both were blind, red with blood, and so exhausted that they frequently fell down. Yet they would not give up, neither would they die. The negro and the white man would pick them up every few seconds, wipe them off, blow cold water on them in a fine spray, and take their heads in their mouths and hold them there a moment—to warm back the perishing life perhaps; I do not know. Then, being set down again, the dying creatures would totter gropingly about, with dragging wings, find each other, strike a guess-work blow or two, and fall exhausted once more.

I did not see the end of the battle. I forced myself to endure it as long as I could, but it was too pitiful a sight; so made frank confession to that effect, and we retired. W heard afterward that the black cock died in the ring, and fighting to the last.

Evidently there is abundant fascination about this "sport for such as have had a degree of familiarity with it. I never saw people enjoy anything more than this gathering enjoyed this fight. The case was the same with old gray-heads and with boys of ten. They lost themselves in frenzies of delight The "cocking-main" is an inhuman sort of entertainment there is no question about that; still, it seems a much more respectable and far less cruel sport than fox-hunting—for the cocks like it; they experience, as well as confer enjoyment which is not the fox's case.

We assisted—in the French sense—at a mule race, one day. I believe I enjoyed this contest more than any other mule there. I enjoyed it more than I remember having enjoyed any other animal race I ever saw. The grand stand was well filled with the beauty and the chivalry of New Orleans. That phrase is not original with me. It is the Southern reporter's. He has used it for two generations. He uses it twenty times a day, or twenty thousand times a day; or a million times a day—according to the exigencies. He is obliged to use it a million times a day, if he have occasion to speak of respectable men and women that often; for he has no other phrase for such service except that single one. He never tires of it; it always has a fine sound to him. There is a kind of swell mediæval bulliness and tinsel about it that pleases his gaudy barbaric soul. If he had been in Palestine in the early times, we should have had no references to "much people" out of him. No, he would have said "the beauty and the chivalry of Galilee" assembled to hear the Sermon on the Mount. It is likely that the men and women of the South are sick enough of that phrase by this time, and would like a change, but there is no immediate prospect of their getting it.

The New Orleans editor has a strong, compact, direct, un-flowery style; wastes no words, and does not gush. Not so with his average correspondent. In the Appendix I have quoted a good letter, penned by a trained hand; but the av-

erage correspondent hurls a style which differs from that. For
instance:—

The "Times-Democrat" sent a relief-steamer up one of the
bayous, last April. This steamer landed at a village, up there
somewhere, and the Captain invited some of the ladies of the
village to make a short trip with him. They accepted and came
aboard, and the steamboat shoved out up the creek. That was
all there was "to it." And that is all that the editor of the
"Times-Democrat" would have got out of it. There was nothing in the thing but statistics, and he would have got nothing
else out of it. He would probably have even tabulated them,
partly to secure perfect clearness of statement, and partly to
save space. But his special correspondent knows other methods of handling statistics. He just throws off all restraint and
wallows in them:—

> "On Saturday, early in the morning, the beauty of the
> place graced our cabin, and proud of her fair freight the
> gallant little boat glided up the bayou."

Twenty-two words to say the ladies came aboard and the
boat shoved out up the creek, is a clean waste of ten good
words, and is also destructive of compactness of statement.

The trouble with the Southern reporter is—Women. They
unsettle him; they throw him off his balance. He is plain, and
sensible, and satisfactory, until a woman heaves in sight. Then
he goes all to pieces; his mind totters, he becomes flowery
and idiotic. From reading the above extract, you would imagine that this student of Sir Walter Scott is an apprentice, and
knows next to nothing about handling a pen. On the contrary, he furnishes plenty of proofs, in his long letter, that he
knows well enough how to handle it when the women are
not around to give him the artificial-flower complaint. For
instance:—

> "At 4 o'clock ominous clouds began to gather in the
> southeast, and presently from the Gulf there came a blow
> which increased in severity every moment. It was not safe
> to leave the landing then, and there was a delay. The oaks
> shook off long tresses of their mossy beards to the tugging

of the wind, and the bayou in its ambition put on minia
ture waves in mocking of much larger bodies of water. A
lull permitted a start, and homewards we steamed, an ink
sky overhead and a heavy wind blowing. As darkness crep
on, there were few on board who did not wish themselve
nearer home."

There is nothing the matter with that. It is good descrip
tion, compactly put. Yet there was great temptation, there, t
drop into lurid writing.

But let us return to the mule. Since I left him, I have rum
maged around and found a full report of the race. In it I fine
confirmation of the theory which I broached just now—
namely, that the trouble with the Southern reporter i
Women: Women, supplemented by Walter Scott and hi
knights and beauty and chivalry, and so on. This is an excel
lent report, as long as the women stay out of it. But whee
they intrude, we have this frantic result:—

"It will be probably a long time before the ladies' stand
presents such a sea of foam-like loveliness as it did yester
day. The New Orleans women are always charming, bu
never so much so as at this time of the year, when in thei
dainty spring costumes they bring with them a breath o
balmy freshness and an odor of sanctity unspeakable. The
stand was so crowded with them that, walking at their fee
and seeing no possibility of approach, many a man appre
ciated as he never did before the Peri's feeling at the Gate
of Paradise, and wondered what was the priceless boon tha
would admit him to their sacred presence. Sparkling or
their white-robed breasts or shoulders were the colors o
their favorite knights, and were it not for the fact that the
doughty heroes appeared on unromantic mules, it woul
have been easy to imagine one of King Arthur's gala-days."

There were thirteen mules in the first heat; all sorts o
mules, they were; all sorts of complexions, gaits, dispositions
aspects. Some were handsome creatures, some were not
some were sleek, some had n't had their fur brushed lately
some were innocently gay and frisky; some were full of malice
and all unrighteousness; guessing from looks, some of them

hought the matter on hand was war, some thought it was a
ark, the rest took it for a religious occasion. And each mule
cted according to his convictions. The result was an absence
f harmony well compensated by a conspicuous presence of
ariety—variety of a picturesque and entertaining sort.

All the riders were young gentlemen in fashionable society.
f the reader has been wondering why it is that the ladies of
New Orleans attend so humble an orgy as a mule-race, the
hing is explained now. It is a fashion-freak; all connected
vith it are people of fashion.

It is great fun, and cordially liked. The mule-race is one of
he marked occasions of the year. It has brought some pretty
fast mules to the front. One of these had to be ruled out,
because he was so fast that he turned the thing into a one-
mule contest, and robbed it of one of its best features—variety. But every now and then somebody disguises him with a
new name and a new complexion, and rings him in again.

The riders dress in full jockey costumes of bright-colored
silks, satins, and velvets.

The thirteen mules got away in a body, after a couple of
false starts, and scampered off with prodigious spirit. As each
mule and each rider had a distinct opinion of his own as to
how the race ought to be run, and which side of the track
was best in certain circumstances, and how often the track
ought to be crossed, and when a collision ought to be accomplished, and when it ought to be avoided, these twenty-six
conflicting opinions created a most fantastic and picturesque
confusion, and the resulting spectacle was killingly comical.

Mile heat; time, 2:22. Eight of the thirteen mules distanced.
I had a bet on a mule which would have won if the procession had been reversed. The second heat was good fun; and
so was the "consolation race for beaten mules," which followed later; but the first heat was the best in that respect.

I think that much the most enjoyable of all races is a steamboat race; but, next to that, I prefer the gay and joyous mule-
rush. Two red-hot steamboats raging along, neck-and-neck,
straining every nerve—that is to say, every rivet in the boilers—quaking and shaking and groaning from stem to stern,
spouting white steam from the pipes, pouring black smoke
from the chimneys, raining down sparks, parting the river

into long breaks of hissing foam—this is sport that makes body's very liver curl with enjoyment. A horse-race is pret tame and colorless in comparison. Still, a horse-race might well enough, in its way, perhaps, if it were not for the tir some false starts. But then, nobody is ever killed. At leas nobody was ever killed when I was at a horse-race. They ha been crippled, it is true; but this is little to the purpose.

XLVI.

Enchantments and Enchanters

THE LARGEST ANNUAL EVENT in New Orleans is a something which we arrived too late to sample—the Mardi-Gras festivities. I saw the procession of the Mystic Crew of Comus there, twenty-four years ago—with knights and nobles and so on, clothed in silken and golden Paris-made gorgeousnesses, planned and bought for that single night's use; and in their train all manner of giants, dwarfs, monstrosities, and other diverting grotesquerie—a startling and wonderful sort of show, as it filed solemnly and silently down the street in the light of its smoking and flickering torches; but it is said that in these latter days the spectacle is mightily augmented, as to cost, splendor, and variety. There is a chief personage—"Rex;" and if I remember rightly, neither this king nor any of his great following of subordinates is known to any outsider. All these people are gentlemen of position and consequence; and it is a proud thing to belong to the organization; so the mystery in which they hide their personality is merely for romance's sake, and not on account of the police.

Mardi-Gras is of course a relic of the French and Spanish occupation; but I judge that the religious feature has been pretty well knocked out of it now. Sir Walter has got the advantage of the gentlemen of the cowl and rosary, and he will stay. His mediæval business, supplemented by the monsters and the oddities, and the pleasant creatures from fairyland, is finer to look at than the poor fantastic inventions and performances of the revelling rabble of the priest's day, and serves quite as well, perhaps, to emphasize the day and admonish men that the grace-line between the worldly season and the holy one is reached.

This Mardi-Gras pageant was the exclusive possession of New Orleans until recently. But now it has spread to Memphis and St. Louis and Baltimore. It has probably reached its limit. It is a thing which could hardly exist in the practical North; would certainly last but a very brief time; as brief a time as it would last in London. For the soul of it is the romantic, not the funny and the grotesque. Take away the romantic mysteries, the kings and knights and big-sounding titles, and Mardi-Gras would die, down there in the South. The very feature that keeps it alive in the South—girly-girly romance—would kill it in the North or in London. Puck and Punch, and the press universal, would fall upon it and make merciless fun of it, and its first exhibition would be also its last.

Against the crimes of the French Revolution and of Bonaparte may be set two compensating benefactions: the Revolution broke the chains of the *ancien régime* and of the Church, and made of a nation of abject slaves a nation of freemen; and Bonaparte instituted the setting of merit above birth, and also so completely stripped the divinity from royalty, that whereas crowned heads in Europe were gods before, they are only men, since, and can never be gods again, but only figure-heads, and answerable for their acts like common clay. Such benefactions as these compensate the temporary harm which Bonaparte and the Revolution did, and leave the world in debt to them for these great and permanent services to liberty, humanity, and progress.

Then comes Sir Walter Scott with his enchantments, and by his single might checks this wave of progress, and even turns it back; sets the world in love with dreams and phantoms; with decayed and swinish forms of religion; with decayed and degraded systems of government; with the sillinesses and emptinesses, sham grandeurs, sham gauds, and sham chivalries of a brainless and worthless long-vanished society. He did measureless harm; more real and lasting harm, perhaps, than any other individual that ever wrote. Most of the world has now outlived good part of these harms, though by no means all of them; but in our South they flourish pretty forcefully still. Not so forcefully as half a generation ago, perhaps, but still forcefully. There, the genuine and wholesome civilization of the nineteenth century is curiously confused and commingled with the Walter Scott Middle-Age sham civilization and so you have practical, common-sense, progressive ideas, and progressive works, mixed up with the duel, the inflated speech, and the jejune romanticism of an absurd past that is dead, and out of charity ought to be buried. But for the Sir Walter disease, the character of the Southerner—or Southron, according to Sir Walter's starchier way of phrasing it—would be wholly modern, in place of modern and mediæval mixed, and the South would be fully a generation further advanced than it is. It was Sir Walter that made every gentleman in the South a Major or a Colonel, or a General or a Judge, before the war; and it was he, also, that made these gentlemen value these bogus decorations. For it was he that created rank and caste down there, and also reverence for rank and caste, and pride and pleasure in them. Enough is laid on slavery, without fathering upon it these creations and contributions of Sir Walter.

Sir Walter had so large a hand in making Southern character, as it existed before the war, that he is in great measure responsible for the war. It seems a little harsh toward a dead man to say that we never should have had any war but for Sir Walter; and yet something of a plausible argument might, perhaps, be made in support of that wild proposition. The Southerner of the American revolution owned slaves; so did the Southerner of the Civil War: but the former resembles the latter as an Englishman resembles a Frenchman. The change of character can be traced rather more easily to Sir Walter's influence than to that of any other thing or person.

One may observe, by one or two signs, how deeply that influence penetrated, and how strongly it holds. If one take up a Northern or Southern literary periodical of forty or fifty years ago, he will find it filled with wordy, windy, flowery "eloquence," romanticism, sentimentality—all imitated from Sir Walter, and sufficiently badly done, too—innocent travesties of his style and methods, in fact. This sort of literature being the fashion in both sections of the country, there was opportunity for the fairest competition; and as a consequence, the South was able to show as many well-known literary names, proportioned to population, as the North could.

But a change has come, and there is no opportunity now for a fair competition between North and South. For the North has thrown out that old inflated style, whereas the Southern writer still clings to it—clings to it and has a restricted market for his wares, as a consequence. There is as much literary talent in the South, now, as ever there was, of course; but its work can gain but slight currency under present conditions; the authors write for the past, not the present; they use obsolete forms, and a dead language. But when a Southerner of genius writes modern English, his book goes upon crutches no longer, but upon wings; and they carry it swiftly all about America and England, and through the great English reprint publishing houses of Germany—as witness the experience of Mr. Cable and Uncle Remus, two of the very few Southern authors who do not write in the southern style. Instead of three or four widely-known literary names, the South ought to have a dozen or two—and will have them when Sir Walter's time is out.

A curious exemplification of the power of a single book for good or harm is shown in the effects wrought by Don Quixote and those wrought by Ivanhoe. The first swept the world's admiration for the mediæval chivalry-silliness out of existence; and the other restored it. As far as our South is concerned, the good work done by Cervantes is pretty nearly a dead letter, so effectually has Scott's pernicious work undermined it.

XLVII.

Uncle Remus and Mr. Cable

M R. JOEL CHANDLER HARRIS ("Uncle Remus") was to arrive from Atlanta at seven o'clock Sunday morning; so we got up and received him. We were able to detect him among the crowd of arrivals at the hotel-counter by his correspondence with a description of him which had been furnished us from a trustworthy source. He was said to be undersized, red-haired, and somewhat freckled. He was the only man in the party whose outside tallied with this bill of particulars. He was said to be very shy. He is a shy man. Of this there is no doubt. It may not show on the surface, but the shyness is there. After days of intimacy one wonders to see that it is still in about as strong force as ever. There is a fine and beautiful nature hidden behind it, as all know who have read the Uncle Remus book; and a fine genius, too, as all know by the same sign. I seem to be talking quite freely about this neighbor; but in talking to the public I am but talking to his personal friends, and these things are permissible among friends.

He deeply disappointed a number of children who had flocked eagerly to Mr. Cable's house to get a glimpse of the illustrious sage and oracle of the nation's nurseries. They said: —

"Why, he 's white!"

They were grieved about it. So, to console them, the book was brought, that they might hear Uncle Remus's Tar-Baby story from the lips of Uncle Remus himself—or what, in their outraged eyes, was left of him. But it turned out that he had never read aloud to people, and was too shy to venture the attempt now. Mr. Cable and I read from books of ours, to show him what an easy trick it was; but his immortal shyness was proof against even this sagacious strategy, so we had to read about Brer Rabbit ourselves.

Mr. Harris ought to be able to read the negro dialect better than anybody else, for in the matter of writing it he is the only master the country has produced. Mr. Cable is the only master in the writing of French dialects that the country has produced; and he reads them in perfection. It was a great treat to hear him read about Jean-ah Poquelin, and about Innerarity and his famous "pigshoo" representing "Louisihanna *Rif*-fusing to Hanter the Union," along with passages of nicely-shaded German dialect from a novel which was still in manuscript.

It came out in conversation, that in two different instances Mr. Cable got into grotesque trouble by using, in his books, next-to-impossible French names which nevertheless happened to be borne by living and sensitive citizens of New Orleans. His names were either inventions or were borrowed from the ancient and obsolete past, I do not now remember which; but at any rate living bearers of them turned up, and were a good deal hurt at having attention directed to themselves and their affairs in so excessively public a manner.

Mr. Warner and I had an experience of the same sort when we wrote the book called "The Gilded Age." There is a character in it called "Sellers." I do not remember what his first name was, in the beginning; but anyway, Mr. Warner did not like it, and wanted it improved. He asked me if I was able to imagine a person named "Eschol Sellers." Of course I said I could not, without stimulants. He said that away out West, once, he had met, and contemplated, and actually shaken hands with a man bearing that impossible name—"Eschol Sellers." He added,—

"It was twenty years ago; his name has probably carried him off before this; and if it has n't, he will never see the book anyhow. We will confiscate his name. The name you are using is common, and therefore dangerous; there are probably a thousand Sellerses bearing it, and the whole horde will come after us; but Eschol Sellers is a safe name—it is a rock.'

So we borrowed that name; and when the book had been out about a week, one of the stateliest and handsomest and most aristocratic looking white men that ever lived, called around, with the most formidable libel suit in his pocket that ever—well, in brief, we got his permission to suppress an edition of ten million[1] copies of the book and change that name to "Mulberry Sellers" in future editions.

---

[1]Figures taken from memory, and probably incorrect. Think it was more.

XLVIII.

Sugar and Postage

O NE DAY, on the street, I encountered the man whom, of all men, I most wished to see—Horace Bixby; formerly pilot under me—or rather, over me—now captain of the great steamer "City of Baton Rouge," the latest and swiftest addition to the Anchor Line. The same slender figure, the same tight curls, the same springy step, the same alertness, the same decision of eye and answering decision of hand, the same erect military bearing; not an inch gained or lost in girth, not an ounce gained or lost in weight, not a hair turned. It is a curious thing, to leave a man thirty-five years old, and come back at the end of twenty-one years and find him still only thirty-five. I have not had an experience of this kind before, I believe. There were some crow's-feet, but they counted for next to nothing, since they were inconspicuous.

His boat was just in. I had been waiting several days for her, purposing to return to St. Louis in her. The captain and I joined a party of ladies and gentlemen, guests of Major Wood, and went down the river fifty-four miles, in a swift tug, to ex-Governor Warmouth's sugar plantation. Strung along below the city, were a number of decayed, ram-shackly, superannuated old steamboats, not one of which had I ever seen before. They had all been built, and worn out, and thrown aside, since I was here last. This gives one a realizing sense of the frailness of a Mississippi boat and the briefness of its life.

Six miles below town a fat and battered brick chimney, sticking above the magnolias and live-oaks, was pointed out as the monument erected by an appreciative nation to celebrate the battle of New Orleans—Jackson's victory over the British, January 8, 1815. The war had ended, the two nations were at peace, but the news had not yet reached New Orleans. If we had had the cable telegraph in those days, this blood would not have been spilt, those lives would not have been wasted; and better still, Jackson would probably never have been president. We have gotten over the harms done us

by the war of 1812, but not over some of those done us by
Jackson's presidency.

The Warmouth plantation covers a vast deal of ground, and
the hospitality of the Warmouth mansion is graduated to the
same large scale. We saw steam-plows at work, here, for the
first time. The traction engine travels about on its own
wheels, till it reaches the required spot; then it stands still and
by means of a wire rope pulls the huge plow toward itself
two or three hundred yards across the field, between the rows
of cane. The thing cuts down into the black mould a foot and
a half deep. The plow looks like a fore-and-aft brace of a
Hudson river steamer, inverted. When the negro steersman
sits on one end of it, that end tilts down near the ground,
while the other sticks up high in air. This great see-saw goes
rolling and pitching like a ship at sea, and it is not every circus rider that could stay on it.

The plantation contains two thousand six hundred acres;
six hundred and fifty are in cane; and there is a fruitful orange
grove of five thousand trees. The cane is cultivated after a
modern and intricate scientific fashion, too elaborate and
complex for me to attempt to describe; but it lost $40,000
last year. I forget the other details. However, this year's crop
will reach ten or twelve hundred tons of sugar, consequently
last year's loss will not matter. These troublesome and expensive scientific methods achieve a yield of a ton and a half, and
from that to two tons, to the acre; which is three or four
times what the yield of an acre was in my time.

The drainage-ditches were everywhere alive with little
crabs—"fiddlers." One saw them scampering sidewise in
every direction whenever they heard a disturbing noise. Expensive pests, these crabs; for they bore into the levees, and
ruin them.

The great sugar-house was a wilderness of tubs and tanks
and vats and filters, pumps, pipes, and machinery. The process of making sugar is exceedingly interesting. First, you
heave your cane into the centrifugals and grind out the juice;
then run it through the evaporating pan to extract the fibre;
then through the bone-filter to remove the alcohol; then
through the clarifying tanks to discharge the molasses; then
through the granulating pipe to condense it; then through

the vacuum pan to extract the vacuum. It is now ready for market. I have jotted these particulars down from memory. The thing looks simple and easy. Do not deceive yourself. To make sugar is really one of the most difficult things in the world. And to make it right, is next to impossible. If you will examine your own supply every now and then for a term of years, and tabulate the result, you will find that not two men in twenty can make sugar without getting sand into it.

We could have gone down to the mouth of the river and visited Captain Eads' great work, the "jetties," where the river has been compressed between walls, and thus deepened to twenty-six feet; but it was voted useless to go, since at this stage of the water everything would be covered up and invisible.

We could have visited that ancient and singular burg, "Pilot-town," which stands on stilts in the water—so they say; where nearly all communication is by skiff and canoe, even to the attending of weddings and funerals; and where the littlest boys and girls are as handy with the oar as unamphibious children are with the velocipede.

We could have done a number of other things; but on account of limited time, we went back home. The sail up the breezy and sparkling river was a charming experience, and would have been satisfyingly sentimental and romantic but for the interruptions of the tug's pet parrot, whose tireless comments upon the scenery and the guests were always this-worldly, and often profane. He had also a superabundance of the discordant, ear-splitting, metallic laugh common to his breed,—a machine-made laugh, a Frankenstein laugh, with the soul left out of it. He applied it to every sentimental remark, and to every pathetic song. He cackled it out with hideous energy after "Home again, home again, from a foreign shore," and said he "wouldn't give a damn for a tug-load of such rot." Romance and sentiment cannot long survive this sort of discouragement; so the singing and talking presently ceased; which so delighted the parrot that he cursed himself hoarse for joy.

Then the male members of the party moved to the forecastle, to smoke and gossip. There were several old steamboatmen along, and I learned from them a great deal of what had been happening to my former river friends during my long absence. I learned that a pilot whom I used to steer for is become a spiritualist, and for more than fifteen years has been receiving a letter every week from a deceased relative, through a New York spiritualistic medium named Manchester—postage graduated by distance: from the local post-office in Paradise to New York, five dollars; from New York to St. Louis, three cents. I remember Mr. Manchester very well. I called on him once, ten years ago, with a couple of friends, one of whom wished to inquire after a deceased uncle. This uncle had lost his life in a peculiarly violent and unusual way, half a dozen years before: a cyclone blew him some three miles and knocked a tree down with him which was four feet through at the butt and sixty-five feet high. He did not survive this triumph. At the *séance* just referred to, my friend questioned his late uncle, through Mr. Manchester, and the late uncle wrote down his replies, using Mr. Manchester's hand and pencil for that purpose. The following is a fair example of the questions asked, and also of the sloppy twaddle in the way of answers, furnished by Manchester under the pretence that it came from the spectre. If this man is not the paltriest fraud that lives, I owe him an apology:—

Question. Where are you?

Answer. In the spirit world.

Q. Are you happy?

A. Very happy. Perfectly happy.

Q. How do you amuse yourself?

A. Conversation with friends, and other spirits.

Q. What else?

A. Nothing else. Nothing else is necessary.

Q. What do you talk about?

A. About how happy we are; and about friends left behind in the earth, and how to influence them for their good.

Q. When your friends in the earth all get to the spirit land, what shall you have to talk about then?—nothing but about how happy you all are?

No reply. It is explained that spirits will not answer frivolous questions.

Q. How is it that spirits that are content to spend an eternity in frivolous employments, and accept it as happiness, are so fastidious about frivolous questions upon the subject?

No reply.

Q. Would you like to come back?

A. No.

Q. Would you say that under oath?

A. Yes.

Q. What do you eat there?

A. We do not eat.

Q. What do you drink?

A. We do not drink.

Q. What do you smoke?

A. We do not smoke.

Q. What do you read?

A. We do not read.

Q. Do all the good people go to your place?

A. Yes.

Q. You know my present way of life. Can you suggest any additions to it, in the way of crime, that will reasonably insure my going to some other place?

A. No reply.

Q. When did you die?

A. I did not die, I passed away.

Q. Very well, then, when did you pass away? How long have you been in the spirit land?

A. We have no measurements of time here.

Q. Though you may be indifferent and uncertain as to dates and times in your present condition and environment, this has nothing to do with your former condition. You had dates then. One of these is what I ask for. You departed on a certain day in a certain year. Is not this true?

A. Yes.

Q. Then name the day of the month.

(Much fumbling with pencil, on the part of the medium, accompanied by violent spasmodic jerkings of his head and body, for some little time. Finally, explanation to the effect that spirits often forget dates, such things being without importance to them.)

Q. Then this one has actually forgotten the date of its translation to the spirit land?

This was granted to be the case.

Q. This is very curious. Well, then, what year was it?

(More fumbling, jerking, idiotic spasms, on the part of the medium. Finally, explanation to the effect that the spirit has forgotten the year.)

Q. This is indeed stupendous. Let me put one more question, one last question, to you, before we part to meet no more;—for even if I fail to avoid your asylum, a meeting there will go for nothing *as* a meeting, since by that time you will easily have forgotten me and my name: did you die a natural death, or were you cut off by a catastrophe?

A. (After long hesitation and many throes and spasms.) *Natural death.*

This ended the interview. My friend told the medium that when his relative was in this poor world, he was endowed with an extraordinary intellect and an absolutely defectless memory, and it seemed a great pity that he had not been allowed to keep some shred of these for his amusement in the realms of everlasting contentment, and for the amazement and admiration of the rest of the population there.

This man had plenty of clients—has plenty yet. He receives letters from spirits located in every part of the spirit world, and delivers them all over this country through the United States mail. These letters are filled with advice—advice from "spirits" who don't know as much as a tadpole—and this advice is religiously followed by the receivers. One of these clients was a man whom the spirits (if one may thus plurally describe the ingenious Manchester) were teaching how to contrive an improved railway car-wheel. It is coarse employment for a spirit, but it is higher and wholesomer activity than talking forever about "how happy we are."

XLIX.

Episodes in Pilot Life

IN THE COURSE of the tug-boat gossip, it came out that out of every five of my former friends who had quitted the river, four had chosen farming as an occupation. Of course this was not because they were peculiarly gifted, agriculturally, and thus more likely to succeed as farmers than in other industries: the reason for their choice must be traced to some other source. Doubtless they chose farming because that life is private and secluded from irruptions of undesirable strangers,—like the pilot-house hermitage. And doubtless they also chose it because on a thousand nights of black storm and danger they had noted the twinkling lights of solitary farmhouses, as the boat swung by, and pictured to themselves the serenity and security and cosiness of such refuges at such times, and so had by and by come to dream of that retired and peaceful life as the one desirable thing to long for, anticipate, earn, and at last enjoy.

But I did not learn that any of these pilot-farmers had astonished anybody with their successes. Their farms do not support them: they support their farms. The pilot-farmer disappears from the river annually, about the breaking of spring, and is seen no more till next frost. Then he appears again, in damaged homespun, combs the hay-seed out of his hair, and takes a pilot-house berth for the winter. In this way he pays the debts which his farming has achieved during the agricultural season. So his river bondage is but half broken; he is still the river's slave the hardest half of the year.

One of these men bought a farm, but did not retire to it. He knew a trick worth two of that. He did not propose to pauperize his farm by applying his personal ignorance to working it. No, he put the farm into the hands of an agricultural expert to be worked on shares—out of every three loads of corn the expert to have two and the pilot the third. But at the end of the season the pilot received no corn. The expert explained that *his* share was not reached. The farm produced only two loads.

Some of the pilots whom I had known had had adventures;—the outcome fortunate, sometimes, but not in all cases. Captain Montgomery, whom I had steered for when he was a pilot, commanded the Confederate fleet in the great battle before Memphis; when his vessel went down, he swam ashore, fought his way through a squad of soldiers, and made a gallant and narrow escape. He was always a cool man; nothing could disturb his serenity. Once when he was captain of the "Crescent City," I was bringing the boat into port at New Orleans, and momently expecting orders from the hurricane deck, but received none. I had stopped the wheels, and there my authority and responsibility ceased. It was evening—dim twilight—the captain's hat was perched upon the big bell, and I supposed the intellectual end of the captain was in it, but such was not the case. The captain was very strict; therefore I knew better than to touch a bell without orders. My duty was to hold the boat steadily on her calamitous course, and leave the consequences to take care of themselves—which I did. So we went plowing past the sterns of steamboats and getting closer and closer—the crash was bound to come very soon—and still that hat never budged; for alas, the captain was napping in the texas. . . . Things were becoming exceedingly nervous and uncomfortable. It seemed to me that the captain was not going to appear in time to see the entertainment. But he did. Just as we were walking into the stern of a steamboat, he stepped out on deck, and said, with heavenly serenity, "Set her back on both"—which I did; but a trifle late, however, for the next moment we went smashing through that other boat's flimsy outer works with a most prodigious racket. The captain never said a word to me about the matter afterwards, except to remark that I had done right, and that he hoped I would not hesitate to act in the same way again in like circumstances.

One of the pilots whom I had known when I was on the river had died a very honorable death. His boat caught fire, and he remained at the wheel until he got her safe to land. Then he went out over the breast-board with his clothing in flames, and was the last person to get ashore. He died from his injuries in the course of two or three hours, and his was the only life lost.

The history of Mississippi piloting affords six or seven instances of this sort of martyrdom, and half a hundred instances of escapes from a like fate which came within a second or two of being fatally too late; *but there is no instance of a pilot deserting his post to save his life while by remaining and sacrificing it he might secure other lives from destruction.* It is well worth while to set down this noble fact, and well worth while to put it in italics, too.

The "cub" pilot is early admonished to despise all perils connected with a pilot's calling, and to prefer any sort of death to the deep dishonor of deserting his post while there is any possibility of his being useful in it. And so effectively are these admonitions inculcated, that even young and but half-tried pilots can be depended upon to stick to the wheel, and die there when occasion requires. In a Memphis graveyard is buried a young fellow who perished at the wheel a great many years ago, in White River, to save the lives of other men. He said to the captain that if the fire would give him time to reach a sand bar, some distance away, all could be saved, but that to land against the bluff bank of the river would be to insure the loss of many lives. He reached the bar and grounded the boat in shallow water; but by that time the flames had closed around him, and in escaping through them he was fatally burned. He had been urged to fly sooner, but had replied as became a pilot to reply:—

"I will not go. If I go, nobody will be saved; if I stay, no one will be lost but me. I will stay."

There were two hundred persons on board, and no life was lost but the pilot's. There used to be a monument to this young fellow, in that Memphis graveyard. While we tarried in Memphis on our down trip, I started out to look for it, but our time was so brief that I was obliged to turn back before my object was accomplished.

The tug-boat gossip informed me that Dick Kennet was dead—blown up, near Memphis, and killed; that several others whom I had known had fallen in the war—one or two of them shot down at the wheel; that another and very particular friend, whom I had steered many trips for, had stepped out of his house in New Orleans, one night years ago, to collect some money in a remote part of the city, and had never been seen again,—was murdered and thrown into the river, it was thought; that Ben Thornburgh was dead long ago; also his wild "cub" whom I used to quarrel with, all through every daylight watch. A heedless, reckless creature he was, and always in hot water, always in mischief. An Arkansas passenger brought an enormous bear aboard, one day, and chained him to a life-boat on the hurricane deck. Thornburgh's "cub" could not rest till he had gone there and unchained the bear, to "see what he would do." He was promptly gratified. The bear chased him around and around the deck, for miles and miles, with two hundred eager faces grinning through the railings for audience, and finally snatched off the lad's coat-tail and went into the texas to chew it. The off-watch turned out with alacrity, and left the bear in sole possession. He presently grew lonesome, and started out for recreation. He ranged the whole boat—visited every part of it, with an advance guard of fleeing people in front of him and a voiceless vacancy behind him; and when his owner captured him at last, those two were the only visible beings anywhere; everybody else was in hiding, and the boat was a solitude.

I was told that one of my pilot friends fell dead at the wheel, from heart disease, in 1869. The captain was on the roof at the time. He saw the boat breaking for the shore; shouted, and got no answer; ran up, and found the pilot lying dead on the floor.

Mr. Bixby had been blown up, in Madrid bend; was not injured, but the other pilot was lost.

George Ritchie had been blown up near Memphis—blown into the river from the wheel, and disabled. The water was very cold; he clung to a cotton bale—mainly with his teeth—and floated until nearly exhausted, when he was rescued by some deck hands who were on a piece of the wreck. They tore open the bale and packed him in the cotton, and warmed the life back into him, and got him safe to Memphis. He is one of Bixby's pilots on the "Baton Rouge" now.

Into the life of a steamboat clerk, now dead, had dropped a bit of romance,—somewhat grotesque romance, but romance nevertheless. When I knew him he was a shiftless young spendthrift, boisterous, good-hearted, full of careless generosities, and pretty conspicuously promising to fool his possibilities away early, and come to nothing. In a Western city lived a rich and childless old foreigner and his wife; and in their family was a comely young girl—sort of friend, sort of servant. The young clerk of whom I have been speaking,— whose name was not George Johnson, but who shall be called George Johnson for the purposes of this narrative,— got acquainted with this young girl, and they sinned; and the old foreigner found them out, and rebuked them. Being ashamed, they lied, and said they were married; that they had been privately married. Then the old foreigner's hurt was healed, and he forgave and blessed them. After that, they were able to continue their sin without concealment. By and by the foreigner's wife died; and presently he followed after her. Friends of the family assembled to mourn; and among the mourners sat the two young sinners. The will was opened and solemnly read. It bequeathed every penny of that old man's great wealth to *Mrs. George Johnson*!

And there was no such person. The young sinners fled forth then, and did a very foolish thing: married themselves before an obscure Justice of the Peace, and got him to ante-date the thing. That did no sort of good. The distant relatives flocked in and exposed the fraudful date with extreme suddenness and surprising ease, and carried off the fortune, leaving the Johnsons very legitimately, and legally, and irre-vocably chained together in honorable marriage, but with not so much as a penny to bless themselves withal. Such are the actual facts; and not all novels have for a base so telling a situation.

L.

The "Original Jacobs"

WE HAD SOME TALK about Captain Isaiah Sellers, now
many years dead. He was a fine man, a high-minded
man, and greatly respected both ashore and on the river. He
was very tall, well built, and handsome; and in his old age—
as I remember him—his hair was as black as an Indian's, and
his eye and hand were as strong and steady and his nerve and
judgment as firm and clear as anybody's, young or old,
among the fraternity of pilots. He was the patriarch of the
craft; he had been a keelboat pilot before the day of steamboats; and a steamboat pilot before any other steamboat pilot
still surviving at the time I speak of, had ever turned a wheel.
Consequently his brethren held him in the sort of awe in
which illustrious survivors of a bygone age are always held by
their associates. He knew how he was regarded, and perhaps
this fact added some trifle of stiffening to his natural dignity,
which had been sufficiently stiff in its original state.

He left a diary behind him; but apparently it did not date
back to his first steamboat trip, which was said to be 1811, the
year the first steamboat disturbed the waters of the Mississippi. At the time of his death a correspondent of the "St.
Louis Republican" culled the following items from the
diary:—

> "In February, 1825, he shipped on board the steamer
> 'Rambler,' at Florence, Ala., and made during that year
> three trips to New Orleans and back,—this on the 'Gen.
> Carrol,' between Nashville and New Orleans. It was during
> his stay on this boat that Captain Sellers introduced the tap
> of the bell as a signal to heave the lead, previous to which
> time it was the custom for the pilot to speak to the men
> below when soundings were wanted. The proximity of the
> forecastle to the pilot-house, no doubt, rendered this an
> easy matter; but how different on one of our palaces of the
> present day.
>
> "In 1827 we find him on board the 'President,' a boat of

two hundred and eighty-five tons burden, and plying between Smithland and New Orleans. Thence he joined the 'Jubilee' in 1828, and on this boat he did his first piloting in the St. Louis trade; his first watch extending from Herculaneum to St. Genevieve. On May 26, 1836, he completed and left Pittsburg in charge of the steamer 'Prairie,' a boat of four hundred tons, and the first steamer with a *state-room cabin* ever seen at St. Louis. In 1857 he introduced the signal for meeting boats, and which has, with some slight change, been the universal custom of this day; in fact, is rendered obligatory by act of Congress.

"As general items of river history, we quote the following marginal notes from his general log:—

"In March, 1825, Gen. Lafayette left New Orleans for St. Louis on the low-pressure steamer 'Natchez.'

"In January, 1828, twenty-one steamers left the New Orleans wharf to celebrate the occasion of Gen. Jackson's visit to that city.

"In 1830 the 'North American' made the run from New Orleans to Memphis in six days—best time on record to that date. It has since been made in two days and ten hours.

"In 1831 the Red River cut-off formed.

"In 1832 steamer 'Hudson' made the run from White River to Helena, a distance of seventy-five miles, in twelve hours. This was the source of much talk and speculation among parties directly interested.

"In 1839 Great Horseshoe cut-off formed.

"Up to the present time, a term of thirty-five years, we ascertain, by reference to the diary, he has made four hundred and sixty round trips to New Orleans, which gives a distance of one million one hundred and four thousand miles, or an average of eighty-six miles a day."

Whenever Captain Sellers approached a body of gossiping pilots, a chill fell there, and talking ceased. For this reason: whenever six pilots were gathered together, there would always be one or two newly fledged ones in the lot, and the elder ones would be always "showing off" before these poor fellows; making them sorrowfully feel how callow they were, how recent their nobility, and how humble their degree, by talking largely and vaporously of old-time experiences on the river; always making it a point to date everything back as fa as they could, so as to make the new men feel their newness to the sharpest degree possible, and envy the old stagers in the like degree. And how these complacent bald-heads *would* swell, and brag, and lie, and date back—ten, fifteen, twenty years,—and how they did enjoy the effect produced upon the marvelling and envying youngsters!

And perhaps just at this happy stage of the proceedings the stately figure of Captain Isaiah Sellers, that real and only genuine Son of Antiquity, would drift solemnly into the midst. Imagine the size of the silence that would result on the instant. And imagine the feelings of those bald-heads, and the exultation of their recent audience when the ancient captain would begin to drop casual and indifferent remarks of a reminiscent nature,—about islands that had disappeared, and cut-offs that had been made, a generation before the oldest bald-head in the company had ever set his foot in a pilot-house!

Many and many a time did this ancient mariner appear on the scene in the above fashion, and spread disaster and humiliation around him. If one might believe the pilots, he always dated his islands back to the misty dawn of river history; and he never used the same island twice; and never did he employ an island that still existed, or give one a name which anybody present was old enough to have heard of before. If you might believe the pilots, he was always conscientiously particular about little details; never spoke of "the State of Mississippi," for instance,—no, he would say, "When the State of Mississippi was where Arkansas now is;" and would never speak of Louisiana or Missouri in a general way, and leave an incorrect impression on your mind,—no, he would say, "When Louisiana was up the river farther," or "When Missouri was on the Illinois side."

The old gentleman was not of literary turn or capacity, but he used to jot down brief paragraphs of plain practical information about the river, and sign them "MARK TWAIN," and give them to the "New Orleans Picayune." They related to the stage and condition of the river, and were accurate and aluable; and thus far, they contained no poison. But in speaking of the stage of the river to-day, at a given point, the captain was pretty apt to drop in a little remark about this being the first time he had seen the water so high or so low at that particular point for forty-nine years; and now and then he would mention Island so and so, and follow it, in parentheses, with some such observation as "disappeared in 1807, if I remember rightly." In these antique interjections lay poison and bitterness for the other old pilots, and they used to chaff the "Mark Twain" paragraphs with unsparing mockery.

It so chanced that one of these paragraphs[1] became the text for my first newspaper article. I burlesqued it broadly, very broadly, stringing my fantastics out to the extent of eight hundred or a thousand words. I was a "cub" at the time. I showed my performance to some pilots, and they eagerly rushed it into print in the "New Orleans True Delta." It was a great pity; for it did nobody any worthy service, and it sent a pang deep into a good man's heart. There was no malice in my rubbish; but it laughed at the captain. It laughed at a man to whom such a thing was new and strange and dreadful. I did not know then, though I do now, that there is no suffering comparable with that which a private person feels when he is for the first time pilloried in print.

Captain Sellers did me the honor to profoundly detest me from that day forth. When I say he did me the honor, I am not using empty words. It was a very real honor to be in the thoughts of so great a man as Captain Sellers, and I had wit enough to appreciate it and be proud of it. It was distinction to be loved by such a man; but it was a much greater distinction to be hated by him, because he loved scores of people; but he did n't sit up nights to hate anybody but me.

He never printed another paragraph while he lived, and he

[1] The original MS. of it, in the captain's own hand, has been sent to me from New Orleans. It reads as follows:—

"VICKSBURG, May 4, 1859.

"My opinion for the benefit of the citizens of New Orleans: The water is higher this far up than it has been since 1815. My opinion is that the water will be 4 feet deep in Canal street before the first of next June. Mrs. Turner's plantation at the head of Big Black Island is all under water, and it has not been since 1815.

"I. SELLERS."

never again signed "Mark Twain" to anything. At the time that the telegraph brought the news of his death, I was on the Pacific coast. I was a fresh new journalist, and needed a *nom de guerre*; so I confiscated the ancient mariner's discarded one, and have done my best to make it remain what it was in his hands—a sign and symbol and warrant that whatever is found in its company may be gambled on as being the petrified truth; how I have succeeded, it would not be modest in me to say.

The captain had an honorable pride in his profession and an abiding love for it. He ordered his monument before he died, and kept it near him until he did die. It stands over his grave now, in Bellefontaine cemetery, St. Louis. It is his image, in marble, standing on duty at the pilot wheel; and worthy to stand and confront criticism, for it represents a man who in life would have staid there till he burned to a cinder if duty required it.

The finest thing we saw on our whole Mississippi trip, we saw as we approached New Orleans in the steam-tug. This was the curving frontage of the crescent city lit up with the white glare of five miles of electric lights. It was a wonderful sight, and very beautiful.

LI.

Reminiscences

W E LEFT for St. Louis in the "City of Baton Rouge," on a delightfully hot day, but with the main purpose of my visit but lamely accomplished. I had hoped to hunt up and talk with a hundred steamboatmen, but got so pleasantly involved in the social life of the town that I got nothing more than mere five-minute talks with a couple of dozen of the craft.

I was on the bench of the pilot-house when we backed out and "straightened up" for the start—the boat pausing for a "good ready," in the old-fashioned way, and the black smoke piling out of the chimneys equally in the old-fashioned way. Then we began to gather momentum, and presently were fairly under way and booming along. It was all as natural and familiar—and so were the shoreward sights—as if there had been no break in my river life. There was a "cub," and I judged that he would take the wheel now; and he did. Captain Bixby stepped into the pilot-house. Presently the cub closed up on the rank of steamships. He made me nervous, for he allowed too much water to show between our boat and the ships. I knew quite well what was going to happen, because I could date back in my own life and inspect the record. The captain looked on, during a silent half-minute, then took the wheel himself, and crowded the boat in, till she went scraping along within a hand-breadth of the ships. It was exactly the favor which he had done me, about a quarter of a century before, in that same spot, the first time I ever steamed out of the port of New Orleans. It was a very great and sincere pleasure to me to see the thing repeated—with somebody else as victim.

We made Natchez (three hundred miles) in twenty-two hours and a half,—much the swiftest passage I have ever made over that piece of water.

The next morning I came on with the four o'clock watch, and saw Ritchie successfully run half a dozen crossings in a fog, using for his guidance the marked chart devised and patented by Bixby and himself. This sufficiently evidenced the great value of the chart.

By and by, when the fog began to clear off, I noticed that the reflection of a tree in the smooth water of an overflowed bank, six hundred yards away, was stronger and blacker than the ghostly tree itself. The faint spectral trees, dimly glimpsed through the shredding fog, were very pretty things to see.

We had a heavy thunder-storm at Natchez, another at Vicksburg, and still another about fifty miles below Memphis. They had an old-fashioned energy which had long been unfamiliar to me. This third storm was accompanied by a raging wind. We tied up to the bank when we saw the tempest coming, and everybody left the pilot-house but me. The wind bent the young trees down, exposing the pale underside of the leaves; and gust after gust followed, in quick succession, thrashing the branches violently up and down, and to this side and that, and creating swift waves of alternating green and white according to the side of the leaf that was exposed, and these waves raced after each other as do their kind over a wind-tossed field of oats. No color that was visible anywhere was quite natural,—all tints were charged with a leaden tinge from the solid cloud-bank overhead. The river was leaden; all distances the same; and even the far-reaching ranks of combing white-caps were dully shaded by the dark, rich atmosphere through which their swarming legions marched. The thunder-peals were constant and deafening; explosion followed explosion with but inconsequential intervals between, and the reports grew steadily sharper and higher-keyed, and more trying to the ear; the lightning was as diligent as the thunder, and produced effects which enchanted the eye and sent electric ecstasies of mixed delight and apprehension shivering along every nerve in the body in unintermittent procession. The rain poured down in amazing volume; the ear-splitting thunder-peals broke nearer and nearer; the wind increased in fury and began to wrench off boughs and tree-tops and send them sailing away through space; the pilot-house fell to rocking and straining and cracking and surging, and I went down in the hold to see what time it was.

People boast a good deal about Alpine thunder-storms; but

the storms which I have had the luck to see in the Alps were not the equals of some which I have seen in the Mississippi Valley. I may not have seen the Alps do their best, of course, and if they can beat the Mississippi, I don't wish to.

On this up trip I saw a little towhead (infant island) half a mile long, which had been formed during the past nineteen years. Since there was so much time to spare that nineteen years of it could be devoted to the construction of a mere towhead, where was the use, originally, in rushing this whole globe through in six days? It is likely that if more time had been taken, in the first place, the world would have been made right, and this ceaseless improving and repairing would not be necessary now. But if you hurry a world or a house, you are nearly sure to find out by and by, that you have left out a towhead, or a broom-closet, or some other little convenience, here and there, which has got to be supplied, no matter how much expense and vexation it may cost.

We had a succession of black nights, going up the river, and it was observable that whenever we landed, and suddenly inundated the trees with the intense sunburst of the electric light, a certain curious effect was always produced: hundreds of birds flocked instantly out from the masses of shining green foliage, and went careering hither and thither through the white rays, and often a song-bird tuned up and fell to singing. We judged that they mistook this superb artificial day for the genuine article.

We had a delightful trip in that thoroughly well-ordered steamer, and regretted that it was accomplished so speedily. By means of diligence and activity, we managed to hunt out nearly all the old friends. One was missing, however; he went to his reward, whatever it was, two years ago. But I found out all about him. His case helped me to realize how lasting can be the effect of a very trifling occurrence. When he was an apprentice-blacksmith in our village, and I a schoolboy, a couple of young Englishmen came to the town and sojourned a while; and one day they got themselves up in cheap royal finery and did the Richard III. sword-fight with maniac energy and prodigious powwow, in the presence of the village boys. This blacksmith cub was there, and the histrionic poison entered his bones. This vast, lumbering, ignorant, dull-witted lout was stage-struck, and irrecoverably. He disappeared, and presently turned up in St. Louis. I ran across him there, by and by. He was standing musing on a street corner, with his right hand on his hip, the thumb of his left supporting his chin, face bowed and frowning, slouch hat pulled down over his forehead—imagining himself to be Othello or some such character, and imagining that the passing crowd marked his tragic bearing and were awestruck.

I joined him, and tried to get him down out of the clouds, but did not succeed. However, he casually informed me, presently, that he was a member of the Walnut Street theatre company,—and he tried to say it with indifference, but the indifference was thin, and a mighty exultation showed through it. He said he was cast for a part in Julius Cæsar, for that night, and if I should come I would see him. *If* I should come! I said I would n't miss it if I were dead.

I went away stupefied with astonishment, and saying to myself, "How strange it is! *we* always thought this fellow a fool; yet the moment he comes to a great city, where intelligence and appreciation abound, the talent concealed in this shabby napkin is at once discovered, and promptly welcomed and honored."

But I came away from the theatre that night disappointed and offended; for I had had no glimpse of my hero, and his name was not in the bills. I met him on the street the next morning, and before I could speak, he asked:—

"Did you see me?"

"No, you were n't there."

He looked surprised and disappointed. He said:—

"Yes, I was. Indeed I was. I was a Roman soldier."

"Which one?"

"Why, did n't you see them Roman soldiers that stood back there in a rank, and sometimes marched in procession around the stage?"

"Do you mean the Roman army?—those six sandalled roustabouts in nightshirts, with tin shields and helmets, that marched around treading on each other's heels, in charge of a spider-legged consumptive dressed like themselves?"

"That 's it! that 's it! I was one of them Roman soldiers. I was the next to the last one. A half a year ago I used to always be the last one; but I 've been promoted."

Well, they told me that that poor fellow remained a Roman soldier to the last—a matter of thirty-four years. Sometimes they cast him for a "speaking part," but not an elaborate one. He could be trusted to go and say, "My lord, the carriage waits," but if they ventured to add a sentence or two to this, his memory felt the strain and he was likely to miss fire. Yet, poor devil, he had been patiently studying the part of Hamlet for more than thirty years, and he lived and died in the belief that some day he would be invited to play it!

And this is what came of that fleeting visit of those young Englishmen to our village such ages and ages ago! What noble horseshoes this man might have made, but for those Englishmen; and what an inadequate Roman soldier he *did* make!

A day or two after we reached St. Louis, I was walking along Fourth Street when a grizzly-headed man gave a sort of start as he passed me, then stopped, came back, inspected me narrowly, with a clouding brow, and finally said with deep asperity:—

"Look here, *have you got that drink yet?*"

A maniac, I judged, at first. But all in a flash I recognized him. I made an effort to blush that strained every muscle in me, and answered as sweetly and winningly as ever I knew how:—

"Been a little slow, but am just this minute closing in on the place where they keep it. Come in and help."

He softened, and said make it a bottle of champagne and he was agreeable. He said he had seen my name in the papers, and had put all his affairs aside and turned out, resolved to find me or die; and make me answer that question satisfactorily, or kill me; though the most of his late asperity had been rather counterfeit than otherwise.

This meeting brought back to me the St. Louis riots of about thirty years ago. I spent a week there, at that time, in a boarding-house, and had this young fellow for a neighbor across the hall. We saw some of the fightings and killings; and by and by we went one night to an armory where two hundred young men had met, upon call, to be armed and go forth against the rioters, under command of a military man. We drilled till about ten o'clock at night; then news came that the mob were in great force in the lower end of the town, and were sweeping everything before them. Our column moved at once. It was a very hot night, and my musket was very heavy. We marched and marched; and the nearer we approached the seat of war, the hotter I grew and the thirstier I got. I was behind my friend; so, finally, I asked him to hold my musket while I dropped out and got a drink. Then I branched off and went home. I was not feeling any solicitude about *him* of course, because I knew he was so well armed, now, that he could take care of himself without any trouble. If I had had any doubts about that, I would have borrowed another musket for him. I left the city pretty early the next morning, and if this grizzled man had not happened to encounter my name in the papers the other day in St. Louis, and felt moved to seek me out, I should have carried to my grave a heart-torturing uncertainty as to whether he ever got out of the riots all right or not. I ought to have inquired, thirty years ago; I know that. And I would have inquired, if I had had the muskets; but, in the circumstances, he seemed better fixed to conduct the investigations than I was.

One Monday, near the time of our visit to St. Louis, the "Globe-Democrat" came out with a couple of pages of Sunday statistics, whereby it appeared that 119,448 St. Louis people attended the morning and evening church services the day before, and 23,102 children attended Sunday-school. Thus 142,550 persons, out of the city's total of 400,000 population, respected the day religious-wise. I found these statistics, in a condensed form, in a telegram of the Associated Press, and preserved them. They made it apparent that St. Louis was in a higher state of grace than she could have claimed to be in my time. But now that I canvass the figures narrowly, I suspect that the telegraph mutilated them. It cannot be that there are more than 150,000 Catholics in the town; the other 250,000 must be classified as Protestants. Out of these 250,000, according to this questionable telegram, only 26,362 attended church and Sunday-school, while out of the 150,000 Catholics, 116,118 went to church and Sunday-school.

LII.

A Burning Brand

A LL AT ONCE the thought came into my mind, "I have not sought out Mr. Brown."

Upon that text I desire to depart from the direct line of my subject, and make a little excursion. I wish to reveal a secret which I have carried with me nine years, and which has become burdensome.

Upon a certain occasion, nine years ago, I had said, with strong feeling, "If ever I see St. Louis again, I will seek out Mr. Brown, the great grain merchant, and ask of him the privilege of shaking him by the hand."

The occasion and the circumstances were as follows. A friend of mine, a clergyman, came one evening and said: —

"I have a most remarkable letter here, which I want to read to you, if I can do it without breaking down. I must preface it with some explanations, however. The letter is written by an ex-thief and ex-vagabond of the lowest origin and basest rearing, a man all stained with crime and steeped in ignorance; but, thank God, with a mine of pure gold hidden away in him, as you shall see. His letter is written to a burglar named Williams, who is serving a nine-year term in a certain State prison, for burglary. Williams was a particularly daring burglar, and plied that trade during a number of years; but he was caught at last and jailed, to await trial in a town where he had broken into a house at night, pistol in hand, and forced the owner to hand over to him $8,000 in government bonds. Williams was not a common sort of person, by any means; he was a graduate of Harvard College, and came of good New England stock. His father was a clergyman. While lying in jail, his health began to fail, and he was threatened with consumption. This fact, together with the opportunity for reflection afforded by solitary confinement, had its effect—its natural effect. He fell into serious thought; his early training asserted itself with power, and wrought with strong influence upon his mind and heart. He put his old life behind him, and became an earnest Christian. Some ladies in

527

the town heard of this, visited him, and by their encouraging words supported him in his good resolutions and strengthened him to continue in his new life. The trial ended in his conviction and sentence to the State prison for the term of nine years, as I have before said. In the prison he became acquainted with the poor wretch referred to in the beginning of my talk, Jack Hunt, the writer of the letter which I am going to read. You will see that the acquaintanceship bore fruit for Hunt. When Hunt's time was out, he wandered to St. Louis; and from that place he wrote his letter to Williams. The letter got no further than the office of the prison warden, of course; prisoners are not often allowed to receive letters from outside. The prison authorities read this letter, but did not destroy it. They had not the heart to do it. They read it to several persons, and eventually it fell into the hands of those ladies of whom I spoke a while ago. The other day I came across an old friend of mine—a clergyman—who had seen this letter, and was full of it. The mere remembrance of it so moved him that he could not talk of it without his voice breaking. He promised to get a copy of it for me; and here it is,—an exact copy, with all the imperfections of the original preserved. It has many slang expressions in it—thieves' *argot*—but their meaning has been interlined, in parentheses, by the prison authorities:"—

ST. LOUIS, JUNE 9th, 1872.

MR. W——friend Charlie if i may call you so: i no you are surprised to get a letter from me, but i hope you won't be mad at my writing to you. i want to tell you my thanks for the way you talked to me when i was in prison—it has led me to try and be a better man; i guess you thought i did not cair for what you said, & at the first go off I did n't, but i noed you was a man who had don big work with good men & want no sucker, nor want gasing & all the boys knod it.

I used to think at nite what you said, & for it i nocked off swearing 5 months before my time was up, for i saw it want no good, nohow—the day my time was up you told me if i would shake the cross, *(quit stealing)* & live on the square for 3 months, it would be the best job i ever done in my life. The state agent give me a ticket to here, & on the car i thought more of what you said to me, but didn't make up my mind. When we got to Chicago on the cars from there to here, I pulled off an old woman's leather; *(robbed her of her pocketbook)* i had n't no more than got it off when i wished i had n't done it, for awhile before that i made up my mind to be a square bloke, for 3 months on your word, but forgot it when i saw the leather was a grip *(easy to get)* — but i kept clos to her & when she got out of the cars at a way place i said, marm have you lost anything? & she tumbled *(discovered)* her leather was off *(gone)* — is this it says i, giving it to her — well if you aint honest, says she, but i had nt got cheak enough to stand that sort of talk, so i left her in a hurry. When i got here i had $1 and 25 cents left & i did n't get no work for 3 days as i aint strong enough for roust about on a steam bote *(for a deck hand)* — The afternoon of the 3rd day I spent my last 10 cts for 2 moons *(large, round sea-biscuit)* & cheese & i felt pretty rough & was thinking i would have to go on the dipe *(picking pockets)* again, when i thought of what you once said about a fellows calling on the Lord when he was in hard luck, & i thought i would try it once anyhow, but when i tryed it i got stuck on the start, & all i could get off wos, Lord give a poor fellow a chance to square it for 3 months for Christ's sake, amen; & i kept a thinking, of it over and over as i went along — about an hour after that i was in 4th St. & this is what happened & is the cause of my being where i am now & about which i will tell you before i get done writing. As i was walking along i herd a big noise & saw a horse running away with a carriage with 2 children in it, & I grabed up a peace of box cover from the side walk & run in the middle of the street, & when the horse came up i smashed him over the head as hard as i could drive — the bord split to peces & the horse checked up a little & i grabbed the reigns & pulled his head down until he stopped — the gentleman what owned him came running up & soon as he saw the children were all rite, he shook hands with me & gave me a $50 green back, & my asking the Lord to help me come into my head, & i was so thunderstruck i could n't drop the reigns nor say nothing —

he saw something was up, & coming back to me said, my
boy are you hurt? & the thought come into my head just
then to ask him for work; & i asked him to take back the
bill and give me a job—says he, jump in here & lets talk
about it, but keep the money—he asked me if i could take
care of horses & i said yes, for i used to hang round livery
stables & often would help clean & drive horses, he told
me he wanted a man for that work, & would give me $16.
a month & bord me. You bet i took that chance at once.
that nite in my little room over the stable i sat a long time
thinking over my past life & of what had just happened &
i just got down on my nees & thanked the Lord for the job
& to help me to square it, & to bless you for putting me
up to it, & the next morning i done it again & got me
some new togs *(clothes)* & a bible for i *made up my mind*
after what the Lord had done for me i would read the bible
every nite and morning, & ask him to keep an eye on me.
When I had been there about a week Mr Brown (that 's his
name) came in my room one nite & saw me reading the
bible—he asked me if i was a Christian & i told him no—
he asked me how it was i read the bible instead of papers
& books—Well Charlie i thought i had better give him a
square deal in the start, so i told him all about my being in
prison & about you, & how i had almost done give up
looking for work & how the Lord got me the job when i
asked him; & the only way i had to pay him back was to
read the bible & square it, & i asked him to give me a
chance for 3 months—he talked to me like a father for a
long time, & told me i could stay & then i felt better than
ever i had done in my life, for i had given Mr. Brown a fair
start with me & now i did n't fear no one giving me a back
cap *(exposing his past life)* & running me off the job—the
next morning he called me into the library & gave me another square talk, & advised me to study some every day,
& he would help me one or 2 hours every nite, & he gave
me a Arithmetic, a spelling book, a Geography & a writing
book, & he hers me every nite—he lets me come into the
house to prayers every morning, & got me put in a bible
class in the Sunday School which i likes very much for it
helps me to understand my bible better.

Now, Charlie the 3 months on the square are up 2 months ago, & as you said, it is the best job i ever did in my life, & i commenced another of the same sort right away, only it is to God helping me to last a lifetime Charlie—i wrote this letter to tell you I do think God has forgiven my sins & herd your prayers, for you told me you should pray for me—i no i love to read his word & tell him all my troubles & he helps me i know for i have plenty of chances to steal but i don't feel to as i once did & now i take more pleasure in going to church than to the theatre & that wasnt so once—our minister and others often talk with me & a month ago they wanted me to join the church, but I said no, not now, i may be mistaken in my feelings, i will wait awhile, but now i feel that God has called me & on the first Sunday in July i will join the church—dear friend i wish i could write to you as i feel, but i cant do it yet—you no i learned to read and write while in prisons & i aint got well enough along to write as i would talk; i no i aint spelled all the words rite in this & lots of other mistakes but you will excuse it i no, for you no i was brought up in a poor house until i run away, & that i never new who my father and mother was & i dont no my rite name, & i hope you wont be mad at me, but i have as much rite to one name as another & i have taken your name, for you wont use it when you get out i no, & you are the man i think most of in the world; so i hope you wont be mad—I am doing well, i put $10 a month in bank with $25 of the $50—if you ever want any or all of it let me know, & it is yours. i wish you would let me send you some now. I send you with this a receipt for a year of Littles Living Age, i did n't know what you would like & i told Mr Brown & he said he thought you would like it— i wish i was nere you so i could send you chuck *(refreshments)* on holidays; it would spoil this weather from here, but i will send you a box next thanksgiving any way—next week Mr Brown takes me into his store as lite porter & will advance me as soon as i know a little more—he keeps a big granary store, wholesale—i forgot to tell you of my mission school, sunday school class—the school is in the sunday afternoon, i went out two sunday afternoons, and

picked up seven kids *(little boys)* & got them to come in
two of them new as much as i did & i had them put in a
class where they could learn something. i dont no much
myself, but as these kids cant read i get on nicely with
them. i make sure of them by going after them every Sun
day ½ hour before school time, i also got 4 girls to come
tell Mack and Harry about me, if they will come out here
when their time is up i will get them jobs at once. i hope
you will excuse this long letter & all mistakes, i wish i could
see you for i cant write as i would talk—i hope the warm
weather is doing your lungs good—i was afraid when you
was bleeding you would die—give my respects to all the
boys and tell them how i am doing—i am doing well and
every one here treats me as kind as they can—Mr Brown is
going to write to you sometime—i hope some day you will
write to me, this letter is from your very true friend

C——W——

who you know as Jack Hunt.
   I send you Mr Brown's card. Send my letter to him.

Here was true eloquence; irresistible eloquence; and without a single grace or ornament to help it out. I have seldom
been so deeply stirred by any piece of writing. The reader of
it halted, all the way through, on a lame and broken voice;
yet he had tried to fortify his feelings by several private readings of the letter before venturing into company with it. He
was practising upon me to see if there was any hope of his
being able to read the document to his prayer-meeting with
anything like a decent command over his feelings. The result
was not promising. However, he determined to risk it; and
did. He got through tolerably well; but his audience broke
down early, and stayed in that condition to the end.

The fame of the letter spread through the town. A brother
minister came and borrowed the manuscript, put it bodily
into a sermon, preached the sermon to twelve hundred people
on a Sunday morning, and the letter drowned them in their
own tears. Then my friend put it into a sermon and went
before his Sunday morning congregation with it. It scored
another triumph. The house wept as one individual.

My friend went on summer vacation up into the fishing

egions of our northern British neighbors, and carried this sermon with him, since he might possibly chance to need a ermon. He was asked to preach, one day. The little church was full. Among the people present were the late Dr. J. G. Holland, the late Mr. Seymour of the "New York Times," Mr. Page, the philantropist and temperance advocate, and, I think, Senator Frye, of Maine. The marvellous letter did its wonted work; all the people were moved, all the people wept; the tears flowed in a steady stream down Dr. Holland's cheeks, and nearly the same can be said with regard to all who were there. Mr. Page was so full of enthusiasm over the letter that he said he would not rest until he made pilgrimage to that prison, and had speech with the man who had been able to inspire a fellow-unfortunate to write so priceless a tract.

Ah, that unlucky Page!—and another man. If they had only been in Jericho, that letter would have rung through the world and stirred all the hearts of all the nations for a thousand years to come, and nobody might ever have found out that it was the confoundedest, brazenest, ingeniousest piece of fraud and humbuggery that was ever concocted to fool poor confiding mortals with!

The letter was a pure swindle, and that is the truth. And take it by and large, it was without a compeer among swindles. It was perfect, it was rounded, symmetrical, complete, colossal!

The reader learns it at this point; but we did n't learn it till some miles and weeks beyond this stage of the affair. My friend came back from the woods, and he and other clergymen and lay missionaries began once more to inundate audiences with their tears and the tears of said audiences; I begged hard for permission to print the letter in a magazine and tell the watery story of its triumphs; numbers of people got copies of the letter, with permission to circulate them in writing, but not in print; copies were sent to the Sandwich Islands and other far regions.

Charles Dudley Warner was at church, one day, when the worn letter was read and wept over. At the church door, afterward, he dropped a peculiarly cold iceberg down the clergyman's back with the question,—

"Do you know that letter to be genuine?"

It was the first suspicion that had ever been voiced; but i
had that sickening effect which first-uttered suspicions agains
one's idol always have. Some talk followed:—

"Why—what should make you suspect that it is n't gen
uine?"

"Nothing that I know of, except that it is too neat, anc
compact, and fluent, and nicely put together for an ignoran
person, an unpractised hand. I think it was done by an edu
cated man."

The literary artist had detected the literary machinery. I
you will look at the letter now, you will detect it yourself—i
is observable in every line.

Straightway the clergyman went off, with this seed of sus
picion sprouting in him, and wrote to a minister residing ir
that town where Williams had been jailed and converted,
asked for light; and also asked if a person in the literary line
(meaning me) might be allowed to print the letter and tell its
history. He presently received this answer:—

Rev. —— ——.

MY DEAR FRIEND,—In regard to that "convict's letter"
there can be no doubt as to its genuineness. "Williams," tc
whom it was written, lay in our jail and professed to have
been converted, and Rev. Mr.——, the chaplain, had great
faith in the genuineness of the change—as much as one
can have in any such case.

The letter was sent to one of our ladies, who is a Sunday-
school teacher,—sent either by Williams himself, or the
chaplain of the State's prison, probably. She has been
greatly annoyed in having so much publicity, lest it might
seem a breach of confidence, or be an injury to Williams.
In regard to its publication, I can give no permission;
though if the names and places were omitted, and especially
if sent out of the country, I think you might take the responsibility and do it.

It is a wonderful letter, which no Christian genius, much
less one unsanctified, could ever have written. As showing
the work of grace in a human heart, and in a very degraded
and wicked one, it proves its own origin and reproves our

weak faith in its power to cope with any form of wickedness.

"Mr. Brown" of St. Louis, some one said, was a Hartford man. Do all whom you send from Hartford serve their
Master as well?

P. S. Williams is still in the State's prison, serving out a
long sentence—of nine years, I think. He has been sick and
threatened with consumption, but I have not inquired after
him lately. This lady that I speak of corresponds with him,
I presume, and will be quite sure to look after him.

This letter arrived a few days after it was written—and up
went Mr. Williams's stock again. Mr. Warner's low-down
suspicion was laid in the cold, cold grave, where it apparently
belonged. It was a suspicion based upon mere internal evidence, anyway; and when you come to internal evidence, it
's a big field and a game that two can play at: as witness this
other internal evidence, discovered by the writer of the note
above quoted, that "it is a wonderful letter—which no Christian genius, much less one unsanctified, could ever have
written."

I had permission now to print—provided I suppressed
names and places and sent my narrative out of the country.
So I chose an Australian magazine for vehicle, as being far
enough out of the country, and set myself to work on my
article. And the ministers set the pumps going again, with the
letter to work the handles.

But meantime Brother Page had been agitating. He had
not visited the penitentiary, but he had sent a copy of the
illustrious letter to the chaplain of that institution, and accompanied it with—apparently—inquiries. He got an answer, dated four days later than that other Brother's reassur-
ing epistle; and before my article was complete, it wandered
into my hands. The original is before me, now, and I here
append it. It is pretty well loaded with internal evidence of
the most solid description:—

State's Prison, Chaplain's Office, July 11, 1873.
Dear Bro. Page,—Herewith please find the letter
kindly loaned me. I am afraid its genuineness cannot be
established. It purports to be addressed to some prisoner

here. No such letter ever came to a prisoner here. All letters received are carefully read by officers of the prison before they go into the hands of the convicts, and any such letter could not be forgotten. Again, Charles Williams is not a Christian man, but a dissolute, cunning prodigal, whose father is a minister of the gospel. His name is an assumed one. I am glad to have made your acquaintance. I am preparing a lecture upon life seen through prison bars, and should like to deliver the same in your vicinity.

And so ended that little drama. My poor article went into the fire; for whereas the materials for it were now more abundant and infinitely richer than they had previously been, there were parties all around me, who, although longing for the publication before, were a unit for suppression at this stage and complexion of the game. They said,—"Wait—the wound is too fresh, yet." All the copies of the famous letter except mine, disappeared suddenly; and from that time onward, the aforetime same old drought set in in the churches. As a rule, the town was on a spacious grin for a while, but there were places in it where the grin did not appear, and where it was dangerous to refer to the ex-convict's letter.

A word of explanation. "Jack Hunt," the professed writer of the letter, was an imaginary person. The burglar Williams—Harvard graduate, son of a minister—wrote the letter himself, *to* himself: got it smuggled out of the prison; got it conveyed to persons who had supported and encouraged him in his conversion—where he knew two things would happen: the genuineness of the letter would not be doubted or inquired into; and the nub of it would be noticed, and would have valuable effect—the effect, indeed, of starting a movement to get Mr. Williams pardoned out of prison.

That "nub" is so ingeniously, so casually, flung in, and immediately left there in the tail of the letter, undwelt upon, that an indifferent reader would never suspect that it was the heart and core of the epistle, if he even took note of it at all. This is the "nub":—

"i hope the warm weather is doing your lungs good—*i was afraid when you was bleeding you would die*—give my respects," etc.

That is all there is of it—simply touch and go—no dwelling upon it. Nevertheless it was intended for an eye that would be swift to see it; and it was meant to move a kind heart to try to effect the liberation of a poor reformed and purified fellow lying in the fell grip of consumption.

When I for the first time heard that letter read, nine years ago, I felt that it was the most remarkable one I had ever encountered. And it so warmed me toward Mr. Brown of St. Louis that I said that if ever I visited that city again, I would seek out that excellent man and kiss the hem of his garment if it was a new one. Well, I visited St. Louis, but I did not hunt for Mr. Brown; for, alas! the investigations of long ago had proved that the benevolent Brown, like "Jack Hunt," was not a real person, but a sheer invention of that gifted rascal, Williams—burglar, Harvard graduate, son of a clergyman.

LIII.

My Boyhood's Home

WE TOOK PASSAGE in one of the fast boats of the S
Louis and St. Paul Packet Company, and started ι
the river.

When I, as a boy, first saw the mouth of the Missou
River, it was twenty-two or twenty-three miles above S
Louis, according to the estimate of pilots; the wear and te
of the banks has moved it down eight miles since then; ar
the pilots say that within five years the river will cut throug
and move the mouth down five miles more, which will brir
it within ten miles of St. Louis.

About nightfall we passed the large and flourishing tow
of Alton, Illinois; and before daylight next morning the tow
of Louisiana, Missouri, a sleepy village in my day, but a bris
railway centre now; however, all the towns out there are rai
way centres now. I could not clearly recognize the place. Th
seemed odd to me, for when I retired from the rebel army i
'61 I retired upon Louisiana in good order; at least in goo
enough order for a person who had not yet learned how t
retreat according to the rules of war, and had to trust to na
tive genius. It seemed to me that for a first attempt at a retrea
it was not badly done. I had done no advancing in all tha
campaign that was at all equal to it.

There was a railway bridge across the river here well sprir
kled with glowing lights, and a very beautiful sight it was.

At seven in the morning we reached Hannibal, Missour
where my boyhood was spent. I had had a glimpse of it fif
teen years ago, and another glimpse six years earlier, but bot
were so brief that they hardly counted. The only notion c
the town that remained in my mind was the memory of it a
I had known it when I first quitted it twenty-nine years age
That picture of it was still as clear and vivid to me as a pho
tograph. I stepped ashore with the feeling of one who return
out of a dead-and-gone generation. I had a sort of realizin;
sense of what the Bastille prisoners must have felt when the
used to come out and look upon Paris after years of captivity

nd note how curiously the familiar and the strange were mixed together before them. I saw the new houses—saw them plainly enough—but they did not affect the older picture in my mind, for through their solid bricks and mortar I saw the vanished houses, which had formerly stood there, with perfect distinctness.

It was Sunday morning, and everybody was abed yet. So I passed through the vacant streets, still seeing the town as it was, and not as it is, and recognizing and metaphorically shaking hands with a hundred familiar objects which no longer exist; and finally climbed Holiday's Hill to get a comprehensive view. The whole town lay spread out below me then, and I could mark and fix every locality, every detail. Naturally, I was a good deal moved. I said, "Many of the people I once knew in this tranquil refuge of my childhood are now in heaven; some, I trust, are in the other place."

The things about me and before me made me feel like a boy again—convinced me that I was a boy again, and that I had simply been dreaming an unusually long dream; but my reflections spoiled all that; for they forced me to say, "I see fifty old houses down yonder, into each of which I could enter and find either a man or a woman who was a baby or unborn when I noticed those houses last, or a grandmother who was a plump young bride at that time."

From this vantage ground the extensive view up and down the river, and wide over the wooded expanses of Illinois, is very beautiful,—one of the most beautiful on the Mississippi, I think; which is a hazardous remark to make, for the eight hundred miles of river between St. Louis and St. Paul afford an unbroken succession of lovely pictures. It may be that my affection for the one in question biases my judgment in its favor; I cannot say as to that. No matter, it was satisfyingly beautiful to me, and it had this advantage over all the other friends whom I was about to greet again: it had suffered no change; it was as young and fresh and comely and gracious as ever it had been; whereas, the faces of the others would be old, and scarred with the campaigns of life, and marked with their griefs and defeats, and would give me no upliftings of spirit.

An old gentleman, out on an early morning walk, came

along, and we discussed the weather, and then drifted int
other matters. I could not remember his face. He said he ha
been living here twenty-eight years. So he had come after n
time, and I had never seen him before. I asked him variou
questions; first about a mate of mine in Sunday school—
what became of him?

"He graduated with honor in an Eastern college, wandere
off into the world somewhere, succeeded at nothing, passe
out of knowledge and memory years ago, and is supposed t
have gone to the dogs."

"He was bright, and promised well when he was a boy."

"Yes, but the thing that happened is what became of it all

I asked after another lad, altogether the brightest in ou
village school when I was a boy.

"He, too, was graduated with honors, from an Eastern co
lege; but life whipped him in every battle, straight along, an
he died in one of the Territories, years ago, a defeated man.

I asked after another of the bright boys.

"He is a success, always has been, always will be, I think.

I inquired after a young fellow who came to the town t
study for one of the professions when I was a boy.

"He went at something else before he got through—wer
from medicine to law, or from law to medicine—then t
some other new thing; went away for a year, came back wit
a young wife; fell to drinking, then to gambling behind th
door; finally took his wife and two young children to he
father's, and went off to Mexico; went from bad to wors
and finally died there, without a cent to buy a shroud, an
without a friend to attend the funeral."

"Pity, for he was the best-natured, and most cheery an
hopeful young fellow that ever was."

I named another boy.

"Oh, he is all right. Lives here yet; has a wife and childrer
and is prospering."

Same verdict concerning other boys.

I named three school-girls.

"The first two live here, are married and have children; th
other is long ago dead—never married."

I named, with emotion, one of my early sweethearts.

"She is all right. Been married three times; buried two hus

bands, divorced from the third, and I hear she is getting ready to marry an old fellow out in Colorado somewhere. She 's got children scattered around here and there, most everywheres."

The answer to several other inquiries was brief and simple,—

"Killed in the war."

I named another boy.

"Well, now, his case *is* curious! There was n't a human being in this town but knew that that boy was a perfect chucklehead; perfect dummy; just a stupid ass, as you may say. Everybody knew it, and everybody said it. Well, if that very boy is n't the first lawyer in the State of Missouri to-day, I 'm a Democrat!"

"Is that so?"

"It 's actually so. I 'm telling you the truth."

"How do you account for it?"

"Account for it? There ain't any accounting for it, except that if you send a damned fool to St. Louis, and you don't tell them he 's a damned fool *they 'll* never find it out. There 's one thing sure—if I had a damned fool I should know what to do with him: ship him to St. Louis—it 's the noblest market in the world for that kind of property. Well, when you come to look at it all around, and chew at it and think it over, *don't* it just bang anything you ever heard of?"

"Well, yes, it does seem to. But don't you think maybe it was the Hannibal people who were mistaken about the boy, and not the St. Louis people?"

"Oh, nonsense! The people here have known him from the very cradle—they knew him a hundred times better than the St. Louis idiots *could* have known him. No, if you have got any damned fools that you want to realize on, take my advice—send them to St. Louis."

I mentioned a great number of people whom I had formerly known. Some were dead, some were gone away, some had prospered, some had come to naught; but as regarded a dozen or so of the lot, the answer was comforting:

"Prosperous—live here yet—town littered with their children."

I asked about Miss ——.

"Died in the insane asylum three or four years ago—never was out of it from the time she went in; and was always suffering, too; never got a shred of her mind back."

If he spoke the truth, here was a heavy tragedy, indeed. Thirty-six years in a madhouse, that some young fools might have some fun! I was a small boy, at the time; and I saw those giddy young ladies come tiptoeing into the room where Miss —— sat reading at midnight by a lamp. The girl at the head of the file wore a shroud and a doughface; she crept behind the victim, touched her on the shoulder, and she looked up and screamed, and then fell into convulsions. She did not recover from the fright, but went mad. In these days it seems incredible that people believed in ghosts so short a time ago. But they did.

After asking after such other folk as I could call to mind, I finally inquired about *myself*:

"Oh, he succeeded well enough—another case of damned fool. If they 'd sent him to St. Louis, he 'd have succeeded sooner."

It was with much satisfaction that I recognized the wisdom of having told this candid gentleman, in the beginning, that my name was Smith.

LIV.

Past and Present

BEING LEFT TO MYSELF, up there, I went on picking out old houses in the distant town, and calling back their former inmates out of the mouldy past. Among them I presently recognized the house of the father of Lem Hackett (fictitious name). It carried me back more than a generation in a moment, and landed me in the midst of a time when the happenings of life were not the natural and logical results of great general laws, but of special orders, and were freighted with very precise and distinct purposes—partly punitive in intent, partly admonitory; and usually local in application.

When I was a small boy, Lem Hackett was drowned—on a Sunday. He fell out of an empty flat-boat, where he was playing. Being loaded with sin, he went to the bottom like an anvil. He was the only boy in the village who slept that night. We others all lay awake, repenting. We had not needed the information, delivered from the pulpit that evening, that Lem's was a case of special judgment—we knew that, already. There was a ferocious thunder-storm, that night, and it raged continuously until near dawn. The winds blew, the windows rattled, the rain swept along the roof in pelting sheets, and at the briefest of intervals the inky blackness of the night vanished, the houses over the way glared out white and blinding for a quivering instant, then the solid darkness shut down again and a splitting peal of thunder followed which seemed to rend everything in the neighborhood to shreds and splinters. I sat up in bed quaking and shuddering, waiting for the destruction of the world, and expecting it. To me there was nothing strange or incongruous in heaven's making such an uproar about Lem Hackett. Apparently it was the right and proper thing to do. Not a doubt entered my mind that all the angels were grouped together, discussing this boy's case and observing the awful bombardment of our beggarly little village with satisfaction and approval. There was one thing which disturbed me in the most serious way; that was the thought that this centering of the celestial inter-

est on our village could not fail to attract the attention of th
observers to people among us who might otherwise have es
caped notice for years. I felt that I was not only one of thos
people, but the very one most likely to be discovered. Tha
discovery could have but one result: I should be in the fir
with Lem before the chill of the river had been fairly warme
out of him. I knew that this would be only just and fair.
was increasing the chances against myself all the time, by feel
ing a secret bitterness against Lem for having attracted thi
fatal attention to me, but I could not help it—this sinfu
thought persisted in infesting my breast in spite of me. Ever
time the lightning glared I caught my breath, and judged
was gone. In my terror and misery, I meanly began to sugges
other boys, and mention acts of theirs which were wickede
than mine, and peculiarly needed punishment—and I tried t
pretend to myself that I was simply doing this in a casua
way, and without intent to divert the heavenly attention t
them for the purpose of getting rid of it myself. With dee
sagacity I put these mentions into the form of sorrowing rec
ollections and left-handed sham-supplications that the sins o
those boys might be allowed to pass unnoticed—"Possibl
they may repent." "It is true that Jim Smith broke a window
and lied about it—but maybe he did not mean any harm
And although Tom Holmes says more bad words than an
other boy in the village, he probably intends to repent—
though he has never said he would. And whilst it is a fac
that John Jones did fish a little on Sunday, once, he did n
really catch anything but only just one small useless mud-cat
and maybe that would n't have been so awful if he ha
thrown it back—as he says he did, but he did n't. Pity bu
they would repent of these dreadful things—and maybe the
will yet."

But while I was shamefully trying to draw attention t
these poor chaps—who were doubtless directing the celestia
attention to me at the same moment, though I never onc
suspected that—I had heedlessly left my candle burning. I
was not a time to neglect even trifling precautions. There wa
no occasion to add anything to the facilities for attracting no
tice to me—so I put the light out.

It was a long night to me, and perhaps the most distressfu

ɔne I ever spent. I endured agonies of remorse for sins which
: knew I had committed, and for others which I was not cer-
ain about, yet was sure that they had been set down against
ne in a book by an angel who was wiser than I and did not
rust such important matters to memory. It struck me, by and
ɔy, that I had been making a most foolish and calamitous
mistake, in one respect: doubtless I had not only made my
ɔwn destruction sure by directing attention to those other
ɔoys, but had already accomplished theirs!—Doubtless the
lightning had stretched them all dead in their beds by this
time! The anguish and the fright which this thought gave me
made my previous sufferings seem trifling by comparison.

Things had become truly serious. I resolved to turn over a
new leaf instantly; I also resolved to connect myself with the
church the next day, if I survived to see its sun appear. I resolved to cease from sin in all its forms, and to lead a high
and blameless life forever after. I would be punctual at church
and Sunday-school; visit the sick; carry baskets of victuals to
the poor (simply to fulfil the regulation conditions, although
I knew we had none among us so poor but they would smash
the basket over my head for my pains); I would instruct other
boys in right ways, and take the resulting trouncings meekly;
I would subsist entirely on tracts; I would invade the rum
shop and warn the drunkard—and finally, if I escaped the
fate of those who early become too good to live, I would go
for a missionary.

The storm subsided toward daybreak, and I dozed gradually to sleep with a sense of obligation to Lem Hackett for
going to eternal suffering in that abrupt way, and thus pre-
venting a far more dreadful disaster—my own loss.

But when I rose refreshed, by and by, and found that those
other boys were still alive, I had a dim sense that perhaps the
whole thing was a false alarm; that the entire turmoil had
been on Lem's account and nobody's else. The world looked
so bright and safe that there did not seem to be any real occasion to turn over a new leaf. I was a little subdued, during
that day, and perhaps the next; after that, my purpose of reforming slowly dropped out of my mind, and I had a peaceful, comfortable time again, until the next storm.

That storm came about three weeks later; and it was the

most unaccountable one, to me, that I had ever experienced
for on the afternoon of that day, "Dutchy" was drowned
Dutchy belonged to our Sunday-school. He was a German
lad who did not know enough to come in out of the rain
but he was exasperatingly good, and had a prodigious mem
ory. One Sunday he made himself the envy of all the youth
and the talk of all the admiring village, by reciting three thou
sand verses of Scripture without missing a word; then he
went off the very next day and got drowned.

Circumstances gave to his death a peculiar impressiveness
We were all bathing in a muddy creek which had a deep hole
in it, and in this hole the coopers had sunk a pile of green
hickory hoop poles to soak, some twelve feet under water
We were diving and "seeing who could stay under longest."
We managed to remain down by holding on to the hoop
poles. Dutchy made such a poor success of it that he was
hailed with laughter and derision every time his head ap
peared above water. At last he seemed hurt with the taunts
and begged us to stand still on the bank and be fair with him
and give him an honest count—"be friendly and kind just
this once, and not miscount for the sake of having the fun of
laughing at him." Treacherous winks were exchanged, and all
said "All right, Dutchy—go ahead, we'll play fair."

Dutchy plunged in, but the boys, instead of beginning to
count, followed the lead of one of their number and scam
pered to a range of blackberry bushes close by and hid behind
it. They imagined Dutchy's humiliation, when he should rise
after a superhuman effort and find the place silent and vacant
nobody there to applaud. They were "so full of laugh" with
the idea, that they were continually exploding into muffled
cackles. Time swept on, and presently one who was peeping
through the briers, said, with surprise:—

"Why, he has n't come up, yet!"

The laughing stopped.

"Boys, it's a splendid dive," said one.

"Never mind that," said another, "the joke on him is all the
better for it."

There was a remark or two more, and then a pause. Talking
ceased, and all began to peer through the vines. Before long
the boys' faces began to look uneasy, then anxious, then ter

ified. Still there was no movement of the placid water. Hearts began to beat fast, and faces to turn pale. We all glided out, silently, and stood on the bank, our horrified eyes wandering back and forth from each other's countenances to the water.

"Somebody must go down and see!"

Yes, that was plain; but nobody wanted that grisly task.

"Draw straws!"

So we did—with hands which shook so, that we hardly knew what we were about. The lot fell to me, and I went down. The water was so muddy I could not see anything, but felt around among the hoop poles, and presently grasped a limp wrist which gave me no response—and if it had I should not have known it, I let it go with such a frightened suddenness.

The boy had been caught among the hoop poles and entangled there, helplessly. I fled to the surface and told the awful news. Some of us knew that if the boy were dragged out at once he might possibly be resuscitated, but we never thought of that. We did not think of anything; we did not know what to do, so we did nothing—except that the smaller lads cried, piteously, and we all struggled frantically into our clothes, putting on anybody's that came handy, and getting them wrong-side-out and upside-down, as a rule. Then we scurried away and gave the alarm, but none of us went back to see the end of the tragedy. We had a more important thing to attend to: we all flew home, and lost not a moment in getting ready to lead a better life.

The night presently closed down. Then came on that tremendous and utterly unaccountable storm. I was perfectly dazed; I could not understand it. It seemed to me that there must be some mistake. The elements were turned loose, and they rattled and banged and blazed away in the most blind and frantic manner. All heart and hope went out of me, and the dismal thought kept floating through my brain, "If a boy who knows three thousand verses by heart is not satisfactory, what chance is there for anybody else?"

Of course I never questioned for a moment that the storm was on Dutchy's account, or that he or any other inconsequential animal was worthy of such a majestic demonstration

from on high; the lesson of it was the only thing that trou
bled me; for it convinced me that if Dutchy, with all his per
fections, was not a delight, it would be vain for me to turn
over a new leaf, for I must infallibly fall hopelessly short o
that boy, no matter how hard I might try. Nevertheless I did
turn it over—a highly educated fear compelled me to do
that—but succeeding days of cheerfulness and sunshine came
bothering around, and within a month I had so drifted back
ward that again I was as lost and comfortable as ever.

Breakfast time approached while I mused these musing
and called these ancient happenings back to mind; so I got
me back into the present and went down the hill.

On my way through town to the hotel, I saw the house
which was my home when I was a boy. At present rates, the
people who now occupy it are of no more value than I am
but in my time they would have been worth not less than five
hundred dollars apiece. They are colored folk.

After breakfast, I went out alone again, intending to hunt
up some of the Sunday-schools and see how this generation
of pupils might compare with their progenitors who had sat
with me in those places and had probably taken me as a
model—though I do not remember as to that now. By the
public square there had been in my day a shabby little brick
church called the "Old Ship of Zion," which I had attended
as a Sunday-school scholar; and I found the locality easily
enough, but not the old church; it was gone, and a trig and
rather hilarious new edifice was in its place. The pupils were
better dressed and better looking than were those of my time.
consequently they did not resemble their ancestors; and consequently there was nothing familiar to me in their faces. Still
I contemplated them with a deep interest and a yearning wist-
fulness, and if I had been a girl I would have cried; for they
were the offspring, and represented, and occupied the places
of boys and girls some of whom I had loved to love, and
some of whom I had loved to hate, but all of whom were
dear to me for the one reason or the other, so many years
gone by—and, Lord, where be they now!

I was mightily stirred, and would have been grateful to be
allowed to remain unmolested and look my fill; but a bald-
summited superintendent who had been a tow-headed Sun-

lay-school mate of mine on that spot in the early ages, recognized me, and I talked a flutter of wild nonsense to those
children to hide the thoughts which were in me, and which
could not have been spoken without a betrayal of feeling that
would have been recognized as out of character with me.

Making speeches without preparation is no gift of mine;
and I was resolved to shirk any new opportunity, but in the
next and larger Sunday-school I found myself in the rear of
the assemblage; so I was very willing to go on the platform a
moment for the sake of getting a good look at the scholars.
On the spur of the moment I could not recall any of the old
idiotic talks which visitors used to insult me with when I was
a pupil there; and I was sorry for this, since it would have
given me time and excuse to dawdle there and take a long
and satisfying look at what I feel at liberty to say was an array
of fresh young comeliness not matchable in another Sunday-
school of the same size. As I talked merely to get a chance to
inspect; and as I strung out the random rubbish solely to prolong the inspection, I judged it but decent to confess these
low motives, and I did so.

If the Model Boy was in either of these Sunday-schools, I
did not see him. The Model Boy of my time—we never had
but the one—was perfect: perfect in manners, perfect in
dress, perfect in conduct, perfect in filial piety, perfect in exterior godliness; but at bottom he was a prig; and as for the
contents of his skull, they could have changed place with the
contents of a pie and nobody would have been the worse off
for it but the pie. This fellow's reproachlessness was a standing reproach to every lad in the village. He was the admiration of all the mothers, and the detestation of all their sons.
I was told what became of him, but as it was a disappointment to me, I will not enter into details. He succeeded in life.

LV.

A Vendetta and Other Things

URING MY THREE DAYS' STAY in the town, I woke up every morning with the impression that I was a boy—for in my dreams the faces were all young again, and looked as they had looked in the old times—but I went to bed a hundred years old, every night—for meantime I had been seeing those faces as they are now.

Of course I suffered some surprises, along at first, before I had become adjusted to the changed state of things. I met young ladies who did not seem to have changed at all; but they turned out to be the daughters of the young ladies I had in mind—sometimes their grand-daughters. When you are told that a stranger of fifty is a grandmother, there is nothing surprising about it; but if, on the contrary, she is a person whom you knew as a little girl, it seems impossible. You say to yourself, "How can a little girl be a grandmother?" It takes some little time to accept and realize the fact that while you have been growing old, your friends have not been standing still, in that matter.

I noticed that the greatest changes observable were with the women, not the men. I saw men whom thirty years had changed but slightly; but their wives had grown old. These were good women; it is very wearing to be good.

There was a saddler whom I wished to see; but he was gone. Dead, these many years, they said. Once or twice a day, the saddler used to go tearing down the street, putting on his coat as he went; and then everybody knew a steamboat was coming. Everybody knew, also, that John Stavely was not expecting anybody by the boat—or any freight, either; and Stavely must have known that everybody knew this, still it made no difference to him; he liked to seem to himself to be expecting a hundred thousand tons of saddles by this boat, and so he went on all his life, enjoying being faithfully on hand to receive and receipt for those saddles, in case by any miracle they should come. A malicious Quincy paper used always to refer to this town, in derision as "Stavely's Landing." Stavely was one of my earliest admirations; I envied him his rush of imaginary business, and the display he was able to make of it, before strangers, as he went flying down the street struggling with his fluttering coat.

But there was a carpenter who was my chiefest hero. He was a mighty liar, but I did not know that; I believed everything he said. He was a romantic, sentimental, melodramatic fraud, and his bearing impressed me with awe. I vividly remember the first time he took me into his confidence. He was planing a board, and every now and then he would pause and heave a deep sigh; and occasionally mutter broken sentences—confused and not intelligible—but out of their midst an ejaculation sometimes escaped which made me shiver and did me good: one was, "O God, it is his blood!" I sat on the tool-chest and humbly and shudderingly admired him; for I judged he was full of crime. At last he said in a low voice:—

"My little friend, can you keep a secret?"

I eagerly said I could.

"A dark and dreadful one?"

I satisfied him on that point.

"Then I will tell you some passages in my history; for oh, I *must* relieve my burdened soul, or I shall die!"

He cautioned me once more to be "as silent as the grave;" then he told me he was a "red-handed murderer." He put down his plane, held his hands out before him, contemplated them sadly, and said:—

"Look—with these hands I have taken the lives of thirty human beings!"

The effect which this had upon me was an inspiration to him, and he turned himself loose upon his subject with interest and energy. He left generalizing, and went into details,—began with his first murder; described it, told what measures he had taken to avert suspicion; then passed to his second homicide, his third, his fourth, and so on. He had always done his murders with a bowie-knife, and he made all my hairs rise by suddenly snatching it out and showing it to me.

At the end of this first *séance* I went home with six of his fearful secrets among my freightage, and found them a great help to my dreams, which had been sluggish for a while back.

I sought him again and again, on my Saturday holidays; in fact I spent the summer with him—all of it which was valuable to me. His fascinations never diminished, for he threw something fresh and stirring, in the way of horror, into each successive murder. He always gave names, dates, places—everything. This by and by enabled me to note two things: that he had killed his victims in every quarter of the globe, and that these victims were always named Lynch. The destruction of the Lynches went serenely on, Saturday after Saturday, until the original thirty had multiplied to sixty,—and more to be heard from yet; then my curiosity got the better of my timidity, and I asked how it happened that these justly punished persons all bore the same name.

My hero said he had never divulged that dark secret to any living being; but felt that he could trust me, and therefore he would lay bare before me the story of his sad and blighted life. He had loved one "too fair for earth," and she had reciprocated "with all the sweet affection of her pure and noble nature." But he had a rival, a "base hireling" named Archibald Lynch, who said the girl should be his, or he would "dye his hands in her heart's best blood." The carpenter, "innocent and happy in love's young dream," gave no weight to the threat, but led his "golden-haired darling to the altar," and there, the two were made one; there also, just as the minister's hands were stretched in blessing over their heads, the fell deed was done—with a knife—and the bride fell a corpse at her husband's feet. And what did the husband do? He plucked forth that knife, and kneeling by the body of his lost one, swore to "consecrate his life to the extermination of all the human scum that bear the hated name of Lynch."

That was it. He had been hunting down the Lynches and slaughtering them, from that day to this—twenty years. He had always used that same consecrated knife; with it he had murdered his long array of Lynches, and with it he had left upon the forehead of each victim a peculiar mark—a cross, deeply incised. Said he:—

"The cross of the Mysterious Avenger is known in Europe, in America, in China, in Siam, in the Tropics, in the Polar Seas, in the deserts of Asia, in all the earth. Wherever in the uttermost parts of the globe, a Lynch has penetrated, there

1as the Mysterious Cross been seen, and those who have seen
t have shuddered and said, 'it is his mark, he has been here.'
You have heard of the Mysterious Avenger—look upon him,
'or before you stands no less a person! But beware—breathe
1ot a word to any soul. Be silent, and wait. Some morning
this town will flock aghast to view a gory corpse; on its brow
will be seen the awful sign, and men will tremble and whisper, 'he has been here,—it is the Mysterious Avenger's mark!'
You will come here, but I shall have vanished; you will see
me no more."

This ass has been reading the "Jibbenainosay," no doubt,
and had had his poor romantic head turned by it; but as I
had not yet seen the book then, I took his inventions for
truth, and did not suspect that he was a plagiarist.

However, we had a Lynch living in the town; and the more
I reflected upon his impending doom, the more I could not
sleep. It seemed my plain duty to save him, and a still plainer
and more important duty to get some sleep for myself, so at
last I ventured to go to Mr. Lynch and tell him what was
about to happen to him—under strict secrecy. I advised him
to "fly," and certainly expected him to do it. But he laughed
at me; and he did not stop there; he led me down to the
carpenter's shop, gave the carpenter a jeering and scornful
lecture upon his silly pretensions, slapped his face, made him
get down on his knees and beg—then went off and left me
to contemplate the cheap and pitiful ruin of what, in my eyes,
had so lately been a majestic and incomparable hero. The carpenter blustered, flourished his knife, and doomed this Lynch
in his usual volcanic style, the size of his fateful words undi-
minished; but it was all wasted upon me; he was a hero to
me no longer but only a poor, foolish, exposed humbug. I
was ashamed of him, and ashamed of myself; I took no further interest in him, and never went to his shop any more.
He was a heavy loss to me, for he was the greatest hero I had
ever known. The fellow must have had some talent; for some
of his imaginary murders were so vividly and dramatically described that I remember all their details yet.

The people of Hannibal are not more changed than is the
town. It is no longer a village; it is a city, with a mayor, and
a council, and water-works, and probably a debt. It has fifteen

thousand people, is a thriving and energetic place, and is paved like the rest of the west and south—where a well-paved street and a good sidewalk are things so seldom seen, that one doubts them when he does see them. The customary half-dozen railways centre in Hannibal now, and there is a new depot which cost a hundred thousand dollars. In my time the town had no specialty, and no commercial grandeur; the daily packet usually landed a passenger and bought a cat-fish, and took away another passenger and a hatful of freight; but now a huge commerce in lumber has grown up and a large miscellaneous commerce is one of the results. A deal of money changes hands there now.

Bear Creek—so called, perhaps, because it was always so particularly bare of bears—is hidden out of sight now, under islands and continents of piled lumber, and nobody but an expert can find it. I used to get drowned in it every summer regularly, and be drained out, and inflated and set going again by some chance enemy; but not enough of it is unoc-cupied now to drown a person in. It was a famous breeder of chills and fever in its day. I remember one summer when ev-erybody in town had this disease at once. Many chimneys were shaken down, and all the houses were so racked that the town had to be rebuilt. The chasm or gorge between Lover's Leap and the hill west of it is supposed by scientists to have been caused by glacial action. This is a mistake.

There is an interesting cave a mile or two below Hannibal, among the bluffs. I would have liked to revisit it, but had not time. In my time the person who then owned it turned it into a mausoleum for his daughter, aged fourteen. The body of this poor child was put into a copper cylinder filled with al-cohol, and this was suspended in one of the dismal avenues of the cave. The top of the cylinder was removable; and it was said to be a common thing for the baser order of tourists to drag the dead face into view and examine it and comment upon it.

LVI.

A Question of Law

T HE SLAUGHTER-HOUSE is gone from the mouth of Bear Creek and so is the small jail (or "calaboose") which once stood in its neighborhood. A citizen asked, "Do you remember when Jimmy Finn, the town drunkard, was burned to death in the calaboose?"

Observe, now, how history becomes defiled, through lapse of time and the help of the bad memories of men. Jimmy Finn was not burned in the calaboose, but died a natural death in a tan vat, of a combination of delirium tremens and spontaneous combustion. When I say natural death, I mean it was a natural death for Jimmy Finn to die. The calaboose victim was not a citizen; he was a poor stranger, a harmless whiskey-sodden tramp. I know more about his case than anybody else; I knew too much of it, in that bygone day, to relish speaking of it. That tramp was wandering about the streets one chilly evening, with a pipe in his mouth, and begging for a match; he got neither matches nor courtesy; on the contrary, a troop of bad little boys followed him around and amused themselves with nagging and annoying him. I assisted; but at last, some appeal which the wayfarer made for forbearance, accompanying it with a pathetic reference to his forlorn and friendless condition, touched such sense of shame and remnant of right feeling as were left in me, and I went away and got him some matches, and then hied me home and to bed, heavily weighted as to conscience, and unbuoyant in spirit. An hour or two afterward, the man was arrested and locked up in the calaboose by the marshal—large name for a constable, but that was his title. At two in the morning, the church bells rang for fire, and everybody turned out, of course—I with the rest. The tramp had used his matches disastrously: he had set his straw bed on fire, and the oaken sheathing of the room had caught. When I reached the ground, two hundred men, women, and children stood massed together, transfixed with horror, and staring at the grated windows of the jail. Behind the iron bars, and tuggin, frantically at them, and screaming for help, stood the tramp he seemed like a black object set against a sun, so white an intense was the light at his back. That marshal could not b found, and he had the only key. A battering-ram was quickl improvised, and the thunder of its blows upon the door ha so encouraging a sound that the spectators broke into wil cheering, and believed the merciful battle won. But it was no so. The timbers were too strong; they did not yield. It wa said that the man's death-grip still held fast to the bars afte he was dead; and that in this position the fires wrapped hin about and consumed him. As to this, I do not know. Wha was seen after I recognized the face that was pleading throug the bars was seen by others, not by me.

I saw that face, so situated, every night for a long tim afterward; and I believed myself as guilty of the man's deat as if I had given him the matches purposely that he migh burn himself up with them. I had not a doubt that I shoulc be hanged if my connection with this tragedy were found out The happenings and the impressions of that time are burn into my memory, and the study of them entertains me a much now as they themselves distressed me then. If anybod spoke of that grisly matter, I was all ears in a moment, anc alert to hear what might be said, for I was always dreading and expecting to find out that I was suspected; and so fin and so delicate was the perception of my guilty conscience that it often detected suspicion in the most purposeless re marks, and in looks, gestures, glances of the eye which hac no significance, but which sent me shivering away in a panic of fright, just the same. And how sick it made me when some body dropped, howsoever carelessly and barren of intent, the remark that "murder will out!" For a boy of ten years, I was carrying a pretty weighty cargo.

All this time I was blessedly forgetting one thing—the fact that I was an inveterate talker in my sleep. But one night I awoke and found my bed-mate—my younger brother—sitting up in bed and contemplating me by the light of the moon. I said:—

"What is the matter?"

"You talk so much I can't sleep."

I came to a sitting posture in an instant, with my kidneys in my throat and my hair on end.

"What did I say? Quick—out with it—what did I say?"

"Nothing much."

"It 's a lie—you know everything."

"Everything about what?"

"You know well enough. About *that*."

"About *what?*—I don't know what you are talking about. I think you are sick or crazy or something. But anyway, you 're awake, and I 'll get to sleep while I 've got a chance."

He fell asleep and I lay there in a cold sweat, turning this new terror over in the whirling chaos which did duty as my mind. The burden of my thought was, How much did I divulge? How much does he know?—what a distress is this uncertainty! But by and by I evolved an idea—I would wake my brother and probe him with a supposititious case. I shook him up, and said—

"Suppose a man should come to you drunk—"

"This is foolish—I never get drunk."

"I don't mean you, idiot—I mean the man. Suppose a *man* should come to you drunk, and borrow a knife, or a tomahawk, or a pistol, and you forgot to tell him it was loaded, and—"

"How could you load a tomahawk?"

"I don't mean the tomahawk, and I did n't *say* the tomahawk; I said the pistol. Now don't you keep breaking in that way, because this is serious. There 's been a man killed."

"What! In this town?"

"Yes, in this town."

"Well, go on—I won't say a single word."

"Well, then, suppose you forgot to tell him to be careful with it, because it was loaded, and he went off and shot himself with that pistol,—fooling with it, you know, and probably doing it by accident, being drunk. Well, would it be murder?"

"No—suicide."

"No, no. I don't mean *his* act, I mean yours: would you be a murderer for letting him have that pistol?"

After deep thought came this answer,—

"Well, I should think I was guilty of something—maybe

murder—yes, probably murder, but I don't quite know."

This made me very uncomfortable. However, it was not a decisive verdict. I should have to set out the real case—there seemed to be no other way. But I would do it cautiously, and keep a watch out for suspicious effects. I said:—

"I was supposing a case, but I am coming to the real one now. Do you know how the man came to be burned up in the calaboose?"

"No."

"Have n't you the least idea?"

"Not the least."

"Wish you may die in your tracks if you have?"

"Yes, wish I may die in my tracks."

"Well, the way of it was this. The man wanted some matches to light his pipe. A boy got him some. The man set fire to the calaboose with those very matches, and burnt himself up."

"Is that so?"

"Yes, it is. Now, is that boy a murderer, do you think?"

"Let me see. The man was drunk?"

"Yes, he was drunk."

"Very drunk?"

"Yes."

"And the boy knew it?"

"Yes, he knew it."

There was a long pause. Then came this heavy verdict:—

"If the man was drunk, and the boy knew it, the boy murdered that man. This is certain."

Faint, sickening sensations crept along all the fibres of my body, and I seemed to know how a person feels who hears his death sentence pronounced from the bench. I waited to hear what my brother would say next. I believed I knew what it would be, and I was right. He said,—

"I know the boy."

I had nothing to say; so I said nothing. I simply shuddered. Then he added,—

"Yes, before you got half through telling about the thing, I knew perfectly well who the boy was; it was Ben Coontz!"

I came out of my collapse as one who rises from the dead. I said, with admiration:—

"Why, how in the world did you ever guess it?"

"You told it in your sleep."

I said to myself, "How splendid that is! This is a habit which must be cultivated."

My brother rattled innocently on: —

"When you were talking in your sleep, you kept mumbling something about 'matches,' which I could n't make anything out of; but just now, when you began to tell me about the man and the calaboose and the matches, I remembered that in your sleep you mentioned Ben Coontz two or three times; so I put this and that together, you see, and right away I knew it was Ben that burnt that man up."

I praised his sagacity effusively. Presently he asked, —

"Are you going to give him up to the law?"

"No," I said; "I believe that this will be a lesson to him. I shall keep an eye on him, of course, for that is but right; but if he stops where he is and reforms, it shall never be said that I betrayed him."

"How good you are!"

"Well, I try to be. It is all a person can do in a world like this."

And now, my burden being shifted to other shoulders, my terrors soon faded away.

The day before we left Hannibal, a curious thing fell under my notice, — the surprising spread which longitudinal time undergoes there. I learned it from one of the most unostentatious of men, — the colored coachman of a friend of mine, who lives three miles from town. He was to call for me at the Park Hotel at 7.30 P.M., and drive me out. But he missed it considerably, — did not arrive till ten. He excused himself by saying: —

"De time is mos' an hour en a half slower in de country en what it is in de town; you 'll be in plenty time, boss. Sometimes we shoves out early for church, Sunday, en fetches up dah right plum in de middle er de sermon. Diffunce in de time. A body can't make no calculations 'bout it."

I had lost two hours and a half; but I had learned a fact worth four.

LVII.

An Archangel

FROM ST. LOUIS northward there are all the enlivening signs of the presence of active, energetic, intelligent, prosperous, practical nineteenth-century populations. The people don't dream, they work. The happy result is manifest all around in the substantial outside aspect of things, and the suggestions of wholesome life and comfort that everywhere appear.

Quincy is a notable example,—a brisk, handsome, well ordered city; and now, as formerly, interested in art, letters, and other high things.

But Marion City is an exception. Marion City has gone backwards in a most unaccountable way. This metropolis promised so well that the projectors tacked "city" to its name in the very beginning, with full confidence; but it was bad prophecy. When I first saw Marion City, thirty-five years ago, it contained one street, and nearly or quite six houses. It contains but one house now, and this one, in a state of ruin, is getting ready to follow the former five into the river.

Doubtless Marion City was too near to Quincy. It had another disadvantage: it was situated in a flat mud bottom, below high-water mark, whereas Quincy stands high up on the slope of a hill.

In the beginning Quincy had the aspect and ways of a model New England town: and these she has yet: broad, clean streets, trim, neat dwellings and lawns, fine mansions, stately blocks of commercial buildings. And there are ample fair-grounds, a well kept park, and many attractive drives; library, reading-rooms, a couple of colleges, some handsome and costly churches, and a grand court-house, with grounds which occupy a square. The population of the city is thirty thousand. There are some large factories here, and manufacturing, of many sorts, is done on a great scale.

La Grange and Canton are growing towns, but I missed Alexandria; was told it was under water, but would come up to blow in the summer.

Keokuk was easily recognizable. I lived there in 1857,—an
:traordinary year there in real-estate matters. The "boom"
as something wonderful. Everybody bought, everybody
ld,—except widows and preachers; they always hold on;
d when the tide ebbs, they get left. Anything in the sem-
ance of a town lot, no matter how situated, was salable, and
a figure which would still have been high if the ground had
en sodded with greenbacks.

The town has a population of fifteen thousand now, and is
ogressing with a healthy growth. It was night, and we
uld not see details, for which we were sorry, for Keokuk
as the reputation of being a beautiful city. It was a pleasant
e to live in long ago, and doubtless has advanced, not ret-
graded, in that respect.

A mighty work which was in progress there in my day is
nished now. This is the canal over the Rapids. It is eight
iles long, three hundred feet wide, and is in no place less
an six feet deep. Its masonry is of the majestic kind which
e War Department usually deals in, and will endure like a
oman aqueduct. The work cost four or five millions.

After an hour or two spent with former friends, we started
p the river again. Keokuk, a long time ago, was an occa-
onal loafing-place of that erratic genius, Henry Clay Dean.
believe I never saw him but once; but he was much talked
f when I lived there. This is what was said of him:—

He began life poor and without education. But he educated
imself—on the curb-stones of Keokuk. He would sit down
n a curb-stone with his book, careless or unconscious of the
latter of commerce and the tramp of the passing crowds, and
ury himself in his studies by the hour, never changing his
osition except to draw in his knees now and then to let a
ray pass unobstructed; and when his book was finished, its
ontents, however abstruse, had been burnt into his memory,
nd were his permanent possession. In this way he acquired
vast hoard of all sorts of learning, and had it pigeon-holed
n his head where he could put his intellectual hand on it
henever it was wanted.

His clothes differed in no respect from a "wharf-rat's," ex-
:ept that they were raggeder, more ill-assorted and inharmo-
ious (and therefore more extravagantly picturesque), and

several layers dirtier. Nobody could infer the master-mind
the top of that edifice from the edifice itself.

He was an orator,—by nature in the first place, and la‹
by the training of experience and practice. When he was o
on a canvass, his name was a loadstone which drew the farم
ers to his stump from fifty miles around. His theme was ‹
ways politics. He used no notes, for a volcano does not ne
notes. In 1862, a son of Keokuk's late distinguished citiz‹
Mr. Claggett, gave me this incident concerning Dean:

The war feeling was running high in Keokuk (in '61), aم
a great mass meeting was to be held on a certain day in t‹
new Athenæum. A distinguished stranger was to address t‹
house. After the building had been packed to its utmost capaci
with sweltering folk of both sexes, the stage still remain‹
vacant,—the distinguished stranger had failed to connect. T‹
crowd grew impatient, and by and by indignant and rebelliou
About this time a distressed manager discovered Dean on a cur
stone, explained the dilemma to him, took his book away fro‹
him, rushed him into the building the back way, and told hi
to make for the stage and save his country.

Presently a sudden silence fell upon the grumbling auc‹
ence, and everybody's eyes sought a single point,—the wid‹
empty, carpetless stage. A figure appeared there whose aspe‹
was familiar to hardly a dozen persons present. It was t‹
scarecrow Dean,—in foxy shoes, down at the heels; socks ‹
odd colors, also "down;" damaged trousers, relics of anti‹
uity, and a world too short, exposing some inches of nak‹
ankle; an unbuttoned vest, also too short, and exposing ‹
zone of soiled and wrinkled linen between it and the wais‹
band; shirt bosom open; long black handkerchief, woun‹
round and round the neck like a bandage; bob-tailed bl‹
coat, reaching down to the small of the back, with sleev‹
which left four inches of forearm unprotected; small, stif‹
brimmed soldier-cap hung on a corner of the bump of–
whichever bump it was. This figure moved gravely out upo‹
the stage and, with sedate and measured step, down to th‹
front, where it paused, and dreamily inspected the house, sa‹
ing no word. The silence of surprise held its own for a m‹
ment, then was broken by a just audible ripple of merrime‹
which swept the sea of faces like the wash of a wave. Th‹

figure remained as before, thoughtfully inspecting. Another wave started,—laughter, this time. It was followed by another, then a third,—this last one boisterous.

And now the stranger stepped back one pace, took off his soldier-cap, tossed it into the wing, and began to speak, with deliberation, nobody listening, everybody laughing and whispering. The speaker talked on unembarrassed, and presently delivered a shot which went home, and silence and attention resulted. He followed it quick and fast, with other telling things; warmed to his work and began to pour his words out, instead of dripping them; grew hotter and hotter, and fell to discharging lightnings and thunder,—and now the house began to break into applause, to which the speaker gave no heed, but went hammering straight on; unwound his black bandage and cast it away, still thundering; presently discarded the bob-tailed coat and flung it aside, firing up higher and higher all the time; finally flung the vest after the coat; and then for an untimed period stood there, like another Vesuvius, spouting smoke and flame, lava and ashes, raining pumice-stone and cinders, shaking the moral earth with intellectual crash upon crash, explosion upon explosion, while the mad multitude stood upon their feet in a solid body, answering back with a ceaseless hurricane of cheers, through a thrashing snow-storm of waving handkerchiefs.

"When Dean came," said Claggett, "the people thought he was an escaped lunatic; but when he went, they thought he was an escaped archangel."

Burlington, home of the sparkling Burdette, is another hill city; and also a beautiful one; unquestionably so; a fine and flourishing city, with a population of twenty-five thousand, and belted with busy factories of nearly every imaginable description. It was a very sober city, too—for the moment—for a most sobering bill was pending; a bill to forbid the manufacture, exportation, importation, purchase, sale, borrowing, lending, stealing, drinking, smelling, or possession, by conquest, inheritance, intent, accident, or otherwise, in the State of Iowa, of each and every deleterious beverage known to the human race, except water. This measure was approved by all the rational people in the State; but not by the bench of Judges.

Burlington has the progressive modern city's full equip ment of devices for right and intelligent government; includ ing a paid fire department, a thing which the great city of New Orleans is without, but still employs that relic of antiq uity, the independent system.

In Burlington, as in all these Upper-River towns, one breathes a go-ahead atmosphere which tastes good in the nos trils. An opera-house has lately been built there which is in strong contrast with the shabby dens which usually do duty as theatres in cities of Burlington's size.

We had not time to go ashore in Muscatine, but had a daylight view of it from the boat. I lived there awhile, many years ago, but the place, now, had a rather unfamiliar look; so I suppose it has clear outgrown the town which I used to know. In fact, I know it has; for I remember it as a small place—which it is n't now. But I remember it best for a lu- natic who caught me out in the fields, one Sunday, and ex- tracted a butcher-knife from his boot and proposed to carve me up with it, unless I acknowledged him to be the only son of the Devil. I tried to compromise on an acknowledgment that he was the only member of the family I had met; but that did not satisfy him; he would n't have any half-measures; I must say he was the sole and only son of the Devil—and he whetted his knife on his boot. It did not seem worth while to make trouble about a little thing like that; so I swung round to his view of the matter and saved my skin whole. Shortly afterward, he went to visit his father; and as he has not turned up since, I trust he is there yet.

And I remember Muscatine—still more pleasantly—for its summer sunsets. I have never seen any, on either side of the ocean, that equalled them. They used the broad smooth river as a canvas, and painted on it every imaginable dream of color, from the mottled daintinesses and delicacies of the opal, all the way up, through cumulative intensities, to blind- ing purple and crimson conflagrations which were enchanting to the eye, but sharply tried it at the same time. All the Upper Mississippi region has these extraordinary sunsets as a familiar spectacle. It is the true Sunset Land: I am sure no other coun- try can show so good a right to the name. The sunrises are also said to be exceedingly fine. I do not know.

LVIII.

On the Upper River

THE BIG TOWNS drop in, thick and fast, now: and between stretch processions of thrifty farms, not desolate
solitude. Hour by hour, the boat plows deeper and deeper
into the great and populous Northwest; and with each successive section of it which is revealed, one's surprise and respect gather emphasis and increase. Such a people, and such
achievements as theirs, compel homage. This is an independent race who think for themselves, and who are competent
to do it, because they are educated and enlightened; they
read, they keep abreast of the best and newest thought, they
fortify every weak place in their land with a school, a college,
a library, and a newspaper; and they live under law. Solicitude
for the future of a race like this is not in order.

This region is new; so new that it may be said to be still in
its babyhood. By what it has accomplished while still teeth-
ing, one may forecast what marvels it will do in the strength
of its maturity. It is so new that the foreign tourist has not
heard of it yet; and has not visited it. For sixty years, the
foreign tourist has steamed up and down the river between
St. Louis and New Orleans, and then gone home and written
his book, believing he had seen all of the river that was worth
seeing or that had anything to see. In not six of all these
books is there mention of these Upper-River towns—
for the reason that the five or six tourists who penetrated this
region did it before these towns were projected. The latest
tourist of them all (1878) made the same old regulation trip—
he had not heard that there was anything north of St. Louis.

Yet there was. There was this amazing region, bristling
with great towns, projected day before yesterday, so to speak,
and built next morning. A score of them number from fifteen
hundred to five thousand people. Then we have Muscatine,
ten thousand; Winona, ten thousand; Moline, ten thousand;
Rock Island, twelve thousand; La Crosse, twelve thousand;
Burlington, twenty-five thousand; Dubuque, twenty-five

thousand; Davenport, thirty thousand; St. Paul, fifty-eight thousand; Minneapolis, sixty thousand and upward.

The foreign tourist has never heard of these; there is no note of them in his books. They have sprung up in the night, while he slept. So new is this region, that I, who am comparatively young, am yet older than it is. When I was born, St. Paul had a population of three persons, Minneapolis had just a third as many. The then population of Minneapolis died two years ago; and when he died he had seen himself undergo an increase, in forty years, of fifty-nine thousand nine hundred and ninety-nine persons. He had a frog's fertility.

I must explain that the figures set down above, as the population of St. Paul and Minneapolis, are several months old. These towns are far larger now. In fact, I have just seen a newspaper estimate which gives the former seventy-one thousand, and the latter seventy-eight thousand. This book will not reach the public for six or seven months yet; none of the figures will be worth much then.

We had a glimpse of Davenport, which is another beautiful city, crowning a hill—a phrase which applies to all these towns; for they are all comely, all well built, clean, orderly, pleasant to the eye, and cheering to the spirit; and they are all situated upon hills. Therefore we will give that phrase a rest. The Indians have a tradition that Marquette and Joliet camped where Davenport now stands, in 1673. The next white man who camped there, did it about a hundred and seventy years later—in 1834. Davenport has gathered its thirty thousand people within the past thirty years. She sends more children to her schools now, than her whole population numbered twenty-three years ago. She has the usual Upper-River quota of factories, newspapers, and institutions of learning; she has telephones, local telegraphs, an electric alarm, and an admirable paid fire department, consisting of six hook and ladder companies, four steam fire engines, and thirty churches. Davenport is the official residence of two bishops— Episcopal and Catholic.

Opposite Davenport is the flourishing town of Rock Island, which lies at the foot of the Upper Rapids. A great railroad bridge connects the two towns—one of the thirteen which fret the Mississippi and the pilots, between St. Louis and St. Paul.

The charming island of Rock Island, three miles long and half a mile wide, belongs to the United States, and the Government has turned it into a wonderful park, enhancing its natural attractions by art, and threading its fine forests with many miles of drives. Near the centre of the island one catches glimpses, through the trees, of ten vast stone four-story buildings, each of which covers an acre of ground. These are the Government workshops; for the Rock Island establishment is a national armory and arsenal.

We move up the river—always through enchanting scenery, there being no other kind on the Upper Mississippi—and pass Moline, a centre of vast manufacturing industries; and Clinton and Lyons, great lumber centres; and presently reach Dubuque, which is situated in a rich mineral region. The lead mines are very productive, and of wide extent. Dubuque has a great number of manufacturing establishments; among them a plough factory which has for customers all Christendom in general. At least so I was told by an agent of the concern who was on the boat. He said:—

"You show me any country under the sun where they really know *how* to plough, and if I don't show you our mark on the plough they use, I 'll eat that plough; and I won't ask for any Woostershyre sauce to flavor it up with, either."

All this part of the river is rich in Indian history and traditions. Black Hawk's was once a puissant name hereabouts; as was Keokuk's, further down. A few miles below Dubuque is the Tête de Mort—Death's-head rock, or bluff—to the top of which the French drove a band of Indians, in early times, and cooped them up there, with death for a certainty, and only the manner of it matter of choice—to starve, or jump off and kill themselves. Black Hawk adopted the ways of the white people, toward the end of his life; and when he died he was buried, near Des Moines, in Christian fashion, modified by Indian custom; that is to say, clothed in a Christian military uniform, and with a Christian cane in his hand, but deposited in the grave in a sitting posture. Formerly, a horse had always been buried with a chief. The substitution of the cane shows that Black Hawk's haughty nature was really humbled, and he expected to walk when he got over.

We noticed that above Dubuque the water of the Mississippi was olive-green—rich and beautiful and semi-transparent, with the sun on it. Of course the water was nowhere as clear or of as fine a complexion as it is in some other seasons of the year; for now it was at flood stage, and therefore dimmed and blurred by the mud manufactured from caving banks.

The majestic bluffs that overlook the river, along through this region, charm one with the grace and variety of their forms, and the soft beauty of their adornment. The steep verdant slope, whose base is at the water's edge, is topped by a lofty rampart of broken, turreted rocks, which are exquisitely rich and mellow in color—mainly dark browns and dull greens, but splashed with other tints. And then you have the shining river, winding here and there and yonder, its sweep interrupted at intervals by clusters of wooded islands threaded by silver channels; and you have glimpses of distant villages, asleep upon capes; and of stealthy rafts slipping along in the shade of the forest walls; and of white steamers vanishing around remote points. And it is all as tranquil and reposeful as dreamland, and has nothing this-worldly about it—nothing to hang a fret or a worry upon.

Until the unholy train comes tearing along—which it presently does, ripping the sacred solitude to rags and tatters with its devil's warwhoop and the roar and thunder of its rushing wheels—and straightway you are back in this world, and with one of its frets ready to hand for your entertainment: for you remember that this is the very road whose stock always goes down after you buy it, and always goes up again as soon as you sell it. It makes me shudder to this day, to remember that I once came near not getting rid of my stock at all. It must be an awful thing to have a railroad left on your hands.

The locomotive is in sight from the deck of the steamboat almost the whole way from St. Louis to St. Paul—eight hundred miles. These railroads have made havoc with the steamboat commerce. The clerk of our boat was a steamboat clerk before these roads were built. In that day the influx of population was so great, and the freight business so heavy, that the boats were not able to keep up with the demands made upon their carrying capacity; consequently the captains were very independent and airy—pretty "biggity," as Uncle Remus would say. The clerk nut-shelled the contrast between the former time and the present, thus:—

"Boat used to land—captain on hurricane roof—mighty stiff and straight—iron ramrod for a spine—kid gloves, plug tile, hair parted behind—man on shore takes off hat and says:—

" 'Got twenty-eight tons of wheat, cap'n—be great favor if you can take them.'

"Captain says:—

" ''ll take two of them'—and don't even condescend to look at him.

"But now-a-days the captain takes off his old slouch, and smiles all the way around to the back of his ears, and gets off a bow which he has n't got any ramrod to interfere with, and says:—

" 'Glad to see you, Smith, glad to see you—you 're looking well—have n't seen you looking so well for years—what you got for us?'

" 'Nuth'n', says Smith; and keeps his hat on, and just turns his back and goes to talking with somebody else.

"Oh, yes, eight years ago, the captain was on top; but it 's Smith's turn now. Eight years ago a boat used to go up the river with every stateroom full, and people piled five and six deep on the cabin floor; and a solid deck-load of immigrants and harvesters down below, into the bargain. To get a first-class stateroom, you 'd got to prove sixteen quarterings of nobility and four hundred years of descent, or be personally acquainted with the nigger that blacked the captain's boots. But it 's all changed now; plenty staterooms above, no harvesters below—there 's a patent self-binder now, and they don't have harvesters any more; they 've gone where the woodbine twineth—and they did n't go by steamboat, either; went by the train."

Up in this region we met massed acres of lumber rafts coming down—but not floating leisurely along, in the old-fashioned way, manned with joyous and reckless crews of fiddling, song-singing, whiskey-drinking, breakdown-dancing rapscallions; no, the whole thing was shoved swiftly along by a powerful stern-wheeler, modern fashion, and the small crews were quiet, orderly men, of a sedate business aspect, with not a suggestion of romance about them anywhere.

Along here, somewhere, on a black night, we ran some exceedingly narrow and intricate island-chutes by aid of the electric light. Behind was solid blackness—a crackless bank of it; ahead, a narrow elbow of water, curving between dense walls of foliage that almost touched our bows on both sides; and here every individual leaf, and every individual ripple stood out in its natural color, and flooded with a glare as of noonday intensified. The effect was strange, and fine, and very striking.

We passed Prairie du Chien, another of Father Marquette's camping-places; and after some hours of progress through varied and beautiful scenery, reached La Crosse. Here is a town of twelve or thirteen thousand population, with electric lighted streets, and with blocks of buildings which are stately enough, and also architecturally fine enough, to command respect in any city. It is a choice town, and we made satisfactory use of the hour allowed us, in roaming it over, though the weather was rainier than necessary.

LIX.

Legends and Scenery

WE ADDED several passengers to our list, at La Crosse; among others an old gentleman who had come to this northwestern region with the early settlers, and was familiar with every part of it. Pardonably proud of it, too. He said:—

"You 'll find scenery between here and St. Paul that can give the Hudson points. You 'll have the Queen's Bluff— seven hundred feet high, and just as imposing a spectacle as you can find anywheres; and Trempeleau Island, which is n't like any other island in America, I believe, for it is a gigantic mountain, with precipitous sides, and is full of Indian traditions, and used to be full of rattlesnakes; if you catch the sun just right there, you will have a picture that will stay with you. And above Winona you 'll have lovely prairies; and then come the Thousand Islands, too beautiful for anything; green? why you never saw foliage so green, nor packed so thick; it 's like a thousand plush cushions afloat on a looking-glass—when the water 's still; and then the monstrous bluffs on both sides of the river—ragged, rugged, dark-complected—just the frame that 's wanted; you always want a strong frame, you know, to throw up the nice points of a delicate picture and make them stand out."

The old gentleman also told us a touching Indian legend or two—but not very powerful ones.

After this excursion into history, he came back to the scenery, and described it, detail by detail, from the Thousand Islands to St. Paul; naming its names with such facility, tripping along his theme with such nimble and confident ease, slamming in a three-ton word, here and there, with such a complacent air of 't is n't-anything,-I-can-do-it-any-time-I-want-to, and letting off fine surprises of lurid eloquence at such judicious intervals, that I presently began to suspect—

But no matter what I began to suspect. Hear him:—

"Ten miles above Winona we come to Fountain City, nestling sweetly at the feet of cliffs that lift their awful fronts,

Jovelike, toward the blue depths of heaven, bathing them in virgin atmospheres that have known no other contact save that of angels' wings.

"And next we glide through silver waters, amid lovely and stupendous aspects of nature that attune our hearts to adoring admiration, about twelve miles, and strike Mount Vernon, six hundred feet high, with romantic ruins of a once first-class hotel perched far among the cloud shadows that mottle its dizzy heights—sole remnant of once-flourishing Mount Vernon, town of early days, now desolate and utterly deserted.

"And so we move on. Past Chimney Rock we fly—noble shaft of six hundred feet; then just before landing at Minnieska our attention is attracted by a most striking promontory rising over five hundred feet—the ideal mountain pyramid. Its conic shape—thickly-wooded surface girding its sides, and its apex like that of a cone, cause the spectator to wonder at nature's workings. From its dizzy heights superb views of the forests, streams, bluffs, hills and dales below and beyond for miles are brought within its focus. What grander river scenery can be conceived, as we gaze upon this enchanting landscape, from the uppermost point of these bluffs upon the valleys below? The primeval wildness and awful loneliness of these sublime creations of nature and nature's God, excite feelings of unbounded admiration, and the recollection of which can never be effaced from the memory, as we view them in any direction.

"Next we have the Lion's Head and the Lioness's Head, carved by nature's hand, to adorn and dominate the beauteous stream; and then anon the river widens, and a most charming and magnificent view of the valley before us suddenly bursts upon our vision; rugged hills, clad with verdant forests from summit to base, level prairie lands, holding in their lap the beautiful Wabasha, City of the Healing Waters, puissant foe of Bright's disease, and that grandest conception of nature's works, incomparable Lake Pepin—these constitute a picture whereon the tourist's eye may gaze uncounted hours, with rapture unappeased and unappeasable.

"And so we glide along; in due time encountering those majestic domes, the mighty Sugar Loaf, and the sublime Maiden's Rock—which latter, romantic superstition has invested with a voice; and oft-times as the birch canoe glides near, at twilight, the dusky paddler fancies he hears the soft sweet music of the long-departed Winona, darling of Indian song and story.

"Then Frontenac looms upon our vision, delightful resort of jaded summer tourists; then progressive Red Wing; and Diamond Bluff, impressive and preponderous in its lone sublimity; then Prescott and the St. Croix; and anon we see bursting upon us the domes and steeples of St. Paul, giant young chief of the North, marching with seven-league stride in the van of progress, banner-bearer of the highest and newest civilization, carving his beneficent way with the tomahawk of commercial enterprise, sounding the warwhoop of Christian culture, tearing off the reeking scalp of sloth and superstition to plant there the steam-plow and the school-house— ever in his front stretch arid lawlessness, ignorance, crime, despair; ever in his wake bloom the jail, the gallows, and the pulpit; and ever—"

"Have you ever travelled with a panorama?"

"I have formerly served in that capacity."

My suspicion was confirmed.

"Do you still travel with it?"

"No, she is laid up till the fall season opens. I am helping now to work up the materials for a Tourist's Guide which the St. Louis and St. Paul Packet Company are going to issue this summer for the benefit of travellers who go by that line."

"When you were talking of Maiden's Rock, you spoke of the long-departed Winona, darling of Indian song and story. Is she the maiden of the rock?—and are the two connected by legend?"

"Yes, and a very tragic and painful one. Perhaps the most celebrated, as well as the most pathetic, of all the legends of the Mississippi."

We asked him to tell it. He dropped out of his conversational vein and back into his lecture-gait without an effort, and rolled on as follows:—

"A little distance above Lake City is a famous point known as Maiden's Rock, which is not only a picturesque spot, but is full of romantic interest from the event which gave it its name. Not many years ago this locality was a favorite resort

for the Sioux Indians on account of the fine fishing and hunting to be had there, and large numbers of them were always
to be found in this locality. Among the families which used
to resort here, was one belonging to the tribe of Wabasha.
We-no-na (first-born) was the name of a maiden who had
plighted her troth to a lover belonging to the same band. But
her stern parents had promised her hand to another, a famous
warrior, and insisted on her wedding him. The day was fixed
by her parents, to her great grief. She appeared to accede to
the proposal and accompany them to the rock, for the purpose of gathering flowers for the feast. On reaching the rock,
We-no-na ran to its summit and standing on its edge up-
braided her parents who were below, for their cruelty, and
then singing a death-dirge, threw herself from the precipice
and dashed them in pieces on the rock below."

"Dashed who in pieces—her parents?"

"Yes."

"Well, it certainly was a tragic business, as you say. And
moreover, there is a startling kind of dramatic surprise about
it which I was not looking for. It is a distinct improvement
upon the threadbare form of Indian legend. There are fifty
Lover's Leaps along the Mississippi from whose summit disappointed Indian girls have jumped, but this is the only jump
in the lot that turned out in the right and satisfactory way.
What became of Winona?"

"She was a good deal jarred up and jolted: but she got
herself together and disappeared before the coroner reached
the fatal spot; and 't is said she sought and married her true
love, and wandered with him to some distant clime, where
she lived happy ever after, her gentle spirit mellowed and
chastened by the romantic incident which had so early deprived her of the sweet guidance of a mother's love and a
father's protecting arm, and thrown her, all unfriended, upon
the cold charity of a censorious world."

I was glad to hear the lecturer's description of the scenery,
for it assisted my appreciation of what I saw of it, and enabled me to imagine such of it as we lost by the intrusion of
night.

As the lecturer remarked, this whole region is blanketed
with Indian tales and traditions. But I reminded him that

people usually merely mentioned this fact—doing it in a way to make a body's mouth water—and judiciously stopped there. Why? Because the impression left, was that these tales were full of incident and imagination—a pleasant impression which would be promptly dissipated if the tales were told. I showed him a lot of this sort of literature which I had been collecting, and he confessed that it was poor stuff, exceedingly sorry rubbish; and I ventured to add that the legends which he had himself told us were of this character, with the single exception of the admirable story of Winona. He granted these facts, but said that if I would hunt up Mr. Schoolcraft's book, published near fifty years ago, and now doubtless out of print, I would find some Indian inventions in it that were very far from being barren of incident and imagination; that the tales in Hiawatha were of this sort, and they came from Schoolcraft's book; and that there were others in the same book which Mr. Longfellow could have turned into verse with good effect. For instance, there was the legend of "The Undying Head." He could not tell it, for many of the details had grown dim in his memory; but he would recommend me to find it and enlarge my respect for the Indian imagination. He said that this tale, and most of the others in the book, were current among the Indians along this part of the Mississippi when he first came here; and that the contributors to Schoolcraft's book had got them directly from Indian lips, and had written them down with strict exactness, and without embellishments of their own.

I have found the book. The lecturer was right. There are several legends in it which confirm what he said. I will offer two of them—"The Undying Head," and "Peboan and Seegwun, an Allegory of the Seasons." The latter is used in Hiawatha; but it is worth reading in the original form, if only that one may see how effective a genuine poem can be without the helps and graces of poetic measure and rhythm:—

PEBOAN AND SEEGWUN

An old man was sitting alone in his lodge, by the side of a frozen stream. It was the close of winter, and his fire was almost out. He appeared very old and very desolate. His locks were white with age, and he trembled in every joint. Day after day passed in solitude, and he heard nothing but the sound of the tempest, sweeping before it the new-fallen snow.

One day, as his fire was just dying, a handsome young man approached and entered his dwelling. His cheeks were red with the blood of youth, his eyes sparkled with animation, and a smile played upon his lips. He walked with a light and quick step. His forehead was bound with a wreath of sweet grass, in place of a warrior's frontlet, and he carried a bunch of flowers in his hand.

"Ah, my son," said the old man, "I am happy to see you. Come in. Come and tell me of your adventures, and what strange lands you have been to see. Let us pass the night together. I will tell you of my prowess and exploits, and what I can perform. You shall do the same, and we will amuse ourselves."

He then drew from his sack a curiously wrought antique pipe, and having filled it with tobacco, rendered mild by a mixture of certain leaves, handed it to his guest. When this ceremony was concluded they began to speak.

"I blow my breath," said the old man, "and the stream stands still. The water becomes stiff and hard as clear stone."

"I breathe," said the young man, "and flowers spring up over the plain."

"I shake my locks," retorted the old man, "and snow covers the land. The leaves fall from the trees at my command, and my breath blows them away. The birds get up from the water, and fly to a distant land. The animals hide themselves from my breath, and the very ground becomes as hard as flint."

"I shake my ringlets," rejoined the young man, "and warm showers of soft rain fall upon the earth. The plants lift up their heads out of the earth, like the eyes of children glistening with delight. My voice recalls the birds. The warmth of my breath unlocks the streams. Music fills the groves wherever I walk, and all nature rejoices."

At length the sun began to rise. A gentle warmth came over the place. The tongue of the old man became silent.

The robin and bluebird began to sing on the top of the lodge. The stream began to murmur by the door, and the fragrance of growing herbs and flowers came softly on the vernal breeze.

Daylight fully revealed to the young man the character of his entertainer. When he looked upon him, he had the icy visage of *Peboan*.[1] Streams began to flow from his eyes. As the sun increased, he grew less and less in stature, and anon had melted completely away. Nothing remained on the place of his lodge-fire but the *miskodeed*,[2] a small white flower, with a pink border, which is one of the earliest species of northern plants.

"The Undying Head" is a rather long tale, but it makes up in weird conceits, fairy-tale prodigies, variety of incident, and energy of movement, for what it lacks in brevity.[3]

[1] Winter.
[2] The *trailing arbutus*.
[3] See Appendix D.

LX.

Speculations and Conclusions

W E REACHED ST. PAUL, at the head of navigation of the
Mississippi, and there our voyage of two thousand
miles from New Orleans ended. It is about a ten-day trip by
steamer. It can probably be done quicker by rail. I judge so
because I know that one may go by rail from St. Louis to
Hannibal—a distance of at least a hundred and twenty
miles—in seven hours. This is better than walking; unless one
is in a hurry.

The season being far advanced when we were in New Orleans, the roses and magnolia blossoms were falling; but here
in St. Paul it was the snow. In New Orleans we had caught
an occasional withering breath from over a crater, apparently;
here in St. Paul we caught a frequent benumbing one from
over a glacier, apparently.

I am not trying to astonish by these statistics. No, it is only
natural that there should be a sharp difference between climates which lie upon parallels of latitude which are one or
two thousand miles apart. I take this position, and I will hold
it and maintain it in spite of the newspapers. The newspaper
thinks it is n't a natural thing; and once a year, in February,
it remarks, with ill-concealed exclamation points, that while
we, away up here are fighting snow and ice, folks are having
new strawberries and peas down South; callas are blooming
out of doors, and the people are complaining of the warm
weather. The newspaper never gets done being surprised
about it. It is caught regularly every February. There must be
a reason for this; and this reason must be change of hands at
the editorial desk. You cannot surprise an individual more
than twice with the same marvel—not even with the February miracles of the Southern climate; but if you keep putting
new hands at the editorial desk every year or two, and forget
to vaccinate them against the annual climatic surprise, that
same old thing is going to occur right along. Each year one
new hand will have the disease, and be safe from its recur-
rence; but this does not save the newspaper. No, the news-

paper is in as bad case as ever; it will forever have its new
hand; and so, it will break out with the strawberry surprise
every February as long as it lives. The new hand is curable;
the newspaper itself is incurable. An act of Congress—no,
Congress could not prohibit the strawberry surprise without
questionably stretching its powers. An amendment to the
Constitution might fix the thing, and that is probably the best
and quickest way to get at it. Under authority of such an
amendment, Congress could then pass an act inflicting imprisonment for life for the first offence, and some sort of lingering death for subsequent ones; and this, no doubt, would
presently give us a rest. At the same time, the amendment
and the resulting act and penalties might easily be made to
cover various cognate abuses, such as the Annual-Veteran-
who-has-Voted-for-Every-President-from-Washington-down,
-and-Walked-to-the-Polls-Yesterday-with-as-Bright-an-Eye-
and-as-Firm-a-Step-as-Ever, and ten or eleven other weary
yearly marvels of that sort, and of the Oldest-Freemason, and
Oldest-Printer, and Oldest-Baptist-Preacher, and Oldest-
Alumnus sort, and Three-Children-Born-at-a-Birth sort, and
so on, and so on. And then England would take it up and
pass a law prohibiting the further use of Sidney Smith's jokes,
and appointing a commissioner to construct some new ones.
Then life would be a sweet dream of rest and peace, and the
nations would cease to long for heaven.

But I wander from my theme. St. Paul is a wonderful town.
It is put together in solid blocks of honest brick and stone,
and has the air of intending to stay. Its post-office was established thirty-six years ago; and by and by, when the postmaster received a letter, he carried it to Washington, horseback,
to inquire what was to be done with it. Such is the legend.
Two frame houses were built that year, and several persons
were added to the population. A recent number of the leading
St. Paul paper, the "Pioneer Press," gives some statistics
which furnish a vivid contrast to that old state of things, to
wit: Population, autumn of the present year (1882), 71,000;
number of letters handled, first half of the year, 1,209,387;
number of houses built during three-quarters of the year, 989;
their cost, $3,186,000. The increase of letters over the corre-
sponding six months of last year was fifty per cent. Last year

the new buildings added to the city cost above $4,500,000 St. Paul's strength lies in her commerce—I mean his commerce. He is a manufacturing city, of course—all the cities of that region are—but he is peculiarly strong in the matter of commerce. Last year his jobbing trade amounted to upwards of $52,000,000.

He has a custom-house, and is building a costly capitol to replace the one recently burned—for he is the capital of the State. He has churches without end; and not the cheap poor kind, but the kind that the rich Protestant puts up, the kind that the poor Irish "hired-girl" delights to erect. What a passion for building majestic churches the Irish hired-girl has. It is a fine thing for our architecture; but too often we enjoy her stately fanes without giving her a grateful thought. In fact, instead of reflecting that "every brick and every stone in this beautiful edifice represents an ache or a pain, and a handful of sweat, and hours of heavy fatigue, contributed by the back and forehead and bones of poverty," it is our habit to forget these things entirely, and merely glorify the mighty temple itself, without vouchsafing one praiseful thought to its humble builder, whose rich heart and withered purse it symbolizes.

This is a land of libraries and schools. St. Paul has three public libraries, and they contain, in the aggregate, some forty thousand books. He has one hundred and sixteen schoolhouses, and pays out more than seventy thousand dollars a year in teachers' salaries.

There is an unusually fine railway station; so large is it, in fact, that it seemed somewhat overdone, in the matter of size, at first; but at the end of a few months it was perceived that the mistake was distinctly the other way. The error is to be corrected.

The town stands on high ground; it is about seven hundred feet above the sea level. It is so high that a wide view of river and lowland is offered from its streets.

It is a very wonderful town indeed, and is not finished yet. All the streets are obstructed with building material, and this is being compacted into houses as fast as possible, to make room for more—for other people are anxious to build, as soon as they can get the use of the streets to pile up their bricks and stuff in.

How solemn and beautiful is the thought, that the earliest pioneer of civilization, the van-leader of civilization, is never the steamboat, never the railroad, never the newspaper, never the Sabbath-school, never the missionary—but always whiskey! Such is the case. Look history over; you will see. The missionary comes after the whiskey—I mean he arrives after the whiskey has arrived; next comes the poor immigrant, with axe and hoe and rifle; next, the trader; next, the miscellaneous rush; next, the gambler, the desperado, the highwayman, and all their kindred in sin of both sexes; and next, the smart chap who has bought up an old grant that covers all the land; this brings the lawyer tribe; the vigilance committee brings the undertaker. All these interests bring the newspaper; the newspaper starts up politics and a railroad; all hands turn to and build a church and a jail,—and behold, civilization is established forever in the land. But whiskey, you see, was the van-leader in this beneficent work. It always is. It was like a foreigner—and excusable in a foreigner—to be ignorant of this great truth, and wander off into astronomy to borrow a symbol. But if he had been conversant with the facts, he would have said,—

Westward the Jug of Empire takes its way.

This great van-leader arrived upon the ground which St. Paul now occupies, in June, 1837. Yes, at that date, Pierre Parrant, a Canadian, built the first cabin, uncorked his jug, and began to sell whiskey to the Indians. The result is before us.

All that I have said of the newness, briskness, swift progress, wealth, intelligence, fine and substantial architecture, and general slash and go, and energy of St. Paul, will apply to his near neighbor, Minneapolis—with the addition that the latter is the bigger of the two cities.

These extraordinary towns were ten miles apart, a few months ago, but were growing so fast that they may possibly be joined now, and getting along under a single mayor. At any rate, within five years from now there will be at least such a substantial ligament of buildings stretching between them and uniting them that a stranger will not be able to tell where the one Siamese twin leaves off and the other begins. Combined, they will then number a population of two hundred and fifty thousand, if they continue to grow as they are now growing. Thus, this centre of population at the head of Mississippi navigation, will then begin a rivalry as to numbers with that centre of population at the foot of it—New Orleans.

Minneapolis is situated at the falls of St. Anthony, which stretch across the river, fifteen hundred feet, and have a fall of eighty-two feet—a waterpower which, by art, has been made of inestimable value, business-wise, though somewhat to the damage of the Falls as a spectacle, or as a background against which to get your photograph taken.

Thirty flouring mills turn out two million barrels of the very choicest of flour every year; twenty sawmills produce two hundred million feet of lumber annually; then there are woollen mills, cotton mills, paper and oil mills; and sash, nail, furniture, barrel, and other factories, without number, so to speak. The great flouring-mills here and at St. Paul use the "new process" and mash the wheat by rolling, instead of grinding it.

Sixteen railroads meet in Minneapolis, and sixty-five passenger trains arrive and depart daily.

In this place, as in St. Paul, journalism thrives. Here there are three great dailies, ten weeklies, and three monthlies.

There is a university, with four hundred students—and, better still, its good efforts are not confined to enlightening the one sex. There are sixteen public schools, with buildings which cost $500,000; there are six thousand pupils and one hundred and twenty-eight teachers. There are also seventy churches existing, and a lot more projected. The banks aggregate a capital of $3,000,000, and the wholesale jobbing trade of the town amounts to $50,000,000 a year.

Near St. Paul and Minneapolis are several points of interest—Fort Snelling, a fortress occupying a river-bluff a hundred feet high; the falls of Minnehaha; White-bear Lake, and so forth. The beautiful falls of Minnehaha are sufficiently celebrated—they do not need a lift from me, in that direction. The White-bear Lake is less known. It is a lovely sheet of water, and is being utilized as a summer resort by the wealth and fashion of the State. It has its club-house, and its hotel, with the modern improvements and conveniences; its fine summer residences; and plenty of fishing, hunting, and pleasant drives. There are a dozen minor summer resorts around about St. Paul and Minneapolis, but the White-bear Lake is *the* resort. Connected with White-bear Lake is a most idiotic Indian legend. I would resist the temptation to print it here, if I could, but the task is beyond my strength. The guide-book names the preserver of the legend, and compliments his "facile pen." Without further comment or delay then, let us turn the said facile pen loose upon the reader:—

A LEGEND OF WHITE-BEAR LAKE

Every spring, for perhaps a century, or as long as there has been a nation of red men, an island in the middle of White-bear Lake has been visited by a band of Indians for the purpose of making maple sugar.

Tradition says that many springs ago, while upon this island, a young warrior loved and wooed the daughter of his chief, and it is said, also, the maiden loved the warrior. He had again and again been refused her hand by her parents, the old chief alleging that he was no brave, and his old consort called him a woman!

The sun had again set upon the "sugar-bush," and the bright moon rose high in the bright blue heavens, when the young warrior took down his flute and went out alone, once more to sing the story of his love, the mild breeze gently moved the two gay feathers in his head-dress, and as he mounted on the trunk of a leaning tree, the damp snow fell from his feet heavily. As he raised his flute to his lips, his blanket slipped from his well-formed shoulders, and lay partly on the snow beneath. He began his weird, wild love-song, but soon felt that he was cold, and as he reached back for his blanket, some unseen hand laid it gently on his shoulders; it was the hand of his love, his guardian angel. She took her place beside him, and for the present they

were happy; for the Indian has a heart to love, and in thi
pride he is as noble as in his own freedom, which make
him the child of the forest. As the legend runs, a larg
white-bear, thinking, perhaps, that polar snows and disma
winter weather extended everywhere, took up his journe
southward. He at length approached the northern shore o
the lake which now bears his name, walked down the ban
and made his way noiselessly through the deep heavy snow
toward the island. It was the same spring ensuing that th
lovers met. They had left their first retreat, and were now
seated among the branches of a large elm which hung fa
over the lake. (The same tree is still standing, and excite
universal curiosity and interest.) For fear of being detected
they talked almost in a whisper, and now, that they migh
get back to camp in good time and thereby avoid suspicion
they were just rising to return, when the maiden uttered a
shriek which was heard at the camp, and bounding toward
the young brave, she caught his blanket, but missed the
direction of her foot and fell, bearing the blanket with her
into the great arms of the ferocious monster. Instantly
every man, woman, and child of the band were upon the
bank, but all unarmed. Cries and wailings went up from
every mouth. What was to be done? In the meantime this
white and savage beast held the breathless maiden in his
huge grasp, and fondled with his precious prey as if he
were used to scenes like this. One deafening yell from the
lover warrior is heard above the cries of hundreds of his
tribe, and dashing away to his wigwam he grasps his faithful knife, returns almost at a single bound to the scene of
fear and fright, rushes out along the leaning tree to the spot
where his treasure fell, and springing with the fury of a
mad panther, pounced upon his prey. The animal turned,
and with one stroke of his huge paw brought the lovers
heart to heart, but the next moment the warrior, with one
plunge of the blade of his knife, opened the crimson sluices
of death, and the dying bear relaxed his hold.

   That night there was no more sleep for the band or the
lovers, and as the young and the old danced about the carcass of the dead monster, the gallant warrior was presented
with another plume, and ere another moon had set he had

a living treasure added to his heart. Their children for many years played upon the skin of the white-bear—from which the lake derives its name—and the maiden and the brave remembered long the fearful scene and rescue that made them one, for Kis-se-me-pa and Ka-go-ka could never forget their fearful encounter with the huge monster that came so near sending them to the happy hunting-ground.

It is a perplexing business. First, she fell down out of the tree—she and the blanket; and the bear caught her and fondled her—her and the blanket; then she fell up into the tree again—leaving the blanket; meantime the lover goes warwhooping home and comes back "heeled," climbs the tree, jumps down on the bear, the girl jumps down after him— apparently, for she was up the tree—resumes her place in the bear's arms along with the blanket, the lover rams his knife into the bear, and saves—whom, the blanket? No—nothing of the sort. You get yourself all worked up and excited about that blanket, and then all of a sudden, just when a happy climax seems imminent, you are let down flat—nothing saved but the girl. Whereas, one is not interested in the girl; she is not the prominent feature of the legend. Nevertheless, there you are left, and there you must remain; for if you live a thousand years you will never know who got the blanket. A dead man could get up a better legend than this one. I don't mean a fresh dead man either; I mean a man that's been dead weeks and weeks.

We struck the home-trail now, and in a few hours were in that astonishing Chicago—a city where they are always rubbing the lamp, and fetching up the genii, and contriving and achieving new impossibilities. It is hopeless for the occasional visitor to try to keep up with Chicago—she outgrows his prophecies faster than he can make them. She is always a novelty; for she is never the Chicago you saw when you passed through the last time. The Pennsylvania road rushed us to New York without missing schedule time ten minutes anywhere on the route; and there ended one of the most enjoyable five-thousand-mile journeys I have ever had the good fortune to make.

Appendix

A.

[*From the New-Orleans Times-Democrat, of March* 29, 1882.]

VOYAGE OF THE TIMES-DEMOCRAT'S RELIEF BOAT THROUGH THE INUNDATED REGIONS.

IT WAS NINE O'CLOCK Thursday morning when the "Susie" left the Mississippi and entered Old River, or what is now called the mouth of the Red. Ascending on the left, a flood was pouring in through and over the levees on the Chandler plantation, the most northern point in Pointe Coupée parish. The water completely covered the place, although the levees had given way but a short time before. The stock had been gathered in a large flat-boat, where, without food, as we passed, the animals were huddled together, waiting for a boat to tow them off. On the right-hand side of the river is Turnbull's Island, and on it is a large plantation which formerly was pronounced one of the most fertile in the State. The water has hitherto allowed it to go scot-free in usual floods, but now broad sheets of water told only where fields were. The top of the protecting levee could be seen here and there, but nearly all of it was submerged.

The trees have put on a greener foliage since the water has poured in, and the woods look bright and fresh, but this pleasant aspect to the eye is neutralized by the interminable waste of water. We pass mile after mile, and it is nothing but trees standing up to their branches in water. A water-turkey now and again rises and flies ahead into the long avenue of silence. A pirogue sometimes flits from the bushes and crosses the Red River on its way out to the Mississippi, but the sad-faced paddlers never turn their heads to look at our boat. The puffing of the boat is music in this gloom, which affects one most curiously. It is not the gloom of deep forests or dark caverns, but a peculiar kind of solemn silence and impressive

586

awe that holds one perforce to its recognition. We passed two negro families on a raft tied up in the willows this morning. They were evidently of the well-to-do class, as they had a supply of meal and three or four hogs with them. Their rafts were about twenty feet square, and in front of an improvised shelter earth had been placed, on which they built their fire.

The current running down the Atchafalaya was very swift, the Mississippi showing a predilection in that direction, which needs only to be seen to enforce the opinion of that river's desperate endeavors to find a short way to the Gulf. Small boats, skiffs, pirogues, etc., are in great demand, and many have been stolen by piratical negroes, who take them where they will bring the greatest price. From what was told me by Mr. C. P. Ferguson, a planter near Red River Landing, whose place has just gone under, there is much suffering in the rear of that place. The negroes had given up all thoughts of a crevasse there, as the upper levee had stood so long, and when it did come they were at its mercy. On Thursday a number were taken out of trees and off of cabin roofs and brought in, many yet remaining.

One does not appreciate the sight of earth until he has travelled through a flood. At sea one does not expect or look for it, but here, with fluttering leaves, shadowy forest aisles, house-tops barely visible, it is expected. In fact a grave-yard, if the mounds were above water, would be appreciated. The river here is known only because there is an opening in the trees, and that is all. It is in width, from Fort Adams on the left bank of the Mississippi to the bank of Rapides Parish, a distance of about sixty miles. A large portion of this was under cultivation, particularly along the Mississippi and back of the Red. When Red River proper was entered, a strong current was running directly across it, pursuing the same direction as that of the Mississippi.

After a run of some hours, Black River was reached. Hardly was it entered before signs of suffering became visible. All the willows along the banks were stripped of their leaves. One man, whom your correspondent spoke to, said that he had had one hundred and fifty head of cattle and one hundred head of hogs. At the first appearance of water he had started to drive them to the high lands of Avoyelles, thirty-five miles off, but he lost fifty head of the beef cattle and sixty hogs. Black River is quite picturesque, even if its shores are under water. A dense growth of ash, oak, gum, and hickory make the shores almost impenetrable, and where one can get a view down some avenue in the trees, only the dim outlines of distant trunks can be barely distinguished in the gloom.

A few miles up this river, the depth of water on the banks was fully eight feet, and on all sides could be seen, still holding against the strong current, the tops of cabins. Here and there one overturned was surrounded by drift-wood, forming the nucleus of possibly some future island.

In order to save coal, as it was impossible to get that fuel at any point to be touched during the expedition, a lookout was kept for a wood-pile. On rounding a point a pirogue, skilfully paddled by a youth, shot out, and in its bow was a girl of fifteen, of fair face, beautiful black eyes, and demure manners. The boy asked for a paper, which was thrown to him, and the couple pushed their tiny craft out into the swell of the boat.

Presently a little girl, not certainly over twelve years, paddled out in the smallest little canoe and handled it with all the deftness of an old voyageur. The little one looked more like an Indian than a white child, and laughed when asked if she were afraid. She had been raised in a pirogue and could go anywhere. She was bound out to pick willow leaves for the stock, and she pointed to a house near by with water three inches deep on the floors. At its back door was moored a raft about thirty feet square, with a sort of fence built upon it, and inside of this some sixteen cows and twenty hogs were standing. The family did not complain, except on account of losing their stock, and promptly brought a supply of wood in a flat.

From this point to the Mississippi River, fifteen miles, there is not a spot of earth above water, and to the westward for thirty-five miles there is nothing but the river's flood. Black River had risen during Thursday, the 23d, 1¾ inches, and was going up at night still. As we progress up the river habitations become more frequent, but are yet still miles apart. Nearly all of them are deserted, and the out-houses floated off. To add to the gloom, almost every living thing seems to have departed, and not a whistle of a bird nor the bark of the squirrel can be heard in this solitude. Sometimes a morose gar will throw his tail aloft and disappear in the river, but beyond this everything is quiet—the quiet of dissolution. Down the river floats now a neatly whitewashed hen-house, then a cluster of neatly split fence-rails, or a door and a bloated carcass, solemnly guarded by a pair of buzzards, the only bird to be seen, which feast on the carcass as it bears them along. A picture-frame in which there was a cheap lithograph of a soldier on horseback, as it floated on told of some hearth invaded by the water and despoiled of this ornament.

At dark, as it was not prudent to run, a place alongside the woods was hunted and to a tall gum-tree the boat was made fast for the night.

A pretty quarter of the moon threw a pleasant light over forest and river, making a picture that would be a delightful piece of landscape study, could an artist only hold it down to his canvas. The motion of the engines had ceased, the puffing of the escaping steam was stilled, and the enveloping silence closed upon us, and such silence it was! Usually in a forest at night one can hear the piping of frogs, the hum of insects, or the dropping of limbs; but here nature was dumb. The dark recesses, those aisles into this cathedral, gave forth no sound, and even the ripplings of the current die away.

At daylight Friday morning all hands were up, and up the Black we started. The morning was a beautiful one, and the river, which is remarkably straight, put on its loveliest garb. The blossoms of the haw perfumed the air deliciously, and a few birds whistled blithely along the banks. The trees were larger, and the forest seemed of older growth than below. More fields were passed than nearer the mouth, but the same scene presented itself—smoke-houses drifting out in the pastures, negro quarters anchored in confusion against some oak, and the modest residence just showing its eaves above water. The sun came up in a glory of carmine, and the trees were brilliant in their varied shades of green. Not a foot of soil is to be seen anywhere, and the water is apparently growing deeper and deeper, for it reaches up to the branches of the largest trees. All along, the bordering willows have been denuded of leaves, showing how long the people have been at work gathering this fodder for their animals. An old man in a pirogue was asked how the willow leaves agreed with his cattle. He stopped in his work, and with an ominous shake of his head replied: "Well, sir, it 's enough to keep warmth in their bodies and that 's all we expect, but it 's hard on the hogs, particularly the small ones. They is dropping off powerful fast. But what can you do? It 's all we 've got."

At thirty miles above the mouth of Black River the water extends from Natchez on the Mississippi across to the pine hills of Louisiana, a distance of seventy-three miles, and there is hardly a spot that is not ten feet under it. The tendency of the current up the Black is toward the west. In fact, so much is this the case, the waters of Red River have been driven down from toward the Calcasieu country, and the waters of the Black enter the Red some fifteen miles above the mouth of the former, a thing never before seen by even the oldest steamboatmen. The water now in sight of us is entirely from the Mississippi.

Up to Trinity, or rather Troy, which is but a short distance below, the people have nearly all moved out, those remaining having enough for their present personal needs. Their cattle, though, are suffering and dying off quite fast, as the confinement on rafts and the food they get breeds disease.

After a short stop we started, and soon came to a section where there were many open fields and cabins thickly scattered about. Here were seen more pictures of distress. On the inside of the houses the inmates had built on boxes a scaffold on which they placed the furniture. The bed-posts were sawed off on top, as the ceiling was not more than four feet from the improvised floor. The buildings looked very insecure, and threaten every moment to float off. Near the houses were cattle standing breast high in the water, perfectly impassive. They did not move in their places, but stood patiently waiting for help to come. The sight was a distressing one, and the poor creatures will be sure to die unless speedily rescued. Cattle differ from horses in this peculiar quality. A horse, after finding no relief comes, will swim off in search of food, whereas a beef will stand in its tracks until with exhaustion it drops in the water and drowns.

At half-past twelve o'clock a hail was given from a flat-boat inside the line of the bank. Rounding to we ran alongside, and General York stepped aboard. He was just then engaged in getting off stock, and welcomed the "Times-Democrat Boat" heartily, as he said there was much need for her. He said that the distress was not exaggerated in the least. People were in a condition it was difficult even for one to imagine. The water was so high there was great danger of their houses being swept away. It had already risen so high that it was approaching the eaves, and when it reaches this point there is always imminent risk of their being swept away. If this occurs, there will be great loss of life. The General spoke of the gallant work of many of the people in their attempts to save their stock, but thought that fully twenty-five per cent had perished. Already twenty-five hundred people had received rations from Troy, on Black River, and he had towed out a great many cattle, but a very great quantity remained and were in dire need. The water was now eighteen inches higher than in 1874, and there was no land between Vidalia and the hills of Catahoula.

At two o'clock the "Susie" reached Troy, sixty-five miles above the mouth of Black River. Here on the left comes in Little River; just beyond that the Ouachita, and on the right the Tensas. These three rivers form the Black River. Troy, or a portion of it, is situated on and around three large Indian mounds, circular in shape, which rise above the present water about twelve feet. They are about one hundred and fifty feet in diameter and are about two hundred yards apart. The houses are all built between these mounds, and hence are all flooded to a depth of eighteen inches on their floors.

These elevations, built by the aborigines hundreds of years ago, are the only points of refuge for miles. When we arrived we found them crowded with stock, all of which was thin and hardly able to stand up. They were mixed together, sheep, hogs, horses, mules, and cattle. One of these mounds has been used for many years as the grave-yard, and to-day we saw attenuated cows lying against the marble tomb-stones, chewing their cud in contentment, after a meal of corn furnished by General York. Here, as below, the remarkable skill of the women and girls in the management of the smaller pirogues was noticed. Children were paddling about in these most ticklish crafts with all the nonchalance of adepts.

General York has put into operation a perfect system in regard to furnishing relief. He makes a personal inspection of the place where it is asked, sees what is necessary to be done, and then, having two boats chartered, with flats, sends them promptly to the place, when the cattle are loaded and towed to the pine hills and uplands of Catahoula. He has made Troy his headquarters, and to this point boats come for their supply of feed for cattle. On the opposite side of Little River, which branches to the left out of Black, and between it and the Ouachita, is situated the town of Trinity, which is hourly threatened with destruction. It is much lower than Troy, and the water is eight and nine feet deep in the houses. A strong current sweeps through it, and it is remarkable that all of its houses have not gone before. The residents of both Troy and Trinity have been cared for, yet some of their stock have to be furnished with food.

As soon as the "Susie" reached Troy, she was turned over to General York and placed at his disposition to carry out the work of relief more rapidly. Nearly all her supplies were landed on one of the mounds to lighten her, and she was headed down stream to relieve those below. At Tom Hooper's place, a few miles from Troy, a large flat, with about fifty head of stock on board, was taken in tow. The animals were fed, and soon regained some strength. To-day we go on Little River, where the suffering is greatest.

DOWN BLACK RIVER.

SATURDAY EVENING, March 25.

We started down Black River quite early, under the direction of General York, to bring out what stock could be reached. Going down river a flat in tow was left in a central locality, and from there men poled her back in the rear of plantations, picking up the animals wherever found. In the loft of a gin-house there were seventeen head found, and after a gangway was built they were led down into the flat without difficulty. Taking a skiff with the General, your reporter was pulled up to a little house of two rooms, in which the water was standing two feet on the floors. In one of the large rooms were huddled the horses and cows of the place, while in the other the Widow Taylor and her son were seated on a scaffold raised on the floor. One or two dug-outs were drifting about in the room ready to be put in service at any time. When the flat was brought up, the side of the house was cut away as the only means of getting the animals out, and the cattle were driven on board the boat. General York, in this as in every case, inquired if the family desired to leave, informing them that Major Burke, of "The Times-Democrat," has sent the "Susie" up for that purpose. Mrs. Taylor said she thanked Major Burke, but she would try and hold out. The remarkable tenacity of the people here to their homes is beyond all comprehension. Just below, at a point sixteen miles from Troy, information was received that the house of Mr. Tom Ellis was in danger, and his family were all in it. We steamed there immediately, and a sad picture was presented. Looking out of the half of the window left above water was Mrs. Ellis, who is in feeble health, whilst at the door were her seven children, the oldest not fourteen years. One side of the house was given up to the work animals, some twelve head, besides hogs. In the next room the family lived, the water coming within two inches of the bed-rail. The stove was below water, and the cooking was done on a fire on top of it. The house threatened to give way at any moment: one end of it was sinking, and, in fact, the building looked a mere shell. As the boat rounded to, Mr. Ellis came out in a dug-out, and General York told him that he had come to his relief; that "The Times-Democrat" boat was at his service, and would remove his family at once to the hills, and on Monday a flat would take out his stock, as, until that time, they would be busy. Notwithstanding the deplorable situation himself and family were in, Mr. Ellis did not want to leave. He said he thought he would wait until Monday, and take the risk of his house falling. The children around the door looked perfectly contented, seeming to care little for the danger they were in.

These are but two instances of the many. After weeks of privation and suffering, people still cling to their houses and leave only when there is not room between the water and the ceiling to build a scaffold on which to stand. It seemed to be incomprehensible, yet the love for the old place was stronger than that for safety.

After leaving the Ellis place, the next spot touched at was the Oswald place. Here the flat was towed alongside the ginhouse where there were fifteen head standing in water; and yet, as they stood on scaffolds, their heads were above the top of the entrance. It was found impossible to get them out without cutting away a portion of the front; and so axes were brought into requisition and a gap made. After much labor the horses and mules were securely placed on the flat.

At each place we stop there are always three, four, or more dug-outs arriving, bringing information of stock in other places in need. Notwithstanding the fact that a great many had driven a part of their stock to the hills some time ago, there yet remains a large quantity, which General York, who is working with indomitable energy, will get landed in the pine hills by Tuesday.

All along Black River the "Susie" has been visited by scores of planters, whose tales are the repetition of those already heard of suffering and loss. An old planter, who has lived on the river since 1844, said there never was such a rise, and he was satisfied more than one quarter of the stock has been lost. Luckily the people cared first for their work stock, and when they could find it horses and mules were housed in a place of safety. The rise which still continues, and was two inches last night, compels them to get them out to the hills; hence it is that the work of General York is of such a great value. From daylight to late at night he is going this way and that, cheering by his kindly words and directing with calm judgment what is to be done. One unpleasant story, of a certain merchant in New Orleans, is told all along the river. It appears for some years past the planters have been dealing with this individual, and many of them had balances in his hands. When the overflow came they wrote for coffee, for meal, and, in fact, for such little necessities as were required. No response to these letters came, and others were written, and yet

hese old customers, with plantations under water, were re-
used even what was necessary to sustain life. It is needless to
ay he is not popular now on Black River.

The hills spoken of as the place of refuge for the people
and stock on Black River are in Catahoula parish, twenty-four
miles from Black River.

After filling the flat with cattle we took on board the family
of T. S. Hooper, seven in number, who could not longer
remain in their dwelling, and we are now taking them up
Little River to the hills.

THE FLOOD STILL RISING.

TROY, March 27, 1882, noon.

The flood here is rising about three and a half inches every
twenty-four hours, and rains have set in which will increase
this. General York feels now that our efforts ought to be directed towards saving life, as the increase of the water has
jeopardized many houses. We intend to go up the Tensas in
a few minutes, and then we will return and go down Black
River to take off families. There is a lack of steam transportation here to meet the emergency. The General has three
boats chartered, with flats in tow, but the demand for these
to tow out stock is greater than they can meet with prompt-
ness. All are working night and day, and the "Susie" hardly
stops for more than an hour anywhere. The rise has placed
Trinity in a dangerous plight, and momentarily it is expected
that some of the houses will float off. Troy is a little higher,
yet all are in the water. Reports have come in that a woman
and child have been washed away below here, and two cabins
floated off. Their occupants are the same who refused to
come off day before yesterday. One would not believe the
utter passiveness of the people.

As yet no news has been received of the steamer "Delia,"
which is supposed to be the one sunk in yesterday's storm on
Lake Catahoula. She is due here now, but has not arrived.
Even the mail here is most uncertain, and this I send by skiff
to Natchez to get it to you. It is impossible to get accurate
data as to past crops, etc., as those who know much about

the matter have gone, and those who remain are not we.
versed in the production of this section.

General York desires me to say that the amount of ration
formerly sent should be duplicated and sent at once. It is im
possible to make any estimate, for the people are fleeing t
the hills, so rapid is the rise. The residents here are in a stat
of commotion that can only be appreciated when seen, an
complete demoralization has set in.

If rations are drawn for any particular section hereabouts
they would not be certain to be distributed, so everythin
should be sent to Troy as a centre, and the General will hav
it properly disposed of. He has sent for one hundred tents
and, if all go to the hills who are in motion now, tw
hundred will be required.

B.

The condition of this rich valley of the Lower Mississipp
immediately after and since the war, constituted one of th
disastrous effects of war most to be deplored. Fictitious prop
erty in slaves was not only righteously destroyed, but ver
much of the work which had depended upon the slave labo
was also destroyed or greatly impaired, especially the leve
system.

It might have been expected by those who have not inves
tigated the subject, that such important improvements as th
construction and maintenance of the levees would have bee
assumed at once by the several States. But what can the Stat
do where the people are under subjection to rates of interes
ranging from 18 to 30 per cent, and are also under the neces
sity of pledging their crops in advance even of planting, a
these rates, for the privilege of purchasing all of their supplie
at 100 per cent profit?

It has needed but little attention to make it perfectly ob
vious that the control of the Mississippi River, if undertake
at all, must be undertaken by the national government, an
cannot be compassed by States. The river must be treated a
a unit; its control cannot be compassed under a divided o
separate system of administration.

Neither are the States especially interested competent t

combine among themselves for the necessary operations. The work must begin far up the river; at least as far as Cairo, if not beyond; and must be conducted upon a consistent general plan throughout the course of the river.

It does not need technical or scientific knowledge to comprehend the elements of the case if one will give a little time and attention to the subject, and when a Mississippi River commission has been constituted, as the existing commission is, of thoroughly able men of different walks in life, may it not be suggested that their verdict in the case should be accepted as conclusive, so far as any *a priori* theory of construction or control can be considered conclusive?

It should be remembered that upon this board are General Gilmore, General Comstock, and General Suter, of the United States Engineers; Professor Henry Mitchell (the most competent authority on the question of hydrography), of the United States Coast Survey; B. B. Harrod, the State Engineer of Louisiana; Jas. B. Eads, whose success with the jetties at New Orleans is a warrant of his competency, and Judge Taylor, of Indiana.

It would be presumption on the part of any single man, however skilled, to contest the judgment of such a board as this.

The method of improvement proposed by the commission is at once in accord with the results of engineering experience and with observations of nature where meeting our wants. As in nature the growth of trees and their proneness where undermined to fall across the slope and support the bank secures at some points a fair depth of channel and some degree of permanence, so in the project of the engineer the use of timber and brush and the encouragement of forest growth are the main features. It is proposed to reduce the width where excessive by brushwood dykes, at first low, but raised higher and higher as the mud of the river settles under their shelter, and finally slope them back at the angle upon which willows will grow freely. In this work there are many details connected with the forms of these shelter dykes, their arrangements so as to present a series of settling basins, etc., a description of which would only complicate the conception. Through the larger part of the river works of contraction will not be required, but nearly all the banks on the concave side of the bends must be held against the wear of the stream, and much of the opposite banks defended at critical points. The works having in view this conservative object may be generally designated works of revetment; and these also will be largely of brushwood, woven in continuous carpets, or twined into wire-netting. This veneering process has been successfully employed on the Missouri River; and in some cases they have so covered themselves with sediments, and have become so overgrown with willows, that they may be regarded as permanent. In securing these mats rubble-stone is to be used in small quantities, and in some instances the dressed slope between high and low river will have to be more or less paved with stone.

Any one who has been on the Rhine will have observed operations not unlike those to which we have just referred; and, indeed, most of the rivers of Europe flowing among their own alluvia have required similar treatment in the interest of navigation and agriculture.

The levee is the crowning work of bank revetment, although not necessarily in immediate connection. It may be set back a short distance from the revetted bank; but it is, in effect, the requisite parapet. The flood river and the low river cannot be brought into register, and compelled to unite in the excavation of a single permanent channel, without a complete control of all the stages; and even the abnormal rise must be provided against, because this would endanger the levee, and once in force behind the works of revetment would tear them also away.

Under the general principle that the local slope of a river is the result and measure of the resistance of its bed, it is evident that a narrow and deep stream should have less slope, because it has less frictional surface in proportion to capacity; i.e., less perimeter in proportion to area of cross section. The ultimate effect of levees and revetments confining the floods and bringing all the stages of the river into register is to deepen the channel and let down the slope. The first effect of the levees is to raise the surface; but this, by inducing greater velocity of flow, inevitably causes an enlargement of section, and if this enlargement is prevented from being made at the expense of the banks, the bottom must give way and the form of the waterway be so improved as to admit this flow with less rise. The actual experience with levees upon the Mississippi River, with no attempt to hold the banks, has been favorable, and no one can doubt, upon the evidence furnished in the reports of the commission, that if the earliest levees had been accompanied by revetment of banks, and made complete, we should have to-day a river navigable at low water and an adjacent country safe from inundation.

Of course it would be illogical to conclude that the constrained river can ever lower its flood slope so as to make levees unnecessary, but it is believed that, by this lateral constraint, the river as a conduit may be so improved in form that even those rare floods which result from the coincident rising of many tributaries will find vent without destroying levees of ordinary height. That the actual capacity of a channel through alluvium depends upon its service during floods has been often shown, but this capacity does not include anomalous, but recurrent, floods.

It is hardly worth while to consider the projects for relieving the Mississippi River floods by creating new outlets, since these sensational propositions have commended themselves only to unthinking minds, and have no support among engineers. Were the river bed cast-iron, a resort to openings for surplus waters might be a necessity; but as the bottom is yielding, and the best form of outlet is a single deep channel, as realizing the least ratio of perimeter to area of cross section, there could not well be a more unphilosophical method of treatment than the multiplication of avenues of escape.

In the foregoing statement the attempt has been made to condense in as limited a space as the importance of the subject would permit, the general elements of the problem, and the general features of the proposed method of improvement which has been adopted by the Mississippi River Commission.

The writer cannot help feeling that it is somewhat presumptuous on his part to attempt to present the facts relating to an enterprise which calls for the highest scientific skill; but it is a matter which interests every citizen of the United States, and is one of the methods of reconstruction which ought to be approved. It is a war claim which implies no private gain, and no compensation except for one of the cases of destruction incident to war, which may well be repaired by the people of the whole country.

EDWARD ATKINSON.

Boston, April 14, 1882.

C.

RECEPTION OF CAPTAIN BASIL HALL'S BOOK IN THE UNITED STATES.

Having now arrived nearly at the end of our travels, I am induced, ere I conclude, again to mention what I consider as one of the most remarkable traits in the national character of the Americans; namely, their exquisite sensitiveness and soreness respecting everything said or written concerning them. Of this, perhaps, the most remarkable example I can give is the effect produced on nearly every class of readers by the appearance of Captain Basil Hall's "Travels in North America." In fact, it was a sort of moral earthquake, and the vibration it occasioned through the nerves of the republic, from one corner of the Union to the other, was by no means over when I left the country in July, 1831, a couple of years after the shock.

I was in Cincinnati when these volumes came out, but it was not till July, 1830, that I procured a copy of them. One bookseller to whom I applied told me that he had had a few copies before he understood the nature of the work, but that, after becoming acquainted with it, nothing should induce him to sell another. Other persons of his profession must, however, have been less scrupulous; for the book was read in city, town, village, and hamlet, steamboat, and stage-coach, and a sort of war-whoop was sent forth perfectly unprecedented in my recollection upon any occasion whatever.

An ardent desire for approbation, and a delicate sensitiveness under censure, have always, I believe, been considered as amiable traits of character; but the condition into which the appearance of Captain Hall's work threw the republic shows plainly that these feelings, if carried to excess, produce a weakness which amounts to imbecility.

It was perfectly astonishing to hear men who, on other subjects, were of some judgment utter their opinions upon this. I never heard of any instance in which the common-sense generally found in national criticism was so overthrown by passion. I do not speak of the want of justice, and of fair and liberal interpretation: these, perhaps, were hardly to be expected. Other nations have been called thin-skinned, but the citizens of the Union have, apparently, no skins at all; they wince if a breeze blows over them, unless it be tempered with adulation. It was not, therefore, very surprising that the acute and forcible observations of a traveller they knew would be listened to should be received testily. The extraordinary features of the business were, first, the excess of the rage into which they lashed themselves; and, secondly, the puerility of the inventions by which they attempted to account for the severity with which they fancied they had been treated.

Not content with declaring that the volumes contained no word of truth from beginning to end (which is an assertion I heard made very nearly as often as they were mentioned), the whole country set to work to discover the causes why Captain Hall had visited the United States, and why he had published his book.

I have heard it said with as much precision and gravity as if the statement had been conveyed by an official report, that Captain Hall had been sent out by the British government expressly for the purpose of checking the growing admiration of England for the government of the United States,—that it was by a commission from the treasury he had come, and that it was only in obedience to orders that he had found anything to object to.

I do not give this as the gossip of a coterie; I am persuaded that it is the belief of a very considerable portion of the coun-try. So deep is the conviction of this singular people that they cannot be seen without being admired, that they will not ad-mit the possibility that any one should honestly and sincerely find aught to disapprove in them or their country.

The American Reviews are, many of them, I believe, well known in England; I need not, therefore, quote them here, but I sometimes wondered that they, none of them, ever thought of translating Obadiah's curse into classic American;

if they had done so, on placing (he, Basil Hall,) between brackets, instead of (he, Obadiah,) it would have saved them a world of trouble.

I can hardly describe the curiosity with which I sat down at length to peruse these tremendous volumes; still less can do justice to my surprise at their contents. To say that I found not one exaggerated statement throughout the work is by no means saying enough. It is impossible for any one who knows the country not to see that Captain Hall earnestly sought out things to admire and commend. When he praises, it is with evident pleasure; and when he finds fault, it is with evident reluctance and restraint, excepting where motives purely patriotic urge him to state roundly what it is for the benefit of his country should be known.

In fact, Captain Hall saw the country to the greatest possible advantage. Furnished, of course, with letters of introduction to the most distinguished individuals, and with the still more influential recommendation of his own reputation, he was received in full drawing-room style and state from one end of the Union to the other. He saw the country in full dress, and had little or no opportunity of judging of it unhouselled, unanointed, unannealed, with all its imperfection on its head, as I and my family too often had.

Captain Hall had certainly excellent opportunities of making himself acquainted with the form of the government and the laws; and of receiving, moreover, the best oral commentary upon them, in conversation with the most distinguished citizens. Of these opportunities he made excellent use; nothing important met his eye which did not receive that sort of analytical attention which an experienced and philosophical traveller alone can give. This has made his volumes highly interesting and valuable; but I am deeply persuaded, that were a man of equal penetration to visit the United States with no other means of becoming acquainted with the national character than the ordinary working-day intercourse of life, he would conceive an infinitely lower idea of the moral atmosphere of the country than Captain Hall appears to have done; and the internal conviction on my mind is strong, that if Captain Hall had not placed a firm restraint on himself, he must have given expression to far deeper indignation than any

1e has uttered against many points in the American character, with which he shows from other circumstances that he was well acquainted. His rule appears to have been to state just so much of the truth as would leave on the mind of his readers a correct impression, at the least cost of pain to the sensitive folks he was writing about. He states his own opinions and feelings, and leaves it to be inferred that he has good grounds for adopting them; but he spares the Americans the bitterness which a detail of the circumstances would have produced.

If any one chooses to say that some wicked antipathy to twelve millions of strangers is the origin of my opinion, I must bear it; and were the question one of mere idle speculation, I certainly would not court the abuse I must meet for stating it. But it is not so.

. . . .

The candor which he expresses, and evidently feels, they mistake for irony, or totally distrust; his unwillingness to give pain to persons from whom he has received kindness, they scornfully reject as affectation, and although they must know right well, in their own secret hearts, how infinitely more they lay at his mercy than he has chosen to betray; they pretend, even to themselves, that he has exaggerated the bad points of their character and institutions; whereas, the truth is, that he has let them off with a degree of tenderness which may be quite suitable for him to exercise, however little merited; while, at the same time, he has most industriously magnified their merits, whenever he could possibly find anything favorable.

D.

THE UNDYING HEAD.

In a remote part of the North lived a man and his sister, who had never seen a human being. Seldom, if ever, had the man any cause to go from home; for, as his wants demanded food, he had only to go a little distance from the lodge, and there, in some particular spot, place his arrows, with their barbs in the ground. Telling his sister where they had been placed, every morning she would go in search, and never fail of find-

ing each stuck through the heart of a deer. She had then onl
to drag them into the lodge and prepare their food. Thus sh
lived till she attained womanhood, when one day her brothe
whose name was Iamo, said to her: "Sister, the time is a
hand when you will be ill. Listen to my advice. If you do no
it will probably be the cause of my death. Take the impl
ments with which we kindle our fires. Go some distance fror
our lodge and build a separate fire. When you are in want c
food, I will tell you where to find it. You must cook for your
self, and I will for myself. When you are ill, do not attemp
to come near the lodge, or bring any of the utensils you use
Be sure always to fasten to your belt the implements yo
need, for you do not know when the time will come. As fo
myself, I must do the best I can." His sister promised to obe
him in all he had said.

Shortly after, her brother had cause to go from home. Sh
was alone in her lodge, combing her hair. She had just untie
the belt to which the implements were fastened, when sud
denly the event, to which her brother had alluded, occurred
She ran out of the lodge, but in her haste forgot the belt
Afraid to return, she stood for some time thinking. Finally
she decided to enter the lodge and get it. For, thought she
my brother is not at home, and I will stay but a moment t
catch hold of it. She went back. Running in suddenly, she
caught hold of it, and was coming out when her brother cam
in sight. He knew what was the matter. "Oh," he said, "di
I not tell you to take care? But now you have killed me." She
was going on her way, but her brother said to her, "Wha
can you do there now? The accident has happened. Go in
and stay where you have always stayed. And what will be
come of you? You have killed me."

He then laid aside his hunting-dress and accoutrements
and soon after both his feet began to turn black, so that he
could not move. Still he directed his sister where to place the
arrows, that she might always have food. The inflammatior
continued to increase, and had now reached his first rib; and
he said: "Sister, my end is near. You must do as I tell you
You see my medicine-sack, and my war-club tied to it. It contains all my medicines, and my war-plumes, and my paints of
all colors. As soon as the inflammation reaches my breast, you

will take my war-club. It has a sharp point, and you will cut off my head. When it is free from my body, take it, place its neck in the sack, which you must open at one end. Then hang it up in its former place. Do not forget my bow and arrows. One of the last you will take to procure food. The remainder, tie in my sack, and then hang it up, so that I can look towards the door. Now and then I will speak to you, but not often." His sister again promised to obey.

In a little time his breast was affected. "Now," said he, "take the club and strike off my head." She was afraid, but he told her to muster courage. "*Strike*," said he, and a smile was on his face. Mustering all her courage, she gave the blow and cut off the head. "Now," said the head, "place me where I told you." And fearfully she obeyed it in all its commands. Retaining its animation, it looked around the lodge as usual, and it would command its sister to go in such places as it thought would procure for her the flesh of different animals she needed. One day the head said: "The time is not distant when I shall be freed from this situation, and I shall have to undergo many sore evils. So the superior manito decrees, and I must bear all patiently." In this situation we must leave the head.

In a certain part of the country was a village inhabited by a numerous and warlike band of Indians. In this village was a family of ten young men—brothers. It was in the spring of the year that the youngest of these blackened his face and fasted. His dreams were propitious. Having ended his fast, he went secretly for his brothers at night, so that none in the village could overhear or find out the direction they intended to go. Though their drum was heard, yet that was a common occurrence. Having ended the usual formalities, he told how favorable his dreams were, and that he had called them together to know if they would accompany him in a war excursion. They all answered they would. The third brother from the eldest, noted for his oddities, coming up with his war-club when his brother had ceased speaking, jumped up. "Yes," said he, "I will go, and this will be the way I will treat those I am going to fight;" and he struck the post in the centre of the lodge, and gave a yell. The others spoke to him, saying: "Slow, slow, Mudjikewis, when you are in other peo-

ple's lodges." So he sat down. Then, in turn, they took th
drum, and sang their songs, and closed with a feast. Th
youngest told them not to whisper their intention to thei
wives, but secretly to prepare for their journey. They a
promised obedience, and Mudjikewis was the first to say so.

The time for their departure drew near. Word was given t
assemble on a certain night, when they would depart imme
diately. Mudjikewis was loud in his demands for his mocca
sins. Several times his wife asked him the reason. "Besides,
said she, "you have a good pair on." "Quick, quick," said he
"since you must know, we are going on a war excursion; s
be quick." He thus revealed the secret. That night they me
and started. The snow was on the ground, and they travelle
all night, lest others should follow them. When it was day
light, the leader took snow and made a ball of it, then tossin
it into the air, he said: "It was in this way I saw snow fall i
a dream, so that I could not be tracked." And he told then
to keep close to each other for fear of losing themselves, a
the snow began to fall in very large flakes. Near as the
walked, it was with difficulty they could see each other. Th
snow continued falling all that day and the following night
so it was impossible to track them.

They had now walked for several days, and Mudjikewis wa
always in the rear. One day, running suddenly forward, h
gave the *saw-saw-quan*,[1] and struck a tree with his war-club
and it broke into pieces as if struck with lightning. "Broth
ers," said he, "this will be the way I will serve those we ar
going to fight." The leader answered, "Slow, slow, Mudjike
wis, the one I lead you to is not to be thought of so lightly.
Again he fell back and thought to himself: "What! what! wh
can this be he is leading us to?" He felt fearful and was silent
Day after day they travelled on, till they came to an extensiv
plain, on the borders of which human bones were bleachin
in the sun. The leader spoke: "They are the bones of thos
who have gone before us. None has ever yet returned to te
the sad tale of their fate." Again Mudjikewis became restless
and, running forward, gave the accustomed yell. Advancin
to a large rock which stood above the ground, he struck it
and it fell to pieces. "See, brothers," said he, "thus will I trea

[1]War-whoop.

hose whom we are going to fight." "Still, still," once more said the leader; "he to whom I am leading you is not to be compared to the rock."

Mudjikewis fell back thoughtful, saying to himself: "I wonder who this can be that he is going to attack;" and he was afraid. Still they continued to see the remains of former warriors, who had been to the place where they were now going, some of whom had retreated as far back as the place where they first saw the bones, beyond which no one had ever escaped. At last they came to a piece of rising ground, from which they plainly distinguished, sleeping on a distant mountain, a mammoth bear.

The distance between them was very great, but the size of the animal caused him to be plainly seen. "There," said the leader, "it is he to whom I am leading you; here our troubles will commence, for he is a mishemokwa and a manito. It is he who has that we prize so dearly (*i.e.* wampum), to obtain which, the warriors whose bones we saw, sacrificed their lives. You must not be fearful; be manly. We shall find him asleep." Then the leader went forward and touched the belt around the animal's neck. "This," said he, "is what we must get. It contains the wampum." Then they requested the eldest to try and slip the belt over the bear's head, who appeared to be fast asleep, as he was not in the least disturbed by the attempt to obtain the belt. All their efforts were in vain, till it came to the one next the youngest. He tried, and the belt moved nearly over the monster's head, but he could get it no farther. Then the youngest one, and the leader, made his attempt, and succeeded. Placing it on the back of the oldest, he said, "Now we must run," and off they started. When one became fatigued with its weight, another would relieve him. Thus they ran till they had passed the bones of all former warriors, and were some distance beyond, when, looking back, they saw the monster slowly rising. He stood some time before he missed his wampum. Soon they heard his tremendous howl, like distant thunder, slowly filling all the sky; and then they heard him speak and say, "Who can it be that has dared to steal my wampum? earth is not so large but that I can find them;" and he descended from the hill in pursuit. As if convulsed, the earth shook with every jump he made. Very soon he approached the party. They, however, kept the belt, exchanging it from one to another, and encouraging each other; but h gained on them fast. "Brothers," said the leader, "has neve any one of you, when fasting, dreamed of some friendly spiri who would aid you as a guardian?" A dead silence followed "Well," said he, "fasting, I dreamed of being in danger o instant death, when I saw a small lodge, with smoke curling from its top. An old man lived in it, and I dreamed he helped me; and may it be verified soon," he said, running forward and giving the peculiar yell, and a howl as if the sounds came from the depths of his stomach, and what is called *checaudum* Getting upon a piece of rising ground, behold! a lodge, with smoke curling from its top, appeared. This gave them all new strength, and they ran forward and entered it. The leader spoke to the old man who sat in the lodge, saying, "Ne mesho, help us; we claim your protection, for the great bear will kill us." "Sit down and eat, my grandchildren," said the old man. "Who is a great manito?" said he. "There is none but me; but let me look," and he opened the door of the lodge, when, lo! at a little distance he saw the enraged animal coming on, with slow but powerful leaps. He closed the door. "Yes," said he, "he is indeed a great manito: my grand children, you will be the cause of my losing my life; you asked my protection, and I granted it; so now, come what may, will protect you. When the bear arrives at the door, you must run out of the other door of the lodge." Then putting his hand to the side of the lodge where he sat, he brought out a bag which he opened. Taking out two small black dogs, he placed them before him. "These are the ones I use when I fight," said he; and he commenced patting with both hands the sides of one of them, and he began to swell out, so that he soon filled the lodge by his bulk; and he had great strong teeth. When he attained his full size he growled, and from that moment, as from instinct, he jumped out at the door and met the bear, who in another leap would have reached the lodge. A terrible combat ensued. The skies rang with the howls of the fierce monsters. The remaining dog soon took the field. The brothers, at the onset, took the advice of the old man, and escaped through the opposite side of the lodge. They had not proceeded far before they heard the dying cry f one of the dogs, and soon after of the other. "Well," said ʌe leader, "the old man will share their fate: so run; he will ɔon be after us." They started with fresh vigor, for they had ₂ceived food from the old man: but very soon the bear came ₁ sight, and again was fast gaining upon them. Again the ₂ader asked the brothers if they could do nothing for their afety. All were silent. The leader, running forward, did as efore. "I dreamed," he cried, "that, being in great trouble, ʌ old man helped me who was a manito; we shall soon see ɩs lodge." Taking courage, they still went on. After going a hort distance they saw the lodge of the old manito. They ntered immediately and claimed his protection, telling him a ıanito was after them. The old man, setting meat before hem, said: "Eat! who is a manito? there is no manito but ʌe; there is none whom I fear;" and the earth trembled as he monster advanced. The old man opened the door and saw ɩim coming. He shut it slowly, and said: "Yes, my grandchil-Iren, you have brought trouble upon me." Procuring his nedicine-sack, he took out his small war-clubs of black stone, ɪnd told the young men to run through the other side of the ɔdge. As he handled the clubs, they became very large, and he old man stepped out just as the bear reached the door. ˉhen striking him with one of the clubs, it broke in pieces; he bear stumbled. Renewing the attempt with the other war-lub, that also was broken, but the bear fell senseless. Each ɪlow the old man gave him sounded like a clap of thunder, ɪnd the howls of the bear ran along till they filled the heavens.

The young men had now run some distance, when they ɔoked back. They could see that the bear was recovering ₹om the blows. First he moved his paws, and soon they saw ɪim rise on his feet. The old man shared the fate of the first, ɔr they now heard his cries as he was torn in pieces. Again he monster was in pursuit, and fast overtaking them. Not yet Iiscouraged, the young men kept on their way; but the bear vas now so close, that the leader once more applied to his ɪrothers, but they could do nothing. "Well," said he, "my Ireams will soon be exhausted; after this I have but one nore." He advanced, invoking his guardian spirit to aid him. ˙Once," said he, "I dreamed that, being sorely pressed, I came ɔ a large lake, on the shore of which was a canoe, partly out

of water, having ten paddles all in readiness. Do not fear," h
cried, "we shall soon get it." And so it was, even as he ha
said. Coming to the lake, they saw the canoe with ten pac
dles, and immediately they embarked. Scarcely had the
reached the centre of the lake, when they saw the bear arriv
at its borders. Lifting himself on his hind legs, he looked a
around. Then he waded into the water; then losing his foo
ing he turned back, and commenced making the circuit of th
lake. Meantime the party remained stationary in the centre t
watch his movements. He travelled all around, till at last h
came to the place from whence he started. Then he com
menced drinking up the water, and they saw the current fa
setting in towards his open mouth. The leader encourage
them to paddle hard for the opposite shore. When only
short distance from land, the current had increased so mucl
that they were drawn back by it, and all their efforts to reac
it were in vain.

Then the leader again spoke, telling them to meet the
fates manfully. "Now is the time, Mudjikewis," said he, "t
show your prowess. Take courage and sit at the bow of th
canoe; and when it approaches his mouth, try what effe
your club will have on his head." He obeyed, and stood read
to give the blow; while the leader, who steered, directed th
canoe for the open mouth of the monster.

Rapidly advancing, they were just about to enter h
mouth, when Mudjikewis struck him a tremendous blow o
the head, and gave the *saw-saw-quan*. The bear's limbs dou
bled under him, and he fell, stunned by the blow. But befor
Mudjikewis could renew it, the monster disgorged all the wa
ter he had drank, with a force which sent the canoe with grea
velocity to the opposite shore. Instantly leaving the canoe
again they fled, and on they went till they were completel
exhausted. The earth again shook, and soon they saw th
monster hard after them. Their spirits drooped, and they fe
discouraged. The leader exerted himself, by actions an
words, to cheer them up; and once more he asked them
they thought of nothing, or could do nothing for their res
cue; and, as before, all were silent. "Then," he said, "this i
the last time I can apply to my guardian spirit. Now, if we d
not succeed, our fates are decided." He ran forward, invokin

his spirit with great earnestness, and gave the yell. "We shall soon arrive," said he to his brothers, "at the place where my last guardian spirit dwells. In him I place great confidence. Do not, do not be afraid, or your limbs will be fear-bound. We shall soon reach his lodge. Run, run," he cried.

Returning now to Iamo, he had passed all the time in the same condition we had left him, the head directing his sister, in order to procure food, where to place the magic arrows, and speaking at long intervals. One day the sister saw the eyes of the head brighten, as if with pleasure. At last it spoke. "Oh, sister," it said, "in what a pitiful situation you have been the cause of placing me! Soon, very soon, a party of young men will arrive and apply to me for aid; but alas! How can I give what I would have done with so much pleasure? Nevertheless, take two arrows, and place them where you have been in the habit of placing the others, and have meat prepared and cooked before they arrive. When you hear them coming and calling on my name, go out and say, 'Alas! it is long ago that an accident befell him. I was the cause of it.' If they still come near, ask them in, and set meat before them. And now you must follow my directions strictly. When the bear is near, go out and meet him. You will take my medicine-sack, bows and arrows, and my head. You must then untie the sack, and spread out before you my paints of all colors, my war-eagle feathers, my tufts of dried hair, and whatever else it contains. As the bear approaches, you will take all these articles, one by one, and say to him, 'This is my deceased brother's paint,' and so on with all the other articles, throwing each of them as far as you can. The virtues contained in them will cause him to totter; and, to complete his destruction, you will take my head, and that too you will cast as far off as you can, crying aloud, 'See, this is my deceased brother's head.' He will then fall senseless. By this time the young men will have eaten, and you will call them to your assistance. You must then cut the carcass into pieces, yes, into small pieces, and scatter them to the four winds; for, unless you do this, he will again revive." She promised that all should be done as he said. She had only time to prepare the meat, when the voice of the leader was heard calling upon Iamo for aid. The woman went out and said as her brother had directed. But the war party being closely pursued, came up to the lodge. She invited them in, and placed the meat before them. While they were eating, they heard the bear approaching. Untying the medicine-sack and taking the head, she had all in readiness for his approach. When he came up she did as she had been told; and, before she had expended the paints and feathers, the bear began to totter, but, still advancing, came close to the woman. Saying as she was commanded, she then took the head, and cast it as far from her as she could. As it rolled along the ground, the blood, excited by the feelings of the head in this terrible scene, gushed from the nose and mouth. The bear, tottering, soon fell with a tremendous noise. Then she cried for help, and the young men came rushing out, having partially re-gained their strength and spirits.

Mudjikewis, stepping up, gave a yell and struck him a blow upon the head. This he repeated, till it seemed like a mass of brains, while the others, as quick as possible, cut him into very small pieces, which they then scattered in every direction. While thus employed, happening to look around where they had thrown the meat, wonderful to behold, they saw starting up and running off in every direction small black bears, such as are seen at the present day. The country was soon over-spread with these black animals. And it was from this monster that the present race of bears derived their origin.

Having thus overcome their pursuer, they returned to the lodge. In the mean time, the woman, gathering the imple-ments she had used, and the head, placed them again in the sack. But the head did not speak again, probably from its great exertion to overcome the monster.

Having spent so much time and traversed so vast a country in their flight, the young men gave up the idea of ever return-ing to their own country, and game being plenty, they deter-mined to remain where they now were. One day they moved off some distance from the lodge for the purpose of hunting, having left the wampum with the woman. They were very successful, and amused themselves, as all young men do when alone, by talking and jesting with each other. One of them spoke and said, "We have all this sport to ourselves; let us go and ask our sister if she will not let us bring the head to this place, as it is still alive. It may be pleased to hear us talk, and

be in our company. In the mean time take food to our sister."
They went and requested the head. She told them to take it,
and they took it to their hunting-grounds, and tried to amuse
it, but only at times did they see its eyes beam with pleasure.
One day, while busy in their encampment, they were unex-
pectedly attacked by unknown Indians. The skirmish was
long contested and bloody; many of their foes were slain, but
still they were thirty to one. The young men fought desperately till they were all killed. The attacking party then retreated to a height of ground, to muster their men, and to
count the number of missing and slain. One of their young
men had stayed away, and, in endeavoring to overtake them,
came to the place where the head was hung up. Seeing that
alone retain animation, he eyed it for some time with fear and
surprise. However, he took it down and opened the sack, and
was much pleased to see the beautiful feathers, one of which
he placed on his head.

Starting off, it waved gracefully over him till he reached his
party, when he threw down the head and sack, and told them
how he had found it, and that the sack was full of paints and
feathers. They all looked at the head and made sport of it.
Numbers of the young men took the paint and painted themselves, and one of the party took the head by the hair and
said: —

"Look, you ugly thing, and see your paints on the faces of
warriors."

But the feathers were so beautiful, that numbers of them
also placed them on their heads. Then again they used all
kinds of indignity to the head, for which they were in turn
repaid by the death of those who had used the feathers. Then
the chief commanded them to throw away all except the head.
"We will see," said he, "when we get home, what we can do
with it. We will try to make it shut its eyes."

When they reached their homes they took it to the council-
lodge, and hung it up before the fire, fastening it with raw
hide soaked, which would shrink and become tightened by
the action of the fire. "We will then see," they said, "if we
cannot make it shut its eyes."

Meantime, for several days, the sister had been waiting for
the young men to bring back the head; till, at last, getting

impatient, she went in search of it. The young men she found lying within short distances of each other, dead, and covered with wounds. Various other bodies lay scattered in different directions around them. She searched for the head and sack, but they were nowhere to be found. She raised her voice and wept, and blackened her face. Then she walked in different directions, till she came to the place from whence the head had been taken. Then she found the magic bow and arrows where the young men, ignorant of their qualities, had left them. She thought to herself that she would find her brother's head, and came to a piece of rising ground, and there saw some of his paints and feathers. These she carefully put up, and hung upon the branch of a tree till her return.

At dusk she arrived at the first lodge of a very extensive village. Here she used a charm, common among Indians when they wish to meet with a kind reception. On applying to the old man and woman of the lodge, she was kindly received. She made known her errand. The old man promised to aid her, and told her the head was hung up before the council-fire, and that the chiefs of the village, with their young men, kept watch over it continually. The former are considered as manitoes. She said she only wished to see it, and would be satisfied if she could only get to the door of the lodge. She knew she had not sufficient power to take it by force. "Come with me," said the Indian, "I will take you there." They went, and they took their seats near the door. The council-lodge was filled with warriors, amusing themselves with games, and constantly keeping up a fire to smoke the head, as they said, to make dry meat. They saw the head move, and not knowing what to make of it, one spoke and said: "Ha! ha! It is beginning to feel the effects of the smoke." The sister looked up from the door, and her eyes met those of her brother, and tears rolled down the cheeks of the head. "Well," said the chief, "I thought we would make you do something at last. Look! look at it—shedding tears," said he to those around him; and they all laughed and passed their jokes upon it. The chief, looking around, and observing the woman, after some time said to the man who came with her: "Who have you got there? I have never seen that woman before in our village." "Yes," replied the man, "you have seen her; she is a relation of mine, and seldom goes out. She stays at my lodge, and asked me to allow her to come with me to this place." In the centre of the lodge sat one of those young men who are always forward, and fond of boasting and displaying themselves before others. "Why," said he, "I have seen her often, and it is to this lodge I go almost every night to court her." All the others laughed and continued their games. The young man did not know he was telling a lie to the woman's advantage, who by that means escaped.

She returned to the man's lodge, and immediately set out for her own country. Coming to the spot where the bodies of her adopted brothers lay, she placed them together, their feet toward the east. Then taking an axe which she had, she cast it up into the air, crying out, "Brothers, get up from under it, or it will fall on you." This she repeated three times, and the third time the brothers all arose and stood on their feet.

Mudjikewis commenced rubbing his eyes and stretching himself. "Why," said he, "I have overslept myself." "No, indeed," said one of the others, "do you not know we were all killed, and that it is our sister who has brought us to life?" The young men took the bodies of their enemies and burned them. Soon after, the woman went to procure wives for them, in a distant country, they knew not where; but she returned with ten young women, which she gave to the ten young men, beginning with the eldest. Mudjikewis stepped to and fro, uneasy lest he should not get the one he liked. But he was not disappointed, for she fell to his lot. And they were well matched, for she was a female magician. They then all moved into a very large lodge, and their sister told them that the women must now take turns in going to her brother's head every night, trying to untie it. They all said they would do so with pleasure. The eldest made the first attempt, and with a rushing noise she fled through the air.

Toward daylight she returned. She had been unsuccessful, as she succeeded in untying only one of the knots. All took their turns regularly, and each one succeeded in untying only one knot each time. But when the youngest went, she commenced the work as soon as she reached the lodge; although it had always been occupied, still the Indians never could see any one. For ten nights now, the smoke had not ascended, but filled the lodge and drove them out. This last night they were all driven out, and the young woman carried off the head.

The young people and the sister heard the young woman coming high through the air, and they heard her saying: "Prepare the body of our brother." And as soon as they heard it, they went to a small lodge where the black body of Iamo lay. His sister commenced cutting the neck part, from which the neck had been severed. She cut so deep as to cause it to bleed; and the others who were present, by rubbing the body and applying medicines, expelled the blackness. In the mean time the one who brought it, by cutting the neck of the head, caused that also to bleed.

As soon as she arrived, they placed that close to the body, and, by aid of medicines and various other means, succeeded in restoring Iamo to all his former beauty and manliness. All rejoiced in the happy termination of their troubles, and they had spent some time joyfully together, when Iamo said: "Now I will divide the wampum;" and getting the belt which contained it, he commenced with the eldest, giving it in equal portions. But the youngest got the most splendid and beautiful, as the bottom of the belt held the richest and rarest.

They were told that, since they had all once died, and were restored to life, they were no longer mortal, but spirits, and they were assigned different stations in the invisible world. Only Mudjikewis's place was, however, named. He was to direct the west wind, hence generally called Kebeyun, there to remain forever. They were commanded, as they had it in their power, to do good to the inhabitants of the earth, and, forgetting their sufferings in procuring the wampum, to give all things with a liberal hand. And they were also commanded that it should also be held by them sacred; those grains or shells of the pale hue to be emblematic of peace, while those of the darker hue would lead to evil and war.

The spirits then, amid songs and shouts, took their flight to their respective abodes on high; while Iamo, with his sister Iamoqua, descended into the depths below.

ADVENTURES OF
HUCKLEBERRY FINN

NOTICE.

PERSONS attempting to find a motive in this narrative will be prosecuted; persons attempting to find a moral in it will be banished; persons attempting to find a plot in it will be shot.

BY ORDER OF THE AUTHOR
PER G. G., CHIEF OF ORDANCE.

EXPLANATORY.

In this book a number of dialects are used, to wit: the Missouri negro dialect; the extremest form of the back-woods South-Western dialect; the ordinary "Pike-County" dialect; and four modified varieties of this last. The shadings have not been done in a hap-hazard fashion, or by guess-work; but pains-takingly, and with the trustworthy guidance and support of personal familiarity with these several forms of speech.

I make this explanation for the reason that without it many readers would suppose that all these characters were trying to talk alike and not succeeding.

The Author.

Contents

I

You don't know about me, without you have read a book by the name of "The Adventures of Tom Sawyer," but that ain't no matter. That book was made by Mr. Mark Twain, and he told the truth, mainly. There was things which he stretched, but mainly he told the truth. That is nothing. I never seen anybody but lied, one time or another, without it was Aunt Polly, or the widow, or maybe Mary. Aunt Polly—Tom's Aunt Polly, she is—and Mary, and the Widow Douglas, is all told about in that book—which is mostly a true book; with some stretchers, as I said before.

Now the way that the book winds up, is this: Tom and me found the money that the robbers hid in the cave, and it made us rich. We got six thousand dollars apiece—all gold. It was an awful sight of money when it was piled up. Well, Judge Thatcher, he took it and put it out at interest, and it fetched us a dollar a day apiece, all the year round—more than a body could tell what to do with. The Widow Douglas, she took me for her son, and allowed she would sivilize me; but it was rough living in the house all the time, considering how dismal regular and decent the widow was in all her ways; and so when I couldn't stand it no longer, I lit out. I got into my old rags, and my sugar-hogshead again, and was free and satisfied. But Tom Sawyer, he hunted me up and said he was going to start a band of robbers, and I might join if I would go back to the widow and be respectable. So I went back.

The widow she cried over me, and called me a poor lost lamb, and she called me a lot of other names, too, but she never meant no harm by it. She put me in them new clothes again, and I couldn't do nothing but sweat and sweat, and feel all cramped up. Well, then, the old thing commenced again. The widow rung a bell for supper, and you had to come to time. When you got to the table you couldn't go right to eating, but you had to wait for the widow to tuck down her head and grumble a little over the victuals, though there warn't really anything the matter with them. That is, nothing only everything was cooked by itself. In a barrel of odds and ends it is different; things get mixed up, and the juice kind of swaps around, and the things go better.

After supper she got out her book and learned me about Moses and the Bulrushers; and I was in a sweat to find out all about him; but by-and-by she let it out that Moses had been dead a considerable long time; so then I didn't care no more about him; because I don't take no stock in dead people.

Pretty soon I wanted to smoke, and asked the widow to let me. But she wouldn't. She said it was a mean practice and wasn't clean, and I must try to not do it any more. That is just the way with some people. They get down on a thing when they don't know nothing about it. Here she was a bothering about Moses, which was no kin to her, and no use to anybody, being gone, you see, yet finding a power of fault with me for doing a thing that had some good in it. And she took snuff too; of course that was all right, because she done it herself.

Her sister, Miss Watson, a tolerable slim old maid, with goggles on, had just come to live with her, and took a set at me now, with a spelling-book. She worked me middling hard for about an hour, and then the widow made her ease up. I couldn't stood it much longer. Then for an hour it was deadly dull, and I was fidgety. Miss Watson would say, "Dont put your feet up there, Huckleberry;" and "dont scrunch up like that, Huckleberry—set up straight;" and pretty soon she would say, "Don't gap and stretch like that, Huckleberry—why don't you try to behave?" Then she told me all about the bad place, and I said I wished I was there. She got mad then, but I didn't mean no harm. All I wanted was to go somewheres; all I wanted was a change, I warn't particular. She said it was wicked to say what I said; said she wouldn't say it for the whole world; *she* was going to live so as to go to the good place. Well, I couldn't see no advantage in going where she was going, so I made up my mind I wouldn't try for it. But I never said so, because it would only make trouble, and wouldn't do no good.

Now she had got a start, and she went on and told me all about the good place. She said all a body would have to do there was to go around all day long with a harp and sing, forever and ever. So I didn't think much of it. But I never said so. I asked her if she reckoned Tom Sawyer would go there, and, she said, not by a considerable sight. I was glad about that, because I wanted him and me to be together.

Miss Watson she kept pecking at me, and it got tiresome and lonesome. By-and-by they fetched the niggers in and had prayers, and then everybody was off to bed. I went up to my room with a piece of candle and put it on the table. Then I set down in a chair by the window and tried to think of something cheerful, but it warn't no use. I felt so lonesome I most wished I was dead. The stars was shining, and the leaves rustled in the woods ever so mournful; and I heard an owl, away off, who-whooing about somebody that was dead, and a whippowill and a dog crying about somebody that was going to die; and the wind was trying to whisper something to me and I couldn't make out what it was, and so it made the cold shivers run over me. Then away out in the woods I heard that kind of a sound that a ghost makes when it wants to tell about something that's on its mind and can't make itself understood, and so can't rest easy in its grave and has to go about that way every night grieving. I got so down-hearted and scared, I did wish I had some company. Pretty soon a spider went crawling up my shoulder, and I flipped it off and it lit in the candle; and before I could budge it was all shriveled up. I didn't need anybody to tell me that that was an awful bad sign and would fetch me some bad luck, so I was scared and most shook the clothes off of me. I got up and turned around in my tracks three times and crossed my breast every time; and then I tied up a little lock of my hair with a thread to keep witches away. But I hadn't no confidence. You do that when you've lost a horse-shoe that you've found, instead of nailing it up over the door, but I hadn't ever heard anybody say it was any way to keep off bad luck when you'd killed a spider.

I set down again, a shaking all over, and got out my pipe for a smoke; for the house was all as still as death, now, and so the widow wouldn't know. Well, after a long time I heard the clock away off in the town go boom—boom—boom— twelve licks—and all still again—stiller than ever. Pretty soon I heard a twig snap, down in the dark amongst the trees—

something was a stirring. I set still and listened. Directly
could just barely hear a "*me-yow! me-yow!*" down there. Tha
was good! Says I, "*me-yow! me-yow!*" as soft as I could, an
then I put out the light and scrambled out of the windov
onto the shed. Then I slipped down to the ground an
crawled in amongst the trees, and sure enough there was Ton
Sawyer waiting for me.

II

WE WENT TIP-TOEING along a path amongst the trees back towards the end of the widow's garden, stooping down so as the branches wouldn't scrape our heads. When we was passing by the kitchen I fell over a root and made a noise. We scrouched down and laid still. Miss Watson's big nigger, named Jim, was setting in the kitchen door; we could see him pretty clear, because there was a light behind him. He got up and stretched his neck out about a minute, listening. Then he says,

"Who dah?"

He listened some more; then he come tip-toeing down and stood right between us; we could a touched him, nearly. Well, likely it was minutes and minutes that there warn't a sound, and we all there so close together. There was a place on my ankle that got to itching; but I dasn't scratch it; and then my ear begun to itch; and next my back, right between my shoulders. Seemed like I'd die if I couldn't scratch. Well, I've noticed that thing plenty of times since. If you are with the quality, or at a funeral, or trying to go to sleep when you ain't sleepy—if you are anywheres where it won't do for you to scratch, why you will itch all over in upwards of a thousand places. Pretty soon Jim says:

"Say—who is you? Whar is you? Dog my cats ef I didn' hear sumf'n. Well, I knows what I's gwyne to do. I's gwyne to set down here and listen tell I hears it agin."

So he set down on the ground betwixt me and Tom. He leaned his back up against a tree, and stretched his legs out till one of them most touched one of mine. My nose begun to itch. It itched till the tears come into my eyes. But I dasn't scratch. Then it begun to itch on the inside. Next I got to itching underneath. I didn't know how I was going to set still. This miserableness went on as much as six or seven minutes; but it seemed a sight longer than that. I was itching in eleven different places now. I reckoned I couldn't stand it more'n a minute longer, but I set my teeth hard and got ready to try. Just then Jim begun to breathe heavy; next he

begun to snore—and then I was pretty soon comfortabl
again.

Tom he made a sign to me—kind of a little noise with hi
mouth—and we went creeping away on our hands and knees
When we was ten foot off, Tom whispered to me and wantec
to tie Jim to the tree for fun; but I said no; he might wake
and make a disturbance, and then they'd find out I warn't in
Then Tom said he hadn't got candles enough, and he woulc
slip in the kitchen and get some more. I didn't want him tc
try. I said Jim might wake up and come. But Tom wanted tc
resk it; so we slid in there and got three candles, and Tom
laid five cents on the table for pay. Then we got out, and
was in a sweat to get away; but nothing would do Tom bu
he must crawl to where Jim was, on his hands and knees, anc
play something on him. I waited, and it seemed a good while
everything was so still and lonesome.

As soon as Tom was back, we cut along the path, arounc
the garden fence, and by-and-by fetched up on the steep tof
of the hill the other side of the house. Tom said he slippec
Jim's hat off of his head and hung it on a limb right ove:
him, and Jim stirred a little, but he didn't wake. Afterward:
Jim said the witches bewitched him and put him in a trance
and rode him all over the State, and then set him under the
trees again and hung his hat on a limb to show who done it
And next time Jim told it he said they rode him down tc
New Orleans; and after that, every time he told it he spreac
it more and more, till by-and-by he said they rode him al
over the world, and tired him most to death, and his back
was all over saddle-boils. Jim was monstrous proud about it
and he got so he wouldn't hardly notice the other niggers
Niggers would come miles to hear Jim tell about it, and he
was more looked up to than any nigger in that country
Strange niggers would stand with their mouths open anc
look him all over, same as if he was a wonder. Niggers is
always talking about witches in the dark by the kitchen fire:
but whenever one was talking and letting on to know all
about such things, Jim would happen in and say, "Hm! What
you know 'bout witches?" and that nigger was corked up and
had to take a back seat. Jim always kept that five-center piece

around his neck with a string and said it was a charm the devil give to him with his own hands and told him he could cure anybody with it and fetch witches whenever he wanted to, just by saying something to it; but he never told what it was he said to it. Niggers would come from all around there and give Jim anything they had, just for a sight of that five-center piece; but they wouldn't touch it, because the devil had had his hands on it. Jim was most ruined, for a servant, because he got so stuck up on account of having seen the devil and been rode by witches.

Well, when Tom and me got to the edge of the hill-top, we looked away down into the village and could see three or four lights twinkling, where there was sick folks, may be; and the stars over us was sparkling ever so fine; and down by the village was the river, a whole mile broad, and awful still and grand. We went down the hill and found Jo Harper, and Ben Rogers, and two or three more of the boys, hid in the old tanyard. So we unhitched a skiff and pulled down the river two mile and a half, to the big scar on the hillside, and went ashore.

We went to a clump of bushes, and Tom made everybody swear to keep the secret, and then showed them a hole in the hill, right in the thickest part of the bushes. Then we lit the candles and crawled in on our hands and knees. We went about two hundred yards, and then the cave opened up. Tom poked about amongst the passages and pretty soon ducked under a wall where you wouldn't a noticed that there was a hole. We went along a narrow place and got into a kind of room, all damp and sweaty and cold, and there we stopped. Tom says:

"Now we'll start this band of robbers and call it Tom Sawyer's Gang. Everybody that wants to join has got to take an oath, and write his name in blood."

Everybody was willing. So Tom got out a sheet of paper that he had wrote the oath on, and read it. It swore every boy to stick to the band, and never tell any of the secrets; and if anybody done anything to any boy in the band, whichever boy was ordered to kill that person and his family must do it, and he mustn't eat and he mustn't sleep till he had killed them and hacked a cross in their breasts, which was the sign of the band. And nobody that didn't belong to the band could use that mark, and if he did he must be sued; and if he done it again he must be killed. And if anybody that belonged to the band told the secrets, he must have his throat cut, and then have his carcass burnt up and the ashes scattered all around, and his name blotted off of the list with blood and never mentioned again by the gang, but have a curse put on it and be forgot, forever.

Everybody said it was a real beautiful oath, and asked Tom if he got it out of his own head. He said, some of it, but the rest was out of pirate books, and robber books, and every gang that was high-toned had it.

Some thought it would be good to kill the *families* of boys that told the secrets. Tom said it was a good idea, so he took a pencil and wrote it in. Then Ben Rogers says:

"Here's Huck Finn, he hain't got no family—what you going to do 'bout him?"

"Well, hain't he got a father?" says Tom Sawyer.

"Yes, he's got a father, but you can't never find him, these days. He used to lay drunk with the hogs in the tanyard, but he hain't been seen in these parts for a year or more."

They talked it over, and they was going to rule me out, because they said every boy must have a family or somebody to kill, or else it wouldn't be fair and square for the others. Well, nobody could think of anything to do—everybody was stumped, and set still. I was most ready to cry; but all at once I thought of a way, and so I offered them Miss Watson—they could kill her. Everybody said:

"Oh, she'll do, she'll do. That's all right. Huck can come in."

Then they all stuck a pin in their fingers to get blood to sign with, and I made my mark on the paper.

"Now," says Ben Rogers, "what's the line of business of this Gang?"

"Nothing only robbery and murder," Tom said.

"But who are we going to rob? houses—or cattle—or——"

"Stuff! stealing cattle and such things ain't robbery, it's burglary," says Tom Sawyer. "We ain't burglars. That ain't no sort of style. We are highwaymen. We stop stages and carriages on the road, with masks on, and kill the people and take their watches and money."

"Must we always kill the people?"

"Oh, certainly. It's best. Some authorities think different, but mostly it's considered best to kill them. Except some that you bring to the cave here and keep them till they're ransomed."

"Ransomed? What's that?"

"I don't know. But that's what they do. I've seen it in books; and so of course that's what we've got to do."

"But how can we do it if we don't know what it is?"

"Why blame it all, we've *got* to do it. Don't I tell you it's in the books? Do you want to go to doing different from what's in the books, and get things all muddled up?"

"Oh, that's all very fine to *say*, Tom Sawyer, but how in the nation are these fellows going to be ransomed if we don't know how to do it to them? that's the thing *I* want to get at. Now what do you *reckon* it is?"

"Well I don't know. But per'aps if we keep them till they're ransomed, it means that we keep them till they're dead."

"Now, that's something *like*. That'll answer. Why couldn't you said that before? We'll keep them till they're ransomed to death—and a bothersome lot they'll be, too, eating up everything and always trying to get loose."

"How you talk, Ben Rogers. How can they get loose when there's a guard over them, ready to shoot them down if they move a peg?"

"A guard. Well, that *is* good. So somebody's got to set up all night and never get any sleep, just so as to watch them. I think that's foolishness. Why can't a body take a club and ransom them as soon as they get here?"

"Because it ain't in the books so—that's why. Now Ben Rogers, do you want to do things regular, or don't you?— that's the idea. Don't you reckon that the people that made the books knows what's the correct thing to do? Do you reckon *you* can learn 'em anything? Not by a good deal. No, sir, we'll just go on and ransom them in the regular way."

"All right. I don't mind; but I say it's a fool way, anyhow. Say—do we kill the women, too?"

"Well, Ben Rogers, if I was as ignorant as you I wouldn't let on. Kill the women? No—nobody ever saw anything in the books like that. You fetch them to the cave, and you're always as polite as pie to them; and by-and-by they fall in love with you and never want to go home any more."

"Well, if that's the way, I'm agreed, but I don't take no stock in it. Mighty soon we'll have the cave so cluttered up with women, and fellows waiting to be ransomed, that there won't be no place for the robbers. But go ahead, I ain't got nothing to say."

Little Tommy Barnes was asleep, now, and when they waked him up he was scared, and cried, and said he wanted to go home to his ma, and didn't want to be a robber any more.

So they all made fun of him, and called him cry-baby, and that made him mad, and he said he would go straight and tell all the secrets. But Tom give him five cents to keep quiet, and said we would all go home and meet next week and rob somebody and kill some people.

Ben Rogers said he couldn't get out much, only Sundays, and so he wanted to begin next Sunday; but all the boys said it would be wicked to do it on Sunday, and that settled the thing. They agreed to get together and fix a day as soon as they could, and then we elected Tom Sawyer first captain and Jo Harper second captain of the Gang, and so started home.

I clumb up the shed and crept into my window just before day was breaking. My new clothes was all greased up and clayey, and I was dog-tired.

III

WELL, I got a good going-over in the morning, from old Miss Watson, on account of my clothes; but the widow she didn't scold, but only cleaned off the grease and clay and looked so sorry that I thought I would behave a while if I could. Then Miss Watson she took me in the closet and prayed, but nothing come of it. She told me to pray every day, and whatever I asked for I would get it. But it warn't so. I tried it. Once I got a fish-line, but no hooks. It warn't any good to me without hooks. I tried for the hooks three or four times, but somehow I couldn't make it work. By-and-by, one day, I asked Miss Watson to try for me, but she said I was a fool. She never told me why, and I couldn't make it out no way.

I set down, one time, back in the woods, and had a long think about it. I says to myself, if a body can get anything they pray for, why don't Deacon Winn get back the money he lost on pork? Why can't the widow get back her silver snuff-box that was stole? Why can't Miss Watson fat up? No, says I to myself, there ain't nothing in it. I went and told the widow about it, and she said the thing a body could get by praying for it was "spiritual gifts." This was too many for me, but she told me what she meant—I must help other people, and do everything I could for other people, and look out for them all the time, and never think about myself. This was including Miss Watson, as I took it. I went out in the woods and turned it over in my mind a long time, but I couldn't see no advantage about it—except for the other people—so at last I reckoned I wouldn't worry about it any more, but just let it go. Sometimes the widow would take me one side and talk about Providence in a way to make a body's mouth water; but maybe next day Miss Watson would take hold and knock it all down again. I judged I could see that there was two Providences, and a poor chap would stand considerable show with the widow's Providence, but if Miss Watson's got him there warn't no help for him any more. I thought it all out, and reckoned I would belong to the widow's, if he wanted me, though I couldn't make out how he was agoing to be any better off then than what he was before, seeing I was so ignorant and so kind of low-down and ornery.

Pap he hadn't been seen for more than a year, and that was comfortable for me; I didn't want to see him no more. He used to always whale me when he was sober and could get his hands on me; though I used to take to the woods most of the time when he was around. Well, about this time he was found in the river drowned, about twelve mile above town, so people said. They judged it was him, anyway; said this drowned man was just his size, and was ragged, and had uncommon long hair—which was all like pap—but they couldn't make nothing out of the face, because it had been in the water so long it warn't much like a face at all. They said he was floating on his back in the water. They took him and buried him on the bank. But I warn't comfortable long, because I happened to think of something. I knowed mighty well that a drownded man don't float on his back, but on his face. So I knowed, then, that this warn't pap, but a woman dressed up in a man's clothes. So I was uncomfortable again. I judged the old man would turn up again by-and-by, though I wished he wouldn't.

We played robber now and then about a month, and then I resigned. All the boys did. We hadn't robbed nobody, we hadn't killed any people, but only just pretended. We used to hop out of the woods and go charging down on hog-drovers and women in carts taking garden stuff to market, but we never hived any of them. Tom Sawyer called the hogs "ingots," and he called the turnips and stuff "julery" and we would go to the cave and pow-wow over what we had done and how many people we had killed and marked. But I couldn't see no profit in it. One time Tom sent a boy to run about town with a blazing stick, which he called a slogan (which was the sign for the Gang to get together), and then he said he had got secret news by his spies that next day a whole parcel of Spanish merchants and rich A-rabs was going to camp in Cave Hollow with two hundred elephants, and six hundred camels, and over a thousand "sumter" mules, all loaded down with di'monds, and they didn't have only a guard of four hundred soldiers, and so we would lay in ambuscade, as he called it, and kill the lot and scoop the things. He said we must slick up our swords and guns, and get ready. He never could go after even a turnip-cart but he must have the swords and guns all scoured up for it; though they was only lath and broom-sticks, and you might scour at them till you rotted and then they warn't worth a mouthful of ashes more than what they was before. I didn't believe we could lick such a crowd of Spaniards and A-rabs, but I wanted to see the camels and elephants, so I was on hand next day, Saturday, in the ambuscade; and when we got the word, we rushed out of the woods and down the hill. But there warn't no Spaniards and A-rabs, and there warn't no camels nor no elephants. It warn't anything but a Sunday-school picnic, and only a primer-class at that. We busted it up, and chased the children up the hollow; but we never got anything but some doughnuts and jam, though Ben Rogers got a rag doll, and Jo Harper got a hymn-book and a tract; and then the teacher charged in and made us drop everything and cut. I didn't see no di'monds, and I told Tom Sawyer so. He said there was loads of them there, anyway; and he said there was A-rabs there, too, and elephants and things. I said, why couldn't we see them, then? He said if I warn't so ignorant, but had read a book called "Don Quixote," I would know without asking. He said it was all done by enchantment. He said there was hundreds of soldiers there, and elephants and treasure, and so on, but we had enemies which he called magicians, and they had turned the whole thing into an infant Sunday school, just out of spite. I said, all right, then the thing for us to do was to go for the magicians. Tom Sawyer said I was a numskull.

"Why," says he, "a magician could call up a lot of genies, and they would hash you up like nothing before you could say Jack Robinson. They are as tall as a tree and as big around as a church."

"Well," I says, "s'pose we got some genies to help *us*—can't we lick the other crowd then?"

"How you going to get them?"

"I don't know. How do *they* get them?"

"Why they rub an old tin lamp or an iron ring, and then the genies come tearing in, with the thunder and lightning a-ripping around and the smoke a-rolling, and everything

they're told to do they up and do it. They don't think noth
ing of pulling a shot tower up by the roots, and belting a
Sunday-school superintendent over the head with it—or any
other man."

"Who makes them tear around so?"

"Why, whoever rubs the lamp or the ring. They belong to
whoever rubs the lamp or the ring, and they've got to do
whatever he says. If he tells them to build a palace forty mile
long, out of di'monds, and fill it full of chewing gum, or
whatever you want, and fetch an emperor's daughter from
China for you to marry, they've got to do it—and they've
got to do it before sun-up next morning, too. And more—
they've got to waltz that palace around over the country
wherever you want it, you understand."

"Well," says I, "I think they are a pack of flatheads for not
keeping the palace themselves 'stead of fooling them away like
that. And what's more—if I was one of them I would see a
man in Jericho before I would drop my business and come to
him for the rubbing of an old tin lamp."

"How you talk, Huck Finn. Why, you'd *have* to come
when he rubbed it, whether you wanted to or not."

"What, and I as high as a tree and as big as a church? All
right, then; I *would* come; but I lay I'd make that man climb
the highest tree there was in the country."

"Shucks, it ain't no use to talk to you, Huck Finn. You
don't seem to know anything, somehow—perfect sap-head."

I thought all this over for two or three days, and then I
reckoned I would see if there was anything in it. I got an old
tin lamp and an iron ring and went out in the woods and
rubbed and rubbed till I sweat like an Injun, calculating to
build a palace and sell it; but it warn't no use, none of the
genies come. So then I judged that all that stuff was only just
one of Tom Sawyer's lies. I reckoned he believed in the Arabs
and the elephants, but as for me I think different. It had all
the marks of a Sunday school.

IV

WELL, three or four months run along, and it was well into the winter, now. I had been to school most all the time, and could spell, and read, and write just a little, and could say the multiplication table up to six times seven is thirty-five, and I don't reckon I could ever get any further than that if I was to live forever. I don't take no stock in mathematics, anyway.

At first I hated the school, but by-and-by I got so I could stand it. Whenever I got uncommon tired I played hookey, and the hiding I got next day done me good and cheered me up. So the longer I went to school the easier it got to be. I was getting sort of used to the widow's ways, too, and they warn't so raspy on me. Living in a house, and sleeping in a bed, pulled on me pretty tight, mostly, but before the cold weather I used to slide out and sleep in the woods, sometimes, and so that was a rest to me. I liked the old ways best, but I was getting so I liked the new ones, too, a little bit. The widow said I was coming along slow but sure, and doing very satisfactory. She said she warn't ashamed of me.

One morning I happened to turn over the salt-cellar at breakfast. I reached for some of it as quick as I could, to throw over my left shoulder and keep off the bad luck, but Miss Watson was in ahead of me, and crossed me off. She says, "Take your hands away, Huckleberry—what a mess you are always making." The widow put in a good word for me, but that warn't going to keep off the bad luck, I knowed that well enough. I started out, after breakfast, feeling worried and shaky, and wondering where it was going to fall on me, and what it was going to be. There is ways to keep off some kinds of bad luck, but this wasn't one of them kind; so I never tried to do anything, but just poked along low-spirited and on the watch-out.

I went down the front garden and clumb over the stile, where you go through the high board fence. There was an inch of new snow on the ground, and I seen somebody's tracks. They had come up from the quarry and stood around the stile a while, and then went on around the garden fence. It was funny they hadn't come in, after standing around so. I couldn't make it out. It was very curious, somehow. I was going to follow around, but I stooped down to look at the tracks first. I didn't notice anything at first, but next I did. There was a cross in the left boot-heel made with big nails, to keep off the devil.

I was up in a second and shinning down the hill. I looked over my shoulder every now and then, but I didn't see nobody. I was at Judge Thatcher's as quick as I could get there. He said:

"Why, my boy, you are all out of breath. Did you come for your interest?"

"No sir," I says; "is there some for me?"

"Oh, yes, a half-yearly is in, last night. Over a hundred and fifty dollars. Quite a fortune for you. You better let me invest it along with your six thousand, because if you take it you'll spend it."

"No sir," I says, "I don't want to spend it. I don't want it at all—nor the six thousand, nuther. I want you to take it; I want to give it to you—the six thousand and all."

He looked surprised. He couldn't seem to make it out. He says:

"Why, what can you mean, my boy?"

I says, "Don't you ask me no questions about it, please. You'll take it—won't you?"

He says:

"Well I'm puzzled. Is something the matter?"

"Please take it," says I, "and don't ask me nothing—then I won't have to tell no lies."

He studied a while, and then he says:

"Oho-o. I think I see. You want to *sell* all your property to me—not give it. That's the correct idea."

Then he wrote something on a paper and read it over, and says:

"There—you see it says 'for a consideration.' That means I have bought it of you and paid you for it. Here's a dollar for you. Now, you sign it."

So I signed it, and left.

* * *

Miss Watson's nigger, Jim, had a hair-ball as big as your fist, which had been took out of the fourth stomach of an ox, and he used to do magic with it. He said there was a spirit inside of it, and it knowed everything. So I went to him that night and told him pap was here again, for I found his tracks in the snow. What I wanted to know, was, what he was going to do, and was he going to stay? Jim got out his hair-ball, and said something over it, and then he held it up and dropped it on the floor. It fell pretty solid, and only rolled about an inch. Jim tried it again, and then another time, and it acted just the same. Jim got down on his knees and put his ear against it and listened. But it warn't no use; he said it wouldn't talk. He said sometimes it wouldn't talk without money. I told him I had an old slick counterfeit quarter that warn't no good because the brass showed through the silver a little, and it wouldn't pass nohow, even if the brass didn't show, because it was so slick it felt greasy, and so that would tell on it every time. (I reckoned I wouldn't say nothing about the dollar I got from the judge.) I said it was pretty bad money, but maybe the hair-ball would take it, because maybe it wouldn't know the difference. Jim smelt it, and bit it, and rubbed it, and said he would manage so the hair-ball would think it was good. He said he would split open a raw Irish potato and stick the quarter in between and keep it there all night, and next morning you couldn't see no brass, and it wouldn't feel greasy no more, and so anybody in town would take it in a minute, let alone a hair-ball. Well, I knowed a potato would do that, before, but I had forgot it.

Jim put the quarter under the hair-ball and got down and listened again. This time he said the hair-ball was all right. He said it would tell my whole fortune if I wanted it to. I says, go on. So the hair-ball talked to Jim, and Jim told it to me. He says:

"Yo' ole father doan' know, yit, what he's a-gwyne to do. Sometimes he spec he'll go 'way, en den agin he spec he'll stay. De bes' way is to res' easy en let de ole man take his own way. Dey's two angels hoverin' roun' 'bout him. One uv 'em is white en shiny, en 'tother one is black. De white one gits him to go right, a little while, den de black one sail in en bust it all up. A body can't tell, yit, which one gwyne to fetch him at de las'. But you is all right. You gwyne to have considable trouble in yo' life, en considable joy. Sometimes you gwyne to git hurt, en sometimes you gwyne to git sick; but every time you's gwyne to git well agin. Dey's two gals flyin' 'bout you in yo' life. One uv 'em's light en 'tother one is dark. One is rich en 'tother is po'. You's gwyne to marry de po' one fust en de rich one by-en-by. You wants to keep 'way fum de water as much as you kin, en don't run no resk, 'kase it's down in de bills dat you's gwyne to git hung."

When I lit my candle and went up to my room that night, there set pap, his own self!

V

I HAD shut the door to. Then I turned around, and there he was. I used to be scared of him all the time, he tanned me so much. I reckoned I was scared now, too; but in a minute I see I was mistaken. That is, after the first jolt, as you may say, when my breath sort of hitched—he being so unexpected; but right away after, I see I warn't scared of him worth bothering about.

He was most fifty, and he looked it. His hair was long and tangled and greasy, and hung down, and you could see his eyes shining through like he was behind vines. It was all black, no gray; so was his long, mixed-up whiskers. There warn't no color in his face, where his face showed; it was white; not like another man's white, but a white to make a body sick, a white to make a body's flesh crawl—a tree-toad white, a fish-belly white. As for his clothes—just rags, that was all. He had one ankle resting on 'tother knee; the boot on that foot was busted, and two of his toes stuck through, and he worked them now and then. His hat was laying on the floor; an old black slouch with the top caved in, like a lid.

I stood a-looking at him; he set there a-looking at me, with his chair tilted back a little. I set the candle down. I noticed the window was up; so he had clumb in by the shed. He kept a-looking me all over. By-and-by he says:

"Starchy clothes—very. You think you're a good deal of a big-bug, *don't* you?"

"Maybe I am, maybe I ain't," I says.

"Don't you give me none o' your lip," says he. "You've put on considerble many frills since I been away. I'll take you down a peg before I get done with you. You're educated, too, they say; can read and write. You think you're better'n your father, now, don't you, because he can't? *I'll* take it out of you. Who told you you might meddle with such hifalut'n foolishness, hey?—who told you you could?"

"The widow. She told me."

"The widow, hey?—and who told the widow she could put in her shovel about a thing that ain't none of her business?"

"Nobody never told her."

"Well, I'll learn her how to meddle. And looky here—you drop that school, you hear? I'll learn people to bring up a boy to put on airs over his own father and let on to be better'n what *he* is. You lemme catch you fooling around that school again, you hear? Your mother couldn't read, and she couldn't write, nuther, before she died. None of the family couldn't before *they* died. *I* can't; and here you're a-swelling yourself up like this. I ain't the man to stand it—you hear? Say— lemme hear you read."

I took up a book and begun something about General Washington and the wars. When I'd read about a half a minute, he fetched the book a whack with his hand and knocked it across the house. He says:

"It's so. You can do it. I had my doubts when you told me. Now looky here; you stop that putting on frills. I won't have it. I'll lay for you, my smarty; and if I catch you about that school I'll tan you good. First you know you'll get religion, too. I never see such a son."

He took up a little blue and yaller picture of some cows and a boy, and says:

"What's this?"

"It's something they give me for learning my lessons good."

He tore it up, and says—

"I'll give you something better—I'll give you a cowhide."

He set there a-mumbling and a-growling a minute, and then he says—

"*Ain't* you a sweet-scented dandy, though? A bed; and bedclothes; and a look'n-glass; and a piece of carpet on the floor—and your own father got to sleep with the hogs in the tanyard. I never see such a son. I bet I'll take some o' these frills out o' you before I'm done with you. Why there ain't no end to your airs—they say you're rich. Hey?—how's that?"

"They lie—that's how."

"Looky here—mind how you talk to me; I'm a-standing about all I can stand, now—so don't gimme no sass. I've been in town two days, and I hain't heard nothing but about you bein' rich. I heard about it away down the river, too.

hat's why I come. You git me that money to-morrow—I
ant it."

"I hain't got no money."

"It's a lie. Judge Thatcher's got it. You git it. I want it."

"I hain't got no money, I tell you. You ask Judge Thatcher;
e'll tell you the same."

"All right. I'll ask him; and I'll make him pungle, too, or
'll know the reason why. Say—how much you got in your
ocket? I want it."

"I hain't got only a dollar, and I want that to——"

"It don't make no difference what you want it for—you
ust shell it out."

He took it and bit it to see if it was good, and then he said
e was going down town to get some whisky; said he hadn't
ad a drink all day. When he had got out on the shed, he put
is head in again, and cussed me for putting on frills and
rying to be better than him; and when I reckoned he was
gone, he come back and put his head in again, and told me
o mind about that school, because he was going to lay for
ne and lick me if I didn't drop that.

Next day he was drunk, and he went to Judge Thatcher's
nd bullyragged him and tried to make him give up the
noney, but he couldn't, and then he swore he'd make the law
orce him.

The judge and the widow went to law to get the court to
ake me away from him and let one of them be my guardian;
ut it was a new judge that had just come, and he didn't
now the old man; so he said courts mustn't interfere and
eparate families if they could help it; said he'd druther not
ake a child away from its father. So Judge Thatcher and the
vidow had to quit on the business.

That pleased the old man till he couldn't rest. He said he'd
owhide me till I was black and blue if I didn't raise some
noney for him. I borrowed three dollars from Judge
Thatcher, and pap took it and got drunk and went a-blowing
round and cussing and whooping and carrying on; and he
kept it up all over town, with a tin pan, till most midnight;
hen they jailed him, and next day they had him before court,
nd jailed him again for a week. But he said *he* was satisfied;
aid he was boss of his son, and he'd make it warm for *him*.

When he got out the new judge said he was agoing to
make a man of him. So he took him to his own house, an
dressed him up clean and nice, and had him to breakfast an
dinner and supper with the family, and was just old pie to
him, so to speak. And after supper he talked to him abou
temperance and such things till the old man cried, and sai
he'd been a fool, and fooled away his life; but now he wa
agoing to turn over a new leaf and be a man nobody wouldn
be ashamed of, and he hoped the judge would help him an
not look down on him. The judge said he could hug him fo
them words; so *he* cried, and his wife she cried again; pa
said he'd been a man that had always been misunderstood be
fore, and the judge said he believed it. The old man said tha
what a man wanted that was down, was sympathy; and th
judge said it was so; so they cried again. And when it was bec
time, the old man rose up and held out his hand, and says:

"Look at it gentlemen, and ladies all; take ahold of it; shak
it. There's a hand that was the hand of a hog; but it ain't s
no more; it's the hand of a man that's started in on a ne
life, and 'll die before he'll go back. You mark them words—
don't forget I said them. It's a clean hand now; shake it—
don't be afeard."

So they shook it, one after the other, all around, and crie
The judge's wife she kissed it. Then the old man he signed
pledge—made his mark. The judge said it was the holie
time on record, or something like that. Then they tucked th
old man into a beautiful room, which was the spare roon
and in the night sometime he got powerful thirsty and clum
out onto the porch-roof and slid down a stanchion and trade
his new coat for a jug of forty-rod, and clumb back again an
had a good old time; and towards daylight he crawled ou
again, drunk as a fiddler, and rolled off the porch and brok
his left arm in two places and was most froze to death whe
somebody found him after sun-up. And when they come t
look at that spare room, they had to take soundings befor
they could navigate it.

The judge he felt kind of sore. He said he reckoned a bod
could reform the ole man with a shot-gun, maybe, but h
didn't know no other way.

VI

WELL, pretty soon the old man was up and around again, and then he went for Judge Thatcher in the courts to make him give up that money, and he went for me, too, for not stopping school. He catched me a couple of times and thrashed me, but I went to school just the same, and dodged him or out-run him most of the time. I didn't want to go to school much, before, but I reckoned I'd go now to spite pap. That law trial was a slow business; appeared like they warn't ever going to get started on it; so every now and then I'd borrow two or three dollars off of the judge for him, to keep from getting a cowhiding. Every time he got money he got drunk; and every time he got drunk he raised Cain around town; and every time he raised Cain he got jailed. He was just suited—this kind of thing was right in his line.

He got to hanging around the widow's too much, and so she told him at last, that if he didn't quit using around there she would make trouble for him. Well, *wasn't* he mad? He said he would show who was Huck Finn's boss. So he watched out for me one day in the spring, and catched me, and took me up the river about three mile, in a skiff, and crossed over to the Illinois shore where it was woody and there warn't no houses but an old log hut in a place where the timber was so thick you couldn't find it if you didn't know where it was.

He kept me with him all the time, and I never got a chance to run off. We lived in that old cabin, and he always locked the door and put the key under his head, nights. He had a gun which he had stole, I reckon, and we fished and hunted, and that was what we lived on. Every little while he locked me in and went down to the store, three miles, to the ferry, and traded fish and game for whisky and fetched it home and got drunk and had a good time, and licked me. The widow she found out where I was, by-and-by, and she sent a man over to try to get hold of me, but pap drove him off with the gun, and it warn't long after that till I was used to being where I was, and liked it, all but the cowhide part.

It was kind of lazy and jolly, laying off comfortable all day
smoking and fishing, and no books nor study. Two month
or more run along, and my clothes got to be all rags and dir
and I didn't see how I'd ever got to like it so well at th
widow's, where you had to wash, and eat on a plate, an
comb up, and go to bed and get up regular, and be foreve
bothering over a book and have old Miss Watson pecking a
you all the time. I didn't want to go back no more. I ha
stopped cussing, because the widow didn't like it; but now
took to it again because pap hadn't no objections. It wa
pretty good times up in the woods there, take it all around.

But by-and-by pap got too handy with his hick'ry, and
couldn't stand it. I was all over welts. He got to going awa
so much, too, and locking me in. Once he locked me in an
was gone three days. It was dreadful lonesome. I judged h
had got drowned and I wasn't ever going to get out an
more. I was scared. I made up my mind I would fix up som
way to leave there. I had tried to get out of that cabin man
a time, but I couldn't find no way. There warn't a window t
it big enough for a dog to get through. I couldn't get up th
chimbly, it was too narrow. The door was thick solid oa
slabs. Pap was pretty careful not to leave a knife or anythin
in the cabin when he was away; I reckon I had hunted th
place over as much as a hundred times; well, I was 'most a
the time at it, because it was about the only way to put in th
time. But this time I found something at last; I found an ol
rusty wood-saw without any handle; it was laid in between
rafter and the clapboards of the roof. I greased it up and wen
to work. There was an old horse-blanket nailed against th
logs at the far end of the cabin behind the table, to keep th
wind from blowing through the chinks and putting the can
dle out. I got under the table and raised the blanket and wen
to work to saw a section of the big bottom log out, big
enough to let me through. Well, it was a good long job, bu
I was getting towards the end of it when I heard pap's gui
in the woods. I got rid of the signs of my work, and dropped
the blanket and hid my saw, and pretty soon pap come in.

Pap warn't in a good humor—so he was his natural self
He said he was down to town, and everything was going
wrong. His lawyer said he reckoned he would win his lawsui

nd get the money, if they ever got started on the trial; but
hen there was ways to put it off a long time, and Judge
Thatcher knowed how to do it. And he said people allowed
here'd be another trial to get me away from him and give me
o the widow for my guardian, and they guessed it would
vin, this time. This shook me up considerable, because I
lidn't want to go back to the widow's any more and be so
cramped up and sivilized, as they called it. Then the old man
got to cussing, and cussed everything and everybody he could
hink of, and then cussed them all over again to make sure he
hadn't skipped any, and after that he polished off with a kind
of a general cuss all round, including a considerable parcel of
people which he didn't know the names of, and so called
hem what's-his-name, when he got to them, and went right
along with his cussing.

He said he would like to see the widow get me. He said he
would watch out, and if they tried to come any such game on
him he knowed of a place six or seven mile off, to stow me
n, where they might hunt till they dropped and they couldn't
find me. That made me pretty uneasy again, but only for a
minute; I reckoned I wouldn't stay on hand till he got that
chance.

The old man made me go to the skiff and fetch the things
he had got. There was a fifty-pound sack of corn meal, and a
side of bacon, ammunition, and a four-gallon jug of whisky,
and an old book and two newspapers for wadding, besides
some tow. I toted up a load, and went back and set down on
the bow of the skiff to rest. I thought it all over, and I reckoned I would walk off with the gun and some lines, and take
to the woods when I run away. I guessed I wouldn't stay in
one place, but just tramp right across the country, mostly
night times, and hunt and fish to keep alive, and so get so far
away that the old man nor the widow couldn't ever find me
any more. I judged I would saw out and leave that night if
pap got drunk enough, and I reckoned he would. I got so full
of it I didn't notice how long I was staying, till the old man
hollered and asked me whether I was asleep or drownded.

I got the things all up to the cabin, and then it was about
dark. While I was cooking supper the old man took a swig or
two and got sort of warmed up, and went to ripping again.

He had been drunk over in town, and laid in the gutter a
night, and he was a sight to look at. A body would a though
he was Adam, he was just all mud. Whenever his liquor be
gun to work, he most always went for the govment. This tim
he says:

"Call this a govment! why, just look at it and see what it'
like. Here's the law a-standing ready to take a man's son awa
from him—a man's own son, which he has had all the troubl
and all the anxiety and all the expense of raising. Yes, just a
that man has got that son raised at last, and ready to go t
work and begin to do suthin' for *him* and give him a rest, th
law up and goes for him. And they call *that* govment! Tha
ain't all, nuther. The law backs that old Judge Thatcher u
and helps him to keep me out o' my property. Here's wha
the law does. The law takes a man worth six thousand dollar
and upards, and jams him into an old trap of a cabin like this
and lets him go round in clothes that ain't fitten for a hog
They call that govment! A man can't get his rights in a gov
ment like this. Sometimes I've a mighty notion to just leav
the country for good and all. Yes, and I *told* 'em so; I tol
old Thatcher so to his face. Lots of 'em heard me, and ca
tell what I said. Says I, for two cents I'd leave the blame
country and never come anear it agin. Them's the very words
I says, look at my hat—if you call it a hat—but the lid raise
up and the rest of it goes down till it's below my chin, an
then it ain't rightly a hat at all, but more like my head wa
shoved up through a jint o' stove-pipe. Look at it, says I—
such a hat for me to wear—one of the wealthiest men in thi
town, if I could git my rights.

"Oh, yes, this is a wonderful govment, wonderful. Why
looky here. There was a free nigger there, from Ohio; a mu
latter, most as white as a white man. He had the whitest shir
on you ever see, too, and the shiniest hat; and there ain't
man in that town that's got as fine clothes as what he had
and he had a gold watch and chain, and a silver-heade
cane—the awfulest old gray-headed nabob in the State. An
what do you think? they said he was a p'fessor in a college
and could talk all kinds of languages, and knowed everything
And that ain't the wust. They said he could *vote*, when he wa
at home. Well, that let me out. Thinks I, what is the countr

a-coming to? It was 'lection day, and I was just about to go and vote, myself, if I warn't too drunk to get there; but when they told me there was a State in this country where they'd let that nigger vote, I drawed out. I says I'll never vote agin. Them's the very words I said; they all heard me; and the country may rot for all me—I'll never vote agin as long as I live. And to see the cool way of that nigger—why, he wouldn't a give me the road if I hadn't shoved him out o' the way. I says to the people, why ain't this nigger put up at auction and sold?—that's what I want to know. And what do you reckon they said? Why, they said he couldn't be sold till he'd been in the State six months, and he hadn't been there that long yet. There, now—that's a specimen. They call that a govment that can't sell a free nigger till he's been in the State six months. Here's a govment that calls itself a govment, and lets on to be a govment, and thinks it is a govment, and yet's got to set stock-still for six whole months before it can take ahold of a prowling, thieving, infernal, white-shirted free nigger, and——"

Pap was agoing on so, he never noticed where his old limber legs was taking him to, so he went head over heels over the tub of salt pork, and barked both shins, and the rest of his speech was all the hottest kind of language—mostly hove at the nigger and the govment, though he give the tub some, too, all along, here and there. He hopped around the cabin considerable, first on one leg and then on the other, holding first one shin and then the other one, and at last he let out with his left foot all of a sudden and fetched the tub a rattling kick. But it warn't good judgment, because that was the boot that had a couple of his toes leaking out of the front end of it; so now he raised a howl that fairly made a body's hair raise, and down he went in the dirt, and rolled there, and held his toes; and the cussing he done then laid over anything he had ever done previous. He said so his own self, afterwards. He had heard old Sowberry Hagan in his best days, and he said it laid over him, too; but I reckon that was sort of piling it on, maybe.

After supper pap took the jug, and said he had enough whisky there for two drunks and one delirium tremens. That was always his word. I judged he would be blind drunk in

about an hour, and then I would steal the key, or saw mysel
out, one or 'tother. He drank, and drank, and tumbled dowr
on his blankets, by-and-by; but luck didn't run my way. He
didn't go sound asleep, but was uneasy. He groaned, anc
moaned, and thrashed around this way and that, for a long
time. At last I got so sleepy I couldn't keep my eyes open, al
I could do, and so before I knowed what I was about I was
sound asleep, and the candle burning.

I don't know how long I was asleep, but all of a sudder
there was an awful scream and I was up. There was pap, looking wild and skipping around every which way and yelling
about snakes. He said they was crawling up his legs; and ther
he would give a jump and scream, and say one had bit him
on the cheek—but I couldn't see no snakes. He started anc
run round and round the cabin, hollering "take him off! take
him off! he's biting me on the neck!" I never see a man look
so wild in the eyes. Pretty soon he was all fagged out, and fel
down panting; then he rolled over and over, wonderful fast.
kicking things every which way, and striking and grabbing at
the air with his hands, and screaming, and saying there was
devils ahold of him. He wore out, by-and-by, and laid still a
while, moaning. Then he laid stiller, and didn't make a sound.
I could hear the owls and the wolves, away off in the woods.
and it seemed terrible still. He was laying over by the corner.
By-and-by he raised up, part way, and listened, with his head
to one side. He says very low:

"Tramp—tramp—tramp; that's the dead; tramp—tramp
—tramp; they're coming after me; but I won't go— Oh,
they're here! don't touch me—don't! hands off—they're cold;
let go— Oh, let a poor devil alone!"

Then he went down on all fours and crawled off begging
them to let him alone, and he rolled himself up in his blanket
and wallowed in under the old pine table, still a-begging; and
then he went to crying. I could hear him through the blanket.

By-and-by he rolled out and jumped up on his feet looking
wild, and he see me and went for me. He chased me round
and round the place, with a clasp-knife, calling me the Angel
of Death and saying he would kill me and then I couldn't
come for him no more. I begged, and told him I was only
Huck, but he laughed *such* a screechy laugh, and roared and

cussed, and kept on chasing me up. Once when I turned short and dodged under his arm he made a grab and got me by the jacket between my shoulders, and I thought I was gone; but I slid out of the jacket quick as lightning, and saved myself. Pretty soon he was all tired out, and dropped down with his back against the door, and said he would rest a minute and then kill me. He put his knife under him, and said he would sleep and get strong, and then he would see who was who.

So he dozed off, pretty soon. By-and-by I got the old split-bottom chair and clumb up, as easy as I could, not to make any noise, and got down the gun. I slipped the ramrod down it to make sure it was loaded, and then I laid it across the turnip barrel, pointing towards pap, and set down behind it to wait for him to stir. And how slow and still the time did drag along.

VII

G IT UP! what you 'bout!"
     I opened my eyes and looked around, trying to make
out where I was. It was after sun-up, and I had been sound
asleep. Pap was standing over me, looking sour—and sick,
too. He says—

"What you doin' with this gun?"

I judged he didn't know nothing about what he had been
doing, so I says:

"Somebody tried to get in, so I was laying for him."

"Why didn't you roust me out?"

"Well I tried to, but I couldn't; I couldn't budge you."

"Well, all right. Don't stand there palavering all day, but
out with you and see if there's a fish on the lines for breakfast.
I'll be along in a minute."

He unlocked the door and I cleared out, up the river bank.
I noticed some pieces of limbs and such things floating down,
and a sprinkling of bark; so I knowed the river had begun to
rise. I reckoned I would have great times, now, if I was over
at the town. The June rise used to be always luck for me;
because as soon as that rise begins, here comes cord-wood
floating down, and pieces of log rafts—sometimes a dozen
logs together; so all you have to do is to catch them and sell
them to the wood yards and the sawmill.

I went along up the bank with one eye out for pap and
'tother one out for what the rise might fetch along. Well, all
at once, here comes a canoe; just a beauty, too, about thirteen
or fourteen foot long, riding high like a duck. I shot head
first off of the bank, like a frog, clothes and all on, and struck
out for the canoe. I just expected there'd be somebody laying
down in it, because people often done that to fool folks, and
when a chap had pulled a skiff out most to it they'd raise up
and laugh at him. But it warn't so this time. It was a drift-
canoe, sure enough, and I clumb in and paddled her ashore.
Thinks I, the old man will be glad when he sees this—she's
worth ten dollars. But when I got to shore pap wasn't in sight
yet, and as I was running her into a little creek like a gully,

ll hung over with vines and willows, I struck another idea;
judged I'd hide her good, and then, stead of taking to the
woods when I run off, I'd go down the river about fifty mile
and camp in one place for good, and not have such a rough
ime tramping on foot.

It was pretty close to the shanty, and I thought I heard the
old man coming, all the time; but I got her hid; and then I
out and looked around a bunch of willows, and there was the
old man down the path apiece just drawing a bead on a bird
with his gun. So he hadn't seen anything.

When he got along, I was hard at it taking up a "trot" line.
He abused me a little for being so slow, but I told him I fell
in the river and that was what made me so long. I knowed he
would see I was wet, and then he would be asking questions.
We got five cat-fish off of the lines and went home.

While we laid off, after breakfast, to sleep up, both of us
being about wore out, I got to thinking that if I could fix up
some way to keep pap and the widow from trying to follow
me, it would be a certainer thing than trusting to luck to get
far enough off before they missed me; you see, all kinds of
things might happen. Well, I didn't see no way for a while,
but by-and-by pap raised up a minute, to drink another barrel
of water, and he says:

"Another time a man comes a-prowling round here, you
roust me out, you hear? That man warn't here for no good.
I'd a shot him. Next time, you roust me out, you hear?"

Then he dropped down and went to sleep again—but what
he had been saying give me the very idea I wanted. I says to
myself, I can fix it now so nobody won't think of following me.

About twelve o'clock we turned out and went along up the
bank. The river was coming up pretty fast, and lots of drift-
wood going by on the rise. By-and-by, along comes part of a
log raft—nine logs fast together. We went out with the skiff
and towed it ashore. Then we had dinner. Anybody but pap
would a waited and seen the day through, so as to catch more
stuff; but that warn't pap's style. Nine logs was enough for
one time; he must shove right over to town and sell. So he
locked me in and took the skiff and started off towing the raft
about half-past three. I judged he wouldn't come back that

night. I waited till I reckoned he had got a good start, then I out with my saw and went to work on that log again. Before he was 'tother side of the river I was out of the hole; him and his raft was just a speck on the water away off yonder.

I took the sack of corn meal and took it to where the cano was hid, and shoved the vines and branches apart and put i in; then I done the same with the side of bacon; then th whisky jug; I took all the coffee and sugar there was, and al the ammunition; I took the wadding; I took the bucket and gourd, I took a dipper and a tin cup, and my old saw and two blankets, and the skillet and the coffee-pot. I took fish lines and matches and other things—everything that wa worth a cent. I cleaned out the place. I wanted an axe, bu there wasn't any, only the one out at the wood pile, and knowed why I was going to leave that. I fetched out the gun and now I was done.

I had wore the ground a good deal, crawling out of the hole and dragging out so many things. So I fixed that as good as I could from the outside by scattering dust on the place which covered up the smoothness and the sawdust. Then fixed the piece of log back into its place, and put two rock under it and one against it to hold it there,—for it was ben up at that place, and didn't quite touch ground. If you stood four or five foot away and didn't know it was sawed, you wouldn't ever notice it; and besides, this was the back of the cabin and it warn't likely anybody would go fooling around there.

It was all grass clear to the canoe; so I hadn't left a track I followed around to see. I stood on the bank and looked ou over the river. All safe. So I took the gun and went up a piece into the woods and was hunting around for some birds, when I see a wild pig; hogs soon went wild in them bottoms afte they had got away from the prairie farms. I shot this fellov and took him into camp.

I took the axe and smashed in the door—I beat it and hacked it considerable, a-doing it. I fetched the pig in and took him back nearly to the table and hacked into his throa with the ax, and laid him down on the ground to bleed— say ground, because it *was* ground—hard packed, and n boards. Well, next I took an old sack and put a lot of big rocks in it,—all I could drag—and I started it from the pig and dragged it to the door and through the woods down to the river and dumped it in, and down it sunk, out of sight. You could easy see that something had been dragged over the ground. I did wish Tom Sawyer was there. I knowed he would take an interest in this kind of business, and throw in the fancy touches. Nobody could spread himself like Tom Sawyer in such a thing as that.

Well, last I pulled out some of my hair, and bloodied the ax good, and stuck it on the back side, and slung the ax in the corner. Then I took up the pig and held him to my breast with my jacket (so he couldn't drip) till I got a good piece below the house and then dumped him into the river. Now I thought of something else. So I went and got the bag of meal and my old saw out of the canoe and fetched them to the house. I took the bag to where it used to stand, and ripped a hole in the bottom of it with the saw, for there warn't no knives and forks on the place—pap done everything with his clasp-knife, about the cooking. Then I carried the sack about a hundred yards across the grass and through the willows east of the house, to a shallow lake that was five mile wide and full of rushes—and ducks too, you might say, in the season. There was a slough or a creek leading out of it on the other side, that went miles away, I don't know where, but it didn't go to the river. The meal sifted out and made a little track all the way to the lake. I dropped pap's whetstone there too, so as to look like it had been done by accident. Then I tied up the rip in the meal sack with a string, so it wouldn't leak no more, and took it and my saw to the canoe again.

It was about dark, now; so I dropped the canoe down the river under some willows that hung over the bank, and waited for the moon to rise. I made fast to a willow; then I took a bite to eat, and by-and-by laid down in the canoe to smoke a pipe and lay out a plan. I says to myself, they'll follow the track of that sackful of rocks to the shore and then drag the river for me. And they'll follow that meal track to the lake and go browsing down the creek that leads out of it to find the robbers that killed me and took the things. They won't ever hunt the river for anything but my dead carcass.

They'll soon get tired of that, and won't bother no more about me. All right; I can stop anywhere I want to. Jackson's Island is good enough for me; I know that island pretty well, and nobody ever comes there. And then I can paddle over to town, nights, and slink around and pick up things I want. Jackson's Island's the place.

I was pretty tired, and the first thing I knowed, I was asleep. When I woke up I didn't know where I was, for a minute. I set up and looked around, a little scared. Then I remembered. The river looked miles and miles across. The moon was so bright I could a counted the drift logs that went a slipping along, black and still, hundred of yards out from shore. Everything was dead quiet, and it looked late, and *smelt* late. You know what I mean—I don't know the words to put it in.

I took a good gap and a stretch, and was just going to unhitch and start, when I heard a sound away over the water. I listened. Pretty soon I made it out. It was that dull kind of a regular sound that comes from oars working in rowlocks when it's a still night. I peeped out through the willow branches, and there it was—a skiff, away across the water. I couldn't tell how many was in it. It kept a-coming, and when it was abreast of me I see there warn't but one man in it. Thinks I, maybe it's pap, though I warn't expecting him. He dropped below me, with the current, and by-and-by he come a-swinging up shore in the easy water, and he went by so close I could a reached out the gun and touched him. Well, it *was* pap, sure enough—and sober, too, by the way he laid to his oars.

I didn't lose no time. The next minute I was a-spinning down stream soft but quick in the shade of the bank. I made two mile and a half, and then struck out a quarter of a mile or more towards the middle of the river, because pretty soon I would be passing the ferry landing and people might see me and hail me. I got out amongst the drift-wood and then laid down in the bottom of the canoe and let her float. I laid there and had a good rest and a smoke out of my pipe, looking away into the sky, not a cloud in it. The sky looks ever so deep when you lay down on your back in the moonshine; I never knowed it before. And how far a body can hear on the water such nights! I heard people talking at the ferry landing. I heard what they said, too, every word of it. One man said it was getting towards the long days and the short nights, now. 'Tother one said *this* warn't one of the short ones, he reckoned—and then they laughed, and he said it over again and they laughed again; then they waked up another fellow and told him, and laughed, but he didn't laugh; he ripped out something brisk and said let him alone. The first fellow said he 'lowed to tell it to his old woman—she would think it was pretty good; but he said that warn't nothing to some things he had said in his time. I heard one man say it was nearly three o'clock, and he hoped daylight wouldn't wait more than about a week longer. After that, the talk got further and further away, and I couldn't make out the words any more, but I could hear the mumble; and now and then a laugh, too, but it seemed a long ways off.

I was away below the ferry now. I rose up and there was Jackson's Island, about two mile and a half down stream, heavy-timbered and standing up out of the middle of the river, big and dark and solid, like a steamboat without any lights. There warn't any signs of the bar at the head—it was all under water, now.

It didn't take me long to get there. I shot past the head at a ripping rate, the current was so swift, and then I got into the dead water and landed on the side towards the Illinois shore. I run the canoe into a deep dent in the bank that I knowed about; I had to part the willow branches to get in; and when I made fast nobody could a seen the canoe from the outside.

I went up and set down on a log at the head of the island and looked out on the big river and the black driftwood, and away over to the town, three mile away, where there was three or four lights twinkling. A monstrous big lumber raft was about a mile up stream, coming along down, with a lantern in the middle of it. I watched it come creeping down, and when it was most abreast of where I stood I heard a man say, "Stern oars, there! heave her head to stabboard!" I heard that just as plain as if the man was by my side.

There was a little gray in the sky, now; so I stepped into the woods and laid down for a nap before breakfast.

VIII

THE SUN was up so high when I waked, that I judged it was after eight o'clock. I laid there in the grass and the cool shade, thinking about things and feeling rested and ruther comfortable and satisfied. I could see the sun out at one or two holes, but mostly it was big trees all about, and gloomy in there amongst them. There was freckled places on the ground where the light sifted down through the leaves, and the freckled places swapped about a little, showing there was a little breeze up there. A couple of squirrels set on a limb and jabbered at me very friendly.

I was powerful lazy and comfortable—didn't want to get up and cook breakfast. Well, I was dozing off again, when I thinks I hears a deep sound of "boom!" away up the river. I rouses up and rests on my elbow and listens; pretty soon I hears it again. I hopped up and went and looked out at a hole in the leaves, and I see a bunch of smoke laying on the water a long ways up—about abreast the ferry. And there was the ferry-boat full of people, floating along down. I knowed what was the matter, now. "Boom!" I see the white smoke squirt out of the ferry-boat's side. You see, they was firing cannon over the water, trying to make my carcass come to the top.

I was pretty hungry, but it warn't going to do for me to start a fire, because they might see the smoke. So I set there and watched the cannon-smoke and listened to the boom. The river was a mile wide, there, and it always looks pretty on a summer morning—so I was having a good enough time seeing them hunt for my remainders, if I only had a bite to eat. Well, then I happened to think how they always put quicksilver in loaves of bread and float them off because they always go right to the drownded carcass and stop there. So says I, I'll keep a lookout, and if any of them's floating around after me, I'll give them a show. I changed to the Illinois edge of the island to see what luck I could have, and I warn't disappointed. A big double loaf come along, and I most got it, with a long stick, but my foot slipped and she floated out further. Of course I was where the current set in the closest to the shore—I knowed enough for that. But by-and-by along comes another one, and this time I won. I took out the plug and shook out the little dab of quicksilver, and set my teeth in. It was "baker's bread"—what the quality eat—none of your low-down corn-pone.

I got a good place amongst the leaves, and set there on a log, munching the bread and watching the ferry-boat, and very well satisfied. And then something struck me. I says, now I reckon the widow or the parson or somebody prayed that this bread would find me, and here it has gone and done it. So there ain't no doubt but there is something in that thing. That is, there's something in it when a body like the widow or the person prays, but it don't work for me, and I reckon it don't work for only just the right kind.

I lit a pipe and had a good long smoke and went on watching. The ferry-boat was floating with the current, and I allowed I'd have a chance to see who was aboard when she come along, because she would come in close, where the bread did. When she'd got pretty well along down towards me, I put out my pipe and went to where I fished out the bread, and laid down behind a log on the bank in a little open place. Where the log forked I could peep through.

By-and-by she come along, and she drifted in so close that they could a run out a plank and walked ashore. Most everybody was on the boat. Pap, and Judge Thatcher, and Bessie Thatcher, and Jo Harper, and Tom Sawyer, and his old Aunt Polly, and Sid and Mary, and plenty more. Everybody was talking about the murder, but the captain broke in and says:

"Look sharp, now; the current sets in the closest here, and maybe he's washed ashore and got tangled amongst the brush at the water's edge. I hope so, anyway."

I didn't hope so. They all crowded up and leaned over the rails, nearly in my face, and kept still, watching with all their might. I could see them first-rate, but they couldn't see me. Then the captain sung out:

"Stand away!" and the cannon let off such a blast right before me that it made me deef with the noise and pretty near blind with the smoke, and I judged I was gone. If they'd a had some bullets in, I reckon they'd a got the corpse they was after. Well, I see I warn't hurt, thanks to goodness. The boat floated on and went out of sight around the shoulder of the island. I could hear the booming, now and then, further and further off, and by-and-by after an hour, I didn't hear it no more. The island was three mile long. I judged they had got to the foot, and was giving it up. But they didn't yet a while. They turned around the foot of the island and started up the channel on the Missouri side, under steam, and booming once in a while as they went. I crossed over to that side and watched them. When they got abreast the head of the island they quit shooting and dropped over to the Missouri shore and went home to the town.

I knowed I was all right now. Nobody else would come a-hunting after me. I got my traps out of the canoe and made me a nice camp in the thick woods. I made a kind of a tent out of my blankets to put my things under so the rain couldn't get at them. I catched a cat-fish and haggled him open with my saw, and towards sundown I started my camp fire and had supper. Then I set out a line to catch some fish for breakfast.

When it was dark I set by my camp fire smoking, and feeling pretty satisfied; but by-and-by it got sort of lonesome, and so I went and set on the bank and listened to the currents washing along, and counted the stars and drift-logs and rafts that come down, and then went to bed; there ain't no better way to put in time when you are lonesome; you can't stay so, you soon get over it.

And so for three days and nights. No difference—just the same thing. But the next day I went exploring around down through the island. I was boss of it; it all belonged to me, so to say, and I wanted to know all about it; but mainly I wanted to put in the time. I found plenty strawberries, ripe and prime; and green summer-grapes, and green razberries; and the green blackberries was just beginning to show. They would all come handy by-and-by, I judged.

Well, I went fooling along in the deep woods till I judged I warn't far from the foot of the island. I had my gun along, but I hadn't shot nothing; it was for protection; thought I would kill some game nigh home. About this time I mighty near stepped on a good sized snake, and it went sliding off hrough the grass and flowers, and I after it, trying to get a shot at it. I clipped along, and all of a sudden I bounded right on to the ashes of a camp fire that was still smoking.

My heart jumped up amongst my lungs. I never waited for to look further, but uncocked my gun and went sneaking back on my tip-toes as fast as ever I could. Every now and then I stopped a second, amongst the thick leaves, and listened; but my breath come so hard I couldn't hear nothing else. I slunk along another piece further, then listened again; and so on, and so on; if I see a stump, I took it for a man; if I trod on a stick and broke it, it made me feel like a person had cut one of my breaths in two and I only got half, and the short half, too.

When I got to camp I warn't feeling very brash, there warn't much sand in my craw; but I says, this ain't no time to be fooling around. So I got all my traps into my canoe again so as to have them out of sight, and I put out the fire and scattered the ashes around to look like an old last year's camp, and then clumb a tree.

I reckon I was up in the tree two hours; but I didn't see nothing, I didn't hear nothing—I only *thought* I heard and seen as much as a thousand things. Well, I couldn't stay up there forever; so at last I got down, but I kept in the thick woods and on the lookout all the time. All I could get to eat was berries and what was left over from breakfast.

By the time it was night I was pretty hungry. So when it was good and dark, I slid out from shore before moonrise and paddled over to the Illinois bank—about a quarter of a mile. I went out in the woods and cooked a supper, and I had about made up my mind I would stay there all night, when I hear a *plunkety-plunk*, *plunkety-plunk*, and says to myself, horses coming; and next I hear people's voices. I got everything into the canoe as quick as I could, and then went creeping through the woods to see what I could find out. I hadn't got far when I hear a man say:

"We better camp here, if we can find a good place; the horses is about beat out. Let's look around."

I didn't wait, but shoved out and paddled away easy. I tied up in the old place, and reckoned I would sleep in the canoe.

I didn't sleep much. I couldn't, somehow, for thinking. And every time I waked up I thought somebody had me by the neck. So the sleep didn't do me no good. By-and-by I says to myself, I can't live this way; I'm agoing to find out who it is that's here on the island with me; I'll find it out or bust. Well, I felt better, right off.

So I took my paddle and slid out from shore just a step or two, and then let the canoe drop along down amongst the shadows. The moon was shining, and outside of the shadows it made it most as light as day. I poked along well onto an hour, everything still as rocks and sound asleep. Well by this time I was most down to the foot of the island. A little ripply cool breeze begun to blow, and that was as good as saying the night was about done. I give her a turn with the paddle and brung her nose to shore; then I got my gun and slipped out and into the edge of the woods. I set down there on a log and looked out through the leaves. I see the moon go off watch and the darkness begin to blanket the river. But in a little while I see a pale streak over the tree-tops, and knowed the day was coming. So I took my gun and slipped off towards where I had run across that camp fire, stopping every minute or two to listen. But I hadn't no luck, somehow; I couldn't seem to find the place. But by-and-by, sure enough, I catched a glimpse of fire, away through the trees. I went for it, cautious and slow. By-and-by I was close enough to have a look, and there laid a man on the ground. It most give me the fan-tods. He had a blanket around his head, and his head was nearly in the fire. I set there behind a clump of bushes, in about six foot of him, and kept my eyes on him steady. It was getting gray daylight, now. Pretty soon he gapped, and stretched himself, and hove off the blanket, and it was Miss Watson's Jim! I bet I was glad to see him. I says:

"Hello, Jim!" and skipped out.

He bounced up and stared at me wild. Then he drops down on his knees, and puts his hands together and says:

"Doan' hurt me—don't! I hain't ever done no harm to a ghos'. I awluz liked dead people, en done all I could for 'em. You go en git in de river agin, whah you b'longs, en doan' do nuffin to Ole Jim, 'at 'uz awluz yo' fren'."

Well, I warn't long making him understand I warn't dead.

I was ever so glad to see Jim. I warn't lonesome, now. I told him I warn't afraid of *him* telling the people where I was. I talked along, but he only set there and looked at me; never said nothing. Then I says:

"It's good daylight. Le's get breakfast. Make up your camp fire good."

"What's de use er makin' up de camp fire to cook straw-bries en sich truck? But you got a gun, hain't you? Den we kin git sumfn better den strawbries."

"Strawberries and such truck," I says. "Is that what you live on?"

"I couldn' git nuffn else," he says.

"Why, how long you been on the island, Jim?"

"I come heah de night arter you's killed."

"What, all that time?"

"Yes-indeedy."

"And ain't you had nothing but that kind of rubbage to eat?"

"No, sah—nuffn else."

"Well, you must be most starved, ain't you?'

"I reck'n I could eat a hoss. I think I could. How long you ben on de islan'?"

"Since the night I got killed."

"No! W'y, what has you lived on? But you got a gun. Oh, yes, you got a gun. Dat's good. Now you kill sumfn en I'll make up de fire."

So we went over to where the canoe was, and while he built a fire in a grassy open place amongst the trees, I fetched meal and bacon and coffee, and coffee-pot and frying-pan, and sugar and tin cups, and the nigger was set back consid-erable, because he reckoned it was all done with witchcraft. I catched a good big cat-fish, too, and Jim cleaned him with his knife, and fried him.

When breakfast was ready, we lolled on the grass and eat it smoking hot. Jim laid it in with all his might, for he was most about starved. Then when we had got pretty well stuffed, we laid off and lazied.

By-and-by Jim says:

"But looky here, Huck, who wuz it dat 'uz killed in dat shanty, ef it warn't you?"

Then I told him the whole thing, and he said it was
He said Tom Sawyer couldn't get up no better plan
what I had. Then I says:

"How do you come to be here, Jim, and how'd y
here?"

He looked pretty uneasy, and didn't say nothing for
ute. Then he says:

"Maybe I better not tell."

"Why, Jim?"

"Well, dey's reasons. But you wouldn' tell on me e
to tell you, would you, Huck?"

"Blamed if I would, Jim."

"Well, I b'lieve you, Huck. I—I *run off.*"

"Jim!"

"But mind, you said you wouldn't tell—you know yc
you wouldn't tell, Huck."

"Well, I did. I said I wouldn't, and I'll stick to it. I
injun I will. People would call me a low down Abli
and despise me for keeping mum—but that don't ma
difference. I ain't agoing to tell, and I ain't agoing back
anyways. So now, le's know all about it."

"Well, you see, it 'uz dis way. Ole Missus—dat's
Watson—she pecks on me all de time, en treats me
rough, but she awluz said she wouldn' sell me down t
leans. But I noticed dey wuz a nigger trader roun' de
considable, lately, en I begin to git oneasy. Well, one n
creeps to de do', pooty late, en de do' warn't quite she
hear ole missus tell de widder she gwyne to sell me do
Orleans, but she didn' want to, but she could git eight h
dollars for me, en it 'uz sich a big stack o' money she c
resis'. De widder she try to git her to say she wouldn'
but I never waited to hear de res'. I lit out mighty qu
tell you.

"I tuck out en shin down de hill en 'spec to steal a
'long de sho' som'ers 'bove de town, but dey wuz peo
stirrin' yit, so I hid in de ole tumble-down cooper shop
bank to wait for everybody to go 'way. Well, I wuz d
night. Dey wuz somebody roun' all de time. 'Long 'bo
in de mawnin', skifts begin to go by, en 'bout eight e

every skift dat went 'long wuz talkin' 'bout how yo' pap come over to de town en say you's killed. Dese las' skifts wuz full o' ladies en genlmen agoin' over for to see de place. Sometimes dey'd pull up at de sho' en take a res' b'fo' dey started acrost, so by de talk I got to know all 'bout de killin'. I 'uz powerful sorry you's killed, Huck, but I ain't no mo', now.

"I laid dah under de shavins all day. I 'uz hungry, but I warn't afeared; bekase I knowed ole missus en de widder wuz goin' to start to de camp-meetn' right arter breakfas' en be gone all day, en dey knows I goes off wid de cattle 'bout daylight, so dey wouldn' 'spec to see me roun' de place, en so dey wouldn' miss me tell arter dark in de evenin'. De yuther servants wouldn' miss me, kase dey'd shin out en take holiday, soon as de ole folks 'uz out'n de way.

"Well, when it come dark I tuck out up de river road, en went 'bout two mile er more to whah dey warn't no houses. I'd made up my mine 'bout what I's agwyne to do. You see ef I kep' on tryin' to git away afoot, de dogs 'ud track me; ef I stole a skift to cross over, dey'd miss dat skift, you see, en dey'd know 'bout what I'd lan' on de yuther side en whah to pick up my track. So I says, a raff is what I's arter; it doan' *make* no track.

"I see a light a-comin' roun' de p'int, bymeby, so I wade' in en shove' a log ahead o' me, en swum more'n half-way acrost de river, en got in 'mongst de drift-wood, en kep' my head down low, en kinder swum agin de current tell de raff come along. Den I swum to de stern uv it, en tuck aholt. It clouded up en 'uz pooty dark for a little while. So I clumb up en laid down on de planks. De men 'uz all 'way yonder in de middle, whah de lantern wuz. De river wuz arisin' en dey wuz a good current; so I reck'n'd 'at by fo' in de mawnin' I'd be twenty-five mile down de river, en den I'd slip in, jis' b'fo' daylight, en swim asho' en take to de woods on de Illinoi side.

"But I didn' have no luck. When we 'uz mos' down to de head er de islan', a man begin to come aft wid de lantern. I see it warn't no use fer to wait, so I slid overboad, en struck out fer de islan'. Well, I had a notion I could lan' mos' any-whers, but I couldn't—bank too bluff. I 'uz mos' to de foot er de islan' b'fo' I foun' a good place. I went into de woods en jedged I wouldn' fool wid raffs no mo', long as dey move de lantern roun' so. I had my pipe en a plug er dog-leg, en some matches in my cap, en dey warn't wet, so I 'uz all right."

"And so you ain't had no meat nor bread to eat all this time? Why didn't you get mud-turkles?"

"How you gwyne to git'm? You can't slip up on um en grab um; en how's a body gwyne to hit um wid a rock? How could a body do it in de night? en I warn't gwyne to show myself on de bank in de daytime."

"Well, that's so. You've had to keep in the woods all the time, of course. Did you hear 'em shooting the cannon?"

"Oh, yes. I knowed dey was arter you. I see um go by heah; watched um thoo de bushes."

Some young birds come along, flying a yard or two at a time and lighting. Jim said it was a sign it was going to rain. He said it was a sign when young chickens flew that way, and so he reckoned it was the same way when young birds done it. I was going to catch some of them, but Jim wouldn't let me. He said it was death. He said his father laid mighty sick once, and some of them catched a bird, and his old granny said his father would die, and he did.

And Jim said you musn't count the things you are going to cook for dinner, because that would bring bad luck. The same if you shook the table-cloth after sundown. And he said if a man owned a bee-hive, and that man died, the bees must be told about it before sun-up next morning, or else the bees would all weaken down and quit work and die. Jim said bees wouldn't sting idiots; but I didn't believe that, because I had tried them lots of times myself, and they wouldn't sting me.

I had heard about some of these things before, but not all of them. Jim knowed all kinds of signs. He said he knowed most everything. I said it looked to me like all the signs was about bad luck, and so I asked him if there warn't any good-luck signs. He says:

"Mighty few—an' *dey* ain' no use to a body. What you want to know when good luck's a-comin' for? want to keep it off?" And he said: "Ef you's got hairy arms en a hairy breas', it's a sign dat you's agwyne to be rich. Well, dey's some use in a sign like dat, 'kase it's so fur ahead. You see, maybe you's got to be po' a long time fust, en so you might git discourage' en kill yo'sef 'f you did n' know by de sign dat you gwyne to be rich bymeby."

"Have you got hairy arms and a hairy breast, Jim?"

"What's de use to ax dat question? don' you see I has?"

"Well, are you rich?"

"No, but I ben rich wunst, and gwyne to be rich agin. Wunst I had foteen dollars, but I tuck to specalat'n', en got busted out."

"What did you speculate in, Jim?"

"Well, fust I tackled stock."

"What kind of stock?"

"Why, live stock. Cattle, you know. I put ten dollars in a cow. But I ain' gwyne to resk no mo' money in stock. De cow up 'n' died on my han's."

"So you lost the ten dollars."

"No, I didn' lose it all. I on'y los' 'bout nine of it. I sole de hide en taller for a dollar en ten cents."

"You had five dollars and ten cents left. Did you speculate any more?"

"Yes. You know dat one-laigged nigger dat b'longs to old Misto Bradish? well, he sot up a bank, en say anybody dat put in a dollar would git fo' dollars mo' at de en' er de year. Well, all de niggers went in, but dey didn' have much. I wuz de on'y one dat had much. So I stuck out for mo' dan fo' dollars, en I said 'f I didn' git it I'd start a bank mysef. Well o' course dat nigger want' to keep me out er de business, bekase he say dey warn't business 'nough for two banks, so he say I could put in my five dollars en he pay me thirty-five at de en' er de year.

"So I done it. Den I reck'n'd I'd inves' de thirty-five dollars right off en keep things a-movin'. Dey wuz a nigger name' Bob, dat had ketched a wood-flat, en his marster didn' know it; en I bought it off'n him en told him to take de thirty-five dollars when de en' er de year come; but somebody stole de wood-flat dat night, en nex' day de one-laigged nigger say de bank 's busted. So dey didn' none uv us git no money."

"What did you do with the ten cents, Jim?"

"Well, I 'uz gwyne to spen' it, but I had a dream, en de dream tole me to give it to a nigger name' Balum—Balum's

Ass dey call him for short, he's one er dem chuckle-heads, you know. But he's lucky, dey say, en I see I warn't lucky. De dream say let Balum inves' de ten cents en he'd make a raise for me. Well, Balum he tuck de money, en when he wuz in church he hear de preacher say dat whoever give to de po' len' to de Lord, en boun' to git his money back a hund'd times. So Balum he tuck en give de ten cents to de po', en laid low to see what wuz gwyne to come of it."

"Well, what did come of it, Jim?"

"Nuffn' never come of it. I couldn' manage to k'leck dat money no way; en Balum he couldn'. I ain' gwyne to len' no mo' money 'dout I see de security. Boun' to git yo' money back a hund'd times, de preacher says! Ef I could git de ten *cents* back, I'd call it squah, en be glad er de chanst."

"Well, it's all right, anyway, Jim, long as you're going to be rich again some time or other."

"Yes—en I's rich now, come to look at it. I owns mysef en I's wuth eight hund'd dollars. I wisht I had de money, I wouldn' want no mo'."

IX

I WANTED to go and look at a place right about the middle of the island, that I'd found when I was exploring; so we started, and soon got to it, because the island was only three miles long and a quarter of a mile wide.

This place was a tolerable long steep hill or ridge, about forty foot high. We had a rough time getting to the top, the sides was so steep and the bushes so thick. We tramped and clumb around all over it, and by-and-by found a good big cavern in the rock, most up to the top on the side towards Illinois. The cavern was as big as two or three rooms bunched together, and Jim could stand up straight in it. It was cool in there. Jim was for putting our traps in there, right away, but I said we didn't want to be climbing up and down there all the time.

Jim said if we had the canoe hid in a good place, and had all the traps in the cavern, we could rush there if anybody was to come to the island, and they would never find us without dogs. And besides, he said them little birds had said it was going to rain, and did I want the things to get wet?

So we went back and got the canoe and paddled up abreast the cavern, and lugged all the traps up there. Then we hunted up a place close by to hide the canoe in, amongst the thick willows. We took some fish off of the lines and set them again, and begun to get ready for dinner.

The door of the cavern was big enough to roll a hogshead in, and on one side of the door the floor stuck out a little bit and was flat and a good place to build a fire on. So we built it there and cooked dinner.

We spread the blankets inside for a carpet, and eat our dinner in there. We put all the other things handy at the back of the cavern. Pretty soon it darkened up and begun to thunder and lighten; so the birds was right about it. Directly it begun to rain, and it rained like all fury, too, and I never see the wind blow so. It was one of these regular summer storms. It would get so dark that it looked all blue-black outside, and lovely; and the rain would thrash along by so thick that the trees off a little ways looked dim and spider-webby; and here would come a blast of wind that would bend the trees down and turn up the pale underside of the leaves; and then a perfect ripper of a gust would follow along and set the branches to tossing their arms as if they was just wild; and next, when it was just about the bluest and blackest—*fst!* it was as bright as glory and you'd have a little glimpse of tree-tops a-plunging about, away off yonder in the storm, hundreds of yards further than you could see before; dark as sin again in a second, and now you'd hear the thunder let go with an awful crash and then go rumbling, grumbling, tumbling down the sky towards the under side of the world, like rolling empty barrels down stairs, where it's long stairs and they bounce a good deal, you know.

"Jim, this is nice," I says. "I wouldn't want to be nowhere else but here. Pass me along another hunk of fish and some hot corn-bread."

"Well, you wouldn't a ben here, 'f it hadn't a ben for Jim. You'd a ben down dah in de woods widout any dinner, en gittn' mos' drownded, too, dat you would, honey. Chickens knows when its gwyne to rain, en so do de birds, chile."

The river went on raising and raising for ten or twelve days, till at last it was over the banks. The water was three or four foot deep on the island in the low places and on the Illinois bottom. On that side it was a good many miles wide; but on the Missouri side it was the same old distance across— a half a mile—because the Missouri shore was just a wall of high bluffs.

Daytimes we paddled all over the island in the canoe. It was mighty cool and shady in the deep woods even if the sun was blazing outside. We went winding in and out amongst the trees; and sometimes the vines hung so thick we had to back away and go some other way. Well, on every old broken-down tree, you could see rabbits, and snakes, and such things; and when the island had been overflowed a day or two, they got so tame, on account of being hungry, that you could paddle right up and put your hand on them if you wanted to; but not the snakes and turtles—they would slide off in the water. The ridge our cavern was in, was full of them. We could a had pets enough if we'd wanted them.

One night we catched a little section of a lumber raft—nice pine planks. It was twelve foot wide and about fifteen or sixteen foot long, and the top stood above water six or seven inches, a solid level floor. We could see saw-logs go by in the daylight, sometimes, but we let them go; we didn't show ourselves in daylight.

Another night, when we was up at the head of the island, just before daylight, here comes a frame house down, on the west side. She was a two-story, and tilted over, considerable. We paddled out and got aboard—clumb in at an up-stairs window. But it was too dark to see yet, so we made the canoe fast and set in her to wait for daylight.

The light begun to come before we got to the foot of the island. Then we looked in at the window. We could make out a bed, and a table, and two old chairs, and lots of things around about on the floor; and there was clothes hanging against the wall. There was something laying on the floor in the far corner that looked like a man. So Jim says:

"Hello, you!"

But it didn't budge. So I hollered again, and then Jim says:

"De man ain't asleep—he's dead. You hold still—I'll go en see."

He went and bent down and looked, and says:

"It's a dead man. Yes, indeedy; naked, too. He's been shot in de back. I reck'n he's been dead two er three days. Come in, Huck, but doan' look at his face—it's too gashly."

I didn't look at him at all. Jim throwed some old rags over him, but he needn't done it; I didn't want to see him. There was heaps of old greasy cards scattered around over the floor, and old whisky bottles, and a couple of masks made out of black cloth; and all over the walls was the ignorantest kind of words and pictures, made with charcoal. There was two old dirty calico dresses, and a sun-bonnet, and some women's under-clothes, hanging against the wall, and some men's clothing, too. We put the lot into the canoe; it might come good. There was a boy's old speckled straw hat on the floor; I took that too. And there was a bottle that had had milk in it; and it had a rag stopper for a baby to suck. We would a took the bottle, but it was broke. There was a seedy old chest, and an old hair trunk with the hinges broke. They stood open, but

there warn't nothing left in them that was any account. Th
way things was scattered about, we reckoned the people le
in a hurry and warn't fixed so as to carry off most of thei
stuff.

We got an old tin lantern, and a butcher knife without an
handle, and a bran-new Barlow knife worth two bits in an
store, and a lot of tallow candles, and a tin candlestick, and
gourd, and a tin cup, and a ratty old bed-quilt off the bec
and a reticule with needles and pins and beeswax and button
and thread and all such truck in it, and a hatchet and som
nails, and a fish-line as thick as my little finger, with som
monstrous hooks on it, and a roll of buckskin, and a leathe
dog-collar, and a horse-shoe, and some vials of medicine tha
didn't have no label on them; and just as we was leaving
found a tolerable good curry-comb, and Jim he found a ratt
old fiddle-bow, and a wooden leg. The straps was broke o
of it, but barring that, it was a good enough leg, though i
was too long for me and not long enough for Jim, and w
couldn't find the other one, though we hunted all around.

And so, take it all around, we made a good haul. When w
was ready to shove off, we was a quarter of a mile below th
island, and it was pretty broad day; so I made Jim lay dow
in the canoe and cover up with the quilt, because if he set up
people could tell he was a nigger a good ways off. I paddle
over to the Illinois shore, and drifted down most a half a mil
doing it. I crept up the dead water under the bank, and hadn'
no accidents and didn't see nobody. We got home all safe.

X

AFTER BREAKFAST I wanted to talk about the dead man and guess out how he come to be killed, but Jim didn't want to. He said it would fetch bad luck; and besides, he said, he might come and ha'nt us; he said a man that warn't buried was more likely to go a-ha'nting around than one that was planted and comfortable. That sounded pretty reasonable, so I didn't say no more; but I couldn't keep from studying over it and wishing I knowed who shot the man, and what they done it for.

We rummaged the clothes we'd got, and found eight dollars in silver sewed up in the lining of an old blanket overcoat. Jim said he reckoned the people in that house stole the coat, because if they'd a knowed the money was there they wouldn't a left it. I said I reckoned they killed him, too; but Jim didn't want to talk about that. I says:˙

"Now you think it's bad luck; but what did you say when I fetched in the snake-skin that I found on the top of the ridge day before yesterday? You said it was the worst bad luck in the world to touch a snake-skin with my hands. Well, here's your bad luck! We've raked in all this truck and eight dollars besides. I wish we could have some bad luck like this every day, Jim."

"Never you mind, honey, never you mind. Don't you git too peart. It's a-comin'. Mind I tell you, it's a-comin'."

It did come, too. It was a Tuesday that we had that talk. Well, after dinner Friday, we was laying around in the grass at the upper end of the ridge, and got out of tobacco. I went to the cavern to get some, and found a rattlesnake in there. I killed him, and curled him up on the foot of Jim's blanket, ever so natural, thinking there'd be some fun when Jim found him there. Well, by night I forgot all about the snake, and when Jim flung himself down on the blanket while I struck a light, the snake's mate was there, and bit him.

He jumped up yelling, and the first thing the light showed was the varmint curled up and ready for another spring. I laid him out in a second with a stick, and Jim grabbed pap's whisky jug and begun to pour it down.

He was barefooted, and the snake bit him right on the heel. That all comes of my being such a fool as to not remember that wherever you leave a dead snake its mate always comes there and curls around it. Jim told me to chop off the snake's head and throw it away, and then skin the body and roast a piece of it. I done it, and he eat it and said it would help cure him. He made me take off the rattles and tie them around his wrist, too. He said that that would help. Then I slid out quiet and throwed the snakes clear away amongst the bushes; for I warn't going to let Jim find out it was all my fault, not if I could help it.

Jim sucked and sucked at the jug, and now and then he got out of his head and pitched around and yelled; but every time he come to himself he went to sucking at the jug again. His foot swelled up pretty big, and so did his leg; but by-and-by the drunk begun to come, and so I judged he was all right; but I'd druther been bit with a snake than pap's whisky.

Jim was laid up for four days and nights. Then the swelling was all gone and he was around again. I made up my mind I wouldn't ever take aholt of a snake-skin again with my hands, now that I see what had come of it. Jim said he reckoned I would believe him next time. And he said that handling a snake-skin was such awful bad luck that maybe we hadn't got to the end of it yet. He said he druther see the new moon over his left shoulder as much as a thousand times than take up a snake-skin in his hand. Well, I was getting to feel that way myself, though I've always reckoned that looking at the new moon over your left shoulder is one of the carelessest and foolishest things a body can do. Old Hank Bunker done it once, and bragged about it; and in less than two years he got drunk and fell off of the shot tower and spread himself out so that he was just a kind of a layer, as you may say; and they slid him edgeways between two barn doors for a coffin, and buried him so, so they say, but I didn't see it. Pap told me. But anyway, it all come of looking at the moon that way, like a fool.

Well, the days went along, and the river went down between its banks again; and about the first thing we done was

to bait one of the big hooks with a skinned rabbit and set it
and catch a cat-fish that was as big as a man, being six foot
two inches long, and weighed over two hundred pounds. We
couldn't handle him, of course; he would a flung us into Illinois. We just set there and watched him rip and tear around
till he drownded. We found a brass button in his stomach,
and a round ball, and lots of rubbage. We split the ball open
with the hatchet, and there was a spool in it. Jim said he'd
had it there a long time, to coat it over so and make a ball of
it. It was as big a fish as was ever catched in the Mississippi,
I reckon. Jim said he hadn't ever seen a bigger one. He would
a been worth a good deal over at the village. They peddle out
such a fish as that by the pound in the market house there;
everybody buys some of him; his meat's as white as snow and
makes a good fry.

Next morning I said it was getting slow and dull, and I
wanted to get a stirring up, some way. I said I reckoned I
would slip over the river and find out what was going on.
Jim liked that notion; but he said I must go in the dark and
look sharp. Then he studied it over and said, couldn't I put
on some of them old things and dress up like a girl? That was
a good notion, too. So we shortened up one of the calico
gowns and I turned up my trowser-legs to my knees and got
into it. Jim hitched it behind with the hooks, and it was a fair
fit. I put on the sun-bonnet and tied it under my chin, and
then for a body to look in and see my face was like looking
down a joint of stove-pipe. Jim said nobody would know me,
even in the daytime, hardly. I practiced around all day to get
the hang of the things, and by-and-by I could do pretty well
in them, only Jim said I didn't walk like a girl; and he said I
must quit pulling up my gown to get at my britches pocket.
I took notice, and done better.

I started up the Illinois shore in the canoe just after dark.

I started across to the town from a little below the ferry
landing, and the drift of the current fetched me in at the bottom of the town. I tied up and started along the bank. There
was a light burning in a little shanty that hadn't been lived in
for a long time, and I wondered who had took up quarters
there. I slipped up and peeped in at the window. There was
a woman about forty year old in there, knitting by a candle

that was on a pine table. I didn't know her face; she was a
stranger, for you couldn't start a face in that town that I
didn't know. Now this was lucky, because I was weakening;
I was getting afraid I had come; people might know my voice
and find me out. But if this woman had been in such a little
town two days she could tell me all I wanted to know; so I
knocked at the door, and made up my mind I wouldn't forget
I was a girl.

XI

"OME IN," says the woman, and I did. She says:
"Take a cheer."

I done it. She looked me all over with her little shiny eyes, and says:

"What might your name be?"

"Sarah Williams."

"Where 'bouts do you live? In this neighborhood?"

"No'm. In Hookerville, seven mile below. I've walked all the way and I'm all tired out."

"Hungry, too, I reckon. I'll find you something."

"No'm, I ain't hungry. I was so hungry I had to stop two mile below here at a farm; so I ain't hungry no more. It's what makes me so late. My mother's down sick, and out of money and everything, and I come to tell my uncle Abner Moore. He lives at the upper end of the town, she says. I hain't ever been here before. Do you know him?"

"No; but I don't know everybody yet. I haven't lived here quite two weeks. It's a considerable ways to the upper end of the town. You better stay here all night. Take off your bonnet."

"No," I says, "I'll rest a while, I reckon, and go on. I ain't afeard of the dark."

She said she wouldn't let me go by myself, but her husband would be in by-and-by, maybe in a hour and a half, and she'd send him along with me. Then she got to talking about her husband, and about her relations up the river, and her relations down the river, and about how much better off they used to was, and how they didn't know but they'd made a mistake coming to our town, instead of letting well alone—and so on and so on, till I was afeard *I* had made a mistake coming to her to find out what was going on in the town; but by-and-by she dropped onto pap and the murder, and then I was pretty willing to let her clatter right along. She told about me and Tom Sawyer finding the six thousand dollars (only she got it ten) and all about pap and what a hard lot he was, and what a hard lot I

was, and at last she got down to where I was murdered. I
says:

"Who done it? We've heard considerable about these
goings on, down in Hookerville, but we don't know who
'twas that killed Huck Finn."

"Well, I reckon there's a right smart chance of people *here*
that 'd like to know who killed him. Some thinks old Finn
done it himself."

"No—is that so?"

"Most everybody thought it at first. He'll never know how
nigh he come to getting lynched. But before night they
changed around and judged it was done by a runaway nigger
named Jim."

"Why *he*——"

I stopped. I reckoned I better keep still. She run on, and
never noticed I had put in at all.

"The nigger run off the very night Huck Finn was killed.
So there's a reward out for him—three hundred dollars. And
there's a reward out for old Finn too—two hundred dollars.
You see, he come to town the morning after the murder, and
told about it, and was out with 'em on the ferry-boat hunt,
and right away after he up and left. Before night they wanted
to lynch him, but he was gone, you see. Well, next day they
found out the nigger was gone; they found out he hadn't ben
seen sence ten o'clock the night the murder was done. So
then they put it on him, you see, and while they was full of
it, next day back comes old Finn and went boo-hooing to
Judge Thatcher to get money to hunt for the nigger all over
Illinois with. The judge give him some, and that evening he
got drunk and was around till after midnight with a couple of
mighty hard looking strangers, and then went off with them.
Well, he hain't come back sence, and they ain't looking for
him back till this thing blows over a little, for people thinks
now that he killed his boy and fixed things so folks would
think robbers done it, and then he'd get Huck's money without
having to bother a long time with a lawsuit. People do say he
warn't any too good to do it. Oh, he's sly, I reckon. If he don't
come back for a year, he'll be all right. You can't prove anything
on him, you know; everything will be quieted down then, and
he'll walk into Huck's money as easy as nothing."

"Yes, I reckon so, 'm. I don't see nothing in the way of it. Has everybody quit thinking the nigger done it?"

"Oh, no, not everybody. A good many thinks he done it. But they'll get the nigger pretty soon, now, and maybe they can scare it out of him."

"Why, are they after him yet?"

"Well, you're innocent, ain't you! Does three hundred dollars lay round every day for people to pick up? Some folks thinks the nigger ain't far from here. I'm one of them—but I hain't talked it around. A few days ago I was talking with an old couple that lives next door in the log shanty, and they happened to say hardly anybody ever goes to that island over yonder that they call Jackson's Island. Don't anybody live there? says I. No, nobody, says they. I didn't say any more, but I done some thinking. I was pretty near certain I'd seen smoke over there, about the head of the island, a day or two before that, so I says to myself, like as not that nigger's hiding over there; anyway, says I, it's worth the trouble to give the place a hunt. I hain't seen any smoke sence, so I reckon maybe he's gone, if it was him; but husband's going over to see—him and another man. He was gone up the river; but he got back to-day and I told him as soon as he got here two hours ago."

I had got so uneasy I couldn't set still. I had to do something with my hands; so I took up a needle off of the table and went to threading it. My hands shook, and I was making a bad job of it. When the woman stopped talking, I looked up, and she was looking at me pretty curious, and smiling a little. I put down the needle and thread and let on to be interested—and I was, too—and says:

"Three hundred dollars is a power of money. I wish my mother could get it. Is your husband going over there to-night?"

"Oh, yes. He went up town with the man I was telling you of, to get a boat and see if they could borrow another gun. They'll go over after midnight."

"Couldn't they see better if they was to wait till daytime?"

"Yes. And couldn't the nigger see better, too? After midnight he'll likely be asleep, and they can slip around through the woods and hunt up his camp fire all the better for the dark, if he's got one."

"I didn't think of that."

The woman kept looking at me pretty curious, and I didn't feel a bit comfortable. Pretty soon she says:

"What did you say your name was, honey?"

"M—Mary Williams."

Somehow it didn't seem to me that I said it was Mary before, so I didn't look up; seemed to me I said it was Sarah; so I felt sort of cornered, and was afeared maybe I was looking it, too. I wished the woman would say something more; the longer she set still, the uneasier I was. But now she says:

"Honey, I thought you said it was Sarah when you first come in?"

"Oh, yes'm, I did. Sarah Mary Williams. Sarah's my first name. Some calls me Sarah, some calls me Mary."

"Oh, that's the way of it?"

"Yes'm."

I was feeling better, then, but I wished I was out of there, anyway. I couldn't look up yet.

Well, the woman fell to talking about how hard times was, and how poor they had to live, and how the rats was as free as if they owned the place, and so forth, and so on, and then I got easy again. She was right about the rats. You'd see one stick his nose out of a hole in the corner every little while. She said she had to have things handy to throw at them when she was alone, or they wouldn't give her no peace. She showed me a bar of lead, twisted up into a knot, and said she was a good shot with it generly, but she'd wrenched her arm a day or two ago, and didn't know whether she could throw true, now. But she watched for a chance, and directly she banged away at a rat, but she missed him wide, and said "Ouch!" it hurt her arm so. Then she told me to try for the next one. I wanted to be getting away before the old man got back, but of course I didn't let on. I got the thing, and the first rat that showed his nose I let drive, and if he'd a stayed where he was he'd a been a tolerable sick rat. She said that that was first-rate, and she reckoned I would hive the next one. She went and got the lump of lead and fetched it back and brought along a hank of yarn, which she wanted me to help her with. I held up my two hands and she put the hank over them and went on talking about her and her husband's matters. But she broke off to say:

"Keep your eye on the rats. You better have the lead in your lap, handy."

So she dropped the lump into my lap, just at that moment, and I clapped my legs together on it and she went on talking. But only about a minute. Then she took off the hank and looked me straight in the face, but very pleasant, and says:

"Come, now—what's your real name?"

"Wh-what, mum?"

"What's your real name? Is it Bill, or Tom, or Bob?—or what is it?"

I reckon I shook like a leaf, and I didn't know hardly what to do. But I says:

"Please to don't poke fun at a poor girl like me, mum. If I'm in the way, here, I'll——"

"No, you won't. Set down and stay where you are. I ain't going to hurt you, and I ain't going to tell on you, nuther. You just tell me your secret, and trust me. I'll keep it; and what's more, I'll help you. So'll my old man, if you want him to. You see, you're a runaway 'prentice—that's all. It ain't anything. There ain't any harm in it. You've been treated bad, and you made up your mind to cut. Bless you, child, I wouldn't tell on you. Tell me all about it, now—that's a good boy."

So I said it wouldn't be no use to try to play it any longer, and I would just make a clean breast and tell her everything, but she mustn't go back on her promise. Then I told her my father and mother was dead, and the law had bound me out to a mean old farmer in the country thirty mile back from the river, and he treated me so bad I couldn't stand it no longer; he went away to be gone a couple of days, and so I took my chance and stole some of his daughter's old clothes, and cleared out, and I had been three nights coming the thirty miles; I traveled nights, and hid day-times and slept, and the bag of bread and meat I carried from home lasted me all the

way and I had a plenty. I said I believed my uncle Abner
Moore would take care of me, and so that was why I struck
out for this town of Goshen.

"Goshen, child? This ain't Goshen. This is St. Petersburg.
Goshen's ten mile further up the river. Who told you this was
Goshen?"

"Why, a man I met at day-break this morning, just as I was
going to turn into the woods for my regular sleep. He told
me when the roads forked I must take the right hand, and
five mile would fetch me to Goshen."

"He was drunk I reckon. He told you just exactly wrong."

"Well, he did act like he was drunk, but it ain't no matter
now. I got to be moving along. I'll fetch Goshen before daylight."

"Hold on a minute. I'll put you up a snack to eat. You
might want it."

So she put me up a snack, and says:

"Say—when a cow's laying down, which end of her gets
up first? Answer up prompt, now—don't stop to study over
it. Which end gets up first?"

"The hind end, mum."

"Well, then, a horse?"

"The for'rard end, mum."

"Which side of a tree does the most moss grow on?"

"North side."

"If fifteen cows is browsing on a hillside, how many of
them eats with their heads pointed the same direction?"

"The whole fifteen, mum."

"Well, I reckon you *have* lived in the country. I thought
maybe you was trying to hocus me again. What's your real
name, now?"

"George Peters, mum."

"Well, try to remember it, George. Don't forget and tell
me it's Elexander before you go, and then get out by saying
it's George-Elexander when I catch you. And don't go about
women in that old calico. You do a girl tolerable poor, but
you might fool men, maybe. Bless you, child, when you set
out to thread a needle, don't hold the thread still and fetch
the needle up to it; hold the needle still and poke the thread
at it—that's the way a woman most always does; but a man

always does 'tother way. And when you throw at a rat or anything, hitch yourself up a tip-toe, and fetch your hand up over your head as awkard as you can, and miss your rat about six or seven foot. Throw stiff-armed from the shoulder, like there was a pivot there for it to turn on—like a girl; not from the wrist and elbow, with your arm out to one side, like a boy. And mind you, when a girl tries to catch anything in her lap, she throws her knees apart; she don't clap them together, the way you did when you catched the lump of lead. Why, I spotted you for a boy when you was threading the needle; and I contrived the other things just to make certain. Now trot along to your uncle, Sarah Mary Williams George Elexander Peters, and if you get into trouble you send word to Mrs. Judith Loftus, which is me, and I'll do what I can to get you out of it. Keep the river road, all the way, and next time you tramp, take shoes and socks with you. The river road's a rocky one, and your feet 'll be in a condition when you get to Goshen, I reckon."

I went up the bank about fifty yards, and then I doubled on my tracks and slipped back to where my canoe was, a good piece below the house. I jumped in and was off in a hurry. I went up stream far enough to make the head of the island, and then started across. I took off the sun-bonnet, for I didn't want no blinders on, then. When I was about the middle, I hear the clock begin to strike; so I stops and listens; the sound come faint over the water, but clear—eleven. When I struck the head of the island I never waited to blow, though I was most winded, but I shoved right into the timber where my old camp used to be, and started a good fire there on a high-and-dry spot.

Then I jumped in the canoe and dug out for our place a mile and a half below, as hard as I could go. I landed, and slopped through the timber and up the ridge and into the cavern. There Jim laid, sound asleep on the ground. I roused him out and says:

"Git up and hump yourself, Jim! There ain't a minute to lose. They're after us!"

Jim never asked no questions, he never said a word; but the way he worked for the next half an hour showed about how he was scared. By that time everything we had in the world was on our raft and she was ready to be shoved out from the willow cove where she was hid. We put out the camp fire at the cavern the first thing, and didn't show a candle outside after that.

I took the canoe out from shore a little piece and took a look, but if there was a boat around I couldn't see it, for stars and shadows ain't good to see by. Then we got out the raft and slipped along down in the shade, past the foot of the island dead still, never saying a word.

XII

IT MUST a been close onto one o'clock when we got below the island at last, and the raft did seem to go mighty slow. If a boat was to come along, we was going to take to the canoe and break for the Illinois shore; and it was well a boat didn't come, for we hadn't ever thought to put the gun into the canoe, or a fishing-line or anything to eat. We was in ruther too much of a sweat to think of so many things. It warn't good judgment to put *everything* on the raft.

If the men went to the island, I just expect they found the camp fire I built, and watched it all night for Jim to come. Anyways, they stayed away from us, and if my building the fire never fooled them it warn't no fault of mine. I played it as low-down on them as I could.

When the first streak of day begun to show, we tied up to a tow-head in a big bend on the Illinois side, and hacked off cotton-wood branches with the hatchet and covered up the raft with them so she looked like there had been a cave-in in the bank there. A tow-head is a sand-bar that has cotton-woods on it as thick as harrow-teeth.

We had mountains on the Missouri shore and heavy timber on the Illinois side, and the channel was down the Missouri shore at that place, so we warn't afraid of anybody running across us. We laid there all day and watched the rafts and steamboats spin down the Missouri shore, and up-bound steamboats fight the big river in the middle. I told Jim all about the time I had jabbering with that woman; and Jim said she was a smart one, and if she was to start after us herself *she* wouldn't set down and watch a camp fire—no, sir, she'd fetch a dog. Well, then, I said, why couldn't she tell her husband to fetch a dog? Jim said he bet she did think of it by the time the men was ready to start, and he believed they must a gone up town to get a dog and so they lost all that time, or else we wouldn't be here on a tow-head sixteen or seventeen mile below the village—no, indeedy, we would be in that same old town again. So I said I didn't care what was the reason they didn't get us, as long as they didn't.

When it was beginning to come on dark, we poked our heads out of the cottonwood thicket and looked up, and down, and across; nothing in sight; so Jim took up some of the top planks of the raft and built a snug wigwam to get under in blazing weather and rainy, and to keep the things dry. Jim made a floor for the wigwam, and raised it a foot or more above the level of the raft, so now the blankets and all the traps was out of the reach of steamboat waves. Right in the middle of the wigwam we made a layer of dirt about five or six inches deep with a frame around it for to hold it to its place; this was to build a fire on in sloppy weather or chilly; the wigwam would keep it from being seen. We made an extra steering oar, too, because one of the others might get broke, on a snag or something. We fixed up a short forked stick to hang the old lantern on; because we must always light the lantern whenever we see a steamboat coming down stream, to keep from getting run over; but we wouldn't have to light it for up-stream boats unless we see we was in what they call a "crossing;" for the river was pretty high yet, very low banks being still a little under water; so up-bound boats didn't always run the channel, but hunted easy water.

This second night we run between seven and eight hours, with a current that was making over four mile an hour. We catched fish, and talked, and we took a swim now and then to keep off sleepiness. It was kind of solemn, drifting down the big still river, laying on our backs looking up at the stars, and we didn't ever feel like talking loud, and it warn't often that we laughed, only a little kind of a low chuckle. We had mighty good weather, as a general thing, and nothing ever happened to us at all, that night, nor the next, nor the next.

Every night we passed towns, some of them away up on black hillsides, nothing but just a shiny bed of lights, not a house could you see. The fifth night we passed St. Louis, and it was like the whole world lit up. In St. Petersburg they used to say there was twenty or thirty thousand people in St. Louis, but I never believed it till I see that wonderful spread of lights at two o'clock that still night. There warn't a sound there; everybody was asleep.

Every night, now, I used to slip ashore, towards ten o'clock, at some little village, and buy ten or fifteen cents' worth of meal or bacon or other stuff to eat; and sometimes I lifted a chicken that warn't roosting comfortable, and took him along. Pap always said, take a chicken when you get a chance, because if you don't want him yourself you can easy find somebody that does, and a good deed ain't ever forgot. I never see pap when he didn't want the chicken himself, but that is what he used to say, anyway.

Mornings, before daylight, I slipped into corn fields and borrowed a watermelon, or a mushmelon, or a punkin, or some new corn, or things of that kind. Pap always said it warn't no harm to borrow things, if you was meaning to pay them back, sometime; but the widow said it warn't anything but a soft name for stealing, and no decent body would do it. Jim said he reckoned the widow was partly right and pap was partly right; so the best way would be for us to pick out two or three things from the list and say we wouldn't borrow them any more—then he reckoned it wouldn't be no harm to borrow the others. So we talked it over all one night, drifting along down the river, trying to make up our minds whether to drop the watermelons, or the cantelopes, or the mush-melons, or what. But towards daylight we got it all settled satisfactory, and concluded to drop crabapples and p'simmons. We warn't feeling just right, before that, but it was all comfortable now. I was glad the way it come out, too, because crabapples ain't ever good, and the p'simmons wouldn't be ripe for two or three months yet.

We shot a water-fowl, now and then, that got up too early in the morning or didn't go to bed early enough in the evening. Take it all around, we lived pretty high.

The fifth night below St. Louis we had a big storm after midnight, with a power of thunder and lightning, and the rain poured down in a solid sheet. We stayed in the wigwam and let the raft take care of itself. When the lightning glared out we could see a big straight river ahead, and high rocky bluffs on both sides. By-and-by says I, "Hel-*lo*, Jim, looky yonder!" It was a steamboat that had killed herself on a rock. We was drifting straight down for her. The lightning showed her very distinct. She was leaning over, with part of her upper deck above water, and you could see every little chimbly-guy clean and clear, and a chair by the big bell, with an old slouch hat hanging on the back of it wher the flashes come.

Well, it being away in the night, and stormy, and all sc mysterious-like, I felt just the way any other boy would a felt when I see that wreck laying there so mournful and lonesome in the middle of the river. I wanted to get aboard of her and slink around a little, and see what there was there. So I says:

"Le's land on her, Jim."

But Jim was dead against it, at first. He says:

"I doan' want to go fool'n 'long er no wrack. We's doin' blame' well, en we better let blame' well alone, as de good book says. Like as not dey's a watchman on dat wrack."

"Watchman your grandmother," I says; "there ain't nothing to watch but the texas and the pilot-house; and do you reckon anybody's going to resk his life for a texas and a pilot-house such a night as this, when it's likely to break up and wash off down the river any minute?" Jim couldn't say nothing to that, so he didn't try. "And besides," I says, "we might borrow something worth having, out of the captain's state-room. Seegars, *I* bet you—and cost five cents apiece, solid cash. Steamboat captains is always rich, and get sixty dollars a month, and *they* don't care a cent what a thing costs, you know, long as they want it. Stick a candle in your pocket; I can't rest, Jim, till we give her a rummaging. Do you reckon Tom Sawyer would ever go by this thing? Not for pie, he wouldn't. He'd call it an adventure—that's what he'd call it; and he'd land on that wreck if it was his last act. And wouldn't he throw style into it?—wouldn't he spread himself, nor nothing? Why, you'd think it was Christopher C'lumbus discovering Kingdom-Come. I wish Tom Sawyer *was* here."

Jim he grumbled a little, but give in. He said we mustn't talk any more than we could help, and then talk mighty low. The lightning showed us the wreck again, just in time, and we fetched the starboard derrick, and made fast there.

The deck was high out, here. We went sneaking down the slope of it to labboard, in the dark, towards the texas, feeling our way slow with our feet, and spreading our hands out to fend off the guys, for it was so dark we couldn't see no sign of them. Pretty soon we struck the forward end of the skylight, and clumb onto it; and the next step fetched us in front of the captain's door, which was open, and by Jimminy, away down through the texas-hall we see a light! and all in the same second we seem to hear low voices in yonder!

Jim whispered and said he was feeling powerful sick, and told me to come along. I says, all right; and was going to start for the raft; but just then I heard a voice wail out and say:

"Oh, please don't, boys; I swear I won't ever tell!"

Another voice said, pretty loud:

"It's a lie, Jim Turner. You've acted this way before. You always want more'n your share of the truck, and you've always got it, too, because you've swore 't if you didn't you'd tell. But this time you've said it jest one time too many. You're the meanest, treacherousest hound in this country."

By this time Jim was gone for the raft. I was just a-biling with curiosity; and I says to myself, Tom Sawyer wouldn't back out now, and so I won't either; I'm agoing to see what's going on here. So I dropped on my hands and knees, in the little passage, and crept aft in the dark, till there warn't but about one stateroom betwixt me and the cross-hall of the texas. Then, in there I see a man stretched on the floor and tied hand and foot, and two men standing over him, and one of them had a dim lantern in his hand, and the other one had a pistol. This one kept pointing the pistol at the man's head on the floor and saying—

"I'd *like* to! And I orter, too, a mean skunk!"

The man on the floor would shrivel up, and say: "Oh, please don't. Bill—I hain't ever goin' to tell."

And every time he said that, the man with the lantern would laugh, and say:

"'Deed you *ain't*! You never said no truer thing 'n that, you bet you." And once he said: "Hear him beg! and yit if we hadn't got the best of him and tied him, he'd a killed us both. And what *for*? Jist for noth'n. Jist because we stood on our *rights*—that's what for. But I lay you ain't agoin' to threaten nobody any more, Jim Turner. Put *up* that pistol, Bill."

Bill says:

"I don't want to, Jake Packard. I'm for killin' him—and

didn't he kill old Hatfield jist the same way—and don't he deserve it?"

"But I don't *want* him killed, and I've got my reasons for it."

"Bless yo' heart for them words, Jake Packard! I'll never forget you, long's I live!" says the man on the floor, sort o' blubbering.

Packard didn't take no notice of that, but hung up his lantern on a nail, and started towards where I was, there in the dark, and motioned Bill to come. I crawfished as fast as I could, about two yards, but the boat slanted so that I couldn't make very good time; so to keep from getting run over and catched I crawled into a stateroom on the upper side. The man come a-pawing along in the dark, and when Packard got to my stateroom, he says:

"Here—come in here."

And in he come, and Bill after him. But before they got in I was up in the upper berth, cornered, and sorry I come. Then they stood there, with their hands on the ledge of the berth, and talked. I couldn't see them, but I could tell where they was, by the whisky they'd been having. I was glad I didn't drink whisky; but it wouldn't made much difference anyway, because most of the time they couldn't a treed me because I didn't breathe. I was too scared. And besides, a body *couldn't* breathe, and hear such talk. They talked low and earnest. Bill wanted to kill Turner. He says:

"He's said he'll tell, and he will. If we was to give both our shares to him *now*, it wouldn't make no difference after the row, and the way we've served him. Shore's you're born, he'll turn State's evidence; now you hear *me*. I'm for putting him out of his troubles."

"So'm I," says Packard, very quiet.

"Blame it, I'd sorter begun to think you wasn't. Well, then, that's all right. Les' go and do it."

"Hold on a minute; I hain't had my say yit. You listen to me. Shooting's good, but there's quieter ways if the thing's *got* to be done. But what *I* say, is this; it ain't good sense to go court'n around after a halter, if you can git at what you're up to in some way that's jist as good and at the same time don't bring you into no resks. Ain't that so?"

"You bet it is. But how you goin' to manage it this time?"

"Well, my idea is this: we'll rustle around and gether up whatever pickins we've overlooked in the staterooms, and shove for shore and hide the truck. Then we'll wait. Now I say it ain't agoin' to be more 'n two hours befo' this wrack breaks up and washes off down the river. See? He'll be drownded, and won't have nobody to blame for it but his own self. I reckon that's a considerble sight better'n killin' of him. I'm unfavorable to killin' a man as long as you can git around it; it ain't good sense, it ain't good morals. Ain't I right?"

"Yes—I reck'n you are. But s'pose she *don't* break up and wash off?"

"Well, we can wait the two hours, anyway, and see, can't we?"

"All right, then; come along."

So they started, and I lit out, all in a cold sweat, and scrambled forward. It was dark as pitch there; but I said in a kind of a coarse whisper, "Jim!" and he answered up, right at my elbow, with a sort of a moan, and I says:

"Quick, Jim, it ain't no time for fooling around and moaning; there's a gang of murderers in yonder, and if we don't hunt up their boat and set her drifting down the river so these fellows can't get away from the wreck, there's one of 'em going to be in a bad fix. But if we find their boat we can put *all* of 'em in a bad fix—for the Sheriff 'll get 'em. Quick—hurry! I'll hunt the labboard side, you hunt the stabboard. You start at the raft, and——"

"Oh, my lordy, lordy! *Raf'*? Dey ain' no raf' no mo', she done broke loose en gone!—'en here we is!"

XIII

WELL, I catched my breath and most fainted. Shut up on a wreck with such a gang as that! But it warn't no time to be sentimentering. We'd *got* to find that boat, now—had to have it for ourselves. So we went a-quaking and shaking down the stabboard side, and slow work it was, too—seemed a week before we got to the stern. No sign of a boat. Jim said he didn't believe he could go any further—so scared he hadn't hardly any strength left, he said. But I said come on, if we get left on this wreck, we are in a fix, sure. So on we prowled, again. We struck for the stern of the texas, and found it, and then scrabbled along forwards on the skylight, hanging on from shutter to shutter, for the edge of the skylight was in the water. When we got pretty close to the cross-hall door, there was the skiff, sure enough! I could just barely see her. I felt ever so thankful. In another second I would a been aboard of her; but just then the door opened. One of the men stuck his head out only about a couple of foot from me, and I thought I was gone; but he jerked it in again, and says:

"Heave that blame lantern out o' sight, Bill!"

He flung a bag of something into the boat, and then got in himself, and set down. It was Packard. Then Bill *he* come out and got in. Packard says, in a low voice:

"All ready—shove off!"

I couldn't hardly hang onto the shutters, I was so weak. But Bill says:

"Hold on—'d you go through him?"

"No. Didn't you?"

"No. So he's got his share o' the cash, yet."

"Well, then, come along—no use to take truck and leave money."

"Say—won't he suspicion what we're up to?"

"Maybe he won't. But we got to have it anyway. Come along."

So they got out and went in.

The door slammed to, because it was on the careened side; and in a half second I was in the boat, and Jim come a tum-

oling after me. I out with my knife and cut the rope, and
away we went!

We didn't touch an oar, and we didn't speak nor whisper,
nor hardly even breathe. We went gliding swift along, dead
silent, past the tip of the paddle-box, and past the stern; then
in a second or two more we was a hundred yards below the
wreck, and the darkness soaked her up, every last sign of her,
and we was safe, and knowed it.

When we was three or four hundred yards down stream,
we see the lantern show like a little spark at the texas door,
for a second, and we knowed by that that the rascals had
missed their boat, and was beginning to understand that they
was in just as much trouble, now, as Jim Turner was.

Then Jim manned the oars, and we took out after our raft.
Now was the first time that I begun to worry about the
men—I reckon I hadn't had time to before. I begun to think
how dreadful it was, even for murderers, to be in such a fix.
I says to myself, there ain't no telling but I might come to be
a murderer myself, yet, and then how would *I* like it? So says
I to Jim:

"The first light we see, we'll land a hundred yards below it
or above it, in a place where it's a good hiding-place for you
and the skiff, and then I'll go and fix up some kind of a yarn,
and get somebody to go for that gang and get them out of
their scrape, so they can be hung when their time comes."

But that idea was a failure; for pretty soon it begun to
storm again, and this time worse than ever. The rain poured
down, and never a light showed; everybody in bed, I reckon.
We boomed along down the river, watching for lights and
watching for our raft. After a long time the rain let up, but
the clouds staid, and the lightning kept whimpering, and by-
and-by a flash showed us a black thing ahead, floating, and
we made for it.

It was the raft, and mighty glad was we to get aboard of it
again. We seen a light, now, away down to the right, on
shore. So I said I would go for it. The skiff was half full of
plunder which that gang had stole, there on the wreck. We
hustled it onto the raft in a pile, and I told Jim to float along
down, and show a light when he judged he had gone about
two mile, and keep it burning till I come; then I manned my

oars and shoved for the light. As I got down towards it, three
or four more showed—up on a hillside. It was a village. I
closed in above the shore-light, and laid on my oars and
floated. As I went by, I see it was a lantern hanging on the
jackstaff of a double-hull ferry-boat. I skimmed around for
the watchman, a-wondering whereabouts he slept: and by-
and-by I found him roosting on the bitts, forward, with his
head down between his knees. I give his shoulder two or
three little shoves, and begun to cry.

He stirred up, in a kind of a startlish way; but when he see it
was only me, he took a good gap and stretch, and then he says:
"Hello, what's up? Don't cry, bub. What's the trouble?"
I says:
"Pap, and mam, and sis, and——"
Then I broke down. He says:
"Oh, dang it, now, *don't* take on so, we all has to have our
troubles and this'n 'll come out all right. What's the matter
with 'em?"
"They're—they're—are you the watchman of the boat?"
"Yes," he says, kind of pretty-well-satisfied like. "'I'm the
captain and the owner, and the mate, and the pilot, and
watchman, and head deck-hand; and sometimes I'm the
freight and passengers. I ain't as rich as old Jim Hornback,
and I can't be so blame' generous and good to Tom, Dick
and Harry as what he is, and slam around money the way he
does; but I've told him a many a time 't I wouldn't trade
places with him; for, says I, a sailor's life's the life for me, and
I'm derned if *I'd* live two mile out o' town, where there ain't
nothing ever goin' on, not for all his spondulicks and as much
more on top of it. Says I——"
I broke in and says:
"They're in an awful peck of trouble, and——"
"*Who* is?"
"Why, pap, and mam, and sis, and Miss Hooker; and if
you'd take your ferry-boat and go up there——"
"Up where? Where are they?"
"On the wreck."
"What wreck?"
"Why, there ain't but one."
"What, you don't mean the *Walter Scott*?"

"Yes."

"Good land! what are they doin' *there*, for gracious sakes?"

"Well, they didn't go there a-purpose."

"I bet they didn't! Why, great goodness, there ain't no chance for 'em if they don't git off mighty quick! Why, how in the nation did they ever git into such a scrape?"

"Easy enough. Miss Hooker was a-visiting, up there to the town——"

"Yes, Booth's Landing—go on."

"She was a-visiting, there at Booth's Landing, and just in the edge of the evening she started over with her nigger woman in the horse-ferry, to stay all night at her friend's house, Miss What-you-may-call-her, I disremember her name, and they lost their steering-oar, and swung around and went a-floating down, stern-first, about two mile, and saddle-baggsed on the wreck, and the ferry man and the nigger woman and the horses was all lost, but Miss Hooker she made a grab and got aboard the wreck. Well, about an hour after dark, we come along down in our trading-scow, and it was so dark we didn't notice the wreck till we was right on it; and so *we* saddle-baggsed; but all of us was saved but Bill Whipple—and oh, he *was* the best cretur!—I most wish't it had been me, I do."

"My George! It's the beatenest thing I ever struck. And *then* what did you all do?"

"Well, we hollered and took on, but it's so wide there, we couldn't make nobody hear. So pap said somebody got to get ashore and get help somehow. I was the only one that could swim, so I made a dash for it, and Miss Hooker she said if I didn't strike help sooner, come here and hunt up her uncle, and he'd fix the thing. I made the land about a mile below, and been fooling along ever since, trying to get people to do something, but they said, 'What, in such a night and such a current? there ain't no sense in it; go for the steam-ferry.' Now if you'll go, and——"

"By Jackson, I'd *like* to, and blame it I don't know but I will; but who in the dingnation's agoin' to *pay* for it? Do you reckon your pap——"

"Why *that's* all right. Miss Hooker she told me, *particular*, that her uncle Hornback——"

"Great guns! is *he* her uncle? Looky here, you break for that light over yonder-way, and turn out west when you git there, and about a quarter of a mile out you'll come to the tavern; tell 'em to dart you out to Jim Hornback's and he'll foot the bill. And don't you fool around any, because he'll want to know the news. Tell him I'll have his niece all safe before he can get to town. Hump yourself, now; I'm agoing up around the corner here, to roust out my engineer."

I struck for the light, but as soon as he turned the corner I went back and got into my skiff and bailed her out and then pulled up shore in the easy water about six hundred yards, and tucked myself in among some woodboats; for I couldn't rest easy till I could see the ferry-boat start. But take it all around, I was feeling ruther comfortable on accounts of taking all this trouble for that gang, for not many would a done it. I wished the widow knowed about it. I judged she would be proud of me for helping these rapscallions, because rapscallions and dead beats is the kind the widow and good people takes the most interest in.

Well, before long, here comes the wreck, dim and dusky, sliding along down! A kind of cold shiver went through me, and then I struck out for her. She was very deep, and I see in a minute there warn't much chance for anybody being alive in her. I pulled all around her and hollered a little, but there wasn't any answer; all dead still. I felt a little bit heavy-hearted about the gang, but not much, for I reckoned if they could stand it, I could.

Then here comes the ferry-boat; so I shoved for the middle of the river on a long down-stream slant; and when I judged I was out of eye-reach, I laid on my oars, and looked back and see her go and smell around the wreck for Miss Hooker's remainders, because the captain would know her uncle Hornback would want them; and then pretty soon the ferry-boat give it up and went for shore, and I laid into my work and went a-booming down the river.

It did seem a powerful long time before Jim's light showed up; and when it did show, it looked like it was a thousand mile off. By the time I got there the sky was beginning to get a little gray in the east; so we struck for an island, and hid the raft, and sunk the skiff, and turned in and slept like dead people.

XIV

B Y-AND-BY, when we got up, we turned over the truck the gang had stole off of the wreck, and found boots, and blankets, and clothes, and all sorts of other things, and a lot of books, and a spyglass, and three boxes of seegars. We hadn't ever been this rich before, in neither of our lives. The seegars was prime. We laid off all the afternoon in the woods talking, and me reading the books, and having a general good time. I told Jim all about what happened inside the wreck, and at the ferry-boat; and I said these kinds of things was adventures; but he said he didn't want no more adventures. He said that when I went in the texas and he crawled back to get on the raft and found her gone, he nearly died; because he judged it was all up with *him*, anyway it could be fixed; for if he didn't get saved he would get drownded; and if he did get saved, whoever saved him would send him back home so as to get the reward, and then Miss Watson would sell him South, sure. Well, he was right; he was most always right; he had an uncommon level head, for a nigger.

I read considerable to Jim about kings, and dukes, and earls, and such, and how gaudy they dressed, and how much style they put on, and called each other your majesty, and your grace, and your lordship, and so on, 'stead of mister; and Jim's eyes bugged out, and he was interested. He says:

"I didn' know dey was so many un um. I hain't hearn 'bout none un um, skasely, but ole King Sollermun, onless you counts dem kings dat's in a pack er k'yards. How much do a king git?"

"Get?" I says; "why, they get a thousand dollars a month if they want it; they can have just as much as they want; everything belongs to them."

"*Ain'* dat gay? En what dey got to do, Huck?"

"*They* don't do nothing! Why how you talk. They just set around."

"No—is dat so?"

"Of course it is. They just set around. Except maybe when there's a war; then they go to the war. But other times they

just lazy around; or go hawking—just hawking and sp—
Sh!—d' you hear a noise?"

We skipped out and looked; but it warn't nothing but the
flutter of a steamboat's wheel, away down coming around the
point; so we come back.

"Yes," says I, "and other times, when things is dull, they
fuss with the parlyment; and if everybody don't go just so he
whacks their heads off. But mostly they hang round the
harem."

"Roun' de which?"

"Harem."

"What's de harem?"

"The place where he keep his wives. Don't you know about
the harem? Solomon had one; he had about a million wives."

"Why, yes, dat's so; I—I'd done forgot it. A harem's a
bo'd'n-house, I reck'n. Mos' likely dey has rackety times in de
nussery. En I reck'n de wives quarrels considable; en dat
'crease de racket. Yit dey say Sollermun de wises' man dat
ever live'. I doan' take no stock in dat. Bekase why: would a
wise man want to live in de mids' er sich a blimblammin' all
de time? No—'deed he wouldn't. A wise man 'ud take en
buil' a biler-factry; en den he could shet *down* de biler-factry
when he want to res'."

"Well, but he *was* the wisest man, anyway; because the
widow she told me so, her own self."

"I doan k'yer what de widder say, he *warn't* no wise man,
nuther. He had some er de dad-fetchedes' ways I ever see.
Does you know 'bout dat chile dat he 'uz gwyne to chop in
two?"

"Yes, the widow told me all about it."

"*Well*, den! Warn' dat de beatenes' notion in de worl'? You
jes' take en look at it a minute. Dah's de stump, dah—dat's
one er de women; heah's you—dat's de yuther one; I's Sollermun; en dish-yer dollar bill's de chile. Bofe un you claims
it. What does I do? Does I shin aroun' mongs' de neighbors
en fine out which un you de bill *do* b'long to, en han' it over
to de right one, all safe en soun', de way dat anybody dat had
any gumption would? No—I take en whack de bill in *two*, en
give half un it to you, en de yuther half to de yuther woman.

Dat's de way Sollermun was gwyne to do wid de chile. Now I want to ast you: what's de use er dat half a bill?—can't buy noth'n wid it. En what use is a half a chile? I would'n give a dern for a million un um."

"But hang it, Jim, you've clean missed the point—blame it, you've missed it a thousand mile."

"Who? Me? Go 'long. Doan' talk to *me* 'bout yo' pints. I reck'n I knows sense when I sees it; en dey ain' no sense in sich doin's as dat. De 'spute warn't 'bout a half a chile, de 'spute was 'bout a whole chile; en de man dat think he kin settle a 'spute 'bout a whole chile wid a half a chile, doan' know enough to come in out'n de rain. Doan' talk to me 'bout Sollermun, Huck, I knows him by de back."

"But I tell you you don't get the point."

"Blame de pint! I reck'n I knows what I knows. En mine you, de *real* pint is down furder—it's down deeper. It lays in de way Sollermun was raised. You take a man dat's got on'y one er two chillen; is dat man gwyne to be waseful o' chillen? No, he ain't; he can't 'ford it. *He* know how to value 'em. But you take a man dat's got 'bout five million chillen runnin' roun' de house, en it's diffunt. *He* as soon chop a chile in two as a cat. Dey's plenty mo'. A chile er two, mo' er less, warn't no consekens to Sollermun, dad fetch him!"

I never see such a nigger. If he got a notion in his head once, there warn't no getting it out again. He was the most down on Solomon of any nigger I ever see. So I went to talking about other kings, and let Solomon slide. I told about Louis Sixteenth that got his head cut off in France long time ago; and about his little boy the dolphin, that would a been a king, but they took and shut him up in jail, and some say he died there.

"Po' little chap."

"But some says he got out and got away, and come to America."

"Dat's good! But he'll be pooty lonesome—dey ain' no kings here, is dey, Huck?"

"No."

"Den he cain't git no situation. What he gwyne to do?"

"Well, I don't know. Some of them gets on the police, and some of them learns people how to talk French."

"Why, Huck, doan' de French people talk de same way we does?"

"*No*, Jim; you couldn't understand a word they said—not a single word."

"Well, now, I be ding-busted! How do dat come?"

"*I* don't know; but it's so. I got some of their jabber out of a book. Spose a man was to come to you and say *Polly-voo-franzy*—what would you think?"

"I wouldn' think nuff'n; I'd take en bust him over de head. Dat is, if he warn't white. I wouldn't 'low no nigger to call me dat."

"Shucks, it ain't calling you anything. It's only saying do you know how to talk French."

"Well, den, why couldn't he *say* it?"

"Why, he *is* a-saying it. That's a Frenchman's *way* of saying it."

"Well, it's a blame' ridicklous way, en I doan' want to hear no mo' 'bout it. Dey ain' no sense in it."

"Looky here, Jim; does a cat talk like we do?"

"No, a cat don't."

"Well, does a cow?"

"No, a cow don't, nuther."

"Does a cat talk like a cow, or a cow talk like a cat?"

"No, dey don't."

"It's natural and right for 'em to talk different from each other, ain't it?"

" 'Course."

"And ain't it natural and right for a cat and a cow to talk different from *us*?"

"Why, mos' sholy it is."

"Well, then, why ain't it natural and right for a *Frenchman* to talk different from us? You answer me that."

"Is a cat a man, Huck?"

"No."

"Well, den, dey ain' no sense in a cat talkin' like a man. Is a cow a man?—er is a cow a cat?"

"No, she ain't either of them."

"Well, den, she ain' got no business to talk like either one er the yuther of 'em. Is a Frenchman a man?"

"Yes."

"*Well*, den! Dad blame it, why doan' he *talk* like a man? You answer me *dat!*"

I see it warn't no use wasting words—you can't learn a nigger to argue. So I quit.

XV

WE JUDGED that three nights more would fetch us to Cairo, at the bottom of Illinois, where the Ohio River comes in, and that was what we was after. We would sell the raft and get on a steamboat and go way up the Ohio amongst the free States, and then be out of trouble.

Well, the second night a fog begun to come on, and we made for a tow-head to tie to, for it wouldn't do to try to run in fog; but when I paddled ahead in the canoe, with the line, to make fast, there warn't anything but little saplings to tie to. I passed the line around one of them right on the edge of the cut bank, but there was a stiff current, and the raft come booming down so lively she tore it out by the roots and away she went. I see the fog closing down, and it made me so sick and scared I couldn't budge for most a half a minute it seemed to me—and then there warn't no raft in sight; you couldn't see twenty yards. I jumped into the canoe and run back to the stern and grabbed the paddle and set her back a stroke. But she didn't come. I was in such a hurry I hadn't untied her. I got up and tried to untie her, but I was so excited my hands shook so I couldn't hardly do anything with them.

As soon as I got started I took out after the raft, hot and heavy, right down the tow-head. That was all right as far as it went, but the tow-head warn't sixty yards long, and the minute I flew by the foot of it I shot out into the solid white fog, and hadn't no more idea which way I was going than a dead man.

Thinks I, it won't do to paddle; first I know I'll run into the bank or a tow-head or something; I got to set still and float, and yet it's mighty fidgety business to have to hold your hands still at such a time. I whooped and listened. Away down there, somewheres, I hears a small whoop, and up comes my spirits. I went tearing after it, listening sharp to hear it again. The next time it come, I see I warn't heading for it but heading away to the right of it. And the next time, I was heading away to the left of it—and not gaining on it

much, either, for I was flying around, this way and that and
'tother, but it was going straight ahead all the time.

I did wish the fool would think to beat a tin pan, and beat
it all the time, but he never did, and it was the still places
between the whoops that was making the trouble for me.
Well, I fought along, and directly I hears the whoop *behind*
me. I was tangled good, now. That was somebody else's
whoop, or else I was turned around.

I throwed the paddle down. I heard the whoop again; it
was behind me yet, but in a different place; it kept coming,
and kept changing its place, and I kept answering, till by-and-
by it was in front of me again and I knowed the current had
swung the canoe's head down stream and I was all right, if
that was Jim and not some other raftsman hollering. I
couldn't tell nothing about voices in a fog, for nothing don't
look natural nor sound natural in a fog.

The whooping went on, and in about a minute I come a
booming down on a cut bank with smoky ghosts of big trees
on it, and the current throwed me off to the left and shot by,
amongst a lot of snags that fairly roared, the current was tearing by them so swift.

In another second or two it was solid white and still again.
I set perfectly still, then, listening to my heart thump, and I
reckon I didn't draw a breath while it thumped a hundred.

I just give up, then. I knowed what the matter was. That
cut bank was an island, and Jim had gone down 'tother side
of it. It warn't no tow-head, that you could float by in ten
minutes. It had the big timber of a regular island; it might be
five or six mile long and more than a half a mile wide.

I kept quiet, with my ears cocked, about fifteen minutes, I
reckon. I was floating along, of course, four or five mile an
hour; but you don't ever think of that. No, you *feel* like you
are laying dead still on the water; and if a little glimpse of a
snag slips by, you don't think to yourself how fast *you're*
going, but you catch your breath and think, my! how that
snag's tearing along. If you think it ain't dismal and lonesome
out in a fog that way, by yourself, in the night, you try it
once—you'll see.

Next, for about a half an hour, I whoops now and then; at
last I hears the answer a long ways off, and tries to follow it,

but I couldn't do it, and directly I judged I'd got into a nest of tow-heads, for I had little dim glimpses of them on both sides of me, sometimes just a narrow channel between; and some that I couldn't see, I knowed was there, because I'd hear the wash of the current against the old dead brush and trash that hung over the banks. Well, I warn't long losing the whoops, down amongst the tow-heads; and I only tried to chase them a little while, anyway, because it was worse than chasing a Jack-o-lantern. You never knowed a sound dodge around so, and swap places so quick and so much.

I had to claw away from the bank pretty lively, four or five times, to keep from knocking the islands out of the river; and so I judged the raft must be butting into the bank every now and then, or else it would get further ahead and clear out of hearing—it was floating a little faster than what I was.

Well, I seemed to be in the open river again, by-and-by, but I couldn't hear no sign of a whoop nowheres. I reckoned Jim had fetched up on a snag, maybe, and it was all up with him. I was good and tired, so I laid down in the canoe and said I wouldn't bother no more. I didn't want to go to sleep, of course; but I was so sleepy I couldn't help it; so I thought I would take just one little cat-nap.

But I reckon it was more than a cat-nap, for when I waked up the stars was shining bright, the fog was all gone, and I was spinning down a big bend stern first. First I didn't know where I was; I thought I was dreaming; and when things begun to come back to me, they seemed to come up dim out of last week.

It was a monstrous big river here, with the tallest and the thickest kind of timber on both banks; just a solid wall, as well as I could see, by the stars. I looked away down stream, and seen a black speck on the water. I took out after it; but when I got to it it warn't nothing but a couple of saw-logs made fast together. Then I see another speck, and chased that; then another, and this time I was right. It was the raft.

When I got to it Jim was setting there with his head down between his knees, asleep, with his right arm hanging over the steering oar. The other oar was smashed off, and the raft was littered up with leaves and branches and dirt. So she'd had a rough time.

I made fast and laid down under Jim's nose on the raft, and begun to gap, and stretch my fists out against Jim, and says:

"Hello, Jim, have I been asleep? Why didn't you stir me up?"

"Goodness gracious, is dat you, Huck? En you ain' dead— you ain' drownded—you's back agin? It's too good for true, honey, it's too good for true. Lemme look at you, chile, lemme feel o' you. No, you ain' dead! you's back agin, 'live en soun', jis de same ole Huck—de same ole Huck, thanks to goodness!"

"What's the matter with you, Jim? You been a drinking?"

"Drinkin'? Has I ben a drinkin'? Has I had a chance to be a drinkin'?"

"Well, then, what makes you talk so wild?"

"How does I talk wild?"

"*How?* why, hain't you been talking about my coming back, and all that stuff, as if I'd been gone away?"

"Huck—Huck Finn, you look me in de eye; look me in de eye. *Hain't* you ben gone away?"

"Gone away? Why, what in the nation do you mean? *I* hain't been gone anywheres. Where would I go to?"

"Well, looky here, boss, dey's sumf'n wrong, dey is. Is I *me*, or who *is* I? Is I heah, or whah *is* I? Now dat's what I wants to know?"

"Well, I think you're here, plain enough, but I think you're a tangle-headed old fool, Jim."

"I is, is I? Well you answer me dis. Didn't you tote out de line in de canoe, fer to make fas' to de tow-head?"

"No, I didn't. What tow-head? I hain't seen no tow-head."

"You hain't seen no tow-head? Looky here—didn't de line pull loose en de raf' go a hummin' down de river, en leave you en de canoe behine in de fog?"

"What fog?"

"Why *de* fog. De fog dat's ben aroun' all night. En didn't you whoop, en didn't I whoop, tell we got mix' up in de islands en one un us got los' en 'tother one was jis' as good

as los', 'kase he didn' know whah he wuz? En didn't I bust up
agin a lot er dem islands en have a turrible time en mos' git
drownded? Now ain' dat so, boss—ain't it so? You answer
me dat."

"Well, this is too many for me, Jim. I hain't seen no fog,
nor no islands, nor no troubles, nor nothing. I been setting
here talking with you all night till you went to sleep about
ten minutes ago, and I reckon I done the same. You couldn't
a got drunk in that time, so of course you've been dreaming."

"Dad fetch it, how is I gwyne to dream all dat in ten
minutes?"

"Well, hang it all, you did dream it, because there didn't
any of it happen."

"But Huck, it's all jis' as plain to me as——"

"It don't make no difference how plain it is, there ain't
nothing in it. I know, because I've been here all the time."

Jim didn't say nothing for about five minutes, but set there
studying over it. Then he says:

"Well, den, I reck'n I did dream it, Huck; but dog my cats
ef it ain't de powerfullest dream I ever see. En I hain't ever
had no dream b'fo' dat's tired me like dis one."

"Oh, well, that's all right, because a dream does tire a body
like everything, sometimes. But this one was a staving
dream—tell me all about it, Jim."

So Jim went to work and told me the whole thing right
through, just as it happened, only he painted it up considerable. Then he said he must start in and "'terpret" it, because
it was sent for a warning. He said the first tow-head stood
for a man that would try to do us some good, but the current
was another man that would get us away from him. The
whoops was warnings that would come to us every now and
then, and if we didn't try hard to make out to understand
them they'd just take us into bad luck, 'stead of keeping us
out of it. The lot of tow-heads was troubles we was going to
get into with quarrelsome people and all kinds of mean folks,
but if we minded our business and didn't talk back and aggravate them, we would pull through and get out of the fog
and into the big clear river, which was the free States, and
wouldn't have no more trouble.

It had clouded up pretty dark just after I got onto the raft, but it was clearing up again, now.

"Oh, well, that's all interpreted well enough, as far as it goes, Jim," I says; "but what does *these* things stand for?"

It was the leaves and rubbish on the raft, and the smashed oar. You could see them first rate, now.

Jim looked at the trash, and then looked at me, and back at the trash again. He had got the dream fixed so strong in his head that he couldn't seem to shake it loose and get the facts back into its place again, right away. But when he did get the thing straightened around, he looked at me steady, without ever smiling, and says:

"What do dey stan' for? I's gwyne to tell you. When I got all wore out wid work, en wid de callin' for you, en went to sleep, my heart wuz mos' broke bekase you wuz los', en I didn' k'yer no mo' what become er me en de raf'. En when I wake up en fine you back agin', all safe en soun', de tears come en I could a got down on my knees en kiss' yo' foot I's so thankful. En all you wuz thinkin 'bout wuz how you could make a fool uv ole Jim wid a lie. Dat truck dah is *trash*; en trash is what people is dat puts dirt on de head er dey fren's en makes 'em ashamed."

Then he got up slow, and walked to the wigwam, and went in there, without saying anything but that. But that was enough. It made me feel so mean I could almost kissed *his* foot to get him to take it back.

It was fifteen minutes before I could work myself up to go and humble myself to a nigger—but I done it, and I warn't ever sorry for it afterwards, neither. I didn't do him no more mean tricks, and I wouldn't done that one if I'd a knowed it would make him feel that way.

XVI

W<small>E SLEPT</small> most all day, and started out at night, a little ways behind a monstrous long raft that was as long going by as a procession. She had four long sweeps at each end, so we judged she carried as many as thirty men, likely. She had five big wigwams aboard, wide apart, and an open camp fire in the middle, and a tall flag-pole at each end. There was a power of style about her. It *amounted* to something being a raftsman on such a craft as that.

We went drifting down into a big bend, and the night clouded up and got hot. The river was very wide, and was walled with solid timber on both sides; you couldn't see a break in it hardly ever, or a light. We talked about Cairo, and wondered whether we would know it when we got to it. I said likely we wouldn't, because I had heard say there warn't but about a dozen houses there, and if they didn't happen to have them lit up, how was we going to know we was passing a town? Jim said if the two big rivers joined together there, that would show. But I said maybe we might think we was passing the foot of an island and coming into the same old river again. That disturbed Jim—and me too. So the question was, what to do? I said, paddle ashore the first time a light showed, and tell them pap was behind, coming along with a trading-scow, and was a green hand at the business, and wanted to know how far it was to Cairo. Jim thought it was a good idea, so we took a smoke on it and waited.

There warn't nothing to do, now, but to look out sharp for the town, and not pass it without seeing it. He said he'd be mighty sure to see it, because he'd be a free man the minute he seen it, but if he missed it he'd be in the slave country again and no more show for freedom. Every little while he jumps up and says:

"Dah she is!"

But it warn't. It was Jack-o-lanterns, or lightning-bugs; so he set down again, and went to watching, same as before. Jim said it made him all over trembly and feverish to be so close to freedom. Well, I can tell you it made me all over trembly

nd feverish, too, to hear him, because I begun to get it
hrough my head that he *was* most free—and who was to
lame for it? Why, *me*. I couldn't get that out of my con-
cience, no how nor no way. It got to troubling me so I
ouldn't rest; I couldn't stay still in one place. It hadn't ever
ome home to me before, what this thing was that I was
oing. But now it did; and it staid with me, and scorched me
ore and more. I tried to make out to myself that *I* warn't
o blame, because *I* didn't run Jim off from his rightful
wner; but it warn't no use, conscience up and says, every
ime, "But you knowed he was running for his freedom, and
ou could a paddled ashore and told somebody." That was
o—I couldn't get around that, noway. That was where it
inched. Conscience says to me, "What had poor Miss Wat-
on done to you, that you could see her nigger go off right
nder your eyes and never say one single word? What did
hat poor old woman do to you, that you could treat her so
ean? Why, she tried to learn you your book, she tried to
arn you your manners, she tried to be good to you every
ay she knowed how. *That's* what she done."

I got to feeling so mean and so miserable I most wished I
was dead. I fidgeted up and down the raft, abusing myself to
myself, and Jim was fidgeting up and down past me. We nei-
her of us could keep still. Every time he danced around and
ays, "Dah's Cairo!" it went through me like a shot, and I
hought if it *was* Cairo I reckoned I would die of miserable-
ess.

Jim talked out loud all the time while I was talking to my-
elf. He was saying how the first thing he would do when he
ot to a free State he would go to saving up money and never
pend a single cent, and when he got enough he would buy
is wife, which was owned on a farm close to where Miss
Vatson lived; and then they would both work to buy the two
hildren, and if their master wouldn't sell them, they'd get an
b'litionist to go and steal them.

It most froze me to hear such talk. He wouldn't ever dared
o talk such talk in his life before. Just see what a difference
t made in him the minute he judged he was about free. It
vas according to the old saying, "give a nigger an inch and
e'll take an ell." Thinks I, this is what comes of my not

thinking. Here was this nigger which I had as good as helpe
to run away, coming right out flat-footed and saying h
would steal his children—children that belonged to a man
didn't even know; a man that hadn't ever done me no harm

I was sorry to hear Jim say that, it was such a lowering c
him. My conscience got to stirring me up hotter than eve
until at last I says to it, "Let up on me—it ain't too late
yet—I'll paddle ashore at the first light, and tell." I felt eas
and happy, and light as a feather, right off. All my trouble
was gone. I went to looking out sharp for a light, and sort c
singing to myself. By-and-by one showed. Jim sings out:

"We's safe, Huck, we's safe! Jump up and crack yo' heel
dat's de good ole Cairo at las', I jis knows it!"

I says:

"I'll take the canoe and go see, Jim. It mightn't be, yo
know."

He jumped and got the canoe ready, and put his old coa
in the bottom for me to set on, and give me the paddle; an
as I shoved off, he says:

"Pooty soon I'll be a-shout'n for joy, en I'll say, it's all o
accounts o' Huck; I's a free man, en I couldn't ever ben fre
ef it hadn' ben for Huck; Huck done it. Jim won't ever forg
you, Huck; you's de bes' fren' Jim's ever had; en you's d
only fren' ole Jim's got now."

I was paddling off, all in a sweat to tell on him; but whe
he says this, it seemed to kind of take the tuck all out of me
I went along slow then, and I warn't right down certai
whether I was glad I started or whether I warn't. When I wa
fifty yards off, Jim says:

"Dah you goes, de ole true Huck; de on'y white genlma
dat ever kep' his promise to ole Jim."

Well, I just felt sick. But I says, I *got* to do it—I can't ge
out of it. Right then, along comes a skiff with two men in i
with guns, and they stopped and I stopped. One of ther
says:

"What's that, yonder?"

"A piece of a raft," I says.

"Do you belong on it?"

"Yes, sir."

"Any men on it?"

"Only one, sir."

"Well, there's five niggers run off to-night, up yonder above the head of the bend. Is your man white or black?"

I didn't answer up prompt. I tried to, but the words wouldn't come. I tried, for a second or two, to brace up and out with it, but I warn't man enough—hadn't the spunk of a rabbit. I see I was weakening; so I just give up trying, and up and says—

"He's white."

"I reckon we'll go and see for ourselves."

"I wish you would," says I, "because it's pap that's there, and maybe you'd help me tow the raft ashore where the light is. He's sick—and so is mam and Mary Ann."

"Oh, the devil! we're in a hurry, boy. But I s'pose we've got to. Come—buckle to your paddle, and let's get along."

I buckled to my paddle and they laid to their oars. When we had made a stroke or two, I says:

"Pap'll be mighty much obleeged to you, I can tell you. Everybody goes away when I want them to help me tow the raft ashore, and I can't do it by myself."

"Well, that's infernal mean. Odd, too. Say, boy, what's the matter with your father?"

"It's the—a—the—well, it ain't anything, much."

They stopped pulling. It warn't but a mighty little ways to the raft, now. One says:

"Boy, that's a lie. What *is* the matter with your pap? Answer up square, now, and it'll be the better for you."

"I will, sir, I will, honest—but don't leave us, please. It's the—the—gentlemen, if you'll only pull ahead, and let me heave you the head-line, you won't have to come a-near the raft—please do."

"Set her back, John, set her back!" says one. They backed water. "Keep away, boy—keep to looard. Confound it, I just expect the wind has blowed it to us. Your pap's got the small-pox, and you know it precious well. Why didn't you come out and say so? Do you want to spread it all over?"

"Well," says I, a-blubbering, "I've told everybody before, and then they just went away and left us."

"Poor devil, there's something in that. We are right down
sorry for you, but we—well, hang it, we don't want the
small-pox, you see. Look here, I'll tell you what to do. Don't
you try to land by yourself, or you'll smash everything to
pieces. You float along down about twenty miles and you'l
come to a town on the left-hand side of the river. It will be
long after sun-up, then, and when you ask for help, you tel
them your folks are all down with chills and fever. Don't be
a fool again, and let people guess what is the matter. Now
we're trying to do you a kindness; so you just put twenty
miles between us, that's a good boy. It wouldn't do any good
to land yonder where the light is—it's only a wood-yard
Say—I reckon your father's poor, and I'm bound to say he's
in pretty hard luck. Here—I'll put a twenty dollar gold piece
on this board, and you get it when it floats by. I feel mighty
mean to leave you, but my kingdom! it won't do to fool with
small-pox, don't you see?"

"Hold on, Parker," says the other man, "here's a twenty to
put on the board for me. Good-bye, boy, you do as Mr. Parker told you, and you'll be all right."

"That's so, my boy—good-bye, good-bye. If you see any
runaway niggers, you get help and nab them, and you car
make some money by it."

"Good-bye, sir," says I, "I won't let no runaway niggers get
by me if I can help it."

They went off, and I got aboard the raft, feeling bad and
low, because I knowed very well I had done wrong, and I see
it warn't no use for me to try to learn to do right; a body
that don't get *started* right when he's little, ain't got no
show—when the pinch comes there ain't nothing to back
him up and keep him to his work, and so he gets beat. Then
I thought a minute, and says to myself, hold on,—s'pose
you'd a done right and give Jim up; would you felt better
than what you do now? No, says I, I'd feel bad—I'd feel just
the same way I do now. Well, then, says I, what's the use you
learning to do right, when it's troublesome to do right and
ain't no trouble to do wrong, and the wages is just the same?
I was stuck. I couldn't answer that. So I reckoned I wouldn't
bother no more about it, but after this always do whichever
come handiest at the time.

I went into the wigwam; Jim warn't there. I looked all around; he warn't anywhere. I says:

"Jim!"

"Here I is, Huck. Is dey out o' sight yit? Don't talk loud."

He was in the river, under the stern oar, with just his nose out. I told him they was out of sight, so he come aboard. He says:

"I was a-listenin' to all de talk, en I slips into de river en was gwyne to shove for sho' if dey come aboard. Den I was gwyne to swim to de raf' agin when dey was gone. But lawsy, how you did fool 'em, Huck! Dat *wuz* de smartes' dodge! I tell you, chile, I 'speck it save' ole Jim—ole Jim ain't gwyne to forgit you for dat, honey."

Then we talked about the money. It was a pretty good raise, twenty dollars apiece. Jim said we could take deck passage on a steamboat now, and the money would last us as far as we wanted to go in the free States. He said twenty mile more warn't far for the raft to go, but he wished we was already there.

Towards daybreak we tied up, and Jim was mighty particular about hiding the raft good. Then he worked all day fixing things in bundles, and getting all ready to quit rafting.

That night about ten we hove in sight of the lights of a town away down in a left-hand bend.

I went off in the canoe, to ask about it. Pretty soon I found a man out in the river with a skiff, setting a trot-line. I ranged up and says:

"Mister, is that town Cairo?"

"Cairo? no. You must be a blame' fool."

"What town is it, mister?"

"If you want to know, go and find out. If you stay here botherin' around me for about a half a minute longer, you'll get something you won't want."

I paddled to the raft. Jim was awful disappointed, but I said never mind, Cairo would be the next place, I reckoned.

We passed another town before daylight, and I was going out again; but it was high ground, so I didn't go. No high ground about Cairo, Jim said. I had forgot it. We laid up for the day, on a tow-head tolerable close to the left-hand bank. I begun to suspicion something. So did Jim. I says:

"Maybe we went by Cairo in the fog that night."

He says:

"Doan' less' talk about it, Huck. Po' niggers can't have no luck. I awluz 'spected dat rattle-snake skin warn't done wid it's work."

"I wish I'd never seen that snake-skin, Jim—I do wish I'd never laid eyes on it."

"It ain't yo' fault, Huck; you didn' know. Don't you blame yo'self 'bout it."

When it was daylight, here was the clear Ohio water in shore, sure enough, and outside was the old regular Muddy. So it was all up with Cairo.

We talked it all over. It wouldn't do to take to the shore; we couldn't take the raft up the stream, of course. There warn't no way but to wait for dark, and start back in the canoe and take the chances. So we slept all day amongst the cotton-wood thicket, so as to be fresh for the work, and when we went back to the raft about dark the canoe was gone!

We didn't say a word for a good while. There warn't any thing to say. We both knowed well enough it was some more work of the rattle-snake skin; so what was the use to talk about it? It would only look like we was finding fault, and that would be bound to fetch more bad luck—and keep on fetching it, too, till we knowed enough to keep still.

By-and-by we talked about what we better do, and found there warn't no way but just to go along down with the raft till we got a chance to buy a canoe to go back in. We warn't going to borrow it when there warn't anybody around, the way pap would do, for that might set people after us.

So we shoved out, after dark, on the raft.

Anybody that don't believe yet, that it's foolishness to handle a snake-skin, after all that that snake-skin done for us, will believe it now, if they read on and see what more it done for us.

The place to buy canoes is off of rafts laying up at shore. But we didn't see no rafts laying up; so we went along during three hours and more. Well, the night got gray, and ruther thick, which is the next meanest thing to fog. You can't tell the shape of the river, and you can't see no distance. It got to be very late and still, and then along comes a steamboat up

he river. We lit the lantern, and judged she would see it. Up-
stream boats didn't generly come close to us; they go out and
follow the bars and hunt for easy water under the reefs; but
nights like this they bull right up the channel against the
whole river.

We could hear her pounding along, but we didn't see her
good till she was close. She aimed right for us. Often they do
that and try to see how close they can come without touching; sometimes the wheel bites off a sweep, and then the pilot
sticks his head out and laughs, and thinks he's mighty smart.
Well, here she comes, and we said she was going to try to
shave us; but she didn't seem to be sheering off a bit. She
was a big one, and she was coming in a hurry, too, looking
like a black cloud with rows of glow-worms around it; but all
of a sudden she bulged out, big and scary, with a long row
of wide-open furnace doors shining like red-hot teeth, and
her monstrous bows and guards hanging right over us. There
was a yell at us, and a jingling of bells to stop the engines, a
pow-wow of cussing, and whistling of steam—and as Jim
went overboard on one side and I on the other, she come
smashing straight through the raft.

I dived—and I aimed to find the bottom, too, for a thirty-
foot wheel had got to go over me, and I wanted it to have
plenty of room. I could always stay under water a minute;
this time I reckon I staid under water a minute and a half.
Then I bounced for the top in a hurry, for I was nearly bust-
ing. I popped out to my arm-pits and blowed the water out
of my nose, and puffed a bit. Of course there was a booming
current; and of course that boat started her engines again ten
seconds after she stopped them, for they never cared much
for raftsmen; so now she was churning along up the river,
out of sight in the thick weather, though I could hear her.

I sung out for Jim about a dozen times, but I didn't get
any answer; so I grabbed a plank that touched me while I was
"treading water," and struck out for shore, shoving it ahead
of me. But I made out to see that the drift of the current was
towards the left-hand shore, which meant that I was in a
crossing; so I changed off and went that way.

It was one of these long, slanting, two-mile crossings; so I
was a good long time in getting over. I made a safe landing,

and clum up the bank. I couldn't see but a little ways, but
went poking along over rough ground for a quarter of a mile
or more, and then I run across a big old-fashioned double log
house before I noticed it. I was going to rush by and get
away, but a lot of dogs jumped out and went to howling and
barking at me, and I knowed better than to move another
peg.

XVII

IN ABOUT HALF A MINUTE somebody spoke out of a window, without putting his head out, and says:

"Be done, boys! Who's there?"

I says:

"It's me."

"Who's me?"

"George Jackson, sir."

"What do you want?"

"I don't want nothing, sir. I only want to go along by, but the dogs won't let me."

"What are you prowling around here this time of night, for—hey?"

"I warn't prowling around, sir; I fell overboard off of the steamboat."

"Oh, you did, did you? Strike a light there, somebody. What did you say your name was?"

"George Jackson, sir. I'm only a boy."

"Look here; if you're telling the truth, you needn't be afraid—nobody 'll hurt you. But don't try to budge; stand right where you are. Rouse out Bob and Tom, some of you, and fetch the guns. George Jackson, is there anybody with you?"

"No, sir, nobody."

I heard the people stirring around in the house, now, and see a light. The man sung out:

"Snatch that light away, Betsy, you old fool—ain't you got any sense? Put it on the floor behind the front door. Bob, if you and Tom are ready, take your places."

"All ready."

"Now, George Jackson, do you know the Shepherdsons?"

"No, sir—I never heard of them."

"Well, that may be so, and it mayn't. Now, all ready. Step forward, George Jackson. And mind, don't you hurry—come mighty slow. If there's anybody with you, let him keep back—if he shows himself he'll be shot. Come along, now.

Come slow; push the door open, yourself—just enough to squeeze in, d' you hear?"

I didn't hurry, I couldn't if I'd a wanted to. I took one slow step at a time, and there warn't a sound, only I thought I could hear my heart. The dogs were as still as the humans, but they followed a little behind me. When I got to the three log door-steps, I heard them unlocking and unbarring and unbolting. I put my hand on the door and pushed it a little and a little more, till somebody said, "There, that's enough—put your head in." I done it, but I judged they would take it off.

The candle was on the floor, and there they all was, looking at me, and me at them, for about a quarter of a minute. Three big men with guns pointed at me, which made me wince, I tell you; the oldest, gray and about sixty, the other two thirty or more—all of them fine and handsome—and the sweetest old gray-headed lady, and back of her two young women which I couldn't see right well. The old gentleman says:

"There—I reckon it's all right. Come in."

As soon as I was in, the old gentleman he locked the door and barred it and bolted it, and told the young men to come in with their guns, and they all went in a big parlor that had a new rag carpet on the floor, and got together in a corner that was out of range of the front windows—there warn't none on the side. They held the candle, and took a good look at me, and all said, "Why *he* ain't a Shepherdson—no, there ain't any Shepherdson about him." Then the old man said he hoped I wouldn't mind being searched for arms, because he didn't mean no harm by it—it was only to make sure. So he didn't pry into my pockets, but only felt outside with his hands, and said it was all right. He told me to make myself easy and at home, and tell all about myself; but the old lady says:

"Why bless you, Saul, the poor thing's as wet as he can be; and don't you reckon it may be he's hungry?"

"True for you, Rachel—I forgot."

So the old lady says:

"Betsy" (this was a nigger woman), "you fly around and get him something to eat, as quick as you can, poor thing; and one of you girls go and wake up Buck and tell him— Oh, here he is himself. Buck, take this little stranger and get the wet clothes off from him and dress him up in some of yours that's dry."

Buck looked about as old as me—thirteen or fourteen or along there, though he was a little bigger than me. He hadn't on anything but a shirt, and he was very frowsy-headed. He come in gaping and digging one fist into his eyes, and he was dragging a gun along with the other one. He says:

"Ain't they no Shepherdsons around?"

They said, no, 'twas a false alarm.

"Well," he says, "if they'd a ben some, I reckon I'd a got one."

They all laughed, and Bob says:

"Why, Buck, they might have scalped us all, you've been so slow in coming."

"Well, nobody come after me, and it ain't right. I'm always kep' down; I don't get no show."

"Never mind, Buck, my boy," says the old man, "you'll have show enough, all in good time, don't you fret about that. Go 'long with you now, and do as your mother told you."

When we got up stairs to his room, he got me a coarse shirt and a roundabout and pants of his, and I put them on. While I was at it he asked me what my name was, but before I could tell him, he started to telling me about a blue jay and a young rabbit he had catched in the woods day before yesterday, and he asked me where Moses was when the candle went out. I said I didn't know; I hadn't heard about it before, no way.

"Well, guess," he says.

"How'm I going to guess," says I, "when I never heard tell about it before?"

"But you can guess, can't you? It's just as easy."

"*Which* candle?" I says.

"Why, any candle," he says.

"I don't know where he was," says I; "where was he?"

"Why he was in the *dark*! That's where he was!"

"Well, if you knowed where he was, what did you ask me for?"

"Why, blame it, it's a riddle, don't you see? Say, how long are you going to stay here? You got to stay always. We can just have booming times—they don't have no school now. Do you own a dog? I've got a dog—and he'll go in the river and bring out chips that you throw in. Do you like to comb up, Sundays, and all that kind of foolishness? You bet I don't, but ma she makes me. Confound these ole britches, I reckon I'd better put 'em on, but I'd ruther not, it's so warm. Are you all ready? All right—come along, old hoss."

Cold corn-pone, cold corn-beef, butter and butter-milk—that is what they had for me down there, and there ain't nothing better that ever I've come across yet. Buck and his ma and all of them smoked cob pipes, except the nigger woman, which was gone, and the two young women. They all smoked and talked, and I eat and talked. The young women had quilts around them, and their hair down their backs. They all asked me questions, and I told them how pap and me and all the family was living on a little farm down at the bottom of Arkansaw, and my sister Mary Ann run off and got married and never was heard of no more, and Bill went to hunt them and he warn't heard of no more, and Tom and Mort died, and then there warn't nobody but just me and pap left, and he was just trimmed down to nothing, on account of his troubles; so when he died I took what there was left, because the farm didn't belong to us, and started up the river, deck passage, and fell overboard; and that was how I come to be here. So they said I could have a home there as long as I wanted it. Then it was most daylight, and everybody went to bed, and I went to bed with Buck, and when I waked up in the morning, drat it all, I had forgot what my name was. So I laid there about an hour trying to think, and when Buck waked up, I says:

"Can you spell, Buck?"

"Yes," he says.

"I bet you can't spell my name," says I.

"I bet you what you dare I can," says he.

"All right," says I, "go ahead."

"G-o-r-g-e J-a-x-o-n—there now," he says.

"Well," says I, "you done it, but I didn't think you could. It ain't no slouch of a name to spell—right off without studying."

I set it down, private, because somebody might want *me* to

spell it, next, and so I wanted to be handy with it and rattle it off like I was used to it.

It was a mighty nice family, and a mighty nice house, too. I hadn't seen no house out in the country before that was so nice and had so much style. It didn't have an iron latch on the front door, nor a wooden one with a buckskin string, but a brass knob to turn, the same as houses in a town. There warn't no bed in the parlor, not a sign of a bed; but heaps of parlors in towns has beds in them. There was a big fireplace that was bricked on the bottom, and the bricks was kept clean and red by pouring water on them and scrubbing them with another brick; sometimes they washed them over with red water-paint that they call Spanish-brown, same as they do in town. They had big brass dog-irons that could hold up a saw-log. There was a clock on the middle of the mantel-piece, with a picture of a town painted on the bottom half of the glass front, and a round place in the middle of it for the sun, and you could see the pendulum swing behind it. It was beautiful to hear that clock tick; and sometimes when one of these peddlers had been along and scoured her up and got her in good shape, she would start in and strike a hundred and fifty before she got tuckered out. They wouldn't took any money for her.

Well, there was a big outlandish parrot on each side of the clock, made out of something like chalk, and painted up gaudy. By one of the parrots was a cat made of crockery, and a crockery dog by the other; and when you pressed down on them they squeaked, but didn't open their mouths nor look different nor interested. They squeaked through underneath. There was a couple of big wild-turkey-wing fans spread out behind those things. On a table in the middle of the room was a kind of a lovely crockery basket that had apples and oranges and peaches and grapes piled up in it which was much redder and yellower and prettier than real ones is, but they warn't real because you could see where pieces had got chipped off and showed the white chalk or whatever it was, underneath.

This table had a cover made out of beautiful oil-cloth, with a red and blue spread-eagle painted on it, and a painted border all around. It come all the way from Philadelphia, they said. There was some books too, piled up perfectly exact, on each corner of the table. One was a big family Bible, full of pictures. One was "Pilgrim's Progress," about a man that left his family it didn't say why. I read considerable in it now and then. The statements was interesting, but tough. Another was "Friendship's Offering," full of beautiful stuff and poetry; but I didn't read the poetry. Another was Henry Clay's Speeches, and another was Dr. Gunn's Family Medicine, which told you all about what to do if a body was sick or dead. There was a Hymn Book, and a lot of other books. And there was nice split-bottom chairs, and perfectly sound, too—not bagged down in the middle and busted, like an old basket.

They had pictures hung on the walls—mainly Washingtons and Lafayettes, and battles, and Highland Marys, and one called "Signing the Declaration." There was some that they called crayons, which one of the daughters which was dead made her own self when she was only fifteen years old. They was different from any pictures I ever see before; blacker, mostly, than is common. One was a woman in a slim black dress, belted small under the arm-pits, with bulges like a cabbage in the middle of the sleeves, and a large black scoop-shovel bonnet with a black veil, and white slim ankles crossed about with black tape, and very wee black slippers, like a chisel, and she was leaning pensive on a tombstone on her right elbow, under a weeping willow, and her other hand hanging down her side holding a white handkerchief and a reticule, and underneath the picture it said "Shall I Never See Thee More Alas." Another one was a young lady with her hair all combed up straight to the top of her head, and knotted there in front of a comb like a chair-back, and she was crying into a handkerchief and had a dead bird laying on its back in her other hand with its heels up, and underneath the picture it said "I Shall Never Hear Thy Sweet Chirrup More Alas." There was one where a young lady was at a window looking up at the moon, and tears running down her cheeks; and she had an open letter in one hand with black sealing-wax showing on one edge of it, and she was mashing a locket with a chain to it against her mouth, and underneath the picture it said "And Art Thou Gone Yes Thou Art Gone Alas." These was all nice pictures, I reckon, but I didn't somehow seem to take to them, because if ever I was down a little, they always give me the fan-tods. Everybody was sorry she died, because she had laid out a lot more of these pictures to do, and a body could see by what she had done what they had lost. But I reckoned, that with her disposition, she was having a better time in the graveyard. She was at work on what they said was her greatest picture when she took sick, and every day and every night it was her prayer to be allowed to live till she got it done, but she never got the chance. It was a picture of a young woman in a long white gown, standing on the rail of a bridge all ready to jump off, with her hair all down her back, and looking up to the moon, with the tears running down her face, and she had two arms folded across her breast, and two arms stretched out in front, and two more reaching up towards the moon—and the idea was, to see which pair would look best and then scratch out all the other arms; but, as I was saying, she died before she got her mind made up, and now they kept this picture over the head of the bed in her room, and every time her birthday come they hung flowers on it. Other times it was hid with a little curtain. The young woman in the picture had a kind of a nice sweet face, but there was so many arms it made her look too spidery, seemed to me.

This young girl kept a scrap-book when she was alive, and used to paste obituaries and accidents and cases of patient suffering in it out of the *Presbyterian Observer*, and write poetry after them out of her own head. It was very good poetry. This is what she wrote about a boy by the name of Stephen Dowling Bots that fell down a well and was drownded:

ODE TO STEPHEN DOWLING BOTS, DEC'D.

And did young Stephen sicken,
    And did young Stephen die?
And did the sad hearts thicken,
    And did the mourners cry?

No; such was not the fate of
    Young Stephen Dowling Bots;
Though sad hearts round him thickened,
    'Twas not from sickness' shots.

No whooping-cough did rack his frame,
Nor measles drear, with spots;
Not these impaired the sacred name
Of Stephen Dowling Bots.

Despised love struck not with woe
That head of curly knots,
Nor stomach troubles laid him low,
Young Stephen Dowling Bots.

O no. Then list with tearful eye,
Whilst I his fate do tell.
His soul did from this cold world fly,
By falling down a well.

They got him out and emptied him;
Alas it was too late;
His spirit was gone for to sport aloft
In the realms of the good and great.

If Emmeline Grangerford could make poetry like that before she was fourteen, there ain't no telling what she could a done by-and-by. Buck said she could rattle off poetry like nothing. She didn't ever have to stop to think. He said she would slap down a line, and if she couldn't find anything to rhyme with it she would just scratch it out and slap down another one, and go ahead. She warn't particular, she could write about anything you choose to give her to write about, just so it was sadful. Every time a man died, or a woman died, or a child died, she would be on hand with her "tribute" before he was cold. She called them tributes. The neighbors said it was the doctor first, then Emmeline, then the undertaker—the undertaker never got in ahead of Emmeline but once, and then she hung fire on a rhyme for the dead person's name, which was Whistler. She warn't ever the same, after that; she never complained, but she kind of pined away and did not live long. Poor thing, many's the time I made myself go up to the little room that used to be hers and get out her poor old scrap-book and read in it when her pictures had been aggravating me and I had soured on her a little. I liked all that family, dead ones and all, and warn't going to let any-thing come between us. Poor Emmeline made poetry about all the dead people when she was alive, and it didn't seem right that there warn't nobody to make some about her, now she was gone; so I tried to sweat out a verse or two myself, but I couldn't seem to make it go, somehow. They kept Emmeline's room trim and nice and all the things fixed in it just the way she liked to have them when she was alive, and nobody ever slept there. The old lady took care of the room herself, though there was plenty of niggers, and she sewed there a good deal and read her Bible there, mostly.

Well, as I was saying about the parlor, there was beautiful curtains on the windows: white, with pictures painted on them, of castles with vines all down the walls, and cattle com-ing down to drink. There was a little old piano, too, that had tin pans in it, I reckon, and nothing was ever so lovely as to hear the young ladies sing, "The Last Link is Broken" and play "The Battle of Prague" on it. The walls of all the rooms was plastered, and most had carpets on the floors, and the whole house was whitewashed on the outside.

It was a double house, and the big open place betwixt them was roofed and floored, and sometimes the table was set there in the middle of the day, and it was a cool, comfortable place. Nothing couldn't be better. And warn't the cooking good, and just bushels of it too!

XVIII

C OL. GRANGERFORD was a gentleman, you see. He was a gentleman all over; and so was his family. He was well born, as the saying is, and that's worth as much in a man as it is in a horse, so the Widow Douglas said, and nobody ever denied that she was of the first aristocracy in our town; and pap he always said it, too, though he warn't no more quality than a mud-cat, himself. Col. Grangerford was very tall and very slim, and had a darkish-paly complexion, not a sign of red in it anywheres; he was clean-shaved every morning, all over his thin face, and he had the thinnest kind of lips, and the thinnest kind of nostrils, and a high nose, and heavy eyebrows, and the blackest kind of eyes, sunk so deep back that they seemed like they was looking out of caverns at you, as you may say. His forehead was high, and his hair was black and straight, and hung to his shoulders. His hands was long and thin, and every day of his life he put on a clean shirt and a full suit from head to foot made out of linen so white it hurt your eyes to look at it; and on Sundays he wore a blue tail-coat with brass buttons on it. He carried a mahogany cane with a silver head to it. There warn't no frivolishness about him, not a bit, and he warn't ever loud. He was as kind as he could be—you could feel that, you know, and so you had confidence. Sometimes he smiled, and it was good to see; but when he straightened himself up like a liberty-pole, and the lightning begun to flicker out from under his eyebrows you wanted to climb a tree first, and find out what the matter was afterwards. He didn't ever have to tell anybody to mind their manners—everybody was always good mannered where he was. Everybody loved to have him around, too; he was sunshine most always—I mean he made it seem like good weather. When he turned into a cloud-bank it was awful dark for a half a minute and that was enough; there wouldn't nothing go wrong again for a week.

When him and the old lady come down in the morning, all the family got up out of their chairs and give them good-day, and didn't set down again till they had set down. Then Tom and Bob went to the sideboard where the decanters was, and mixed a glass of bitters and handed it to him, and he held it in his hand and waited till Tom's and Bob's was mixed, and then they bowed and said "Our duty to you, sir, and madam;" and *they* bowed the least bit in the world and said thank you, and so they drank, all three, and Bob and Tom poured a spoonful of water on the sugar and the mite of whisky or apple brandy in the bottom of their tumblers, and give it to me and Buck, and we drank to the old people too.

Bob was the oldest, and Tom next. Tall, beautiful men with very broad shoulders and brown faces, and long black hair and black eyes. They dressed in white linen from head to foot, like the old gentleman, and wore broad Panama hats.

Then there was Miss Charlotte, she was twenty-five, and tall and proud and grand, but as good as she could be, when she warn't stirred up; but when she was, she had a look that would make you wilt in your tracks, like her father. She was beautiful.

So was her sister, Miss Sophia, but it was a different kind. She was gentle and sweet, like a dove, and she was only twenty.

Each person had their own nigger to wait on them—Buck, too. My nigger had a monstrous easy time, because I warn't used to having anybody do anything for me, but Buck's was on the jump most of the time.

This was all there was of the family, now; but there used to be more—three sons; they got killed; and Emmeline that died.

The old gentleman owned a lot of farms, and over a hundred niggers. Sometimes a stack of people would come there, horseback, from ten or fifteen mile around, and stay five or six days, and have such junketings round about and on the river, and dances and picnics in the woods, day-times, and balls at the house, nights. These people was mostly kin-folks of the family. The men brought their guns with them. It was a handsome lot of quality, I tell you.

There was another clan of aristocracy around there—five or six families—mostly of the name of Shepherdson. They was as high-toned, and well born, and rich and grand, as the tribe of Grangerfords. The Shepherdsons and the Granger-

fords used the same steamboat landing, which was about two
mile above our house; so sometimes when I went up there
with a lot of our folks I used to see a lot of the Shepherdsons
there, on their fine horses.

One day Buck and me was away out in the woods, hunting
and heard a horse coming. We was crossing the road. Buck
says:

"Quick! Jump for the woods!"

We done it, and then peeped down the woods through the
leaves. Pretty soon a splendid young man come galloping
down the road, setting his horse easy and looking like a soldier. He had his gun across his pommel. I had seen him before. It was young Harney Shepherdson. I heard Buck's gun
go off at my ear, and Harney's hat tumbled off from his head.
He grabbed his gun and rode straight to the place where we
was hid. But we didn't wait. We started through the woods
on a run. The woods warn't thick, so I looked over my shoulder, to dodge the bullet, and twice I seen Harney cover Buck
with his gun; and then he rode away the way he come—to
get his hat, I reckon, but I couldn't see. We never stopped
running till we got home. The old gentleman's eyes blazed a
minute—'twas pleasure, mainly, I judged—then his face sort
of smoothed down, and he says, kind of gentle:

"I don't like that shooting from behind a bush. Why didn't
you step into the road, my boy?"

"The Shepherdsons don't, father. They always take advantage."

Miss Charlotte she held her head up like a queen while
Buck was telling his tale, and her nostrils spread and her eyes
snapped. The two young men looked dark, but never said
nothing. Miss Sophia she turned pale, but the color come
back when she found the man warn't hurt.

Soon as I could get Buck down by the corn-cribs under the
trees by ourselves, I says:

"Did you want to kill him, Buck?"

"Well, I bet I did."

"What did he do to you?"

"Him? He never done nothing to me."

"Well, then, what did you want to kill him for?"

"Why nothing—only it's on account of the feud."

"What's a feud?"

"Why, where was you raised? Don't you know what a feud is?"

"Never heard of it before—tell me about it."

"Well," says Buck, "a feud is this way. A man has a quarrel with another man, and kills him; then that other man's brother kills *him*; then the other brothers, on both sides, goes for one another; then the *cousins* chip in—and by-and-by everybody's killed off, and there ain't no more feud. But it's kind of slow, and takes a long time."

"Has this one been going on long, Buck?"

"Well I should *reckon*! it started thirty year ago, or som'ers along there. There was trouble 'bout something and then a lawsuit to settle it; and the suit went agin one of the men, and so he up and shot the man that won the suit—which he would naturally do, of course. Anybody would."

"What was the trouble about, Buck?—land?"

"I reckon maybe—I don't know."

"Well, who done the shooting?—was it a Grangerford or a Shepherdson?"

"Laws, how do *I* know? it was so long ago."

"Don't anybody know?"

"Oh, yes, pa knows, I reckon, and some of the other old folks; but they don't know, now, what the row was about in the first place."

"Has there been many killed, Buck?"

"Yes—right smart chance of funerals. But they don't always kill. Pa's got a few buck-shot in him; but he don't mind it 'cuz he don't weigh much anyway. Bob's been carved up some with a bowie, and Tom's been hurt once or twice."

"Has anybody been killed this year, Buck?"

"Yes, we got one and they got one. 'Bout three months ago, my cousin Bud, fourteen year old, was riding through the woods, on t'other side of the river, and didn't have no weapon with him, which was blame' foolishness, and in a lonesome place he hears a horse a-coming behind him, and sees old Baldy Shepherdson a-linkin' after him with his gun in his hand and his white hair a-flying in the wind; and 'stead of jumping off and taking to the brush, Bud 'lowed he could outrun him; so they had it, nip and tuck, for five mile or more, the old man a-gaining all the time; so at last Bud seen it warn't any use, so he stopped and faced around so as to have the bullet holes in front, you know, and the old man he rode up and shot him down. But he didn't git much chance to enjoy his luck, for inside of a week our folks laid *him* out."

"I reckon that old man was a coward, Buck."

"I reckon he *warn't* a coward. Not by a blame' sight. There ain't a coward amongst them Shepherdsons—not a one. And there ain't no cowards amongst the Grangerfords, either. Why, that old man kep' up his end in a fight one day, for a half an hour, against three Grangerfords, and come out winner. They was all a-horseback; he lit off of his horse and got behind a little wood-pile, and kep' his horse before him to stop the bullets; but the Grangerfords staid on their horses and capered around the old man, and peppered away at him, and he peppered away at them. Him and his horse both went home pretty leaky and crippled, but the Grangerfords had to be *fetched* home—and one of 'em was dead, and another died the next day. No, sir, if a body's out hunting for cowards, he don't want to fool away any time amongst them Shepherdsons, becuz they don't breed any of that *kind*."

Next Sunday we all went to church, about three mile, everybody a-horseback. The men took their guns along, so did Buck, and kept them between their knees or stood them handy against the wall. The Shepherdsons done the same. It was pretty ornery preaching—all about brotherly love, and such-like tiresomeness; but everybody said it was a good sermon, and they all talked it over going home, and had such a powerful lot to say about faith, and good works, and free grace, and preforeordestination, and I don't know what all, that it did seem to me to be one of the roughest Sundays I had run across yet.

About an hour after dinner everybody was dozing around, some in their chairs and some in their rooms, and it got to be pretty dull. Buck and a dog was stretched out on the grass in the sun, sound asleep. I went up to our room, and judged I would take a nap myself. I found that sweet Miss Sophia standing in her door, which was next to ours, and she took me in her room and shut the door very soft, and asked me if I liked her, and I said I did; and she asked me if I would do something for her and not tell anybody, and I said I would. Then she said she'd forgot her Testament, and left it in the seat at church, between two other books and would I slip out quiet and go there and fetch it to her, and not say nothing to nobody. I said I would. So I slid out and slipped off up the road, and there warn't anybody at the church, except maybe a hog or two, for there warn't any lock on the door, and hogs likes a puncheon floor in summer-time because it's cool. If you notice, most folks don't go to church only when they've got to; but a hog is different.

Says I to myself something's up—it ain't natural for a girl to be in such a sweat about a Testament; so I give it a shake, and out drops a little piece of paper with "*Half-past two*" wrote on it with a pencil. I ransacked it, but couldn't find anything else. I couldn't make anything out of that, so I put the paper in the book again, and when I got home and up stairs, there was Miss Sophia in her door waiting for me. She pulled me in and shut the door; then she looked in the Testament till she found the paper, and as soon as she read it she looked glad; and before a body could think, she grabbed me and give me a squeeze, and said I was the best boy in the world, and not to tell anybody. She was mighty red in the face, for a minute, and her eyes lighted up and it made her powerful pretty. I was a good deal astonished, but when I got my breath I asked her what the paper was about, and she asked me if I had read it, and I said no, and she asked me if I could read writing, and I told her "no, only coarse-hand," and then she said the paper warn't anything but a book-mark to keep her place, and I might go and play now.

I went off down to the river, studying over this thing, and pretty soon I noticed that my nigger was following along behind. When we was out of sight of the house, he looked back and around a second, and then comes a-running, and says:

"Mars Jawge, if you'll come down into de swamp, I'll show you a whole stack o' water-moccasins."

Thinks I, that's mighty curious; he said that yesterday. He oughter know a body don't love water-moccasins enough to go around hunting for them. What is he up to anyway? So I says—

"All right, trot ahead."

I followed a half a mile, then he struck out over the swamp and waded ankle deep as much as another half mile. We come to a little flat piece of land which was dry and very thick with trees and bushes and vines, and he says—

"You shove right in dah, jist a few steps, Mars Jawge, dah's whah dey is. I's seed 'm befo', I don't k'yer to see 'em no mo'."

Then he slopped right along and went away, and pretty soon the trees hid him. I poked into the place a-ways, and come to a little open patch as big as a bedroom, all hung around with vines, and found a man laying there asleep—and by jings it was my old Jim!

I waked him up, and I reckoned it was going to be a grand surprise to him to see me again, but it warn't. He nearly cried, he was so glad, but he warn't surprised. Said he swum along behind me, that night, and heard me yell every time, but dasn't answer, because he didn't want nobody to pick *him* up, and take him into slavery again. Says he—

"I got hurt a little, en couldn't swim fas', so I wuz a con-sidable ways behine you, towards de las'; when you landed I reck'ned I could ketch up wid you on de lan' 'dout havin' to shout at you, but when I see dat house I begin to go slow. I 'uz off too fur to hear what dey say to you—I wuz 'fraid o' de dogs—but when it 'uz all quiet agin, I knowed you's in de house, so I struck out for de woods to wait for day. Early in de mawnin' some er de niggers come along, gwyne to de fields, en dey tuck me en showed me dis place, whah de dogs can't track me on accounts o' de water, en dey brings me truck to eat every night, en tells me how you's a gitt'n along."

"Why didn't you tell my Jack to fetch me here sooner, Jim?"

"Well, 'twarn't no use to 'sturb you, Huck, tell we could do sumfn—but we's all right, now. I ben a-buyin' pots en pans en vittles, as I got a chanst, en a patchin' up de raf', nights, when——"

"*What* raft, Jim?"

"Our ole raf'."

"You mean to say our old raft warn't smashed all to flin-ders?"

"No, she warn't. She was tore up a good deal—one en' of

ner was—but dey warn't no great harm done, on'y our traps was mos' all los'. Ef we hadn' dive' so deep en swum so fur under water, en de night hadn' ben so dark, en we warn't so sk'yerd, en ben sich punkin-heads, as de sayin' is, we'd a seed de raf'. But it's jis' as well we didn't, 'kase now she's all fixed up agin mos' as good as new, en we's got a new lot o' stuff, too, in de place o' what 'uz los'."

"Why, how did you get hold of the raft again, Jim—did you catch her?"

"How I gwyne to ketch her, en I out in de woods? No, some er de niggers foun' her ketched on a snag, along heah in de ben', en dey hid her in a crick, 'mongst de willows, en dey wuz so much jawin' 'bout which un 'um she b'long to de mos', dat I come to heah 'bout it pooty soon, so I ups en settles de trouble by tellin' 'um she don't b'long to none uv um, but to you en me; en I ast 'm if dey gwyne to grab a young white genlman's propaty, en git a hid'n for it? Den I gin 'm ten cents apiece, en dey 'uz mighty well satisfied, en wisht some mo' raf's 'ud come along en make 'm rich agin. Dey's mighty good to me, dese niggers is, en whatever I wants 'm to do fur me, I doan' have to ast 'm twice, honey. Dat Jack's a good nigger, en pooty smart."

"Yes, he is. He ain't ever told me you was here; told me to come, and he'd show me a lot of water-moccasins. If anything happens, *he* ain't mixed up in it. He can say he never seen us together, and it'll be the truth."

I don't want to talk much about the next day. I reckon I'll cut it pretty short. I waked up about dawn, and was agoing to turn over and go to sleep again, when I noticed how still it was—didn't seem to be anybody stirring. That warn't usual. Next I noticed that Buck was up and gone. Well, I gets up, a-wondering, and goes down stairs—nobody around; everything as still as a mouse. Just the same outside; thinks I, what does it mean? Down by the wood-pile I comes across my Jack, and says:

"What's it all about?"

Says he:

"Don't you know, Mars Jawge?"

"No," says I, "I don't."

"Well, den, Miss Sophia's run off! 'deed she has. She run

off in de night, sometime—nobody don't know jis' when—
run off to git married to dat young Harney Shepherdson, you
know—leastways, so dey 'spec. De fambly foun' it out, 'bout
half an hour ago—maybe a little mo'—en' I *tell* you dey
warn't no time los'. Sich another hurryin' up guns en hosse
you never see! De women folks has gone for to stir up d
relations, en ole Mars Saul en de boys tuck dey guns en rod
up de river road for to try to ketch dat young man en kill him
'fo' he kin git acrost de river wid Miss Sophia. I reck'n dey'
gwyne to be mighty rough times."

"Buck went off 'thout waking me up."

"Well I reck'n he *did*! Dey warn't gwyne to mix you up in
it. Mars Buck he loaded up his gun en 'lowed he's gwyne to
fetch home a Shepherdson or bust. Well, dey'll be plenty un
'm dah, I reck'n, en you bet you he'll fetch one ef he gits a
chanst."

I took up the river road as hard as I could put. By-and-by
I begin to hear guns a good ways off. When I come in sight
of the log store and the wood-pile where the steamboat
lands, I worked along under the trees and brush till I got to
a good place, and then I clumb up into the forks of a cotton
wood that was out of reach, and watched. There was a wood
rank four foot high, a little ways in front of the tree, and first
I was going to hide behind that; but maybe it was luckier I
didn't.

There was four or five men cavorting around on their
horses in the open place before the log store, cussing and
yelling, and trying to get at a couple of young chaps that was
behind the wood-rank alongside of the steamboat landing—
but they couldn't come it. Every time one of them showed
himself on the river side of the wood-pile he got shot at. The
two boys was squatting back to back behind the pile, so they
could watch both ways.

By-and-by the men stopped cavorting around and yelling.
They started riding towards the store; then up gets one of the
boys, draws a steady bead over the wood-rank, and drops one
of them out of his saddle. All the men jumped off of their
horses and grabbed the hurt one and started to carry him to
the store; and that minute the two boys started on the run.
They got half-way to the tree I was in before the men noticed.

Then the men see them, and jumped on their horses and took out after them. They gained on the boys, but it didn't do no good, the boys had too good a start; they got to the wood-pile that was in front of my tree, and slipped in behind it, and so they had the bulge on the men again. One of the boys was Buck, and the other was a slim young chap about nineteen years old.

The men ripped around awhile, and then rode away. As soon as they was out of sight, I sung out to Buck and told him. He didn't know what to make of my voice coming out of the tree, at first. He was awful surprised. He told me to watch out sharp and let him know when the men come in sight again; said they was up to some devilment or other—wouldn't be gone long. I wished I was out of that tree, but I dasn't come down. Buck begun to cry and rip, and 'lowed that him and his cousin Joe (that was the other young chap) would make up for this day, yet. He said his father and his two brothers was killed, and two or three of the enemy. Said the Shepherdsons laid for them, in ambush. Buck said his father and brothers ought to waited for their relations—the Shepherdsons was too strong for them. I asked him what was become of young Harney and Miss Sophia. He said they'd got across the river and was safe. I was glad of that; but the way Buck did take on because he didn't manage to kill Harney that day he shot at him—I hain't ever heard anything like it.

All of a sudden, bang! bang! bang! goes three or four guns—the men had slipped around through the woods and come in from behind without their horses! The boys jumped for the river—both of them hurt—and as they swum down the current the men run along the bank shooting at them and singing out, "Kill them, kill them!" It made me so sick I most fell out of the tree. I ain't agoing to tell *all* that happened—it would make me sick again if I was to do that. I wished I hadn't ever come ashore that night, to see such things. I ain't ever going to get shut of them—lots of times I dream about them.

I staid in the tree till it begun to get dark, afraid to come down. Sometimes I heard guns away off in the woods; and twice I seen little gangs of men gallop past the log store with

guns; so I reckoned the trouble was still agoing on. I wa
mighty down-hearted; so I made up my mind I wouldn't eve
go anear that house again, because I reckoned I was to blame
somehow. I judged that that piece of paper meant that Mis
Sophia was to meet Harney somewheres at half-past two an
run off; and I judged I ought to told her father about tha
paper and the curious way she acted, and then maybe h
would a locked her up and this awful mess wouldn't ever hap
pened.

When I got down out of the tree, I crept along down th
river bank a piece, and found the two bodies laying in th
edge of the water, and tugged at them till I got them ashore
then I covered up their faces, and got away as quick as
could. I cried a little when I was covering up Buck's face, fo
he was mighty good to me.

It was just dark, now. I never went near the house, bu
struck through the woods and made for the swamp. Jin
warn't on his island, so I tramped off in a hurry for the crick
and crowded through the willows, red-hot to jump aboar
and get out of that awful country—the raft was gone! My
souls, but I was scared! I couldn't get my breath for most
minute. Then I raised a yell. A voice not twenty-five foo
from me, says—

"Good lan'! is dat you, honey? Doan' make no noise."

It was Jim's voice—nothing ever sounded so good before
I run along the bank a piece and got aboard, and Jim he
grabbed me and hugged me, he was so glad to see me. He
says—

"Laws bless you, chile, I 'uz right down sho' you's dead
agin. Jack's been heah, he say he reck'n you's ben shot, kase
you didn' come home no mo'; so I's jes' dis minute a startin
de raf' down towards de mouf er de crick, so's to be all ready
for to shove out en leave soon as Jack comes agin en tells me
for certain you *is* dead. Lawsy, I's mighty glad to git you back
agin, honey."

I says—

"All right—that's mighty good; they won't find me, and
they'll think I've been killed, and floated down the river—
there's something up there that'll help them to think so—sc

don't you lose no time, Jim, but just shove off for the big
water as fast as ever you can."

I never felt easy till the raft was two mile below there and
out in the middle of the Mississippi. Then we hung up our
signal lantern, and judged that we was free and safe once
more. I hadn't had a bite to eat since yesterday; so Jim he got
out some corn-dodgers and buttermilk, and pork and cabbage, and greens—there ain't nothing in the world so good,
when it's cooked right—and whilst I eat my supper we
talked, and had a good time. I was powerful glad to get away
from the feuds, and so was Jim to get away from the swamp.
We said there warn't no home like a raft, after all. Other
places do seem so cramped up and smothery, but a raft don't.
You feel mighty free and easy and comfortable on a raft.

XIX

TWO OR THREE DAYS and nights went by; I reckon I might say they swum by, they slid along so quiet and smooth and lovely. Here is the way we put in the time. It was a monstrous big river down there—sometimes a mile and a half wide; we run nights, and laid up and hid day-times; soon as night was most gone, we stopped navigating and tied up—nearly always in the dead water under a tow-head; and then cut young cotton-woods and willows and hid the raft with them. Then we set out the lines. Next we slid into the river and had a swim, so as to freshen up and cool off; then we set down on the sandy bottom where the water was about knee deep, and watched the daylight come. Not a sound, anywheres—perfectly still—just like the whole world was asleep, only sometimes the bull-frogs a-cluttering, maybe. The first thing to see, looking away over the water, was a kind of dull line—that was the woods on t'other side—you couldn't make nothing else out; then a pale place in the sky; then more paleness, spreading around; then the river softened up, away off, and warn't black any more, but gray; you could see little dark spots drifting along, ever so far away—trading scows, and such things; and long black streaks—rafts; sometimes you could hear a sweep screaking; or jumbled up voices, it was so still, and sounds come so far; and by-and-by you could see a streak on the water which you know by the look of the streak that there's a snag there in a swift current which breaks on it and makes that streak look that way; and you see the mist curl up off of the water, and the east reddens up, and the river, and you make out a log cabin in the edge of the woods, away on the bank on t'other side of the river, being a wood-yard, likely, and piled by them cheats so you can throw a dog through it anywheres; then the nice breeze springs up, and comes fanning you from over there, so cool and fresh, and sweet to smell, on account of the woods and the flowers; but sometimes not that way, because they've left dead fish laying around, gars, and such, and they do get pretty rank; and next you've got the full day, and everything smiling in the sun, and the song-birds just going it!

A little smoke couldn't be noticed, now, so we would take some fish off of the lines, and cook up a hot breakfast. And afterwards we would watch the lonesomeness of the river, and kind of lazy along, and by-and-by lazy off to sleep. Wake up, by-and-by, and look to see what done it, and maybe see a steamboat, coughing along up stream, so far off towards the other side you couldn't tell nothing about her only whether she was stern-wheel or side-wheel; then for about an hour there wouldn't be nothing to hear nor nothing to see—just solid lonesomeness. Next you'd see a raft sliding by, away off yonder, and maybe a galoot on it chopping, because they're most always doing it on a raft; you'd see the ax flash, and come down—you don't hear nothing; you see that ax go up again, and by the time it's above the man's head, then you hear the *k'chunk!*—it had took all that time to come over the water. So we would put in the day, lazying around, listening to the stillness. Once there was a thick fog, and the rafts and things that went by was beating tin pans so the steamboats wouldn't run over them. A scow or a raft went by so close we could hear them talking and cussing and laughing—heard them plain; but we couldn't see no sign of them; it made you feel crawly, it was like spirits carrying on that way in the air. Jim said he believed it was spirits; but I says:

"No, spirits wouldn't say, 'dern the dern fog.'"

Soon as it was night, out we shoved; when we got her out to about the middle, we let her alone, and let her float wherever the current wanted her to; then we lit the pipes, and dangled our legs in the water and talked about all kinds of things—we was always naked, day and night, whenever the mosquitoes would let us—the new clothes Buck's folks made for me was too good to be comfortable, and besides I didn't go much on clothes, nohow.

Sometimes we'd have that whole river all to ourselves for the longest time. Yonder was the banks and the islands, across the water; and maybe a spark—which was a candle in a cabin window—and sometimes on the water you could see a spark or two—on a raft or a scow, you know; and maybe you could hear a fiddle or a song coming over from one of them crafts. It's lovely to live on a raft. We had the sky, up there, all speckled with stars, and we used to lay on our backs and look up at them, and discuss about whether they was made, or only just happened—Jim he allowed they was made, but I allowed they happened; I judged it would have took too long to *make* so many. Jim said the moon could a *laid* them; well, that looked kind of reasonable, so I didn't say nothing against it, because I've seen a frog lay most as many, so of course it could be done. We used to watch the stars that fell, too, and see them streak down. Jim allowed they'd got spoiled and was hove out of the nest.

Once or twice of a night we would see a steamboat slipping along in the dark, and now and then she would belch a whole world of sparks up out of her chimbleys, and they would rain down in the river and look awful pretty; then she would turn a corner and her lights would wink out and her pow-wow shut off and leave the river still again; and by-and-by her waves would get to us, a long time after she was gone, and joggle the raft a bit, and after that you wouldn't hear nothing for you couldn't tell how long, except maybe frogs or something.

After midnight the people on shore went to bed, and then for two or three hours the shores was black—no more sparks in the cabin windows. These sparks was our clock—the first one that showed again meant morning was coming, so we hunted a place to hide and tie up, right away.

One morning about day-break, I found a canoe and crossed over a chute to the main shore—it was only two hundred yards—and paddled about a mile up a crick amongst the cypress woods, to see if I couldn't get some berries. Just as I was passing a place where a kind of a cow-path crossed the crick, here comes a couple of men tearing up the path as tight as they could foot it. I thought I was a goner, for whenever anybody was after anybody I judged it was *me*—or maybe Jim. I was about to dig out from there in a hurry, but they was pretty close to me then, and sung out and begged me to save their lives—said they hadn't been doing nothing, and was being chased for it—said there was men and dogs a-coming. They wanted to jump right in, but I says—

"Don't you do it. I don't hear the dogs and horses yet; you've got time to crowd through the brush and get up the crick a little ways; then you take to the water and wade down to me and get in—that'll throw the dogs off the scent."

They done it, and soon as they was aboard I lit out for our tow-head, and in about five or ten minutes we heard the dogs and the men away off, shouting. We heard them come along towards the crick, but couldn't see them; they seemed to stop and fool around a while; then, as we got further and further away all the time, we couldn't hardly hear them at all; by the time we had left a mile of woods behind us and struck the river, everything was quiet, and we paddled over to the tow-head and hid in the cotton-woods and was safe.

One of these fellows was about seventy, or upwards, and had a bald head and very gray whiskers. He had an old battered-up slouch hat on, and a greasy blue woolen shirt, and ragged old blue jeans britches stuffed into his boot tops, and home-knit galluses—no, he only had one. He had an old long-tailed blue jeans coat with slick brass buttons, flung over his arm, and both of them had big fat ratty-looking carpet-bags.

The other fellow was about thirty and dressed about as ornery. After breakfast we all laid off and talked, and the first thing that come out was that these chaps didn't know one another.

"What got you into trouble?" says the baldhead to t'other chap.

"Well, I'd been selling an article to take the tartar off the teeth—and it does take it off, too, and generly the enamel along with it—but I staid about one night longer than I ought to, and was just in the act of sliding out when I ran across you on the trail this side of town, and you told me they were coming, and begged me to help you to get off. So I told you I was expecting trouble myself and would scatter out *with* you. That's the whole yarn—what's yourn?"

"Well, I'd ben a-runnin' a little temperance revival thar, 'bout a week, and was the pet of the women-folks, big and little, for I was makin' it mighty warm for the rummies, I *tell* you, and takin' as much as five or six dollars a night—ten cents a head, children and niggers free—and business a growin' all the time; when somehow or another a little report got around, last night, that I had a way of puttin' in my time with a private jug, on the sly. A nigger rousted me out this mornin', and told me the people was getherin' on the quiet, with their dogs and horses, and they'd be along pretty soon and give me 'bout half an hour's start, and then run me down, if they could; and if they got me they'd tar and feather me and ride me on a rail, sure. I didn't wait for no breakfast—I warn't hungry."

"Old man," says the young one, "I reckon we might double-team it together; what do you think?"

"I ain't undisposed. What's your line—mainly?"

"Jour printer, by trade; do a little in patent medicines; theatre-actor—tragedy, you know; take a turn at mesmerism and phrenology when there's a chance; teach singing-geography school for a change; sling a lecture, sometimes—oh, I do lots of things—most anything that comes handy, so it ain't work. What's your lay?"

"I've done considerble in the doctoring way in my time. Layin' on o' hands is my best holt—for cancer, and paralysis, and sich things; and I k'n tell a fortune pretty good, when I've got somebody along to find out the facts for me. Preachin's my line, too; and workin' camp-meetin's; and missionaryin' around."

Nobody never said anything for a while; then the young man hove a sigh and says—

"Alas!"

"What 're you alassin' about?" says the baldhead.

"To think I should have lived to be leading such a life, and be degraded down into such company." And he begun to wipe the corner of his eye with a rag.

"Dern your skin, ain't the company good enough for you?" says the baldhead, pretty pert and uppish.

"Yes, it *is* good enough for me; it's as good as I deserve; for who fetched me so low, when I was so high? *I* did myself. I don't blame *you*, gentlemen—far from it; I don't blame anybody. I deserve it all. Let the cold world do its worst; one thing I know—there's a grave somewhere for me. The world may go on just as it's always done, and take everything from me—loved ones, property, everything—but it can't take that. Some day I'll lie down in it and forget it all, and my poor broken heart will be at rest." He went on a-wiping.

"Drot your pore broken heart," says the baldhead; "what are you heaving your pore broken heart at *us* f'r? *We* hain't done nothing."

"No, I know you haven't. I ain't blaming you, gentlemen. I brought myself down—yes, I did it myself. It's right I should suffer—perfectly right—I don't make any moan."

"Brought you down from whar? Whar was you brought down from?"

"Ah, you would not believe me; the world never believes—let it pass—'tis no matter. The secret of my birth——"

"The secret of your birth? Do you mean to say——"

"Gentlemen," says the young man, very solemn, "I will reveal it to you, for I feel I may have confidence in you. By rights I am a duke!"

Jim's eyes bugged out when he heard that; and I reckon mine did, too. Then the baldhead says: "No! you can't mean it?"

"Yes. My great-grandfather, eldest son of the Duke of Bridgewater, fled to this country about the end of the last century, to breathe the pure air of freedom; married here, and died, leaving a son, his own father dying about the same time. The second son of the late duke seized the title and estates— the infant real duke was ignored. I am the lineal descendant of that infant—I am the rightful Duke of Bridgewater; and here am I, forlorn, torn from my high estate, hunted of men, despised by the cold world, ragged, worn, heart-broken, and degraded to the companionship of felons on a raft!"

Jim pitied him ever so much, and so did I. We tried to comfort him, but he said it warn't much use, he couldn't be much comforted; said if we was a mind to acknowledge him, that would do him more good than most anything else; so we said we would, if he would tell us how. He said we ought to bow, when we spoke to him, and say "Your Grace," or "My Lord," or "Your Lordship"—and he wouldn't mind it if we called him plain "Bridgewater," which he said was a title, anyway, and not a name; and one of us ought to wait on him at dinner, and do any little thing for him he wanted done.

Well, that was all easy, so we done it. All through dinner Jim stood around and waited on him, and says, "Will yo'

Grace have some o' dis, or some o' dat?" and so on, and a body could see it was mighty pleasing to him.

But the old man got pretty silent, by-and-by—didn't have much to say, and didn't look pretty comfortable over all that petting that was going on around that duke. He seemed to have something on his mind. So, along in the afternoon, he says:

"Looky here, Bilgewater," he says, "I'm nation sorry for you, but you ain't the only person that's had troubles like that."

"No?"

"No, you ain't. You ain't the only person that's ben snaked down wrongfully out'n a high place."

"Alas!"

"No, you ain't the only person that's had a secret of his birth." And by jings, *he* begins to cry.

"Hold! What do you mean?"

"Bilgewater, kin I trust you?" says the old man, still sort of sobbing.

"To the bitter death!" He took the old man by the hand and squeezed it, and says, "The secret of your being: speak!"

"Bilgewater, I am the late Dauphin!"

You bet you Jim and me stared, this time. Then the duke says:

"You are what?"

"Yes, my friend, it is too true—your eyes is lookin' at this very moment on the pore disappeared Dauphin, Looy the Seventeen, son of Looy the Sixteen and Marry Antonette."

"You! At your age! No! You mean you're the late Charlemagne; you must be six or seven hundred years old, at the very least."

"Trouble has done it, Bilgewater, trouble has done it; trouble has brung these gray hairs and this premature balditude. Yes, gentlemen, you see before you, in blue jeans and misery, the wanderin', exiled, trampled-on and sufferin' rightful King of France."

Well, he cried and took on so, that me and Jim didn't know hardly what to do, we was so sorry—and so glad and proud we'd got him with us, too. So we set in, like we done before with the duke, and tried to comfort *him*. But he said it warn't no use, nothing but to be dead and done with it all could do him any good; though he said it often made him feel easier and better for a while if people treated him according to his rights, and got down on one knee to speak to him, and always called him "Your Majesty," and waited on him first at meals, and didn't set down in his presence till he asked them. So Jim and me set to majestying him, and doing this and that and t'other for him, and standing up till he told us we might set down. This done him heaps of good, and so he got cheerful and comfortable. But the duke kind of soured on him, and didn't look a bit satisfied with the way things was going; still, the king acted real friendly towards him, and said the duke's great-grandfather and all the other Dukes of Bilgewater was a good deal thought of by *his* father and was allowed to come to the palace considerable; but the duke staid huffy a good while, till by-and-by the king says:

"Like as not we got to be together a blamed long time, on this h-yer raft, Bilgewater, and so what's the use o' your bein' sour? It'll only make things oncomfortable. It ain't my fault I warn't born a duke, it ain't your fault you warn't born a king—so what's the use to worry? Make the best o' things the way you find 'em, says I—that's my motto. This ain't no bad thing that we've struck here—plenty grub and an easy life—come, give us your hand, Duke, and less all be friends."

The duke done it, and Jim and me was pretty glad to see it. It took away all the uncomfortableness, and we felt mighty good over it, because it would a been a miserable business to have any unfriendliness on the raft; for what you want, above all things, on a raft, is for everybody to be satisfied, and feel right and kind towards the others.

It didn't take me long to make up my mind that these liars warn't no kings nor dukes, at all, but just low-down humbugs and frauds. But I never said nothing, never let on; kept it to myself; it's the best way; then you don't have no quarrels, and don't get into no trouble. If they wanted us to call them kings and dukes, I hadn't no objections, 'long as it would keep peace in the family; and it warn't no use to tell Jim, so I didn't tell him. If I never learnt nothing else out of pap, I learnt that the best way to get along with his kind of people is to let them have their own way.

XX

THEY ASKED us considerable many questions; wanted to know what we covered up the raft that way for, and laid by in the day-time instead of running—was Jim a runaway nigger? Says I—

"Goodness sakes, would a runaway nigger run *south*?"

No, they allowed he wouldn't. I had to account for things some way, so I says:

"My folks was living in Pike County, in Missouri, where I was born, and they all died off but me and pa and my brother Ike. Pa, he 'lowed he'd break up and go down and live with Uncle Ben, who's got a little one-horse place on the river, forty-four mile below Orleans. Pa was pretty poor, and had some debts; so when he'd squared up there warn't nothing left but sixteen dollars and our nigger, Jim. That warn't enough to take us fourteen hundred mile, deck passage nor no other way. Well, when the river rose, pa had a streak of luck one day; he ketched this piece of a raft; so we reckoned we'd go down to Orleans on it. Pa's luck didn't hold out; a steamboat run over the forrard corner of the raft, one night, and we all went overboard and dove under the wheel; Jim and me come up, all right, but pa was drunk, and Ike was only four years old, so they never come up no more. Well, for the next day or two we had considerable trouble, because people was always coming out in skiffs and trying to take Jim away from me, saying they believed he was a runaway nigger. We don't run day-times no more, now; nights they don't bother us."

The duke says—

"Leave me alone to cipher out a way so we can run in the day-time if we want to. I'll think the thing over—I'll invent a plan that'll fix it. We'll let it alone for to-day, because of course we don't want to go by that town yonder in daylight—it mightn't be healthy."

Towards night it begun to darken up and look like rain; the heat lightning was squirting around, low down in the sky, and the leaves was beginning to shiver—it was going to be pretty ugly, it was easy to see that. So the duke and the king went to overhauling our wigwam, to see what the beds was like. My bed was a straw tick—better than Jim's, which was a corn-shuck tick; there's always cobs around about in a shuck tick, and they poke into you and hurt; and when you roll over, the dry shucks sound like you was rolling over in a pile of dead leaves; it makes such a rustling that you wake up. Well, the duke allowed he would take my bed; but the king allowed he wouldn't. He says—

"I should a reckoned the difference in rank would a sejested to you that a corn-shuck bed warn't just fitten for me to sleep on. Your Grace'll take the shuck bed yourself."

Jim and me was in a sweat again, for a minute, being afraid there was going to be some more trouble amongst them; so we was pretty glad when the duke says—

" 'Tis my fate to be always ground into the mire under the iron heel of oppression. Misfortune has broken my once haughty spirit; I yield, I submit; 'tis my fate. I am alone in the world—let me suffer; I can bear it."

We got away as soon as it was good and dark. The king told us to stand well out towards the middle of the river, and not show a light till we got a long ways below the town. We come in sight of the little bunch of lights by-and-by—that was the town, you know—and slid by, about a half a mile out, all right. When we was three-quarters of a mile below, we hoisted up our signal lantern; and about ten o'clock it come on to rain and blow and thunder and lighten like every-thing; so the king told us to both stay on watch till the weather got better; then him and the duke crawled into the wigwam and turned in for the night. It was my watch below, till twelve, but I wouldn't a turned in, anyway, if I'd had a bed; because a body don't see such a storm as that every day in the week, not by a long sight. My souls, how the wind did scream along! And every second or two there'd come a glare that lit up the white-caps for a half a mile around, and you'd see the islands looking dusty through the rain, and the trees thrashing around in the wind; then comes a *h-wack!*—bum! bum! bumble-umble-um-bum-bum-bum-bum—and the thunder would go rumbling and grumbling away, and quit—and then *rip* comes another flash and another sockdolager. The waves most washed me off the raft, sometimes, but I hadn't any clothes on, and didn't mind. We didn't have no trouble about snags; the lightning was glaring and flittering around so constant that we could see them plenty soon enough to throw her head this way or that and miss them.

I had the middle watch, you know, but I was pretty sleepy by that time, so Jim he said he would stand the first half of it for me; he was always mighty good, that way, Jim was. I crawled into the wigwam, but the king and the duke had their legs sprawled around so there warn't no show for me; so I laid outside—I didn't mind the rain, because it was warm, and the waves warn't running so high, now. About two they come up again, though, and Jim was going to call me, but he changed his mind because he reckoned they warn't high enough yet to do any harm; but he was mistaken about that, for pretty soon all of a sudden along comes a regular ripper, and washed me overboard. It most killed Jim a-laughing. He was the easiest nigger to laugh that ever was, anyway.

I took the watch, and Jim he laid down and snored away; and by-and-by the storm let up for good and all; and the first cabin-light that showed, I rousted him out and we slid the raft into hiding-quarters for the day.

The king got out an old ratty deck of cards, after breakfast, and him and the duke played seven-up a while, five cents a game. Then they got tired of it, and allowed they would "lay out a campaign," as they called it. The duke went down into his carpet-bag and fetched up a lot of little printed bills, and read them out loud. One bill said "The celebrated Dr. Armand de Montalban of Paris," would "lecture on the Science of Phrenology" at such and such a place, on the blank day of blank, at ten cents admission, and "furnish charts of character at twenty-five cents apiece." The duke said that was *him*. In another bill he was the "world renowned Shaksperean trage- dian, Garrick the Younger, of Drury Lane, London." In other bills he had a lot of other names and done other wonderful things, like finding water and gold with a "divining rod," "dissipating witch-spells," and so on. By-and-by he says—

"But the histrionic muse is the darling. Have you ever trod the boards, Royalty?"

"No," says the king.

"You shall, then, before you're three days older, Fallen Grandeur," says the duke. "The first good town we come to, we'll hire a hall and do the sword-fight in Richard III. and the balcony scene in Romeo and Juliet. How does that strike you?"

"I'm in, up to the hub, for anything that will pay, Bilgewater, but you see I don't know nothing about play-actn', and hain't ever seen much of it. I was too small when pap used to have 'em at the palace. Do you reckon you can learn me?"

"Easy!"

"All right. I'm jist a-freezn' for something fresh, anyway. Less commence, right away."

So the duke he told him all about who Romeo was, and who Juliet was, and said he was used to being Romeo, so the king could be Juliet.

"But if Juliet's such a young gal, Duke, my peeled head and my white whiskers is goin' to look oncommon odd on her, maybe."

"No, don't you worry—these country jakes won't ever think of that. Besides, you know, you'll be in costume, and that makes all the difference in the world; Juliet's in a balcony, enjoying the moonlight before she goes to bed, and she's got on her night-gown and her ruffled night-cap. Here are the costumes for the parts."

He got out two or three curtain-calico suits, which he said was meedyevil armor for Richard III. and t'other chap, and a long white cotton night-shirt and a ruffled night-cap to match. The king was satisfied; so the duke got out his book and read the parts over in the most splendid spread-eagle way, prancing around and acting at the same time, to show how it had got to be done; then he give the book to the king and told him to get his part by heart.

There was a little one-horse town about three mile down the bend, and after dinner the duke said he had ciphered out his idea about how to run in daylight without it being dangersome for Jim; so he allowed he would go down to the town and fix that thing. The king allowed he would go too, and see if he couldn't strike something. We was out of coffee, so Jim said I better go along with them in the canoe and get some.

When we got there, there warn't nobody stirring; streets empty, and perfectly dead and still, like Sunday. We found a sick nigger sunning himself in a back yard, and he said everybody that warn't too young or too sick or too old, was gone to camp-meeting, about two mile back in the woods. The king got the directions, and allowed he'd go and work that camp-meeting for all it was worth, and I might go, too.

The duke said what he was after was a printing office. We found it; a little bit of a concern, up over a carpenter shop— carpenters and printers all gone to the meeting, and no doors locked. It was a dirty, littered-up place, and had ink marks, and handbills with pictures of horses and runaway niggers on them, all over the walls. The duke shed his coat and said he was all right, now. So me and the king lit out for the camp-meeting.

We got there in about a half an hour, fairly dripping, for it was a most awful hot day. There was as much as a thousand people there, from twenty mile around. The woods was full of teams and wagons, hitched everywheres, feeding out of the wagon troughs and stomping to keep off the flies. There was sheds made out of poles and roofed over with branches, where they had lemonade and gingerbread to sell, and piles of watermelons and green corn and such-like truck.

The preaching was going on under the same kinds of sheds, only they was bigger and held crowds of people. The benches was made out of outside slabs of logs, with holes bored in the round side to drive sticks into for legs. They didn't have no backs. The preachers had high platforms to stand on, at one end of the sheds. The women had on sun-bonnets; and some had linsey-woolsey frocks, some gingham ones, and a few of the young ones had on calico. Some of the young men was barefooted, and some of the children didn't have on any clothes but just a tow-linen shirt. Some of the old women was knitting, and some of the young folks was courting on the sly.

The first shed we come to, the preacher was lining out a hymn. He lined out two lines, everybody sung it, and it was kind of grand to hear it, there was so many of them and they done it in such a rousing way; then he lined out two more for them to sing—and so on. The people woke up more and more, and sung louder and louder; and towards the end, some begun to groan, and some begun to shout. Then the preacher begun to preach; and begun in earnest, too; and went weaving first to one side of the platform and then the other, and then a leaning down over the front of it, with his arms and his body going all the time, and shouting his words out with all his might; and every now and then he would hold up his Bible and spread it open, and kind of pass it around this way and that, shouting, "It's the brazen serpent in the wilderness! Look upon it and live!" And people would shout out, "Glory!—A-a-*men*!" And so he went on, and the people groaning and crying and saying amen:

"Oh, come to the mourners' bench! come, black with sin! *(amen!)* come, sick and sore! *(amen!)* come, lame and halt, and blind! *(amen!)* come, pore and needy, sunk in shame! *(a-a-men!)* come all that's worn, and soiled, and suffering!— come with a broken spirit! come with a contrite heart! come in your rags and sin and dirt! the waters that cleanse is free, the door of heaven stands open—oh, enter in and be at rest!" *(a-a-men! glory, glory hallelujah!)*

And so on. You couldn't make out what the preacher said, any more, on account of the shouting and crying. Folks got up, everywheres in the crowd, and worked their way, just by main strength, to the mourners' bench, with the tears running down their faces; and when all the mourners had got up there to the front benches in a crowd, they sung, and shouted, and flung themselves down on the straw, just crazy and wild.

Well, the first I knowed, the king got agoing; and you could hear him over everybody; and next he went a-charging up on to the platform and the preacher he begged him to speak to the people, and he done it. He told them he was a pirate—been a pirate for thirty years, out in the Indian Ocean, and his crew was thinned out considerable, last spring, in a fight, and he was home now, to take out some fresh men, and thanks to goodness he'd been robbed last night, and put ashore off of a steamboat without a cent, and he was glad of it, it was the blessedest thing that ever happened to him, because he was a changed man now, and happy for the first time in his life; and poor as he was, he was going to start right off and work his way back to the Indian Ocean and put in the rest of his life trying to turn the pirates into the true path; for he could do it better than anybody else, being acquainted with all the pirate crews in that ocean; and though it would take him a long time to get there, without money, he would get there anyway, and every time he convinced a pirate he would say to him, "Don't you thank me, don't you give me no credit, it all belongs to them dear people in Pokeville camp-meeting, natural brothers and benefactors of the race—and that dear preacher there, the truest friend a pirate ever had!"

And then he busted into tears, and so did everybody. Then somebody sings out, "Take up a collection for him, take up a collection!" Well, a half a dozen made a jump to do it, but somebody sings out, "Let *him* pass the hat around!" Then everybody said it, the preacher too.

So the king went all through the crowd with his hat, swabbing his eyes, and blessing the people and praising them and thanking them for being so good to the poor pirates away off there; and every little while the prettiest kind of girls, with the tears running down their cheeks, would up and ask him would he let them kiss him, for to remember him by; and he always done it; and some of them he hugged and kissed as many as five or six times—and he was invited to stay a week; and everybody wanted him to live in their houses, and said they'd think it was an honor; but he said as this was the last day of the camp-meeting he couldn't do no good, and besides he was in a sweat to get to the Indian Ocean right off and go to work on the pirates.

When we got back to the raft and he come to count up, he found he had collected eighty-seven dollars and seventy-five cents. And then he had fetched away a three-gallon jug of whisky, too, that he found under a wagon when we was starting home through the woods. The king said, take it all around, it laid over any day he'd ever put in in the missionarying line. He said it warn't no use talking, heathens don't amount to shucks, alongside of pirates, to work a camp-meeting with.

The duke was thinking *he'd* been doing pretty well, till the king come to show up, but after that he didn't think so so much. He had set up and printed off two little jobs for farmers, in that printing office—horse bills—and took the money, four dollars. And he had got in ten dollars worth of advertisements for the paper, which he said he would put in for four dollars if they would pay in advance—so they done it. The price of the paper was two dollars a year, but he took in three subscriptions for half a dollar apiece on condition of them paying him in advance; they were going to pay in cordwood and onions, as usual, but he said he had just bought the concern and knocked down the price as low as he could afford it, and was going to run it for cash. He set up a little piece of poetry, which he made, himself, out of his own head—three verses—kind of sweet and saddish—the name of it was, "Yes, crush, cold world, this breaking heart"—and he left that all set up and ready to print in the paper and didn't charge nothing for it. Well, he took in nine dollars and a half, and said he'd done a pretty square day's work for it.

Then he showed us another little job he'd printed and hadn't charged for, because it was for us. It had a picture of a runaway nigger, with a bundle on a stick, over his shoulder, and "$200 reward" under it. The reading was all about Jim, and just described him to a dot. It said he run away from St. Jacques' plantation, forty mile below New Orleans, last winter, and likely went north, and whoever would catch him and send him back, he could have the reward and expenses.

"Now," says the duke, "after to-night we can run in the daytime if we want to. Whenever we see anybody coming, we can tie Jim hand and foot with a rope, and lay him in the wigwam and show this handbill and say we captured him up the river, and were too poor to travel on a steamboat, so we got this little raft on credit from our friends and are going down to get the reward. Handcuffs and chains would look still better on Jim, but it wouldn't go well with the story of us being so poor. Too much like jewelry. Ropes are the correct thing—we must preserve the unities, as we say on the boards."

We all said the duke was pretty smart, and there couldn't

be no trouble about running daytimes. We judged we could make miles enough that night to get out of the reach of the pow-wow we reckoned the duke's work in the printing office was going to make in that little town—then we could boom right along, if we wanted to.

We laid low and kept still, and never shoved out till nearly ten o'clock; then we slid by, pretty wide away from the town, and didn't hoist our lantern till we was clear out of sight of it.

When Jim called me to take the watch at four in the morning, he says—

"Huck, does you reck'n we gwyne to run acrost any mo kings on dis trip?"

"No," I says, "I reckon not."

"Well," says he, "dat's all right, den. I doan' mine one er two kings, but dat's enough. Dis one's powerful drunk, en de duke ain' much better."

I found Jim had been trying to get him to talk French, so he could hear what it was like; but he said he had been in this country so long, and had so much trouble, he'd forgot it.

XXI

I T WAS AFTER SUN-UP, now, but we went right on, and
didn't tie up. The king and the duke turned out, by-and-
by, looking pretty rusty; but after they'd jumped overboard
and took a swim, it chippered them up a good deal. After
breakfast the king he took a seat on a corner of the raft, and
pulled off his boots and rolled up his britches, and let his legs
dangle in the water, so as to be comfortable, and lit his pipe,
and went to getting his Romeo and Juliet by heart. When he
had got it pretty good, him and the duke begun to practice it
together. The duke had to learn him over and over again,
how to say every speech; and he made him sigh, and put his
hand on his heart, and after while he said he done it pretty
well; "only," he says, "you mustn't bellow out *Romeo!* that
way, like a bull—you must say it soft, and sick, and lan-
guishy, so—R-o-o-meo! that is the idea; for Juliet's a dear
sweet mere child of a girl, you know, and she don't bray like
a jackass."

Well, next they got out a couple of long swords that the
duke made out of oak laths, and begun to practice the sword-
fight—the duke called himself Richard III.; and the way they
laid on, and pranced around the raft was grand to see. But
by-and-by the king tripped and fell overboard, and after that
they took a rest, and had a talk about all kinds of adventures
they'd had in other times along the river.

After dinner, the duke says:

"Well, Capet, we'll want to make this a first-class show, you
know, so I guess we'll add a little more to it. We want a little
something to answer encores with, anyway."

"What's onkores, Bilgewater?"

The duke told him, and then says:

"I'll answer by doing the Highland fling or the sailor's
hornpipe; and you—well, let me see—oh, I've got it—you
can do Hamlet's soliloquy."

"Hamlet's which?"

"Hamlet's soliloquy, you know; the most celebrated thing
in Shakespeare. Ah, it's sublime, sublime! Always fetches the

house. I haven't got it in the book—I've only got one vol
ume—but I reckon I can piece it out from memory. I'll jus
walk up and down a minute, and see if I can call it back from
recollection's vaults."

So he went to marching up and down, thinking, and
frowning horrible every now and then; then he would hois
up his eyebrows; next he would squeeze his hand on his fore
head and stagger back and kind of moan; next he would sigh
and next he'd let on to drop a tear. It was beautiful to see
him. By-and-by he got it. He told us to give attention. Then
he strikes a most noble attitude, with one leg shoved for
wards, and his arms stretched away up, and his head tilted
back, looking up at the sky; and then he begins to rip and
rave and grit his teeth; and after that, all through his speech
he howled, and spread around, and swelled up his chest, and
just knocked the spots out of any acting ever *I* see before
This is the speech—I learned it, easy enough, while he was
learning it to the king:

To be, or not to be; that is the bare bodkin
That makes calamity of so long life;
For who would fardels bear, till Birnam Wood do come to
    Dunsinane,
But that the fear of something after death
Murders the innocent sleep,
Great nature's second course,
And makes us rather sling the arrows of outrageous fortune
Than fly to others that we know not of.
There's the respect must give us pause:
Wake Duncan with thy knocking! I would thou couldst;
For who would bear the whips and scorns of time,
The oppressor's wrong, the proud man's contumely,
The law's delay, and the quietus which his pangs might take,
In the dead waste and middle of the night, when
    churchyards yawn
In customary suits of solemn black,
But that the undiscovered country from whose bourne no
    traveler returns,
Breathes forth contagion on the world,

And thus the native hue of resolution, like the poor cat i' the
    adage,
Is sicklied o'er with care,
And all the clouds that lowered o'er our housetops,
With this regard their currents turn awry,
And lose the name of action.
Tis a consummation devoutly to be wished. But soft you,
    the fair Ophelia:
Ope not thy ponderous and marble jaws,
But get thee to a nunnery—go!

Well, the old man he liked that speech, and he mighty soon
got it so he could do it first rate. It seemed like he was just
born for it; and when he had his hand in and was excited, it
was perfectly lovely the way he would rip and tear and rair
up behind when he was getting it off.

The first chance we got, the duke he had some show bills
printed; and after that, for two or three days as we floated
along, the raft was a most uncommon lively place, for there
warn't nothing but sword-fighting and rehearsing—as the
duke called it—going on all the time. One morning, when
we was pretty well down the State of Arkansaw, we come in
sight of a little one-horse town in a big bend; so we tied up
about three-quarters of a mile above it, in the mouth of a
crick which was shut in like a tunnel by the cypress trees, and
all of us but Jim took the canoe and went down there to see
if there was any chance in that place for our show.

We struck it mighty lucky; there was going to be a circus
there that afternoon, and the country people was already beginning to come in, in all kinds of old shackly wagons, and
on horses. The circus would leave before night, so our show
would have a pretty good chance. The duke he hired the
court house, and we went around and stuck up our bills.
They read like this:

Shaksperean Revival ! ! !
Wonderful Attraction !
For One Night Only !
The world renowned tragedians,
David Garrick the younger, of Drury Lane Theatre, London,

and
Edmund Kean the elder, of the Royal Haymarket Theatre,
Whitechapel, Pudding Lane, Piccadilly, London, and
the Royal Continental Theatres, in their sublime
Shaksperean Spectacle entitled
The Balcony Scene
in
Romeo and Juliet ! ! !

Romeo. . . . . Mr. Garrick.
Juliet. . . . . Mr. Kean.
Assisted by the whole strength of the company !
New costumes, new scenery, new appointments !
Also:
The thrilling, masterly, and blood-curdling
Broad-sword conflict
In Richard III. ! ! !

Richard III. . . . . Mr. Garrick.
Richmond. . . . . Mr. Kean.
also:
(by special request,)
Hamlet's Immortal Soliloquy ! !
By the Illustrious Kean !
Done by him 300 consecutive nights in Paris!
For One Night Only,
On account of imperative European engagements!
Admission 25 cents; children and servants, 10 cents.

Then we went loafing around the town. The stores and
houses was most all old shackly dried-up frame concerns that
hadn't ever been painted; they was set up three or four foot
above ground on stilts, so as to be out of reach of the water
when the river was overflowed. The houses had little gardens
around them, but they didn't seem to raise hardly anything in
them but jimpson weeds, and sunflowers, and ash-piles, and
old curled-up boots and shoes, and pieces of bottles, and rags,
and played-out tin-ware. The fences was made of different
kinds of boards, nailed on at different times; and they leaned
every which-way, and had gates that didn't generly have but
one hinge—a leather one. Some of the fences had been
whitewashed, some time or another, but the duke said it was

in Clumbus's time, like enough. There was generly hogs in the garden, and people driving them out.

All the stores was along one street. They had white-domestic awnings in front, and the country people hitched their horses to the awning-posts. There was empty dry-goods boxes under the awnings, and loafers roosting on them all day long, whittling them with their Barlow knives; and chawing tobacco, and gaping and yawning and stretching—a mighty ornery lot. They generly had on yellow straw hats most as wide as an umbrella, but didn't wear no coats nor waistcoats; they called one another Bill, and Buck, and Hank, and Joe, and Andy, and talked lazy and drawly, and used considerable many cuss-words. There was as many as one loafer leaning up against every awning-post, and he most always had his hands in his britches pockets, except when he fetched them out to lend a chaw of tobacco or scratch. What a body was hearing amongst them, all the time was—

"Gimme a chaw 'v tobacker, Hank."

"Cain't—I hain't got but one chaw left. Ask Bill."

Maybe Bill he gives him a chaw; maybe he lies and says he ain't got none. Some of them kinds of loafers never has a cent in the world, nor a chaw of tobacco of their own. They get all their chawing by borrowing—they say to a fellow, "I wisht you'd len' me a chaw, Jack, I jist this minute give Ben Thompson the last chaw I had"—which is a lie, pretty much every time; it don't fool nobody but a stranger; but Jack ain't no stranger, so he says—

"*You* give him a chaw, did you? so did your sister's cat's grandmother. You pay me back the chaws you've awready borry'd off'n me, Lafe Buckner, then I'll loan you one or two ton of it, and won't charge you no back intrust, nuther."

"Well, I *did* pay you back some of it wunst."

"Yes, you did—'bout six chaws. You borry'd store tobacker and paid back nigger-head."

Store tobacco is flat black plug, but these fellows mostly chaws the natural leaf twisted. When they borrow a chaw, they don't generly cut it off with a knife, but they set the plug in between their teeth, and gnaw with their teeth and tug at the plug with their hands till they get it in two—then sometimes the one that owns the tobacco looks mournful at it when it's handed back, and says, sarcastic—

"Here, gimme the *chaw*, and you take the *plug*."

All the streets and lanes was just mud, they warn't nothing else *but* mud—mud as black as tar, and nigh about a foot deep in some places; and two or three inches deep in *all* the places. The hogs loafed and grunted around, everywheres. You'd see a muddy sow and a litter of pigs come lazying along the street and whollop herself right down in the way where folks had to walk around her, and she'd stretch out and shut her eyes, and wave her ears, whilst the pigs was milking her, and look as happy as if she was on salary. And pretty soon you'd hear a loafer sing out, "Hi! *so* boy! sick him, Tige!" and away the sow would go, squealing most horrible, with a dog or two swinging to each ear, and three or four dozen more a-coming; and then you would see all the loafers get up and watch the thing out of sight, and laugh at the fun and look grateful for the noise. Then they'd settle back again till there was a dog-fight. There couldn't anything wake them up all over, and make them happy all over, like a dog-fight—unless it might be putting turpentine on a stray dog and setting fire to him, or tying a tin pan to his tail and see him run himself to death.

On the river front some of the houses was sticking out over the bank, and they was bowed and bent, and about ready to tumble in. The people had moved out of them. The bank was caved away under one corner of some others, and that corner was hanging over. People lived in them yet, but it was dangersome, because sometimes a strip of land as wide as a house caves in at a time. Sometimes a belt of land a quarter of a mile deep will start in and cave along and cave along till it all caves into the river in one summer. Such a town as that has to be always moving back, and back, and back, because the river's always gnawing at it.

The nearer it got to noon that day, the thicker and thicker was the wagons and horses in the streets, and more coming all the time. Families fetched their dinners with them, from the country, and eat them in the wagons. There was considerable whiskey drinking going on, and I seen three fights. By-and-by somebody sings out—

"Here comes old Boggs!—in from the country for his little old monthly drunk—here he comes, boys!"

All the loafers looked glad—I reckoned they was used to having fun out of Boggs. One of them says—

"Wonder who he's a gwyne to chaw up this time. If he'd a chawed up all the men he's ben a gwyne to chaw up in the last twenty year, he'd have considerble ruputation, now."

Another one says, "I wisht old Boggs 'd threaten me, 'cuz then I'd know I warn't gwyne to die for a thousan' year."

Boggs comes a-tearing along on his horse, whooping and yelling like an Injun, and singing out—

"Cler the track, thar. I'm on the waw-path, and the price uv coffins is a gwyne to raise."

He was drunk, and weaving about in his saddle; he was over fifty year old, and had a very red face. Everybody yelled at him, and laughed at him, and sassed him, and he sassed back, and said he'd attend to them and lay them out in their regular turns, but he couldn't wait now, because he'd come to town to kill old Colonel Sherburn, and his motto was, "meat first, and spoon vittles to top off on."

He see me, and rode up and says—

"Whar'd you come f'm, boy? You prepared to die?"

Then he rode on. I was scared; but a man says—

"He don't mean nothing; he's always a carryin' on like that, when he's drunk. He's the best-naturedest old fool in Arkansaw—never hurt nobody, drunk nor sober."

Boggs rode up before the biggest store in town and bent his head down so he could see under the curtain of the awning, and yells—

"Come out here, Sherburn! Come out and meet the man you've swindled. You're the houn' I'm after, and I'm a gwyne to have you, too!"

And so he went on, calling Sherburn everything he could lay his tongue to, and the whole street packed with people listening and laughing and going on. By-and-by a proud-looking man about fifty-five—and he was a heap the best dressed man in that town, too—steps out of the store, and the crowd drops back on each side to let him come. He says to Boggs, mighty ca'm and slow—he says:

"I'm tired of this; but I'll endure it till one o'clock. Till one o'clock, mind—no longer. If you open your mouth against me only once, after that time, you can't travel so far but I will find you."

Then he turns and goes in. The crowd looked mighty sober; nobody stirred, and there warn't no more laughing. Boggs rode off blackguarding Sherburn as loud as he could yell, all down the street; and pretty soon back he comes and stops before the store, still keeping it up. Some men crowded around him and tried to get him to shut up, but he wouldn't; they told him it would be one o'clock in about fifteen minutes, and so he *must* go home—he must go right away. But it didn't do no good. He cussed away, with all his might, and throwed his hat down in the mud and rode over it, and pretty soon away he went a-raging down the street again, with his gray hair a-flying. Everybody that could get a chance at him tried their best to coax him off of his horse so they could lock him up and get him sober; but it warn't no use—up the street he would tear again, and give Sherburn another cussing. By-and-by somebody says—

"Go for his daughter!—quick, go for his daughter; sometimes he'll listen to her. If anybody can persuade him, she can."

So somebody started on a run. I walked down street a ways, and stopped. In about five or ten minutes, here comes Boggs again—but not on his horse. He was a-reeling across the street towards me, bareheaded, with a friend on both sides of him aholt of his arms and hurrying him along. He was quiet, and looked uneasy; and he warn't hanging back any, but was doing some of the hurrying himself. Somebody sings out—

"Boggs!"

I looked over there to see who said it, and it was that Colonel Sherburn. He was standing perfectly still, in the street, and had a pistol raised in his right hand—not aiming it, but holding it out with the barrel tilted up towards the sky. The same second I see a young girl coming on the run, and two men with her. Boggs and the men turned round, to see who called him, and when they see the pistol the men jumped to one side, and the pistol barrel come down slow and steady to a level—both barrels cocked. Boggs throws up both of his

ands, and says, "O Lord, don't shoot!" Bang! goes the first
shot, and he staggers back clawing at the air—bang! goes the
second one, and he tumbles backwards onto the ground,
heavy and solid, with his arms spread out. That young girl
screamed out, and comes rushing, and down she throws herself on her father, crying, and saying, "Oh, he's killed him,
he's killed him!" The crowd closed up around them, and
shouldered and jammed one another, with their necks
stretched, trying to see, and people on the inside trying to
shove them back, and shouting, "Back, back! give him air,
give him air!"

Colonel Sherburn he tossed his pistol onto the ground, and
turned around on his heels and walked off.

They took Boggs to a little drug store, the crowd pressing
around, just the same, and the whole town following, and I
rushed and got a good place at the window, where I was
close to him and could see in. They laid him on the floor, and
put one large Bible under his head, and opened another one
and spread it on his breast—but they tore open his shirt first,
and I seen where one of the bullets went in. He made about
a dozen long gasps, his breast lifting the Bible up when he
drawed in his breath, and letting it down again when he
breathed it out—and after that he laid still; he was dead.
Then they pulled his daughter away from him, screaming and
crying, and took her off. She was about sixteen, and very
sweet and gentle-looking, but awful pale and scared.

Well, pretty soon the whole town was there, squirming and
scrouging and pushing and shoving to get at the window and
have a look, but people that had the places wouldn't give
them up, and folks behind them was saying all the time, "Say,
now, you've looked enough, you fellows; 'taint right and
'taint fair, for you to stay thar all the time, and never give
nobody a chance; other folks has their rights as well as you."

There was considerable jawing back, so I slid out, thinking
maybe there was going to be trouble. The streets was full,
and everybody was excited. Everybody that seen the shooting
was telling how it happened, and there was a big crowd
packed around each one of these fellows, stretching their
necks and listening. One long lanky man, with long hair and
a big white fur stove-pipe hat on the back of his head, and a

crooked-handled cane, marked out the places on the ground
where Boggs stood, and where Sherburn stood, and the people following him around from one place to t'other and
watching everything he done, and bobbing their heads to
show they understood, and stooping a little and resting their
hands on their thighs to watch him mark the places on the
ground with his cane; and then he stood up straight and stiff
where Sherburn had stood, frowning and having his hat-brim
down over his eyes, and sung out, "Boggs!" and then fetched
his cane down slow to a level, and says "Bang!" staggered
backwards, says "Bang!" again, and fell down flat on his back.
The people that had seen the thing said he done it perfect;
said it was just exactly the way it all happened. Then as much
as a dozen people got out their bottles and treated him.

Well, by-and-by somebody said Sherburn ought to be
lynched. In about a minute everybody was saying it; so away
they went, mad and yelling, and snatching down every
clothes-line they come to, to do the hanging with.

XXII

THEY SWARMED up the street towards Sherburn's house, a-whooping and yelling and raging like Injuns, and everything had to clear the way or get run over and tromped to mush, and it was awful to see. Children was heeling it ahead of the mob, screaming and trying to get out of the way; and every window along the road was full of women's heads, and there was nigger boys in every tree, and bucks and wenches looking over every fence; and as soon as the mob would get nearly to them they would break and skaddle back out of reach. Lots of the women and girls was crying and taking on, scared most to death.

They swarmed up in front of Sherburn's palings as thick as they could jam together, and you couldn't hear yourself think for the noise. It was a little twenty-foot yard. Some sung out "Tear down the fence! tear down the fence!" Then there was a racket of ripping and tearing and smashing, and down she goes, and the front wall of the crowd begins to roll in like a wave.

Just then Sherburn steps out on to the roof of his little front porch, with a double-barrel gun in his hand, and takes his stand, perfectly ca'm and deliberate, not saying a word. The racket stopped, and the wave sucked back.

Sherburn never said a word—just stood there, looking down. The stillness was awful creepy and uncomfortable. Sherburn run his eye slow along the crowd; and wherever it struck, the people tried a little to outgaze him, but they couldn't; they dropped their eyes and looked sneaky. Then pretty soon Sherburn sort of laughed; not the pleasant kind, but the kind that makes you feel like when you are eating bread that's got sand in it.

Then he says, slow and scornful:

"The idea of *you* lynching anybody! It's amusing. The idea of you thinking you had pluck enough to lynch a *man*! Because you're brave enough to tar and feather poor friendless cast-out women that come along here, did that make you think you had grit enough to lay your hands on a *man*? Why, a *man's* safe in the hands of ten thousand of your kind—as long as it's day-time and you're not behind him.

"Do I know you? I know you clear through. I was born and raised in the South, and I've lived in the North; so I know the average all around. The average man's a coward. In the North he lets anybody walk over him that wants to, and goes home and prays for a humble spirit to bear it. In the South one man, all by himself, has stopped a stage full of men, in the day-time, and robbed the lot. Your newspapers call you a brave people so much that you think you *are* braver than any other people—whereas you're just *as* brave, and no braver. Why don't your juries hang murderers? Because they're afraid the man's friends will shoot them in the back, in the dark—and it's just what they *would* do.

"So they always acquit; and then a *man* goes in the night, with a hundred masked cowards at his back, and lynches the rascal. Your mistake is, that you didn't bring a man with you; that's one mistake, and the other is that you didn't come in the dark, and fetch your masks. You brought *part* of a man— Buck Harkness, there—and if you hadn't had him to start you, you'd a taken it out in blowing.

"You didn't want to come. The average man don't like trouble and danger. *You* don't like trouble and danger. But if only *half* a man—like Buck Harkness, there—shouts 'Lynch him, lynch him!' you're afraid to back down—afraid you'll be found out to be what you are— *cowards*—and so you raise a yell, and hang yourselves onto that half-a-man's coat tail, and come raging up here, swearing what big things you're going to do. The pitifulest thing out is a mob; that's what an army is—a mob; they don't fight with courage that's born in them, but with courage that's borrowed from their mass, and from their officers. But a mob without any *man* at the head of it, is *beneath* pitifulness. Now the thing for *you* to do, is to droop your tails and go home and crawl in a hole. If any real lynching's going to be done, it will be done in the dark, Southern fashion; and when they come they'll bring their masks, and fetch a *man* along. Now *leave*—and take your half-a-man with you"—tossing his gun up across his left arm and cocking it, when he says this.

The crowd washed back sudden, and then broke all apart

and went tearing off every which way, and Buck Harkness he heeled it after them, looking tolerable cheap. I could a staid, if I'd a wanted to, but I didn't want to.

I went to the circus, and loafed around the back side till the watchman went by, and then dived in under the tent. I had my twenty-dollar gold piece and some other money, but I reckoned I better save it, because there ain't no telling how soon you are going to need it, away from home and amongst strangers, that way. You can't be too careful. I ain't opposed to spending money on circuses, when there ain't no other way, but there ain't no use in *wasting* it on them.

It was a real bully circus. It was the splendidest sight that ever was, when they all come riding in, two and two, a gentleman and lady, side by side, the men just in their drawers and under-shirts, and no shoes nor stirrups, and resting their hands on their thighs, easy and comfortable—there must a' been twenty of them—and every lady with a lovely complexion, and perfectly beautiful, and looking just like a gang of real sure-enough queens, and dressed in clothes that cost millions of dollars, and just littered with diamonds. It was a powerful fine sight; I never see anything so lovely. And then one by one they got up and stood, and went a-weaving around the ring so gentle and wavy and graceful, the men looking ever so tall and airy and straight, with their heads bobbing and skimming along, away up there under the tent-roof, and every lady's rose-leafy dress flapping soft and silky around her hips, and she looking like the most loveliest parasol.

And then faster and faster they went, all of them dancing, first one foot stuck out in the air and then the other, the horses leaning more and more, and the ring-master going round and round the centre-pole, cracking his whip and shouting "hi!—hi!" and the clown cracking jokes behind him; and by-and-by all hands dropped the reins, and every lady put her knuckles on her hips and every gentleman folded his arms, and then how the horses did lean over and hump themselves! And so, one after the other they all skipped off into the ring, and made the sweetest bow I ever see, and then scampered out, and everybody clapped their hands and went just about wild.

Well, all through the circus they done the most astonishing things; and all the time that clown carried on so it most killed the people. The ring-master couldn't ever say a word to him but he was back at him quick as a wink with the funniest things a body ever said; and how he ever *could* think of so many of them, and so sudden and so pat, was what I couldn't noway understand. Why, I couldn't a thought of them in a year. And by-and-by a drunk man tried to get into the ring—said he wanted to ride; said he could ride as well as anybody that ever was. They argued and tried to keep him out, but he wouldn't listen, and the whole show come to a standstill. Then the people begun to holler at him and make fun of him, and that made him mad, and he begun to rip and tear; so that stirred up the people, and a lot of men begun to pile down off of the benches and swarm towards the ring, saying, "Knock him down! throw him out!" and one or two women begun to scream. So, then, the ring-master he made a little speech, and said he hoped there wouldn't be no disturbance, and if the man would promise he wouldn't make no more trouble, he would let him ride, if he thought he could stay on the horse. So everybody laughed and said all right, and the man got on. The minute he was on, the horse begun to rip and tear and jump and cavort around, with two circus men hanging onto his bridle trying to hold him, and the drunk man hanging onto his neck, and his heels flying in the air every jump, and the whole crowd of people standing up shouting and laughing till the tears rolled down. And at last, sure enough, all the circus men could do, the horse broke loose, and away he went like the very nation, round and round the ring, with that sot laying down on him and hanging to his neck, with first one leg hanging most to the ground on one side, and then t'other one on t'other side, and the people just crazy. It warn't funny to me, though; I was all of a tremble to see his danger. But pretty soon he struggled up astraddle and grabbed the bridle, a-reeling this way and that; and the next minute he sprung up and dropped the bridle and stood! and the horse agoing like a house afire too. He just stood up there, a-sailing around as easy and comfortable as if he warn't ever drunk in his life—and then he begun to pull off his clothes and sling them. He shed them so thick they kind of clogged up the air, and altogether he shed seventeen suits. And then, there he was, slim and handsome, and dressed the gaudiest and prettiest you ever saw, and he lit into that horse with his whip and made him fairly hum—and finally skipped off, and made his bow and danced off to the dressing-room, and everybody just a-howling with pleasure and astonishment.

Then the ring-master he see how he had been fooled, and he *was* the sickest ring-master you ever see, I reckon. Why, it was one of his own men! He had got up that joke all out of his own head, and never let on to nobody. Well, I felt sheepish enough, to be took in so, but I wouldn't a been in that ring-master's place, not for a thousand dollars. I don't know; there may be bullier circuses than what that one was, but I never struck them yet. Anyways it was plenty good enough for *me*; and wherever I run across it, it can have all of *my* custom, every time.

Well, that night we had *our* show; but there warn't only about twelve people there; just enough to pay expenses. And they laughed all the time, and that made the duke mad; and everybody left, anyway, before the show was over, but one boy which was asleep. So the duke said these Arkansaw lunkheads couldn't come up to Shakspeare; what they wanted was low comedy—and may be something ruther worse than low comedy, he reckoned. He said he could size their style. So next morning he got some big sheets of wrapping-paper and some black paint, and drawed off some handbills and stuck them up all over the village. The bills said:

AT THE COURT HOUSE!
FOR 3 NIGHTS ONLY!
The World-Renowned Tragedians
DAVID GARRICK THE YOUNGER!
AND
EDMUND KEAN THE ELDER!
Of the London and Continental Theatres,
In their Thrilling Tragedy of
THE KING'S CAMELOPARD
OR
THE ROYAL NONESUCH ! ! !
Admission 50 cents.

Then at the bottom was the biggest line of all—which said

LADIES AND CHILDREN NOT ADMITTED.

"There," says he, "if that line don't fetch them, I don't know Arkansaw!"

XXIII

WELL, all day him and the king was hard at it, rigging up a stage, and a curtain, and a row of candles for footlights; and that night the house was jam full of men in no time. When the place couldn't hold no more, the duke he quit tending door and went around the back way and come onto the stage and stood up before the curtain, and made a little speech, and praised up this tragedy, and said it was the most thrillingest one that ever was; and so he went on a-bragging about the tragedy and about Edmund Kean the Elder, which was to play the main principal part in it; and at last when he'd got everybody's expectations up high enough, he rolled up the curtain, and the next minute the king come a-prancing out on all fours, naked; and he was painted all over, ring-streaked-and-striped, all sorts of colors, as splendid as a rainbow. And—but never mind the rest of his outfit, it was just wild, but it was awful funny. The people most killed themselves laughing; and when the king got done capering, and capered off behind the scenes, they roared and clapped and stormed and haw-hawed till he come back and done it over again; and after that, they made him do it another time. Well, it would a made a cow laugh to see the shines that old idiot cut.

Then the duke he lets the curtain down, and bows to the people, and says the great tragedy will be performed only two nights more, on accounts of pressing London engagements, where the seats is all sold aready for it in Drury Lane; and then he makes them another bow, and says if he has succeeded in pleasing them and instructing them, he will be deeply obleeged if they will mention it to their friends and get them to come and see it.

Twenty people sings out:

"What, is it over? Is that *all?*"

The duke says yes. Then there was a fine time. Everybody sings out "sold," and rose up mad, and was agoing for that stage and them tragedians. But a big fine-looking man jumps up on a bench, and shouts:

"Hold on! Just a word, gentlemen." They stopped to listen. "We are sold—mighty badly sold. But we don't want to be the laughing-stock of this whole town, I reckon, and never hear the last of this thing as long as we live. *No*. What we want, is to go out of here quiet, and talk this show up, and sell the *rest* of the town! Then we'll all be in the same boat. Ain't that sensible?" ("You bet it is!—the jedge is right!" everybody sings out.) "All right, then—not a word about any sell. Go along home, and advise everybody to come and see the tragedy."

Next day you couldn't hear nothing around that town but how splendid that show was. House was jammed again, that night, and we sold this crowd the same way. When me and the king and the duke got home to the raft we all had a supper; and by-and-by, about midnight, they made Jim and me back her out and float her down the middle of the river and fetch her in and hide her about two mile below town.

The third night the house was crammed again—and they warn't new-comers, this time, but people that was at the show the other two nights. I stood by the duke at the door, and see that every man that went in had his pockets bulging, or something muffled up under his coat—and I see it warn't no perfumery neither, not by a long sight. I smelt sickly eggs by the barrel, and rotten cabbages, and such things; and if I know the signs of a dead cat being around, and I bet I do, there was sixty-four of them went in. I shoved in there for a minute, but it was too various for me, I couldn't stand it. Well, when the place couldn't hold no more people, the duke he give a fellow a quarter and told him to tend door for him a minute, and then he started around for the stage door, I after him; but the minute we turned the corner and was in the dark, he says:

"Walk fast, now, till you get away from the houses, and then shin for the raft like the dickens was after you!"

I done it, and he done the same. We struck the raft at the same time, and in less than two seconds we was gliding down stream, all dark and still, and edging towards the middle of the river, nobody saying a word. I reckoned the poor king was in for a gaudy time of it with the audience; but nothing of the sort; pretty soon he crawls out from under the wig-wam, and says:

"Well, how'd the old thing pan out this time, Duke?"

He hadn't been up town at all.

We never showed a light till we was about ten mile below that village. Then we lit up and had a supper, and the king and the duke fairly laughed their bones loose over the way they'd served them people. The duke says:

"Greenhorns, flatheads! *I* knew the first house would keep mum and let the rest of the town get roped in; and I knew they'd lay for us the third night, and consider it was *their* turn now. Well, it *is* their turn, and I'd give something to know how much they'd take for it. I *would* just like to know how they're putting in their opportunity. They can turn it into a picnic, if they want to—they brought plenty provisions."

Them rapscallions took in four hundred and sixty-five dollars in that three nights. I never see money hauled in by the wagon-load like that, before.

By-and-by, when they was asleep and snoring, Jim says:

"Don't it 'sprise you, de way dem kings carries on, Huck?"

"No," I says, "it don't."

"Why don't it, Huck?"

"Well, it don't, because it's in the breed. I reckon they're all alike."

"But, Huck, dese kings o' ourn is regular rapscallions; dat's jist what dey is; dey's reglar rapscallions."

"Well, that's what I'm a-saying; all kings is mostly rapscallions, as fur as I can make out."

"Is dat so?"

"You read about them once—you'll see. Look at Henry the Eight; this'n 's a Sunday-School Superintendent to *him*. And look at Charles Second, and Louis Fourteen, and Louis Fifteen, and James Second, and Edward Second, and Richard Third, and forty more; besides all them Saxon heptarchies that used to rip around so in old times and raise Cain. My, you ought to seen old Henry the Eight when he was in bloom. He *was* a blossom. He used to marry a new wife every day, and chop off her head next morning. And he would do it just as indifferent as if he was ordering up eggs. 'Fetch up

Nell Gwynn,' he says. They fetch her up. Next mornin,
'Chop off her head!' And they chop it off. 'Fetch up Ja
Shore,' he says; and up she comes. Next morning 'Chop o
her head'—and they chop it off. 'Ring up Fair Rosamur
Fair Rosamun answers the bell. Next morning, 'Chop off h
head.' And he made every one of them tell him a tale eve
night; and he kept that up till he had hogged a thousand an
one tales that way, and then he put them all in a book, an
called it Domesday Book—which was a good name an
stated the case. You don't know kings, Jim, but I know then
and this old rip of ourn is one of the cleanest I've struck i
history. Well, Henry he takes a notion he wants to get u
some trouble with this country. How does he go at it—giv
notice?—give the country a show? No. All of a sudden h
heaves all the tea in Boston Harbor overboard, and whacl
out a declaration of independence, and dares them to con
on. That was *his* style—he never give anybody a chance. H
had suspicions of his father, the Duke of Wellington. We
what did he do?—ask him to show up? No—drownded hir
in a butt of mamsey, like a cat. Spose people left money lay
ing around where he was—what did he do? He collared i
Spose he contracted to do a thing; and you paid him, an
didn't set down there and see that he done it—what did h
do? He always done the other thing. Spose he opened h
mouth—what then? If he didn't shut it up powerful quicl
he'd lose a lie, every time. That's the kind of a bug Henr
was; and if we'd a had him along 'stead of our kings, he'd
fooled that town a heap worse than ourn done. I don't sa
that ourn is lambs, because they ain't, when you come righ
down to the cold facts; but they ain't nothing to *that* ol
ram, anyway. All I say is, kings is kings, and you got to mak
allowances. Take them all around, they're a mighty orner
lot. It's the way they're raised."

"But dis one do *smell* so like de nation, Huck."

"Well, they all do, Jim. *We* can't help the way a kin
smells; history don't tell no way."

"Now de duke, he's a tolerble likely man, in some ways."

"Yes, a duke's different. But not very different. This one'
a middling hard lot, for a duke. When he's drunk, there ain'
no near-sighted man could tell him from a king."

"Well, anyways, I doan' hanker for no mo' un um, Huck. Dese is all I kin stan'."

"It's the way I feel, too, Jim. But we've got them on our hands, and we got to remember what they are, and make allowances. Sometimes I wish we could hear of a country that's out of kings."

What was the use to tell Jim these warn't real kings and dukes? It wouldn't a done no good; and besides, it was just as I said; you couldn't tell them from the real kind.

I went to sleep, and Jim didn't call me when it was my turn. He often done that. When I waked up, just at daybreak, he was setting there with his head down betwixt his knees, moaning and mourning to himself. I didn't take notice, nor let on. I knowed what it was about. He was thinking about his wife and his children, away up yonder, and he was low and homesick; because he hadn't ever been away from home before in his life; and I do believe he cared just as much for his people as white folks does for their'n. It don't seem natural, but I reckon it's so. He was often moaning and mourning that way, nights, when he judged I was asleep, and saying, "Po' little 'Lizabeth! po' little Johnny! its mighty hard; I spec' I ain't ever gwyne to see you no mo', no mo'!" He was a mighty good nigger, Jim was.

But this time I somehow got to talking to him about his wife and young ones; and by-and-by he says:

"What makes me feel so bad dis time, 'uz bekase I hear sumpn over yonder on de bank like a whack, er a slam, while ago, en it mine me er de time I treat my little 'Lizabeth so ornery. She warn't on'y 'bout fo' year ole, en she tuck de sk'yarlet-fever, en had a powful rough spell; but she got well, en one day she was a-stannin' aroun', en I says to her, I says:

"'Shet de do'.'

"She never done it; jis' stood dah, kiner smilin' up at me. It make me mad; en I says agin, mighty loud, I says:

"'Doan' you hear me?—shet de do'!'

"She jis' stood de same way, kiner smilin' up. I was a-bilin'! I says:

"'I lay I *make* you mine!'

"En wid dat I fetch' her a slap side de head dat sont her a-sprawlin'. Den I went into de yuther room, en 'uz gone 'bout

ten minutes; en when I come back, dah was dat do' a-standii
open *yit*, en dat chile stannin' mos' right in it, a-lookin' dow
and mournin', en de tears runnin' down. My, but I *wuz* ma
I was agwyne for de chile, but jis' den—it was a do' dat ope
innerds—jis' den, 'long come de wind en slam it to, behin
de chile, ker-*blam!*—en my lan', de chile never move'! M
breff mos' hop outer me; en I feel so—so—I doan' know
how I feel. I crope out, all a-tremblin', en crope aroun' e
open de do' easy en slow, en poke my head in behine de chil
sof' en still, en all uv a sudden, I says *pow!* jis' as loud as
could yell. *She never budge!* Oh, Huck, I bust out a-cryin' e
grab her up in my arms, en say, 'Oh, de po' little thing! d
Lord God Amighty fogive po' ole Jim, kaze he never gwyn
to fogive hisself as long's he live!' Oh, she was plumb deef e
dumb, Huck, plumb deef en dumb—en I'd ben a-treat'n he
so!"

XXIV

NEXT DAY, towards night, we laid up under a little willow tow-head out in the middle, where there was a village on each side of the river, and the duke and the king begun to lay out a plan for working them towns. Jim he spoke to the duke, and said he hoped it wouldn't take but a few hours, because it got mighty heavy and tiresome to him when he had to lay all day in the wigwam tied with the rope. You see, when we left him all alone we had to tie him, because if anybody happened on him all by himself and not tied, it wouldn't look much like he was a runaway nigger, you know. So the duke said it *was* kind of hard to have to lay roped all day, and he'd cipher out some way to get around it.

He was uncommon bright, the duke was, and he soon struck it. He dressed Jim up in King Lear's outfit—it was a long curtain-calico gown, and a white horse-hair wig and whiskers; and then he took his theatre-paint and painted Jim's face and hands and ears and neck all over a dead dull solid blue, like a man that's been drownded nine days. Blamed if he warn't the horriblest looking outrage I ever see. Then the duke took and wrote out a sign on a shingle so—

Sick Arab—but harmless when not out of his head.

And he nailed that shingle to a lath, and stood the lath up four or five foot in front of the wigwam. Jim was satisfied. He said it was a sight better than laying tied a couple of years every day and trembling all over every time there was a sound. The duke told him to make himself free and easy, and if anybody ever come meddling around, he must hop out of the wigwam, and carry on a little, and fetch a howl or two like a wild beast, and he reckoned they would light out and leave him alone. Which was sound enough judgment; but you take the average man, and he wouldn't wait for him to howl. Why, he didn't only look like he was dead, he looked considerable more than that.

These rapscallions wanted to try the Nonesuch again, because there was so much money in it, but they judged it wouldn't be safe, because maybe the news might a worked along down by this time. They couldn't hit no project that suited, exactly; so at last the duke said he reckoned he'd lay off and work his brains an hour or two and see if he couldn't put up something on the Arkansaw village; and the king he allowed he would drop over to t'other village, without any plan, but just trust in Providence to lead him the profitable way—meaning the devil, I reckon. We had all bought store clothes where we stopped last; and now the king put his'n on, and he told me to put mine on. I done it, of course. The king's duds was all black, and he did look real swell and starchy. I never knowed how clothes could change a body before. Why, before, he looked like the orneriest old rip that ever was; but now, when he'd take off his new white beaver and make a bow and do a smile, he looked that grand and good and pious that you'd say he had walked right out of the ark, and maybe was old Leviticus himself. Jim cleaned up the canoe, and I got my paddle ready. There was a big steamboat laying at the shore away up under the point, about three mile above town—been there a couple of hours, taking on freight. Says the king:

"Seein' how I'm dressed, I reckon maybe I better arrive down from St. Louis or Cincinnati, or some other big place. Go for the steamboat, Huckleberry; we'll come down to the village on her."

I didn't have to be ordered twice, to go and take a steamboat ride. I fetched the shore a half a mile above the village, and then went scooting along the bluff bank in the easy water. Pretty soon we come to a nice innocent-looking young country jake setting on a log swabbing the sweat off of his face, for it was powerful warm weather; and he had a couple of big carpet-bags by him.

"Run her nose in shore," says the king. I done it. "Wher' you bound for, young man?"

"For the steamboat; going to Orleans."

"Git aboard," says the king. "Hold on a minute, my servant 'll he'p you with them bags. Jump out and he'p the gentleman, Adolphus"—meaning me, I see.

I done so, and then we all three started on again. The young chap was mighty thankful; said it was tough work toting his baggage such weather. He asked the king where he

,as going, and the king told him he'd come down the river
nd landed at the other village this morning, and now he was
'oing up a few mile to see an old friend on a farm up there.
he young fellow says:

"When I first see you, I says to myself, 'It's Mr. Wilks,
ure, and he come mighty near getting here in time.' But then
says again, 'No, I reckon it ain't him, or else he wouldn't be
•addling up the river.' You *ain't* him, are you?"

"No, my name's Blodgett—Elexander Blodgett—*Reverend*
Elexander Blodgett, I spose I must say, as I'm one o' the
Lord's poor servants. But still I'm jist as able to be sorry for
Mr. Wilks for not arriving in time, all the same, if he's missed
anything by it—which I hope he hasn't."

"Well, he don't miss any property by it, because he'll get
that all right; but he's missed seeing his brother Peter die—
which he mayn't mind, nobody can tell as to that—but his
brother would a give anything in this world to see *him* before
he died; never talked about nothing else all these three weeks;
hadn't seen him since they was boys together—and hadn't
ever seen his brother William at all—that's the deef and
dumb one—William ain't more than thirty or thirty-five. Peter and George was the only ones that come out here; George
was the married brother; him and his wife both died last year.
Harvey and William's the only ones that's left now; and, as
was saying, they haven't got here in time."

"Did anybody send 'em word?"

"Oh, yes; a month or two ago, when Peter was first took;
because Peter said then that he sorter felt like he warn't going
o get well this time. You see, he was pretty old, and George's
g'yirls was too young to be much company for him, except
Mary Jane the red-headed one; and so he was kinder lonesome after George and his wife died, and didn't seem to care
much to live. He most desperately wanted to see Harvey—
and William too, for that matter—because he was one of
them kind that can't bear to make a will. He left a letter behind for Harvey, and said he'd told in it where his money was
hid, and how he wanted the rest of the property divided up
o George's g'yirls would be all right—for George didn't
leave nothing. And that letter was all they could get him to
put a pen to."

"Why do you reckon Harvey don't come? Wher' does he live?"

"Oh, he lives in England—Sheffield—preaches there— hasn't ever been in this country. He hasn't had any too much time—and besides he mightn't a got the letter at all, you know."

"Too bad, too bad he couldn't a lived to see his brothers poor soul. You going to Orleans, you say?"

"Yes, but that ain't only a part of it. I'm going in a ship next Wednesday, for Ryo Janeero, where my uncle lives."

"It's a pretty long journey. But it'll be lovely; I wisht I was agoing. Is Mary Jane the oldest? How old is the others?"

"Mary Jane's nineteen, Susan's fifteen, and Joanna's about fourteen—that's the one that gives herself to good works and has a hare-lip."

"Poor things! to be left alone in the cold world so."

"Well, they could be worse off. Old Peter had friends, and they ain't going to let them come to no harm. There's Hobson, the Babtis' preacher; and Deacon Lot Hovey, and Ben Rucker, and Abner Shackleford, and Levi Bell, the lawyer; and Dr. Robinson, and their wives, and the widow Bartley, and—well, there's a lot of them; but these are the ones that Peter was thickest with, and used to write about sometimes, when he wrote home; so Harvey 'll know where to look for friends when he gets here."

Well, the old man he went on asking questions till he just fairly emptied that young fellow. Blamed if he didn't inquire about everybody and everything in that blessed town, and all about all the Wilkses; and about Peter's business—which was a tanner; and about George's—which was a carpenter; and about Harvey's—which was a dissentering minister; and so on, and so on. Then he says:

"What did you want to walk all the way up to the steamboat for?"

"Because she's a big Orleans boat, and I was afeard she mightn't stop there. When they're deep they won't stop for a hail. A Cincinnati boat will, but this is a St. Louis one."

"Was Peter Wilks well off?"

"Oh, yes, pretty well off. He had houses and land, and it's reckoned he left three or four thousand in cash hid up som'ers."

"When did you say he died?"

"I didn't say, but it was last night."

"Funeral to-morrow, likely?"

"Yes, 'bout the middle of the day."

"Well, it's all terrible sad; but we've all got to go, one time or another. So what we want to do is to be prepared; then we're all right."

"Yes, sir, it's the best way. Ma used to always say that."

When we struck the boat, she was about done loading, and pretty soon she got off. The king never said nothing about going aboard, so I lost my ride, after all. When the boat was gone, the king made me paddle up another mile to a lonesome place, and then he got ashore, and says:

"Now hustle back, right off, and fetch the duke up here, and the new carpet-bags. And if he's gone over to t'other side, go over there and git him. And tell him to git himself up regardless. Shove along, now."

I see what *he* was up to; but I never said nothing, of course. When I got back with the duke, we hid the canoe and then they set down on a log, and the king told him everything, just like the young fellow had said it—every last word of it. And all the time he was a doing it, he tried to talk like an Englishman; and he done it pretty well too, for a slouch. I can't imitate him, and so I ain't agoing to try to; but he really done it pretty good. Then he says:

"How are you on the deef and dumb, Bilgewater?"

The duke said, leave him alone for that; said he had played a deef and dumb person on the histrionic boards. So then they waited for a steamboat.

About the middle of the afternoon a couple of little boats come along, but they didn't come from high enough up the river; but at last there was a big one, and they hailed her. She sent out her yawl, and we went aboard, and she was from Cincinnati; and when they found we only wanted to go four or five mile, they was booming mad, and give us a cussing, and said they wouldn't land us. But the king was ca'm. He says:

"If gentlemen kin afford to pay a dollar a mile apiece, to be took on and put off in a yawl, a steamboat kin afford to carry 'em, can't it?"

So they softened down and said it was all right; and when we got to the village, they yawled us ashore. About two dozen men flocked down, when they see the yawl a coming; and when the king says—

"Kin any of you gentlemen tell me wher' Mr. Peter Wilks lives?" they give a glance at one another, and nodded their heads, as much as to say, "What d' I tell you?" Then one of them says, kind of soft and gentle:

"I'm sorry, sir, but the best we can do is to tell you where he *did* live yesterday evening."

Sudden as winking, the ornery old cretur went all to smash, and fell up against the man, and put his chin on his shoulder, and cried down his back, and says:

"Alas, alas, our poor brother—gone, and we never got to see him; oh, it's too, *too* hard!"

Then he turns around, blubbering, and makes a lot of idiotic signs to the duke on his hands, and blamed if *he* didn't drop a carpet-bag and bust out a-crying. If they warn't the beatenest lot, them two frauds, that ever I struck.

Well, the men gethered around, and sympathized with them, and said all sorts of kind things to them, and carried their carpet-bags up the hill for them, and let them lean on them and cry, and told the king all about his brother's last moments, and the king he told it all over again on his hands to the duke, and both of them took on about that dead tanner like they'd lost the twelve disciples. Well, if ever I struck anything like it, I'm a nigger. It was enough to make a body ashamed of the human race.

XXV

T HE NEWS was all over town in two minutes, and you could see the people tearing down on the run, from every which way, some of them putting on their coats as they come. Pretty soon we was in the middle of a crowd, and the noise of the tramping was like a soldier-march. The windows and dooryards was full; and every minute somebody would say, over a fence:

"Is it *them*?"

And somebody trotting along with the gang would answer back and say,

"You bet it is."

When we got to the house, the street in front of it was packed, and the three girls was standing in the door. Mary Jane *was* red-headed, but that don't make no difference, she was most awful beautiful, and her face and her eyes was all lit up like glory, she was so glad her uncles was come. The king he spread his arms, and Mary Jane she jumped for them, and the hare-lip jumped for the duke, and there they *had* it! Everybody most, leastways women, cried for joy to see them meet again at last and have such good times.

Then the king he hunched the duke, private—I see him do it—and then he looked around and see the coffin, over in the corner on two chairs; so then, him and the duke, with a hand across each other's shoulder, and t'other hand to their eyes, walked slow and solemn over there, everybody dropping back to give them room, and all the talk and noise stopping, people saying "Sh!" and all the men taking their hats off and drooping their heads, so you could a heard a pin fall. And when they got there, they bent over and looked in the coffin, and took one sight, and then they bust out a crying so you could a heard them to Orleans, most; and then they put their arms around each other's necks, and hung their chins over each other's shoulders; and then for three minutes, or maybe four, I never see two men leak the way they done. And mind you, everybody was doing the same; and the place was that damp I never see anything like it. Then one of them got on

one side of the coffin, and t'other on t'other side, and they
kneeled down and rested their foreheads on the coffin, and let
on to pray all to theirselves. Well, when it come to that, it
worked the crowd like you never see anything like it, and so
everybody broke down and went to sobbing right out loud—
the poor girls, too; and every woman, nearly, went up to the
girls, without saying a word, and kissed them, solemn, on the
forehead, and then put their hand on their head, and looked
up towards the sky, with the tears running down, and then
busted out and went off sobbing and swabbing, and give the
next woman a show. I never see anything so disgusting.

Well, by-and-by the king he gets up and comes forward a
little, and works himself up and slobbers out a speech, all full
of tears and flapdoodle about its being a sore trial for him
and his poor brother to lose the diseased, and to miss seeing
diseased alive, after the long journey of four thousand mile,
but its a trial that's sweetened and sanctified to us by this dear
sympathy and these holy tears, and so he thanks them out of
his heart and out of his brother's heart, because out of their
mouths they can't, words being too weak and cold, and all
that kind of rot and slush, till it was just sickening; and then
he blubbers out a pious goody-goody Amen, and turns himself loose and goes to crying fit to bust.

And the minute the words was out of his mouth somebody
over in the crowd struck up the doxolojer, and everybody
joined in with all their might, and it just warmed you up and
made you feel as good as church letting out. Music *is* a good
thing; and after all that soul-butter and hogwash, I never see
it freshen up things so, and sound so honest and bully.

Then the king begins to work his jaw again, and says how
him and his nieces would be glad if a few of the main principal friends of the family would take supper here with them
this evening, and help set up with the ashes of the diseased;
and says if his poor brother laying yonder could speak, he
knows who he would name, for they was names that was very
dear to him, and mentioned often in his letters; and so he will
name the same, to-wit, as follows, vizz:—Rev. Mr. Hobson,
and Deacon Lot Hovey, and Mr. Ben Rucker, and Abner
Shackleford, and Levi Bell, and Dr. Robinson, and their
wives, and the widow Bartley.

Rev. Hobson and Dr. Robinson was down to the end of the town, a-hunting together; that is, I mean the doctor was shipping a sick man to t'other world, and the preacher was pinting him right. Lawyer Bell was away up to Louisville on some business. But the rest was on hand, and so they all come and shook hands with the king and thanked him and talked to him; and then they shook hands with the duke, and didn't say nothing but just kept a-smiling and bobbing their heads like a passel of sapheads whilst he made all sorts of signs with his hands and said "Goo-goo—goo-goo-goo," all the time, like a baby that can't talk.

So the king he blatted along, and managed to inquire about pretty much everybody and dog in town, by his name, and mentioned all sorts of little things that happened one time or another in the town, or to George's family, or to Peter; and he always let on that Peter wrote him the things, but that was a lie, he got every blessed one of them out of that young flathead that we canoed up to the steamboat.

Then Mary Jane she fetched the letter her father left behind, and the king he read it out loud and cried over it. It give the dwelling-house and three thousand dollars, gold, to the girls; and it give the tanyard (which was doing a good business), along with some other houses and land (worth about seven thousand), and three thousand dollars in gold to Harvey and William, and told where the six thousand cash was hid, down cellar. So these two frauds said they'd go and fetch it up, and have everything square and above-board; and told me to come with a candle. We shut the cellar door behind us, and when they found the bag they spilt it out on the floor, and it was a lovely sight, all them yaller-boys. My, the way the king's eyes did shine! He slaps the duke on the shoulder, and says:

"Oh, *this* ain't bully, nor noth'n! Oh, no, I reckon not! Why, Biljy, it beats the Nonesuch, *don't* it!"

The duke allowed it did. They pawed the yaller-boys, and sifted them through their fingers and let them jingle down on the floor; and the king says:

"It ain't no use talkin'; bein' brothers to a rich dead man, and representatives of furrin heirs that's got left, is the line for you and me, Bilge. Thish-yer comes of trust'n to Providence. It's the best way, in the long run. I've tried 'em all, and ther' ain't no better way."

Most everybody would a been satisfied with the pile, and took it on trust; but no, they must count it. So they counts it, and it comes out four hundred and fifteen dollars short. Says the king:

"Dern him, I wonder what he done with that four hunderd and fifteen dollars?"

They worried over that a while, and ransacked all around for it. Then the duke says:

"Well, he was a pretty sick man, and likely he made a mistake—I reckon that's the way of it. The best way's to let it go, and keep still about it. We can spare it."

"Oh, shucks, yes, we can *spare* it. I don't k'yer noth'n 'bout that—it's the *count* I'm thinkin' about. We want to be awful square and open and above-board, here, you know. We want to lug this h-yer money up stairs and count it before everybody—then ther' ain't noth'n suspicious. But when the dead man says ther's six thous'n dollars, you know, we don't want to——"

"Hold on," says the duke. "Less make up the deffisit"—and he begun to haul out yaller-boys out of his pocket.

"It's a most amaz'n' good idea, duke—you *have* got a rattlin' clever head on you," says the king. "Blest if the old Nonesuch ain't a heppin' us out agin"—and *he* begun to haul out yaller-jackets and stack them up.

It most busted them, but they made up the six thousand clean and clear.

"Say," says the duke. "I got another idea. Le's go up stairs and count this money, and then take and *give it to the girls*."

"Good land, duke, lemme hug you! It's the most dazzling idea 'at ever a man struck. You have cert'nly got the most astonishin' head I ever see. Oh, this is the boss dodge, ther' ain't no mistake 'bout it. Let 'em fetch along their suspicions now, if they want to—this'll lay 'em out."

When we got up stairs, everybody gethered around the table, and the king he counted it and stacked it up, three hundred dollars in a pile—twenty elegant little piles. Everybody looked hungry at it, and licked their chops. Then they raked it into the bag again, and I see the king begin to swell himself up for another speech. He says:

"Friends all, my poor brother that lays yonder, has done generous by them that's left behind in the vale of sorrers. He has done generous by these-yer poor little lambs that he loved and sheltered, and that's left fatherless and motherless. Yes, and we that knowed him, knows that he would a done *more* generous by 'em if he hadn't ben afeard o' woundin' his dear William and me. Now, *wouldn't* he? Ther' ain't no question 'bout it, in *my* mind. Well, then—what kind o' brothers would it be, that 'd stand in his way at sech a time? And what kind o' uncles would it be that 'd rob—yes, *rob*—sech poor sweet lambs as these 'at he loved so, at sech a time? If I know William—and I *think* I do—he—well, I'll jest ask him." He turns around and begins to make a lot of signs to the duke with his hands; and the duke he looks at him stupid and leather-headed a while, then all of a sudden he seems to catch his meaning, and jumps for the king, goo-gooing with all his might for joy, and hugs him about fifteen times before he lets up. Then the king says, "I knowed it; I reckon *that* 'll convince anybody the way *he* feels about it. Here, Mary Jane, Susan, Joanner, take the money—take it *all*. It's the gift of him that lays yonder, cold but joyful."

Mary Jane she went for him, Susan and the hare-lip went for the duke, and then such another hugging and kissing I never see yet. And everybody crowded up with the tears in their eyes, and most shook the hands off of them frauds, saying all the time:

"You *dear* good souls!—how *lovely!*—how *could* you!"

Well, then, pretty soon all hands got to talking about the diseased again, and how good he was, and what a loss he was, and all that; and before long a big iron-jawed man worked himself in there from outside, and stood a listening and looking, and not saying anything; and nobody saying anything to him either, because the king was talking and they was all busy listening. The king was saying—in the middle of something he'd started in on—

"—they bein' partickler friends o' the diseased. That's why they're invited here this evenin'; but to-morrow we want *all* to come—everybody; for he respected everybody, he liked everybody, and so it's fitten that his funeral orgies sh'd be public."

And so he went a-mooning on and on, liking to hear himself talk, and every little while he fetched in his funeral orgies again, till the duke he couldn't stand it no more; so he writes on a little scrap of paper, "*obsequies*, you old fool," and folds it up and goes to goo-gooing and reaching it over people's heads to him. The king he reads it, and puts it in his pocket, and says:

"Poor William, afflicted as he is, his *heart's* aluz right. Asks me to invite everybody to come to the funeral—wants me to make 'em all welcome. But he needn't a worried—it was jest what I was at."

Then he weaves along again, perfectly ca'm, and goes to dropping in his funeral orgies again every now and then, just like he done before. And when he done it the third time, he says:

"I say orgies, not because it's the common term, because it ain't—obsequies bein' the common term—but because orgies is the right term. Obsequies ain't used in England no more, now—it's gone out. We say orgies now, in England. Orgies is better, because it means the thing you're after, more exact. It's a word that's made up out'n the Greek *orgo*, outside, open, abroad; and the Hebrew *jeesum*, to plant, cover up; hence in *ter*. So, you see, funeral orgies is an open er public funeral."

He was the *worst* I ever struck. Well, the iron-jawed man he laughed right in his face. Everybody was shocked. Everybody says, "Why *doctor!*" and Abner Shackleford says:

"Why, Robinson, hain't you heard the news? This is Harvey Wilks."

The king he smiled eager, and shoved out his flapper, and says:

"*Is* it my poor brother's dear good friend and physician? I——"

"Keep your hands off of me!" says the doctor. "*You* talk like an Englishman—*don't* you? It's the worse imitation I ever heard. *You* Peter Wilks's brother. You're a fraud, that's what you are!"

Well, how they all took on! They crowded around the doctor, and tried to quiet him down, and tried to explain to him,
and tell him how Harvey'd showed in forty ways that he *was*
Harvey, and knowed everybody by name, and the names of
the very dogs, and begged and *begged* him not to hurt
Harvey's feelings and the poor girls' feelings, and all that; but
it warn't no use, he stormed right along, and said any man
that pretended to be an Englishman and couldn't imitate the
lingo no better than what he did, was a fraud and a liar. The
poor girls was hanging to the king and crying; and all of a
sudden the doctor ups and turns on *them*. He says:

"I was your father's friend, and I'm your friend; and I warn
you *as* a friend, and an honest one, that wants to protect you
and keep you out of harm and trouble, to turn your backs on
that scoundrel, and have nothing to do with him, the ignorant tramp, with his idiotic Greek and Hebrew as he calls it.
He is the thinnest kind of an impostor—has come here with
a lot of empty names and facts which he has picked up somewheres, and you take them for *proofs*, and are helped to fool
yourselves by these foolish friends here, who ought to know
better. Mary Jane Wilks, you know me for your friend, and
for your unselfish friend, too. Now listen to me; turn this
pitiful rascal out—I *beg* you to do it. Will you?"

Mary Jane straightened herself up, and my, but she was
handsome! She says:

"*Here* is my answer." She hove up the bag of money and
put it in the king's hands, and says, "Take this six thousand
dollars, and invest it for me and my sisters any way you want
to, and don't give us no receipt for it."

Then she put her arm around the king on one side, and
Susan and the hare-lip done the same on the other. Everybody clapped their hands and stomped on the floor like a
perfect storm, whilst the king held up his head and smiled
proud. The doctor says:

"All right. I wash *my* hands of the matter. But I warn you
all that a time's coming when you're going to feel sick whenever you think of this day"—and away he went.

"All right, doctor," says the king, kinder mocking him,
"we'll try and get 'em to send for you"—which made them
all laugh, and they said it was a prime good hit.

XXVI

WELL when they was all gone, the king he asks Mary Jane how they was off for spare rooms, and she said she had one spare room, which would do for Uncle William, and she'd give her own room to Uncle Harvey, which was a little bigger, and she would turn into the room with her sisters and sleep on a cot; and up garret was a little cubby, with a pallet in it. The king said the cubby would do for his valley—meaning me.

So Mary Jane took us up, and she showed them their rooms, which was plain but nice. She said she'd have her frocks and a lot of other traps took out of her room if they was in Uncle Harvey's way, but he said they warn't. The frocks was hung along the wall, and before them was a curtain made out of calico that hung down to the floor. There was an old hair trunk in one corner, and a guitar box in another, and all sorts of little knick-knacks and jim-cracks around, like girls brisken up a room with. The king said it was all the more homely and more pleasanter for these fixings, and so don't disturb them. The duke's room was pretty small, but plenty good enough, and so was my cubby.

That night they had a big supper, and all them men and women was there, and I stood behind the king and the duke's chairs and waited on them, and the niggers waited on the rest. Mary Jane she set at the head of the table, with Susan along side of her, and said how bad the biscuits was, and how mean the preserves was, and how ornery and tough the fried chickens was—and all that kind of rot, the way women always do for to force out compliments; and the people all knowed everything was tip-top, and said so—said "How *do* you get biscuits to brown so nice?" and "Where, for the land's sake *did* you get these amaz'n pickles?" and all that kind of humbug talky-talk, just the way people always does at a supper, you know.

And when it was all done, me and the hare-lip had supper in the kitchen off of the leavings, whilst the others was help-

ng the niggers clean up the things. The hare-lip she got to
)umping me about England, and blest if I didn't think the ice
vas getting mighty thin, sometimes. She says:

"Did you ever see the king?"

"Who? William Fourth? Well, I bet I have—he goes to our
:hurch." I knowed he was dead years ago, but I never let on.
)o when I says he goes to our church, she says:

"What—regular?"

"Yes—regular. His pew's right over opposite ourn—on
tother side the pulpit."

"I thought he lived in London?"

"Well, he does. Where *would* he live?"

"But I thought *you* lived in Sheffield?"

I see I was up a stump. I had to let on to get choked with
a chicken bone, so as to get time to think how to get down
again. Then I says:

"I mean he goes to our church regular when he's in Sheffield. That's only in the summer-time, when he comes there
to take the sea baths."

"Why, how you talk—Sheffield ain't on the sea."

"Well, who said it was?"

"Why, you did."

"I *didn't*, nuther."

"You did!"

"I didn't."

"You did."

"I never said nothing of the kind."

"Well, what *did* you say, then?"

"Said he come to take the sea *baths*—that's what I said."

"Well, then! how's he going to take the sea baths if it ain't
on the sea?"

"Looky here," I says; "did you ever see any Congress water?"

"Yes."

"Well, did you have to go to Congress to get it?"

"Why, no."

"Well, neither does William Fourth have to go to the sea
to get a sea bath."

"How does he get it, then?"

"Gets it the way people down here gets Congress-water—

in barrels. There in the palace at Sheffield they've got furnaces, and he wants his water hot. They can't bile that amount of water away off there at the sea. They haven't got no conveniences for it."

"Oh, I see, now. You might a said that in the first place and saved time."

When she said that, I see I was out of the woods again, and so I was comfortable and glad. Next, she says:

"Do you go to church, too?"

"Yes—regular."

"Where do you set?"

"Why, in our pew."

"*Whose* pew?"

"Why, *ourn*—your Uncle Harvey's."

"His'n? What does *he* want with a pew?"

"Wants it to set in. What did you *reckon* he wanted with it?"

"Why, I thought he'd be in the pulpit."

Rot him, I forgot he was a preacher. I see I was up a stump again, so I played another chicken bone and got another think. Then I says:

"Blame it, do you suppose there ain't but one preacher to a church?"

"Why, what do they want with more?"

"What!—to preach before a king? I never see such a girl as you. They don't have no less than seventeen."

"Seventeen! My land! Why, I wouldn't set out such a string as that, not if I *never* got to glory. It must take 'em a week."

"Shucks, they don't *all* of 'em preach the same day—only *one* of 'em."

"Well, then, what does the rest of 'em do?"

"Oh, nothing much. Loll around, pass the plate—and one thing or another. But mainly they don't do nothing."

"Well, then, what are they *for*?"

"Why, they're for *style*. Don't you know nothing?"

"Well, I don't *want* to know no such foolishness as that. How is servants treated in England? Do they treat 'em better 'n we treat our niggers?"

"*No!* A servant ain't nobody there. They treat them worse than dogs."

"Don't they give 'em holidays, the way we do, Christmas and New Year's week, and Fourth of July?"

"Oh, just listen! A body could tell *you* hain't ever been to England, by that. Why, Hare-l—why, Joanna, they never see a holiday from year's end to year's end; never go to the circus, nor theatre, nor nigger shows, nor nowheres."

"Nor church?"

"Nor church."

"But *you* always went to church."

Well, I was gone up again. I forgot I was the old man's servant. But next minute I whirled in on a kind of an explanation how a valley was different from a common servant, and *had* to go to church whether he wanted to or not, and set with the family, on account of it's being the law. But I didn't do it pretty good, and when I got done I see she warn't satisfied. She says:

"Honest injun, now, hain't you been telling me a lot of lies?"

"Honest injun," says I.

"None of it at all?"

"None of it at all. Not a lie in it," says I.

"Lay your hand on this book and say it."

I see it warn't nothing but a dictionary, so I laid my hand on it and said it. So then she looked a little better satisfied, and says:

"Well, then, I'll believe some of it; but I hope to gracious if I'll believe the rest."

"What is it you won't believe, Joe?" says Mary Jane, stepping in with Susan behind her. "It ain't right nor kind for you to talk so to him, and him a stranger and so far from his people. How would you like to be treated so?"

"That's always your way, Maim—always sailing in to help somebody before they're hurt. I hain't done nothing to him. He's told some stretchers, I reckon; and I said I wouldn't swallow it all; and that's every bit and grain I *did* say. I reckon he can stand a little thing like that, can't he?"

"I don't care whether 'twas little or whether 'twas big, he's here in our house and a stranger, and it wasn't good of you to say it. If you was in his place, it would make you feel ashamed; and so you oughtn't to say a thing to another person that will make *them* feel ashamed."

"Why, Maim, he said——"

"It don't make no difference what he *said*—that ain't the thing. The thing is for you to treat him *kind*, and not be saying things to make him remember he ain't in his own country and amongst his own folks."

I says to myself, *this* is a girl that I'm letting that old reptle rob her of her money!

Then Susan *she* waltzed in; and if you'll believe me, she did give Hare-lip hark from the tomb!

Says I to myself, And this is *another* one that I'm letting him rob her of her money!

Then Mary Jane she took another inning, and went in sweet and lovely again—which was her way—but when she got done there warn't hardly anything left o' poor Hare-lip. So she hollered.

"All right, then," says the other girls, "you just ask his pardon."

She done it, too. And she done it beautiful. She done it so beautiful it was good to hear; and I wished I could tell her a thousand lies, so she could do it again.

I says to myself, this is *another* one that I'm letting him rob her of her money. And when she got through, they all jest laid theirselves out to make me feel at home and know I was amongst friends. I felt so ornery and low down and mean that I says to myself, My mind's made up; I'll hive that money for them or bust.

So then I lit out—for bed, I said, meaning some time or another. When I got by myself, I went to thinking the thing over. I says to myself, shall I go to that doctor, private, and blow on these frauds? No—that won't do. He might tell who told him; then the king and the duke would make it warm for me. Shall I go, private, and tell Mary Jane? No—I dasn't do it. Her face would give them a hint, sure; they've got the money, and they'd slide right out and get away with it. If she was to fetch in help, I'd get mixed up in the business, before it was done with, I judge. No, there ain't no good way but one. I got to steal that money, somehow; and I got to steal it some way that they won't suspicion that I done it. They've got a good thing, here; and they ain't agoing to leave till they've played this family and this town for all they're worth, so I'll find a chance time enough. I'll steal it, and hide it; and by-and-by, when I'm away down the river, I'll write a letter and tell Mary Jane where it's hid. But I better hive it to-night, if I can, because the doctor maybe hasn't let up as much as he lets on he has; he might scare them out of here, yet.

So, thinks I, I'll go and search them rooms. Up stairs the hall was dark, but I found the duke's room, and started to paw around it with my hands; but I recollected it wouldn't be much like the king to let anybody else take care of that money but his own self; so then I went to his room and begun to paw around there. But I see I couldn't do nothing without a candle, and I dasn't light one, of course. So I judged I'd got to do the other thing—lay for them, and eavesdrop. About that time, I hears their footsteps coming, and was going to skip under the bed; I reached for it, but it wasn't where I thought it would be; but I touched the curtain that hid Mary Jane's frocks, so I jumped in behind that and snuggled in amongst the gowns, and stood there perfectly still.

They come in and shut the door; and the first thing the duke done was to get down and look under the bed. Then I was glad I hadn't found the bed when I wanted it. And yet, you know, it's kind of natural to hide under the bed when you are up to anything private. They sets down, then, and the king says:

"Well, what is it? and cut it middlin' short, because it's better for us to be down there a whoopin'-up the mournin', than up here givin' 'em a chance to talk us over."

"Well, this is it, Capet. I ain't easy; I ain't comfortable. That doctor lays on my mind. I wanted to know your plans. I've got a notion, and I think it's a sound one."

"What is it, duke?"

"That we better glide out of this, before three in the morning, and clip it down the river with what we've got. Specially, seeing we got it so easy—*given* back to us, flung at our heads, as you may say, when of course we allowed to have to steal it back. I'm for knocking off and lighting out."

That made me feel pretty bad. About an hour or two ago,

it would a been a little different, but now it made me feel bad and disappointed. The king rips out and says:

"What! And not sell out the rest o' the property? March off like a passel o' fools and leave eight or nine thous'n' dollars' worth o' property layin' around jest sufferin' to be scooped in?—and all good salable stuff, too."

The duke he grumbled; said the bag of gold was enough, and he didn't want to go no deeper—didn't want to rob a lot of orphans of *everything* they had.

"Why, how you talk!" says the king. "We shan't rob 'em of nothing at all but jest this money. The people that *buys* the property is the suff'rers; because as soon's it's found out 'at we didn't own it—which won't be long after we've slid—the sale won't be valid, and it'll all go back to the estate. These-yer orphans 'll git their house back agin, and that's enough for *them*; they're young and spry, and k'n easy earn a livin'. *They* ain't agoing to suffer. Why, jest think—there's thous'n's and thous'n's that ain't nigh so well off. Bless you, *they* ain't got noth'n to complain of."

Well, the king he talked him blind; so at last he give in, and said all right, but said he believed it was blame foolishness to stay, and that doctor hanging over them. But the king says:

"Cuss the doctor! What do we k'yer for *him*? Hain't we got all the fools in town on our side? and ain't that a big enough majority in any town?"

So they got ready to go down stairs again. The duke says:

"I don't think we put that money in a good place."

That cheered me up. I'd begun to think I warn't going to get a hint of no kind to help me. The king says:

"Why?"

"Because Mary Jane 'll be in mourning from this out; and first you know the nigger that does up the rooms will get an order to box these duds up and put 'em away; and do you reckon a nigger can run across money and not borrow some of it?"

"Your head's level, agin, duke," says the king; and he come a fumbling under the curtain two or three foot from where I was. I stuck tight to the wall, and kept mighty still, though quivery; and I wondered what them fellows would say to me if they catched me; and I tried to think what I'd better do if they did catch me. But the king he got the bag before I could think more than about a half a thought, and he never suspicioned I was around. They took and shoved the bag through a rip in the straw tick that was under the feather bed, and crammed it in a foot or two amongst the straw and said it was all right, now, because a nigger only makes up the feather bed, and don't turn over the straw tick only about twice a year, and so it warn't in no danger of getting stole, now.

But I knowed better. I had it out of there before they was half-way down stairs. I groped along up to my cubby, and hid it there till I could get a chance to do better. I judged I better hide it outside of the house somewheres, because if they missed it they would give the house a good ransacking. I knowed that very well. Then I turned in, with my clothes all on; but I couldn't a gone to sleep, if I'd a wanted to, I was in such a sweat to get through with the business. By-and-by I heard the king and the duke come up; so I rolled off of my pallet and laid with my chin at the top of my ladder and waited to see if anything was going to happen. But nothing did.

So I held on till all the late sounds had quit and the early ones hadn't begun, yet; and then I slipped down the ladder.

XXVII

I CREPT to their doors and listened; they was snoring, so
I tip-toed along, and got down stairs all right. There warn'
a sound anywheres. I peeped through a crack of the dining
room door, and see the men that was watching the corpse al
sound asleep on their chairs. The door was open into the par
lor, where the corpse was laying, and there was a candle ir
both rooms. I passed along, and the parlor door was open
but I see there warn't nobody in there but the remainders o
Peter; so I shoved on by; but the front door was locked, anc
the key wasn't there. Just then I heard somebody coming
down the stairs, back behind me. I run in the parlor, and took
a swift look around, and the only place I see to hide the bag
was in the coffin. The lid was shoved along about a foot
showing the dead man's face down in there, with a wet cloth
over it, and his shroud on. I tucked the money-bag in under
the lid, just down beyond where his hands was crossed, which
made me creep, they was so cold, and then I run back across
the room and in behind the door.

The person coming was Mary Jane. She went to the coffin,
very soft, and kneeled down and looked in; then she put up
her handkerchief and I see she begun to cry, though I
couldn't hear her, and her back was to me. I slid out, and as
I passed the dining-room I thought I'd make sure them
watchers hadn't seen me; so I looked through the crack and
everything was all right. They hadn't stirred.

I slipped up to bed, feeling ruther blue, on accounts of the
thing playing out that way after I had took so much trouble
and run so much resk about it. Says I, if it could stay where
it is, all right; because when we get down the river a hundred
mile or two, I could write back to Mary Jane, and she could
dig him up again and get it; but that ain't the thing that's
going to happen; the thing that's going to happen is, the
money 'll be found when they come to screw on the lid. Then
the king 'll get it again, and it 'll be a long day before he gives
anybody another chance to smouch it from him. Of course I
wanted to slide down and get it out of there, but I dasn't try

it. Every minute it was getting earlier, now, and pretty soon some of them watchers would begin to stir, and I might get catched—catched with six thousand dollars in my hands that nobody hadn't hired me to take care of. I don't wish to be mixed up in no such business as that, I says to myself.

When I got down stairs in the morning, the parlor was shut up, and the watchers was gone. There warn't nobody around but the family and the widow Bartley and our tribe. I watched their faces to see if anything had been happening, but I couldn't tell.

Towards the middle of the day the undertaker come, with his man, and they set the coffin in the middle of the room on a couple of chairs, and then set all our chairs in rows, and borrowed more from the neighbors till the hall and the parlor and the dining-room was full. I see the coffin lid was the way it was before, but I dasn't go to look in under it, with folks around.

Then the people begun to flock in, and the beats and the girls took seats in the front row at the head of the coffin, and for a half an hour the people filed around slow, in single rank, and looked down at the dead man's face a minute, and some dropped in a tear, and it was all very still and solemn, only the girls and the beats holding handkerchiefs to their eyes and keeping their heads bent, and sobbing a little. There warn't no other sound but the scraping of the feet on the floor, and blowing noses—because people always blows them more at a funeral than they do at other places except church.

When the place was packed full, the undertaker he slid around in his black gloves with his softy soothering ways, putting on the last touches, and getting people and things all ship-shape and comfortable, and making no more sound than a cat. He never spoke; he moved people around, he squeezed in late ones, he opened up passage-ways, and done it all with nods, and signs with his hands. Then he took his place over against the wall. He was the softest, glidingest, stealthiest man I ever see; and there warn't no more smile to him than there is to a ham.

They had borrowed a melodeum—a sick one; and when everything was ready, a young woman set down and worked it, and it was pretty skreeky and colicky, and everybody joined

in and sung, and Peter was the only one that had a goo
thing, according to my notion. Then the Reverend Hobso
opened up, slow and solemn, and begun to talk; and straigh
off the most outrageous row busted out in the cellar a bod
ever heard; it was only one dog, but he made a most powerfu
racket, and he kept it up, right along; the parson he had to
stand there, over the coffin, and wait—you couldn't hea
yourself think. It was right down awkward, and nobod
didn't seem to know what to do. But pretty soon they se
that long-legged undertaker make a sign to the preacher a
much as to say, "Don't you worry—just depend on me.
Then he stooped down and begun to glide along the wal
just his shoulders showing over the people's heads. So h
glided along, and the pow-wow and racket getting more an
more outrageous all the time; and at last, when he had gon
around two sides of the room, he disappears down cellar
Then, in about two seconds we heard a whack, and the do
he finished up with a most amazing howl or two, and the
everything was dead still, and the parson begun his solem
talk where he left off. In a minute or two here comes thi
undertaker's back and shoulders gliding along the wall again
and so he glided, and glided, around three sides of the roon
and then rose up, and shaded his mouth with his hands, an
stretched his neck out towards the preacher, over the people'
heads, and says, in a kind of a coarse whisper, *"He had a rat!*
Then he drooped down and glided along the wall again to hi
place. You could see it was a great satisfaction to the people
because naturally they wanted to know. A little thing like tha
don't cost nothing, and it's just the little things that makes
man to be looked up to and liked. There warn't no mor
popular man in town than what that undertaker was.

Well, the funeral sermon was very good, but pison long
and tiresome; and then the king he shoved in and got of
some of his usual rubbage, and at last the job was through
and the undertaker begun to sneak up on the coffin with hi
screw-driver. I was in a sweat then, and watched him prett
keen. But he never meddled at all; just slid the lid along, a
soft as mush, and screwed it down tight and fast. So there
was! I didn't know whether the money was in there, or not

So, says I, spose somebody has hogged that bag on the sly?—now how do *I* know whether to write to Mary Jane or not? 'Spose she dug him up and didn't find nothing—what would she think of me? Blame it, I says, I might get hunted up and jailed; I'd better lay low and keep dark, and not write at all; the thing's awful mixed, now; trying to better it, I've worsened it a hundred times, and I wish to goodness I'd just let it alone, dad fetch the whole business!

They buried him, and we come back home, and I went to watching faces again—I couldn't help it, and I couldn't rest easy. But nothing come of it; the faces didn't tell me nothing.

The king he visited around, in the evening, and sweetened every body up, and made himself ever so friendly; and he give out the idea that his congregration over in England would be in a sweat about him, so he must hurry and settle up the estate right away, and leave for home. He was very sorry he was so pushed, and so was everybody; they wished he could stay longer, but they said they could see it couldn't be done. And he said of course him and William would take the girls home with them; and that pleased everybody too, because then the girls would be well fixed, and amongst their own relations; and it pleased the girls, too—tickled them so they clean forgot they ever had a trouble in the world; and told him to sell out as quick as he wanted to, they would be ready. Them poor things was that glad and happy it made my heart ache to see them getting fooled and lied to so, but I didn't see no safe way for me to chip in and change the general tune.

Well, blamed if the king didn't bill the house and the niggers and all the property for auction straight off—sale two days after the funeral; but anybody could buy private beforehand if they wanted to.

So the next day after the funeral, along about noontime, the girls' joy got the first jolt; a couple of nigger traders come along, and the king sold them the niggers reasonable, for three-day drafts as they called it, and away they went, the two sons up the river to Memphis, and their mother down the river to Orleans. I thought them poor girls and them niggers would break their hearts for grief; they cried around each other, and took on so it most made me down sick to see it. The girls said they hadn't ever dreamed of seeing the family separated or sold away from the town. I can't ever get it out of my memory, the sight of them poor miserable girls and niggers hanging around each other's necks and crying; and I reckon I couldn't a stood it all but would a had to bust out and tell on our gang if I hadn't knowed the sale warn't no account and the niggers would be back home in a week or two.

The thing made a big stir in the town, too, and a good many come out flat-footed and said it was scandalous to separate the mother and the children that way. It injured the frauds some; but the old fool he bulled right along, spite of all the duke could say or do, and I tell you the duke was powerful uneasy.

Next day was auction day. About broad-day in the morning, the king and the duke come up in the garret and woke me up, and I see by their look that there was trouble. The king says:

"Was you in my room night before last?"

"No, your majesty"—which was the way I always called him when nobody but our gang warn't around.

"Was you in there yisterday er last night?"

"No, your majesty."

"Honor bright, now—no lies."

"Honor bright, your majesty, I'm telling you the truth. I hain't been anear your room since Miss Mary Jane took you and the duke and showed it to you."

The duke says:

"Have you seen anybody else go in there?"

"No, your grace, not as I remember, I believe."

"Stop and think."

I studied a while, and see my chance, then I says:

"Well, I see the niggers go in there several times."

Both of them give a little jump; and looked like they hadn't ever expected it, and then like they *had*. Then the duke says:

"What, *all* of them?"

"No—leastways not all at once. That is, I don't think I ever see them all come *out* at once but just one time."

"Hello—when was that?"

"It was the day we had the funeral. In the morning. It warn't early, because I overslept. I was just starting down the ladder, and I see them."

"Well, go on, *go* on—what did they do? How'd they act?"

"They didn't do nothing. And they didn't act anyway, much, as fur as I see. They tip-toed away; so I seen, easy enough, that they'd shoved in there to do up your majesty's room, or something, sposing you was up; and found you *warn't* up, and so they was hoping to slide out of the way of trouble without waking you up, if they hadn't already waked you up."

"Great guns, *this* is a go!" says the king; and both of them looked pretty sick, and tolerable silly. They stood there a thinking and scratching their heads, a minute, and then the duke he bust into a kind of a little raspy chuckle, and says:

"It does beat all, how neat the niggers played their hand. They let on to be *sorry* they was going out of this region! and I believed they *was* sorry. And so did you, and so did everybody. Don't ever tell *me* any more that a nigger ain't got any histrionic talent. Why, the way they played that thing, it would fool *anybody*. In my opinion there's a fortune in 'em. If I had capital and a theatre, I wouldn't want a better lay out than that—and here we've gone and sold 'em for a song. Yes, and ain't privileged to sing the song, yet. Say, where *is* that song?—that draft."

"In the bank for to be collected. Where *would* it be?"

"Well, *that's* all right then, thank goodness."

Says I, kind of timid-like:

"Is something gone wrong?"

The king whirls on me and rips out:

"None o' your business! You keep your head shet, and mind y'r own affairs—if you got any. Long as you're in this town, don't you forgit *that*, you hear?" Then he says to the duke, "We got to jest swaller it, and say noth'n: mum's the word for *us*."

As they was starting down the ladder, the duke he chuckles again, and says:

"Quick sales *and* small profits! It's a good business—yes."

The king snarls around on him and says,

"I was trying to do for the best, in sellin' 'm out so quick.

If the profits has turned out to be none, lackin' considable, and none to carry, is it my fault any more'n it's yourn?"

"Well, *they'd* be in this house yet, and we *wouldn't* if I could a got my advice listened to."

The king sassed back, as much as was safe for him, and then swapped around and lit into *me* again. He give me down the banks for not coming and *telling* him I see the niggers come out of his room acting that way—said any fool would a *knowed* something was up. And then waltzed in and cussed *himself* a while; and said it all come of him not laying late and taking his natural rest that morning, and he'd be blamed if he'd ever do it again. So they went off a jawing; and I felt dreadful glad I'd worked it all off onto the niggers and yet hadn't done the niggers no harm by it.

XXVIII

B Y-AND-BY it was getting-up time; so I come down the
ladder and started for down stairs, but as I come to the
girls' room, the door was open, and I see Mary Jane setting
by her old hair trunk, which was open and she'd been packing
things in it—getting ready to go to England. But she had
stopped now, with a folded gown in her lap, and had her face
in her hands, crying. I felt awful bad to see it; of course anybody would. I went in there, and says:

"Miss Mary Jane, you can't abear to see people in trouble,
and I can't—most always. Tell me about it."

So she done it. And it was the niggers—I just expected it.
She said the beautiful trip to England was most about spoiled
for her; she didn't know *how* she was ever going to be happy
there, knowing the mother and the children warn't ever going
to see each other no more—and then busted out bitterer than
ever, and flung up her hands, and says:

"Oh, dear, dear, to think they ain't *ever* going to see each
other any more!"

"But they *will*—and inside of two weeks—and I *know* it!"
says I.

Laws it was out before I could think!—and before I could
budge, she throws her arms around my neck, and told me to
say it *again*, say it *again*, say it *again*!

I see I had spoke too sudden, and said too much, and was
in a close place. I asked her to let me think a minute; and she
set there, very impatient and excited, and handsome, but
looking kind of happy and eased-up, like a person that's had
a tooth pulled out. So I went to studying it out. I says to
myself, I reckon a body that ups and tells the truth when he
is in a tight place, is taking considerable many resks, though
I ain't had no experience, and can't say for certain; but it
looks so to me, anyway; and yet here's a case where I'm blest
if it don't look to me like the truth is better, and actuly *safer*,
than a lie. I must lay it by in my mind, and think it over some
time or other, it's so kind of strange and unregular. I never
see nothing like it. Well, I says to myself at last, I'm agoing

to chance it; I'll up and tell the truth this time, though it does seem most like setting down on a kag of powder and touching it off just to see where you'll go to. Then I says:

"Miss Mary Jane, is there any place out of town a little ways, where you could go and stay three or four days?"

"Yes—Mr. Lothrop's. Why?"

"Never mind why, yet. If I'll tell you how I know the niggers will see each other again—inside of two weeks—here in this house—and *prove* how I know it—will you go to Mr. Lothrop's and stay four days?"

"Four days!" she says; "I'll stay a year!"

"All right," I says, "I don't want nothing more out of *you* than just your word—I druther have it than another man's kiss-the-Bible." She smiled, and reddened up very sweet, and I says, "If you don't mind it, I'll shut the door—and bolt it."

Then I come back and set down again, and says:

"Don't you holler. Just set still, and take it like a man. I got to tell the truth, and you want to brace up, Miss Mary, because it's a bad kind, and going to be hard to take, but there ain't no help for it. These uncles of yourn ain't no uncles at all—they're a couples of frauds—regular dead-beats. There, now we're over the worst of it—you can stand the rest middling easy."

It jolted her up like everything, of course; but I was over the shoal water now, so I went right along, her eyes a blazing higher and higher all the time, and told her every blame thing, from where we first struck that young fool going up to the steamboat, clear through to where she flung herself onto the king's breast at the front door and he kissed her sixteen or seventeen times—and then up she jumps, with her face afire like sunset, and says:

"The brute! Come—don't waste a minute—not a *second*—we'll have them tarred and feathered, and flung in the river!"

Says I:

"Cert'nly. But do you mean, *before* you go to Mr. Lothrop's, or——"

"Oh," she says, "what am I *thinking* about!" she says, and set right down again. "Don't mind what I said—please don't—you *won't*, now, *will* you?" Laying her silky hand on mine in that kind of a way that I said I would die first. "I never thought, I was so stirred up," she says; "now go on, and I won't do so any more. You tell me what to do, and whatever you say, I'll do it."

"Well," I says, "it's a rough gang, them two frauds, and I'm fixed so I got to travel with them a while longer, whether I want to or not—I druther not tell you why—and if you was to blow on them this town would get me out of their claws, and I'd be all right, but there'd be another person that you don't know about who'd be in big trouble. Well, we got to save *him*, hain't we? Of course. Well, then, we won't blow on them."

Saying them words put a good idea in my head. I see how maybe I could get me and Jim rid of the frauds; get them jailed here, and then leave. But I didn't want to run the raft in day-time, without anybody aboard to answer questions but me; so I didn't want the plan to begin working till pretty late to-night. I says:

"Miss Mary Jane, I'll tell you what we'll do—and you won't have to stay at Mr. Lothrop's so long, nuther. How fur is it?"

"A little short of four miles—right out in the country, back here."

"Well, that'll answer. Now you go along out there, and lay low till nine or half-past, to-night, and then get them to fetch you home again—tell them you've thought of something. If you get here before eleven, put a candle in this window, and if I don't turn up, wait *till* eleven, and *then* if I don't turn up it means I'm gone, and out of the way, and safe. Then you come out and spread the news around, and get these beats jailed."

"Good," she says, "I'll do it."

"And if it just happens so that I don't get away, but get took up along with them, you must up and say I told you the whole thing beforehand, and you must stand by me all you can."

"Stand by you, indeed I will. They sha'n't touch a hair of your head!" she says, and I see her nostrils spread and her eyes snap when she said it, too.

"If I get away, I sha'n't be here," I says, "to prove these rapscallions ain't your uncles, and I couldn't do it if I *was*

here. I could swear they was beats and bummers, that's all;
though that's worth something. Well, there's others can do
that better than what I can—and they're people that ain't
going to be doubted as quick as I'd be. I'll tell you how to
find them. Gimme a pencil and a piece of paper. There—
'*Royal Nonesuch, Bricksville.*' Put it away, and don't lose it.
When the court wants to find out something about these two,
let them send up to Bricksville and say they've got the men
that played the Royal Nonesuch, and ask for some witnesses—why, you'll have that entire town down here before
you can hardly wink, Miss Mary. And they'll come a-biling,
too."

I judged we had got everything fixed about right, now. So
I says:

"Just let the auction go right along, and don't worry. Nobody don't have to pay for the things they buy till a whole
day after the auction, on accounts of the short notice, and
they ain't going out of this till they get that money—and the
way we've fixed it the sale ain't going to count, and they ain't
going to *get* no money. It's just like the way it was with the
niggers—it warn't no sale, and the niggers will be back before long. Why, they can't collect the money for the *niggers*,
yet—they're in the worst kind of a fix, Miss Mary."

"Well," she says, "I'll run down to breakfast now, and then
I'll start straight for Mr. Lothrop's."

" 'Deed, *that* ain't the ticket, Miss Mary Jane," I says, "by
no manner of means; go *before* breakfast."

"Why?"

"What did you reckon I wanted you to go at all for, Miss
Mary?"

"Well, I never thought—and come to think, I don't know.
What was it?"

"Why, it's because you ain't one of these leather-face people. I don't want no better book than what your face is. A
body can set down and read it off like coarse print. Do you
reckon you can go and face your uncles, when they come to
kiss you good-morning, and never——"

"There, there, don't! Yes, I'll go before breakfast—I'll be
glad to. And leave my sisters with them?"

"Yes—never mind about them. They've got to stand it yet

a while. They might suspicion something if all of you was to go. I don't want you to see them, nor your sisters, nor nobody in this town—if a neighbor was to ask how is your uncles this morning, your face would tell something. No, you go right along, Miss Mary Jane, and I'll fix it with all of them. I'll tell Miss Susan to give your love to your uncles and say you've went away for a few hours for to get a little rest and change, or to see a friend, and you'll be back to-night or early in the morning."

"Gone to see a friend is all right, but I won't have my love given to them."

"Well, then, it sha'n't be." It was well enough to tell *her* so—no harm in it. It was only a little thing to do, and no trouble; and it's the little things that smoothes people's roads the most, down here below; it would make Mary Jane comfortable, and it wouldn't cost nothing. Then I says: "There's one more thing—that bag of money."

"Well, they've got that; and it makes me feel pretty silly to think *how* they got it."

"No, you're out, there. They hain't got it."

"Why, who's got it?"

"I wish I knowed, but I don't. I *had* it, because I stole it from them: and I stole it to give to you; and I know where I hid it, but I'm afraid it ain't there no more. I'm awful sorry, Miss Mary Jane, I'm just as sorry as I can be; but I done the best I could; I did, honest. I come nigh getting caught, and I had to shove it into the first place I come to, and run—and it warn't a good place."

"Oh, stop blaming yourself—it's too bad to do it, and I won't allow it—you couldn't help it; it wasn't your fault. Where did you hide it?"

I didn't want to set her to thinking about her troubles again; and I couldn't seem to get my mouth to tell her what would make her see that corpse laying in the coffin with that bag of of money on his stomach. So for a minute I didn't say nothing—then I says:

"I'd ruther not *tell* you where I put it, Miss Mary Jane, if you don't mind letting me off; but I'll write it for you on a piece of paper, and you can read it along the road to Mr. Lothrop's, if you want to. Do you reckon that'll do?"

"Oh, yes."

So I wrote: "I put it in the coffin. It was in there when you was crying there, away in the night. I was behind the door, and I was mighty sorry for you, Miss Mary Jane."

It made my eyes water a little, to remember her crying there all by herself in the night, and them devils laying there right under her own roof, shaming her and robbing her; and when I folded it up and give it to her, I see the water come into her eyes, too; and she shook me by the hand, hard, and says:

"*Good*-bye—I'm going to do everything just as you've told me; and if I don't ever see you again, I sha'n't ever forget you, and I'll think of you a many and a many a time, and I'll *pray* for you, too!"—and she was gone.

Pray for me! I reckoned if she knowed me she'd take a job that was more nearer her size. But I bet she done it, just the same—she was just that kind. She had the grit to pray for Judus if she took the notion—there warn't no backdown to her, I judge. You may say what you want to, but in my opinion she had more sand in her than any girl I ever see; in my opinion she was just full of sand. It sounds like flattery, but it ain't no flattery. And when it comes to beauty—and goodness too—she lays over them all. I hain't ever seen her since that time that I see her go out of that door; no, I hain't ever seen her since, but I reckon I've thought of her a many and a many a million times, and of her saying she would pray for me; and if ever I'd a thought it would do any good for me to pray for *her*, blamed if I wouldn't a done it or bust.

Well, Mary Jane she lit out the back way, I reckon; because nobody see her go. When I struck Susan and the hare-lip, I says:

"What's the name of them people over on t'other side of the river that you all goes to see sometimes?"

They says:

"There's several; but it's the Proctors, mainly."

"That's the name," I says; "I most forgot it. Well, Miss Mary Jane she told me to tell you she's gone over there in a dreadful hurry—one of them's sick."

"Which one?"

"I don't know; leastways I kinder forget; but I think it's——"

"Sakes alive, I hope it ain't *Hanner*?"

"I'm sorry to say it," I says, "but Hanner's the very one."

"My goodness—and she so well only last week! Is she took bad?"

"It ain't no name for it. They set up with her all night, Miss Mary Jane said, and they don't think she'll last many hours."

"Only think of that, now! What's the matter with her!"

I couldn't think of anything reasonable, right off that way, so I says:

"Mumps."

"Mumps your granny! They don't set up with people that's got the mumps."

"They don't, don't they? You better bet they do with *these* mumps. These mumps is different. It's a new kind, Miss Mary Jane said."

"How's it a new kind?"

"Because it's mixed up with other things."

"What other things?"

"Well, measles, and whooping-cough and erysiplas, and consumption, and yaller janders, and brain fever, and I don't know what all."

"My land! And they call it the *mumps*?"

"That's what Miss Mary Jane said."

"Well, what in the nation do they call it the *mumps* for?"

"Why, because it *is* the mumps. That's what it starts with."

"Well, ther' ain't no sense in it. A body might stump his toe, and take pison, and fall down the well, and break his neck, and bust his brains out, and somebody come along and ask what killed him, and some numskull up and say, 'Why, he stumped his *toe*.' Would ther' be any sense in that? *No*. And ther' ain't no sense in *this*, nuther. Is it ketching?"

"Is it *ketching*? Why, how you talk. Is a *harrow* catching?— in the dark? If you don't hitch onto one tooth, you're bound to on another, ain't you? And you can't get away with that tooth without fetching the whole harrow along, can you? Well, these kind of mumps is a kind of a harrow, as you may say—and it ain't no slouch of a harrow, nuther, you come to get it hitched on good."

"Well, it's awful, *I* think," says the hare-lip. "I'll go to Uncle Harvey and——"

"Oh, yes," I says, "I *would*. Of *course* I would. I wouldn't
lose no time."

"Well, why wouldn't you?"

"Just look at it a minute, and maybe you can see. Hain't
your uncles obleeged to get along home to England as fast as
they can? And do you reckon they'd be mean enough to go
off and leave you to go all that journey by yourselves? *You*
know they'll wait for you. So fur, so good. Your uncle
Harvey's a preacher, ain't he? Very well, then; is a *preacher*
going to deceive a steamboat clerk? is he going to deceive a
ship clerk?—so as to get them to let Miss Mary Jane go
aboard? Now *you* know he ain't. What *will* he do, then? Why,
he'll say, 'It's a great pity, but my church matters has got to
get along the best way they can; for my niece has been exposed to the dreadful pluribus-unum mumps, and so it's my
bounden duty to set down here and wait the three months it
takes to show on her if she's got it.' But never mind, if you
think it's best to tell your uncle Harvey——"

"Shucks, and stay fooling around here when we could all
be having good times in England whilst we was waiting to
find out whether Mary Jane's got it or not? Why, you talk
like a muggins."

"Well, anyway, maybe you better tell some of the neighbors."

"Listen at that, now. You do beat all, for natural stupid-
ness. Can't you *see* that *they'd* go and tell? Ther' ain't no way
but just to not tell anybody at *all*."

"Well, maybe you're right—yes, I judge you *are* right."

"But I reckon we ought to tell Uncle Harvey she's gone
out a while, anyway, so he wont be uneasy about her?"

"Yes, Miss Mary Jane she wanted you to do that. She says,
'Tell them to give Uncle Harvey and William my love and a
kiss, and say I've run over the river to see Mr.—Mr.—what
is the name of that rich family your uncle Peter used to think
so much of?—I mean the one that——"

"Why, you must mean the Apthorps, ain't it?"

"Of course; bother them kind of names, a body can't ever
seem to remember them, half the time, somehow. Yes, she

said, say she has run over for to ask the Apthorps to be sure and come to the auction and buy this house, because she allowed her uncle Peter would ruther they had it than anybody else; and she's going to stick to them till they say they'll come, and then, if she ain't too tired, she's coming home; and if she is, she'll be home in the morning anyway. She said, don't say nothing about the Proctors, but only about the Apthorps—which'll be perfectly true, because she *is* going there to speak about their buying the house; I know it, because she told me so, herself."

"All right," they said, and cleared out to lay for their uncles, and give them the love and the kisses, and tell them the message.

Everything was all right now. The girls wouldn't say nothing because they wanted to go to England; and the king and the duke would ruther Mary Jane was off working for the auction than around in reach of Doctor Robinson. I felt very good; I judged I had done it pretty neat—I reckoned Tom Sawyer couldn't a done it no neater himself. Of course he would a throwed more style into it, but I can't do that very handy, not being brung up to it.

Well, they held the auction in the public square, along towards the end of the afternoon, and it strung along, and strung along, and the old man he was on hand and looking his level pisonest, up there longside of the auctioneer, and chipping in a little Scripture, now and then, or a little goody-goody saying, of some kind, and the duke he was around goo-gooing for sympathy all he knowed how, and just spreading himself generly.

But by-and-by the thing dragged through, and everything was sold. Everything but a little old trifling lot in the graveyard. So they'd got to work *that* off—I never see such a giraft as the king was for wanting to swallow *everything*. Well, whilst they was at it, a steamboat landed, and in about two minutes up comes a crowd a whooping and yelling and laughing and carrying on, and singing out:

"*Here's* your opposition line! here's your two sets o' heirs to old Peter Wilks—and you pays your money and you takes your choice!"

XXIX

THEY WAS FETCHING a very nice looking old gentleman along, and a nice looking younger one, with his right arm in a sling. And my souls, how the people yelled, and laughed, and kept it up. But I didn't see no joke about it, and I judged it would strain the duke and the king some to see any. I reckoned they'd turn pale. But no, nary a pale did *they* turn. The duke he never let on he suspicioned what was up, but just went a goo-gooing around, happy and satisfied, like a jug that's googling out buttermilk; and as for the king, he just gazed and gazed down sorrowful on them new-comers like it give him the stomach-ache in his very heart to think there could be such frauds and rascals in the world. Oh, he done it admirable. Lots of the principal people gethered around the king, to let him see they was on his side. That old gentleman that had just come looked all puzzled to death. Pretty soon he begun to speak, and I see, straight off, he pronounced *like* an Englishman, not the king's way, though the king's *was* pretty good, for an imitation. I can't give the old gent's words, nor I can't imitate him; but he turned around to the crowd, and says, about like this:

"This is a surprise to me which I wasn't looking for; and I'll acknowledge, candid and frank, I ain't very well fixed to meet it and answer it; for my brother and me has had misfortunes, he's broke his arm, and our baggage got put off at a town above here, last night in the night by a mistake. I am Peter Wilks's brother Harvey, and this is his brother William, which can't hear nor speak—and can't even make signs to amount to much, now 't he's only got one hand to work them with. We are who we say we are; and in a day or two, when I get the baggage, I can prove it. But, up till then, I won't say nothing more, but go to the hotel and wait."

So him and the new dummy started off; and the king he laughs, and blethers out:

"Broke his arm— *very* likely *ain't* it?—and very convenient, too, for a fraud that's got to make signs, and hain't learnt how. Lost their baggage! That's *mighty* good!—and mighty ingenious—under the *circumstances*!"

So he laughed again; and so did everybody else, except three or four, or maybe half a dozen. One of these was that doctor; another one was a sharp looking gentleman, with a carpet-bag of the old-fashioned kind made out of carpet-stuff, that had just come off of the steamboat and was talking to him in a low voice, and glancing towards the king now and then and nodding their heads—it was Levi Bell, the lawyer that was gone up to Louisville; and another one was a big rough husky that come along and listened to all the old gentleman said, and was listening to the king now. And when the king got done, this husky up and says:

"Say, looky here; if you are Harvey Wilks, when'd you come to this town?"

"The day before the funeral, friend," says the king.

"But what time o' day?"

"In the evenin'—'bout an hour er two before sundown."

"*How'd* you come?"

"I come down on the *Susan Powell*, from Cincinnati."

"Well, then, how'd you come to be up at the Pint in the *mornin'*—in a canoe?"

"I warn't up at the Pint in the mornin'."

"It's a lie."

Several of them jumped for him and begged him not to talk that way to an old man and a preacher.

"Preacher be hanged, he's a fraud and a liar. He was up at the Pint that mornin'. I live up there, don't I? Well, I was up there, and he was up there. I *see* him there. He come in a canoe, along with Tim Collins and a boy."

The doctor he up and says:

"Would you know the boy again if you was to see him, Hines?"

"I reckon I would, but I don't know. Why, yonder he is, now. I know him perfectly easy."

It was me he pointed at. The doctor says:

"Neighbors, I don't know whether the new couple is frauds or not; but if *these* two ain't frauds, I am an idiot, that's all. I think it's our duty to see that they don't get away from here till we've looked into this thing. Come along, Hines; come along, the rest of you. We'll take these fellows to the tavern and affront them with t'other couple, and I reckon we'll find out *something* before we get through."

It was nuts for the crowd, though maybe not for the king', friends; so we all started. It was about sundown. The docto he led me along by the hand, and was plenty kind enough but he never let *go* my hand.

We all got in a big room in the hotel, and lit up some candles, and fetched in the new couple. First, the doctor says

"I don't wish to be too hard on these two men, but *I* think they're frauds, and they may have complices that we don' know nothing about. If they have, won't the complices get away with that bag of gold Peter Wilks left? It ain't unlikely If these men ain't frauds, they won't object to sending for that money and letting us keep it till they prove they're all right—ain't that so?"

Everybody agreed to that. So I judged they had our gang in a pretty tight place, right at the outstart. But the king he only looked sorrowful, and says:

"Gentlemen, I wish the money was there, for I ain't got no disposition to throw anything in the way of a fair, open, out-and-out investigation o' this misable business; but alas, the money ain't there; you k'n send and see, if you want to."

"Where is it, then?"

"Well, when my niece give it to me to keep for her, I took and hid it inside o' the straw tick o' my bed, not wishin' to bank it for the few days we'd be here, and considerin' the bed a safe place, we not bein' used to niggers, and suppos'n' 'em honest, like servants in England. The niggers stole it the very next mornin' after I had went down stairs; and when I sold 'em, I hadn't missed the money yit, so they got clean away with it. My servant here k'n tell you 'bout it gentlemen."

The doctor and several said "Shucks!" and I see nobody didn't altogether believe him. One man asked me if I see the niggers steal it. I said no, but I see them sneaking out of the room and hustling away, and I never thought nothing, only I reckoned they was afraid they had waked up my master and was trying to get away before he made trouble with them. That was all they asked me. Then the doctor whirls on me and says:

"Are *you* English too?"

I says yes; and him and some others laughed, and said, "Stuff!"

Well, then they sailed in on the general investigation, and there we had it, up and down, hour in, hour out, and nobody never said a word about supper, nor ever seemed to think about it—and so they kept it up, and kept it up; and it *was* the worst mixed-up thing you ever see. They made the king tell his yarn, and they made the old gentleman tell his'n; and anybody but a lot of prejudiced chuckleheads would a *seen* that the old gentleman was spinning truth and t'other one lies. And by-and-by they had me up to tell what I knowed. The king he give me a left-handed look out of the corner of his eye, and so I knowed enough to talk on the right side. I begun to tell about Sheffield, and how we lived there, and all about the English Wilkses, and so on; but I didn't get pretty fur till the doctor begun to laugh; and Levi Bell, the lawyer, says:

"Set down, my boy, I wouldn't strain myself, if I was you. I reckon you ain't used to lying, it don't seem to come handy; what you want is practice. You do it pretty awkward."

I didn't care nothing for the compliment, but I was glad to be let off, anyway.

The doctor he started to say something, and turns and says:

"If you'd been in town at first, Levi Bell——"

The king broke in and reached out his hand, and says:

"Why, is this my poor dead brother's old friend that he's wrote so often about?"

The lawyer and him shook hands, and the lawyer smiled and looked pleased, and they talked right along a while, and then got to one side and talked low; and at last the lawyer speaks up and says:

"That'll fix it. I'll take the order and send it, along with your brother's, and then they'll know it's all right."

So they got some paper and a pen, and the king he set down and twisted his head to one side, and chawed his tongue, and scrawled off something; and then they give the pen to the duke—and then for the first time, the duke looked sick. But he took the pen and wrote. So then the lawyer turns to the new old gentleman and says:

"You and your brother please write a line or two and sign your names."

The old gentleman wrote, but nobody couldn't read it. The lawyer looked powerful astonished, and says:

"Well, it beats *me*"—and snaked a lot of old letters out of his pocket, and examined them, and then examined the old man's writing, and then *them* again; and then says: "These old letters is from Harvey Wilks; and here's *these* two's handwritings, and anybody can see *they* didn't write them" (the king and the duke looked sold and foolish, I tell you, to see how the lawyer had took them in), "and here's *this* old gentleman's handwriting, and anybody can tell, easy enough, *he* didn't write them—fact is, the scratches he makes ain't properly *writing*, at all. Now here's some letters from——"

The new old gentleman says:

"If you please, let me explain. Nobody can read my hand but my brother there—so he copies for me. It's *his* hand you've got there, not mine."

"*Well!*" says the lawyer, "this *is* a state of things. I've got some of William's letters too; so if you'll get him to write a line or so we can com——"

"He *can't* write with his left hand," says the old gentleman. "If he could use his right hand, you would see that he wrote his own letters and mine too. Look at both, please—they're by the same hand."

The lawyer done it, and says:

"I believe it's so—and if it ain't so, there's a heap stronger resemblance than I'd noticed before, anyway. Well, well, well! I thought we was right on the track of a slution, but it's gone to grass, partly. But anyway, *one* thing is proved—*these* two ain't either of 'em Wilkses"—and he wagged his head towards the king and the duke.

Well, what do you think?—that muleheaded old fool wouldn't give in *then*! Indeed he wouldn't. Said it warn't no fair test. Said his brother William was the cussedest joker in the world, and hadn't *tried* to write—*he* see William was going to play one of his jokes the minute he put the pen to paper. And so he warmed up and went warbling and warbling right along, till he was actuly beginning to believe what he was saying, *himself*—but pretty soon the new old gentle-man broke in, and says:

"I've thought of something. Is there anybody here that helped to lay out my br—helped to lay out the late Peter Wilks for burying?"

"Yes," says somebody, "me and Ab Turner done it. We're both here."

Then the old man turns towards the king, and says:

"Peraps this gentleman can tell me what was tatooed on his breast?"

Blamed if the king didn't have to brace up mighty quick, or he'd a squshed down like a bluff bank that the river has cut under, it took him so sudden—and mind you, it was a thing that was calculated to make most *anybody* sqush to get fetched such a solid one as that without any notice—because how was *he* going to know what was tatooed on the man? He whitened a little; he couldn't help it; and it was mighty still in there, and everybody bending a little forwards and gaz-ing at him. Says I to myself, *Now* he'll throw up the sponge—there ain't no more use. Well, did he? A body can't hardly believe it, but he didn't. I reckon he thought he'd keep the thing up till he tired them people out, so they'd thin out, and him and the duke could break loose and get away. Anyway, he set there, and pretty soon he begun to smile, and says:

"Mf! It's a *very* tough question, *ain't* it! *Yes*, sir, I k'n tell you what's tatooed on his breast. It's jest a small, thin, blue arrow—that's what it is; and if you don't look clost, you can't see it. *Now* what do you say—hey?"

Well, *I* never see anything like that old blister for clean out-and-out cheek.

The new old gentleman turns brisk towards Ab Turner and his pard, and his eye lights up like he judged he'd got the king *this* time, and says:

"There—you've heard what he said! Was there any such mark on Peter Wilks's breast?"

Both of them spoke up and says:

"We didn't see no such mark."

"Good!" says the old gentleman. "Now, what you *did* see on his breast was a small dim P, and a B (which is an initial he dropped when he was young), and a W, with dashes be-

tween them, so: P—B—W"—and he marked them that way
on a piece of paper. "Come—ain't that what you saw?"

Both of them spoke up again, and says:

"No, we *didn't*. We never seen any marks at all."

Well, everybody *was* in a state of mind, now; and they
sings out:

"The whole *bilin'* of 'm 's frauds! Le's duck 'em! le's drown
'em! le's ride 'em on a rail!" and everybody was whooping at
once, and there was a rattling pow-wow. But the lawyer he
jumps on the table and yells, and says:

"Gentlemen—gentle*men*! Hear me just a word—just a *single* word—if you PLEASE! There's one way yet—let's go and
dig up the corpse and look."

That took them.

"Hooray!" they all shouted, and was starting right off; but
the lawyer and the doctor sung out:

"Hold on, hold on! Collar all these four men and the boy,
and fetch *them* along, too!"

"We'll do it!" they all shouted: "and if we don't find them
marks we'll lynch the whole gang!"

I *was* scared, now, I tell you. But there warn't no getting
away, you know. They gripped us all, and marched us right
along, straight for the graveyard, which was a mile and a half
down the river, and the whole town at our heels, for we made
noise enough, and it was only nine in the evening.

As we went by our house I wished I hadn't sent Mary Jane
out of town; because now if I could tip her the wink, she'd
light out and save me, and blow on our dead-beats.

Well, we swarmed along down the river road, just carrying
on like wild-cats; and to make it more scary, the sky was dark-
ing up, and the lightning beginning to wink and flitter, and
the wind to shiver amongst the leaves. This was the most
awful trouble and most dangersome I ever was in; and I was
kinder stunned; everything was going so different from what
I had allowed for; stead of being fixed so I could take my
own time, if I wanted to, and see all the fun, and have Mary
Jane at my back to save me and set me free when the close-fit
come, here was nothing in the world betwixt me and sudden
death but just them tatoo-marks. If they didn't find them—

I couldn't bear to think about it; and yet, somehow, I couldn't think about nothing else. It got darker and darker, and it was a beautiful time to give the crowd the slip; but that big husky had me by the wrist—Hines—and a body might as well try to give Goliar the slip. He dragged me right along, he was so excited; and I had to run to keep up.

When they got there they swarmed into the graveyard and washed over it like an overflow. And when they got to the grave, they found they had about a hundred times as many shovels as they wanted, but nobody hadn't thought to fetch a lantern. But they sailed into digging, anyway, by the flicker of the lightning, and sent a man to the nearest house a half a mile off, to borrow one.

So they dug and dug, like everything; and it got awful dark, and the rain started, and the wind swished and swushed along, and the lightning come brisker and brisker, and the thunder boomed; but them people never took no notice of it, they was so full of this business; and one minute you could see everything and every face in that big crowd, and the shovelfuls of dirt sailing up out of the grave, and the next second the dark wiped it all out, and you couldn't see nothing at all.

At last they got out the coffin, and begun to unscrew the lid, and then such another crowding, and shouldering, and shoving as there was, to scrouge in and get a sight, you never see; and in the dark, that way, it was awful. Hines he hurt my wrist dreadful, pulling and tugging so, and I reckon he clean forgot I was in the world, he was so excited and panting.

All of a sudden the lightning let go a perfect sluice of white glare, and somebody sings out:

"By the living jingo, here's the bag of gold on his breast!"

Hines let out a whoop, like everybody else, and dropped my wrist and give a big surge to bust his way in and get a look, and the way I lit out and shinned for the road in the dark, there ain't nobody can tell.

I had the road all to myself, and I fairly flew—leastways I had it all to myself except the solid dark, and the now-and-then glares, and the buzzing of the rain, and the thrashing of the wind, and the splitting of the thunder; and sure as you are born I did clip it along!

When I struck the town, I see there warn't nobody out in the storm, so I never hunted for no back streets, but humped it straight through the main one; and when I begun to get towards our house I aimed my eye and set it. No light there; the house all dark—which made me feel sorry and disappointed, I didn't know why. But at last, just as I was sailing by, *flash* comes the light in Mary Jane's window! and my heart swelled up sudden, like to bust; and the same second the house and all was behind me in the dark, and wasn't ever going to be before me no more in this world. She *was* the best girl I ever see, and had the most sand.

The minute I was far enough above the town to see I could make the towhead, I begun to look sharp for a boat to borrow; and the first time the lightning showed me one that wasn't chained, I snatched it and shoved. It was a canoe, and warn't fastened with nothing but a rope. The towhead was a rattling big distance off, away out there in the middle of the river, but I didn't lose no time; and when I struck the raft at last, I was so fagged I would a just laid down to blow and gasp if I could afforded it. But I didn't. As I sprung aboard I sung out:

"Out with you Jim, and set her loose! Glory be to goodness, we're shut of them!"

Jim lit out, and was a coming for me with both arms spread, he was so full of joy; but when I glimpsed him in the lightning, my heart shot up in my mouth, and I went overboard backwards; for I forgot he was old King Lear and a drownded A-rab all in one, and it most scared the livers and lights out of me. But Jim fished me out, and was going to hug me and bless me, and so on, he was so glad I was back and we was shut of the king and the duke, but I says:

"Not now—have it for breakfast, have it for breakfast! Cut loose and let her slide!"

So, in two seconds, away we went, a sliding down the river, and it *did* seem so good to be free again and all by ourselves on the big river and nobody to bother us. I had to skip around a bit, and jump up and crack my heels a few times, I couldn't help it; but about the third crack, I noticed a sound that I knowed mighty well—and held my breath and listened and waited—and sure enough, when the next flash busted out over the water, here they come!—and just a laying to their oars and making their skiff hum! It was the king and the duke.

So I wilted right down onto the planks, then, and give up; and it was all I could do to keep from crying.

XXX

WHEN THEY GOT ABOARD, the king went for me, and shook me by the collar, and says:

"Tryin' to give us the slip, was ye, you pup! Tired of our company—hey?"

I says:

"No, your majesty, we warn't—*please* don't, your majesty!"

"Quick, then, and tell us what *was* your idea, or I'll shake the insides out o' you!"

"Honest, I'll tell you everything, just as it happened, your majesty. The man that had aholt of me was very good to me, and kept saying he had a boy about as big as me that died last year, and he was sorry to see a boy in such a dangerous fix; and when they was all took by surprise by finding the gold, and made a rush for the coffin, he lets go of me and whispers, 'Heel it, now, or they'll hang ye, sure!' and I lit out. It didn't seem no good for *me* to stay—*I* couldn't do nothing, and I didn't want to be hung if I could get away. So I never stopped running till I found the canoe; and when I got here I told Jim to hurry, or they'd catch me and hang me yet, and said I was afeard you and the duke wasn't alive, now, and I was awful sorry, and so was Jim, and was awful glad when we see you coming, you may ask Jim if I didn't."

Jim said it was so; and the king told him to shut up, and said, "Oh, yes, it's *mighty* likely!" and shook me up again, and said he reckoned he'd drownd me. But the duke says:

"Leggo the boy, you old idiot! Would *you* a done any different? Did you inquire around for *him*, when you got loose? *I* don't remember it."

So the king let go of me, and begun to cuss that town and everybody in it. But the duke says:

"You better a blame sight give *yourself* a good cussing, for you're the one that's entitled to it most. You hain't done a thing, from the start, that had any sense in it, except coming out so cool and cheeky with that imaginary blue-arrow mark. That *was* bright—it was right down bully; and it was the thing that saved us. For if it hadn't been for that, they'd a jailed us till them Englishmen's baggage come—and then—the penitentiary, you bet! But that trick took 'em to the graveyard, and the gold done us a still bigger kindness; for if the excited fools hadn't let go all holts and made that rush to get a look, we'd a slept in our cravats to-night—cravats warranted to *wear*, too—longer than *we'd* need 'em."

They was still a minute—thinking—then the king says, kind of absent-minded like:

"Mf! And we reckoned the *niggers* stole it!"

That made me squirm!

"Yes," says the duke, kinder slow, and deliberate, and sarcastic, "*We* did."

After about a half a minute, the king drawls out:

"Leastways—*I* did."

The duke says, the same way:

"On the contrary—*I* did."

The king kind of ruffles up, and says:

"Looky here, Bilgewater, what'r you referrin' to?"

The duke says, pretty brisk:

"When it comes to that, maybe you'll let me ask, what was *you* referring to?"

"Shucks!" says the king, very sarcastic; "but *I* don't know—maybe you was asleep, and didn't know what you was about."

The duke bristles right up, now, and says:

"Oh, let *up* on this cussed nonsense—do you take me for a blame' fool? Don't you reckon *I* know who hid that money in that coffin?"

"*Yes*, sir! I know you *do* know—because you done it yourself!"

"It's a lie!"—and the duke went for him. The king sings out:

"Take y'r hands off!—leggo my throat!—I take it all back!"

The duke says:

"Well, you just own up, first, that you *did* hide that money there, intending to give me the slip one of these days, and come back and dig it up, and have it all to yourself."

"Wait jest a minute, duke—answer me this one question,

honest and fair; if you didn't put the money there, say it, and I'll b'lieve you, and take back everything I said."

"You old scoundrel, I didn't, and you know I didn't. There, now!"

"Well, then, I b'lieve you. But answer me only jest this one more—now *don't* git mad; didn't you have it in your *mind* to hook the money and hide it?"

The duke never said nothing for a little bit; then he says:

"Well—I don't care if I *did*, I didn't *do* it, anyway. But you not only had it in mind to do it, but you *done* it."

"I wisht I may never die if I done it, duke, and that's honest. I won't say I warn't *goin'* to do it, because I *was*; but you—I mean somebody—got in ahead o' me."

"It's a lie! You done it, and you got to *say* you done it, or——"

The king begun to gurgle, and then he gasps out:

"'Nough!—*I own up!*"

I was very glad to hear him say that, it made me feel much more easier than what I was feeling before. So the duke took his hands off, and says:

"If you ever deny it again, I'll drown you. It's *well* for you to set there and blubber like a baby—it's fitten for you, after the way you've acted. I never see such an old ostrich for wanting to gobble everything—and I a trusting you all the time, like you was my own father. You ought to been ashamed of yourself to stand by and hear it saddled onto a lot of poor niggers and you never say a word for 'em. It makes me feel ridiculous to think I was soft enough to *believe* that rubbage. Cuss you, I can see, now, why you was so anxious to make up the deffesit—you wanted to get what money I'd got out of the Nonesuch and one thing or another, and scoop it *all*!"

The king says, timid, and still a snuffling:

"Why, duke, it was you that said make up the deffersit, it warn't me."

"Dry up! I don't want to hear no more *out* of you!" says the duke. "And *now* you see what you *got* by it. They've got all their own money back, and all of *ourn* but a shekel or two, *besides*. G'long to bed—and don't you deffersit *me* no more deffersits, long 's *you* live!"

So the king sneaked into the wigwam, and took to his bottle for comfort; and before long the duke tackled *his* bottle; and so in about a half an hour they was as thick as thieves again, and the tighter they got, the lovinger they got; and went off a snoring in each other's arms. They both got powerful mellow, but I noticed the king didn't get mellow enough to forget to remember to not deny about hiding the money-bag again. That made me feel easy and satisfied. Of course when they got to snoring, we had a long gabble, and I told Jim everything.

XXXI

WE DASN'T stop again at any town, for days and days; kept right along down the river. We was down south in the warm weather, now, and a mighty long ways from home. We begun to come to trees with Spanish moss on them, hanging down from the limbs like long gray beards. It was the first I ever see it growing, and it made the woods look solemn and dismal. So now the frauds reckoned they was out of danger, and they begun to work the villages again.

First they done a lecture on temperance; but they didn't make enough for them both to get drunk on. Then in another village they started a dancing school; but they didn't know no more how to dance than a kangaroo does; so the first prance they made, the general public jumped in and pranced them out of town. Another time they tried a go at yellocution; but they didn't yellocute long till the audience got up and give them a solid good cussing and made them skip out. They tackled missionarying, and mesmerizering, and doctoring, and telling fortunes, and a little of everything; but they couldn't seem to have no luck. So at last they got just about dead broke, and laid around the raft, as she floated along, thinking, and thinking, and never saying nothing, by the half a day at a time, and dreadful blue and desperate.

And at last they took a change, and begun to lay their heads together in the wigwam and talk low and confidential two or three hours at a time. Jim and me got uneasy. We didn't like the look of it. We judged they was studying up some kind of worse deviltry than ever. We turned it over and over, and at last we made up our minds they was going to break into somebody's house or store, or was going into the counterfeit-money business, or something. So then we was pretty scared, and made up an agreement that we wouldn't have nothing in the world to do with such actions, and if we ever got the least show we would give them the cold shake, and clear out and leave them behind. Well, early one morning we hid the raft in a good safe place about two mile below a little bit of a shabby village, named Pikesville, and the king he

830

went ashore, and told us all to stay hid whilst he went up to town and smelt around to see if anybody had got any wind of the Royal Nonesuch there yet. ("House to rob, you *mean*," says I to myself; "and when you get through robbing it you'll come back here and wonder what's become of me and Jim and the raft—and you'll have to take it out in wondering.") And he said if he warn't back by midday, the duke and me would know it was all right, and we was to come along.

So we staid where we was. The duke he fretted and sweated around, and was in a mighty sour way. He scolded us for everything, and we couldn't seem to do nothing right; he found fault with every little thing. Something was a-brewing, sure. I was good and glad when midday come and no king; we could have a change, anyway—and maybe a chance for *the* change, on top of it. So me and the duke went up to the village, and hunted around there for the king, and by-and-by we found him in the back room of a little low doggery, very tight, and a lot of loafers bullyragging him for sport, and he a cussing and threatening with all his might, and so tight he couldn't walk, and couldn't do nothing to them. The duke he begun to abuse him for an old fool, and the king begun to sass back; and the minute they was fairly at it, I lit out, and shook the reefs out of my hind legs, and spun down the river road like a deer—for I see our chance; and I made up my mind that it would be a long day before they ever see me and Jim again. I got down there all out of breath but loaded up with joy, and sung out—

"Set her loose, Jim, we're all right, now!"

But there warn't no answer, and nobody come out of the wigwam. Jim was gone! I set up a shout—and then another—and then another one; and run this way and that in the woods, whooping and screeching; but it warn't no use—old Jim was gone. Then I set down and cried; I couldn't help it. But I couldn't set still long. Pretty soon I went out on the road, trying to think what I better do, and I run across a boy walking, and asked him if he'd seen a strange nigger, dressed so and so, and he says:

"Yes."

"Wherebouts?" says I.

"Down to Silas Phelps's place, two mile below here. He's a runaway nigger, and they've got him. Was you looking for him?"

"You bet I ain't! I run across him in the woods about an hour or two ago, and he said if I hollered he'd cut my livers out—and told me to lay down and stay where I was; and I done it. Been there ever since; afeard to come out."

"Well," he says, "you needn't be afeard no more, becuz they've got him. He run off f'm down South, som'ers."

"It's a good job they got him."

"Well, I *reckon*! There's two hunderd dollars reward on him. It's like picking up money out'n the road."

"Yes, it is—and *I* could a had it if I'd been big enough; I see him *first*. Who nailed him?"

"It was an old fellow—a stranger—and he sold out his chance in him for forty dollars, becuz he's got to go up the river and can't wait. Think o' that, now! You bet *I'd* wait, if it was seven year."

"That's me, every time," says I. "But maybe his chance ain't worth no more than that, if he'll sell it so cheap. Maybe there's something ain't straight about it."

"But it *is*, though—straight as a string. I see the handbill myself. It tells all about him, to a dot—paints him like a picture, and tells the plantation he's frum, below Newr*leans*. No-sirree-*bob*, they ain't no trouble 'bout *that* speculation, you bet you. Say, gimme a chaw tobacker, won't ye?"

I didn't have none, so he left. I went to the raft, and set down in the wigwam to think. But I couldn't come to nothing. I thought till I wore my head sore, but I couldn't see no way out of the trouble. After all this long journey, and after all we'd done for them scoundrels, here was it all come to nothing, everything all busted up and ruined, because they could have the heart to serve Jim such a trick as that, and make him a slave again all his life, and amongst strangers, too, for forty dirty dollars.

Once I said to myself it would be a thousand times better for Jim to be a slave at home where his family was, as long as he'd *got* to be a slave, and so I'd better write a letter to Tom Sawyer and tell him to tell Miss Watson where he was. But I soon give up that notion, for two things: she'd be mad and disgusted at his rascality and ungratefulness for leaving her, and so she'd sell him straight down the river again; and if she didn't, everybody naturally despises an ungrateful nigger, and they'd make Jim feel it all the time, and so he'd feel ornery and disgraced. And then think of *me*! It would get all around, that Huck Finn helped a nigger to get his freedom; and if I was to ever see anybody from that town again, I'd be ready to get down and lick his boots for shame. That's just the way: a person does a low-down thing, and then he don't want to take no consequences of it. Thinks as long as he can hide it, it ain't no disgrace. That was my fix exactly. The more I studied about this, the more my conscience went to grinding me, and the more wicked and low-down and ornery I got to feeling. And at last, when it hit me all of a sudden that here was the plain hand of Providence slapping me in the face and letting me know my wickedness was being watched all the time from up there in heaven, whilst I was stealing a poor old woman's nigger that hadn't ever done me no harm, and now was showing me there's One that's always on the lookout, and ain't agoing to allow no such miserable doings to go only just so fur and no further, I most dropped in my tracks I was so scared. Well, I tried the best I could to kinder soften it up somehow for myself, by saying I was brung up wicked, and so I warn't so much to blame; but something inside of me kept saying, "There was the Sunday school, you could a gone to it; and if you'd a done it they'd a learnt you, there, that people that acts as I'd been acting about that nigger goes to everlasting fire."

It made me shiver. And I about made up my mind to pray; and see if I couldn't try to quit being the kind of a boy I was, and be better. So I kneeled down. But the words wouldn't come. Why wouldn't they? It warn't no use to try and hide it from Him. Nor from *me*, neither. I knowed very well why they wouldn't come. It was because my heart warn't right; it was because I warn't square; it was because I was playing double. I was letting *on* to give up sin, but away inside of me I was holding on to the biggest one of all. I was trying to make my mouth *say* I would do the right thing and the clean thing, and go and write to that nigger's owner and tell where he was; but deep down in me

I knowed it was a lie—and He knowed it. You can't pray a lie—I found that out.

So I was full of trouble, full as I could be; and didn't know what to do. At last I had an idea; and I says, I'll go and write the letter—and *then* see if I can pray. Why, it was astonishing, the way I felt as light as a feather, right straight off, and my troubles all gone. So I got a piece of paper and a pencil, all glad and excited, and set down and wrote:

> Miss Watson your runaway nigger Jim is down here two mile below Pikesville and Mr. Phelps has got him and he will give him up for the reward if you send.
>
> HUCK FINN.

I felt good and all washed clean of sin for the first time I had ever felt so in my life, and I knowed I could pray now. But I didn't do it straight off, but laid the paper down and set there thinking—thinking how good it was all this happened so, and how near I come to being lost and going to hell. And went on thinking. And got to thinking over our trip down the river; and I see Jim before me, all the time, in the day, and in the night-time, sometimes moonlight, sometimes storms, and we a floating along, talking, and singing, and laughing. But somehow I couldn't seem to strike no places to harden me against him, but only the other kind. I'd see him standing my watch on top of his'n, stead of calling me, so I could go on sleeping; and see him how glad he was when I come back out of the fog; and when I come to him again in the swamp, up there where the feud was; and suchlike times; and would always call me honey, and pet me, and do everything he could think of for me, and how good he always was; and at last I struck the time I saved him by telling the men we had small-pox aboard, and he was so grateful, and said I was the best friend old Jim ever had in the world, and the *only* one he's got now; and then I happened to look around, and see that paper.

It was a close place. I took it up, and held it in my hand. I was a trembling, because I'd got to decide, forever, betwixt two things, and I knowed it. I studied a minute, sort of holding my breath, and then says to myself:

"All right, then, I'll *go* to hell"—and tore it up.

It was awful thoughts, and awful words, but they was said. And I let them stay said; and never thought no more about reforming. I shoved the whole thing out of my head; and said I would take up wickedness again, which was in my line, being brung up to it, and the other warn't. And for a starter, I would go to work and steal Jim out of slavery again; and if I could think up anything worse, I would do that, too; because as long as I was in, and in for good, I might as well go the whole hog.

Then I set to thinking over how to get at it, and turned over considerable many ways in my mind; and at last fixed up a plan that suited me. So then I took the bearings of a woody island that was down the river a piece, and as soon as it was fairly dark I crept out with my raft and went for it, and hid it there, and then turned in. I slept the night through, and got up before it was light, and had my breakfast, and put on my store clothes, and tied up some others and one thing or another in a bundle, and took the canoe and cleared for shore. I landed below where I judged was Phelps's place, and hid my bundle in the woods, and then filled up the canoe with water, and loaded rocks into her and sunk her where I could find her again when I wanted her, about a quarter of a mile below a little steam sawmill that was on the bank.

Then I struck up the road, and when I passed the mill I see a sign on it, "Phelps's Sawmill," and when I come to the farm-houses, two or three hundred yards further along, I kept my eyes peeled, but didn't see nobody around, though it was good daylight, now. But I didn't mind, because I didn't want to see nobody just yet—I only wanted to get the lay of the land. According to my plan, I was going to turn up there from the village, not from below. So I just took a look, and shoved along, straight for town. Well, the very first man I see, when I got there, was the duke. He was sticking up a bill for the Royal Nonesuch—three-night performance—like that other time. *They* had the cheek, them frauds! I was right on him, before I could shirk. He looked astonished, and says:

"Hel-*lo!* Where'd *you* come from?" Then he says, kind of glad and eager, "Where's the raft?—got her in a good place?"

I says:

"Why, that's just what I was agoing to ask your grace."

Then he didn't look so joyful—and says:

"What was your idea for asking *me*?" he says.

"Well," I says, "when I see the king in that doggery yesterday I says to myself, we can't get him home for hours, till he's soberer; so I went a loafing around town to put in the time, and wait. A man up and offered me ten cents to help him pull a skiff over the river and back to fetch a sheep, and so I went along; but when we was dragging him to the boat, and the man left me aholt of the rope and went behind him to shove him along, he was too strong for me, and jerked loose and run, and we after him. We didn't have no dog, and so we had to chase him all over the country till we tired him out. We never got him till dark then we fetched him over, and I started down for the raft. When I got there and see it was gone, I says to myself, 'they've got into trouble and had to leave; and they've took my nigger, which is the only nigger I've got in the world, and now I'm in a strange country, and ain't got no property no more, nor nothing, and no way to make my living;' so I set down and cried. I slept in the woods all night. But what *did* become of the raft then?—and Jim, poor Jim!"

"Blamed if *I* know—that is, what's become of the raft. That old fool had made a trade and got forty dollars, and when we found him in the doggery the loafers had matched half dollars with him and got every cent but what he'd spent for whisky; and when I got him home late last night and found the raft gone, we said, 'That little rascal has stole our raft and shook us, and run off down the river.'"

"I wouldn't shake my *nigger*, would I?—the only nigger I had in the world, and the only property."

"We never thought of that. Fact is, I reckon we'd come to consider him *our* nigger; yes, we did consider him so—goodness knows we had trouble enough for him. So when we see the raft was gone, and we flat broke, there warn't anything for it but to try the Royal Nonesuch another shake. And I've pegged along ever since, dry as a powder-horn. Where's that ten cents? Give it here."

I had considerable money, so I give him ten cents, but

egged him to spend it for something to eat, and give me ome, because it was all the money I had, and I hadn't had othing to eat since yesterday. He never said nothing. The ext minute he whirls on me and says:

"Do you reckon that nigger would blow on us? We'd skin im if he done that!"

"How can he blow? Hain't he run off?"

"No! That old fool sold him, and never divided with me, nd the money's gone."

"*Sold* him?" I says, and begun to cry; "why, he was *my* igger, and that was my money. Where is he?—I want my igger."

"Well, you can't *get* your nigger, that's all—so dry up your lubbering. Looky here—do you think *you'd* venture to blow on us? Blamed if I think I'd trust you. Why, if you *was* to low on us——"

He stopped, but I never see the duke look so ugly out of is eyes before. I went on a-whimpering, and says:

"I don't want to blow on nobody; and I ain't got no time o blow, nohow. I got to turn out and find my nigger."

He looked kinder bothered, and stood there with his bills luttering on his arm, thinking, and wrinkling up his fore-ead. At last he says:

"I'll tell you something. We got to be here three days. If ou'll promise you won't blow, and won't let the nigger low, I'll tell you where to find him."

So I promised, and he says:

"A farmer by the name of Silas Ph——" and then he topped. You see he started to tell me the truth; but when e stopped, that way, and begun to study and think again, I eckoned he was changing his mind. And so he was. He vouldn't trust me; he wanted to make sure of having me out of the way the whole three days. So pretty soon he says: "The nan that bought him is named Abram Foster—Abram G. Foster—and he lives forty mile back here in the country, on he road to Lafayette."

"All right," I says, "I can walk it in three days. And I'll start his very afternoon."

"No you won't, you'll start *now*; and don't you lose any

time about it, neither, nor do any gabbling by the way. Ju
keep a tight tongue in your head and move right along, ar
then you won't get into trouble with *us*, d'ye hear?"

That was the order I wanted, and that was the one I play
for. I wanted to be left free to work my plans.

"So clear out," he says; "and you can tell Mr. Foster wha
ever you want to. Maybe you can get him to believe that Ji
is your nigger—some idiots don't require documents—leas
ways I've heard there's such down South here. And when yc
tell him the handbill and the reward's bogus, maybe he'll b
lieve you when you explain to him what the idea was f
getting 'em out. Go 'long, now, and tell him anything yc
want to; but mind you don't work your jaw any *between* he
and there."

So I left, and struck for the back country. I didn't loc
around, but I kinder felt like he was watching me. But
knowed I could tire him out at that. I went straight out i
the country as much as a mile, before I stopped; then I dot
bled back through the woods towards Phelps's. I reckoned
better start in on my plan straight off, without foolin
around, because I wanted to stop Jim's mouth till these fe
lows could get away. I didn't want no trouble with their kin
I'd seen all I wanted to of them, and wanted to get entire
shut of them.

XXXII

WHEN I GOT THERE it was all still and Sunday-like, and hot and sunshiny—the hands was gone to the fields; and there was them kind of faint dronings of bugs and flies in the air that makes it seem so lonesome and like everybody's dead and gone; and if a breeze fans along and quivers the leaves, it makes you feel mournful, because you feel like it's spirits whispering—spirits that's been dead ever so many years—and you always think they're talking about *you*. As a general thing it makes a body wish *he* was dead, too, and done with it all.

Phelps's was one of these little one-horse cotton plantations; and they all look alike. A rail fence round a two-acre yard; a stile, made out of logs sawed off and up-ended, in steps, like barrels of a different length, to climb over the fence with, and for the women to stand on when they are going to jump onto a horse; some sickly grass-patches in the big yard, but mostly it was bare and smooth, like an old hat with the nap rubbed off; big double log house for the white folks—hewed logs, with the chinks stopped up with mud or mortar, and these mud-stripes been whitewashed some time or another; round-log kitchen, with a big broad, open but roofed passage joining it to the house; log smoke-house back of the kitchen; three little log nigger-cabins in a row t'other side the smoke-house; one little hut all by itself away down against the back fence, and some out-buildings down a piece the other side; ash-hopper, and big kettle to bile soap in, by the little hut; bench by the kitchen door, with bucket of water and a gourd; hound asleep there, in the sun; more hounds asleep, round about; about three shade-trees away off in a corner; some currant bushes and gooseberry bushes in one place by the fence; outside of the fence a garden and a water-melon patch; then the cotton fields begins; and after the fields, the woods.

I went around and clumb over the back stile by the ash-hopper, and started for the kitchen. When I got a little ways, I heard the dim hum of a spinning-wheel wailing along up and sinking along down again; and then I knowed for certain I wished I was dead—for that *is* the lonesomest sound in the whole world.

I went right along, not fixing up any particular plan, but just trusting to Providence to put the right words in my mouth when the time come; for I'd noticed that Providence always did put the right words in my mouth, if I left it alone.

When I got half-way, first one hound and then another got up and went for me, and of course I stopped and faced them, and kept still. And such another pow-wow as they made! In a quarter of a minute I was a kind of a hub of a wheel, as you may say—spokes made out of dogs—circle of fifteen of them packed together around me, with their necks and noses stretched up towards me, a barking and howling; and more a coming; you could see them sailing over fences and around corners from everywheres.

A nigger woman come tearing out of the kitchen with a rolling-pin in her hand, singing out, "Begone! *you* Tige! you Spot! begone, sah!" and she fetched first one and then another of them a clip and sent him howling, and then the rest followed; and the next second, half of them come back, wagging their tails around me and making friends with me. There ain't no harm in a hound, nohow.

And behind the woman comes a little nigger girl and two little nigger boys, without anything on but tow-linen shirts, and they hung onto their mother's gown, and peeped out from behind her at me, bashful, the way they always do. And here comes the white woman running from the house, about forty-five or fifty year old, bareheaded, and her spinning-stick in her hand; and behind her comes her little white children, acting the same way the little niggers was doing. She was smiling all over so she could hardly stand—and says:

"It's *you*, at last!—*ain't* it?"

I out with a "Yes'm," before I thought.

She grabbed me and hugged me tight; and then gripped me by both hands and shook and shook; and the tears come in her eyes, and run down over; and she couldn't seem to hug and shake enough, and kept saying, "You don't look as much like your mother as I reckoned you would, but law sakes, I don't care for that, I'm *so* glad to see you! Dear, dear, it does seem like I could eat you up! Children, it's your cousin Tom!—tell him howdy."

But they ducked their heads, and put their fingers in their mouths, and hid behind her. So she run on:

"Lize, hurry up and get him a hot breakfast, right away— or did you get your breakfast on the boat?"

I said I had got it on the boat. So then she started for the house, leading me by the hand, and the children tagging after. When we got there, she set me down in a split-bottomed chair, and set herself down on a little low stool in front of me, holding both of my hands, and says:

"Now I can have a *good* look at you: and laws-a-me, I've been hungry for it a many and a many a time, all these long years, and it's come at last! We been expecting you a couple of days and more. What's kep' you?—boat get aground?"

"Yes'm—she——"

"Don't say yes'm—say Aunt Sally. Where'd she get aground?"

I didn't rightly know what to say, because I didn't know whether the boat would be coming up the river or down. But I go a good deal on instinct; and my instinct said she would be coming up—from down towards Orleans. That didn't help me much, though; for I didn't know the names of bars down that way. I see I'd got to invent a bar, or forget the name of the one we got aground on—or— Now I struck an idea, and fetched it out:

"It warn't the grounding—that didn't keep us back but a little. We blowed out a cylinder-head."

"Good gracious! anybody hurt?"

"No'm. Killed a nigger."

"Well, it's lucky; because sometimes people do get hurt. Two years ago last Christmas, your uncle Silas was coming up from Newrleans on the old *Lally Rook*, and she blowed out a cylinder-head and crippled a man. And I think he died afterwards. He was a Babtist. Your uncle Silas knowed a family in Baton Rouge that knowed his people very well. Yes, I remember, now he *did* die. Mortification set in, and they had to amputate him. But it didn't save him. Yes, it was mortification—that was it. He turned blue all over, and died in the hope of a glorious resurrection. They say he was a sight to

look at. Your uncle's been up to the town every day to fetch
you. And he's gone again, not more'n an hour ago; he'll be
back any minute, now. You must a met him on the road,
didn't you?—oldish man, with a———"

"No, I didn't see nobody, Aunt Sally. The boat landed just
at daylight, and I left my baggage on the wharf-boat and
went looking around the town and out a piece in the country,
to put in the time and not get here too soon; and so I come
down the back way."

"Who'd you give the baggage to?"

"Nobody."

"Why, child, it'll be stole!"

"Not where *I* hid it I reckon it won't," I says.

"How'd you get your breakfast so early on the boat?"

It was kinder thin ice, but I says:

"The captain see me standing around, and told me I better
have something to eat before I went ashore; so he took me in
the texas to the officers' lunch, and give me all I wanted."

I was getting so uneasy I couldn't listen good. I had my
mind on the children all the time; I wanted to get them out
to one side, and pump them a little, and find out who I was.
But I couldn't get no show, Mrs. Phelps kept it up and run
on so. Pretty soon she made the cold chills streak all down
my back, because she says:

"But here, we're a running on this way, and you hain't told
me a word about Sis, nor any of them. Now I'll rest my
works a little, and you start up yourn; just tell me *everything*—tell me all about 'm all—every one of 'm; and how
they are, and what they're doing, and what they told you to
tell me; and every last thing you can think of."

Well, I see I was up a stump—and up it good. Providence
had stood by me this fur, all right, but I was hard and tight
aground, now. I see it warn't a bit of use to try to go ahead—
I'd *got* to throw up my hand. So I says to myself, here's another place where I got to resk the truth. I opened my mouth
to begin; but she grabbed me and hustled me in behind the
bed, and says:

"Here he comes! stick your head down lower—there,
that'll do; you can't be seen, now. Don't you let on you're
here. I'll play a joke on him. Childern, don't you say a word."

I see I was in a fix, now. But it warn't no use to worry; there warn't nothing to do but just hold still, and try and be ready to stand from under when the lightning struck.

I had just one little glimpse of the old gentleman when he come in, then the bed hid him. Mrs. Phelps she jumps for him and says:

"Has he come?"

"No," says her husband.

"Good-*ness* gracious!" she says, "what in the world *can* have become of him?"

"I can't imagine," says the old gentleman; "and I must say, it makes me dreadful uneasy."

"Uneasy!" she says, "I'm ready to go distracted! He *must* a come; and you've missed him along the road. I *know* it's so— something *tells* me so."

"Why Sally, I *couldn't* miss him along the road—*you* know that."

"But oh, dear, dear, what *will* Sis say! He must a come! You must a missed him. He——"

"Oh, don't distress me any more'n I'm already distressed. I don't know what in the world to make of it. I'm at my wit's end, and I don't mind acknowledging 't I'm right down scared. But there's no hope that he's come; for he *couldn't* come and me miss him. Sally, it's terrible—just terrible— something's happened to the boat, sure!"

"Why, Silas! Look yonder!—up the road!—ain't that somebody coming?"

He sprung to the window at the head of the bed, and that give Mrs. Phelps the chance she wanted. She stooped down quick, at the foot of the bed, and give me a pull, and out I come; and when he turned back from the window, there she stood, a-beaming and a-smiling like a house afire, and I stand- ing pretty meek and sweaty alongside. The old gentleman stared, and says:

"Why, who's that?"

"Who do you reckon 't is?"

"I haint no idea. Who *is* it?"

"It's *Tom Sawyer!*"

By jings, I most slumped through the floor. But there warn't no time to swap knives; the old man grabbed me by the hand and shook, and kept on shaking; and all the time, how the woman did dance around and laugh and cry; and then how they both did fire off questions about Sid, and Mary, and the rest of the tribe.

But if they was joyful, it warn't nothing to what I was; for it was like being born again, I was so glad to find out who I was. Well, they froze to me for two hours; and at last when my chin was so tired it couldn't hardly go, any more, I had told them more about my family—I mean the Sawyer family—than ever happened to any six Sawyer families. And I explained all about how we blowed out a cylinder-head at the mouth of White River and it took us three days to fix it. Which was all right, and worked first rate; because *they* didn't know but what it would take three days to fix it. If I'd a called it a bolt-head it would a done just as well.

Now I was feeling pretty comfortable all down one side, and pretty uncomfortable all up the other. Being Tom Sawyer was easy and comfortable; and it stayed easy and comfortable till by-and-by I hear a steamboat coughing along down the river—then I says to myself, spose Tom Sawyer come down on that boat?—and spose he steps in here, any minute, and sings out my name before I can throw him a wink to keep quiet? Well, I couldn't *have* it that way—it wouldn't do at all. I must go up the road and waylay him. So I told the folks I reckoned I would go up to the town and fetch down my baggage. The old gentleman was for going along with me, but I said no, I could drive the horse myself, and I druther he wouldn't take no trouble about me.

XXXIII

So I STARTED for town, in the wagon, and when I was half-way I see a wagon coming, and sure enough it was Tom Sawyer, and I stopped and waited till he come along. I says "Hold on!" and it stopped alongside, and his mouth opened up like a trunk, and staid so; and he swallowed two or three times like a person that's got a dry throat, and then says:

"I hain't ever done you no harm. You know that. So then, what you want to come back and ha'nt *me* for?"

I says:

"I hain't come back—I hain't been *gone*."

When he heard my voice, it righted him up some, but he warn't quite satisfied yet. He says:

"Don't you play nothing on me, because I wouldn't on you. Honest injun, now, you ain't a ghost?"

"Honest injun, I ain't," I says.

"Well—I—I—well, that ought to settle it, of course; but I can't somehow seem to understand it, no way. Looky here, warn't you ever murdered *at all*?"

"No. I warn't ever murdered at all—I played it on them. You come in here and feel of me if you don't believe me."

So he done it; and it satisfied him; and he was that glad to see me again, he didn't know what to do. And he wanted to know all about it right off; because it was a grand adventure, and mysterious, and so it hit him where he lived. But I said, leave it alone till by-and-by; and told his driver to wait, and we drove off a little piece, and I told him the kind of a fix I was in, and what did he reckon we better do? He said, let him alone a minute, and don't disturb him. So he thought and thought, and pretty soon he says:

"It's all right, I've got it. Take my trunk in your wagon, and let on it's your'n; and you turn back and fool along slow, so as to get to the house about the time you ought to; and I'll go towards town a piece, and take a fresh start, and get there a quarter or a half an hour after you; and you needn't let on to know me, at first."

I says:

"All right; but wait a minute. There's one more thing—a thing that *nobody* don't know but me. And that is, there's a nigger here that I'm a trying to steal out of slavery—and his name is *Jim*—old Miss Watson's Jim."

He says:

"What! Why Jim is——"

He stopped and went to studying. I says:

"*I* know what you'll say. You'll say it's dirty low-down business; but what if it is?—*I'm* low down; and I'm agoing to steal him, and I want you to keep mum and not let on. Will you?"

His eye lit up, and he says:

"I'll *help* you steal him!"

Well, I let go all holts then, like I was shot. It was the most astonishing speech I ever heard—and I'm bound to say Tom Sawyer fell, considerable, in my estimation. Only I couldn't believe it. Tom Sawyer a *nigger stealer*!

"Oh, shucks," I says, "you're joking."

"I ain't joking, either."

"Well, then," I says, "joking or no joking, if you hear anything said about a runaway nigger, don't forget to remember that *you* don't know nothing about him, and *I* don't know nothing about him."

Then we took the trunk and put it in my wagon, and he drove off his way, and I drove mine. But of course I forgot all about driving slow, on accounts of being glad and full of thinking; so I got home a heap too quick for that length of a trip. The old gentleman was at the door, and he says:

"Why, this is wonderful. Who ever would a thought it was in that mare to do it. I wish we'd a timed her. And she hain't sweated a hair—not a hair. It's wonderful. Why, I wouldn't take a hunderd dollars for that horse now; I wouldn't, honest; and yet I'd a sold her for fifteen before, and thought 'twas all she was worth."

That's all he said. He was the innocentest, best old soul I ever see. But it warn't surprising; because he warn't only just a farmer, he was a preacher, too, and had a little one-horse log church down back of the plantation, which he built it himself at his own expense, for a church and school-house,

nd never charged nothing for his preaching, and it was
worth it, too. There was plenty other farmer-preachers like
hat, and done the same way, down South.

In about half an hour Tom's wagon drove up to the front
tile, and Aunt Sally she see it through the window because
t was only about fifty yards, and says:

"Why, there's somebody come! I wonder who 'tis? Why, I
do believe it's a stranger. Jimmy" (that's one of the children),
"run and tell Lize to put on another plate for dinner."

Everybody made a rush for the front door, because, of
ourse, a stranger don't come *every* year, and so he lays over
he yaller fever, for interest, when he does come. Tom was
over the stile and starting for the house; the wagon was spin-
ing up the road for the village, and we was all bunched in
he front door. Tom had his store clothes on, and an audi-
nce—and that was always nuts for Tom Sawyer. In them
ircumstances it warn't no trouble to him to throw in an
mount of style that was suitable. He warn't a boy to meeky
long up that yard like a sheep; no, he come ca'm and impor-
ant, like the ram. When he got afront of us, he lifts his hat
ver so gracious and dainty, like it was the lid of a box that
had butterflies asleep in it and he didn't want to disturb them,
nd says:

"Mr. Archibald Nichols, I presume?"

"No, my boy," says the old gentleman, "I'm sorry to say 't
your driver has deceived you; Nichols's place is down a mat-
er of three mile more. Come in, come in."

Tom he took a look back over his shoulder, and says, "Too
ate—he's out of sight."

"Yes, he's gone, my son, and you must come in and eat
your dinner with us; and then we'll hitch up and take you
down to Nichols's."

"Oh, I *can't* make you so much trouble; I couldn't think of
t. I'll walk—I don't mind the distance."

"But we won't *let* you walk—it wouldn't be Southern hospitality to do it. Come right in."

"Oh, *do*," says Aunt Sally; "it ain't a bit of trouble to us,
not a bit in the world. You *must* stay. It's a long, dusty three
mile, and we *can't* let you walk. And besides, I've already told
em to put on another plate, when I see you coming; so you

mustn't disappoint us. Come right in, and make yourself a home."

So Tom he thanked them very hearty and handsome, and let himself be persuaded, and come in; and when he was in he said he was a stranger from Hicksville, Ohio, and his name was William Thompson—and he made another bow.

Well, he run on, and on, and on, making up stuff about Hicksville and everybody in it he could invent, and I getting a little nervous, and wondering how this was going to help me out of my scrape; and at last, still talking along, he reached over and kissed Aunt Sally right on the mouth, and then settled back again in his chair, comfortable, and was going on talking; but she jumped up and wiped it off with the back of her hand, and says:

"You owdacious puppy!"

He looked kind of hurt, and says:

"I'm surprised at you, m'am."

"You're s'rp— Why, what do you reckon *I* am? I've a good notion to take and—say, what do you mean by kissing me?"

He looked kind of humble, and says:

"I didn't mean nothing, m'am. I didn't mean no harm. I—I—thought you'd like it."

"Why, you born fool!" She took up the spinning-stick, and it looked like it was all she could do to keep from giving him a crack with it. "What made you think I'd like it?"

"Well, I don't know. Only, they—they—told me you would."

"*They* told you I would. Whoever told you 's *another* lunatic. I never heard the beat of it. Who's *they*?"

"Why—everybody. They all said so, m'am."

It was all she could do to hold in; and her eyes snapped, and her fingers worked like she wanted to scratch him; and she says:

"Who's 'everybody?' Out with their names—or ther'll be an idiot short."

He got up and looked distressed, and fumbled his hat, and says:

"I'm sorry, and I warn't expecting it. They told me to. They all told me to. They all said kiss her; and said she'll like it.

'hey all said it—every one of them. But I'm sorry, m'am, nd I won't do it no more—I won't, honest."

"You won't, won't you? Well, I sh'd *reckon* you won't!"

"No'm, I'm honest about it; I won't ever do it again. Till ou ask me."

"Till I *ask* you! Well, I never see the beat of it in my born ays! I lay you'll be the Methusalem-numskull of creation be- ore ever *I* ask you—or the likes of you."

"Well," he says, "it does surprise me so. I can't make it out, omehow. They said you would, and I thought you would. But—" He stopped and looked around slow, like he wished .e could run across a friendly eye, somewhere's; and fetched ıp on the old gentleman's, and says, "Didn't *you* think she'd ke me to kiss her, sir?"

"Why, no, I—I—well, no, I b'lieve I didn't."

Then he looks on around, the same way, to me—and says:

"Tom, didn't *you* think Aunt Sally 'd open out her arms nd say, 'Sid Sawyer——' "

"My land!" she says, breaking in and jumping for him, you impudent young rascal, to fool a body so—" and was ;oing to hug him, but he fended her off, and says:

"No, not till you've asked me, first."

So she didn't lose no time, but asked him; and hugged him nd kissed him, over and over again, and then turned him ›ver to the old man, and he took what was left. And after hey got a little quiet again, she says:

"Why, dear me, I never see such a surprise. We warn't ooking for *you*, at all, but only Tom. Sis never wrote to me ıbout anybody coming but him."

"It's because it warn't *intended* for any of us to come but Tom," he says; "but I begged and begged, and at the last ninute she let me come, too; so, coming down the river, me ınd Tom thought it would be a first-rate surprise for him to :ome here to the house first, and for me to by-and-by tag dlong and drop in and let on to be a stranger. But it was a nistake, Aunt Sally. This ain't no healthy place for a stranger o come."

"No—not impudent whelps, Sid. You ought to had your aws boxed; I hain't been so put out since I don't know when. But I don't care, I don't mind the terms—I'd be willing to

stand a thousand such jokes to have you here. Well, to thin
of that performance! I don't deny it, I was most putrified wit
astonishment when you give me that smack."

We had dinner out in that broad open passage betwixt th
house and the kitchen; and there was things enough on tha
table for seven families—and all hot, too; none of your flabb
tough meat that's laid in a cupboard in a damp cellar all nigh
and tastes like a hunk of old cold cannibal in the morning
Uncle Silas he asked a pretty long blessing over it, but it wa
worth it; and it didn't cool it a bit, neither, the way I've see
them kind of interruptions do, lots of times.

There was a considerable good deal of talk, all the after
noon, and me and Tom was on the lookout all the time, bu
it warn't no use, they didn't happen to say nothing about an
runaway nigger, and we was afraid to try to work up to it
But at supper, at night, one of the little boys says:

"Pa, mayn't Tom and Sid and me go to the show?"

"No," says the old man, "I reckon there ain't going to b
any; and you couldn't go if there was; because the runawa
nigger told Burton and me all about that scandalous show
and Burton said he would tell the people; so I reckon they'v
drove the owdacious loafers out of town before this time."

So there it was!—but I couldn't help it. Tom and me wa
to sleep in the same room and bed; so, being tired, we bi
good-night and went up to bed, right after supper, and clum
out of the window and down the lightning-rod, and shovee
for the town; for I didn't believe anybody was going to giv
the king and the duke a hint, and so, if I didn't hurry up an
give them one they'd get into trouble sure.

On the road Tom he told me all about how it was reckone
I was murdered, and how pap disappeared, pretty soon, an
didn't come back no more, and what a stir there was whe
Jim run away; and I told Tom all about our Royal Nonesuc
rapscallions, and as much of the raft-voyage as I had time to
and as we struck into the town and up through the middle o
it—it was as much as half-after eight, then—here comes
raging rush of people, with torches, and an awful whooping
and yelling, and banging tin pans and blowing horns: and we
jumped to one side to let them go by; and as they went by
I see they had the king and the duke astraddle of a rail—tha

is, I knowed it *was* the king and the duke, though they was all over tar and feathers, and didn't look like nothing in the world that was human—just looked like a couple of monstrous big soldier-plumes. Well, it made me sick to see it; and I was sorry for them poor pitiful rascals, it seemed like I couldn't ever feel any hardness against them any more in the world. It was a dreadful thing to see. Human beings *can* be awful cruel to one another.

We see we was too late—couldn't do no good. We asked some stragglers about it, and they said everybody went to the show looking very innocent; and laid low and kept dark till the poor old king was in the middle of his cavortings on the stage; then somebody give a signal, and the house rose up and went for them.

So we poked along back home, and I warn't feeling so brash as I was before, but kind of ornery, and humble, and to blame, somehow—though *I* hadn't done nothing. But that's always the way; it don't make no difference whether you do right or wrong, a person's conscience ain't got no sense, and just goes for him *anyway*. If I had a yaller dog that didn't know no more than a person's conscience does, I would pison him. It takes up more room than all the rest of a person's insides, and yet ain't no good, nohow. Tom Sawyer he says the same.

XXXIV

W E STOPPED TALKING, and got to thinking.
By-and-by Tom says:

"Looky here, Huck, what fools we are, to not think of it before! I bet I know where Jim is."

"No! Where?"

"In that hut down by the ash-hopper. Why, looky here. When we was at dinner, didn't you see a nigger man go in there with some vittles?"

"Yes."

"What did you think the vittles was for?"

"For a dog."

"So'd I. Well, it wasn't for a dog."

"Why?"

"Because part of it was watermelon."

"So it was—I noticed it. Well, it does beat all, that I never thought about a dog not eating watermelon. It shows how a body can see and don't see at the same time."

"Well, the nigger unlocked the padlock when he went in, and he locked it again when he come out. He fetched uncle a key, about the time we got up from table—same key, I bet. Watermelon shows man, lock shows prisoner; and it ain't likely there's two prisoners on such a little plantation, and where the people's all so kind and good. Jim's the prisoner. All right—I'm glad we found it out detective fashion; I wouldn't give shucks for any other way. Now you work your mind and study out a plan to steal Jim, and I will study out one, too; and we'll take the one we like the best."

What a head for just a boy to have! If I had Tom Sawyer's head, I wouldn't trade it off to be a duke, nor mate of a steamboat, nor clown in a circus, nor nothing I can think of. I went to thinking out a plan, but only just to be doing something; I knowed very well where the right plan was going to come from. Pretty soon, Tom says:

"Ready?"

"Yes," I says.

"All right—bring it out."

"My plan is this," I says. "We can easy find out if it's Jim in there. Then get up my canoe to-morrow night, and fetch my raft over from the island. Then the first dark night that comes, steal the key out of the old man's britches, after he goes to bed, and shove off down the river on the raft, with Jim, hiding day-times and running nights, the way me and Jim used to do before. Wouldn't that plan work?"

"*Work?* Why cert'nly, it would work, like rats a fighting. But it's too blame' simple; there ain't nothing *to* it. What's the good of a plan that ain't no more trouble than that? It's as mild as goose-milk. Why, Huck, it wouldn't make no more talk than breaking into a soap factory."

I never said nothing, because I warn't expecting nothing different; but I knowed mighty well that whenever he got *his* plan ready it wouldn't have none of them objections to it.

And it didn't. He told me what it was, and I see in a minute it was worth fifteen of mine, for style, and would make Jim just as free a man as mine would, and maybe get us all killed besides. So I was satisfied, and said we would waltz in on it. I needn't tell what it was, here, because I knowed it wouldn't stay the way it was. I knowed he would be changing it around, every which way, as we went along, and heaving in new bullinesses wherever he got a chance. And that is what he done.

Well, one thing was dead sure; and that was, that Tom Sawyer was in earnest and was actuly going to help steal that nigger out of slavery. That was the thing that was too many for me. Here was a boy that was respectable, and well brung up; and had a character to lose; and folks at home that had characters; and he was bright and not leather-headed; and knowing and not ignorant; and not mean, but kind; and yet here he was, without any more pride, or rightness, or feeling, than to stoop to this business, and make himself a shame, and his family a shame, before everybody. I *couldn't* understand it, no way at all. It was outrageous, and I knowed I ought to just up and tell him so; and so be his true friend, and let him quit the thing right where he was, and save himself. And I *did* start to tell him; but he shut me up, and says:

"Don't you reckon I know what I'm about? Don't I generly know what I'm about?"

"Yes."

"Didn't I *say* I was going to help steal the nigger?"

"Yes."

"*Well* then."

That's all he said, and that's all I said. It warn't no use to say any more; because when he said he'd do a thing, he always done it. But *I* couldn't make out how he was willing to go into this thing; so I just let it go, and never bothered no more about it. If he was bound to have it so, *I* couldn't help it.

When we got home, the house was all dark and still; so we went on down to the hut by the ash-hopper, for to examine it. We went through the yard, so as to see what the hounds would do. They knowed us, and didn't make no more noise than country dogs is always doing when anything comes by in the night. When we got to the cabin, we took a look at the front and the two sides; and on the side I warn't acquainted with—which was the north side—we found a square window-hole, up tolerable high, with just one stout board nailed across it. I says:

"Here's the ticket. This hole's big enough for Jim to get through, if we wrench off the board."

Tom says:

"It's as simple as tit-tat-toe, three-in-a-row, and as easy as playing hooky. I should *hope* we can find a way that's a little more complicated than *that*, Huck Finn."

"Well then," I says, "how'll it do to saw him out, the way I done before I was murdered, that time?"

"That's more *like*," he says. "It's real mysterious, and troublesome, and good," he says; "but I bet we can find a way that's twice as long. There ain't no hurry; le's keep on looking around."

Betwixt the hut and the fence, on the back side, was a lean-to, that joined the hut at the eaves, and was made out of plank. It was as long as the hut, but narrow—only about six foot wide. The door to it was at the south end, and was padlocked. Tom he went to the soap kettle, and searched around and fetched back the iron thing they lift the lid with; so he took it and prized out one of the staples. The chain fell down, and we opened the door and went in, and shut it, and struck a match, and see the shed was only built against the cabin and hadn't no connection with it; and there warn't no floor to the shed, nor nothing in it but some old rusty played-out hoes, and spades, and picks, and a crippled plow. The match went out, and so did we, and shoved in the staple again, and the door was locked as good as ever. Tom was joyful. He says:

"Now we're all right. We'll *dig* him out. It'll take about a week!"

Then we started for the house, and I went in the back door—you only have to pull a buckskin latch-string, they don't fasten the doors—but that warn't romantical enough for Tom Sawyer: no way would do him but he must climb up the lightning-rod. But after he got up half-way about three times, and missed fire and fell every time, and the last time most busted his brains out, he thought he'd got to give it up; but after he was rested, he allowed he would give her one more turn for luck, and this time he made the trip.

In the morning we was up at break of day, and down to the nigger cabins to pet the dogs and make friends with the nigger that fed Jim—if it *was* Jim that was being fed. The niggers was just getting through breakfast and starting for the fields; and Jim's nigger was piling up a tin pan with bread and meat and things; and whilst the others was leaving, the key come from the house.

This nigger had a good-natured, chuckle-headed face, and his wool was all tied up in little bunches with thread. That was to keep witches off. He said the witches was pestering him awful, these nights, and making him see all kinds of strange things, and hear all kinds of strange words and noises, and he didn't believe he was ever witched so long, before, in his life. He got so worked up, and got to running on so about his troubles, he forgot all about what he'd been agoing to do. So Tom says:

"What's the vittles for? Going to feed the dogs?"

The nigger kind of smiled around gradully over his face, like when you heave a brickbat in a mud puddle, and he says:

"Yes, Mars Sid, *a* dog. Cur'us dog, too. Does you want to go en look at 'im?"

"Yes."

I hunched Tom, and whispers:

"You going, right here in the day-break? *That* warn't the plan."

"No, it warn't—but it's the plan *now*."

So, drat him, we went along, but I didn't like it much. When we got in, we couldn't hardly see anything, it was so dark; but Jim was there, sure enough, and could see us; and he sings out:

"Why, *Huck*! En good *lan'*! ain' dat Misto Tom?"

I just knowed how it would be; I just expected it. *I* didn't know nothing to do; and if I had, I couldn't a done it; because that nigger busted in and says:

"Why, de gracious sakes! do he know you genlmen?"

We could see pretty well, now. Tom he looked at the nigger, steady and kind of wondering, and says:

"Does *who* know us?"

"Why, dish-yer runaway nigger."

"I don't reckon he does; but what put that into your head?"

"What *put* it dar? Didn' he jis' dis minute sing out like he knowed you?"

Tom says, in a puzzled-up kind of way:

"Well, that's mighty curious. *Who* sung out? *When* did he sing out? *What* did he sing out?" And turns to me, perfectly c'am, and says, "Did *you* hear anybody sing out?"

Of course there warn't nothing to be said but the one thing; so I says:

"No; *I* ain't heard nobody say nothing."

Then he turns to Jim, and looks him over like he never see him before; and says:

"Did you sing out?"

"No, sah," says Jim; "*I* hain't said nothing, sah."

"Not a word?"

"No, sah, I hain't said a word."

"Did you ever see us before?"

"No, sah; not as *I* knows on."

So Tom turns to the nigger, which was looking wild and distressed, and says, kind of severe:

"What do you reckon's the matter with you, anyway? What made you think somebody sung out?"

"Oh, it's de dad-blame' witches, sah, en I wisht I was dead, I do. Dey's awluz at it, sah, en dey do mos' kill me, dey

sk'yers me so. Please to don't tell nobody 'bout it sah, er ole
Mars Silas he'll scole me; 'kase he say dey *ain't* no witches. I
jis' wish to goodness he was heah now—*den* what would he
say! I jis' bet he couldn' fine no way to git aroun' it *dis* time.
But it's awluz jis' so; people dat's *sot*, stays sot; dey won't
look into nothin' en fine it out f'r deyselves, en when *you* fine
it out en tell um 'bout it, dey doan' b'lieve you."

Tom give him a dime, and said we wouldn't tell nobody;
and told him to buy some more thread to tie up his wool
with; and then looks at Jim, and says:

"I wonder if Uncle Silas is going to hang this nigger. If I
was to catch a nigger that was ungrateful enough to run
away, *I* wouldn't give him up, I'd hang him." And whilst the
nigger stepped to the door to look at the dime and bite it to
see if it was good, he whispers to Jim, and says:

"Don't ever let on to know us. And if you hear any digging
going on nights, it's us: we're going to set you free."

Jim only had time to grab us by the hand and squeeze it,
then the nigger come back, and we said we'd come again
some time if the nigger wanted us to; and he said he would,
more particular if it was dark, because the witches went for
him mostly in the dark, and it was good to have folks around
then.

XXXV

IT WOULD BE most an hour, yet, till breakfast, so we left, and struck down into the woods; because Tom said we got to have *some* light to see how to dig by, and a lantern makes too much, and might get us into trouble; what we must have was a lot of them rotten chunks that's called fox-fire and just makes a soft kind of a glow when you lay them in a dark place. We fetched an armful and hid it in the weeds, and set down to rest, and Tom says, kind of dissatisfied:

"Blame it, this whole thing is just as easy and awkard as it can be. And so it makes it so rotten difficult to get up a difficult plan. There ain't no watchman to be drugged—now there *ought* to be a watchman. There ain't even a dog to give a sleeping-mixture to. And there's Jim chained by one leg, with a ten-foot chain, to the leg of his bed: why, all you got to do is to lift up the bedstead and slip off the chain. And Uncle Silas he trusts everybody; sends the key to the punkin-headed nigger, and don't send nobody to watch the nigger. Jim could a got out of that window hole before this, only there wouldn't be no use trying to travel with a ten-foot chain on his leg. Why, drat it, Huck, it's the stupidest arrangement I ever see. You got to invent *all* the difficulties. Well, we can't help it, we got to do the best we can with the materials we've got. Anyhow, there's one thing—there's more honor in getting him out through a lot of difficulties and dangers, where there warn't one of them furnished to you by the people who it was their duty to furnish them, and you had to contrive them all out of your own head. Now look at just that one thing of the lantern. When you come down to the cold facts, we simply got to *let on* that a lantern's resky. Why, we could work with a torchlight procession if we wanted to, *I* believe. Now, whilst I think of it, we got to hunt up something to make a saw out of, the first chance we get."

"What do we want of a saw?"

"What do we *want* of it? Hain't we got to saw the leg of Jim's bed off, so as to get the chain loose?"

"Why, you just said a body could lift up the bedstead and lip the chain off."

"Well, if that ain't just like you, Huck Finn. You *can* get ip the infant-schooliest ways of going at a thing. Why, hain't 'ou ever read any books at all?—Baron Trenck, nor Casa-10va, nor Benvenuto Chelleeny, nor Henri IV., nor none of hem heroes? Whoever heard of getting a prisoner loose in iuch an old-maidy way as that? No; the way all the best au-:horities does, is to saw the bed-leg in two, and leave it just io, and swallow the sawdust, so it can't be found, and put iome dirt and grease around the sawed place so the very keen-:st seneskal can't see no sign of it's being sawed, and thinks the bed-leg is perfectly sound. Then, the night you're ready, fetch the leg a kick, down she goes; slip off your chain, and there you are. Nothing to do but hitch your rope-ladder to the battlements, shin down it, break your leg in the moat—because a rope-ladder is nineteen foot too short, you know—and there's your horses and your trusty vassles, and they scoop you up and fling you across a saddle and away you go, to your native Langudoce, or Navarre, or wherever it is. It's gaudy, Huck. I wish there was a moat to this cabin. If we get time, the night of the escape, we'll dig one."

I says:

"What do we want of a moat, when we're going to snake him out from under the cabin?"

But he never heard me. He had forgot me and everything else. He had his chin in his hand, thinking. Pretty soon, he sighs, and shakes his head; then sighs again, and says:

"No, it wouldn't do—there ain't necessity enough for it."

"For what?" I says.

"Why, to saw Jim's leg off," he says.

"Good land!" I says, "why, there ain't *no* necessity for it. And what would you want to saw his leg off for, anyway?"

"Well, some of the best authorities has done it. They couldn't get the chain off, so they just cut their hand off, and shoved. And a leg would be better still. But we got to let that go. There ain't necessity enough in this case; and besides, Jim's a nigger and wouldn't understand the reasons for it, and how it's the custom in Europe; so we'll let it go. But there's one thing—he can have a rope-ladder; we can tear up our sheets and make him a rope-ladder easy enough. And we can send it to him in a pie; it's mostly done that way. And I've et worse pies."

"Why, Tom Sawyer, how you talk," I says; "Jim ain't got no use for a rope-ladder."

"He *has* got use for it. How *you* talk, you better say; you don't know nothing about it. He's *got* to have a rope ladder they all do."

"What in the nation can he *do* with it?"

"*Do* with it? He can hide it in his bed, can't he? That's what they all do; and *he's* got to, too. Huck, you don't ever seem to want to do anything that's regular; you want to be starting something fresh all the time. Spose he *don't* do nothing with it? ain't it there in his bed, for a clew, after he's gone? and don't you reckon they'll want clews? Of course they will. And you wouldn't leave them any? That would be a *pretty* howdy-do, *wouldn't* it! I never heard of such a thing."

"Well," I says, "if it's in the regulations, and he's got to have it, all right, let him have it; because I don't wish to go back on no regulations; but there's one thing, Tom Sawyer— if we go to tearing up our sheets to make Jim a rope-ladder, we're going to get into trouble with Aunt Sally, just as sure as you're born. Now, the way I look at it, a hickry-bark ladder don't cost nothing, and don't waste nothing, and is just as good to load up a pie with, and hide in a straw tick, as any rag ladder you can start; and as for Jim, he ain't had no experience, and so *he* don't care what kind of a——"

"Oh, shucks, Huck Finn, if I was as ignorant as you, I'd keep still—that's what *I'd* do. Who ever heard of a state prisoner escaping by a hickry-bark ladder? Why, it's perfectly ridiculous."

"Well, all right, Tom, fix it your own way; but if you'll take my advice, you'll let me borrow a sheet off of the clothesline."

He said that would do. And that give him another idea, and he says:

"Borrow a shirt, too."

"What do we want of a shirt, Tom?"

"Want it for Jim to keep a journal on."

"Journal your granny—*Jim* can't write."

"Spose he *can't* write—he can make marks on the shirt, can't he, if we make him a pen out of an old pewter spoon or a piece of an old iron barrel-hoop?"

"Why, Tom, we can pull a feather out of a goose and make him a better one; and quicker, too."

"*Prisoners* don't have geese running around the donjon-keep to pull pens out of, you muggins. They *always* make their pens out of the hardest, toughest, troublesomest piece of old brass candlestick or something like that they can get their hands on; and it takes them weeks and weeks, and months and months to file it out, too, because they've got to do it by rubbing it on the wall. *They* wouldn't use a goose-quill if they had it. It ain't regular."

"Well, then, what'll we make him the ink out of?"

"Many makes it out of iron-rust and tears; but that's the common sort and women; the best authorities uses their own blood. Jim can do that; and when he wants to send any little common ordinary mysterious message to let the world know where he's captivated, he can write it on the bottom of a tin plate with a fork and throw it out of the window. The Iron Mask always done that, and it's a blame' good way, too."

"Jim ain't got no tin plates. They feed him in a pan."

"That ain't anything; we can get him some."

"Can't nobody *read* his plates."

"That ain't got nothing to *do* with it, Huck Finn. All *he's* got to do is to write on the plate and throw it out. You don't *have* to be able to read it. Why, half the time you can't read anything a prisoner writes on a tin plate, or anywhere else."

"Well, then, what's the sense in wasting the plates?"

"Why, blame it all, it ain't the *prisoner's* plates."

"But it's *somebody's* plates, ain't it?"

"Well, spos'n it is? What does the *prisoner* care whose——"

He broke off there, because we heard the breakfast-horn blowing. So we cleared out for the house.

Along during that morning I borrowed a sheet and a white shirt off of the clothes-line; and I found an old sack and put them in it, and we went down and got the fox-fire, and put that in too. I called it borrowing, because that was what pap always called it, but Tom said it warn't borrowing, it was stealing. He said we was representing prisoners; and prisoners

don't care how they get a thing so they get it, and nobody
don't blame them for it, either. It ain't no crime in a prisoner
to steal the thing he needs to get away with, Tom said; it's
his right; and so, as long as we was representing a prisoner
we had a perfect right to steal anything on this place we had
the least use for, to get ourselves out of prison with. He said
if we warn't prisoners it would be a very different thing, and
nobody but a mean ornery person would steal when he warn't
a prisoner. So we allowed we would steal everything there
was that come handy. And yet he made a mighty fuss, one
day, after that, when I stole a watermelon out of the nigger
patch and eat it; and he made me go and give the niggers a
dime, without telling them what it was for. Tom said that
what he meant was, we could steal anything we *needed*. Well,
I says, I needed the watermelon. But he said I didn't need it
to get out of prison with, there's where the difference was.
He said if I'd a wanted it to hide a knife in, and smuggle it
to Jim to kill the seneskal with, it would a been all right. So
I let it go at that, though I couldn't see no advantage in my
representing a prisoner, if I got to set down and chaw over a
lot of gold-leaf distinctions like that, every time I see a chance
to hog a watermelon.

Well, as I was saying, we waited that morning till everybody was settled down to business, and nobody in sight
around the yard; then Tom he carried the sack into the lean-
to whilst I stood off a piece to keep watch. By-and-by he
come out, and we went and set down on the wood-pile, to
talk. He says:

"Everything's all right, now, except tools: and that's easy
fixed."

"Tools?" I says.

"Yes."

"Tools for what?"

"Why, to dig with. We ain't agoing to *gnaw* him out, are
we?"

"Ain't them old crippled picks and things in there good
enough to dig a nigger out with?" I says.

He turns on me looking pitying enough to make a body
cry, and says:

"Huck Finn, did you *ever* hear of a prisoner having picks

and shovels, and all the modern conveniences in his wardrobe
to dig himself out with? Now I want to ask you—if you got
any reasonableness in you at all—what kind of a show would
that give him to be a hero? Why, they might as well lend him
the key, and done with it. Picks and shovels—why they
wouldn't furnish 'em to a king."

"Well, then," I says, "if we don't want the picks and shovels, what do we want?"

"A couple of case-knives."

"To dig the foundations out from under that cabin with?"

"Yes."

"Confound it, it's foolish, Tom."

"It don't make no difference how foolish it is, it's the *right*
way—and it's the regular way. And there ain't no *other* way,
that ever *I* heard of, and I've read all the books that gives any
information about these things. They always dig out with a
case-knife—and not through dirt, mind you; generly it's
through solid rock. And it takes them weeks and weeks and
weeks, and for ever and ever. Why, look at one of them prisoners in the bottom dungeon of the Castle Deef, in the harbor of Marseilles, that dug himself out that way; how long
was *he* at it, you reckon?"

"I don't know."

"Well, guess."

"I don't know. A month and a half?"

"*Thirty-seven year*—and he come out in China. *That's* the
kind. I wish the bottom of *this* fortress was solid rock."

"*Jim* don't know nobody in China."

"What's *that* got to do with it? Neither did that other fellow. But you're always a-wandering off on a side issue. Why
can't you stick to the main point?"

"All right—*I* don't care where he comes out, so he *comes*
out; and Jim don't, either, I reckon. But there's one thing,
anyway—Jim's too old to be dug out with a case-knife. He
won't last."

"Yes he will *last*, too. You don't reckon it's going to take
thirty-seven years to dig out through a *dirt* foundation, do
you?"

"How long will it take, Tom?"

"Well, we can't resk being as long as we ought to, because

it mayn't take very long for Uncle Silas to hear from down there by New Orleans. He'll hear Jim ain't from there. Then his next move will be to advertise Jim, or something like that. So we can't resk being as long digging him out as we ought to. By rights I reckon we ought to be a couple of years; but we can't. Things being so uncertain, what I recommend is this: that we really dig right in, as quick as we can; and after that, we can *let on*, to ourselves, that we was at it thirty-seven years. Then we can snatch him out and rush him away the first time there's an alarm. Yes, I reckon that'll be the best way."

"Now, there's *sense* in that," I says. "Letting on don't cost nothing; letting on ain't no trouble; and if it's any object, I don't mind letting on we was at it a hundred and fifty year. It wouldn't strain me none, after I got my hand in. So I'll mosey along now, and smouch a couple of case-knives."

"Smouch three," he says; "we want one to make a saw out of."

"Tom, if it ain't unregular and irreligious to sejest it," I says, "there's an old rusty saw-blade around yonder sticking under the weatherboarding behind the smoke-house."

He looked kind of weary and discouraged-like, and says:

"It ain't no use to try to learn you nothing, Huck. Run along and smouch the knives—three of them." So I done it.

XXXVI

As soon as we reckoned everybody was asleep, that night, we went down the lightning-rod, and shut ourselves up in the lean-to, and got out our pile of fox-fire, and went to work. We cleared everything out of the way, about four or five foot along the middle of the bottom log. Tom said he was right behind Jim's bed now, and we'd dig in under it, and when we got through there couldn't nobody in the cabin ever know there was any hole there, because Jim's counterpin hung down most to the ground, and you'd have to raise it up and look under to see the hole. So we dug and dug, with the case-knives, till most midnight; and then we was dog-tired, and our hands was blistered, and yet you couldn't see we'd done anything, hardly. At last I says:

"This ain't no thirty-seven year job, this is a thirty-eight year job, Tom Sawyer."

He never said nothing. But he sighed, and pretty soon he stopped digging, and then for a good little while I knowed he was thinking. Then he says:

"It ain't no use, Huck, it ain't agoing to work. If we was prisoners it would, because then we'd have as many years as we wanted, and no hurry; and we wouldn't get but a few minutes to dig, every day, while they was changing watches, and so our hands wouldn't get blistered, and we could keep it up right along, year in and year out, and do it right, and the way it ought to be done. But *we* can't fool along, we got to rush; we ain't got no time to spare. If we was to put in another night this way, we'd have to knock off for a week to let our hands get well—couldn't touch a case-knife with them sooner."

"Well, then, what we going to do, Tom?"

"I'll tell you. It ain't right, and it ain't moral, and I wouldn't like it to get out—but there ain't only just the one way; we got to dig him out with the picks, and *let on* it's case-knives."

"*Now* you're *talking!*" I says; "your head gets leveler and leveler all the time, Tom Sawyer," I says. "Picks is the thing, moral or no moral; and as for me, I don't care shucks for the morality of it, nohow. When I start in to steal a nigger, or a watermelon, or a Sunday-school book, I ain't no ways particular how it's done so it's done. What I want is my nigger; or what I want is my watermelon; or what I want is my Sunday-school book; and if a pick's the handiest thing, that's the thing I'm agoing to dig that nigger or that watermelon or that Sunday-school book out with; and I don't give a dead rat what the authorities thinks about it nuther."

"Well," he says, "there's excuse for picks and letting-on in a case like this; if it warn't so, I wouldn't approve of it, nor I wouldn't stand by and see the rules broke—because right is right, and wrong is wrong, and a body ain't got no business doing wrong when he ain't ignorant and knows better. It might answer for *you* to dig Jim out with a pick, *without* any letting-on, because you don't know no better; but it wouldn't for me, because I do know better. Gimme a case-knife."

He had his own by him, but I handed him mine. He flung it down, and says:

"Gimme a *case-knife*."

I didn't know just what to do—but then I thought. I scratched around amongst the old tools, and got a pick-ax and give it to him, and he took it and went to work, and never said a word.

He was always just that particular. Full of principle.

So then I got a shovel, and then we picked and shoveled, turn about, and made the fur fly. We stuck to it about a half an hour, which was as long as we could stand up; but we had a good deal of a hole to show for it. When I got up stairs, I looked out at the window and see Tom doing his level best with the lightning-rod, but he couldn't come it, his hands was so sore. At last he says:

"It ain't no use, it can't be done. What you reckon I better do? Can't you think up no way?"

"Yes," I says, "but I reckon it ain't regular. Come up the stairs, and let on it's a lightning-rod."

So he done it.

Next day Tom stole a pewter spoon and a brass candlestick in the house, for to make some pens for Jim out of, and six tallow candles; and I hung around the nigger cabins, and laid for a chance, and stole three tin plates. Tom said it wasn't enough; but I said nobody wouldn't ever see the plates that Jim throwed out, because they'd fall in the dog-fennel and jimpson weeds under the window-hole—then we could tote them back and he could use them over again. So Tom was satisfied. Then he says:

"Now, the thing to study out is, how to get the things to Jim."

"Take them in through the hole," I says, "when we get it done."

He only just looked scornful, and said something about nobody ever heard of such an idiotic idea, and then he went to studying. By-and-by he said he had ciphered out two or three ways, but there warn't no need to decide on any of them yet. Said we'd got to post Jim first.

That night we went down the lightning-rod a little after ten, and took one of the candles along, and listened under the window-hole, and heard Jim snoring; so we pitched it in, and it didn't wake him. Then we whirled in with the pick and shovel, and in about two hours and a half the job was done. We crept in under Jim's bed and into the cabin, and pawed around and found the candle and lit it, and stood over Jim a while, and found him looking hearty and healthy, and then we woke him up gentle and gradual. He was so glad to see us he most cried; and called us honey, and all the pet names he could think of; and was for having us hunt up a cold chisel to cut the chain off of his leg with, right away, and clearing out without losing any time. But Tom he showed him how unregular it would be, and set down and told him all about our plans, and how we could alter them in a minute any time there was an alarm; and not to be the least afraid, because we would see he got away, *sure*. So Jim he said it was all right, and we set there and talked over old times a while, and then Tom asked a lot of questions, and when Jim told him Uncle Silas come in every day or two to pray with him, and Aunt Sally come in to see if he was comfortable and had plenty to eat, and both of them was kind as they could be, Tom says:

"*Now* I know how to fix it. We'll send you some things by them."

I said, "Don't·do nothing of the kind; it's one of the most jackass ideas I ever struck;" but he never paid no attention to me; went right on. It was his way when he'd got his plans set.

So he told Jim how we'd have to smuggle in the rope-ladder pie, and other large things, by Nat, the nigger that fed him, and he must be on the lookout, and not be surprised, and not let Nat see him open them; and we would put small things in uncle's coat pockets and he must steal them out; and we would tie things to aunt's apron strings or put them in her apron pocket, if we got a chance; and told him what they would be and what they was for. And told him how to keep a journal on the shirt with his blood, and all that. He told him everything. Jim he couldn't see no sense in the most of it, but he allowed we was white folks and knowed better than him; so he was satisfied, and said he would do it all just as Tom said.

Jim had plenty corn-cob pipes and tobacco; so we had a right down good sociable time; then we crawled out through the hole, and so home to bed, with hands that looked like they'd been chawed. Tom was in high spirits. He said it was the best fun he ever had in his life, and the most intellectural; and said if he only could see his way to it we would keep it up all the rest of our lives and leave Jim to our children to get out; for he believed Jim would come to like it better and better the more he got used to it. He said that in that way it could be strung out to as much as eighty year, and would be the best time on record. And he said it would make us all celebrated that had a hand in it.

In the morning we went out to the wood-pile and chopped up the brass candlestick into handy sizes, and Tom put them and the pewter spoon in his pocket. Then we went to the nigger cabins, and while I got Nat's notice off, Tom shoved a piece of candlestick into the middle of a corn-pone that was in Jim's pan, and we went along with Nat to see how it would work, and it just worked noble; when Jim bit into it it most mashed all his teeth out; and there warn't ever anything could a worked better. Tom said so himself. Jim he never let on but what it was only just a piece of rock or something like that that's always getting into bread, you know; but after that he never bit into nothing but what he jabbed his fork into it in three or four places, first.

And whilst we was a standing there in the dimmish light, here comes a couple of the hounds bulging in, from under Jim's bed; and they kept on piling in till there was eleven of them, and there warn't hardly room in there to get your breath. By jings, we forgot to fasten that lean-to door. The nigger Nat he only just hollered "witches!" once, and keeled over onto the floor amongst the dogs, and begun to groan like he was dying. Tom jerked the door open and flung out a slab of Jim's meat, and the dogs went for it, and in two seconds he was out himself and back again and shut the door, and I knowed he'd fixed the other door too. Then he went to work on the nigger, coaxing him and petting him, and asking him if he'd been imagining he saw something again. He raised up, and blinked his eyes around, and says:

"Mars Sid, you'll say I's a fool, but if I didn't b'lieve I see most a million dogs, er devils, er some'n, I wisht I may die right heah in dese tracks. I did, mos' sholy. Mars Sid, I *felt* um—I *felt* um, sah; dey was all over me. Dad fetch it, I jis' wisht I could git my han's on one er dem witches jis' wunst— on'y jis' wunst—it's all *I'*d ast. But mos'ly I wisht dey'd lemme 'lone, I does."

Tom says:

"Well, I tell you what *I* think. What makes them come here just at this runaway nigger's breakfast-time? It's because they're hungry; that's the reason. You make them a witch pie; that's the thing for *you* to do."

"But my lan', Mars Sid, how's *I* gwyne to make 'm a witch pie? I doan' know how to make it. I hain't ever hearn er sich a thing b'fo.' "

"Well, then, I'll have to make it myself."

"Will you do it, honey?—will you? I'll wusshup de groun' und' yo' foot, I will!"

"All right, I'll do it, seeing it's you, and you've been good to us and showed us the runaway nigger. But you got to be mighty careful. When we come around, you turn your back; and then whatever we've put in the pan, don't you let on you see it at all. And don't you look, when Jim unloads the pan—

something might happen, I don't know what. And above all, don't you *handle* the witch-things."

"*Hannel* 'm Mars Sid? What *is* you a talkin' 'bout? I wouldn' lay de weight er my finger on um, not f'r ten hund'd thous'n' billion dollars, I wouldn't."

XXXVII

THAT was all fixed. So then we went away and went to the rubbage-pile in the back yard where they keep the old boots, and rags, and pieces of bottles, and wore-out tin things, and all such truck, and scratched around and found an old tin washpan and stopped up the holes as well as we could, to bake the pie in, and took it down cellar and stole it full of flour, and started for breakfast and found a couple of shingle-nails that Tom said would be handy for a prisoner to scrabble his name and sorrows on the dungeon walls with, and dropped one of them in Aunt Sally's apron pocket which was hanging on a chair, and t'other we stuck in the band of Uncle Silas's hat, which was on the bureau, because we heard the children say their pa and ma was going to the runaway nigger's house this morning, and then went to breakfast, and Tom dropped the pewter spoon in Uncle Silas's coat pocket, and Aunt Sally wasn't come yet, so we had to wait a little while.

And when she come she was hot, and red, and cross, and couldn't hardly wait for the blessing; and then she went to sluicing out coffee with one hand and cracking the handiest child's head with her thimble with the other, and says:

"I've hunted high, and I've hunted low, and it does beat all, what *has* become of your other shirt."

My heart fell down amongst my lungs and livers and things, and a hard piece of corn-crust started down my throat after it and got met on the road with a cough and was shot across the table and took one of the children in the eye and curled him up like a fishing-worm, and let a cry out of him the size of a war-whoop, and Tom he turned kinder blue around the gills, and it all amounted to a considerable state of things for about a quarter of a minute or as much as that, and I would a sold out for half price if there was a bidder. But after that we was all right again—it was the sudden surprise of it that knocked us so kind of cold. Uncle Silas he says:

"It's most uncommon curious, I can't understand it. I know perfectly well I took it *off*, because——"

"Because you hain't got but one *on*. Just *listen* at the man! *I* know you took it off, and know it by a better way than your wool-gethering memory, too, because it was on the clo'es-line yesterday—I see it there myself. But it's gone—that's the long and the short of it, and you'll just have to change to a red flann'l one till I can get time to make a new one. And it'll be the third I've made in two years; it just keeps a body on the jump to keep you in shirts; and whatever you do manage to *do* with 'm all, is more'n *I* can make out. A body'd think you *would* learn to take some sort of care of 'em, at your time of life."

"I know it, Sally, and I do try all I can. But it oughtn't to be altogether my fault, because you know I don't see them nor have nothing to do with them except when they're on me; and I don't believe I've ever lost one of them *off* of me."

"Well, it ain't *your* fault if you haven't, Silas—you'd a done it if you could, I reckon. And the shirt ain't all that's gone, nuther. Ther's a spoon gone; and *that* ain't all. There was ten, and now ther's only nine. The calf got the shirt I reckon, but the calf never took the spoon, *that's* certain."

"Why, what else is gone, Sally?"

"Ther's six *candles* gone—that's what. The rats could a got the candles, and I reckon they did; I wonder they don't walk off with the whole place, the way you're always going to stop their holes and don't do it; and if they warn't fools they'd sleep in your hair, Silas—*you'd* never find it out; but you can't lay the *spoon* on the rats, and that I *know*."

"Well, Sally, I'm in fault, and I acknowledge it; I've been remiss; but I won't let to-morrow go by without stopping up them holes."

"Oh, I wouldn't hurry, next year'll do. Matilda Angelina Araminta *Phelps!*"

Whack comes the thimble, and the child snatches her claws out of the sugar-bowl without fooling around any. Just then, the nigger woman steps onto the passage, and says:

"Missus, dey's a sheet gone."

"A *sheet* gone! Well, for the land's sake!"

"I'll stop up them holes *to-day*," says Uncles Silas, looking sorrowful.

"Oh, *do* shet up!—spose the rats took the *sheet*? *Where's* it gone, Lize?"

"Clah to goodness I hain't no notion, Miss Sally. She wuz on de clo's-line yistiddy, but she done gone; she ain' dah no mo', now."

"I reckon the world *is* coming to an end. I *never* see the beat of it, in all my born days. A shirt, and a sheet, and a spoon, and six can——"

"Missus," comes a young yaller wench, "dey's a brass can-nelstick miss'n."

"Cler out from here, you hussy, or I'll take a skillet to ye!"

Well, she was just a biling. I begun to lay for a chance; I reckoned I would sneak out and go for the woods till the weather moderated. She kept a raging right along, running her insurrection all by herself, and everybody else mighty meek and quiet; and at last Uncle Silas, looking kind of foolish, fishes up that spoon out of his pocket. She stopped, with her mouth open and her hands up; and as for me, I wished I was in Jerusalem or somewheres. But not long; because she says:

"It's *just* as I expected. So you had it in your pocket all the time; and like as not you've got the other things there, too. How'd it get there?"

"I reely don't know, Sally," he says, kind of apologizing, "or you know I would tell. I was a-studying over my text in Acts Seventeen, before breakfast, and I reckon I put it in there, not noticing, meaning to put my Testament in, and it must be so, because my Testament ain't in, but I'll go and see, and if the Testament is where I had it, I'll know I didn't put it in, and that will show that I laid the Testament down and took up the spoon, and——"

"Oh, for the land's sake! Give a body a rest! Go 'long now, the whole kit and biling of ye; and don't come nigh me again till I've got back my peace of mind."

I'd a heard her, if she'd a said it to herself, let alone speaking it out; and I'd a got up and obeyed her, if I'd a been dead. As we was passing through the setting-room, the old man he took up his hat, and the shingle-nail fell out on the floor, and he just merely picked it up and laid it on the mantel-shelf, and never said nothing, and went out. Tom see him do it, and remembered about the spoon, and says:

"Well, it ain't no use to send things by *him* no more, he ain't reliable." Then he says: "But he done us a good turn with the spoon, anyway, without knowing it, and so we'll go and do him one without *him* knowing it—stop up his rat-holes."

There was a noble good lot of them, down cellar, and it took us a whole hour, but we done the job tight and good, and ship-shape. Then we heard steps on the stairs, and blowed out our light, and hid; and here comes the old man, with a candle in one hand and a bundle of stuff in t'other, looking as absent-minded as year before last. He went a mooning around, first to one rat-hole and then another, till he'd been to them all. Then he stood about five minutes, picking tallow-drip off his candle and thinking. Then he turns off slow and dreamy towards the stairs, saying:

"Well, for the life of me I can't remember when I done it. I could show her now that I warn't to blame on account of the rats. But never mind—let it go. I reckon it wouldn't do no good."

And so he went on a mumbling up stairs, and then we left. He was a mighty nice old man. And always is.

Tom was a good deal bothered about what to do for a spoon, but he said we'd got to have it; so he took a think. When he had ciphered it out, he told me how we was to do; then we went and waited around the spoon-basket till we see Aunt Sally coming, and then Tom went to counting the spoons and laying them out to one side, and I slid one of them up my sleeve, and Tom says:

"Why, Aunt Sally, there ain't but nine spoons, *yet*."

She says:

"Go 'long to your play, and don't bother me. I know better, I counted 'm myself."

"Well, I've counted them twice, Aunty, and *I* can't make but nine."

She looked out of all patience, but of course she come to count—anybody would.

"I declare to gracious ther' *ain't* but nine!" she says. "Why, what in the world—plague *take* the things, I'll count 'm again."

So I slipped back the one I had, and when she got done counting, she says:

"Hang the troublesome rubbage, ther's *ten*, now!" and she looked huffy and bothered both. But Tom says:

"Why, Aunty, *I* don't think there's ten."

"You numskull, didn't you see me *count* 'm?"

"I know, but——"

"Well, I'll count 'm *again*."

So I smouched one, and they come out nine same as the other time. Well, she *was* in a tearing way—just a trembling all over, she was so mad. But she counted and counted, till she got that addled she'd start to count-in the *basket* for a spoon, sometimes; and so, three times they come out right, and three times they come out wrong. Then she grabbed up the basket and slammed it across the house and knocked the cat galley-west; and she said cle'r out and let her have some peace, and if we come bothering around her again betwixt that and dinner, she'd skin us. So we had the odd spoon; and dropped it in her apron pocket whilst she was a giving us our sailing-orders, and Jim got it all right, along with her shingle-nail, before noon. We was very well satisfied with this business, and Tom allowed it was worth twice the trouble it took, because he said *now* she couldn't ever count them spoons twice alike again to save her life; and wouldn't believe she'd counted them right, if she *did*; and said that after she'd about counted her head off, for the next three days, he judged she'd give it up and offer to kill anybody that wanted her to ever count them any more.

So we put the sheet back on the line, that night, and stole one out of her closet; and kept on putting it back and stealing it again, for a couple of days, till she didn't know how many sheets she had, any more, and said she didn't *care*, and warn't agoing to bullyrag the rest of her soul out about it, and wouldn't count them again not to save her life, she druther die first.

So we was all right now, as to the shirt and the sheet and the spoon and the candles, by the help of the calf and the rats

and the mixed-up counting; and as to the candlestick, i
warn't no consequence, it would blow over by-and-by.

But that pie was a job; we had no end of trouble with tha
pie. We fixed it up away down in the woods, and cooked i
there; and we got it done at last, and very satisfactory, too
but not all in one day; and we had to use up three washpan:
full of flour, before we got through, and we got burnt pretty
much all over, in places, and eyes put out with the smoke.
because, you see, we didn't want nothing but a crust, and we
couldn't prop it up right, and she would always cave in. But
of course we thought of the right way at last; which was to
cook the ladder, too, in the pie. So then we laid in with Jim,
the second night, and tore up the sheet all in little strings,
and twisted them together, and long before daylight we had
a lovely rope, that you could a hung a person with. We let on
it took nine months to make it.

And in the forenoon we took it down to the woods, but it
wouldn't go in the pie. Being made of a whole sheet, that
way, there was rope enough for forty pies, if we'd a wanted
them, and plenty left over for soup, or sausage, or anything
you choose. We could a had a whole dinner.

But we didn't need it. All we needed was just enough for
the pie, and so we throwed the rest away. We didn't cook
none of the pies in the washpan, afraid the solder would melt;
but Uncle Silas he had a noble brass warming-pan which he
thought considerable of, because it belonged to one of his
ancestors with a long wooden handle that come over from
England with William the Conqueror in the *Mayflower* or one
of them early ships and was hid away up garret with a lot of
other old pots and things that was valuable, not on account
of being any account because they warn't, but on account of
them being relicts, you know, and we snaked her out, private,
and took her down there, but she failed on the first pies, because we didn't know how, but she come up smiling on the
last one. We took and lined her with dough, and set her in
the coals, and loaded her up with rag-rope, and put on a
dough roof, and shut down the lid, and put hot embers on
top, and stood off five foot, with the long handle, cool and
comfortable, and in fifteen minutes she turned out a pie that

was a satisfaction to look at. But the person that et it would want to fetch a couple of kags of toothpicks along, for if that rope-ladder wouldn't cramp him down to business, I don't know nothing what I'm talking about, and lay him in enough stomach-ache to last him till next time, too.

Nat didn't look, when we put the witch-pie in Jim's pan; and we put the three tin plates in the bottom of the pan under the vittles; and so Jim got everything all right, and as soon as he was by himself he busted into the pie and hid the rope-ladder inside of his straw tick, and scratched some marks on a tin plate and throwed it out of the window-hole.

XXXVIII

MAKING THEM PENS was a distressid-tough job, and so was the saw; and Jim allowed the inscription was going to be the toughest of all. That's the one which the prisoner has to scrabble on the wall. But we had to have it; Tom said we'd *got* to; there warn't no case of a state prisoner not scrabbling his inscription to leave behind, and his coat of arms.

"Look at Lady Jane Grey," he says; "look at Gilford Dudley; look at old Northumberland! Why, Huck, spose it *is* considerble trouble?—what you going to do?—how you going to get around it? Jim's *got* to do his inscription and coat of arms. They all do."

Jim says:

"Why, Mars Tom, I hain't got no coat o' arms; I hain't got nuffn but dish-yer ole shirt, en you knows I got to keep de journal on dat."

"Oh, you don't understand, Jim; a coat of arms is very different."

"Well," I says, "Jim's right, anyway, when he says he hain't got no coat of arms, because he hain't."

"I reckon *I* knowed that," Tom says, "but you bet he'll have one before he goes out of this—because he's going out *right*, and there ain't going to be no flaws in his record."

So whilst me and Jim filed away at the pens on a brickbat apiece, Jim a making his'n out of the brass and I making mine out of the spoon, Tom set to work to think out the coat of arms. By-and-by he said he'd struck so many good ones he didn't hardly know which to take, but there was one which he reckoned he'd decide on. He says:

"On the scutcheon we'll have a bend *or* in the dexter base, a saltire *murrey* in the fess, with a dog, couchant, for common charge, and under his foot a chain embattled, for slavery, with a chevron *vert* in a chief engrailed, and three invected lines on a field *azure*, with the nombril points rampant on a dancette indented; crest, a runaway nigger, *sable*, with his bundle over his shoulder on a bar sinister: and a couple of gules for supporters, which is you and me; motto, *Maggiore fretta, mi-nore atto*. Got it out of a book—means, the more haste, the less speed."

"Geewhillikins," I says, "but what does the rest of it mean?"

"We ain't got no time to bother over that," he says, "we got to dig in like all git-out."

"Well, anyway," I says, "what's *some* of it? What's a fess?"

"A fess—a fess is—*you* don't need to know what a fess is. I'll show him how to make it when he gets to it."

"Shucks, Tom," I says, "I think you might tell a person. What's a bar sinister?"

"Oh, *I* don't know. But he's got to have it. All the nobility does."

That was just his way. If it didn't suit him to explain a thing to you, he wouldn't do it. You might pump at him a week, it wouldn't make no difference.

He'd got all that coat of arms business fixed, so now he started in to finish up the rest of that part of the work, which was to plan out a mournful inscription—said Jim got to have one, like they all done. He made up a lot, and wrote them out on a paper, and read them off, so:

1. *Here a captive heart busted.*

2. *Here a poor prisoner, forsook by the world and friends, fret-ted out his sorrowful life.*

3. *Here a lonely heart broke, and a worn spirit went to its rest, after thirty-seven years of solitary captivity.*

4. *Here, homeless and friendless, after thirty-seven years of bit-ter captivity, perished a noble stranger, natural son of Louis XIV.*

Tom's voice trembled, whilst he was reading them, and he most broke down. When he got done, he couldn't no way make up his mind which one for Jim to scrabble onto the wall, they was all so good; but at last he allowed he would let him scrabble them all on. Jim said it would take him a year to scrabble such a lot of truck onto the logs with a nail, and he didn't know how to make letters, besides; but Tom said he would block them out for him, and then he wouldn't have nothing to do but just follow the lines. Then pretty soon he says:

"Come to think, the logs ain't agoing to do; they don' have log walls in a dungeon: we got to dig the inscription into a rock. We'll fetch a rock."

Jim said the rock was worse than the logs; he said it would take him such a pison long time to dig them into a rock, he wouldn't ever get out. But Tom said he would let me help him do it. Then he took a look to see how me and Jim was getting along with the pens. It was most pesky tedious hard work and slow, and didn't give my hands no show to get well of the sores, and we didn't seem to make no headway, hardly. So Tom says:

"I know how to fix it. We got to have a rock for the coat of arms and mournful inscriptions, and we can kill two birds with that same rock. There's a gaudy big grindstone down at the mill, and we'll smouch it, and carve the things on it, and file out the pens and the saw on it, too."

It warn't no slouch of an idea; and it warn't no slouch of a grindstone nuther; but we allowed we'd tackle it. It warn't quite midnight, yet, so we cleared out for the mill, leaving Jim at work. We smouched the grindstone, and set out to roll her home, but it was a most nation tough job. Sometimes, do what we could, we couldn't keep her from falling over, and she come mighty near mashing us, every time. Tom said she was going to get one of us, sure, before we got through. We got her half way; and then we was plumb played out, and most drownded with sweat. We see it warn't no use, we got to go and fetch Jim. So he raised up his bed and slid the chain off of the bed-leg, and wrapt it round and round his neck, and we crawled out through our hole and down there, and Jim and me laid into that grindstone and walked her along like nothing; and Tom superintended. He could out-superintend any boy I ever see. He knowed how to do everything.

Our hole was pretty big, but it warn't big enough to get the grindstone through; but Jim he took the pick and soon made it big enough. Then Tom marked out them things on it with the nail, and set Jim to work on them, with the nail for a chisel and an iron bolt from the rubbage in the lean-to for a hammer, and told him to work till the rest of his candle quit on him, and then he could go to bed, and hide the grind-

stone under his straw tick and sleep on it. Then we helped
him fix his chain back on the bed-leg, and was ready for bed
ourselves. But Tom thought of something, and says:

"You got any spiders in here, Jim?"

"No, sah, thanks to goodness I hain't, Mars Tom."

"All right, we'll get you some."

"But bless you, honey, I doan' *want* none. I's afeard un
um. I jis' 's soon have rattlesnakes aroun'.'"

Tom thought a minute or two, and says:

"It's a good idea. And I reckon it's been done. It *must* a
been done; it stands to reason. Yes, it's a prime good idea.
Where could you keep it?"

"Keep what, Mars Tom?"

"Why, a rattlesnake."

"De goodness gracious alive, Mars Tom! Why, if dey was
a rattlesnake to come in heah, I'd take en bust right out thoo
dat log wall, I would, wid my head."

"Why, Jim, you wouldn't be afraid of it, after a little. You
could tame it."

"*Tame* it!"

"Yes—easy enough. Every animal is grateful for kindness
and petting, and they wouldn't *think* of hurting a person
that pets them. Any book will tell you that. You try—
that's all I ask; just try for two or three days. Why, you
can get him so, in a little while, that he'll love you; and
sleep with you; and won't stay away from you a minute;
and will let you wrap him round your neck and put his
head in your mouth."

"*Please*, Mars Tom—*doan'* talk so! I can't *stan'* it! He'd *let*
me shove his head in my mouf—fer a favor, hain't it? I lay
he'd wait a pow'ful long time 'fo' I *ast* him. En mo' en dat,
I doan' *want* him to sleep wid me."

"Jim, don't act so foolish. A prisoner's *got* to have some
kind of a dumb pet, and if a rattlesnake hain't ever been tried,
why, there's more glory to be gained in your being the first
to ever try it than any other way you could ever think of to
save your life."

"Why, Mars Tom, I doan' *want* no sich glory. Snake take
'n bite Jim's chin off, den *whah* is de glory? No, sah, I doan'
want no sich doin's."

"Blame it, can't you *try*? I only *want* you to try—yo needn't keep it up if it don't work."

"But de trouble all *done*, ef de snake bite me while I's tryin' him. Mars Tom, I's willin' to tackle mos' anything 'a ain't onreasonable, but ef you en Huck fetches a rattlesnak in heah for me to tame, I's gwyne to *leave*, dat's *shore*."

"Well, then, let it go, let it go, if you're so bullheade about it. We can get you some garter-snakes and you can ti some buttons on their tails, and let on they're rattlesnakes and I reckon that'll have to do."

"I k'n stan' *dem*, Mars Tom, but blame' 'f I couldn't ge along widout um, I tell you dat. I never knowed b'fo', 't wa so much bother and trouble to be a prisoner."

"Well, it *always* is, when it's done right. You got any rat around here?"

"No, sah, I hain't seed none."

"Well, we'll get you some rats."

"Why, Mars Tom, I doan' *want* no rats. Dey's de dad blamedest creturs to sturb a body, en rustle roun' over 'im, er bite his feet, when he's tryin' to sleep, I ever see. No, sah gimme g'yarter-snakes, 'f I's got to have 'm, but doan' gimme no rats, I ain't got no use f'r um, skasely."

"But Jim, you *got* to have 'em—they all do. So don't make no more fuss about it. Prisoners ain't ever without rats. There ain't no instance of it. And they train them, and pet them and learn them tricks, and they get to be as sociable as flies But you got to play music to them. You got anything to play music on?"

"I ain' got nuffin but a coase comb en a piece o' paper, en a juice-harp; but I reck'n dey wouldn' take no stock in a juice-harp."

"Yes they would. *They* don't care what kind of music 'tis. A jews-harp's plenty good enough for a rat. All animals like music—in a prison they dote on it. Specially, painful music; and you can't get no other kind out of a jews-harp. It always interests them; they come out to see what's the matter with you. Yes, you're all right; you're fixed very well. You want to set on your bed, nights, before you go to sleep, and early in the mornings, and play your jews-harp; play The Last Link is Broken—that's the thing that'll scoop a rat, quicker'n any-

thing else: and when you've played about two minutes, you'll
see all the rats, and the snakes, and spiders, and things begin
to feel worried about you, and come. And they'll just fairly
swarm over you, and have a noble good time."

"Yes, *dey* will, I reck'n, Mars Tom, but what kine er time
is *Jim* havin'? Blest if I kin see de pint. But I'll do it ef I got
to. I reck'n I better keep de animals satisfied, en not have no
trouble in de house."

Tom waited to think over, and see if there wasn't nothing
else; and pretty soon he says:

"Oh—there's one thing I forgot. Could you raise a flower
here, do you reckon?"

"I doan' know but maybe I could, Mars Tom; but it's tol-
able dark in heah, en I ain' got no use f'r no flower, nohow,
en she'd be a pow'ful sight o' trouble."

"Well, you try it, anyway. Some other prisoners has done
it."

"One er dem big cat-tail-lookin' mullen-stalks would grow
in heah, Mars Tom, I reck'n, but she wouldn' be wuth half
de trouble she'd coss."

"Don't you believe it. We'll fetch you a little one, and you
plant it in the corner, over there, and raise it. And don't call
it mullen, call it Pitchiola—that's its right name, when it's in
a prison. And you want to water it with your tears."

"Why, I got plenty spring water, Mars Tom."

"You don't *want* spring water; you want to water it with
your tears. It's the way they always do."

"Why, Mars Tom, I lay I kin raise one er dem mullen-stalks
twyste wid spring water whiles another man's a *start'n* one
wid tears."

"That ain't the idea. You *got* to do it with tears."

"She'll die on my han's, Mars Tom, she sholy will; kase I
doan' skasely ever cry."

So Tom was stumped. But he studied it over, and then said
Jim would have to worry along the best he could with an
onion. He promised he would go to the nigger cabins and
drop one, private, in Jim's coffee-pot, in the morning. Jim
said he would "jis' 's soon have tobacker in his coffee;" and
found so much fault with it, and with the work and bother
of raising the mullen, and jews-harping the rats, and petting

and flattering up the snakes and spiders and things, on top of all the other work he had to do on pens, and inscriptions, and journals, and things, which made it more trouble and worry and responsibility to be a prisoner than anything he ever undertook, that Tom most lost all patience with him; and said he was just loadened down with more gaudier chances than a prisoner ever had in the world to make a name for himself, and yet he didn't know enough to appreciate them, and they was just about wasted on him. So Jim he was sorry, and said he wouldn't behave so no more, and then me and Tom shoved for bed.

XXXIX

In the morning we went up to the village and bought a wire rat trap and fetched it down, and unstopped the best rat hole, and in about an hour we had fifteen of the bulliest kind of ones; and then we took it and put it in a safe place under Aunt Sally's bed. But while we was gone for spiders, little Thomas Franklin Benjamin Jefferson Elexander Phelps found it there, and opened the door of it to see if the rats would come out, and they did; and Aunt Sally she come in, and when we got back she was a standing on top of the bed raising Cain, and the rats was doing what they could to keep off the dull times for her. So she took and dusted us both with the hickry, and we was as much as two hours catching another fifteen or sixteen, drat that meddlesome cub, and they warn't the likeliest, nuther, because the first haul was the pick of the flock. I never see a likelier lot of rats than what that first haul was.

We got a splendid stock of sorted spiders, and bugs, and frogs, and caterpillars, and one thing or another; and we like-to got a hornet's nest, but we didn't. The family was at home. We didn't give it right up, but staid with them as long as we could; because we allowed we'd tire them out or they'd got to tire us out, and they done it. Then we got allycumpain and rubbed on the places, and was pretty near all right again, but couldn't set down convenient. And so we went for the snakes, and grabbed a couple of dozen garters and house-snakes, and put them in a bag, and put it in our room, and by that time it was supper time, and a rattling good honest day's work; and hungry?—oh, no, I reckon not! And there warn't a blessed snake up there, when we went back—we didn't half tie the sack, and they worked out, somehow, and left. But it didn't matter much, because they was still on the premises somewheres. So we judged we could get some of them again. No, there warn't no real scarcity of snakes about the house for a considerble spell. You'd see them dripping from the rafters and places, every now and then; and they generly landed in your plate, or down the back of your neck, and most of

the time where you didn't want them. Well, they was handsome, and striped, and there warn't no harm in a million of
them; but that never made no difference to Aunt Sally, she
despised snakes, be the breed what they might, and she
couldn't stand them no way you could fix it; and every time
one of them flopped down on her, it didn't make no difference what she was doing, she would just lay that work down
and light out. I never see such a woman. And you could hear
her whoop to Jericho. You couldn't get her to take aholt of
one of them with the tongs. And if she turned over and found
one in bed, she would scramble out and lift a howl that you
would think the house was afire. She disturbed the old man
so, that he said he could most wish there hadn't ever been no
snakes created. Why, after every last snake had been gone
clear out of the house for as much as a week, Aunt Sally
warn't over it yet; she warn't near over it; when she was setting thinking about something, you could touch her on the
back of her neck with a feather and she would jump right out
of her stockings. It was very curious. But Tom said all women
was just so. He said they was made that way; for some reason
or other.

We got a licking every time one of our snakes come in her
way; and she allowed these lickings warn't nothing to what
she would do if we ever loaded up the place again with them.
I didn't mind the lickings, because they didn't amount to
nothing; but I minded the trouble we had, to lay in another
lot. But we got them laid in, and all the other things; and
you never see a cabin as blithesome as Jim's was when they'd
all swarm out for music and go for him. Jim didn't like the
spiders, and the spiders didn't like Jim; and so they'd lay for
him and make it mighty warm for him. And he said that between the rats, and the snakes, and the grindstone, there
warn't no room in bed for him, skasely; and when there was,
a body couldn't sleep, it was so lively, and it was always lively,
he said, because *they* never all slept at one time, but took turn
about, so when the snakes was asleep the rats was on deck,
and when the rats turned in the snakes come on watch, so he
always had one gang under him, in his way, and t'other gang
having a circus over him, and if he got up to hunt a new
place, the spiders would take a chance at him as he crossed

over. He said if he ever got out, this time, he wouldn't ever be a prisoner again, not for a salary.

Well, by the end of three weeks, everything was in pretty good shape. The shirt was sent in early, in a pie, and every time a rat bit Jim he would get up and write a little in his journal whilst the ink was fresh; the pens was made, the inscriptions and so on was all carved on the grindstone; the bed-leg was sawed in two, and we had et up the sawdust, and it give us a most amazing stomach-ache. We reckoned we was all going to die, but didn't. It was the most undigestible sawdust I ever see; and Tom said the same. But as I was saying, we'd got all the work done, now, at last; and we was all pretty much fagged out, too, but mainly Jim. The old man had wrote a couple of times to the plantation below Orleans to come and get their runaway nigger, but hadn't got no answer, because there warn't no such plantation; so he allowed he would advertise Jim in the St. Louis and New Orleans papers; and when he mentioned the St. Louis ones, it give me the cold shivers, and I see we hadn't no time to lose. So Tom said, now for the nonnamous letters.

"What's them?" I says.

"Warnings to the people that something is up. Sometimes it's done one way, sometimes another. But there's always somebody spying around, that gives notice to the governor of the castle. When Louis XVI. was going to light out of the Tooleries, a servant girl done it. It's a very good way, and so is the nonnamous letters. We'll use them both. And it's usual for the prisoner's mother to change clothes with him, and she stays in, and he slides out in her clothes. We'll do that too."

"But looky here, Tom, what do we want to *warn* anybody for, that something's up? Let them find it out for themselves—it's their lookout."

"Yes, I know; but you can't depend on them. It's the way they've acted from the very start—left us to do *everything*. They're so confiding and mullet-headed they don't take notice of nothing at all. So if we don't *give* them notice, there won't be nobody nor nothing to interfere with us, and so after all our hard work and trouble this escape 'll go off perfectly flat: won't amount to nothing—won't be nothing *to* it."

"Well, as for me, Tom, that's the way I'd like."

"Shucks," he says, and looked disgusted. So I says:

"But I ain't going to make no complaint. Anyway that suits you suits me. What you going to do about the servant-girl?"

"You'll be her. You slide in, in the middle of the night, and hook that yaller girl's frock."

"Why, Tom, that'll make trouble next morning; because of course she prob'bly hain't got any but that one."

"I know; but you don't want it but fifteen minutes, to carry the nonnamous letter and shove it under the front door."

"All right, then, I'll do it; but I could carry it just as handy in my own togs."

"You wouldn't look like a servant-girl *then*, would you?"

"No, but there won't be nobody to see what I look like, *anyway*."

"That ain't got nothing to do with it. The thing for us to do, is just to do our *duty*, and not worry about whether anybody *sees* us do it or not. Hain't you got no principle at all?"

"All right, I ain't saying nothing; I'm the servant-girl. Who's Jim's mother?"

"I'm his mother. I'll hook a gown from Aunt Sally."

"Well, then, you'll have to stay in the cabin when me and Jim leaves."

"Not much. I'll stuff Jim's clothes full of straw and lay it on his bed to represent his mother in disguise, and Jim 'll take the nigger woman's gown off of me and wear it, and we'll all evade together. When a prisoner of style escapes, it's called an evasion. It's always called so when a king escapes, f'rinstance. And the same with a king's son; it don't make no difference whether he's a natural one or an unnatural one."

So Tom he wrote the nonnamous letter, and I smouched the yaller wench's frock, that night, and put it on, and shoved it under the front door, the way Tom told me to. It said:

Beware. Trouble is brewing. Keep a sharp lookout.
UNKNOWN FRIEND.

Next night we stuck a picture which Tom drawed in blood, of a skull and crossbones, on the front door; and next night another one of a coffin, on the back door. I never see a family in such a sweat. They couldn't a been worse scared if the place had a been full of ghosts laying for them behind everything and under the beds and shivering through the air. If a door banged, Aunt Sally she jumped, and said "ouch!" if anything fell, she jumped and said "ouch!" if you happened to touch her, when she warn't noticing, she done the same; she couldn't face noway and be satisfied, because she allowed there was something behind her every time—so she was always a whirling around, sudden, and saying "ouch," and before she'd get two-thirds around, she'd whirl back again, and say it again; and she was afraid to go to bed, but she dasn't set up. So the thing was working very well, Tom said; he said he never see a thing work more satisfactory. He said it showed it was done right.

So he said, now for the grand bulge! So the very next morning at the streak of dawn we got another letter ready, and was wondering what we better do with it, because we heard them say at supper they was going to have a nigger on watch at both doors all night. Tom he went down the lightning-rod to spy around; and the nigger at the back door was asleep, and he stuck it in the back of his neck and come back. This letter said:

> *Don't betray me, I wish to be your friend. There is a desprate gang of cutthroats from over in the Ingean Territory going to steal your runaway nigger to-night, and they have been trying to scare you so as you will stay in the house and not bother them. I am one of the gang, but have got religgion and wish to quit it and lead a honest life again, and will betray the helish design. They will sneak down from northards, along the fence, at midnight exact, with a false key, and go in the nigger's cabin to get him. I am to be off a piece and blow a tin horn if I see any danger; but stead of that, I will* BA *like a sheep soon as they get in and not blow at all; then whilst they are getting his chains loose, you slip there and lock them in, and can kill them at your leisure. Don't do anything but just the way I am telling you, if you do they will suspicion something and raise whoopjamboreehoo. I do not wish any reward but to know I have done the right thing.*
>
> UNKNOWN FRIEND.

XL

WE WAS FEELING pretty good, after breakfast, and took my canoe and went over the river a fishing, with a lunch, and had a good time, and took a look at the raft and found her all right, and got home late to supper, and found them in such a sweat and worry they didn't know which end they was standing on, and made us go right off to bed the minute we was done supper, and wouldn't tell us what the trouble was, and never let on a word about the new letter, but didn't need to, because we knowed as much about it as anybody did, and as soon as we was half up stairs and her back was turned, we slid for the cellar cubboard and loaded up a good lunch and took it up to our room and went to bed, and got up about half-past eleven, and Tom put on Aunt Sally's dress that he stole and was going to start with the lunch, but says:

"Where's the butter?"

"I laid out a hunk of it," I says, "on a piece of a corn-pone."

"Well, you *left* it laid out, then—it ain't here."

"We can get along without it," I says.

"We can get along *with* it, too," he says; "just you slide down cellar and fetch it. And then mosey right down the lightning-rod and come along. I'll go and stuff the straw into Jim's clothes to represent his mother in disguise, and be ready to *ba* like a sheep and shove soon as you get there."

So out he went, and down cellar went I. The hunk of butter, big as a person's fist, was where I had left it, so I took up the slab of corn-pone with it on, and blowed out my light, and started up stairs, very stealthy, and got up to the main floor all right, but here comes Aunt Sally with a candle, and I clapped the truck in my hat, and clapped my hat on my head, and the next second she see me; and she says:

"You been down cellar?"

"Yes'm."

"What you been doing down there?"

"Noth'n!"

"*Noth'n!*"

"No'm."

"Well, then, what possessed you to go down there, this time of night?"

"I don't know'm."

"You don't *know*? Don't answer me that way, Tom, I want to know what you been *doing* down there?"

"I hain't been doing a single thing, Aunt Sally, I hope to gracious if I have."

I reckoned she'd let me go, now, and as a generl thing she would; but I spose there was so many strange things going on she was just in a sweat about every little thing that warn't yard-stick straight; so she says, very decided:

"You just march into that setting-room and stay there till I come. You been up to something you no business to, and I lay I'll find out what it is before *I'm* done with you."

So she went away as I opened the door and walked into the setting-room. My, but there was a crowd there! Fifteen farmers, and every one of them had a gun. I was most powerful sick, and slunk to a chair and set down. They was setting around, some of them talking a little, in a low voice, and all of them fidgety and uneasy, but trying to look like they warn't; but I knowed they was, because they was always taking off their hats, and putting them on, and scratching their heads, and changing their seats, and fumbling with their buttons. I warn't easy myself, but I didn't take my hat off, all the same.

I did wish Aunt Sally would come, and get done with me, and lick me, if she wanted to, and let me get away and tell Tom how we'd overdone this thing, and what a thundering hornet's nest we'd got ourselves into, so we could stop fooling around, straight off, and clear out with Jim before these rips got out of patience and come for us.

At last she come, and begun to ask me questions, but I *couldn't* answer them straight, I didn't know which end of me was up; because these men was in such a fidget now, that some was wanting to start right *now* and lay for them desperadoes, and saying it warn't but a few minutes to midnight; and others was trying to get them to hold on and wait for the sheep-signal; and here was aunty pegging away at the questions, and me a shaking all over and ready to sink down in my tracks I was that scared; and the place getting hotter and hotter, and the butter beginning to melt and run down my neck and behind my ears; and pretty soon, when one of them says, "*I'm* for going and getting in the cabin *first*, and right *now*, and catching them when they come," I most dropped; and a streak of butter come a trickling down my forehead, and Aunt Sally she see it, and turns white as a sheet, and says:

"For the land's sake what *is* the matter with the child!— he's got the brain fever as shore as you're born, and they're oozing out!"

And everybody runs to see, and she snatches off my hat, and out comes the bread, and what was left of the butter, and she grabbed me, and hugged me, and says:

"Oh, what a turn you did give me! and how glad and grateful I am it ain't no worse; for luck's against us, and it never rains but it pours, and when I see that truck I thought we'd lost you, for I knowed by the color and all, it was just like your brains would be if— Dear, dear, whydn't you *tell* me that was what you'd been down there for, *I* wouldn't a cared. Now cler out to bed, and don't lemme see no more of you till morning!"

I was up stairs in a second, and down the lightning-rod in another one, and shining through the dark for the lean-to. I couldn't hardly get my words out, I was so anxious; but I told Tom as quick as I could, we must jump for it, now, and not a minute to lose—the house full of men, yonder, with guns!

His eyes just blazed; and he says:

"No!—is that so? *Ain't* it bully! Why, Huck, if it was to do over again, I bet I could fetch two hundred! If we could put it off till——"

"Hurry! *hurry!*" I says. "Where's Jim?"

"Right at your elbow; if you reach out your arm you can touch him. He's dressed, and everything's ready. Now we'll slide out and give the sheep-signal."

But then we heard the tramp of men, coming to the door, and heard them begin to fumble with the padlock; and heard a man say:

"I *told* you we'd be too soon; they haven't come—the door
s locked. Here, I'll lock some of you into the cabin and you
ay for 'em in the dark and kill 'em when they come; and the
·est scatter around a piece, and listen if you can hear 'em
:oming."

So in they come, but couldn't see us in the dark, and most
·rod on us whilst we was hustling to get under the bed. But
,ve got under all right, and out through the hole, swift but
,oft—Jim first, me next, and Tom last, which was according
:o Tom's orders. Now we was in the lean-to, and heard
:rampings close by outside. So we crept to the door, and Tom
;topped us there and put his eye to the crack, but couldn't
nake out nothing, it was so dark; and whispered and said he
,vould listen for the steps to get further, and when he nudged
ıs Jim must glide out first, and him last. So he set his ear to
:he crack and listened, and listened, and listened, and the
;teps a scraping around, out there, all the time; and at last he
nudged us, and we slid out, and stooped down, not breathing, and not making the least noise, and slipped stealthy towards the fence, in Injun file, and got to it, all right, and me
and Jim over it; but Tom's britches catched fast on a splinter
on the top rail, and then he hear the steps coming, so he had
to pull loose, which snapped the splinter and made a noise;
and as he dropped in our tracks and started, somebody sings
out:

"Who's that? Answer, or I'll shoot!"

But we didn't answer; we just unfurled our heels and
shoved. Then there was a rush, and a *bang, bang, bang!* and
the bullets fairly whizzed around us! We heard them sing out:

"Here they are! They've broke for the river! after 'em,
boys! And turn loose the dogs!"

So here they come, full tilt. We could hear them, because
they wore boots, and yelled, but we didn't wear no boots,
and didn't yell. We was in the path to the mill; and when
they got pretty close onto us, we dodged into the bush and
let them go by, and then dropped in behind them. They'd
had all the dogs shut up, so they wouldn't scare off the robbers; but by this time somebody had let them loose, and here
they come, making pow-wow enough for a million; but they
was our dogs; so we stopped in our tracks till they catched

up; and when they see it warn't nobody but us, and no ex
citement to offer them, they only just said howdy, and tor
right ahead towards the shouting and clattering; and then w
up steam again and whizzed along after them till we wa
nearly to the mill, and then struck up through the bush to
where my canoe was tied, and hopped in and pulled for dea
life towards the middle of the river, but didn't make no more
noise than we was obleeged to. Then we struck out, easy and
comfortable, for the island where my raft was; and we could
hear them yelling and barking at each other all up and dowr
the bank, till we was so far away the sounds got dim and died
out. And when we stepped onto the raft, I says:

"*Now*, old Jim, you're a free man *again*, and I bet you
won't ever be a slave no more."

"En a mighty good job it wuz, too, Huck. It 'uz planned
beautiful, en it *done* beautiful; en dey ain't *nobody* kin git
up a plan dat's mo' mixed-up en splendid den what dat one
wuz."

We was all as glad as we could be, but Tom was the glad-
dest of all, because he had a bullet in the calf of his leg.

When me and Jim heard that, we didn't feel so brash as
what we did before. It was hurting him considerble, and
bleeding; so we laid him in the wigwam and tore up one of
the duke's shirts for to bandage him, but he says:

"Gimme the rags. I can do it myself. Don't stop, now;
don't fool around here, and the evasion booming along so
handsome; man the sweeps, and set her loose! Boys, we done
it elegant!—'deed we did. I wish *we'd* a had the handling of
Louis XVI., there wouldn't a been no 'Son of Saint Louis,
ascend to heaven!' wrote down in *his* biography: no, sir, we'd
a whooped him over the *border*—that's what we'd a done
with *him*—and done it just as slick as nothing at all, too.
Man the sweeps—man the sweeps!"

But me and Jim was consulting—and thinking. And after
we'd thought a minute, I says:

"Say it, Jim."

So he says:

"Well, den, dis is de way it look to me, Huck. Ef it wuz
him dat 'uz bein' set free, en one er de boys wuz to git shot,
would he say, 'Go on en save me, nemmine 'bout a doctor f'r

to save dis one?' Is dat like Mars Tom Sawyer? Would he say
dat? You *bet* he wouldn't! *Well*, den, is *Jim* gwyne to say it?
No, sah—I doan' budge a step out'n dis place, 'dout a *doctor*;
not if it's forty year!"

I knowed he was white inside, and I reckoned he'd say
what he did say—so it was all right, now, and I told Tom I
was agoing for a doctor. He raised considerble row about it,
but me and Jim stuck to it and wouldn't budge; so he was for
crawling out and setting the raft loose himself; but we
wouldn't let him. Then he give us a piece of his mind—but
it didn't do no good.

So when he see me getting the canoe ready, he says:

"Well, then, if you're bound to go, I'll tell you the way to
do, when you get to the village. Shut the door, and blindfold
the doctor tight and fast, and make him swear to be silent as
the grave, and put a purse full of gold in his hand, and then
take and lead him all around the back alleys and everywheres,
in the dark, and then fetch him here in the canoe, in a round-
about way amongst the islands, and search him and take his
chalk away from him, and don't give it back to him till you
get him back to the village, or else he will chalk this raft so
he can find it again. It's the way they all do."

So I said I would, and left, and Jim was to hide in the
woods when he see the doctor coming, till he was gone again.

XLI

T HE DOCTOR was an old man; a very nice, kind-looking old man, when I got him up. I told him me and my brother was over on Spanish Island hunting, yesterday afternoon, and camped on a piece of a raft we found, and about midnight he must a kicked his gun in his dreams, for it went off and shot him in the leg, and we wanted him to go over there and fix it and not say nothing about it, nor let anybody know, because we wanted to come home this evening, and surprise the folks.

"Who is your folks?" he says.

"The Phelpses, down yonder."

"Oh," he says. And after a minute, he says: "How'd you say he got shot?"

"He had a dream," I says, "and it shot him."

"Singular dream," he says.

So he lit up his lantern, and got his saddle-bags, and we started. But when he see the canoe, he didn't like the look of her—said she was big enough for one, but didn't look pretty safe for two. I says:

"Oh, you needn't be afeard, sir, she carried the three of us, easy enough."

"What three?"

"Why, me and Sid, and—and—and *the guns*; that's what I mean."

"Oh," he says.

But he put his foot on the gunnel, and rocked her; and shook his head, and said he reckoned he'd look around for a bigger one. But they was all locked and chained; so he took my canoe, and said for me to wait till he come back, or I could hunt around further, or maybe I better go down home and get them ready for the surprise, if I wanted to. But I said I didn't; so I told him just how to find the raft, and then he started.

I struck an idea, pretty soon. I says to myself, spos'n he can't fix that leg just in three shakes of a sheep's tail, as the saying is? spos'n it takes him three or four days? What are we going to do?—lay around there till he lets the cat out of the bag? No, sir, I know what *I'll* do. I'll wait, and when he comes back, if he says he's got to go any more, I'll get down there, too, if I swim; and we'll take and tie him, and keep him, and shove out down the river; and when Tom's done with him, we'll give him what it's worth, or all we got, and then let him get shore.

So then I crept into a lumber pile to get some sleep; and next time I waked up the sun was away up over my head! I shot out and went for the doctor's house, but they told me he'd gone away in the night, some time or other, and warn't back yet. Well, thinks I, that looks powerful bad for Tom, and I'll dig out for the island, right off. So away I shoved, and turned the corner, and nearly rammed my head into Uncle Silas's stomach! He says:

"Why, *Tom*! Where you been, all this time, you rascal?"

"*I* hain't been nowheres," I says, "only just hunting for the runaway nigger—me and Sid."

"Why, where ever did you go?" he says. "Your aunt's been mighty uneasy."

"She needn't," I says, "because we was all right. We followed the men and the dogs, but they out-run us, and we lost them; but we thought we heard them on the water, so we got a canoe and took out after them, and crossed over but couldn't find nothing of them; so we cruised along up-shore till we got kind of tired and beat out; and tied up the canoe and went to sleep, and never waked up till about an hour ago, then we paddled over here to hear the news, and Sid's at the post-office to see what he can hear, and I'm a branching out to get something to eat for us, and then we're going home."

So then we went to the post-office to get "Sid"; but just as I suspicioned, he warn't there; so the old man he got a letter out of the office, and we waited a while longer but Sid didn't come; so the old man said come along, let Sid foot it home, or canoe-it, when he got done fooling around—but we would ride. I couldn't get him to let me stay and wait for Sid; and he said there warn't no use in it, and I must come along, and let Aunt Sally see we was all right.

When we got home, Aunt Sally was that glad to see me she laughed and cried both, and hugged me, and give me one of them lickings of hern that don't amount to shucks, and said she'd serve Sid the same when he come.

And the place was plumb full of farmers and farmers' wives, to dinner; and such another clack a body never heard. Old Mrs. Hotchkiss was the worst; her tongue was agoing all the time. She says:

"Well, Sister Phelps, I've ransacked that-air cabin over an' I b'lieve the nigger was crazy. I says so to Sister Damrell—didn't I, Sister Damrell?—s'I, he's crazy, s'I—them's the very words I said. You all hearn me: he's crazy, s'I; everything shows it, s'I. Look at that-air grindstone, s'I; want to tell *me*'t any cretur 'ts in his right mind 's agoin' to scrabble all them crazy things onto a grindstone, s'I? Here sich 'n' sich a person busted his heart; 'n' here so 'n' so pegged along for thirty-seven year, 'n' all that—natcherl son o' Louis somebody, 'n' sich everlast'n rubbage. He's plumb crazy, s'I; it's what I says in the fust place, it's what I says in the middle, 'n' it's what I says last 'n' all the time—the nigger's crazy—crazy 's Nebo-koodneezer, s'I."

"An' look at that-air ladder made out'n rags, Sister Hotch-kiss," says old Mrs. Damrell, "what in the name o' goodness *could* he ever want of——"

"The very words I was a-sayin' no longer ago th'n this min-ute to Sister Utterback, 'n' she'll tell you so herself. Sh-she, look at that-air rag ladder, sh-she; 'n' s'I, yes, *look* at it, s'I—what *could* he a wanted of it, s'I. Sh-she, Sister Hotchkiss, sh-she——"

"But how in the nation'd they ever *git* that grindstone *in* there, *any*way? 'n' who dug that-air *hole*? 'n' who——"

"My very *words*, Brer Penrod! I was a-sayin'—pass that-air sasser o' m'lasses, won't ye?—I was a-sayin' to Sister Dunlap, jist this minute, how *did* they git that grindstone in there, s'I. Without *help*, mind you—'thout *help*! *Thar's* wher' 'tis. Don't tell *me*, s'I; there *wuz* help, s'I; 'n' ther' wuz a *plenty* help, too, s'I; ther's ben a *dozen* a-helpin' that nigger, 'n' I lay I'd skin every last nigger on this place, but *I'd* find out who done it, s'I; 'n' moreover, s'I——"

"A *dozen* says you!—*forty* couldn't a done everything that's been done. Look at them case-knife saws and things, how tedious they've been made; look at that bed-leg sawed off with 'm, a week's work for six men; look at that nigger made out'n straw on the bed; and look at——"

"You may *well* say it, Brer Hightower! It's jist as I was a-sayin' to Brer Phelps, his own self. S'e, what do *you* think of it, Sister Hotchkiss, s'e? think o' what, Brer Phelps, s'I? think o' that bed-leg sawed off that a way, s'e? *think* of it, s'I? I lay it never sawed *itself* off, s'I—somebody *sawed* it, s'I; that's my opinion, take it or leave it, it mayn't be no 'count, s'I, but sich as 't is, it's my opinion, s'I, 'n' if anybody k'n start a better one, s'I, let him *do* it, s'I, that's all. I says to Sister Dunlap, s'I——"

"Why, dog my cats, they must a ben a house-full o' niggers in there every night for four weeks, to a done all that work, Sister Phelps. Look at that shirt—every last inch of it kivered over with secret African writ'n done with blood! Must a ben a raft uv 'm at it right along, all the time, amost. Why, I'd give two dollars to have it read to me; 'n' as for the niggers that wrote it, I 'low I'd take 'n' lash 'm t'll——"

"People to *help* him, Brother Marples! Well, I reckon you'd *think* so, if you'd a been in this house for a while back. Why, they've stole everything they could lay their hands on—and we a watching, all the time, mind you. They stole that shirt right off o' the line! and as for that sheet they made the rag ladder out of ther' ain't no telling how many times they *didn't* steal that; and flour, and candles, and candlesticks, and spoons, and the old warming-pan, and most a thousand things that I disremember, now, and my new calico dress; and me, and Silas, and my Sid and Tom on the constant watch day *and* night, as I was a telling you, and not a one of us could catch hide nor hair, nor sight nor sound of them; and here at the last minute, lo and behold you, they slides right in under our noses, and fools us, and not only fools *us* but the Injun Territory robbers too, and actuly gets *away* with that nigger, safe and sound, and that with sixteen men and twenty-two dogs right on their very heels at that very time! I tell you, it just bangs anything I ever *heard* of. Why, *sperits* couldn't a done better, and been no smarter. And I reckon they must a *been* sperits—because, *you* know our dogs, and ther' ain't no better; well, them dogs never even got on the *track* of 'm, once! You explain *that* to me, if you can!—*any* of you!"

"Well, it does beat——"

"Laws alive, I never——"

"So help me, I wouldn't a be——"

"*House*-thieves as well as——"

"Goodnessgracioussakes, I'd a ben afeard to *live* in sich a——"

"'Fraid to *live*!—why, I was that scared I dasn't hardly go to bed, or get up, or lay down, or *set* down, Sister Ridgeway. Why, they'd steal the very—why, goodness sakes, you can guess what kind of a fluster *I* was in by the time midnight come, last night. I hope to gracious if I warn't afraid they'd steal some o' the family! I was just to that pass, I didn't have no reasoning faculties no more. It looks foolish enough, *now*, in the day-time; but I says to myself, there's my two poor boys asleep, 'way up stairs in that lonesome room, and I declare to goodness I was that uneasy 't I crep' up there and locked 'em in! I *did*. And anybody would. Because, you know, when you get scared, that way, and it keeps running on, and getting worse and worse, all the time, and your wits gets to addling, and you get to doing all sorts o' wild things, and by-and-by you think to yourself, spos'n *I* was a boy, and was away up there, and the door ain't locked, and you——" She stopped, looking kind of wondering, and then she turned her head around slow, and when her eye lit on me—I got up and took a walk.

Says I to myself, I can explain better how we come to not be in that room this morning, if I go out to one side and study over it a little. So I done it. But I dasn't go fur, or she'd a sent for me. And when it was late in the day, the people all went, and then I come in and told her the noise and shooting waked up me and "Sid," and the door was locked, and we wanted to see the fun, so we went down the lightning-rod, and both of us got hurt a little, and we didn't never want to try *that* no more. And then I went on and told her all what I told Uncle Silas before; and then she said she'd forgive us, and maybe it was all right enough anyway, and about what a body might expect of boys, for all boys was a pretty harum-scarum lot, as fur as she could see; and so, as long as no harm hadn't come of it, she judged she better put in her time being grateful we was alive and well and she had us still, stead of fretting over what was past and done. So then she kissed me, and patted me on the head, and dropped into a kind of a brown study; and pretty soon jumps up, and says:

"Why, lawsamercy, it's most night, and Sid not come yet! What *has* become of that boy?"

I see my chance; so I skips up and says:

"I'll run right up to town and get him," I says.

"No you won't," she says. "You'll stay right wher' you are; *one's* enough to be lost at a time. If he ain't here to supper, your uncle 'll go."

Well, he warn't there to supper; so right after supper uncle went.

He come back about ten, a little bit uneasy; hadn't run across Tom's track. Aunt Sally was a good *deal* uneasy; but Uncle Silas he said there warn't no occasion to be—boys will be boys, he said, and you'll see this one turn up in the morning, all sound and right. So she had to be satisfied. But she said she'd set up for him a while, anyway, and keep a light burning, so he could see it.

And then when I went up to bed she come up with me and fetched her candle, and tucked me in, and mothered me so good I felt mean, and like I couldn't look her in the face; and she set down on the bed and talked with me a long time, and said what a splendid boy Sid was, and didn't seem to want to ever stop talking about him; and kept asking me every now and then, if I reckoned he could a got lost, or hurt, or maybe drownded, and might be laying at this minute, somewheres, suffering or dead, and she not by him to help him, and so the tears would drip down, silent, and I would tell her that Sid was all right, and would be home in the morning, sure; and she would squeeze my hand, or maybe kiss me, and tell me to say it again, and keep on saying it, because it done her good, and she was in so much trouble. And when she was going away, she looked down in my eyes, so steady and gentle, and says:

"The door ain't going to be locked, Tom; and there's the window and the rod; but you'll be good, *won't* you? And you won't go? For *my* sake."

Laws knows I *wanted* to go, bad enough, to see about Tom, and was all intending to go; but after that, I wouldn't a went, not for kingdoms.

But she was on my mind, and Tom was on my mind; so I slept very restless. And twice I went down the rod, away in the night, and slipped around front, and see her setting there by her candle in the window with her eyes towards the road and the tears in them; and I wished I could do something for her, but I couldn't, only to swear that I wouldn't never do nothing to grieve her any more. And the third time, I waked up at dawn, and slid down, and she was there yet, and her candle was most out, and her old gray head was resting on her hand, and she was asleep.

XLII

THE OLD MAN was up town again, before breakfast, but couldn't get no track of Tom; and both of them set at the table, thinking, and not saying nothing, and looking mournful, and their coffee getting cold, and not eating anything. And by-and-by the old man says:

"Did I give you the letter?"

"What letter?"

"The one I got yesterday out of the post-office."

"No, you didn't give me no letter."

"Well, I must a forgot it."

So he rummaged his pockets, and then went off somewheres where he had laid it down, and fetched it, and give it to her. She says:

"Why, it's from St. Petersburg—it's from Sis."

I allowed another walk would do me good; but I couldn't stir. But before she could break it open, she dropped it and run—for she see something. And so did I. It was Tom Sawyer on a mattress; and that old doctor; and Jim, in *her* calico dress, with his hands tied behind him; and a lot of people. I hid the letter behind the first thing that come handy, and rushed. She flung herself at Tom, crying, and says:

"Oh, he's dead, he's dead, I know he's dead!"

And Tom he turned his head a little, and muttered something or other, which showed he warn't in his right mind; then she flung up her hands, and says:

"He's alive, thank God! And that's enough!" and she snatched a kiss of him, and flew for the house to get the bed ready, and scattering orders right and left at the niggers and everybody else, as fast as her tongue could go, every jump of the way.

I followed the men to see what they was going to do with Jim; and the old doctor and Uncle Silas followed after Tom into the house. The men was very huffy, and some of them wanted to hang Jim, for an example to all the other niggers around there, so they wouldn't be trying to run away, like Jim done, and making such a raft of trouble, and keeping a

whole family scared most to death for days and nights. But
the others said, don't do it, it wouldn't answer at all, he ain't
our nigger, and his owner would turn up and make us pay
for him, sure. So that cooled them down a little, because the
people that's always the most anxious for to hang a nigger
that hain't done just right, is always the very ones that ain't
the most anxious to pay for him when they've got their satisfaction out of him.

They cussed Jim considerble, though, and give him a cuff
or two, side the head, once in a while, but Jim never said
nothing, and he never let on to know me, and they took him
to the same cabin, and put his own clothes on him, and
chained him again, and not to no bed-leg, this time, but to a
big staple drove into the bottom log, and chained his hands,
too, and both legs, and said he warn't to have nothing but
bread and water to eat, after this, till his owner come or he
was sold at auction, because he didn't come in a certain length
of time, and filled up our hole, and said a couple of farmers
with guns must stand watch around about the cabin every
night, and a bull-dog tied to the door in the day-time; and
about this time they was through with the job and was taper-
ing off with a kind of generl good-bye cussing, and then the
old doctor comes and takes a look, and says:

"Don't be no rougher on him than you're obleeged to, because he ain't a bad nigger. When I got to where I found the
boy, I see I couldn't cut the bullet out without some help,
and he warn't in no condition for me to leave, to go and get
help; and he got a little worse and a little worse, and after a
long time he went out of his head, and wouldn't let me come
anigh him, any more, and said if I chalked his raft he'd kill
me, and no end of wild foolishness like that, and I see I
couldn't do anything at all with him; so I says, I got to have
help, somehow; and the minute I says it, out crawls this nigger from somewheres, and says he'll help, and he done it, too,
and done it very well. Of course I judged he must be a runaway nigger, and there I *was*! and there I had to stick, right
straight along all the rest of the day, and all night. It was a
fix, I tell you! I had a couple of patients with the chills, and
of course I'd of liked to run up to town and see them, but I
dasn't, because the nigger might get away, and then I'd be to

blame; and yet never a skiff come close enough for me to hail. So there I had to stick, plumb till daylight this morning; and I never see a nigger that was a better nuss or faithfuller, and yet he was resking his freedom to do it, and was all tired out, too, and I see plain enough he'd been worked main hard, lately. I liked the nigger for that; I tell you, gentlemen, a nigger like that is worth a thousand dollars—and kind treatment, too. I had everything I needed, and the boy was doing as well there as he would a done at home—better, maybe, because it was so quiet; but there I *was*, with both of 'm on my hands; and there I had to stick, till about dawn this morning; then some men in a skiff come by, and as good luck would have it, the nigger was setting by the pallet with his head propped on his knees, sound asleep; so I motioned them in, quiet, and they slipped up on him and grabbed him and tied him before he knowed what he was about, and we never had no trouble. And the boy being in a kind of a flighty sleep, too, we muffled the oars and hitched the raft on, and towed her over very nice and quiet, and the nigger never made the least row nor said a word, from the start. He ain't no bad nigger, gentlemen; that's what I think about him."

Somebody says:

"Well, it sounds very good, doctor, I'm obleeged to say."

Then the others softened up a little, too, and I was mighty thankful to that old doctor for doing Jim that good turn; and I was glad it was according to my judgment of him, too; because I thought he had a good heart in him and was a good man, the first time I see him. Then they all agreed that Jim had acted very well, and was deserving to have some notice took of it, and reward. So every one of them promised, right out and hearty, that they wouldn't cuss him no more.

Then they come out and locked him up. I hoped they was going to say he could have one or two of the chains took off, because they was rotten heavy, or could have meat and greens with his bread and water, but they didn't think of it, and I reckoned it warn't best for me to mix in, but I judged I'd get the doctor's yarn to Aunt Sally, somehow or other, as soon as I'd got through the breakers that was laying just ahead of me. Explanations, I mean, of how I forgot to mention about Sid being shot, when I was telling how him and me put in that dratted night paddling around hunting the runaway nigger.

But I had plenty time. Aunt Sally she stuck to the sick-room all day and all night; and every time I see Uncle Silas mooning around, I dodged him.

Next morning I heard Tom was a good deal better, and they said Aunt Sally was gone to get a nap. So I slips to the sick-room, and if I found him awake I reckoned we could put up a yarn for the family that would wash. But he was sleeping, and sleeping very peaceful, too; and pale, not fire-faced the way he was when he come. So I set down and laid for him to wake. In about a half an hour, Aunt Sally comes gliding in, and there I was, up a stump again! She motioned me to be still, and set down by me, and begun to whisper, and said we could all be joyful now, because all the symptoms was first rate, and he'd been sleeping like that for ever so long, and looking better and peacefuller all the time, and ten to one he'd wake up in his right mind.

So we set there watching, and by-and-by he stirs a bit, and opened his eyes very natural, and takes a look, and says:

"Hello, why I'm at *home*! How's that? Where's the raft?"

"It's all right," I says.

"And *Jim*?"

"The same," I says, but couldn't say it pretty brash. But he never noticed, but says:

"Good! Splendid! *Now* we're all right and safe! Did you tell Aunty?"

I was going to say yes; but she chipped in and says:

"About what, Sid?"

"Why, about the way the whole thing was done."

"What whole thing?"

"Why, *the* whole thing. There ain't but one; how we set the runaway nigger free—me and Tom."

"Good land! Set the run— What *is* the child talking about! Dear, dear, out of his head again!"

"*No*, I ain't out of my HEAD; I know all what I'm talking about. We *did* set him free—me and Tom. We laid out to do it, and we *done* it. And we done it elegant, too." He'd got a start, and she never checked him up, just set and stared and

tared, and let him clip along, and I see it warn't no use for
me to put in. "Why, Aunty, it cost us a power of work—
weeks of it—hours and hours, every night, whilst you was all
asleep. And we had to steal candles, and the sheet, and the
shirt, and your dress, and spoons, and tin plates, and case-
knives, and the warming-pan, and the grindstone, and flour,
and just no end of things, and you can't think what work it
was to make the saws, and pens, and inscriptions, and one
thing or another, and you can't think *half* the fun it was.
And we had to make up the pictures of coffins and things,
and nonnamous letters from the robbers, and get up and
down the lightning-rod, and dig the hole into the cabin, and
make the rope-ladder and send it in cooked up in a pie, and
send in spoons and things to work with, in your apron
pocket"——

"Mercy sakes!"

——"and load up the cabin with rats and snakes and so on,
for company for Jim; and then you kept Tom here so long
with the butter in his hat that you come near spiling the
whole business, because the men come before we was out of
the cabin, and we had to rush, and they heard us and let drive
at us, and I got my share, and we dodged out of the path and
let them go by, and when the dogs come they warn't interested in us, but went for the most noise, and we got our
canoe, and made for the raft, and was all safe, and Jim was a
free man, and we done it all by ourselves, and *wasn't* it bully,
Aunty!"

"Well, I never heard the likes of it in all my born days! So
it was *you*, you little rapscallions, that's been making all this
trouble, and turned everybody's wits clean inside out and
scared us all most to death. I've as good a notion as ever I
had in my life, to take it out o' you this very minute. To
think, here I've been, night after night, a—*you* just get well
once, you young scamp, and I lay I'll tan the Old Harry out
o' both o' ye!"

But Tom, he *was* so proud and joyful, he just *couldn't* hold
in, and his tongue just *went* it—she a-chipping in, and spitting fire all along, and both of them going it at once, like a
cat-convention; and she says:

"*Well*, you get all the enjoyment you can out of it *now* for mind I tell you if I catch you meddling with him again——"

"Meddling with *who*?" Tom says, dropping his smile and looking surprised.

"With *who*? Why, the runaway nigger, of course. Who'd you reckon?"

Tom looks at me very grave, and says:

"Tom, didn't you just tell me he was all right? Hasn't he got away?"

"*Him?*" says Aunt Sally; "the runaway nigger? 'Deed he hasn't. They've got him back, safe and sound, and he's in that cabin again, on bread and water, and loaded down with chains, till he's claimed or sold!"

Tom rose square up in bed, with his eye hot, and his nostrils opening and shutting like gills, and sings out to me:

"They hain't no *right* to shut him up! *Shove!*—and don't you lose a minute. Turn him loose! he ain't no slave; he's as free as any cretur that walks this earth!"

"What *does* the child mean?"

"I mean every word I *say*, Aunt Sally, and if somebody don't go, *I*'ll go. I've knowed him all his life, and so has Tom, there. Old Miss Watson died two months ago, and she was ashamed she ever was going to sell him down the river, and *said* so; and she set him free in her will."

"Then what on earth did *you* want to set him free for, seeing he was already free?"

"Well, that *is* a question, I must say; and *just* like women! Why, I wanted the *adventure* of it; and I'd a waded neck-deep in blood to—goodness alive, AUNT POLLY!"

If she warn't standing right there, just inside the door, looking as sweet and contented as an angel half-full of pie, I wish I may never!

Aunt Sally jumped for her, and most hugged the head off of her, and cried over her, and I found a good enough place for me under the bed, for it was getting pretty sultry for *us*, seemed to me. And I peeped out, and in a little while Tom's Aunt Polly shook herself loose and stood there looking across at Tom over her spectacles—kind of grinding him into the earth, you know. And then she says:

"Yes, you *better* turn y'r head away—I would if I was you, Tom."

"Oh, deary me!" says Aunt Sally; "*is* he changed so? Why, hat ain't *Tom* it's Sid; Tom's—Tom's—why, where is Tom? He was here a minute ago."

"You mean where's Huck *Finn*—that's what you mean! I reckon I hain't raised such a scamp as my Tom all these years, not to know him when I *see* him. That *would* be a pretty howdy-do. Come out from under that bed, Huck Finn."

So I done it. But not feeling brash.

Aunt Sally she was one of the mixed-upset looking persons I ever see; except one, and that was Uncle Silas, when he come in, and they told it all to him. It kind of made him drunk, as you may say, and he didn't know nothing at all the rest of the day, and preached a prayer-meeting sermon that night that give him a rattling reputation, because the oldest man in the world couldn't a understood it. So Tom's Aunt Polly, she told all about who I was, and what; and I had to up and tell how I was in such a tight place that when Mrs. Phelps took me for Tom Sawyer—she chipped in and says, "Oh, go on and call me Aunt Sally, I'm used to it, now, and 'tain't no need to change"—that when Aunt Sally took me for Tom Sawyer, I had to stand it—there warn't no other way, and I knowed he wouldn't mind, because it would be nuts for him, being a mystery, and he'd make an adventure out of it and be perfectly satisfied. And so it turned out, and he let on to be Sid, and made things as soft as he could for me.

And his Aunt Polly she said Tom was right about old Miss Watson setting Jim free in her will; and so, sure enough, Tom Sawyer had gone and took all that trouble and bother to set a free nigger free! and I couldn't ever understand, before, until that minute and that talk, how he *could* help a body set a nigger free, with his bringing-up.

Well, Aunt Polly she said that when Aunt Sally wrote to her that Tom and *Sid* had come, all right and safe, she says to herself:

"Look at that, now! I might have expected it, letting him go off that way without anybody to watch him. So now I got to go and trapse all the way down the river, eleven hundred mile, and find out what that creetur's up to, *this* time; as long as I couldn't seem to get any answer out of you about it."

"Why, I never heard nothing from you," says Aunt Sally.

"Well, I wonder! Why, I wrote to you twice, to ask you what you could mean by Sid being here."

"Well, I never got 'em, Sis."

Aunt Polly, she turns around slow and severe, and says:

"You, Tom!"

"Well— *what?*" he says, kind of pettish.

"Don't you what *me*, you impudent thing—hand out them letters."

"What letters?"

"*Them* letters. I be bound, if I have to take aholt of you I'll——"

"They're in the trunk. There, now. And they're just the same as they was when I got them out of the office. I hain't looked into them, I hain't touched them. But I knowed they'd make trouble, and I thought if you warn't in no hurry, I'd——"

"Well, you *do* need skinning, there ain't no mistake about it. And I wrote another one to tell you I was coming; and I spose he——"

"No, it come yesterday; I hain't read it yet, but *it's* all right, I've got that one."

I wanted to offer to bet two dollars she hadn't, but I reckoned maybe it was just as safe to not to. So I never said nothing.

Chapter the Last

THE FIRST TIME I catched Tom, private, I asked him what was his idea, time of the evasion?—what it was he'd planned to do if the evasion worked all right and he managed to set a nigger free that was already free before? And he said, what he had planned in his head, from the start, if we got Jim out all safe, was for us to run him down the river, on the raft, and have adventures plumb to the mouth of the river, and then tell him about his being free, and take him back up home on a steamboat, in style, and pay him for his lost time, and write word ahead and get out all the niggers around, and have them waltz him into town with a torch-light procession and a brass band, and then he would be a hero, and so would we. But I reckened it was about as well the way it was.

We had Jim out of the chains in no time, and when Aunt Polly and Uncle Silas and Aunt Sally found out how good he helped the doctor nurse Tom, they made a heap of fuss over him, and fixed him up prime, and give him all he wanted to eat, and a good time, and nothing to do. And we had him up to the sick-room; and had a high talk; and Tom give Jim forty dollars for being prisoner for us so patient, and doing it up so good, and Jim was pleased most to death, and busted out, and says:

"*Dah*, now, Huck, what I tell you?—what I tell you up dah on Jackson islan'? I *tole* you I got a hairy breas', en what's de sign un it; en I *tole* you I ben rich wunst, en gwineter to be rich *agin*; en it's come true; en heah she *is*! *Dah*, now! doan' talk to *me*—signs is *signs*, mine I tell you; en I knowed jis' 's well 'at I 'uz gwineter be rich agin as I's a stannin' heah dis minute!"

And then Tom he talked along, and talked along, and says, le's all three slide out of here, one of these nights, and get an outfit, and go for howling adventures amongst the Injuns, over in the Territory, for a couple of weeks or two; and I says, all right, that suits me, but I aint got no money for to buy the outfit, and I reckon I couldn't get none from home, because it's likely pap's been back before now, and got it all away from Judge Thatcher and drunk it up.

"No he hain't," Tom says; "it's all there, yet—six thousand dollars and more; and your pap hain't ever been back since. Hadn't when I come away, anyhow."

Jim says, kind of solemn:

"He ain't a comin' back no mo', Huck."

I says:

"Why, Jim?"

"Nemmine why, Huck—but he ain't comin' back no mo'."

But I kept at him; so at last he says:

"Doan' you 'member de house dat was float'n down de river, en dey wuz a man in dah, kivered up, en I went in en unkivered him and didn' let you come in? Well, den, you k'n git yo' money when you wants it; kase dat wuz him."

Tom's most well, now, and got his bullet around his neck on a watch-guard for a watch, and is always seeing what time it is, and so there ain't nothing more to write about, and I am rotten glad of it, because if I'd a knowed what a trouble it was to make a book I wouldn't a tackled it and ain't agoing to no more. But I reckon I got to light out for the Territory ahead of the rest, because Aunt Sally she's going to adopt me and sivilize me and I can't stand it. I been there before.

PUDD'NHEAD WILSON

A Tale

A Whisper to the Reader

THERE is no character, howsoever good and fine, but it can be destroyed by ridicule, howsoever poor and witless. Observe the ass, for instance: his character is about perfect, he is the choicest spirit among all the humbler animals, yet see what ridicule has brought him to. Instead of feeling complimented when we are called an ass, we are left in doubt.

— Pudd'nhead Wilson's Calendar.

A PERSON who is ignorant of legal matters is always liable to make mistakes when he tries to photograph a court scene with his pen; and so I was not willing to let the law chapters in this book go to press without first subjecting them to rigid and exhausting revision and correction by a trained barrister—if that is what they are called. These chapters are right, now, in every detail, for they were rewritten under the immediate eye of William Hicks, who studied law part of a while in southwest Missouri thirty-five years ago and then came over here to Florence for his health and is still helping for exercise and board in Macaroni Vermicelli's horse-feed shed which is up the back alley as you turn around the corner out of the Piazza del Duomo just beyond the house where that stone that Dante used to sit on six hundred years ago is let into the wall when he let on to be watching them build Giotto's campanile and yet always got tired looking as soon as Beatrice passed along on her way to get a chunk of chestnut cake to defend herself with in case of a Ghibelline outbreak before she got to school, at the same old stand where they sell the same old cake to this day and it is just as light and good as it was then, too, and this is not flattery, far from it. He was a little rusty on his law, but he rubbed up for this book, and those two or three legal chapters are right and straight, now. He told me so himself.

Given under my hand this second day of January, 1893, at the Villa Viviani, village of Settignano, three miles back of Florence, on the hills—the same certainly affording the most charming view to be found on this planet, and with it the most dream-like and enchanting sunsets to be found in any planet or even in any solar system—and given, too, in the swell room of the house, with the busts of Cerretani senators and other grandees of this line looking approvingly down upon me as they used to look down upon Dante, and mutely asking me to adopt them into my family, which I do with pleasure, for my remotest ancestors are but spring chickens compared with these robed and stately antiques, and it will be a great and satisfying lift for me, that six hundred years will.

Mark Twain.

I

THE SCENE of this chronicle is the town of Dawson's Landing, on the Missouri side of the Mississippi, half a day's journey, per steamboat, below St. Louis.

In 1830 it was a snug little collection of modest one- and two-story frame dwellings whose whitewashed exteriors were almost concealed from sight by climbing tangles of rose vines, honeysuckles and morning-glories. Each of these pretty homes had a garden in front fenced with white palings and opulently stocked with hollyhocks, marigolds, touch-me-nots, prince's-feathers and other old-fashioned flowers; while on the window-sills of the houses stood wooden boxes containing moss-rose plants and terra-cotta pots in which grew a breed of geranium whose spread of intensely red blossoms accented the prevailing pink tint of the rose-clad house-front like an explosion of flame. When there was room on the ledge outside of the pots and boxes for a cat, the cat was there—in sunny weather—stretched at full length, asleep and blissful, with her furry belly to the sun and a paw curved over her nose. Then that house was complete, and its contentment and peace were made manifest to the world by this symbol, whose testimony is infallible. A home without a cat—and a well-fed, well-petted and properly revered cat—may be a perfect home, perhaps, but how can it prove title?

All along the streets, on both sides, at the outer edge of the brick sidewalks, stood locust-trees with trunks protected by wooden boxing, and these furnished shade for summer and a sweet fragrance in spring when the clusters of buds came forth. The main street, one block back from the river, and running parallel with it, was the sole business street. It was six blocks long, and in each block two or three brick stores three stories high towered above interjected bunches of little frame shops. Swinging signs creaked in the wind, the street's whole length. The candy-striped pole which indicates nobility proud and ancient along the palace-bordered canals of Ven-

ice, indicated merely the humble barber-shop along the main
street of Dawson's Landing. On a chief corner stood a lofty
unpainted pole wreathed from top to bottom with tin pots
and pans and cups, the chief tinmonger's noisy notice to the
world (when the wind blew) that his shop was on hand for
business at that corner.

The hamlet's front was washed by the clear waters of the
great river; its body stretched itself rearward up a gentle in-
cline; its most rearward border fringed itself out and scattered
its houses about the base-line of the hills; the hills rose high,
inclosing the town in a half-moon curve, clothed with forests
from foot to summit.

Steamboats passed up and down every hour or so. Those
belonging to the little Cairo line and the little Memphis line
always stopped; the big Orleans liners stopped for hails only,
or to land passengers or freight; and this was the case also
with the great flotilla of "transients." These latter came out of
a dozen rivers—the Illinois, the Missouri, the Upper Mississippi, the Ohio, the Monongahela, the Tennessee, the Red
River, the White River, and so on; and were bound every
whither and stocked with every imaginable comfort or necessity which the Mississippi's communities could want, from
the frosty Falls of St. Anthony down through nine climates
to torrid New Orleans.

Dawson's Landing was a slaveholding town, with a rich
slave-worked grain and pork country back of it. The town
was sleepy and comfortable and contented. It was fifty years
old, and was growing slowly—very slowly, in fact, but still it
was growing.

The chief citizen was York Leicester Driscoll, about forty
years old, judge of the county court. He was very proud of
his old Virginian ancestry, and in his hospitalities and his
rather formal and stately manners he kept up its traditions.
He was fine and just and generous. To be a gentleman—a
gentleman without stain or blemish—was his only religion,
and to it he was always faithful. He was respected, esteemed
and beloved by all the community. He was well off, and was
gradually adding to his store. He and his wife were very
nearly happy, but not quite, for they had no children. The
longing for the treasure of a child had grown stronger and

stronger as the years slipped away, but the blessing never came—and was never to come.

With this pair lived the Judge's widowed sister, Mrs. Rachel Pratt, and she also was childless—childless, and sorrowful for that reason, and not to be comforted. The women were good and commonplace people, and did their duty and had their reward in clear consciences and the community's approbation. They were Presbyterians, the Judge was a freethinker.

Pembroke Howard, lawyer and bachelor, aged about forty, was another old Virginian grandee with proved descent from the First Families. He was a fine, brave, majestic creature, a gentleman according to the nicest requirements of the Virginian rule, a devoted Presbyterian, an authority on the "code," and a man always courteously ready to stand up before you in the field if any act or word of his had seemed doubtful or suspicious to you, and explain it with any weapon you might prefer from brad-awls to artillery. He was very popular with the people, and was the Judge's dearest friend.

Then there was Colonel Cecil Burleigh Essex, another F. F. V. of formidable caliber—however, with him we have no concern.

Percy Northumberland Driscoll, brother to the Judge, and younger than he by five years, was a married man, and had had children around his hearthstone; but they were attacked in detail by measles, croup and scarlet fever, and this had given the doctor a chance with his effective antediluvian methods; so the cradles were empty. He was a prosperous man, with a good head for speculations, and his fortune was growing. On the 1st of February, 1830, two boy babes were born in his house: one to him, the other to one of his slave girls, Roxana by name. Roxana was twenty years old. She was up and around the same day, with her hands full, for she was tending both babies.

Mrs. Percy Driscoll died within the week. Roxy remained in charge of the children. She had her own way, for Mr. Driscoll soon absorbed himself in his speculations and left her to her own devices.

In that same month of February, Dawson's Landing gained a new citizen. This was Mr. David Wilson, a young fellow of

Scotch parentage. He had wandered to this remote region from his birthplace in the interior of the State of New York to seek his fortune. He was twenty-five years old, college-bred, and had finished a post-college course in an Eastern law school a couple of years before.

He was a homely, freckled, sandy-haired young fellow with an intelligent blue eye that had frankness and comradeship in it and a covert twinkle of a pleasant sort. But for an unfortunate remark of his, he would no doubt have entered at once upon a successful career at Dawson's Landing. But he made his fatal remark the first day he spent in the village, and it "gaged" him. He had just made the acquaintance of a group of citizens when an invisible dog began to yelp and snarl and howl and make himself very comprehensively disagreeable, whereupon young Wilson said, much as one who is thinking aloud—

"I wished I owned half of that dog."

"Why?" somebody asked.

"Because I would kill my half."

The group searched his face with curiosity, with anxiety even, but found no light there, no expression that they could read. They fell away from him as from something uncanny, and went into privacy to discuss him. One said:

"'Pears to be a fool."

"'Pears?" said another. "*Is*, I reckon you better say."

"Said he wished he owned *half* of the dog, the idiot," said a third. "What did he reckon would become of the other half if he killed his half? Do you reckon he thought it would live?"

"Why, he must have thought it, unless he *is* the downrightest fool in the world; because if he had n't thought it, he would have wanted to own the whole dog, knowing that if he killed his half and the other half died, he would be responsible for that half just the same as if he had killed that half instead of his own. Don't it look that way to you, gents?"

"Yes, it does. If he owned one half of the general dog, it would be so; if he owned one end of the dog and another person owned the other end, it would be so, just the same; particularly in the first case, because if you kill one half of a general dog, there ain't any man that can tell whose half it was, but if he owned one end of the dog, maybe he could kill his end of it and—"

"No, he could n't, either: he could n't and not be responsible if the other end died, which it would. In my opinion the man ain't in his right mind."

"In my opinion he hain't *got* any mind."

No. 3 said: "Well, he 's a lummox, anyway."

"That 's what he is," said No. 4, "he 's a labrick—just a Simon-pure labrick, if ever there was one."

"Yes, sir, he 's a dam fool, that 's the way I put him up," said No. 5. "Anybody can think different that wants to, but those are my sentiments."

"I 'm with you, gentlemen," said No. 6. "Perfect jackass—yes, and it ain't going too far to say he is a pudd'nhead. If he ain't a pudd'nhead, I ain't no judge, that 's all."

Mr. Wilson stood elected. The incident was told all over the town, and gravely discussed by everybody. Within a week he had lost his first name; Pudd'nhead took its place. In time he came to be liked, and well liked too; but by that time the nickname had got well stuck on, and it stayed. That first day's verdict made him a fool, and he was not able to get it set aside, or even modified. The nickname soon ceased to carry any harsh or unfriendly feeling with it, but it held its place, and was to continue to hold its place for twenty long years.

II

ADAM was but human—this explains it all. He did not want
the apple for the apple's sake, he wanted it only because it was
forbidden. The mistake was in not forbidding the serpent; then
he would have eaten the serpent.

— *Pudd'nhead Wilson's Calendar.*

PUDD'NHEAD WILSON had a trifle of money when he arrived, and he bought a small house on the extreme western verge of the town. Between it and Judge Driscoll's house
there was only a grassy yard, with a paling fence dividing the
properties in the middle. He hired a small office down in the
town and hung out a tin sign with these words on it:

DAVID WILSON.
ATTORNEY AND COUNSELOR-AT-LAW.
SURVEYING, CONVEYANCING, ETC.

But his deadly remark had ruined his chance—at least in
the law. No clients came. He took down his sign, after a
while, and put it up on his own house with the law features
knocked out of it. It offered his services now in the humble
capacities of land-surveyor and expert accountant. Now and
then he got a job of surveying to do, and now and then a
merchant got him to straighten out his books. With Scotch
patience and pluck he resolved to live down his reputation
and work his way into the legal field yet. Poor fellow, he
could not foresee that it was going to take him such a weary
long time to do it.

He had a rich abundance of idle time, but it never hung
heavy on his hands, for he interested himself in every new
thing that was born into the universe of ideas, and studied it
and experimented upon it at his house. One of his pet fads
was palmistry. To another one he gave no name, neither
would he explain to anybody what its purpose was, but
merely said it was an amusement. In fact he had found that
his fads added to his reputation as a pudd'nhead; therefore he
was growing chary of being too communicative about them.

The fad without a name was one which dealt with people's finger-marks. He carried in his coat pocket a shallow box with grooves in it, and in the grooves strips of glass five inches long and three inches wide. Along the lower edge of each strip was pasted a slip of white paper. He asked people to pass their hands through their hair (thus collecting upon them a thin coating of the natural oil) and then make a thumb-mark on a glass strip, following it with the mark of the ball of each finger in succession. Under this row of faint grease-prints he would write a record on the strip of white paper—thus:

JOHN SMITH, *right hand*—

and add the day of the month and the year, then take Smith's left hand on another glass strip, and add name and date and the words "left hand." The strips were now returned to the grooved box, and took their place among what Wilson called his "records."

He often studied his records, examining and poring over them with absorbing interest until far into the night; but what he found there—if he found anything—he revealed to no one. Sometimes he copied on paper the involved and delicate pattern left by the ball of a finger, and then vastly enlarged it with a pantograph so that he could examine its web of curving lines with ease and convenience.

One sweltering afternoon—it was the first day of July, 1830—he was at work over a set of tangled account-books in his workroom, which looked westward over a stretch of vacant lots, when a conversation outside disturbed him. It was carried on in yells, which showed that the people engaged in it were not close together:

"Say, Roxy, how does yo' baby come on?" This from the distant voice.

"Fust-rate; how does *you* come on, Jasper?" This yell was from close by.

"Oh, I 's middlin'; hain't go noth'n' to complain of. I 's gwine to come a-court'n' you bimeby, Roxy."

"*You* is, you black mud-cat! Yah—yah—yah! I got somep'n' better to do den 'sociat'n' wid niggers as black as you is. Is ole Miss Cooper's Nancy done give you de mitten?" Roxy followed this sally with another discharge of care-free laughter.

"You 's jealous, Roxy, dat 's what 's de matter wid *you*, you hussy—yah—yah—yah! Dat 's de time I got you!"

"Oh, yes, *you* got me, hain't you. 'Clah to goodness if dat conceit o' yo'n strikes in, Jasper, it gwine to kill you sho'. If you b'longed to me I 'd sell you down de river 'fo' you git too fur gone. Fust time I runs acrost yo' marster, I 's gwine to tell him so."

This idle and aimless jabber went on and on, both parties enjoying the friendly duel and each well satisfied with his own share of the wit exchanged—for wit they considered it.

Wilson stepped to the window to observe the combatants; he could not work while their chatter continued. Over in the vacant lots was Jasper, young, coal-black and of magnificent build, sitting on a wheelbarrow in the pelting sun—at work, supposably, whereas he was in fact only preparing for it by taking an hour's rest before beginning. In front of Wilson's porch stood Roxy, with a local hand-made baby-wagon, in which sat her two charges—one at each end and facing each other. From Roxy's manner of speech, a stranger would have expected her to be black, but she was not. Only one sixteenth of her was black, and that sixteenth did not show. She was of majestic form and stature, her attitudes were imposing and statuesque, and her gestures and movements distinguished by a noble and stately grace. Her complexion was very fair, with the rosy glow of vigorous health in the cheeks, her face was full of character and expression, her eyes were brown and liquid, and she had a heavy suit of fine soft hair which was also brown, but the fact was not apparent because her head was bound about with a checkered handkerchief and the hair was concealed under it. Her face was shapely, intelligent and comely—even beautiful. She had an easy, independent carriage—when she was among her own caste—and a high and "sassy" way, withal; but of course she was meek and humble enough where white people were.

To all intents and purposes Roxy was as white as anybody, but the one sixteenth of her which was black outvoted the other fifteen parts and made her a negro. She was a slave, and salable as such. Her child was thirty-one parts white, and he, too, was a slave, and by a fiction of law and custom a negro. He had blue eyes and flaxen curls like his white comrade, but even the father of the white child was able to tell the children apart—little as he had commerce with them—by their clothes: for the white babe wore ruffled soft muslin and a coral necklace, while the other wore merely a coarse tow-linen shirt which barely reached to its knees, and no jewelry.

The white child's name was Thomas à Becket Driscoll, the other's name was Valet de Chambre: no surname—slaves had n't the privilege. Roxana had heard that phrase somewhere, the fine sound of it had pleased her ear, and as she had supposed it was a name, she loaded it on to her darling. It soon got shortened to "Chambers," of course.

Wilson knew Roxy by sight, and when the duel of wit began to play out, he stepped outside to gather in a record or two. Jasper went to work energetically, at once, perceiving that his leisure was observed. Wilson inspected the children and asked—

"How old are they, Roxy?"

"Bofe de same age, sir—five months. Bawn de fust o' Feb'uary."

"They 're handsome little chaps. One 's just as handsome as the other, too."

A delighted smile exposed the girl's white teeth, and she said:

"Bless yo' soul, Misto Wilson, it 's pow'ful nice o' you to say dat, 'ca'se one of 'em ain't on'y a nigger. Mighty prime little nigger, I al'ays says, but dat 's 'ca'se it 's mine, o' course."

"How do you tell them apart, Roxy, when they have n't any clothes on?"

Roxy laughed a laugh proportioned to her size, and said:

"Oh, I kin tell 'em 'part, Misto Wilson, but I bet Marse Percy could n't, not to save his life."

Wilson chatted along for a while, and presently got Roxy's finger-prints for his collection—right hand and left—on a couple of his glass strips; then labeled and dated them, and took the "records" of both children, and labeled and dated them also.

Two months later, on the 3d of September, he took this trio of finger-marks again. He liked to have a "series," two or three "takings" at intervals during the period of childhood, these to be followed by others at intervals of several years.

The next day—that is to say, on the 4th of September— something occurred which profoundly impressed Roxana. Mr. Driscoll missed another small sum of money—which is a way of saying that this was not a new thing, but had happened before. In truth it had happened three times before. Driscoll's patience was exhausted. He was a fairly humane man toward slaves and other animals; he was an exceedingly humane man toward the erring of his own race. Theft he could not abide, and plainly there was a thief in his house. Necessarily the thief must be one of his negroes. Sharp measures must be taken. He called his servants before him. There were three of these, besides Roxy: a man, a woman, and a boy twelve years old. They were not related. Mr. Driscoll said:

"You have all been warned before. It has done no good. This time I will teach you a lesson. I will sell the thief. Which of you is the guilty one?"

They all shuddered at the threat, for here they had a good home, and a new one was likely to be a change for the worse. The denial was general. None had stolen anything—not money, anyway—a little sugar, or cake, or honey, or something like that, that "Marse Percy would n't mind or miss," but not money—never a cent of money. They were eloquent in their protestations, but Mr. Driscoll was not moved by them. He answered each in turn with a stern "Name the thief!"

The truth was, all were guilty but Roxana; she suspected that the others were guilty, but she did not know them to be so. She was horrified to think how near she had come to being guilty herself; she had been saved in the nick of time by a revival in the colored Methodist Church, a fortnight before, at which time and place she "got religion." The very next day after that gracious experience, while her change of style was fresh upon her and she was vain of her purified condition, her master left a couple of dollars lying unprotected on his desk, and she happened upon that temptation when she was polishing around with a dust-rag. She looked at the money a while with a steadily rising resentment, then she burst out with—

"Dad blame dat revival, I wisht it had 'a' be'n put off till to-morrow!"

Then she covered the tempter with a book, and another member of the kitchen cabinet got it. She made this sacrifice as a matter of religious etiquette; as a thing necessary just now, but by no means to be wrested into a precedent; no, a week or two would limber up her piety, then she would be rational again, and the next two dollars that got left out in the cold would find a comforter—and she could name the comforter.

Was she bad? Was she worse than the general run of her race? No. They had an unfair show in the battle of life, and they held it no sin to take military advantage of the enemy— in a small way; in a small way, but not in a large one. They would smouch provisions from the pantry whenever they got a chance; or a brass thimble, or a cake of wax, or an emery bag, or a paper of needles, or a silver spoon, or a dollar bill, or small articles of clothing, or any other property of light value; and so far were they from considering such reprisals sinful, that they would go to church and shout and pray their loudest and sincerest with their plunder in their pockets. A farm smoke-house had to be kept heavily padlocked, for even the colored deacon himself could not resist a ham when Providence showed him in a dream, or otherwise, where such a thing hung lonesome and longed for some one to love. But with a hundred hanging before him the deacon would not take two—that is, on the same night. On frosty nights the humane negro prowler would warm the end of a plank and put it up under the cold claws of chickens roosting in a tree; a drowsy hen would step on to the comfortable board, softly clucking her gratitude, and the prowler would dump her into his bag, and later into his stomach, perfectly sure that in taking this trifle from the man who daily robbed him of an inestimable treasure—his liberty—he was not committing any sin that God would remember against him in the Last Great Day.

"Name the thief!"

For the fourth time Mr. Driscoll had said it, and always in the same hard tone. And now he added these words of awful import:

"I give you one minute"—he took out his watch. "If at the end of that time you have not confessed, I will not only sell all four of you, but—I will sell you DOWN THE RIVER!"

It was equivalent to condemning them to hell! No Missouri negro doubted this. Roxy reeled in her tracks and the color vanished out of her face; the others dropped to their knees as if they had been shot; tears gushed from their eyes, their supplicating hands went up, and three answers came in the one instant:

"I done it!"

"I done it!"

"I done it!—have mercy, marster—Lord have mercy on us po' niggers!"

"Very good," said the master, putting up his watch, "I will sell you *here*, though you don't deserve it. You ought to be sold down the river."

The culprits flung themselves prone, in an ecstasy of gratitude, and kissed his feet, declaring that they would never forget his goodness and never cease to pray for him as long as they lived. They were sincere, for like a god he had stretched forth his mighty hand and closed the gates of hell against them. He knew, himself, that he had done a noble and gracious thing, and was privately well pleased with his magnanimity; and that night he set the incident down in his diary, so that his son might read it in after years, and be thereby moved to deeds of gentleness and humanity himself.

III

WHOEVER has lived long enough to find out what life is, knows how deep a debt of gratitude we owe to Adam, the first great benefactor of our race. He brought death into the world.

— *Pudd'nhead Wilson's Calendar.*

PERCY DRISCOLL slept well the night he saved his house-minions from going down the river, but no wink of sleep visited Roxy's eyes. A profound terror had taken possession of her. Her child could grow up and be sold down the river! The thought crazed her with horror. If she dozed and lost herself for a moment, the next moment she was on her feet and flying to her child's cradle to see if it was still there. Then she would gather it to her heart and pour out her love upon it in a frenzy of kisses, moaning, crying, and saying "Dey sha'n't, oh, dey *sha'n't!*—yo' po' mammy will kill you fust!"

Once, when she was tucking it back in its cradle again, the other child nestled in its sleep and attracted her attention. She went and stood over it a long time, communing with herself: "What has my po' baby done, dat he could n't have yo' luck? He hain't done noth'n'. God was good to you; why war n't he good to him? Dey can't sell *you* down de river. I hates yo' pappy; he ain't got no heart—for niggers he hain't, anyways. I hates him, en I could kill him!" She paused a while, thinking; then she burst into wild sobbings again, and turned away, saying, "Oh, I got to kill my chile, dey ain't no yuther way,—killin' *him* would n't save de chile fum goin' down de river. Oh, I got to do it, yo' po' mammy's got to kill you to save you, honey"—she gathered her baby to her bosom, now, and began to smother it with caresses—"Mammy 's got to kill you—how *kin* I do it! But yo' mammy ain't gwine to desert you,—no, no; *dah*, don't cry—she gwine *wid* you, she gwine to kill herself too. Come along, honey, come along wid mammy; we gwine to jump in de river, den de troubles o' dis worl' is all over—dey don't sell po' niggers down the river over *yonder*."

She started toward the door, crooning to the child and hushing it; midway she stopped, suddenly. She had caught

929

sight of her new Sunday gown—a cheap curtain-calico thing, a conflagration of gaudy colors and fantastic figures. She surveyed it wistfully, longingly.

"Hain't ever wore it yet," she said, "en it 's jist lovely." Then she nodded her head in response to a pleasant idea, and added, "No, I ain't gwine to be fished out, wid everybody lookin' at me, in dis mis'able ole linsey-woolsey."

She put down the child and made the change. She looked in the glass and was astonished at her beauty. She resolved to make her death-toilet perfect. She took off her handkerchief-turban and dressed her glossy wealth of hair "like white folks"; she added some odds and ends of rather lurid ribbon and a spray of atrocious artificial flowers; finally she threw over her shoulders a fluffy thing called a "cloud" in that day, which was of a blazing red complexion. Then she was ready for the tomb.

She gathered up her baby once more; but when her eye fell upon its miserably short little gray tow-linen shirt and noted the contrast between its pauper shabbiness and her own volcanic irruption of infernal splendors, her mother-heart was touched, and she was ashamed.

"No, dolling, mammy ain't gwine to treat you so. De angels is gwine to 'mire you jist as much as dey does yo' mammy. Ain't gwine to have 'em putt'n' dey han's up 'fo' dey eyes en sayin' to David en Goliah en dem yuther prophets, 'Dat chile is dress' too indelicate fo' dis place.' "

By this time she had stripped off the shirt. Now she clothed the naked little creature in one of Thomas à Becket's snowy long baby-gowns, with its bright blue bows and dainty flummery of ruffles.

"Dah—now you 's fixed." She propped the child in a chair and stood off to inspect it. Straightway her eyes began to widen with astonishment and admiration, and she clapped her hands and cried out, "Why, it do beat all!—I *never* knowed you was so lovely. Marse Tommy ain't a bit puttier—not a single bit."

She stepped over and glanced at the other infant; she flung a glance back at her own; then one more at the heir of the house. Now a strange light dawned in her eyes, and in a moment she was lost in thought. She seemed in a trance; when she came out of it she muttered, "When I 'uz a-washin' 'em in de tub, yistiddy, his own pappy asked me which of 'em was his'n."

She began to move about like one in a dream. She undressed Thomas à Becket, stripping him of everything, and put the tow-linen shirt on him. She put his coral necklace on her own child's neck. Then she placed the children side by side, and after earnest inspection she muttered—

"Now who would b'lieve clo'es could do de like o' dat? Dog my cats if it ain't all *I* kin do to tell t' other fum which, let alone his pappy."

She put her cub in Tommy's elegant cradle and said—

"You 's young Marse *Tom* fum dis out, en I got to practise and git used to 'memberin' to call you dat, honey, or I 's gwine to make a mistake some time en git us bofe into trouble. Dah—now you lay still en don't fret no mo', Marse Tom—oh, thank de good Lord in heaven, you 's saved, you 's saved!—dey ain't no man kin ever sell mammy's po' little honey down de river now!"

She put the heir of the house in her own child's unpainted pine cradle, and said, contemplating its slumbering form uneasily—

"I 's sorry for you, honey; I 's sorry, God knows I is,—but what *kin* I do, what *could* I do? Yo' pappy would sell him to somebody, some time, en den he' d go down de river, sho', en I could n't, could n't, *could n't* stan' it."

She flung herself on her bed and began to think and toss, toss and think. By and by she sat suddenly upright, for a comforting thought had flown through her worried mind—

" 'T ain't no sin—*white* folks has done it! It ain't no sin, glory to goodness it ain't no sin! *Dey 's* done it—yes, en dey was de biggest quality in de whole bilin', too—*kings!*"

She began to muse; she was trying to gather out of her memory the dim particulars of some tale she had heard some time or other. At last she said—

"Now I 's got it; now I 'member. It was dat ole nigger preacher dat tole it, de time he come over here fum Illinois en preached in de nigger church. He said dey ain't nobody kin save his own self—can't do it by faith, can't do it by works, can't do it no way at all. Free grace is de *on'y* way, en dat don't come fum nobody but jis' de Lord; en *he* kin give it to anybody he please, saint or sinner—*he* don't kyer. He do jis' as he 's a mineter. He s'lect out anybody dat suit him, en put another one in his place, en make de fust one happy forever en leave t' other one to burn wid Satan. De preacher said it was jist like dey done in Englan' one time, long time ago. De queen she lef' her baby layin' aroun' one day, en went out callin'; en one o' de niggers roun' 'bout de place dat was 'mos' white, she come in en see de chile layin' aroun', en tuck en put her own chile's clo'es on de queen's chile, en put de queen's chile's clo'es on her own chile, en den lef' her own chile layin' aroun' en tuck en toted de queen's chile home to de nigger-quarter, en nobody ever foun' it out, en her chile was de king bimeby, en sole de queen's chile down de river one time when dey had to settle up de estate. Dah, now—de preacher said it his own self, en it ain't no sin, 'ca'se white folks done it. *Dey* done it—yes, *dey* done it; en not on'y jis' common white folks nuther, but de biggest quality dey is in de whole bilin'. Oh, I 's *so* glad I 'member 'bout dat!"

She got up light-hearted and happy, and went to the cradles and spent what was left of the night "practising." She would give her own child a light pat and say humbly, "Lay still, Marse Tom," then give the real Tom a pat and say with severity, "Lay *still*, Chambers!—does you want me to take somep'n' *to* you?"

As she progressed with her practice, she was surprised to see how steadily and surely the awe which had kept her tongue reverent and her manner humble toward her young master was transferring itself to her speech and manner toward the usurper, and how similarly handy she was becoming in transferring her motherly curtness of speech and peremptoriness of manner to the unlucky heir of the ancient house of Driscoll.

She took occasional rests from practising, and absorbed herself in calculating her chances.

"Dey 'll sell dese niggers to-day fo' stealin' de money, den dey 'll buy some mo' dat don't know de chillen—so *dat 's* all right. When I takes de chillen out to git de air, de minute I 's roun' de corner I 's gwine to gaum dey mouths all roun'

thing he wanted, particularly things that would give him the stomach-ache.

When he got to be old enough to begin to toddle about and say broken words and get an idea of what his hands were for, he was a more consummate pest than ever. Roxy got no rest while he was awake. He would call for anything and everything he saw, simply saying "Awnt it!" (want it), which was a command. When it was brought, he said in a frenzy, and motioning it away with his hands, "Don't awnt it! don't awnt it!" and the moment it was gone he set up frantic yells of "Awnt it! awnt it! awnt it!" and Roxy had to give wings to her heels to get that thing back to him again before he could get time to carry out his intention of going into convulsions about it.

What he preferred above all other things was the tongs. This was because his "father" had forbidden him to have them lest he break windows and furniture with them. The moment Roxy's back was turned he would toddle to the presence of the tongs and say "Like it!" and cock his eye to one side to see if Roxy was observing; then, "Awnt it!" and cock his eye again; then, "Hab it!" with another furtive glance; and finally, "Take it!"—and the prize was his. The next moment the heavy implement was raised aloft; the next, there was a crash and a squall, and the cat was off on three legs to meet an engagement; Roxy would arrive just as the lamp or a window went to irremediable smash.

Tom got all the petting, Chambers got none. Tom got all the delicacies, Chambers got mush and milk, and clabber without sugar. In consequence Tom was a sickly child and Chambers was n't. Tom was "fractious," as Roxy called it, and overbearing; Chambers was meek and docile.

With all her splendid common sense and practical everyday ability, Roxy was a doting fool of a mother. She was this toward her child—and she was also more than this: by the fiction created by herself, he was become her master; the necessity of recognizing this relation outwardly and of perfecting herself in the forms required to express the recognition, had moved her to such diligence and faithfulness in practising these forms that this exercise soon concreted itself into habit; it became automatic and unconscious; then a natural result followed: deceptions intended solely for others gradually grew practically into self-deceptions as well; the mock reverence became real reverence, the mock obsequiousness real obsequiousness, the mock homage real homage; the little counterfeit rift of separation between imitation-slave and imitation-master widened and widened, and became an abyss, and a very real one—and on one side of it stood Roxy, the dupe of her own deceptions, and on the other stood her child, no longer a usurper to her, but her accepted and recognized master. He was her darling, her master, and her deity all in one, and in her worship of him she forgot who she was and what he had been.

In babyhood Tom cuffed and banged and scratched Chambers unrebuked, and Chambers early learned that between meekly bearing it and resenting it, the advantage all lay with the former policy. The few times that his persecutions had moved him beyond control and made him fight back had cost him very dear at headquarters; not at the hands of Roxy, for if she ever went beyond scolding him sharply for "forgitt'n' who his young master was," she at least never extended her punishment beyond a box on the ear. No, Percy Driscoll was the person. He told Chambers that under no provocation whatever was he privileged to lift his hand against his little master. Chambers overstepped the line three times, and got three such convincing canings from the man who was his father and did n't know it, that he took Tom's cruelties in all humility after that, and made no more experiments.

Outside of the house the two boys were together all through their boyhood. Chambers was strong beyond his years, and a good fighter; strong because he was coarsely fed and hard worked about the house, and a good fighter because Tom furnished him plenty of practice—on white boys whom he hated and was afraid of. Chambers was his constant body-guard, to and from school; he was present on the playground at recess to protect his charge. He fought himself into such a formidable reputation, by and by, that Tom could have changed clothes with him, and "ridden in peace," like Sir Kay in Launcelot's armor.

He was good at games of skill, too. Tom staked him with marbles to play "keeps" with, and then took all the winnings away from him. In the winter season Chambers was on hand, in Tom's worn-out clothes, with "holy" red mittens, and "holy" shoes, and pants "holy" at the knees and seat, to drag a sled up the hill for Tom, warmly clad, to ride down on; but he never got a ride himself. He built snow men and snow fortifications under Tom's directions. He was Tom's patient target when Tom wanted to do some snowballing, but the target could n't fire back. Chambers carried Tom's skates to the river and strapped them on him, then trotted around after him on the ice, so as to be on hand when wanted; but he was n't ever asked to try the skates himself.

In summer the pet pastime of the boys of Dawson's Landing was to steal apples, peaches, and melons from the farmers' fruit-wagons,—mainly on account of the risk they ran of getting their head laid open with the butt of the farmer's whip. Tom was a distinguished adept at these thefts—by proxy. Chambers did his stealing, and got the peach-stones, apple-cores, and melon-rinds for his share.

Tom always made Chambers go in swimming with him, and stay by him as a protection. When Tom had had enough, he would slip out and tie knots in Chambers's shirt, dip the knots in the water to make them hard to undo, then dress himself and sit by and laugh while the naked shiverer tugged at the stubborn knots with his teeth.

Tom did his humble comrade these various ill turns partly out of native viciousness, and partly because he hated him for his superiorities of physique and pluck, and for his manifold clevernesses. Tom could n't dive, for it gave him splitting headaches. Chambers could dive without inconvenience, and was fond of doing it. He excited so much admiration, one day, among a crowd of white boys, by throwing back somersaults from the stern of a canoe, that it wearied Tom's spirit, and at last he shoved the canoe underneath Chambers while he was in the air—so he came down on his head in the canoe-bottom; and while he lay unconscious, several of Tom's ancient adversaries saw that their long-desired opportunity was come, and they gave the false heir such a drubbing that with Chambers's best help he was hardly able to drag himself home afterward.

When the boys were fifteen and upward, Tom was "showing off" in the river one day, when he was taken with a cramp, and shouted for help. It was a common trick with the boys—particularly if a stranger was present—to pretend a cramp and howl for help; then when the stranger came tearing hand over hand to the rescue, the howler would go on struggling and howling till he was close at hand, then replace the howl with a sarcastic smile and swim blandly away, while the town boys assailed the dupe with a volley of jeers and laughter. Tom had never tried this joke as yet, but was supposed to be trying it now, so the boys held warily back; but Chambers believed his master was in earnest, therefore he swam out, and arrived in time, unfortunately, and saved his life.

This was the last feather. Tom had managed to endure everything else, but to have to remain publicly and permanently under such an obligation as this to a nigger, and to this nigger of all niggers—this was too much. He heaped insults upon Chambers for "pretending" to think he was in earnest in calling for help, and said that anybody but a blockheaded nigger would have known he was funning and left him alone.

Tom's enemies were in strong force here, so they came out with their opinions quite freely. They laughed at him, and called him coward, liar, sneak, and other sorts of pet names, and told him they meant to call Chambers by a new name after this, and make it common in the town—"Tom Driscoll's niggerpappy,"—to signify that he had had a second birth into this life, and that Chambers was the author of his new being. Tom grew frantic under these taunts, and shouted—

"Knock their heads off, Chambers! knock their heads off! What do you stand there with your hands in your pockets for?"

Chambers expostulated, and said, "But, Marse Tom, dey 's too many of 'em—dey 's—"

"Do you hear me?"

"Please, Marse Tom, don't make me! Dey 's so many of 'em dat—"

Tom sprang at him and drove his pocket-knife into him two or three times before the boys could snatch him away and give the wounded lad a chance to escape. He was considerably hurt, but not seriously. If the blade had been a little longer his career would have ended there.

Tom had long ago taught Roxy "her place." It had been many a day now since she had ventured a caress or a fondling epithet in his quarter. Such things, from a "nigger," were repulsive to him, and she had been warned to keep her distance and remember who she was. She saw her darling gradually cease from being her son, she saw *that* detail perish utterly; all that was left was master—master, pure and simple, and it was not a gentle mastership, either. She saw herself sink from the sublime height of motherhood to the somber deeps of unmodified slavery. The abyss of separation between her and her boy was complete. She was merely his chattel, now, his convenience, his dog, his cringing and helpless slave, the humble and unresisting victim of his capricious temper and vicious nature.

Sometimes she could not go to sleep, even when worn out with fatigue, because her rage boiled so high over the day's experiences with her boy. She would mumble and mutter to herself—

"He struck me, en I war n't no way to blame—struck me in de face, right before folks. En he 's al'ays callin' me nigger-wench, en hussy, en all dem mean names, when I 's doin' de very bes' I kin. Oh, Lord, I done so much for him—I lift' him away up to what he is—en dis is what I git for it."

Sometimes when some outrage of peculiar offensiveness stung her to the heart, she would plan schemes of vengeance and revel in the fancied spectacle of his exposure to the world as an impostor and a slave; but in the midst of these joys fear would strike her: she had made him too strong; she could prove nothing, and—heavens, she might get sold down the river for her pains! So her schemes always went for nothing, and she laid them aside in impotent rage against the fates, and against herself for playing the fool on that fatal September day in not providing herself with a witness for use in the day when such a thing might be needed for the appeasing of her vengeance-hungry heart.

And yet the moment Tom happened to be good to her, and kind,—and this occurred every now and then,—all her sore places were healed, and she was happy; happy and proud, for this was her son, her nigger son, lording it among the whites and securely avenging their crimes against her race.

There were two grand funerals in Dawson's Landing that fall—the fall of 1845. One was that of Colonel Cecil Burleigh Essex, the other that of Percy Driscoll.

On his death-bed Driscoll set Roxy free and delivered his idolized ostensible son solemnly into the keeping of his brother the Judge and his wife. Those childless people were glad to get him. Childless people are not difficult to please.

Judge Driscoll had gone privately to his brother, a month before, and bought Chambers. He had heard that Tom had been trying to get his father to sell the boy down the river, and he wanted to prevent the scandal—for public sentiment did not approve of that way of treating family servants for light cause or for no cause.

Percy Driscoll had worn himself out in trying to save his great speculative landed estate, and had died without succeeding. He was hardly in his grave before the boom collapsed and left his hitherto envied young devil of an heir a pauper. But that was nothing; his uncle told him he should be his heir and have all his fortune when he died; so Tom was comforted.

Roxy had no home, now; so she resolved to go around and say good-by to her friends and then clear out and see the world—that is to say, she would go chambermaiding on a steamboat, the darling ambition of her race and sex.

Her last call was on the black giant, Jasper. She found him chopping Pudd'nhead Wilson's winter provision of wood. Wilson was chatting with him when Roxy arrived. He asked her how she could bear to go off chambermaiding and leave her boys; and chaffingly offered to copy off a series of their finger-prints, reaching up to their twelfth year, for her to remember them by; but she sobered in a moment, wondering if he suspected anything; then she said she believed she did n't want them. Wilson said to himself, "The drop of black blood in her is superstitious; she thinks there 's some devilry, some witch-business about my glass mystery somewhere; she used to come here with an old horseshoe in her hand; it could have been an accident, but I doubt it."

V

TRAINING is everything. The peach was once a bitter almond;
cauliflower is nothing but cabbage with a college education.
— *Pudd'nhead Wilson's Calendar.*

REMARK of Dr. Baldwin's, concerning up-starts: We don't care
to eat toadstools that think they are truffles.
— *Pudd'nhead Wilson's Calendar.*

MRS. YORK DRISCOLL enjoyed two years of bliss with
that prize, Tom—bliss that was troubled a little at
times, it is true, but bliss nevertheless; then she died, and her
husband and his childless sister, Mrs. Pratt, continued the
bliss-business at the old stand. Tom was petted and indulged
and spoiled to his entire content—or nearly that. This went
on till he was nineteen, then he was sent to Yale. He went
handsomely equipped with "conditions," but otherwise he
was not an object of distinction there. He remained at Yale
two years, and then threw up the struggle. He came home
with his manners a good deal improved; he had lost his sur-
liness and brusqueness, and was rather pleasantly soft and
smooth, now; he was furtively, and sometimes openly, ironical of speech, and given to gently touching people on the
raw, but he did it with a good-natured semiconscious air that
carried it off safely, and kept him from getting into trouble.
He was as indolent as ever and showed no very strenuous
desire to hunt up an occupation. People argued from this that
he preferred to be supported by his uncle until his uncle's
shoes should become vacant. He brought back one or two
new habits with him, one of which he rather openly practised—tippling—but concealed another, which was gambling. It would not do to gamble where his uncle could hear
of it; he knew that quite well.

Tom's Eastern polish was not popular among the young
people. They could have endured it, perhaps, if Tom had
stopped there; but he wore gloves, and that they could n't
stand, and would n't; so he was mainly without society. He
brought home with him a suit of clothes of such exquisite
style and cut and fashion,—Eastern fashion, city fashion,—

that it filled everybody with anguish and was regarded as a peculiarly wanton affront. He enjoyed the feeling which he was exciting, and paraded the town serene and happy all day; but the young fellows set a tailor to work that night, and when Tom started out on his parade next morning he found the old deformed negro bell-ringer straddling along in his wake tricked out in a flamboyant curtain-calico exaggeration of his finery, and imitating his fancy Eastern graces as well as he could.

Tom surrendered, and after that clothed himself in the local fashion. But the dull country town was tiresome to him, since his acquaintanceship with livelier regions, and it grew daily more and more so. He began to make little trips to St. Louis for refreshment. There he found companionship to suit him, and pleasures to his taste, along with more freedom, in some particulars, than he could have at home. So, during the next two years his visits to the city grew in frequency and his tarryings there grew steadily longer in duration.

He was getting into deep waters. He was taking chances, privately, which might get him into trouble some day—in fact, *did*.

Judge Driscoll had retired from the bench and from all business activities in 1850, and had now been comfortably idle three years. He was president of the Free-thinkers' Society, and Pudd'nhead Wilson was the other member. The society's weekly discussions were now the old lawyer's main interest in life. Pudd'nhead was still toiling in obscurity at the bottom of the ladder, under the blight of that unlucky remark which he had let fall twenty-three years before about the dog.

Judge Driscoll was his friend, and claimed that he had a mind above the average, but that was regarded as one of the Judge's whims, and it failed to modify the public opinion. Or rather, that was one of the reasons why it failed, but there was another and better one. If the judge had stopped with bare assertion, it would have had a good deal of effect; but he made the mistake of trying to prove his position. For some years Wilson had been privately at work on a whimsical almanac, for his amusement—a calendar, with a little dab of ostensible philosophy, usually in ironical form, appended to each date; and the Judge thought that these quips and fancies of Wilson's were neatly turned and cute; so he carried a handful of them around, one day, and read them to some of the chief citizens. But irony was not for those people; their mental vision was not focussed for it. They read those playful trifles in the solidest earnest, and decided without hesitancy that if there had ever been any doubt that Dave Wilson was a pudd'nhead—which there had n't—this revelation removed that doubt for good and all. That is just the way in this world; an enemy can partly ruin a man, but it takes a good-natured injudicious friend to complete the thing and make it perfect. After this the Judge felt tenderer than ever toward Wilson, and surer than ever that his calendar had merit.

Judge Driscoll could be a free-thinker and still hold his place in society because he was the person of most consequence in the community, and therefore could venture to go his own way and follow out his own notions. The other member of his pet organization was allowed the like liberty because he was a cipher in the estimation of the public, and nobody attached any importance to what he thought or did. He was liked, he was welcome enough all around, but he simply did n't count for anything.

The widow Cooper—affectionately called "aunt Patsy" by everybody—lived in a snug and comely cottage with her daughter Rowena, who was nineteen, romantic, amiable, and very pretty, but otherwise of no consequence. Rowena had a couple of young brothers—also of no consequence.

The widow had a large spare room which she let to a lodger, with board, when she could find one, but this room had been empty for a year now, to her sorrow. Her income was only sufficient for the family support, and she needed the lodging-money for trifling luxuries. But now, at last, on a flaming June day, she found herself happy; her tedious wait was ended; her year-worn advertisement had been answered; and not by a village applicant, oh, no!—this letter was from away off yonder in the dim great world to the North; it was from St. Louis. She sat on her porch gazing out with unseeing eyes upon the shining reaches of the mighty Mississippi, her thoughts steeped in her good fortune. Indeed it was specially good fortune, for she was to have two lodgers instead of one.

She had read the letter to the family, and Rowena had danced away to see to the cleaning and airing of the room by the slave woman Nancy, and the boys had rushed abroad in the town to spread the great news, for it was matter of public interest, and the public would wonder and not be pleased if not informed. Presently Rowena returned, all ablush with joyous excitement, and begged for a re-reading of the letter. It was framed thus:

HONORED MADAM: My brother and I have seen your advertisement, by chance, and beg leave to take the room you offer. We are twenty-four years of age and twins. We are Italians by birth, but have lived long in the various countries of Europe, and several years in the United States. Our names are Luigi and Angelo Capello. You desire but one guest; but dear Madam, if you will allow us to pay for two, we will not incommode you. We shall be down Thursday.

"Italians! How romantic! Just think, ma—there 's never been one in this town, and everybody will be dying to see them, and they 're all *ours*! Think of that!"

"Yes, I reckon they 'll make a grand stir."

"Oh, indeed they will. The whole town will be on its head! Think—they 've been in Europe and everywhere! There 's never been a traveler in this town before. Ma, I should n't wonder if they 've seen kings!"

"Well, a body can't tell; but they 'll make stir enough, without that."

"Yes, that 's of course. Luigi—Angelo. They 're lovely names; and so grand and foreign—not like Jones and Robinson and such. Thursday they are coming, and this is only Tuesday; it 's a cruel long time to wait. Here comes Judge Driscoll in at the gate. He 's heard about it. I 'll go and open the door."

The judge was full of congratulations and curiosity. The letter was read and discussed. Soon Justice Robinson arrived with more congratulations, and there was a new reading and a new discussion. This was the beginning. Neighbor after neighbor, of both sexes, followed, and the procession drifted in and out all day and evening and all Wednesday and Thursday. The letter was read and re-read until it was nearly worn out; everybody admired its courtly and gracious tone, and smooth and practised style, everybody was sympathetic and excited, and the Coopers were steeped in happiness all the while.

The boats were very uncertain in low water, in these primitive times. This time the Thursday boat had not arrived at ten at night—so the people had waited at the landing all day for nothing; they were driven to their homes by a heavy storm without having had a view of the illustrious foreigners.

Eleven o'clock came; and the Cooper house was the only one in the town that still had lights burning. The rain and thunder were booming yet, and the anxious family were still waiting, still hoping. At last there was a knock at the door and the family jumped to open it. Two negro men entered, each carrying a trunk, and proceeded up-stairs toward the guest-room. Then entered the twins—the handsomest, the best dressed, the most distinguished-looking pair of young fellows the West had ever seen. One was a little fairer than the other, but otherwise they were exact duplicates.

VI

LET US endeavor so to live that when we come to die even the
undertaker will be sorry.

— *Pudd'nhead Wilson's Calendar.*

HABIT is habit, and not to be flung out of the window by any
man, but coaxed down-stairs a step at a time.

— *Pudd'nhead Wilson's Calendar.*

AT BREAKFAST in the morning the twins' charm of manner
and easy and polished bearing made speedy conquest of
the family's good graces. All constraint and formality quickly
disappeared, and the friendliest feeling succeeded. Aunt Patsy
called them by their Christian names almost from the beginning. She was full of the keenest curiosity about them, and
showed it; they responded by talking about themselves,
which pleased her greatly. It presently appeared that in their
early youth they had known poverty and hardship. As the talk
wandered along the old lady watched for the right place to
drop in a question or two concerning that matter, and when
she found it she said to the blond twin, who was now doing
the biographies in his turn while the brunette one rested—

"If it ain't asking what I ought not to ask, Mr. Angelo,
how did you come to be so friendless and in such trouble
when you were little? Do you mind telling? But don't if
you do."

"Oh, we don't mind it at all, madam; in our case it was
merely misfortune, and nobody's fault. Our parents were well
to do, there in Italy, and we were their only child. We were
of the old Florentine nobility"—Rowena's heart gave a great
bound, her nostrils expanded, and a fine light played in her
eyes—"and when the war broke out my father was on the
losing side and had to fly for his life. His estates were confiscated, his personal property seized, and there we were, in
Germany, strangers, friendless, and in fact paupers. My
brother and I were ten years old, and well educated for that
age, very studious, very fond of our books, and well
grounded in the German, French, Spanish, and English lan-

guages. Also, we were marvelous musical prodigies—if you will allow me to say it, it being only the truth.

"Our father survived his misfortunes only a month, our mother soon followed him, and we were alone in the world. Our parents could have made themselves comfortable by exhibiting us as a show, and they had many and large offers; but the thought revolted their pride, and they said they would starve and die first. But what they would n't consent to do we had to do without the formality of consent. We were seized for the debts occasioned by their illness and their funerals, and placed among the attractions of a cheap museum in Berlin to earn the liquidation money. It took us two years to get out of that slavery. We traveled all about Germany, receiving no wages, and not even our keep. We had to be exhibited for nothing, and beg our bread.

"Well, madam, the rest is not of much consequence. When we escaped from that slavery at twelve years of age, we were in some respects men. Experience had taught us some valuable things; among others, how to take care of ourselves, how to avoid and defeat sharks and sharpers, and how to conduct our own business for our own profit and without other people's help. We traveled everywhere—years and years—picking up smatterings of strange tongues, familiarizing ourselves with strange sights and strange customs, accumulating an education of a wide and varied and curious sort. It was a pleasant life. We went to Venice—to London, Paris, Russia, India, China, Japan—"

At this point Nancy the slave woman thrust her head in at the door and exclaimed:

"Ole Missus, de house is plum' jam full o' people, en dey 's jes a-spi'lin' to see de gen'lmen!" She indicated the twins with a nod of her head, and tucked it back out of sight again.

It was a proud occasion for the widow, and she promised herself high satisfaction in showing off her fine foreign birds before her neighbors and friends—simple folk who had hardly ever seen a foreigner of any kind, and never one of any distinction or style. Yet her feeling was moderate indeed when contrasted with Rowena's. Rowena was in the clouds, she walked on air; this was to be the greatest day, the most romantic episode, in the colorless history of that dull country

town. She was to be familiarly near the source of its glory
and feel the full flood of it pour over her and about her; the
other girls could only gaze and envy, not partake.

The widow was ready, Rowena was ready, so also were the
foreigners.

The party moved along the hall, the twins in advance, and
entered the open parlor door, whence issued a low hum of
conversation. The twins took a position near the door, the
widow stood at Luigi's side, Rowena stood beside Angelo,
and the march-past and the introductions began. The widow
was all smiles and contentment. She received the procession
and passed it on to Rowena.

"Good mornin', Sister Cooper"—hand-shake.

"Good morning, Brother Higgins—Count Luigi Capello,
Mr. Higgins"—hand-shake, followed by a devouring stare
and "I 'm glad to see ye," on the part of Higgins, and a courteous inclination of the head and a pleasant "Most happy!"
on the part of Count Luigi.

"Good mornin', Roweny"—hand-shake.

"Good morning, Mr. Higgins—present you to Count Angelo Capello." Hand-shake, admiring stare, "Glad to see
ye,"—courteous nod, smily "Most happy!" and Higgins
passes on.

None of these visitors was at ease, but, being honest people, they did n't pretend to be. None of them had ever seen
a person bearing a title of nobility before, and none had been
expecting to see one now, consequently the title came upon
them as a kind of pile-driving surprise and caught them un-
prepared. A few tried to rise to the emergency, and got out
an awkward "My lord," or "Your lordship," or something of
that sort, but the great majority were overwhelmed by the
unaccustomed word and its dim and awful associations with
gilded courts and stately ceremony and anointed kingship, so
they only fumbled through the hand-shake and passed on,
speechless. Now and then, as happens at all receptions everywhere, a more than ordinarily friendly soul blocked the
procession and kept it waiting while he inquired how the
brothers liked the village, and how long they were going to
stay, and if their families were well, and dragged in the
weather, and hoped it would get cooler soon, and all that sort

of thing, so as to be able to say, when they got home, "I had quite a long talk with them"; but nobody did or said anything of a regrettable kind, and so the great affair went through to the end in a creditable and satisfactory fashion.

General conversation followed, and the twins drifted about from group to group, talking easily and fluently and winning approval, compelling admiration and achieving favor from all. The widow followed their conquering march with a proud eye, and every now and then Rowena said to herself with deep satisfaction, "And to think they are ours—all ours!"

There were no idle moments for mother or daughter. Eager inquiries concerning the twins were pouring into their enchanted ears all the time; each was the constant center of a group of breathless listeners; each recognized that she knew now for the first time the real meaning of that great word Glory, and perceived the stupendous value of it, and understood why men in all ages had been willing to throw away meaner happinesses, treasure, life itself, to get a taste of its sublime and supreme joy. Napoleon and all his kind stood accounted for—and justified.

When Rowena had at last done all her duty by the people in the parlor, she went up-stairs to satisfy the longings of an overflow-meeting there, for the parlor was not big enough to hold all the comers. Again she was besieged by eager questioners and again she swam in sunset seas of glory. When the forenoon was nearly gone, she recognized with a pang that this most splendid episode of her life was almost over, that nothing could prolong it, that nothing quite its equal could ever fall to her fortune again. But never mind, it was sufficient unto itself, the grand occasion had moved on an ascending scale from the start, and was a noble and memorable success. If the twins could but do some crowning act, now, to climax it, something unusual, something startling, something to concentrate upon themselves the company's loftiest admiration, something in the nature of an electric surprise—

Here a prodigious slam-banging broke out below, and everybody rushed down to see. It was the twins knocking out a classic four-handed piece on the piano, in great style. Rowena was satisfied—satisfied down to the bottom of her heart.

The young strangers were kept long at the piano. The villagers were astonished and enchanted with the magnificence of their performance, and could not bear to have them stop. All the music that they had ever heard before seemed spiritless prentice-work and barren of grace or charm when compared with these intoxicating floods of melodious sound. They realized that for once in their lives they were hearing masters.

VII

ONE of the most striking differences between a cat and a lie is that a cat has only nine lives.

— Pudd'nhead Wilson's Calendar.

THE COMPANY broke up reluctantly, and drifted toward their several homes, chatting with vivacity, and all agreeing that it would be many a long day before Dawson's Landing would see the equal of this one again. The twins accepted several invitations while the reception was in progress, and had also volunteered to play some duets at an amateur entertainment for the benefit of a local charity. Society was eager to receive them to its bosom. Judge Driscoll had the good fortune to secure them for an immediate drive, and to be the first to display them in public. They entered his buggy with him, and were paraded down the main street, everybody flocking to the windows and sidewalks to see.

The Judge showed the strangers the new graveyard, and the jail, and where the richest man lived, and the Freemasons' hall, and the Methodist church, and the Presbyterian church, and where the Baptist church was going to be when they got some money to build it with, and showed them the town hall and the slaughter-house, and got out the independent fire company in uniform and had them put out an imaginary fire; then he let them inspect the muskets of the militia company, and poured out an exhaustless stream of enthusiasm over all these splendors, and seemed very well satisfied with the responses he got, for the twins admired his admiration, and paid him back the best they could, though they could have done better if some fifteen or sixteen hundred thousand previous experiences of this sort in various countries had not already rubbed off a considerable part of the novelty of it.

The Judge laid himself out hospitably to make them have a good time, and if there was a defect anywhere it was not his fault. He told them a good many humorous anecdotes, and always forgot the nub, but they were always able to furnish it, for these yarns were of a pretty early vintage, and they had had many a rejuvenating pull at them before. And he told

them all about his several dignities, and how he had held this
and that and the other place of honor or profit, and had once
been to the legislature, and was now president of the Society
of Free-thinkers. He said the society had been in existence
four years, and already had two members, and was firmly established. He would call for the brothers in the evening if
they would like to attend a meeting of it.

Accordingly he called for them, and on the way he told
them all about Pudd'nhead Wilson, in order that they might
get a favorable impression of him in advance and be prepared
to like him. This scheme succeeded—the favorable impression was achieved. Later it was confirmed and solidified when
Wilson proposed that out of courtesy to the strangers the
usual topics be put aside and the hour be devoted to conversation upon ordinary subjects and the cultivation of friendly
relations and good-fellowship,—a proposition which was put
to vote and carried.

The hour passed quickly away in lively talk, and when it
was ended the lonesome and neglected Wilson was richer by
two friends than he had been when it began. He invited the
twins to look in at his lodgings, presently, after disposing of
an intervening engagement, and they accepted with pleasure.

Toward the middle of the evening they found themselves
on the road to his house. Pudd'nhead was at home waiting
for them and putting in his time puzzling over a thing which
had come under his notice that morning. The matter was this:
He happened to be up very early—at dawn, in fact, and he
crossed the hall which divided his cottage through the center,
and entered a room to get something there. The window of
the room had no curtains, for that side of the house had long
been unoccupied, and through this window he caught sight
of something which surprised and interested him. It was a
young woman—a young woman where properly no young
woman belonged; for she was in Judge Driscoll's house, and
in the bedroom over the Judge's private study or sitting-
room. This was young Tom Driscoll's bedroom. He and the
Judge, the Judge's widowed sister Mrs. Pratt and three negro
servants were the only people who belonged in the house.
Who, then, might this young lady be? The two houses were
separated by an ordinary yard, with a low fence running back

through its middle from the street in front to the lane in the rear. The distance was not great, and Wilson was able to see the girl very well, the window-shades of the room she was in being up and the window also. The girl had on a neat and trim summer dress, patterned in broad stripes of pink and white, and her bonnet was equipped with a pink veil. She was practising steps, gaits and attitudes, apparently; she was doing the thing gracefully, and was very much absorbed in her work. Who could she be, and how came she to be in young Tom Driscoll's room?

Wilson had quickly chosen a position from which he could watch the girl without running much risk of being seen by her, and remained there hoping she would raise her veil and betray her face. But she disappointed him. After a matter of twenty minutes she disappeared, and although he stayed at his post half an hour longer, she came no more.

Toward noon he dropped in at the Judge's and talked with Mrs. Pratt about the great event of the day, the levee of the distinguished foreigners at Aunt Patsy Cooper's. He asked after her nephew Tom, and she said he was on his way home, and that she was expecting him to arrive a little before night; and added that she and the Judge were gratified to gather from his letters that he was conducting himself very nicely and creditably—at which Wilson winked to himself privately. Wilson did not ask if there was a newcomer in the house, but he asked questions that would have brought light-throwing answers as to that matter if Mrs. Pratt had had any light to throw; so he went away satisfied that he knew of things that were going on in her house of which she herself was not aware.

He was now waiting for the twins, and still puzzling over the problem of who that girl might be, and how she happened to be in that young fellow's room at daybreak in the morning.

VIII

THE holy passion of Friendship is of so sweet and steady and loyal and enduring a nature that it will last through a whole lifetime, if not asked to lend money.

— Pudd'nhead Wilson's Calendar.

CONSIDER well the proportions of things. It is better to be a young June-bug than an old bird of paradise.

— Pudd'nhead Wilson's Calendar.

IT IS NECESSARY now, to hunt up Roxy.

At the time she was set free and went away chambermaiding, she was thirty-five. She got a berth as second chambermaid on a Cincinnati boat in the New Orleans trade, the *Grand Mogul*. A couple of trips made her wonted and easy-going at the work, and infatuated her with the stir and adventure and independence of steamboat life. Then she was promoted and became head chambermaid. She was a favorite with the officers, and exceedingly proud of their joking and friendly ways with her.

During eight years she served three parts of the year on that boat, and the winters on a Vicksburg packet. But now for two months she had had rheumatism in her arms, and was obliged to let the wash-tub alone. So she resigned. But she was well fixed—rich, as she would have described it; for she had lived a steady life, and had banked four dollars every month in New Orleans as a provision for her old age. She said in the start that she had "put shoes on one bar'footed nigger to tromple on her with," and that one mistake like that was enough; she would be independent of the human race thenceforth forevermore if hard work and economy could accomplish it. When the boat touched the levee at New Orleans she bade good-by to her comrades on the *Grand Mogul* and moved her kit ashore.

But she was back in an hour. The bank had gone to smash and carried her four hundred dollars with it. She was a pauper, and homeless. Also disabled bodily, at least for the present. The officers were full of sympathy for her in her trouble, and made up a little purse for her. She resolved to go to her birthplace; she had friends there among the negroes, and the unfortunate always help the unfortunate, she was well aware of that; those lowly comrades of her youth would not let her starve.

She took the little local packet at Cairo, and now she was on the home-stretch. Time had worn away her bitterness against her son, and she was able to think of him with serenity. She put the vile side of him out of her mind, and dwelt only on recollections of his occasional acts of kindness to her. She gilded and otherwise decorated these, and made them very pleasant to contemplate. She began to long to see him. She would go and fawn upon him, slave-like—for this would have to be her attitude, of course—and maybe she would find that time had modified him, and that he would be glad to see his long-forgotten old nurse and treat her gently. That would be lovely; that would make her forget her woes and her poverty.

Her poverty! That thought inspired her to add another castle to her dream: maybe he would give her a trifle now and then—maybe a dollar, once a month, say; any little thing like that would help, oh, ever so much.

By the time she reached Dawson's Landing she was her old self again; her blues were gone, she was in high feather. She would get along, surely; there were many kitchens where the servants would share their meals with her, and also steal sugar and apples and other dainties for her to carry home—or give her a chance to pilfer them herself, which would answer just as well. And there was the church. She was a more rabid and devoted Methodist than ever, and her piety was no sham, but was strong and sincere. Yes, with plenty of creature comforts and her old place in the amen-corner in her possession again, she would be perfectly happy and at peace thenceforward to the end.

She went to Judge Driscoll's kitchen first of all. She was received there in great form and with vast enthusiasm. Her wonderful travels, and the strange countries she had seen and the adventures she had had, made her a marvel, and a heroine of romance. The negroes hung enchanted upon the great story of her experiences, interrupting her all along with eager questions, with laughter, exclamations of delight and expres-

sions of applause; and she was obliged to confess to herself
that if there was anything better in this world than steamboating, it was the glory to be got by telling about it. The
audience loaded her stomach with their dinners and then stole
the pantry bare to load up her basket.

Tom was in St. Louis. The servants said he had spent the
best part of his time there during the previous two years.
Roxy came every day, and had many talks about the family
and its affairs. Once she asked why Tom was away so much.
The ostensible "Chambers" said:

"De fac' is, ole marster kin git along better when young
marster 's away den he kin when he 's in de town; yes, en
he love him better, too; so he gives him fifty dollahs a
month—"

"No, is dat so? Chambers, you 's a-jokin', ain't you?"

" 'Clah to goodness I ain't, mammy; Marse Tom tole me
so his own self. But nemmine, 't ain't enough."

"My lan', what de reason 't ain't enough?"

"Well, I 's gwine to tell you, if you gimme a chanst,
mammy. De reason it ain't enough is 'ca'se Marse Tom gam-
bles."

Roxy threw up her hands in astonishment and Chambers
went on—

"Ole marster found it out, 'ca'se he had to pay two hunderd
dollahs for Marse Tom 's gamblin' debts, en dat 's true,
mammy, jes as dead certain as you 's bawn."

"Two—hund'd—dollahs! Why, what is you talkin' 'bout?
Two—hund'd—dollahs. Sakes alive, it 's 'mos' enough to
buy a tol'able good second-hand nigger wid. En you ain't
lyin', honey?—you would n't lie to yo' ole mammy?"

"It 's God's own truth, jes as I tell you—two hund'd dollahs—I wisht I may never stir outen my tracks if it ain't so.
En, oh, my lan', ole Marse was jes a-hoppin'! he was b'ilin'
mad, I tell you! He tuck 'n' dissenhurrit him."

He licked his chops with relish after that stately word.
Roxy struggled with it a moment, then gave it up and
said—

"Dissen *whiched* him?"

"Dissenhurrit him."

"What 's dat? What do it mean?"

"Means he bu'sted de will."

"Bu's—ted de will! He would n't *ever* treat him so! Take
it back, you mis'able imitation nigger dat I bore in sorrow en
ribbilation."

Roxy's pet castle—an occasional dollar from Tom's
pocket—was tumbling to ruin before her eyes. She could not
abide such a disaster as that; she could n't endure the thought
of it. Her remark amused Chambers:

"Yah-yah-yah! jes listen to dat! If I 's imitation, what is
you? Bofe of us is imitation *white*—dat 's what we is—en
pow'ful good imitation, too—yah-yah-yah!—we don't
'mount to noth'n' as imitation *niggers*; en as for—"

"Shet up yo' foolin', 'fo' I knock you side de head, en tell
me 'bout de will. Tell me 't ain't bu'sted—do, honey, en I 'll
never forgit you."

"Well, *'tain't*—'ca'se dey 's a new one made, en Marse
Tom 's all right ag'in. But what is you in such a sweat 'bout
it for, mammy? 'T ain't none o' your business I don't reckon."

" 'T ain't none o' my business? Whose business is it den, I
'd like to know? Wuz I his mother tell he was fifteen years
old, or wus n't I?—you answer me dat. En you speck I could
see him turned out po' en ornery on de worl' en never care
noth'n' 'bout it? I reckon if you 'd ever be'n a mother yo'self,
Valet de Chambers, you would n't talk sich foolishness
as dat."

"Well, den, ole Marse forgive him en fixed up de will
ag'in—do dat satisfy you?"

Yes, she was satisfied now, and quite happy and sentimental over it. She kept coming daily, and at last she was
told that Tom had come home. She began to tremble with
emotion, and straightway sent to beg him to let his "po'
ole nigger mammy have jes one sight of him en die for
joy."

Tom was stretched at his lazy ease on a sofa when Chambers brought the petition. Time had not modified his ancient
detestation of the humble drudge and protector of his boyhood; it was still bitter and uncompromising. He sat up and
bent a severe gaze upon the fair face of the young fellow
whose name he was unconsciously using and whose family
rights he was enjoying. He maintained the gaze until the vic-

tim of it had become satisfactorily pallid with terror, then he said—

"What does the old rip want with me?"

The petition was meekly repeated.

"Who gave you permission to come and disturb me with the social attentions of niggers?"

Tom had risen. The other young man was trembling now, visibly. He saw what was coming, and bent his head sideways, and put up his left arm to shield it. Tom rained cuffs upon the head and its shield, saying no word; the victim received each blow with a beseeching "Please, Marse Tom!—oh, please, Marse Tom!" Seven blows—then Tom said, "Face the door—march!" He followed behind with one, two, three solid kicks. The last one helped the pure-white slave over the door-sill, and he limped away mopping his eyes with his old ragged sleeve. Tom shouted after him, "Send her in!"

Then he flung himself panting on the sofa again, and rasped out the remark, "He arrived just at the right moment; I was full to the brim with bitter thinkings, and nobody to take it out of. How refreshing it was! I feel better."

Tom's mother entered now, closing the door behind her, and approached her son with all the wheedling and supplicating servilities that fear and interest can impart to the words and attitudes of the born slave. She stopped a yard from her boy and made two or three admiring exclamations over his manly stature and general handsomeness, and Tom put an arm under his head and hoisted a leg over the sofa-back in order to look properly indifferent.

"My lan', how you is growed, honey! 'Clah to goodness, I would n't a-knowed you, Marse Tom! 'deed I would n't! Look at me good; does you 'member old Roxy?—does you know yo' old nigger mammy, honey? Well now, I kin lay down en die in peace, 'ca'se I 's seed—"

"Cut it short,——it, cut it short! What is it you want?"

"You heah dat? Jes de same old Marse Tom, al'ays so gay and funnin' wid de ole mammy. I 'uz jes as shore—"

"Cut it short, I tell you, and get along! What do you want?"

This was a bitter disappointment. Roxy had for so many days nourished and fondled and petted her notion that Tom would be glad to see his old nurse, and would make her proud and happy to the marrow with a cordial word or two, that it took two rebuffs to convince her that he was not funning, and that her beautiful dream was a fond and foolish vanity, a shabby and pitiful mistake. She was hurt to the heart, and so ashamed that for a moment she did not quite know what to do or how to act. Then her breast began to heave, the tears came, and in her forlornness she was moved to try that other dream of hers—an appeal to her boy's charity; and so, upon the impulse, and without reflection, she offered her supplication:

"Oh, Marse Tom, de po' ole mammy is in sich hard luck dese days; en she 's kinder crippled in de arms en can't work, en if you could gimme a dollah—on'y jes one little dol—"

Tom was on his feet so suddenly that the supplicant was startled into a jump herself.

"A dollar!—give you a dollar! I've a notion to strangle you! Is *that* your errand here? Clear out! and be quick about it!"

Roxy backed slowly toward the door. When she was half-way she stopped, and said mournfully:

"Marse Tom, I nussed you when you was a little baby, en I raised you all by myself tell you was 'most a young man; en now you is young en rich, en I is po' en gitt'n' ole, en I come heah b'lievin' dat you would he'p de ole mammy 'long down de little road dat 's lef' 'twix' her en de grave, en—"

Tom relished this tune less than any that had preceded it, for it began to wake up a sort of echo in his conscience; so he interrupted and said with decision, though without asperity, that he was not in a situation to help her, and was n't going to do it.

"Ain't you ever gwine to he'p me, Marse Tom?"

"No! Now go away and don't bother me any more."

Roxy's head was down, in an attitude of humility. But now the fires of her old wrongs flamed up in her breast and began to burn fiercely. She raised her head slowly, till it was well up, and at the same time her great frame unconsciously assumed an erect and masterful attitude, with all the majesty and grace of her vanished youth in it. She raised her finger and punctuated with it:

"You has said de word. You has had yo' chance, en you has trompled it under yo' foot. When you git another one, you 'll git down on yo' knees en *beg* for it!"

A cold chill went to Tom's heart, he did n't know why; for he did not reflect that such words, from such an incongruous source, and so solemnly delivered, could not easily fail of that effect. However, he did the natural thing: he replied with bluster and mockery:

"*You* 'll give me a chance —*you!* Perhaps I 'd better get down on my knees now! But in case I don't—just for argument's sake—what 's going to happen, pray?"

"Dis is what is gwine to happen. I 's gwine as straight to yo' uncle as I kin walk, en tell him every las' thing I knows 'bout you."

Tom's cheek blenched, and she saw it. Disturbing thoughts began to chase each other through his head. "How can she know? And yet she must have found out—she looks it. I 've had the will back only three months, and am already deep in debt again, and moving heaven and earth to save myself from exposure and destruction, with a reasonably fair show of getting the thing covered up if I 'm let alone, and now this fiend has gone and found me out somehow or other. I wonder how much she knows? Oh, oh, oh, it 's enough to break a body's heart! But I 've got to humor her—there 's no other way."

Then he worked up a rather sickly sample of a gay laugh and a hollow chipperness of manner, and said:

"Well, well, Roxy dear, old friends like you and me must n't quarrel. Here 's your dollar—now tell me what you know."

He held out the wild-cat bill; she stood as she was, and made no movement. It was her turn to scorn persuasive foolery, now, and she did not waste it. She said, with a grim implacability in voice and manner which made Tom almost realize that even a former slave can remember for ten minutes insults and injuries returned for compliments and flatteries received, and can also enjoy taking revenge for them when the opportunity offers:

"What does I know? I 'll tell you what I knows. I knows enough to bu'st dat will to flinders—en more, mind you, *more!*"

Tom was aghast.

"More?" he said. "What do you call more? Where 's there any room for more?"

Roxy laughed a mocking laugh, and said scoffingly, with a toss of her head, and her hands on her hips—

"Yes!—oh, I reckon! Co'se you 'd like to know—wid yo' po' little ole rag dollah. What you reckon I 's gwine to tell *you* for?—you ain't got no money. I 's gwine to tell yo' uncle—en I 'll do it dis minute, too—he 'll gimme *five* dollahs for de news, en mighty glad, too."

She swung herself around disdainfully, and started away. Tom was in a panic. He seized her skirts, and implored her to wait. She turned and said, loftily—

"Look-a-heah, what 'uz it I tole you?"

"You—you—I don't remember anything. What was it you told me?"

"I tole you dat de next time I give you a chance you 'd git down on yo' knees en beg for it."

Tom was stupefied for a moment. He was panting with excitement. Then he said:

"Oh, Roxy, you would n't require your young master to do such a horrible thing. You can't mean it."

"I 'll let you know mighty quick whether I means it or not! You call me names, en as good as spit on me when I comes here po' en ornery en 'umble, to praise you for bein' growed up so fine en handsome, en tell you how I used to nuss you en tend you en watch you when you 'uz sick en had n't no mother but me in de whole worl', en beg you to give de po' ole nigger a dollah for to git her sum'n' to eat, en you call me names—*names*, dad blame you! Yassir, I gives you jes one chance mo', and dat's *now*, en it las' on'y a half a second—you hear?"

Tom slumped to his knees and began to beg, saying—

"You see I 'm begging, and it 's honest begging, too! Now tell me, Roxy, tell me."

The heir of two centuries of unatoned insult and outrage looked down on him and seemed to drink in deep draughts of satisfaction. Then she said—

"Fine nice young white gen'l'man kneelin' down to a nigger-wench! I 's wanted to see dat jes once befo' I 's called. Now, Gabr'el, blow de hawn, I 's ready . . . Git up!"

Tom did it. He said, humbly—

"Now, Roxy, don't punish me any more. I deserved what I've got, but be good and let me off with that. Don't go to uncle. Tell me—I'll give you the five dollars."

"Yes, I bet you will; en you won't stop dah, nuther. But I ain't gwine to tell you heah—"

"Good gracious, no!"

"Is you 'feared o' de ha'nted house?"

"N-no."

"Well, den, you come to de ha'nted house 'bout ten or 'leven to-night, en climb up de ladder, 'ca'se de sta'r-steps is broke down, en you'll fine me. I's a-roostin' in de ha'nted house 'ca'se I can't 'ford to roos' nowher's else." She started toward the door, but stopped and said, "Gimme de dollah bill!" He gave it to her. She examined it and said, "H'm— like enough de bank 's bu'sted." She started again, but halted again. "Has you got any whisky?"

"Yes, a little."

"Fetch it!"

He ran to his room overhead and brought down a bottle which was two thirds full. She tilted it up and took a drink. Her eyes sparkled with satisfaction, and she tucked the bottle under her shawl, saying, "It's prime. I'll take it along."

Tom humbly held the door for her, and she marched out as grim and erect as a grenadier.

IX

TOM FLUNG HIMSELF on the sofa, and put his throbbing head in his hands, and rested his elbows on his knees. He rocked himself back and forth and moaned.

"I 've knelt to a nigger-wench!" he muttered. "I thought I had struck the deepest depths of degradation before, but oh, dear, it was nothing to this. . . . Well, there is one consolation, such as it is—I 've struck bottom this time; there 's nothing lower."

But that was a hasty conclusion.

At ten that night he climbed the ladder in the haunted house, pale, weak, and wretched. Roxy was standing in the door of one of the rooms, waiting, for she had heard him.

This was a two-story log house which had acquired the reputation a few years before of being haunted, and that was the end of its usefulness. Nobody would live in it afterward, or go near it by night, and most people even gave it a wide berth in the daytime. As it had no competition, it was called *the* haunted house. It was getting crazy and ruinous, now, from long neglect. It stood three hundred yards beyond Pudd'nhead Wilson's house, with nothing between but vacancy. It was the last house in the town at that end.

Tom followed Roxy into the room. She had a pile of clean straw in the corner for a bed, some cheap but well-kept clothing was hanging on the wall, there was a tin lantern freckling the floor with little spots of light, and there were various soap- and candle-boxes scattered about, which served for chairs. The two sat down. Roxy said—

"Now den, I 'll tell you straight off, en I 'll begin to k'leck

de money later on; I ain't in no hurry. What does you reckon
I 's gwine to tell you?"

"Well, you—you—oh, Roxy, don't make it too hard for
me! Come right out and tell me you 've found out somehow
what a shape I 'm in on account of dissipation and foolishness."

"Disposition en foolishness! *No* sir, dat ain't it. Dat jist
ain't nothin' at all, 'longside o' what *I* knows."

Tom stared at her, and said—

"Why, Roxy, what do you mean?"

She rose, and gloomed above him like a Fate.

"I means dis—en it 's de Lord's truth. You ain't no more
kin to ole Marse Driscoll den I is!—*dat 's* what I means!"
and her eyes flamed with triumph.

"What!"

"Yassir, en *dat* ain't all! You 's a *nigger!*—*bawn* a nigger
en a *slave!*—en you 's a nigger en a slave dis minute; en if I
opens my mouf ole Marse Driscoll 'll sell you down de river
befo' you is two days older den what you is now!"

"It 's a thundering lie, you miserable old blatherskite!"

"It ain't no lie, nuther. It 's jes de truth, en nothin' *but* de
truth, so he'p me. Yassir—you 's my *son*—"

"You devil!"

"En dat po' boy dat you 's be'n a-kickin' en a-cuffin' to-day
is Percy Driscoll's son en yo' *marster*—"

"You beast!"

"En *his* name 's Tom Driscoll, en *yo'* name 's Valet de
Chambers, en you ain't *got* no fambly name, beca'se niggers
don't *have* 'em!"

Tom sprang up and seized a billet of wood and raised it;
but his mother only laughed at him, and said—

"Set down, you pup! Does you think you kin skyer me? It
ain't in you, nor de likes of you. I reckon you 'd shoot me in
de back, maybe, if you got a chance, for dat 's jist yo' style—
I knows you, thoo en thoo—but I don't mind gitt'n' killed,
beca'se all dis is down in writin', en it 's in safe hands, too,
en de man dat 's got it knows whah to look for de right man
when I gits killed. Oh, bless yo' soul, if you puts yo' mother
up for as big a fool as *you* is, you 's pow'ful mistaken, I kin

tell you! Now den, you set still en behave yo'self; en don't you git up ag'in till I tell you!"

Tom fretted and chafed awhile in a whirlwind of disorganizing sensations and emotions, and finally said, with something like settled conviction—

"The whole thing is moonshine; now then, go ahead and do your worst; I 'm done with you."

Roxy made no answer. She took the lantern and started toward the door. Tom was in a cold panic in a moment.

"Come back, come back!" he wailed. "I did n't mean it, Roxy; I take it all back, and I 'll never say it again! Please come back, Roxy!"

The woman stood a moment, then she said gravely:

"Dah 's one thing you 's got to stop, Valet de Chambers. You can't call me *Roxy*, same as if you was my equal. Chillen don't speak to dey mammies like dat. You 'll call me ma or mammy, dat 's what you 'll call me—leastways when dey ain't nobody aroun'. *Say* it!"

It cost Tom a struggle, but he got it out.

"Dat 's all right. Don't you ever forgit it ag'in, if you knows what 's good for you. Now den, you has said you would n't ever call it lies en moonshine ag'in. I 'll tell you dis, for a warnin': if you ever does say it ag'in, it 's de *las'* time you 'll ever say it to me; I 'll tramp as straight to de Judge as I kin walk, en tell him who you is, en *prove* it. Does you b'lieve me when I says dat?"

"Oh," groaned Tom, "I more than believe it; I *know* it."

Roxy knew her conquest was complete. She could have proved nothing to anybody, and her threat about the writings was a lie; but she knew the person she was dealing with, and had made both statements without any doubt as to the effect they would produce.

She went and sat down on her candle-box, and the pride and pomp of her victorious attitude made it a throne. She said—

"Now den, Chambers, we 's gwine to talk business, en dey ain't gwine to be no mo' foolishness. In de fust place, you gits fifty dollahs a month; you 's gwine to han' over half of it to yo' ma. Plank it out!"

But Tom had only six dollars in the world. He gave her that, and promised to start fair on next month's pension.

"Chambers, how much is you in debt?"

Tom shuddered, and said—

"Nearly three hundred dollars."

"How is you gwine to pay it?"

Tom groaned out—

"Oh, I don't know; don't ask me such awful questions."

But she stuck to her point until she wearied a confession out of him: he had been prowling about in disguise, stealing small valuables from private houses; in fact, had made a good deal of a raid on his fellow-villagers a fortnight before, when he was supposed to be in St. Louis; but he doubted if he had sent away enough stuff to realize the required amount, and was afraid to make a further venture in the present excited state of the town. His mother approved of his conduct, and offered to help, but this frightened him. He tremblingly ventured to say that if she would retire from the town he should feel better and safer, and could hold his head higher—and was going on to make an argument, but she interrupted and surprised him pleasantly by saying she was ready; it did n't make any difference to her where she stayed, so that she got her share of the pension regularly. She said she would not go far, and would call at the haunted house once a month for her money. Then she said—

"I don't hate you so much now, but I 've hated you a many a year—and anybody would. Did n't I change you off, en give you a good fambly en a good name, en made you a white gen'l'man en rich, wid store clothes on—en what did I git for it? You despised me all de time, en was al'ays sayin' mean hard things to me befo' folks, en would n't ever let me forgit I 's a nigger—en—en—"

She fell to sobbing, and broke down. Tom said—

"But you know I did n't know you were my mother; and besides—"

"Well, nemmine 'bout dat, now; let it go. I 's gwine to fo'git it." Then she added fiercely, "En don't you ever make me remember it ag'in, or you 'll be sorry, *I* tell you."

When they were parting, Tom said, in the most persuasive way he could command—

"Ma, would you mind telling me who was my father?"

He had supposed he was asking an embarrassing question. He was mistaken. Roxy drew herself up with a proud toss of her head, and said—

"Does I mine tellin' you? No, dat I don't! You ain't got no 'casion to be shame' o' yo' father, *I* kin tell you. He wuz de highest quality in dis whole town—ole Virginny stock. Fust famblies, he wuz. Jes as good stock as de Driscolls en de Howards, de bes' day dey ever seed." She put on a little prouder air, if possible, and added impressively: "Does you 'member Cunnel Cecil Burleigh Essex, dat died de same year yo' young Marse Tom Driscoll's pappy died, en all de Masons en Odd Fellers en Churches turned out en give him de bigges' funeral dis town ever seed? Dat 's de man."

Under the inspiration of her soaring complacency the departed graces of her earlier days returned to her, and her bearing took to itself a dignity and state that might have passed for queenly if her surroundings had been a little more in keeping with it.

"Dey ain't another nigger in dis town dat 's as high-bawn as you is. Now den, go 'long! En jes you hold yo' head up as high as you want to—you has de right, en dat I kin swah."

X

ALL say, "How hard it is that we have to die"—a strange complaint to come from the mouths of people who have had to live.
— *Pudd'nhead Wilson's Calendar.*

WHEN angry, count four; when very angry, swear.
— *Pudd'nhead Wilson's Calendar.*

EVERY NOW AND THEN, after Tom went to bed, he had
sudden wakings out of his sleep, and his first thought
was, "Oh, joy, it was all a dream!" Then he laid himself heavily down again, with a groan and the muttered words, "A
nigger! I am a nigger! Oh, I wish I was dead!"

He woke at dawn with one more repetition of this horror,
and then he resolved to meddle no more with that treacherous sleep. He began to think. Sufficiently bitter thinkings
they were. They wandered along something after this fashion:

"Why were niggers *and* whites made? What crime did the
uncreated first nigger commit that the curse of birth was decreed for him? And why is this awful difference made between white and black? . . . How hard the nigger's fate
seems, this morning!—yet until last night such a thought
never entered my head."

He sighed and groaned an hour or more away. Then
"Chambers" came humbly in to say that breakfast was nearly
ready. "Tom" blushed scarlet to see this aristocratic white
youth cringe to him, a nigger, and call him "Young Marster."
He said roughly—

"Get out of my sight!" and when the youth was gone, he
muttered, "He has done me no harm, poor wretch, but he is
an eyesore to me now, for he is Driscoll the young gentleman, and I am a—oh, I wish I was dead!"

A gigantic irruption, like that of Krakatoa a few years ago,
with the accompanying earthquakes, tidal waves, and clouds
of volcanic dust, changes the face of the surrounding landscape beyond recognition, bringing down the high lands, ele-
vating the low, making fair lakes where deserts had been, and
deserts where green prairies had smiled before. The tremen-

dous catastrophe which had befallen Tom had changed his moral landscape in much the same way. Some of his low places he found lifted to ideals, some of his ideals had sunk to the valleys, and lay there with the sackcloth and ashes of pumice-stone and sulphur on their ruined heads.

For days he wandered in lonely places, thinking, thinking, thinking—trying to get his bearings. It was new work. If he met a friend, he found that the habit of a lifetime had in some mysterious way vanished—his arm hung limp, instead of involuntarily extending the hand for a shake. It was the "nigger" in him asserting its humility, and he blushed and was abashed. And the "nigger" in him was surprised when the white friend put out his hand for a shake with him. He found the "nigger" in him involuntarily giving the road, on the sidewalk, to the white rowdy and loafer. When Rowena, the dearest thing his heart knew, the idol of his secret worship, invited him in, the "nigger" in him made an embarrassed excuse and was afraid to enter and sit with the dread white folks on equal terms. The "nigger" in him went shrinking and skulking here and there and yonder, and fancying it saw suspicion and maybe detection in all faces, tones, and gestures. So strange and uncharacteristic was Tom's conduct that people noticed it, and turned to look after him when he passed on; and when he glanced back as he could not help doing, in spite of his best resistance—and caught that puzzled expression in a person's face, it gave him a sick feeling, and he took himself out of view as quickly as he could. He presently came to have a hunted sense and a hunted look, and then he fled away to the hilltops and the solitudes. He said to himself that the curse of Ham was upon him.

He dreaded his meals; the "nigger" in him was ashamed to sit at the white folks' table, and feared discovery all the time; and once when Judge Driscoll said, "What 's the matter with you? You look as meek as a nigger," he felt as secret murderers are said to feel when the accuser says, "Thou art the man!" Tom said he was not well, and left the table.

His ostensible "aunt's" solicitudes and endearments were become a terror to him, and he avoided them.

And all the time, hatred of his ostensible "uncle" was steadily growing in his heart; for he said to himself, "He is white;

and I am his chattel, his property, his goods, and he can sell me, just as he could his dog."

For as much as a week after this, Tom imagined that his character had undergone a pretty radical change. But that was because he did not know himself.

In several ways his opinions were totally changed, and would never go back to what they were before, but the main structure of his character was not changed, and could not be changed. One or two very important features of it were altered, and in time effects would result from this, if opportunity offered—effects of a quite serious nature, too. Under the influence of a great mental and moral upheaval his character and habits had taken on the appearance of complete change, but after a while with the subsidence of the storm both began to settle toward their former places. He dropped gradually back into his old frivolous and easy-going ways and conditions of feeling and manner of speech, and no familiar of his could have detected anything in him that differentiated him from the weak and careless Tom of other days.

The theft-raid which he had made upon the village turned out better than he had ventured to hope. It produced the sum necessary to pay his gaming-debts, and saved him from exposure to his uncle and another smashing of the will. He and his mother learned to like each other fairly well. She could n't love him, as yet, because there "war n't nothing *to* him," as she expressed it, but her nature needed something or somebody to rule over, and he was better than nothing. Her strong character and aggressive and commanding ways compelled Tom's admiration in spite of the fact that he got more illustrations of them than he needed for his comfort. However, as a rule her conversation was made up of racy tattle about the privacies of the chief families of the town (for she went harvesting among their kitchens every time she came to the village), and Tom enjoyed this. It was just in his line. She always collected her half of his pension punctually, and he was always at the haunted house to have a chat with her on these occasions. Every now and then she paid him a visit there on between-days also.

Occasionally he would run up to St. Louis for a few weeks,

and at last temptation caught him again. He won a lot of money, but lost it, and with it a deal more besides, which he promised to raise as soon as possible.

For this purpose he projected a new raid on his town. He never meddled with any other town, for he was afraid to venture into houses whose ins and outs he did not know and the habits of whose households he was not acquainted with. He arrived at the haunted house in disguise on the Wednesday before the advent of the twins—after writing his aunt Pratt that he would not arrive until two days after—and lay in hiding there with his mother until toward daylight Friday morning, when he went to his uncle's house and entered by the back way with his own key, and slipped up to his room, where he could have the use of mirror and toilet articles. He had a suit of girl's clothes with him in a bundle as a disguise for his raid, and was wearing a suit of his mother's clothing, with black gloves and veil. By dawn he was tricked out for his raid, but he caught a glimpse of Pudd'nhead Wilson through the window over the way, and knew that Pudd'n-head had caught a glimpse of him. So he entertained Wilson with some airs and graces and attitudes for a while, then stepped out of sight and resumed the other disguise, and by and by went down and out the back way and started down town to reconnoiter the scene of his intended labors.

But he was ill at ease. He had changed back to Roxy's dress, with the stoop of age added to the disguise, so that Wilson would not bother himself about a humble old woman leaving a neighbor's house by the back way in the early morning, in case he was still spying. But supposing Wilson had seen him leave, and had thought it suspicious, and had also followed him? The thought made Tom cold. He gave up the raid for the day, and hurried back to the haunted house by the obscurest route he knew. His mother was gone; but she came back, by and by, with the news of the grand reception at Patsy Cooper's, and soon persuaded him that the opportunity was like a special providence, it was so inviting and perfect. So he went raiding, after all, and made a nice success of it while everybody was gone to Patsy Cooper's. Success gave him nerve and even actual intrepidity; insomuch, indeed, that after he had conveyed his harvest to his mother in a back alley, he went to the reception himself, and added several of the valuables of that house to his takings.

AFTER this long digression we have now arrived once more at the point where Pudd'nhead Wilson, while waiting for the arrival of the twins on that same Friday evening, sat puzzling over the strange apparition of that morning—a girl in young Tom Driscoll's bedroom; fretting, and guessing, and puzzling over it, and wondering who the shameless creature might be.

XI

THERE ARE three infallible ways of pleasing an author, and the three form a rising scale of compliment: 1, to tell him you have read one of his books; 2, to tell him you have read all of his books; 3, to ask him to let you read the manuscript of his forthcoming book. No. 1 admits you to his respect; No. 2 admits you to his admiration; No. 3 carries you clear into his heart.
— *Pudd'nhead Wilson's Calendar.*

As to the Adjective: when in doubt, strike it out.
— *Pudd'nhead Wilson's Calendar.*

THE TWINS arrived presently, and talk began. It flowed along chattily and sociably, and under its influence the new friendship gathered ease and strength. Wilson got out his Calendar, by request, and read a passage or two from it, which the twins praised quite cordially. This pleased the author so much that he complied gladly when they asked him to lend them a batch of the work to read at home. In the course of their wide travels they had found out that there are three sure ways of pleasing an author; they were now working the best of the three.

There was an interruption, now. Young Tom Driscoll appeared, and joined the party. He pretended to be seeing the distinguished strangers for the first time when they rose to shake hands; but this was only a blind, as he had already had a glimpse of them at the reception, while robbing the house. The twins made mental note that he was smooth-faced and rather handsome, and smooth and undulatory in his movements—graceful, in fact. Angelo thought he had a good eye; Luigi thought there was something veiled and sly about it. Angelo thought he had a pleasant free-and-easy way of talking; Luigi thought it was more so than was agreeable. Angelo thought he was a sufficiently nice young man; Luigi reserved his decision. Tom's first contribution to the conversation was a question which he had put to Wilson a hundred times before. It was always cheerily and good-naturedly put, and always inflicted a little pang, for it touched a secret sore; but this time the pang was sharp, since strangers were present.

"Well, how does the law come on? Had a case yet?"

Wilson bit his lip, but answered, "No—not yet," with as much indifference as he could assume. Judge Driscoll had generously left the law feature out of the Wilson biography which he had furnished to the twins. Young Tom laughed pleasantly, and said:

"Wilson 's a lawyer, gentlemen, but he does n't practise now."

The sarcasm bit, but Wilson kept himself under control, and said without passion:

"I don't practise, it is true. It is true that I have never had a case, and have had to earn a poor living for twenty years as an expert accountant in a town where I can't get hold of a set of books to untangle as often as I should like. But it is also true that I did fit myself well for the practice of the law. By the time I was your age, Tom, I had chosen a profession, and was soon competent to enter upon it." Tom winced. "I never got a chance to try my hand at it, and I may never get a chance; and yet if I ever do get it I shall be found ready, for I have kept up my law-studies all these years."

"That 's it; that 's good grit! I like to see it. I 've a notion to throw all my business your way. My business and your law-practice ought to make a pretty gay team, Dave," and the young fellow laughed again.

"If you will throw—" Wilson had thought of the girl in Tom's bedroom, and was going to say, "If you will throw the surreptitious and disreputable part of your business my way, it may amount to something"; but thought better of it and said, "However, this matter does n't fit well in a general conversation."

"All right, we 'll change the subject; I guess you were about to give me another dig, anyway, so I'm willing to change. How 's the Awful Mystery flourishing these days? Wilson 's got a scheme for driving plain window-glass out of the market by decorating it with greasy finger-marks, and getting rich by selling it at famine prices to the crowned heads over in Europe to outfit their palaces with. Fetch it out, Dave."

Wilson brought three of his glass strips, and said—

"I get the subject to pass the fingers of his right hand through his hair, so as to get a little coating of the natural oil on them, and then press the balls of them on the glass. A fine and delicate print of the lines in the skin results, and is permanent, if it does n't come in contact with something able to rub it off. You begin, Tom."

"Why, I think you took my finger-marks once or twice before."

"Yes; but you were a little boy the last time, only about twelve years old."

"That 's so. Of course I 've changed entirely since then, and variety is what the crowned heads want, I guess."

He passed his fingers through his crop of short hair, and pressed them one at a time on the glass. Angelo made a print of his fingers on another glass, and Luigi followed with the third. Wilson marked the glasses with names and date, and put them away. Tom gave one of his little laughs, and said—

"I thought I would n't say anything, but if variety is what you are after, you have wasted a piece of glass. The hand-print of one twin is the same as the hand-print of the fellow-twin."

"Well, it 's done now, and I like to have them both, anyway," said Wilson, returning to his place.

"But look here, Dave," said Tom, "you used to tell people's fortunes, too, when you took their finger-marks. Dave 's just an all-round genius—a genius of the first water, gentlemen; a great scientist running to seed here in this village, a prophet with the kind of honor that prophets generally get at home— for here they don't give shucks for his scientifics, and they call his skull a notion-factory—hey, Dave, ain't it so? But never mind; he 'll make his mark some day—finger-mark, you know, he-he! But really, you want to let him take a shy at your palms once; it 's worth twice the price of admission or your money 's returned at the door. Why, he 'll read your wrinkles as easy as a book, and not only tell you fifty or sixty things that 's going to happen to you, but fifty or sixty thousand that ain't. Come, Dave, show the gentlemen what an inspired Jack-at-all-science we 've got in this town, and don't know it."

Wilson winced under this nagging and not very courteous chaff, and the twins suffered with him and for him. They rightly judged, now, that the best way to relieve him would be to take the thing in earnest and treat it with respect, ignoring Tom's rather overdone raillery; so Luigi said—

"We have seen something of palmistry in our wanderings, and know very well what astonishing things it can do. If it is n't a science, and one of the greatest of them, too, I don't know what its other name ought to be. In the Orient—"

Tom looked surprised and incredulous. He said—

"That juggling a science? But really, you ain't serious, are you?"

"Yes, entirely so. Four years ago we had our hands read out to us as if our palms had been covered with print."

"Well, do you mean to say there was actually anything in it?" asked Tom, his incredulity beginning to weaken a little.

"There was this much in it," said Angelo; "what was told us of our characters was minutely exact—we could not have bettered it ourselves. Next, two or three memorable things that had happened to us were laid bare—things which no one present but ourselves could have known about."

"Why, it 's rank sorcery!" exclaimed Tom, who was now becoming very much interested. "And how did they make out with what was going to happen to you in the future?"

"On the whole, quite fairly," said Luigi. "Two or three of the most striking things foretold have happened since; much the most striking one of all happened within that same year. Some of the minor prophecies have come true; some of the minor and some of the major ones have not been fulfilled yet, and of course may never be: still, I should be more surprised if they failed to arrive than if they did n't."

Tom was entirely sobered, and profoundly impressed. He said, apologetically—

"Dave, I was n't meaning to belittle that science; I was only chaffing—chattering, I reckon I 'd better say. I wish you would look at their palms. Come, won't you?"

"Why, certainly, if you want me to; but you know I 've had no chance to become an expert, and don't claim to be one. When a past event is somewhat prominently recorded in the palm I can generally detect that, but minor ones often escape me,—not always, of course, but often,—but I have n't much confidence in myself when it comes to reading the future. I am talking as if palmistry was a daily study with me, but that is not so. I have n't examined half a dozen hands in the last half dozen years; you see, the people got to joking about it, and I stopped to let the talk die down. I 'll tell you what we 'll do, Count Luigi: I 'll make a try at your past, and if I have any success there—no, on the whole, I 'll let the future alone; that 's really the affair of an expert."

He took Luigi's hand. Tom said—

"Wait—don't look yet, Dave! Count Luigi, here 's paper and pencil. Set down that thing that you said was the most striking one that was foretold to you, and happened less than a year afterward, and give it to me so I can see if Dave finds it in your hand."

Luigi wrote a line privately, and folded up the piece of paper, and handed it to Tom, saying—

"I 'll tell you when to look at it, if he finds it."

Wilson began to study Luigi's palm, tracing life lines, heart lines, head lines, and so on, and noting carefully their relations with the cobweb of finer and more delicate marks and lines that enmeshed them on all sides; he felt of the fleshy cushion at the base of the thumb, and noted its shape; he felt of the fleshy side of the hand between the wrist and the base of the little finger, and noted its shape also; he painstakingly examined the fingers, observing their form, proportions, and natural manner of disposing themselves when in repose. All this process was watched by the three spectators with absorbing interest, their heads bent together over Luigi's palm, and nobody disturbing the stillness with a word. Wilson now entered upon a close survey of the palm again, and his revelations began.

He mapped out Luigi's character and disposition, his tastes, aversions, proclivities, ambitions, and eccentricities in a way which sometimes made Luigi wince and the others laugh, but both twins declared that the chart was artistically drawn and was correct.

Next, Wilson took up Luigi's history. He proceeded cautiously and with hesitation, now, moving his finger slowly along the great lines of the palm, and now and then halting it at a "star" or some such landmark, and examining that neighborhood minutely. He proclaimed one or two past events, Luigi confirmed his correctness, and the search went on. Presently Wilson glanced up suddenly with a surprised expression—

"Here is record of an incident which you would perhaps not wish me to—"

"Bring it out," said Luigi, good-naturedly; "I promise you it sha'n't embarrass me."

But Wilson still hesitated, and did not seem quite to know what to do. Then he said—

"I think it is too delicate a matter to—to—I believe I would rather write it or whisper it to you, and let you decide for yourself whether you want it talked out or not."

"That will answer," said Luigi; "write it."

Wilson wrote something on a slip of paper and handed it to Luigi, who read it to himself and said to Tom—

"Unfold your slip and read it, Mr. Driscoll."

Tom read:

"It was prophesied that I would kill a man. It came true before the year was out."

Tom added, "Great Scott!"

Luigi handed Wilson's paper to Tom, and said—

"Now read this one."

Tom read:

"You have killed some one, but whether man, woman or child, I do not make out."

"Cæsar's ghost!" commented Tom, with astonishment. "It beats anything that was ever heard of! Why, a man's own hand is his deadliest enemy! Just think of that—a man's own hand keeps a record of the deepest and fatalest secrets of his life, and is treacherously ready to expose him to any black-magic stranger that comes along. But what do you let a person look at your hand for, with that awful thing printed in it?"

"Oh," said Luigi, reposefully, "I don't mind it. I killed the man for good reasons, and I don't regret it."

"What were the reasons?"

"Well, he needed killing."

"I 'll tell you why he did it, since he won't say himself," said Angelo, warmly. "He did it to save my life, that 's what he did it for. So it was a noble act, and not a thing to be hid in the dark."

"So it was, so it was," said Wilson; "to do such a thing to save a brother's life is a great and fine action."

"Now come," said Luigi, "it is very pleasant to hear you say these things, but for unselfishness, or heroism, or magnanimity, the circumstances won't stand scrutiny. You overlook one detail: suppose I had n't saved Angelo's life, what would have become of mine? If I had let the man kill him, would n't he have killed me, too? I saved my own life, you see."

"Yes; that is your way of talking," said Angelo, "but I know you—I don't believe you thought of yourself at all. I keep that weapon yet that Luigi killed the man with, and I 'll show it to you some time. That incident makes it interesting, and it had a history before it came into Luigi's hands which adds to its interest. It was given to Luigi by a great Indian prince, the Gaikowar of Baroda, and it had been in his family two or three centuries. It killed a good many disagreeable people who troubled that hearthstone at one time and another. It is n't much to look at, except that it is n't shaped like other knives, or dirks, or whatever it may be called— here, I 'll draw it for you." He took a sheet of paper and made a rapid sketch. "There it is—a broad and murderous blade, with edges like a razor for sharpness. The devices engraved on it are the ciphers or names of its long line of possessors—I had Luigi's name added in Roman letters myself with our coat of arms, as you see. You notice what a curious handle the thing has. It is solid ivory, polished like a mirror, and is four or five inches long—round, and as thick as a large man's wrist, with the end squared off flat, for your thumb to rest on; for you grasp it, with your thumb resting on the blunt end—so—and lift it aloft and strike downward. The Gaikowar showed us how the thing was done when he gave it to Luigi, and before that night was ended Luigi had used the knife, and the Gaikowar was a man short by reason of it. The sheath is magnificently ornamented with gems of great value. You will find the sheath more worth looking at than the knife itself, of course."

Tom said to himself—

"It's lucky I came here. I would have sold that knife for a song; I supposed the jewels were glass."

"But go on; don't stop," said Wilson. "Our curiosity is up now, to hear about the homicide. Tell us about that."

"Well, briefly, the knife was to blame for that, all around. A native servant slipped into our room in the palace in the night, to kill us and steal the knife on account of the fortune incrusted on its sheath, without a doubt. Luigi had it under his pillow; we were in bed together. There was a dim night-light burning. I was asleep, but Luigi was awake, and he thought he detected a vague form nearing the bed. He slipped the knife out of the sheath and was ready, and unembarrassed by hampering bed-clothes, for the weather was hot and we had n't any. Suddenly that native rose at the bedside, and bent over me with his right hand lifted and a dirk in it aimed at my throat; but Luigi grabbed his wrist, pulled him downward, and drove his own knife into the man's neck. That is the whole story."

Wilson and Tom drew deep breaths, and after some general chat about the tragedy, Pudd'nhead said, taking Tom's hand—

"Now, Tom, I 've never had a look at your palms, as it happens; perhaps you 've got some little questionable privacies that need—hel-lo!"

Tom had snatched away his hand, and was looking a good deal confused.

"Why, he 's blushing!" said Luigi.

Tom darted an ugly look at him, and said sharply—

"Well, if I am, it ain't because I 'm a murderer!" Luigi's dark face flushed, but before he could speak or move, Tom added with anxious haste: "Oh, I beg a thousand pardons. I did n't mean that; it was out before I thought, and I 'm very, very sorry—you must forgive me!"

Wilson came to the rescue, and smoothed things down as well as he could; and in fact was entirely successful as far as the twins were concerned, for they felt sorrier for the affront put upon him by his guest's outburst of ill manners than for the insult offered to Luigi. But the success was not so pronounced with the offender. Tom tried to seem at his ease, and he went through the motions fairly well, but at bottom

e felt resentful toward all the three witnesses of his exhibi-
ion; in fact, he felt so annoyed at them for having witnessed
: and noticed it that he almost forgot to feel annoyed at him-
elf for placing it before them. However, something presently
happened which made him almost comfortable, and brought
him nearly back to a state of charity and friendliness. This was
. little spat between the twins; not much of a spat, but still a
pat; and before they got far with it they were in a decided
condition of irritation with each other. Tom was charmed; so
pleased, indeed, that he cautiously did what he could to increase the irritation while pretending to be actuated by more
respectable motives. By his help the fire got warmed up to
he blazing-point, and he might have had the happiness of
seeing the flames show up, in another moment, but for the
interruption of a knock on the door—an interruption which
fretted him as much as it gratified Wilson. Wilson opened the
door.

The visitor was a good-natured, ignorant, energetic, middle-aged Irishman named John Buckstone, who was a great
politician in a small way, and always took a large share in
public matters of every sort. One of the town's chief excite-
ments, just now, was over the matter of rum. There was a
strong rum party and a strong anti-rum party. Buckstone was
training with the rum party, and he had been sent to hunt up
the twins and invite them to attend a mass-meeting of that
faction. He delivered his errand, and said the clans were already gathering in the big hall over the market-house. Luigi
accepted the invitation cordially, Angelo less cordially, since
he disliked crowds, and did not drink the powerful intoxi-
cants of America. In fact, he was even a teetotaler sometimes—when it was judicious to be one.

The twins left with Buckstone, and Tom Driscoll joined
company with them uninvited.

In the distance one could see a long wavering line of
torches drifting down the main street, and could hear the
throbbing of the bass drum, the clash of cymbals, the squeaking of a fife or two, and the faint roar of remote hurrahs. The
tail-end of this procession was climbing the market-house
stairs when the twins arrived in its neighborhood; when they
reached the hall it was full of people, torches, smoke, noise,

and enthusiasm. They were conducted to the platform b' Buckstone—Tom Driscoll still following—and were deliv'ered to the chairman in the midst of a prodigious explosion of welcome. When the noise had moderated a little, the chai' proposed that "our illustrious guests be at once elected, b' complimentary acclamation, to membership in our ever-glo'rious organization, the paradise of the free and the perdition of the slave."

This eloquent discharge opened the flood-gates of enthusi'asm again, and the election was carried with thundering una'nimity. Then arose a storm of cries:

"Wet them down! Wet them down! Give them a drink!"

Glasses of whisky were handed to the twins. Luigi waved his aloft, then brought it to his lips; but Angelo set his down There was another storm of cries:

"What 's the matter with the other one?" "What is the blond one going back on us for?" "Explain! Explain!"

The chairman inquired, and then reported—

"We have made an unfortunate mistake, gentlemen. I find that the Count Angelo Cappello is opposed to our creed—is a teetotaler, in fact, and was not intending to apply for mem-bership with us. He desires that we reconsider the vote by which he was elected. What is the pleasure of the house?"

There was a general burst of laughter, plentifully accented with whistlings and cat-calls, but the energetic use of the gavel presently restored something like order. Then a man spoke from the crowd, and said that while he was very sorry that the mistake had been made, it would not be possible to rectify it at the present meeting. According to the by-laws it must go over to the next regular meeting for action. He would not offer a motion, as none was required. He desired to apologize to the gentleman in the name of the house, and begged to assure him that as far as it might lie in the power of the Sons of Liberty, his temporary membership in the or-der would be made pleasant to him.

This speech was received with great applause, mixed with cries of—

"That 's the talk!" "He 's a good fellow, any way, if he *is* a teetotaler!" "Drink his health!" "Give him a rouser, and no heel-taps!"

Glasses were handed around, and everybody on the platform drank Angelo's health, while the house bellowed forth
in song:

> For he 's a jolly good fel-low,
> For he 's a jolly good fel-low,
> For he 's a jolly good fe-el-low,—
> Which nobody can deny.

Tom Driscoll drank. It was his second glass, for he had
drunk Angelo's the moment that Angelo had set it down. The
two drinks made him very merry—almost idiotically so—and
he began to take a most lively and prominent part in the proceedings, particularly in the music and cat-call and side-
remarks.

The chairman was still standing at the front, the twins at
his side. The extraordinarily close resemblance of the brothers
to each other suggested a witticism to Tom Driscoll, and just
as the chairman began a speech he skipped forward and said
with an air of tipsy confidence to the audience—

"Boys, I move that he keeps still and lets this human philopena snip you out a speech."

The descriptive aptness of the phrase caught the house, and
a mighty burst of laughter followed.

Luigi's southern blood leaped to the boiling-point in a moment under the sharp humiliation of this insult delivered in
the presence of four hundred strangers. It was not in the
young man's nature to let the matter pass, or to delay the
squaring of the account. He took a couple of strides and
halted behind the unsuspecting joker. Then he drew back and
delivered a kick of such titanic vigor that it lifted Tom clear
over the footlights and landed him on the heads of the front
row of the Sons of Liberty.

Even a sober person does not like to have a human being
emptied on him when he is not doing any harm; a person
who is not sober cannot endure such an attention at all. The
nest of Sons of Liberty that Driscoll landed in had not a sober
bird in it; in fact there was probably not an entirely sober one
in the auditorium. Driscoll was promptly and indignantly
flung on to the heads of Sons in the next row, and these Sons

passed him on toward the rear, and then immediately began to pummel the front-row Sons who had passed him to them. This course was strictly followed by bench after bench as Driscoll traveled in his tumultuous and airy flight toward the door; so he left behind him an ever lengthening wake of raging and plunging and fighting and swearing humanity. Down went group after group of torches, and presently above the deafening clatter of the gavel, roar of angry voices, and crash of succumbing benches, rose the paralyzing cry of

"FIRE!"

The fighting ceased instantly; the cursing ceased; for one distinctly defined moment there was a dead hush, a motionless calm, where the tempest had been; then with one impulse the multitude awoke to life and energy again, and went surging and struggling and swaying, this way and that, its outer edges melting away through windows and doors and gradually lessening the pressure and relieving the mass.

The fire-boys were never on hand so suddenly before; for there was no distance to go, this time, their quarters being in the rear end of the market-house. There was an engine company and a hook-and-ladder company. Half of each was composed of rummies and the other half of anti-rummies, after the moral and political share-and-share-alike fashion of the frontier town of the period. Enough anti-rummies were loafing in quarters to man the engine and the ladders. In two minutes they had their red shirts and helmets on—they never stirred officially in unofficial costume—and as the mass meeting overhead smashed through the long row of windows and poured out upon the roof of the arcade, the deliverers were ready for them with a powerful stream of water which washed some of them off the roof and nearly drowned the rest. But water was preferable to fire, and still the stampede from the windows continued, and still the pitiless drenchings assailed it until the building was empty; then the fire-boys mounted to the hall and flooded it with water enough to annihilate forty times as much fire as there was there; for a village fire-company does not often get a chance to show off, and so when it does get a chance it makes the most of it. Such citizens of that village as were of a thoughtful and judicious temperament did not insure against fire; they insured against the fire-company.

XII

COURAGE is resistance to fear, mastery of fear—not absence of fear. Except a creature be part coward it is not a compliment to say it is brave; it is merely a loose misapplication of the word. Consider the flea!—incomparably the bravest of all the creatures of God, if ignorance of fear were courage. Whether you are asleep or awake he will attack you, caring nothing for the fact that in bulk and strength you are to him as are the massed armies of the earth to a sucking child; he lives both day and night and all days and nights in the very lap of peril and the immediate presence of death, and yet is no more afraid than is the man who walks the streets of a city that was threatened by an earthquake ten centuries before. When we speak of Clive, Nelson, and Putnam as men who "did n't know what fear was," we ought always to add the flea—and put him at the head of the procession.

— Pudd'nhead Wilson's Calendar.

JUDGE DRISCOLL was in bed and asleep by ten o'clock on Friday night, and he was up and gone a-fishing before daylight in the morning with his friend Pembroke Howard. These two had been boys together in Virginia when that State still ranked as the chief and most imposing member of the Union, and they still coupled the proud and affectionate adjective "old" with her name when they spoke of her. In Missouri a recognized superiority attached to any person who hailed from Old Virginia; and this superiority was exalted to supremacy when a person of such nativity could also prove descent from the First Families of that great commonwealth. The Howards and Driscolls were of this aristocracy. In their eyes it was a nobility. It had its unwritten laws, and they were as clearly defined and as strict as any that could be found among the printed statutes of the land. The F. F. V. was born a gentleman; his highest duty in life was to watch over that great inheritance and keep it unsmirched. He must keep his honor spotless. Those laws were his chart; his course was marked out on it; if he swerved from it by so much as half a point of the compass it meant shipwreck to his honor; that is to say, degradation from his rank as a gentleman. These laws required certain things of him which his religion might forbid: then his religion must yield—the laws could not be relaxed to accommodate religions or anything else. Honor stood first; and the laws defined what it was and wherein it differed in certain details from honor as defined by church creeds and by the social laws and customs of some of the minor divisions of the globe that had got crowded out when the sacred boundaries of Virginia were staked out.

If Judge Driscoll was the recognized first citizen of Dawson's Landing, Pembroke Howard was easily its recognized second citizen. He was called "the great lawyer"—an earned title. He and Driscoll were of the same age—a year or two past sixty.

Although Driscoll was a free-thinker and Howard a strong and determined Presbyterian, their warm intimacy suffered no impairment in consequence. They were men whose opinions were their own property and not subject to revision and amendment, suggestion or criticism, by anybody, even their friends.

The day's fishing finished, they came floating down stream in their skiff, talking national politics and other high matters, and presently met a skiff coming up from town, with a man in it who said:

"I reckon you know one of the new twins gave your nephew a kicking last night, Judge?"

"Did *what*?"

"Gave him a kicking."

The old Judge's lips paled, and his eyes began to flame. He choked with anger for a moment, then he got out what he was trying to say—

"Well—well—go on! Give me the details."

The man did it. At the finish the Judge was silent a minute, turning over in his mind the shameful picture of Tom's flight over the footlights; then he said, as if musing aloud—

"H'm—I don't understand it. I was asleep at home. He didn't wake me. Thought he was competent to manage his affair without my help, I reckon." His face lit up with pride and pleasure at that thought, and he said with a cheery complacency, "I like that—it 's the true old blood—hey, Pembroke?"

Howard smiled an iron smile, and nodded his head approvingly. Then the news-bringer spoke again—

"But Tom beat the twin on the trial."

The Judge looked at the man wonderingly, and said—

"The trial? What trial?"

"Why, Tom had him up before Judge Robinson for assault and battery."

The old man shrank suddenly together like one who has received a death-stroke. Howard sprang for him as he sank forward in a swoon, and took him in his arms, and bedded him on his back in the boat. He sprinkled water in his face, and said to the startled visitor—

"Go, now—don't let him come to and find you here. You see what an effect your heedless speech has had; you ought to have been more considerate than to blurt out such a cruel piece of slander as that."

"I 'm right down sorry I did it now, Mr. Howard, and I would n't have done it if I had thought: but it ain't a slander; it 's perfectly true, just as I told him."

He rowed away. Presently the old Judge came out of his faint and looked up piteously into the sympathetic face that was bent over him.

"Say it ain't true, Pembroke; tell me it ain't true!" he said in a weak voice.

There was nothing weak in the deep organ-tones that responded—

"You know it 's a lie as well as I do, old friend. He is of the best blood of the Old Dominion."

"God bless you for saying it!" said the old gentleman, fervently. "Ah, Pembroke, it was such a blow!"

Howard stayed by his friend, and saw him home, and entered the house with him. It was dark, and past supper-time, but the Judge was not thinking of supper; he was eager to hear the slander refuted from headquarters, and as eager to have Howard hear it, too. Tom was sent for, and he came immediately. He was bruised and lame, and was not a happy-looking object. His uncle made him sit down, and said—

"We have been hearing about your adventure, Tom, with a handsome lie added to it for embellishment. Now pulverize that lie to dust! What measures have you taken? How does the thing stand?"

Tom answered guilelessly: "It don't stand at all; it 's all over. I had him up in court and beat him. Pudd'nhead Wilson defended him—first case he ever had, and lost it. The judge fined the miserable hound five dollars for the assault."

Howard and the Judge sprang to their feet with the opening sentence—why, neither knew; then they stood gazing vacantly at each other. Howard stood a moment, then sat mournfully down without saying anything. The Judge's wrath began to kindle, and he burst out—

"You cur! You scum! You vermin! Do you mean to tell me that blood of my race has suffered a blow and crawled to a court of law about it? Answer me!"

Tom's head drooped, and he answered with an eloquent silence. His uncle stared at him with a mixed expression of amazement and shame and incredulity that was sorrowful to see. At last he said—

"Which of the twins was it?"

"Count Luigi."

"You have challenged him?"

"N—no," hesitated Tom, turning pale.

"You will challenge him to-night. Howard will carry it."

Tom began to turn sick, and to show it. He turned his hat round and round in his hand, his uncle glowering blacker and blacker upon him as the heavy seconds drifted by; then at last he began to stammer, and said piteously—

"Oh, please don't ask me to do it, uncle! He is a murderous devil—I never could—I—I 'm afraid of him!"

Old Driscoll's mouth opened and closed three times before he could get it to perform its office; then he stormed out—

"A coward in my family! A Driscoll a coward! Oh, what have I done to deserve this infamy!" He tottered to his secretary in the corner repeating that lament again and again in heartbreaking tones, and got out of a drawer a paper, which he slowly tore to bits scattering the bits absently in his track as he walked up and down the room, still grieving and lamenting. At last he said—

"There it is, shreds and fragments once more—my will. Once more you have forced me to disinherit you, you base son of a most noble father! Leave my sight! Go—before I spit on you!"

The young man did not tarry. Then the Judge turned to Howard:

"You will be my second, old friend?"

"Of course."

"There is pen and paper. Draft the cartel, and lose no time."

"The Count shall have it in his hands in fifteen minutes," said Howard.

Tom was very heavy-hearted. His appetite was gone with his property and his self-respect. He went out the back way and wandered down the obscure lane grieving, and wondering if any course of future conduct, however discreet and carefully perfected and watched over, could win back his uncle's favor and persuade him to reconstruct once more that generous will which had just gone to ruin before his eyes. He finally concluded that it could. He said to himself that he had accomplished this sort of triumph once already, and that what had been done once could be done again. He would set about it. He would bend every energy to the task, and he would score that triumph once more, cost what it might to his convenience, limit as it might his frivolous and liberty-loving life.

"To begin," he said to himself, "I 'll square up with the proceeds of my raid, and then gambling has got to be stopped—and stopped short off. It 's the worst vice I 've got—from my standpoint, anyway, because it 's the one he can most easily find out, through the impatience of my creditors. He thought it expensive to have to pay two hundred dollars to them for me once. Expensive—*that!* Why, it cost me the whole of his fortune—but of course he never thought of that; some people can't think of any but their own side of a case. If he had known how deep I am in, now, the will would have gone to pot without waiting for a duel to help. Three hundred dollars! It 's a pile! But he 'll never hear of it, I 'm thankful to say. The minute I 've cleared it off, I 'm safe; and I 'll never touch a card again. Anyway, I won't while he lives, I make oath to that. I 'm entering on my last reform— I know it—yes, and I 'll win; but after that, if I ever slip again I 'm gone."

XIII

THUS MOURNFULLY COMMUNING with himself Tom moped along the lane past Pudd'nhead Wilson's house, and still on and on between fences inclosing vacant country on each hand till he neared the haunted house, then he came moping back again, with many sighs and heavy with trouble. He sorely wanted cheerful company. Rowena! His heart gave a bound at the thought, but the next thought quieted it—the detested twins would be there.

He was on the inhabited side of Wilson's house, and now as he approached it he noticed that the sitting-room was lighted. This would do; others made him feel unwelcome sometimes, but Wilson never failed in courtesy toward him, and a kindly courtesy does at least save one's feelings, even if it is not professing to stand for a welcome. Wilson heard footsteps at his threshold, then the clearing of a throat.

"It's that fickle-tempered, dissipated young goose—poor devil, he finds friends pretty scarce to-day, likely, after the disgrace of carrying a personal-assault case into a law-court."

A dejected knock. "Come in!"

Tom entered, and drooped into a chair, without saying anything. Wilson said kindly—

"Why, my boy, you look desolate. Don't take it so hard. Try and forget you have been kicked."

"Oh, dear," said Tom, wretchedly, "it 's not that, Pudd'n-head—it 's not that. It's a thousand times worse than that—oh, yes, a million times worse."

"Why, Tom, what do you mean? Has Rowena—"

"Flung me? No, but the old man has."

Wilson said to himself, "Aha!" and thought of the mysterious girl in the bedroom. "The Driscolls have been making discoveries!" Then he said aloud, gravely:

"Tom, there are some kinds of dissipation which—"

"Oh, shucks, this has n't got anything to do with dissipation. He wanted me to challenge that derned Italian savage, and I would n't do it."

"Yes, of course he would do that," said Wilson in a meditative matter-of-course way; "but the thing that puzzled me was, why he did n't look to that last night, for one thing, and why he let you carry such a matter into a court of law at all, either before the duel or after it. It 's no place for it. It was not like him. I could n't understand it. How did it happen?"

"It happened because he did n't know anything about it. He was asleep when I got home last night."

"And you did n't wake him? Tom, is that possible?"

Tom was not getting much comfort here. He fidgeted a moment, then said:

"I did n't choose to tell him—that 's all. He was going a-fishing before dawn, with Pembroke Howard, and if I got the twins into the common calaboose—and I thought sure I could—I never dreamed of their slipping out on a paltry fine for such an outrageous offense—well, once in the calaboose they would be disgraced, and uncle would n't want any duels with that sort of characters, and would n't allow any."

"Tom, I am ashamed of you! I don't see how you could treat your good old uncle so. I am a better friend of his than you are; for if I had known the circumstances I would have kept that case out of court until I got word to him and let him have a gentleman's chance."

"You would?" exclaimed Tom, with lively surprise. "And it your first case! And you know perfectly well there never would have been any case if he had got that chance, don't you? And you 'd have finished your days a pauper nobody, instead of being an actually launched and recognized lawyer to-day. And you would really have done that, would you?"

"Certainly."

Tom looked at him a moment or two, then shook his head sorrowfully and said—

"I believe you—upon my word I do. I don't know why I do, but I do. Pudd'nhead Wilson, I think you 're the biggest fool I ever saw."

"Thank you."

"Don't mention it."

"Well, he has been requiring you to fight the Italian and you have refused. You degenerate remnant of an honorable line! I 'm thoroughly ashamed of you, Tom!"

"Oh, that 's nothing! I don't care for anything, now that the will 's torn up again."

"Tom, tell me squarely—did n't he find any fault with you for anything but those two things—carrying the case into court and refusing to fight?"

He watched the young fellow's face narrowly, but it was entirely reposeful, and so also was the voice that answered:

"No, he did n't find any other fault with me. If he had had any to find, he would have begun yesterday, for he was just in the humor for it. He drove that jack-pair around town and showed them the sights, and when he came home he could n't find his father's old silver watch that don't keep time and he thinks so much of, and could n't remember what he did with it three or four days ago when he saw it last; and so when I arrived he was all in a sweat about it, and when I suggested that it probably was n't lost but stolen, it put him in a regular passion and he said I was a fool—which convinced me, without any trouble, that that was just what he was afraid *had* happened, himself, but did not want to believe it, because lost things stand a better chance of being found again than stolen ones."

"Whe-ew!" whistled Wilson; "score another on the list."

"Another what?"

"Another theft!"

"Theft?"

"Yes, theft. That watch is n't lost, it 's stolen. There 's been another raid on the town—and just the same old mysterious sort of thing that has happened once before, as you remember."

"You don't mean it!"

"It 's as sure as you are born! Have you missed anything yourself?"

"No. That is, I did miss a silver pencil-case that Aunt Mary Pratt gave me last birthday—"

"You 'll find it 's stolen—that 's what you 'll find."

"No, I sha'n't; for when I suggested theft about the watch and got such a rap, I went and examined my room, and the pencil-case was missing, but it was only mislaid, and I found it again."

"You are sure you missed nothing else?"

"Well, nothing of consequence. I missed a small plain gold ring worth two or three dollars, but that will turn up. I 'll look again."

"In my opinion you 'll not find it. There 's been a raid, I tell you. Come *in!*"

Mr. Justice Robinson entered, followed by Buckstone and the town-constable, Jim Blake. They sat down, and after some wandering and aimless weather-conversation Wilson said—

"By the way, we 've just added another to the list of thefts, maybe two. Judge Driscoll's old silver watch is gone, and Tom here has missed a gold ring."

"Well, it is a bad business," said the Justice, "and gets worse the further it goes. The Hankses, the Dobsons, the Pilligrews, the Ortons, the Grangers, the Hales, the Fullers, the Holcombs, in fact everybody that lives around about Patsy Cooper's has been robbed of little things like trinkets and teaspoons and such-like small valuables that are easily carried off. It 's perfectly plain that the thief took advantage of the reception at Patsy Cooper's, when all the neighbors were in her house and all their niggers hanging around her fence for a look at the show, to raid the vacant houses undisturbed. Patsy is miserable about it; miserable on account of the neighbors, and particularly miserable on account of her foreigners, of course; so miserable on their account that she has n't any room to worry about her own little losses."

"It 's the same old raider," said Wilson. "I suppose there is n't any doubt about that."

"Constable Blake does n't think so."

"No, you 're wrong there," said Blake; "the other times it was a man; there was plenty of signs of that, as we know, in the profession, though we never got hands on him; but this time it 's a woman."

Wilson thought of the mysterious girl straight off. She was always in his mind now. But she failed him again. Blake continued:

"She 's a stoop-shouldered old woman with a covered basket on her arm, in a black veil, dressed in mourning. I saw her going aboard the ferry-boat yesterday. Lives in Illinois, I reckon; but I don't care where she lives, I 'm going to get her—she can make herself sure of that."

"What makes you think she 's the thief?"

"Well, there ain't any other, for one thing; and for another, some of the nigger draymen that happened to be driving along saw her coming out of or going into houses, and told me so—and it just happens that they was *robbed* houses, every time."

It was granted that this was plenty good enough circumstantial evidence. A pensive silence followed, which lasted some moments, then Wilson said—

"There 's one good thing, anyway. She can't either pawn or sell Count Luigi's costly Indian dagger."

"My!" said Tom, "is *that* gone?"

"Yes."

"Well, that was a haul! But why can't she pawn it or sell it?"

"Because when the twins went home from the Sons of Liberty meeting last night, news of the raid was sifting in from everywhere, and Aunt Patsy was in distress to know if they had lost anything. They found that the dagger was gone, and they notified the police and pawnbrokers everywhere. It was a great haul, yes, but the old woman won't get anything out of it, because she 'll get caught."

"Did they offer a reward?" asked Buckstone.

"Yes; five hundred dollars for the knife, and five hundred more for the thief."

"What a leather-headed idea!" exclaimed the constable. "The thief da's n't go near them, nor send anybody. Whoever goes is going to get himself nabbed, for there ain't any pawnbroker that 's going to lose the chance to—"

If anybody had noticed Tom's face at that time, the gray-green color of it might have provoked curiosity; but nobody did. He said to himself: "I 'm gone! I never can square up;

the rest of the plunder won't pawn or sell for half of the bill. Oh, I know it—I 'm gone, I 'm gone—and this time it 's for good. Oh, this is awful—I don't know what to do, nor which way to turn!"

"Softly, softly," said Wilson to Blake. "I planned their scheme for them at midnight last night, and it was all finished up shipshape by two this morning. They 'll get their dagger back, and then I 'll explain to you how the thing was done."

There were strong signs of a general curiosity, and Buckstone said—

"Well, you have whetted us up pretty sharp, Wilson, and I 'm free to say that if you don't mind telling us in confidence—"

"Oh, I 'd as soon tell as not, Buckstone, but as long as the twins and I agreed to say nothing about it, we must let it stand so. But you can take my word for it you won't be kept waiting three days. Somebody will apply for that reward pretty promptly, and I 'll show you the thief and the dagger both very soon afterward."

The constable was disappointed, and also perplexed. He said—

"It may all be—yes, and I hope it will, but I 'm blamed if I can see my way through it. It 's too many for yours truly."

The subject seemed about talked out. Nobody seemed to have anything further to offer. After a silence the justice of the peace informed Wilson that he and Buckstone and the constable had come as a committee, on the part of the Democratic party, to ask him to run for mayor—for the little town was about to become a city and the first charter election was approaching. It was the first attention which Wilson had ever received at the hands of any party; it was a sufficiently humble one, but it was a recognition of his début into the town's life and activities at last; it was a step upward, and he was deeply gratified. He accepted, and the committee departed, followed by young Tom.

XIV

THE true Southern watermelon is a boon apart, and not to be mentioned with commoner things. It is chief of this world's luxuries, king by the grace of God over all the fruits of the earth. When one has tasted it, he knows what the angels eat. It was not a Southern watermelon that Eve took: we know it because she repented.

— *Pudd'nhead Wilson's Calendar.*

ABOUT THE TIME that Wilson was bowing the committee out, Pembroke Howard was entering the next house to report. He found the old Judge sitting grim and straight in his chair, waiting.

"Well, Howard—the news?"

"The best in the world."

"Accepts, does he?" and the light of battle gleamed joyously in the Judge's eye.

"Accepts? Why, he jumped at it."

"Did, did he? Now that 's fine—that 's very fine. I like that. When is it to be?"

"Now! Straight off! To-night! An admirable fellow—admirable!"

"Admirable? He 's a darling! Why, it 's an honor as well as a pleasure to stand up before such a man. Come—off with you! Go and arrange everything—and give him my heartiest compliments. A rare fellow, indeed; an admirable fellow, as you have said!"

Howard hurried away, saying—

"I 'll have him in the vacant stretch between Wilson's and the haunted house within the hour, and I 'll bring my own pistols."

Judge Driscoll began to walk the floor in a state of pleased excitement; but presently he stopped, and began to think—began to think of Tom. Twice he moved toward the secretary, and twice he turned away again; but finally he said—

"This may be my last night in the world—I must not take the chance. He is worthless and unworthy, but it is largely my fault. He was intrusted to me by my brother on his dying

996

bed, and I have indulged him to his hurt, instead of training him up severely, and making a man of him. I have violated my trust, and I must not add the sin of desertion to that. I have forgiven him once already, and would subject him to a long and hard trial before forgiving him again, if I could live; but I must not run that risk. No, I must restore the will. But if I survive the duel, I will hide it away, and he will not know, and I will not tell him until he reforms and I see that his reformation is going to be permanent."

He re-drew the will, and his ostensible nephew was heir to a fortune again. As he was finishing his task, Tom, wearied with another brooding tramp, entered the house and went tiptoeing past the sitting-room door. He glanced in, and hurried on, for the sight of his uncle had nothing but terrors for him to-night. But his uncle was writing! That was unusual at this late hour. What could he be writing? A chill of anxiety settled down upon Tom's heart. Did that writing concern him? He was afraid so. He reflected that when ill luck begins, it does not come in sprinkles, but in showers. He said he would get a glimpse of that document or know the reason why. He heard some one coming, and stepped out of sight and hearing. It was Pembroke Howard. What could be hatching?

Howard said, with great satisfaction:

"Everything 's right and ready. He's gone to the battle-ground with his second and the surgeon—also with his brother. I 've arranged it all with Wilson—Wilson 's his second. We are to have three shots apiece."

"Good! How is the moon?"

"Bright as day, nearly. Perfect, for the distance—fifteen yards. No wind—not a breath; hot and still."

"All good; all first-rate. Here, Pembroke, read this, and witness it."

Pembroke read and witnessed the will, then gave the old man's hand a hearty shake and said:

"Now that 's right, York—but I knew you would do it. You could n't leave that poor chap to fight along without means or profession, with certain defeat before him, and I knew you would n't, for his father's sake if not for his own."

"For his dead father's sake I could n't, I know; for poor

Percy—but you know what Percy was to me. But mind— Tom is not to know of this unless I fall to-night."

"I understand. I 'll keep the secret."

The Judge put the will away, and the two started for the battle-ground. In another minute the will was in Tom's hands. His misery vanished, his feelings underwent a tremendous revulsion. He put the will carefully back in its place, and spread his mouth and swung his hat once, twice, three times around his head, in imitation of three rousing huzzas, no sound issuing from his lips. He fell to communing with himself excitedly and joyously, but every now and then he let off another volley of dumb hurrahs.

He said to himself: "I 've got the fortune again, but I 'll not let on that I know about it. And this time I 'm going to hang on to it. I take no more risks. I 'll gamble no more, I 'll drink no more, because—well, because I 'll not go where there is any of that sort of thing going on, again. It 's the sure way, and the only sure way; I might have thought of that sooner—well, yes, if I had wanted to. But now—dear me, I 've had a bad scare this time, and I 'll take no more chances. Not a single chance more. Land! I persuaded myself this evening that I could fetch him around without any great amount of effort, but I 've been getting more and more heavy-hearted and doubtful straight along, ever since. If he tells me about this thing, all right; but if he does n't, I sha'n't let on. I—well, I 'd like to tell Pudd'nhead Wilson, but—no, I 'll think about that; perhaps I won't." He whirled off another dead huzza, and said, "I 'm reformed, and this time I 'll stay so, sure!"

He was about to close with a final grand silent demonstration, when he suddenly recollected that Wilson had put it out of his power to pawn or sell the Indian knife, and that he was once more in awful peril of exposure by his creditors for that reason. His joy collapsed utterly, and he turned away and moped toward the door moaning and lamenting over the bitterness of his luck. He dragged himself upstairs, and brooded in his room a long time disconsolate and forlorn, with Luigi's Indian knife for a text. At last he sighed and said:

"When I supposed these stones were glass and this ivory bone, the thing had n't any interest for me because it had n't any value, and could n't help me out of my trouble. But now—why, now it is full of interest; yes, and of a sort to break a body's heart. It 's a bag of gold that has turned to dirt and ashes in my hands. It could save me, and save me so easily, and yet I 've got to go to ruin. It 's like drowning with a life-preserver in my reach. All the hard luck comes to me, and all the good luck goes to other people—Pudd'nhead Wilson, for instance; even his career has got a sort of a little start at last, and what has he done to deserve it, I should like to know? Yes, he has opened his own road, but he is n't content with that, but must block mine. It 's a sordid, selfish world, and I wish I was out of it." He allowed the light of the candle to play upon the jewels of the sheath, but the flashings and sparklings had no charm for his eye; they were only just so many pangs to his heart. "I must not say anything to Roxy about this thing," he said, "she is too daring. She would be for digging these stones out and selling them, and then—why, she would be arrested and the stones traced, and then—" The thought made him quake, and he hid the knife away, trembling all over and glancing furtively about, like a criminal who fancies that the accuser is already at hand.

Should he try to sleep? Oh, no, sleep was not for him; his trouble was too haunting, too afflicting for that. He must have somebody to mourn with. He would carry his despair to Roxy.

He had heard several distant gunshots, but that sort of thing was not uncommon, and they had made no impression upon him. He went out at the back door, and turned westward. He passed Wilson's house and proceeded along the lane, and presently saw several figures approaching Wilson's place through the vacant lots. These were the duelists returning from the fight; he thought he recognized them, but as he had no desire for white people's company, he stooped down behind the fence until they were out of his way.

Roxy was feeling fine. She said:

"Whah was you, child? Warn't you in it?"

"In what?"

"In de duel."

"Duel? Has there been a duel?"

" 'Co'se dey has. De ole Jedge has be'n havin' a duel wid one o' dem twins."

"Great Scott!" Then he added to himself: "That 's what made him re-make the will; he thought he might get killed, and it softened him toward me. And that 's what he and Howard were so busy about . . . Oh dear, if the twin had only killed him, I should be out of my—"

"What is you mumblin' 'bout, Chambers? Whah was you? Did n't you know dey was gwyne to be a duel?"

"No. I did n't. The old man tried to get me to fight one with Count Luigi, but he did n't succeed, so I reckon he concluded to patch up the family honor himself."

He laughed at the idea, and went rambling on with a detailed account of his talk with the Judge, and how shocked and ashamed the Judge was to find that he had a coward in his family. He glanced up at last, and got a shock himself. Roxana's bosom was heaving with suppressed passion, and she was glowering down upon him with measureless contempt written in her face.

"En you refuse' to fight a man dat kicked you, 'stid o' jumpin' at de chance! En you ain't got no mo' feelin' den to come en tell me, dat fetched sich a po' low-down ornery rabbit into de worl'! Pah! it make me sick! It 's de nigger in you, dat 's what it is. Thirty-one parts o' you is white, en on'y one part nigger, en dat po' little one part is yo' *soul*. Tain't wuth savin'; tain't wuth totin' out on a shovel en thowin in de gutter. You has disgraced yo' birth. What would yo' pa think o' you? It 's enough to make him turn in his grave."

The last three sentences stung Tom into a fury, and he said to himself that if his father were only alive and in reach of assassination his mother would soon find that he had a very clear notion of the size of his indebtedness to that man, and was willing to pay it up in full, and would do it too, even at risk of his life; but he kept his thought to himself; that was safest in his mother's present state.

"Whatever has come o' yo' Essex blood? Dat 's what I can't understand. En it ain't on'y jist Essex blood dat 's in you, not by a long sight—'deed it ain't. My great-great-great-gran'father en yo' great-great-great-great-gran'father was ole Cap'n John Smith, de highest blood dat Ole Virginny ever turned out, en *his* great-great-gran'mother or somers along back dah, was Pocahontas de Injun queen, en her husbun' was a nigger king outen Africa—en yit here you is, a slinkin' outen a duel en disgracin' our whole line like a ornery low-down hound! Yes, it 's de nigger in you!"

She sat down on her candle-box and fell into a reverie. Tom did not disturb her; he sometimes lacked prudence, but it was not in circumstances of this kind. Roxana's storm went gradually down, but it died hard, and even when it seemed to be quite gone, it would now and then break out in a distant rumble, so to speak, in the form of muttered ejaculations. One of these was, "Ain't nigger enough in him to show in his finger-nails, en dat takes mighty little—yit dey 's enough to paint his soul."

Presently she muttered, "Yassir, enough to paint a whole thimbleful of 'em." At last her ramblings ceased altogether, and her countenance began to clear—a welcome sign to Tom, who had learned her moods, and knew she was on the threshold of good-humor, now. He noticed that from time to time she unconsciously carried her finger to the end of her nose. He looked closer and said:

"Why, mammy, the end of your nose is skinned. How did that come?"

She sent out the sort of whole-hearted peal of laughter which God has vouchsafed in its perfection to none but the happy angels in heaven and the bruised and broken black slave on the earth, and said:

"Dad fetch dat duel, I be'n in it myself."

"Gracious! did a bullet do that?"

"Yassir, you bet it did!"

"Well, I declare! Why, how did that happen?"

"Happen dis-away. I 'uz a-sett'n' here kinder dozin' in de dark, en *che-bang!* goes a gun, right out dah. I skips along out towards t' other end o' de house to see what 's gwyne on, en stops by de ole winder on de side towards Pudd'nhead Wilson's house dat ain't got no sash in it,—but dey ain't none of 'em got any sashes, fur as dat 's concerned,—en I stood dah in de dark en look out, en dar in de moonlight, right down under me 'uz one o' de twins a-cussin'—not much, but jist a-cussin' soft—it 'uz de brown one dat 'uz cussin', 'ca'se he 'uz hit in de shoulder. En Doctor Claypool he 'uz a-workin' at him, en Pudd'nhead Wilson he 'uz a-he'pin', en ole Jedge Driscoll en Pem Howard 'uz a-standin' out yonder a little piece waitin' for 'em to git ready agin. En treckly dey squared off en give de word, en *bang-bang* went de pistols, en de twin he say, 'Ouch!'—hit him on de han' dis time,—en I hear dat same bullet go *spat!* ag'in' de logs under de winder; en de nex' time dey shoot, de twin say, 'Ouch!' ag'in, en I done it too, 'ca'se de bullet glance' on his cheek-bone en skip up here en glance on de side o' de winder en whiz right acrost my face en tuck de hide off'n my nose— why, if I 'd 'a' be'n jist a inch or a inch en a half furder 't would 'a' tuck de whole nose en disfigger me. Here 's de bul-let; I hunted her up."

"Did you stand there all the time?"

"Dat 's a question to ask, ain't it! What else would I do? Does I git a chance to see a duel every day?"

"Why, you were right in range! Were n't you afraid?"

The woman gave a sniff of scorn.

" 'Fraid! De Smith-Pocahontases ain't 'fraid o' nothin', let alone bullets."

"They 've got pluck enough, I suppose; what they lack is judgment. *I* would n't have stood there."

"Nobody 's accusin' you!"

"Did anybody else get hurt?"

"Yes, we all got hit 'cep' de blon' twin en de doctor en de seconds. De Jedge did n't git hurt, but I hear Pudd'nhead say de bullet snip some o' his ha'r off."

" 'George!" said Tom to himself, "to come so near being out of my trouble, and miss it by an inch. Oh dear, dear, he will live to find me out and sell me to some nigger-trader yet—yes, and he would do it in a minute." Then he said aloud, in a grave tone—

"Mother, we are in an awful fix."

Roxana caught her breath with a spasm, and said—

"Chile! What you hit a body so sudden for, like dat? What 's be'n en gone en happen'?"

"Well, there 's one thing I did n't tell you. When I would n't fight, he tore up the will again, and—"

Roxana's face turned a dead white, and she said—

"Now you 's *done!*—done forever! Dat 's de end. Bofe un us is gwyne to starve to—"

"Wait and hear me through, can't you! I reckon that when he resolved to fight, himself, he thought he might get killed and not have a chance to forgive me any more in this life, so he made the will again, and I 've seen it, and it 's all right. But—"

"Oh, thank goodness, den we 's safe agin!—safe! en so what did you want to come here en talk sich dreadful—"

"Hold *on*, I tell you, and let me finish. The swag I gathered won't half square me up, and the first thing we know, my creditors—well, you know what 'll happen."

Roxana dropped her chin, and told her son to leave her alone—she must think this matter out. Presently she said impressively:

"You got to go mighty keerful now, I tell you! En here 's what you got to do. He did n't git killed, en if you gives him de least reason, he 'll bust de will ag'in, en dat 's de *las'* time, now you hear me! So—you 's got to show him what you kin do in de nex' few days. You 's got to be pison good, en let him see it; you got to do everything dat 'll make him b'lieve in you, en you got to sweeten aroun' ole Aunt Pratt, too,—she 's pow'ful strong wid de Jedge, en de bes' frien' you got. Nex', you 'll go 'long away to Sent Louis, en dat 'll *keep* him in yo' favor. Den you go en make a bargain wid dem people. You tell 'em he ain't gwyne to live long—en dat 's de fac', too,—en tell 'em you 'll pay 'em intrust, en big intrust, too,—ten per—what you call it?"

"Ten per cent. a month?"

"Dat 's it. Den you take and sell yo' truck aroun', a little at a time, en pay de intrust. How long will it las'?"

"I think there 's enough to pay the interest five or six months."

"Den you 's all right. If he don't die in six months, dat don't make no diff'rence—Providence 'll provide. You 's gwyne to be safe—if you behaves." She bent an austere eye on him and added, "En you *is* gwyne to behave—does you know dat?"

He laughed and said he was going to try, anyway. She did not unbend. She said gravely:

"Tryin' ain't de thing. You 's gwyne to *do* it. You ain't gwyne to steal a pin—'ca'se it ain't safe no mo'; en you ain't gwyne into no bad comp'ny—not even once, you understand; en you ain't gwyne to drink a drop—nary single drop; en you ain't gwyne to gamble one single gamble—not one! Dis ain't what you 's gwyne to *try* to do, it 's what you 's gwyne to *do*. En I 'll tell you how I knows it. Dis is how. I 's gwyne to foller along to Sent Louis my own self; en you 's gwyne to come to me every day o' yo' life, en I 'll look you over; en if you fails in one single one o' dem things—jist *one*—I take my oath I 'll come straight down to dis town en tell de Jedge you 's a nigger en a slave—en *prove* it!" She paused to let her words sink home. Then she added, "Chambers, does you b'lieve me when I says dat?"

Tom was sober enough now. There was no levity in his voice when he answered:

"Yes, mother. I know, now, that I am reformed—and permanently. Permanently—and beyond the reach of any human temptation."

"Den g' long home en begin!"

XV

WHAT A TIME OF IT Dawson's Landing was having! All
its life it had been asleep, but now it hardly got a
chance for a nod, so swiftly did big events and crashing surprises come along in one another's wake: Friday morning,
first glimpse of Real Nobility, also grand reception at Aunt
Patsy Cooper's, also great robber-raid; Friday evening, dramatic kicking of the heir of the chief citizen in presence of
four hundred people; Saturday morning, emergence as practising lawyer of the long-submerged Pudd'nhead Wilson; Saturday night, duel between chief citizen and titled stranger.

The people took more pride in the duel than in all the
other events put together, perhaps. It was a glory to their
town to have such a thing happen there. In their eyes the
principals had reached the summit of human honor. Everybody paid homage to their names; their praises were in all
mouths. Even the duelists' subordinates came in for a handsome share of the public approbation: wherefore Pudd'nhead
Wilson was suddenly become a man of consequence. When
asked to run for the mayoralty Saturday night he was risking
defeat, but Sunday morning found him a made man and his
success assured.

The twins were prodigiously great, now; the town took
them to its bosom with enthusiasm. Day after day, and night
after night, they went dining and visiting from house to
house, making friends, enlarging and solidifying their popularity, and charming and surprising all with their musical
prodigies, and now and then heightening the effects with
samples of what they could do in other directions, out of
their stock of rare and curious accomplishments. They were

so pleased that they gave the regulation thirty days' notice, the required preparation for citizenship, and resolved to finish their days in this pleasant place. That was the climax. The delighted community rose as one man and applauded; and when the twins were asked to stand for seats in the forthcoming aldermanic board, and consented, the public contentment was rounded and complete.

Tom Driscoll was not happy over these things; they sunk deep, and hurt all the way down. He hated the one twin for kicking him, and the other one for being the kicker's brother.

Now and then the people wondered why nothing was heard of the raider, or of the stolen knife or the other plunder, but nobody was able to throw any light on that matter. Nearly a week had drifted by, and still the thing remained a vexed mystery.

On Saturday Constable Blake and Pudd'nhead Wilson met on the street, and Tom Driscoll joined them in time to open their conversation for them. He said to Blake—

"You are not looking well, Blake; you seem to be annoyed about something. Has anything gone wrong in the detective business? I believe you fairly and justifiably claim to have a pretty good reputation in that line, is n't it so?"—which made Blake feel good, and look it; but Tom added, "for a country detective"—which made Blake feel the other way, and not only look it, but betray it in his voice—

"Yes, sir, I *have* got a reputation; and it 's as good as anybody's in the profession, too, country or no country."

"Oh, I beg pardon; I did n't mean any offense. What I started out to ask was only about the old woman that raided the town—the stoop-shouldered old woman, you know, that you said you were going to catch; and I knew you would, too, because you have the reputation of never boasting, and—well, you—you 've caught the old woman?"

"D—— the old woman!"

"Why, sho! you don't mean to say you have n't caught her?"

"No; I have n't caught her. If anybody could have caught her, I could; but nobody could n't, I don't care who he is."

"I am sorry, real sorry—for your sake; because, when it

gets around that a detective has expressed himself so confidently, and then—"

"Don't you worry, that 's all—don't you worry; and as for the town, the town need n't worry, either. She 's my meat—make yourself easy about that. I 'm on her track; I 've got clues that—"

"That 's good! Now if you could get an old veteran detective down from St. Louis to help you find out what the clues mean, and where they lead to, and then—"

"I 'm plenty veteran enough myself, and I don't need anybody's help. I 'll have her inside of a we—inside of a month. That I 'll swear to!"

Tom said carelessly—

"I suppose that will answer—yes, that will answer. But I reckon she is pretty old, and old people don't often outlive the cautious pace of the professional detective when he has got his clues together and is out on his still-hunt."

Blake's dull face flushed under this gibe, but before he could set his retort in order Tom had turned to Wilson, and was saying, with placid indifference of manner and voice—

"Who got the reward, Pudd'nhead?"

Wilson winced slightly, and saw that his own turn was come.

"What reward?"

"Why, the reward for the thief, and the other one for the knife."

Wilson answered—and rather uncomfortably, to judge by his hesitating fashion of delivering himself—

"Well, the—well, in fact, nobody has claimed it yet."

Tom seemed surprised.

"Why, is that so?"

Wilson showed a trifle of irritation when he replied—

"Yes, it 's so. And what of it?"

"Oh, nothing. Only I thought you had struck out a new idea, and invented a scheme that was going to revolutionize the time-worn and ineffectual methods of the—" He stopped, and turned to Blake, who was happy now that another had taken his place on the gridiron: "Blake, did n't you understand him to intimate that it would n't be necessary for you to hunt the old woman down?"

"B'George, he said he 'd have thief and swag both inside of three days—he did, by hokey! and that 's just about a week ago. Why, I said at the time that no thief and no thief's pal was going to try to pawn or sell a thing where he knowed the pawnbroker could get both rewards by taking *him* into camp *with* the swag. It was the blessedest idea that ever *I* struck!"

"You 'd change your mind," said Wilson, with irritated bluntness, "if you knew the entire scheme instead of only part of it."

"Well," said the constable, pensively, "I had the idea that it would n't work, and up to now I 'm right, anyway."

"Very well, then, let it stand at that, and give it a further show. It has worked at least as well as your own methods, you perceive."

The constable had n't anything handy to hit back with, so he discharged a discontented sniff, and said nothing.

After the night that Wilson had partly revealed his scheme at his house, Tom had tried for several days to guess out the secret of the rest of it, but had failed. Then it occurred to him to give Roxana's smarter head a chance at it. He made up a supposititious case, and laid it before her. She thought it over, and delivered her verdict upon it. Tom said to himself, "She 's hit it, sure!" He thought he would test that verdict, now, and watch Wilson's face; so he said reflectively—

"Wilson, you 're not a fool—a fact of recent discovery. Whatever your scheme was, it had sense in it, Blake's opinion to the contrary notwithstanding. I don't ask you to reveal it, but I will suppose a case—a case which will answer as a starting-point for the real thing I am going to come at, and that 's all I want. You offered five hundred dollars for the knife, and five hundred for the thief. We will suppose, for argument's sake, that the first reward is *advertised*, and the second offered by *private letter* to pawnbrokers and—"

Blake slapped his thigh, and cried out—

"By Jackson, he 's got you, Pudd'nhead! Now why could n't I or *any* fool have thought of that?"

Wilson said to himself, "Anybody with a reasonably good head would have thought of it. I am not surprised that Blake did n't detect it; I am only surprised that Tom did. There is more to him than I supposed." He said nothing aloud, and Tom went on:

"Very well. The thief would not suspect that there was a trap, and he would bring or send the knife, and say he bought it for a song, or found it in the road, or something like that, and try to collect the reward, and be arrested—would n't he?"

"Yes," said Wilson.

"I think so," said Tom. "There can't be any doubt of it. Have you ever seen that knife?"

"No."

"Has any friend of yours?"

"Not that I know of."

"Well, I begin to think I understand why your scheme failed."

"What do you mean, Tom? What are you driving at?" asked Wilson, with a dawning sense of discomfort.

"Why, that there *is n't* any such knife."

"Look here, Wilson," said Blake, "Tom Driscoll 's right, for a thousand dollars—if I had it."

Wilson's blood warmed a little, and he wondered if he had been played upon by those strangers; it certainly had something of that look. But what could they gain by it? He threw out that suggestion. Tom replied:

"Gain? Oh, nothing that you would value, maybe. But they are strangers making their way in a new community. Is it nothing to them to appear as pets of an Oriental prince—at no expense? Is it nothing to them to be able to dazzle this poor little town with thousand-dollar rewards—at no expense? Wilson, there is n't any such knife, or your scheme would have fetched it to light. Or if there is any such knife, they 've got it yet. I believe, myself, that they 've seen such a knife, for Angelo pictured it out with his pencil too swiftly and handily for him to have been inventing it, and of course I can't swear that they 've never had it; this I 'll go bail for—if they had it when they came to this town, they 've got it yet."

Blake said—

"It looks mighty reasonable, the way Tom puts it; it most certainly does."

Tom responded, turning to leave—

"You find the old woman, Blake, and if she can't furnish the knife, go and search the twins!"

Tom sauntered away. Wilson felt a good deal depressed. He hardly knew what to think. He was loth to withdraw his faith from the twins, and was resolved not to do it on the present indecisive evidence; but—well, he would think, and then decide how to act.

"Blake, what do you think of this matter?"

"Well, Pudd'nhead, I 'm bound to say I put it up the way Tom does. They had n't the knife; or if they had it, they 've got it yet."

The men parted. Wilson said to himself:

"I believe they had it; if it had been stolen, the scheme would have restored it, that is certain. And so I believe they 've got it yet."

Tom had no purpose in his mind when he encountered those two men. When he began his talk he hoped to be able to gall them a little and get a trifle of malicious entertainment out of it. But when he left, he left in great spirits, for he perceived that just by pure luck and no troublesome labor he had accomplished several delightful things: he had touched both men on a raw spot and seen them squirm; he had modified Wilson's sweetness for the twins with one small bitter taste that he would n't be able to get out of his mouth right away; and, best of all, he had taken the hated twins down a peg with the community; for Blake would gossip around freely, after the manner of detectives, and within a week the town would be laughing at them in its sleeve for offering a gaudy reward for a bauble which they either never possessed or had n't lost. Tom was very well satisfied with himself.

Tom's behavior at home had been perfect during the entire week. His uncle and aunt had seen nothing like it before. They could find no fault with him anywhere.

Saturday evening he said to the Judge—

"I 've had something preying on my mind, uncle, and as I am going away, and might never see you again, I can't bear it any longer. I made you believe I was afraid to fight that Italian adventurer. I had to get out of it on some pretext or other, and maybe I chose badly, being taken unawares, but no honorable person could consent to meet him in the field, knowing what I knew about him."

"Indeed? What was that?"

"Count Luigi is a confessed assassin."

"Incredible!"

"It is perfectly true. Wilson detected it in his hand, by palmistry, and charged him with it, and cornered him up so close that he had to confess; but both twins begged us on their knees to keep the secret, and swore they would lead straight lives here; and it was all so pitiful that we gave our word of honor never to expose them while they kept that promise. You would have done it yourself, uncle."

"You are right, my boy; I would. A man's secret is still his own property, and sacred, when it has been surprised out of him like that. You did well, and I am proud of you." Then he added mournfully, "But I wish I could have been saved the shame of meeting an assassin on the field of honor."

"It could n't be helped, uncle. If I had known you were going to challenge him I should have felt obliged to sacrifice my pledged word in order to stop it, but Wilson could n't be expected to do otherwise than keep silent."

"Oh no; Wilson did right, and is in no way to blame. Tom, Tom, you have lifted a heavy load from my heart; I was stung to the very soul when I seemed to have discovered that I had a coward in my family."

"You may imagine what it cost *me* to assume such a part, uncle."

"Oh, I know it, poor boy, I know it. And I can understand how much it has cost you to remain under that unjust stigma to this time. But it is all right now, and no harm is done. You have restored my comfort of mind, and with it your own; and both of us had suffered enough."

The old man sat a while plunged in thought; then he looked up with a satisfied light in his eye, and said: "That this assassin should have put the affront upon me of letting me meet him on the field of honor as if he were a gentleman is a matter which I will presently settle—but not now. I will not shoot him until after election. I see a way to ruin them both before; I will attend to that first. Neither of them shall be elected, that I promise. You are sure that the fact that he is an assassin has not got abroad?"

"Perfectly certain of it, sir."

"It will be a good card. I will fling a hint at it from the stump on the polling-day. It will sweep the ground from under both of them."

"There 's not a doubt of it. It will finish them."

"That and outside work among the voters will, to a certainty. I want you to come down here by and by and work privately among the rag-tag and bobtail. You shall spend money among them; I will furnish it."

Another point scored against the detested twins! Really it was a great day for Tom. He was encouraged to chance a parting shot, now, at the same target, and did it.

"You know that wonderful Indian knife that the twins have been making such a to-do about? Well, there 's no track or trace of it yet; so the town is beginning to sneer and gossip and laugh. Half the people believe they never had any such knife, the other half believe they had it and have got it still. I 've heard twenty people talking like that to-day."

Yes, Tom's blemishless week had restored him to the favor of his aunt and uncle.

His mother was satisfied with him, too. Privately, she believed she was coming to love him, but she did not say so. She told him to go along to St. Louis, now, and she would get ready and follow. Then she smashed her whisky bottle and said—

"Dah now! I 's a-gwyne to make you walk as straight as a string, Chambers, en so I 's bown' you ain't gwyne to git no bad example out o' yo' mammy. I tole you you could n't go into no bad comp'ny. Well, you 's gwyne into my comp'ny, en I 's gwyne to fill de bill. Now, den, trot along, trot along!"

Tom went aboard one of the big transient boats that night with his heavy satchel of miscellaneous plunder, and slept the sleep of the unjust, which is serener and sounder than the other kind, as we know by the hanging-eve history of a million rascals. But when he got up in the morning, luck was against him again: A brother-thief had robbed him while he slept, and gone ashore at some intermediate landing.

point of even half believing he was doing Roxy a splendid surreptitious service in selling her "down the river." And then he kept diligently saying to himself all the time: "It 's for only a year. In a year I buy her free again; she 'll keep that in mind, and it 'll reconcile her." Yes; the little deception could do no harm, and everything would come out right and pleasant in the end, any way. By agreement, the conversation in Roxy's presence was all about the man's "up-country" farm, and how pleasant a place it was, and how happy the slaves were there; so poor Roxy was entirely deceived; and easily, for she was not dreaming that her own son could be guilty of treason to a mother who, in voluntarily going into slavery— slavery of any kind, mild or severe, or of any duration, brief or long—was making a sacrifice for him compared with which death would have been a poor and commonplace one. She lavished tears and loving caresses upon him privately, and then went away with her owner—went away broken-hearted, and yet proud of what she was doing, and glad that it was in her power to do it.

Tom squared his accounts, and resolved to keep to the very letter of his reform, and never to put that will in jeopardy again. He had three hundred dollars left. According to his mother's plan, he was to put that safely away, and add her half of his pension to it monthly. In one year this fund would buy her free again.

For a whole week he was not able to sleep well, so much the villainy which he had played upon his trusting mother preyed upon his rag of a conscience; but after that he began to get comfortable again, and was presently able to sleep like any other miscreant.

THE boat bore Roxy away from St. Louis at four in the afternoon, and she stood on the lower guard abaft the paddle-box and watched Tom through a blur of tears until he melted into the throng of people and disappeared; then she looked no more, but sat there on a coil of cable crying till far into the night. When she went to her foul steerage-bunk at last, between the clashing engines, it was not to sleep, but only to wait for the morning, and, waiting, grieve.

It had been imagined that she "would not know," and

would think she was traveling up stream. She! Why, she had been steamboating for years. At dawn she got up and went listlessly and sat down on the cable-coil again. She passed many a snag whose "break" could have told her a thing to break her heart, for it showed a current moving in the same direction that the boat was going; but her thoughts were else-where, and she did not notice. But at last the roar of a bigger and nearer break than usual brought her out of her torpor, and she looked up, and her practised eye fell upon that tell-tale rush of water. For one moment her petrified gaze fixed itself there. Then her head dropped upon her breast, and she said—

"Oh, de good Lord God have mercy on po' sinful me— *I 's sole down de river!*"

XVII

THE SUMMER WEEKS dragged by, and then the political campaign opened—opened in pretty warm fashion, and waxed hotter and hotter daily. The twins threw themselves into it with their whole heart, for their self-love was engaged. Their popularity, so general at first, had suffered afterward; mainly because they had been *too* popular, and so a natural reaction had followed. Besides, it had been diligently whispered around that it was curious—indeed, *very* curious—that that wonderful knife of theirs did not turn up—*if* it was so valuable, or *if* it had ever existed. And with the whisperings went chucklings and nudgings and winks, and such things have an effect. The twins considered that success in the election would reinstate them, and that defeat would work them irreparable damage. Therefore they worked hard, but not harder than Judge Driscoll and Tom worked against them in the closing days of the canvass. Tom's conduct had remained so letter-perfect during two whole months, now, that his uncle not only trusted him with money with which to persuade voters, but trusted him to go and get it himself out of the safe in the private sitting-room.

The closing speech of the campaign was made by Judge Driscoll, and he made it against both of the foreigners. It was disastrously effective. He poured out rivers of ridicule upon them, and forced the big mass-meeting to laugh and applaud. He scoffed at them as adventurers, mountebanks, side-show riff-raff, dime-museum freaks; he assailed their showy titles with measureless derision; he said they were back-alley barbers disguised as nobilities, peanut pedlers masquerading as gentlemen, organ-grinders bereft of their brother-monkey. At last he stopped and stood still. He waited until the place had become absolutely silent and expectant, then he delivered his deadliest shot; delivered it with ice-cold seriousness and deliberation, with a significant emphasis upon the closing words: he said he believed that the reward offered for the lost knife was humbug and buncombe, and that its owner would know where to find it whenever he should have occasion *to assassinate somebody.*

Then he stepped from the stand, leaving a startled and impressive hush behind him instead of the customary explosion of cheers and party cries.

The strange remark flew far and wide over the town and made an extraordinary sensation. Everybody was asking, "What could he mean by that?" And everybody went on asking that question, but in vain; for the Judge only said he knew what he was talking about, and stopped there; Tom said he had n't any idea what his uncle meant, and Wilson, whenever he was asked what he thought it meant, parried the question by asking the questioner what *he* thought it meant.

Wilson was elected, the twins were defeated—crushed, in fact, and left forlorn and substantially friendless. Tom went back to St. Louis happy.

Dawson's Landing had a week of repose, now, and it needed it. But it was in an expectant state, for the air was full of rumors of a new duel. Judge Driscoll's election labors had prostrated him, but it was said that as soon as he was well enough to entertain a challenge he would get one from Count Luigi.

The brothers withdrew entirely from society, and nursed their humiliation in privacy. They avoided the people, and went out for exercise only late at night, when the streets were deserted.

XVIII

GRATITUDE and treachery are merely the two extremities of the same procession. You have seen all of it that is worth staying for when the band and the gaudy officials have gone by.
— *Pudd'nhead Wilson's Calendar.*

THANKSGIVING DAY. Let all give humble, hearty, and sincere thanks, now, but the turkeys. In the island of Fiji they do not use turkeys; they use plumbers. It does not become you and me to sneer at Fiji.
— *Pudd'nhead Wilson's Calendar.*

THE FRIDAY after the election was a rainy one in St. Louis. It rained all day long, and rained hard, apparently trying its best to wash that soot-blackened town white, but of course not succeeding. Toward midnight Tom Driscoll arrived at his lodgings from the theater in the heavy downpour, and closed his umbrella and let himself in; but when he would have shut the door, he found that there was another person entering—doubtless another lodger; this person closed the door and tramped up-stairs behind Tom. Tom found his door in the dark, and entered it and turned up the gas. When he faced about, lightly whistling, he saw the back of a man. The man was closing and locking his door for him. His whistle faded out and he felt uneasy. The man turned around, a wreck of shabby old clothes sodden with rain and all a-drip, and showed a black face under an old slouch hat. Tom was frightened. He tried to order the man out, but the words refused to come, and the other man got the start. He said, in a low voice—

"Keep still—I 's yo' mother!"

Tom sunk in a heap on a chair, and gasped out—

"It was mean of me, and base—I know it; but I meant it for the best, I did indeed—I can swear it."

Roxana stood awhile looking mutely down on him while he writhed in shame and went on incoherently babbling self-accusations mixed with pitiful attempts at explanation and palliation of his crime; then she seated herself and took off her hat, and her unkempt masses of long brown hair tumbled down about her shoulders.

"It ain't no fault o' yo'n dat dat ain't gray," she said sadly, noticing the hair.

"I know it, I know it! I 'm a scoundrel. But I swear I meant for the best. It was a mistake, of course, but I thought it was for the best, I truly did."

Roxy began to cry softly, and presently words began to find their way out between her sobs. They were uttered lamentingly, rather than angrily—

"Sell a pusson down de river— *down de river!*—for de bes'! I would n't treat a dog so! I is all broke down en wore out, now, en so I reckon it ain't in me to storm aroun' no mo', like I used to when I 'uz trompled on en 'bused. I don't know—but maybe it 's so. Leastways, I 's suffered so much dat mournin' seem to come mo' handy to me now den stormin'."

These words should have touched Tom Driscoll, but if they did, that effect was obliterated by a stronger one—one which removed the heavy weight of fear which lay upon him, and gave his crushed spirit a most grateful rebound, and filled all his small soul with a deep sense of relief. But he kept prudently still, and ventured no comment. There was a voiceless interval of some duration, now, in which no sounds were heard but the beating of the rain upon the panes, the sighing and complaining of the winds, and now and then a muffled sob from Roxana. The sobs became more and more infrequent, and at last ceased. Then the refugee began to talk again:

"Shet down dat light a little. More. More yit. A pusson dat is hunted don't like de light. Dah—dat 'll do. I kin see whah you is, en dat 's enough. I 's gwine to tell you de tale, en cut it jes as short as I kin, en den I 'll tell you what you 's got to do. Dat man dat bought me ain't a bad man; he 's good enough, as planters goes; en if he could 'a' had his way I 'd 'a' be'n a house servant in his fambly en be'n comfortable: but his wife she was a Yank, en not right down good lookin', en she riz up agin me straight off; so den dey sent me out to de quarter 'mongst de common fiel' han's. Dat woman war n't satisfied even wid dat, but she worked up de overseer ag'in' me, she 'uz dat jealous en hateful; so de overseer he had me out befo' day in de mawnin's en worked me de whole long day as long as dey 'uz any light to see by; en many 's de lashin's I got 'ca'se I could n't come up to de work o' de stronges'. Dat overseer wuz a Yank, too, outen New Englan', en anybody down South kin tell you what dat mean. *Dey* knows how to work a nigger to death, en dey knows how to whale 'em, too—whale 'em till dey backs is welted like a washboard. 'Long at fust my marster say de good word for me to de overseer, but dat 'uz bad for me; for de mistis she fine it out, en arter dat I jist ketched it at every turn—dey war n't no mercy for me no mo'."

Tom's heart was fired—with fury against the planter's wife; and he said to himself, "But for that meddlesome fool, everything would have gone all right." He added a deep and bitter curse against her.

The expression of this sentiment was fiercely written in his face, and stood thus revealed to Roxana by a white glare of lightning which turned the somber dusk of the room into dazzling day at that moment. She was pleased—pleased and grateful; for did not that expression show that her child was capable of grieving for his mother's wrongs and of feeling resentment toward her persecutors?—a thing which she had been doubting. But her flash of happiness was only a flash, and went out again and left her spirit dark; for she said to herself, "He sole me down de river—he can't feel for a body long; dis 'll pass en go." Then she took up her tale again.

" 'Bout ten days ago I 'uz sayin' to myself dat I could n't las' many mo' weeks I 'uz so wore out wid de awful work en de lashin's, en so downhearted en misable. En I did n't care no mo', nuther—life war n't wuth noth'n' to me if I got to go on like dat. Well, when a body is in a frame o' mine like dat, what do a body care what a body do? Dey was a little sickly nigger wench 'bout ten year ole dat 'uz good to me, en had n't no mammy, po' thing, en I loved her en she loved me; en she come out whah I 'uz workin' en she had a roasted tater, en tried to slip it to me,—robbin' herself, you see, 'ca'se she knowed de overseer did n't gimme enough to eat,—en he ketched her at it, en give her a lick acrost de back wid his stick, which 'uz as thick as a broom-handle, en she drop'

screamin' on de groun', en squirmin' en wallerin' aroun' in de
dust like a spider dat 's got crippled. I could n't stan' it. All
de hell-fire dat 'uz ever in my heart flame' up, en I snatch de
stick outen his han' en laid him flat. He laid dah moanin' en
cussin', en all out of his head, you know, en de niggers 'uz
plumb sk'yerd to death. Dey gathered roun' him to he'p him,
en I jumped on his hoss en took out for de river as tight as I
could go. I knowed what dey would do wid me. Soon as he
got well he would start in en work me to death if marster let
him; en if dey did n't do dat, they 'd sell me furder down de
river, en dat 's de same thing. So I 'lowed to drown myself en
git out o' my troubles. It 'uz gitt'n' towards dark. I 'uz at de
river in two minutes. Den I see a canoe, en I says dey ain't
no use to drown myself tell I got to; so I ties de hoss in de
edge o' de timber en shove out down de river, keepin' in
under de shelter o' de bluff bank en prayin' for de dark to
shet down quick. I had a pow'ful good start, 'ca'se de big
house 'uz three mile back f'om de river en on'y de work-
mules to ride dah on, en on'y niggers to ride 'em, en *dey* war
n't gwine to hurry—dey 'd gimme all de chance dey could.
Befo' a body could go to de house en back it would be long
pas' dark, en dey could n't track de hoss en fine out which
way I went tell mawnin', en de niggers would tell 'em all de
lies dey could 'bout it.

"Well, de dark come, en I went on a-spinnin' down de
river. I paddled mo'n two hours, den I war n't worried no
mo', so I quit paddlin', en floated down de current, considerin' what I 'uz gwine to do if I did n't have to drown myself.
I made up some plans, en floated along, turnin' 'em over in
my mine. Well, when it 'uz a little pas' midnight, as I reckoned, en I had come fifteen or twenty mile, I see de lights o'
a steamboat layin' at de bank, whah dey war n't no town en
no woodyard, en putty soon I ketched de shape o' de chim-
bly-tops ag'in' de stars, en de good gracious me, I 'most
jumped out o' my skin for joy! It 'uz de *Gran' Mogul*—I 'uz
chambermaid on her for eight seasons in de Cincinnati en
Orleans trade. I slid 'long pas'—don't see nobody stirrin' no-
whah—hear 'em a-hammerin' away in de engine-room, den
I knowed what de matter was—some o' de machinery 's
broke. I got asho' below de boat and turn' de canoe loose,

den I goes 'long up, en dey 'uz jes one plank out, en I step' 'board de boat. It 'uz pow'ful hot, deckhan's en roustabouts 'uz sprawled aroun' asleep on de fo'cas'l', de second mate, Jim Bangs, he sot dah on de bitts wid his head down, asleep— 'ca'se dat 's de way de second mate stan' de cap'n's watch!— en de ole watchman, Billy Hatch, he 'uz a-noddin' on de companionway;—en I knowed 'em all; 'en, lan', but dey did look good! I says to myself, I wished old marster 'd come along *now* en try to take me—bless yo' heart, I 's 'mong frien's, I is. So I tromped right along 'mongst 'em, en went up on de b'iler deck en 'way back aft to de ladies' cabin guard, en sot down dah in de same cheer dat I 'd sot in 'mos' a hund'd million times, I reckon; en it 'uz jist home ag'in, I tell you!

"In 'bout an hour I heard de ready-bell jingle, en den de racket begin. Putty soon I hear de gong strike. 'Set her back on de outside,' I says to myself—'I reckon I knows dat music!' I hear de gong ag'in. 'Come ahead on de inside,' I says. Gong ag'in. 'Stop de outside.' Gong ag'in. 'Come ahead on de outside—now we 's pinted for Sent Louis, en I 's outer de woods en ain't got to drown myself at all.' I knowed de *Mogul* 'uz in de Sent Louis trade now, you see. It 'uz jes fair daylight when we passed our plantation, en I seed a gang o' niggers en white folks huntin' up en down de sho', en troublin' deyselves a good deal 'bout me; but I war n't troublin' myself none 'bout dem.

" 'Bout dat time Sally Jackson, dat used to be my second chambermaid en 'uz head chambermaid now, she come out on de guard, en 'uz pow'ful glad to see me, en so 'uz all de officers; en I tole 'em I 'd got kidnapped en sole down de river, en dey made me up twenty dollahs en give it to me, en Sally she rigged me out wid good clo'es, en when I got here I went straight to whah you used to wuz, en den I come to dis house, en dey say you 's away but 'spected back every day; so I did n't dast to go down de river to Dawson's, 'ca'se I might miss you.

"Well, las' Monday I 'uz pass'n' by one o' dem places in Fourth street whah dey sticks up runaway-nigger bills, en he'ps to ketch 'em, en I seed my marster! I 'mos' flopped down on de groun', I felt so gone. He had his back to me, en 'uz talkin' to de man en givin' him some bills—nigger-bills, I reckon, en I 's de nigger. He 's offerin' a reward—dat 's it. Ain't I right, don't you reckon?"

Tom had been gradually sinking into a state of ghastly terror, and he said to himself, now: "I 'm lost, no matter what turn things take! This man has said to me that he thinks there was something suspicious about that sale. He said he had a letter from a passenger on the *Grand Mogul* saying that Roxy came here on that boat and that everybody on board knew all about the case; so he says that her coming here instead of flying to a free State looks bad for me, and that if I don't find her for him, and that pretty soon, he will make trouble for me. I never believed that story; I could n't believe she would be so dead to all motherly instincts as to come here, knowing the risk she would run of getting me into irremediable trouble. And after all, here she is! And I stupidly swore I would help him find her, thinking it was a perfectly safe thing to promise. If I venture to deliver her up, she—she—but how can I help myself? I 've got to do that or pay the money, and where 's the money to come from? I—I—well, I should think that if he would swear to treat her kindly hereafter— and she says, herself, that he is a good man—and if he would swear to never allow her to be overworked, or ill fed, or—"

A flash of lightning exposed Tom's pallid face, drawn and rigid with these worrying thoughts. Roxana spoke up sharply now, and there was apprehension in her voice—

"Turn up dat light! I want to see yo' face better. Dah now—lemme look at you. Chambers, you 's as white as yo' shirt! Has you seen dat man? Has he be'n to see you?"

"Ye-s."

"When?"

"Monday noon."

"Monday noon! Was he on my track?"

"He—well, he thought he was. That is, he hoped he was. This is the bill you saw." He took it out of his pocket.

"Read it to me!"

She was panting with excitement, and there was a dusky glow in her eyes that Tom could not translate with certainty, but there seemed to be something threatening about it. The handbill had the usual rude woodcut of a turbaned negro woman running, with the customary bundle on a stick over her shoulder, and the heading in bold type, "$100 REWARD." Tom read the bill aloud—at least the part that described Roxana and named the master and his St. Louis address and the address of the Fourth-street agency; but he left out the item that applicants for the reward might also apply to Mr. Thomas Driscoll.

"Gimme de bill!"

Tom had folded it and was putting it in his pocket. He felt a chilly streak creeping down his back, but said as carelessly as he could—

"The bill? Why, it is n't any use to you; you can't read it. What do you want with it?"

"Gimme de bill!" Tom gave it to her, but with a reluctance which he could not entirely disguise. "Did you read it *all* to me?"

"Certainly I did."

"Hole up yo' han' en swah to it."

Tom did it. Roxana put the bill carefully away in her pocket, with her eyes fixed upon Tom's face all the while; then she said—

"You 's lyin'!"

"What would I want to lie about it for?"

"I don't know—but you is. Dat 's my opinion, anyways. But nemmine 'bout dat. When I seed dat man I 'uz dat sk'yerd dat I could sca'cely wobble home. Den I give a nigger man a dollar for dese clo'es, en I ain't be'n in a house sence, night ner day, till now. I blacked my face en laid hid in de cellar of a ole house dat 's burnt down, daytimes, en robbed de sugar hogsheads en grain sacks on de wharf, nights, to git somethin' to eat, en never dast to try to buy noth'n', en I 's 'mos' starved. En I never dast to come near dis place till dis rainy night, when dey ain't no people roun' sca'cely. But to-night I be'n a-stannin' in de dark alley ever sence night come, waitin' for you to go by. En here I is."

She fell to thinking. Presently she said—

"You seed dat man at noon, las' Monday?"

"Yes."

"I seed him de middle o' dat arternoon. He hunted you up, did n't he?"

"Yes."

"Did he give you de bill dat time?"

"No, he had n't got it printed yet."

Roxana darted a suspicious glance at him.

"Did you he'p him fix up de bill?"

Tom cursed himself for making that stupid blunder, and tried to rectify it by saying he remembered, now, that it *was* at noon Monday that the man gave him the bill. Roxana said—

"You 's lyin' ag'in, sho." Then she straightened up and raised her finger:

"Now den! I 's gwine to ast you a question, en I wants to know how you 's gwine to git aroun' it. You knowed he 'uz arter me; en if you run off, 'stid o' stayin' here to he'p him, he 'd know dey 'uz somethin' wrong 'bout dis business, en den he would inquire 'bout you, en dat would take him to yo' uncle, en yo' uncle would read de bill en see dat you be'n sellin' a free nigger down de river, en you know *him*, I reckon! He 'd t'ar up de will en kick you outen de house. Now, den, you answer me dis question: hain't you tole dat man dat I would be sho' to come here, en den you would fix it so he could set a trap en ketch me?"

Tom recognized that neither lies nor arguments could help him any longer—he was in a vise, with the screw turned on, and out of it there was no budging. His face began to take on an ugly look, and presently he said, with a snarl—

"Well, what could I do? You see, yourself, that I was in his grip and could n't get out."

Roxy scorched him with a scornful gaze awhile, then she said—

"What could you do? You could be Judas to yo' own mother to save yo' wuthless hide! Would anybody b'lieve it? No—a dog could n't! You is de low-downest orneriest hound dat was ever pup'd into dis worl'—en I 's 'sponsible for it!"—and she spat on him.

He made no effort to resent this. Roxy reflected a moment, then she said—

"Now I 'll tell you what you 's gwine to do. You 's gwine to give dat man de money dat you 's got laid up, en make him wait till you kin go to de Jedge en git de res' en buy me free agin."

"Thunder! what are you thinking of? Go and ask him for three hundred dollars and odd? What would I tell him I want with it, pray?"

Roxy's answer was delivered in a serene and level voice—

"You 'll tell him you 's sole me to pay yo' gamblin' debts en dat you lied to me en was a villain, en dat I 'quires you to git dat money en buy me back ag'in."

"Why, you 've gone stark mad! He would tear the will to shreds in a minute—don't you know that?"

"Yes, I does."

"Then you don't believe I 'm idiot enough to go to him, do you?"

"I don't b'lieve nothin' 'bout it—I *knows* you 's a-goin', I knows it 'ca'se you knows dat if you don't raise dat money I 'll go to him myself, en den he 'll sell *you* down de river, en you kin see how you like it!"

Tom rose, trembling and excited, and there was an evil light in his eye. He strode to the door and said he must get out of this suffocating place for a moment and clear his brain in the fresh air so that he could determine what to do. The door would n't open. Roxy smiled grimly, and said—

"I 's got de key, honey—set down. You need n't cle'r up yo' brain none to fine out what you gwine to do—*I* knows what you 's gwine to do." Tom sat down and began to pass his hands through his hair with a helpless and desperate air. Roxy said, "Is dat man in dis house?"

Tom glanced up with a surprised expression, and asked—

"What gave you such an idea?"

"You done it. Gwine out to cle'r yo' brain! In de fust place you ain't got none to cle'r, en in de second place yo' ornery eye tole on you. You 's de low-downest hound dat ever—but I done tole you dat befo'. Now den, dis is Friday. You kin fix it up wid dat man, en tell him you 's gwine away to git de res' o' de money, en dat you 'll be back wid it nex' Tuesday, or maybe Wednesday. You understan'?"

Tom answered sullenly—

"Yes."

"En when you gits de new bill o' sale dat sells me to my own self, take en send it in de mail to Mr. Pudd'nhead Wilson, en write on de back dat he 's to keep it tell I come. You understan'?"

"Yes."

"Dat 's all, den. Take yo' umbreller, en put on yo' hat."

"Why?"

"Beca'se you 's gwine to see me home to de wharf. You see dis knife? I 's toted it aroun' sence de day I seed dat man en bought dese clo'es en it. If he ketched me, I 'uz gwine to kill myself wid it. Now start along, en go sof', en lead de way; en if you gives a sign in dis house, or if anybody comes up to you in de street, I 's gwine to jam it into you. Chambers, does you b'lieve me when I says dat?"

"It 's no use to bother me with that question. I know your word 's good."

"Yes, it 's diff'rent from yo'n! Shet de light out en move along—here 's de key."

They were not followed. Tom trembled every time a late straggler brushed by them on the street, and half expected to feel the cold steel in his back. Roxy was right at his heels and always in reach. After tramping a mile they reached a wide vacancy on the deserted wharves, and in this dark and rainy desert they parted.

As Tom trudged home his mind was full of dreary thoughts and wild plans; but at last he said to himself, wearily—

"There is but the one way out. I must follow her plan. But with a variation—I will not ask for the money and ruin myself; I will *rob* the old skinflint."

XIX

Few things are harder to put up with than the annoyance of a good example.

— Pudd'nhead Wilson's Calendar.

It were not best that we should all think alike; it is difference of opinion that makes horse-races.

— Pudd'nhead Wilson's Calendar.

DAWSON'S LANDING was comfortably finishing its season of dull repose and waiting patiently for the duel. Count Luigi was waiting, too; but not patiently, rumor said. Sunday came, and Luigi insisted on having his challenge conveyed. Wilson carried it. Judge Driscoll declined to fight with an assassin—"that is," he added significantly, "in the field of honor."

Elsewhere, of course, he would be ready. Wilson tried to convince him that if he had been present himself when Angelo told about the homicide committed by Luigi, he would not have considered the act discreditable to Luigi; but the obstinate old man was not to be moved.

Wilson went back to his principal and reported the failure of his mission. Luigi was incensed, and asked how it could be that the old gentleman, who was by no means dull-witted, held his trifling nephew's evidence and inferences to be of more value than Wilson's. But Wilson laughed, and said—

"That is quite simple; that is easily explicable. I am not his doll—his baby—his infatuation: his nephew is. The Judge and his late wife never had any children. The Judge and his wife were past middle age when this treasure fell into their lap. One must make allowances for a parental instinct that has been starving for twenty-five or thirty years. It is famished, it is crazed with hunger by that time, and will be entirely satisfied with anything that comes handy; its taste is atrophied, it can't tell mud-cat from shad. A devil born to a young couple is measurably recognizable by them as a devil before long, but a devil adopted by an old couple is an angel to them, and remains so, through thick and thin. Tom is this old man's angel; he is infatuated with him. Tom can persuade him into

things which other people can 't—not all things; I don't
mean that, but a good many—particularly one class of things:
the things that create or abolish personal partialities or prej-
udices in the old man's mind. The old man liked both of you.
Tom conceived a hatred for you. That was enough; it turned
the old man around at once. The oldest and strongest friendship must go to the ground when one of these late-adopted
darlings throws a brick at it."

"It 's a curious philosophy," said Luigi.

"It ain't a philosophy at all—it 's a fact. And there is something pathetic and beautiful about it, too. I think there is
nothing more pathetic than to see one of these poor old
childless couples taking a menagerie of yelping little worthless
dogs to their hearts; and then adding some cursing and
squawking parrots and a jackass-voiced macaw; and next a
couple of hundred screeching song-birds, and presently some
fetid guinea-pigs and rabbits, and a howling colony of cats. It
is all a groping and ignorant effort to construct out of base
metal and brass filings, so to speak, something to take the
place of that golden treasure denied them by Nature, a child.
But this is a digression. The unwritten law of this region requires you to kill Judge Driscoll on sight, and he and the
community will expect that attention at your hands—though
of course your own death by his bullet will answer every purpose. Look out for him! Are you heeled—that is, fixed?"

"Yes; he shall have his opportunity. If he attacks me I will
respond."

As Wilson was leaving, he said—

"The Judge is still a little used up by his campaign work,
and will not get out for a day or so; but when he does get
out, you want to be on the alert."

About eleven at night the twins went out for exercise, and
started on a long stroll in the veiled moonlight.

Tom Driscoll had landed at Hackett's Store, two miles below Dawson's, just about half an hour earlier, the only passenger for that lonely spot, and had walked up the shore road
and entered Judge Driscoll's house without having encountered any one either on the road or under the roof.

He pulled down his window-blinds and lighted his candle.
He laid off his coat and hat and began his preparations. He

unlocked his trunk and got his suit of girl's clothes out from under the male attire in it, and laid it by. Then he blacked his face with burnt cork and put the cork in his pocket. His plan was, to slip down to his uncle's private sitting-room below, pass into the bed-room, steal the safe-key from the old gentleman's clothes, and then go back and rob the safe. He took up his candle to start. His courage and confidence were high, up to this point, but both began to waver a little, now. Suppose he should make a noise, by some accident, and get caught— say, in the act of opening the safe? Perhaps it would be well to go armed. He took the Indian knife from its hiding-place, and felt a pleasant return of his waning courage. He slipped stealthily down the narrow stair, his hair rising and his pulses halting at the slightest creak. When he was half-way down, he was disturbed to perceive that the landing below was touched by a faint glow of light. What could that mean? Was his uncle still up? No, that was not likely; he must have left his night-taper there when he went to bed. Tom crept on down, pausing at every step to listen. He found the door standing open, and glanced in. What he saw pleased him beyond measure. His uncle was asleep on the sofa; on a small table at the head of the sofa a lamp was burning low, and by it stood the old man's small tin cash-box, closed. Near the box was a pile of bank-notes and a piece of paper covered with figures in pencil. The safe-door was not open. Evidently the sleeper had wearied himself with work upon his finances, and was taking a rest.

Tom set his candle on the stairs, and began to make his way toward the pile of notes, stooping low as he went. When he was passing his uncle, the old man stirred in his sleep, and Tom stopped instantly—stopped, and softly drew the knife from its sheath, with his heart thumping, and his eyes fastened upon his benefactor's face. After a moment or two he ventured forward again—one step—reached for his prize and seized it, dropping the knife-sheath. Then he felt the old man's strong grip upon him, and a wild cry of "Help! help!" rang in his ear. Without hesitation he drove the knife home— and was free. Some of the notes escaped from his left hand and fell in the blood on the floor. He dropped the knife and snatched them up and started to fly; transferred them to his

left hand, and seized the knife again, in his fright and confusion, but remembered himself and flung it from him, as being
a dangerous witness to carry away with him.

He jumped for the stair-foot, and closed the door behind
him; and as he snatched his candle and fled upward, the stillness of the night was broken by the sound of urgent footsteps
approaching the house. In another moment he was in his
room and the twins were standing aghast over the body of
the murdered man!

Tom put on his coat, buttoned his hat under it, threw on
his suit of girl's clothes, dropped the veil, blew out his light,
locked the room door by which he had just entered, taking
the key, passed through his other door into the back hall,
locked that door and kept the key, then worked his way along
in the dark and descended the back stairs. He was not expecting to meet anybody, for all interest was centered in the other
part of the house, now; his calculation proved correct. By the
time he was passing through the back yard, Mrs. Pratt, her
servants, and a dozen half-dressed neighbors had joined the
twins and the dead, and accessions were still arriving at the
front door.

As Tom, quaking as with a palsy, passed out at the gate,
three women came flying from the house on the opposite side
of the lane. They rushed by him and in at the gate, asking
him what the trouble was there, but not waiting for an answer. Tom said to himself, "Those old maids waited to
dress—they did the same thing the night Stevens's house
burned down next door." In a few minutes he was in the
haunted house. He lighted a candle and took off his girl-
clothes. There was blood on him all down his left side, and
his right hand was red with the stains of the blood-soaked
notes which he had crushed in it; but otherwise he was free
from this sort of evidence. He cleansed his hand on the straw,
and cleaned most of the smut from his face. Then he burned
his male and female attire to ashes, scattered the ashes, and
put on a disguise proper for a tramp. He blew out his light,
went below, and was soon loafing down the river road with
the intent to borrow and use one of Roxy's devices. He
found a canoe and paddled off down-stream, setting the
canoe adrift as dawn approached, and making his way by land

to the next village, where he kept out of sight till a transient steamer came along, and then took deck passage for St. Louis. He was ill at ease until Dawson's Landing was behind him; then he said to himself, "All the detectives on earth could n't trace me now; there 's not a vestige of a clue left in the world; that homicide will take its place with the permanent mysteries, and people won't get done trying to guess out the secret of it for fifty years."

In St. Louis, next morning, he read this brief telegram in the papers—dated at Dawson's Landing:

> Judge Driscoll, an old and respected citizen, was assassinated here about midnight by a profligate Italian nobleman or barber on account of a quarrel growing out of the recent election. The assassin will probably be lynched.

"One of the twins!" soliloquized Tom; "how lucky! It is the knife that has done him this grace. We never know when fortune is trying to favor us. I actually cursed Pudd'nhead Wilson in my heart for putting it out of my power to sell that knife. I take it back, now."

Tom was now rich and independent. He arranged with the planter, and mailed to Wilson the new bill of sale which sold Roxana to herself; then he telegraphed his Aunt Pratt:

> Have seen the awful news in the papers and am almost prostrated with grief. Shall start by packet to-day. Try to bear up till I come.

When Wilson reached the house of mourning and had gathered such details as Mrs. Pratt and the rest of the crowd could tell him, he took command as mayor, and gave orders that nothing should be touched, but everything left as it was until Justice Robinson should arrive and take the proper measures as coroner. He cleared everybody out of the room but the twins and himself. The sheriff soon arrived and took the twins away to jail. Wilson told them to keep heart, and promised to do his best in their defense when the case should come to trial. Justice Robinson came presently, and with him Constable Blake. They examined the room thoroughly. They found the knife and the sheath. Wilson noticed that there were finger-prints on the knife-handle. That pleased him, for

the twins had required the earliest comers to make a scrutiny
of their hands and clothes, and neither these people nor Wilson himself had found any blood-stains upon them. Could
there be a possibility that the twins had spoken the truth
when they said they found the man dead when they ran into
the house in answer to the cry for help? He thought of that
mysterious girl at once. But this was not the sort of work for
a girl to be engaged in. No matter; Tom Driscoll's room must
be examined.

After the coroner's jury had viewed the body and its surroundings, Wilson suggested a search up-stairs, and he went
along. The jury forced an entrance to Tom's room, but found
nothing, of course.

The coroner's jury found that the homicide was committed
by Luigi, and that Angelo was accessory to it.

The town was bitter against the unfortunates, and for the
first few days after the murder they were in constant danger
of being lynched. The grand jury presently indicted Luigi for
murder in the first degree, and Angelo as accessory before the
fact. The twins were transferred from the city jail to the
county prison to await trial.

Wilson examined the finger-marks on the knife-handle and
said to himself, "Neither of the twins made those marks."
Then manifestly there was another person concerned, either
in his own interest or as hired assassin.

But who could it be? That, he must try to find out. The
safe was not open, the cash-box was closed, and had three
thousand dollars in it. Then robbery was not the motive, and
revenge was. Where had the murdered man an enemy except
Luigi? There was but that one person in the world with a
deep grudge against him.

The mysterious girl! The girl was a great trial to Wilson.
If the motive had been robbery, the girl might answer; but
there was n't any girl that would want to take this old
man's life for revenge. He had no quarrels with girls; he
was a gentleman.

Wilson had perfect tracings of the finger-marks of the
knife-handle; and among his glass-records he had a great array of the finger-prints of women and girls, collected during
the last fifteen or eighteen years, but he scanned them in vain,

they successfully withstood every test; among them were no duplicates of the prints on the knife.

The presence of the knife on the stage of the murder was a worrying circumstance for Wilson. A week previously he had as good as admitted to himself that he believed Luigi had possessed such a knife, and that he still possessed it notwithstanding his pretense that it had been stolen. And now here was the knife, and with it the twins. Half the town had said the twins were humbugging when they claimed that they had lost their knife, and now these people were joyful, and said, "I told you so!"

If their finger-prints had been on the handle—but it was useless to bother any further about that; the finger-prints on the handle were *not* theirs—that he knew perfectly.

Wilson refused to suspect Tom; for first, Tom could n't murder anybody—he had n't character enough; secondly, if he could murder a person he would n't select his doting benefactor and nearest relative; thirdly, self-interest was in the way; for while the uncle lived, Tom was sure of a free support and a chance to get the destroyed will revived again, but with the uncle gone, that chance was gone, too. It was true the will had really been revived, as was now discovered, but Tom could not have been aware of it, or he would have spoken of it, in his native talky, unsecretive way. Finally, Tom was in St. Louis when the murder was done, and got the news out of the morning journals, as was shown by his telegram to his aunt. These speculations were unemphasized sensations rather than articulated thoughts, for Wilson would have laughed at the idea of seriously connecting Tom with the murder.

Wilson regarded the case of the twins as desperate—in fact, about hopeless. For he argued that if a confederate was not found, an enlightened Missouri jury would hang them, sure; if a confederate was found, that would not improve the matter, but simply furnish one more person for the sheriff to hang. Nothing could save the twins but the discovery of a person who did the murder on his sole personal account—an undertaking which had all the aspect of the impossible. Still, the person who made the finger-prints must be sought. The twins might have no case *with* him, but they certainly would have none without him.

So Wilson mooned around, thinking, thinking, guessing, guessing, day and night, and arriving nowhere. Whenever he ran across a girl or a woman he was not acquainted with, he got her finger-prints, on one pretext or another; and they always cost him a sigh when he got home, for they never tallied with the finger-marks on the knife-handle.

As to the mysterious girl, Tom swore he knew no such girl, and did not remember ever seeing a girl wearing a dress like the one described by Wilson. He admitted that he did not always lock his room, and that sometimes the servants forgot to lock the house doors; still, in his opinion the girl must have made but few visits or she would have been discovered. When Wilson tried to connect her with the stealing-raid, and thought she might have been the old woman's confederate, if not the very thief herself disguised as an old woman, Tom seemed struck, and also much interested, and said he would keep a sharp eye out for this person or persons, although he was afraid that she or they would be too smart to venture again into a town where everybody would now be on the watch for a good while to come.

Everybody was pitying Tom, he looked so quiet and sorrowful, and seemed to feel his great loss so deeply. He was playing a part, but it was not all a part. The picture of his alleged uncle, as he had last seen him, was before him in the dark pretty frequently, when he was awake, and called again in his dreams, when he was asleep. He would n't go into the room where the tragedy had happened. This charmed the doting Mrs. Pratt, who realized now, "as she had never done before," she said, what a sensitive and delicate nature her darling had, and how he adored his poor uncle.

XX

EVEN the clearest and most perfect circumstantial evidence is likely to be at fault, after all, and therefore ought to be received with great caution. Take the case of any pencil, sharpened by any woman: if you have witnesses, you will find she did it with a knife; but if you take simply the aspect of the pencil, you will say she did it with her teeth.

— *Pudd'nhead Wilson's Calendar.*

THE WEEKS dragged along, no friend visiting the jailed twins but their counsel and Aunt Patsy Cooper, and the day of trial came at last—the heaviest day in Wilson's life; for with all his tireless diligence he had discovered no sign or trace of the missing confederate. "Confederate" was the term he had long ago privately accepted for that person—not as being unquestionably the right term, but as being at least possibly the right one, though he was never able to understand why the twins did not vanish and escape, as the confederate had done, instead of remaining by the murdered man and getting caught there.

The court-house was crowded, of course, and would remain so to the finish, for not only in the town itself, but in the country for miles around, the trial was the one topic of conversation among the people. Mrs. Pratt, in deep mourning, and Tom with a weed on his hat, had seats near Pembroke Howard, the public prosecutor, and back of them sat a great array of friends of the family. The twins had but one friend present to keep their counsel in countenance, their poor old sorrowing landlady. She sat near Wilson, and looked her friendliest. In the "nigger corner" sat Chambers; also Roxy, with good clothes on, and her bill of sale in her pocket. It was her most precious possession, and she never parted with it, day or night. Tom had allowed her thirty-five dollars a month ever since he came into his property, and had said that he and she ought to be grateful to the twins for making them rich; but had roused such a temper in her by this speech that he did not repeat the argument afterward. She said the old Judge had treated her child a thousand times better than he deserved, and had never done her an unkindness in his life; so she hated these outlandish devils for killing him, and should n't ever sleep satisfied till she saw them hanged for it. She was here to watch the trial, now, and was going to lift up just one "hooraw" over it if the County Judge put her in jail a year for it. She gave her turbaned head a toss and said, "When dat verdic' comes, I 's gwine to lif' dat *roof*, now, I *tell* you."

Pembroke Howard briefly sketched the State's case. He said he would show by a chain of circumstantial evidence without break or fault in it anywhere, that the principal prisoner at the bar committed the murder; that the motive was partly revenge, and partly a desire to take his own life out of jeopardy, and that his brother, by his presence, was a consenting accessory to the crime; a crime which was the basest known to the calendar of human misdeeds—assassination; that it was conceived by the blackest of hearts and consummated by the cowardliest of hands; a crime which had broken a loving sister's heart, blighted the happiness of a young nephew who was as dear as a son, brought inconsolable grief to many friends, and sorrow and loss to the whole community. The utmost penalty of the outraged law would be exacted, and upon the accused, now present at the bar, that penalty would unquestionably be executed. He would reserve further remark until his closing speech.

He was strongly moved, and so also was the whole house; Mrs. Pratt and several other women were weeping when he sat down, and many an eye that was full of hate was riveted upon the unhappy prisoners.

Witness after witness was called by the State, and questioned at length; but the cross-questioning was brief. Wilson knew they could furnish nothing valuable for his side. People were sorry for Pudd'nhead; his budding career would get hurt by this trial.

Several witnesses swore they heard Judge Driscoll say in his public speech that the twins would be able to find their lost knife again when they needed it to assassinate somebody with. This was not news, but now it was seen to have been sorrowfully prophetic, and a profound sensation quivered through the hushed court-room when those dismal words were repeated.

The public prosecutor rose and said that it was within his knowledge, through a conversation held with Judge Driscoll on the last day of his life, that counsel for the defense had brought him a challenge from the person charged at this bar with murder; that he had refused to fight with a confessed assassin—"that is, on the field of honor," but had added significantly, that he would be ready for him elsewhere. Presumably the person here charged with murder was warned that he must kill or be killed the first time he should meet Judge Driscoll. If counsel for the defense chose to let the statement stand so, he would not call him to the witness stand. Mr. Wilson said he would offer no denial. [Murmurs in the house—"It is getting worse and worse for Wilson's case."]

Mrs. Pratt testified that she heard no outcry, and did not know what woke her up, unless it was the sound of rapid footsteps approaching the front door. She jumped up and ran out in the hall just as she was, and heard the footsteps flying up the front steps and then following behind her as she ran to the sitting-room. There she found the accused standing over her murdered brother. [Here she broke down and sobbed. Sensation in the court.] Resuming, she said the persons entering behind her were Mr. Rogers and Mr. Buckstone.

Cross-examined by Wilson, she said the twins proclaimed their innocence; declared that they had been taking a walk, and had hurried to the house in response to a cry for help which was so loud and strong that they had heard it at a considerable distance; that they begged her and the gentlemen just mentioned to examine their hands and clothes— which was done, and no blood-stains found.

Confirmatory evidence followed from Rogers and Buckstone.

The finding of the knife was verified, the advertisement minutely describing it and offering a reward for it was put in evidence, and its exact correspondence with that description proved. Then followed a few minor details, and the case for the State was closed.

Wilson said that he had three witnesses, the Misses Clarkson, who would testify that they met a veiled young woman leaving Judge Driscoll's premises by the back gate a few minutes after the cries for help were heard, and that their evidence, taken with certain circumstantial evidence which he would call the court's attention to, would in his opinion convince the court that there was still one person concerned in this crime who had not yet been found, and also that a stay of proceedings ought to be granted, in justice to his clients, until that person should be discovered. As it was late, he would ask leave to defer the examination of his three witnesses until the next morning.

The crowd poured out of the place and went flocking away in excited groups and couples, talking the events of the session over with vivacity and consuming interest, and everybody seemed to have had a satisfactory and enjoyable day except the accused, their counsel, and their old-lady friend. There was no cheer among these, and no substantial hope.

In parting with the twins Aunt Patsy did attempt a goodnight with a gay pretense of hope and cheer in it, but broke down without finishing.

Absolutely secure as Tom considered himself to be, the opening solemnities of the trial had nevertheless oppressed him with a vague uneasiness, his being a nature sensitive to even the smallest alarms; but from the moment that the poverty and weakness of Wilson's case lay exposed to the court, he was comfortable once more, even jubilant. He left the court-room sarcastically sorry for Wilson. "The Clarksons met an unknown woman in the back lane," he said to himself— "*that* is his case! I'll give him a century to find her in—a couple of them if he likes. A woman who does n't exist any longer, and the clothes that gave her her sex burnt up and the ashes thrown away—oh, certainly, he'll find *her* easy enough!" This reflection set him to admiring, for the hundredth time, the shrewd ingenuities by which he had insured himself against detection—more, against even suspicion.

"Nearly always in cases like this there is some little detail or other overlooked, some wee little track or trace left behind, and detection follows; but here there's not even the faintest suggestion of a trace left. No more than a bird leaves when it flies through the air—yes, through the night, you may say.

The man that can track a bird through the air in the dark and find that bird is the man to track me out and find the Judge's assassin—no other need apply. And that is the job that has been laid out for poor Pudd'nhead Wilson, of all people in the world! Lord, it will be pathetically funny to see him grubbing and groping after that woman that don't exist, and the right person sitting under his very nose all the time!" The more he thought the situation over, the more the humor of it struck him. Finally he said, "I'll never let him hear the last of that woman. Every time I catch him in company, to his dying day, I 'll ask him in the guileless affectionate way that used to gravel him so when I inquired how his unborn law-business was coming along, 'Got on her track yet—hey, Pudd'nhead?' " He wanted to laugh, but that would not have answered; there were people about, and he was mourning for his uncle. He made up his mind that it would be good entertainment to look in on Wilson that night and watch him worry over his barren law-case and goad him with an exasperating word or two of sympathy and commiseration now and then.

Wilson wanted no supper, he had no appetite. He got out all the finger-prints of girls and women in his collection of records and pored gloomily over them an hour or more, trying to convince himself that that troublesome girl's marks were there somewhere and had been overlooked. But it was not so. He drew back his chair, clasped his hands over his head, and gave himself up to dull and arid musings.

Tom Driscoll dropped in, an hour after dark, and said with a pleasant laugh as he took a seat—

"Hello, we 've gone back to the amusements of our days of neglect and obscurity for consolation, have we?" and he took up one of the glass strips and held it against the light to inspect it. "Come, cheer up, old man; there 's no use in losing your grip and going back to this child's-play merely because this big sun-spot is drifting across your shiny new disk. It 'll pass, and you 'll be all right again"—and he laid the glass down. "Did you think you could win always?"

"Oh, no," said Wilson, with a sigh, "I did n't expect that, but I can't believe Luigi killed your uncle, and I feel very sorry for him. It makes me blue. And you would feel as I do,

Tom, if you were not prejudiced against those young fellows."

"I don't know about that," and Tom's countenance darkened, for his memory reverted to his kicking; "I owe them no good will, considering the brunette one's treatment of me that night. Prejudice or no prejudice, Pudd'nhead, I don't like them, and when they get their deserts you 're not going to find me sitting on the mourner's bench."

He took up another strip of glass, and exclaimed—

"Why, here 's old Roxy's label! Are you going to ornament the royal palaces with nigger paw-marks, too? By the date here, I was seven months old when this was done, and she was nursing me and her little nigger cub. There 's a line straight across her thumb-print. How comes that?" and Tom held out the piece of glass to Wilson.

"That is common," said the bored man, wearily. "Scar of a cut or a scratch, usually"—and he took the strip of glass indifferently, and raised it toward the lamp.

All the blood sunk suddenly out of his face; his hand quaked, and he gazed at the polished surface before him with the glassy stare of a corpse.

"Great Heavens, what 's the matter with you, Wilson? Are you going to faint?"

Tom sprang for a glass of water and offered it, but Wilson shrank shuddering from him and said—

"No, no!—take it away!" His breast was rising and falling, and he moved his head about in a dull and wandering way, like a person who has been stunned. Presently he said, "I shall feel better when I get to bed; I have been overwrought to-day; yes, and overworked for many days."

"Then I 'll leave you and let you get to your rest. Goodnight, old man." But as Tom went out he could n't deny himself a small parting gibe: "Don't take it so hard; a body can't win every time; you 'll hang somebody yet."

Wilson muttered to himself, "It is no lie to say I am sorry I have to begin with you, miserable dog though you are!"

He braced himself up with a glass of cold whisky, and went to work again. He did not compare the new finger-marks unintentionally left by Tom a few minutes before on Roxy's glass with the tracings of the marks left on the knife-handle, there being no need of that (for his trained eye), but busied himself with another matter, muttering from time to time, "Idiot that I was!—Nothing but a *girl* would do me—a man in girl's clothes never occurred to me." First, he hunted out the plate containing the finger-prints made by Tom when he was twelve years old, and laid it by itself; then he brought forth the marks made by Tom's baby fingers when he was a suckling of seven months, and placed these two plates with the one containing this subject's newly (and unconsciously) made record.

"Now the series is complete," he said with satisfaction, and sat down to inspect these things and enjoy them.

But his enjoyment was brief. He stared a considerable time at the three strips, and seemed stupefied with astonishment. At last he put them down and said, "I can't make it out at all—hang it, the baby's don't tally with the others!"

He walked the floor for half an hour puzzling over his enigma, then he hunted out two other glass plates.

He sat down and puzzled over these things a good while, but kept muttering, "It 's no use; I can't understand it. They don't tally right, and yet I 'll swear the names and dates are right, and so of course they *ought* to tally. I never labeled one of these things carelessly in my life. There is a most extraordinary mystery here."

He was tired out, now, and his brains were beginning to clog. He said he would sleep himself fresh, and then see what he could do with this riddle. He slept through a troubled and unrestful hour, then unconsciousness began to shred away, and presently he rose drowsily to a sitting posture. "Now what was that dream?" he said, trying to recall it; "what was that dream?—it seemed to unravel that puz—"

He landed in the middle of the floor at a bound, without finishing the sentence, and ran and turned up his light and seized his "records." He took a single swift glance at them and cried out—

"It 's so! Heavens, what a revelation! And for twenty-three years no man has ever suspected it!"

XXI

He is useless on top of the ground; he ought to be under it, inspiring the cabbages.

— *Pudd'nhead Wilson's Calendar.*

April 1. This is the day upon which we are reminded of what we are on the other three hundred and sixty-four.

— *Pudd'nhead Wilson's Calendar.*

WILSON PUT ON enough clothes for business purposes and went to work under a high pressure of steam. He was awake all over. All sense of weariness had been swept away by the invigorating refreshment of the great and hopeful discovery which he had made. He made fine and accurate reproductions of a number of his "records," and then enlarged them on a scale of ten to one with his pantograph. He did these pantograph enlargements on sheets of white cardboard, and made each individual line of the bewildering maze of whorls or curves or loops which constituted the "pattern" of a "record" stand out bold and black by reinforcing it with ink. To the untrained eye the collection of delicate originals made by the human finger on the glass plates looked about alike; but when enlarged ten times they resembled the markings of a block of wood that has been sawed across the grain, and the dullest eye could detect at a glance, and at a distance of many feet, that no two of the patterns were alike. When Wilson had at last finished his tedious and difficult work, he arranged its results according to a plan in which a progressive order and sequence was a principal feature; then he added to the batch several pantograph enlargements which he had made from time to time in bygone years.

The night was spent and the day well advanced, now. By the time he had snatched a trifle of breakfast it was nine o'clock, and the court was ready to begin its sitting. He was in his place twelve minutes later with his "records."

Tom Driscoll caught a slight glimpse of the records, and nudged his nearest friend and said, with a wink, "Pudd'n-head's got a rare eye to business—thinks that as long as he can't win his case it's at least a noble good chance to advertise his palace-window decorations without any expense." Wilson was informed that his witnesses had been delayed, but would arrive presently; but he rose and said he should probably not have occasion to make use of their testimony. [An amused murmur ran through the room—"It 's a clean back-down! he gives up without hitting a lick!"] Wilson continued—"I have other testimony—and better. [This compelled interest, and evoked murmurs of surprise that had a detectible ingredient of disappointment in them.] If I seem to be springing this evidence upon the court, I offer as my justification for this, that I did not discover its existence until late last night, and have been engaged in examining and classifying it ever since, until half an hour ago. I shall offer it presently; but first I wish to say a few preliminary words.

"May it please the Court, the claim given the front place, the claim most persistently urged, the claim most strenuously and I may even say aggressively and defiantly insisted upon by the prosecution, is this—that the person whose hand left the blood-stained finger-prints upon the handle of the Indian knife is the person who committed the murder." Wilson paused, during several moments, to give impressiveness to what he was about to say, and then added tranquilly, *"We grant that claim."*

It was an electrical surprise. No one was prepared for such an admission. A buzz of astonishment rose on all sides, and people were heard to intimate that the overworked lawyer had lost his mind. Even the veteran judge, accustomed as he was to legal ambushes and masked batteries in criminal procedure, was not sure that his ears were not deceiving him, and asked counsel what it was he had said. Howard's impassive face betrayed no sign, but his attitude and bearing lost something of their careless confidence for a moment. Wilson resumed:

"We not only grant that claim, but we welcome it and strongly endorse it. Leaving that matter for the present, we will now proceed to consider other points in the case which we propose to establish by evidence, and shall include that one in the chain in its proper place."

He had made up his mind to try a few hardy guesses, in mapping out his theory of the origin and motive of the murder—guesses designed to fill up gaps in it—guesses which could help if they hit, and would probably do no harm if they did n't.

"To my mind, certain circumstances of the case before the court seem to suggest a motive for the homicide quite different from the one insisted on by the State. It is my conviction that the motive was not revenge, but robbery. It has been urged that the presence of the accused brothers in that fatal room, just after notification that one of them must take the life of Judge Driscoll or lose his own the moment the parties should meet, clearly signifies that the natural instinct of self-preservation moved my clients to go there secretly and save Count Luigi by destroying his adversary.

"Then why did they stay there, after the deed was done? Mrs. Pratt had time, although she did not hear the cry for help, but woke up some moments later, to run to that room—and there she found these men standing, and making no effort to escape. If they were guilty, they ought to have been running out of the house at the same time that she was running to that room. If they had had such a strong instinct toward self-preservation as to move them to kill that unarmed man, what had become of it now, when it should have been more alert than ever? Would any of us have remained there? Let us not slander our intelligence to that degree.

"Much stress has been laid upon the fact that the accused offered a very large reward for the knife with which this murder was done; that no thief came forward to claim that extraordinary reward; that the latter fact was good circumstantial evidence that the claim that the knife had been stolen was a vanity and a fraud; that these details taken in connection with the memorable and apparently prophetic speech of the deceased concerning that knife, and the final discovery of that very knife in the fatal room where no living person was found present with the slaughtered man but the owner of the knife and his brother, form an indestructible chain of evidence which fixes the crime upon those unfortunate strangers.

"But I shall presently ask to be sworn, and shall testify that there was a large reward offered for the *thief*, also; that it was offered secretly and not advertised; that this fact was indiscreetly mentioned—or at least tacitly admitted—in what was supposed to be safe circumstances, but may *not* have been. The thief may have been present himself. [Tom Driscoll had been looking at the speaker, but dropped his eyes at this point.] In that case he would retain the knife in his possession, not daring to offer it for sale, or for pledge in a pawn-shop. [There was a nodding of heads among the audience by way of admission that this was not a bad stroke.] I shall prove to the satisfaction of the jury that there *was* a person in Judge Driscoll's room several minutes before the accused entered it. [This produced a strong sensation; the last drowsy-head in the court-room roused up, now, and made preparation to listen.] If it shall seem necessary, I will prove by the Misses Clarkson that they met a veiled person—ostensibly a woman—coming out of the back gate a few minutes after the cry for help was heard. This person was not a woman, but a man dressed in woman's clothes." Another sensation. Wilson had his eye on Tom when he hazarded this guess, to see what effect it would produce. He was satisfied with the result, and said to himself, "It was a success—he 's hit!"

"The object of that person in that house was robbery, not murder. It is true that the safe was not open, but there was an ordinary tin cash-box on the table, with three thousand dollars in it. It is easily supposable that the thief was concealed in the house; that he knew of this box, and of its owner's habit of counting its contents and arranging his accounts at night—if he had that habit, which I do not assert, of course;—that he tried to take the box while its owner slept, but made a noise and was seized, and had to use the knife to save himself from capture; and that he fled without his booty because he heard help coming.

"I have now done with my theory, and will proceed to the evidences by which I propose to try to prove its soundness." Wilson took up several of his strips of glass. When the audience recognized these familiar mementos of Pudd'nhead's old-time childish "puttering" and folly, the tense and funereal interest vanished out of their faces, and the house burst into volleys of relieving and refreshing laughter, and Tom chirked up and joined in the fun himself; but Wilson was apparently not disturbed. He arranged his records on the table before him, and said—

"I beg the indulgence of the court while I make a few remarks in explanation of some evidence which I am about to
introduce, and which I shall presently ask to be allowed to
verify under oath on the witness stand. Every human being
carries with him from his cradle to his grave certain physical
marks which do not change their character, and by which he
can always be identified—and that without shade of doubt or
question. These marks are his signature, his physiological autograph, so to speak, and this autograph cannot be counterfeited, nor can he disguise it or hide it away, nor can it become illegible by the wear and the mutations of time. This
signature is not his face—age can change that beyond recognition; it is not his hair, for that can fall out; it is not his
height, for duplicates of that exist; it is not his form, for duplicates of that exist also, whereas this signature is each man's
very own—there is no duplicate of it among the swarming
populations of the globe! [The audience were interested once
more.]

"This autograph consists of the delicate lines or corruga-
tions with which Nature marks the insides of the hands and
the soles of the feet. If you will look at the balls of your
fingers,—you that have very sharp eyesight,—you will observe that these dainty curving lines lie close together, like
those that indicate the borders of oceans in maps, and that
they form various clearly defined patterns, such as arches, circles, long curves, whorls, etc., and that these patterns differ
on the different fingers. [Every man in the room had his hand
up to the light, now, and his head canted to one side, and
was minutely scrutinizing the balls of his fingers; there were
whispered ejaculations of "Why, it's so—I never noticed that
before!"] The patterns on the right hand are not the same as
those on the left. [Ejaculations of "Why, that's so, too!"]
Taken finger for finger, your patterns differ from your neighbor's. [Comparisons were made all over the house—even the
judge and jury were absorbed in this curious work.] The patterns of a twin's right hand are not the same as those on his
left. One twin's patterns are never the same as his fellow-
twin's patterns—the jury will find that the patterns upon the
finger-balls of the accused follow this rule. [An examination
of the twins' hands was begun at once.] You have often heard

of twins who were so exactly alike that when dressed alike their own parents could not tell them apart. Yet there was never a twin born into this world that did not carry from birth to death a sure identifier in this mysterious and marvelous natal autograph. That once known to you, his fellow-twin could never personate him and deceive you."

Wilson stopped and stood silent. Inattention dies a quick and sure death when a speaker does that. The stillness gives warning that something is coming. All palms and finger-balls went down, now, all slouching forms straightened, all heads came up, all eyes were fastened upon Wilson's face. He waited yet one, two, three moments, to let his pause complete and perfect its spell upon the house; then, when through the profound hush he could hear the ticking of the clock on the wall, he put out his hand and took the Indian knife by the blade and held it aloft where all could see the sinister spots upon its ivory handle; then he said, in a level and passionless voice—

"Upon this haft stands the assassin's natal autograph, written in the blood of that helpless and unoffending old man who loved you and whom you all loved. There is but one man in the whole earth whose hand can duplicate that crimson sign,"—he paused and raised his eyes to the pendulum swinging back and forth,—"and please God we will produce that man in this room before the clock strikes noon!"

Stunned, distraught, unconscious of its own movement, the house half rose, as if expecting to see the murderer appear at the door, and a breeze of muttered ejaculations swept the place. "Order in the court!—sit down!" This from the sheriff. He was obeyed, and quiet reigned again. Wilson stole a glance at Tom, and said to himself, "He is flying signals of distress, now; even people who despise him are pitying him; they think this is a hard ordeal for a young fellow who has lost his benefactor by so cruel a stroke—and they are right." He resumed his speech:

"For more than twenty years I have amused my compulsory leisure with collecting these curious physical signatures in this town. At my house I have hundreds upon hundreds of them. Each and every one is labeled with name and date; not labeled the next day or even the next hour, but in the very minute that the impression was taken. When I go upon the witness stand I will repeat under oath the things which I am now saying. I have the finger-prints of the court, the sheriff, and every member of the jury. There is hardly a person in this room, white or black, whose natal signature I cannot produce, and not one of them can so disguise himself that I cannot pick him out from a multitude of his fellow-creatures and unerringly identify him by his hands. And if he and I should live to be a hundred I could still do it! [The interest of the audience was steadily deepening, now.]

"I have studied some of these signatures so much that I know them as well as the bank cashier knows the autograph of his oldest customer. While I turn my back now, I beg that several persons will be so good as to pass their fingers through their hair, and then press them upon one of the panes of the window near the jury, and that among them the accused may set *their* finger-marks. Also, I beg that these ex-perimenters, or others, will set their finger-marks upon an-other pane, and add again the marks of the accused, but not placing them in the same order or relation to the other sig-natures as before—for, by one chance in a million, a person might happen upon the right marks by pure guess-work *once*, therefore I wish to be tested twice."

He turned his back, and the two panes were quickly cov-ered with delicately-lined oval spots, but visible only to such persons as could get a dark background for them—the foliage of a tree, outside, for instance. Then, upon call, Wilson went to the window, made his examination, and said—

"This is Count Luigi's right hand; this one, three signa-tures below, is his left. Here is Count Angelo's right; down here is his left. Now for the other pane: here and here are Count Luigi's, here and here are his brother's." He faced about. "Am I right?"

A deafening explosion of applause was the answer. The Bench said—

"This certainly approaches the miraculous!"

Wilson turned to the window again and remarked, point-ing with his finger—

"This is the signature of Mr. Justice Robinson. [Applause.] This, of Constable Blake. [Applause.] This, of John Mason, juryman. [Applause.] This, of the sheriff. [Applause.] I cannot name the others, but I have them all at home, named and dated, and could identify them all by my finger-print records."

He moved to his place through a storm of applause— which the sheriff stopped, and also made the people sit down, for they were all standing and struggling to see, of course. Court, jury, sheriff, and everybody had been too absorbed in observing Wilson's performance to attend to the audience earlier.

"Now, then," said Wilson, "I have here the natal autographs of two children—thrown up to ten times the natural size by the pantograph, so that any one who can see at all can tell the markings apart at a glance. We will call the children *A* and *B*. Here are *A's* finger-marks, taken at the age of five months. Here they are again, taken at seven months. [Tom started.] They are alike, you see. Here are *B's* at five months, and also at seven months. They, too, exactly copy each other, but the patterns are quite different from *A's*, you observe. I shall refer to these again presently, but we will turn them face down, now.

"Here, thrown up ten sizes, are the natal autographs of the two persons who are here before you accused of murdering Judge Driscoll. I made these pantograph copies last night, and will so swear when I go upon the witness stand. I ask the jury to compare them with the finger-marks of the accused upon the window-panes, and tell the court if they are the same."

He passed a powerful magnifying-glass to the foreman.

One juryman after another took the cardboard and the glass and made the comparison. Then the foreman said to the judge—

"Your honor, we are all agreed that they are identical."

Wilson said to the foreman—

"Please turn that cardboard face down, and take this one, and compare it searchingly, by the magnifier, with the fatal signature upon the knife-handle, and report your findings to the court."

Again the jury made minute examination, and again reported—

"We find them to be exactly identical, your honor."

Wilson turned toward the counsel for the prosecution, and there was a clearly recognizable note of warning in his voice when he said—

"May it please the court, the State has claimed, strenuously and persistently, that the blood-stained finger-prints upon that knife-handle were left there by the assassin of Judge Driscoll. You have heard us grant that claim, and welcome it." He turned to the jury: "Compare the finger-prints of the accused with the finger-prints left by the assassin—and report."

The comparison began. As it proceeded, all movement and all sound ceased, and the deep silence of an absorbed and waiting suspense settled upon the house; and when at last the words came—

"*They do not even resemble,*" a thunder-crash of applause followed and the house sprang to its feet, but was quickly repressed by official force and brought to order again. Tom was altering his position every few minutes, now, but none of his changes brought repose nor any small trifle of comfort. When the house's attention was become fixed once more, Wilson said gravely, indicating the twins with a gesture—

"These men are innocent—I have no further concern with them. [Another outbreak of applause began, but was promptly checked.] We will now proceed to find the guilty. [Tom's eyes were starting from their sockets—yes, it was a cruel day for the bereaved youth, everybody thought.] We will return to the infant autographs of *A* and *B*. I will ask the jury to take these large pantograph facsimiles of *A's*, marked five months and seven months. Do they tally?

The foreman responded—

"Perfectly."

"Now examine this pantograph, taken at eight months, and also marked *A*. Does it tally with the other two?"

The surprised response was—

"*No—they differ widely!*"

"You are quite right. Now take these two pantographs of *B's* autograph, marked five months and seven months. Do they tally with each other?"

"Yes—perfectly."

"Take this third pantograph marked *B*, eight months. Does it tally with *B's* other two?"

"By no means!"

"Do you know how to account for those strange discrepancies? I will tell you. For a purpose unknown to us, but probably a selfish one, somebody changed those children in the cradle."

This produced a vast sensation, naturally; Roxana was astonished at this admirable guess, but not disturbed by it. To guess the exchange was one thing, to guess who did it quite another. Pudd'nhead Wilson could do wonderful things, no doubt, but he could n't do impossible ones. Safe? She was perfectly safe. She smiled privately.

"Between the ages of seven months and eight months those children were changed in the cradle"—he made one of his effect-collecting pauses, and added—"and the person who did it is in this house!"

Roxy's pulses stood still! The house was thrilled as with an electric shock, and the people half rose as if to seek a glimpse of the person who had made that exchange. Tom was growing limp; the life seemed oozing out of him. Wilson resumed:

"*A* was put into *B's* cradle in the nursery; *B* was transferred to the kitchen and became a negro and a slave [Sensation—confusion of angry ejaculations]—but within a quarter of an hour he will stand before you white and free! [Burst of applause, checked by the officers.] From seven months onward until now, *A* has still been a usurper, and in my finger-records he bears *B's* name. Here is his pantograph at the age of twelve. Compare it with the assassin's signature upon the knife-handle. Do they tally?"

The foreman answered—

"To the minutest detail!"

Wilson said, solemnly—

"The murderer of your friend and mine—York Driscoll of the generous hand and the kindly spirit—sits in among you. Valet de Chambre, negro and slave,—falsely called Thomas à Becket Driscoll,—make upon the window the finger-prints that will hang you!"

Tom turned his ashen face imploringly toward the speaker,

made some impotent movements with his white lips, then slid limp and lifeless to the floor.

Wilson broke the awed silence with the words—

"There is no need. He has confessed."

Roxy flung herself upon her knees, covered her face with her hands, and out through her sobs the words struggled—

"De Lord have mercy on me, po' misable sinner dat I is!"

The clock struck twelve.

The court rose; the new prisoner, hand-cuffed, was removed.

Conclusion

IT is often the case that the man who can't tell a lie thinks he is the best judge of one.

— Pudd'nhead Wilson's Calendar.

October 12, the Discovery. It was wonderful to find America, but it would have been more wonderful to miss it.

— Pudd'nhead Wilson's Calendar.

T HE TOWN sat up all night to discuss the amazing events of the day and swap guesses as to when Tom's trial would begin. Troop after troop of citizens came to serenade Wilson, and require a speech, and shout themselves hoarse over every sentence that fell from his lips—for all his sentences were golden, now, all were marvelous. His long fight against hard luck and prejudice was ended; he was a made man for good.

And as each of these roaring gangs of enthusiasts marched away, some remorseful member of it was quite sure to raise his voice and say—

"And this is the man the likes of us have called a pudd'nhead for more than twenty years. He has resigned from that position, friends."

"Yes, but it is n't vacant—we 're elected."

THE twins were heroes of romance, now, and with rehabilitated reputations. But they were weary of Western adventure, and straightway retired to Europe.

Roxy's heart was broken. The young fellow upon whom she had inflicted twenty-three years of slavery continued the false heir's pension of thirty-five dollars a month to her, but her hurts were too deep for money to heal; the spirit in her eye was quenched, her martial bearing departed with it, and the voice of her laughter ceased in the land. In her church and its affairs she found her only solace.

The real heir suddenly found himself rich and free, but in a most embarrassing situation. He could neither read nor write, and his speech was the basest dialect of the negro quarter. His gait, his attitudes, his gestures, his bearing, his laugh—all were vulgar and uncouth; his manners were the manners of a slave. Money and fine clothes could not mend these defects or cover them up; they only made them the more glaring and the more pathetic. The poor fellow could not endure the terrors of the white man's parlor, and felt at home and at peace nowhere but in the kitchen. The family pew was a misery to him, yet he could nevermore enter into the solacing refuge of the "nigger gallery"—that was closed to him for good and all. But we cannot follow his curious fate further—that would be a long story.

The false heir made a full confession and was sentenced to imprisonment for life. But now a complication came up. The Percy Driscoll estate was in such a crippled shape when its owner died that it could pay only sixty per cent. of its great indebtedness, and was settled at that rate. But the creditors came forward, now, and complained that inasmuch as through an error for which *they* were in no way to blame the false heir was not inventoried at that time with the rest of the property, great wrong and loss had thereby been inflicted upon them. They rightly claimed that "Tom" was lawfully their property and had been so for eight years; that they had already lost sufficiently in being deprived of his services during that long period, and ought not to be required to add anything to that loss; that if he had been delivered up to them in the first place, they would have sold him and he could not have murdered Judge Driscoll; therefore it was not he that had really committed the murder, the guilt lay with the erroneous inventory. Everybody saw that there was reason in this. Everybody granted that if "Tom" were white and free it would be unquestionably right to punish him—it would be no loss to anybody; but to shut up a valuable slave for life—that was quite another matter.

As soon as the Governor understood the case, he pardoned Tom at once, and the creditors sold him down the river.

Chronology

1835   Samuel Langhorne Clemens born November 30 in Florida, Missouri, third of the four children of John Marshall Clemens (1798–1847) and Jane Lampton Clemens (1803–90) who survived into adulthood. The other children were: Orion (1825–97); Pamela (1827–1904); and Henry (1838–58). The Clemenses, of slaveholding but struggling Virginia farming stock, arrived about June 1 in Florida after unsuccessful efforts to establish themselves in Kentucky and Tennessee. Martha Ann Quarles, sister of Jane Clemens, and her husband, John Quarles, were already in Florida.

1839   John Clemens—austere, industrious, luckless—moves his family thirty miles from inland Florida to Hannibal, a port village about 116 miles by road (or about 130 miles by water) north of St. Louis.

1847   Unsuccessful as storekeeper, farmer, lawyer, and landowner, John Clemens dies on March 24. A few months later, Sam begins part-time work but probably receives intermittent schooling for two additional years. During the autumn is employed in the printshop of Joseph P. Ament.

1848   Works in the office of Ament's *Missouri Courier* and lives meagerly in Ament's house as an apprentice.

1851   On January 16 publishes first known sketch, the humorous anecdote "A Gallant Fireman," in the Hannibal *Western Union*. The newspaper is owned and edited by his brother Orion. Receives little or no pay as printer and editorial assistant.

1852   Writes squibs for Orion's new paper, the *Journal*, and publishes a brief example of Southwestern humor, "The Dandy Frightening the Squatter," in the Boston *Carpet Bag*, May 1. On September 9 signs a sketch "W. Epaminondas Adrastus Perkins," probably the first of his many pseudonyms.

1853–57   Leaves Hannibal at the end of May, 1853, to work as a printer in St. Louis, New York, Philadelphia, Keokuk, and Cincinnati. Publishes humorous travel letters in the Muscatine, Iowa, *Journal*.

1857–61   About April, 1857, becomes a cub pilot on the Mississippi under tutelage of Horace Bixby. Henry Clemens, a much-loved brother, dies (1858) as a result of an explosion on the steamboat *Pennsylvania*. Publishes May 17, 1859, in the New Orleans *Crescent* a widely read lampoon of Captain Isaiah Sellers, a senior pilot, from whom Clemens later claimed (though unconvincingly) he borrowed the pseudonym "Mark Twain." License as a pilot granted him on September 9, 1859. Continues on the river until approximately April 25, 1861, when river traffic is disrupted.

1861   Member of the Marion Rangers, a small Confederate militia group, for perhaps two weeks. Through the influence of Edward Bates of St. Louis, Attorney General under Lincoln, Orion is appointed Secretary to the Nevada Territory. Sam accompanies Orion with some prospect of assisting him. They arrive in Carson City by stage on August 14. Sam is clerk of the Territorial Legislature October 1 through November 29. Enters timber claims, speculates in mining stock, and prospects for silver.

1862   Contributes letters and sketches to the Keokuk, Iowa, *Gate City*; the Carson City, Nevada, *Silver Age*; the Virginia City, Nevada, *Territorial Enterprise*; and the Sacramento, California, *Union*. Probably late in September joins the staff of the *Enterprise* as local reporter and reports on the proceedings of the legislature when it is in session. Quickly masters such popular forms of newspaper comedy as the satirical sketch, the tall tale, the hoax, and the burlesque; gains a reputation with Western readers.

1863   On February 3, in a letter from Carson City to the *Enterprise* reporting legislative proceedings, signs himself for the first time as "Mark Twain." Vacations in San Francisco during May and June. Becomes a correspondent for the San Francisco *Morning Call*. Contributes to the *Golden Era*, a literary weekly.

1864   Leaves Virginia City on May 29, 1864, for San Francisco. Works about four months as a local reporter for the *Morning Call* but dislikes the restraints of straight reporting. Contributes to the *Californian*, a literary weekly edited by Bret Harte. Joins storytelling prospectors in the Tuolumne hills and hears, perhaps from Ben Coon of Angel's Camp, a tale about a jumping frog.

1865   Returns to San Francisco on February 25 and remains for a year writing for newspapers and literary periodicals. Publishes "Jim Smiley and His Jumping Frog"—often called his earliest masterpiece—in the New York *Saturday Press* for November 18, 1865.

1866   Leaves San Francisco for Sacramento at the end of February, then takes five-month journey to the Sandwich Islands (Hawaii) to report in letters to the Sacramento *Union* on prospects for industry and trade. October 2 enters the lucrative business of public lecturing and reading by delivering first of many lectures on the Islands. Already he is taking on the attributes of a charismatic public figure and metaphoric Western hero. Publicized as the best of the Western humorists, he sails, with conquest in mind, for New York on December 15 as roving correspondent for the San Francisco *Alta California*.

1867   Is commissioned by the *Alta* to sail June 10 on the first cruise ship, the *Quaker City*, for Europe and the Holy Land in order to send back entertaining travel letters. Dislikes most of his affluent, religiously minded fellow passengers, but accepts from Mrs. Abel W. Fairbanks ("Mother Fairbanks") correction of his manners and purification of his prose. Young Charles Jervis Langdon (born 1849), another passenger, is said to have shown him a miniature of his sister, Olivia Lewis Langdon (born 1845). Returns to United States on November 19. Meets Olivia (Livy) in New York on December 27. Her parents, the Jervis Langdons of Elmira, New York, are newly rich from mining and marketing coal. Serves briefly in Washington as private secretary to Senator William M. Stewart of Nevada. In collaboration with Charles Henry Webb publishes *The Celebrated Jumping Frog of Calaveras County and Other Sketches*.

1868   Lectures widely. Assists in support of his mother, sister, and his always aspiring, always indigent brother, Orion. Begins courtship of the semi-invalid Livy Langdon. Re-works and expands his *Quaker City* letters. At his insistence, Livy begins her career as chief among his many editors and censors. Livy's influence, like that of the East in general, is toward the serious and genteel, away from the vulgar and comic.

1869   With a loan from Livy's father, buys a one-third interest in the Buffalo *Express*. The thoroughly reworked *Quaker City* travel letters, published as *The Innocents Abroad*, are a great financial success and set patterns for a number of his later books.

1870   Marries Livy on February 2. The next day goes with members of the bridal party by private train to Buffalo, where he and Livy are installed in the handsome house Jervis Langdon has bought and furnished for them. Langdon dies on August 16. Son, Langdon, born to Livy November 7.

1871   Hating the tedium of newspaper work, sells house and interest in the *Express*, both at losses. Begins residence of twenty-one years in Hartford, Connecticut, interspersed with periods abroad and working summers at Quarry Farm, near Elmira, home of Susan Crane (Mrs. Theodore Crane), Livy's sister-by-adoption.

1872   Susan Olivia Clemens (Susy), born March 19. First-born, sickly Langdon dies in June. Clemens publishes *Roughing It*.

1873   Takes family for the first of several stays in Europe, some of long duration. Economy in living is often the chief object, as speculations and lavish expenditures consume his and Livy's income and a substantial portion of Livy's inheritance. Publishes *The Gilded Age* with co-author Charles Dudley Warner, friend and Hartford neighbor.

1874   Clara Langdon Clemens born June 8 in Elmira. In September the family moves into their not-quite-complete, architecturally bizarre, extremely costly, luxuriously furnished mansion in the "Nook Farm" area of Hartford. Clemens increasingly in demand as a speaker at breakfasts, lunches, dinners, political rallies, reunions, fund raisings, and celebrations of all kinds.

1875 Publishes "Old Times on the Mississippi" (later part of *Life on the Mississippi*) in the *Atlantic Monthly*, then edited by his friend, admirer, and sometimes literary adviser and censor, William Dean Howells.

1876 In summer receives proofs of *The Adventures of Tom Sawyer* and begins writing *Adventures of Huckleberry Finn*. Is becoming deeply engaged in exploiting boyhood and the vernacular in a partly remembered, partly imagined Mississippi River valley, the post-frontier. Publishes *The Adventures of Tom Sawyer*.

1877 On December 17 delivers the "Whittier Birthday Speech," a burlesque treating the New Englanders Longfellow, Emerson, and Holmes in a way that shocks a number of listeners and is at times to be deeply regretted by Clemens.

1878–79 Travels in Europe, turns again to the writing of *Huckleberry Finn*.

1880 In this or the following year begins "investing" in the Paige typesetter, the most monetarily and psychically costly of his many speculations. Expends approximately $190,000 and untold hours before abandoning hope for this machine in January, 1895. Between late 1880 and early 1883 works once more on *Huckleberry Finn*. Publishes *A Tramp Abroad* and permits the private publication of the best known and most reprinted of his scatological writings, *1601. Conversation, as It Was by the Social Fireside, in the Time of the Tudors*. Jane Lampton Clemens (called Jean) born July 26.

1882 Makes trip on the Mississippi with James R. Osgood (at this time his publisher) and a stenographer to refresh his recollections, form new impressions, and collect information useful in completing *Life on the Mississippi*. Leaves New York on April 18, returns to Hartford on May 24. Publishes *The Prince and the Pauper,* a favorite with Livy and the children.

1883 Once again returns to writing *Huckleberry Finn*. Publishes *Life on the Mississippi*.

1884–85   Makes successful reading tour with George W. Cable, Louisiana writer and civil rights advocate (November 5–February 28). On December 10, 1884, publishes *Adventures of Huckleberry Finn* in England; on February 18, 1885, through his own publishing house, Charles L. Webster & Company, in the United States.

1889   Publishes *A Connecticut Yankee in King Arthur's Court*. Annoyed by its mixed reception in England.

1890   Jane Clemens (his mother) and Olivia L. Langdon (Livy's mother) both die.

1891   Sails for Europe in June and lives there for most of the next decade.

1894   Charles L. Webster & Company declares itself bankrupt in April. Clemens loses roughly $110,000 of his own money and $60,000 of Livy's. With the encouragement of Livy and the shrewd assistance of Henry H. Rogers, a vice-president of the Standard Oil Company, begins the difficult task of setting his tangled affairs in order, making his copyrights secure, and paying off his creditors. His inclination toward pessimism and determinism is heightened. Publishes *Pudd'nhead Wilson, A Tale* in the *Century Magazine*. (In book form the novel is entitled *The Tragedy of Pudd'nhead Wilson*.)

1895   In August begins a lecture trip around the world to raise money to repay creditors. Has become a public figure world-wide. Tour ends in Europe in July, 1896.

1896   Publishes *Personal Recollections of Joan of Arc*. Daughter Susy dies in Hartford of meningitis, August 18, while Clemens is in London, Livy and Clara are en route home. Clemens characteristically blames himself, then inveighs against fate and a God whom he increasingly depicts as malevolent. Jean Clemens diagnosed as epileptic; thereafter often in rest homes and clinics.

1897   Publishes *Following the Equator*.

1898   In March Henry Rogers notifies Clemens in Vienna that his undisputed creditors have been repaid. Within days Clemens attempts to engage in new, grandiose speculative ventures. During these last years he places increased emphasis on the monetary value of his writings, which he has always treated as marketable products. At the same time he is strongly moved to write "seriously," to set down what he deems unprintable truths about God, religious institutions, man, politicians, tycoons, business associates, friends, and relatives.

1900   Returns to New York from England in October. Makes anti-missionary and anti-imperialist statements in connection with actions of the United States in China and the Philippines.

1901   Receives honorary degree from Yale.

1902   Receives honorary degree from the University of Missouri. Isabel Lyon, who comes into the household to be secretary to Livy, becomes Clemens' secretary and general family factotum until forced out, April, 1909, following bitter quarrels, especially with Clara. Their fortunes partly restored, the Clemenses' combined incomes for the year amount to more than $100,000.

1903   Takes a villa in Florence for the benefit of Livy's health.

1904   Olivia Clemens dies in Florence on June 5, and her body is taken to Elmira for burial. Clara enters a sanitarium in July; later undergoes a number of restorative treatments. Clemens' pleasure in the companionship of little girls becomes marked and continues until his death.

1906   Publishes *What Is Man?* privately and anonymously. In January accepts as his biographer Albert Bigelow Paine. A close association begins that lasts until Clemens' death and results in the publication of a massive biography and miscellaneous additional volumes.

1907   Receives honorary degree from Oxford University; enjoys displaying himself then and later in his crimson gown.

1908   John Howells (architect son of William Dean Howells) and Isabel Lyon supervise the building of a mansion called Stormfield near Redding, Connecticut. Clemens moves there from New York.

1909   Clara marries Ossip Gabrilowitsch, pianist and conductor, at Stormfield on October 6. Jean dies in bathtub, apparently during a seizure, on the morning of Christmas Eve.

1910   Clemens dies at Stormfield on April 21. Joseph Twichell of Hartford, one of Clemens' oldest friends, and Henry Van Dyck conduct services at the Presbyterian Brick Church in New York. Buried in Elmira on April 24 in the Langdon family plot, where little Langdon, Susy, Livy, and Jean had been interred before him. Left behind an enormous quantity of unpublished papers: autobiographical dictations, notebooks, letters, finished and unfinished sketches, essays, stories, polemics, and incomplete drafts of "The Mysterious Stranger," generally considered even in its unfinished state to be the most powerful of his later writings. For literary executors and editors, sifting and publishing these literary remains becomes almost at once a major, long-continuing enterprise.

Note on the Texts

Each of the four books reprinted in this volume is presented in the best text now available. The text for *The Adventures of Tom Sawyer* (Berkeley, 1980) reprinted here was prepared for the Iowa Center for Textual Studies by Paul Baender and his associates according to the standards established by the Center for Editions of American Authors of the Modern Language Association of America and has received the approval of the Center. It uses as copy-text Samuel Clemens' original ink holograph manuscript (now at the Riggs Memorial Library of Georgetown University), which was printer's copy for the first American edition, and accepts certain variants from a secretarial copy (in the Mark Twain Birthplace Memorial Shrine, Florida, Missouri) and from different printings of the first American edition.

Clemens' manuscript had a gestation of at least five years. In working through Clemens' papers after his death, A. B. Paine found a manuscript of fifty-eight half-sheets numbered 3–60 (the first two pages were missing) and wrote on page 3: "Boy's Manuscript. Probably written about 1870." Paine also discovered a single page of a holograph manuscript that dramatizes the opening of Tom Sawyer, with "Aunt Winny" ("Aunt Polly" in the book) calling for Tom. Bernard DeVoto, who succeeded Paine as editor of the Mark Twain Papers, recognized the "Boy's Manuscript" as containing characters and incidents leading toward *Tom Sawyer* and accepted 1870 as the probable year of composition but argued against Paine's belief that the dramatized version, which Paine dated "about 1872," was the predecessor of *Tom Sawyer*. The dramatization, DeVoto believed, was attempted after the completion of a version of the novel. Editors of the Iowa edition, however, date the dramatized page and the first 118 pages of what became the complete manuscript version of the novel at approximately the same time—late in 1872 or early in 1873.

During the early months of 1873, Clemens set *Tom Sawyer* aside and worked on *The Gilded Age*. He next took up *Tom Sawyer* in earnest while at Quarry Farm in April, 1874, and worked on it intermittently until September, finishing about 400 manuscript pages. He returned to it in the spring or summer of 1875, completing the book early in July. As Hamlin Hill has shown, the original manuscript indicates that during those last months Clemens developed his ideas about character and structure and rearranged large sections of manuscript.

Revision went on in several stages. Clemens made numerous changes in the manuscript (see pp. 555–600 of the Iowa text) and nearly half as many in an amanuensis copy (pp. 601–619 of the Iowa text), some of the changes in the latter predating changes in the holograph original. William Dean Howells finished correcting and commenting on the revised secretarial copy in November, 1875. The book was published in England in June, 1876, and in America, after many delays, on December 8.

As early as January, 1866, Clemens had contemplated writing a travel book about the Mississippi River. Five years later, he told his wife that he proposed to spend two months on the river and take notes, but the actual beginning of "the Mississippi book" did not come until William Dean Howells, editor of the *Atlantic Monthly*, pressed Clemens for a contribution to follow "A True Story" (November, 1874). Clemens wrote twice to Howells on October 24, 1874, first to say "my head won't 'go,' " next to propose a topic. While walking in the woods with his friend and pastor, Joseph Twichell, he explained, he "got to telling him about old Mississippi days of steamboating glory & grandeur" as he had seen them from the pilot house. Twichell exclaimed, "What a virgin subject to hurl into a magazine!" The work that resulted went into seven issues of the *Atlantic*, January through August, 1875, omitting July.

The contribution to the *Atlantic* was not nearly enough to make a subscription book, however, and only after a series of efforts to persuade Howells or some other friend to accompany him on a note-taking visit to the Mississippi did Clemens at last undertake the journey in 1882. By the terms of his contract for the book with James R. Osgood, Clemens became in effect his own publisher, Osgood—who had no experience in the publishing of subscription books—his agent.

Clemens redivided chapters, revised chapter titles, added "The Record of Some Famous Trips" (334–36), made perhaps forty-five other changes, and the *Atlantic* material became chapters IV through XVII of the book. In composing the additional forty-six chapters—a wearying task—Clemens made voluminous use of his own travel notes and padded the work with previously written but unpublished tales, such as "The Professor's Yarn" (chapter XXXVI). He also borrowed perhaps 11,000 words from other writers. Most interestingly, he took the "raft passage" from his manuscript for what later became *Adventures of Huckleberry Finn* and incorporated it in "Frescoes from the Past" (chapter III). Indeed, he crowded so many pages into his manuscript that some became superfluous; he was able to omit some 13,000 to 15,000 words and to move other material to appendices.

The first American edition (1883) is reprinted here. Ultimately, the methodically prepared text of the future will involve a comparison of the first American edition and the holograph manuscript held since 1909 by the J. Pierpont Morgan Library. The manuscript contains matter not in the book, and the book, matter not in the manuscript. Except for a few pages that Clemens called "the eighth batch" and—because of the illness of his typist—sent to Osgood in holograph form, the first American edition was set from a typescript made from the Morgan manuscript. Only a few pages of the typescript survive (at the Morgan Library and at the Houghton Library, Harvard). Clemens revised both the typescript and printer's proofs. That collating the manuscript with the first American edition will reveal errors in the book text has been shown by Willis Wager in "A Critical Edition of the Morgan Manuscript of Mark Twain's *Life on the Mississippi*," a dissertation submitted at New York University, Washington Square College, 1942. A few original manuscript readings are given in the notes that follow at 233.3, 380.14, 451.32, and 516.27–28.

Adventures of Huckleberry Finn was probably begun early in July, 1876, for on August 9 Clemens wrote to tell Howells that he had started another boys' book. Soon afterwards, however, he set aside the approximately 400 pages of manuscript that he had composed. He may have taken it up again in the winter of 1879–80; probably he prepared some working notes in 1882; and he went seriously to work in 1883. On August 22, 1883, he informed Howells that he had almost finished; on April 8, 1884, he thanked Howells for offering to read proof for him; and on August 7 he mailed proofs to Howells.

The first American edition of February 18, 1885, is at present the best available text. A holograph manuscript of about 700 sheets of octavo-size paper representing approximately three-fifths of the book, preserved at the Buffalo Public Library, is fragmentary and in important respects unlike the finished book. It begins in the middle of chapter XII, continues through chapter XIV, resumes again with chapter XXII, and continues to the end. Howells had part of a manuscript re-typed in May, 1884, and somewhat more than one-fourth of the book, much edited by Richard Watson Gilder, appeared in the *Century Magazine*. Existing proof sheets for the book (preserved among the Mark Twain Papers at Berkeley) cover a part of the text that is missing from the manuscript. Following editing of a typescript by Howells, the novel was printed by Clemens' own publishing house under the eye of his manager, Charles L. Webster. Webster added the table of contents, the running heads, and the captions for illustrations. Some printer's proofs were read by Howells; Clemens wrote, "I cursed my way through the rest and survived."

Clemens once commented that writing *Pudd'nhead Wilson* cost him little effort but that revising it almost killed him. In actuality his revisions were less than scrupulously made, yet the novel that he published was radically different from the one that he started to write some time after December, 1891, when conjoined Italian twins began to tour the United States. He worked on the story in Europe early in 1892, a time of great personal financial stress, in Nauheim and in Florence. An incomplete manuscript of perhaps 10,000 words called "Those Extraordinary Twins," now preserved in the Berg Collection of the New York Public Library, records this early stage. But the farce about Siamese twins that Clemens originally had in mind began to sprawl as he added characters and themes. During the summer of 1892 he made an effort to re-cast it, ending in December with a long, mainly holograph, partly typescript text that was unfavorably criticized by his wife and by readers in New York. This extended version, now preserved in the J. Pierpont Morgan Library, represents the last stage in composition before Clemens made large shifts, exclusions, and additions, and produced a publishable text.

During June and July of 1893, Clemens separated the twins, subordinated non-essential characters, and centered the story, he said, on the murder and the trial. The resulting text, prob-ably mainly typescript, was ready on August 14 to send to the *Century Magazine,* which bought the serial rights in Septem-ber, 1893, and published the story from December, 1893, through June, 1894, under the title *Pudd'nhead Wilson, A Tale.* This *Century* text, for which Clemens himself read at least part of the proof, is reprinted here.

For book publication Clemens turned to the American Publishing Company, from which he had parted in anger a dozen years earlier, and to Chatto & Windus, in England. The American publisher used the *Century* text for printer's copy of *Pudd'nhead Wilson* and added what Clemens called "refuse matter," a patched-together version of the excluded story of Siamese twins, to enlarge the volume. This edition was almost surely not proofread by Clemens, nor was the En-glish first edition (which does not include the "refuse matter," *Those Extraordinary Twins*).

There are numerous small differences among comparable passages in the *Century* text, the first American edition, the Berg manuscript, and the Morgan manuscript; but, except for subtractions and additions, most of them, whether in acciden-tals or in substantive distinctions, are minor. Readers who wish to examine lists of variants may consult the text estab-lished by Sidney E. Berger, *Pudd'nhead Wilson and Those Ex-traordinary Twins* (New York: W. W. Norton & Co., 1980).

The standards for American English continue to fluctuate and in some ways were different in earlier periods from what they are now. In nineteenth-century writings, for example, a word might be spelled in more than one way, even in the same work. Commas could be used expressively to suggest the movements of voice, and capitals sometimes gave significances to a word beyond those it might have in its lower-case form. Since modernization would remove these effects, this volume has preserved the spelling, punctuation, capitalization, and wording of the editions reprinted here.

The present edition is concerned only with presenting the texts of these editions; it does not attempt to reproduce features of the typographic design—such as the display capitalization of chapter openings. Footnotes within the text are those supplied by Clemens. Open contractions are retained if they appeared in the original edition. Corrections have been made in *The Adventures of Tom Sawyer* based on "The Note on the Text" in the Mark Twain Library edition (Berkeley, 1982) of that text, signed by Robert H. Hirst, General Editor, Mark Twain Project. Typographical errors in the other editions used here have also been corrected. The following is a list of those errors, cited by page and line number: 9.9, them; 25.16, what're; 26.32, o'clock; 47.26, been; 64.14, aunt; 67.2, devils; 74.8, hopes; 77.4, Who?; 89.14, two; 130.1, longer; 143.37, been; 185.34, before; 194.8, gratified; 210.21, cent,; 212.9, pears; 213.19, in.; 213.22, they're; 265.5, What; 285.9, beeen; 389.32–33, a number; 392.36, R.N.; 641.19, I I; 657.17, was; 669.7, agin; 684.3, Goshen."; 690.12, wrack.'; 695.3, didn'; 701.30, age; 705.25, then; 728.5, Douglass; 729.21, twenty; 744.37, its; 767.35, you re; 775.20, By-and by; 777.32, "Shet; 781.4, says·; 782.24, get's; 790.2, orgiess h'd; 791.27, invest for; 807.17, says; 808.40, mind; 810.34, that; 833.35, is; 841.22, did'nt; 855.31, runinng; 864.11, way"; 873.7, mo,'; 882.33, jew-sharp's; 895.1, one?; 900.9, das'nt; 912.20, aint't; 974.1, yet?; 985.32, F. F. V.   Errors corrected third printing: 670.7, po,'.

Notes

In the notes below, numbers refer to page and line of the present volume (line count includes chapter headings). For fuller informational notes on *Tom Sawyer* and on *Huckleberry Finn*, see (1) John C. Gerber, Paul Baender, and Terry Firkins, eds., *The Adventures of Tom Sawyer; Tom Sawyer Abroad; Tom Sawyer, Detective* (Berkeley: University of California Press, 1980) and (2) Leo Marx, ed., *Adventures of Huckleberry Finn* (Indianapolis: Bobbs-Merrill, 1967). Extremely helpful, too, are: Robert L. Ramsay and Frances Guthrie Emberson, *A Mark Twain Lexicon* (University of Missouri Studies, 13, January 1, 1930); Alan Gribben, *Mark Twain's Library: A Reconstruction* (Boston: G. K. Hall, 1980), 2 vols.; and the three volumes thus far in print—the several editors are Frederick Anderson, Michael B. Frank, Kenneth M. Sanderson; Frederick Anderson, Lin Salamo, Bernard L. Stein; Robert Pack Browning, Michael B. Frank, and Lin Salamo—of *Mark Twain's Notebooks & Journals* (Berkeley: University of California Press, 1975–79). No note is made for material included in a standard desk-reference book.

THE ADVENTURES OF TOM SAWYER

3.4–8   Huck . . . architecture.]   In 1895 Clemens told an interviewer that he did not believe an author ever lived who created a character, that characters are always drawn from someone the writer has known. Characters may be composites taken from life or may come from books. "We mortals can't create, we can only copy." More often than Clemens indicates in the Preface, his figures are composites, partly imaginary, partly drawn from life and literature. Places in the story, too, have their corresponding locations in actuality: Hannibal is St. Petersburg; Holiday's Hill is Cardiff Hill; McDowell's cave becomes McDougal's cave; in Clemens' manuscript, Palmyra, Missouri, is first called Coonville and then revised to Constantinople. Sunday schools that Clemens attended in the Old Ship of Zion Methodist church and in the North Fourth Street Presbyterian church are merged.

16.19   tree-box]   A wooden frame to protect the trunk of a tree.

16.21   "Buffalo Gals."]   Minstrel show performers changed the place reference in "Lubly Fan Will You Cum Out To Night" (by "Cool White"— John Hodges—copyrighted 1844) as they moved from town to town. The most popular version was known as "Buffalo Gals" (copyrighted in 1848 by the "Ethiopian Serenaders" and mentioned also in *Life on the Mississippi*, 317.11–12).

18.6   "Big Missouri,"] Probably meaning the largest of a number of steamboats named "Missouri" or with "Missouri" in their names, a side-wheeler which made St. Louis its home port.

29.15   "Barlow" knife] A cheap, strong jacknife supposed to have been designed in England by a cutler named Barlow some time in the seventeenth century. The knife became popular in America before 1779. John Russell, of Massachusetts, has been credited with being the first American cutler to man-ufacture the knives, beginning about 1834, and their mention by Clemens is supposed to have helped perpetuate the name.

30.6   a man . . . brother] The allusion is to "Am I not a man and a brother?" This inscription appears on a medallion by Wedgwood (1787) rep-resenting a Negro in chains with one knee on the ground and both hands lifted up to heaven. The design was adopted as a seal by the Antislavery Society of London and was used in jewelry. Whittier made it an epigraph for his poem "My Countrymen in Chains!" It was sometimes played upon for humorous purposes, as in *The Smoker's Guide, Philosopher, and Friend* (1876), by Andrew Steinmetz: "Am I not—a smoker and a brother?"

37.2   cracked bell] The cracked bell from the wrecked steamboat *Chester* hung in the steeple of the Presbyterian church on North Fourth Street, Han-nibal.

38.10–13   Shall . . . seas?] Isaac Watts, "Am I a Soldier of the Cross?" (1709). Clemens knew at least some of Watts's hymns well, mentioning them in a jesting letter of January 30, 1862, to his mother as among the luxuries (Dickens' *Dombey and Son* and fourteen decks of cards were others) that he and his comrades packed into their wagon in Nevada. Here he changes the first word of the first line of the second stanza from "Must" to "Shall" and the first word of what is properly line 3 from "While" to "Whilst" and makes several small changes to indicate the regional pronunciation.

46.12   spunk-water] "Spunk" often means "rotten wood"; thus "spunk-water" may be water held in a rotten stump. Folklorists record a wide variety of charms and procedures that have been believed to be useful in removing warts.

48.9   Lord's Prayer back'ards."] Perhaps the idea that conditions in Hades are reversed from those in heaven suggested to early Christian magi-cians the reversal of the normal mass (addressed to heaven). Twentieth-cen-tury witches in the Ozark mountains have been alleged to recite the Lord's Prayer backwards; and a travesty of the mass is asserted by some folklorists to have been for centuries a fundamental part of performances of the Black Mass by witches.

48.11   Hoss Williams] True W. Williams, illustrator of the first American edition, put his own name on a gravestone in a drawing showing the opened grave of Hoss Williams.

58.1   over . . . away,]   With "over" or "o'er," the expression has been in common use and could have been heard anywhere by Clemens. As a refrain, it may have been alluded to as early as 1549; it appears in a black-letter ballad, *The Wind hath blown my Plaid away* (ca. 1670). Relevant verses from the second part of chapbooks entitled *Tom, the Piper's Son* run:

> Tom, he was a piper's son,
> He learnt to play when he was young,
> And all the tune that he could play
> Was, "Over the hills and far away" . . .

60.27   Black . . . Main!"]   The allusion is to the titular hero of *The Black Avenger of the Spanish Main, or the Fiend of Blood* (1847), by "Ned Buntline" (Edward Z. C. Judson), one of the more prolific American dime novelists of the nineteenth century.

62.22   "by the book,"]   The book has been shown to be Joseph Cundall's popular, often-reprinted *Robin Hood and His Merry Foresters* (London, 1841).

81.6   "whistle . . . wind,"]   The expression may be explained by turning to *Othello*, III, iii, 262, where the imagery is from falconry. Made suspicious of Desdemona's virtue, Othello says that if she prove "wild," "I'd whistle her off and let her down the wind, / To prey at fortune." According to Samuel Johnson, if the falconer lets the hawk fly with the wind behind her, she will seldom return; therefore, if a hawk was to be dismissed, she was let fly down wind.

81.33–34   pale . . . after."]   Loosely quoted from Rev. 6:8.

82.21   Pain-Killer]   "Perry Davis's Pain Killer" was advertised in Hannibal newspapers but was intended for external use only.

86.21–22   "two . . . thought."]   "Two souls with but a single thought, / Two hearts that beat as one," are lines from *Der Sohn der Wildnis* (1843?), by Eligius F. J. von Münch-Bellinghausen, translated and adapted to the English stage by Maria Anne Lovell as *Ingomar, the Barbarian* (2:1). Clemens clearly is citing *Ingomar*, for he reviewed and burlesqued a performance of that drama given in Virginia City, Nevada, in November, 1863.

87.12   Jackson's Island]   Actually Glasscock's Island, later washed away by the Mississippi.

96.20   shoot a cannon]   A variously explained superstition that appears also in *Adventures of Huckleberry Finn*, chapter VIII. The supposition below, that mercury placed in a loaf of bread and set afloat will seek out the spot where a corpse lies, was another popular belief.

109.22   Spirit . . . Night]   Clemens is probably not being specifically allusive. In Homer the feminine personification of night was so powerful that she could subdue Zeus. Systematizing mythographers portrayed her as living in Hades, dressed in dark clothes, accompanied by stars, either winged or riding in a chariot. Shelley begins his poem "To Night" (1821) with the lines: "Swiftly walk over the western wave, / Spirit of Night!"

115.34 Old Hundred] Often in Protestant churches called "the Doxology," meaning the stanza beginning "Praise God from whom all blessings flow," sung to a tune of ancient and uncertain origins that was set in metrical versions of the Psalms to the hundredth as early as 1563. Its swelling, joyous sound has made it a favorite. In *The Biglow Papers*, second series (1867), James Russell Lowell struck somewhat the same chord as does Clemens here: "My! when he made Old Hundred ring, / She *knowed* the Lord was nigher." In English as opposed to American usage the psalm with tune is called "Old Hundredth."

120.2 Milum apple] Milam apple, a medium-sized dessert apple formerly popular in some portions of the Middle West.

134.14–15 "You'd . . . stage,"] From David Everett (1770–1813), "Lines Written for a School Declamation by a Little Boy of Seven" at New Ipswich, New Hampshire—a poem that was reprinted many times in anthologies. Everett was a teacher, lawyer, journalist, and author of plays, political essays, and orations.

134.35 "The Boy . . . Deck"] The first line of "Casabianca," one of the best-known poems by the very popular, prolific English poet Felicia Dorothea Hemans (1793–1835).

134.36 "The Assyrian Came Down,"] From Byron, "The Destruction of Sennacherib" (1815), a poem that Clemens liked to quote.

135.31 the "Examination."] For all of the compositions given by the young ladies, Clemens used as copy-text pages ripped from *Prose and Poetry*, "by a Georgia lady," published for the author in Nashville, Tennessee, in 1858. The author was Mary Ann Harris Gay. The book went through at least eleven editions, under three or more imprints. The expanded title became *The Pastor's Story and Other Pieces; or, Prose and Poetry*. Clemens in his note (138.39–40) attributed the volume to "a Western lady."

162.21 Murrel's gang] John A. Murrell (1804?–44) was the chief of a powerful, widely scattered association of river pirates, slave-stealers, and cut-throats. Clemens writes on Murrell and his activities in *Life on the Mississippi*, chapter XXIX.

170.17 good as wheat!"] As good as gold or corn or some other article of value that may be used as a medium of exchange.

171.7–8 "hi-spy" . . . "gully keeper"] More conventionally, "I spy" and "goalie-keeper."

LIFE ON THE MISSISSIPPI

217.1   LIFE ON THE MISSISSIPPI]   Clemens considered, then rejected, titles that would relate this book to *The Innocents Abroad*, his early, successful travel volume: *Abroad on the Great River; Abroad on the Father of Waters;* and *Abroad on the Mississippi.*

230.34   burnt Fisher]   John Fisher (1459–1535), Bishop of Rochester, was convicted of treason against Henry VIII and was beheaded.

233.3   La Salle himself sued]   The manuscript reading here is: La Salle humbly sued.

235.1   rude . . . paintings]   Francis Parkman, whose *La Salle and the Discovery of the Great West* (1869; rev. ed. 1879) Clemens uses extensively in chapters I and II, mentions that the sighting of these paintings by Louis Joliet, Jacques Marquette, and their party "reminded them that the Devil was still lord paramount of this wilderness." A pair of monsters painted in red, black, and green—each as large as a calf and visible from the river—were painted on a flat rock. These paintings, later called the Piasa Bird or Thunder Bird, were destroyed during blasting operations in 1870 but were reproduced in 1934.

238.26   Natchez-under-the-hill]   The chief part of Natchez, Mississippi, was on high ground, but at the foot of the bluff there grew up around 1800 a small settlement notorious during much of the nineteenth century for its vices. Its decline began with the Civil War. For a comment by Clemens, see p. 463.

239.20–24   By . . . more.]   The "raft passage" that follows was composed in 1876 for a manuscript that later became *Adventures of Huckleberry Finn*. Clemens considered restoring the passage to chapter XVI of *Huckleberry Finn* (beginning 710.27), but he never did so.

239.33   bound for Cairo]   The Ohio river joins the Mississippi at Cairo, and the runaway slave, Jim, intended to go up the Ohio to safety.

240.22   it . . . song]   Clemens incorporated a version of this ballad in an incomplete farce that probably belongs to his San Francisco period, put it into the *Prince and the Pauper* in bowdlerized form, and sang it when he played a role in a dramatization by his children and their friends at Christmas time in 1884.

253.2   *The Boys' Ambition*]   Here begins what was called "Old Times on the Mississippi," first published in the *Atlantic Monthly*.

256.21   "mud clerks;"]   A mud-clerk, the second or third clerk of a steamer, so called because it was his duty to go ashore, often at a mere mudbank, to receive or check off freight.

260.27   wildcat literature]   Unrealistic, unbelievable, in the same way that
wildcat banks and wildcat currency were not to be depended on.

264.23   "Father . . . declining,"]   From what has been published as an
anonymous hymn in two stanzas. The first stanza begins: "Fading, still fading, the last beam is shining, / Father in Heaven, the day is declining" (*Plym-
outh Collection of Hymns, for the use of Christian Congregations,* ed. H. W.
Beecher [New York: A. S. Barnes and Co., 1855], p. 822. Under the title "The
Last Beam," words and music are given by Roswell Dwight Hitchcock, et
al., eds., *Carmina Sanctorum: A Selection of Hymns and Songs of Praise* [New
York: A. S. Barnes and Co., 1886], p. 33).

317.11−12   'Buffalo Gals,]   See entry at 16.21.

319.21−22   organization . . . guild]   A Louisville Pilots' Benevolent Association was organized in 1841, a Little Rock Pilots' Association in 1845−49.
Soon after 1854 the St. Louis−New Orleans association was formed. In 1870
associations of pilots were active on the runs between Cincinnati and St.
Louis, Cincinnati and New Orleans, and St. Louis and New Orleans. The
Steamboat Inspection Act of 1852 included a stringent system for licensing
engineers and pilots. (In 1842 associations of engineers were formed in Cincinnati and St. Louis.)

331.35   "doctor"]   An independent steam pump with a working beam,
used on western river steamers.

334.26   *Commodore Rollingpin's Almanac*]   John Henton Carter, a reporter of river news for St. Louis newspapers and an acquaintance of Clemens', used the pseudonym "Commodore Rollingpin."

361.2   *I . . . Muttons*]   *Revenons à nos moutons*: let us get back to our
subject; a line from the anonymous *La Farce de maître Pathelin* (ca. 1464).

361.6   a poet . . . stenographer]   James R. Osgood, of Boston, at this
time Clemens' publisher, and not a poet; and Roswell H. Phelps, a stenographer of Hartford, who made part of the trip with Clemens and Osgood.
Clemens refers to him below as "Rogers."

365.30   Charles Augustus Murray]   Author of *Travels in North America
during the Years 1834, 1835 & 1836 . . .* (2 vols., 1839). Clemens made use of
eighteen or more travel books in writing *Life on the Mississippi,* including at
least two not identified in his text. Among the writers made use of are: Captain Basil Hall, *Travels in North America in the Years 1827 and 1828* (3 vols.,
1828); Mrs. Frances Trollope, *Domestic Manners of the Americans* (1832); and
Alexander Mackay, *Western World, or Travels in the United States in 1846−47*
(3 vols., 1849).

380.14   dress-reform period]   Manuscript reading here is: achieved by the
dress-reform. This error suggests that Clemens' typist may have had parts of
the holograph manuscript read to her.

382.26   Mr. Dickens's]   In his *American Notes for General Circulation* (2 vols., 1842), Charles Dickens took a frequently condemnatory look at American towns, manners, and mores. Slavery distressed him, and he was disgusted by what he saw of semi-frontier conditions.

392.15   images . . . Bolgia]   That is, of another ditch like the ten ditches of Malebolge, the eighth circle of Dante's *Inferno*; of a place of extreme disorder.

399.29–30   Ecclesiastes vii.13]   "Consider the work of God: for who can make *that* straight, which he hath made crooked?"

402.15–16   ask . . . numbers,]   More accurately, "Tell me not, in mournful numbers," from "A Psalm of Life," by Henry Wadsworth Longfellow.

402.31   Mr. Edward Atkinson]   Atkinson (1827–1905), named here and below (438.39–40; 439.5–6; 600.5), a Bostonian, published books on such topics as labor and capital, cotton manufacturing, and railways. He recommended diversified agriculture for the South.

404.32   Jesse James]   The well-known desperado (1847–82) who served as a Confederate guerilla under William Clarke Quantrill and, in 1866, formed a band of brigands that operated for approximately fifteen years.

422.21   A . . . CONFESSION]   James R. Osgood, who at the request of Clemens helped him with revisions, suggested that this story be condensed. Clemens decided against the suggestion, but he did condense or delete other passages at the suggestion of Osgood.

451.32   short stout bag]   The manuscript reading here is: shot-bag.

458.12   "Alonzo and Melissa;"]   Clemens is almost surely referring to *Alonzo and Melissa; or The Unfeeling Father* (1811), a plagiarized version by Daniel Jackson, Jr., of Isaac Mitchell's *The Asylum; or Alonzo and Melissa* (1810), first published as "Alonzo and Melissa, A Tale," in weekly installments (1804) in the *Political Barometer* of Poughkeepsie, New York.

485.25   author . . . "The Grandissimes."]   George Washington Cable. He and Clemens made a successful joint reading tour, November 5, 1884, through February 28, 1885.

488.33–36   I . . . South.]   Florida and Hannibal, Missouri, were usually called West, but they were slaveholding communities; and upon occasion Clemens considered them to have been in the South and himself to have been, like his parents, Southern.

494.30   "much people"]   St. Mark 5:21.

504.17   Mr. Warner]   Charles Dudley Warner, a Hartford neighbor.

507.10   Captain Eads' . . . jetties,"]   James Buchanan Eads (1820–87) constructed ironclad steamers and mortar boats for the Federal Government during the Civil War, built the Eads bridge (1874) across the Mississippi at

St. Louis, and, his greatest work, by means of jetties deepened and fixed the mouths of the Mississippi.

516.3   Captain Isaiah Sellers]   Clemens said and wrote repeatedly, as he does below, that he borrowed the pseudonym "Mark Twain" from Captain Sellers (who supposedly had contributed river news over that signature to a New Orleans newspaper) at the death of Sellers. It has been established, however, that Clemens first used the pseudonym on February 3, 1863, and that Sellers did not die until March 6, 1864. It is possible, moreover, that Sellers never used the pseudonym.

516.27–28   Orleans . . . Orleans.]   Apparently the copyist missed a line here. The manuscript reads: Orleans and back—this boat was 115 tons burthen. In 1826 he was engaged on the 'Gen. Carrol,' between Nashville and New Orleans.

553.11   the "Jibbenainosay,"]   Robert Montgomery Bird, *Nick of the Woods, or the Jibbenainosay, a Tale of Kentucky* (2 vols., 1837).

561.23   Henry Clay Dean]   Dean was a Methodist circuit rider, lawyer, and Chaplain of the United States Senate.

562.8–9   a son . . . Claggett,]   William H. Claggett served in both houses of the Nevada legislature, was notary public for Unionville, Nevada, and later was in the Congress from Montana. He prospected for silver with Clemens.

563.28   the sparkling Burdette]   Robert J. Burdette (1844–1914), a platform lecturer, Baptist clergyman, newspaper humorist, and acquaintance of Clemens. He worked for the Peoria *Daily Transcript*, the Burlington *Daily Hawkeye*, and contributed columns to the Brooklyn *Daily Eagle*. Known as "the Burlington Hawkeye Man," he published *The Rise and Fall of the Mustache and Other "Hawk-Eyetems"* (1877).

575.11   Mr. Schoolcraft's book]   Clemens is probably referring to Henry Rowe Schoolcraft's *Algic Researches* . . . (2 vols., 1839), the first volume of which contains "Peboan and Seegwun" and "Iamo; or, the Undying Head."

581.24   Westward . . . way.]   George Berkeley (1685–1753), bishop of Cloyne, in "Verses, on the Prospect of Planting Arts and Learning in America" (1752), wrote, "Westward the course of empire takes its way."

601.40   Obadiah's curse]   The allusion is to Obadiah, shortest book in the Old Testament. A judgment is promised on the nations, including the Edomites, who gave aid to the Babylonians and gloated over Israel when Jerusalem fell in 586 B.C.

602.21–22   unhouselled, unanointed, unannealed]   *Hamlet*, I, i, 77. The "unanointed" is Pope's emendation; the line should read: "Unhousel'd, disappointed, unaneled."

ADVENTURES OF HUCKLEBERRY FINN

619.7   Per G. G.]   Probably a joking reference to General Ulysses S. Grant, whom Clemens greatly admired. Early in 1885, Charles L. Webster & Co., which belonged to Clemens, contracted to publish Grant's memoirs.

620.2–12   In . . . succeeding.]   Although Clemens did make numerous revisions directed toward some kind of accuracy, his use of dialect was not as systematic as he claimed.

626.4   Moses . . . Bulrushers]   Exodus 2:3.

635.6   took . . . closet]   Matthew 6:6: "But thou, when thou prayest, enter into thy closet."

636.28   hived]   Here means "captured."

636.33   slogan]   One of many mistaken or garbled words, phrases, names, and episodes, usually drawn from Tom Sawyer's reading as remembered by Huck. "Slogan," which means a battle-cry in Sir Walter Scott's "The Lay of the Last Minstrel," Canto IV, is confused with the fiery cross sent about to call the clans together in *The Lady of the Lake*, Canto III.

650.31   a free nigger]   There were free Negroes in Hannibal during the 1840s, but Missouri passed increasingly strict laws intended to exclude them.

652.37–38   Angel of Death]   Azrael, from Mohammedan iconology and mythology. The phrase appears in *The Arabian Nights* and in Byron's "The Destruction of Sennacherib," both of which were well known to Clemens. Clemens quoted often from Byron's poem.

660.21–22   firing . . . water]   A folk belief held that the concussion would bring the body to the surface.

660.30   quicksilver in loaves]   That the loaves would seek out the corpse of a drowned person was widely believed.

661.25–26   Bessie Thatcher]   Clemens forgot repeatedly what names he had given to characters or, for that matter, to books. Here he means "Becky Thatcher."

663.26–37   By the . . . around."]   This passage, like several others, may be a fragment from a plot sequence which was deleted before the novel was published.

701.30   dolphin]   The Dauphin, Louis Charles (1785–95?), almost certainly died in prison; but legends of his escape persisted, and imposters appeared in Europe and in America. In early English usage "dolphin" was one of several alternative variants of "dauphin," in France the name of the cetacean and also, from the fourteenth century to 1830, the appellation of the eldest son of the King of France.

704.5–6   up . . . trouble]   In August, 1876, Clemens seems to have completed this chapter and most of the following one before running into difficulties and setting the manuscript aside. The book was developing into something more than an episodic, lighthearted tale for boys, and, besides, he knew nothing of the Ohio River country that Jim should have turned toward. In October, 1879, he took up the manuscript again and began to introduce new themes, new characters, and somewhat casual explanations for not taking Huck and Jim up the Ohio toward freedom but on down the Mississippi into territory where slavery existed in some of its worst aspects.

710.26   waited.]   Clemens was asked in a letter of April 21, 1884, by Charles L. Webster, husband of his niece and manager of his publishing company, whether it would not be better to omit from *Huckleberry Finn* "the raft passage," which began at this point but had already been removed from the manuscript and published in chapter III of *Life on the Mississippi*. The book was, he complained, "so *much* larger than *Tom Sawyer*." Clemens readily agreed. For the "raft passage," see chapter III, p. 239, of *Life on the Mississippi*.

716.10–11   clear . . . Muddy!]   The Missouri River is frequently called "the Muddy" because the Mississippi is the clearer of the two at their juncture just above St. Louis. Clemens has the Mississippi become "the Muddy," because at Cairo, where the Ohio and the Mississippi come together, the Ohio is the clearer.

717.21   raft.]   Clemens set his manuscript aside at about this point in the summer of 1876.

724.14   Highland Marys]   Pictures of Mary Campbell, briefly before her death the sweetheart of Robert Burns, about whom Burns wrote several poems, best known of which is "Highland Mary."

733.27   coarse-hand]   Apparently a rare Americanism meaning written in capital letters.

736.22–23   wood-rank]   Usually means about half a cord of neatly laid-up wood.

750.34   Garrick the Younger]   The duke confuses David Garrick and Charles John Kean, son of Edmund Kean and called "the Younger." Clemens introduces similar blunders later.

758.19–759.10   To . . . go!]   Extraneous passages from *Macbeth* and *Richard III* are jumbled together with lines from *Hamlet*, mainly from the soliloquy, III, ii. Comparable literary burlesques written by American humorists were familiar to Clemens.

759.22   little one-horse town]   Clemens has in mind Napoleon, Arkansas. Arkansas was notoriously given to violence.

764.32–765.13   I . . . off.]   John Marshall Clemens, J. P., took depositions in 1845 relative to the shooting on January 24, of Samuel Smarr, a farmer, by William Owsley of Hannibal. The shooting of Boggs by Sherburn follows closely the details of the actual killing as recorded in these depositions. Owsley was tried and acquitted on March 14, 1846, in Palmyra, Missouri.

771.37   THE KING'S CAMELOPARD]   The dramatic hoax introduced under this title was called "The Burning Shame" in the manuscript of *Huckleberry Finn* and was probably based on a story told to Clemens by Dick Stoker, a miner, in a cabin at Jackass Gulch, Calaveras County, California, where Clemens spent part of the winter of 1864–65. A reviewer of *Huckleberry Finn* called "The King's Camelopard" a polite version of the "Giascutus" (usually spelled "gyascutus") story, a hoaxing story of a fabulous animal which was circulated in multiple versions in oral tradition and in newspapers and was presumably given various portrayals on the stage. It has usually been supposed that the part of the king's outfit which Huck refers to as "just wild" was a false phallus. An alternative explanation suggests that, as in comic scenes over the centuries, the king, during his prancing and capering, has a lighted candle protruding from his anus. The candle would account for the original title, "The Burning Shame," or, as Clemens says it was called by its narrator at Jackass Gulch, "The Tragedy of the Burning Shame." "The Burning Shame" could be a version of the gyascutus story, as Clemens' use of the word "Camelopard" may indicate.

796.11   hark . . . tomb!]   "Hark from the tombs, a doleful sound," from Isaac Watts, bk. ii, Hymn 63, used as a socially acceptable substitute for an obscene or profane expression.

806.6–7   down the banks]   A substitute expression analogous to "down the country," meaning a chiding.

847.18   meeky]   To skulk or sneak along. Cf. meach, meech, miche.

861.20–21   Iron Mask]   The masked prisoner in Alexandre Dumas' romance, *Dix ans plus, ou le Vicomte de Bragelonne* (1845–50), part of which was translated as *The Man in the Iron Mask*. The prisoner is said to have died in the Bastille in 1703.

863.20   Castle Deef]   The Chateau d'If, a state prison where the hero of Dumas' *Le Comte de Monte Cristo* (1844) was imprisoned.

883.23   Pitchiola]   In the romance *Picciola* (1836) by Joseph-Xavier Boniface ("Xavier Saintine") a plant enables a noble prisoner to survive.

885.23   allycumpain]   Elecampane, a perennial composite with large yellow radiate flowers; formerly used as a tonic and stimulant; here used to relieve pain.

889.22   *Ingean Territory*]   The federal land grant to Indians in what became Oklahoma; also a base for desperadoes.

894.29–30   'Son . . . heaven!'] The quotation is from Thomas Carlyle's *The French Revolution*, III, 2, viii.

898.18–19   Nebokoodneezer] Nebuchadnezzar, Chaldean King of Babylon (reigned ca. 605–562 B.C.), is represented in Daniel 4:33 as becoming insane.

906.20   opened] Probably should be corrected to "opens." The other verbs in the series are in the present tense.

PUDD'NHEAD WILSON

915.8   *Pudd'nhead Wilson's Calendar.*] Clemens set down in notes and notebooks perhaps three hundred examples—most of them written during the 1890s and some in two or more versions—of aphoristic expressions such as were popularly used in calendars and almanacs. During the serial publication of *Pudd'nhead Wilson* in the *Century Magazine*, the *Century* printed a miniature calendar with maxims from among those used as epigraphs at the head of each chapter. Early in 1894, after entering into an agreement, soon cancelled, with L. Prang & Co., an almanac maker, permitting the use of appropriate passages from his writings, Clemens spent several days composing compact witticisms, writing "special squibs for 10 of the months & all the national holidays." He later made use of previously unprinted maxims— over the inscription "Pudd'nhead Wilson's New Calendar"—at the heads of chapters in *Following the Equator* (1897).

915.34   the Villa Viviani] Although much concerned about approaching bankruptcy, beginning on September 26, 1892, the Clemenses settled for a prolonged stay in this handsome, twenty-eight-room villa approximately three miles outside of the center of Florence.

917.4–5   Dawson's Landing] The name is taken from J. D. Dawson, master of one of the schools that Clemens attended.

918.23   Falls . . . St. Anthony] At Minneapolis, Minnesota, supplying the water power which determined the development of that city as a manufacturing center.

919.8–9   the Judge . . . free-thinker] In his working notes Clemens made Judge Driscoll the father of the slave woman Roxy's child.

919.14   the "code,"] Meaning not the legal code but the "code duello."

921.23   Percy Northumberland Driscoll] Percy Driscoll is more exemplary of the dehumanizing effect of slavery on slaveholders in the J. Pierpont Morgan Library manuscript version of *Pudd'nhead Wilson* than he is in the published text. In the earlier version Percy Driscoll travels miles to collect a debt but lets it go uncollected because the debtor is in unfortunate circumstances. On the other hand, Driscoll sells a slave because the slave is a nuisance to travel with. This omitted episode parallels closely at key points an episode in the life of John Clemens, who, when virtually bankrupt, made a long, expensive trip during the winter of 1841–42 trying to collect an old debt.

919.32   Roxana]   The name may come from Daniel Defoe's *Roxana, or the Fortunate Mistress* (1724), a novel urgently recommended to Clemens by William Dean Howells in 1885.

920.17   "I . . . dog."]   The witticism appears in many versions, including the story of Solomon as told in chapter XIV of *Huckleberry Finn* and the story of an elephant with two proprietors as recounted in *The Life of P. T. Barnum, Written by Himself* (1854), a book that Clemens read with pleasure.

921.8   labrick]   U. S. (Missouri) slang: a fool, an ass.

923.2   finger-marks]   Clemens used the device of fingerprinting for the discovery of identity in chapter XXXI of *Life on the Mississippi* (1883), but at that time little was accurately known about the regularity of these markings. In an earlier version of *Pudd'nhead Wilson*, he planned to use footprints as a means for establishing identity; then in 1892 Sir Francis Galton published *Finger Prints*, the first book on the subject, and Clemens requested a copy from his London publishers. Galton, he later declared, changed the whole plot and plan of his book. The use by Clemens of fingerprints for identification in 1830 has been questioned as an anachronism, but Galton refers to a University Thesis on the subject at Breslau in 1823.

934.7–9   In . . . children.]   How two she bears "tare forty and two" of the children who mocked Elisha. II Kings 2:23–25.

936.37–38   Sir . . . armor]   Clemens knew Sir Thomas Malory's *Le Morte Darthur* in a printing of the Globe edition and in the version for boys edited by Sidney Lanier. Sir Lancelot takes the armor, shield, and horse of Sir Kay while Kay sleeps, leaving his own in their place. Upon waking, Kay says that knights will be bold against Lancelot, whereas because of Lancelot's armor and shield, he will ride in peace. (In the Globe text, London, 1868, bk. 6, chap. 11; in *The Boy's King Arthur*, New York, 1880, bk. 2, chap. 8.)

941.15   "conditions,"]   Courses or subjects in which Tom did not satisfy the entrance requirements of the college.

941.35–942.9   He . . . could.]   The passage is transcribed from memory of life in Hannibal. In "Villagers of 1840–3," written around 1897, Clemens describes an envied rich boy, Neil Moss: "Was sent to Yale—a mighty journey and an incomparable distinction. Came back in swell eastern clothes, and the young men dressed up the warped negro bell ringer in a travesty of him—which made him descend to village fashions."

944.6   ablush]   Manuscript reading here is "aflush."

944.11   twins]   Clemens was acquainted with twins and doubles in literature ranging from Shakespeare to Charlotte M. Yonge and Sarah Grand. His interest in duality, disguises, and the problem of identity appears in his notes for writing and in his published works. Clemens' interest in Siamese twins was not new. Chang and Eng (1811–74), born in Siam of mainly

Chinese parentage, were exhibited in the United States, settled in North Carolina, and married sisters. In August, 1869, Clemens published "Personal Habits of the Siamese Twins" in *Packard's Monthly*, and on September 2, 1869, he published in the Buffalo *Express* a sketch about a two-headed girl. The immediate suggestion for a tale about Siamese twins probably came from an article (with accompanying illustration) in the *Scientific Monthly* for December 12, 1891, on the Italian twins, Giovanni and Giacomo Tocci, who had two heads, four arms, and one body. The Toccis were then appearing in the United States. In early versions of what became *Pudd'nhead Wilson*, the twins Luigi and Angelo are congenitally united. Clemens later separated them, but because his revising was inadequate, indications of their united origins remain in the published text. See, for example, 946.27; 947.11; 979.9−10; and 1017.35−36.

945.19   the West] In American usage, "West" has been a relative term. Not only could St. Louis and Cincinnati be referred to as Western cities in this period, but parts of Georgia could be spoken of as "the West."

949.25   sunset . . . glory] Possibly an allusion to a sonnet called "Miracles" by Clemens' friend Thomas Bailey Aldrich, published in his *Poems* (1865). The sonnet includes these lines (later revised): "The fading alps and archipelagoes, / And great cloud-continents of sunset-seas."

983.19−20   human . . . speech."] In the Morgan Library manuscript of *Pudd'nhead Wilson*, Clemens wrote "human pair of scissors" because of the visual image presented at that moment by the (still Siamese) twins. After deleting the image and separating the twins, he revised the description to "human philopena," referring to the twin kernels of a nut, but neglected to change the no longer appropriate "snip."

992.18   that jack-pair] Perhaps two meanings are intended: a pair of rascals; and (Siamese) twins, like the reversible figure of a jack, or knave, in a deck of playing cards.

1000.39−1001.3   ole . . . Africa] In an early draft Clemens wrote: "My father en yo' gran'father was ole John Randolph of Roanoke, de highes' blood dat ole Virginny ever turned out . . ." The revision was probably made to spare the feelings of existing Randolphs.

1001.12−13   "Ain't . . . finger-nails] It has been widely believed that Negro blood in a person who otherwise appears to be white may be detected by the distinctive appearance of the fingernails. About 1884 Clemens made notes for a story about a mulatto who decides to pass for white: "At last, seeing even the best educated negro is at a disadvantage, besides always being insulted, clips his wiry hair close, wears gloves always (to conceal his telltale nails,) & passes for a white man, in a northern city."

1053.35   sits in among you] The phrase was revised from the manuscript reading: "in your midst," and the apparently extraneous "in" was overlooked.

1056.33−34   As . . . river.] In an earlier version Tom, instead of being sold down the river, makes use of his suspenders to hang himself.

Library of Congress Cataloging in Publication Data

Clemens, Samuel Langhorne (Mark Twain) 1835–1910.
  Mississippi writings.

  (The Library of America, 5)
  Edited by Guy Cardwell.
  Contents: The adventures of Tom Sawyer—Life on the Mississippi—
Adventures of Huckleberry Finn—Pudd'nhead Wilson.
  1. Mississippi River—Literary collections. I. Cardwell, Guy, 1905–
II. Title. III. Twain, Mark. IV. The adventures of Tom Sawyer. 1982.
V. Life on the Mississippi. 1982. VI. Adventures of Huckleberry Finn.
1982. VII. Pudd'nhead Wilson. 1982. VIII. Series: The Library of
America.
PS1302 1982   813'.4   82–9917
ISBN 0-940450-07-0   AACR2

For a list of titles in The Library of America, write to:
The Library of America
14 East 60th Street
New York, NY 10022

This book is set in 10 point Linotron Galliard,
a face designed for photocomposition by Matthew Carter
and based on the sixteenth-century face Granjon. The paper
is acid-free Ecusta Nyalite and meets the requirements for perma-
nence of the American National Standards Institute. The binding
material is Brillianta, a 100% woven rayon cloth made by
Van Heek-Scholco Textielfabrieken, Holland. The com-
position is by Haddon Craftsmen, Inc., and The
Clarinda Company. Printing and binding
by R. R. Donnelley & Sons Company.
Designed by Bruce Campbell.

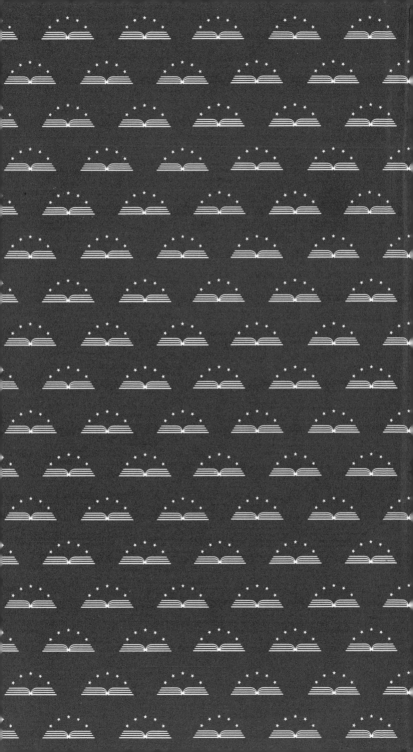